COLORADO MOUNTAIN COLLEGE
PZ3.L81146RAI
SP
Lockridge, Ross Fran
S0-ALC-458
LOCKRIDGE, JR., ROSS
Raintree County

Erven T. Larson

Raintree County

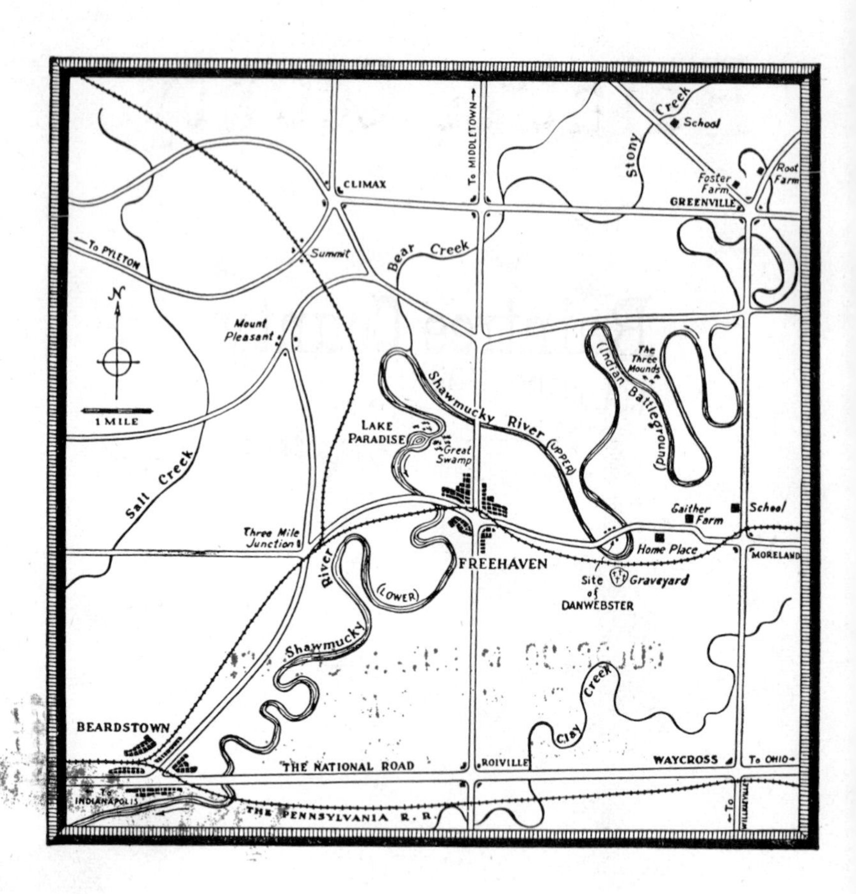

To MIDDLETOWN
CLIMAX
Stony Creek
School
Foster Farm
Root Farm
GREENVILLE
To PYLETON
Summit
Bear Creek
N
Mount Pleasant
The Three Mounds
(Indian Battleground)
Shawmucky River (UPPER)
1 MILE
LAKE PARADISE
Great Swamp
Sall Creek
Gaither Farm
School
Three Mile Junction
Home Place
MORELAND
River
FREEHAVEN
Site of DANWEBSTER
Graveyard
(LOWER)
Shawmucky
Clay Creek
BEARDSTOWN
THE NATIONAL ROAD
ROIVILLE
WAYCROSS
To OHIO
To INDIANAPOLIS
THE PENNSYLVANIA R. R.

Raintree County

...which had no boundaries in time and space, where lurked musical and strange names and mythical and lost peoples, and which was itself only a name musical and strange.

ROSS LOCKRIDGE, Jr.

HOUGHTON MIFFLIN COMPANY

The Riverside Press Cambridge
BOSTON 1948

THERE IS NO INTENDED RESEMBLANCE
BETWEEN THE CHARACTERS OF THIS
NOVEL AND ANY PEOPLE LIVING OR DEAD

Hard roads and wide will run through Raintree County.
You will hunt it on the map, and it won't be there.

For Raintree County is not the country of the perishable fact. It is the country of the enduring fiction. The clock in the Court House Tower on page five of the *Raintree County Atlas* is always fixed at nine o'clock, and it is summer and the days are long.

PRINTED IN THE UNITED STATES OF AMERICA BY
KINGSPORT PRESS, INC., KINGSPORT, TENNESSEE

For My Mother

Elsie Shockley Lockridge

This book of lives, loves, and antiquities.

I wish to acknowledge the assistance of my wife, VERNICE BAKER LOCKRIDGE, whose devotion to this book over our joint seven-year period of unintermitted labor upon it was equal to my own. Without her, *Raintree County* would never have come into being.

Ross Lockridge, Jr.

For the Reader

Raintree County is the story of a single day in which are imbedded a series of flashbacks. The chronologies printed here may assist the reader in understanding the structure of the novel. At the back of the book may be found a chronology of historical events with bearing on the story.

Chronology of *A GREAT DAY* for RAINTREE COUNTY July 4, 1892

Morning

Dawn — *MR. JOHN WICKLIFF SHAWNESSY* awakens in the town of Waycross. (*page 3*)

6:00 — The Shawnessy family leaves Waycross by surrey.

6:45 — In the Court House Square of Freehaven, Mr. Shawnessy enters a Museum of Raintree County Antiquities.

7:45 — Across the site of the vanished town of Danwebster, Mr. Shawnessy carries a sickle and a box of cut flowers.

8:30 — Approaching the town of Moreland, *EVA* Alice Shawnessy reads the last page of *Barriers Burned Away*. (*page 235*)

8:45 — Re-entering *THE GREAT ROAD OF THE REPUBLIC* in Waycross, Mr. Shawnessy is engulfed in wheels and faces. (*page 253*)

9:30 — Senator Garwood B. Jones arrives by special train in Waycross Station.

10:00 — Three men tip their chairs back against the General Store for a talk.

10:05 — Esther Root Shawnessy enters the Revival Tent to hear *THE OLDEST STORY IN THE WORLD*, the Reverend Lloyd G. Jarvey officiating. (*page 358*)

10:30 — Mr. Shawnessy hands Professor Jerusalem Webster Stiles a copy of the *News-Historian*, containing the legend of a *HOUSE DIVIDED*. (*page 421*)

11:15 — A photographer, a preacher, a lady in a Victorian mansion, a chorus of men only, and *A WHITE BULL* prepare respectively to take pictures, glorify God, distribute pamphlets, see an Exhibition for Men Only, and affirm life. (*page 553*)

Afternoon

12:30 — In the intersection of Waycross, General Jacob J. Jackson presents Mr. Shawnessy with a copy of a manuscript entitled *FIGHTING FOR FREEDOM*, and the G.A.R. parade forms to march on the schoolhouse for a banquet. (*page 595*)

2:30 — The Grand Patriotic Program begins in the schoolhouse yard.

4:30 — Eva Alice Shawnessy muses in *WAYCROSS STATION*, where Statesmen, Soldiers, Financiers, and Poets arrive and depart by train. (*page 753*)

4:35 — As Senator Garwood B. Jones prepares to entrain for the City, Mr. Shawnessy recalls a *SPHINX RECUMBENT* in his gilded years. (*page 765*)

5:05 — Financier Cassius P. Carney descends from the Eastbound Express in Waycross Station.

6:00 — *BETWEEN TWO WORLDS* in contest for her soul, Esther Root Shawnessy passes the intersection in Waycross as a train bears Financier Cassius P. Carney from Waycross Station. (*page 869*)

Evening

7:30 — On the porchswing at Mrs. Evelina Brown's mansion, an informal meeting of the Waycross Literary Society opens a discussion on *THE GOLDEN BOUGH.*

(*page 885*)

9:30 — Esther Root Shawnessy watches a cluster of torches approach the garden east of Waycross.

9:35 — From the tower of Mrs. Brown's mansion, Eva Alice Shawnessy beholds a celestial conflict.

10:50 — The last Fourth of July rocket explodes over Waycross.

Midnight — Professor Jerusalem Webster Stiles departs by train from Waycross Station.

CHRONOLOGICAL ORDER OF FLASHBACKS

(Page numbers show actual order in text.)

Raintree County

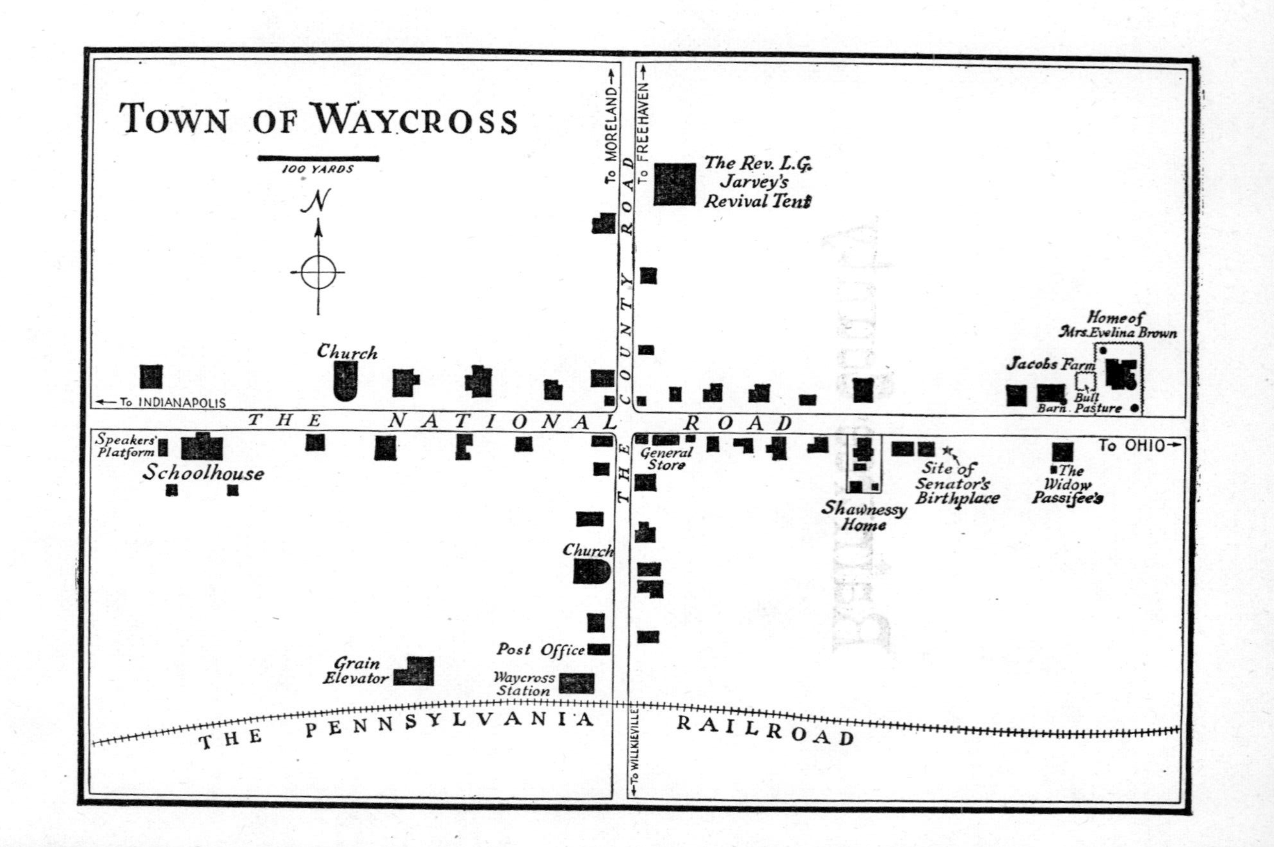
TOWN OF WAYCROSS
100 YARDS
N
To MORELAND
To FREEHAVEN
The Rev. L.G. Jarvey's Revival Tent
COUNTY ROAD
Church
Home of Mrs. Evelina Brown
Jacobs Farm
Bull
Barn
Pasture
To INDIANAPOLIS
THE NATIONAL ROAD
Speakers' Platform
Schoolhouse
General Store
To OHIO
Site of Senator's Birthplace
The Widow Passifee's
Shawnessy Home
THE
Church
Post Office
Grain Elevator
Waycross Station
THE PENNSYLVANIA RAILROAD
To WILLKIEVILLE

A Great Day

FOR RAINTREE COUNTY

(Epic Fragment from the *Free Enquirer,* July 4, 1892)

YES, SIR, here's the Glorious Fourth again. And here's our special Semicentennial Edition of the *Free Enquirer,* fifty pages crowded with memories of fifty years since we published the first copy of this newspaper in 1842. And, friends, what a half-century it has been! While the *Enquirer* has been growing from a little four-page weekly to a daily paper of twice the size, the population of these United States has quadrupled and the territory governed under the Institutions of Freedom has been extended from sea to shining sea. In those fifty years the Great West has been conquered, and the Frontier has been closed. The Union has been preserved in the bloodiest war of all time. The Black Man has been emancipated. Giant new industries have been created. The Golden Spike has been driven at Promontory Point, binding ocean to ocean in bands of steel. Free Education has been brought to the masses. Cities have blossomed from the desert. Inventions of all kinds, from telephones to electric lights, have put us in a world that Jules Verne himself couldn't have foreseen in 1842.

Folks, it has been an Era of Progress unexampled in the annals of mankind, and all of it has been made possible by the great doctrines on which this Republic was founded on July 4, 1776.

During those fifty years, we haven't exactly stood still here in Raintree County. Freehaven has grown from a little country town to a bustling city of ten thousand. The Old Court House of 1842 could be put into the court room of the present imposing edifice, one of the finest in the State of Indiana. And we challenge any section of comparable size in this Republic to show a more distinguished progeny of great men than our own little county has produced.

If anybody doubts the above statement, let him take a look at what is going on in the little town of Waycross down in good old Shortwater Township. The eyes of the whole nation are fixed on that little rural community today. The celebration there to honor the homecoming of Senator Garwood B. Jones is a striking testimonial to the vitality of our democratic institutions. While we have often opposed Senator Jones on political grounds, we would be the last to diminish the lustre of his name or the distinction he has brought upon the county of his birth. We had hoped that the Senator would see fit to make his homecoming address here in the County Seat, but no one can doubt the political wisdom of Garwood's decision to speak in his birthplace, a town of two hundred inhabitants, as the opening move in his campaign for reelection. It's a dramatic gesture, and the Senior Senator from Indiana needs all his vote-winning sagacity, not only to defeat the rising tide of Populism this year, but to further his well-known ambition to achieve the Presidency in 1896.

Nor is the Senator the only nationally known figure in Waycross today. His friend and ours, another Raintree County boy, Mr. Cassius P. Carney, the famous multimillionaire, is expected to be there. And our own great war hero, General Jacob J. Jackson, is going to lead a march of G.A.R. veterans to point up the pension issue. There are rumors of other celebrities coming on the Senator's special train, and all in all it looks like the little town of Waycross will have dern near as many famous people in it today as Washington, D. C. If the celebrated Stanley set out to explore this dark continent tomorrow for the Greatest Living American, he could do worse than get off a train in Waycross to ask his famous question. . . .

Mr. John Wickliff Shawnessy

I PRESUME?

—Yes?

His voice was tentative as he looked for the woman who had spoken from the dusk of the little post office. The whole thing seemed vaguely implausible. A short while ago, he had left his house to take part in the welcoming exercises for the Senator, whose train was expected momentarily in the Waycross Station. Walking west on the National Road, he had joined the crowd that poured from three directions into the south arm of the cross formed by the County and National roads. A swollen tide of parasols and derby hats blurred and brightened around the Station. Except on Sundays, he had never seen over ten people at once along this street, and he had been afraid that he might not be able to reach the platform where he was to greet the Senator. Near the Station, the crowd had been so dense that he could hardly move. Women in dowdy summer gowns jockeyed his nervous loins. Citizens with gold fobs and heavy canes thrust, butted, cursed. A band blared fitfully. Firecrackers crumped under skirts of women, rumps of horses. From the struggling column of bodies, bared teeth and bulgy eyes stuck suddenly.

Then he had found himself looking into the glass doorpane of the Post Office, where his own face had looked back at him, youthfully innocent for his fifty-three years, brows lifted in discovery, long blue eyes narrowed in the sunlight, dark hair smouldering with inherent redness. He had just begun to smooth his big mustaches and adjust the poet's tie at his throat when the crowd shoved him against the door. It had opened abruptly, and stepping inside on a sudden impulse, he had heard the woman's question.

Now he shut the door, drowning the noise of the crowd to a confused murmur.

—I was expecting you, Johnny, the woman said in the same husky voice. Where have you been?

—I was just on my way to greet the Senator, he said. Is there—is there some mail for me?

He walked slowly toward the distribution window, where in the darkness a face was looking out at him.

—Some letters carved on stone, the voice said. The fragments of forgotten language. I take my pen in hand and seat myself——

The woman was lying on a stone slab that extended dimly into the space where the window usually was. She lay on her stomach, chin propped on hands. Her hair was a dark gold, unloosened. Her eyes were a great cat's, feminine, fountain-green, enigmatic. A dim smile curved her lips.

She was naked, her body palely flowing back from him in an attitude of languor.

He was disturbed by this unexpected, this triumphant nakedness. He was aroused to memory and desire by the stately back and generously sculptured flanks.

—How do you like my costume, Johnny? she asked, her voice tinged with mockery.

—Very becoming, he said.

Her husky laughter filled the room, echoing down the vague recess into which she lay. He hadn't noticed before that the slab was a stone couch, curling into huge paws under her head. He was trying to understand what her reappearance meant on this memorial day.

Watching him with wistful eyes, she had begun to bind up her hair, fastening it behind her ears with silver coins.

—What creature is it that in the morning of its life——

She paused and opened her left hand, color of the pallid stone on which she lay. The hand was excitingly feminine, though perhaps too broad, too fleshy for perfect beauty. She put her arm on his shoulder. Then with her hand gently plucking and pulling at the base of his neck, like one wishing to uproot a little tree without hurting it, she pressed his head down to hers. Reminding himself that she was an old friend of the family and perhaps even a relative, he was about to kiss her.

Just then she turned her face aside and handed him a rolled newspaper.

—Our Semicentennial Edition, dear, she said, with a special column devoted to the history of the County. The fragments from your own unfinished epic occupy a prominent place on page one. You'll find a picture of the authentic Raintree——

Opened, the paper was a parchment warm to the touch, engraved with a map of Raintree County so exquisitely made that the principal landmarks showed in relief with living colors. In the middle of the County, Paradise Lake was a pool of shimmering green. Its shore eastward where the river entered dissolved into the steaming substance of the Great Swamp. The roads crisscrossing on the flat earth were brown and gravelly. Tiny shiny carriages moved on the National Road, which, side by side with the Pennsylvania Railroad, cut across the County close to the southern border. Westward on the railroad, a darkly lovely little locomotive pulled a chain of coaches covered with patriotic bunting. The intersection at Waycross was dense with human faces. All over the County, the bladed corn swayed softly in the fields. In the Square of Freehaven, a mile and a half southeast of the lake, the Court House stood in a lawn of slender trees. A flag fluttered from the brave brick tower, and the four clock faces told the time of day. From the northeastern to the southwestern corner of the County, the Shawmucky River lay in loops of green, halved into upper and lower segments by the lake. On the road east from Freehaven two bridges spanned the upper river's great south loop, and in the halfcircle formed by the road and the river, relics of the vanished town of Danwebster lay in deep grass. Across the river was the graveyard, a mound of pale stones. And somewhat beyond the bridge on the south side of the road was the Old Home Place, a little collection of farmbuildings on a gentle hill, the ancestral Shawnessy home in Raintree County, where Mr. Shawnessy had been born fifty-three years before. So precise was the map that he could see the great rock halfsunk in the earth at the limit of the South Field.

He was certain that in the pattern of its lines and letters this map contained the answer to the old conundrum of his life in Raintree County. It was all warm and glowing with the secret he had sought for half a century. The words inscribed on the deep paper were dawnwords, each one disclosing the origin and essence of the thing named. But as he sought to read them, they dissolved into the substance of the map.

With a feeling suspended between erotic hunger and intellectual curiosity, he looked for the young woman. She was no longer lying on the stone couch. Her voice was passionate, musical, receding.

—Johnny! Tall one! Shakamak!

He could see her pale form turning over and over in a slow spiral floating away on green waters. From time to time, one hand rose beckoning while the other untwined her hair. The loose gold cord of her hair was at last all he saw of her, untwisting, prolonged in the water to a single shimmering thread.

Holding a branch of maize loaded with one ripe ear, he stood on the threshold of the door, about to lunge into the delirious crowd. The ceremonial day that he had spent a lifetime preparing, a web of faces and festive rites, trembled before him. The girls in their summer dresses were twirling their parasols and shouting hymen. The official starter of the Fourth of July Race was raising his pistol. A path was opening through the crowd to a platform erected in a distant square. Beyond, beside a sky-reflecting pool, he saw white pillars and a shrine. He heard a far voice calling. The sound was shrill, appealing, with a note of sadness. . . .

He awoke. The whistle of a train at the crossing had at last pressed its way into his sleep. It was early dawn. He lay in bed, among the glowing fragments of the dream. The dream had been vivid with the promise of adventure, consummation. He rewove its tantalizing web, contrasting it with the simple reality into which he had awakened.

His wife, Esther, eighteen years younger than he, lay beside him, her Indianblack hair screwed into curlpapers, her regular features composed by sleep into a look of stony, almost mournful serenity. In the next room slept the three children, Wesley, Eva, and Will, thirteen, twelve, and seven years old. The family slept in the two upstairs rooms of the plain white wooden house. There were four main rooms down—parlor, middle room, dining room, and kitchen, running in that order from front to back. A pumproom adjoined the kitchen, and a small spare bedroom was annexed to the dining room. A cellar with outside entrance was under the kitchen. A porch extended along the front and halfway down the east side of the house. The house was set well forward in a trimly kept yard, fenced in with white pickets in front and on the two sides. Almost against the house behind was a small frame building of two parts, smokehouse and woodshed. A path started at the backdoor and ran along a garden to the outhouse. At the rear of the lawn was a small barn. A narrow field planted in corn extended a hundred yards back to the railroad.

The town of Waycross, where Mr. Shawnessy had lived for two years, had an equally austere pattern. The business buildings were at the intersection of the roads—general store, barber shop, bank, feedstore, blacksmith shop. Half a hundred houses were scattered along the four arms of the cross. On the south arm were a church, the Post Office, and the Railroad Station. The Schoolhouse, where Mr. Shawnessy and his wife were the only teachers, was on the west arm. On the north arm was a huge tent where the Reverend Lloyd G. Jarvey had been conducting his Summer Revival Series. Among the dwellings on the east arm were the Shawnessy house, lying on the south side of the National Road, and the mansion of Mrs. Evelina Brown somewhat beyond the town proper.

In the naked pallor of dawn, Waycross seemed to him devoid of visual complexity, as if to reduce the problem of place to its basic ingredients. And Raintree County also aspired to spatial symmetry, being a perfect square twelve miles to the side. What could be more certain than the location of Raintree County, whose western border was sixty miles from Indianapolis and whose eastern border was fifty miles from the neighboring state of Ohio? And yet, the dream had left him with an uneasy feeling of being anchorless, adrift on an unknown substance. The formal map of Raintree County had been laid down like a mask on something formless, warm, recumbent, convolved with rivers, undulous with flowering hills, blurred with motion, green with life.

He mused upon this mingling of man's linear dream with the curved earth, couched in mystery like a sphinx.

Had the woman of his dream, whose face had been teasingly familiar, known the answer to this riddle? And what token could she have given him of himself, he who also escaped name and definition in his long journey through time, a traveller from dawn to darkness, and all at once a child, a man, an old man?

He should have asked this gracious lady about time past. He should have followed her beckoning hand down the mystic river of the years back to the gates of time, the beginning of himself. He should have traced a tangled thread to the source of a life on the breast of the land.

It was dawn on Raintree County, and in a little while he would have to yield himself to the ritual day. Past midnight, he had lain awake thinking about the big Fourth of July Program, in which, as principal of the local school and an old friend of the Senator, he had a leading responsibility. First he would drive to Freehaven, where he had some matters to see to before the Senator arrived. Despite the necessarily early hour of the trip, the whole family planned to go along as usual. On the way back, he would stop at the Danwebster Graveyard for his annual visit to the family lot. At nine-thirty the Senator's special train was due in Waycross, and the substance of Mr. Shawnessy's dream would be repeated—minus, no doubt, the interesting lady in the Post Office. Then he would entertain the Senator until the G.A.R. parade and banquet at twelve-thirty. The main program was planned for two-thirty, and after that he would see the Senator off at the Station. In the evening there was to be a lawn party sponsored by the Literary Society at the home of Mrs. Evelina Brown. It promised to be the most exciting day since his second marriage fourteen years ago.

He could still hear the thunder of the train on distant rails receding. Its passing echoed in the eastern valleys of his sleep. The lone shriek of it at the crossing had been like a calling of his name. The sound of it ebbing down gray lanes of dawn into the west was the lonely music of a century, awakening memories of himself and the Republic. He would lie awhile and chase a phantom of himself that was always passing on a road from east to west. He would hunt for the earliest mask of an elusive person, a forgotten child named Johnny, the father of a man.

What creature is it that in the morning of its life . . .

It was dawn now on Raintree County, and he would begin with things of the dawn. He would pursue awhile his ancient pastime of looking for the mystic shape of a life upon the land, the legend of a face of stone, a happy valley, an extinct republic, a memory of

Election Day— How —1844

ON THE MORNING OF ELECTION DAY

THE MOTHER AND THE LITTLE CHILD WERE WAITING

before the cabin. At the bottom of the yard, a rudely sculptured head stood on the gatepost by the road. Johnny had helped T. D. make it, and they called it Henry Clay, maybe because it had been made out of clay from the river bank.

—Henry Clay, T. D. had said, is the Greatest Living American.

T. D. had also said that Henry Clay was running for President, a matter of interest to Johnny, who for his age was considered a very fast runner himself.

The head on the gatepost had had an ugly, eyeless look when T. D. and Johnny first made it, but now at this distance it had an expression of greatness and distinction.

A few days ago when Johnny was in the yard by himself, a man had driven past in a covered wagon. He was a bearded man in a big hat, his wagon was pulled by two big oxen, it was all stuffed up with things, there was a thinfaced woman on the seat beside him, and a pretty little girl with vivid brown eyes kept peeping out of the wagon and shaking her pigtails at Johnny.

—Hello, son, the man said, stopping the wagon.

Big white teeth flashed through the thick bush of his beard.

—Hello, Mister.

—You look like a smart boy, son. Maybe you could tell me if this here is the road to Freehaven.

—Yes, sir, this here is it.

—How fer is it, son?

—You go on down the road, Johnny said, pointing west, and you git there after a while. They's a court house and a lots of people.

—Ain't he a smart boy! the man said, winking at his wife. Maybe you can tell me, son, what that there head is on the fence there.

—Henry Clay, Johnny said.

—Who's he?

—The Greatest Living American, Johnny said.

—You don't say, the man said. Who tole you so?

—T. D. did.

—Who's T. D.?

—My pa. He's a doctor and a preacher.

—Well, you go tell T. D. that that there head ain't Clay. It's mud. Anyhow it'll be mud after the Election.

—It ain't mud, Johnny said. It's clay. It was made out of clay, and it's Henry Clay.

—It's mud, dad burn it! the man said. You tell your pappy somethin' else. You tell him a man passed said Henry Clay *ain't* the Greatest Livin' American. He's nothin' but a goddern Whig protectionist. Can you say that?

—Yessir. A goddern Whig protectionist.

The man roared, and the woman said something to him. The man leaned out again.

—You tell your pa you saw a man, and he told you the Greatest Livin' American was James K. Polk. Yessiree, James K. Polk is the man that's goin' to win that election. James K. Polk.

The man was motioning big and violent with a whip.

—James K. Polk. The Lone Star Republic and the Oregon Trail. Can you say that, son?

—The Lone Star Republic and the Oregon Trail, Johnny recited.

—Listen to him say that, the man said. How old are you, son?

—Five.

—You're a smart boy, son. You'll amount to somethin' some day. Don't fergit that slogan. James K. Polk is the man that'll win the Election, and he'll make Clay's name mud.

—It ain't mud, Johnny said. We got it down along the river. Mud's black. This here's red, and it's clay.

—O.K., son, the man said. But all the same, don't fergit to tell your pa what I said. The Oregon Trail. That's where I'm a-headin' right now, and if your pappy was half a man, he'd be a-goin' there with me to settle out there and git that land fer America instead of votin' fer Harry Clay and Protection.

The man made his whip lash over the backs of the oxen.

—Oregon, here we come!

As the oxen pulled away, the girl with the pigtails leaned from the wagon and waved her hand. She waved a long time, and Johnny waved back.

It seemed to him then that he had always been a small boy who stood beside a road and waved to people going west.

Later when he had told his father about it, T. D. had laughed and said to his mother,

—I wonder what they were doing off the main road.

—Where is the Lone Star Republic and the Oregon Trail? Johnny had asked.

His father told him something about them.

—Are there Indians out there?

—Yes, I reckon there are, T. D. said.

The Indians used to live right around the Home Place before T. D. and Ellen Shawnessy had come there in 1820. The Indians were naked and had red skins, and they lived in tepees, and they killed and scalped you with tomahawks. They were marvellous people, and they had lived all over America before the pioneers came and made the stumps. Now all the Indians had gone out West, where the man in the covered wagon was heading.

Next to the Indians, the most interesting people were probably the Negroes. Men would get together in front rooms and around the Court House at Freehaven, shake fists, spit tobacco, and talk in loud voices about the Negroes and the Election and Polk and Clay and Texas and the West.

The Negroes were black slaves in the South. It was a bad thing to keep them slaves and make them work. Johnny had walked through the South Field once and had gone a long way back hoping to see a Negro. He never did see one.

But that same day he kept on going and wound around back north until he crossed a road and came out at the Gaither farm. Nell Gaither was playing in the orchard under an appletree. She was a thin, serious girl with long golden hair, big blue-green eyes, and a freckled nose. She had a quiet, grave way of talking in contrast with Johnny's older sisters, who were very giggly and loud.

—You're Johnny Shawnessy, she said.

—Yes, I am.

—I'm Nell.

—Is the river back of your house?

—Yes. I'll show you.

The river was a big mystery to Johnny. Now he and Nell walked a piece and pushed through some trees and came right out at the edge of the river. It was wide and pale green, and it had a cold green odor. He and Nell had played a long time by the river building little mud and stick huts. They both waded out looking for crawdads and frogs. Johnny forgot all about the time until he noticed that long shadows were falling on the river.

—Your folks'll be after you, Johnny, Nell said.

—Let 'em, Johnny said.

You had to run away from home to have a good time like that.

When he started down the road that evening, he ran into a lot of people, and they all rushed at him and grabbed him and took him home.

Later his mother had come home on a horse, all hot and dusty and her dark red hair in strings down her face. She began to cry when she saw Johnny in the front yard surrounded by people. She hugged him very hard and kept saying, Thank God! and laughing and crying at the same time. Johnny cried too from sheer excitement. It appeared that he had been lost and found again. People said that his mother had ridden all over Raintree County looking for him.

—Poor Ellen! people said. Johnny, you pretty near killed your poor mother.

They never let him go back and play along the river again with Nell because it was too much fun.

That was when he learned that he was a person of great importance and that his exact location in Raintree County was a matter of intense concern to everyone.

Ellen Shawnessy, his mother, was short and slight. Though not pretty, she had a young girlish look. Her hair, dark with glints of red like Johnny's, was entirely ungrayed. Johnny was the last of her nine children, four boys and five girls. Two of the girls had died in an epidemic that swept through Raintree County in the early forties, and they lay beneath two stones with letters on them in the Danwebster Graveyard, across the river from the board church where T. D. preached.

—What is a great man, Mamma? Johnny asked as they waited in front of the cabin for T. D.

—A great man is somebody everyone looks up to. He's a good man who does things for other people.

—Like Pa?

Ellen Shawnessy smiled. Her smile was like Johnny's, quick and affectionate. More often than not she smiled for no other reason than that she felt animated and happy.

—Well, T. D. is a mighty good man, she said, and he's smart too. But usually a great man is a wellknown man. That is, he's famous.

Johnny's father, T. D. Shawnessy, preached and wrote poetry and delivered babies and made sick people well. He was very tall and thin, and his head looking down at Johnny from a great height always nodded blondly and benignly and smiled confidently and spoke very hopefully of God and the future.

—I aim to be a great man, Johnny said. Is God a great man?

—God isn't exactly a man, Ellen Shawnessy said. He's—well—he's just God. He's a divine being. That is, he's greater than any human being.

God was the biggest puzzle of all to Johnny. He had begun to worry about God during the summer when the Millerites were camping out in Raintree County. When the family would be riding down the road, they would see at night the bonfires burning on a distant hill.

—There's them plaguey Millerites, T. D. would say.

The Millerites were out there on the hill waiting for the End of the World. T. D. said that in his opinion it wouldn't come for quite a while yet.

In those days, God was a whitebearded giant who lived up in Heaven but had a sneaky way of being everywhere else at the same time. He could do anything he wanted and just waited around for you to make a mistake, whereupon he would land on you and whop you good. Johnny used to wonder if it would do any good to go out and hunt for God. But God was just as scarce as the Indians and the Negroes in Raintree County. There were times when Johnny wondered if God was just a big story, the kind that big people were always telling little people.

Later on that day when T. D. came home, they all got into the wagon, the older ones sitting on chairs in the wagon bed, and went into Freehaven. There was a big crowd around the Court House Square, people talking loud and waving banners. Later the older children took Johnny down to the Polls. Johnny looked around for some tall sticks, but it turned out that the Polls was a place where a lot of people were trying to put papers into a box.

Several big barrels were hoisted on sawhorses and wedged into the crotches of trees, and men kept going over and turning on the taps and getting brown stuff out of the barrels. Johnny got lost from the other children for a while and was swept up in a crowd of people marching and chanting:

—Vote, vote, for James K. Polk!
The Lone Star Republic and the Oregon Trail!

Johnny marched and chanted too, until T. D. spied him and striding into the middle of the parade carried him off.

—Don't you know them's Democrats, John? he said.

A lot of men went around swatting people on the back and laughing fiercely. T. D. put a paper in the ballot box. Things got louder as the night came on. Bonfires burned on the Court House Square. The family had a big feed in the wagon, and after that Johnny slipped off into the crowd with his brother Ezekiel, who was two years older than he and a lot bigger. They watched some men hitting each other and yelling things about God, Polk, and Clay over in front of the Saloon. A man was knocked down and had his coat torn off. A woman came up shrieking and grabbed at the man lying on the sidewalk, so that Johnny didn't see how he could get up if he wanted to. Zeke disappeared for a while, and when he turned up again, he was grinning all over his face and said he had just beaten up on a goddern kid that admitted he was a Democrat. Zeke showed his knuckles all skinned and bruised.

Late at night, the family started back to the Home Place in the wagon. Johnny lay for a long time awake with his head in his mother's lap, looking up at the stars. He hunted the heavens until he saw one big star low in the west. He thought it might be the Lone Star. Somewhere out there in the Far West, under the night and the shining stars and across the Great Plains, was the Lone Star Republic and the Oregon Trail. Right now maybe the little girl with the pigtails was out there.

Johnny Shawnessy decided that some day when he was big enough to go away from home by himself, he would go over and get Nell Gaither, and they would get into a big covered wagon and go down and find the National Pike, and they would ride off together toward those big plains and those far western mountains beneath the shining stars, where the land was fair and free, where the Indians lived in tepees, and the streams were full of fish, in the country called the United States of America, which was somewhere in Raintree County.

For in those days, he didn't very well understand the boundaries of Raintree County or of his own life. Raintree County was simply the place where people lived, it was the earth, and you might go anywhere and never leave it. He had heard people talk of a time when there was no Raintree County. He used to think back and back to see if he could remember such a time, and he would come to a place where all his memories fading reached a green wall of summer. Sometimes he would attempt to cross that wall, vaguely wondering at the murmurous world beyond it from which his being had been ferried up some summer long ago to be deposited in Raintree County. He had some dim intuitions and memories of it, all drenched in green and gold. Nameless, and neither child nor man, he had lived in a beautiful garden where stately trees dripped flowers on the ground. And somehow that life was longer than all the rest of his life together. But long ago that summer of wordless forms had been lost to him, or rather the forms had been subtly changed and hidden by a veil of words.

Now in the still night, Johnny Shawnessy was carried in a wagon over the dark earth of Raintree County, which had no boundaries in time and space, where lurked musical and strange names and mythical and lost peoples, and which was itself only a name musical and strange.

And lying in his mother's arms, he went to sleep and dreamed that he was riding in a ribbed and canvascovered wagon down a road at night toward a lone star palely shining over fields of summer.

—Look there! everyone said. The Greatest Living American!

In the red far light of the star, he saw an immense face of clay, and he and all the other people were running for President as fast as they could go. So in the still night

HE DREAMED A FAIR YOUNG

DREAM OF

GOING

WESTWARD, the National Road pursued its way, a streak of straightness to the flat horizon. As the surrey approached the intersection, Mr. Shawnessy was thinking of his dream. Although he had since risen, dressed, eaten breakfast, and set out for Freehaven, he was still haunted by the riddle of a naked woman in the Waycross Post Office. The dream had distilled the conundrum of his life into one image, delightful and disturbing.

She had reminded him of his plural being. He had presented to her Mr. Shawnessy, a dutiful citizen of the Republic calling for his mail. She had addressed herself to mr. shawnessy, a faunlike hero, poised on the verge of festive adventures.

Mr. Shawnessy, meet mr. shawnessy. Hail and farewell! Farewell and hail!

Just now, the majuscular twin, Mr. Shawnessy, was sitting upright in the front seat of the surrey beside his wife, Esther, while the three children, Wesley, Eva, and Will, occupied the back seat. It was a characteristic Mr. Shawnessy attitude, for Mr. Shawnessy was eminently a family man and a respectable citizen. When he called at the Waycross Post Office later in the morning, he wouldn't find a naked woman on a stone. Instead he would receive the *Indianapolis News-Historian* from a fat-faced functionary named Bob.

Only the adventurous twin, mr. shawnessy, could achieve naked women in post offices. For mr. shawnessy was a lower-case person, disowning all proper names, including his own, and many other proprieties. Yet it was convenient to call him mr. shawnessy since he was always moving in and out of Mr. Shawnessy with pleasant alacrity, using his obliging companion as a kind of depot for incessant arrivals and departures. In fact, mr. shawnessy used Mr. Shawnessy as a straw man, a large comfortable mask that he had spent a lifetime adapting for public performances.

Mr. Shawnessy, the straw man, was now driving the family westward through Waycross, an inseparable part of the Shawnessy landscape. At the intersection, he would turn due north, being a creature bounded by severe alignments.

He was bounded by the Nineteenth Century and knew only one way to escape—by living his way out moment by moment.

He was bounded by a box, the County, inside a box, the State, inside a box, the Nation, inside a box inside a box inside a box.

He was sartorially bounded by his one good suit, a cloth of light black wool, newly pressed for the day, a white shirt, a black poet's tie, knobtoed black shoes, dark soft hat. A hundred dollars would not have persuaded him to walk down the street of Waycross in an Elizabethan doublet, a woman's bonnet, or naked.

He was linguistically bounded by the English language, which he spoke with a Hoosier accent, though, when he pleased, with precision, wit, and eloquence.

He was morally bounded by a certain code of right and wrong that Moses had brought down from Sinai into Raintree County. He had a way of lingering wistfully on thresholds without crossing.

He was a completely legal person. On April 23, 1839, his birth had been accomplished from an inkwell in the Raintree County Court House. His marriage to Esther Root in 1878 had achieved a whole column of print on the first page of the Raintree County *Free Enquirer*. The children who occupied the back seat of his surrey on trips around the County were what was known as legitimate. He enjoyed certain rights of citizenship under the Constitution of the United States and certain inalienable rights under the Declaration of Independence, among them, Life, Liberty, and the Pursuit of Happiness.

He was a creature of amazing certainties. He had his infallible Saturdays and his relentless Mondays. He almost never went to bed in the middle of the night or rose at noon. And every year the Fourth of July came and bestowed on him firecrackers, patriotic programs, and a drive with the family to the middle of Raintree County where he placed some flowers on a grave.

He lived in a precariously poised world of taboos, pomps, and games called American Society—with no spectacular triumphs, it is true, but in a manner to inspire confidence and respect. In fact he was one of the priests of the temple, being responsible for teaching the communion to others, for he had spent a lifetime instructing the young of Raintree County in what is known as the rudiments of education.

In a world convulsed with war, famine, industrial unrest, and public and private vice, Mr. Shawnessy was a citizen of the American Republic, living quietly on the National Road of life where it intersected with Raintree County, and tacitly involved in a confused course of human events that the newspapers and people in general agreed to call American History.

The versatile twin, mr. shawnessy, on the other hand, was a fugitive from boundaries. No sooner did he appear to be caught in a definition than he somehow turned inside out to include the includer. He was always pressing beyond the confines of himself, yet could never go anywhere that wasn't himself.

His seeming foothold in the Nineteenth Century was illusory. His face peered furtively from a frieze of the Parthenon, passed in mob scenes in the reign of Justinian, crossed with crowds on Brooklyn Ferry ever so many centuries hence.

His landscape was an infinitely potential number of Raintree Counties past, present, and to be. He was always arriving in train stations from parts unknown to meet himself departing for unknown parts.

In him, the word and the thing almost rejoined each other at the source. His words were dreams of things; his dreams were things of words.

He had a way of joyfully crossing the thresholds at which Mr. Shawnessy lingered.

He had no legal existence whatsoever. His birth was recorded, if anywhere, in the first chapter of Genesis and his death was foreseen only in Revelation. Eve was his mother, his daughter, and his wife, and he was the citizen of a republic that never was on sea or land.

Of course, his being was all tangled up in that of Mr. Shawnessy. The two were always colliding with each other as Mr. Shawnessy went his ritual way through conversations and thoroughfares, and mr. shawnessy carried on his eternal vagabondage through a vast reserve of memories and dreams. But even in dreams the carefree twin had to do devotion in strange ways to Raintree County and its gods. It was clearly the whim of mr. shawnessy to prepare a naked woman on a stone slab in the Post Office, but it was Mr. Shawnessy who timidly asked for a newspaper, trying his best to adapt himself and his puritan conscience to the bizarre world of his twin.

Yet doubtless there was really only one John Wickliff Shaw
one Raintree County, one Republic, one riddle with plural n
That was what the young woman with the catlike eyes had mea
the half-given line from a legend of antiquity:

What creature is it that in the morning of its life . . .

Mr. Shawnessy had made the turn north onto the County R
But the insouciant twin had kept the westward bias.

Westward the star of empire. Westward the Great Compan
takes his way. Shirt open at the neck, broad hat pushed back
matted, vital hair, he walks the boulevards of westward cities, cros
the wide windrippled plains, ferries the Mississippi, and strikes c
strongly through the sagebrush mesas. He climbs the sunblaze su
mits of the Rockies, descends deep passes to the Golden Shore.

> O, Californy!
> That's the place for me!
> I'm off for . . .

Firecrackers crumped in backyards. A smell of patriotism tinged the early morning air.

—How long before we get back, Papa? Wesley asked.

—About nine o'clock. We have to be back by then.

—What yuh readin', Eva? little Will asked.

—Book, Eva muttered, absorbed.

—I want to be back in time for the service, Esther Shawnessy said, as the surrey passed the Revival Tent.

—We'll be in time, Mr. Shawnessy said. We won't be stopping in Freehaven long. And I only mean to leave a few flowers at Mamma's grave.

—Papa, what's Senator Jones look like? Will asked.

—I haven't seen him for twenty years. When I last saw him, he was a big heavyset man, broadshouldered, deepchested, with blue eyes, dark brown hair, and a voice like a bull.

—What's General Jackson like?

—The General looks like a fighting man. Of course, he's pretty old now, but in his prime he was a fine figure of a man.

—Will he have his uniform on?

—I imagine so.

—Will he have a sword?

nessy,
asks.
nt by

oad.

ion
on
ses
ut
n-

e.

sword! How many wars did he fight in?

xican War and the Civil War.

. When was that?

x to eighteen forty-eight. I was about your

hawnessy? Yes, sir. Can you read, son? Yes, then.

a Fourth of July when you were a boy, Papa?

e firecrackers and things?

rd, boys, all along the line! Kill the damn greasers! tar of empire.

of July was the memory of a lone white rocket rising sky above a town in Raintree County long ago. The and feathered into burning spray and floated softly on night. The Fourth of July was the memory of a new bloody babe of destiny, waiting to be filled with soul. of July was a war on sunbaked plains, a fighting in the es and in California. It was the pasteboard red of fire- the blue of armies charging stiffranked in steel engravings, e of flowers flung by girls in summer dresses for the boys ight at Buena Vista. It was the fury and the fighting heart of g republic, fledgling of the nations, conceived in battle and ned in battle. It was a lone star rising in the east and westward ng. It was a million faces pressing westward, the harshvoiced ners of a strange, disordered dream.

Ir. Shawnessy jingled the reins over President's back, passing the houses of Waycross. Meanwhile mr. shawnessy roamed on other ads. There had been a wagon shrugging down a road to westward ears ago. It had gone on for days creaking across the vast plain. Where were all the days of the travellers in that wagon?

But those days had passed, and the girl with the pigtails had grown up, no doubt had married and borne children. The burly charioteer of the westward sun, who had driven his oxdrawn car through Johnny Shawnessy's life, had died long ago, and the wagon itself was ribs of weathering wood in a far lone valley of the West.

A small boy had wandered out into the morning of America and down far ways seeking the Lone Star Republic and the Oregon Trail. A small boy had dreamed forever westward, and the dream had drawn a visible mark across the earth. But the boy had never gone that way. He had only dreamed it.

He saw the face of a girl fading among the vehicular tangle of the years. All the evenings of a life in the West dyed the sunset peaks with purple—the lost years ebbed with waning voices in the cuts where the little trains passed, crying. Yes, he had been fated to stay after all, chosen for a task that called for more than ordinary strength. He and only he had stood on the earth of Raintree County in an early summer dawn and had had that deep vision of the Republic, the passionate, westward dream.

I had a dream the other night,
When . . .

July 20— EVERYTHING —1848

WAS STILL ON THE WIDE FIELDS

AND SLEEPY STREAM OF SUMMER, AND THE DAYS

were long in the hot weather that summer, and the world of Raintree County seemed fixed around him like paintings on a wall. Then one day a horse thundered up the road from Freehaven and into the yard of the Home Place, and a young man got off. He had long blond hair under a broad hat.

—This where Doctor Shawnessy lives?

—Yes, sir, Johnny said.

He and the man went to the Office behind the house.

—What's the trouble, son? T. D. said.

—Why, my wife's gonna have a baby, sir, the man said. We got into this here town of Danwebster over here last night, and she was took sudden and before her time. Some fellers in town said as how you was the best baby doctor around here. I'd be mighty obliged to git some help for my wife.

While T. D. was getting his medical kit, Ellen came out and talked with the young man, who said that he was from Tennessee and was on his way to California. He and his wife had left the National Pike intending to stop with friends in Middletown, but the woman had come down unexpectedly with labor pains. It was her first baby.

Johnny was pleased when he was permitted to go along with his mother and father to Danwebster.

—It's the house right aside of the General Store, the man said, getting up on his horse. Name is Alec Doniphant.

While they were driving to Danwebster, Ellen said,

—Courteous young feller. It must be awful hard on 'em having their first baby on the road thisaway. There's so many of 'em these days. Anything to get out West.

When they got to Danwebster, T. D. and Ellen went into the house with Mr. Doniphant. There were several men sitting on a bench in front of the General Store. Just as Johnny got settled on the bench, he heard a low sound from the house, musical like a mouth rounded. The men on the bench listened without turning their heads.

—She ain't a-hollerin' loud enough yet, a man said.

He was a fat old man everyone called Grampa Peters. Those days, he always seemed to be sitting on the bench before the General Store in Danwebster. A Democrat of the old Jacksonian breed, he was reported to have Southern sympathies and was the only person in town who received a newspaper regularly.

—I seen them come in last night, a thin man said. She was in considerable pain then and kept a-cryin' out all night.

There was another low moan from the house.

—She'll have to bear down harder than that, Grampa Peters said. She ain't puttin' herself into it yet. She'll have to make up her mind to have that baby.

A cry of pain lay suddenly on the quiet street.

—That's the first real loud one I've heard her give, Grampa Peters said. That was a good loud one.

His flesh stirred a little as if pleasantly goaded by this fierce contact with life. He fumbled around in a coat pocket and drew out a newspaper.

—Son, can you read?

—Yes, sir, Johnny said.

—I heard you could, Grampa Peters said. They say you read as good as a grown person. Well, I want you to read me somethin' here. I fergot my specs.

Grampa Peters spread out a copy of a newspaper. At the top it said

THE INDIANA COURIER

—Read that there righthand colyum for me, Grampa Peters said.

Johnny read outloud how the Whig Nominating Convention meeting on June 7 had nominated General Zachary Taylor for the Presidency. While he was reading, T. D. and Mr. Doniphant came out of the house.

—How's she comin'? Grampa Peters asked.

—She's pretty little and of course it's her first one, T. D. said absently. But she's young and strong, and I take a hopeful view of the situation. After all, having a baby is the most natural thing in the world.

—I hope it comes soon, young Mr. Doniphant said.

—I think it'll be a while, T. D. said. My wife's going to stay with her. You look fagged out, young feller. You better relax awhile.

—Git us that there banjo of yours, the thin man said, and play us some music.

—I reckon it might take my mind off of it, the young man said, and he went back of the house.

—What about it, T. D.? Grampa Peters said, when Mr. Doniphant was gone.

—It's a hard case, T. D. said. She hasn't really got anywhere with it yet, and she's very narrow. There isn't anything to do but wait. However, as I said before——

His voice trailed off.

—What you got there, John?

—Newspaper.

—The boy was just readin' it to us, the thin man said. He's a bright boy.

—How'd you learn to read, son? Grampa Peters said.

—I learned at school.

—John learned at this here school in Danwebster, T. D. said. He can read anything. What's in the news these days? I haven't seen a paper for mighty near a month.

—I see where your danged Whigs nominated old Blood and Thunder, Grampa Peters said.

—Yes, so I hear, T. D. said. Well, I guess he'd make a good President.

—Maybe that's what we need, a military man, the thin man said. The country's so all tore up. Winnin' the war pretty near wrecked us.

—Pretty near wrecked us! Grampa Peters snorted. What are you talkin' about, boy? Some folks don't reason things out. Who made this glorious victory possible and added all this here new land to the Republic? The Democratic Administration—that's who.

—Couldn't have done it, hadn't of been fer ole Zach Taylor whippin' the damn greasers, the thin man said.

—What's Taylor's stand on the slavery question? T. D. said.

—Probly, he ain't got no stand, Grampa Peters said. Call it a straddle rather.

Johnny read some more from the paper. It appeared that General Taylor had avoided the slavery question. There was a good deal in the paper about the old veteran of many a hardfought campaign who had personally inspired his stalwart troops on the windy plains of Buena Vista.

Johnny was glad that General Zachary Taylor was going to be the Whig candidate for President because he was the Greatest Living American.

Zachary Taylor was a rugged, whitehaired old man standing in the middle of a wall engraving. Stiff ranks of soldiers dressed in blue advanced across a plain through volleys of bounding cannonballs. In the background of the picture a darkskinned horde, color of the earth, dissolved in flight.

The War with Mexico was a pageant of names that made your flesh tingle. The names were Rio Grande, Monterey, Buena Vista, Vera Cruz, Cerro Gordo, Cherubusco, Molino del Rey, Chapultepec, Mexico City. The names were Zachary Taylor, Winfield Scott, John C. Frémont. The names were the Santa Fe Trail, Oregon, New Mexico, and California. The names were color of the sun on deserts and treeless mountains, color of buckskin breeches and blue coats, streaming South and West in a perpetual Fourth of July.

The Mexican War was a memory of orators, long hair combed back lush behind their ears, frock coats flapping, standing on the platform in the Court House Square, raising and dropping their arms and bellowing the names of battles and heroes. Johnny remembered the recent Fourth in Freehaven, when the County had turned out to welcome back its boys who had fought in Mexico. Marching at their head was the young hero, Captain Jake Jackson, who had distinguished himself in the attack on Chapultepec and been three times wounded as he led his men over impregnable defenses. The girls of Raintree County had flung flowers on the marching soldiers.

Johnny wished the men in front of the General Store would talk more about the real war, but instead, as usual, they talked about slavery.

Grampa Peters kept saying that the best thing to do was just to leave the whole question alone and not get the South all excited about it and that the territories to be carved out of the new land would settle the question of slavery for themselves. He said there never would have been all this fuss and fidget if it hadn't been for the Wilmot Proviso. The thin man said that the South was all for throwing over the Missouri Compromise and that they never would be satisfied to let California come in as a free state.

—Damn them! the thin man said, getting excited, as people always did sooner or later when they talked about the new lands and slavery, that's what they fought the damn war for—slavery.

T. D. was inclined to take a hopeful view of the situation.

—It was destiny, he said. We was going in that direction.

Mr. Doniphant came back, carrying his banjo. He sat down and sang some songs in a soft whanging voice, and while he was singing, Ellen came out of the house to listen, and some other people gathered around.

—Sing that one you sang last night, Grampa Peters said.

Mr. Doniphant sang:

—I come from Alabama
With my banjo on my knee,
I'se gwine to Louisiana,
My true love for to see.
It rained all day the night I left;
The weather it was dry.
The sun so hot, I froze to death,
Susanna, don't you cry.

The chorus went:

—O, Susanna,
Do not cry for me;
I come from Alabama
With my banjo on my knee.

The best verse was the second:

—I had a dream the other night,
When everything was still;
I thought I saw Susanna dear,
A-comin' down the hill.

The buckwheat cake was in her mouth,
The tear was in her eye.
Says I, I'se comin' from the south,
Susanna, don't you cry.

—That's a good one, Grampa Peters said.

They had him sing it again.

—Where'd you learn it? T. D. said. I don't recollect ever hearing it before.

—O, I picked it up in a camp of folks over in Ohio. We had a different way of singin' it too that they made up around there. They was some of 'em singin' it thisaway:

—O, Californy!
That's the place for me!
I'm off for Sacramento
With my washbowl on my knee.

—Reckon you intend to git some gold out there, eh, son? Grampa Peters said.

—Well, sir, Mr. Doniphant said. I didn't know if all them stories about there bein' gold there was true. Most people just said they heerd it from somebody else. I thought I'd git me some land. If they is gold to be got, maybe I could git some of it too. I ain't worryin' none about it. All I want is to git out there.

—What d'yuh think about this here slavery question, son? Grampa Peters said. Do you think they'd ought to keep slavery out of them new lands?

Young Mr. Doniphant strummed softly on his banjo.

—Well, he said softly, I don't know how you folks feel about it around here. Me and the folks I been travellin' with goin' West don't want no slave labor to compete with in the new lands.

—But have they a constitutional right to prohibit it? Grampa Peters said. That's the question. There ain't any right under the Constitution to prohibit it. That's all I say.

—Maybe they ain't, the young man said. But I don't figger there'll be any slavery in the new lands.

He strummed softly on the banjo, humming,

—O, Californy!
There's the land for me.

I've tooken quite a journey from
My home in Tennessee.

—If we keep slavery from spreading, T. D. said, it will die natural of its own accord. Slavery's a wrong, and nothing can make it right. I take a more or less hope——

Something bit and tore the mildly spoken words. Young Mr. Doniphant stood up, ashamed and scared.

—D'yuh think——

—She's all right, T. D. said. It's natural. The pains are getting sharper.

—No good baby was ever got without a lot of yellin', Grampa Peters said.

Ellen and some other women went back into the house.

—Take it easy, son, T. D. said. This may go on all day.

—By the way, T. D., Grampa Peters said, could you let me have another bottle of them pokeberry bitters sometime? My stummick's been actin' up on me agin. Sometimes I think I can't hardly stand it.

Mr. Doniphant sat down slowly and kept picking nervously at the banjo and humming,

—O, Californy!
That's the place for me!

—What route do you figure on takin' to git out there? the thin man said.

—Why, I don't know yet. I aim to take the safest.

—After what happened to them Donners, Grampa Peters said, I reckon you can't be too careful. I wonder if you ain't goin' to have to winter over somewhere before you try it.

—Maybe so, the young man said.

—Have you seen any Mormons along the way? T. D. said.

—Not as I know of. They say the Mormons has all gone out and got them a place out there somewheres.

—I seen a book, Grampa Peters said, and it had a picture in it of a Mormon goin' to bed with his wives. That there bed was simply swarmin' with women pullin' each other's hair and feedin' babies.

—One woman's more'n enough fer me, the thin man said. They'd ought to take and burn all them Mormons at the stake.

Those days, people were always going West. Johnny had heard it said that along the National Pike there was a wagon every hour regular and at times a whole train. Nothing could stop the people from going West. They had babies along the way, like Mr. and Mrs. Doniphant. They died in the snow on the mountains and ate each other to keep from starving, like the Donners. They had a scad of wives in one bed like the Mormons. Most of them were slightly crazy some way. But they kept right on going. Perhaps it had something to do with the sun that made an arc day after day above the National Pike. Johnny thought of the western land under the far setting of the sun, wide plains in purple evening through which on softly thundering hooves the buffalo herds were running, he thought of Indians, riding swift ponies toward the flanks of purple mountains, wagontrains streaming thinly westward, he thought of shining rivers, green slopes, blue ocean on the distant shore of evening.

Those days, Johnny thought much of gold, Indians, great rivers, buffalo, and men who carried guns. Before the war, the West was a vagueness, a direction, a place of few names that belonged mostly to someone else. Now, however, it was good to think that the Nation extended from sea to shining sea.

—Here's an interesting item, T. D. said, shaking the newspaper. It tells here how they laid the cornerstone for the Washington Monument.

—I wonder will they ever git that thing built, Grampa Peters said. Seems to me I've heard talk of it for a long time now.

—O, I guess they'll get it built some——

A cry cut across T. D.'s sentence. This time it lasted longer than usual, and Mr. Doniphant got up and went into the house.

—Now that's what I call a good loud one, Grampa Peters said. Sounds like the real business, T. D.

—How do you stand listenin' to 'em all the time, T. D.? Just this one's drivin' me crazy, the thin man said. But I suppose you git use to it.

—I never will get use to it, T. D. said. But the Lord requires it of Woman for her Sin, and so it must be.

—I guess it must hurt 'em somethin' awful, the thin man said.

Grampa Peters belched complacently.

—By God, I got to git me another bottle a them bitters.

Each time the woman cried, Johnny wanted to crawl off somewhere and hide. His pleasant landscape of Raintree County revolved dizzily, running with rivers of blood. Life was not what he had supposed it to be. When his mother appeared at the door, he turned his face away. He and all his brothers and sisters had entered life by an incredible wound inflicted on that slight beloved form. This was what the word 'woman' really meant.

—Daniel Webster, Grampa Peters was saying, much as I oppose him in most questions, has the right idea about this whole slavery thing. Stand upon the Constitution, and all will be well.

In those days, people were always standing on the Constitution. The Constitution was like the Bible. When you appealed to the Constitution, you had made the ultimate appeal. If you could quote the Constitution to support your argument, you had quoted God. People who quoted the Constitution always did so solemnly and as if that finished the matter. The majority of arguments ended by each man appealing to the Constitution, and the man who did it oftenest and in the loudest voice was adjudged the winner.

Not that anyone ever really won.

It seemed as though Grampa Peters' remark about the Constitution set the argument going again. More men gathered around, and as the woman in the house cried more often, the men talked more loudly and profanely about slavery, westward expansion, and presidential candidates. There appeared to be a contest between the men before the General Store and the woman in the house to see which could get the best of a furious debate in which the two contestants were determined to ignore each other. But to Johnny, only the cry of pain was real. It filled up the street. It drew a bloodred streak across the day. And at last it compelled silence and respect.

After a particularly loud cry, Ellen came to the door and said,

—You better come now, T. D.

—Must be the breakin' of the waters, Grampa Peters said.

—O, my God! a woman's voice cried from the house. O, dear God!

—That's all right, honey, Ellen Shawnessy was heard saying. Go right on and holler, honey. Just holler as loud as you want to, if it helps.

The men sat cowed. Johnny hated them and himself. He hated

especially Grampa Peters. He hated the portly bulk of Grampa Peters, squatting majestically before the General Store; he hated the male complacency of Grampa Peters, which never had to be torn open and rent by such an anguish, the trousered fatness of Grampa Peters, who only sat before the General Store on his big dumb behind and made words about politics while life shrieked in an upstairs room. He hated all men in the person of Grampa Peters, because men caused this awful thing to happen and then could do nothing about it.

After the screaming had gone on for a while, the men began to curse softly.

—Well, Jesus God, I wish she'd hurry up and git it over with.

—Goddammit! Grampa Peters said once. I don't remember my wife yelled that loud, though God and Jesus knows she always yelled loud enough.

—They sure git the raw end of things, the thin man said.

After a particularly frightful yell,

—Well, Jeeeeeeeeeesus God in Heaven, Dear Lord! said Grampa Peters, git rid of it, sister!

The men began to act as though they were being abused in some way. As for Johnny, each time the shrieking came, the skin of his face drew tight, his chest heaved, tears came to his eyes, he wanted to scream, roll on the ground, and yell with laughter. The desire to laugh became so strong that he had to get up and walk away. He went to the big wagon that was in back of the house where Mr. Doniphant had gone for the banjo. He got behind the wagon and tried to laugh, but instead he was sobbing. Apparently that was what he had been wanting to do.

After a while, the shrieking stopped and was followed by a series of moans and then a silence. The men got up and stood looking at the house. Johnny felt strangely calm. He dried his eyes and walked back to the road and stood with the men.

There was a new sound, which was like an echo of the other, a piping, insistent little echo, helpless and shameless as the other. But after that sound began, the other sound never did return.

The men in front of the General Store began to smile, at first a little sheepishly, then broadly.

—By God, listen to that little pipsqueak howl a hisn.

—That ain't no pipsqueak howl. He's got a good loud yell fer a baby.

—He ought to have, if he takes after his maw.

After a while, the door opened, and Ellen Shawnessy came out.

—They want you all to come in and see it, she said.

—I reckon they'd *better* leave us see it, said Grampa Peters. I never worked harder to have a baby in my life.

The men all removed their hats and walked sheepishly into the house. Johnny brought up the rear. In a room upstairs, a woman was lying on the bed. Her cheeks were flushed, and her hair was all strung around on the pillow. She was looking at something lying on her arm. Her husband was standing beside the bed looking at it too.

It was a little hairless monkey with a scalded skin, the ugliest thing Johnny had ever seen.

—It's a boy, said Mr. Doniphant tentatively.

—It's a *fine* boy, Grampa Peters said, lying magnificently.

The mother only lay looking at the baby. The baby was yelling again, and T. D. said,

—A perfect baby. The beginnings of a fine family, my boy.

Some of the men hit Mr. Doniphant solidly between the shoulders, and others pumped his hand. He looked bewildered and kept saying,

—Thank ye, sir, thank ye.

—Well, Missus, Grampa Peters said, how do you feel?

—All right, said the woman on the bed. I'm sorry if I caused y'all trouble by carryin' on so. I never knowed what it'd be like.

All of them lied, saying they didn't notice a thing, and anyway it didn't bother them the least bit.

—What you goin' to call it, Missus? Grampa Peters asked.

—Well, the young woman said very slowly, looking at it, we was aimin' to call it, iffen it was a boy, Zachary Taylor Doniphant, but I done change my mind, and my husband and I would like to give him the name of this kind gentleman here who help us out and maybe save my life and the baby's.

—O, I assure you—— T. D. started to say.

—No, sir, Mr. Doniphant said, we talked about it while you was all out of the room just now, and we're a-goin' to christen 'im Timothy Shawnessy Doniphant, if the doctor don't mind.

—Mind! T. D. said. I would be delighted. But I assure you——

Johnny thought it was a terrible insult to his father because the baby was a monstrous-looking object, but T. D. seemed to be delighted.

—T. D., one of the women said, I think that calls for a little prayer.

T. D. blew his nose and put his head down. The baby kept on crying.

—Dear Father in Heaven, T. D. said, these good young people have come a long way across the great continent of America and have suffered many hardships. So far Your kind providence has been upon them. We ask You now to continue to favor them with the benign light of Your countenance and take a hopeful view of their future, far-wandering across the land. May this little child that is this day born unto them live and prosper in the far land to which they are journeying. Dear Lord, preserve him and his father and his mother in the trials that await them. May they reach that far-off beautiful land of California and may they find all of their desires fulfilled until they arrive as all of us must, after much wandering, on that Golden Shore where there is no distinction between here and hereafter. We ask it, Lord, in Jesus' name. Amen.

Outside, everyone made a little contribution for the new baby, and T. D., who had already donated his services, gave two dollars. The baby was yelling again when they went in to give the money to the Doniphants. One thing you could say for it: it had a lot of life in it.

Johnny was very quiet until they were on their way home. Then he found that he was humming a song:

—O, Susanna,
Do not cry for me.

—I wish I could get the words to that song, Ellen said. How much do you remember, Johnny?

Johnny started in, and it turned out that he knew the whole song.

—It pays to have a good memory, T. D. said. With your mind for remembering things, John, you ought to go far.

The tune had a fine gaiety, but the words filled Johnny Shawnessy with delicious sadness, and the name Susanna haunted him even into his sleep, for that night he dreamed that he was hunting through the

Court House Square for a mysterious woman, whose stately name he couldn't remember. Meanwhile the Square darkened; people were rushing by him in wagons going west.

—It's the breaking of the waters, they said solemnly.

And indeed he could see the cold waters of the Shawmucky rising in the cornfields. He himself, trying to escape, wandered all night through familiar landscapes. They had an empty, joyless look

LIKE PAINTINGS ON A WALL

OR PICTURES

IN

AN
ILLUSTRATED HISTORICAL
ATLAS
OF
RAINTREE COUNTY
INDIANA
1875

In the back seat of the surrey little Will had the book open.

—Who is that lady above the door, Papa?

He pushed the book over into Mr. Shawnessy's lap. The title was stamped in gold on a black clothbound cover, eighteen by fifteen inches. The *Atlas* was an inch deep, corners and spine reinforced in tooled black leather. The fullpage lithograph of the Court House showed a rectangular brick and stone building. A tall tower set into the west end contained the Main Entrance, an American flag stood stiff out from the peak of the tower, and two clock faces visible in the sloped roof read nine o'clock. Two ladies, bustled, bearing parasols, walked on symmetrical paths of the court house lawn. Over the Main Entrance a draperied woman stood in a niche, blindfolded, leaning on a sheathèd sword, holding bronze scales.

—Justice, Mr. Shawnessy said.

—What are those things in her hands?

—Scales. To measure the exact difference between right and wrong.

—Why do they call it an atlas? Will asked.

—An atlas, Mr. Shawnessy said, is a book with maps—pictures of the earth. In the old Greek stories, a giant named Atlas held the world on his shoulders.

—Hercules came and held the world for him once, Wesley said, while Atlas went to the Garden of the Hesperides and got the golden apples for Hercules.

—What did Hercules want with the apples? Will asked.

—It was one of his twelve labors. And when Atlas came back, he just laughed at Hercules and said he was going to leave Hercules there holding the world forever. He didn't want to take the world back.

—You can't exactly blame him, Mr. Shawnessy said.

—But, Wesley said, Hercules played a trick on him. He fooled Atlas into taking the world back just long enough so he could fix his lion skin on his shoulders to keep the world from chafing them. And as soon as Atlas had the world back on his shoulders, Hercules just laughed at Atlas and took the apples and beat it, leaving Atlas to hold the world.

—He isn't still holding it, is he? Will asked.

—No, of course he isn't, Wesley said. It's just a Greek myth.

The *Illustrated Historical Atlas of Raintree County* was not, however, just a myth. It was a very substantial piece of work. A Chicago firm had sent its own compilers, surveyors, and delineators to make a verbal and pictorial record of Raintree County. Fifteen years ago Mr. Shawnessy had bought a copy of the *Atlas* for ten dollars and put it on the parlor table with the Family Bible and the Photograph Album. The *Atlas* was printed on paper of excellent quality, great grainy sheets, some forty-eight in all. There was an illustrated title-page, colored fullpage maps of the County and each of its twelve townships, and smaller maps of the principal communities, including Waycross. At the back were unfolding maps of Indiana, the United States, and the Eastern and Western Hemispheres. The reading matter provided a history of the County, statistical tables, and descriptions of churches, eminent public buildings, newspapers, and schools. Ten whole pages were given over to a list of over five hundred prominent citizens, each of whom had given satisfactory proof of prestige and good taste by subscribing to the *Atlas* in advance.

The name Shawnessy, J. W. appeared on page 44.

The *Atlas* was remarkable for its illustrations, fullpage lithographs of the New Court House, Freehaven's leading hotel, the south side of the Square; and half a hundred pictures—some fullpage and some two and four to the page—of Raintree County homes, mostly farms.

Into the faintly golden texture of the great soft sheets, an unknown artist had touched the earth of Raintree County with a sensitive pencil. In the sketches of farm homes, the principal building was seen as from a slight elevation so as to include a generous setting of outbuildings and the land around. Walks, lanes, roads, forests, gardens, pastures, cornfields appeared in accurate perspective. People played croquet on lawns; children skipped ropes, rolled hoops, pulled wagons; families passed in surreys, spring wagons, buggies; mare and colt scampered in the pasture; the great bull passively grazed behind the barn; the farmer engaged in his characteristic occupations—feeding, mowing, raking, plowing.

The earth had the effect of being a massy substance continuous under all traces of humanity. Through page after page, this earth of Raintree County appeared in an unvaried summer morning, radiant and precise to a depth of miles, until sky touched horizon with a frieze of soft clouds.

One played with the idea that the artist had been a gifted young man forced to hack for a living but leaving the stamp of genius even on his routine assignments.

—How come you're taking the *Atlas* to town, Papa? Wesley asked.

—What's that? O, to exchange it for one at the Museum, which is slightly different. They can use mine while I have theirs.

—How is the one at the Museum different? Wesley asked.

—It's an earlier edition, Mr. Shawnessy said evasively. What's Eva reading?

He didn't listen to the answer. He was thinking of Senator Jones's letter in his pocket and the quaint mission that he was undertaking to Freehaven.

The letter had come to him a week before. Everyone who knew the Senator well, knew that he had two distinct styles—sacred and profane. His informal letters to close friends favored the second vein.

Dear John:

. . . By the way, on top of all your painful responsibilities for the success of my homecoming, I want to pile one more that ought to be a pure joy to you.

As you know, I haven't been back to the County for twenty years, but I still have good contacts there and keep up pretty well. Now, here's a story I picked up in '75 when I received a copy of a Raintree County Atlas. I was told that the artist who drew the pictures for it was on his last job for the company before getting the axe. It seems he fancied himself a Raphael without a patron and was going nutty from so much hack work. Anyway, he got even with his firm and the world in general for years of artistic frustration by letting his imagination run hogwild on the plates he did for the Atlas. So when old Waldo Mays, who founded and ran the Historical Museum and was the leading spirit in getting the Atlas commissioned, received his advance copy, he took one look and beat it the hell up to Chicago, where he demanded the plates and had them altered or destroyed in his presence. All the rest of the subscription was castrated, including your copy and mine.

Meanwhile old Waldo kept the unique copy under lock and key in the Museum and never let anyone see it. Harve Watkins, who gave me the story, says Waldo kept hinting that the damage hadn't been all cleaned up, so that people kept scurrying to their Atlases to see if they could see anything. My own copy is ragged.

I've heard several hot tips about Waldo's unique copy, to wit: A lovely dame is standing in her pelt, ankledeep in the river under the railroad trestle on the titlepage. The lady going into the dry goods store on the south side of the Square, page 37, is stark naked, except for a parasol. On page 65, Bob Ray's prize bull, Mr. Jocko the Strong, blue ribbon at the State Fair in '74, is pictured showing prizewinning form in an intimate domestic scene. On page 53, Titian's Venus and Adonis are romping in the forest background. Adam and Eve are under an apple tree on page 57. A pair of country lovers are surprised in a haystack on page 17. The fountain in the front yard of John J. Jubal's palatial home in Beardstown features an ithyphallic Aztec god instead of a cast-iron triton. The sign reading Burke House on Freehaven's leading hotel has been altered to something more pungent. And Jesus Christ surrounded by the Twelve Apostles is getting ready to jump to Zion from the observation platform of the house on page 61. You can see the possibilities.

Now, I've been using this story for years with great éclat in the smokefilled rooms of the Nation's Capital, Washington, D. C. I adapt it for the company. It's good for lusty laughter at the stag banquet, and in a daintier version it fetches a giggle from the most cultivated females in Washington.

I'm sure there's some truth in it because I once wrote old Waldo myself in my best senatorial style, stating that I understood he had in his possession a unique copy of the Atlas containing some interesting variations, and as I was collecting books of all kinds on the old home county out of a sentimental interest, I would be glad to buy his copy—and he could name the price.

The old bastard wrote back that the variations to which I referred were of such a profane character that he had sworn never to allow the copy to get into the hands of another human being, where it might expose a character less staunchly fortified than his own, to overwhelming temptations. He said that he planned to destroy the book before his death and delayed now only because the presence of it in his museum brought hundreds of folks every year who bent bug-eyed over the glass case in his private office, where he kept the book locked up and covers closed. He said he considered this an excellent training in self-denial, not to say that it encouraged people to explore the Museum and its other treasures (all those goddamned stinking stuffed possums and Indian skulls).

That Atlas has become an obsession with me. I have the same feeling about it that a collector would have for the famous Satan's Bible with the misprint in the seventh commandment or a hitherto undiscovered Shakespeare play published with the author's face engraved from life in the frontispiece and an autobiographical preface.

Now, just last week I got word from Harve that old Waldo was found stiff and stone-cold at six in the morning on the front steps of the Museum with his key in the lock. Apparently, feeling that his hour had come, he'd staggered down in the dead of the night to get that book and destroy it. And they say his niece by marriage and only heir (who's been East and got married and widowed) was visiting the old man in his last illness and immediately took over the estate and the Museum lock, stock, and barrel and closed it up for adjustments.

In other words, John, that cussed book is in the hands of a woman, young, pretty they say, and therefore impressionable—instead of an old he-frump who has been lusting over it in secret for seventeen years.

Someone is going to get hold of that book now—and fast. If I were in the County, I'd be willing to bet my chances for the Presidency in '96 that I'd get access to the lady and the book in a matter of hours. But since I can't do it, my first thought is you. We all know, John, that where a skirt is involved, you carry a golden key.

Sprout, I'm personally counting on you to put the hex on that woman and get that book and have it in Waycross when I arrive. My letter to her is already in the mail, blazing the trail, and I leave the rest up to you. I'll personally lay out a cold hundred dollars for the privilege of adding that book to my private collection of prints by the old masters.

Of course, I didn't give my birthyell yesterday, and I know the whole thing may have been just a figment of the old man's mind. We all know that Waldo has been off his nut ever since he cracked his marbles on a wagontongue as a boy on his father's farm. But I don't want to go to my grave without satisfying my curiosity as to what that two-bit Michelangelo did to Raintree County.

By the way, John, not a word on this subject where it might diminish that splendid image of decorum which the hoi polloi entertain for a U. S. Senator. Of course, in the right quarters it will give my character that touch of humanity which woos the beauteous ballot to the box—and after all, this is an Election Year. . . .

Cordially yours,

GARWOOD B. JONES

Mr. Shawnessy had in his pocket another letter received two days before.

My dear Mr. Shawnessy,

Your kind note in hand, I hasten to reply. The book of which you speak and in which Senator Jones has expressed an interest is in my possession. Apparently my revered uncle placed a great value on it, but I would be glad to see you and talk with you about it.

I am opening the Museum for Independence Day, as many people like to visit. If you come early, before seven, as you suggest, I will meet you there on the Fourth.

By the way, you are wrong—I remember you quite well. As a little girl of ten, I was a doting protégée of yours. You trained me and some other girls for a patriotic pageant on the Court House lawn in 1868. I had the part of the Productive Institutions and wore a skirt made out of corn husks which came off halfway through my speech.

So you see, you are not forgotten after all. Remember me kindly to your family.

Sincerely,

PERSEPHONE R. MAYS

The surrey had turned west at Moreland and was approaching the Old Home Place. Granite boulders were strewn on the earth here, negligent droppings of the great ice sheet whose southernmost rim had lain on Raintree County aeons before, leaving its load of alien rocks and glacial dirt.

Fleshed with loam, tufted with groves, and dense with corn, the earth swam beneath him and away to distant summer. The sky built a vault pillared with far clouds over the floor of Raintree County.

What made the earth of Raintree County? Who holds up the earth? *What creature is it that in the morning of its life . . .*

Man made an atlas for the earth and tried to get a lasting place among the Prominent Citizens. With straight lines—ranks of corn, telegraph poles, rectangular walls—he tried to overcome its feminine evasions. Across its mapflattened face, devoid of contour, he drew the unwavering legends of his names. But he had never caught the naked goddess in his net.

Mr. John Atlas Shawnessy had reluctantly taken the world back on his shoulders, releasing his heroic twin, Mr. John Hercules Shawnessy, who ran off bearing a branch of golden apples. With fleet thighs, he fled up and down the corridors of a mythical Raintree County. He laughed. His gold hair hung long on his shoulders. He had held the world for a little while, or rather he had drawn it with a sensitive pencil and had made a delightful legend of it, had sketched forbidden beauty into a puritan landscape, achieved Acropolis in the Court House Square, Shakespeare at the County Fair, Venus risen from the Shawmucky, Eden in an apple orchard.

Take back the world a minute while I adjust my lion skin. There, you poor benighted bonehead, you can keep it. Did you build yourself a respectable world and bound yourself beneath it, friend, and call it Raintree County? Well, I will tell you what it is—your Raintree County—to reward you for plucking me these golden and forbidden apples.

I will give you back the world neatly bound in tooled leather and black cloth by the firm of Jackson, Higgs, and Company, Lakeside Building, Corner Clark and Adams Streets, Chicago, but with a few special additions of my own. As the anonymous artist sent down from headquarters, I don't hesitate to say that I have improved a little on the work of God in making you this legendary Raintree County. The universe never did sufficiently reward me for my intuitive perspectives.

Ladies and gentlemen, let's take off on our conducted tour of Raintree County. Look sharp! There's more naked here than meets the eye. These sentimental landscapes are full of sly gods. And from the back of our book, we unveil you the earth, our lady of the stately hemispheres. Look sharp, ladies and gentlemen! This little magic world within a world is strewn with the memories of all mankind.

—There's the Old Home Place, Wesley said. Look, they've been cutting clover in the South Field.

A plain white farmhouse, surrounded by weathered outbuildings, stood on a slight elevation leftward of the road. Scarred and strange, it lay on the immemorial way to Freehaven; and passing it, Mr. Shawnessy passed again through an invisible great gate and into the garden of a Hesperian memory, seeking

1848— A —1852

FABULOUS AND FORGOTTEN SECRET WAS WRITTEN IN A LOST LANGUAGE UPON THE EARTH

of Raintree County. This he had known from the beginning, and he had known too that the secret was for him to unriddle; he alone could one day find the answer. For this secret was not only the secret of the earth in which he lived but also the secret of himself and what he was. Who and what are you, little manchild? Whence have you come and whither are you going? What are you doing upon this ancient, stream-divided earth?

Many devious paths seemed to lead backward to the secret.

There was the secret of the County's origin and naming. The County seemed to Johnny an eternal thing, and yet only some twenty years before his birth, it had been an indivisible part of central Indiana, then a new State, admitted to the Union in 1816. In 1818, the central region was opened up for white settlement, and counties were created by an act of the state legislature meeting in the new capital, Indianapolis. After that, the settlers came, mostly Scotch-Irish and English stock from the coastal states. They poured into the southeastern corner of the County by way of the National Pike, among them young T. D. Shawnessy and his wife, Ellen.

The way in which the County got its name was a subject involved in mystery. The first state legislature had called it after a hero of the Revolution, but later, when a legal county government had been formed and a site selected for a county seat, a petition was accepted for changing the name to Raintree County. Clearly enough, a sentiment had grown up in the County for the new name, but exactly why was never fully understood.

According to a popular legend, the earliest settlers found a ragged preacher wandering in the neighborhood of a lake in the middle of the County. He told them that in his youth he had had a vision of Heaven in which he beheld a green land full of fruitbearing trees and pleasant waters and had gone seeking for its earthly counterpart through the wilderness of America, carrying with him the seed of an oriental tree never before planted in America. Now he had found, as he believed, the land of his vision.

—Lo! I have sowed the seed, he cried. The Raintree will blossom in the western earth. The tree of life will drop its golden fruit in the new earthly Paradise.

The mad preacher had worked so strongly on the imagination of the first settlers around Freehaven that they began to refer to the neighborhood, a little facetiously, as the Land of the Raintree. From this source came at length the names Paradise Lake and Raintree County.

Some people insisted that the preacher had been no other than the celebrated John Chapman, better known as Johnny Appleseed. A ragged, quaint, beloved form, he had spent his life travelling through the pioneer West, planting apple orchards in the wilderness and preaching a Swedenborgian gospel of the teeming, sacred earth. If the man who planted the Raintree was Johnny Appleseed, then it seemed likely that the seed he planted was only apple seed. Perhaps he had merely established one of his famous tree nurseries somewhere in what was to become Raintree County.

At any rate, no one had ever found the eponymous tree of Raintree County, and after a passage of years people in general began to assume that there was no such tree as a Raintree.

Then something happened that seemed strangely to confirm the legend of the County's naming.

In the year 1826, the Scotch philanthropist Robert Owen founded New Harmony on the Wabash River in southern Indiana. Down the Ohio and up the Wabash came a Boatload of Knowledge—scientists, artists, and educators imported from the East and from overseas to found a New Moral World in the western wilderness. People were invited to come and join a paradise regained by innate human goodness. The noble experiment lasted two years and collapsed in the usual picturesque wreckage of innate human selfishness and inefficiency. But many gifted people remained and fostered an interest in science and art so much advanced for the place and the period that New Harmony came to be known as the Athens of the West. Among the New Harmonians were students of natural science, and it was one of these who brought to New Harmony the seeds of an exotic tree, which he planted by the gate of his house. This tree, bearing the scientific name of Koelreuteria paniculata, had been called the Golden Raintree in its native China. From these parent seeds the Golden Raintree—or the Gate Tree, as it was commonly known in Indiana—spread all over New Harmony and more slowly through other parts of the State. It bore no fruit in the popular meaning of the word, but in late June or early July the mature trees, which seldom grew taller than twenty or thirty feet, bloomed with a delicate yellow flower and dropped a rain of yellow pollendust and petals.

Thus, by chance, the State of Indiana did acquire a mysterious seedling of Asia, a true Raintree. But for a long time this tree flourished only in a little town in the southwestern corner of the State, while the county named for such a tree had not a single specimen within its boundaries, as far as anyone knew.

Not that anyone in Raintree County was ever much disturbed by the paradox. No one ever challenged New Harmony's claim to having introduced the Asiatic Raintree to America. Scarcely anyone knew about the gate trees of New Harmony, and no one except one or two garrulous gaffers and Johnny Shawnessy cared how the County got its name anyway. The earth had taken back one of its legends—that was all.

Nothing would remain at last except the name itself, itself a legend beautiful and talismanic, a sound of magic and of recollection, a phrase of music and of strangeness—Raintree County.

Johnny Shawnessy never doubted the truth of the legend. He felt sure that a wondrous tree grew in secret somewhere in the County. People might have passed beside it a hundred times and never realized that it was the tree planted by the fabulous preacher, whose name was also Johnny.

Johnny Shawnessy used to imagine that someday he would be walking in a wild, rarely visited part of the County and in the late afternoon would come upon a tree rising jetlike from the earth and spreading to a fountain spray of dense leaves, among which was a fruit of delectable flavor. He used to imagine the stately trunk of the tree and the clean isolation of it from the other trees of the forest. Or perhaps it was standing lonely in a field of grass. Once Johnny had asked T. D. where such a tree could grow unseen in the County, and T. D. said,

—They's a regular wilderness around Paradise Lake, especially where the Shawmucky flows into it. Folks call it the Great Swamp. Why, a man went in there once and never come out again. There could be a whole slew of such trees in there and no one ever know about them.

Johnny felt that there was only one tree, one sacred trunk standing in the druid silence of woodlands in the middle County. Someday, perhaps he would find that tree and thus become the hero of the County, the Alexander who cut the Gordian knot, the Hercules who obtained the Golden Apples of the Hesperides, the Oedipus who solved the Riddle of the Sphinx.

The secret of the tree was blended strangely with the whole secret of his life and the mystery from which he had sprung.

In T. D.'s Office, the little building behind the house, there hung a big picture of a tree with a black printed legend beneath:

THE LEAVES OF THE TREE WERE FOR
THE HEALING OF THE NATIONS

When he was very young, Johnny had thought this tree had something to do with the mythical tree of Raintree County. Later he understood why T. D. had the picture.

The Office was nearly as old as the log cabin which had been the original Shawnessy Home in Raintree County. A shrine of memories, it had its own peculiar incense. If from all the herbs of Raintree County a scent had been distilled, that quintessential fragrance would have been the scent of T. D.'s Office.

When he was very young, Johnny had supposed that all things in the Office gave off the scent, the varnished chart of a man's anatomy, the ancient, papery skull on the threelegged table in the corner, the rows of scuffed books behind the bookcase glass, the littered desk, the bottles on the shelves, the tree engraving, and T. D. himself. But later he knew that the scent was from the bottles only.

The Botanical Medicines in the square glass-stoppered bottles were made by T. D. from roots, barks, grasses, fruits, and flowers of the County. Barkybrown, rivergreen, color of blood, they were the bottled lifejuice of the County and the aroma of all its withered summers.

It was in the Office, oddly appendent to the house itself, that

Johnny had come closest to the buried secret of his father's life.

One day when he was about ten years old, he had gone into the Office during his father's absence and had found lying on the desk a ledger that T. D. had always before kept carefully locked up and to which he referred for purposes that Johnny had never understood. Now, Johnny picked up the ledger and read on the outside

BOOK OF MISCELLANIES

T. D. SHAWNESSY

Inside, Johnny found many strange things. The whole first part of the book contained recipes for the Botanical Medicines. One read:

An Indian Remmady. Cure for Ague Cakes.

Take of the bark of black Haw Root Wild Cherry Root Bitter Sweet Root and Skunk Root of each one hand full put in one gallon of soft water and boil down to one quart. To be drank in one day, and so continue making and drinking for severl days if necessary.

Another:

Take of Gambage	— 2 oz
Blood-Root	— 2 oz
Labelia Seeds	— 1 oz
Cayenne pepper	— 2 drams
Rhubarb	— 4 drams
Penlash	— 1 dram

All made fine well mixed and formed into pills with butternut syrup. Dose—take one every hour—until they purg or take 4 and they will puke.

There followed many testimonials of people who had been cured by the Botanical Medicines. One read:

This may certify to all whome it may concern that I David Farnsworth of the County of Raintree in the State of Indiana have ben for years subject to repeted attacts of the pleurecy and have ben brought (as I and others have thought) very near the gates of death.

In April of 1822 I had another attact of this distressing and painful complaint. I was taken on Satterday with cold chills and flashes of heat with pains in my bones and headach and a severe pain in my left side, with other disagreeable symtoms which continued until monday with increasing rapidity, when I sent for T. D. Shawnessy to cum and bring with him sum medicines and when he had examened me he stated that I had better be taken through a corse ot medicine without delay. Prepperation was made and I began to drink of the hot medicine to rase the internel heat. I was then steemed, and an emettic of Labelia with its appendents was afterwards administered and then steemed again and showered with cold water and vinnegar then wiped off dry and put to bed with a warm rock to my feet still drinking of the warm teas to keep up a perspiration and by the blessing of kind providence through the means of those medicines administered and good nursing I was soon restored to health, and will further add that I never was cured in so short a time of so vilent atact of this complaint. My family has also used his medicine in other complaints and find them to answer the purpose in all cases and are so well convinced of their suppererorety over those used by the medical docters that they seek for no other then the Botanical Medicines.

DANIEL FARNSWORTH
ELIZABETH FARNSWORTH

August 5th, 1822

Farther over in the book were some original poems—hymns and moral diatribes. One poem, inserted on a separate sheet of paper, had been written in purple ink, and although it was in T. D.'s hand, the letters were more carefully formed than usual and the capitals had ornamental flourishes. It seemed to Johnny perhaps a hymn—but a strange one.

It was a morning in the Spring.
Beneeth a hawthorn tree we lade,
Drunk with the od'rous blosoming,
Togather, kissing in the shade.
Heaven! how lustily we played!

It was a day of frollic wind.
We heard the insecks drone and buz.
God's purest angle would have sinned
And i, no angle, did becaus
My God! how bewtifull she was!

It was a morning in the prime.
I struv the bewteus prize to win,

> And if our gaming was a crime,
> And if our luving was a sin,
> Dear Jesus! let me err agin!

On a few pages in the back of the book were recorded some baffling particulars about the Shawnessy family tree. One entry read:

> Eliza Shawnessy, mother of Timothy Duff Shawnessy, came from Scotland to the State of Delaware in 1805 and departed this life in 1820 at the age of forty-six.

> Fair from my natif place
> A strainger in this Land was I.
> I go to my eturnel rest
> And shall live no more to die.
> From Scottish earth I came to this.
> From here I go to endless bliss.

There was no mention of a Grandfather Shawnessy. Johnny knew that T. D. had come over from Scotland with his mother when he was a boy. T. D. would say only that his own father had 'passed on' before mother and son had left Scotland. But there must have been an interesting family connection there, for when Johnny—by far the most gifted of the children—would show a flash of precocity in memory or expression, T. D. would say,

—Well, the boy ought to amount to something some day. He's related on my father's side to one of the greatest living writers of the English language. Some day maybe he will make the name of Shawnessy as great in America as the name of Carlyle has become in England.

Then T. D.'s blue eyes would flash, his thin shoulders would snap back, and he would walk rapidly back and forth, coattails flapping, showing the restless energy that had brought him all the way from Scotland to the middle of America.

T. D. himself was a famous man in Raintree County. Whether driving about with a buggyload of the Botanical Medicines or standing in the pulpit of the Methodist Church in Danwebster, rocking back on his heels, he had but one aim—to improve the spiritual and physical welfare of the County. Devoid equally of grammar and guile, he had become known beyond the borders of the County for his sermons, which were sometimes composed in spirited doggerel.

He got continual requests from other parts of the State for his poems, especially the one about the Evils of Tobacco, which Johnny had heard so many times that he knew it by heart, including the two celebrated lines:

Some do it chew and some it smoke
Whilst some it up their nose do poke.

There was no special mystery about this everyday T. D., but Johnny was always discovering secrets where no one else could and was endlessly curious about the origin of things and their occult relationships to one another. For him the mystery of his father's origin and his own was signed and sealed into a ledger of recipes and poems and into a legend of a tree of golden rain.

T. D. Shawnessy, his father, was a tall tree with a golden top, the carrier of a strange seed from the East planted deep in Raintree County. That was why a tree with a black legend beneath, taken from the Bible, grew in the little shrinelike office. T. D. Shawnessy was a tall, windshaken tree of life, and from the branches and the leaves thereof was a healing balsam shaken on the minds and bodies of men. And the seed of this tree had fallen on the County in secret for many years, but none there was who could say the place and the purpose and the meaning thereof.

There was also the secret of his mother, Ellen Shawnessy. His earliest memories, archaic fragments saved out of otherwise razed eras of his life, were all pervaded with the presence of his mother. These memories appeared to have been plucked out of an eternal summer and preserved by an access of strong light that burned the images more lastingly on his awareness. Perhaps the oldest memory of all was one of his mother's face bending down to him from a vague tumult of sound and color. Painted by the strong light, it was a slender face, the cheek and jawlines emphatic, the skin fair but freckled, the nose pert, the mouth large and mobile, the eyes a vivid blue in dark lashes, the hair a dark, smouldering mass. A smile suffused this precise small face with beauty and warmth. The lips moved; there was a sound, beautiful and talismanic,

—Johnny!

With this word, spoken in his mother's quick, girlish voice, he had been called from the murmurous world where he had been lulled so long in the prehistoric age before there was any Raintree County. Thus his origin was a kind of virgin birth, as if a word had touched him into being.

Later it never ceased to disturb him that he had been a somewhat belated accident in his mother's life, the last of nine children.

Ellen was universally beloved in the County, more so even than T. D., who, because he was a Methodist minister and an advocate of reform, stirred up antagonisms. In both manner and appearance she had a young charm that made her more like an older sister than a typical Raintree County mother. She was quick to laugh and joke, having an infectious gaiety lacking in T. D.'s amiable but unhumorous nature. Her enjoyments were spontaneous like a child's, and it was always fun to go with her to one of the typical Raintree County gatherings—family reunions, Saturdays at the Court House Square, church picnics, ice cream socials, patriotic celebrations. She entered into the pastimes of the younger people, even played at the running games. It was a common saying in the County that Johnny had got his great fleetness of foot from his mother. Men would say,

—When your mother first come to this county, son, she could outfoot most of the men.

Among the fairest images of his life were the occasions when Ellen Shawnessy would take some younger person's challenge to a footrace and sitting down would slip off her shoes and stockings. With shyness and wonder, Johnny saw the white feet, slender and elfin, appear suddenly where he was accustomed to see the prim-buckled shoes.

Ellen was also an excellent horsewoman, never bothering to saddle a horse but jumping on like a man and riding away bareback. This she often did, leaving at a moment's notice for the home of a friend or relative. In the supreme emergencies of life—childbirth, marriage, death—she was as much in demand as T. D., her small radiant person arriving like an omen of good luck and good hope.

Together she and T. D. were like two invulnerable angels as they went about the County dealing in life and death.

One of Johnny's most poignant early memories was of standing in the yard of the Home Place waiting for Ellen Shawnessy to come back from one of her sudden missions at a distant home. The girls had prepared both dinner and supper and had left Johnny to his own devices. He heard the talking from time to time in the house and yard.

—I wonder what can be keeping Mamma so long.

It was nearly nightfall. He couldn't remember when she had stayed away so long. He walked back and forth before the gate, looking east along the road in the direction she had taken. He had never before felt so miserable and lonely. The house, the fields surrounding, and the road had lost all purpose and significance, seeming empty and forlorn at the top of the world. At last, in the fading day, he saw Ellen's erect form riding swiftly up the road. He ran from the gate, his voice shrill:

—Mamma! Mamma! It's me—Johnny!

She rode up to him and leaped lightly off the horse, her face flushed, her hair blown and tangled.

—Why, Johnny! she said. Why haven't you gone to bed?

He was very happy to walk with her into the house and see the usual bustle and excitement on her arrival as she began to tell in her fast, crowded speech some narrative of birth, of life hanging by a thread, of what people said out there in the limitless, enchanted world of Raintree County.

His mother's being was woven into the substance of his surroundings, unchanging essence of a changing earth. There had been two distinct Home Places. Johnny's first memories preserved the earlier Home Place, the pioneer Shawnessy dwelling in Raintree County. The central shrine had been the log cabin, a sturdy, competent dwelling well floored and chinked, with two partitions downstairs and a loft above for sleeping. Behind the cabin were T. D.'s office, an outhouse, and the small barn where a few horses and cows were kept: T. D. wasn't primarily a farmer and had only twenty acres of land. Some distance from the house was a spring welling up from a small rocky hollow to form a trickling branch that made its way circuitously across the field and northward to the river. Back of the house was the main pasture, the South Field, its grassy undulations strewn with firescarred rocks, negligent droppings of some condor-winged bird of time in the ages before the first human beings had come to Raintree County. The South Field rose to a gentle summit behind the Home Place and then fell like a wave of waning strength to the limit of the Shawnessy earth. There, just inside the railfence, was the greatest of the glacial boulders, a rock much taller than Johnny, egg-shaped, faintly red, half sunken in the earth, immovable and lonely. Beyond it was the oak forest, a place of tranquil and great trunks. Johnny could remember when the South Field was stubbled with stumps, having been, some years before his birth, part of the great oak forest which apparently had covered several square miles of the land around the Home Place when T. D. first came to the County, being itself a remnant of that legendary great forest which extended clear across the Mississippi Valley and of which there were still some dim recollections handed down from the earliest settlers and explorers.

In this simple setting of cabin, road, railfences, pasturefield, cornland, forest, spring and branch, the infant Johnny Shawnessy had grown up. Then one day in his ninth year, the family returned from a Saturday on the Court House Square to find the log cabin in flames. From its ashes rose the new Home Place, a plain board farmhouse built in the fashion of the middle forties. Slowly, too, the land lost its raw unfinished look. New outbuildings and a larger barn were built. The farm was entirely fenced in. The road was widened and corduroyed.

But under the thin veil of the new Home Place, under the tidal rhythm of the seasons, Johnny seemed always to be trying to remember and restore a pattern primitive and simple, of which only tantalizing traces remained.

Once in his tenth year he went a long way back of the land and entered the great oak forest and walked a long way through its druid aisles, wondering if he might not find in it somewhere the fabulous Raintree. He stayed longer away than he had intended. Darkness came suddenly among the broad trunks, which even at noon were steeped in a kind of twilight. He hurried back through expiring noises of the day. It seemed to him that he was going much farther than necessary to find the railfence at the limit of the land. A feeling possessed him of the fragility of his life on the earth and of the transiency of all human habitation. He had a sensation of long absence and return, or as if he had reawakened into some earlier time. Suppose he should come out of the forest and find the Home Place as it was in its early and now all but forgotten form. Nay, suppose it wasn't there at all, the road, the railfence, and the log cabin having been erased by the backward-travelling years. The primeval forest might extend once more in majestic solitude all over the lost earth of Raintree County. He was suddenly afraid, uprooted from his familiar world. He ran like mad between the trees, lashed by branches and weeds.

Abruptly, he came out at the railfence. The rock was there, faintly red in the declining light. He sprang over the fence and ran up the slow bulge of the field. Below him, across the long earth, were the yellow windows of the Home Place. A bell sounded, calling for supper. It was not so late as he had thought. His small fleet legs found a new strength. He ran on slow, floating strides down the slow hill watching for his mother's form across the land.

He then dimly understood that every memory of his life, like every journey of his body, returned at last to the same mysterious place which had nothing to do with space. And he wondered at the miracle by which he had been spun out of the substance of his mother's flesh in some prehistoric era that had nothing to do with time. Somehow he had sprung without a pollution into the world of names. And the names made all the difference and rescued him from the feeling of being lost in a void of earth and night—the names, the omnipotent words, Johnny, father, mother, Raintree County.

For Johnny always had a curious feeling that he would one day find the meaning of himself and Raintree County locked up in words. He himself had sprung into being from words in an immense blackboarded book on the parlor table.

This book was the Family Bible. On its first page the beginning of all things was recorded in the inspired word of God. On its last page Johnny's beginning was recorded in T. D.'s handwriting:

John Wickliff Shawnessy, Borned in Raintree
County at the Home Place, April 23, 1839

It early seemed to Johnny that his whole life had been woven from the pages of this august book. Over and over, at church and in the home, he heard its stories of beginnings, its dreadful dooms, and its beautiful lives and deaths. His very substance was shaped from its archaic language. In a way, even his Christian name had come from the Bible. T. D. had called his last child after the great English Reformer who had been one of the first to attempt a translation of the

Bible into English. The name, variously spelled and misspelled in the old texts, was further misspelled 'Wickliff' by T. D., and Wickliff it became in the middle of Johnny's name.

John Wickliff—this name had been set upon him like a badge. Perhaps he too was fated to rewrite the great book of God in a new land and in a new tongue.

Some of the legends of the Bible became as much a part of him as his own life in the County. His mother had early read him the story of Adam and Eve and the Garden of Eden, of God and the guileful Serpent, and of the Tree that bore the Forbidden Fruit.

The story of Adam and Eve was the oldest story in the world, sealed with the seal of primal mystery. What earth was more secret than the Garden of Eden? Where was this garden in which the father and mother of mankind had wandered naked? At first, Johnny had supposed that because Raintree County was the whole world, therefore Eden was somewhere in Raintree County, especially since there was a lake in the center of the County called Paradise Lake. But T. D. laughed pleasantly at this misconception and cleared it up.

The greatest mystery of all was the Forbidden Tree. What kind of tree was it and why was it forbidden? And where was that other tree, the Tree of Life, that Adam and Eve might also have eaten of to live forever? And why had God forbidden them to eat the fruit of the trees at all?

Yes, that story had a light of dawn like an early memory of the County. Much of the mystery came from the fact that Adam and Eve were the only people who lived naked. He had seen a picture of them in the frontispiece of the Family Bible, tasting the Forbidden Fruit, Eve having her long hair down and a figleaf over the vital spot. This story was the boldest and truest of all the stories and the most marvellous and exciting because in it the father and mother of mankind had been naked. And the wonderful word 'naked' was used, and it meant 'without clothes.'

In the Danwebster Church, where T. D. preached about God and the Bible, everyone wore clothes, a mysterious result of the sin which Adam and Eve had committed in the garden. The divine disease of curiosity that burned in the vitals of Johnny Shawnessy ended for most Raintree County citizens when they entered the church. To it they came for the same answer to life's riddle that had been given to their fathers before them.

One of the dominant images of Johnny's childhood was the approach to the Danwebster Church. Following the road from the Home Place, the family wagon would make a sharp turn, dip down through trees across the river bridge, and clattering over and through the screening foliage on the far side, would bring suddenly into view the form of the Danwebster Church standing on a hill above the river, a white frame building with a steeple holding a bell. It was like a revelation austere and tranquil. The doors would open, and the bell would ring, and from miles around the dwellers of Raintree County would gather to raise their voices in song and prayer.

What was the thing to which they prayed?

It was a rather appalling mystery called God. Toward the little church of Danwebster, Johnny had a divided emotion. He always associated it with sunshine, a gentle boredom, the image of T. D. pleasantly rocking in the pulpit. But over it there hovered too the memory of a crime, the old unlucky error by which the history of mankind had been darkened. The mystery of Raintree County was all stained and bloody and confused with this crime. The whole mournful affair was only slightly relieved by the worship of God's gentle son, who, after all, had been nailed to a cross for being good.

More satisfying to Johnny's yearning for definite answers was the little schoolhouse at Danwebster where he learned to read and write and cipher. Here he studied a legend called American History, bloody, irrational, and exciting like the Bible, and was told that he lived in the greatest republic since the beginning of time, a place where all men were created equal and where they were all entitled to Life, Liberty, and the Pursuit of Happiness. Though the school at Danwebster was only spasmodically in operation under a succession of itinerant teachers, Johnny here began to show his phenomenal memory. In Class Day exercises he recited gems of oratory and rhetoric, including the peroration of Webster's famous reply to Hayne. He emerged from his schooling with the conviction that Liberty and Union were one and inseparable, that George Washington was the greatest man who ever lived, and that two plus two equalled four in Raintree County and throughout the universe. Above all, he acquired a holy faith in the printed word.

After he had learned to read, Johnny read newspapers, books, magazines, or just odd pieces of anything covered with words. He believed that some day, if he read fast and far enough, he would strip away the thin black veil of words and behold the great mystery that dwelt at the beginning of himself. He read with complete absorption, and when he was lost in a book, he was truly and completely lost, so much so that sometimes his mother was obliged to call several times before he heard.

And as he read and didn't find the answer to the secret, he made a resolution that he would someday write the book that would unlock the riddle of the earth of Raintree County, of his mother and father, and himself. Thus when he was very young, only about seven years old, he decided upon his life work.

Most of the words that he read as a boy only carried him farther from the secret, but a few stories were filled with revelation.

In the summer of 1852, T. D. got hold of a two-volume copy of the novel *Uncle Tom's Cabin* by Harriet Beecher Stowe. He gave sermons about it, and people discussed it for weeks pro and con. It was one of the great spiritual events of Raintree County, having as much effect on the County's mind as a National Election or even a minor war. Long after Johnny had read the book, a permanent residue of simple images remained, and this residue was the great American legend of Uncle Tom's Cabin.

The legend of Uncle Tom's Cabin was a legend of the South, but not the South which was below the Ohio River, a hundred and fifty miles from Johnny's home in Indiana. It was the South of Stephen Foster's songs. It was way down upon the Swanee Ribber, far far away in the Old Kentucky Home. There beneath a scented beauty lay a black evil called slavery. There the good and the poor and the humble and the enslaved of the earth were set clearly apart by God in black skins and patiently awaited their deliverance. Uncle Tom's Cabin was the story of a few enduring characters, too simple to be real and thus more true than life: little Eva, that good, goldenhaired child, destroyed somehow by the noxious blight of slavery:

> Farewell, beloved child! the bright eternal doors have closed after thee; we shall see thy sweet face no more. . . .

Eliza running across the icefloes on the river from slave land into free with the bloodhounds roaring after; Topsy, the puckish Negro child who wasn't born but just growed; Simon Legree, whose fist had got hard as iron from knocking down niggers; and Uncle Tom himself, the good old woollytopped Negro, who died like Christ that a people might be saved.

> Think of your freedom, every time you see UNCLE TOM'S CABIN; and let it be a memorial to put you all in mind to follow in his steps, and be as honest and faithful and Christian as he was.

Uncle Tom's Cabin was a legend eternally true because it was eternally good. It spoke directly to the heart of Johnny Shawnessy and became blended in his being with Raintree County and America. After he read *Uncle Tom's Cabin,* he was never confused again about the question of slavery. He knew where and what slavery was, he knew that it was bad, he knew also that it would one day be destroyed.

There was a time during which Johnny read and reread all the Greek myths he could get hold of. It seemed to him that in these stories of human forms woven from the teeming earth, of women flying from the love-pursuit of gods beside the river, of monsters that mingled beast and god, of combat, love, and epic quests and everlasting godlike games, he had perhaps recovered the lost prehistoric summer of his own life.

At about the same time he read some of the stories of Nathaniel Hawthorne, the great American mythmaker. One of these filled him again with the old sense of mystery and seemed to have a special meaning for his own life. This was the story of 'The Great Stone Face.' Johnny read it over and over until he had it almost by heart. The austere language seemed imbued with a mystical meaning beyond the literal phrase. To him it seemed the most wonderful story ever told.

The story opened with a description of a mother and a little child named Ernest sitting at their cottage door and gazing at a Great Stone Face. High above the populous valley where they lived, a colossal face of stone had been shaped in a cliff by some remote convulsion of the earth and transformed to human aspect by the weathering touch of time. *It was a happy lot for children to grow up to manhood or womanhood with the Great Stone Face before their eyes, for all the features were noble, and the expression was at once grand and sweet, as if it were the glow of a vast, warm heart, that embraced all mankind in its affections.* Gazing at the Great Stone Face, the mother repeated to the little child a legend of the valley, older even than the Indian peoples who had formerly lived there. The purport was that some day a child would be born in the valley who would become *the greatest and noblest personage of his time,* and whose face in manhood would bear an exact resemblance to the Great Stone Face.

The boy Ernest grew up in the valley, having no teacher except the Great Stone Face. While he was yet a child, *an exceedingly rich merchant* returned to the valley, hailed as the one who fulfilled the ancient prophecy. He had great wealth and was known by the name of Gathergold. As the rich man passed in his carriage among the applauding people, Ernest caught a glimpse of a withered yellow face that bore no resemblance at all to the Great Stone Face, having none of its benignity and wisdom. And yet the people seemed actually to believe that here was the likeness of the Great Stone Face.

But as time passed, the episode was forgotten, and Ernest growing now to manhood continued to hope that he might live to see the fulfillment of the prophecy. Then there came back to the valley of his birth *an illustrious commander,* who was affectionately called Old Blood-and-Thunder and who the people asserted was the exact likeness of the Great Stone Face. Obtaining a view of the famous soldier, Ernest beheld *a war-worn and weather-beaten countenance, full of energy, and expressive of an iron will,* but lacking the gentle wisdom and humane sympathy of the Great Stone Face.

Years passed. Ernest became a preacher, remaining in the valley and hoping that he might yet see the man who would resemble the beloved Face. Then there came back to the valley of his birth *a certain eminent statesman,* who was so wonderfully eloquent that he had *finally persuaded his countrymen to select him for the Presidency.* He was known by the name of Old Stony Phiz, so much was he thought to resemble the Great Stone Face, but once again Ernest was disappointed.

Ernest was now aged and had ceased to be obscure. Meanwhile, *a bountiful Providence had granted a new poet to this earth.* Likewise a native of the valley, he had spent most of his life *a distance from that romantic region, pouring out his sweet music amid the bustle and din of cities.* Now he took passage by railroad and returned to the valley in order to speak with Ernest, because he deemed nothing so desirable as to meet this man, *whose untaught wisdom walked hand in hand with the noble simplicity of his life* and *who made great truths so familiar by his simple utterance of them.* Ernest hoped that the poet would fulfill the prophecy, but the poet himself declined the nomination, insisting that while he had dreamed great dreams, he had lived by his own choice among poor and mean realities.

Then at the story's end, Ernest had gone out to address the people, and the light of the setting sun had shone for a brief while in mist and splendor on the distant image of the Great Stone Face. And the poet had called out:

'Behold! Behold! Ernest is himself the likeness of the Great Stone Face!'. . .

But Ernest, having finished what he had to say, took the poet's arm, and walked slowly homeward, still hoping that some wiser and better man than himself would by and by appear, bearing a resemblance to the GREAT STONE FACE.

Here was the secret that Johnny Shawnessy was hunting. In this story the earth itself acquired the mystical dimensions of a human face. An ideal being appeared in distant splendor above the valley of human years. Here was the meaning of man's aspiration woven into the very substance of the earth.

His sensation on first reading this famous American fable was much like the thrill he felt when he went one day into an office of the Court House with T. D. and saw hanging on the wall a map of Raintree County, colored and varnished, like the human anatomy in T. D.'s Office. It was the first time he had seen a map of his home earth, and he had a Columbian moment of discovery. The earth acquired shape, coherence, meaning. The road travelling before his house joined other roads, was part of an integrated system. The river coiled like the body of a snake, cutting from corner to corner of the County. The lake was a pool of green concentric circles in the very center of the County.

He had suddenly achieved a world. The dearly bought victory of man over the increate and stubborn earth was his. He had gazed at a map of his own life, the pattern of himself, securely bounded by the four walls of Raintree County. He held the whole great riddle in the focus of his eyes—naked, imminent, perfect.

He left the Court House feeling that he had almost discovered the eternal meaning buried in the debris of all his memories, in the changing seasons of Raintree County, in the streamdivided earth, in the faces of his father and mother, and in his own elusive self that had wandered out from the brightness of an everlasting summer and hunted for itself across the everlasting earth.

And so Johnny Shawnessy passed through the years of his childhood steeping himself in legends old and new. From this preoccupation came a dream that he dreamed repeatedly just before awakening and which he relinquished always with an emotion of regret. The dream itself was apparently the memory of a dream, an archetypal dream; perhaps that was why it was always much the same.

Dreaming, he was trying to recover the memory of a sacred place. He couldn't remember now in what summer he had been there. He must have been a child, though he had possessed vigor and desire more than a child's. He remembered only vaguely the temple whose circular roof was open to the summer so that the tree within might live. For a long time, he had possessed a golden bough and had meant to keep it for a token, all heavy with seed and fruit. He could not even remember the face of one whom he had known there in that tranquil summer. She had been beautiful, and, yes, assuredly, his desire had been more than a child's. And were not the morals of that maternal deity delightfully suspect? He had even forgotten all the names—the names equally of the tree, the goddess, and the shrine, the singular names which he knew he must have heard over and over. He had forgotten the name of the curious and curving pathway to the place. And he had even forgotten his own name, the special name that they had given him because he was the only one who had found the way. He had been amazed by the vast extent of the forest around him, the immense and silent grove steeped in twilight, through which weak sunrays filtering fell, and he remembered the distant and soft floor of the forest, and the trunks of trees, all oaks of an extinct species. Through that forest he had walked, and in its shadow he had lived, and there he had discovered the place of sacred waters. But then all this must have been a memory of something he had read or heard. If only once again he might return and stand where the slant rays touched with fire the topmost branches of the tree! Then perhaps a golden warmth would descend his body, and he would discover in the twilight of the trunk a goddess exquisitely formed, whose gold hair lay along the earth and whose precise face would stir him to recognition. Then perhaps he would recapture the word which had been from the beginning, which had awakened him from sleep and touched his ears with music and ecstasy, a word that quivered through the grove

AND CAUSED THE TREE TO SHIVER AND SEND DOWN

A RAIN OF YELLOW AND

UNUSUAL

DUST bloomed and drifted from President's hooves as the surrey drew abreast of the Old Home Place and went by without stopping. Distant explosions, linked and separate, began to intrude through the steady noise of hooves and wheels.

—Listen to them in town, Wesley said.

—We could always hear them on the Fourth from here, Mr. Shawnessy said.

—Was the Fourth any fun when you were a boy, Papa?

—It was a good Fourth. We took it even harder than you do today. We usually went into Freehaven early in the morning. Of course, the town was very different then. The Old Court House was there then and——

—What happened to it? Wesley asked.

—It burned down during the Civil War.

—What was it like?

—Well, it was a rather plain brick building, not nearly so big as the present court house. It was a rectangle in shape with some white wooden columns in front, Southern style, and a little wooden cupola.

—Did it have a clock and a flag?

—A flag, yes. But no clock.

Mr. Shawnessy remembered the Old Court House. It stood soft and clear in the air of a remembered summer, the young earth of Raintree County was beneath it, the ancient buildings of the Square enclosed it, the Court House Square was filled with people, the fronts of stores were gay with bunting, firecrackers burst. And the Old Court House was there, a flag was flying from the cupola, but there was no clock to tell the time of day.

The surrey was well past the Old Home Place. He could see the treebordered fringe of the Shawmucky, where the road made its immemorial jog and straightened out for the run into Freehaven.

Listen, it was all a dream, I know, of the Great War and of growing older and of all the faces of the children. The river crosses there under the bridge, the road jogs, firecrackers are crumping in the distant morning.

I must hurry down the road to the County Seat. I must hurry through the young morning of America. I must be there early and walk ceaselessly around the clockless Court House. I must press my eager young face close to the faces of the crowd. I must see my young tousled head reflected in the store windows. I must also go somewhere and get something hot and strong to eat.

I must find you there, too. I must look wistfully from a distance at your little puritan face with freckles on it. I must hunt you out in the strong light of the Court House Square. I shall not look you straight in the eye and say, I love you, because you will be taller than I.

In the Court House Square, the vender of tonics bestows lush and fragrant locks on all the true believers. The Professor puts his pointer to the Phrenological Chart. The band plays 'Yankee Doodle,' and a small boy sets off a big cracker under the Speaker of the Day.

In the Court House Square, the athlete stands with cocked arms bulging. By God, he will run any man in the County! By God, none shall beat him!

But I will walk swiftly and ceaselessly in the fringes of the crowd. My faunlike being shall be woven through the fabric of the crowd. They shall not any of them die or change.

And somewhere in the crowd, the harshvoiced, fierce, exciting crowd, I shall walk holding the little black book in which my name is written. And I shall hear words spoken in the Square, thin syllables of vanished summers, I shall hear the words before the words became Events, before the words became History. I didn't know it then, but the words were really the seeds of battles and of marches, the words were also love that is a shy flower opening beside remembered waters, the words were also dead men lying in the rain, bloated bodies between the cornrows in the beautiful July earth of America. I didn't know it then, but the words were seeds, falling at random in the Court House Square, falling through the summer air of Raintree County, and the strange fruit of the little seeding words was always love and death. But now I must hasten to the Square, for in Freehaven it is the Fourth of July, they are hanging out the flag with one and thirty stars, the band is playing 'Yankee Doodle' for

July 4— A —1854

BIG CROWD OF PEOPLE

HAD POURED INTO THE COURT HOUSE SQUARE

of Freehaven for the Fourth of July Celebration. Among them was Johnny Shawnessy, fifteen years old, bony and angular and beginning to bust out of his kneepants. His head looked too big for his body, his hair was a tangled mat of brightness, his cheeks and chin showed the beginnings of a beard and were sprinkled with little pimples. From a platform erected on the court house yard, a military band blasted out number after number, while the people came streaming from every corner of the County, into the foursided, sunflooded morning of the Square. There they walked with shining eyes, looking over their shoulders, craning their necks, bobbing out from behind buildings as if they were hunting for something.

Johnny Shawnessy was hunting for something too. Whenever he came to the Court House Square on festive days, he vaguely hoped for two things: that he would stand before the crowd a hero and be rocked with a thunder of hands; and that he would find in the crowd a lovely girl he had never seen before, who, perceiving at once his great soul through the callow veil of his fifteen years, would go with him to a place remote from the crowd, where she would take off her dress and all her petticoats for him, and he would be her impetuous lover, kneepants and all.

—Hello, Johnny.

The name was said in a manner softly personal. He turned around. A strange girl, half a head taller than he, was standing on the sidewalk with a boy he had never seen before.

—Nell!

Johnny hadn't seen Nell Gaither for years. When he was much smaller, he had gone to school with her and had seen her often at the Danwebster Church with her father and mother. Mrs. Gaither had been a fragile, lovely woman from a Connecticut family of means and culture. She had come with her husband in the great migration West, and they had settled in Raintree County in the late thirties to the hard existence of making a living from the earth. Nell had been the first child, and for a long time the only one. Johnny remembered how Nell had always seemed so much more ladylike than the other girls he knew, probably because of her mother's influence. Then when Nell was seven, Mrs. Gaither had died after the birth of a stillborn child, and Mr. Gaither had sent the girl back to her mother's family in the East. And that was the last Johnny had heard of her until now.

—Where did you come from, Nell? he asked.

—I'm back with Daddy, Nell said. He's married again, you know, and I'm going to live here for a while. O, by the way, Johnny, I want you to meet a friend of mine, Garwood Jones.

Garwood Jones was a large, sleek, florid boy, perhaps a year older than Johnny. He had a broad, smooth face, dark, wavy hair fragrant with oil, and blue eyes filled with faint amusement. He thrust out his hand and said in an incredibly big voice,

—Happy to make your acquaintance, John.

The greeting was both personal and patronizing.

—Pleased to meet you, Johnny said.

—What part of the County are you from, John?

Johnny told him, and the boy said that he used to live at Waycross in the southeast corner but that his family had long ago moved to Freehaven.

—Garwood is speaking on the program today, Johnny, Nell said.

—Just a few patriotic recitations, the boy said with arrogant humility.

Johnny didn't dislike Garwood Jones, but he envied the smooth, newly razored face, the deep voice, the long trousers, and the place on the Program of the Day.

—How did you and Nell get to know each other? Johnny said.

—O, I get to know all the pretty girls, John, Garwood said.

He laughed a throaty laugh. The flat of his hand fell affectionately between Johnny's shoulderblades.

In the old days, Johnny had never thought of Nell as especially pretty. Now he looked at her a little more closely. The thin, serious child was gone. Nell had her hair bound up like a woman's, showing her long white neck. A sort of small crazy hat teetered on her suncolored curls. Her face, which was rather small, was studiedly serene, the chin held high, the unusual, fleshy mouth primly closed. The very wide-apart green eyes, her most attractive feature, looked calmly down at him a little sideways past her nose, which was pert and covered with freckles. She had on a white shortsleeved dress. She had the steep breasts of a budding girl and was getting somewhat wide in the hips, although her waist was very slender and her arms were long, angular, and childlike.

She stood, right hand on hip and left hand over right hand, dangling a parasol, while her left foot was toed out to show her new shoe.

Johnny thought she looked a little dowdy and ridiculous, but when she spoke, her voice was very husky, grave, and sweet. He noticed especially the soft, personal way in which she said his name, as if she had practiced it.

—I'll see you at church, Sunday, Johnny, she said.

The small lofty face smiled. Nell suddenly shot her parasol open. The interview was at an end.

—Well, John, Garwood Jones said, I trust I will have the pleasure of seeing you again.

He removed his straw hat and made a stately bow, and he and Nell walked away toward a lemonade stand. Johnny stood watching Nell walk, her hips softly moving as if revolving around a center, while her long, slender back and primly held shoulders were motionless.

—Hey, Johnny!

His brother Zeke was waving from in front of the Saloon. In the middle of a crowd there, a young man stood, white teeth flashing from a brown bearded face. In one hand he held a beermug, and with the other he kept pushing back the brown shag of his hair. His skintight pants showed off the hard length of his legs and the great breadth of his whiteshirted chest and shoulders. The young man laughed and said in a harsh, high voice, as Johnny approached,

—I can beat any man or boy in the County, and here's five dollars says I can.

He buried his white teeth in the mug and came up, mouth and beard shining. A gold coin glinted in his free hand. A hush fell on the crowd. Two men removed their hats, perhaps to see better. Johnny joined Zeke on the edges of the crowd.

—I said I can lick any man or boy in this County.

—And he can do it too, a solemn, sharpfaced man confided to Johnny. Just like he says, can't none of 'em touch 'im. Flash Perkins kin outrun 'em all.

From this remark, Johnny gathered that the talk was about the annual Fourth of July Footrace by which the fastest runner in Raintree County was determined.

—Our boy from Prairie Township'll make yuh eat them words this afternoon, a voice in the crowd said.

—Who said that? Flash Perkins said.

His forehead shot up into ridges, his mouth went on smiling, his eyes never changed from the childlike, excited look. He shoved his way into the crowd.

—Hot darn! Zeke said. A fight!

The crowd withdrew leaving one man alone in a ring of red faces. The man, a tall gawky fellow, looked embarrassed and put upon. He extended his arm, his finger almost touching Flash Perkins' nose.

—Take it easy now, brother, he said. Better not start nothin' you cain't finish.

His voice was high and nervous.

—You the man that said that? Flash Perkins asked.

—Yes, I am. I said it, and I stick by it.

—Reckon you wouldn't want to cover that there statement with a little coin?

The man looked relieved.

—I cain't cover it by myself, but they's a bunch of us from Prairie will make up a pot for Pud Foster.

—Git a hat, said a voice.

—Here's a hat, said a voice.

—Who's here'll back Pud Foster from Prairie?

—I'll put in, a man said. He can beat any beersot from town any day.

Several men shoved their way in and began to talk bets. There was a frightful blast of sound. It was the band starting up again. They were playing 'Yankee Doodle.'

—Shucks, Zeke said. No fight.

—But that sure ought to be some race, Johnny said.

—What's going on, boys?

It was T. D. He was taller than anyone else in the crowd. His blond pointed beard was bobbing up and down. He was rubbing his hands together and smacking his lips.

—They're betting on a race, Johnny said.

—That's what I thought, T. D. said.

He pushed his way into the crowd.

—Gambling is a sin before the Lord, gentlemen. Put up your money.

—Put up your lip, you old she-goat, a man said.

The crowd roared.

—Pa's gittin' hisself into something, Zeke said. Looks like they might be a fight after all, and us in it.

—No harm done, Pop, Flash Perkins said. Here, give the old guy a drink.

—Who is that crazy old bastard, anyway? the solemn, sharpfaced citizen said to Zeke.

—That's my pa, Zeke said.

Zeke was seventeen and looked a man. His red hair bristled all directions.

—What's that? the man said.

—I said that's my father.

—O, the man said. Is that a fact?

He looked thoughtful and began to move away through the crowd.

—Young man, T. D. said to Flash Perkins, who was holding his beermug in one hand and a hatful of money in the other, don't you know that your body is a temple of the spirit and you defile it and pollute it with that devil's brew you have there?

Flash's forehead made ridges.

—If you say so, Pappy.

—Hello, Johnny.

It was Ellen Shawnessy, her face excited and curious, her small body straining on tiptoes to see over the shoulders of the crowd.

—What's T. D. doing? she asked.

—Pa's preaching a little at them.

T. D. went on talking awhile about the lusts of the flesh and the wages of sin. He clasped his hands behind his back in the usual way and teetered back and forth from heels to toes, smiling amiably at the crowd, his long blue eyes a little absent and noticing things that went on some distance away. His closing remarks were delivered in some haste, like a child's recitation.

—What are they betting about? Ellen whispered to Johnny.

—The Footrace, Johnny said.

—When is it?

—I don't know.

—Be sure not to let me miss it, she said.

—O.K., O.K., Reverend, I get it, Flash Perkins said. We were just foolin'.

T. D. bowed pleasantly, straightened his tie, and walked serenely down the street with Ellen. The crowd went right on arguing and making bets, only now they all moved into the Saloon and got drinks. Johnny could see through the batwing doors how they laughed and swatted each other's backs and how they kept wiping beer out of their mustaches.

—I hope he loses that race, Zeke said.

But Johnny somehow felt that Flash Perkins would win the race. He looked like the winner type.

—Ladies and Gentlemen, spare me a little of your precious time, boomed a rich voice from the court house lawn.

Behind a table loaded with brightcolored bottles, stood a man with noble black mane and heavy beard, unshorn, lustrous, magnificent.

—I trust you all perceive the object which I hold in my hand, the man said, as the boys joined the crowd.

—Yes, we see it, Perfessor.

—What is it?

—Well, what of it?

—It is nothing, the man said, but a bottle, a simple, unadorned, ordinary bottle. And yet, friends, this simple, plain, unadorned, and ordinary bottle contains in it a secret preparation, the miracle-worker of our age. Ladies and Gentlemen, may I have just a little of your precious time to describe to you the extree-ordinary virtues of the elixir contained in this bottle?

—Sure. Go on.

—Get to the point, Perfessor.

—I am getting to the point, the man said serenely, and judging, my good sir, from the condition of *your* scalp and hair, you would be wise to pay special heed to what I have to say.

The man who had said, Get to the point, was standing right beside Johnny. He was a short man, genteelly dressed. Singled out, he put his hand up and smoothed a wreath of hair fitted down on his bare dome.

—Now then, the speaker continued, I trust you will all permit me to indulge in a little personal reminiscence. I am sure that few of you will believe me when I tell you that not many years ago my head was fast approaching the condition of hairlessness that you behold in the gentleman on the front row and in several other domes which I see about me here and which are, in the words of the poet,

> Open unto the fields and to the sky,
> All bright and glittering in the smokeless air.

Now I think we will all agree that the good Lord never does anything without a purpose, and if he meant mankind to go about with his skull naked of hair, why did he bestow upon us this lush and luxuriant foliage that in our natural state starts and stands triumphantly, according to the words of the poet,

> With all its fronds in air?

Fellow Americans, the good Lord intended each and every one of us to have his hair and all of it too, for as the fellow said about his wife, She ain't much, but I mean to hang on to her if I can.

The crowd whahwhahed.

—Yes, Ladies and Gentlemen, I was once in the condition of several of you here. For about twenty years, my hair had been turning gray and had become very stiff and unpliant. Bald patches were appearing on my scalp, and the skin scaled off. Each time I brushed my hair, I found the brush matted with dry tufts of hair. I tried all the famous hair restoratives on the market, but they seemed to only aggravate my condition. Then a friend told me about Mrs. Allen's World Hair Restorer and reported to me the marvellous recoveries effected thereby. I will confess to you that I was very skeptical at first, but on the repeated importunities of my friend, I finally gave in and purchased a bottle of Mrs. Allen's World Hair Restorer. Ladies and Gentlemen, need I say more? Within a week or two, a noticeable change was apparent. My hair began to recover the black lustre it had in my younger days when a boy in the hills of western Virginia. My head became entirely clear of dandruff, and new hair grew where the old had been. You see before you today, Ladies and Gentlemen, a man whose pride and hair have been restored together and general health improved. Butler, my acquaintances often remark to me, where did you get the fine wig? But I assure you, friends, it is no wig.

—It looks like a wig to me, friend, the baldheaded man said.

—Pull it, friend, the vender said.

The baldheaded man walked right out of the crowd and carefully examined the speaker's head. He pulled hard.

—No sir, he said, that's no wig.

—You bet it isn't, the speaker said. It's hair, friend, live and lusty, and you can have a head like that too, friend.

—How can I, friend? said the baldheaded man, now standing beside the speaker.

—Very simple, friend. Purchase one bottle of Mrs. Allen's World Hair Restorer for one dollar and fifty cents, and I will personally guarantee that you will have the beginnings of a fine head of hair in a week or two.

—I'll take a bottle of that, the baldheaded man said.

He pulled out a dollar and a half and gave it to the speaker.

—And just to be sure that you get your money's worth, the speaker said, I am going to give away to you free, gratis, and for no extra charge this large bottle of Doctor Hostetter's Celebrated Stomach Waters, guaranteed to cure any and all diseases of the alimentary tract, nervous, respiratory, muscular, and circulatory systems—to wit, stomach ache, heartburn, dyspepsia, diarrhea, dysentery, dizziness, fainting spells, biliousness, piles, pimples, arthritis, lumbago, rheumatism, jaundice, kidney trouble, female complaints, and organic weaknesses caused by youthful indiscretion or the approach of old age. For the next ten minutes, to everyone who can get up here with a dollar and fifty cents, I will make this extra-special-gigantic-double-for-your-money offer of two bottles. Mrs. Allen's World Hair Restorer is also an excellent hair-dressing for the ladies.

—I'll take *two* orders, Perfessor, said the baldheaded man, who was still holding his money and had not yet got his hands on the bottle.

—Here you are, my friend, the man said.

He gave the baldheaded man four bottles and put the money in his pocket.

The baldheaded man opened a bottle of the hair-restorer, shot a little of the brown liquid into the cup of his hand, and rubbed it on his head. There was a silence. A hundred eager faces watched the little man with the shiny bald head.

—It tingles, said the baldheaded man.

—You bet it does, friend, the vender said. It tingles, and that means it's taking already. Use that bottle religiously, friend, and I predict the barbers of this community will get a lot of your money before the year is out.

—But he ain't from this community, a man next to Johnny said.

—Where's he from? another man said.

—I dunno, the first man said, but I never seen him before.

—And, said the vender, let me be the first to congratulate you on the great discovery which you have just made. Your wife will be a happy woman, friend.

—I'm not married, friend, said the baldheaded man.

—You will be, friend, you will be! said the vender magnificently. No woman in town will be able to resist you when you grow the shiny, black, and vigorous head of hair that will spring up in response to the stimulating power of this wonderful hair restorative.

Johnny Shawnessy felt happy because the baldheaded man had discovered the secret for getting back his hair; he was very happy, too, to see how people flocked up and bought bottle after bottle from the vender. He could not remember ever having seen so much money in so short a time.

—How can he make any money, giving that other bottle away? Johnny asked.

—I reckon he does it for fun, Zeke said. Look how he's enjoyed hisself.

—I wish I had a dollar and fifty cents, Johnny said. I'd like to get a couple of bottles.

—But you got all your hair, and you ain't sick, Zeke said.

—Just the same—— Johnny said.

Just then the band struck up again, and the two boys moved reluctantly away. They watched the baldheaded man withdraw from the crowd. Moving along close to this person whose scalp now seemed to shine with the promise of reviving hair, they were a little surprised when he stopped at a small tent on the other side of the Square and went in. They waited, and in a moment, he came out again, carrying a large board frame, which he hung over a nail on a maple tree beside the tent. The frame bore a huge picture of a head, seen in profile and with all the upper part, beginning on a level with the eye, divided into sections, in each of which a word was written. Some of the words were Acquisitiveness, Alimentativeness, Amativeness, Cautiousness, Sublimity, Spirituality, Self-Esteem, Approbativeness. Above the picture were the words

PROFESSOR GLADSTONE, WORLD-RENOWNED PHRENOLOGIST.

At the bottom were the words

KNOW THYSELF.

The little man re-entered the tent and reappeared with a pointer, an armload of small clothbound books, and a cowbell, which he began to ring. A large crowd gathered.

—Allow me, said the baldheaded man, to introduce myself, Ladies and Gentlemen. I am Professor Horace Gladstone. Those of you who may have heard me lecture lately in the great city of Cincinnati will pardon me if I repeat some of the things I said there to the distinguished company which assembled in the great lecture hall of that metropolis of the West.

Now I have a question to ask each and every intelligent person gathered here. Friend, are you everything today that you would like to be? Are you as rich as you wish? Do you excel in the social graces? Do you radiate that personal magnetism which makes the great to respect you and the humble to acknowledge your superiority? Why, friends, *why* are there so many blighted and unhappy lives, so many stunted souls, so many men and women today in this great and glorious country of ours who are something less than they had hoped to be in the blithe optimism of their youth?

Ladies and Gentlemen, I can answer that question. It is through a simple ignorance of the scientific principles that regulate human life. O, you say, Perfessor, don't go giving me any high-falutin' language about science because I can't understand it. Friends, it is my happy good fortune to have it within my power to open up to each and every one of you all the marvellous secrets of a great new science, by which you can achieve, like thousands before you, complete self-knowledge and self-control. That science, Ladies and Gentlemen, is the great new science of Phrenology.

Now we all agree, do we not, that no man can or does exist in rational society without a brain. May I say that in Kentucky, whence I have lately come, I felt some disposition to modify that statement, but——

The Professor waited for the applause and laughter of the crowd to subside.

—But I see no need to do so for the intelligent and enlightened concourse that I see before my eyes. Now, we all know that the brain is the instrument of every mental act, just as every movement of the body has to be performed by a muscle. Certain areas of the brain control certain human faculties and are large or small in proportion to the development of the faculties they control. Thanks to the great experiments and studies of Professors Gall, Spurheiz, and Fowler, it is now possible to say with the strictest accuracy which part of the brain controls which faculty. These facts are now available to all. Nothing is simpler, once these principles are known, than to apply them.

I have myself become a specialist in the science of Phrenology. I have examined the heads of three Presidents and many other great and distinguished heads here and abroad, not excepting the crowned heads of Europe. By helping people to become better acquainted with their strong and weak points, I have been able to direct them to a fuller exercise or restraint of certain faculties. Many hundreds and thousands of people have already benefited from this instruction. Penniless paupers have become the possessors of uncounted pelf. Timid and backward souls have sought and won the hands of the richest and most ravishing maidens. Old men have recovered the lost joys of their juvenescence. Gentlemen and Ladies, I am here in your fair little city of Middletown——

—This ain't Middletown, said a voice in the crowd. It's Freehaven.

—Freehaven, said the Professor. Thank you, friend, for the correction. I am here in this fair little city of Freehaven for a limited time. I have a small stock of books left over from my travels in the great cities of the West, and I should like to get rid of them as rapidly as I can. Now I wish I could give each and every one of you a private and personal analysis of your phrenological faculties. Alas, my friends, due to the small time I have at my disposal, I must forego this signal pleasure. But I have here between my two hands a little book that contains all the advice needful. It is perfectly within the comprehension of every one and each of you. On the inside page of this book is a copy of the chart which you see hanging here, and a table of the phrenological faculties. Now the book is entirely self-explanatory, but I am willing to give a little demonstration here of Phrenological Analysis, if someone in the crowd will be so kind as to volunteer.

There was a silence.

—Come, don't be embarrassed, the Professor said. It's absolutely free of charge, and furthermore I will give to anyone who so volunteers for the instruction of this amiable and enlightened company one of these books at half-price instead of the usual price of one dollar and fifty cents.

Johnny Shawnessy felt himself propelled from behind out of the crowd. He heard Zeke laughing, and he was about to duck back, but the Professor was tapping him smartly on the shoulder with his pointer.

—Yes, my boy. Step right up here. I am about to do you a great favor, my boy. O, that I had had the inestimable blessing of a Phrenological Analysis when I was your age! How old are you, my boy?

—Fifteen, Johnny said. I didn't mean to——

—Perfectly all right, my boy. Just come up on this platform and sit down here on the edge of this table.

A firecracker exploded, and the band struck up a number. The Professor waved his hands to indicate that nothing could be accomplished until the band was through. For the first time in his life, Johnny had the sensation of being extracted from the crowd and placed above it in naked isolation. The Court House Square was converging upon him; he was being absorbed by its manifold bright eyes. The band stopped playing.

—Ladies and Gentlemen, said the little man, we have an interesting head here, a very interesting head. To you, this may be only another head, more or less, but to the practiced eye of the phrenologist, this boy's character and potentialities—nay, his whole past, present, and future—are legible in the geography of his skull. Now, then, just cast your eyes on this chart a moment, friends, and notice this section of the head below the eye.

The pointer touched the glazed, segmented head and underlined the word LANGUAGE.

—According to phrenological principles, friends, we are to measure the degree of prominence which these various areas of the skull possess and we can determine thereby the capabilities of the person we are dealing with. Now then——

A fat hand touched moistly the region below Johnny's eyes.

—Open your eyes, boy. Don't sit there blinking like an owl.

As usual the sun hurt his eyes; there was much light in the Square.

—Extraordinary, the man said. Very.

The crowd drew closer. People gathered from far back.

—Very, very interesting. Please observe, folks. Very long eyes and set somewhat forward in the head. Cheekbones prominent. In a boy of fifteen, the development is quite unusual. Now, then, let us turn to the book.

The man expertly thumbed the book.

—Here we are. 'Such people are (I quote) exceedingly expressive in all they say and do, have a most expressive countenance, eye, and manner in everything; have a most emphatic way of saying and doing everything, and thoroughly impress the various operations of their own minds on the minds of others; use the very word required by the occasion; are intuitively grammatical, even without study, and say oratorically whatever they attempt to say at all; commit to memory by reading or hearing once or twice; learn languages with remarkable facility; are both fluent and copious, even redundant and verbose,' and so forth, and so forth.

There was a stir in the crowd.

—Here, the man said, are pictures illustrating these developments. An engraving of the great English author Charles Dickens, whose linguistic characteristics are excessively developed.

—Say, Perfessor, Zeke said from the crowd, you ain't fer wrong about that boy. He's got a head for memorizing like nothin' you ever seen.

—There you are, the little bald man said, Phrenology never lies. And I was about to say that even if the boy hadn't shown any faculty in that direction, it was high time he cultivated his natural aptitude for it. But to pass on.

The Professor went all over Johnny's head, pointing out interesting hills and hollows and putting numbers in a chart that was in the front of one of the books. Finally, the Professor had worked clear over the top of Johnny's head and down to the base of his skull behind.

—Mirthfulness, the Professor said. Very large. This boy ought to be the fiddle of the company.

—Ain't that T. D. Shawnessy's son? a man said.

—Smart little cuss, someone said.

—What a cute boy! a woman said.

The band blew up; it was another march. Everyone began talking very loud and strong. People were laughing violently. Somebody set off a firecracker under a fat man in the crowd and blew his hat off. A horse got scared and began dragging a buggy down the street. The band finished its number, and by that time the Professor had made another discovery.

—Very remarkable! the Professor said in a loud voice. For a boy of his age too. Most extree-ordinary! Unusual, to say the least.

—What is it, Perfessor?

The crowd was now participating freely in the examination.

—Let us in on it, too, Perfessor.

—Has he got lice?

—Ladies and Gentlemen, the Professor said, please observe the remarkable development of this boy's head at the base of the skull. The lump of AMATIVENESS is remarkably distended.

—What does that mean, Perfessor?

—What does that mean, friend? To put it bluntly, this young gentleman is going to be an extra-special catch for the ladies.

The Professor winked and rubbed his hands jovially together. People in the crowd sniggered. Various men felt the back of their skulls.

—Hey, girls, Zeke said, I got a lump back there big as a duck's egg.

—Say, Perfessor, said a little man thrusting forward, and presenting his head for inspection. Feel that there. What do you think of that?

With obliging hand the Professor palped the back of the little man's skull and whistled.

—Hey, Perfessor, how about me? another man said. Feel that.

—Now, wait a minute, folks, the Professor said, suddenly walking back to the platform and grabbing an armload of books. Much as I would like to, I can't subject each and all of you to a personal scrutiny, but this book here will answer all your questions. For those whose various organs and faculties are underdeveloped, rules for enlargement are given. Know thyself, said the great philosopher Socrates to the Athenians in the Golden Age of Greece. And I say to you, Know thyself, fellow Americans, in this great age of Progress and Perfection, in this greatest and fairest republic the world has ever known. God bless her on the day of her birth and glorious founding! One dollar, folks, just one round dollar—reduced from a dollar and a half!

As if by prearrangement, the band exploded with 'Hail, Columbia! Happy Land!' and with moisture in his eyes, the Professor began to distribute books as fast as he could, at the same time dropping dollars into a box on the table. Johnny sat for a while watching from the platform how the people all rushed up and pulled dollars out of their pockets, rudely grabbing for books in their haste.

—While they last! While they last! the Professor said. One dollar, friends, while they last! One hundred and fifty-four illustrations. *Phrenological Self-Instructor.*

People who hadn't even heard what the Professor said fought their way through and bought a book. The pile was almost gone, and Johnny Shawnessy began to feel alarmed.

—Know thyself! Know thyself! One dollar. While they last.

The pile was gone.

—One moment, folks, the Professor said. I have a small reserve supply that I had hoped to save for sale in the great city of St. Louis.

He disappeared in the tent and reappeared immediately with another armload of books. When the last sale had been made, there were still some books left. Johnny went up to the man and put down seventy-five cents.

—It's a dollar, my friend, the Professor said.

—But you said I could have it half-price. Half of a dollar and a half is——

—Unusual development of the bumps of Calculation and Eventuality, the Professor said.

He laughed at his own good joke.

—Here's your book, boy, all marked. You've a good head on your shoulders there, son. What is your name, my boy?

Johnny told him, and the Professor took a pencil from his coat pocket and on the title page where it said THE CHART AND CHARACTER OF he wrote on blank lines provided for the purpose:

John Wickliff Shawnessy

As Marked By

Professor Horace Gladstone,

July 4, 1854

—I predict a great future for you, my boy, the Professor said, tossing the three quarters deftly into the air.

He bit the tip off a cigar.

—Smoke?

—No, thanks, sir.

—Never start it, said the Professor. Filthy habit. Yes, a great future, my boy. Tell me, son, is there a place around here where one can obtain a little liquid refreshment for the stimulation of a jaded physique?

—The Saloon is right over there.

—Good day, boy, the Professor said and walked off briskly, landing smartly on his heels, his toes turned slightly up and out.

—Ladies and Gentlemen, said at that moment a rich, oily voice from the other side of the Square, spare me a little of your precious——

Johnny walked away holding the little book in his hand. For a few bright coins, dropped in a wooden cigar box, a future of wonderful self-mastery had been opened up. In the presence of the people he had become a child of prophecy; his consecration had been sanctified by the majestic adjective 'scientific' and the formidable epithet 'phrenological.' Here, suddenly and by accident on the Court House Square, there had been a confirmation of something Johnny Shawnessy had always secretly believed—that he was destined to be a great man and to find one day the key to all knowledge. For a while, he felt jealous of all the other people who had purchased the same cheap ticket to intellectual beatitude, but when he saw the innocent, shy joy on their faces, as they wandered somewhat confusedly like himself in the Court House Square, clutching their *Self-Instructors,* he was thrilled to think that he was to be one of a whole community of Americans working together toward the creation of a perfect republic.

He didn't have time to look over the book at all, because the Program for the Day was beginning. He and Zeke went over and found seats in a big space in the assembly ground south of the Court House, and all the people sat and listened to a man read the Declaration of Independence. Then the chairman of the program introduced the outstanding boy orator Garwood Jones. Talking in a thundering, artificial way and waving his arms, Garwood brought the crowd down with gems of American oratory, including the peroration of Webster's Reply to Hayne.

Wearing his Mexican War uniform and all his medals, Captain Jake Jackson, Raintree County's war hero, got up and gave a very dramatic speech about the security of the Nation. He was a virile young man, of open, fearless countenance. He stood very straight with one leg slightly forward and spoke with chest expanded. He said that the Union was threatened from within and without, but he reminded his hearers that the last bunch who tangled with the sovereign authority of the United States of America had got one devil of a drubbing, in which he, Jake Jackson, had taken, as they knew, a humble part. And he was there to say that although he was a man who loved peace, he, Jacob J. Jackson, would personally Gird on the Sword and once more Bare his Patriot Breast to the Sleet of Battle ere he would permit one corner of the Dear Old Flag to be Dragged in the Dirt. Johnny applauded violently and was angry when an older man close by said he was getting goddam tired of young Jackson's heroics and fuh Christ's sake, did he think he fought the Mexican War singlehanded?

The Honorable Somebody or Other was introduced for the Address of the Day. He spoke for two hours, beginning in the usual vein but getting louder, hoarser, and more eloquent all the time as he talked about slavery and the South.

In those days everyone was excited about the Kansas-Nebraska Bill. The word had come through only a day or so before that Congress had made the bill a law. Johnny wasn't exactly certain what the bill said, but it appeared that land once saved for freedom was going to be opened up for slavery. The Orator of the Day made it out so that you thought of a poisonous black flood boiling up out of the South, and here were people trying to build walls against it, and then one of the people—and a Northerner to boot—Stephen A. Douglas, had gone yellow on them, and let the flood come through, and now there was nothing to stop it anywhere.

Those days, there was a strange spirit abroad in the land. It was not uncommon for families to stop talking to each other over political questions. T. D., who was always fighting some kind of evil or other, talked with a singular fierceness about certain people who were perfectly willing that part of the human race should be in chains, if it meant a few more dollars in *their* pockets or if they didn't have to see it happen under *their* noses. The problem was spatial, geographical—like Phrenology. In a section of the country below a certain line people kept slaves. You could draw a line across the Nation, and half of it was white and half was black. And now that they had passed the Kansas-Nebraska Bill, it was all right for the black part to go over into the white part if it could.

The man on the platform said that that was exactly what would happen.

—Fellow Americans, he said, I am addressing you in one of the darkest hours that has confronted our great republic since those glorious days when Washington was nursing the tiny flickering flame of our freedom in a tattered tent in the windy wilderness of Valley Forge. It is a time when, if necessary, a man should put aside wife and child, leave the hearth of his home, and go resolutely forth to do battle for the preservation of those great principles upon which this republic was founded and which we have just heard read to us from that immortal document, the Declaration of Independence.

—Let them alone, and they'll leave us alone, shouted a voice from the crowd.

—Throw that guy out! yelled other voices.

—It is a time, said the speaker, to gird on armor and the sword. Our most pious blessing and our most fervent hopes must go with those courageous spirits who are at this moment giving up all they have to rush into the newly opened territories of Kansas and Nebraska to insure that when those territories are petitioning for membership in the Union of the States, no shadow of that cursed blight whose ancient crime has stained the otherwise perfect beauty of our institutions shall sully the virginal banners of their statehood.

The orator went on and on, and the afternoon waned, and when he finished, the formal program was over. But men kept on making speeches. One of them said that he was just passing through on his way to Jackson, Michigan, where a gathering of publichearted citizens was going to talk very seriously about the growing threat to our free institutions and consider the feasibility of creating a new political party. Another man got up and said that the existing Whig party was adequate to meet the threat to the security of the Nation, but he was booed and heckled by Democrats all the way through. A Democrat who succeeded him could not get halfway through his speech and became so angry that he leaped off the platform and got into a fight with one of his persecutors.

Johnny and Zeke rushed over to the neighborhood of the disturbance, and the crowd stormed and shouted. Johnny got lost from Zeke and never did get close enough to see the fight, but he saw some people leading off a man with a bloody mouth, who was weeping and shaking his fist and yelling,

—I'll beat his goddam head off, goddamn him!

Johnny finally found Zeke, who showed where his knuckles were skinned and said earnestly,

—I just got that there from beating up on a damn Democrat.

Later they saw T. D. standing in the middle of a group of men, including the man who was on his way to Jackson, Michigan.

—Friends, the man was saying, I am not just using a figure of speech when I say to you that here in the North we are going to all hang together or hang separately. The South has opened this question up, and they mean to keep it open. It has become a sectional issue. Men, there will be bloodshed before this thing is over.

—God forbid! T. D. said. Personally, I take a hopeful view of the situation. I don't think it will ever come to that. Americans will never fight one another.

—Pardon me, my friend, said the man, a sober white-faced person in a tailcoat and a high black hat. But I'm afraid you take too bright a view of the whole thing. They're fighting now in Kansas, and the whole nation will be at war unless something is done to keep the hotheads of the South in check. It's getting to be all or nothing with them.

—Personally, said another man, whose face was working with anger, I think we'll just have to go down there and beat the hell out of 'em.

—That's just what they're saying about us, the man said. How long do you think we can exist as a nation, pulling two separate ways and fighting over the new territory? Something has got into the life-blood of the Nation. It's a poison, and a black one, and it has diseased the whole body politic. What it will come to I don't know, but I see dark days ahead.

—Say what you will, T. D. said, speaking calmly and brightly, but Americans will never fight each other. We will resolve our difficulties peacefully.

—I hope so, friend, said the man in the top hat. But what will you do if the South prefers to secede from the Union rather than submit to laws that don't protect her peculiar institution?

—They may talk of it, T. D. said, but they will never do it.

Johnny agreed with his father. It really didn't seem possible that a part of the country could separate and not be a part of the country. How could that be? Could an amputated leg grow a new body? T. D. was right. Yes, it was all only words spoken in the Court House Square. None of those words seemed so important as the word 'Phrenology,' which provided a clearcut, scientific route to individual and social perfection. He was hoping to get an opportunity to read his *Self-Instructor* and see what all the words meant that were parts of his head, but the next thing he knew, Zeke ran up, yelling,

—The race is starting!

Naked to the waist and barefooted, Flash Perkins stood in the middle of a crowd at a street intersection one block from the Square.

—What do you think this is, Flash—a prize fight? someone yelled as the two boys came up.

For answer, Flash struck a pose, balled fists up. The muscles of his cocked arms bulged circularly. The afternoon bathed his body with a young radiance. He seemed stronger and more real than anything else in the exploding vortex of the Fourth of July.

—God, don't he think he's some punkins! said a man next to Johnny.

—Struttin' aroun' like a damn bull on show, said another man. I hope to hell he gets beat and beat proper.

—Pud Foster'll beat 'im, damn 'im, said the first man. They say this here Perkins has been drinkin' his guts full all day and can't hardly walk.

—Seems to me he walks all right, the first man said.

—Yeh, but can he run?

—If he's drunk, maybe it'd be smart to take some of his money, said the first man.

—Damn right it would be!

It got around the crowd that Perkins was filled to the ears and could hardly stand, and a lot of men began to take some of the Perkins money.

Meanwhile Flash Perkins had gone over to a nearby buggy and then back to the starting line. His hairline jumped up each time he smiled. His eyes, full of drunkenness and goodnatured insolence, had never lost the childlike, excited look.

—They's a young lady over here, he said, wants to bet somebody five dollars a certain galoot name of Orville Perkins, better known as Flash, will win this here race. Person'ly, I respect the sex too much to doubt this young lady's opinion, and I'll add another five dollars to her bet and bet anybody here that I can beat any man in Raintree County—or anywhere else, by God!—and let's see the color of his coin.

—Christ amighty! he's drunk! the first man said.

A rather dowdy girl in the buggy fanned herself vigorously.

—It must be her, that one over there, Zeke said. She's some looker.

—I'll bet he gets her regular, a man in the crowd said.

Those days, there was always someone in the crowd who took a cynical view of things.

All of a sudden a man walked into the street with a pistol in his hand.

—Ladies and Gentlemen, he yelled, the Annual Fourth of July Footrace is ready to start. The contestants are . . .

The runners lined up, the crowd began pushing out of the street, the starter's pistol went off, and everyone yelled and pushed and shoved down toward the Square where the race was to end. Johnny got a passing glimpse of Flash Perkins, white teeth bared, fists churning, far ahead of his competitors as he ran toward a distant string.

There was a vast yelling in the Court House Square, and several cannon crackers blew up simultaneously. The band played 'Hail to the Chief.'

When Johnny and Zeke got to the Square, they saw Flash Perkins on the shoulders of a throng. He was borne toward a platform where a girl sat holding a ring of oakleaves. Bare to the waist, sweating, magnificent, he accepted the circlet of victory and fitted it down over his tangled hair. His teeth were clenched on an unlit cigar.

—Speech! yelled the crowd.

—It was easy, folks, Flash said. They give me a good race, but like I said, I can beat any man in Raintree County.

—Hello, Johnny.

It was his mother. She had been standing at the finish line. Her eyes were still shining with the excitement of the race.

—That Perkins boy is the fastest runner I ever seen, she said.

She looked a little wistfully at the broadshouldered victor sitting on top of a crowd of men and boys, puffing his cigar. Perhaps she was remembering her own fleetfooted days. It had been a long time since Johnny had seen his mother run a race.

Everyone was crazy with excitement. Johnny and several other halfgrown boys organized races on the court house lawn. Johnny ran wildly through the crowd, hoping someone would notice how fast he was for his size.

Later he saw a man who was walking through the streets with a big sign saying,

GIVE A PENNY FOR WASHINGTON'S MONUMENT!
MAKE YOUR COUNTRY BEAUTIFUL!

The man gave a short speech:

—The Washington Monument has reached a height of 154 feet of the projected 500. A national appeal is being made to the people to finance the erection of this beautiful and costly monument. Contribution boxes will be found here and there all over the Square. Remember the Father of Our Country on the day of our Country's birth, and let us all contribute generously and freely to the erection of this great shaft. First in War, First in Peace, and First in the Hearts of his Countrymen.

That night there was a fireworks display on the court house yard. Rockets rose over the dark town, burst into sparks, and went down, feebly flaming, in distant fields. Some exhibition pieces were hung on trees, and the climax of the whole day came with a contraption called 'The Glorious Union.' It was supposed to burn like a lot of stars and stripes in the shape of a shield, but it fizzled at first.

—It ain't goin' to go, everyone said.

Then it did go after all; in fact it caught on fire and blew up all at once with a terrific bang.

As they drove home that night, Johnny told T. D. about the book on Phrenology.

—What do you think about it, Pa? Is it any good?

—Sounds scientific, T. D. said. I seen the man giving you a going-over. Of course, it might of been a fraud. You shouldn't of spent all that money for it, John. You could of looked at someone else's book.

Rob, the oldest boy, said he heard a fellow say that the phrenology man and the vender of hair tonic had both been at Middletown just a day or two before and that they had put on the same act they did in Freehaven. The baldheaded man had pretended to buy hair tonic from the vender just the same way, and they made the same remarks, and the baldheaded man was just as bald now as he was then, no more and no less. Johnny was a little disturbed at this, but T. D. took a serene view of the matter.

—Probably just a story, he said. Why would anybody want to do that? Besides, he was practically giving those bottles away at that price. I have spent my life studying the beneficent effects of botanical medicines, and the ingredients in those bottles sounded good.

T. D. talked a good deal about the condition of the country.

—This here new party they plan to form up there in Michigan may be just what we need, he said. I've voted the Whig ticket faithful for twenty-five years, but it seems to me we need stronger stuff now.

If they can just get some big man to head the new party up, someone, say, like John C. Frémont, who is, in my opinion, the Greatest Living American, why, we might bring the country right out of the fix it's in.

—Things will work out all right, Ellen said.

Johnny Shawnessy looked up at the purple night thicksown with stars that brooded warm and yellow over Raintree County. Yes, things would work out all right. He closed his eyes and seemed to see, ascending in a starless night, the thin, bright streaks of rockets. So would the years go speeding through the purple night of time and bring him all good things before they dropped, feebly flaming, in the distant meadows of the future. So would he too some day know fame and fortune and a great love, and the people in the Court House Square would cheer him. Time and the secret earth of Raintree County would bring all good fruits to him who knew the secret. One day, he would be the fastest runner in Raintree County, because he willed it to be so. One day he would stand with breast expanded, bright with medals, and the crowds would cheer the savior of the Nation. One day he would have the lucid self-understanding that would enable him to say and do everything that he desired, and he would become greater than Charles Dickens or Thomas Carlyle or even William Shakespeare, and he would speak and write words that would resound along the corridors of time forever. And the Court House Square would give place to a more spacious arena, there would be domed tremendous buildings, steps ascending, a platform bigger than was ever seen in Freehaven. And a tall monument would pierce the sky, erected in his memory. All things could be accomplished by him who had the key, who knew the secret, who could pronounce the talismanic word. And in that shining future, he would stand among the greathearted citizens of a perfect America, their heads would be bright with lush and streaming locks, they would all be superbly phrenological in the greatest republic the world had ever seen. And somewhere too in that golden day a vaguely beautiful girl was waiting, her bright hair streamed on delicate shoulders and steep breasts, and on her fruity lips was the highly personal and softly uttered word 'Johnny.'

When they went to get out of the wagon at the Home Place, Johnny knocked something over.

—Careful there, John, T. D. said. Here, let me have that stuff.
It was a couple of bottles of

MRS. ALLEN'S WORLD HAIR RESTORER AND
DR. HOSTETTER'S CELEBRATED
STOMACH

WATERS of the Shawmucky River flowed beneath the clattering board bridge. The surrey passed over and, jogging southwest, started along the quarter-mile stretch through the valleyground in the great bend of the river. Reeds, swampgrass, thistles grew where the town of Danwebster had been before the War. Across the river, due south, Mr. Shawnessy could see the hill and the white stones of the graveyard.

—Well, children, he said, feeling old and inarticulate, here's where I used to shine when I was a boy. Here's where the old town was.

—I don't see a thing of it, Will said.

Weeds, swampgrass, thistles, and the river. All is gone. And where is the young Shawnessy, the lover of the river, the budding bard of Raintree County? Where are the *Complete Works* in a single volume, with biographical preface and notes? Where are the pilgrim thousands and the graven stone beside the river? *Good friend, for Jesus' sake forbear——*

—All around here, Mr. Shawnessy was saying, motioning vaguely with his hand, his voice fading, was the little town of . . .

DANWEBSTER ON THE SHAWMUCKY

(Epic Fragment from Preface to *The Complete Works of John Wickliff Shawnessy*)

A vague rapture fills the breast of the pilgrim, as he approaches the very earth which was the birthplace and burial spot of the greatest bard of all time. And indeed these pastoral glades seem as undesecrated by the hand of man as erst they did, so many years ago, when an obscure stripling sauntered through the rural glades, never dreaming that one day his name would be the brightest and loftiest star in all the constellations of the great.

Let us follow a little with reverent feet and pensive tread the windings of this little stream. Each bend and shallow is sanctified to the memory of a great name. In this deep pool beneath a hoary oak, we muse, the young Shawnessy perhaps did plunge and swim. Here his shouts mingled with those of his village companions. Perhaps he came to this haunt sometimes to escape the vigilant eye and stout ferule of the village scholarch, never dreaming that his own name would become both bane and blessing to generations of schoolboys. On the limb of this ancient oak, beside the circling waters of the Shawmucky, perhaps he swung in sportive play. In this open space, he urged the festive ball. How often, too, did he not walk, solitary and pensive, beside the river, bearing perchance a few stray leaves of paper and a quill, stopping now and then to indite the first utterances of a muse that has had no peer in all the annals of mankind!

Then let us proceed farther until we reach the thrice-enchanted ground where stood in ancient days the little village of Danwebster, in whose purlieus the young bard must often have walked, a beardless stripling upon whom, even then, we must believe there dwelt some halo of potential greatness. What unrecorded words, flung random on the ears of laughing comrades, betokened the genial humor, which, running the entire gamut from rude and ridiculous to subtle and sophisticate, was destined to be a perpetual wonder and entertainment for the generations of mankind?

Here, too, along the meanderings of the dulcet Shawmucky, he must have felt the first raptures of love—love, the most holy passion of the human breast, love, which he was later to express in the immortal verses of his great productions.

Aye, it is sacred ground, every inch of it. And we are happy indeed to make one with the thousands of reverent pilgrims who pay each year this tribute to the eternal greatness of the human spirit, which can cause to flower unexpectedly the rarest growth of all the ages on the banks of . . .

The Shawmucky River went south from the road, making its great bend, and returned to meet the surrey at the second bridge. The river flowed beneath the bridge, it was choked with bushes and mudbars, it was a length of savage, swarming life through the cornlands of the County.

—I thought you were going to stop at the graveyard, Wesley said.

—On the way back.

He looked up and down the river, sniffing. The bridge was like a crossroads. The lazy highway of the river beckoned, luring down banks and shoals of memory. Now briefly, the river lay again across his life, opaque and green, a serpent water.

On the banks of the Shawmucky, I had a vision of beauty. I held the river deity between my hands, it was a white flesh and lovely, its eyes were green, but this was long ago.

Little river of the blurred and murmurous name, you still rise from your Delphic cavern in the northeastern corner of the County and come uncoiling to the lake, with greater and greater divagations. Curious fleshes squawk, shriek, spout seed, die, and decay in your reedy marge. But where is the brighthaired boy who lay beside your waters, beholder of beauty in the antique summertime before the War? Where is the innocent young man, beloved of the gods, whose name was secret like your own and carried from afar?

On the banks of the Shawmucky River, I had a vision of beauty. I slept near the earth of the three mounds. I slept and dreamed beside the Indian river.

Yes, I remember now how I came down from haying in the long summers before the War—the smell of the clover was sweet on the upland meadows—and gave my body to your cold arms. O, circling goddess tracing a word of prophecy on the earth of Raintree County, you took the warm seed and the sweat from my body, you loved the plunge of mortals in your cool waters.

I had a vision of beauty on the banks of the Shawmucky River. What dream was that I dreamed of summertime and cities far away, and of corn growing in the valleyplains? What civilization of the maize did I introspect beside the little snakeriver of Raintree County?

On the banks of the Shawmucky, I had a vision of beauty. I lay at the brink of the river. I shut my eyes against the greening brightness. I lay in soft grass. I was sleeping.

I had a vision of beauty

Summer— FLOWING —1856

FROM DISTANT

TO DISTANT SUMMER, THE RIVER

was a place of archaic lifeforms and primitive sounds, and it was a cold green flowing and a place for beautiful nakedness that summer. That summer Johnny Shawnessy was seventeen years old. His body shot up like a stalk of July corn, he got his man's height of six feet, his shoulders widened, his arms and legs lengthened and were covered with light hair, his beard had to be shaved. Often in the afternoon, when he had finished working on the farm, he would go barefooted, dressed in blue jeans, shirt, and straw hat down the road to where the river approached from the north, and then cutting across a field would come out on the bank of the Shawmucky. He was free then from the geometry of fences, roads, and railroads, and he plunged naked into the river, re-entering some ancestral part of himself.

The river was the oldest pathway of the County, a place of frogs, fish, waterbirds, turtles, muskrats, coons, wildcats, groundhogs. The life within and upon its banks had not changed for centuries. And the river's name was the oldest name in Raintree County.

In fact, 'Shawmucky' was the only Indian name left in the County. No one knew for sure what the original Indian word was or meant. Some agent of the first land-office in the County, writing the name of the river on the earliest land-deeds, spelled it Shawmucky. In this disguise of English misspelling and mispronunciation lurked a vagrant Indian word, a name never spelled but only spoken, a relic of pure language, the utterance of a vanished people. For within two or three years after the settlers came to the County, the Indians were forever gone.

Johnny Shawnessy probably had a better guess about the river's name than anyone else as he was the only person in the County for years who made any research into the Indian culture. He finally decided that the river's name was related to the Indian word 'Shakamak,' meaning long fish or eel. There was a Shakamak River in southern Indiana; and in the northern part of the state, an Eel River, which in the Miami tongue had been called the Kenapocomoko, or River of Snake Fish.

The only drawback to Johnny's theory was the fact that he never found an eel in the Shawmucky River.

Johnny's interest in the Indians was stimulated by the poem *Hiawatha,* which he read not long after its publication in 1855. He wished to emulate Longfellow by writing an epic of the people who had given his state a name and who had left the music of their forest language on most of the important rivers of the Middle West, from the Ohio to the Mississippi. Yet the Indians, who had lived less than fifty years before in Raintree County, had vanished utterly, leaving only a few traces, almost all, as it happened, along the Shawmucky River and close to Johnny's home.

In that summer when he acquired the form of a man, Johnny found a favorite place on the river where it veered away from the road not far from the Shawnessy farm and ran northerly more than a mile as if it intended to flow out of the top of the County. Here on both banks of the stream, he used to find arrowheads and stone heads of tomahawks. As there was no record that the Indians had ever had a city on the banks of the Shawmucky, it was believed that these were relics of a battle that had been fought beside the stream perhaps long before the white men came. Johnny called the place the Indian Battleground.

Still more mysterious were the three symmetrical mounds on the right bank of the river near this place, relics of a much older people than the Indians, who were known simply as the Mound Dwellers.

Hardly anyone visited this part of the river except Johnny Shawnessy. The spot to which he came most often was halfway up the long northerly arm, on the right bank, close to the lowermost of the mounds. There was a place near-by where he would ford the river, book in hand. He would undress and swim in a deep, quiet pool under an oak, whose gnarled roots reached down into the water and fixed themselves in the bank like a giant hand clutched in the coil of a snake. Lying in the shade, he could see up and down the water a halfmile either way. And here he lay and thought about the river.

Then, indeed, he seemed closest to the secret of the County.

It was, he was certain, a water secret in the beginning. What secret lurked in the reedy, fishy, muddy word 'Shawmucky'? Was this name the memory of a strange creature that the first man discovered in the river? For the river had been there before any man had come. The river was there when the great icesheet withdrew and left the land virginal, dripping, devoid of life. The river was there when the first green life surged up from the south. The river was full of shining fleshes when the first man came wandering into the forest country that was now called Raintree County. And with him man brought names, and the river became a name.

Who was the first man who named the river? Ancestor of the Indian, he had come from those obscure migrations in which mankind, rootless wanderers on the earth, had left their Asian homeland and wandered east and west. They had come across the island bridge from Asia to America and down into a manless continent, bringing the already complex tongue and culture of their homeland. The first man who named the river was not an Indian, nor perhaps even a Mound Dweller. He was, however, a man. He made a husky sound as he saw in the river—or imagined that he saw—a fabulous creature. But the first man standing by the river was himself a fabulous creature. And the word that he pronounced was, like all words, a fabulous sound. He had brought it with him from the far-off source of humanity, which, like the Shawmucky River, had risen from a mysterious place and flowed down between widening banks in huge divagations, seeking for a lake. Words were the music of this murmurous water. All language was a stream flowing from distant to distant summer. Perhaps it all was sprung from some parent word, the first word uttered by the lips of man in the oriental garden of his birth. And the name of Raintree County's Indian river was thus a palimpsest upon a palimpsest, a wandering, ancient, mutilated sound, a pilgrim from remote shores like man himself.

As the boy lay dreaming beside the river that summer, he thought of the miracle of names. What was his own name, Shawnessy? What did it mean? Whence had it come? It too had come a devious way, and if the sounds and the meanings that it once had were traced back far enough, it too perhaps would return into the primitive garden of the race, back to the parent Word.

For Johnny had always been vaguely aware of the likeness of his name to the name of the Indian river of Raintree County. Perhaps he was only a more belated wanderer from the Biblical homeland of humanity, who had found here in Raintree County an echo of himself, a murmurous reminder of the common source and common destiny of man.

East and West had met on the earth of Raintree County. Language had flowed around the world and met in intermingling waves. The men who had no spelling had given a sound to the men who spelled. And now in summer afternoons a youth named John Wickliff Shawnessy stretched his white body beside a river called the Shawmucky, in the central, streamdivided earth of America.

The Indians had left in Raintree County one other memorial of their vanished culture, its proudest achievement. This was the plant called maize, or, as it was known to America, corn. It was the County's chief crop. Even T. D., who never seriously turned his hand to farming, put in a field of corn each year. In May the first tender tips were through the black loam. In June the little plants were a hand high. Kneehigh by the Fourth of July in a good year, the stalks were thick as a child's arm, and the few blades were inchbroad. During the hot July the corn grew with fantastic speed, sometimes four inches in a single day. By August, the stalks were higher than a man, not rarely shooting ten feet up. Leaves like voluptuous swords stirred in the moist air, drinking light. The bared roots grappled manyfingered at the crusted soil, tassels formed at the tall tips, the stalks made ears. Warm rains of late July and August fattened the kernels. In early fall the ears broke at the stalk, hung heavy for harvest. Then came the cutting of the corn and the piling in shocks. The huskers ripped the sheath and the silk from the hard ears. And the bared fruit was piled yellow in cribs.

This was the great festival of the corn in Raintree County, perhaps the County's richest image, bequeathed it by a vanished race.

In these years when Johnny Shawnessy became a man, he spent a great part of his summers working on his father's land and helping with his brothers on neighboring farms. For the big harvests, the ablebodied men in the County travelled about in work gangs. Harvest, of wheat or corn, was a prodigious festival of hard work, huge dinners, rude fun. Day after day, Johnny helped at taking the County's bountiful yield and loading its cribs. In this work, he developed a body hard and swift, capable of daylong exertion in the hot sun. No one was faster at shucking the corn than he.

He lost himself in this work with pagan identification, came home from it drunk with the good fatigue of a strong young man, his mind full of the tranquil images of harvest—the great mounds of shucked ears, the fodderstacks, the creaking wagons, the loaded harvest tables.

What did it mean, this immense ritual of growth and harvest, this rending of ripe seed from the earth? Perhaps the secret of life reached its climax in the festival moment when armies of harvesters attacked the standing corn.

Properly enough, the season of the harvest in Raintree County was called for the people who had discovered and nurtured the corn. In Indian Summer, the blue bright days flooded the harvest fields with mellow warmth. And at such times Johnny Shawnessy, student of the County's vanished cultures, bethought him of a legended Indian goddess whose bare, bright limbs slipped deeper and deeper into the nodding leaves as the cornknives felled her guardians one by one. Perhaps the low shriek of an ear of corn cleanly husked was the wail of her spirit as it suffered at last the delicious rape. Then he would wonder at the immense achievement of that old race who named the river, and of all primitive humanity as well, which had somehow learned the lesson of the seasons and the seed. And as he saw the swollen ocean of the corn sweeping to the very rim of the river, as he smelled the rank odor of the green corn's milky juices, he knew that the cultivating stick had been greater than the tomahawk.

He would always remember homecoming at evening with his brothers, Zeke, Rob, and Bill. Ellen Shawnessy would have a big hot supper waiting, and while the boys ate, telling the feats and pranks of the day, she hovered over them, the maternal spirit of the feast, loading the table with pork, roasting ears, butter, mashed potatoes, apple pie, milk.

Such was the harvest in Raintree County, that ancient valley threaded by an ancient water.

When he came to the river in summer afternoons from working on the farm, Johnny would strip off his clothes and plunge matted with seed and caked with dust into the water. After a swim, he would lie naked in soft grass reading or writing. His skin felt itchy from the hot air and the touch of the tingling grass. His youth was in his blood and on his skin and in the burgeoning parts of his body like a low fever.

That summer, he brought only one book to the banks of the Shawmucky, a copy of *The Complete Works of William Shakespeare* in a single volume. Summer light ate fiercely around the finely printed words; the little words in turn ate fiercely into Johnny's being. Like the river itself, this book was a place of life, the columns of the bordered pages were full of streaming, vivid forms, the little words were seeds proceeding from a lifeplace, a magical productive name —William Shakespeare. So on the banks of the Shawmucky the naked American boy, seventeen years old, read in the pages of the greatest poet of all time. He was drunk in the sunlight of Raintree County. He was drunk too with the creative fury of the book, which was for him a book of prophecy revealing himself to himself.

As he read and wrote and mused beside the river in summer afternoons, he thought much of that other gifted child of nature, Willie Shakespeare. Willie Shakespeare, living at Stratford-on-Avon, had been a boy like Johnny Shawnessy, familiar with the course of country waters, growing unheeded like a flower beside a little river whose name was then unknown beyond the speech of those who lived and loved and died along it. Doubtless this Willie Shakespeare had the same stripling form, the adolescent beard and blemishes, the hair long, unshorn, mussed by wind. Doubtless, he felt the fevered, mute desires of youth, had the same inquisitive, beautyseeking mind, made the same shout of sound when he meant mother, father, sun, seed, water, love, and beauty, smiled by the same wrinkling of the face, shook with the same spasmed laughter. Doubtless he yearned after the maids who lived on neighboring farms, lay often tossing on his bed at night, thinking of their saucy breasts, sleek buttocks, velvet-muscled thighs. Doubtless he found, when first he tried to make words in rhythmed sequence, that the world rushed in upon him and peopled his mind with images and filled his ears with rich, strange language. And as he lay beside the sinuous river, Willie Shakespeare must have dreamed how one day he would go to the City and be famous and tup the most exciting woman and make much gold and come back at last to Stratford-on-Avon and buy the finest house in town.

Sometimes it seemed that in some occult way Johnny Shawnessy was Willie Shakespeare, and that the Plays were still waiting to be written and that everyone was somehow Willie Shakespeare and everyone and everything was Johnny Shawnessy, and that life was discovery and not creation—it was permitting oneself to be a great poet and not forcing oneself to be a great poet.

For as he lay on the bank of the Shawmucky, he knew that he too would be a great poet. It seemed to him that he must be a greater poet even than Shakespeare because there was some essence of what he was that Elizabethan England couldn't possibly compose. He, John Wickliff Shawnessy, was perhaps the bearer of the sacred fire of poetic genius that is given from mind to mind like a regenerating torch. It was he, child of the sunlight, the corndense earth, the simple beliefs of Raintree County, who would become the great American poet. Son of his greathearted mother, of his energetic, sanguine father, he was perhaps a chosen seed, brought from far places.

Johnny Shawnessy didn't so much read Shakespeare as he read a vaguely imagined book of himself. In Shakespeare's luxuriant language, strong rhythms, terrific metaphors, Johnny was groping toward a new language of himself, a vocabulary equal to the dramas, characters, ideas, events that only America could produce. In Shakespeare, he discovered not the created but the creating thing. From a source fruitful like the earth, the crowding creatures of the dramas came. Their language was life itself, had life's variety and rhythm, and at times its senselessness, fury, imperfection. The tears, the terrors, the ecstatic loves, the vast, vulgar laughters were of life itself. And under the lavish veil of Shakespeare's words, the secret shape of beauty was more truly shown than anywhere else.

Johnny Shawnessy didn't think he would have to wait long to become the great poet. A whole world of creation seemed waiting. He had only to set pencil to paper in the sunlight of the Shawmucky. And wandlike, the pencil would touch immortal poems into being. Putting a pencil to the coarsegrained paper of a notebook was exciting to him like the touch of a young man's flowering nakedness to the body of a pretty girl. His whole being then was drained into feeling at one quickening point. Through the wand of the pencil he would jet the rivering lines of life.

He had already discovered that he had a gift for verse. Without effort, he could shape the language of his fancies in any of the English meters. The very resistance of the poetic medium seemed to stir up his word-horde. During that first summer of his great desire to be a poet, he wrote hundreds of verses that seemed to him no less good than Shakespeare's. In the summer of his body's maturity, he had become expressive like a god, and like a god, he would ravish beauty by the mere wishing. He already contemplated a lifetime of immortal words, which would one day be treasured by the world in a single volume entitled *The Complete Works of John Wickliff Shawnessy.*

This was a season of gorgeous dreams by day and night. Achieving all at once a man's full vigor of body and mind, Johnny Shawnessy lived in a continual torment of desire—desire to know, to possess, to make. He memorized whole books of poetry, read everything he could find, aspired to have all human knowledge, allowing himself a few years at most to accomplish it all. At night, his dreams, always vivid, were enriched with his bardic obsession. He wandered in a world of old enchantments, peopled a sleeptime Raintree County with the memories of all mankind, enacted dramas that seemed to him more passionate and fanciful than Shakespeare's. What did it signify, this world of sleep? Who was this protean being who borrowed the semblance of a waking self and strove through a self-created world in quest of beauty and high achievement? He didn't know, but to these sleeptime visions he resigned himself with eager yearning, hoping that they would yield him the consummations denied him during the day.

At this time he began to write a column for the *Free Enquirer,* one of Raintree County's two weekly newspapers. He called his articles *Meditations from the Upper Shawmucky,* and in the pen name Will Westward managed to conceal his identity from everyone, including his own family and the editor of the paper, Niles Foster. The column soon awakened great interest in the County. It contained everything from philosophical musings to political disputation, and in it from time to time Johnny imbedded the poems that he had been writing. The most popular feature was a fictitious rustic philosopher, poet, and amateur politician whom Johnny called Seth Twigs. The scholarly author of the articles, Will Westward, talked frequently with this denizen from the banks of the Shawmucky and reported his sayings in their unvarnished Hoosier dialect. The political bias of Johnny's articles was Republican, like that of the newspaper itself. Eighteen fifty-six was an election year, the rising young Republican Party was making a strong bid for the Presidency behind the candidacy of John C. Frémont, and partisan feeling ran high in Raintree County. Soon in the Democratic paper of the County, the Freehaven *Clarion,* a column similar to Johnny's began to appear, purporting to be written by one Dan Populus and retailing from time to time the wit and wisdom of a backwoods raconteur Rube Shucks. Dan Populus was no mean antagonist for Will Westward, and after a while the rumor went that Dan Populus was none other than the rising young orator Garwood Jones.

Wanting to keep his authorship of the articles a secret, Johnny always composed them at his favorite haunt beside the Shawmucky. For the river drew him to itself. All that came from it fascinated him. Whenever he hooked a fish and jerked it wriggling from the water, he had a momentous feeling of discovery. Was it the sacred being of the river, the Shawmucky itself, goggle-eyed, scaly, gilled, panting in the thin, destroying air? But it always turned out to be a familiar variety of fish and seldom larger than a man's hand. And yet people said that in the river a catfish had been seen big as a man.

Or he would watch cranes standing in the shallow water. Now and then, he managed to get very close to one, and it seemed to him that if he could catch in his arms the great kingcrane, rank-feathered, gaunt, bony, and throw him down, it would be as if he caught a colossal birdgod, who belonged only to the river.

Or he would hunt for frogs in swamps and shallows of the river. For a while he sought them with as much passion as a prospector hunting gold in California waters. Sometimes at night, he would hear, sounding all the way across the fields to the Home Place, the deep belch of a frog. It was perhaps the biggest frog of all time, hundreds of years old, as big as a man's head. Whoever caught that frog would have in his hand the rinded, mossy secret of the river. Once Johnny saw a big frog wedged in among rushes near a place where he was swimming. Furiously excited, he grabbed the torpid thing and plucked it from the river. For a moment he felt as though he had the legendary Shawmucky. Held in both hands with legs extended, the frog was shaped grotesquely like a man, had the long slender legs, the toed feet, the tight rump, the white belly, the wide shoulders, the two arms with spread hands, the head. Part for part, it was a man in a forgotten shape. It was an antique man who had stayed too long in the Shawmucky River and had never suffered the air change.

But the river itself was the most mysterious creature of all. It lay like a coiled body on the land. It had its secret source in distant summer and its sinklike goal in distant summer. Johnny had always had a wish to explore the Upper Shawmucky up and down its length, and in that summer, he nearly had his wish fulfilled.

One day, setting out by himself, he walked northeastward along the river to see if he could find the source. He went for miles, following the river as it grew smaller until it was only a few feet wide. But it kept flowing on strongly between fields and past rockstrewn hills, cutting its deep sharp trace through the County. The sun went steeply up at noon and down its western arc, dying at evening in clouds of purple fire, and still Johnny Shawnessy hadn't reached the source of the Shawmucky River. At dusk, he asked a farmer in a field how far it was to the river's source, and the farmer said he didn't recollect ever hearing anybody say. At this, Johnny cut over to the closest road and started home. It was ten o'clock at night and he was weak all over when he staggered into the yard of the Home Place.

Sometime later, he discovered an old boat, foundered in the river. In secret he repaired it, proposing to row down the river to Paradise Lake, which he had never seen. One day in late June, early in the morning, he started out near his favorite haunt beneath the oak. Rowing strongly, he went up the long northward-flowing stroke of the river to where it bent sharply back upon itself. From there on, he was amazed at the great slow vistas of the Shawmucky. After rowing nearly four miles he crossed under the two bridges at Danwebster, only a mile by crowflight from the place where he had started. When he got beyond the town and was veering northwest toward the lake, it was already afternoon. The air seemed more moist and heavy with the rank scent of the widening river and its flowers. The boat grounded many times on mudbars, and Johnny had to get out and shove it loose. Water and air were dense with life. He had never seen so many birds, fish, turtles, frogs, bugs in all his life before. The country too was savage, with acres of forest and swampland on every side. The river spread out among islands so that the main current was hard to follow. Bushes, waterweeds, willows, swampoaks were so dense in places that they nearly choked off the river's course. The water seemed to Johnny to be flowing the other way in places, as if the lake were the river's real source.

Meanwhile, he kept looking about him to see if he could see any unusual tree that might be the celebrated Raintree, but he gave up the hunt as hopeless, so thick and various was the thrust of life in the last mile. The boat leaked more and more, and finally in the hot blaze of midafternoon, it stove and foundered in the very middle of the shallow river. Johnny swam and waded toward the shore, but there seemed to be only swampland and water everywhere. He felt that he must be very close to Paradise Lake, but he was so exhausted with coming down the river that he wished only to get home again. Blundering through banks of waterweeds, he tried to find firm ground. More and more, the solid substance of the earth dissolved with life. The creatures of the river swarmed, shrieked, swam, coupled, seeded, bloomed, died, stank around him. He appeared to be in the very source of life, a womblike center. River and shore were one; leaf and flesh, blossom and genitalia, seed and egg were one cruel impulse. All the creatures of the river were fecund, shining, perfect, each one a paragon of the image that all the members of its race embodied. Farther away in the summer afternoon, this furious fecundity became enfeebled—there was a genteel creature called man. But here there was no man, except only Johnny Shawnessy, half naked, an intruder, his body scratched and itchy, his shirt torn by branches, his pants ripped half off, his hair stiff with seed.

Suddenly, as he lurched and stumbled through this vortex of life, his foot slipped through a mesh of vines and he dropped neckdeep into a pool. A thick net of roots and lily stems laced his body. A bottomless ooze drank his feet and legs heavily, heavily. His young strength twisted and sprang, not for a moment admitting that it was in danger. Yet he moved hardly an inch. His hands clutched and tore at roots and stems.

A gigantic willow presided calmly over his struggle, one root fantastically bared within six inches of his hand.

The pool heaved slowly, enveloped him in constricting coils. He was going down surely. The change was so cruelly slow and his body so completely engaged that his mind ran free with skipping alacrity, observing, recording, and a hundred times over reminding him of the grimness of his situation. Slowly a phrase formed in his memory, writhing in green letters.

The Great Swamp. The words of his father spoken long ago ran sluggish and half-submerged in his memory.

—Folks call it the Great Swamp. Why, a man went in there once and never came out again.

Johnny Shawnessy struggled mutely for life in the embrace of the Great Swamp. A few seconds ago he had been a free, happy, purposeful human being on his way back to one of those little firm brown roads that were so reassuringly frequent on the landscape of Raintree County. He had intended to go home and have a good supper and maybe read a little poetry before he went to bed. Now he gasped and fought for dear life, his head thrown back, drowning in a private universe of mud and light. There was no one to know where he was or what had become of him. If his head disappeared under this shining surface, he would be gone forever from the sunlight of Raintree County, sunk without a trace.

He kept his eyes fastened on the willow root still six inches from his hand. The water was over his chin, touched his mouth, covered it. A thick vine looped his neck and prevented the forward thrust of his body. He made a furious effort catching the vine with both hands, trying to push it over his head. As if all his contortions up to this moment had been a grotesque joke prolonged for the amusement of an immensely superior antagonist and now ended with brutal suddenness, his whole body, head and all, plunged under: the vine twisted muscularly in his hands, and his own strength had driven him out of sight.

That instant, freed from the vine, he made a forward lunge in the deep muck groping under water. His left hand touched the submerged willow root, coated with slime. His hand slid on it, but he had drawn himself forward by inches. Blinded and choked, he shot his right hand from the water and caught something dry and firm.

The white hand of Johnny Shawnessy stuck from the surface of the Great Swamp, holding an exposed willow root.

With ridiculous ease, he drew himself from the pool and lay on the roots of the willow, gasping. The whole thing had lasted perhaps half a minute.

He looked about him. He had almost died in the middle of Raintree County. Hundreds of people who loved him, who would willingly have caught his hands and pulled him out, had gone on securely about their work while he wallowed in the gripe of death.

He clung to the willow, gasping with a fear he hadn't felt during the struggle. Around him, impassive, secret, beautiful, the Great Swamp shimmered and stank. With a brutal indifference, his own earth had nearly killed him.

Finally, he got up from the willow and cautiously hunted for a way out. After a while, he found firm ground and breaking through a screen of rushes, discovered himself on the edge of a lonely, rutted road.

A snappy two-seater spring wagon was coming down the road from the direction of the setting sun. As it approached, the two couples in it giggled and pointed. In the driver's seat a nattily dressed, broadshouldered young man boomed jovially,

—Look! It's Johnny Appleseed!

The girls tittered.

—Why, no, Garwood, said the girl beside him. It's Johnny Shawnessy!

Johnny Shawnessy, who had just come from the Great Swamp, gazed at the improbable creature who had just spoken. Wideapart eyes shone like green jellies in a small white face. The mouth was a red fruit. It moved, made sibilant sounds, lingered huskily on the name 'Johnny.' The yellow hair, blooming rankly around a hairless forehead, was pulled back to show the little shameless ears. The white long neck was a supple stem joining the flower of a human head to a white hairless body.

But, after all, this creature had a name, as nothing in the Great Swamp had a name.

—Hello, Nell, he said.

Everyone was laughing at him except her.

—I was out walking, he said weakly.

He hated them all. He had nearly drowned, and here they sat clothed and tittering.

—I nearly drowned in there, he said.

Garwood roared at this, and even Nell smiled a little. Johnny himself began to feel that he had said something absurd.

—For goodness' sake, what for, Johnny? Nell said.

—A little botanical excursion, he said.

His panic was giving way to a much more human emotion, embarrassment.

—Let's take him in and get him home, Nell said. Goodness gracious, Johnny, how you are mussed up! But come on, you can sit between us if you're dry enough.

Johnny climbed up and sat between Nell and Garwood. He was surprised to see Nell coming from the direction of Paradise Lake. It was well known in the County that a certain type of social activity went on in the wild neighborhood of the lake which was not reported in the society columns of the *Free Enquirer*. Besides, the couple in the back seat were a notorious pair, who had been going steady for some time, and rumor had cast doubt on the chastity of their connection.

—Say, how far is it to the lake, anyway? Johnny said.

—It's right over there, John, Garwood said, pointing into the very region through which Johnny had floundered.

All the way home, Nell was very maternal. She pulled away at Johnny's tangled hair with a comb, blowing her breath like warm mist into his face, while he kept his eyes down in an agony of shyness. He kept noticing her hands. It was as though he had never looked carefully at a pair of human hands before. He marvelled at their five fingers, their naked palms, blunt nails. They were swift, slender hands, woman's hands, knowing and maternal. Suddenly he imagined them like his own, sticking from the surface of the swamp, while below them in the green dusk, enmeshed in vines, a curious white creature lurked. The image made him faint and almost sick.

Nell meanwhile brushed off his shirt, pointing out various rips and tears.

—You poor dear boy, she said, you're nearly undressed!

Her pert face maintained its composure, but the couple in the back seat sniggered vulgarly. Johnny was glad when Garwood stopped the buggy at the Home Place. He felt like a fool and disliked Nell for mothering him. He had hardly looked at her face after that first moment when he came from the swamp and saw her in the buggy.

His mind was still absorbed with the secret that had whirred, sung, buzzed, squawked around him in the fierce sunlight of the swamp. He was afraid to say what the secret was, even to himself; yet he had penetrated almost to its core.

Part of the secret was that all things that came from the Shawmucky River were one thing, and all were subtle reminders of himself, and all were perfect in their way, and all had been forever in the river, and the river was the ancient valley of his being, and everything that came from its waters was intolerably beautiful.

But the river still had its last, most amazing disclosure to make.

One day in late August during a sweltering heatwave, Johnny had gone to his favorite place on the river. As usual he plunged in for a swim. Then he stretched on grass at the water's edge, listening to the spiral music of cicadas. The river burned green in sunlight. He lay on his back and let the notebook and pencil he had brought lie untouched beside him. He shut his eyes and felt heat and light rain like soft arrows on his fluttering lids. He slept.

Awakening, he turned over and looked through the reeds that screened his hiding-place. Not twenty yards from where he lay was a skein of gold hair floating backward on the current.

Then while he watched in sleepy bewilderment, a fabulous creature rose slowly from the Shawmucky, walking from midriver to the far shore. Glistening whitely from the green water, the neck emerged, the long back, the stately buttocks, the smooth-fleshed thighs, the tapering calves, and at last the long slender feet. On the left of the deepfleshed hemispheres was a brown mole, pennysized. Then as the creature half turned a moment and stretched up its arms full length in the sunlight, he saw the brightnippled breasts, the wide, smooth belly, and three gold tufts of hair.

He saw also the precise face, the wideapart eyes warily looking up and down the banks, the pert nose, the mouth panting.

While he watched stonestill, the creature ran quickfooted behind some bushes and a few moments later came out barefoot, wearing a loose summer dress, and disappeared in the barky shadow southward down the river.

Johnny Shawnessy opened and closed his eyes several times and shook the sleep out of his head. A sweet tumult beat in his veins.

He panted with the anguish of a desire that had not even acquired the image of possession.

He had done it with his own eyes. With his eyes, he had suddenly stripped the costume of Raintree County from its most lovely flesh. With his eyes, he had possessed the white secret of Helen and the Greeks. With his young eyes, he had learned the lesson of the deep-fleshed loins of Venus.

For the face had been the face of a Raintree County girl. But the form had been the form of a goddess foamborn and beautiful, sprung from the waters of the inland ocean. That vision of the supple back incurved to the small waist, outcurved to the abundant hips, softly recurved down the greatmuscled thighs to the small knees, gently outcurved to the long calves, distinctly and yet softly returned and tapered to the ankles—that white vision of curves recurrent, so thoroughly unmasculine, so delicately made for erotic and maternal uses, so tranquilly seductive—that vision was Johnny Shawnessy's first overwhelming awareness of Woman. The small bare face of Nell Gaither, a familiar face which had always risen serenely from a Raintree County dress, had appeared on the nakedest, the most seductive creature that he had ever seen.

In that one vision, the old Nell Gaither was gone. In her place was a woman almost cruelly beautiful, seen through the green mesh of the reeds, with the sigil of her uniqueness delicately staining her beauty. She had risen from the little Indian river of Raintree County, and her name now coursed through Johnny's mind with a new music, full of love's precise anguish.

He tried to remind himself of the girl who belonged to the prim world of Raintree County, who wore its highnecked bodice and its formdisguising skirt and petticoats, who spoke its evasive language, worshipped in its little church whitely puritan upon a hill, sedately walked under the taut dome of a parasol. But beneath all these images now, looking warily from under wet gold hair, was the river girl, whose impudent nakedness had stunned him.

Beneath her puritan ways, she was not afraid of life: she had come down to the green prolific river and placed her skin in contact with it. How fortunate would be the hero—how like a young god—who would win for himself the gift of that triumphant nudity, the sweet candors of the river girl!

In the days that followed, Johnny Shawnessy was not quite sane. He wandered around the County in long walks that had no plan and came out nowhere. He lay sometimes all night till dawn without sleeping a wink. Sometimes he could eat nothing at all. Sometimes he stuffed ravenously. But his craziest impulse caused him to write for the *Free Enquirer* the queerest meditation that had yet come from the Upper Shawmucky. It awakened a good deal of comment.

NEW SPECIES FOUND IN THE SHAWMUCKY

WILD EXCITEMENT IN DANWEBSTER

SPECULATION RIFE

(Epic Fragment from the *Free Enquirer*)

August 20. Danwebster has been stirred up with the biggest furore since the Great Comet. A new species of water-creature has been seen in the Shawmucky River. It is well known that the river abounds in rare varieties of flora and fauna that merit the interest of the sauntering naturalist. But judging from the scanty descriptions now available, the new find has never before been classified. A very pretty specimen was observed no longer ago than last Tuesday by the naked eye of a gentleman whose scientific objectivity there is no reason to doubt.

Last Tuesday afternoon, we were lying in our backyard engaged in our favorite pursuit, when suddenly we were awakened by a sound like thunder on the pike. Looking up we saw the form of Seth Twigs flying across a field from the direction of the river. Without a pause, the excellent Seth (whom we do not remember ever seeing run ten steps in his life before) pigeonwinged over the fence and arrived panting in our midst. After resting for half an hour our rural Phidippides was able to gasp out his story. It appears that Seth had been swimming in the Shawmucky and had retired to the bank for a good snooze, when awakening he espied something in the river.

Now precisely what Seth saw is still a question hotly argued these days wherever two minds meet in the northeastern quarter of the County. If Raintree County were ancient Greece and Seth's bony figure resembled that of the noble hunter Actaeon instead of a scarecrow, we would have no hesitation in saying that the strange new visitant in the waters of the Shawmucky was none other than the goddess Diana or at very least the nymphic deity of the river. But as we are living (according to the best authorities) in the middle of the Nineteenth Century, it is pretty certain that nothing in the shape of a woman, goddess or otherwise, will ever be seen by any Raintree County man bathing in the radiant garment of Nature. The creature seen in the waters of the Shawmucky was, according to Seth, definitely devoid of the outer integument that universally adorns human beings of her sex in Raintree County (Seth's exact words were, 'She was nekkid as a shucked ear'). Besides she appeared to have two distinct 'legs,' and everyone knows that no woman in the County has anything of the kind that she will admit to.

Many contend that Seth saw the great white fish for which, some say, the Indians named the river, and others that he saw the famous mudcat, big as a man, that is supposed to lurk in the deepest pools of the river. Others say that Seth Twigs never yet told a plain truth in his life and there's no reason to suppose he deviated into honesty in this particular.

Your correspondent does not intend to let the matter rest here. He is aware that recently in a rival newspaper he was accused of being 'a lazy no-account who made all his reports from Danwebster without exerting himself any further than to walk between his own back porch and the outhouse or occasionally to join the group of retired gentlemen whose principal occupation in life appears to be the self-appointed task of glazing with the seat of their britches the bench in front of the General Store.' This statement not only contains a misspelled word, but is too palpably false to deserve the compliment of a formal refutation. In order to put it in the category of repulsive slander to which it clearly belongs, it is only sufficient to remark that it appeared in the *Clarion* over the name of Dan Populus.

If any doubt can remain in the mind of anyone as to the tireless energy with which at the expense of his own health (not of the strongest) this correspondent pursues the task of reporting the news from the Upper Shawmucky, let it be known that he was the first to catch hold of the exciting development recorded in this article and that he has every intention of devoting his time and his talents, such as they are, to running the whole business to the ground.

As for the ambiguous libeller who imagines that he can with impunity throw his loathsome epithets on an untarnished reputation, be it known that his foul machinations go not unobserved, that his identity is fully known to this correspondent, and that if any further feculence is spewed from that hideous receptacle of filth and fetidness which he possesses in lieu of a mind, this correspondent will openly brand him with the ignominy which he deserves.

Your correspondent intends to keep himself fully informed on this situation, and he hopes to have the whole thing well in hand at the next writing.

WILL WESTWARD

At about the same time, Johnny also told a friend what he had seen and where he had seen it. He concealed the identity of the girl, saying that the distance was too great for recognition, and he exacted an oath of absolute secrecy.

A few days later when he repaired to his favorite nook on the river, he was surprised to find five young men sitting under his oak in such a way as to be able to look up and down the river from ambuscade. One of them was Garwood Jones.

—Hello, John, he said. Sit down and have a smoke.

—No, thanks, Johnny said glumly. I don't smoke.

—Filthy habit, Garwood said. Never start it.

He put a cigar between his moist, full lips, touched a matchflame to the tip, puffed.

—Beautiful view, he said. I love Nature.

Some of the other boys sniggered.

—What brings *you* here, John? Garwood said.

—Just out for a walk, Johnny said. I don't remember seeing you here before.

—My interest in Nature has lately been stimulated, Garwood said, by a certain article appearing in the *Enquirer*. Perhaps you've read it too.

Garwood's blue eyes gazed shrewdly through cigar smoke.

There was a noise of someone walking through bushes across the river.

—Down, men! Garwood barked.

He ground out his cigar and crawled on his belly toward the reeds.

On the other side of the river, three young men appeared, walking stealthily. They approached the bank and looked up and down the river.

—Goddam! Garwood said, sitting up. What the hell is this—a political convention?

The next edition of the Freehaven *Clarion* contained the following article by Dan Populus:

THE NYMPH OF THE SHAWMUCKY
SETH A LIAR
RUBE CHECKS UP IN PERSON
(Epic Fragment from the *Clarion*)

August 27. Well, we have been checking the facts in the sensational report that came out in the *Enquirer* a week ago over the name of Will Westward. The facts are simple and they all add up to one fact: Seth Twigs is the biggest liar since the snake fooled Eve.

We should know better by this time, but we sent our deputy, that lovable rustic, Rube Shucks, out to check the story for us. Rube went to the bank of the Shawmucky, intending to get a glimpse, if he could, of the seraphic creature Seth Twigs says he saw there. Here are Rube's own words for it: 'They wuz a hull goldern army of men and boys along that thar river. I kept a-flushin' one out of ever bush. I reckon they ain't bin sich a scientifick intrust showed in Raintree County since the Widder Black dissolved her faithless husband in a barl of assid. I sot down in a nice private spot with fifty other gennulman and wotched the river. I sot and sot. After a spell, down kum Seth Twigs. He wuz not the least bit drunker than usual, that mutch I will say fer him. "Seth," sez I, "whar's this here mermaid you seen?" "Rube," he sez, "you jist set thar, and I guarantee you'll see her." Well, I sot and I sot. I got stang by skeeters and stuck with nittles, but along about five o'clock in the afternoon, my patience and persistunce wuz rewarded. I hurd a noise in the bushes acrost the river. Hyar it kums! thinks I. "I see suthin white," a man sez. Then and thar we wuz all treated to the excitin' spectacle of Horace Perkins' cow Jessica, who kum down to the ford fer a drink. I wish to report to yure readers, Mr. Populus, that Jessica wuz clad only in the coztoom of Natur and that she is an onusual attracktive and well-preporshuned annimule, whooze daily milk-output is unsurpassed in these parts.'

DAN POPULUS

It was plain from this that Johnny Shawnessy had been found out as the author of the Will Westward articles and therefore also as the beholder of a Raintree County girl naked in the Shawmucky River. In a subsequent article, Will Westward reported that the repentant Seth had confessed the whole thing a fraud, insisting that the vision he saw was caused by 'guzzlin' a pint of pure pizen that Rube Shucks wuz sellin' in the County fer corn likker.' But the hurt was done. Nell Gaither must have guessed that she was the now celebrated nymph of the Shawmucky and must know, as everyone else seemed to, that Johnny was the author of the article in question. For two weeks, Johnny didn't go to church or any other place where he might see Nell.

But this cowardice of his couldn't last long. T. D. had planned a Temperance Rally for September, and the members of the Cold Water Army had enlisted to give a temperance drama. Johnny had agreed to write it, and Nell Gaither and Garwood Jones were both cast in leading parts.

It was on a Sunday at the Danwebster Church that Johnny and Nell met again for the first time since the famous emergence from the river. Johnny was standing at the door of the church handing out some private printings of a new hymn by T. D. called 'Wash me in the Jordan.' Just before time for the service to begin, Nell and her father and stepmother arrived. Nell was in a new green dress. Johny took one look at her getting out of a surrey and then kept his eyes averted. He felt as though he would choke while she climbed the pathway up the steep bank and approached the door.

—Hello, Johnny.

—Hello, Nell. Have a program.

—Thanks, Johnny.

He didn't look at her, but her voice, low and musical, pronounced the word 'Johnny' in her special way. Only now, the touch of her tongue on his name went through him in a tide of sweet anguish. As she went down the aisle, he studied the point where her hair, piled up in a mound, dwindled to a wispy peak on her neck.

While the service was going on, Johnny sat on the front bench, holding a hymnbook. Under his oak on the Shawmucky he had lately memorized the most exciting passages from Shakespeare's *Venus and Adonis.* In his mind he had repeated unweariedly the assault of a sultry goddess on a shy boy, and all the time against all reason he had endowed the goddess with the fullflanked form, small piquant face, and golden hair of Nell Gaither. He, too, on the fierce tide of this new love had tried his hand at an erotic poem, in which a swain beheld a rustic maid bathing in a woodland water. But there was something in the puritan perspectives of Raintree County or his own fledgling inexperience that had prevented a free, fine handling of the subject in the spirit of his lusty precursor.

T. D. had insisted that Johnny lead the singing of the original hymn. While the congregation was in full cry, Johnny stole a glance at Nell. Her mouth was making pleasing O's, her eyes were oval pools of rivergreen, she seemed entirely chaste and inaccessible. An innocent young republic had labored to clothe her in her puritan costume, had given her moral serenity and comely speech, had instructed her in the means of hiding the victorious nudity that the river had bequeathed her. (The river flowing out of distant summers, the river coiling past the beautiful twin mounds, the river twisting in slow anguish by reeds and rushes, tarn and tangling swamp unto the lake where life began.)

Wash me spotless in the Jordan,
  Cleanse my soul of earthly sin,
For I've wandered from the pathway
  That my fathers put me in.
Lead me back unto the river
  Where I strayed in happy youth
And array my limbs forever
  In the radiant robe of truth.

(The river, older than Helen and the Greeks, older than the Indian peoples who left the relics of savage warfare on its banks, older than man himself, and concealing in its course through Raintree County a fabulous, forgotten secret, of life that buzzed, sang, murmured, flapped great rushing wings, and shouted from the shallows.)

O, wash me in the Jordan,
  And I'll climb the happy shore
Where the blessed band of angels
  Bathe in bliss forevermore.

In rehearsals for the temperance play and elsewhere during the next few weeks, Johnny saw Nell often. In no way did she betray the secret that she and Johnny shared. After a while, he wondered if he had seen wrong.

Meanwhile, he returned as often as he could to the banks of the Shawmucky. For his desire was of the river. Those days, through all his waking dreams it ran, rank with curious fleshes, to the lake. It had given him beauty and desire. Some day, he must find again forbidden whiteness in the river and become the joyous fisherman, the proud possessor of the river's most curved and radiant flesh.

He never went to sleep without hoping that he would dream of Nell. And in his sleeping as in his waking dreams, the river ran. He was rowing a rotten boat on the Shawmucky or wading through a fetid swamp. The river shimmered on its mudded floors. Sometimes, he would find a young woman in the reeds. He wanted to look directly into her green eyes, and persuade her to become again the goddess of the river. But in the climax of the dream, as he sought her skin under a green dress, he would find himself entangled in rushes, her slippery body writhed whitebellied and flaggyfooted, escaping in the yellow reeds, and then the spasmed jet of his desire would stream off his body in the night, finding no place for its delicious anguish except the river. He would awaken lying in his bed at the Home Place, drenched with the mystery of his own young seed. Summer night was on the breathing earth. She whom he loved lay somewhere in this night, her curved, pale body stretched in darkness close to the river like his own. They were the children of the rivered earth, meant for each other. And yet there lay between him and this fabled whiteness all the green mesh of Raintree County, a net of names and words, a costume of puritan restraints, and he must be

BOLD LIKE A YOUNG GOD WHO WOULD BREAK
HIS WAY PAST ALL
THOSE

BARRIERS BURNED AWAY

The gilt words were stamped into a green cloth binding.

—Yes, I've read it, Mr. Shawnessy said.

He handed the book back to Eva, who became instantly reabsorbed in the story.

Brief résumé of the Sentimental Epic of America:

Between green cloth covers, on yellow faded pages, an upright young man from the country goes to the wicked city of Chicago to seek his fortune. There he falls in love with a rich girl, innately good but unredeemed by the Christian faith. Scenes of love, misunderstanding, danger, sickness, and death follow each other with dramatic vividness. In the climax of the book, the Great Chicago Fire bursts catastrophically upon the world of private lives and loves. The hero saves the heroine from a villainous rape amid spectacular scenes of fire and death and converts her to Jesus on the shore of the lake while around them the corrupt wealth and social inequalities of the City are leveled by the purging fire, and all barriers between the lovers are forever burned away. The congregation is requested to stand on the last verse.

The river was far behind. The roofs of Freehaven were visible a straight half-mile down the road. The Court House Tower stood in a haze of distance directly from the line of the road, a square stem of red brick, capped with a dull green roof ascending to a blunt point. A clockface recessed in the roofslope was too distant to be read.

He sifted the faded pages of himself.

Beautiful and lost was the secret he had sought to find long ago in a green cloth binding. In the greatest of the sentimental novels, he too had lain beside the river of desire, had been the hero of a sentimental epic—a legend of barriers unburned away. For America was always an education in self-denial. And Raintree County was itself the barrier of form imposed upon a stuff of longing, life-jet of the river.

In a way, all stories, no matter how badly written and printed, were legend—and eternal. Each book was sacred, a unique copy that had somewhere in its crowded pages the famous misprint, the cryptogram, or the lithograph of a beautiful woman whose nudity was signed with the faint signature of her mortality. Wherever paper was covered with print, the papyrus rush shook down its seed again by the river of life, the music of Nilotic reeds was carried on the air of summer. The strange linkage of a sound and its visual symbol was invented by men who lived beside a river, saw a cursive shape written on the earth, heard the continuous sound of flowing water.

And again he was making the memorial journey from the river to the Court House Square, from the random curve of water to the rectilinear stone. It was the pathway of the hero of a legend, of one who rose from the Great Swamp and rode a horse of godlike appetite to the summit of Platonic forms.

Mr. John Wickliff Shawnessy shook the reins over President's back. He took a deep breath to still his big excitement as the surrey passed the red barn at the edge of town where travellers went abruptly from the open road into the shade of a wide, treebordered street.

Instantly, it seemed, the sound of the firecrackers became multitudinous and intimate. A powdersmell drifted up the sleepy streets, incense of holiday. Flagbright, the broad street stretched between diminished tree trunks to the far enclosure of the Square.

Make way, make way for the Hero of Raintree County! For he is coming to pluck the golden apples! Down with the ancient prohibitions! None shall restrain the intemperate young man with the sunlight in his hair! Make way, make way for . . .

Mr. Shawnessy drove the surrey to a place on the east side of the Square and tied President up to the hitching rail. A firecracker burst in the alley near-by, scattering children. The clock in the Court House Tower showed six-forty.

—I've got two or three places to go, Pet, he said. It shouldn't take me over fifteen or twenty minutes. Keep the children around close.

Atlas under arm, he crossed the street toward a tall, sourfaced brick building. Sandstone steps led up to a door over which a legend was carved into the sandstone arch:

HISTORICAL MUSEUM
ANTIQUITIES OF RAINTREE COUNTY

'Footprints on the sands of time'
H. W. Longfellow

He hesitated at the foot of the steps and looked around the Square. The Court House was a recumbent beast couched on the curled paws of its balustraded stairs. The four walls of the Square were holed with a hundred immutable doors to a hundred immutable desires. The old pomps and prohibitions of Raintree County were enacted into the shapes of this enclosure.

Yet all this had been pulled like a mask over the naked beauty of an ancient human want. This mask quivered on the secret thing that it concealed. And soon all the holiday hundreds would be pouring into the enclosure, wearing their ritual costumes. All would enjoy the sacrifice and the incense, the invocation of the sainted names. All would share in the feast and the communion.

But only the consecrated hero could enter the inmost shrine where a young woman waited with a book of revelation.

He mounted the steps to the museum door.

A few mornings before, the body of an old man had lain on these steps, his face pressing the cold stone, his heart exploded, while in the lock stood his unturned key. An imperturbable god had curved cold lips and had forbidden the old man a last cold lust of killing. For Waldo Mays, Custodian of the Raintree County Historical Museum, had meant to kill the shape of beauty. Priestlike, in the name of the dourly orthodox god of Raintree County, he had meant to make a sacrifice most pleasing to his deity.

Now there came one younger, with a golden key, a hero capable of getting golden apples.

Mr. Shawnessy straightened his poet's tie in the mirror of the glass doorpane. His reflection exactly filled the statuary niche over the Main Entrance of the Court House across the street.

Entering a little hallway, he sniffed a faint stink of stuffed pelts. Antiquities of Raintree County filled up the four floors of the narrow building: relics of Indians and Mound Dwellers on the first floor; pioneer relics and implements of agriculture on the second; weapons and other mementoes of four American wars on the third; and an exhibit of natural history on the fourth. Metal stairs ascended in spiral from floor to floor. He stood, waiting and listening, in the place where the accumulated residue of life in Raintree County had been preserved. Relics of more than fifty years were crowded into rows of glass cases that walled the gloomy rooms. They had all achieved (these pistols, books, bundles of beribboned letters, daguerreotypes, pioneer cradles, primitive scythes, tallow lamps, candleholders, slates, spinning wheels, arrowheads, tomahawks, moccasins, stone knives, belts of wampum, firebows, cultivating sticks) the antiquarian repose.

This was the land of shades. An elder American bard, the celebrated Longfellow, had met a young aspirant at the portals and ushered him into these fuscous circles.

A sound of high heels started up and tapped smartly toward him. Peering into the brown dusk of the corridor, he saw a young woman approaching. Her hair was tawny yellow, her figure abundant, her face fair, lightly freckled, with wide blue eyes, a large but pretty mouth, and a look of radiant freshness and health.

—Mr. Shawnessy! I'm so pleased to see you again!

The impulsive gesture with which she took his hand was made with her whole body.

—Well, well, he said, you've grown a good deal since I saw you last, Persephone.

The remark made him more fully aware of the ample yet classic proportions of her figure, which he now saw was clothed in an attractive green dress, asserted by puffs of cloth flowers over the breasts and by a saucy bustle.

—You hardly change at all, Mr. Shawnessy.

—The light isn't very good here, he said, smiling with lifted brows. Is it possible that it's been twenty years!

—Yes. In 1872 I left for the East and haven't been back until Uncle Waldo took ill a few weeks ago.

—I was sorry to hear of your uncle's death, he recited. But it's nice to know that the Museum is to be in such good hands. Do you mean to become our Lady Custodian?

—I really don't know. I haven't any plans. I've been a widow, you know, for two years now.

As he spoke to her of circumstances and changes, he kept wondering at the inexorable rhythms that had fulfilled themselves in her. She had been a lank stick of a girl when last he saw her; now she stood before him, a mature woman who had known vicissitudes of travel, love, marriage, death. But at this instant of reunion, she brought to him the adoring schoolgirl he had last seen, and he brought to her the youthful yet paternal teacher. And this reunion was for both of them a delightful anachronism among the other antiquities of Raintree County.

It required an act of desperate boldness for him to say,

—I know your time is precious, Persephone. What have you decided about the—the book? I'm to meet the Senator around ten o'clock in Waycross. The Senator is a man of curious tastes and has expressed a keen interest, as you know, in this volume because of its—its rarity.

—Let's get it out, she said, and have a look at it.

Mr. Shawnessy's heart paced nimbly after as she walked before him down the corridor, a weaving, fullflanked form, into the office of the defunct Waldo Mays.

In the glass case beside the old man's desk, the *Atlas* lay on a bed of red velvet, its gilded letters brightening in the dark oakpaneled room. The young woman seemed studiedly casual as she turned a key in the back of the case and lifted the book out.

—Well, here it is, she said, opening the cover and laying the *Atlas* on top of the case.

The title-page contained a picture. On the wooded bank of a river, underneath a widebranching tree, a bearded gentleman sighted with a surveyor's level at a pole held by another gentleman some distance off. Seated near-by on a rock, an artist sketched the scene of a train crossing a river trestle in the background.

Mr. Shawnessy was relieved to see no woman standing in her pelt, ankledeep in the river under the bridge. The picture was exactly like the one in his own copy. Then he felt a depression of spirit as if this one refutation of an idle rumor proved the whole story a fraud.

Lifting the heavy load of the leaves between index finger and thumb of her left hand, the young woman let them sift down slowly as she said,

—It's a lovely book, isn't it? I'd never seen a copy until I came back. I've been looking through it since I got your letter. It seems to be in good condition.

He watched the earth of Raintree County blurring past in a shower of familiar images. The eyes of the woman were speculative and distant, he thought, as she closed the *Atlas*. He followed her gaze through the window, which framed a portion of the Court House Tower above the Main Entrance.

Pedestaled in the deep niche thereof, blindfolded, leaning on a sheathèd sword, the Statue of Justice stood, a granite woman sternly pectoral, holding bronze scales, her stony features spattered with pigeondung.

Mr. Shawnessy blushed, bit his lip, fought an irrational desire to grin, then gasped as Mrs. Persephone Mays herself laughed in a clear, bubbling contralto.

—O dear, she said. Pardon me, I—I was just remembering our pageant on the court house lawn in '68. You remember how my corn-costume came off just as I recited the line

> So yearly doth the sturdy husbandman
> Strip the dry husks from ranks of standing corn.

O dear, and just then the belt or whatever it was held it together came loose and left me standing there in my petticoat.

Mr. Shawnessy's answering laugh was too loud. He laid his own copy of the *Raintree County Historical Atlas* on the glass case.

—Shall we exchange worlds?

—Why, yes, she said, handing him the coveted, mysterious book.

He took it gingerly, as if he expected a strong vibration from it, a flood of that dangerous force which primitive man detected in sacred objects.

—The Senator can let me know if he wants it, she said. I *would* be a little reluctant to part with it. But I'll keep yours on display while I'm waiting.

He thought her eyes had a veiled glint as she walked past him down the corridor into the entrance hall. Baffled, he followed her, wondering what treasure he held under his arm. At the door, he took her hand and bowed.

—By the way, he said, three weeks from now I'm conducting a

tour of schoolchildren to scenes of historic interest in the County. May I bring them here on the twenty-fifth?

—Of course, she said. Come often—sometime when you can stay longer. I'd love to talk to someone about the County. I've been away so long, and people back here are so nice.

He was certain as he stepped out of the door that she would stand a moment watching him from behind the glass pane, her hair gorgeously alive against the dusky inward of the Museum.

Cheeks burning, *Atlas* clutched under arm, he picked his way carefully down the steps. A man had died on these steps not many days before, reaching a stiffened claw to destroy the thing that Mr. Shawnessy now carried out into the sunlight of the Fourth.

He had saved a thing golden and strange. He hugged the living myth of Raintree County under his arm.

He made a sudden plan to carry the *Atlas* into the Court House where perhaps he would have leisure to examine it, but he must show no unseemly haste. He crossed the street, walked through the gate onto the court house lawn, approached the Main Entrance, feeling himself watched by thousands of accusing eyes.

Just as he reached the steps, an aging man with white closecropped hair came out of the Court House. It was Niles Foster, founder and editor of the *Free Enquirer*.

—Hello, John! I'm surprised to see you here.

—Hello, Niles. Had a little business to transact.

—With that big program in Waycross, I should think you'd be too busy. John, I'm counting on you to send me the story of the day there. Much as I hate to, I've got to stay here in Freehaven for the program. Say, if you have a minute, come on over to the Office with me, and I'll give you a copy of the Semicentennial Edition.

Mr. Shawnessy turned and walked with Niles to the south side of the Square.

—Be sure to remember me to Garwood, Niles was saying. Say, I see the Saloon's open early today. How about a glass of beer with me in honor of the Old Days? Or are you teetotaling?

Mr. Shawnessy eyed the swinging invitation of the batwing doors. A slow sense of joy and power came over him. He had plucked a forbidden fruit and had achieved the wisdom of a god. Bright rivers of intoxication flowed through the Court House Square. He would enjoy strong temptations, be life's young victor.

—I don't know, Niles. Have to be back by nine. Wife and children waiting in the surrey and——

—I recall, Niles said, gently rambling, how your pa, old T. D., was dead set against drinking. I hadn't thought for years about the big Temperance Rally he put on in '56 and the fire and all that until I read your story of it in the 'History of the County.' Say, that reminds me—they're putting on quite a show at the New Opera House tonight. Anyway, we old-timers call it new.

He thumbsigned at theatre bills pasted on the alleyside of the Saloon.

UNCLE TOM'S CABIN

A Great Experienced Cast

Also

THE GEORGIA JAMBOLIERS

Famous Minstrel Comedians

With

ASSORTED SHORT FEATURES

See Those Burlesque Queens!

Fullfashioned ladies pranced across the poster on tiny toes.

—Sure you won't have a glass of beer with me, John?

The Saloon was a brown dusk beyond curved halves of the door. Clutching a golden bough, the hero twin lunged over a forbidden threshold, through memories of innocent wickedness, intemperate dreams. Voices gaily accusing pursued him singing, O

September 6— 'FATHER, —1856

COME OUT OF

THAT OLD SALOON'

ORIGINAL PLAY AT BIG TEMPERANCE RALLY TONIGHT

FREE ENTERTAINMENT

were the words on the crude sign hanging from the wagon. Johnny Shawnessy drove onward past the exhibits at the County Fair until he reached a point opposite the Saloon on the south side of the Square. There he stopped and as the crowd walled him in stood up on the wagon seat and said:

—Ladies and Gentlemen, come to the Opera House tonight, and bring your friends. The Play is a good one. I ought to know because I wrote it.

The crowd laughed.

—Give the boy a drink, a hoarse voice yelled.

Someone threw a tomato. Johnny ducked and drove on, one street north of the Square to the Opera House, a frame building made with wooden columns in front to resemble a Greek temple.

In front stood T. D. talking with a smartly dressed young man of middle height, who was leaning against the hitching rail, cigar in mouth, thumbs hooked in vest, thin legs crossed. He had a soft dark beard, thoughtful brown eyes, a small derby hat.

—Hello, Pa. Hello, Cash, Johnny said, pulling up.

—John, the young man said, I just been telling your pa that we ought to charge admission to this here Rally. Look at this crowd. We could clean up maybe fifty dollars.

The young man's eyes were christlike as he spoke. He unlipped his cigar and tipped the ash delicately.

—No, T. D. said. We ain't selling reform. We're offering it. Virtue ought not to be priced.

—Just a nominal sum, the young man said. Ten cents a ticket. People are likely to take it more serious if they have to pay for it. Besides you'd keep the undesirable element away.

—The undesirable element is what we desire, T. D. said.

—You got to have money to run your organization, the young man said.

—Cassius, you got natural money sense, T. D. said amiably. No getting around that. But I don't want the taint of money on this purely humanitarian venture.

In those days, Cassius Carney was already known in Raintree County as a comer. Although he wasn't much more than twenty, he had managed to get a controlling interest in the local feedstore. He had been keeping the books for the outfit when the owner died, leaving a business saddled with debt and an attractive widow, age thirty. Cash and the widow exchanged condolence of sundry kinds, and in a few weeks Cash was in the saddle and driving things with a tight rein. At the end of a year the business was his, lock, stock, and barrel.

—That there's a longheaded boy, men said. He'll go fer.

Johnny had met Cash in connection with the Temperance Drive, to which Cash had volunteered his services. One day Cash had said,

—John, you and I are some cuts above the other hicks. Frankly, I like you, and when I like a person I tell him so. Have a cigar?

—No, thanks, Cash, Johnny had said. I don't smoke. My pa would croak if I took up smoking. He's against it, you know.

—Never start it. Filthy habit, Cash had said, lighting up. I like your pa too. With all his contacts and energy, he ought to be rolling in dough. But frankly, he don't know the first thing about money. He isn't hardboiled enough. He can't make collections. I took a look at his books the other day, and I said to him, T. D., what's the use of all these fine columns of figures? You never collect half. He took a hopeful view of the thing, but he'll never see any of that money. Still, he's a nice old guy, and I like him. That's why I agreed to help him out in this Temperance Drive.

Some people said Cash was really in the Drive because he wanted to see the local saloon closed so that he could start a ginstore of his own. But T. D., who was President of the Raintree County Temperance Crusaders, was convinced that Cash had come into the Drive in response to the most virtuous impulses.

—Now that young feller, Cassius Carney, T. D. said, he's gone and joined up to the Crusaders and offered to keep our books for us and be a sort of business manager for us. A fine young feller, and I have no hesitation in saying to you that he's got as long a head on his shoulders for business at twenty as I had when I was thirty.

But Cash's real interest was the railroad. In 1855 a singletrack branch was run from the main line at Beardstown to Freehaven and on east. It passed just below the southernmost bend of the Shawmucky, between the river and the Danwebster Graveyard, running behind the Home Place. Cash would point to the railroad and say,

—There lies the future.

Those days, Johnny didn't think the future lay down the railroad at all. The railroad was a lonely, manmade thing piercing bleakly through halfcleared forests. Once a day a chugging woodburner engine and a few cars went by.

—Where you going now, John? T. D. said, when Johnny had left the wagon behind the Opera House.

—Back to the Square, Johnny said. I thought I'd look the Fair over.

—If you see Nell and Garwood, T. D. said, tell 'em to be sure to get over here at seven-thirty tonight. Wouldn't hurt us to have one more quick rehearsal of the Play.

The Square was a tented town within a town. Excepting a cleared space for the political rallies, tents were everywhere on the court house lawn, and venders had set up stands along the curbs and sidewalks. Barkers for sideshows and amusements advertised their wares. One whole side of the Square was roped off for exhibitions of livestock. Bulls bellowed, cows mooed, chickens clucked, pigs snorted from wooden enclosures in the unpaved streets. Crowds flowed by to see the biggest bulls, the gaudiest cocks, the heaviest ears of corn in Raintree County.

—Ladies and gentlemen, spare me a minute of your precious time.

It was a vaguely familiar voice booming across the tented confusion, pouring bright oils of hope on the Square.

—I trust you all perceive the object that I hold in my hand. It is only a plain, unadorned, ordinary . . .

—Fatima, barked a vibrant voice, is the biggest hunk of human flesh on the face of the globe. And yet, friends, she is as bee-ewtiful as she is big. And along with this, friends, I have inside this tent six other impossible, unbelievable freaks. You can't afford to miss . . .

—Hucko the Strong, a man with a megaphone was shouting from the exhibition ground, is the winner of last year's prize competition in the yearling class. Notice his unusual . . .

Pointer raised, a bespectacled man standing beneath a tree indicated areas on the Phrenological Chart.

—To each and all of you, I want to put this question. Are you all that you hoped to be in the bloom of your youth? Do you possess . . .

FREE SOIL, FREE SPEECH, AND FRÉMONT

were the words printed on a large sign carried by a belligerent man in a stovepipe hat who was leading a snakedance of citizens through the Square. He disappeared among the tents while the trail of his followers dissolved in confusion.

—What's this here line formin' fer? a citizen asked.

—I don't rightly know, a second citizen said. I hear we're gittin' free beer tother end of the Square.

—How's that? said a third citizen. Ain't this a demonstration agin Frémont?

—No, it's *fer* Frémont, the first citizen said.

—Way I heard it, the second citizen persisted, we was goin' to git . . .

A VOTE FOR BUCHANAN IS A VOTE FOR THE UNION

appeared on a placard carried at the head of another line, which mingled with the first.

A man stood on the sidewalk beside a metal chair that dangled from the hook of a weighing apparatus. While a crowd watched, a woman sitting in the chair pulled the pointer up to a hundred and forty-five.

—Sorry, Madame, the man said. No surprise box of Bonafee's Bon Bons for you. Next! Guess your weight! Guess your weight! If I miss by more than three pounds, you get a box of . . .

—Hello, Johnny.

Nell was standing beside him, revealed by a shifting of the crowd. She was wearing the green dress he had seen at the Danwebster Church. Her hair was pulled hard to the shape of her head and was rolled up into a huge bun that rode the back of her neck. It gave her little face a bare look and seemed to magnify the big eyes which, when he turned, gazed thoughtfully into his. Except for the caressing way in which she had said the word 'Johnny'—a word that seemed to invite vocal caresses—she was studiedly proper, as indeed she had been all through the play rehearsals.

—Hello, Nell, he said. Say, I was looking for you.

Along the Shawmucky, the summer reeds are yellow, leaves are falling in the shallows, the waterbirds are crying. I waited by the deep pool close to the twin mounds. I was behind rushes watching all afternoon. But you didn't come again.

—Smoke, John? Garwood Jones said.

He had been standing on the other side of Nell.

—No, thanks, Johnny said.

Garwood made a fat curl of smoke around his fat lips. His face was smooth and creamy.

—Guess your weight, the weightguessing man said.

—How do you tell? Nell asked.

—We can't tell about the ladies, the man said. God made 'em, but Godey did 'em over. We just guess the ladies and hope we get within a hundred miles.

Nell put out her tonguetip and fluttered it between her teeth while her eyes studied the apparatus.

—Well, I'll try, she said.

—Step right up, young lady.

The man was a brash scoundrel with a fox face. He touched Nell's bare arm and turned her in the street.

—In Kentucky, he said, we feel the ladies. But of course, in Indiana——

The crowd laughed. Nell allowed herself to be turned. Nothing seemed to disturb the green composure of her eyes.

—Brother, said Garwood Jones, if you guess it, I'll take it away.

—You get the better end of that deal, the weightguesser said.

Who will guess the weight of the most beautiful exhibit at the County Fair? In Kentucky, we feel the ladies. But in Indiana, we hide behind rushes and watch them in the river. Who will guess the weight of the river nymph? Add in, too, the beautyspot, on the left cheek of her saucy tail. Without that, you'll be a little short.

—Well now, young lady—— the weightguesser said.

He ran eyes of shrewd appraisal all over her body, then back again to her face.

—Chum, I'll bet you a cigar I can guess it closer than you will, Garwood said.

—Taken, chum, the guesser said, unless you have special advantages. Does this young man know this young lady?

—Not that well, Nell said.

—We have to allow a lot for the things we can't see, the weightguesser said. With the women, it's pure magic.

—I say one hundred and thirty pounds, Garwood said.

—I see, my boy, the weightguesser said, that you're a lame hand at this sport.

The crowd laughed.

—All right, the weightguesser said, I guess this young lady's weight to be——

He hesitated.

—Let me guess too, Johnny said impulsively.

—No fair, Nell said.

—One hundred and thirteen pounds, shouted the weightguesser, for the young woman and seven for the accessories. One hundred and twenty pounds. Now, young lady, if you'll just park yourself in this chair and lift your dainty feet off the ground.

Nell sat down, gravely gathering her skirts about her. The pointer squeaked up and stopped at a shade over one hundred and twenty pounds.

—Ha, ha, laughed the weightguesser. Wonder what I left out? Well, do I get to keep her, boy?

The crowd applauded.

—Here's your smoke, chum, Garwood said in his grand manner. Now don't forget to vote for James Buchanan for President.

Nell sat swinging gently a moment under the scales, hands folded in her lap. Her eyes were enigmatic.

Had she at last confessed their naughty secret? But she looked slowly away, patting the bun of hair, and stood up.

Johnny gave the message about the rehearsal and then walked away into the crowd. He had seen the arithmetic of gravity applied to the most beautiful thing in Raintree County. For some reason it made him faint with love.

Weigh me a hundred and thirteen pounds of Raintree County earth. Weigh me the loamy, lively earth from the river valley. Weigh in the river and the color of the river and the lazy curve of the river. Weigh in desire.

Johnny slouched around on the fringes of a crowd listening to a political speaker. The man was a Republican candidate for the State Legislature, but his topic was the State of the Nation. He spoke at some length about the fighting in Kansas between the slavery faction and the free-soilers, who were being led by a man named John Brown. He said that the Republican Party was the defender of the Constitution and didn't seek to kill slavery but only to prevent its spread. He quoted someone he referred to as the Honorable Abraham Lincoln of Illinois as having said,

> —Slavery is founded on the selfishness of man's nature—opposition to it in his love of justice. These principles are in eternal antagonism, and when brought into collision so fiercely as slavery extension brings them, shocks and throes and convulsions must ceaselessly follow.

There was a big crowd in the Opera House at eight o'clock that night when the Temperance Rally began. T. D., Cash Carney, and members of the cast peeked out from between the drawn curtains and were appalled by hundreds of faces.

—If we'd charged fifty cents admission, Cash said, we'd of been able to buy the Saloon and then burn it down.

T. D. had a hard time bringing the crowd to order. Some ladies vocalized a few temperance songs. T. D. gave a speech, but was heckled all the way through by a hoarse voice in the back of the house. When T. D. made the first call for volunteers to come up and take the Total Abstinence Pledge, a young man came down the aisle aided and encouraged by a group of companions. Watching from the wings, Johnny saw that it was Flash Perkins, the undefeated champion runner of the County.

—I wanna take pledge, Flash said in a loud, hoarse voice.

—My dear boy, T. D. said mildly, I want no one but sober men to take this pledge.

—If yuh wan' no one but sober men, what's use havin' 'em take it? Flash said.

The crowd applauded. T. D. tried to explain.

—Then I wanna make testimonial, Flash said. Wanna testify that I been drunk fer two weeks. I have drank beer, wine, whiskey, and hair-ile. Friend, I'm drunk. I defy any man here to drink much as I have and walk straight. I can still outrace any man in this here County.

—Please, T. D. said, you're disturbing the Rally. Will some friend of this young man's please——

—I ain' disturbin' no rally, Flash said. Wanna make lil testimonial. Wanna tell folks how I got into thish disrespectibubble condition so's they can avoid same mistake.

—Well, all right, T. D. said. Go ahead.

—When I small boy, Flash said, I sick of the colic. My parents took me emminunt physician in these parts, I mean respected gennulman now on stage fore y'all, Mr. T. D. Shawnessy. Medicine he give me contained brandy, folks, at least a halfpint. I drank it then, when I small and unsuspectin' infant, and I been drinkin' ever since.

The crowd laughed. Flash laughed too, baring his white bright teeth. He held his hard belly and laughed a high, hooting laugh that ended in an Indian whoop. Laughing with head thrown back, he walked up the aisle. No one touched him.

Cash Carney reached out, caught T. D.'s coattails, and pulled him gently through the curtain.

—Dim the lights, Cash said. Let's have the Play. Meanwhile, I'll go down and get those hoodlums out of here.

T. D. went back out and read the playbill to the audience.

FATHER, COME OUT OF THAT OLD SALOON

or

Drink, Crime, Adultery, Poverty, Death,
and Damnation

by

John Wickliff Shawnessy

BELLE BRAYDON, a beautiful spirited girl........Miss Nell Gaither
WILLIAM WORTH, a virtuous young man from the
country.........................Mr. John Wickliff Shawnessy
FERDIE FAIRWEATHER, a villainous fellow......Mr. Garwood Jones
PEACHES MONROE, a Girl of the Town..........Miss Fanny Rider

MR. WEBSTER WEAKLY, an intemperate
Father.................................Mr. Ezekiel Shawnessy
PHOEBE WEAKLY, his hapless daughter........Miss Faith Shawnessy
BARNEY BILGE, a bartender........................Mr. Jake Dryer
Habitués of the Saloon....................Messers Bob Parsons,
Ezra Joiner, Nat Franklin, and Waldo Pierce
Male Quartette composed of: Messers Jake Dryer, Nat Franklin,
Bob Parsons, and John Wickliff Shawnessy.
Original Lyrics by Mr. John Wickliff Shawnessy and sung by members
of the cast and the Male Quartette.

ACT I
In Barney Bilge's Barroom

ACT II
Scene One: A railroad track in a lonely part of the country
Scene Two: Back at the Barroom

ACT III
Down by the Railroad Track

The hollow womb of the Opera House rumored applause as Johnny Shawnessy walked out of the dressing room and into the darkened wings, wandering vaguely toward the other side of the stage where the ladies' dressing room was.

For weeks, he had envisioned to himself an impossibly beautiful thing. It was that some time he would be hunting behind the scenes in the Opera House, when no one else was there, and he would find his way to a forbidden room where the ladies changed their clothes, a neglected closet where costumes and greasepaints were stored. There through the halfopen door he would see Nell Gaither in among the hanging costumes, river-naked in the glow of the gaslight. Her hair, parted in the middle, would be bound up to show her ears, her face would be smouldering with a thin mask of paint and powder. Invitation would be in her eyes as she looked back at him over her shoulder allowing him to see the supple column of her back.

In fact, he now saw Nell coming out of the door of the ladies' dressing room. She walked over to him.

—Johnny, she said, I'm so scared. Feel my hands.

He took her hands. They were cold and sweating like his own.

—If I remember my first line, I'll be all right.

—Think how I feel, Johnny said. I wrote this darn play. I wish now I never had.

—It's a wonderful play, honest! How do you like my costume, Johnny?

—Very becoming, he said.

—Is my make-up on straight?

She held her face up, tilted toward a weak illumination shed through joints in the scenery. Her face, pertly composed with paint and powder, filled him with despair. It was not the face of the loving one, shy, with averted eyes.

—You look beautiful, Nell, he said, but laughed a little to show he didn't mean anything by it.

Garwood Jones was stomping around through the angles that held up the scenery. He wore a big black mustache with oiled points and a black derby. T. D. was calling from the front. The crowd was applauding. Johnny ran to the left wing. The curtains rolled back. The Play was on.

The scene was the interior of a Saloon, where habitués leaned against the bar, among them an old man who laughed drunkenly and rolled his head on the counter:

WILLIAM WORTH

entering, addressing the old man,

—You seem happy, sir. But consider that there are doubtless those who are rendered desperately unhappy by your behavior.

FATHER

—Ah, yes, alas! Poor little Phoebe! But then I'll not think of that now. Give us another glass, bartender. Fill it up, and let's forget our troubles, boys. Laugh with me, boys, laugh!

WILLIAM

moving to front of stage with piano accompaniment and singing,

—Laugh if you will, and drink your fill
Of the cup that is crowned with foam.
But the day will come when the demon rum
Will lay you in the loam.

Some day a girl with a little curl
Who once to you was dear
Will point to that den of degraded men
And say, as she drops a tear:

From the wings entering came Phoebe, thin, forlorn, her corn-colored hair down and trailing.

PHOEBE

singing in a high sweet voice,

—O Father, come out of that old Saloon.
They say you are full of gin.
They say you've been drinking there since noon,
And are sunk in the sink of sin.
O Father, hearken, dear Father, 'tis I,
And my heart will be breaking soon,
Unless you list to my plaintive cry:—
Come out of that old Saloon!

From this classic opening in the best and purest tradition of the American Temperance Drama, Johnny Shawnessy's play proceeded according to a well-defined formula. So in the Raintree County Opera House, in a box of quaint and timeless postures called a stage, the Honest Country Boy made his visit to the Wicked City to find his beloved engaged in a Menial Capacity. In the name of the Cold Water Army, he refused the Proffered Glass. The Little Golden-haired Girl came seeking her Drunken Father, and the Male Quartette assisted her in captivating waltztime. The Bigamous and Glittering Villain proposed marriage to the Virtuous but Misguided Heroine, who was estranged from her True Love by an Unfortunate Misunderstanding. Down by the Railroad Tracks, the Hissing Villain dragged the Unwilling Heroine into the path of the Approaching Train to Force her Virtue. Meanwhile, the Inept but Upright Hero was tempted by a Girl of the Town to Drown his Sorrows in the Lethean Wine. Warned by the sound of the train whistle, he appeared in time to Foil the Villain, who even with a pistol was no match for the Intrepid Strength of Indignant Virtue. The cardboard train ran swiftly across the scene, missed the Shrieking Heroine, and mangled the Prostrate Villain. And back in the barroom, the Play achieved the classic ending:

WILLIAM

to assembled cast, minus Ferdie,

—And I attribute whatever success I have had to my inflexible resolution never to touch a drop of intoxicating beverage.

Father and others promised to reform, and the two lovers discovered that their correspondence had been intercepted by the bartender.

BARTENDER

—I destroyed all those letters before the young lady had a chance to read them. I am heartily sorry for my nefarious conduct, and in retribution I am going to turn my saloon into a respectable eating house.

WILLIAM

taking Belle's hand and singing,

—I came to the City, a vagrant day,
In the bloom of my blithesome youth,
And I sought in the City great and gray
The beautiful bird of Truth.
I sought her along the wide, wide streets,
The glimmering parks and lawns,
Through all of the City's dim retreats
And under its lonely dawns.

CHORUS

entire cast,

—O beautiful, beautiful singing bird
That I sought in my happy youth.
O marvellous song that touched and stirred
My heart with the love of Truth.

WILLIAM

second verse,

—And many a year I spent at last
In the City's swallowing void,
Till it seemed that my youthful dream were past
And its delicate form destroyed.
Then I decided no more to roam,
And I turned me with a will
Back to the hills of my native home
Where the bird was singing still.

FATHER

coming forward, after second chorus,

—A toast to the lovers!

PHOEBE

—But, Father, you promised!

FATHER

with a subtle smile,

—A toast to the lovers in that most beneficial of all beverages, that most excellent of elixirs, that plenteous and replenishing draft, that transparent restorer of our strength, which God has lavished upon mankind in such copious quantities. Bartender, bring me a glass of water!

Now while the Play lived its brief existence before the footlights, life had pressed darkly around it from behind the scenes. Between the first two acts, while the scenery was being shifted, unknown to the audience who watched the Play, the Playwright and Principal Actor had climbed a winding metal stair hung like a ladder from the loft of the stage. From the crow's nest at the top, in a tangle of old curtains and cables, though well hidden himself, the Playwright had looked down on the whole cluttered world behind the scenes, musing, while puppet-like the figures of the stage crew and the cast moved on grotesquely shortened bodies below.

From his perch he had seen Nell Gaither emerge from the ladies' dressing room in a far corner of the backstage area. The steep angle of his vision had emphasized the feminine bulge of hip and bustle line. Her shoulders and waist had swayed slenderly as she hesitated a moment by the door and then walked slowly toward an obscure corner of the stage, where she appeared to be alone, standing in silhouette against an unused sceneshift of woodland and river scenery. But she had hardly come there when as if by appointment a figure, whose bulky shoulders were hugely enhanced by the downward angle of vision had moved confidently out of a near-by maze of partitions and found its way into the same corner. There the first figure had melted passively into it. The Playwright had heard a stifled giggle and a mellow bass chuckle.

There had been no doubt about it. Garwood Jones was kissing Nell Gaither in that obscure corner of the Opera House, as no doubt he had done many times before during rehearsals. And even at that distance, the Playwright could tell that Garwood's hands were not unfamiliar with the place where a slender back began its downward curve into Raintree County's most beautiful twin mounds.

In greasepaint, bowtie, and straw skimmer, simulating the honest boy from the country, Johnny Shawnessy had clung unhappily to his lofty perch and watched the villain of the Play kiss the willing heroine. So life, an intemperate comedy, had giggled and guffawed at his genteel little temperance farce.

He had felt all along that he had miscast the parts. He had early begun to envy Garwood the role of villain. It was much the more exciting role—or perhaps Garwood himself made it that way with his authoritative baritone and his big sleek body, which was now masterfully pushing and throbbing against the little Venus with a Raintree County face.

And at that moment Johnny Shawnessy's love had reached such a furious peak of unfulfillment that he had felt like shutting his eyes and hurling himself down from his high mast upon the little backstage world to shatter it to bits.

Instead, he had watched until Garwood and Nell separated, then carefully shinnied back to the floor to await the opening of the Second Act.

Now that the Play was over, the curtain opened again to reveal the entire cast singing 'O Father, Come Out of That Old Saloon.' T. D. was out before the crowd exhorting them to come forward and take the Total Abstinence Pledge. The gasyellowed walls of the Opera House rang with young joyous voices. In greasepaint and green gown, Nell Gaither swayed in time to the music between Johnny Shawnessy and Garwood Jones, who were holding each a hand. And for this rhythmical moment, it seemed to Johnny that the anguish of his frustrate love became an ecstasy, as of possession.

—O Father, hearken, dear Father, 'tis I,
And my heart will be breaking soon,
Unless you list to my plaintive cry:—

—Fire! Fire! yelled a red-faced man who had been standing on the stage like an actor, waving his arms and trying to make himself heard above the song.

This too was a dream of something implausible like the Play, and a dream too was the deadheavy hush that fell on the Opera House, and like a dream the lazy drift of smoke from the wings, and like a dream the crackling sheet of flame.

As fire roared from the vague world of the wings, the pit of the Opera House became a whirlpool of faces and frenzied arms. Johnny, Nell, Garwood, and the other performers ran wildly about looking for water. There was nothing but some jugs of colored water that had been used to simulate liquor in the Play. Johnny threw it at the flames, but the next moment he was driven clear off the stage. As he and the other performers climbed out through a rear window, he heard gas explode, wood smash, glass splinter, women scream.

And then there was running to and fro, the sound of firebells ringing, the sight of the firemen coming down the street pulling their new wagon and unrolling hose. The last few people came out of the darkened, roaring womb of the Opera House with singed hair, torn clothes, bleeding faces.

Apparently no one had been seriously hurt, but there was nothing anyone could do about the Opera House except to watch it burn. The whole County seemed to be there in a vast circle filling up streets and yards for blocks back, cheering the newly organized fire department. Everyone looked happy and excited. Men performed prodigies of valor and strength. Flash Perkins, who an hour before had been almost too drunk to stand, risked his life over and over. Everyone was vastly pleased with the new firewagon. It added a great deal to the interest and excitement of the occasion.

Johnny stood close to Nell and several other members of the cast, all talking excitedly.

—Ain't the new firewagon a beauty! someone said.

—It's wonderful, Nell said.

—No building in Raintree County ever burned down so efficiently, Johnny said.

The Opera House was a big broad torch roaring straight-up and casting light down the roads for miles.

—It's like a pillar of fire by night, T. D. said.

Johnny felt that he must devour this spectacle and possess it all, the dense firelit faces of the crowd, the gay terror of the springing fire, the glistening helmets of the firemen, the shining perfection of the new firewagon. The Play itself had been leading to this great torch of flame in which the yellow interiors of the Opera House were consumed forever.

It was late at night before the Opera House collapsed in ash and smoking timbers. People began to go home, agreeing that the fire was by far the most successful exhibit at the County Fair.

—It was a wonderful play, Johnny, Nell said. I enjoyed being in it.

She was leaning out of Garwood's buggy. Her face had rivulets of sweat through the greasepaint, her hair hung wispily around her cheeks, her eyes had stains of darkness under them, and her fruity mouth above her small pointed chin looked particularly luscious.

—Let's go, my proud beauty, Garwood said.

He shook the reins and took her away.

T. D. came up with a small shabby man.

—I want you all to meet Mr. Gruber, T. D. said. He came around after the fire and took the Temperance Pledge. He's the only one that did.

They all looked at Mr. Gruber. He was little, and he had a red nose and watery eyes. He took off his hat and shook hands with Ellen Shawnessy.

—Well, T. D. said, it's a start.

As they were driving home, T. D. said,

—People are more interested now in politics than anything else. And of course the fire broke up the whole shebang just when it was about to do the most good.

In the back seat the young people were singing songs from the Play.

> —I went to the City, a vagrant day,
> In the bloom of my blithesome youth. . . .

Johnny heard the whistle of a train coming along the branch line behind the Home Place and past the south bend of the Shawmucky. He thought of the river running in the night, treebordered, faintly shining; of the alien engine passing close to its waters, screaming alarm, emergency, disaster; of Nell Gaither's pretty calves beneath her dress; of her candid face upturned and smeared with greasepaint. And of Garwood Jones, that enormously competent young man, so vigorous in obtaining his objectives, crowding his face against her face.

Then there came to him a terrible image in which Garwood Jones achieved the very conquest that Johnny Shawnessy had dreamed a hundred times for himself. Strangely, this vision was not entirely unpleasant to him—he had some fierce joy in it, or else why did he repeat it obsessively?

And now it seemed to him that he must never love or pursue Nell Gaither again, for she was certainly another's and laughed at him and cared nothing for him and never could understand his great soul.

And in that thought his love achieved its hopeless climax of desire.

This desire had acquired new backdrops for its tireless make-believe. In the interiors of an extinct Opera House, the ghost of his play lingered, aspiring to be something high, tragic, and meaningful, the Great American Drama, more wondrous than the plays of Shakespeare. It hovered wistfully, all entangled with something confused, remorseless, yet beautiful, the Comedy of Life. Unpencilled and unvocalized, scenes of this greater Play crowded against halfopening curtains of Time. Some day he would write this play, the image of his great desire.

His day would come.

For him, deepfleshed thighs waited in the night under velvet costumes, up stairs that the sceneshifters mount. For him (the intemperate young man), the City great and gray. For him, kisses like alcohol, green inundations of desire.

His desire was of the river, but it was also of the train and its quavering whistle in the night and of the City to which the train was speeding. Desire hunting through the rooms of an old opera house had found its way into a bigger opera house and behind the scenes of an immense stage where the firstnight audience was a lake of murmuring faces. And here Mr. John Wickliff Shawnessy, the greatest playwright of the age, sought a green-eyed girl up the most winding stairs and into the most neglected room, where no one else ever came. Desire was of the river, but the weedy Shawmucky flowed from Raintree County to a joining with greater rivers gemmed with cities in the night! And if not now, then some day, the river nymph would yield herself to a more sophisticated Johnny. He would find on a certain deep, mysterious mound a little hieroglyph, the birthmark of the river. Then, he too would be erring, he too would drink a drink that maddened, a beverage of kisses and of fame, and it would be running in his veins like this fever of the river that he couldn't lose, and it wouldn't be at all like the effect of that purest and most excellent of all beverages,

THAT TRANSPARENT RESTORER OF OUR
STRENGTH, BARTENDER, BRING
ME

—A GLASS OF WATER, Niles, if you don't mind. I'll just step into the office with you and get the paper.

They stepped through the door of the newspaper office, and Niles went to a stack of fresh papers.

—Here you are, he said. I've had a lot of fun putting it together. It stirs up old memories. By the way, thanks for your 'History of the County.' No one else knows it so well.

Mr. Shawnessy took the fat memorial newspaper and turned the pages.

—If I could have four or five extra copies, Niles, I'd like to give them to friends at Waycross. The Senator will want a copy. Cash Carney is going to stop off for a little while on his way to Pittsburgh. I'd like to have a copy for him.

—Help yourself, John. Be sure to give one to General Jackson too. I understand he's going to lead a march of G.A.R. veterans to point up the pension issue.

—Garwood thought of everything.

—Are we ever going to stop fighting that damn war? Niles said from a back room.

He returned with the water.

—I've given nearly the whole front page, he said, to the big doings in Waycross. Did you ever stop to think, John, how many great men Raintree County has given to the Nation? Here's Garwood Jones, a distinguished U.S. Senator for eighteen years and favorably mentioned for the Presidency in the next election, and here's Cassius Carney, a big railroad magnate, one of the richest men in the country, and of course General Jackson, an outstanding hero of the War—all three of them returning to the County today for this big celebration. I don't suppose anything like it ever happened before. And to think that you and I knew all those people in the Old Days!

Niles looked out of the front window at the Court House, through the reversed letters of the paper's name.

—How the face of the County has changed since I founded the *Free Enquirer* fifty years ago! Just take, for example, those illustrations accompanying your article—the Old Court House, the Old Methodist Church, the Old Opera House, and the Academy. All gone now.

—I thought the Academy Building was still up.

—Only half of it. Up to two years ago it was a cheap hotel. Then the railroad decided to extend the yards into that lot. They ripped off the front half of the old building and put a platform on. I think they're using it for storing grain and coal now.

Mr. Shawnessy had found the picture on page eighteen over the words:

THE OLD PEDEE ACADEMY

—Say what you will, John—those were the Good Old Days! I still remember as clear as anything how we brought higher education to Raintree County.

Standing in the office of the *Free Enquirer,* sniffing the odor of damp newsprint, Mr. Shawnessy ran his eye over the manycolumned 'History of Raintree County,' a mist of fine words flowing around the stiff engravings of buildings old and new and scenic views. He remembered then the old Academy Building, a place of young voices and tattered books. He remembered chalked words, light in the little lecture hall, changing with the changing seasons of the County. And he seemed to remember also the frustrate dream of a young republic, an academic dream of pillars and perfection, which had thrust itself to flower in the dark chaos of time and had left a white remembrance on the lips of men. There came to him a noise of waters beating on leaguelong beaches. Undraped forms rose from a shrine in Raintree County, as from a womb of fair and fecund issue.

A forgotten youth sprang toward the forms of that adolescent republic, with a copy of Ovid's *Metamorphoses* in his hand.

He remembered reeds made vocal by the passion and pursuit of nymph and god down by the riverside.

And he remembered especially a winged visitor from the direction of the sun, who had alighted walking on the fields of that republic, teaching a forbidden music on his unusual lyre.

Mr. Shawnessy folded the papers and piled them on the face of the *Raintree County Historical Atlas*.

They were all gone, slain by a smoky dragon, driven from their groves beside the river. The beautiful young gods had abandoned Raintree County. He remembered

1857— How —1859

A QUAINT VISITOR ARRIVED IN THE GARDEN OF RAINTREE COUNTY

bringing much learning from the East. In September of 1857 the following article appeared in the *Free Enquirer:*

AN INSTITUTION OF HIGHER LEARNING

Raintree County is to have an institution of higher learning. This temple of Minerva, which at the request of its financial sponsors will bear the dignified and not unsonorous appellation of Pedee Academy, is to be instituted in the large brick building formerly known as the Taylor Boarding House. The new college is to be conducted upon the most progressive modern principles. Female as well as male students are desiderated. Courses in Latin, English Rhetoric, Philosophy, Natural History, Mathematics, and Ancient and Modern History will be offered with a diploma after two years of study. Also classes will be conducted in which adults may learn to read and write.

The principal of the new college, Professor Jerusalem Webster Stiles, has studied in the best schools of the East, including Harvard, and has spent some years abroad. A native of the County, he was born on the very day, January 28, 1830, on which Webster delivered the classic reply to Hayne. Hence the name bestowed upon him by his pious and patriotic parents. Professor Stiles is conversant with several languages and is a man of great personal amiability.

Republican Institutions cannot be maintained without universal enlightenment. Let all the intellect and enterprise in Raintree County flock to the new Academy and demonstrate to the world that we have as much gray matter under our hats as the next fellow.

Johnny Shawnessy was among the dozen Raintree County citizens who answered this challenge. During the year that had passed since the Temperance Play, he had been teaching at a school—his first—at Summit in the north-central part of the County. He had lost sight of Nell Gaither, but heard that she had returned to live in the East. It seemed unlikely that he would see her again in Raintree County.

Meanwhile, he had gone on writing for the *Enquirer*, reading all the books he could get his hands on, versifying, and in general preparing to be a Great Man. As winter passed and spring and summer came again, he was annoyed at times by an inability to call up a precise image of Nell's face. For diversion he attended the usual taffy pulls, square dances, husking bees, barbecues, and ice-cream socials by means of which the County placed its young people in legitimate proximity. Johnny was popular on these occasions and began to lose a little of his shyness. In fact, he kissed and was kissed by several Raintree County girls, who showed great interest and proficiency in the sport. All of them talked a good deal in his presence about friends of theirs who had been recently married.

On the day of his enrollment in the new college, Johnny walked to the Academy building, two blocks south of the Square, finding a comfortable two-story brick house set in the middle of a wide lawn shaded by elms. He walked up onto the verandah and through the front door into a hall where several prospective students were waiting to see the new professor. Among the young men, Johnny recognized Garwood Jones and Cassius Carney.

—Well, look who's here, boys! Garwood said. High time someone connected with the *Enquirer* learned to read and write.

Just then a door opened, and from a side room where Professor Stiles was interviewing candidates a young woman appeared.

—Hello, Johnny.

The word was softly uttered and highly personal.

Instantly, as if it had only slept to increase its strength, an old passion came alive. The young woman who looked demurely up at him had not changed from his earlier memory of her.

—Hello, Nell, he said. Are you enrolling in the College?

—Yes, I am, Johnny.

—It's awfully nice seeing you again, Nell.

—It's nice seeing you again too, Johnny.

They were shaking hands and smiling in the best Raintree County tradition.

—Next! Come in, my boy! said a pleasant, high-pitched voice.

Blushing from this reunion with desire, Johnny Shawnessy walked through the door to his first meeting with Professor Jerusalem Webster Stiles.

The man who stood in the little office room of the Pedee Academy made Johnny Shawnessy think of a huge, vivid insect that had flown from unknown parts and lit walking in Raintree County. Surely there was nothing else in the County like him. He was tall and thin. Black hair, split exactly in the middle, was slicked flat to a long, narrow head. The nose suggested a cutting instrument. Small piercing black eyes, not quite in focus, peered through pince-nez glasses. From that moment on, Johnny always had an uneasy presentiment that Professor Stiles was not there to stay. Sometime, in the very middle of a sentence, abruptly remembering whence and why he had come, he would rise to the points of his toes, his black coat-tails would erect themselves into shining wings, and his angular brittle body would shoot off the ground and go whirring down the air to some other temporary lodgment on the American earth.

Just now he was holding out a cigar to Johnny.

—Sit down, my boy. Smoke?

—No, thanks, Johnny said. I don't smoke.

—Filthy habit. Never start it. Ah, to be innocent once again, my boy, as you are now, before women, tobacco, and bad whiskey ruined me!

The man behind the desk showed his even white teeth and shook soundlessly as if his body were being subjected to a series of galvanic shocks.

Johnny was quite certain then that he had never in his life seen anything or anybody remotely like the new teacher, and he had no reason to change that opinion in the weeks and months that followed as he became better acquainted with Professor Jerusalem Webster Stiles.

From the beginning Raintree County called him 'the Perfessor.' Johnny Shawnessy, some cuts above the other hicks, as Cassius Carney had said, was careful always to preserve the first syllable pure, but the rest of the County said it perversely wrong; and even to Johnny this quaint distortion had an ideal fitness. For it was the same title that had been applied from time immemorial in the County to all the glib, fraudulent creatures who appeared at carnivals and festive anniversaries to sell hair tonic, quick success, and brand-new sexual potency to the common folk. Each of these egregious fakirs was known to his assistants and to the unschooled yokels as the Perfessor. It was a title of respect for an itinerant wizard who robbed the people by sheer power of language. Johnny had seen it happen a hundred times and never failed to enjoy the magnificently comic spectacle of a victory won by cunning from human hope and greed. So, too, Professor Jerusalem Webster Stiles, most glittering and gifted of all the Perfessors who ever came to Raintree County, understood the aspirations and appetites of mankind. Quack and genius combined, he perpetrated on the citizens of Raintree County a continual farce, whipping and stinging them with the scorn of his incomparably superior intellect, yet in a manner so subtly ironic that they never perceived how entirely they were bilked. As for his Raintree County title, the Perfessor accepted it, as he accepted all things, with tolerant cynicism. In a way he belonged to Raintree County himself, and if he ever had a home, it was there.

For the Perfessor had been born in Raintree County, had left it during his childhood, and had not returned until the opening of the Academy. He still talked the County's tongue, though in some ways his speech had been slightly altered as if through contact with an older, more sophisticated culture. Often the words he used seemed not wholly spontaneous but as if recollected and put quaintly together from the pages of innumerable books. Exceptional was the Perfessor's memory for quotations, which he would toss out in the course of lecture or conversation, with skipping irrelevance and a shy smile from his unfocused eyes. Johnny was not always sure whether the Perfessor was quoting or extemporizing. Once after he and the Perfessor had become well acquainted, Johnny asked him about it, and the Perfessor admitted that he wasn't always sure himself.

—What is all speech, John, but a quotation? When we are not quoting from books, we are quoting from Nature.

Perhaps because of his youth—he was only twenty-seven—the Perfessor placed his students on a basis of entire equality with himself. The boys used to go up to his quarters on the second floor of the Academy and sit around talking literature, philosophy, and politics while the Perfessor presided like a scurrilous and skeptic Greek, sometimes dispensing corn liquor and always cigars. Everyone smoked and drank but Johnny.

The Perfessor imported a great many shocking ideas into Raintree County. In sex, religion, politics, and literature he was a radical departure from everything the County taught. In the classroom, he curbed himself, but in private talk he gave out heretical doctrine. Exchanging his classroom pointer for a cane, he would swing down a country road with one of his disciples—more often Johnny Shawnessy than not—quoting from the incredible grab-bag of his memory, skipping from theme to theme, casting off words and ideas that fell on the County's fertile soil like seeds of exotic, fastgrowing flowers. His private talk was a mixture of the learned and the colloquial. When he was in vein, his speech was a ceaselessly bright torrent of ideas and witticisms. At first Johnny listened as if charmed. Later he found that he himself became more eloquent than usual in conversation with the Perfessor. It was a little like reading Shakespeare and then becoming one himself. For the Perfessor included among his gifts the power to follow the will-o'-the-wisp of ideas without rancor or arrogance wherever the chase might lead. It seemed to Johnny that in the Perfessor he had discovered an alter ego. His teacher's words often came to him like queer half-recollections of something he himself might have been or thought a long time ago. The Perfessor, for his part, regarded Johnny as a special being.

—John, he said once, you don't know how gifted you are. All ideas seem to exist in you already and to await only touching into life. You understand by hints, where someone else must read whole books and live a lifetime. Yours is the poet's mind—but not your little simpering metrist and maker of sweet parlor verse. No, you make me think of the young Plato, eager for ideas. Or Homer, hearkening to legends. Or the genial young Elizabethan himself, steeped in life. But Raintree County has added something American—a touch of innocence that is like the earth, the sunshine, and the river. Never lose, my boy, this eagerness for life and this primitive innocence. As, alas! I did long ago! Perhaps I should never have left the County.

And the Perfessor's eyes acquired a look of fake sadness.

Most of the time his words were curling and crackling around ideas that shocked even such enlightened beings as Garwood Jones, Cash Carney, and Johnny Shawnessy.

—The Christian Religion, the Perfessor remarked once, is the product of a dreadful mistake. Somehow the mind of humanity got obsessed with the bloody Hebrew legends and has been lugging around ever since the burden of this vindictive old man called God, who is equally repulsive in his rages and in his self-glorifying love! Pass the cigars, John.

Slightly stunned, Johnny would pass the cigars.

—Perfessor, Garwood said, if one word of that got out to the wrong parties in the County, you'd go out of town on a rail. In fact, I wouldn't mind daubing on the tar myself.

They all argued with the Perfessor about these matters. Garwood, in particular, appealed to a strict construction of the Bible, as he did of the Constitution in the political debates held at the Academy.

—As for the Bible, said the Perfessor, it's just a lot of old Jewish myths and archives, some of it pretty dull stuff. If we have to believe in myths, what's wrong with selecting something beautiful. I would rather contemplate Venus' cute behind than old Moses' withered puss. Not that the Hebrews didn't toss off some wonderful poetry now and then. They were wise, those old beards, and they knew the wine and the roses of life, as well as the ashes. *Stay me with flagons, comfort me with apples: for I am sick of love.* By the way, did you ever know any Jewish women, Garwood?

—Not since the six I had last New Year's Eve, said Garwood, always a fast man with a comeback.

—Well, did I ever tell you, the Perfessor went on, about the time I outflanked a Jewess in Vienna. She was the original Assyrian harlot—though of quite good family, understand—a vast, dark beauty who mauled your fragile mentor all of a winter's night. Ah, those great Babylonian thighs! Jesus and Jacob, what a woman! John, pass the cigars.

Stunned, Johnny would pass the cigars, and the Perfessor would lean his thin, virile body back in the chair and smoke reflectively.

From the Perfessor, Johnny got his first acquaintance with the teachings of Ralph Waldo Emerson. Fresh from New England, the Perfessor was steeped in Transcendentalism and full of definitions peculiarly his own.

—Study Emerson, lads, he would say, our foremost American.

Sometimes I think he's just an ancient Greek with a bad memory. His philosophy, you know, is anti-Christian. It restores Beauty to Nature and Man. The tree resumes the fatal apple. It is the pre-fall Paradise, boys—America another Eden. Of course, as a person, Waldo lacks warmth and flesh. He's an old woman with a bisected skirt. He may have something lively in his jeans, but I doubt if he ever transcendentalizes it. Still, I consider him by all odds the Greatest Living American. John, dispense some more of the vile weed.

On every subject where Raintree County had a fixed opinion, Professor Stiles could be counted on to express the exact opposite. During the early part of 1859, he came very near getting himself into trouble by his reaction to the celebrated Sickles Murder Case. The principals in the case, as it broke in the newspapers, were the Hon. Daniel Sickles, the Late P. Barton Key, and the Beautiful Young Mrs. Sickles, all prominent in Washington Society. The Hon. Daniel Sickles shot the then not quite Late P. Barton Key for illicit relations with the Beautiful Young Mrs. Sickles. The case made a deep impression on Raintree County, as on the whole nation. For months under the cloak of outraged morality, the County had an excuse for discussing love-making, murder, secret appointments, guilty passion, and other forbidden topics. The judgment of Raintree County was expressed accurately by an editorial in *Harper's Weekly:*

> There can be no excuse for the adulterer. He commits a three-fold crime: a crime against the woman whom he misleads, a crime against the man whom he dishonors, a crime against society which he disorganizes. Each of the three calls for condign punishment. In these latter days experience proves that in all such cases society will justify the infliction of the last penalty by the husband.

Professor Stiles openly flaunted public opinion in the case. Privately, among the young blades of the Academy, he was overheard to say:

—When did two lovers ever really hurt anyone? Because a woman tires of her gamecock of a husband (who, by the way, was fluting around all he could on the side) and lets another man have the enjoyment of her body, shall the husband have a right to kill?

That's lynch law. Besides, Nature puts no premium on chastity. My God, where would the human race be if it weren't for the bastards? Pass the perfectos, John.

Completely stunned, Johnny passed the cigars.

When all the preachers in the community, with the exception of T. D., condoned the murder from the pulpit, the Perfessor remarked that he never saw a clergyman yet who would practice more than one commandment at a time.

It was the Perfessor who taught Johnny Greek and Latin. Here again were secret words, these the oldest Johnny had yet seen, older than the Indian names, older than the word 'Shawmucky.' On the banks of an Indian river, Johnny studied the plastic rhythm of Homer, the togaed majesty of Virgil. What gave these languages their sculpturesque beauty, like words encircling stone columns? They had ceased to be the living speech of men and had acquired the tranquil beauty of ideas. And yet they had once been exclamations of young republics, rhythmical speech of men who loved the earth, the waters, and the sun and peopled their surfsurrounded lands with gods.

Here too in Raintree County was a young republic; here too were shining waters and much sunshine. Here too was a young worshipper of the earth and its inexhaustible life. And it was one of Raintree County's most meaningful conundrums that the tongue spoken there contained manifold reminders of the speech of those extinct republics.

Would this America also produce an epic speech, the language of humane poets, philosophers, and statesmen? Would they include in their number the mystical name of John Wickliff Shawnessy, child of the riverpenetrated earth of Raintree County? And then would the visible world of Raintree County, its boundaries and belongings, crumble into nothingness at last, leaving a legend and a name?

Under the tutelage of Professor Jerusalem Webster Stiles, Johnny Shawnessy discovered classic columns beside the Shawmucky River and a memory of pagan peoples who worshiped the undraped human form beside the inland ocean, that fecund womb of ideas, before man had put on the garments of Hebraic morality.

All this the Perfessor accomplished by his words. For he had brought more words to Raintree County than had been there before.

Those days, the secret of all things still seemed to Johnny to reside in words. No tongue could pronounce the living language of the ancient Greeks and Romans, but the words remained, visual, plastic, like graven coins. The Perfessor himself was a man of words. Ideas seemed often less important to him than the words in which he framed them. He had thousands—and perhaps hundreds of thousands of words. And Johnny believed that if he himself possessed all words, he would possess all things. Then he would be expressive like a god, more expressive even than that parochial deity, Professor Jerusalem Webster Stiles.

As time went on, Johnny learned that in the Perfessor's museum of quaint words there lurked a faunlike, baffled creature. This creature was perhaps the real man, a nameless deeper self, who gave blood and being to the words. It gave a flirt of its tail in wild, witty vulgarities. It showed sometimes its yearning, halfsorrowful face under the Perfessor's pince-nez glasses. It was tender and wistful. It was made distraught by beauty. It was neither good nor evil but was pure feeling and wished to be pure expression.

For curiously, Johnny felt from the beginning—and never quite lost the feeling—that the Perfessor, Raintree County's most unexpurgated talker, wasn't really a wicked person. His excesses of speech and idea had their own vigorous rationale. His gods were simply not the gods of Raintree County. And with all his faults, in all the time Johnny knew him the Perfessor remained a strangely gentle, humane person who never deliberately hurt anyone's feelings and was never vain, hypocritical, petty, or malicious.

During the summer of 1858 Johnny and the Perfessor often went together to the bank of the Shawmucky where they swam, talked, and versified. And because they were close to the river, where life was undisguised, they had few secrets from each other. To the Perfessor, Johnny described the vision he had seen in the Shawmucky and the desire that it awakened. The Perfessor laughed tolerantly.

—My dear boy, he said, you're an incurable idealist. A little country girl with nice breasts and a cute bottom takes a dip in the river on a hot day, and you act as if it's Venus reborn from the foam of the inland ocean.

But later the Perfessor told of a forbidden fruit that he too had seen temptingly displayed in the garden of Raintree County.

Lydia Gray, one of the students at the Pedee Academy, was the wife of the Reverend Ezra Gray, who had come to Raintree County from another state not long before. No one ever knew how this chilly January had got such a blithesome May, for the Reverend Gray was at least fifty and had withered lips and eyes like balls of blue flint, while his wife was young, artless, blonde, and endowed with a conspicuously lush figure.

In the Academy, Mrs. Gray was touchingly eager for knowledge. She adored the Perfessor, as did all women without exception. The Perfessor always addressed her formally as the Reverend Mrs. Gray (although the students called her simply Lydia), and adopted in her presence a sanctimonious air shot with flashes of ribald humor, all lost upon her.

—She's just a bucolic girl, pure and impulsive, the Perfessor said lightly during one of the boarding-house symposiums. Fate loves a paradox and so hitched her to that old frock, her husband, who can't even beget offspring in that fruitful garden of all delight. Have you noticed her bust, boys?

—I've been too busy parsing my Latin, Garwood said, always a fast man with a comeback.

—Plump twins of love, the Perfessor said. Really very nice—and I speak as a connoisseur.

After a while, the Perfessor no longer made fun of Mrs. Gray. He said nothing about her at all.

Then one day on the bank of the Shawmucky, when Johnny was translating from the *Aeneid,* the Perfessor, who had been lying in the sun with nothing on but his pince-nez glasses, suddenly sat up and spoke an irrelevant word.

—Ach! John! Think of her ripe body in bed with that ugly priest.

—Uh—what's that, Professor?

—When she sits there in the front row with those two softnosed fawns trembling under her blouse and her big blue eyes watching me, I melt, boy, like wax in a flame. I lose voice and utterance. I become inarticulate.

—O, Johnny said.

The Perfessor laughed a brief and bitter laugh and adjusted his pince-nez.

—Go on with your Latin, John.

That was the last thing he said to Johnny on the subject for a long time.

Thus for two years Johnny Shawnessy sought the answer to life's riddle in a little shrine of bookish words presided over by the wistfully pagan spirit of Professor Jerusalem Webster Stiles. He had discovered a new place and a new person in Raintree County and at the same time had renewed an old craving. The whole conundrum of the County was now embodied in the person of Nell Gaither.

For Nell was nothing if not Raintree County. It had made her what she was, given her grace, demureness, tenderness, quick sympathies, strong enthusiasms, purity, endeavor, moral delicacy, religious fervor. Yet she was so habitual and easy in the ways of the County that she could doff the whole costume like a dress and return into her passively seductive attitude of Venus in the river. The more demure and sentimental she seemed, the more, by paradox, did she become to him a woman made for erotic and maternal uses, a strange meeting of the eternal feminine river with the illusory rectangle of Raintree County.

To him she was the unconquered paradise called Woman. He had glimpsed only the white gates of it in the river. He had discovered a strange thing—that nakedness is the most mysterious clothing in the world. When Nell Gaither doffed her dress, she put on a garment that concealed, while half suggesting, the secret of life itself.

What gave his whole dream of her a touch of mortal pathos was Johnny's knowledge that the ideal she embodied was subject like all things human to plunder and ruin in the random collisions of life. Johnny was Raintree County's one true aesthete and somehow managed to erect all things beautiful and ugly into an ideal existence. But the rest of the County went on living the old remorseless comedy, and the knife that had been driven into Johnny's heart behind the scenes of the Opera House was cruelly twisted from time to time.

Once during the harvest season of '58, Johnny had gone for a swim in the Shawmucky with some farmhands who along with him had been helping get in wheat on the Gaither farm. The boys were usual rural types, goodhumored, unlettered, lusty. When they had finished washing the seed and sweat off, they stretched out naked on the bank, smoking cigars and chewing tobacco, and the talk turned on girls. Someone mentioned Nell's name. One of the boys was in the act of lighting his cigar.

—D'yuh—puff, puff—spose ole Garwood Jones has—puff, puff—been in there?

The words had the callous brutality with which boys in Raintree County often spoke of girls with whom they weren't very well acquainted.

—Reckon he would if he could, another boy said. If he ain't too busy stayin' on top a that girl what's-her-name over to Summit.

—Lizzie Franklin?

—Yeh, that one.

—Ole Garwood sure gits 'em.

—Garwood thinks he's some punkins.

—You'd think you was some punkins if you'd of had as many pretty janes under you as old Garwood.

—Them girls is all alike. Any of 'em ud lay down fer a guy with money and smart city talk.

—I'd like to roll in a haystack with that there Nell Gaither. I got as much as Garwood Jones any time.

—Hell, she wouldn't let a rube like you touch her little finger. She's too fancy for you.

—Hell she is. Garwood Jones—puff, puff—ain't got a—puff, puff—thing I ain't got.

While Johnny lay and listened, the frogs squawked hoarsely in the reeds, and the dialogue of life along the river went on and on, verbally stripping and pawing his beloved. It seemed cruelly proper that this pillage should occur on the banks of the Shawmucky, where life was conscienceless.

Johnny wasn't the only person who had detected the paradox of Nell Gaither, the image of erotic and spiritual beauty. Professor Jerusalem Webster Stiles had taken special note of his star girl student, helped thereto, no doubt, by Johnny's vivid account of what he had seen in the river.

—There, he said, by your leave, John, is the most passionate little piece in Raintree County. She's so poised and invulnerably pure. Such women are always volcanoes of passion when aroused. There's something about her that reminds me of those old Greek statues which were painted in pure colors. It's marble, and it's also life.

Good thing you've staked out your claim to it. By the way, you don't suppose Garwood's been in there?

Some time later the Perfessor told Johnny that in his, the Perfessor's, opinion he, Johnny, could set all doubts to rest as to Nell's chastity.

—My word for it, he said, the young lady is—if not imperforable—at least imperforate.

—What makes you think so?

—A small bird, the Perfessor said.

He was gaily evasive, and Johnny didn't find out exactly what had given the Perfessor this assurance, unless perhaps he had gained it from some of his very private conversations with Nell in his office, where he sometimes remained closeted with his more promising female students after hours.

Meanwhile, Johnny went on loving in secret, hoping that one day he might find the river girl again. And in fact not long after the comic dialogue with the farmhands, he did see Nell again in the Shawmucky River.

A wave of holiness swept through the County in the summer of 1858 on the tide of a Great Revival Program to bring everyone back to the arms of Jesus. Almost everyone was taken back during this time except Johnny Shawnessy, who was not aware that he had ever left the arms of Jesus, and Professor Stiles, who had apparently never been there in the first place.

The Revival featured a succession of mass baptisms in the Shawmucky. Even T. D. yielded to the popular demand for total immersion and three times under. One Sunday night, almost the whole congregation of the Danwebster Methodist Church went from the church to the near-by river for baptism. Johnny stood on the bank watching with the Perfessor, who delivered a running fire of comment on the operation. Wearing nothing but sheets, a hundred people filed barefoot down the bank to T. D. standing hipdeep in water.

—God is doing his laundry, the Perfessor said.

They all sang 'Wash me in the Jordan,' and what with the flaring torches and swung lanterns, the flickering shape of the church on its high bank, the wild stream of the river, the splashings, gurglings, stampings, snortings, cries of penitence, shouts of hosanna, everyone had reached a state of violent excitement.

Toward the end of the line came Nell Gaither. Her face was meek and mild. Her gold hair hung to her hips. Her long, graceful feet were bare. She carried a taper.

—This is your chance, my boy, the Perfessor said. Take her home after the baptism. When they're christbitten, girls will do practically anything. You might even get a kiss.

—Probably Garwood's waiting around somewhere, Johnny said. She's crazy about him.

The Perfessor held up his hand and recited,

—*I cannot praise a fugitive and cloistered virtue unexercised and unbreathed, that never sallies out and seeks her adversary, but slinks out of the race, where that immortal garland is to be run for, not without dust and heat!*

In the confusion of the night, Nell's voice was perfectly audible as she stepped into the water.

—Dear Jesus, I have sinned and am repentant. O, dear Lordie Jesus, wash my sins away.

After she had come out, the Perfessor and Johnny went around to help her. She was shivering, the sheet was soaked to her body, her hair was plastered to her neck, but she looked happy and excited. The Perfessor arranged it so that Johnny put her in a buggy and took her home.

—Why don't you get baptized, Johnny? she said.

—I don't exactly believe in it, Nell.

—O, I do, Nell said. For sinners, that is. But then I suppose that wouldn't include you, Johnny.

She was tranquil and sincere.

—And are your sins so very great, Nell?

—O, yes, Nell said, smiling up at Johnny with her radiant and innocent smile. I'm afraid I'm not a very good person, Johnny.

She looked out at the warm purple night brooding with mist of stars on Raintree County.

—I feel so wonderful, she said. You have no idea, Johnny, what it will do for you. Garwood was baptized yesterday at my suggestion. But then he needs it more than you.

—I don't know, Johnny said. Maybe not.

That night he lay in his bed at the Home Place and wondered what were the mortal stains that Nell had tried to wash away in the waters of the Shawmucky. Did they include a little misprint on the white nudity with which she had ravaged the heart of Johnny Shawnessy?

Johnny Shawnessy ached with the insufficiency of youth. He was never more erotically in love with Nell Gaither than that night when he saw her soaked in a sheet in the name of Raintree County's puritan religion.

Thus there was too much youth and love and wishing in this whole era of his life. All things were touched with sadness and beauty by this first erotic passion of his young manhood.

The most delicious and frustrating hours were those spent at the Academy, where Johnny and Nell often studied together in the little library. Both spent a great deal of extra time there. It was not unusual for Johnny to come over in the evening and find the library open and only one other person in it—Nell. The Perfessor abetted Johnny's hopeless passion by assigning to his two prize pupils extra readings in the Greek and Latin texts. Garwood Jones was, as everyone knew, too smart for his own good, but he never aspired to be, as the Perfessor once remarked, either a scholar or a gentleman, so that Nell was, next to Johnny, the best student in the Academy, especially in language and rhetoric. Gifted in versification, her muse was not so vigorous and facile as Johnny's, but it was fashionably feminine, specializing in affecting compositions about departed beauty, spent passion, withered roses, tombstones, dewy flowers, and unreturning springs. When she read these verbal confections, her face and voice were pleasingly mournful in the approved fashion of the time.

Sometimes she and Johnny would sit in the library to late hours in the evening studying together. They shared each other's passions in literature, and would sometimes read aloud, but each was too shy to read original poetry to the other. Their great common enthusiasm for a long time was Lord Byron.

—I think Lord Byron was the most fascinating man who ever lived, Nell said once while they were alone in the library. He seemed so much in need of a good woman to love and to love him, and he never really found one. What's your favorite passage in Lord Byron's works, Johnny?

—I like the opening sections of *Don Juan* best, Johnny said.

—I haven't read that yet, Nell said. My favorite is 'Fare Thee Well.' I'll read the opening passages of *Don Juan* if you'll let me have the book.

Johnny had been using the Academy's unique copy for some time past. He gave Nell the book, but as it made him a little uncomfortable to see her sit down and become absorbed in the exquisitely beautiful canto in which the young Don Juan falls from innocence with Julia and is apprehended and sent off on his travels, he got up and left the Academy. Some days later, Nell gave him the book back, with one of her radiant smiles mixed with a trace of bepuzzlement and concern. Inside the book in the Juan passage, he found a note for him.

Dear Johnny,

I'm surprised at *you*. But the poetry *is* very beautiful.

Nell

The happiest hours in Johnny's life during this time were those spent in translating some of the *Metamorphoses* of Ovid with Nell. They were both deeply touched by the myth of Daphne and Apollo. Both had been essaying a translation of it and met one evening to compare their respective efforts. They sat at the table in the library where they had done so much of their work together. The Perfessor, who was usually hovering about somewhere like the resident deity of the place, had obligingly retired to his quarters upstairs. In the gaslight, Nell sat across from Johnny, wearing the green dress that he had come to associate with her in all his daydreams. She seemed more than usual remote and pensive as her hands nervously played in the loose sheets of her manuscript.

—You read yours first, Johnny.

His composition was in blank verse. In the yellow light of the oakpaneled library, walled in with the softly glowing backs of hundreds of classics, his young voice, which understood so perfectly the music of English verse, re-created the legend of the sungod who sought and was denied the love of a river nymph. The little library was peopled with the Ovidian images—the love-pursuit beside the river, the fleeting nymph, the ardent god. Some of the musical passion of the old republic which had given this myth to the world crept into Johnny's voice. He too had known the rhythmed pain of love along the river, had seen a white flesh in the reeds, had felt the barky shadow climb up forbidden limbs and cover them from view. He too had come away with a laurel branch to requite him for a frustrate love. His voice was husky with the poem's music of renunciation and farewell.

He had hardly finished when Nell said in a trembling voice,

—O, Johnny, it's beautiful! Yours is much better than mine.

A sudden moisture in her eyes increased their green brilliance. Her parted mouth was a scarlet stain on her white face, which had two flushes of scarlet high on the cheeks. Her voice was husky with earnestness.

—Johnny, you know what I think? I think you will be a great poet some day.

She sat across from him, her eyes full of admiration and humility.

—You are the best of us all, she said. I know it.

—No, you are the best of all, Nell.

—No, no, Nell said. You have a gift that can't be learned. It's something sacred. To see beauty and to say it—like Byron or Ovid or Shakespeare. It's really so fine to have known you, Johnny.

He was startled by this strangely elegiac expression.

—Well, he said. Which is better—to express beauty or to have it?

She looked puzzled, and he felt that perhaps he had said more than was wise.

—How now! said a voice from the library door. Up so late, children?

It was the Perfessor, leaning into the door. He came in and bent over Nell's shoulder.

—The Ovid—eh? How did it go?

—Johnny has a beautiful translation, Nell said.

She was blushing.

—Our boy John, said the Perfessor, has the golden touch. Let me see.

He picked up Johnny's translation and ran his eyes over it.

—Not bad, not bad, he said. Though rather too full of alliteration.

Garwood came shortly after. Johnny and the Perfessor stood at the gate of the Academy and watched Nell leaning out of Garwood's buggy smiling her radiant, tender smile, full of Ovidian enthusiasm.

—We'll have to work out the next *liber* together, Johnny!

Garwood took Nell away.

—Is there such a thing, Professor, Johnny said, as one man possessing a woman's soul and another her body?

—You read too much, John, the Perfessor said.

Johnny watched the buggy receding. How well that wise old Roman poet of the protean earth and its mixing and mating forms had understood the only possible reward for the lover of ideal beauty! He shall pursue a lovely flesh and be rewarded with a branch of laurel.

During those years the lyrics of Stephen Foster, especially the more romantic ballads such as 'Come Where My Love Lies Dreaming' and 'Jeanie with the Light Brown Hair,' became the musical image of Johnny's love. This love could have existed only in an adolescent republic that tried to dream itself to perfection by ignoring the realities of life's remorseless comedy. This love could have existed only in a sentimental America of bright, running streams and high, grassy lawns, where girls in shimmering gowns walked with their lovers hand in hand till starlight faded into morn.

Meanwhile, the real republic of the slave and free controversy, growing ever closer to open conflict, loomed menacingly on the horizons of Johnny Shawnessy's private universe of Raintree County. The students at Pedee Academy gravely debated the issues of the great struggle. Lincoln and Douglas, the western champions of the opposing camps, were quoted everywhere during their contest for the Senate in 1858. But for Johnny Shawnessy, the issues of that day—slavery and emancipation, free lands in the West, senatorial and presidential candidates, new states, supreme court decisions—were shadows and echoes compared to the image of a girl with enigmatic green eyes in a small piquant face, sitting at a table in the Pedee Academy, making pagan polysyllables with her fullflown mouth.

Her image suffused the whole of Raintree County, until the County was changed from what it had been. Somewhere along the way, the County of Johnny's childhood had been lost. In that County, which would always lie beneath the rest as the parent stratum, his mother, Ellen Shawnessy, had been the dominant image. Then he had been the favored child whose quest was to solve the secret of his origin; and Raintree County was the garden of this quest, an auroral and maternal earth. Now this earlier earth and the myths that embodied its secret (myths not of Eros but of Oedipus) had changed with the changing body and mind of Johnny Shawnessy. He was no longer the child of this earth—he had become its aggressive lover. The old myth of origins—the Raintree in its primitive garden—had temporarily lost its place to the myth of the love-pursuit and conquest of beauty.

Yet the secret of the County was still feminine. It had taken for its image the Venus Callipygos in exchange for Mother Eve in her figleaf.

For this love, which was so intensely ideal that it had absorbed to itself the whole being of Johnny Shawnessy and the whole landscape of Raintree County, was also fiercely erotic, dreaming over and over the image of possession and endlessly inventive in the technique of this possession. And of these dreams the most persistent involved the Academy itself. Pedee Academy enshrined then, as it would forever, the image of his young desire.

Now this was the favorite daydream of Johnny Shawnessy in the days of Pedee Academy and Professor Jerusalem Webster Stiles: He imagined that he came some time of a winter evening to the Academy Building to get a book. Sleet and fine snow were blowing on the fields and roads. He opened the door and found that the Perfessor was not in and that the building was empty. He went back then into the lecture room and along the passageway to the little library where he turned up a lamp and looked for the book. In the Academy the air was close and warm, redolent of ink, varnish, and books. Then he was surprised to see that someone else had entered from the winter night. It was Nell Gaither, who was standing at the library door muffled in her long furcollared coat. As he looked at her, the lamp burned out, and he could see her face, a pale stain in the dark. She held up to him this face with parted lips and unaverted eyes and by a motion of her body invited him to help her off with her wraps. He began with the coat and then, assisted by her, slowly removed her garments one by one. All this they did together without a single word, while she looked back over her shoulder at him. At last her tranquilly seductive form was posed in entire nudity, like a tinted marble in the warm murk of the Academy Building. Her demure face and bound-up hair were strangely in contrast with the pale, deepfleshed mounds, on one of which he saw the tiny imprint of the river. And then among the benches and the books, where their young mouths had said the antique words of the rivered earth, love, death, beauty, and the gods, here in the very center of Raintree County, in its most Delphic cave, here where only a faint light shone, while all around them in the blustering night the fields and roads were swept with sleet, he too became naked, like a young god, and his mouth would touch at last her warm mouth. And love would be tall and imperious, it would be a young man seeking, it would go into the most secret places in Raintree County, where lake and river met and shore and shallow were hardly to be told apart. And his desire, clothed in eager flesh, would find at last the secret source and secret destination, would ache in the anguishingly tight caress of the river girl, her warm breath would beat upon his halfshut lids, her slippery body would writhe in his arms, and she would

DRAIN FROM HIM THE POOLED-UP ANGUISH OF HIS BODY,
TOO YOUNG, TOO AMOROUS, TOO BESET
WITH

—LONGING, said Niles Foster, as he and Mr. Shawnessy stepped out into the street, won't bring those days back. Sure you won't have a glass with me, John?

—Sorry, Niles. Have to be back in Waycross in time to meet that nine-thirty train.

He walked past the Saloon and turned in at the Photographer's. The stair was rickety and dark. The building had a stale smell of tobacco and chemicals.

There was no one on the stair. He stopped, hugged the bundle of papers under one arm, opened the *Atlas,* and flapped the leaves swiftly to page 37. A block of brick business buildings started into life, all the familiar legends and doors of the south side of the Square (including the one he had just entered), little changed in the seventeen years since the artist had drawn the picture.

But the gracefully made lady just stepping into the drygoods store was fully clothed, like all the other precise little figures in the picture.

Nevertheless, this flat, inactual world of light and shadow seemed about to do something, mean something. Buggies passed on wheels of finedrawn spokes, haunches of horses gathered into lumps of muscle, the clock over the jeweler's read eighteen minutes past eleven. Enmeshed in a thin web of pencil marks was a lost America and a departed Raintree County, struggling for expression. And in the middle of this web, an imagined lady stood, clothed in the possibility of all feminine nakedness. The coil of her dark hair swung between bare shoulders, the long furrow of her back was faintly curved with the walking motion of her body, the palm of her right foot was arched and thrusting from the toes.

With a rush of desire, he seemed about to pluck away a veil of light and shadow and lay bare the shape of beauty and forever.

The door banged open, a rush of light blinded him, and a blocky woman in a hideously white dress burst in.

He slapped the book shut and sprang three steps at a time up the stair to the Photographer's Shop. He entered a little reception gallery and laid the *Atlas* on a table, concealing it under the newspapers. He listened as the woman mounted the stair, paused at the landing, breathing audibly, then entered another room.

From oval frames along the wall, the tinted faces of young women looked at him wistfully. He had a mission this day to resurrect the past in pencil sketches and faded photographs.

The door opened at the end of the gallery, and a sallow man of middle age looked out.

—Hello, John. See you made it.

—Morning, Bill. Sorry to get you out so early. Well, what luck?

—I found the plates all right, the man said, preceding him into a room flooded with white light from a glass window slanting from roof to floor.

—I can't thank you enough, Bill, Mr. Shawnessy said. Did you——

—I'm sorry, John, he said. I didn't get the prints made. I didn't have time.

—It was my fault for not writing sooner. The idea occurred to me at the last minute. I'm delighted that you found the plates.

—My father, the first Mr. Huddleston, the man said, kept everything. I dug into some old things in the cellar and found the plates last night stored away with the date of exposure and name of subject on each one.

He opened a package and took out a half-dozen glass plates, three by five inches, each with a strip of paper glued at the bottom edge containing a name and date in ink.

—Perfectly preserved, he said. The old wetplate process. I've used it myself.

Mr. Shawnessy picked them up one at a time and read the captions. They had all been taken on the same day, May 26, 1859.

—These are the six I wanted, he said. I had copies of them once, but lost them all.

He carried them to an open window and held them up to the light. Through a glass darkly, he saw one by one four men and two women, hovering in chemical prisons.

—The Senator and Mr. Carney will be pleased to see themselves as young men, the photographer said. As for Mr. Stiles, I don't remember him, and the two women are unfamiliar. Any relation?

—No, not exactly, Mr. Shawnessy said.

He dwelt a long time on the images of the two women, holding them side by side. Under one picture was the caption N. Gaither; under the other, S. Drake.

Bodies of beautiful women floated in a pale river of remembrance, white flesh dissolving in green acid of years. Traced on the plate of memory with a finger of light, their lost forms wavered, a vaporous smoke on the sullen and triumphant earth.

N. Gaither. Ovidian statue starting into life, Daphne in a mesh of Raintree County reeds. *We parted in the springtime of life, Nell and I.*

A sweet anguish vexed him, and he turned to the other plate.

S. Drake. Little sleepwalker from an alien earth, bearer of a scarlet mark. *O, Susanna! Do not cry for me.*

J. Shawnessy. Lost boy whom girl mouths once called Johnny, just risen from the tumult of the Square where all is sunlight and the greatest athlete in Raintree County stands with cocked arm bulging. O, innocent and unforgotten boy!

But where were all the other images that mixed on the plateglass windows of the Square, each window recording the image of a clockless Court House?

He held a vitreous world, the creature of a god whose radiant finger wrote all the legends that were ever written. Musing, he studied a vanished Raintree County reflected on

May 26— THE —1859

PLATEGLASS WINDOW

OF THE SALOON HELD THE SQUARE

in a golden prism, including the form of Cash Carney, who leaned against the window reading a copy of the *Clarion,* and the form of Johnny Shawnessy, who had just stopped to say hello.

—Had your face friz yet, John?

—My appointment's for three o'clock, Johnny said.

—I've had mine, Cash said. To while away the time, listen to Garwood's latest potshot.

He read aloud:

> —A report comes from the Upper Shawmucky that Seth Twigs got kicked in his think-box by a mule and sustained a slight injury (the mule cracked a hoof). Seth has been having delusions of grandeur since and has got the idea that he can beat any man in this county footracing, including the great Orville (better known as Flash) Perkins of Freehaven. Now we do not want to discourage the roseate dreams of youth. Nor do we wish to underestimate the speed of foot Seth may have acquired keeping away from various citizens he has slandered in the *Enquirer.* But when we mentioned this matter to Rube Shucks, Rube said, 'Seth Twigs is the laziest critter in Raintree County. He never runned a step in his life. Seth Twigs once let a hive of bees swarm on 'im ruthern break out of a shuffle. Flash Perkins kin run faster backways with a pianner on his neck than Seth kin frontways. If Seth Twigs beats Flash Perkins in a footrace, I will personly plunge my haid into the Shawmucky and swaller the fust big ole stinkin' catfish comes along, horns and all.'

—Garwood isn't going to like that catfish, Johnny said.

He had been looking at his reflection in the plateglass window. He was twenty years old and had gained a good deal of weight in the last year. He was six feet tall. His hair was dark and wavy and shot with red. His face had lost its pimply, boyish look. He had on a new suit bought especially for the Graduation Exercises at the

Academy. His legs in the tight pants were lithe and long. The knobs of his new shoes shone. A bowtie was poised on his throat like an irrelevant butterfly. It had been two years since anyone had beat Johnny Shawnessy in a race, and his friends had been encouraging him to try his speed against Flash Perkins, Raintree County's most famous athlete, in the annual Fourth of July Footrace.

This day, a Saturday, he had come into town to get his picture taken. The Graduation Exercises were only two weeks away, and the graduates had all agreed to exchange images of each other in the *carte de visite* size.

Cash unlipped his cigar and tipped the ash. His eyes were soft and visionary.

—It's been five years since anyone laid a bet against Flash Perkins. John, if you could beat Flash, we could clean up the biggest pot a money ever bet in Raintree County.

—I wouldn't want my friends to lose any money on me, Johnny said.

—I got a plan, Cash said. You remember the race two years ago when Flash was so drunk they practickly had to carry him to the starting line?

—He nearly got beat.

—By a secondrate runner too—a man you could whip with your legs tied in a potato sack.

—If Flash Perkins is drunk next Fourth, he's a gone goose, Johnny said. I think I can beat him sober, and I know I can beat him drunk.

The image of Johnny Shawnessy in the window stood with shoulders well back. The bowtie appeared just ready to wing its way off.

—I got a plan, Cash Carney said.

As always when he was dreaming up a good plan, his eyes became soft and christlike.

—I got a sure-fire plan for getting Flash Perkins to the starting line pig-drunk. Listen to this! About an hour before racetime, you go and find Flash. He'll be here at the Saloon showing his muscles and bragging. You go up to him, and you say, Perkins, I've heard enough of your blow about how you can beat any man in Raintree County drunk or sober. I can beat you drinking or running. Now everybody knows Flash Perkins never turned down a dare in his life.

He'll take you up in a second. You and he'll walk into the Saloon here and call for raw whiskey, the barkeep fills them up, and to the amazement of the crowd you drink with Perkins glass for glass.

—Don't forget, Johnny said, I'm a member of the Cold Water Army. I never touched a——

Brown eyes upcast, waving his cigar, Cash ignored the interruption.

—Meanwhile, I and some of the boys will have covered every Perkins bet we can get at odds of two to one. Come racetime, they'll carry Flash Perkins, the Pride of Raintree County, to the starting line, and you'll beat him all holler.

—Who'll carry *me* to the post? Johnny said. Besides, T. D. and Mamma would skin me alive if I did such a thing. I won't touch any alcoholic beverages.

—Who said anything about you touching any alcoholic beverages? Cash said. Suppose that the bartender pours colored water in your glass and straight stuff in Perkins'.

—He'd never do it.

—He *might* do it, Cash said, before he'd lose his job. If the Boss asked him to, he might.

—The Boss?

—I don't want it generly known, John, Cash said, tipping his ash, so keep it under your hat. But I own this joint now.

Johnny argued with Cash about it, but Cash pointed out that T. D. wouldn't have any kick coming if Johnny touched nothing but colored water, and it would be all in favor of the temperance movement if Flash beat himself by drink.

—Serve him right, Cash said. We'll take some of our winnings and put them into the next temperance drive.

Garwood Jones, who also had an appointment at the Photographer's, joined the two in front of the Saloon. He had just come from the barber's and stood a moment glancing at himself in the plateglass. Pleased, he opened his coat, extracted a cigar, and put a foot up on the low windowsill.

—Well, boys, he said, did you see it go by?

He put the cigar in his face. His handsome blue eyes crossed slightly as he touched matchflame to tip. He puffed, laughed gently. His hair was black and wavy. He palped his newly razored faceskin, soft like a baby's. His shoulders were bulky and sleek in his dandy coat. He exhaled fragrance of face lotion and hair oil, aroma of success. He reminded Johnny of a well-groomed prize bull.

—What a lovely pair!

Garwood's voice was deep, and he had a manner of speaking slowly so that every word told.

Professor Jerusalem Webster Stiles crossed the street and joined the group in front of the Saloon.

—Good afternoon, gentlemen. I hope the subject under discussion is sufficiently elevated to engage my interest.

—The Perfessor knows her too, Garwood said.

—Are you referring, the Perfessor said, to our charming little visitor from below the Mason and Dixon Line?

—She just went by the barber shop while I was in the chair, Garwood said. Boy, what a dream!

—Do you think your tone is strictly avuncular? the Perfessor said.

—What's it all about? Johnny said. Let us country boys in on it too.

—We have a new girl in town, the Perfessor said, affecting a stagey Southern accent, from the great and gran' old state of Lou'siana—Noo Orleans, Lou'siana, that is. Son, have you evuh visited in Dixie? Well, Ah'm heah to tail you, son, thet those accustomed tew the pinchin' and penurious weathuh of the Nawth cannot possibly *im*agine, until they have *ex*perienced it, the softness and fragrance of the Southuhn air. Below the Mason and Dixon Lahn, one passes impercetibluh into anothuh——

The Perfessor broke off and resumed in his normal voice.

—The new girl has already been closely scrutinized by the local experts and pronounced a very passable specimen of her sex. Just ask Uncle Garwood here, whose protective arm has so far guarded her against all contact with the raucous elements of the County.

—I'm not her uncle, Garwood said. Just a relative of a relative of hers. When I made that trip to New Orleans recently, I met Susanna, and since some of her relatives call me Uncle, goddamned if she didn't start calling me Uncle too just for a joke.

—Susanna who?

—Susanna Drake, Garwood said.

—Where'd she get all the money? Cash asked.

Apparently Cash knew about her too. Only Johnny Shawnessy was unaware of this exciting new arrival in Raintree County.

—The money, as I understand it, Garwood said, is an independent income which she has received ever since she was a kid and orphaned. Her folks had a big plantation near New Orleans, owned a lot of land and niggers. She was an only child and inherited a pile when they died. Her father's sister came here to Freehaven and built. She brought Susanna with her. Then Susanna grew up a little and went back South and stayed there. But when Auntie died last year, the house became Susanna's. It stayed empty for a while, but now Susanna turns up—just why I don't know.

—By herself? the Perfessor said.

—Couple of nigger girls with her, Garwood said. But I'm surprised at you asking *me,* Perfessor. *You* ought to know all about her.

The Perfessor laughed soundlessly and smoothed his already glue-slick hair with sidelong glance in the plateglass.

—The boys are referring to a little fatherly conversation that I had with the young lady last Saturday.

—Fatherly, hell! Garwood said. A bunch of us went on a swimming party to Lake Paradise and took the Perfessor along for a chaperon. Goddamned if he and Susanna didn't disappear for hours.

—Marvellous swimmer, that girl, the Perfessor said.

—What's she look like? Johnny asked.

—Well, Garwood said, studying his cigar, I sure would like to put *my* head between 'em.

—Don't be crude, Uncle, the Perfessor said. But they are lovely.

—Wish she wouldn't cover 'em up so with those highnecked dresses, Garwood said. It seems a shame to have all that beauty blush unseen. She has jet black hair, John, big round eyes, olive complexion without a blemish——

—You'd be surprised, though, the Perfessor said.

—O, Garwood said, I suppose she showed you her birthmarks and everything on that swim.

The Perfessor tipped his ash with an appraising eye.

—It's a shame, he said. I hate to tell you, boys, but she has a large scarlet scar on her beautiful left breast. It starts right here—

He drew a line with his finger across his skinny chest.

—And it ends right here.

He ended up complacently scratching his left nipple.

Garwood watched through smilingly skeptic eyes.

—What's the diameter of her navel?

The Perfessor contemplated his cigar.

—*There is no excellent beauty,* gentlemen, he said, *that hath not some strangeness in the proportion.*

—She isn't as fast as she acts, Cash said. Rob Peters, that has the big gray and the new spring buggy, took her over to Middletown two nights ago, and when he took her home, he tried to get fresh with her, and she slapped his hat off. He said he never saw anything like her to lead a man on and then give 'im the back of her hand.

—It might interest you guys to know, Garwood said, that it's Uncle Garwood who's taking her to the Decoration Day Program next week.

Garwood paid a sly glance to himself in the plateglass mirror and caressed his backward-flowing mane.

—Boys, he said, that little lady is a fast filly, a high-steppin' little thoroughbred, and Uncle Garwood is just the boy that can ride 'em. You fellas wouldn't believe it if I told you the truth about her. I heard some stories about her down in New Orleans that'd make this County stand up and take note. I'm telling you right now, boys, we're kinda slow stuff around here compared to the set she's been——

—Here's the boy now!

A hoarse, high voice stung Johnny like a slap in the face. Advancing up the street, the first of a throng, came Flash Perkins, Raintree County's greatest athlete.

By this time whenever Flash Perkins walked through the Square, small boys followed at a reverent distance pointing. He was generally in the middle of a gang of secondrate imitators who enjoyed moving in the reflected glory of the man who could outrun, outdrink, outfight, outlove, and outcuss any other man in the County.

It seemed to Johnny that if anyone had found the secret of pure expression, it was Flash Perkins. Everything Flash did was sheer affirmation. He never analyzed, worried, debated. He fought, worked, drank, and talked with the same sublime physical gusto. Johnny had never seen Flash angry. Flash never took the trouble. His motto was, Hit fust and argeefy after. He was a born clown and played to every crowd like a gallery. His blue eyes were those of an excited child, and one had the feeling that if a single moment of tranquillity were to set in, they would become naïve and baffled. He acted always from sheer impulse, but his impulses were predictable, for he had a code.

It was because of this code that everyone in Raintree County, including Johnny Shawnessy, understood and, after a fashion, adulated Flash Perkins. It was the code of the early Hoosier, the backwoodsman or river man, a type already becoming extinct in Indiana. The code of Flash Perkins was the code of a people who had become great fighters and talkers in a wilderness where there was not much else a man could do for diversion except fight and talk. It was the code of the tellers of tall tales who tried to live up to their tales. It was the code of a competitive people, who had fought the Indian and a still greater antagonist, the wilderness itself, the stubborn, root-filled pioneer earth, the beautiful and deadly river, the sheer space of the West. It was the code of breezy, cocky men, who had no fear in heaven or earth they would admit to. The code involved never hitting a man who was down, never turning down a drink, never refusing to take a dare, never backing out of a fight—except with a woman. The code involved contempt for city folks, redskins, varmints of all kinds, atheists, scholars, aristocrats, and the enemies of the United States of America.

Actually, every Raintree County man had a little of the code in him. It was simply the Code of the West, and though the West had already passed over Raintree County and left it far behind, nevertheless the County had once been and would always be a part of the West. As Professor Jerusalem Webster Stiles was wont to say,

—To the true Easterner, everything on the other side of the Alleghenies is the West. And in a way that's right.

Now as Flash Perkins walked toward the Saloon, chest thrust out, arms swung wide from his hips, feet flung strongly forward, teeth bared in the insolent smile that always preceded the fight, the tall tale, or the dare, Johnny Shawnessy realized that he had arrived at one of the mythical encounters of his life. He had always known that one day he would stand chest to chest with Flash Perkins in the Court House Square, and Flash would suddenly take notice of him. For years he had watched Flash win the applause of the County by swiftness and strength, the all-conquering beauty of execution. He, too, Johnny Shawnessy, a child of the word and the dream, had always secretly intended to excel as an athlete. Only so, he felt, did one wholly win the applause of Raintree County and its most beautiful women. Only so did one become the completely affirmative man.

For Johnny Shawnessy too had the West in him, the amiably pugnacious West, where a man wanted and meant to get everything the best he could have, where a man meant to be first if he could in everything—from shucking corn to catching the loveliest girl. And because of his great speed of foot, Johnny Shawnessy had long had a special vision of achievement. One day in the Court House Square he would defeat Flash Perkins, and a beautiful girl would fit the crown of oakleaves on his own suncolored locks.

—Are you Jack Shawnessy? Flash said, coming up and standing hands on hips and feet wide apart.

Johnny continued to lean against the plateglass window with a pretense of unconcern. No one had ever called him Jack before.

—I might be, he said. Who wants to know?

—Hear that, boys? Flash said to his crowd. Shall I tell this here kid who I am?

—Go on and tell 'im, Flash.

—Son, Flash said, it gives me great and pecoolyar satisfication and gratifaction to interduce to you and this handsome and intellygent company that emminunt gentleman, Mister Orville—better known as Flash—Perkins, the fastest runner in Raintree County.

—Never heard of him, Johnny said. Who is he?

—Son, Flash said, I'm the originiffical yellin' Yahoo from the banks of Clay Crick. I'm half horse and half alligator, and rastle bulls in my spare time. I've smashed more skulls, drank more corn pisen, and raped more virgins than any other janejumper on the phiz of the arth. I can run like a horse, fight like a barl of wildcats, yell like a skun cattymount, and make love like a bull. I chaw little boys like you up with my terbaccer and I spit holes in walls. Who're you?

—Son, Johnny said, I'm the cer-tee-fied, gen-u-ine, ripsnortin', ragtearin,' ringtailed, headbustin' mankiller from the banks of the Shawmucky. I fight all the time exceptin' when I'm eatin', and I eat all the time exceptin' when I'm fightin'. I strangle bars with my bar hands fer a livin', I chaw wildcat tails instidder terbaccer, I've slept with ever widder under forty in the County and some of 'em twicet, and I kin run like a colt with a redhot cob under his tail. I use minners like you to bait muh hook with when I go fishin'.

For answer, Flash Perkins jerked off coat and shirt. He threw his hat on the ground. It looked as though he was going to hit Johnny.

—Fight! Fight! someone yelled.

A big crowd had already gathered. But smiling all the time, Flash sat down on the sidewalk and pulled off his shoes.

—Come on, Jack, he said. No use waitin' till Fourth of July. I'll race you right now from here to the Baptist Church, or anywheres else you wanna run to.

—Make it the church, Johnny said.

He pulled off coat, tie, and shirt. He sat down on the ground and pulled off shoes and socks. Bare to the waist, he shoved through the crowd to Flash Perkins.

In the saloon window, the reflections of two young men leaned slightly forward. The sun shone on the hard, broadshouldered body of Flash Perkins, who stood in stocking feet a trifle shorter than Johnny, shone on the shag of his brown hair, his curly beard, his smiling teeth, shone on the lean ribs and sinewy shoulders of Johnny Shawnessy, shone on his massy chestnutcolored hair. There was a faint prismatic light around both figures.

—Sot us off, Fred, Flash said.

—Just a minute, Cash Carney said, stepping up. Put your duds on, John.

—What fer? Flash said.

—This boy ain't racing today, Cash said. He's under contract to me, and he don't race for any but big stakes.

—If he don't race me now, he's a yallerbellied coward.

—He's not racing, Cash said. That's final. You're afraid to run him regular and official, Perkins, because you're afraid of losing money.

—Get a hat! Flash Perkins yelled.

—Here's a hat! somebody yelled.

—I'll give 'im odds of two to one, Flash said.

—You just say that, Perkins, Cash said, because you know nobody'll bet you. If someone came along with a little hard coin, you'd try to weasel out of them odds, and you know it.

—Try me and see, Flash said.

Cash Carney reached in a back pocket and coolly took out a leather snap-purse. The crowd became reverently silent as Cash took five gold coins out of the purse and held them in the cup of his hand.

—That thar's gold, a citizen said.

—It ain't horse manure, a second citizen said.

—Here's fifty dollars says you're a liar, Perkins, Cash said.

—I'll cover it, Flash said, or if I can't, my sidekicks will before the Fourth of July.

—I'll take some of that, myself, Garwood Jones said. Friendship is friendship, John, but a bet on Flash Perkins is a sure thing.

Johnny began to put on his clothes. He fixed his tie in the plate-glass window, where the suncreated images of the crowd mixed incessantly. The hard, high nasal talk rasped in his ears.

—I'll see you racetime, Jack, Flash said. I promise not to beat you more'n a city block.

Flash Perkins walked straight into the batwing doors of the Saloon without bothering to put out his hand. The doors slapped back and forth. Johnny could hear the high, goodhumored voice yelling for a drink, the sound of obsequious laughter.

It was three o'clock as Johnny walked down to a door that had a sign over it reading

PHOTOGRAPHS, DAGUERREOTYPES, and AMBROTYPES

Entering, he climbed a rickety stair to a hall on the second floor. The old building smelled of tobacco, urine, chemicals. Johnny had never been up this stair before, and he didn't know which way to turn for the photographer's. He was half expecting to meet Nell Gaither, as she too had an appointment. Through an open door on the left he saw a dimly lighted gallery, hung with oval pictures. He walked in toward a closed door at the far end, watching his own image grow larger and larger in a full-length mirror hung on the door. He laid his hand on the knob and opened the door.

Light drenched him, a white radiance without warmth, as if he were inside a camera whose shutter had just been opened. He blinked and narrowed his eyes.

The room was bathed in light. A skylight of milky glass slanted almost to the floor on the left wall. The young afternoon flooding in bathed each object in shadowless purity.

A young woman stood posed for a picture. Her jetblack hair was shaken out over her shoulders and down her cloudy white gown, which resembled a nightdress. She leaned against a cardboard column, holding an artificial lily in her left hand. The backdrop showed a riverscene: a landing in the foreground piled up with cottonbales, a steamboat in the middle distance, and in the background pillared ruins beside the river.

The photographer had just slipped the cap over the lens. The girl relaxed from her pose and turning looked right at Johnny. Instantly she gave a little shriek and clutched her throat with her left hand.

—O, it's you! she said.

Her olivecolored skin blushed scarlet and she began to laugh.

—O, hello, Johnny said, and backed out and closed the door.

The girl had spoken as if she had recognized him or had even been waiting for him, but he knew that he had never seen a face like hers before. Seen bare and sudden in the white light, the face in the studio had burned its image so brightly on his memory that it was more like an afterimage than a recollection as he paced in the dark little gallery.

In this face innocence was strangely confused with sensuality. The upper part of the face, the patrician brow, the delicately limned eyebrows and the great blue eyes, childlike and almost unnaturally vivid, suggested purity and romantic sadness. But these qualities were lost in the barbarously lovely lower face. The cheekbones were wide. The jawlines swept in to a precise little chin. The nose flared from a fine bridge to wide nostrils. The mouth though not big was deep-lipped and protrudent, and challenged the eyes for dominance. It was in a perpetual pout, as if about to offer itself for a kiss. Yet it too, this savage little mouth, when he had first seen it, had been touched by an expression childlike and tender.

Later, the door opened, and the girl came out. She was dressed in a white satin gown, chastely high at the neck and completed by a scarlet neckband, matching her parasol. Her hair, bound up to show her ears and brushed down in bangs over her forehead, emphasized the sensual breadth of her face. Her skin was a beautiful smooth olive, firm and free of blemish. Johnny couldn't help thinking that the same olivecolored skin covered her whole body, including the breasts, which had been admired by the local experts. They did indeed command admiration, tilting steeply under the white satin.

—I didn't mean to scream, she said. I saw you all down in the street getting ready to run, and I didn't expect to see you in the studio. Why didn't you run?

Her slight drawl was pleasantly Southern and vaguely querulous.

—We're going to postpone it until the Fourth of July, Johnny said.

—Are you a fast runner?

—Pretty fast, ma'am.

—I'm a good runner myself, the girl said.

—How about a race sometime?

—You don't believe me, do you? the girl purred. You'd be surprised how fast I can run. I'm as quick as a cat.

She gazed candidly into his eyes, her face turned up just at his shoulder, her eyes drinking his. Her lashes were long and coarse. The whites of her eyes were veined with little violet lines.

—I wouldn't be at all surprised, he said.

He would not have been surprised. Doubtless, this olivecolored softness could be curved and sudden with catlike muscles.

The girl was still looking at his face when the voice of the photographer broke in.

—Come in, young man.

Johnny went in and had his picture taken. When he came out ten minutes later, the girl was still in the gallery, posing in front of a portrait with both hands on a femininely thrustout hip.

—Hello, she said.

—Hello.

—You're John Shawnessy, the girl said.

—Thanks for letting me know, Johnny said, grinning.

To his surprise, the girl didn't smile at all.

—You're Susanna Drake, he said.

—How'd you know?

—From Uncle Garwood.

This time the girl laughed. Her laughter was like that of an excited child. While she laughed, she put her left hand on her throat.

—What did he say? she asked.

Johnny began obediently to recite what Garwood had said, omitting certain personalities. They walked down the stair together, and it was natural for Johnny to ask her if he might take her home.

—I'd be hurt if you didn't, she said.

Outside in the Square, her scarlet parasol bloomed suddenly into a taut dome. Johnny was aware of hundreds of eyes turning to watch him. She took his arm, and they walked past the Saloon. She had a cute, bouncy way of walking, moving her shoulders with little thrusts and swaying her hips.

—Hello, Uncle Garwood, she said archly.

Garwood pursed his lips and nodded his head approvingly like a judge at the County Fair appraising a well-proportioned heifer. Cash Carney unlipped his cigar and delicately tipped the ash.

—I think I'll go in and get *my* picture took, Garwood said. They give away such nice prizes.

—That boy is definitely ready to graduate, the Perfessor said.

—By the way, how did you know *my* name? Johnny asked.

—O, I've heard of you, the girl said. You write for the newspapers, and you're very shy around girls, and you're the most gifted boy in this County, and you're very idealistic.

—Who told you?

—A friend of yours.

—Ah, the Professor, Johnny said.

—He's the funniest man!

Susanna Drake began to laugh again, touching her throat with her left hand. Then suddenly serious, she said,

—I'm very idealistic too. Have you read *St. Elmo?*

—Yes, I have.

—Don't you think that's just the most wonderful book! I think it's just marvellous the way she works for the redemption of that man's soul! I could really *love* a man like that marvellous St. Elmo. Isn't Mrs. Evans about your most favorite woman writer?

—I prefer Mrs. Stowe, Johnny said.

The girl stopped short and thrust him away with a violence that shocked him.

—That dirty slut! she hissed.

Fury poured up and down her body as if a big angry snake were coiling and uncoiling inside the satin. Some of his amazement must have shown in his face, for this voluptuous fury subsided as swiftly as it began, and the girl leaned against him affectionately.

—Don't pay any attention to me, honey. I just can't stand to hear that woman's name. It makes my flesh crawl. It really does.

In fact, her whole body went through a quick convulsion beginning at the knees and flowing up through her back and hunching her shoulders. She shivered violently and shook her head. That appeared to end it, for she emerged from her fit smiling sunnily and talking about other things.

—This is where I live, she said, when they had walked a block south of the Square.

They were standing at the bottom of a steep flight of stone steps that led up a high lawn to a house. Johnny thought he must have noticed this house before, as it looked vaguely familiar. It was not like any of the other houses in town. It was three stories high, and the front had five windows on it in the pattern of a five-spot in a deck of cards. The corniced roof had one little round window under the peak. There was a long, low verandah with small pillars.

—I just love this house, Susanna said. I always have ever since Aunt and I came to live here when I was a little girl.

—Do you live here all by yourself?

—I have two Nigro girls to do the work, she said. I'll say good-by now.

She held out her small hand, and he took it, supposing that he was about to say good-by. But she allowed her hand to stay in his and remained standing on the first step, so that her head was on a level with his own. From there, she candidly studied his face, her mouth pouting.

—Where did you get that nice smile? she asked.

—That's my St. Elmo expression, Johnny said, embarrassed.

That was just the beginning of it. It was half an hour before he had trailed her step by step all the way up to the door. Meanwhile they talked of a hundred things, Johnny listening for the most part, enchanted by this alien speech that flowed into his ears like a music vaguely remembered. Every word that she spoke and her manner of speaking, he reflected, was a legend of an alien way of life. This girl had been ferried through languorous days and nights and now stepped down into Raintree County, a barbarous creature with a stately name.

—You must come and visit me sometime.

—I'll do that, Miss Drake.

—I'm Susanna to special friends.

—May I count myself among that select number, ma'am?

—You may.

—Susanna. It's a beautiful name, he said. By the way, people call me Johnny, though it's not special like your name.

—Johnny, she said, pronouncing the name in a special way. It happens to be a name I love, Johnny.

He watched her go in and saw her face a moment looking out at him through the glass doorpane, the pouting mouth touched with an expression of tenderness. As he walked back toward the Square, he remembered the measures of an old tune, racy, yet vaguely unhappy.

> I come from Alabama
> With my banjo on my knee,
> I'se gwine to Louisiana,
> My true love for to see. . . .
>
> O, Susanna,
> Do not cry for me;
> I come from Alabama,
> With my banjo on my knee.

He found himself thinking of those steep breasts nodding a pointed invitation from below the Mason and Dixon Line.

But his yearning wasn't directed toward the girl he had just seen. Those days, all beauty reminded him of Nell. He was entirely faithful to this love that was entirely faithful to him by remaining in the image of unattainable beauty. Soon his innocent love-communion in the polysyllables of an antique tongue would end. Graduation Day was near. And besides there was a report abroad that Garwood Jones and Nell were going to be married.

As for Johnny Shawnessy, he had that day thrown off a garment of shyness. He had stood stripped to the waist in the Court House Square, shoulder to shoulder with the fastest runner in Raintree County. Who could say

WHAT IMMORTAL GARLAND WAS TO BE RUN FOR,

NOT WITHOUT DUST

AND

HEAT of the sun filled up the valleyground of the river. Mr. Shawnessy, climbing out of the surrey, carefully laid the *Atlas* face-down on the seat and covered it with a copy of the *Free Enquirer*.

—Might glance through my article, Pet, while I run over here and have a look at things. You children can amuse yourselves hunting for relics of Danwebster.

He opened a copy of the paper to an inside section. Sunlight on the white sheet smote the fine print into a mist under the headline:

HISTORY OF RAINTREE COUNTY, INDIANA

by Prof. John W. Shawnessy

He took a sickle and a covered cardboard box from the floor of the back seat, opened the gate, and stepped into the deepgrassed field.

In my best historical style, a language of inscriptions.

The origin and early development of Raintree County . . .

He stepped over the ribbed and rotten skeleton of a picket fence. Flies whirled from dried cowpads. Weeds boiled rankly from a filled-in cellar. He walked through a tiny stonehenge, the still vaguely human arrangement of a foundation. He picked his way through tufts of marsh grass approaching the river bank. In a far corner of the field, some cows gazed tranquilly at the intruder.

Quo vadis? Whither goest thou, disturbing this earth? In the marketplace of Rome, we ruminate the summer grass. We drop peaceful dung on the memory of Caesar. *Hic jacet* the noblest Roman of them all.

Among the earliest settlements in Raintree County was a community in the great south bend of the Shawmucky, a thriving town on the eastern approach to the County Seat, quaintly called Danwebster, in honor of the greatest name of the Ante-Bellum Republic. The swift decline and disappearance of this little town during and after the War is perhaps attributable to . . .

A pig thrust snogging and snorting from a hole under the remains of the mill.

Who goes there, bearing a sickle and a box of cut flowers? Where feet of lovers trod, our snouts grub roots.

He walked warily out on the remains of the dam and leaping from rock to rock crossed the river. He climbed the low bank on the other side, pushed into the river's fringe of trees, and plunged through nettles and horseweeds, unsettling mists of mosquitoes. He broke from the cool shadow of the river-bordering leaves. Heat and light dizzied him. The waisthigh weeds clung to his clothes. He leaped a marshy ditch, wetting his heels. He paused for breath at the base of the railroad embankment.

Who goes there with a hook of iron and the damp corpses of flowers?

Historian of a vanished culture. Who lies here, sleeping by the river?

Here lies the memory of a little town, of golden and agrarian days and sainted elders on the porches in the evening talking of the Union. Here lies the white republic, founded foursquare on the doctrine of universal law. Here lies a preflood name, Danwebster. Who goes there, with memorial flowers?

A maker of inscriptions. *Ave atque vale!* Hail and Farewell! What path is this, cutting through the cornlands of the County?

Here lies the clean bright knife that slew an old republic. Here lies the sickle-armed castrater of the elder gods. Tread warily, crossing the pathway of new gods.

He scrambled up the embankment. The slight elevation raised him cleanly above the river-valley. The railroad was a long line rising in a gentle grade from the east to the point where he stood and waning in a gentle grade to the west.

Who goes there hunting for memorial stones?

An archeologist of love. I hunt old mounds beside the river. Who lies there sleeping in a hill of earth?

Level with the railroad, south, some fifty yards away, rising from the waves of a vast cornfield like an island in the corn, was a mound of grass and flowers.

Here lies the enduring bone, more lasting than historians of cultures. Here lies a white bone held in a bracelet of bright hair. Who goes there, bearer of a golden bough?

The hero of a lost inscription, the guardian of a talismanic name, an answerer of riddles. Who lies there buried in the earth of Raintree County?

He saw the stones grayly protruding from the grass and weeds, some nodding to the ground, and on their tranquil forms frail lines of

June 1— LEGENDS —1859
IN A CLASS-DAY ALBUM

IN MEMORY OF HAPPY DAYS TOGETHER

at the Pedee Academy marked the close of Johnny Shawnessy's schooling in Raintree County. The Graduation Ceremonies were the occasion of much sprightly newspaper comment. But no newspaper was ever to record an interesting thing that happened to Johnny on Graduation Day.

That spring, in nights of feathery leaves and sweet odors, Johnny lay awake thinking of the coming Graduation Exercises, the Class Picnic, and the Fourth of July Race. Waves of languor succeeded by waves of tumultuous energy made him mad with a springtime madness, and during these days, he decided that he would reveal to Nell Gaither that he was in love with her.

The way he did it was undoubtedly in the purest Johnny Shawnessy tradition.

The Graduation Exercises were in middle June. Everyone agreed that the write-up the following day in the *Free Enquirer* expressed with unusual felicity the spirit of the occasion. The article went in part as follows:

YOUTH FACES THE WORLD

(Epic Fragment from the *Free Enquirer*)

Frankly, we were touched at the sight of the blooming and blushful company of young academicians gathered for the final exercises in the yard of that little Parnassus of the West, Pedee Academy. We felt our own wasted boyhood resurgent in our breast as we looked upon those faces steeped in the immortal dreams of youth!

Before the conferring of diplomas, each graduate stood up and delivered an original composition. Mr. John Wickliff Shawnessy, Valedictorian and Class Poet, recited by heart a long ode in which he bade farewell to classmates and academy. Friends and relatives of this upright young citizen were pleased to perceive that his poetical maturity has in no wise belied his early promise. Garwood Jones, Class Orator, delivered a bang-up oration in which he promised that the future of the Republic could be safely entrusted to the graduating class of Pedee Academy. Miss Nell Gaither, the Salutatorian, than whom no fairer flower ever adorned with its cernuous and supple stem the bedded banks of the Shawmucky, read an original composition entitled 'A Rose of Remembrance in the Faded Garden of Love.' This verbal bouquet, ornamented with some of the most odorous peonies of rhetoric, acquired no little of its charm from the circumstance of its being uttered by a young woman who unites in her person all the blandishments of beauty with all the witcheries of wit. At the end of this composition was a poem, which, we later learned, had been unexpectedly added by Miss Gaither. As we consider it a flower that ought not to blush unseen, we secured the author's permission to print it.

LINES COMPOSED IN MELANCHOLY REMEMBRANCE

In the day when my heart will cease beating
  In the echoing cell of my breast,
And its music so fervid and fleeting,
  Has forever subsided to rest,
If ever thou look'dest with longing
  On her who has passed from thy ken,
O, believe that her heart was belonging
  To thee, though all secretly, then!

O, then, when thine eyes shall discover,
  Too late, how she doted on thee,
When the turf is upmounded above her,
  And her love-fettered spirit is free,
O, then wilt thou pensively hover
  And beweep by her desolate grave,
Thy pale, yet unpenitent lover,
  Thy rejected, yet passionate slave!

So ardent was Miss Gaither's rendition of this empurpled effusion that both she and the audience were visibly moved, and the young lady delivered the last few lines in a scarcely audible voice before retiring in a pretty confusion amid the plaudits of the crowd.

Finally, from the hands of Professor Jerusalem Stiles, diplomas were dispensed to . . .

The graduates gathered in the Academy Yard after the formal exercises to converse with friends and relatives and to exchange gifts, signatures, photographs, and scraps of sentiment in keepsake books.

In everyone's book, Johnny inscribed the following statement enclosed in a border of ornamental penmarks:

A Concluding Specimen of my Writing with Jerusalem W. Stiles at Pedee Academy, Raintree County, Indiana, June 1, 1859.
John Wickliff Shawnessy

Johnny received a similar inscription from the other graduates. Additional sentiments, original or borrowed, were optional.

The Perfessor signed all the keepsake books. In Johnny's he wrote:

To John Wickliff Shawnessy, the budding bard of Raintree County, Life's eternal young American,
Ave atque vale
J. W. Stiles

The Reverend Mrs. Gray came around sniffling and wrote in Johnny's book a wistfully inappropriate sentiment:

Many the changes since last we met.
Blushes have brightened and tears have been wept.
Friends have been scattered like roses in bloom,
Some to the bridal and some to the tomb.

Johnny retaliated with:

Lydia, now I've heard your accents please,
I know what is meant by Lydian melodies.

In Garwood Jones's book, Johnny wrote:

This is tew surtyfie that I Seth Twigs of the County of Raintree, State of Injianny, in the Yewnited States of Amerikee, am acwainted with the owner of this book, and I have no hezzitation in sayin to all and sundry that he kin read, spel, and rite (tho not ellygant like myself). Single men without funds can employ him with the utmost confidents that they hev nuthin to looze by the transacksshun.
Signed, Seth Twigs

Garwood, always a fast man with a comeback, wrote in Johnny's book:

Tew hoom it may consurn:
The owner of this book is wun of my closest pursonal ennumies. I hev no reluctuntz in recommending him fer enny kind of ordeenary

household work, inclooding ginneral carpentry (his fabreekations are noomerous and unsurpassed), but vurgins over fiftee wood dew well to keep him out of there drawers.

Signed, Rube Shucks

After a half-hour or so, Johnny found that he had collected the following additional posies in his keepsake book or on the backs of photographs:

Remember me as your friend
From now until time shall end. Sarah Peters

. . .

A place in thy memory, Johnny, is all that I claim.
Wilt thou pause and look back when thou hearest the sound
of my name! Matilda Thackett

. . .

Forget me not.
Bob Fraser

. . .

Remember well and bear in mind
A constant friend is hard to find.
And when you find one that is true,
Change not the old one for the new. Cassius Carney

. . .

Remember me, when this you see,
Your righthand man at old Pedee. Thomas Smith

The weakest scholar in the graduating class had polished a special gem for the occasion which he inscribed in all the keepsake books:

O, may your pathway ever gleam
With sincere love and joy supreme.
May Him whose eye is felt, not seen,
Bless you with thousand blessings e'en,
With all that fairest love could dream.
Such is the wish of your friend, T. F. Greene.

Then by prearrangement all the graduates gathered in a ring around Professor Stiles, and Mrs. Lydia Gray blushingly presented him with an ornamental cigarbox, which Johnny and Garwood had driven all the way to Middletown to buy. The graduating class had pooled its resources and paid thirteen dollars for it. Lydia's presentation speech started out bravely enough:

—We the members of the First Graduating Class of Pedee Academy wish to tender to you, Professor Stiles, our beloved mentor and friend, this little token of our deep admiration and abiding esteem. May . . .

From here on Lydia's voice steadily diminished in strength so that Johnny never heard the concluding words.

—Madame and members of the First Graduating Class of the Pedee Academy, the Perfessor said, accepting the box and gingerly peeping into it like Pandora expecting troubles, I am deeply touched by this manifestation of your affection, which I hope I may have deserved. Let me only say . . .

The Perfessor went on with a shameless collection of clichés and delighted everyone with the classic roundness of his periods and the aptness of his sentiments. The applause was loud when he finally concluded his remarks and began to pass out the cigars.

At that moment, standing in the shade of the Academy Yard, a tall youthful form, his brilliant black eyes glancing about him, Professor Jerusalem Webster Stiles reached the summit of his popularity in Raintree County.

In a short time, Johnny himself had collected the following gifts: four beautifully bound and illustrated gift books entitled *Friendship's Album, Autumn Leaves, The Heart's Treasure,* and *Pearls of Memory;* a framed picture of a farmhouse with a mother standing in the doorway and waving to her departing boy, whose earthly belongings were bundled to a stick on his shoulder; a framed picture of a farmhouse with a mother standing in the doorway and waving to her returning boy, whose good success in the world was reflected in the neat city clothes and fine suitcase he held in his hand; a handful of *carte de visite* photographs variously inscribed on the back; and a large blue bowtie. He had also been kissed violently by a young girl graduate, whose great passion had kept itself in hiding until then, and by a dozen female relatives from various corners of the County, some of whom he had never seen before in his life. Most of the girl graduates were weeping here and there on the Academy grounds from emotions of farewell.

Johnny himself had distributed various keepsakes, pictures of himself, and gifts. But the most important sentimental remembrance had not yet been exchanged.

He had watched Nell Gaither all the time after the Exercises were over. It was essential for his plan that he catch her alone and suggest that she come with him to the library where he had something to give her. She had been peculiarly quiet and pale as if she hadn't yet recovered from the emotion that had betrayed her while she was giving her Graduation Composition. At last she walked away from the crowd and stopped under an elm in a remote corner of the yard, but before Johnny could react, Garwood Jones walked across the lawn to join her.

Garwood had something in his hand which he presented with a courtly motion. In her white graduation gown and bonnet trimmed in green, Nell seemed untouchably aloof. Yet she smiled up at Garwood in a very lovely way. Garwood fastened a necklace around her neck, and she gave something to him which Johnny couldn't make out; but whatever it was, he could imagine Garwood's voice mellowly throbbing with gratitude.

At that moment, a relative came up and hit Johnny on the back and shook his hand, and Johnny didn't see the climax of the scene. When next he looked, Nell was alone, walking along the fence. Then abruptly, as if remembering something, she turned and went swiftly to the porch of the Academy. Just before entering, she swept the yard with her eyes, which rested finally on Johnny Shawnessy. She looked at him a long moment with lifted brows, lips parted. Then she turned and went into the Academy Building.

—Excuse me, Johnny said, rudely leaving the group he had been with.

His chance had come, the moment he had rehearsed in fancy so often that the actuality became many times more exciting than an improvisation. Heart pounding, he followed Nell into the building and down the dim corridor to the library. She was inside, sitting at the table with her head on her hands. He picked up a big book which some hours before he had carefully hidden in a corner of a bookshelf. He put the book on the table in front of her.

—Here's a little graduation remembrance, Nell.

It was a brandnew leatherbound giltedged copy of *The Complete*

Works of William Shakespeare. It had cost Johnny seven dollars and fifty cents and weighed six pounds.

—Sort of *in memoriam,* he recited in a hoarse voice, for all the good times studying together, Nell.

Nell raised her head. Her eyes were wet. She picked up the huge book and held it helplessly. It struck Johnny that he had done a touchingly brave and also quite pitiable thing. Nell ran her hands wordlessly a few times over the big book, looking up at Johnny and then down at the gilt words on the cover. She tugged at the book, and it opened suddenly, the pages, newly gilded, sticking. Where it opened, the picture of a young man looked out from a *carte de visite* photograph which had been inserted in the book under the printed words

VENUS AND ADONIS

It was the picture of a youth of twenty in a dandy suit. The shoulders were well back, the chest well forward, the arms fixed at the sides but thrust a little back, the left foot slightly advanced. The head was held high as if forced up by the bowtie at the throat. The eyes were steeped in visions. The mouth was firm but gentle, as if about to smile. The heavy eyebrows were slightly raised as if touched upward with a mild surprise. The whole image had a quality of youthful, affectionate charm.

Johnny winced as he saw this sudden image of himself planted in the immense book of William Shakespeare.

—Please don't let anyone else see what I wrote on the back of that picture, Nell, he said.

Then he walked swiftly out of the door and down the corridor.

On the back of the picture he had written:

ACTAEON

One day a vision was vouchsafed to me,
  That filled my burning heart with bright emotion,
A sight more fair than Venus was when she
  Came streamingly from the Ionian ocean.
I had been lying by a riverside
  And as I lay, I slept and dreamed a dream,

And then awaking, from my covert spied
  A girl—and beautiful—bathed in the stream.
Like one enchanted, swooningly I lay
  And watched her. She was naked. And her bare,
Brightlimbed, and slender body was at play
  With the green water dropping from her hair.
Her name, which even now I dare not tell,
Rang in my stricken heart a lovely kNELL.

John Wickliff Shawnessy,
June 1, 1859.

No one else had yet seen this sonnet, upon which Johnny had expended all his technical resources, except Professor Stiles, who had remarked,

—Shall the Shawmucky be another Avon? I see our rural bard has been *sleeping, by a virgin hand disarmed*. You may get your face slapped for that poem. Undressing Raintree County damsels even in pentameters is a pretty risky business.

The summerclad forms of the graduates and their friends bloomed suddenly on Johnny's vision as he burst from the dusk of the Academy into the sunlight of the yard. The white dresses hurt his eyes; the blithe voices stung his ears. He walked slowly out into the lawn, appalled by the exquisite wickedness of the thing that he had done.

At this very moment, the girl in the Academy Building held in her two hands the soul of Johnny Shawnessy, a throbbing, vulnerable thing. Words were more naked than flesh, and he could never get them back. He had once held her white beauty imprisoned in his cruelly eager eyes; but now she was returning the favor with a vengeance. He had tried to be life's young Greek in Nineteenth Century America. His poem was wellnamed 'Actaeon.' Like the hunter who beheld Diana bathing in the stream and was changed to a stag and hunted by his own dogs, he could hear howling after him already the bloodhounds of Raintree County's puritan conscience.

—Here's the boy now, Garwood said, his booming voice calling everyone's attention to Johnny emerging from the building. Garwood walked importantly through the crowd and taking Johnny by the arm led him to a group of men near the front gate.

—This the boy? one of the men said.

Johnny shifted uneasily. The whole crowd turned to watch.

—Think you got any chance to whip Flash Perkins on the Fourth? the man said.

—I mean to try.

—Garwood here has been offering me odds of three to one Perkins'll beat you. I thought you and Garwood were friends.

—Garwood and I hate each other affectionately, Johnny said.

—Tell 'em how good you are, John, Garwood said. I'll give you half my winnings.

—A bet on John Shawnessy's a sure thing, mister, Johnny said.

—Sure to lose, Garwood said. Ha, Ha, Ha.

—Johnny! Yoo hoo, Johnny! Come here.

It was his mother calling. He walked over to her. As Valedictorian he was a noteworthy object and was expected to show his face and say bright things. Ellen was very proud of him, her great, handsome, likeable Johnny, who had led his class and had been called by the distinguished Professor Stiles 'the most gifted young man I have ever had the good fortune to teach, Madame.'

—This is Cousin Hurlbut Shawnessy from Middletown, Ellen said. He's quite a scholar himself and has similar interests to you, Johnny.

—O, is that so? Pleased to meet you.

—Pleased to meet you, young John, Cousin Hurlbut said.

Cousin Hurlbut obviously favored the bigframed, fatfaced, bucktoothed branch of the Shawnessys. He had jawlength sideburns and a portentous manner.

—Cousin Ellen tells me you're the author of the Will Westward articles in the Freehaven *Enquirer,* young John, Cousin Hurlbut said.

—Yes, I guess so, Johnny said, watching the door of the Academy.

—I have read your inditings with interest, Cousin Hurlbut said. Maybe you've seen some columns appearing in the Middletown *Radiant* under my numdyploom, Peter Patter.

—Uh, yes, I believe so, Johnny said. Very fine.

He had some memory of having seen some clippings from Cousin Hurlbut's muse, which specialized in poems about looking backward down the years and realizing that one's youth was spent.

—John's the scholar of the family, T. D. said, rocking pleasantly.

The boy always had a knack for saying things from the time he was a little shaver.

Johnny excused himself and withdrew from the crowd. He skirted the edges of the yard. He thought of slipping through the side gate and going down to the train station. He had always wanted to go West anyway. In the West, a man could do as he pleased. In Raintree County there were too many barriers and too much beauty.

He was standing alone under the big elm by the side gate when Nell came out of the Academy and picked her way sedately through the yard coming directly toward him. Under her arm was a huge book.

It was clear that she was returning his present.

—Here's something for you, Johnny, she said in her low, soft voice, lingering her mouth along his name.

As she gave him the book, she put her head to one side in one of her unconsciously statuary attitudes, the sidepoised head communicating its evasive gesture musically down the length of her body and somehow suggesting the emotion of farewell.

The book was a brandnew leatherbound giltedged copy of *The Complete Works of Lord Byron.*

—I knew you didn't have a copy, Johnny, and I thought you might want one to keep. Your poem was beautiful.

She turned and walked away with the same undulant, unhurried step and, accepting the arm of Garwood Jones at the gate, climbed into his buggy. As she gathered her dress in, she looked over her right shoulder and her eyes found Johnny's in a lingering look.

Someone was coming toward him. He walked hurriedly to the Academy and ran up onto the verandah and through the door. The library was still empty. He carried the book over to the recessed window. He pulled at the stuck gilt leaves. Where the book opened, the picture of a girl looked up from a *carte de visite* photograph underneath the poem 'Fare Thee Well.'

It was the picture of a young woman standing with her body in profile, so poised that she appeared to be just rising to her toes. Her face was in half-profile, her eyes looking back over her right shoulder and directly out of the picture. The whole pose was an unconsciously classic attitude. It was the river nymph inviting the love-pursuit.

On the back of the photograph were the words

> Johnny, please keep forever this image of her who has been for longer than you guess
>
> Your pale, yet unpenitent lover,
> Your rejected, yet passionate slave.
>
> Nell

To his ears came the distant sound of voices and laughter. They beat softly on the brick walls of the Academy Building, echoing in its empty shell. They were like the sound of surf, a blue surf churning on immemorable shores. They poured languor and sweetness of love over the listening soul of Johnny Shawnessy.

On the way back to the Home Place, T. D. kept talking about the significance of higher education.

—Yessirree, John, he said, I wish I had had just half your advantages when I was your age. I always did want to know a little Latin and Greek. I tell you, with Latin and Greek, and your natural aptitudes and faculties, John, I take a very hopeful view of your future. I'm sure I express and echo the sentiments of your mother too, when I say that we're very proud of you.

YOU HAVE A BRIGHT ROAD AHEAD OF YOU, MY BOY,
AND WE EXPECT YOU TO
GO

FAR around on three sides the ocean of July corn undulated toward the Danwebster Graveyard and broke, a gentle surf, against it, ebbing from the wire fence. Mr. Shawnessy opened the gate and stepped inside.

The graveyard, abandoned like the town, was a hundred stones beside the river. In the middle of orderly cornlands, it was an island of disorder. He kicked up crowds of grasshoppers as he walked through uncut grass, gravemyrtle, wild carrot, white top, blackberries, poison ivy.

He stopped and shaded his eyes, looking for familiar stones. In the place of death he felt overwhelmed by life. Life rushed up from the breasts of the dead in a dense tangle of stems that sprayed seeds and spat bugs. As he thought of other memorial journeys to the graveyard, the stones seemed to him doomed and huddled shapes around which green waters were steadily rising. He stood up to his knees in grass and weeds, holding in one hand a box of peaceful cut flowers and in the other a sickle, his eyes hurting with sunlight.

They lie beside the river, lulled by the music of its waters. They lie beside the river.

Where are the forms and faces of my pagan youth? Where is the hunger of the shockhead boy who saw a white flesh in secret waters? Where are youth and maiden?

They lie beside the immemorial river.

Where are the generations of those who loved beside the river? Where are the generations of grass and flowers that bloomed and seeded by the river?

Bare feet of lovers, thudding on the roofs of mounds, press lightly on these crumbled hearts.

There are many mounds beside the running river, become beautiful and secret by the lapse of years. There are entire eras of lost lovers who have left only mounds full of bright boneshards beside the river. All the people who ever lived here were lovers and the seed of lovers. Where are all those who ever beheld beauty in bright waters?

They lie beside the river. They lie beside the river.

He walked a little farther into the graveyard and bent over a stone that rose slenderly from the grass, completing itself in a tranquil arc. He began to tear at the dense grass with his sickle.

O, beautiful, springing hair from the flesh of the dead! I will remember long gold hair around a face that was like no other. I will remember boats that moved in gala procession far down between widening shores. And oars that made languid wounds in the pale flesh of the river.

What difference now does it make that love was a tall, imperious bloom beside the river? What difference if face touched face beside the river?

There was no guilt or recollection of guilt. There was only love that is desire for beauty. We were like flowers that seduce each other without memory and without guilt.

He stood up leaving the base of the stone softly revealed by the sickle. He had put very far from him, he knew, the anxieties of the coming day. Very far from him now was Waycross, on the periphery of the County, where before long he must participate in patriotic ceremonies. He stood in a place of classic stones. Halfshutting his eyes, he felt his body drenched in sunlight. He listened to the murmur of cornleaves swayed by the wind and the music of the river passing through its vocal reeds.

This was the earth of riddles, this was the earth from which had sprung all myths, memories of passion. He shut his eyes entirely. Something white and graven with a legend was approaching him on a sundrenched water. There were words that he had meant to remember, a legend of his life in one of its memorable springtimes.

Then he had a sharp, clear memory of the lecture room of the old Academy Building. He was sitting at his desk, pencil in hand, among the other students. It was the Final Examination in 1859. Across the board a tall, blacksuited man chalked slantingly

A QUESTION IN RHETORIC

Compose an essay suggested by the following incident:

One day a poet walking on the shores of the Mediterranean picked up a broken oar washed in by the sea. These words were graven on the blade:

Remembering the cryptic line, he heard again a sound of surf—young voices, laughter, beating on brick walls.

I see the blue mass of the seamounds shifting in. O, little blade, naked and smooth, borne in from untumultuous seas, I hear the slanting music of your legend.

My body is whitely reclined on leaguelong beaches. O, plastic Mediterranean forms!

What is this white tower of beauty? I see it slenderly arisen from bright waters.

O, goddess, you were borne to me by a white oar sandward washed in summer. Foamborn, with young unpendulous breasts, far from your ancient shores you came to me, forgetful of your old fruitions. We were together youngly before great wars.

I the child of a young republic reached hands of a young desire to your body clad in the archaic garment of nudity. Did we not weary ourselves in a rhythm of rowing, daylong on the inland waters?

Our arms were interlaced, our sobbing breaths beat on each other's eyelids under the seedenlivening light of eternal day. O, bright annihilator of lines and minutes, o, ceaseless undulator of curves recurrent, o, visual and unvestal goddess, *Oft was I weary when I toiled with*

June 18— THE —1859

ROMANTIC, ILLSTARRED, WONDERFUL,

WICKED CLASS PICNIC WAS IMPARTIALLY REPORTED

only in the *Free Enquirer,* and even then not until several days after the excitement had died down. The article, a remarkable one, was published as coming from an unknown pen. It began:

THE EPIC PICNIC

> Most of those who have written of the late picnic have told nothing but lies, monstrous fabrications on a thin scaffolding of truth. This observer had hoped that the whole thing would escape the pitiless light of the press, which could only serve to keep wounds open and passions inflamed. Since the lid is off, however, he feels incumbent upon him the melancholy duty of giving a full account of the entire episode which, as it happens, he is in a position to know better than anyone else. And as, except for its unhappy dénouement, the picnic will remain a fadelessly blithe memory in the hearts of most of those who were there, let us paint it for posterity with an impartial pen, gay where gaiety is apposite, grave where, alas! the events that transpired upon the banks of the Shawmucky require such a style. So that those who live after us may have the picture in all its light and shadow, long after hearts that are now embittered have ceased to beat, let us for a little withdraw the curtain and then lower it forever on the events of that memorable and melancholy day. Say, then, Muse, what was the beginning of . . .

The picnic began at the Academy Building, where the students assembled and set out noisily in buggyloads. The Perfessor led the way, driving a black spring buggy belonging to the Reverend Ezra Gray, which his wife Lydia had procured for the afternoon. Johnny, Lydia, and Cassius Carney were squeezed into this buggy. Garwood Jones's buggy followed with five people wedged in, including Nell Gaither. The third buggy brought the rest. There were thirteen altogether, counting the Perfessor.

—Thirteen, the Perfessor had said at starting. Which is the marked man?

Startled, Johnny Shawnessy had kept his eyes down. It had been a week since he and Nell Gaither had exchanged certain keepsakes. Two nights after, he had decided on a bold move and had walked down the road to Nell's house. A buggy passed him on the way and turned in at the Gaither drive. When Johnny reached the house, Garwood Jones was giving Nell's father a cigar on the front porch. Johnny walked back home without paying his respects.

At the Academy, Nell had turned up in Garwood's buggy, wearing her green dress, her gold hair pulled back to show her ears under a wide white sunbonnet. Stepping down from the buggy, she had fluttered her hand at Johnny, and a smile touched the corners of her mouth, this mouth with the pointed red tongue, so fullflown and sensual and, alas! so often kissed—but never by Johnny Shawnessy.

—Hello, Johnny, it said, lingering on the word. It's hot, isn't it?

This remark seemed to Johnny somehow the most exciting and subtly meaningful thing he had ever heard.

But Nell's eyes gave no special sign. Johnny felt a cold and not wholly irrational fear. Girls were mawkish sentimentalists and would write almost anything in a keepsake book.

On the way over to Danwebster, where picnic tables had been set out beside the mill, everyone laughed and sang. The Perfessor was full of quips and quotations. Johnny Shawnessy kept leaning out of the Reverend's buggy and yelling things at the Garwood Jones buggy. Each time he did so, Garwood solemnly thumbed his nose, and Nell stuck out her tongue in a very ladylike manner. Johnny deliberately fell out of the Reverend's buggy once and raced the horse for a hundred yards to loud applause.

When they reached the bank of the river, they put their picnic baskets on the tables and engaged in a new sport that the Perfessor had introduced into Raintree County.

THE BASE BALL GAME

(Epic Fragment from the *Free Enquirer*)

Arriving on the banks of the legendary Shawmucky, the young men promptly divested themselves of their coats and laying out a 'base ball diamond' proceeded to urge the sportive ball hither and thither in the somewhat complicated evolutions of this new game only recently imported by Professor Stiles from the East into Raintree County. Cassius Carney demonstrated a baffling speed and precision in the exacting art of wafting the ethereal sphere across the spot denominated 'home plate.' Professor Stiles showed extraordinary agility in snatching the bounding pellet off the ground or stopping it in mid-air, whenas with one graceful sweep of his arm he would propel it to the appropriate spot on the 'diamond.' John Shawnessy, he of the limber legspring, shot around the 'bases' like a comet whenever he got a chance, which, be it remarked in passing, was not often, as he showed a marked inability to engender that contact between bat and ball which is necessary for a 'hit.' The game was marred by a few altercations, at the bottom of which one could invariably expect to find that rising young politician, Garwood Jones, whose ignorance of the rules and regulations of 'base ball' did not in the least diminish his readiness to argue about every moot point.

The final score could not be exactly ascertained for a variety of reasons, especially as the rules were scandalously relaxed from time to time in favor of several young ladies who were invited to play in order to make up two 'teams.' It is believed that about thirty or forty legal 'runs' were scored by each side.

One amusing mishap involved the person of the aforesaid Mr. Jones, who mistook for 'second base' a certain circular adornment that is oftentimes found in places where members of the bovine species ruminate.

After the game of 'base ball' had terminated, several of the young gentlemen were pitted against each other in a test of fleetness of foot. In all these encounters, John Wickliff Shawnessy, that poetic young denizen of the Upper Shawmucky, dismounted from Pegasus long enough to demonstrate to the assembled company a velocity of pedal locomotion not seen in these parts for many a moon. This young man is being groomed by his supporters as a challenger to the honors now so long held by Orville Perkins of Freehaven, better known as 'Flash,' who has been undisputed champion of the County for five years. When asked by your correspondent whether or not he thought he could obtain the victory over the redoubtable Mr. Perkins in the Annual Fourth of July Race in Freehaven, our modest young hero said without a moment's hesitation, 'Shucks, it won't hurt to try. Someone ought to beat that old guy before he trips on his beard.'

Personally, we should like to see the veteran velocipede from Freehaven match his stuff against this brash beanpole from the banks of the Shawmucky. Five dollars will get you one of ours that youth will not be denied and that Mr. Perkins' venerable years (he is now, we understand, a senile twenty-two), if not the fleetness of his challengers, will at last get the better of him.

But now we approach that part of our recital from which the Muse shrinks in trembling anticipation. It was about three o'clock in the afternoon that . . .

It had been Johnny Shawnessy's idea that the picnic include a boating excursion down the Shawmucky River. A half dozen rowboats had been procured and rowed laboriously up the river from Danwebster the day before by Johnny and others to a spot where the river looped behind the Gaither Farm. Here the picnickers could break up into twosomes and row the loops of the river back to the picnic ground at Danwebster, arriving in time for supper and a bonfire before breaking up and going home.

On the mile walk over to the river, the girls collected around Professor Stiles, who led the way, while the young men brought up the rear, falling farther and farther back. Near the river Garwood Jones pulled out a bottle of corn whiskey and passed it around. Everyone took a drink but Johnny. Garwood stopped, passed out cigars, and told a hearty joke, while Johnny lingered uneasily, watching the Perfessor and the girls climbing into boats at the water's edge. Nell hadn't yet entered a boat but stood as if waiting for someone. She shaded her eyes and, as it seemed to Johnny, looked directly at him. She slowly raised her hand and gently beckoned.

While Garwood roared loudly at his own good joke, Johnny began to run. When he reached Nell, he took her hand, which he hadn't held since they were children, and together they stepped into a boat.

—Hey! Garwood yelled. What's the big idea?

He was standing on the bank now, feet wide apart, hands on hips, staring at Nell. Nell bit her lip in confusion and turned her head away. As for Johnny, he stood up, planted the oarblade in the bank squarely between Garwood's legs and with one shove sent the boat skimming to the middle of the river.

ROWING DOWN THE RIVER

(Epic Fragment from the *Free Enquirer*)

Their boats dispread upon the river were like swans on classic waters. With a languorous lifting and falling of oarblades, the gala procession floated on the widening stream. In romantic twosomes, they lingered on between green walls. Did they stop to think, in the midst of their gaiety and laughter, that they were passing burial places and battlegrounds of vanished peoples? Did they think that the winding river was the highway of extinct races, whose skimming light canoes did cleave the same waters in centuries long ago? Did these maidens in wide bonnets, these lads in straw skimmers and bowties, dream of aught but innocent love and beauty and desire as they drifted on languid oars down waters of youth and summertime! Ah! let us behold them this brief while, floating on the classic river of Raintree County, with all their gushing joys in their bloom. . . .

Johnny dug the water with slow oars. On the breast of the slow-flooding river, he was floating with Nell Gaither, who sat in the stern of the boat, her feet together, her hands on the sides of the boat, her wide bonnet buckling with the breeze that freshened fitfully along the river. Languor and desire flowed from the fullbodied river. Looking past Nell, Johnny could see the broad road of water curving distantly in the haze of afternoon. The air was moist with the odor of the river and its flowers. Nell Gaither's body in the green dress was curved like the river; her face in the bonnet was an incredible, lush flower swaying on a supple stem. Her eyes glowed with a curious light in the brightness of the river air. Turning now and then, Johnny saw the other boats spread out upon the water. In the farthest boat Professor Stiles, paired with Lydia Gray, rowed fiercely toward the bend.

Garwood Jones and Cash Carney, forced by the shortage of women to row down the river together, hung around Johnny's boat. Just opposite the place where Johnny had seen Nell in the river, his boat grounded on a mudbar. Everyone else had missed it by yards, but Johnny, who knew that part of the river by heart, drove straight onto it. Garwood, slightly ahead, laughed grimly and stood up in his boat.

—You'll have to push off, John. Need any help?

—I can manage, Garwood. Thanks.

—Be glad to help, Garwood said grimly.

—No, thanks. I can manage.

Johnny, looking over his shoulder, watched the last boat coasting toward the bend. He and Nell were alone on a mudbar in the middle of the Shawmucky.

Eyes thoughtful, Nell sat with her feet primly together. She reached up often to push a wisp of hair off her forehead, and sometimes she trailed her hand in the river.

—This boat is here to stay, Johnny said, until we push it off. I drove it on hard.

Nell laughed.

—You sure did, Johnny, she said. I thought you knew the river.

—I do.

—O.

—You in any hurry to get to Danwebster? Johnny said.

—Not a bit. This is nicer right here.

Johnny raised the oars and laid them up along the sides of the boat. Nell put her hand on the left oar, still dripping from the river.

—I feel so funny, she said, and the sun's so bright.

She ran her fingers along the thin blade of the oar.

—Remember the line from the Final Examination? she said. I don't know why I thought of it.

She took off her wide bonnet and shook her hair. Her eyes were nearly shut in the brilliant sunlight. Johnny watched her mouth as she recited in a low voice, rhythmical and pensive:

—*Oft was I weary when I toiled with thee.* I wonder where the Perfessor got it?

—Probably he made it up, Johnny said.

—*Oft was I weary when I toiled with thee,* Nell said. I wonder what it means. It sounds so—so pagan.

She kept running her hand along the smooth oarblade and trailing her other hand in the river.

—Is it wrong to be pagan, Johnny?

—I hope not, Johnny said.

—*Oft was I weary when I toiled with thee,* Nell said.

Her large, lovely mouth moulding and murmuring these words was itself a legend, a series of plastic attitudes. What she said no longer seemed important. But this flowerlike mouth, against which he wished to press his own mouth with undissuadable hunger, seemed important.

—I feel so strange. Johnny, did you ever see the river so beautiful?

The air seemed filled with a mist, through which nevertheless all things were seen with peculiar distinctness. Johnny Shawnessy felt islanded in languor, as the river flooded past on its journey to the lake. Somewhere far down on the greenwalled waters, boats were floating in a gay procession. He could hardly open his eyes against the greening brightness. He was tired with rowing on the river. He had dipped white oars a long time in the pale stream of the river.

—My hair keeps falling down, Nell said, pushing it back. Did you mean to sit here a long time?

—We might go ashore, Johnny said.

—We'll have to wade, Nell said. But I don't mind. I feel so funny, Johnny.

They took off their shoes and stockings and left them, along with Nell's bonnet, in the boat. They stepped out into shallow water close to the right bank of the river and made for shore, where they sat for a while on the bank under Johnny's oak, their feet trailing in the water. They talked in half sentences about the picnic and graduation. The afternoon ebbed and flooded around them in waves of warmth and stridulous sound. The murmur of the river was constant on its shoals and among its rushes.

It was Nell who suggested that they walk over and see the Indian mounds.

—I've never really gone up on them, she said. I guess they're so close to our own land that they never interested me.

—The two on the river here, I've seen often, Johnny said. And there's another, isn't there, across the field there?

SCENIC VIEWS ALONG THE SHAWMUCKY

(Epic Fragment from the *Free Enquirer*)

The banks of our own not unclassic river vie with any in the world for scenes of historic and poetic charm. To those who celebrate the Tiber, the Euphrates, and the Nile, we say: When Rome first rose in templed splendor on her many hills, this river ran as now upon her centuried pathway to the lake, part of a mighty system of waters going to the gulf. Before the Parthenon was, this river was. When Babylon rose and fell, this river was. Its shores were dense in summer with crowding vegetation. Green frogs and greatwinged birds, more ancient structures than Egyptian columns, peopled its water and the circumambient air. What is older than the antiquity of life itself? We know not what ancient empires rose and flourished on these banks, or how often the syllables of lovers mingled with the vocal passion of the river running in the shallows. This river, too, has its human shards, and we dare to suggest that the true archaeologist of beauty will feel a deep, peculiar charm when he beholds the twin mounds upon the river's banks, lonely undulations, mysterious hummocks, sole relics of races that flowered and faded on the Shawmucky without a Bible or an epic poet to keep their names alive. . . .

Barefoot, they walked downstream to the twin mounds. The mounds were fifty feet apart and almost perfectly round—smooth humps fifty feet in diameter and ten feet high.

—Think how long these have been here! Nell said. Hundreds of years maybe.

A curious light hid living in her narrowed eyes. Pinpoint pupils burned in green pools, fringed by her lashes, each lash shiny and distinct. Scrambling up the slope of the mound, Johnny took her hand. It was warm and responsive. The odor of her hair and skin was in his nostrils.

Thick grass covered the mounds. The dirt on top was brown and looked somehow old and pulverized. As they stood on top of the left mound, Johnny had a feeling that it was slightly resilient, as if roofed. The ticklegrassed earth was warm to the palms of his feet. He watched the river, a shining sheet of greenness.

He started a little, hearing a train on the branch line. For a moment he felt like an anachronistic ghost from the antiquity of human days. He remembered suddenly the County, its fences and its boundaries, its sickleshaped railroad, its orderly farms, and its thousands of figures in suits and bellshaped dresses. He felt faintly sad and uneasy as the train made a quavering, distant cry. The cry expired slowly, drowned in vistas of afternoon. Frogs shouted from the shallows, the rushes swayed, the waterbirds were crying.

When they left the mound, they walked out upon the bulge of a neighboring clover field. The hay was newly cut, but the fresh stubble didn't hurt their feet. It was a small field, and on the far side, tufted with flowering weeds, was the third mound.

They never quite got there.

When they reached the haypile in the middle of the field, they stopped. Johnny was panting as if he had been climbing a steep hill.

Absurdly, he felt as if it was the grass and clover-stubble on the bottom of his feet that took his breath.

—My hair keeps coming down, Nell said.

She stopped and plucking out a pin let the whole left side of her hair down around her face. She put the pin in her mouth and started to bind the hair back up again.

—Let it fall, Johnny said.

His voice was husky with the heat. Nell leaned back against the hay.

—I don't know what to do with it, she said. It's such a nuisance.

She looked directly at him and slowly took the pin out of her mouth. Her lips were parted.

—I haven't played in hay since I was a kid, Johnny said.

—Me neither.

He put his arms around her to lift her up and his hands sliding down to get a better hold felt her smooth flesh in the Raintree County dress. He touched his mouth to hers as she leaned deeply back in the hay. Her mouth was warm and alive. Her eyes were halfshut, watching him, and her breath came and went in little quick gasps, drinking his. He put his arms clear around her and squeezed her hard, feeling her go limp. Suddenly, she was slipping away from him. He saw her bare feet and legs under her dress as she scrambled halfway up the new soft stack of hay.

—Come on up, Johnny, she said, shaking out her hair.

He sprang up and caught her and put his arms around her again. Her hair was all shaken down now, it touched his cheeks and shook around his face. In this dense hair was the warm, kissing mouth of the river girl, her white powderscented skin, her vivid eyes. He was amazed by the passion of her kisses.

She still breathed with the quick little breaths, but when she lay back and shook the hair out of her face and looked up at him, she was strangely serene.

—O, Johnny, she said. This was a long time happening. I thought you didn't care for me.

—I thought you didn't care for me.

—Who wouldn't care for you, Johnny?

She put her warm, bare arms around his neck and drew his face down to hers. She knew ways of kissing that had never occurred to him. He didn't know how long they lay in the warm sunshine. Much later, Nell said,

—I feel so funny, Johnny. I don't know what gets into me sometimes. I want to do crazy things.

—Like swimming in the river with nothing on? Johnny said.

—Yes, Nell said. I've done that a lot. I always liked to swim that way.

—Were you mad when I wrote that thing in the *Enquirer?*

—I should've been. But I wasn't. I wondered if you liked me.

—You were beautiful, Johnny said. You don't need to feel embarrassed.

—It's all right, Nell said. Besides I saw you too.

—Me?

—Yes, Nell said, blushing, with eyes averted. Two can play at that game.

—When? Johnny said, blushing furiously.

—O, several times, Nell said.

—You mean—uh—before I saw you?

—O, don't ask so many questions, Johnny.

Later when they left the haystack and walked back to the river, the sun was far down over the western bank, but the air seemed moister and warmer than before. Johnny's face felt swollen with heat, his body itched, he was covered with haystems.

They sat at the river's edge again and dangled their feet in the water.

—It's so hot, Nell said. Doesn't the water feel good to your feet?

The riverpool was a depth of green and clear. He leaned over the water, aching to plunge his hot face into the river, to hide a thought that was too bold for Raintree County.

—If we could only have a swim now, he said.

—It would be sinful, Nell said. What if someone saw?

The way she said it, he knew that she had said yes.

—No one ever comes down here but us. Everyone else is way down the river by now. We could just go in for a little while and get cool.

—I wouldn't do it with anyone but you, Johnny, Nell said.

When they undressed, she stood on one side of the great oak by the river, he on the other. Undressed, he wished he hadn't done it.

—How are you, Nell?

There was no response behind the tree.

—If you'd rather not——

—Here I go, Nell said.

She stepped down the bank and into the water. And before he himself plunged desire into the cold pool of evening, John Wickliff Shawnessy, the budding bard of Raintree County, intently watched a rippling mark like the stain of a pressed flower on a page of verse, a signature of mortal beauty

ON ONE OF RAINTREE COUNTY'S

MOST EXCITING

TWIN

MOUNDS and a mound and lettered stones, the Danwebster Graveyard was a formal garden of death, which life was slowly reclaiming to formless fecundity.

Mr. Shawnessy listened—he had heard a distant sound and at the same time a rush of voices by the river. Perhaps the children had cried out, but he had thought that the voices called his name, not as he was called today but as he was called in the old days before the War.

—Johnny!

The name had formed suddenly from mixing sound. It had been uttered in a warmly personal way, with a touch of sadness and even of alarm. He listened, his ears still troubled with the sound.

He had remembered love, bare arms embracing, nakedness and young mouths kissing; he had remembered a mythical and seldom remembered boy.

He listened to hear if the imagined call would be repeated, to hear if some voice speaking from the lost days would say again the talismanic, youthawakening word.

But instead there was a troublous sound, a rhythmical and rapid sound across the land.

He watched for the first appearance of the train. Standing among the stones of the Danwebster Graveyard, he was in the attitude of one who listens, a little fearful, for a necessary thing. His heart beat quick and hard, he felt as though the visual impact of the train would be an unendurable violation. He listened, hearing from the archaic valley of the Shawmucky, voices of urgency and faint alarm, calling stopped and held themselves half-submerged, listening. Great birds plunged squawking into flight from feeding places near shore. Frogs sprang among reeds in quick flat leaps.

The name 'Johnny' echoed between the walls of the river, up and down the milelong valley, ebbing and dwindling, renewed, insistent.

The two white ones now swam and waded from the river to the shore. The voices calling 'Johnny' called also now the name 'Nell,' and the names mixing and blending reverberated on the twilight river.

The two from the river now asserted their fundamental difference, the one by pulling a pair of trousers up his legs, the other by pulling a dress down over her head. There were a few moments of panting speechlessness while Johnny Shawnessy and Nell Gaither resumed the garments of Raintree County. Johnny had a brief view of Nell bending over and pulling up pantaloons beneath her gown while from the unfastened top of her bodice, her left breast spilled out silkily. Then for the first time, though almost clothed, she looked to him naughtily nude.

—O, dear! Johnny! she said, in a forlorn small voice, my hair's soaked.

—Get out to the boat, Johnny said. Get yourself wet on the way. We'll upset it and say we couldn't right it.

They waded to the mudded boat, grabbed out their shoes and stockings and Nell's bonnet, pulled the boat off the bar, and tried to upset it. It wouldn't upset.

The calls were close. Johnny recognized the voices of his brother Zeke, Garwood Jones, and Cash Carney. Three figures were barely visible in the fading light walking along the left bank.

—Here we are! Johnny yelled.

He helped Nell into the boat, took the oars, and rowed toward the three boys, who stood waiting on the far shore.

—Where've you been? Garwood said. We thought you were drowned.

Johnny said something about walking back from the river to find the mounds, getting lost, and upsetting the boat.

—We got all wet, Nell said.

She laughed, nervously touching her soaked hair. But Johnny could see that the boys on the shore were not amused.

—Better come out of there, John, Zeke said. Just leave the boat tied here.

—What's the matter? Johnny said.

He heard voices over by the road, men talking, boots in the underbrush.

—What's the matter, anyway? Johnny repeated. What's everyone excited about?

—Come on out, Garwood said, and we'll tell you. I can see you don't know.

—You better take Nell home first, Zeke said.

—We better get out, Nell said.

They had been putting on their shoes and stockings and now climbed out of the boat. Lanterns were flashing in the underbrush. Several men were crashing down a path to the river. A strange voice called out,

—Did you find 'em?

—Here they are! Cash yelled back.

—We better tell 'im now, Garwood said. Nell might as well hear too. Before these guys get here.

However, the men were already there, at least a dozen in the dim light, and they all had guns. A heavy, blunt-featured man thrust a lantern from face to face. Johnny shrank back from the blazing light, hair dripping. He didn't remember ever having seen this man before. He couldn't identify the other men. He blinked sheepishly.

—Is this young Shawnessy? the man said.

—What's the matter? Johnny said.

The man thrust the hot lantern in Johnny's face while the other men all crowded in close, breathing hard.

—Listen, young Shawnessy, the leader said menacingly, if you know anything about this, you better come clean.

Johnny felt the flesh on his face crawl. His fists knotted.

—I haven't told him yet, Garwood said.

—Listen, Shawnessy, the man said, if you had anything to do with this, you'd best tell, or by God, we'll beat the livin'——

—Say, what the hell! Zeke said, shoving the man back with an openhanded blow on the chest. What makes you think the kid had anything to do with it? Lay a hand on that boy, and I'll smash hell out of you.

—Take it easy, Zeke, the man said, angrily, but he stayed back.

—What's the matter? Johnny said.

—It's the Perfessor, Garwood said. He's run off with Lydia.

At first Johnny felt a wild desire to laugh. Then he went all weak in the knees.

—How do you know?

—They were seen, Garwood said. They tried to catch the train at Three Mile Junction. You two disappeared, and some folks thought you might be in on it. We said no, but they had to know for sure. What were you doing anyway?

—I told you, Johnny said. We upset in the river.

—It looks funny to me, the man said. Young Shawnessy, they say you're a good friend of this bastard's. You have any idea where he might've gone?

—If you mean Professor Stiles, Johnny said, no, I haven't the slightest idea. Maybe it's all a mistake.

—It's a mistake all right, the leader said. Nobody can come into this county and run away with a preacher's wife.

—They have sinned, a mournful voice said, and they shall be made to pay for it.

The Reverend Ezra Gray was standing to one side. He had a shotgun on his arm. His eyes glowed with a cold, determined light. He looked strangely happy.

—I don't think this boy knows anything, another man said. Let's git out of here.

The men went away from the river toward the road.

Garwood, Cash, and Zeke stayed with Johnny and Nell.

—The Perfessor's gone and got himself into a hell of a mess, Garwood said. There's at least a hundred men out looking for him.

He listened until the footsteps of the posse were faint.

—You got any idea where he is, John?

—No, Johnny said. Honest.

—I got a plan, Cash said. Let's get another horse at John's and see if we can find him. If he's in the County, he'll be killed sure unless somebody helps him. The Reverend's out for blood.

—They've got every road around Freehaven covered and men planted in the train stations, Garwood said. The Perfessor hasn't got a chance in a hundred of getting out alive. He and Lydia missed the train at Three Mile Junction and went back east from there. That's the last anyone's heard.

—First we got to get Nell home, Johnny said.

—Please don't bother, Nell said. I know the way.

She turned and plunged into the bushes, running.

—Wait, Nell! he cried.

He ran after her and caught up with her.

—Please, he said. I'll take you home.

She whirled around facing him, breaking his hold on her arm.

—Let me go, Johnny! Don't touch me!

The small face with the wet hair plastered around it had an imperious, tragic look, though it was hardly more than a pale stain in the darkness and the eyes pools of shadow.

—I can get home by myself. Good-by, Johnny.

The words were a command. He could hear her running and running in the forest fringe of the river. He rejoined the three boys on the bank.

—Let 'er go, Garwood said. This is serious. We got work to do.

—What'll we do if we find them?

—Try to bring 'em to the Saloon, Cash said. Through the back way. If we can get 'em upstairs there, they'll be perfectly safe. The sheriff's practically in my pay, anyway.

Horsed and galloping in the warm night, the four boys rode into Freehaven, to make inquiries at the Square.

For the first time in Johnny's memory, murderous passions were unleashed in Raintree County. Through this warm night, where the foliage of the young summer shook out moist odors on the air, armed men like blind projectiles thundered through the County, and somewhere in that maze of dark roads a buggy fled toward dark intersections.

And all this was only because love was a flower that wanted to tear its tassel and scatter its ecstasy of seed in spring beside the river.

He remembered certain columns of print in *Harper's Weekly,* stiff engravings, facsimiles of letters.

> Finally, the injured husband may take the life of him who has injured him. This is the American system: and latterly it has been followed in many parts of Europe. Terrible as homicide is, this method must, on the whole, be admitted to be the most effectual, the wisest, and the most natural revenge of an outraged husband.

All the way to Freehaven Johnny carried a singularly vivid image. He kept seeing the two lovers in bed together somewhere in the County, enlaced in their forbidden love. Then in the night heavy-booted feet stamped on boards, a door splintered, blackbearded faces, glittering eyes, hoarse male breath filled up the room suddenly. The lovers, clinging to each other, sat up in bed, blinking in the flare of the torches and the swinging arcs of the lamps. The men stood hushed a moment, fully clothed in thick pants, broadbrimmed hats, heavy boots. Then blast after blast of lead seed tore the frail bodies of the lovers, still warm from each other.

Hundreds of people were in the Square talking about the flight of the two lovers. Johnny had seldom seen so many happy, excited faces. Rumors ran wild everywhere. One man insisted that he had heard someone say that the lovers had been caught in bed together down in the southeastern part of the County and that the Reverend had blown the Perfessor's head off with a shotgun. Another man said, no, he heard that they caught the Perfessor and Mrs. Gray in bed together up in the northwestern part of the County, and that the Perfessor had blown the Reverend's head off with a shotgun. A report came that a man with no clothes on was seen driving a buggy in the western part of the County. Soon a dozen people swore that they had seen the now fabulous buggy with their own eyes in a dozen different parts of the County.

—Godamighty! Garwood said. The Perfessor sure is travelling fast. Why doesn't he just stop somewhere and enjoy what he's got until they catch up with him and blow him to Kingdom Come?

There seemed to be no way of getting the truth from this welter of particulars. Even the original testimony about the buggy's appearance at Three Mile Junction could be collected in a dozen different versions. Meanwhile, parties of pursuers were beating up and down the County like mad. The four boys decided to wait until they had something definite to go on.

The break came around midnight. Most of the posses had come back to the Square by that time to compare results. The main party, including the Reverend Gray himself and the heavy man who had flashed a lantern in Johnny's face, had just ridden up to the Saloon and dismounted. The heavy man had a hempen rope in his hand, and the Reverend still cradled the shotgun. While they were trying to get news, a man came up and said,

—Reverend, is that 'ere buggy of yours black with a scroll on her tailboard?

—It is, brother, the Reverend said.

—Is it a black mare with a white mark on her forehead?

—It is, brother, the Reverend said.

—Well, they's a horse and buggy just like that a-settin' in front a your house right now not two blocks from here. I just came by there and seen it with my own eyes.

No one said anything. The Reverend's dry lips opened and snapped shut. He set off the safety on his shotgun and started walking down the street in the direction of his house, which was just one block west from the Square on the same street. A hundred men formed behind and around him and walked with him in a silent, purposeful wedge. The Reverend's eyes shone like balls of blue flint. He licked his lips. The skin on his forehead jerked.

Suddenly, someone broke into a run. With one impulse the mass of men around the Reverend and the Reverend himself began to run. Without a word, scores of people, mostly men and boys, ran through the Square.

Far ahead was Johnny Shawnessy, who had been the first to think of running. He ran hard, doubling his fists. He felt his coat split at the shoulder seams. He could hear the feet of the crowd behind. He had the sensation that they were chasing him. He kept expecting a blast of gunfire from the voiceless, pursuing crowd. He reached the house. He saw the buggy, covered with dust, one wheel sagging and nearly off, and the horse, lathered and jaded. He bounded to the porch in a single leap and flung open the front door.

—Professor, he yelled. Professor! They're coming!

The downstairs hall in the large frame house was dark, but a faint light came from upstairs. Johnny called again and listened. He thought he heard someone going down a back stair and a door shutting somewhere in the back of the house, but he couldn't be sure, for already twenty men were on the porch and through the front door, shoving and shouldering their way into the hall and pouring through the lower floor.

—Try upstairs! Johnny yelled, to divert the crowd.

He himself ran up the stair.

In a room at the head of the stair, sitting in a chair that faced the door, was Lydia Gray. Her head hung to one side, and her eyes were closed. Her yellow hair was unloosened. Her face was flushed but tearless. She had on the dress that she had worn to the picnic, and in one hand she held her widebrimmed hat trailing to the floor. The room was small, and there was obviously no one there but Lydia.

At the door, Johnny was shoved aside by the Reverend and half a dozen other men armed with shotguns.

—Woman, the Reverend said, where is your lover?

Without changing her position, the woman opened her eyes and said,

—He's not here.

Johnny had expected tears, entreaties, protestations of innocence—anything but this beautiful indifference. The men removed their hats and looked sheepishly at each other.

—Woman, the Reverend said, what can you say for yourself?

—I have nothing to say, she said. I don't want Mr. Stiles hurt. He isn't guilty.

The men shuffled their feet uneasily and began to try to put their guns where they couldn't be seen.

—Ma'am, the heavy man with the rope said in an absurdly courteous voice, could you tell us the whereabouts of Mr. Stiles?

—I don't know, the woman said.

—Yes, ma'am, the heavy man said. Don't trouble yourself, ma'am.

—Let's go, a man said.

All but the Reverend began to bow out of the room. Heavy-booted, they pushed clumsily through the door, replacing their hats. The Reverend stayed in the house, but all the rest of the men went out into the yard. Some of them were giggling like girls with embarrassment and relief.

—Reckon we ought to spread out and comb the town, boys? the heavy man said without conviction.

—Spread out yourself, one of the men said. I'm goin' home.

There was a vague feeling of disappointment in the crowd.

—You reckon he did? a citizen said.

—Does a cat have claws? a second citizen said.

As he rode home, Johnny was remembering the woman in the chair, trying to recall where he had seen such a thing before. Then he remembered. It was a picture that had appeared in a *Harper's Weekly* about the time of the Sickles trial, an engraving of a statue 'Eve Repentant,' by the young American sculptor Bartholomew. The beautiful naked woman was seated, her long hair trailed over her shoulders, her gentle head was bent over and slightly averted, and her eyes were closed. In her hand she held the half-eaten apple, and on the ground beneath the seat coiled the serpent.

Johnny felt a hot, choking sensation that made him want to go off and hide his face, but it was shame for himself and himself only. For Lydia and the Perfessor, he felt only pity. They had been lovers and brave. Now they were discovered. And that was over. No, the shame was for himself, as if the hunt had really been for him, the obscene guns for him, the glaring torches for him.

As for Lydia, she was a woman lost, sitting, it might be, on the chair still, her hat trailing the floor, her hair touching her cheeks, and her husband flapping his withered lips at her.

When Johnny and Zeke got home, they had to tell the whole thing to T. D. and Ellen. Johnny felt the shame come back hot and strong as these things were talked of in the presence of his mother.

—Isn't it terrible! Ellen kept saying. Poor woman! Well, I must say, I blame Perfessor Stiles. Look at all the trouble he caused.

Johnny felt as if he had personally planned and executed the whole thing and as if everyone secretly suspected it.

—If, said T. D., there was only just some way to prove that there wasn't any uh physical uh any—well, people make such a point of such things.

Johnny went outdoors to put up the horses and get the cold night air on his skin. He kept telling himself that he had, after all, only kissed a girl and swum with her in the Shawmucky River. But it was no use. The feeling of guilt persisted strong as ever.

When he stepped into the barn, a tall figure stood in the gloom.

—Hello, John. Fancy meeting you here.

The Perfessor still had his cane, his straw hat, and his glasses, but he was dusty and sweaty, and his clothes were torn. He looked as if he had been crawling and rolling all over Raintree County.

—Professor, Johnny said, you've got to get out of the County!

—This idea has also occurred to me, boy, the Perfessor said. But tell me, what about Lydia?

Johnny told him how they had found her.

—Wonderful woman! the Perfessor said, rapping the barn wall sharply with his cane. I really wanted to carry her away. If we hadn't missed that goddam train at the Junction, we'd've been a hundred miles away by now. Damn buggy wheel nearly came off when we turned in a ditch. We drove all the way down to Beardstown to get the train there. I left the buggy a block from the station and walked in. First man I saw said, You hear about the guy ran away with a preacher's wife in Freehaven? I'm a stranger in these parts, myself, I said. They telegraphed down here to watch for them, he said. I looked out of the window and saw three men with guns marching up and down the platform. On my way back to the buggy, I passed a whole platoon of God's cavalry going by hellbent for the station. I got in the buggy, turned her back to Freehaven, deciding I better take Lydia home and put a good face on the thing before somebody got shot. We rode high and handsome all the way back to Freehaven, and not a soul stopped us. I parked the buggy right in front of the Reverend's house and went upstairs and thought up a beautiful lie to explain the whole thing. Then I heard the yelling and saw that mob of righteous citizens roaring down the street. I hesitated for a minute, and then I heard you yell, and I lit down the backstair. That's about all there is to it. I guess you think I'm a scoundrel—eh, John?

—I don't know what to think, Johnny said slowly.

—Ah, John, John! the Perfessor said in his slightly fake tragic manner, love is a strong thing. I loved that woman, boy. Believe it or not, this skinny breast is capable of a generous emotion. I loved and pitied her, and I wanted to carry her away. Don't think too badly of me, my boy.

—I don't, Professor. Somehow I can't. I want to help you get away, if I can.

—I suppose the heroic thing would have been for me to stay around when that mob came thundering up and let the outraged husband discharge his righteous fury by blowing off various parts of my anatomy with his shotgun. But I hate that sanctimonious bastard too much to give him the satisfaction. Besides, I was scared.

—What are you going to do?

—I haven't decided yet, the Perfessor said. The more I think about this, the madder I get. O, goddamn the injustice of it all!

The Perfessor seated himself in the hay.

—One thing really hurts me, John. I didn't get a thing. But the hell of it is that no one will ever believe that. Every old venom-dripping hag in the County will have it that I raked the lady fore and aft, and her damned old he-whore of a husband will think the same, and dammit, John, if they're going to think it, there might as well have been some truth in it.

—I wish there was some way to prove——

—No chance, the Perfessor said. I could go before the Reverend and make a virtuous denial. I'd get my head blown off, and no one would believe it anyway. Well, I managed the whole thing badly. You see, John, I'm a very impetuous man. It all happened in a flash this afternoon.

—But, couldn't you have waited, Professor, for some legal remedy?

Professor Jerusalem Webster Stiles shook his head sadly and recited,

> —Of guilt or peril do they deem
> In that tumultuous tender dream!

He and Johnny talked a long time, but there seemed nothing to do except that the Perfessor would have to get out of the County and go back East.

And thus, in the early dawn, Johnny Shawnessy and Professor Jerusalem Webster Stiles rose from a ditch at the base of the railroad embankment beside the Danwebster Graveyard. Somewhere down the track they heard the train coming along the branchline on its way out of Freehaven, and they knew it would be moving slow enough for a man to hook on when it reached the top of the upgrade.

The tall, skinny figure of the Perfessor stood up against the eastern sky. His black eyes looked at Johnny intently.

—John, my boy, the Perfessor said, holding out his hand and adopting his rhetorical manner, at this affecting moment I find myself inarticulate. What can I say, my boy, that shall convey to you my deep and genuine fondness and admiration? Let me only say that I expect great things of you. Don't let the world nail you on the cross of respectability. You and I are alike in only a few ways, but those are fundamental. We both love life and beauty. If a series of misadventures have made me a cynic, that need not happen to you, my boy. You have a beautiful girl who loves you and whom you love. By all means, my boy, marry her, love her, beget broods of happy cherubim, go on, my boy, to greater and better things, and in the years that are to come let your mind sometimes revert, not without a feeling of affection, to that amiable miscreant, your misguided but perhaps not wholly misguiding mentor. Your hand, my boy. A scrap of verse may not be unfitting at this moment, if I can lay my tongue to one. Well, perhaps this will do.

The Perfessor winked and, arms gesticulating in his best classroom manner, recited,

—O, may your pathway ever gleam
With sincere love and joy supreme.
May Him whose eye is felt for miles,
Bless you with Nellie's brightest smiles
And all that fairest love can dream:
Such is the wish of your friend, Jerusalem Webster Stiles.

The train was drawing abreast, a lantern swinging from the cowcatcher. The Perfessor climbed the bank. With brittle agility, black coattails flapping, he leaped upon the rear of the ultimate car. Johnny heard a high voice crackling above the sullen rumble of the train:

—*Ave atque vale!*

—Good-by, Professor! Johnny called, waving.

He saw a long, thin arm shaken obscurely against the dull sky. Then the Perfessor was gone in the grayness of the just beginning day.

Johnny's eyes were blurred with tears. It was because a beautiful, mournful dawn was breaking in the sky, it was because he felt that there had just been a great departure in his life, it was because in this parting he knew that he had not only said good-by to the departing one but to a portion of himself as well. An era of his life was ending. He had discovered that the earth of Raintree County was not only full of beauty but of peril, and that its Hesperian fruits were guarded by dragons breathing fire. All this he had learned in part from the gifted but erring creature who had just gone down the track to eastward, but he knew that he had always suspected it himself.

When he finally got back to the Home Place and in bed, beneath his shut eyes the day just passed sprang to life again. Dreaming, he relived it in bizarre distortions. This dream, like many of his dreams, disturbed him with strange, savage encounters and adventures. And yet his dreaming self passed through the dream's protean, erotic landscapes somehow always in the best Johnny Shawnessy tradition, pursuing an eternal quest for beauty and the good. This night, more vividly than usual (and his dreams were always vivid) the remorseless comedy of life streamed on; and just before awakening, he dreamed perhaps the most delicious, if frustrating, dream that he had ever dreamed.

He was, it seemed, coming into Freehaven along the oldest pathway of his childhood. Down the road, he saw the redbrick structure of the Court House in a clearing stubbled with stumps. It was some vision of early times in Indiana when the founders of Raintree County imposed their austere dream of freedom on the forest earth. Riding in the wagon with T. D., Ellen, and the other children, he felt as if the scene had been conceived and colored by his own verbal magic, he the budding bard of Raintree County, who like William Shakespeare would write the epic dramas of his people. For him, lusty dialogues in the manner of the elder poets, bards of deathless dramas!

Everyone was waiting for a certain important personage to arrive so that the program might begin. The sky darkened. Over the roofs of Freehaven shot a fiery streak, perhaps the burning stick of a rocket, descending till it became a train pulling into the station. Someone sprang lightly down, turning a somersault in the air, black coattails stiff out behind, eyes compounded by brilliant lenses, black hair slicked flat to a reptile skull.

PROFESSOR JERUSALEM WEBSTER STILES

bowing gracefully to crowd, twirling malacca cane,

—Greetings, one and all, from foreign parts. As I was about to say before I was so rudely interrupted by the Protestant Reformation, I trust you all perceive the object that I hold in my hand.

THE REVEREND MRS. GRAY

blushing, speaking with grave and sweet decorum,

—Your majesty, as representative of the ladies of Raintree County, I wish to tender you a cordial token of our gratitude for your ardent efforts in our behalf.

PERFESSOR

with malacca cane expertly flipping Mrs. Gray's back skirts up and gravely reading an inscription embroidered across her bloomers,

—When this you see, remember me,
And all our fun at Old Pedee.

Madame, I accept this festive offering in the spirit in which it is tendered. Henceforth it shall occupy a prominent place in my home as a reminder to me of happy days spent in the old Pedee Academy. And now, folks, time for our geography lesson.

He touched his pointer to a phrenological chart hanging on a tree; and as he did so, the chart, changing slowly, became a varnished study of the human anatomy and then a map of Raintree County.

PERFESSOR

in best classroom manner,

—Beware, my boy, the Peak of Penis!
Beware, beware the Mount of Venus,
The Wandering Isles of Genitalia!
Beware the Roman Saturnalia
And all the Paphian Penetralia.

GIRLS

naked, dancing with maenad fury, venereal mounds adorned by the ripe tobacco leaf,

—Some do it chew and some it smoke,
Whilst some it up their nose do poke!

JOHNNY

declining proffered cigars,

—Sorry. No, thanks. You see, my pa—— Besides, they tell me it's against the law.

GARWOOD JONES

bulky and sleek in new suit, handsome blue eyes smiling, exhaling odor of lotion, holding whiskey bottle,

—Pure yellow corn that comes by the cup! Come on, fellers, drink up, drink up!

PERFESSOR

through megaphone,

—Ladies and gentlemen, yes-sir-ee, we're ready to start the huskin' bee! Workin' fast on the middle row is young John Shawnessy. Go, boy, go!

He husked his way down a corn row growing through the court house yard past a series of exhibits while the crowd cheered him on. Nearing the finish line, he was surrounded by girls in costumes of the corn, swaying with cernuous motion.

CORN MAIDENS

—Shakamak! Husky lover! Shawny, shockheaded boy! Reder of riddles!

VOICE

husky and rehearsed, from within a shrine of pillars, walled with stalks of the ripe corn,

—With yellow and unloosened hair,
Clothed in a garment white and fair,
Inside a green and guarded keep,
A lovely lady lies asleep.
No key can turn the twisted lock;
Yet love comes in and tears her smock.

He burst through a wall of laughing girls into the shrine where an ear of corn tall as a maiden grew from a treebroad stalk. He tore the green husk down, laying bare the yellow tresses, ripe redtipped breasts, round white belly of

NELL GAITHER

entangled in green cornstalks, looking back at him with wistful eyes, in low voice, musical, receding,

—Let's do the next *liber* together, Johnny. *Oft was I weary when I toiled with . . .*

He was lying on the bank of the Shawmucky, where he and a great many other young men had been hunting for the fabulous white creature lost in country waters and reported in a famous article of the *Free Enquirer*.

WILLIE SHAKESPEARE

sharpfaced stripling in overalls, straw hat, shirt open at neck, chewing a grass-stem, writing on coarsegrained paper,

—William Shakespeare, his hand and pen.
He will be great—but God knows when.

JOHNNY SHAWNESSY

—Say, Bill, if it's not being too personal, what's the lowdown on your affair with Ann Hathaway? According to the records, she was twenty-six and you were eighteen when the marriage took place, and the first child was born just six months after——

WILLIE

—By cock, John, you're sharp at your sums. Alackalas and welladay, 'twas midsummer madness with too little method that tumbled poor Will in the hay.

As you like it—and what doth it skill—
Ann Hathaway—and also a Will.
Everyone knows poor Will was to blame
For taming the shrew—and for shrewing the dame.

GARWOOD JONES

lying on back, hands under head, blowing smoke rings,

—Ain't Nature grand?

WILLIE

peering through rushes, pointing at a girl standing naked in green sedge across the river,

—Ain't God good to Indiana—fellers, ain't He, ain't He though?

PERFESSOR

—By the way, Bill, do you think John's been in there?

WILLIE

—Don't be banal, boy.

PERFESSOR

standing up, baseball bat in hand,

—It's about time I instructed the local primates in an ingenious game. Now, folks, I trust you all perceive . . .

The bat in the Perfessor's hand had shrunk into a starter's pistol. In the Court House Square, hundreds of people crowded to the starting line.

OFFICIAL STARTER

tall black hat, pistol in air,

—After several delays, folks, we're ready to start this here dash. Emulate Adam, folks. He set sich a blisterin' early pace that he started—and dern near finished—the race. (Struggling with pistol) This doggone shootin' ar'n ain't wuth a dang. I cain't seem exactly to git the——

PISTOL

—BANG!

Everyone was running in the Court House Square. Children and dogs ran under the wheels of carriages. Old men ran, waving crutches and shouting hymen. Grandams ran, holding up petticoats and making bony legs blur with speed. Girls in summer dresses ran, emitting high squeaks of excitement, backs gracefully erect, necks and shoulders held with fashionable stiffness, parasols maintained primly over heads.

FLASH PERKINS

running a shade ahead of Johnny, white teeth clenched in an insolent grin,

—Five times runnin' I won that dash—Perkins, Orville—better known as Flash!

SOUTHERN BELLE

shaking her shoulders and twisting her hips,

—Come on, honey, the weather's fine down below the mixin' and the dazin' line.

GIRLS

flinging ecstatic flowers,

—Goddess, give of your gracious bounty, to the fastest runner in Raintree County!

Running, his feet were all daubed with mud. He seemed unable to stay up with the other contestants. He was ashamed to see that he was running unclothed like the ancient contenders in the Olympic games. Beside him in the fastgathering murk of the Square was his mother, Ellen Shawnessy. Her white feet glimmered beside him, as she tried to lead him along some darkening path at the end of which was a face of stone or perhaps the mythical Raintree. But he had failed her somehow. He had committed an unpardonable crime. He had done and said pagan, fleshly things and he had known desires that were of the flesh only. For this, he dared not look at her.

ELLEN SHAWNESSY

her face a pale stain in the darkness,

—A great man is a man who does good for other people. What's this I hear, Johnny, about you and——

A crowd came by yelling the lustful shout of the mob. At first, Johnny thought that they had come for him, but then he saw that they were full cry in pursuit of a buggy in which a man and woman rode naked.

PERFESSOR

lashing horses, chanting in thin sardonic voice above the sullen fury of the mob,

—Woodman, spare that tree!
For my head am bendin' low!
My country, 'tis of thee!
Goddammit, Dobbin, go!

The whole grostesquely comic vision swept past into darkness, and then with a tidal rhythm came flowing back again from darkness. Now the mob bore aloft the body of the Perfessor tied on crossed rails, dripping hot tar, bestuck with feathers. The lean, terrible body began to change form, flapped vast birdwings, tore loose from its rotting cross, began to rise slowly over the river.

PERFESSOR

beating his condor wings,

—To John Wickliff Shawnessy, life's eternal young American, *ave atque vale*. Awk. Awk. Shawkamawk.

> Green be the grass above thee,
> Friend of my better days.
> None knew thee but to love thee.
> But whiskey never pays.

It was night along the river. Beams of lantern light accused the darkness. He remembered now why he was here. He had stolen a famous statue by a young American sculptor and had hidden it in his favorite nook beside the river. No doubt the whole County knew of it and was coming to chastise him. In deep grass he tugged at the antique stone and slowly unearthed the marble breasts and back and buttocks of the Venus found in Melos. Pulled loose, it seemed to come alive in his hands, a mature young woman. He strove against her warmfleshed nudity, impeded by a white oarblade, broken, which she held between them. Her green eyes watched him, pensively calm. Her hands played with the planed wood, tracing with featherlight fingertips a legend carven in an antique language. Their slight touch on the oar gave him a remote pleasure, but suddenly the visual pain of beholding their delicate caress became the anguish of his own body, betrayed into spasms of desire. Smiling, the young woman leaned her mouth to his, grazed his lips lightly. The very fury with which he seized her drove her from him. Beneath his hands her twisting waist was barky and rough, her hair was a branch of oakleaves. And she was gone beside the dark river in which he swam and stumbled through mucky pools and webs of waterweeds. Shocks of corn in near-by fields were flooded with the gray waters. . . .

He awoke into the risen day, the full sunlight of the morrow. He awoke from the dream with something like relief, for it had been, after all, less innocent than the realities of the day preceding. The Perfessor was safely gone. Best now to laurel this strange being and the memory of his stay in Raintree County with elegiac words and turn resolutely to the future.

HAIL AND FAREWELL

(Epic Fragment from the *Free Enquirer*)

That a foolish lark ended in unnecessary anguish for many cannot be denied. But this commentator will stake his own honor for it that the lady was returned to the bosom of her spouse as chaste as when she left it. The whole thing appears to have been a sudden improvisation, a mad lark, in which, it is true, the lady acquiesced, but which had for its object nothing more serious than a little frolic at the expense of owl-visaged respectability. The open letter which Professor Stiles addressed some days ago from parts unknown to the columns of this and other Raintree County papers should place the integrity of the lady's honor beyond any possible suspicion, except such as will always rankle in base minds. And so let us draw the curtain of merciful oblivion upon the name and memory of a man, who whatever . . .

Professor Jerusalem Webster Stiles left his mark on Raintree County. He left, among other things, columns of print in soon-forgotten newspapers, anguish in some hearts, a dozen pieces of printed skin called diplomas, a defunct institution of higher learning that soon began to be referred to as the Old Academy Building, and some unforeseen complications in the life of Johnny Shawnessy.

But it was still early summer in Raintree County. The Fourth of July Footrace was coming and had awakened more excitement than any athletic event for years because it appeared that at last Orville (better known as Flash) Perkins had met a challenger worthy of his mettle. Soon everyone was talking about the Race, and the Perfessor began to be forgotten. Johnny Shawnessy put the guilty memory of an afternoon on the banks of the Shawmucky in the back of his mind. Great preparations were forward for the Footrace. Susanna Drake, a Lovely Southern Belle, visiting in the County, had been selected to make the award of oakleaves to the winner. And Johnny had heard from a roundabout source that she had secretly expressed a preference between the Champion and the Challenger.

A few days before the Fourth, Cash Carney came around and told Johnny that Miss Drake had expressed a desire to include Johnny Shawnessy in an excursion of young people to Paradise Lake in the afternoon of the Fourth, following the Footrace. After perhaps insufficient reflection, Johnny accepted this invitation, the more readily because a few days after the Class Picnic and the Perfessor's disappearance, he had received a note in the mail, reading:

Johnny,

Never try to speak to me again. I will try to forget you, and I beg you to put from your mind

FOREVER ALL RECOLLECTIONS OF

YOUR UNWORTHY BUT

REPENTANT

NELL

In the timesoftened valley of the Shawmucky, he stood, retracing with his finger a carven name. From the letters, he dug out a hundred little gray cocoons, blind dwellers in a legend unperceived, a hieroglyph that love and sorrow had wrought in stone.

The last car of the train rumbled by.

He opened the cardboard box and laid a handful of cut flowers, roses and lilies, on the mound. Backing away, he gazed at the stone. Its stately form tranquillized the emotion of farewell. Curved whiteness from the river had become a lapidary attitude. By Ovidian magic, young love was changed to stone.

He walked quickly over to the Shawnessy lot, sickled the five mounds, dropped the remnant flowers by the family monument.

The train, westward diminishing, wailed at a crossing. He pulled out his watch and read the dial. Eight-five.

Train doesn't know the earth it passes over. Train thunders daily down the stretch behind the Old Home Place. Train is a tumult passing. Hoarse voice of train wails in the valley of Danwebster.

Sleepers in the earth, do you hear the train passing? Do you any longer hear the sound of its diurnal course, beloved sleepers in the earth of Raintree County?

Listen to the voice of train. The way for it is straight and far across the land. It rushes far and fast across the Nation, passing westward, passing through Raintree County.

(O, blithe days, o, early agrarian days on the breast of the land! O, Eden of bland repose!)

Listen! There is a voice of thunder on the land. It is the voice of years and fates, crying at intersections; it is the bullhead beast, who runs on a Cretan maze of iron roads and chases the naked sacrifices hither and thither. The bullgod comes up fast out of the east, under the churning of his round rear haunches. Smell of a blackened ash, odor of hot metal, the frictioning iron parts, blows across the earth of memories.

(O, sweet young days of the aching but unripped seedpurse. O, tall endeavors. O, innocent, fragrant time.)

Listen! What voice is calling now, voice of the grooved wheels on the roads of the hurrying days! It is the thunder of the big events. They are coming, full of malice and arrogance, they are coming on hooves of iron, wounding the earth of Raintree County. They will travel straight and far, through the light barriers of the corngold days. Lo! they will drive the young gods, the beautiful young gods, from the river's reedy marge.

The day becomes brighter and hotter. In court house squares, the streets of the Nation, the people gather. The train bears its streamer of black smoke, a banner of progress fast and far across the land. Lo! we must keep our appointments. The clock on the Court House Tower is telling the time of day. We have a rendezvous in a train station, there where the thundering express stops a moment in the bright day and lets down out of its smoky womb a procession of remembered faces.

Listen! great voice of thunder and urgency, voice of titan yesterdays and of still more titanic tomorrows! Do you still bring me tidings, have you still a bundle of headlines to throw down for me, will the face of the most beautiful of women look unexpectedly from a window of the trembling coaches for me? Or do you bring again, as so often before, a somber freight for me, who hearken the voice of your passing here on the breast of the land?

He walked back through the tangled grass of the Danwebster Graveyard, trying not to step on graves.

He sighed as he pushed through the gates of the graveyard. He was tired. He had rebuilt the classic stones of a lost republic. He had dreamed again the fabric of an antique Raintree County. His eyes smarted from the sweat of this endeavor.

Hundreds and thousands had travailed at the task. Now they were dead, sleepers in the earth. What did it avail a man, the labor long and hard, the weary road, and many years?

He climbed up the grade of the railroad, plunged longstriding down the far side, retraced his own trail to the riverbank, crossed on the dam, slightly wetting his feet.

In the valley of a vanished name, two boys loitered, hunting for relics. In a surrey by the road, a young woman with grave dark eyes looked down the road in motionless profile.

What creature is it that in the morning of its life . . .

What were the days of a man? Where did the small brown roads lead him at last? Who could preserve the ancient verities of Raintree County?

Mr. John Wickliff Shawnessy replaced a sickle, wet with blood of grass, in the back seat of the surrey, where a girl sat lost in a sentimental legend between green cloth covers. Like the forgotten boy named Johnny, he saw her as given to a quest, believing that all books are somehow legend and eternal, each one containing somewhere the talismanic word, the lost engraving, peace. All the intersections of his life had been necessary so that she too might have her morning on this road of memories and be the child and cherisher of Raintree County, his daughter

Eva

CLOSED THE BOOK. It had been a noble last page. All the barriers had been burned away.

The surrey had left the site of Danwebster and the river far behind. She had meant to get a good look at the Old Home Place, where she had been born twelve years ago and had spent the first five years of her life, but she had been too much absorbed in the climax of the story. Now the surrey was almost to Moreland.

—Through with the book, Eva?

—Yes.

She handed the book to Wesley, feeling how precious was the thing she surrendered in a gilded cover. But she would linger in a golden world.

She would linger in the world of the sentimental novels, where it wasn't necessary to be Eva Alice Shawnessy, a girl of twelve beginning to be ungracefully a woman. She would linger in the world of her namesake, the most famous child of the Nineteenth Century. In this world, unknown to all, she would be the heroine of beautiful adventures and beautiful deaths. By purity, courage, faith, she would save lives, free races, win the deathless admiration and love of all who knew her, and at last expire in a circle of weeping friends and relatives with the sun lighting a halo around her pale, thin face. *Farewell, beloved child! the bright eternal doors have closed after thee; we shall see thy sweet face no more. . . .* Then she would have a hundred resurrections of herself like all those other sunny, deathless little girls who appeared in book after book, narratives grave and gay, intended for the entertainment and instruction of all the wellbroughtup little girls of America.

OUR HEROINE INTRODUCED

(Epic Fragment from the *Eva Series*)

It was a summer's day, and it was summer too in the heart of a certain small person, who at this commencement of our tale, we find sauntering idly by herself along a country road. And who is this girl whose hair is like finespun gold, whose eyes are the color of the cloudless skies? Some of our little readers have already guessed her name. She is, of course, none other than Eva, that delightful child, heroine of so many happy and instructive tales. At the time of our present story she is about twelve years old, her form foretelling already the graceful proportions of the woman, while retaining the delicate lightness of the child. And where is Eva going? That, my inquisitive little dears, will be discovered to you all in good time. . . .

—Have you finished your book, Eva?

—Yes, Mamma.

Austere and vaguely accusing, the question had shattered the golden dream, and instantly Eva remembered the nightmare she had dreamed just before waking up in the morning. Then as now it had been the earth of Raintree County over which she travelled, but she had been alone, walking, forlornly hunting for her home on roads diminishing in mournful silence to the far horizons. Yes, these were surely the small brown roads of Raintree County, and the houses that she saw at a great distance were surely the plain board houses of Raintree County. But she had somehow become lost in her own familiar earth. She couldn't even remember what home the family was living in from among the many homes she had had in Raintree County. And what season was it—summer, winter, autumn, spring? Or was it some seasonless and timeless landscape, one in which it was impossible to return to the right home at the right time? If only she could find a familiar landmark—the plain board buildings of the Old Home Place, or perhaps the brick tower of the Greenville house, or the steeple of the Moreland School, or the lonely structure of Waycross Station—she would have her bearings and be instantly at home. Somehow she had got lost from an earlier dream in which small golden flowers had sifted on her eyes and she had floated on a lake at evening, and it was summer and the days were long. Or was that all the legend of another girl, a fabulous, forgotten little girl, the little dreamer of a summer dream?

Then while she wandered in that dawncolored landscape, she remembered about the crazy woman. Right now, the crazy woman might be hiding behind a hedge watching. Looking over her shoulder, Eva saw a tall woman with black hair and bright black eyes coming swiftly across the field behind her.

—Papa! Papa!

Her screaming was a tortured small moaning in her throat. Her legs were glued with earth. The crazy woman came up behind her and raised the knife in her rigid arm; her indianstraight hair was shaken with fury. . . .

—Eva! Time to get up.

It had been her mother's voice, thrusting into the dream and bringing her back into real life.

Her father shook the reins over President's back.

—How time passes! he said. It seems only yesterday, children, that we walked along this road on the way to school.

—It seems a long time ago to me, Papa, Eva said.

It was clear to her that her father didn't measure time as she did. Already she divided the twelve years of her life into distinct periods, according to where she had lived. It made her uneasy to think that perhaps her father regarded the entire fourteen years since his marriage to Esther Root as a single period, in which Eva was a minor—if somewhat noisy and persistent—accident.

She looked at the green earth swimming by her as the surrey passed like a lazy boat rocking on a lazy river. She was passing down one of the oldest pathways of her childhood, a way to school. She was remembering summers of long, slow trips in the surrey from town to little town. In all these memories, her father was a presence mystical, pervasive. The years of his life—those lost years before there was any Eva, years of his boyhood, his youth, and his young manhood—spoke to her with indistinct, soft voices. The legend of her father waited for her to rediscover it between the green covers of a sentimental novel inscribed with a golden legend. In that story, she too would have a part. Unseen, she must have been there all the time, travelling the little long brown roads of Raintree County, tracing on the earth a vast initial, hunting for her home. A hundred bright eternal doors opened for her. Her ways and times were neither before nor after his, but woven with his own in the same gold myth of summer and the earth. Welcome, beloved child, heroine of an endless series! Yes, she would linger in a golden world, remembering

1880— HOW —1890

ONCE UPON A TIME

A LITTLE GIRL LIVED BESIDE A ROAD

that went somewhere and somewhere and how she had a father and a mother and a brother and had always been a little girl in a house beside a road.

Her great desire was to travel on the road that went somewhere and somewhere. Often the family would go together in the surrey and start along the road, and it would be a long day in the summer, and they would go a long way and visit another house beside a road. And sometimes it was night and she slept as the surrey passed along the road, and always she was back at last in the house beside the road.

Behind the big house was a little house where she and her brother Wesley played. The little house was piled with old things, and it had a strange spicy smell that came from glass-stoppered bottles with black words on them. This little house was taken down when she was still very small. It was called the Office, and it belonged once to T. D., who was dead long ago. She and her brother played Explorer too, and sometimes they went to the end of the South Field and watched the train go by. A few big oaks partly hid the hurrying train on its high embankment. Close to the railfence was a scarred boulder, higher than a man, lying like a big egg halfsunk in the earth.

—This is the oldest thing on the Home Place, Eva, her father told her once. Older than you and I.

—Or T. D.?

—Yes, much older.

—Or the road?

—Yes, even than the road.

She tried to think of the time when there hadn't been a road. But she couldn't do it. She couldn't even remember being a baby.

There was a picture of the baby Eva. The baby Eva was a fat, bald, bugeyed thing that looked something like a toad in a dress. It was too bad, because this baby had been given beautiful names. She had been called Eva from a little girl in a book called *Uncle Tom's Cabin,* and one time her father told her that the word 'Eva' meant Life, and that it was the noblest name a little girl could have. Her other name, Alice, had come from another book called *Alice's Adventures in Wonderland.* It had been written by a grown-up man for a little girl who really lived and whose name was Alice.

Child of the pure unclouded brow
And dreaming eyes of wonder!

It had taken great courage for her father to call the baby Eva by these noble, beautiful names. Eva would have to become a famous and beautiful woman to justify these names.

But when she got bigger, she was still squatty and plump with large staring blue eyes and peculiar brown hair. When people called, they never said, Isn't she pretty! but instead, Well, I'll bet this one isn't sick much! Then Eva would almost cry for rage and shame, and especially for pity of her father, who had given her the names.

People called her father Mr. Shawnessy—or, rarely, John. But one time a woman Eva didn't know called him Johnny. Eva was shocked. Her mother had never called him anything but Mr. Shawnessy in front of other people and had never in her life used his first name in any form. Perhaps that was because she had gone to school to him when she was a little girl, years before they were married.

Eva's father had the school in Moreland, to which he walked every day of the schoolyear. At home he was almost always reading or writing. Eva would think back and back, and it seemed to her that the oldest memories she had were of her father sitting in the yard of the Old Home Place, feet propped on a rock, reading a book or writing in a tablet. She would look over his arm and study the curved, softflowing marks. Her father never got tired of making them. He said that they were poems.

It bothered Eva that she knew so little. The big trouble was that she didn't know where she came from. Once her father said,

—You came from those two photographs on the wall, Eva. They belong to the Pre-Eva Age.

The two photographs on the parlor wall were a picture of the Shawnessy family and a picture of the Root family, grouped in the respective front yards of the Old Home Place and the Old Root Farm.

These pictures had been taken at about the same time, two weeks before a famous Fourth of July in 1878, when Eva's father and mother had run away to get married. In the middle of the Shawnessy group was T. D., Eva's grandfather, a tall brittle old man looking vaguely happy about something, as he sat with his three daughters and four sons. He had died a year before there was any Eva, and they had put him into the ground in a hill by the river. In the Root picture Eva's other grandfather, Gideon Root, sat blackbearded, bigheaded, immense in the middle of his children. On his right, with her hand in his, stood Eva's mother, Esther Root, in half-profile, her eyes like her father's, dark and sad.

For a long time Eva never saw her Grandfather Root except in the picture. Then one day he rode hugely out of the picture—or rather Eva rode into it.

The family had been visiting in an unfamiliar part of the County. As the surrey topped a gentle rise, Eva's mother pointed to a lonely farmhouse on the left, set close to the road.

—That's where I was brought up, children, she said. That's the Old Farm.

Then a fearful thing happened.

A buggy came into view as if it had sprung from the ground. It rolled swiftly along a lane from the barn behind the house to the main road. It was a black shiny buggy pulled by a big black horse. It turned onto the main road and came toward the surrey. There was a low thunder of hooves and a squeaking sound. The buggy came closer and closer, and Eva could see a big face under the hood, and a black beard with jags of gray, and a thickfleshed nose ending in a sensitive tip, and eyes black and big that looked right into her eyes.

A few yards away, the man in the buggy jerked the reins and shouted,

—Whoa!

His voice was so loud and terrible that buggy and surrey stopped side by side. Eva's father could have reached out and touched the man in the buggy.

The big man sat, knees close together. He held the reins in one hand, and in the other the crop of a coiled whip of woven leather. He looked at Eva's mother as if she were the only one in the surrey.

—Esther, he said, the old home's waitin' for you. Come on back.

Eva's mother looked at the man. Her eyes were dark and sad like his own.

—Pa, she said, I'll come back as soon as I can bring Mr. Shawnessy and the children.

There was a dead hush. The man and the woman looked at each other. The man's eyes burned with dark hunger, and the woman's were brooding and sad. The buggy and surrey and their occupants side by side on the narrow road were as still as a photograph. And the lonely little farmhouse was still. And the long acres around it were still.

Then the man's face changed. From deadwhite, it turned red, bloating with blood. The man looked at Eva's father and then at herself and her brothers in the back seat and again at her father. The man's bluntfingered hand bulged on the crop of the black whip, the knuckles of his balled fist turned blue, his mouth opened, he panted, half rose in the buggy, and swung the whip. It went crashing out along the flanks of the black horse. The black horse lunged as if it had been shot, President reared in the stays, and in the same instant, buggy and surrey shot forward and down the road in opposite directions.

After that one meeting with her Grandfather Root, Eva never again felt quite the same sense of peace and security when riding on the County roads. As for why her grandfather hated her father, no one would tell her the reason. It was one of the secrets of the Old Days.

The Old Days were full of maddening secrets. Once while Eva was digging things out of a box in the attic, she found two photographs—one of a woman holding a little boy and another of the same woman holding a doll. The woman was very pretty, but she looked sick or frightened. Eva took the pictures to her father and asked him about them.

—That was my first wife, he said, startled. A long time ago—before I married your mother, Eva.

—Where is she now, Papa?

—She's dead.

—Whose little boy is that?

—That was my little boy, he said. Here, Eva, we'd better put those pictures away. It makes me sad to look at them. You don't want to make Papa sad, do you?

Another secret thing from the Old Days was the biggest book in the family bookcase, the Byron book, which Eva once got down, finding these words on the flyleaf in a pretty hand:

For Johnny,
In memory of happy days together at Pedee Academy,
NELL

Between the pages of the book were wisps of flowers plucked in some summer of her father's youth, weightless little corpses that left faint stains and fragrance on the fine black print.

—Who was Nell, Papa? Eva had asked her father.

—Someone I knew in my youth, Eva, he said, closing the book and putting it back into the top row of the bookcase.

In the Old Days, everything was either Before the War, During the War, or After the War. The War had been fought to free the slaves and save the country. President Lincoln was a kind good man with a sad face and a black beard. He had had a small boy named Tad and had been shot in a theatre. Their own father had come home sick at the end of the War with a scar on his left shoulder.

Before the War her father had been a great runner and had run a famous race against someone named Flash Perkins in the Court House Square. Sometimes the surrey would go by an old brick building in Freehaven, and her father would say that it was the old Pedee Academy, where he went to school when he was a boy Before the War. As for the Old Days After the War, they were more mysterious even than the others. One day Eva and Wesley found in the attic a little red book with black words printed on the outside:

VISITOR'S GUIDE
TO THE
CENTENNIAL EXHIBITION
AND
PHILADELPHIA
1876

Their father said that it was a guidebook he had bought in Philadelphia, where they had a kind of fair like the County Fair, only much bigger.

All through the Old Days her father had taught school in Raintree County. Eva was always meeting people who had gone to school to him, and some of them looked older than he. But then he never changed much, and it was hard to believe that he was eighteen years older than her mother.

Her mother was sallow and slender and had a red smooth mouth and jetblack hair. Her face in repose was sad and almost stern. In her mother's presence, Eva always felt vaguely guilty of something. When Eva was naughty—which was not seldom—it was her mother who punished her, switching her legs with a rattail plaintain while Eva yelled without shame, being unable to take punishment like Wesley.

—Wesley's an Indian like his mother, their father would say. They never show their real feelings.

That was a good one of her father's about Wesley being an Indian. There was something about Indian blood in her mother's family, but Wesley had blond hair and skyblue eyes. He was a boy, and boys had it better than girls. Their mother always favored him, and everyone looked upon him as the bright light and shining star of the family because he had such a wonderful memory.

Her other brother, Will, was born at the Old Home Place when Eva was five. One morning, not long after his birth, their mother was down on her knees going along the edge of the carpet pulling up tacks, and all the time the tears ran down her cheeks and fell on the floor, but she didn't make a sound. It was in the late summer, and all their things were loaded into two big wagons, and they all got into the surrey and rode away down the road that went somewhere and somewhere.

The road brought them by evening to a little town called Greenville, and they took an angling street to the outskirts, and in the declining light, across the pastures and the fences, standing in isolation beside a pond, its redbrick sides glowing with a living warmth, its upper windows reddened by the sun, a house stood waiting.

—Why, it's like a tower! Eva said.

A lonely form, unlike any other in all Raintree County, the house in Greenville where Eva lived for two years was a kind of sixsided brick tower, the whole mass pierced with narrow windows and crowned with a mansard roof rising to an observation platform. A small greenhouse attached to the back of the house and extending to the pond was full of glistening plants. A queer doctor, whom Eva never saw and whose name she couldn't remember, had made the house, the greenhouse, and the pond.

Her father had the school at Greenville, and except for the new house, his life was as before, with reading, writing, and teaching. But for Eva the life at Greenville was a changed life. The dominant image of this new life was the pond mucky and green, full of spooling and spawning forms of fish and frogs and snakes scaringly beautiful. Deeply puzzled by the miracle of life and the mystery of the sexes, Eva was a moody, jealous little girl during the years at Greenville. It was here that she committed the greatest crime of her life, the murder of the boy doll.

This was a lovely doll that was given to her little brother Will on his second birthday. Eva coveted the doll, and when Will wouldn't let her hold it and their mother scolded her for taking it away, Eva wished the destruction of the doll. In the afternoon, taking her old rag doll she dipped it into the pond to baptize it, and as she had hoped, Will dipped his doll. As the beautiful new doll slipped out of his hands into the pond, Eva felt a terrible pang of joy and remorse mingled. She took a stick and snagged the doll and brought it to the surface muddy and ruined. Crying, the children laid the soaked dolls at their mother's feet. As Eva had expected, no one was punished since the harm had come to the doll through a religious motive.

Soon after this, the family left Greenville. But all her life, when she would think of Greenville, Eva would think of how the little blue-eyed human form went down into the green waters of the pond and came up drowned and dead, and then she would think of the house itself with the greenhouse projecting from its base, the house that was like a tower, of a mysterious and significant origin.

And then slowly the image of her father would come to her, prevailing above all the other images, and she would remember her talks with him beside the pond where he had told her the meaning of life and had explained to her the ineffaceable difference that she carried on her small body, source of her darkest speculations and jealousies. She would remember then how she had come home in the evenings from school (for it was at Greenville that she began her schooling) and had seen the house down in its lowlying field far back from the road. The picturesque thrust of it, the piercing uniqueness of it, the quaint distinction that sat upon its lonely form blended somehow with the memory of her father in those ancient years of the life in Greenville. This towerlike house beside a road became with the Old Home Place one of the landmarks of her life, rising mystic and serene above the green pondwoven shapes and passions of her childhood. It was one of the temples of her father's spirit.

From Greenville, the family returned to the Old Home Place and after a year moved into Moreland, where her father had the school again. Now for the first time, Eva went to school to her father.

Moreland. It was a word forlorn and tender, like the sound and aftersound of a distant schoolbell. This word and the meaning that it came to have for Eva pervaded the plain of her life with a sweet and strenuous sound. Moreland. It called into being a new Eva, who, like a princess imprisoned in a toad, had been waiting to shed her drab skin. The blind little creature of the Greenville pond was touched with light and became a human being with divine aspirations. From the moment that she saw her father at the front of the schoolroom and heard his gentle, leisurely voice, a hunger possessed her to press beyond the barriers of her own existence into her father's world. It was the world of eternal life, and it called to Eva, the child of life, in the familiar accents of her father's voice. To find this world, to understand its principles, strong and certain, to learn its language supremely musical and strange, became a religion for Eva.

The temple of this new religion was the Moreland Schoolhouse, standing symmetrical in its wide yard, two equal wings and a tower holding a bell. And the way to school from the Home Place to Moreland became to her the most memorable pathway of her childhood, the most beautiful and secret road in Raintree County, the same road which had gone somewhere and somewhere in her infancy.

She and her father and Wesley would walk together in the early morning to school and in the evening home. The way was very pleasant in the fall, when grass and weeds in the ditches were beginning to toughen and turn color. Later the road froze hard, and sometimes it was snow all the way, so that their eyes hurt, and their faces were red and raw in the soft white world of winter. Then came the first thaws and windy skies of spring, and then gray days of rain and rivulets running, and during this time their father carried a black umbrella. Then blades and buds rushed from the rainsoaked earth, and a faint flush of green lay shimmering down the road from tiny spears of grass in the soft May. Their father always had time to let them loiter and examine things. In season, they would strip the black haw trees while he leaned on a fence, reading a book or perhaps simply regarding the sky as if he owned it and understood it.

During these years of her schooling at Moreland, Eva acquired a clearer image of her father, one that she would never greatly change. He became for her a sacred object toward which she had a special duty greater than that of mere daughter to mere father. The manuscript on which he worked in his spare time contained the most precious words in the world. Her favorite daydream was that the house would catch on fire, and she would climb in through a window, crawl through flame and smoke, grab the huge, sagging pile of her father's poem, fight her way back through smoke and flame, and come staggering out into the yard, where her father would find her pitiful, dead form, with the great manuscript clutched safe on her breast.

The great reverence which she felt for her father was shared by other people in the County, who sought her father's advice on all sorts of things. Whenever the family made a progress through the County in the surrey, they were almost certain to have some quaint encounter that testified to the special reverence in which her father was held. Once a man stopped beside them in a buggy and leaning out said,

—John, I've had two lines of a pome runnin' in my head for days. I can't git rid of it, and I can't finish it. I says to myself, I'll see John Shawnessy, and he'll finish it.

—Let's hear it, her father said.

The man recited:

—Adam, the first of humankind,
He had music on his mind.

Her father thought a moment and recited,

—But in that great and dreadful Fall,
He lost his musicbook and all.

The man sat thoughtful in his buggy a long time, following the surrey with his eyes.

Eva did not entirely conquer her spiteful, envious self during the years at Moreland. It nearly wore her out trying to keep up with her brother Wesley in school. She never hoped to hold her own with him in literature and history, but Wesley had no mind for arithmetic while Eva was a whiz at it.

—Eva has a scientific mind, her father said.

She treasured this statement, a consolation to her in her unending strife with Wesley. The image she made of her brother in this period became fixed like the one she made of her father, and she put it away in her mind along with the shape of the Moreland schoolhouse and other eternal things and never greatly altered it. It was the image of him as going into the contest, whether racing to victory in the schoolyard games or fighting bigger boys to a standstill, his tongue between his teeth, his blue eyes shining with a peculiar light, not anger but more like someone seeing a vision. He was the eternal competitor, ruthless in contest, generous in victory.

Eva must have walked thousands of miles with her father and Wesley on the roads of Raintree County on the way to and from school in the early years of her life. And as always, these roads held for her a promise of strange encounters and discoveries.

One afternoon in the spring, returning without their father from the Moreland School to the Old Home Place, the two children stopped to pick violets and spring beauties where the road turned outside Moreland. Close by in the ditch, Eva saw a pile of trash and right on top the fist-sized bust of a man. But Wesley beat her to it and got the little statuehead, on which as he held it up Eva could see the word BYRON on a scroll at the base. It was a beautiful head, like old marble, virile, with clustering curls, and the only flaw a nick in the left shoulder. Eva, who had seen it first, wanted it more than anything else she had ever seen. She tried to grab it from Wesley, and when he refused to give it up, saying that he planned to put it with his other treasures in a box at the top of a big maple that Eva was afraid to climb, she lost her head completely. There was a scuffle and Wesley broke away and ran down the road with Eva in pursuit, bawling and shrieking. He easily outdistanced her and left her out of breath and blind with tears. At home, she broke out afresh, while Wesley as usual remained stoically calm. Her mother told her to quiet down before they settled the matter. But Eva couldn't quiet down. She went on sobbing and yelling dreadful things about how she hated Wesley and her mother and how they always hung together. At last, her mother switched her, and Eva went into a bedroom and wished outloud that she were dead. When her father got home, he came in to see her, holding her hand and smoothing her hair. She was aware of herself as a small squatty girl, her face dirtied with crying, her hair mussed, her dress stained, her stockings down, her nose running, while her father sat there looking tired from teaching all day and talking with her a little about the value of things. Eva couldn't explain to herself now why it was that she had wanted the little head so badly. But gradually she grew calmer and felt horribly ashamed of the whole affair. At suppertime, Wesley came around and offered her the statuehead, and the strange thing was that now she didn't want it and wouldn't take it and started to cry again. All her sorrow seemed to come back upon her, but without the angry feeling, and she felt as if she could weep whole rivers of tears and never get over the sorrow that she felt.

It was some time after this episode that she dreamed the most terrible nightmare of her life. In her dream she had just left the schoolhouse to go home. In the quiet time of day, alone and homeward going, her schoolbooks in a strap over her shoulder, her lunchbox in her hand, passing the last houses of Moreland, she was tracing on the earth the silent letter of her being. She thought of the jog in the road, the faces of the few houses along the way, arrival in the evening. She had reached the turning, she was about to turn.

Just then across the fading day a single lone, lorn, clear, compelling bell of sorrow sounded, and her gaze was lifted and prolonged by the sound so that it fell just on a place beside the road where she and her brother sometimes picked violets in the spring.

A human head was lying there among the flowers. She walked slowly to the spot, bending over to see more clearly.

It was her father's head, cleanly severed at the neck, eyes shut, mouth open. It had been chewed by dogs. She stood rooted, her tongue glued to the roof of her mouth so that she couldn't scream. Her father's dark reddish hair had been trampled and mussed, the skin had been worried by dogs' teeth, but the face retained its warm coloring against the dank earth.

Unutterable sorrow flooded her with an emotion stronger than any she had ever felt before. She began to moan and shake her head. Hot tears ran down her cheeks. With the absurdity of desperation, she wondered if there might not be some way of sewing the head back on the headless trunk, as one might repair a sawdust doll. But then it was necessary to find her father's body. She turned and with outstretched arms began to run down the road crying,

—Papa! Papa! Papa! . . .

From this dream, her father's own voice awakened her to the knowledge that the thing was not so. Yet her grief could not have been more real if she had really seen her father's head lying on the road. And the dreadful image haunted her for days and even weeks so that she was afraid to go to sleep lest she behold it again, an ambush for her soul lurking on some road of Raintree County. What fate, she wondered, pursued her with this sinister image? What guilt required a self-chastisement so terrible? For after all, she alone was the dreamer of these dreams.

But most of the time during the years at Moreland, she was very happy and seemed to be getting the best of the spiteful, passionate Eva of earlier years. Into her great effort to learn everything and to be good and worthy in the eyes of her father, she threw all her strength. She had a secret hope that if she persevered and never admitted defeat, the time would come when Eva Alice Shawnessy would be a great name, equal to those of the world's most famous women. She would make her father proud, and the name of Shawnessy the equal of any other name down the ages.

Several times she had heard her father say that there would one day be a genius in the family. From time to time, he would have the three children line up, and in a half-humorous way would examine the bumps on their heads. They would all stand solemnly waiting for his pronouncement, and he would say something about Bumps of Calculation, Memory, and the like. Eva would stand with eyes averted while her father examined her head. She hoped that her bumps were right so that some day she might be greatly worthy of her father.

—What do you think, Papa? she would say hopefully.

—A *very* remarkable head, her father would say. Perhaps Eva will be the best of us all.

It was very kind of her father to say it, because secretly he must have known that he was the best of all in the whole world and also he must have known (what she, Eva, secretly knew, but hardly admitted even to herself) that Wesley was smarter, and that everyone expected Wesley to be the bright light and shining star of the family and not Eva, who was, after all, only a girl.

Eva sometimes wondered if she ever got very far beyond the great enlightenment of those first few years when her father was her teacher and she learned that all things were founded on fundamental principles and that the process of knowing was a matter of grasping those principles and keeping them steadfastly in mind.

The feeling of deliverance from a prison of ignorance made the years at Moreland unique among her memories. Then it was that she discovered the plan of an Eva noble and intelligent. This Eva was the Moreland Eva.

The Moreland Eva had lived in a world of time and longing but now remained forever in a world of eternal images, a world of small brown roads and plain board houses.

The Moreland Eva walked on an ancient road between the Home Place and the Moreland School. She made the turn into Moreland, crossed the tracks, went down the street between the houses, turned left into the grassless playground. The Moreland Eva walked through the single door of the Moreland Schoolhouse and hung her wraps in the cloakroom. She sat at her carved familiar desk, she smelled the odor of chalk and children's bodies, she saw through the window a lasting shape of earth. She saw her brother Wesley sitting in his place. And at the front of the room in his old black suit, standing at the blackboard holding a piece of chalk, her father stood and moved his lips, his eyes had a remote and sweet expression, words and numbers grew mystically beneath his hand. And after school, the Moreland Eva (a small stocky girl with large blue eyes, straight, strong features, and indecisive brown hair) would go forth from the Moreland School and set off along the road, tracing again .

AND EVER ON THE EARTH OF RAINTREE COUNTY

THE PATHWAY TO

HER

—HOME in plenty of time to meet the Senator's train, her father said, consulting his watch.

Looking for the roofs of Waycross, Eva saw something like a vast brown bladder swelling on the south horizon. The unfamiliar became instantly a vague fear.

Then she remembered what it was.

She was wondering if she would see her Grandfather Root at the Revival Tent. He had come to some of the earlier meetings, and Eva had even walked past him, almost touching him with her dress once. Of course, as usual, he didn't speak to her, although he did go over and talk with her mother awhile.

There was something ominous about the big Revival Tent. Eva knew that her life had always been pierced with flashes of anxiety, just as sometimes on a blithe summer day a black cloud would roll down on Raintree County, the air would split with jags of fire, thunder would bound in heavy balls up and down the County, and then the rain would fall. Raintree County was itself a vast four-sided tent, under which might rush at times the four winds of the Nation.

Among the few parked buggies, Eva looked for the shiny black horse of her Grandfather Root, or for her grandfather himself, standing massively apart, his beard shot with jags of gray, his big head pivoting slowly on the motionless block of his body.

Just past the Revival Tent the surrey had to stop behind a line of vehicles waiting to enter the National Road.

—The children and I will just get out here, Esther Shawnessy said, and walk down to the Station. Then I'll come back alone for the service at the tent.

She and the children climbed out.

—I'll drive home, their father said, and put President up for the day. I suppose I'll be busy from then on looking after the Senator. Have a good day, children.

—Pshaw! Did you ever see so many people! Eva's mother said.

She walked ahead of the children past the stalled vehicles, her straightbacked form moving with grave purpose, her feet planted exactly parallel.

Eva hadn't stepped on firm ground since they had left home at sun-up. The rocking motion of the surrey still governed her body. She felt languidly aswim in light. For hours, she had floated on the calm ocean of summer and had enjoyed an immense, passive possession of herself and the earth. Now the earth surprised her by its immovable substance. She looked at the sky, walled by far clouds east, but cloudless over Raintree County.

EVA'S ETERNAL HOME

(Epic Fragment from the *Eva Series*)

Yes, little blue-eyed Eva, you raise your eyes toward the eternal sky. What do you see there, Eva, child of the summer day? Look deep and far, Eva, our favorite little girl, and see if you can read upon the face of this ocean of God's universe any tracing of your own life in huge characters. Do you see there the far, beautiful realms of peace and love where joy forever dwells, the cloudbuilt ramparts of your heavenly home awaiting, when all earthly barriers have been burned away? Little tempestuous and tender spirit, our own dear Eva of the childlife series, our little heroine of so many episodes fraught with grave and gay, entertainment and instruction for the well-broughtup little girls of America, do you see there some haven of eternal peace, where all your dreams come true, in the arms of a beneficent Creator, your Father and your God, when the slow-pacing years have carried you home at last along

The Great Road of the Republic

PASSING through Waycross made a sound like a prolonged chord, dissonant but not unmusical. It aroused in Mr. Shawnessy an old excitement. It was the sound of humanity in crowds.

As he drove nearer to the Road, the tonal ingredients of the chord emerged. Bandmusic spouted, firecrackers crumped, wheels ground on gravel, hooves clanged, horses whinnied, human throats bubbled. Beyond the intersection, the long aisle of the street was swollen with parasols, derby hats, flags, blurring and brightening around the railroad station. Stranger even than Mr. Shawnessy's prophetic dream of the early dawn was this glut of people on the wide and quiet crossing.

At the intersection, he felt the pull of the Great Road. It sucked him out of the narrow county road, picked him up, flung him about in a whirlpool of traffic. Engulfed in the Mississippian stream of the Republic, he navigated the surrey carefully against the tide. He reached his own yard, went into it between parked buggies, and drove into the barn, where he quickly unharnessed President and put him into a stall.

He picked up the *Atlas* and the newspapers, planning to run into the house and tidy up before going down to the Station. As he went around to the front porch, he saw a man in a white linen suit sitting on the porchswing.

—Mr. John Wickliff Shawnessy, I presume?

The voice was a pleasant, hissing sound.

—Yes? Mr. Shawnessy said, tentatively.

The man stood up and walked briskly down the steps, plucking the cigar from his mouth and switching it to his canehand.

—Glad to see you again, my boy.

—Professor! Mr. Shawnessy said, taking the thin, strong hand.

Nodding amiably, Professor Jerusalem Webster Stiles exhaled aroma of distant places and metropolitan manners.

—Don't you grow old like other people, my boy?

—You haven't changed much yourself, Professor.

—I grow old, the Perfessor said. Deep scars of thunder have entrenched, and care sits on this faded cheek. But happily I still have my teeth. Both are sound and sometimes leave a signature of senile passion on the shoulders of the most beautiful women in the City of New York.

The Perfessor shook soundlessly. His skull was bonebright under thin hairs that were still defiantly—almost obscenely—black, slicked back from a middle part. His long, narrow face seemed all features and wrinkles. But the tall form was still erect and jaunty, the malacca cane swung with practised ease, the black eyes darted restlessly about. The essential Perfessor was still there, seen as through a frosted glass.

—You fooled me, Professor. Your letter didn't say——

—At exactly seven forty-five this morning, the Perfessor said, trainborne I crossed the borders of Raintree County. I haven't been back since that day thirty-three years ago when the preacher's shotgun goosed me over the border. When did we last see each other, John?

—Fifteen years ago. July of '77. Night of the Grand Ball at Laura Golden's in New York.

—Ah, yes, the Perfessor said. The night you ascended the Great Stair. I envied you that night, John. Tell me the truth, my boy, what did you do up there?

—I was hunting for the exit.

—Hmmmmmmm, the Perfessor said. Won't tell, eh?

He looked around, twirling his cane.

—So this is where the Bard of Raintree County has elected to spend his declining years. Really, John, isn't it a bit bucolic for a man of your talents?

—I have a good pure life here.

—Unavoidably! said the Perfessor. What in the devil is that big book under your arm, John?

The Perfessor peered keenly at the *Atlas,* covered up with newspapers.

—Something I promised to get for the Senator. By the way, is this a professional visit?

—Strictly, the Perfessor said. I persuaded my paper to let me cover this thing. These days, when Garwood moves, the stars zigzag in their orbits, the stock market fluctuates, and the virgins bedew themselves with ecstasy. What an opportunity, I thought, to return unobtrusively to Raintree County, drop a tear once more on the soil that gave me birth, and touch again that magical, mystical time, John, when you and I were young, Maggie.

—Does Evelina know you're coming?

The Perfessor shot a quick glance at Mr. Shawnessy.

—I did write her a letter, he said. How is our little poetess?

—Lovely as ever, Mr. Shawnessy said.

—Where does she live?

—An improbable big brick mansion just outside town, Mr. Shawnessy said, pointing east. You can't quite see it from here.

—I've never forgiven you, John, for luring the little woman away from New York.

—I had nothing to do with it, Mr. Shawnessy said.

—Of course, I blame myself too, the Perfessor said. You two got together in my column. By the way, do you read it these days?

—It's been scintillatingly naughty of late, Professor. How do you get away with it?

—The secret is this: The truth, the real truth, sounds so preposterously false to the average citizen of the Republic that he thinks I'm kidding. So they let me go my lonely way as the New York *Dial*'s Special Reporter on Life, the only man in America who reports the news as it really is.

—Some time, Professor, I want you to publish a newspaper of your own and call it the *Cosmic Enquirer*.

—Right now I'm cosmically thirsty, the Perfessor said. Where's the local hell?

—The town is teetotal.

—How lucky, then, that I happen to have a little on me, no?

From a backpocket, the Perfessor pulled a flat bottle of corn-colored fluid, uncorked, lipped, gurgled.

—Have some?

—No, thanks, Mr. Shawnessy said, looking warily to see who watched.

—By the way, would you conduct me to the Chair of Philosophy?

On the way back, Mr. Shawnessy said,

—The Senator arrives in a few minutes. I'm supposed to be at the Station to meet him.

—What kind of country is it, the Perfessor said, pushing back the crescentcarved door, that permits itself to be run by such bastards! If we're not careful he'll be the next President. Hi, there, Apollo invades the Privy!

The interior walls of the little twoseater were covered with clippings from books and newspapers.

—Wherever Socrates and Plato converse, there is the abode of the Muses, Mr. Shawnessy said.

RURAL PHILOSOPHERS CONGREGATE

(Epic Fragment from the *Cosmic Enquirer*)

> Some of the brainiest savants in this section of the country assembled recently for high metaphysical discourse. The scholarchs are reported to have sought out a meetingplace suitably quiet for their deliberations. Occupying the Boylston Chair of Oratory and Rhetoric was that engaging wiseman and wit . . .

Professor Stiles adjusted his glasses and read aloud from one of the clippings,

> —Government, like dress, is the badge of lost innocence. The palaces of kings are erected upon the bowers of Paradise.

We have a text. Mr. Shawnessy, will you elucidate to the goodly and handsome company assembled?

Mr. Shawnessy consulted his watch.

—To be naked is to be either god or beast, he said. Eden is man's memory of godlike appetite and animal satisfaction, uncurbed by moral law. The forbidden fruit is the act of love resulting in discovery of another and not simply affirmation of oneself. In this act, man becomes man—moral, responsible, parental, and the Republic is born. By the way, Garwood's train is about due. I have to tidy up a little. Meet me in front of the house.

Walking up the back path, he glanced at the sundial. Inside the circular inscription, *I record only the sunshine,* the sharp shadowhand darkened the numeral IX. He reflected that in the *Atlas,* which he carried under his arm, the same hour was fixed forever on the face of the Court House Clock. A radiant god was writing nine o'clock all over Raintree County. With his golden finger he traced a hundred images on great soft sheets of earth, and all proclaimed the magical, morning hour of nine. Without selection or distinction, he traced all legends with a brush of light and shadow. In his bright book of simultaneously existing images, was one thing more forbidden than another?

In the house, Mr. Shawnessy spent a few minutes running through the *Atlas,* but without success. Remembering the Senator's request, he carried the book outdoors, sandwiched in copies of the *Free Enquirer.* On the sidewalk, the Perfessor waited, intoning words for the music which the band at the Station was playing.

—Blow ye the trumpet, blow
  The gladly-solemn sound!
Let all the nations know,
  To earth's remotest bound,
The year of Jubilee has come.

—John Brown's favorite hymn!

—John Brown! the Perfessor said. How well I remember those days! All that summer and fall of '59, when the War was coming on and no one knew it. Those were the days of our paradisal innocence, John. Let me see, what were J. W. Shawnessy and J. W. Stiles doing that summer?

—That summer, Mr. Shawnessy said, J. W. Shawnessy left the estate of youth and innocence and entered upon the estate of manhood and bitter wisdom.

—That summer, the Perfessor said, J. W. Stiles left the County of his Birth lest it become the County of his Demise.

—That summer, J. W. Shawnessy discovered the Source of Life.

—And where is that? said the Perfessor.

—Where the river joins the lake.

—That summer, J. W. Stiles remained a small name and alive, while John Brown prepared to be a great name and dead.

—That summer, J. W. Shawnessy became an agriculturist of love, and worried about his crops.

—Ah, and I remember, too, said the Perfessor,

Summer— How —1859

THAT WAS A SUMMER
OF DROUGHT IN THE MIDDLE STATES.

The crops were dried and stunted. In the dark earth lay the rejected seed. It was a summer, too, of catastrophe and violence. In the prolonged heat men did strange deeds. The deep of the national character was troubled and cast up monsters. The newspaper columns were filled with rape cases. A woman was said to be running about a desolate part of the country naked. Members of a certain religious sect were reported to be waylaying and violating women with organized efficiency. A man fell into the vault of a privy and suffocated. Trains leaped trestles. The crops in the Middle States were stunted. In the dark earth lay the rejected seed.

On the morning after the Fourth of July, Johnny Shawnessy woke up slowly and reluctantly. He was troubled by a pagan memory. There had been a young man bold like a god. He had bestridden a whiteloined horse and had ridden beneath the sun. Winged and triumphant, he had taken no thought of the morrow. He had been naked, and he had no name.

Johnny kept telling himself that he had had one of his vivid dreams, and now he was waking up from it, and everything was all right. But he kept remembering new details. A sequence of sun-drenched images hovered in his mind and refused to be dispelled.

He had a memory of swimming on still waters toward a wooded shore in the region where lake and river met. Of a sleeping in bright sunlight. Of an awakening on a bed of grass. Of a nude form reclined upon his own. Of mouths meeting in more and more perilous kisses. Of a young woman, garmentless, seen running toward an unguessed place. Of a pursuit and of an overtaking. And of a tree with a slender trunk and a shapely roof of foliage from which there sifted a rain of yellow pollen. And it had been as though the two beneath the tree, seizing the supple trunk, had shaken down (at first languorously and then more and more violently) forbidden fruit.

Fully awake, Johnny didn't want to get up. He himself had a name known and respected. He didn't want to have any responsibility for a nameless scamp who had acted as though time and causality didn't exist.

Nevertheless, when the naked ones of that memory had put on their clothes, they had put their names back on too. They were called Johnny Shawnessy and Susanna Drake. They had ridden back from Paradise Lake into Freehaven and had begun to look at each other with thoughtful looks. They were strangers again.

A few weeks before, Johnny Shawnessy had been the most innocent young man in Raintree County. Now he was the most guilty. In the space of a few weeks he had done incredible things. He had told a girl that he loved her and had promptly gone swimming with her naked in the river. Two weeks later he had gone with another girl, an almost total stranger, to a place where he had never been before, and he and she had performed the act of love.

It was useless to point out that by a freak of fate, which was by no means entirely his fault, he had been drunk the second time on whiskey and hard cider. That was merely another crime.

Apparently he had a fatal talent for picking out girls who liked to take off their clothes by lonely waters.

The thing that happened to him at Paradise Lake on the Fourth of July hadn't seemed evil at the time. Indeed, while he was in full career, he had felt like the Hero of the County, life's young American, who had discovered beauty by secret waters. He would no more have plucked himself from that terrific happening than he would have plucked himself out of existence. The feeling of guilt came afterwards when he returned to the familiar part of the County and the effects of the cider wore off. Guilt had not been in the act itself. It was superimposed upon the immutable act, as the map of Raintree County was superimposed upon the immutable earth.

He felt that he had always participated in two worlds. One was the guiltless earth of the river of desire, the earth big with seed, the earth of fruit and flower. The other was the world of memory and sadness, guilt and duty, loyalty and ideas. The two worlds were not antithetical. They were flesh and form, thing and thought, river and map, desire and love. Now the second world had reclaimed him with a vengeance, and he was sincerely penitent.

But his sense of guilt was not religious. If a huge voice had thundered down at him from the summer sky and had said, John Wickliff Shawnessy, thou hast lain with a woman named Susanna Drake for thine own lewd pleasure. Why hast thou done this evil thing, my son? Johnny would have been impressed, of course, but he wouldn't have had any strong sense of guilt. His answer would have been respectful, something like, I'm awfully sorry, Sir. I just drank too much cider and made a slip. I beg Your forgiveness, Sir.

This would be easy. God was impersonal. But Johnny couldn't even imagine a conversation that he might hold with his mother on such a subject. The mere thought of it made him want to climb into a hole and die.

—A great man, Johnny, is a man who does good for other people.

As an innocent child he had understood what Ellen Shawnessy expected of him—to be a good man, to be pure, to combat human suffering and wickedness. During his whole memory of his mother, she had been an angel of purity and good hope, standing at the gates of life and death, secure in the age-old faith that she and T. D. had conferred upon their last child and emphasized by the name they had given him. In his mother's Raintree County, there was no official recognition of the strong desire by which life cunningly furthered itself. There was propagation—but not pleasure. There was love—but not the act of love. Eros and his flametipped arrow had abdicated in favor of Jesus and the cross.

And yet Ellen Shawnessy's most gifted child, John Wickliff, bearing the name of the great reformer and Bible translator like a trumpet-peal of righteousness, had done the Unpardonable Thing. For pleasure, he had stripped the garment of shame from the body of beauty, for pleasure and pastime of his body, had clasped the forbidden whiteness of a young woman in his arms. This he had done in the formrevealing brightness of a July afternoon. Under the circumstances, God, whom T. D. and Ellen were always locating in the sky directly over Raintree County, couldn't have had any trouble seeing the trespass. Johnny might as well have done it on the court house lawn for all the world to see.

The guilt was peculiarly aggravated by the fact that he had committed this trespass with a young woman whom he scarcely knew, an alien from beyond the County. If he had fallen from the path of righteousness with someone like Nell Gaither, a marriage could be quickly gotten up and the fault condoned by official sanction. Johnny had often heard T. D. say,

—High time them youngsters got married.

The truth was that something about the climate of Raintree County or the resilience of its haystacks encouraged the nuptial embrace before the nuptials. And in such cases, the County was inclined to be smilingly tolerant.

—Guess they just couldn't wait, was a common expression when a seven-months' baby had nine months' fingernails.

But there was nothing to condone what Johnny Shawnessy had done. The only rueful satisfaction that he could derive from his sin was that it had the quality of genius about it. An ordinary sinner couldn't have conceived and carried out such a brilliantly successful piece of self-damnation.

For nearly two weeks, Johnny holed up at the Home Place. Then, he received two letters at about the same time. The first said:

> Dear Johnny,
>
> I take my pen in hand and seat myself to say that I am as well as a distressed heart will let me be. Johnny, why haven't you come to see me again? Since a certain afternoon, I have thought about you a great deal. I'll be at home for you next Saturday afternoon, if you care to renew an acquaintance that has already meant more to me, Johnny, than it would be modest in me to say. Johnny, I have been worried and unhappy at not seeing you again. Please come if you can.
>
> Yours trustingly,
>
> SUSANNA

The other letter said:

> Dear Johnny,
>
> I take my pen in hand and seat myself to write you something that a more discreet, but, alas! less wounded heart would not disclose. Johnny, I have paid dearly for my foolish pride since I wrote you a certain note last spring. If I have hurt you, please forgive me, and believe, Johnny, that to see you again would gladden the grieving heart of
>
> Your disconsolate
>
> NELL

All over the County the rain was falling, as he drove through Freehaven to call on Susanna Drake. The rain came down, big drops vertical in dead air, and ran in rivulets on the sunhardened earth. He thought of all the seeds that lay wet in their tombs, beginning to feel an impulse stirring in hard rinds. The rain came as a kind of relief. It was a washing if not a purification.

Susanna's house on its high lawn gleamed palely under vast, rainy skies. Green branches of trees near-by dripped noisily against it. The gutters of the high roof spouted gray water. The house there on its lofty lawn was a shell of riddles, inscrutable against the veined and hovering skies. As he sat a moment bleakly in the raindrenched buggy looking up at it, a strong excitement possessed him. What waited up the stone steps, in the hollow rooms of the house beyond the five front windows to catch the soul of Johnny Shawnessy in a satin snare?

At the door knocking, he had an involuntary image of himself entering a room whose walls were scarved with scarlet; a naked woman whose olive body curved with sleek muscles pounced on him with catlike fury and thrust him upon a couch while her deeplipped mouth purred and stung his face with savage kisses and her black hair lashed his shoulders. He visualized himself as sturdily resisting this assault in the name of his late—and lamented—innocence.

When Susanna's face appeared at the glass doorpane, it was the eyes that dominated the face, those soft childlike eyes with their violet veins, which could be, he knew, all misty with passion. The black hair was now pulled back and chastely bound to show the ears and emphasize the forehead. The lips had their perpetual pout, of course, but suggesting now the wistful child rather than the barbarous little voluptuary who had drunk his kisses with such inexhaustible appetite on the shore of Lake Paradise.

The door opened.

—Hello, Johnny.

The girl in the doorway was chastely attired in black with just a few scarlet ribbons at the neck and shoulders. She held out her hand with a gracious ladylike gesture, and he bowed stiffly into the house.

—Won't you sit down, Johnny, and I'll have the maid bring tea.

A silent little Negress brought tea, while Johnny sat in a deep chair. Demurely lovely, Susanna poured two cups.

—You like tea, don't you, Johnny?

—I hardly ever have it, Johnny said.

—You'll *love* it, she said.

The expression disturbed him. She had said the same thing on the shores of Lake Paradise, and he had wondered about it ever since, though at the time he hadn't stopped to consider what it implied. Since then he had thought more calmly of it, wondering at the history of amorous pastime in which this elegant figure in the black dress must have participated. Perhaps he, Johnny Shawnessy of Raintree County, had merely contributed the latest chapter in a legend with the tantalizing title *You'll Love It.*

He heard the same phrase many more times that afternoon, applied to a variety of things that were not his things, most of them things Southern, from New Orleans architecture to steamboat excursions on the Mississippi River. The phrase was clearly habitual with her; and indeed it did disclose a vivid, lush, romantic world to Johnny, a world he had always wanted to explore. Susanna dominated the conversation, and it soon appeared to Johnny that only thus was conversation between them possible. Her talk was an incessant self-exposure, candid, vivid, artless—yet somehow never giving a satisfactory explanation of anything. No girl in Raintree County, he was sure, had ever talked as Susanna Drake did that afternoon.

Sometimes he was charmed by her romantic views of life and love and, again, shocked by crudities of speech and anecdote, as when she got off on a whole repertoire of stories intended to show that the Negro was not a human being and that there was no use to talk of emancipating him, people who had any other view were just black abolitionists with Negro wives, and hussies like Harriet Beecher Stowe who didn't know a thing about the good old South, you had only to come down there and you would just love it. Some of the most offensive stories concerning black people were told in the presence of the Negro girl who carried the tea service in and out. To Johnny this was an inexcusable breach of good taste, and he blushed for it, but it was clear to him that Susanna didn't regard the Negro girl as a person.

She seemed to have a peculiar relish for sexual atrocities,

—The good Nigroes are just like children, she said. But if they once got equality ideas, we would all be raped in our beds. They're just like beasts in the jungle. Johnny, I could tell you stories about Nigroes assaulting white women that would make your hair stand up. Why, a few years ago a girl in one of the finest families in New Orleans was out riding in a buggy, and she was attacked by a big runaway Nigro, he made her get out of the buggy, and he tore all her clothes off, and she had to submit to him to save her life. And finally he let her go, and the poor thing drove back into town naked.

Johnny winced and put his head down at this torrent of invective against the immorality of the Negro, creature of the jungle and the Great Swamp. All the time he was remembering how he and Susanna Drake had rediscovered the Great Swamp in the middle of Raintree County, steaming in the sunlight.

A more charming manifestation of Susanna's absorption in herself was the album of pictures that she brought out toward the end of the afternoon.

—O, here's the picture taken the day I met you, he said, opening it.

—No, she said, that's another one.

It turned out that the album was full of pictures of Susanna in romantic attitudes like the one in which he had found her in the Freehaven studio. Usually her black hair was unloosened and her body was buried in a cloudy white robe.

Enclosed in the album separately was a daguerreotype of a house, a Southern mansion pillared and stately with a corniced roof. Standing on the porch were three people, a bearded man, a woman, and a little girl. Behind them, half in shadow, was a tall, imperially lovely woman.

—That's my mother and father, Susanna said, and there's me. And there's Henrietta. She was a mulatto, but you couldn't tell it to look at her, could you?

—No, Johnny said, barely able to distinguish the faces of the picture because of the fading light in the parlor.

—We lived right by the Mississippi River, Susanna said. That house burned.

She made her habitual gesture, touching her throat with her left hand.

—That's how I got my scar, she said.

Her voice was low and thrilling and her childlike eyes looked down wistfully at Johnny as she bent over his shoulder.

He was remembering the scar then—how he had awakened on the shore of Lake Paradise and had seen the scar, the whole of it, six inches long, beginning at the base of her neck and making a curious, curving pattern through her olive flesh until it stopped just at the roots of her left breast, as though it shrank from disfiguring anything so exquisitely formed. It was not a deep scar, and there were times when it was hardly visible. There were times too, when the blood beat it crimson, and it glowed and throbbed on the olive smoothness of her body, which had no other blemish.

She had spoken of it then, too, saying simply,

—I hope you don't mind my scar, Johnny.

She had pronounced the words exactly as a woman of good breeding might refer with quiet pride to a costly necklace.

Remembering what had followed her reference to the scar that other time, Johnny blushed.

—I've got to go now, Susanna, he said.

—I'll show you to the door, she said, her voice pensive, her face turned away and lost in shadow.

And so he left the tall house south of the Square. Except for the mention of the scar, no other reference had been made to the wanton encounter on the shores of Lake Paradise. Nor had any word been said either to release him or to bind him more closely to this mysterious girl. He strongly suspected—indeed almost hoped—that he wasn't the first to explore her tawny nudity. Johnny wished he could confide his trespass to his erstwhile mentor and get a frank opinion from the Perfessor, who shared with Johnny precise knowledge of a secret anatomical detail. Had that perceptive young man also discovered a pollendropping tree on the shores of Lake Paradise, and had he too made unexpected forays below the Mason and Dixon Line? But Johnny remembered that the Perfessor, who was nothing if not exact in matters of fact, had in describing the scar prolonged it beyond its actual range. Perhaps he was not so deeply seen in this subject as Johnny Shawnessy after all.

So Johnny went on home through the still falling rain. He was a prisoner now in his own beloved earth of Raintree County. All these corridors through sheets of rain led to and from the person of a darkhaired girl whose body had a hidden scarlet mark. Try as he might, he couldn't fathom her secret. A talented little voluptuary—yes—but she had also been a little girl who once lived in a house beside a river. And in spite of her probable experience, he was convinced that her passion for him had been genuine. It had been tender and undissuadable that afternoon at Lake Paradise; both he and she had been the victims of it and of his own triumphant manhood. She too had fallen—it had been a mutual seduction, and he couldn't force from his mind the feeling that the woman who had taken the first young giving of his love had a powerful, enduring claim upon him.

Meanwhile, he took no action on Nell Gaither's note. But the strangest part of his situation was that his passion for Nell had been intensified by all that had happened. What he had begun with her when they swam together in the Shawmucky had been meant to reach its consummation at the lake. It was a damnable piece of luck that somehow, in the moment of discovering the lake, his true beloved had changed her name and the color of her hair, and instead of an imprint on one of Raintree County's most beautiful twin mounds, there had been a scar like a scarlet letter.

At times, he even indulged the guilty dream of repeating with Nell what he had done with Susanna. He thought of going to the lake and seeking out with Nell the same spot beneath the same tree. He was not at all sure that he could find his way to it, but he played with the fancy that the tree he had only vaguely seen (what with the cider and his amorous excitement) was the celebrated Raintree. At the time it had seemed to him dimly that he had thrust his way to the secret heart of life. And but for a slight error induced by Fate, it would have been so. But now such fancies only added to his sick, unhappy feeling that by one willful act he had cut himself off forever from all the good things of life in Raintree County.

During the next few days, he simply waited for something to happen. He lost all appetite for his usual pursuits. He stayed away from the County Seat. He sent nothing to the newspapers. He did, however, get hold of both the *Clarion* and the *Enquirer* every week. Each time he picked up a copy of the papers, his hands trembled, and his heart beat furiously. Perhaps in this paper he would find the article that told his crime to everyone. He read each paper avidly before any other member of the family got hold of it, devouring column after column and finishing with a feeling of exhaustion and relief, which promptly began to dissolve as he thought of the next issue of the paper, in which the fateful article might really appear and brand him for what he was.

The news in general was not important that summer. The country was apathetic on the great issue of the day. No one seemed to care very much what was to be done about the slaves. Editorials complained a little of the speeches of Alexander Stephens, Jefferson Davis, and other important Southerners, who made it manifest that the South was acquiring a unified point of view on the question of slavery and the Union. There was little doubt that the African slave trade would be renewed and that the South's peculiar institution would continue to expand and require more and more political power and land for its furtherance. But in the heat and stillness of the summer of 1859, the issue was buried in the editorial pages, and nothing indicated that the Republican Party would find the leadership necessary to overthrow the immoral concessions of the Dred Scott Decision and the compromise legislation, or that the South would remain content with them.

In fact, the Republic was deceptively calm, and instead of political explosions as the election of 1860 approached, people concerned themselves with fashions in dress, the Daniel Sickles Murder Trial, rape cases, railroad accidents. The leading news event was the day-by-day account of how a Frenchman named Blondin, balancing himself with a great pole, walked on a tightrope over the chasm of Niagara Falls, defying death again and again in more and more ingenious ways to the shocked delight of thousands of Americans.

Here was danger that could be overcome by skill and determination. But Johnny Shawnessy was up against something that courage couldn't control. For the first time in his life, he had become the fool of time and its blind processes. There was no person he could surpass, no work he could do, no barrier he could leap. He could only wait. This young agrarian had planted some seed, and after that, it was all a question of time and the earth.

About three weeks after the Fourth, the absence of news from the Upper Shawmucky aroused a comment. Johnny read the following note in the *Clarion:*

GREAT MYSTERY!!!

WHERE IS SETH?

Well, we don't hear anything these days emanating from a certain sportive individual who used to contribute to the columns of the *Enquirer*. What has happened to Seth? All his friends and admirers are genuinely alarmed. Both of them admit that they haven't seen or heard anything of Seth since the famous footrace last Fourth of July. Some say he kept right on running, fell into the Shawmucky River, and was swallowed by the mythical beast, which never forgave Seth for the misrepresentations made about it in the *Enquirer* a few years ago. If so, we hope Seth didn't stick in the monster's craw. He always did in ours.

DAN POPULUS

At about this time, Johnny made another visit to the tall house south of the Square.

When he knocked at the door, a plain, workworn woman with a cleaning rag in her hand opened.

—Hello, Johnny said. Is Miss Drake in?

—No, she's gone, the woman said.

—When'll she be in?

—She won't be in. She's gone back South, the woman said.

—You mean she's left town?

—Yeh, she left all of a sudden last Tuesday.

—You—you live here now?

—I'm just to keep the place up for her, the woman said.

—You—you don't know why she left?

—I don't know anything about it, the woman said. But I was here to close up when she left. She and them nigger girls and all the trunks went out a here on three wagons.

—Did she say when she'd be back?

—She said it might be a year or two. I'm to come in every month and dust the place and check up on it. It's a mighty queer house. You ever see it inside?

—No, not especially, Johnny said. Thanks a lot.

He walked back to the Square, where he hadn't been since the Fourth of July. He wanted to see faces. He wanted to shake people by the hand. He wanted to be able to say, Look, it's me, Johnny Shawnessy. He that was dead has risen.

He found Garwood Jones in front of the Saloon. He went up and violently shook Garwood's hand.

—What the hell's the matter? Garwood said.

—Nothing, Johnny said. I'm just glad to see you, that's all.

—I don't know why, Garwood said. I've been giving you one hell of a going over lately. Don't you ever read the newspapers?

—O, that? Johnny said. They were sweet articles, all of them, Garwood. Really sweet—like you.

—What *in* the hell's come over you? You must be saving up something big.

—I'm darn glad to see you again, Garwood. That's all. I really am.

Johnny stood pumping Garwood's hand and hitting him on the back.

—By God, I think he means it, Garwood said several times.

The next issue of the *Free Enquirer* carried the following intelligence from the Upper Shawmucky:

SETH IS BACK

Rejoice, ye virgins, o, make sport, ye maids.
  Bid Error reinvest his dirty den.
Once more a genial shadow haunts the glades:
  Lo! Seth is vocal on his hill again!

Greetings one and all! Your correspondent is glad to report that after a brief sojourn in foreign parts, once more the amiable Mr. Twigs adorns with the tenuous architecture of his frame the shades and shallows of the Upper Shawmucky.

We have been titillated by the several speculations that have come to our ears purporting to explain the disappearance of this kindly bumpkin, and we are frankly at a loss to say exactly what happened to him. Some say that while snoozing in a hedgerow one day, he was discovered by a nearsighted farmer, who mistaking Seth for a scarecrow, tied him to a post, where he dangled helplessly until blown down by the recent storms. Others insist that his well-known weakness for the opposite sex caused him to follow an attractive widow all the way out to California, where, when he at last plucked up nerve enough to make his proposal, the widow replied in the following vein, to wit: that if she were the clinging vine type, she would not know where to find a better beanpole, but that she was more than half persuaded it was not her person so much as her purse the amiable Seth was after, and that she would be willing, if necessary, to dispense all the contents of the second to prevent him from obtaining possession of the first; that she had heard much of the romantic prowess of the gamesome sparrow, but was not under the impression that any poet had composed odes to the amatorial proficiencies of the longshanked crane; and finally that it was better in the whole scheme of things that feckless sorrow should devastate one matronly bosom in California than that it should ravage twenty virginal ones in Raintree County. Acknowledging the cogency of this last argument, it is reported, Seth returned once more to his native haunts.

We cannot in all conscience pretend to be a friend to Mr. Rube Shucks, as though not overly finicky in our tastes we draw some lines, but the sentiment of pity which universally animates the human breast bids us warn him that Seth looks much refreshed, and woe to him who in his absence has taken liberties with the name of Twigs.

WILL WESTWARD

It now seemed to Johnny that he had passed safely through the most dangerous trial that life could offer. He had dreamed a dream of guilt and had awakened to find that it was only a dream. The days and weeks slipped past. By October, hearing no more of Susanna Drake, he became convinced that he had been needlessly alarmed from the beginning. He began even to lose his feeling of uneasiness in the presence of his mother. He now looked back with a certain detachment on the superb young man who in the space of two weeks in early summer had accomplished such notable feats. After a wobbly start, he took up again the unfinished work of becoming life's American, the completely affirmative man, and plunged headlong into plans for composing an epic poem based on American History. A lingering anxiety kept him from making up right away with Nell Gaither, and he was a little nervous when he called for the family mail. But Time, which had been his enemy for a while, was becoming his friend again. And he was beginning to recall with more envy than guilt a pollendropping tree beside the lake, and a companion who had waited for him there as if to teach him

AN INGENIOUS AND FORBIDDEN GAME AND THEN RETURN

TO THE ALIEN EARTH FROM WHICH SHE

HAD

—Come, Mr. Shawnessy said. The Great Man will soon be here.

—I see why you stay here, John, the Perfessor said. One is not confused about human beings on this little crossroads. One has only a few neighbors, and all of them are innocent cretins. It's a good naked life. Perhaps you are trying to regain Paradise here.

—You err, Professor. The Republic is established here in all its sophistication. We are very far from the Edenic nakedness. A Waycross housewife would endure whipping before she'd let the man next door see her bottom bare.

—Thus, the Perfessor said, over Raintree County, the backside of creation, is draped the majestic garb of the Republic.

—Yes, the State is the Individual writ large. The Republic is only people.

Mr. Shawnessy made a vague gesture with his arm at the intersection, which he and the Perfessor had just reached. On foot and wheel, the citizenry of Raintree County converged on the street leading south to the Station. A band of business men, flushed and cherubic, marched in the street bearing a banner:

HOWDY DO, SENATOR!
FROM
THE SOLID MEN'S CLUB OF FREEHAVEN

Behind them marched a deputation of Civil War veterans, falsely vigorous men in faded, tightfitting uniforms, bearing a banner:

HURRAH FOR COLONEL JONES
AND THE SOLDIERS' PENSION

Behind them marched a delegation of healthy ladies, bearing a banner:

THE SITTING AND SEWING SOCIETY
GREETS YOU, SENATOR!

Behind them rolled a score of bicyclists, teetering crazily on their seats atop the huge front wheels, bearing a banner:

WHEELCOME, SENATOR!
FROM
THE WHEELMEN OF MIDDLETOWN

Every now and then a band went by, blaring foggily. And all the time small boys broadcast firecrackers on yards and sidewalks.

—Look at them! the Perfessor said. Aren't they pitiful! All confidently believing that they are going to see the greatest man of the age. Is this your republic of enlightened individuals?

—Here, Professor, are hundreds of republics. And here, too, is one Republic. *E pluribus unum,* as the emblem on the coin has it.

—How is that? the Perfessor asked.

—Show me the man who can solve the problem of the One and the Many, and I will follow in his footsteps as in those of a god.

—If Socrates were living today, the Perfessor said, he'd be reduced to sitting on a crackerbarrel outside Joe's Saloon chewing tobacco and telling dirty stories. That's what America does to greatness. The Greeks were way ahead of us. They never made the mistake of attaching undue importance to the Individual. And they were right. We Americans make the modern error of dignifying the Individual. We do everything we can to butter him up. We give him a name, we assure him that he has certain inalienable rights, we educate him, we let him pass on his name to his brats, and when he dies, we give him a special hole in the ground and a hunk of stone with his name on it. But after all, he's only a seed, a bloom, and a withering stalk among pressing billions. Your Individual is a pretty disgusting, vain, lewd little bastard—with all his puling palaver about his Rights! By God, he has only one right guaranteed to him in Nature, and that is the right to die and stink to Heaven.

Conscious of having come an effective climax, the Perfessor snorted and puffed eloquently on his cigar.

—As for your Republic, he went on, what is it but a brute aggregate of these pointless individuals, all of them worshiping the same illusions, trampling each other in their haste to applaud a fourflusher like Garwood B. Jones!

—You don't get the Republic by adding bodies together, Mr. Shawnessy said, beginning to be pushed about by the crowd. The

Republic is an image that men live by. All life is a self—but in the Republic this self finds a greater self. The Republic begins with love and possibly guilt. In accepting the Republic, man gives up—a little regretfully—brute, naked selfishness. *Government, like dress, is the badge of lost innocence.*

—Well, then, John, isn't it a good thing to lose one's innocence? Is there any virtue in virginity?

The several bands had all taken up their stations around the Station, and in vying with each other all were defeating music.

Blow ye the trumpet, blow!

—Here where the two roads cross, Mr. Shawnessy said gently, I study and study the riddle of the Sphinx, the intersection of my life with the Republic.

—Your little town seems a solid and steadfast institution, the Perfessor said, with its Bank, its Feedstore, and its Post Office. But all this is a frail mist hovering precariously over the Great Swamp. Only Nature with her blind fruitions is finally meaningful. Nothing can save us from the swamp at last.

—Professor, I consider you definitely worth saving, and I won't let you go back into that swamp.

—Thank you very much, the Perfessor said, for keeping me out of that great dismal place.

He made a jaunty movement with his malacca cane.

Near the Station, the crowd was so dense that Mr. Shawnessy and the Perfessor could hardly get through. Women in dowdy summer gowns jockeyed the Perfessor's nervous loins. Citizens with gold fobs and heavy canes thrust, lunged, cursed. The bands blared tunelessly. Firecrackers crumped under skirts of women, rumps of horses. From the struggling column of bodies, bared teeth and bulgy eyes stuck suddenly.

Mr. Shawnessy stopped by a small board building.

—Just a moment, Professor, I see the Post Office is open.

He stepped into the little room and looked into the postmaster's cage.

—Anything for me, Bob?

He studied the fat, steaming face of the postmaster, dispenser of the government mails.

—Just a minute, John.

The postmaster ran his eye along the pigeonholes.

Out of the ocean that beats forever on the walls of my island self, a few words—like manuscripts found in a bottle or a legend graven on a broken oar.

He remembered hundreds of letters and newspapers. He reached into the pigeonholes of hundreds of lost days and pulled out hundreds and hundreds of lost sheets of paper, and the shimmering mist of their words poured over him from the brightness of departed summers.

Dear Johnny, I take my pen in hand to . . . Dear John, I seat myself and . . . My dearest Johnny, It is a painful task for me to . . . John Wickliff Shawnessy, Esq., Dear Sir, We are in receipt of . . . Dear Son, It pleases me to hear that . . . My dear Professor Shawnessy, We wish to bring to your attention a . . . My sweet husband, Do you miss your . . . Shawnessy, you goddam nogood bastard, if you think nobody's on to . . . My Darling, It's been a long time since . . .

Did you want to assure yourself that I was still there? Were you reaching out for me with frail words across the vast spaces of the Republic? (There are no vaster spaces than divide next to next.) But did you want to touch me with words and find me out and reassure yourself that I was there, that I moved somewhere beneath the same day as yourself and that my eyes, falling upon these curved forms dropped on whiteness, would remember you and be touched?

Out of the time that was not my time, out of the world I never knew—fragments of the immense puzzle of myself, letters and newspapers. They brought me tidings of myself and told me what I was and what I must do, brought me the noise of great names and roared them over and over in my ears to be certain I couldn't forget.

—Nice of you to stay open on the Fourth, Bob.

—Just till the train comes in, John. I'm shutting up right away. I want to see the Senator arrive. Here they are. A letter and your newspaper.

Mr. Shawnessy gave a quick glance at the envelope and then stuffed it along with the rolled newspaper into his pocket, for he had heard a distant whistle. Joining the Perfessor, he stood a little apart from the crowd near the station platform.

—John, said the Perfessor, what *in* the hell is that big book under your arm?

—Mr. Shawnessy! Yoohoo!

A woman's voice shrilled at him from the station platform.

—Yes?

—Time for the train. The committee is assembling.

—Hold this for me, Professor. Amuse yourself by examining the beautiful and secret earth of Raintree County. Perhaps you may find something here to delight your pagan soul.

—My God! the Perfessor said, flapping pages. Look at all the pictures of cows, manure piles, and Raintree County citizens.

—Yoohoo, Mr. Shawnessy!

—Coming.

Mr. Shawnessy and the Perfessor pushed through the crowd to the station platform where a place had been reserved for the official Welcoming Committee.

The Perfessor pulled a pencil and a notebook out of his pocket.

—Be sure to say something memorable, John. Something that the world will not willingly let die. I'll see that it appears in tomorrow's *Dial* misquoted and with typographical errors.

They joined the rest of the committee on the platform. A woman from Freehaven, wearing a large badge on her breast, stood holding a horseshoe of flowers. A man in Civil War uniform stood holding a box containing a gold medal. A solid-looking citizen, talltophatted and tailcoated, stood holding a large mantel clock, which showed the time to be nine-twenty-eight.

—My Gracious! Mr. Shawnessy, the woman said, I'm so flustered. How does a person act anyway in the presence of a great man like Senator Jones?

—Just don't accept any cigars, Mr. Shawnessy said. Confidentially, I always found that Garwood's cigars were the worst I ever smoked.

—O, Mr. Shawnessy! You're such a tease, the lady said, arching her back and giving him a sidelong glance. But honestly, I wish the Sitting and Sewing Society had chosen someone else to make the presentation speech.

The man standing there holding the clock said,

—I feel a little silly standing here, holding this clock.

—For my part, I find it much easier to use a pocket watch, Mr. Shawnessy said.

—This is a gift of the Solid Men's Club, the man said. It cost one hundred and thirteen dollars, the best that money could buy in the City of Indianapolis.

—Are you giving him anything? the lady said.

—Just a bouquet of rhetoric, Mr. Shawnessy said.

—When did you last see Garwood, John? the Perfessor asked.

—It's been nearly twenty years. I haven't seen him since '72, when he and I were opponents in the election for Congressional Representative.

Senator Garwood B. Jones impinged from the East in the guise of a blacksnouted locomotive, pulling three special cars, draped with red, white, and blue bunting. When the train was a quarter of a mile distant, the band began to play 'Hail to the Chief.' The crowd strained and stared for a first glimpse of the statesman whose name was a household word throughout the Republic. People moved almost directly into the path of the train, waving the banners of welcome. Professor Stiles was making curves fast in his notebook.

Mr. Shawnessy was deeply unprepared for the man who stood on the platform of the third coach. In a few seconds, he had to make revisions to the form of Garwood Jones that time had taken twenty years to make. The Senator had the belly sag of a fat old man. His hair was a yellow white. He had a stained look as though he had been in too many smokefilled rooms. The famous cigar in the left corner of the mouth pulled the whole face down and left, as if the features, recognizing their true center, were trying to regroup themselves around it. The head was still leonine, but fraudulently so, a mask worn too long without retouching. The eyebrows, thick and black, had a dyed look; and when the Senator, without removing his cigar, smiled his famous smile, his teeth were marmoreal in their chill perfection. It was reported that he had several plates in reserve and that he used now one, now another, depending on his mood and the acoustical situation like an expert violinist changing his Stradivarii.

Only the handsome blue eyes, that always had a faint cynicism in their depths, were unchanged.

The train stopped and left the figure of the Senator gesturing hugely, close to the startled crowd. The head jerked up and down, the teeth clenched hideously on an unlit cigar, the great, grotesque thing smiled, winked, stretched out its arms, incredible in its black senatorial coat and loose black Lincoln tie.

Shocked and disturbed, Mr. Shawnessy stared at the big Greek mask of Senator Garwood B. Jones and wondered about the ego beneath it, putting on this costume with cynical unbelief, no longer caring if the crowds were at first a little shocked by the greasepaint and the theatre hoarseness of the voice, before they slipped into the suspension of unbelief necessary for the enjoyment of the play.

Yet this voice had shaped the future of the Republic from platforms where faces converged in dim banks and shifting masses. And this mask concealed a baffling human being who had come back out of triumphant years to the valley of his humble beginnings, Raintree County.

Briefly the Senator bobbing on the train platform, the environing faces, the little station, the banners, and the bands achieved a pictorial fixity, and over this image was shed the antique, golden light of the Republic.

—Hello, John, the Senator said, stepping down from the platform.

His big voice boomed jovially. His blue eyes had the faint mockery that was neither friendship nor contempt but an indefinable mixture of the two that Mr. Shawnessy had never wholly understood. The Senator's entourage swarmed out of the car, flanking the Great Man and walling out the crowd. A half-dozen reporters pulled out notebooks and began to make notes.

—Glad to see you, Garwood, Mr. Shawnessy said.

He and the Senator clasped hands, as the crowd applauded. Mr. Shawnessy cleared his throat. His voice was high, uncertain, tremulous.

Senator, he said, we have . . .

IMPRESSIVE WELCOMING RITES
FOR THE GREAT JONES

(Epic Fragment from the *Cosmic Enquirer*)

One of the highlights of the Senator's Homecoming Day was the reception in the little station at Waycross. Visibly moved by this return to the haunts of his childhood, the Senator recognized and called by name several old friends and acquaintances. Among these, the local schoolmaster, a Mr. J. P. O'Shaughnessy, who had been a schoolmate of the Senator's in the old Pre-War days, came forward as the head of the Reception Committee and delivered a quaintly humorous address of welcome, most of which could barely be overheard because of the commotion in the Station. The Senator, calling upon his celebrated gift for impromptu discourse . . .

—John, said the Senator, in a hoarse whisper when Mr. Shawnessy had finished his speech, give me a little information, will you? Is there anything left in the town that was here in 1850?

—The church was here then, Mr. Shawnessy whispered.

—Where is the goddam thing?

—Right on this street.

—Ladies and Gentlemen, the Senator said in a great voice. The emotion I feel as I . . .

VIEW OF CHILDHOOD HOME
FILLS STATESMAN WITH
EMOTION

(Epic Fragment from the *Cosmic Enquirer*)

In his reply, the Senator described the emotion in his breast as one that could find no fit utterance in words. He showed an amazing memory for the most minute details of his old stamping grounds, accurately recalling in his speech one of the oldest buildings in the town, the church, which he said he had often passed on his way to buy eggs from an old widow who resided a little way out in the country. The Senator found a few wellchosen words to express his feeling for his parents and especially his mother, than whom, he asserted, no finer or more virtuous woman ever lived. He concluded his short talk by saying that he was tired after his long trip and must be excused from a lengthy address as he intended to speak more fully of the weighty matters on his heart in the Address of the Day, which he would deliver in the Fourth of July Ceremonies that afternoon. Pursuant to this speech, the Senator listened to short addresses by three other members of the welcoming committee, who . . .

—Senator Jones, the Sitting and Sewing Society of Raintree County wish to tender you this token of their esteem, a symbol of good luck from the Gardenspot of Indiana and America, beautiful Raintree County. To a weaver of immortal garlands of eloquence, I give this garland of living and lovely petals, taken from the very soil that sired a great man.

—Madame, said the Perfessor in a low voice, is the Senator a horse or a flower?

—Madame, the Senator said, dropping shy lids on his beautiful eyes, I accept this lovely floral tribute. Believe me, Madame, I shall treasure this beautiful bouquet and shall be by it reminded that no more beautiful flowers grow anywhere in the world than those which are to be plucked in our own Raintree County, Gardenspot of the Universe, home, as you say, Madame, of beautiful flowers and, Madame, with your permission, of beautiful ladies.

—Your Excellency, the man with the clock said, as Delegate of the Solid Men's Club of Raintree County, we have a little gift here we would like to uh tender unto you, in appreciation and uh token of uh our esteem and cordial uh appreciation of uh the uh cordial and friendly uh feeling uh you have always uh manifested and shown and uh demonstrated toward the business men of our county, and which we appreciate it very much.

The Senator accepted the clock and, holding it like a bulky baby with soiled diaper, replied,

—My friend, this beautiful clock will occupy a prominent place on the mantel of my home in the Nation's Capital, Washington, D.C. I assure you, sir—and I wish to extend that assurance to each and every member of your enterprising and forward-looking organization—that I shall never gaze upon this clock without remembering the happy hours which I have spent with old friends, business acquaintances, and rural people in Raintree County. And you may be sure, my friend, that this clock shall record no single second during which my every thought, my every endeavor shall not have been devoted to the furtherance of Raintree County's best interests.

—Colonel Jones, the uniformed man said, the members of the Raintree County Post of the Grand Army of the Republic wish to give you this little medal commemorating your valiant efforts in their behalf. As the poet laureate of this organization, I have composed a little pome I would like to read:

> In the forefront of the battle
> For Union and Freedom and his Nation's Life,
> He fought, nor once was daunted
> In that fierce and bloody strife.

And when the battle's breath was through
And scream of shot and shell,
Did he forget his soldier-comrades true
Who for their country's flag had fought and fell?

The Good Old Cause he fought for
He never did let lag,
But fought right on in Congress and Nation
For the rights of the men who saved the dear old Flag.

Mr. Shawnessy swallowed audibly, and the Perfessor winced visibly.

—Comrade, the Senator said, deeply moved, I am deeply moved. I have no prouder recollection than the fact that I had a small, humble, and inconspicuous part in that Great War for the Preservation of our nation and for the perpetuity of Human Freedom. And you have my word for it, sir, which I hope you will transmit to my comrades-at-arms all over this County, that I do not mean for the Nation to forget the men who saved the Union. You, sir, have touched me more than I can express by the tender lyric which you have seen fit to dedicate to me.

Mr. Shawnessy could not get close to the Senator, who strode down the street shaking hands, swatting backs, and dispensing cigars.

—We have fallen upon degenerate days, John, the Perfessor said. Is this the heir of all the ages?

—Pardon me, gentlemen, said a young attaché of the Senator. I have here some little pictures of the Senator which I would like to circulate unobtrusively during the day. No political motives involved. Only the Senator's desire to gratify old friends who might be interested in a likeness of the most illustrious statesman of our time.

—Let me see, Mr. Shawnessy said, as the Senator's secretary lifted from a briefcase a bundle of cheap prints, three-by-five leaflets bearing a bold engraving of the Senator's face and the simple caption:

GARWOOD B. JONES, THE MAN OF THE PEOPLE

—I'll leave the distribution of these entirely up to you, Mr. Shawnessy said.

—I'll take a pad, the Perfessor said. I am positive I can put them to good use.

When the secretary had moved on, the Perfessor said,

—I have an idea for a vast promotional stunt. Suppose Garwood contracted with leading toilet paper manufacturers to have his likeness faintly impressed upon every sheet of——

The Perfessor began to shake soundlessly.

—Thank you very much, said the President of the Sitting and Sewing Society, accepting a leaflet from the Perfessor. By the way, what does the B stand for?

—Give you one guess, said the Perfessor.

Mr. Shawnessy holding one of the likenesses in his hand walked on, smiling faintly. From the paper in his hand stared vacantly the face of Senator Garwood B. Jones, Bumwiper Candidate for the Presidency of the United States.

A face fluttered down on a republic of his memory, raining grayly on hundreds of court house squares in the time of the prophets and martyrs.

Blow ye the trumpet, blow!

Blow the lone far bugle of the conscience abroad in the Republic in ancient days! Send the hornnotes crowding in the court house squares all over the Republic! Awaken the conscience of the sleeping North! Blow ye the trumpet, blow, and let the blind walls crumble.

I saw the bitten granite of the face. I could not bear the bitter sadness of those eyes in the Court House Square.

Blow ye the trumpet, blow the gladly-solemn sound!

But (you will remember) I was he who lay with one of the daughters of those Babylonian valleys. Let all men everywhere know that I was forgetful of duty. Beneath a tree in summertime, I was held long, long on the flanks of a daughter of Egypt. The precious seed of the chosen I gave to guilty ground stained by the bondsman's blood. Let all men know how I slunk from the bosom of my parents, guilty and afraid.

Let all the nations know, to earth's remotest bound . . .

Let it be repeated by word of mouth, by letter, by items in the corners of the inside pages of the wellthumbed weeklies how I sinned with a daughter of the Philistines.

Who was it then that I took by the supple waist? With whom did I taste of a scarlet fruit close to serpent waters? Whence did they come, those darkskinned patient generations, to bear witness to my guilt? Was my flesh their flesh?

The Year of Jubilee is come! Let it be known all over the Republic. Let it be told by trumpets and by proclamations and by

October 19— A —1859

LETTER AT THE POST OFFICE
WAS ALWAYS A BIG EVENT IN RAINTREE COUNTY,

and on being advised that there was one there for him, Johnny had lost no time getting into Freehaven. But as he came through the Square, he saw the big crowd around the railroad station a half block north. The excitement there seemed so unusual that he went up to see what it was.

At the depot the crowd was even bigger than he had thought. There were scores of people sitting in buggies or standing in little groups. The telegrapher at his table just inside an open window was taking a dispatch. Garwood Jones and Cash Carney were in the group of men crowding around the window.

—It was a fool thing to do, Garwood was saying, and I hope they string him up.

—String who up? Johnny said. What's going on anyway?

Garwood turned and took the cigar out of his mouth. His sleek face was streaked with sweat and flushed with excitement.

—I keep forgetting you hillbillies don't get into town but once a month, he said.

Cash Carney, impeccably dressed as usual, said with an air of detachment,

—There's been a big insurrection of slaves at Harper's Ferry in Virginia. A man named John Brown that used to do all that feudin' in Kansas seems to be at the bottom of it. This old Brown, near as we can find out, got a band of armed men and captured the Federal Arsenal at Harper's Ferry. They plan to give out arms to the slaves and spread a revolt through the South. But according to the last report Federal troops have surrounded the place. Brown and his men have been holding out for two days.

—By God, I hope he succeeds, a citizen said.

—That's talkin', Bill, a second citizen said, thrusting his way into the crowd near the window.

—Say, what do you fellows want, anyway? Garwood said. Civil war?

—Civil war! Shucks! What are you talking about! Civil war!

—Why, man, Garwood said, didn't you hear? He attacked the Federal Arsenal. That's an attack on the People, on the Government of the United States, on the Constitution.

—It ain't an attack on any government I want any part of, a man said.

—Why, man, Garwood said, that's treason. Much as I feel for the lot of the Black Man, I can't see any justification for a deed of bloody violence that will hurl the whole country into civil war. Things can't be settled that way.

—If they won't *give* the niggers their freedom, seems like the niggers ought to have the right to *fight* for it, the man said doggedly.

But Garwood got much the best of the argument, and a majority of the people on the Square seemed to agree reluctantly with his point of view.

Meanwhile Johnny got hold of the latest paper and read the reports of the raid. He remembered how he had read years ago of this same John Brown fighting in Kansas. There had been an undeclared war between slave and free elements, but it had been beyond the Mississippi where men were always fighting something anyway—Indians, buffalo, Mexicans, the earth itself. That wound in the flank of the Republic had closed; the arid West had drunk and dried the gore of those old fights as if they had never been at all. Their distant tumult had dwindled and become lost in the headlines of onward-pressing days. And yet the name 'John Brown' had been a tough seed waiting in darkness. Now it had sprung to bloodier fruition in Virginia, Mother of States and Presidents. It was almost as though the deed had been done in Raintree County, so vast and instantaneous was the shock.

Someone had dared to defy the most anciently rooted wrong in the Republic, a wrong grown sacred in the very measure of its age and enormity. Someone had shed blood on the porch of the Republic.

One man had taken the jawbone of an ass to shatter an army. It was sheer act, founded on sheer faith. It restored the age of miracle. The people of Raintree County waited for word of this amazing madman in the hope that an enterprise of such grandly crazy proportions would have a success equally grand and crazy.

—Say, he's a tough old scoundrel. By God, it wouldn't surprise me any did he cause a lot of trouble, men were saying on the Square.

—A few more men like him, and we'd see about all this talk of slavery and disunion.

—By God, we need more men with gunpowder in their guts.

—Walked right into a United States Arsenal and held the place up. In my opinion, John Brown is the Greatest Living American.

Around four o'clock in the afternoon, Johnny walked back to the Post Office.

—Do you have a letter there for John Shawnessy?

—Just a minute, the postmaster said.

He sorted through some letters and brought one over. It had a New Orleans postmark. Johnny took the letter and started out. There was a dark passageway between the office and the street, where he stopped and turned the letter over and over in his hands.

—One against a thousand, a citizen outside said. But they'll hang him as sure as shootin'!

—What's the latest? a second citizen said.

—Still hemmed in and fightin', I guess. The whole goldern U.S. Army! What's a man to do?

Johnny began to tear the letter open. It was only words, inklines on an envelope. It had come to him from beyond the walls of Raintree County. It had come from a remote earth, jasmine-scented, where it was always summer. He unfolded the letter and read it over once quickly. He felt as though he could have written the words himself, so often had he dreamed them. The words said what he had always feared, what he had known would come to pass.

He didn't want to leave this passageway. Outside there were a thousand eyes. People who had no worries were on the lookout for a tender flesh to crucify. He fumblingly put the letter in his pocket, drew it out again, minutely inspected the outside of the envelope, put it back into his pocket and felt—but conquered—a burning desire to take it out again. He stuffed a handkerchief down on it. He leaned against the wall and waited. Someone would come in and find him leaning insanely against this wall and would know that he was guilty of something. He panted, trying to breathe the hot blush of guilt from his face. Footsteps approached. He walked swiftly out of the door, almost ran into someone.

—Hello, Johnny.

It was his mother.

His mind had just been filled with the exotic image of Susanna Drake. He had been thinking of her young pouting face, her love-talented body in a costly gown. Now suddenly this image was shattered by the apparition of Ellen Shawnessy in her drab little farm-wife's dress. He saw as never before his mother's small weathered face, her bony, workroughened hands, her skyblue eyes, her slender body, which to him was neither masculine nor feminine—but simply maternal, this body which had had its anguish of childbirth many times and which was now saved from it by the blessing of the life-change.

—Any mail?

She peered blithely at him, her face heavily lined in the sunlight. She wore a fussy little hat that she had had for years.

—I—guess not, Johnny said.

—The news is exciting. I suppose you've heard.

He pressed his hand on the letter in his pocket.

—What? he said. You mean——

—The raid. This man Brown.

—O, Johnny said. Sure.

—I'm afraid nothing can be mended that way, Ellen said. Still it was the act of a brave man. God rest his soul.

—Is he—is he dead?

—Dead or dying. News just came over the wire.

As his mother walked slowly away, he saw a picture of an old man dying heroically from gunshot wounds. It was sweet to die a hero for the right, in an absurdly brave act. In the Act there was no remorse for things past. In the Act, there was only the living present.

A throng of people came up the street. In the middle Garwood Jones was shouting, sweating, waving his arms.

—I tell you, Garwood said, they'll hang 'im. What else can they do? The local courts will have jurisdiction since a number of people were killed right there in the town.

—It was a foolish thing to do, Cash said. The old guy didn't have a chance. There's no future in that kind of thing. Seventeen men or so against the country! The niggers'll never revolt. What did he expect to accomplish? It was blood thrown away.

—A few more men like that would blow things wide open in this godforsaken country, a man said.

Garwood Jones began to sound more and more like an orator. He drew apart from the other men, and they turned their faces toward him and formed a group.

—Fellow Americans, Garwood said gravely, it was treason. Technically, legally, what he did was directed as much against the North as the South. It was an affront to the whole country. I personally yield to no man in my desire to see the Negro gradually acquire as many rights as he is capable of exercising intelligently, but just to shove a gun in his hand and say, All right, Sambo, go out and start shooting every white man you see, why, men, that's madness—or—what's worse—coldblooded murder. I'd like to know what the Republicans——

—Who said anything about the Republicans? a man said hotly. The Republicans never had anything to do with this.

—Well, Garwood said hotly, what have they been doing all along but inflaming the minds of people and keeping this issue alive! No, sir, Douglas is right. Let them——

—O, the hell with Douglas! a man said. By God, if we had more politicians from the North with a little of John Brown's guts, we'd not be allays backing down when——

—All I say is, Garwood said, his big handsome face flushed with anger, all I say is that——

—What a story! Niles Foster said in passing. I'm getting out an extra. First time in the paper's history. Folks are demanding it. I guess I can do it.

—What kind of trial will he get down there! a man said.

—If they give him justice, Garwood said, he'll get hanged. Nothing can save that man but a war.

—Justice! a man said. What was he trying to do but free some slaves?

—He killed some people, didn't he? Garwood said. He tried to overturn the Government. He broke into a United States Arsenal. You talk about justice. Why, the man's a murderer!

—Some people have a funny idea of justice, by God!

Words had never been so hot and fierce before in the Court House Square.

—Cash, Johnny said, pulling him aside, I want to talk with you.

He got Cash Carney out of the crowd, took him to a quiet place off the Square, and told him everything.

—I just had to tell someone, he said. What am I going to do?

—Jesus, John, Cash said, you're in a mess!

—I know it, Johnny said.

The muscles of Cash Carney's face twitched. He looked as if he had just got hold of a fat deal for making some money. He rubbed his hands together and puffed happily on his cigar.

—Jesus, John, I didn't know you had it in you.

He gave Johnny a quick look in which respect, sympathy, and a kind of veiled pleasure were mixed. He threw away his halfsmoked cigar, bit off the end of a new cigar, and covered his face with his cupped hands.

—You got raped, he said.

—No, Johnny said. It was both of us.

—By God, I thought there was something queer about that dame. Here, let me see that letter.

He read it over.

—One-Shot Johnny! he said. Why'd she put it off so long, telling you? Three, four months already. My God, she's no right asking a man to marry her after that. She'll stick out.

—I know, Johnny said.

—Now, don't worry, Cash said. We can lick this thing. We'll think of something. What if your folks found out?

—I know, Johnny said.

—But don't worry, Cash said, throwing away his second cigar and biting the tip off a third. Yes, sir, she'll stick right out. What kind of a marriage would that be, John?

—I know, Johnny said.

—That little dress has been off before. You can bet your bottom dollar on that. Say, do you suppose Garwood's been in there?

—I don't know, Johnny said.

Cash finally got the cigar burning. He leaned back against a fence, opened his coat, hooked his thumbs in his waistcoat, and considered the situation calmly. It appealed to his imagination.

—I see just how it happened, John. On top of that whiskey, which under the circumstances wasn't exactly your fault, you drink cider, which happens to be hard. You swim a little, and you're a little tired and dizzy, it's hot, you lie down, you find this girl on top of you, and you——

—I know, Johnny said.

—It could have happened to anyone, John.

—I know, Johnny said.

—Listen, Cash said. Why'nt she write sooner? Why'd she go South? There's something fishy here.

—I don't know, Johnny said.

—Now, listen, John, Cash said, don't worry about this thing. It can be fixed up. There *must* be a way to get you out of this. Does anyone else know?

—Not that I know of, Johnny said.

—Good, Cash said, as if that solved the whole problem. Fine! Now let me think. Jesus, John, you should have been more careful.

—I know.

—Coming back in a couple of weeks, she says. That gives us some time. Now let me see.

Cash chewed his cigar thoughtfully, but he didn't say he had a plan.

Nevertheless, Johnny felt much better to have someone else sharing the burden and thinking about it along with him. Good old Cash! It was good to have a man that bit down hard on his cigar and figured out ways to beat the game and come out on top, a practical man, a business man. Cash Carney would grab hold of a problem like this and whip it. Personally, he, Johnny, was helpless.

In the following days, the only relief Johnny Shawnessy had from the burden of his guilt came from reading about the famous raid and its aftermath. The trial of the wounded old man dragged on for two weeks. The Nation was drenched with rivers of black words in narrow columns—questions, counterquestions, legal jargon, names of witnesses, conspirators, friends, innocent dead. One day Johnny went into Freehaven and heard that John Brown had been sentenced to die. He read the record of the old man's last words to the Court, words that would remain in the Republic's memory after all the hundreds and thousands of words of that year had been washed away in the acid bath of time.

> . . . I say I am yet too young to understand that God is any respecter of persons. I believe that to have interfered as I have done, as I have

> always freely admitted I have done in behalf of His despised poor, I did no wrong, but right. Now, if it is deemed necessary that I should forfeit my life for the furtherance of the ends of justice and mingle my blood further with the blood of my children and with the blood of millions in this slave country whose rights are disregarded by wicked, cruel and unjust enactments, I say, let it be done.

Also at that time, Johnny saw in the Square pictures of John Brown, which could be bought in lots of a dozen for a dollar. During those days the face of the foremost American of the hour loomed above the land like a face of stone. Looking at that face, men knew that the appointed time was nearing when John Brown would go out and the rope would be tied around his neck and the trap would be sprung and his body would drop jerking at the rope's end and the face with the accusing eyes would be the face of a dead man. Men had a little time to wait and think how and why this death was being done. It was only a question of time.

For Johnny Shawnessy, too, it was only a question of time. Time had become again a real duration that had a seed in the past and a flower in the future. In the Court House Square, he had had his being sown with small black words, and they had become a promise he could neither alter nor diminish. They would remain within him and grow upon him in magnitude and terror.

Always and for all men, he knew, time had been bringing dark events to birth. Some men were passive and let time bully them. But brave men acted. John Brown was such a man. He had performed the living Act and had dared the consequence. Like an Old Testament prophet, in whom trembled the fury of an avenging God, he had made the people mindful of themselves, awakened them from slumber. Somewhere now in darkness and agony, jailed, wounded, spat on, lay John Brown's body. It was a tough seed that couldn't be killed. And all men felt that when that body was given to the grave, it would be only that it might go on in darkness preparing for a mightier birth because that name, that body, and that face were chosen.

History had thrust a torch into John Brown's hand. He had become an image-bearer of the Republic.

The night after hearing of John Brown's sentence, Johnny Shawnessy got out of bed and silently putting on his clothes, slipped down to the place beside the tracks where he had said good-by to the Perfessor. A train approached, coming from the east. The lone red eye blinked at him, the train chugged up the grade, flame flared from the smokestack in the dark. Johnny Shawnessy rose and ran toward the embankment, slipping and scrambling through dead vines and withering grasses by the river. For an instant, he saw in the engine's scarlet glare the vision of a new life for him. California, on the Golden Shore! There rushed over him the images of a future of achievement, such as he had always dreamed. He saw himself among the intrepid thousands who went west with the Republic. He would take up again the Quest of the Shawnessys. One of that restless, messianic seed, he would push on and leave the past behind. He would say good-by to Raintree County and go forth and fearless to a land where purple hills were drenched with golden fire at evening.

For a tumultuous instant, the necessary words were rising to his tongue, the words that said farewell and made it possible for him to turn his face from the faces of his people. In that instant, as the last car rolled over the crest of the hill, he looked backward. The river flowed in darkness making its great south loop. On the Home Place leaf-fires were charring in the darkness, and a lonely rock lay at the limit of the land. Then all the summers of his life rushed back upon him. He remembered his mother standing at the back door and calling the boys in from the fields for dinner. He remembered T. D.'s tall, gentle form in the cluttered Office among the squarecornered bottles. Johnny Shawnessy's voice made a hoarse cry in his throat, and at the same time he heard the lonely wail of the departing engine. Then all that he was and all that he had been, like a hundred feminine and pleading hands, held him fast; he lay entangled with the vines and grasses of the autumnal earth beside the river. He knew then that he could no more uproot himself from this memoryhaunted earth than he could pluck body from soul. He lay in wet weeds at the base of the embankment and wondered at the image of himself departing from himself, of the disinherited one whom he had just sent down the tracks to westward and never would behold again.

THE EARTH WAS ODOROUS WITH AUTUMN;
ACROSS THE FIELDS DRIFTED A SCENT
OF

SMOKE curled up from the cigars of three men seated in front of the General Store.

—Let's try page 65, the Senator said.

He was wedged into the middle one of three chairs. The Perfessor on his right and Mr. Shawnessy on his left were bent over to see the *Atlas* lying open in the Senator's lap. The Perfessor licked his lips. His eyes were beady.

—I must say, he said, I never thought I'd take so much interest in the face of Raintree County. What a priceless opportunity that artist had!

—I'm beginning to think that the whole thing was the figment of an old man's diseased mind, Mr. Shawnessy said.

—It must be here somewhere, the Senator said, studying page 65. If there weren't so many interruptions——

Page 65 showed the farm residence of Robert Ray. Hugely passive in the foreground stood Jocko the Strong, blueribbon bull, surrounded by lesser bovine gentry.

—There goes another possibility, the Senator said. Doggone it! Let's see—have we looked through it carefully?

—Let me try for a while, the Perfessor said.

He began to flap through the pages, holding the book at various angles and removes. He had the air of slipping up on the pictures before something could run away.

—I guess that story was too good to be true, the Senator said.

He tipped his chair back against the wall of the General Store, and nodding pleasantly at a group of hovering pedestrians, began to light a new cigar.

—John—puff, puff—how do you stand living in this little—puff, puff—burg? When I was a—puff, puff—kid, I couldn't wait to get out.

He sat back breathing hard, triumphant possessor of a lit cigar.

—These are good smokes, he said. I burn about fifteen every day.

—This is the first smoke I've had for weeks, Mr. Shawnessy said. My wife doesn't like the odor.

—Ten o'clock, the Senator said, consulting his watch. What do I do now, John?

—Just sit here and let the people gaze on the Man of the People.

All three men tipped their chairs back against the wall of the General Store.

—John, I remember how your dad, old T. D., was deadset against tobacco, the Senator said. What was that famous couplet of his?

> Some do it chew, and some it smoke,
> Whilst some it up their nose do poke.

He quaked with senatorial laughter.

Drinking the strong aroma of the cigar, Mr. Shawnessy felt heady and full of words.

Garwood the Great. Occupying the throne. And I in shadow sucking on a borrowed smoke. Well, I was too ambitious to be a great man in this age. We are definitely in the Garwood B. Jones Period of American History.

—Gentlemen, said the Senator, hooking his thumbs under his armpits, where would America be without the cigar?

Mr. Shawnessy watched the crowd go by in the thin mist of his cigar, incense of the Republic.

How will you find this manyness in one, this oneness in many, the Republic? It hovers in the smell of all the pullman cars and diners, and all the lobbies, court rooms, courthouse toilets, and all the senate chambers, hotel rooms, and statehouse corridors. The Republic is rolled up in thin brown leaves and smoked all over the Republic.

I will spend five cents and buy the earth. I will buy the subtle fragrance of sorghum, rum, molasses, dung, and dark flesh from below the Ohio River. For they have taken Alabama, Mississippi, Georgia, Louisiana, and the Carolinas, they have taken Old Virginny, and distilled them into smoke.

I saw a halfburned butt beneath a vaudeville poster. The street outside the drugstore was littered with chewed fragments of the Old Kentucky Home.

Have a smoke, brother. Thank you, Senator. Give me a light, will you? Here's a good cigar. And don't forget, brother, I stand for free soil, free speech, and the rights of men.

Can I get more for a nickel anywhere than the memory of all those great white domes and statehouse yards on Independence Day and summer streets and sainted elders reading their papers in the evening?

The cigar is mightier than the sword. Our thin smokes curl upon the summer air, tracing the legend of an elder day. Our thin smokes curl upon the summer air, our thin smokes curl upon, our thin smokes curl . . .

—By the way, men, the Senator was saying, I am eager to have the opinion of two such erudite gentlemen on a book I am writing. As time and the pressure of public duty permit, I have been working on a little *magnum opus,* a record of my life and the crowding pageant of the Nation's history during my career as a servant of the people.

—Garwood, Mr. Shawnessy said, for goodness' sake, get off the platform and talk English. You're among friends now—not voters. You never got a vote of mine, and by the gods, you never shall.

—That's what I like about you, John, the Senator said. You make me feel right at home again. Remember how we used to maul each other in the partisan weeklies? Well, what I want you two smart bastards to do is to prod me a little, stir up my ideas about these things. I figure on calling the goddam thing

MEMORIES OF THE REPUBLIC IN WAR AND PEACE

What do you think of that?

—Why don't you just call it frankly

WHY I OUGHT TO BE PRESIDENT

the Perfessor said.

—I admit, the Senator said, that the appearance of this book, about two years from now, won't hurt my candidacy for the Presidency in '96. But all joking aside, boys, I have been turning over in my mind the whole question of what the United States of America stands for, and where we have been heading in the last fifty years. Or in the last four hundred years, for that matter. Do you fellows realize that we are in the Quadricentennial Year of the Discovery of America by the well-known Wop?

—America, Mr. Shawnessy said, is still waiting to be discovered.

America is a perpetual adventure in discovery. I've spent my fifty years of life trying to discover America.

—That sounds rather good, the Senator said. Whom are you quoting?

He made a lazy ring, fat breathing of the senatorial lips.

—Well, what is America? Mr. Shawnessy said.

The Senator laughed gently, became silent. At last he said,

—America is the most perfect form of government ever devised by man.

—A lawyer's definition, Mr. Shawnessy said.

—America, said the Perfessor, is where a great many beasts try to live under a government perfectly devised for men.

—A cynic's definition, Mr. Shawnessy said.

—We need a poet's definition, the Perfessor said.

—See my forthcoming opus, Mr. Shawnessy said, which, if the pressure of public duty permits, will appear just in time to strengthen my bid for the Presidency in 1948.

—John, the Senator said, where in Christ's name *is* that great book you were always going to write?

A deputation of citizens approached to greet the Senator, who got out of his chair and began shaking hands.

Mr. Shawnessy drew deeply on the cigar.

America is a memory of my pre-Columbian years. America is a cabin in the clearing and a road that scarcely ruts the earth. It is the face of my mother in the sentimental doorway of our home in Indiana. America is an innocent myth that makes us glad and hopeful each time we read it in the book of our own life. It is the same myth each time with multiple meanings. It has the same homeplace in the county, the doorway and the face in the doorway, the cabin made of logs, the spring and running branch, the fields around the house, and it has the same rock lying at the utmost limit of the land at evening.

—Boys, the Senator said, resuming his chair, whatever America may be, I'm sure of one thing—that in fifty years we have seen a radical change in this country, as much so as if we had adopted a different form of government.

—For good or bad? the Perfessor said.

—Why, for good, the Senator said.

—For my part, the Perfessor said, I think we live in the period of the Great Betrayal.

—How so?

—We've betrayed the martyrs of the Civil War. We've betrayed the Negro. We've betrayed the working man. We've betrayed the immigrant millions. We've betrayed each other. We've betrayed the early dream and promise of America.

Mr. Shawnessy drank the strong aroma of the cigar.

Betrayals. The saddest moment of our life is the moment of betrayal. To love someone is to betray someone.

Anguish welled up, a brackish water from dank cisterns. A thin smoke curling had lured him to this pitfall of memory.

Apostate sucking on a borrowed smoke in the Main Street of the Nation, reclaim your heritage. Decayed shell, incapable of tears. My God, how I wept in the old days! The terrible rivers of remembrance streamed from my eyes. Wandering, I went to the farthest limits of the land at evening.

Listen, I did not betray you. I remember you, though you are many years buried in the seed-dense earth. I remember your purity, your hurt eyes, and how I fled to the verge of our land in the evening. I remember the waning light of autumn day, all the land was a conflagration of the fallen and falling leaves, and I remember

November— How —1859

THE ROCK HAD LAIN

THERE ALWAYS AT THE LIMIT OF THE LAND,

immutable and lonely. Eggshaped, part-sunken in the ground, yet higher than a man, it lay in the South Field just short of the rail-fence. The land rose gently behind the farmhouse and then fell like a wave of waning strength to the limit of the field where the rock lay. The rock's immensely solid mass was tinged with red, and sometimes on summer evenings the great scarred shape would glow dull scarlet after the land had turned to gray. The moveless mass of it had been there before the settlers came, had been there when Columbus saw the flowering shores of western islands, had been there when the first man, wandering through the forests of the middle continent discovered a river winding to a lake. Centuries had flowed and faded around the rock as seasons did around the life of Johnny Shawnessy. And yet it had always seemed a stranger in this earth, a stranded voyager from other climes.

He could be sure that in the periphery of all his memories the rock had lain there at the limit of the land. If he had wished, he could have gone there at any time and put his hand on it. Perhaps he would have found the rough rind of it faintly warm.

But one day it seemed to Johnny that perhaps he discovered why the rock was there and what it waited for.

For the rock had been there too during that triumphant spring when Johnny Shawnessy had thrust himself to the inmost recesses of the County. When he lunged through the pollenous air of Lake Paradise and lay with one beautiful and alien, the rock had been there at the utmost verge of the Home Place though he had never given it a thought or wondered how it could be there at that same instant, or how it could be so abidingly at all.

And the rock had been there too when Susanna Drake went back to her own earth, and it was there when she came back to Raintree County.

In early November, Johnny got a letter that read:

Dearest Johnny,
I'm back.
Your own
SUSANNA

Grass was withering in the fields, and the rock at the limit of the Shawnessy land was a dull dome of color in the gray afternoon when he walked into Freehaven to see Susanna Drake. As he approached the house, standing white and mournful on its high lawn, his imagination involuntarily wished fire upon it, fire that would burn a vacant place against the sky and purge this shape and the memory of it from his life forever.

But after all he wasn't so badly off, if it came to that. He was not going to have his neck wrung like John Brown.

At the door, he was met by the Negro girl, who ushered him into the parlor. He sat down and waited. While he was waiting, he picked up the album and gloomily conned its pages. There were two or three new pictures of Susanna in various romantic attitudes. Susanna with Child, he mused, mournfully.

The daguerreotype of four people before the old Southern mansion was still there. He examined it more closely than before. When held to avoid reflection, this primitive legend of light and shadow had a precision of detail that more modern methods couldn't achieve. There were more than four faces in the picture after all. If you wanted to be pedantic, there were five, for the little girl was hugging a doll whose tiny features were clear like a cameo.

The father was a tall, lanky, bearded man, gentle and distinguished in appearance. The mother appeared to be a brunette, her face oval, her body fattish, her eyes distrustful, her mouth twisted. The little girl was a lovely, eager child, her face all eyes and mouth, as she clutched her doll with one hand and held her father's hand with the other.

Here was a fragment from the lost days of a little girl—innocent, scarless days, bathed in a brown light of arrested time. A secret lurked here in pools of shadow, like the lovely mulatto woman standing on the porch.

—Johnny!

He sprang up just in time to catch Susanna's half-naked body as she fled across the room in a white nightdress.

—O, Johnny! she said, don't leave me. I've been sick.

She was sobbing. It was no ordinary sobbing fit: it lasted a good hour by the clock. She clung to his neck, and when he sat down, she sat on his lap and wept on his coat and face. It was a fit of passion as violent in its way—and as seemingly authentic—as the one at Lake Paradise. Perhaps it was intended to have the same climax, for Susanna kept trying to press her mouth against his between fits of sobbing. But the superb young god of July had given place to a young man with gloomy November scruples. Johnny was terrified to think that he had caused a woman to weep in this way, and he found himself muttering reassuring affirmatives. When at last she seemed a little quieted, he started to say,

—But why didn't you let me know sooner, Susanna? Now it's——

At this point, the sobbing broke out afresh and with it an incoherent tide of explanation. She hadn't wanted to hurt him, she had tried to forget him, she had been very sick and unhappy, mysterious people—her own relatives and friends—had all turned against her in New Orleans, there had been shameful plots to get her property and her good name away from her, he had no idea what she had been through.

It was another half-hour before she subsided again, lying quiet in his arms with her head on his shoulder, like a heartbroken child, soothed but occasionally catching her breath and ready to break out afresh. He decided that the best thing he could do was to get away, if he could, and talk with her when she was calmer.

—I want a little time, he said, to think things out. I'll come back and see you again, Susanna.

The figure in his arms didn't stir, but continued to cling to him. Brusquely decisive, he stood up and lifted her to her feet. She offered no resistance, passively allowing him to use her as he pleased. Her eyes were faraway, mournful, pensive.

—I'll come back and see you again, Susanna.

She didn't say anything. He moved indecisively toward the door as she stood where he had set her, a picture of forlorn resignation. He felt ashamed of himself.

—Good-by, he said. And try not to worry. Things will work out all right.

She didn't say anything but threw herself down as if collapsing on the divan, and lay there, silent, with her face down, and hidden by the tumultuous black hair. In falling, the nightdress somehow was pulled up to show her bare thighs. Her feet were pointed to prolong the olive flowing length of her legs. Even in his distress, Johnny couldn't help noticing how beautifully formed she was. It seemed a little curious that no unsightly bulge marred the slenderness of Susanna's waist.

—Good-by, he said.

The figure on the couch merely drew a long, quavering breath. He went to the door, opened it, and started down the steps. He felt like running, but he took his time until he reached the street. There was no sound from the tall house. He turned his back on it and began to walk away. He turned a corner and drew a deep breath. He must have been holding his breath, for he was panting. He felt as though someone had been slapping his face.

He stopped in town for his mail. There was a letter for him from New York.

> Dear John,
>
> I am personally writing to the proper governmental authority requesting that a bronze medal be struck to commemorate your extraordinary achievement. It shall be engraved with the image of Venus bestowing a garland on the kneeling hero, the circular inscription to read:
>
> *Uno fulmine, terram perturbavit.*
>
> Seriously, my boy, I'm sorry this happened to you, and especially with the female in question. Under the circumstances, I feel I should reply to your highly personal query, if it will set your mind at ease. Yes, I saw that mysterious scar under the following auspices: You will recall that I was acting as duenna to a party of young people at that peculiar little pond in the middle of the County. Everyone was partaking freely of a poisonous compound supplied by Garwood Jones, and after a while I found myself in the water with Miss Drake. The lady is a perfect little hellcat when liquored up—but why tell you. Though I am but an indifferent swimmer, she and I arrived on the far shore, where we amused ourselves by frolicking in the water. The lady swims like a fish and insisted upon ducking me several times and

goddam near drowning me. The last time she pushed me under (squealing with lust) I took a good firm purchase on her bathing costume and ripped it open, whereupon I got a peek at Elysium. I guess I was doing the dress rehearsal for your performance.

Don't believe any other version you may hear of this incident.

As for Miss Drake, I think she's morally, emotionally, and politically problematical—to say the least. I have even darker suspicions. At any rate, boy, don't imagine that you seduced anybody. The seduction, if any, was strictly bilateral. My own impression is that you were the only virgin in that brawl.

Get out of it any way you can. Maybe a money settlement would do the trick, but I doubt it—she seems to have plenty of money.

Why are you so perplexed as to her motives? From among the various candidates for the honor of legitimizing the bulge, she elected you—understandably.

Maybe you could talk her into switching her attentions to someone else. By the way, do you think Garwood's been in there?

Yes, I'm in New York beating up news for the *Dial.* Would you care to have me run an item on your accomplishment? People are getting tired of balloonists and funambulists, and maybe a series on the Hoosier Hotshot (He only fars once, folks!) would titillate the jaded sensibilities of the *polloi.*

Apropos, New York is a nice place to get lost in. Better join me there if things get too hot in Raintree County. I firmly believe that the age of prophets and martyrs is over. Better be live Judas than dead Jesus.

Well, think I'll run along and get Under the Raintree myself. Her name is Agnes, and she stands five ten in her bare feet.

Fraternally yours,

JERUSALEM WEBSTER STILES

Johnny walked down to the Saloon. It was late, but Cash Carney was still standing in front talking with the boys. Johnny hadn't seen him for two weeks. He gave him the sign, and Cash walked over. The two of them went down a sidestreet.

—She's back, Johnny said.

—How's she look?

—You wouldn't know it.

He told Cash about his reunion with Susanna.

—Now, look, John, Cash said, I've given this a lot of time and thought. I've personally milked Garwood for everything I could find out. I got some names of some folks down there to write to. I've wrote some letters and received some replies. The more I see of this thing, the more I don't like it.

—I hope you conducted all this in secret.

Cash was lighting a cigar.

—Naturally, John! Of course, Garwood is a smart—puff, puff—bastard, and I think he smelled a mouse.

He exhaled a quantity of smoke.

—First I tried to draw Garwood out to find out how far he went with the girl himself. He wouldn't tell me a thing. Kept swatting me on the back and saying, Hell, I wouldn't do a thing like that to my own niece, Ha, Ha. There are laws against that, son, Ha, Ha. But I dug up a lot of dirt about the girl. She's only twenty-two years old, but she's been a wild one for years. According to Garwood, she ran off with her cousin's husband a year ago. They disappeared completely, and the rumor in New Orleans had it they'd run off to Jamaica. He come back a month or two later, very contrite, and Susanna come up here for the scandal to blow over. That was when we first saw her last spring. It seems that when she went back there this summer, people forgave her out of curiosity. She went to a lot of balls and parties and was seen everywhere with a lot of different men and there were rumors of engagements and so on, but nothing come of it. Nobody seems to know down there why she come back up here.

—What can I do?

—Just tell her you have no intention of being the sucker in this situation. Tell her she can't prove anything anyway, and the best thing she can do is to go back to her own people and try to catch someone back there.

Johnny felt a lump of sickness forming in his stomach and rising in his throat.

—I couldn't do it, Cash.

—I'll do it for you, Cash said. I'll go talk with her.

—I'd rather you'd not, Johnny said. Wait till you hear from me.

They talked some more, but to no purpose.

When he drove back home, he didn't know what he would do. In the far field of the Home Place under dripping skies, the rock lay, immutable and lonely. And the thought came over him that only the rock and the gray earth were lasting and that the tortured world of conscience, guilt, and consequence in which he lived was really nothing but a kind of mist that passed as seasons did over the immutable and mournful earth.

Meanwhile, the rock lay there lonely at the verge of his ancestral earth; and he didn't know it then, but in a sense it was waiting for him to discover it.

Only a few days later, he was driving his mother home from Freehaven, where he had arranged to meet her after some work at the *Free Enquirer* office. As they drove out of town on the old road east, he noticed that she hadn't said anything but was sitting with her hands folded in her lap and her eyes looking down the road. Ordinarily Ellen would have detailed all the adventures and encounters of the morning in a girlish, ungrammatical narrative. He gave her a quick slantwise glance. Her eyes were hurt, puzzled. She looked aging and pathetic. Her fussy old bonnet was tied on askew, her dark coarse hair had fallen in wisps and strings down her forehead and around her cheeks.

He drove gloomily in silence, waiting. At last, she said,

—Johnny, I want to talk with you about something.

In that one moment, the question was settled forever. He knew then that he would marry Susanna Drake. Thus only could he still the great voice of conscience, which was the voice of Raintree County.

—Yes, Mamma.

—I got a letter from someone today trying to tell me something that I hope isn't true. I got it right here.

She handed him a short note written in an unfamiliar scrawl, huge, childish letters that looked forged. 'Dear Mrs. Shawnessy,' it began, 'I think you should know that your son John . . .' It was signed, 'From a Well-meaning Friend.' It was explicit, accurate, completely damning.

—That isn't true, is it, Johnny?

A bitter emotion welled up in him. He wanted to be able to tell his mother that somehow he hadn't been disloyal to her belief in him, that he was still at heart the virtuous and fortunate Johnny, that there was still possible for him that great, good life to which long ago he had pledged himself on the breast of the land. But as he was aware of her sitting there, waiting, a woman no longer young, her face seamed with the passing of the years, her body clothed in the shapeless mother's garb of the County, when he thought of the shattered image in her heart, he realized that there could be no real explanation or communion between himself and her. He understood her Raintree County, but she could never understand his. She could never understand the young man's omnivorous appetite for life. To her, the young man's pagan world of beauty and desire, which no doubt God had intended for the perpetuation of life, would seem only vulgarity and lewdness.

Johnny Shawnessy bled helplessly in the old tragedy of the son's rebellion and couldn't say a word. But his silence was itself an answer.

—If it's true, Johnny, please tell me so. I want to know.

Now his emotion became so strong that he had to defend himself from it.

—It's none of your business, Mamma. Please stay out of it.

The words were said the only way they could be, short and bitter.

What she said after that and what he said were merely the truncated mouthings of the Oedipean agony. During the last halfmile of the road from Freehaven to the Home Place, mother and son drove in a shocked silence, which grew more and more terrible. When at last they reached the Home Place and he had driven the buggy up the drive, he wanted nothing more than to get out and run. In fact, he did get out and started walking swiftly across the land, striking off through the South Field as if he had a definite place to go. He felt as if he must get away from the Home Place and from his mother forever if he was to achieve manhood and independence. As he reached the curve of the earth, he heard the train passing on its way behind the woods toward the great bend of the river. It made its disconsolate wail of parting and farewell; the naked little engine and one passenger car were cleanly visible through the thinning foliage of the oak forest. It was evening. Leaves were falling in the woods as he approached the limit of the land.

—Johnny!

He turned. Ellen Shawnessy was coming down the long slow hill, an erect small person picking her way, halfrunning to catch up with him. He knew then that she was coming because she feared that in his grief and anger he might do himself some injury.

He had reached the rock that lay solid, faintly tinged with red just short of the railfence. He stopped and bent his head against it and said,

—Please go away, Mamma. I'm all right.

—I just want you to know, Johnny, that anything I've done or said was because I love you. If I done anything wrong, tell me what it was. I know that whatever you do'll be the right thing.

—Please go away, Mamma.

He hid his face against the rock. He was crying. He couldn't control the violent sobs that shook him. He hadn't cried since he was a child, but now he cried and didn't see how he could get hold of himself again.

After a while Ellen had gone back across the land, and it was night. The tears were all gone out of him then, the river of his being had dwindled to its source, the waters had retreated into distant and deep caverns. He stood a long time yet there at the limit of the land, leaning on the rock, and wondering how it was that he had come to be upon this land in the fading evening of the years beside a rock that knew no tears or time or laughter, love or passion or regret. And then he felt deeply stilled and strengthened, and he felt that he could never be hurt again by the world's opinion. Then he turned and walked back across the field

TOWARD THE YELLOW WINDOWS OF THE HOME PLACE

BECAUSE HE KNEW THAT THERE

WAS

—NOWHERE ELSE TO GO, the Perfessor was saying. That's why they came to America. This nation is the love-child of History. Dame Clio bore the others of a paternity known and acknowledged, but America was a lusty by-blow.

—There's a good deal to be said for the bastards of men or of nations, the Senator said. The bar sinister is a badge of vitality.

—All life is casually begot, the Perfessor said, but the bastard birth is less casual than the other kind. A certain amount of resolution goes into the fathering of your bastard. Believe me, as Willie Shakespeare says, some woman has to screw her courage to the sticking place—and vice versa.

The Perfessor leaned over and, using the tip of his malacca cane, began to draw lines in a patch of dusty earth between the store and the sidewalk.

—Behold the diagram of Life! he said. At the base of the diagram, there's an immense swamplike womb, and from this rises a giant tree, the umbilicus, through which saplike pours for aeons the stuff of life. Then dangling from this tree in its maturity would be a tiny seedpod, your post-natal individual, whose separation from the parent tree is, biologically speaking, a brief period. Actually we so-called mature individuals are only the pods of the tree, quaintly contrived to seduce one another so that the precious impulse that we carry, the immortal seed, may again and again be shaken back into the swamp of life.

The Senator got up and shook hands with a large lady from Indianapolis. He bowed, waggled his head, fondled her hand.

—There, said the Perfessor, the seedpod is shaking on its invisible tree. By a million winds of chance, the seed is sprinkled back into the womb of humanity, and the process goes on. Out of this swamplike womb grows the terrific tangle of the family trees and swinging briefly from some branches thereof are those little flowers of life, Jerusalem W. Stiles, John W. Shawnessy, and that big fulsome flower, Garwood B. Jones, the Senator from Indiana.

—Pure Darwinism, Professor. Where is History in this view? What is the life of a nation? And who—or rather what—is God?

—These questions I will leave to you, said the Perfessor.

—You were talking about genealogy, boys, the Senator said, sitting down again. I've been looking back into the family past of the Raintree County Joneses in connection with my forthcoming little opus. I'm proud to say that there isn't an earl or a duke in the family. Just a bunch of barefoot farmers and horsethieves. I recently got a letter from a fourflusher offering to hunt up a suitable coat of arms for me. I told the skunk to go ahead and see what he could find. What would you suggest for a heraldic device, Professor?

The Perfessor thought for a while.

—*An ass ascendant and about to bray,* he said.

—I have one for you, Professor, Mr. Shawnessy said.

—And what's that?

—*A serpent pendent from a branch of bay.*

—And for you, John, the Perfessor said, how about: *A Raintree rampant in a field of hay.*

Golden tree, never labelled by arborealists, I look far down from one of your topmost swinging branches to the shadowy trunk. Here is a good tree, tawny with shocks of shaken flowers, the Shawnessy Tree, spreading on the amorous air of summer the seedburst of its golden bloom. Here is a rare seed, brought overseas in old migrations. Beware, ye virgins! It was made for deep plantings. It will spring in your dark wombs with a fierce leaping, blindly hunting the channels of the future.

Seedtime, summer, and bearded harvest. O, young sporespreader, I lift a wisp of memoryladen smoke to you, fragrant with

November 22— THE —1859

SCENT OF WITHERED SUMMERS

HOVERED IN THE DUSK OF T. D.'S OFFICE,

where Johnny waited for his father to begin. T. D. sat finger-drumming on his desk. After a while he said without looking up,

—John, this marriage that you've announced. I uh ought to tell you that I don't entirely approve of the precipitate but uh under the circumstances necessary haste with which you have gone into it. I have found out something about the whole thing, and I am deeply pained, and——

T. D. looked out of the window at the gray November earth. Johnny stared at the anatomical chart on the wall. He hadn't seen T. D. so incoherent and pedantic since the time many years before when he had ushered Johnny into the Office to tell him the Facts of Life. At that time, he had taken a pointer and made certain indications at the anatomical chart on the wall. Eyes fixed on the chart now, Johnny saw, under the yellowing varnish, a man's body laid open to show the internal organs. The genitalia were a wrecked mass of blood vessels and tubes. Johnny felt only a dry resentment and a wish to get the thing over with.

—John, T. D. was saying, maybe I've got this whole thing wrong. I hope I have.

—I guess it's the way you heard it, Johnny said.

—You mean, T. D. said, stealing a glance at Johnny, you mean that you uh that you and this young woman——

—Yes, Johnny said. Yes, we did. I haven't any excuse. I got drunk on cider. It was after the Fourth of July Race.

—Fourth of July! T. D. said, reflecting. Jerusalem! boy, that was uh—that was——

He tapped his long fingers quickly——

—nearly five months ago!

—Yes, I know, Johnny said. I'd rather not talk about it, Pa. I was wrong. I'm trying to make it right.

—But this young woman uh, I saw her, you know. I went to see her, after someone wrote me an unsigned note and uh I didn't see any visible outward indication that she uh was in that uh shall we say advanced state of uh the gestatory process which reveals itself uh externally—that is, I——

—I know, Johnny said, feeling sorry for T. D. I don't know how to explain it. She *says* she's with child. It doesn't make any difference. I'm going to marry her anyway.

—She's uh she's quite an attractive young woman, you know, T. D. said, drumming on the table. She uh—that is, I understand how a man might—that is uh, given the circumstances, and the fact that, as you say, you had partaken of what I presume you thought was a harmless beverage—uh, I can see that—but of course, you understand, John, nothing can condone your uh headlong behavior. I had thought that of all my sons—that you——

—Yes, Johnny said, I know. I've been a terrible disappointment to you. I'm sorry.

—Not that I entirely blame you, T. D. said. You're after all only a boy—what?—twenty years old? At twenty, I myself—but then that's another matter. Still, I want you to know that I understand your feelings and I wish to express to you my uh——

At this point, T. D.'s verbal process broke down completely, and he stood head down before the lone window. There was a long silence.

—John, he said, more quietly, there's something I might as well tell you right now. I've told the three older boys, and it's been my intention to tell each of my children when they reached the age of twenty-one. Under the circumstances I think I might as well tell you now since you have uh after a manner of speaking reached the age uh—the age where uh——

Johnny had the strange feeling that somehow his own and his father's role had been subtly reversed and that he, Johnny, was now in the position of the judge and his father in that of the accused.

—I have a special reason for being glad, John, that you've done the manly thing in this case—though a bit late—and have decided to make it up to this young woman, whom you have uh—with whom you have——

—Yes, Johnny said.

—You might as well know it, John, T. D. said, turning around and squaring his shoulders. There is a stain on the name of Shawnessy. Do you know what I mean?

—No, I don't, Johnny said.

—You've never heard me speak much of my father, have you, John? I've always told you that he died in Scotland when I was very small and that my mother came to America with me. You don't know much about my life in Scotland, do you?

—No.

—Well, the truth is, T. D. said slowly, that Shawnessy is not the name of my father. My father's name was Carlyle. Shawnessy is my mother's name.

Johnny felt that he ought to understand now, but somehow he couldn't grasp the significance of what T. D. had said.

—No use mincing words, T. D. said. I was the issue of an illegitimate union.

T. D. squared his shoulders and turned around, looking a little belligerent. His blue eyes flashed. His rabbity mouth worked under his immense blond mustache.

—In plain English, my boy, I'm a bastard. Just a good cleancut bastard.

—O, Johnny said. Is that a fact?

It was the strongest word he had ever heard T. D. use. He felt relief and also a new respect for T. D., who was (the word was somehow comforting) a bastard.

—Yes, sir, T. D. said. I bear what men might call a dishonored name. But I have never been ashamed of the name of Shawnessy. It's the name of my mother, a superb woman.

—Yes, sir, Johnny said, coming crisply to attention.

—As for my father, T. D. said, he bore a name which has since become famous in the world.

Then Johnny understood why it was that T. D. had so often told the children that they were related to a name famous in letters. He had never been explicit about the closeness of that connection, saying only that it was through his father's side of the family.

—Yes, sir, T. D. was saying in his old brisk voice, as if he had suddenly got back all his old assurance, yessirree, and when I got to be old enough to understand my situation, I swore I'd make the name of Shawnessy as great as the name of Carlyle. Here in America, in a virgin wilderness, where a man's name and past mean nothing, I meant to make the name of Shawnessy a great one in the world.

Johnny nodded. T. D. began to walk back and forth, vibrant with the preternatural energy that seemed to flow into him at times.

—I can't say, T. D. said, that I've entirely realized all my ambitions. I suppose I've been handicapped by a want of education, and perhaps I lacked the native ability to realize my hopes. Not that I consider my life a misspent one. Not at all.

—Of course not, Johnny said.

—I come west with the country, T. D. said. I married young and had children to support. I've grown up with this great country, and I've been one of those who made it grow. I was one of the first settlers in Raintree County. When I come here, this was a wilderness. I've saved the lives of many Americans. I've done my small part for the spiritual welfare of the people of this republic. And if the name of Shawnessy don't become famous in the land, as famous as the name which by rights I ought to bear is in England, I am not in the least ashamed of it. I'm proud of it. And I want my children to be proud of it. I'd rather be Timothy Duff Shawnessy in America than a king in England.

—Certainly, Johnny said.

—In America, T. D. said, nobody cares about a man's past. If I've not become a great man, I've only myself to blame. But I want my children to know that I pass on to them a great name, my mother's, and I'm still confident that in generations to come people will speak the name of Shawnessy with reverence. I take as yet the most hopeful view of my own future and that of my children.

T. D. paused then, with one long arm outflung, and seemed to reflect upon something that he had forgotten.

—But that brings me to say, John, that there's—well—a kind of curse on the Shawnessys. I've noticed it in myself, and I'm afraid that you and perhaps other members of our family bear the mark of it. We're a passionate people, John, us Shawnessys. We are at one and the same time seekers after knowledge, scholars, poets, teachers, and preachers—and also, alas! lovers of beauty. And this second trait is the fatal one. I know, my boy, that you wrestle under more extreme temptation than most men. I know, because I myself have uh in my youth felt that fatal uh susceptibility. It's hard for a Shawnessy to resist a beautiful woman. It's our curse, my boy, an amiable one—and one, may I say, which I'd be very unhappy not to have, but just the same a curse.

—Yes, sir, Johnny said.

He found it easier to bear his sense of guilt, when he discovered that he had come by it honestly from his grandmother. The fault had acquired a certain dignity and family standing.

—All my younger life, I fought against this legacy of my noble mother, T. D. was saying. I think I may say that I fairly mastered it. By the way, don't breathe a word of this to your mother.

—Of course not, Johnny said.

—Who are we, T. D. said, beginning unconsciously to adopt his pulpit manner, to judge of these moments of weakness? The father and mother of the race sinned. They knew each other in guilty passion after they did eat of the forbidden fruit. 'Tis an ancient curse. Yea, my son, who are we to question the weakness of a woman who surrenders to her desire? No more virtuous woman lived than my mother. She loved and sinned. That was all. But I beg you to take notice, my boy, that if she hadn't, where would you and I be?

T. D. and Johnny looked shyly at each other for a split second and lowered their eyes.

Who shall assign a value to the event or to its consequence? Life has its own inscrutable ends to serve. My grandmother, I am glad that you were once an amorous girl and had the weakness—and the courage—of your love. I am glad, my grandmother, that you allowed yourself to be tumbled in a hayfield beside the little town of Ecclefechan in Scotland years ago. Who knows but even then you fell under the compulsion of the springing impulse that was I! Did you not sin and suffer that I might one day flower and be fair? It was a great gift that you gave that day, my grandmother, in your desirous girlhood. You were one of the makers of America, my gay and guilty paternal grandma. And a woman who gives herself for love only, and without hope of moral security, is she not more courageous than the other kind? O, peerless, antique little Scot, you deserved to give your own great name unto your children and your children's children. Now it can never die. Another of your line has been busy to that end, in your own inimitable style, my wee, unvirginal grandma.

—I hope, T. D. was saying, that you don't take this thing too hard.

—Not at all, Johnny said. I'm glad you told me. It makes me feel a little better.

—As for your own case, my boy, T. D. said, you've done the manly thing. I hope this young lady is all that she appears to be. *Judge not that ye be not judged.*

—Yes, sir.

—Marry her, my boy, T. D. said, standing up erect and tall and holding out his hand, and be happy. Do you need money?

—No, I believe not, Papa.

—When is the wedding?

—December 2, Johnny said. Susanna's choice.

He shook his father's hand and left the Office.

Later on in the evening, he was aware that T. D. was still out in the Office, with no light on. Undoubtedly, he was pacing there in his cluttered cage, a distinguished-looking gentleman with a large blond mustache, marching back and forth surrounded by the Botanical Medicines. He had come to America to make himself famous, and somehow he had got lost in the land. It was strange now to think how some fifty years ago there had been a casting of seed in a putative hayfield in Scotland, and the vital impulse in it was strong, so very strong, that it was carried safely over the sea and so very, very strong that it was carried west and west. Along the way it had lodged in fertile earth, and now there were many vessels, bearers of seed, many and many on the breast of the land.

O, strange little swimmer of so long ago, o, little immortal! What difference is it to you what name you bear! What do you care for a name! O, little lifegiver, you only are eternal. We exist only for you, and you pay us back by faint repetitions of our features, for you never forget anything. You remember us,

YOU REMEMBER OUR FACES, AS YOU PROCEED

UPON YOUR WAY, JETTING

EPHEMERAL

FACES on the Great Road of the Republic floated through the haze of Mr. Shawnessy's cigar, rising out of vacant time and fading into vacant time. He thought of all the faces of mankind that had passed briefly through the world of time and space. Flowerlike they rose—like flowers springing and like dense flowers falling and fading back into the swamp.

—Did you ever stop to consider what a face is, Professor?

—Isn't it bad enough to have one, the Perfessor said, without having to explain it?

—It's a strange fact, Mr. Shawnessy said, that a woman carries her face naked for all the world to see and thinks she's respectable because she hides the rest in clothes. The hidden part is, after all, very simple, but the face is delicate, mobile, passionate. The flesh of it moves, the eyes glance about, the lips make sounds. If like Hawthorne's minister or the Moslem women, we veiled our faces, we'd learn to value the secrecy and mystic beauty of these big lush flowers.

—The face is merely a traffic center for sense organs, the Perfessor said. For economy's sake, it got crammed together. A face is really a pretty loathsome proposition, you know.

—The face is a human discovery, Mr. Shawnessy said. Other animals don't think of themselves as having separate faces. And only human beings make love face to face. What an exciting discovery that must have been for some dawn man!

—An ancestor of yours maybe? the Perfessor said. His name should go down to us along with Cadmus, who invented the alphabet. Perhaps the name Shawnessy is a direct lineal derivative and means He-Who-Made-Love-Face-to-Face.

—A face, Mr. Shawnessy said, is also a memory of a million other faces. Our faces are palimpsests. Like all things human, faces are both synoptic and unique.

—Have you ever stopped to figure, John, how fearfully fouled up our family trees are? Each human being is fifty thousand kinds of cousin to the stranger he passes on the street. Each time we make love to a woman we're committing infinitely multiplied incest. Nothing is more certain.

—How is that? the Senator said. I'm damned if I follow that.

—It's a simple question of arithmetic, the Perfessor said. Each person is the child of two. Each of these was the child of two. That makes four. Each of these was the child of two. That makes eight. Each of these was the child of two. That makes sixteen. Now, go on in that fashion, and assume that there's no intermarriage of relatives back to the time of Charlemagne. That would be about fifty generations only. On that basis, do you know how many human beings were living in the time of Charlemagne to form the base of the pyramid of which you are the apex?

—I give up, the Senator said.

—Roughly about six hundred trillion. Just for you—mind you. That's leaving out of account other human beings now living. Think of all the incest near and far there must have been in order that the few hundred million human beings actually living in Charlemagne's time could sire the much greater number living now. A few generations back and our family trees get so damnably scrambled that individual names and faces no longer have any importance at all, I assure you. Let me remind you, too, that this does not even take us back to the time of Christ. And even two thousand years is only a quarter of a mile in the Mississippi of human descent. Man has been more or less man for two hundred thousand years. In all this muck of human beings, what is an individual face?

The Perfessor adjusted his glasses and stroked his brows with sensitive fingertips.

—Biologically, the Perfessor went on, there's just one face—with the standard fixtures. All the fuss people expend on their damfool faces is part of the fuss they make over themselves as damfool individuals. The life-impulse doesn't really care anything about faces. The ugliest people I know have the most children, and they're all ugly like their parents. Very beautiful women often have no issue, or ugly issue. Ugly and beautiful, like moral and immoral, are unknown to the Republic of the Great Swamp, which really doesn't give a hang who your forebears were. It only cares that the seed be sifted back into the muck so that the little faces will pop out again, year after year, generation after generation, and seduce each other like flowers, innocently and promiscuously.

The Perfessor snorted and puffed on his cigar.

—What do you think of that, John?

—I think that you don't understand faces. Your remorseless logic leaves out the most significant fact about faces.

—What's that?

—That a face is a map.

—You speak in parables.

—It takes some explaining and involves my whole philosophy, but——

He was interrupted by a chord of male voices from the door of the barber shop. A quartet, calling themselves the Freehaven Chanticleers, were beginning a brief program of popular airs to entertain the Senator.

—Don't you remember sweet Alice, Ben Bolt?
Sweet Alice, whose hair was so brown. . . .

Faces of his life rose on the pale stream of the years, like images on cards turning slowly over and over in riverpools. Slowly the white flesh dissolved from the bone. The faces were gone, lost in winter nights. But there had been a republic in which these faces had seemed immortal. Shimmering, it had risen from the Great Swamp, and even the Great Swamp was one of its immortal images. Was this republic really the fool of time? Where was the fading ruin of all its faces?

The Chanticleers had begun another song.

—Beautiful dreamer, wake unto me,
Starlight and dewdrops are waiting for thee. . . .

Wake unto me, faces of an old republic. Where did you come from, children of a golden god? Like big lush flowers, you briefly swayed in white seductions.

—Over the streamlet vapors are borne,
Waiting to fade at the bright coming morn.
Beautiful dreamer, beam on my heart,
E'en as the morn on the streamlet and sea;
Then will all clouds of sorrow depart. . . .

Beautiful dreamer, wake unto me! It was in a cold dawn of the unreturning years, and our tears and kisses mingled on our cheeks. There was a path that time never took, down ribboning rails to the great and golden West. Beside the little river that flows into the lake, on the banks where we played in childhood's golden summer, we two were torn apart long ago, and your pale face glimmered down the vistas of the morn, long ago, long ago, and o, I remember, I remember, your sweet face fading in the mists above the river till the purple haze of morning wreathed it from my view.

The Chanticleers were singing an encore.

—I remember the days of our youth and love. . . .

Mr. Shawnessy ached with love-desire, as there awakened, within the shell of middle-age, the young Shawnessy, the shockheaded boy, tender and sentimental, the adolescent god of early American days.

—Nevermore will come those happy, happy hours,
Whiled away in life's young dawn;
Nevermore we'll roam thro' pleasure's sunny bowers,
For our bright, bright summer days are gone.

Listen! are you there, face of the young Shawnessy, face that is only half of the archetypal human face, seeking for the other half that will make up the sum of ideal beauty, hunting down the lanes and over the cornfields of an infinite number of hypothetical Raintree Counties! I see you momentarily—a young god, tall. Your hair is shaken into sunlight. You hunt a tree beside the river where you will find at last the face that you were seeking.

—How we joyed when we met, and grieved to part,
How we sighed when the night came on;
How I longed for thee in my dreaming heart,
Till the first fair coming of the dawn.

She has risen from the river. Hurry, be fleet, for the bark is closing on her whitemuscled loins, her face is covered up in leaves. And it is dark, dark, dark in the woodlands of all the Raintree Counties that never were, it is a long, long time till the first fair coming of the

December 1–2— DAWN —1859

AND ITS DAY OF

LONG FAREWELL WERE STILL

many hours distant as Johnny Shawnessy rode home from Freehaven to the Home Place, returning from a bachelor's dinner given him by Garwood Jones and Cash Carney. On the morrow he was to be married.

The night was cloudy, raw, and moonless but not dark. He could see the wet road palely dissolving in the bleak night; he could see damp fields, dark masses of forest, and the mute farmhouses, lightless at this late hour.

Crossing the bridge at Danwebster, he looked down at the river, a cold, cheerless water. Around him was the immutable and mournful earth of Raintree County, and beyond, the great plains rolling east and west and north and south, the valleys, mountains, deserts of America; beyond that the limitless, cold oceans, and the whole waste of earth, slowly revolving in the night of human time. Was it his earth? Did he hold lasting title to a single handful of it?

He thought of people wandering in the night or making love or dying—all over the Republic. Was one any more important than another? Did any of them possess anything that they could keep forever? Did the lovers really possess each other in the night? Did they really become one? Did the bride and groom really marry and belong forever to each other?

He was thinking then of John Brown, who had fought for the freedom of a few million nameless black men, shadowy projections of the Southern earth where they toiled. What good had it done John Brown to believe, to labor long and hard, to go up and down in the land? Now he would have one brief, reluctant morning. He would have one long farewell.

Perhaps it was better to make a few concessions and live a little longer than to be once brave and forever dead.

But then did it really matter so much if the neck snapped at a predictable time? Wasn't each sleeper in his bed condemned and merely enjoying a stay of execution? Light was coming always, in great beams up the eastern marches of the earth. No one could keep the old man from the rope. John Brown must die, terribly alone as all men must.

But John Shawnessy was alive. He would go tomorrow to far, strange places. He would escape and pleasure himself with a barbaric love while the old man went down to a dirty grave.

On a clear, cold day in mid-November, Johnny had gone back to the tall house in Freehaven to ask Susanna's hand in marriage. Ushered in by a Negro girl, he had waited on the divan in the parlor. After a very long time, the maid returned.

—Miss Susanna will receive in her room upstairs.

He followed the maid up the stair from the hall and into a huge bedroom occupying most of the secondfloor front.

The room was shaded by gorgeous red curtains closely drawn over the single window, which was the middle one of five on the front of the house. At first Johnny couldn't see very well, but slowly his eyes made out a canopied bedstead scarlet-draperied like the window and closed on all sides. Except for mirrors placed at intervals along the walls, the rest of the room was almost empty of furniture.

The maid stopped at the door.

—Here's the young gentleman to see you, Miss Susanna.

—Come in, Johnny.

It was Susanna's voice, plaintive and remote from the depths of the bed. The draperies faintly stirred on the side nearest him.

Johnny walked over to the bed.

—How does a person get into this thing?

—Just pull that cord there, the voice in the bed said. I haven't been well, Johnny.

—I'm sorry, Johnny said.

He jerked the cord, and the curtains parted and shot back on his side.

In the darkly scarlet depths of the huge bed he could see Susanna's face looking at him from under a sheet. But what startled him was that a hundred other faces were peering at him from the shadowy corners and walls of the bed—tiny, motionless faces, grotesquely fixed at a hundred different angles.

The bed was aswarm with dolls.

Dolls were sitting on the head and foot of the bed, dolls were lying in the corners of the bed, dolls were propped against the head and footboards, dolls were hanging by their coats on hooks. There were all sizes from one as small as a thumb to a monster with a fat, creamy face, leering happily from a sitting position at the foot of the bed. All the dolls stared with a horrible, waxy fixity at nothing at all. Most of them were male.

—My word! Johnny gasped. Are they all friendly?

In the middle of this asylum of hideously diversified little human heads, Susanna lay voluptuously alive, softly moving her shoulders, but only her face showed above the sheet, peculiarly broad and lush in the reclining position. She looked savagely healthy. A shy smile curved her lips.

—Sort of a hobby, she said.

—How—how many are there?

Susanna looked gravely around at the dolls.

—One hundred and sixteen now, counting Jeemie, she said. This is Mr. John Wickliff Shawnessy, children.

—Pleased to meet you, fellows, Johnny said, bowing formally. Nice day, isn't it?

The dolls continued to stare fixedly at nothing at all, a hundred lidded, mysterious little faces.

—They've been sick children today, Susanna said, and they've all had to go to bed.

—My word! Johnny said. Don't tell me you move this gang around with you!

—O, yes, Susanna said. Sometimes we sit on chairs, and sometimes we play on the floor, and sometimes we dress and undress ourselves, don't we, children?

Susanna looked entirely pathetic and adorable in the great bed as she gravely harangued her dolls. Johnny sat down on the edge of the bed and took one of her hands. She allowed him to have it, extending her naked arm from under the sheet.

—Susanna, I have come to ask your hand in marriage.

She lay for a long time merely looking pensively at the dolls, not changing her position. At last she said in a forlorn, low voice,

—You don't have to marry me, Johnny. I release you. As for the child——

—I don't care about the child, Johnny said fiercely. I have asked your hand in marriage, and I expect a reply.

Susanna turned and looked a long time into his eyes with her violet eyes. Then with her free hand she pulled the sheet down a little from the pillow revealing a doll Johnny hadn't yet seen lying with its little head on the pillow beside her. All the other dolls were beautifully clean and newlooking, but this doll had evidently been through a fire. Its clothes were charred and browned, and its head was blistered and blackened.

—What about it, Jeemie? Susanna said to the doll. Shall we marry this gentleman? He's a very lovely young man, and I love him very much, Jeemie. I love him much, much, much more than any of the rest. What do you think, Jeemie?

She looked inquiringly at the firepuffed face on the pillow which in the darkness looked like a little Negro's.

—What does he say? Johnny said, grinning in spite of himself.

—We accept, Susanna said.

Her large lovely eyes were suddenly filled with tears. She squeezed Johnny's hand and let her free arm bend loosely over his neck so that the open hand swung back and forth languidly at his throat. It was surprising how heavy this hand was, pulling his head down toward hers. Her deep lips pouted and parted under his. She was shuddering with sobs.

—O, Johnny, she said, I *do* love you so much.

—And I love you too, Johnny said, thinking that perhaps after all he did love this strange, passionate, wistful, wandering child who had come back to him from the Deep South.

But his position was an awkward one, as he still sat on the bed with his head bent all the way down.

—Here, get in with us, Susanna said, and lying on her side, with a quick motion she flipped the sheet back.

She was completely naked. She touched her hand delicately to the everpresent scarlet scar that burned cruelly into the beginnings of the left breast, which—downtilted, tipped with rose—swung softly from the motion of her shoulders.

Confused, Johnny accidentally put his hand on the burnt doll. He picked it up.

Susanna stopped sobbing and watched intently. Johnny carefully put the doll at the top of the pillow. Susanna looked at him and then looked at the doll, sitting stiffly at the top of the pillow.

—There now, Jeemie, how's that? Johnny said. You can see everything from there.

Susanna smiled sweetly and sank back on the pillow.

—I'm glad the family likes me, Johnny said, feeling as though he had successfully passed an examination of some kind.

—We *love* you, Johnny, Susanna said.

And with her catlike strength she pulled him violently down upon her, where he lay fully dressed in a tweed suit, stiff collar, and shiny knobtoed shoes. Disturbed, the doll population shook on their hooks and nodded vigorously and in unison from their perches on the head and footboards. One fell down and sat astraddle Johnny's neck. The big one at the foot of the bed bent over and tackled him heavily on the calves. Another fell with a faint squeak on the small of his back. For a moment, he felt as though he was being attacked by hideous dwarfs, while his face was only three inches away from the dreadful, seared face of the doll Jeemie.

Suddenly, Susanna began to laugh, and Johnny laughed too, as it was all rather absurd and delightful. Susanna laughed with little high shrieks and sobs, and while she laughed her sinewy arms and legs seemed to envelop him in a net of nudity. She laughed and laughed, and the doll heads laughed too, all gently nodding in happy unison.

That was how Johnny Shawnessy had proposed marriage to Susanna Drake, and that was how his proposal had been accepted.

The day following this adventure with a sick girl and a hundred and sixteen dolls, Johnny had his approaching marriage announced in the newspapers. When he dropped in at the *Clarion* office, Garwood Jones, who had become the editor-in-chief a few weeks before, was busy filling the copy hook.

—Hi, sprout, he said, when Johnny showed up.

Garwood kept on writing. He was in shirt sleeves and bowtie, and his lush dark hair was attractively mussed. His big mobile, sensual mouth pursed at the pencil as he studied for the next word.

—I'm getting married, Garwood, Johnny said casually. Here's an item on it.

Garwood didn't bother to look up.

—Go away and be funny somewhere else, he said. I'm busy as hell.

—I really am, Johnny said. And I expect a little better treatment than this from my in-laws.

—Huh? Garwood said. All right. You're getting married. Who is it?

—This will give you all the needful information, Uncle, Johnny said, dropping the item on Garwood's desk.

—Well, I'll be goddamned! Garwood said, as Johnny went out of the door. Susanna!

In the newspapers, the announcement sounded very official and correct. The *Clarion* in particular laid itself out to do the thing right.

APPROACHING NUPTIALS ANNOUNCED

> The long and happy engagement of Mr. John Wickliff Shawnessy and Miss Susanna Drake will soon be consummated in marital union, the prospective groom disclosed today. This festive event, toward which the friends and relatives of the blissful pair have long been looking with keen anticipation, has been set for December 2 and at the bride's request will be held at the Danwebster Methodist Church, with the groom's father, the Reverend T. D. Shawnessy, presiding. Among the many unusual and romantic features of this genuine love-match is the fact that the bride is a former resident of the Sunny South. Her frequent visits to friends in Freehaven began the friendship which soon ripened into reciprocal esteem and at last achieved the full flower of mutual love. The groom, a young newspaperman and writer of promise, is well-known throughout Raintree County as the author of . . .

A good deal of mischief was circulated at Johnny's expense by his male friends, but the female contingent of his own family bravely conducted a series of parties at which the bride and groom appeared sometimes singly, sometimes together.

The most embarrassing moment in all the hectic days before the marriage, came when Johnny presented Susanna to his parents. At the appointed time, he brought her from town and ushered her into the front parlor of the Home Place, which was always kept cool and closed, with the shades drawn except for special visits. Ellen Shawnessy had on a new dress, and T. D. was togged out in his one good suit. Susanna had been very nervous on the way over, but when she came in she was all grace and loveliness. Her manner toward Johnny's mother was a mixture of girlish humility and ladylike reserve. Johnny could tell that Ellen was pleased, and as for T. D. he rocked violently on his heels, yawned, blinked, smiled, bowed, and chuckled with satisfaction. Susanna insisted upon hearing him recite the famous 'Ode on the Evils of Tobacco' and listened attentively without a single trace of amusement even on the two celebrated lines:

> Some do it chew and some it smoke
> Whilst some it up their nose do poke.

She talked with Ellen very diligently about the preparation of certain Southern dishes, admired her dress, which was too large for her bony little figure, and remarked that she saw now where Johnny got his beautiful smile and hair. She also met some of Johnny's brothers and sisters and was very sweet to them all. There wasn't a single slip on anyone's part, except that Zeke whistled when he first saw Susanna. It was a wonderful performance, and Johnny was as grateful and proud as under the circumstances it was possible for him to be.

After it was over and Johnny was taking Susanna home, she said,

—I just *love* your folks, Johnny. They're awfully sweet. I see now why you're the way you are. Johnny——

She had said the name suddenly and plaintively.

—Yes.

—I want to tell you something.

—Yes.

—I'm not going to have a child after all.

—O.

—I lied about it, Susanna said, dropping her eyes and nervously smoothing her left coat lapel.

—What for?

But he was so immensely relieved that he couldn't feel angry at the imposture.

—Because I wanted you more than anything I can remember since I was a little girl.

As far as Johnny was concerned, this was the perfect excuse. The dmission proved one thing conclusively—that for some reason Suanna Drake was really in love with him. Now, suddenly, he felt ery cheerful and innocent, as if, after all, everything had been crupulously correct from the start.

—Tell me something, Susanna. With your money and looks, you ould have married a lot of different men. Why did you want me?

—I never cared much for the men I met before, except in a passing ort of way. But the minute I laid eyes on you, I fell in love.

—Why? What was it?

—O, I couldn't explain it to you, she said, smoothing and smoothng her left coat lapel. Any woman would know.

She turned and touched his cheek near the mouth with her right and and looked intently at his face with the wistfully childlike look f her photographs.

—But you'd look better with beard and mustaches, Johnny, she aid. More manly.

In the days preceding the marriage, Ellen Shawnessy threw all her nergy into preparations for the event, and in general Raintree County ose heroically to the task of making everything conform to its ancient anons of respectability. There was a great deal to do. Everything vas complicated by Susanna's decision that she wanted to go away mmediately after the marriage ceremony. The happy pair were to atch the train at Freehaven and follow a tight schedule which vould bring them by nightfall to the city of Louisville, Kentucky, on he other side of the Ohio River from Indiana. This was to be the tart of a long honeymoon in the South. The loving pair were going o go by steamboat down the Ohio to the Mississippi, and from there o New Orleans, where Johnny would have a chance to meet Suanna's relatives. It all sounded lustrous and magnificent and helped ive a respectable air to the whole undertaking. In fact, all of ohnny's friends began to consider his precipitate marriage a step up n life for him. He had married money, beauty, and culture. Raintree County's fairhaired boy was making good after all.

There were some clouds, of course. Another letter from the Peressor failed to sound very exultant. One part of it in especial disurbed Johnny.

> As for a dark suspicion you say I mentioned in my last letter, I can't even remember what it was, so it must not have been very important. Forget it, my boy, and be happy. You have a beautiful girl who loves you and whom you love. By all means, my boy, marry her, love her, beget broods of happy cherubim, go on, my boy, to greater and better things. . . .

This stereotype sounded vaguely familiar and thoroughly insincere to Johnny, and besides it was out of tune with the rest of the letter, which made merry at the expense of the sacred human institution of marriage.

As for the evasive remark concerning a dark suspicion, Johnny was perfectly well aware that Professor Jerusalem Webster Stiles never forgot anything.

The worst thing about it all was that Johnny hadn't stopped loving Nell Gaither. Everything he had done with Susanna and even Susanna's beauty had merely inflamed the passion that he had for his own privately created Venus with the Raintree County face. In a way he felt that he had not been unfaithful to her. What had happened to him had been a strange accident of fate, caused by occult events and surroundings.

In that wild taking in deep grass under the tree, where the sun fell steeply slanting on two stones, and the leaves had dropped a thin brightness like sifted sunshine, and the tree had swayed, a slender and great reed, and he had seen not very far away the river where it was hardly to be told from the lake (or the lake where it was hardly to be told from the river—green waters swollen with beautiful lifeforms), then he had known that the secret of Raintree County was indeed a secret of water and earth and tree, stone, and the living golden seed, and he had known too that it was a shared secret and could only be carried in the vessel of a woman's body, and he knew also that it must be brought from afar and bear a rhythmical (though, for the moment, a forgotten) name and that she who brought it must be likewise a creature of the river, though whether her hair was black or brown or golden did not greatly matter, and he had known too that she must bear upon her body a secret imperfection and he had known too, even in that savagely sweet moment, he had known already by anticipation that to learn the secret was also to learn duty and hot tears.

As he rode home in the night to the Home Place after the bachelor party, that secret plagued him with a delicious sorrow. The secret of human love and desire was to discover something that was at once universal and particular—beauty and a person. At Lake Paradise, he had been lost in the universal. It was only later that he realized that all life is personal beyond escape.

Ever since the Fourth of July outing, he had avoided seeing Nell and had allowed her note of reconciliation to go unanswered. Of course, it had been necessary to go to church, where she appeared without fail, imperially calm as usual. When he reminded himself that this person had once been naked in his arms and that her flower-like mouth had clung to his in long, long kisses, he was sick with love.

It was not mere longing of the flesh; it was a total longing to possess someone. To him, Nell Gaither was an entire republic of beauty and nostalgic memory, which now he had to relinquish.

When he reached the Home Place, it was after midnight, and everyone else had gone to bed. He went to his room and undressed in the dark. When he pulled back the covers and lay down, his face touched something pinned to his pillow. It had been concealed under the cover. He lit a lamp and unpinned an envelope addressed, 'To Johnny.' Inside was a piece of letterpaper beautifully inscribed with a message:

> One for whom you once professed affection would esteem it a generous action on your part, though undeserved on hers, if you would see her once again before you leave the County. She will be waiting near a certain spot sanctified to the memory of a profane but sweet encounter. Let your heart and the memory of a blissful hour (perilous, yes, but alas! all the more precious in recollection to one at least who shared its raptures) tell you the name of her who penned these lines.

He reread the note several times, savoring its stylistic beauties, which were as good as a signature. Probably one of his sisters (who were not very happy about the coming marriage) had connived in placing it on his pillow.

With perhaps insufficient reflection, he dressed again and started to slip out of the window, which was on the ground floor. Then he crawled back in and got a big volume out of the bookcase. He hunted among some private papers and keepsakes in a drawer and put something in the book. Then he climbed out of the window again and slipped out to the road. He crossed it and walked through a field following a lane that led to the river. He stayed out of the forest fringe of the river but followed it north along the Indian Battle-ground. Halfway up the long northwardflowing arm, he cut into the forest, walking among the leafless trees. The ground was deep with damp leaves. There was a cold, dripping mist in the air, almost a rain. He could hear the river trickling between dissolving banks. As he neared the bank opposite the Johnny Shawnessy oak and the pool where he and Nell had swum together, he made out the form of a young woman muffled in a long furcollared coat. She stood by the trunk of a big tree. She was hatless, and she had a large dark object under her arm.

—Hello, Nell.

—Hello, Johnny.

—I got the note, he said. It—it was beautifully written. I—I appreciate your thinking of me, especially at this time.

The tree under which they stood had extinguished the smaller trees within its widebranching circumference, and now that it stood in wintry nudity, the space beneath it was less dark than the forest around. The river swirled not five feet below them. He could make out Nell's face, small and piquant at the top of her muffled form. It had a pensive, distant look.

—I have something, Johnny, I feel I ought to return to you, she said. I thought probably you would want it back, now—now that I don't mean anything to you any more.

She held out the big dark object. It was no doubt *The Complete Works of William Shakespeare.*

—And I've left in it your image, she said, which I would like to keep, but considering the poem on the back, feel I am no longer entitled to.

Her voice had a sweet, trailing, rehearsed sound.

—I won't take it, Johnny said. I'm entirely at fault in this thing, and for that reason I feel that I ought in all honor to return something to you which is more precious to me than life itself but of which I have shown myself unworthy.

He held out the book he had brought with him, a large dark volume. Doubtless, it was a copy of *The Complete Poetical Works of Lord Byron.*

—And I've left in it your image, he said, the image of your

beautiful face, which I will always remember with love and admiration.

—I won't take it, Nell said.

They stood in darkness awkwardly presenting these two huge volumes, some twelve pounds of words, Johnny reflected, by two of the greatest poets of the English language, twelve pounds of distilled, passionate, violent, rhythmical, confused language, the outpouring of man's desire for life, beauty, and the good, words of the wonderful tragi-comedy of human life.

—I really don't want to give mine up, Nell said, her voice beginning to sound more and more dim and rehearsed. It's just because I know you don't care for me any more and because you're being married. I just wanted to say to you, Johnny, in the words of that dear book which you gave me and inscribed to me, *If ever thou didst hold me in thy*——

Her voice, which had been getting smaller and higher, suddenly dissolved in a little shriek of anguish. Johnny tossed his book on the ground and put his arms around Nell. He turned her face up to his, and when he did, this face, which he had always seen (except once) so deceptively composed, was all wet with tears, and the flowerlike mouth kept turning down at the corners and emitting cries of sorrow. Then the mouth found his mouth and kissed him again and again as if it would devour him with hunger. *The Complete Works of William Shakespeare* fell on the ground. The two bodies tightened to each other. He kissed her mouth, her eyes, her forehead, her hair, her cheeks, her chin, her throat, and again and again her mouth, which melted into his with a taste of passion and farewell.

The old image of escape flashed into his mind. It would be so easy. He knew with a tempting certainty that he had only to say the word. Together they would slip away in the night. They would catch the early morning train at Three Mile Junction, and by morning they would have left Raintree County far behind. Somewhere in the West, the great and golden West, a man might begin life all over again and——

But he knew that he couldn't say the word. Somehow the whole thing had been decided when he stood by the rock at the limit of the land. One betrayal was enough. Then he had said good-by to an older, sunnier County. Then the borders of his private little earth had dissolved into something called the Republic, full of duty and the memory of a crime.

—Nell, he said, I love you, and will always love you. I tell you now in the most absolute secrecy that my marriage is the result of an error on my part. My wife-to-be is a lovely woman whom I admire and whom I hope I may learn to love, but I wouldn't now be saying good-by to you—forever—if I hadn't made a slip. It was the afternoon of the Fourth of July, I had drunk all that whiskey, which wasn't exactly my fault, and then we went on that picnic and——

—Everyone knows about that, Johnny, Nell said. O, dear! Johnny, why do you have so much conscience!

This remarkably feminine statement, so subtly illogical, startled him and brought him more or less to his senses. If everyone knew, then he was indeed right in pursuing the path of rectitude and in clearing his honor and good name before the County.

—That's just like you, Johnny, Nell said fiercely, beginning to cry again with sharp intakes of breath after every few words. Why can't you be a little bit bad like me! Maybe that's why I love you so much! O, dear heaven, I wish I didn't love you so much! O, Johnny, I *do* love you so much!

The turn of the last phrase twisted a cold knife in his heart. He began trying to get control of the situation. At last, after an interval during which her face had been hidden on his shoulder, Nell stepped back. There was a mournful dignity in her manner.

—We can always be friends, Johnny, she said in the best tradition of Raintree County.

—Sure, he said.

Now he was the one who felt like crying.

—I want to tell you, Johnny, that I haven't lost my faith in you. Some day you will be a great man.

After the events of the last hour, Johnny tacitly agreed.

—Since we won't either one of us take back the things, Nell said, maybe we'd best destroy them.

—Not the books, Johnny said. We'll keep our books.

Even for a romantic gesture, he knew he couldn't do malice on the *Complete Works* of Lord Byron and William Shakespeare. Besides there was nothing incriminating in the books.

That was why Johnny Shawnessy and Nell Gaither, both twenty

years old, standing on a bank over the Shawmucky River at three o'clock of a raw December morning, opened their hands and allowed two stiff little cards to flutter into the cold pool of the river. That was why the eponymous monster of the river, the legendary Shawmucky himself, squatting goggle-eyed at the bottom of that wintry water, perhaps saw the innocent faces of a boy and girl fixed in attitudes of a lost republic, turning over and over and trailing lightly and sadly away in the pale stream.

And that was why Johnny Shawnessy stood in the twilight of early December dawn and watched the figure of a girl in a furcollared coat disappear in the forestfringe of the river.

Then he turned and walked home.

It was somehow in the best Johnny Shawnessy tradition that he was not exactly sad at this moment. He was filled with a young exultation neither joy nor sorrow. A wondrous secret had been almost shown to him. It had come to him out of cold and darkness and across fields of gray December and had thrust itself upon him, feminine and pleading. It said, I waited for you here beside the river, I am still waiting, I will always wait. It said, I love you, I love you, I have always loved you. This secret was a face from which he parted in the springtime of life. It was the bright little smiles of Raintree County that he would never see again. It was millions of such faces in the night, all wishing and waiting for the morrow and trying to find each other in the dark maze of time.

On the morrow he would rise and go forth and marry himself to a strange, wistful girl from the Deep South, and John Brown, too, would go forth to an equally ancient and mysterious wedding. Who were these two men and who were these millions waiting for the dawn, these citizens of the Republic, wounding and loving, losing and finding each other in the human landscape of time and fate? So long as John Wickliff Shawnessy could spring up joyous in the springing day, John Brown could never die, no one could ever die, and one heroic soul was enough to sustain the whole mass and fabric of the world. One hero who had found a white face in the night and had heard warm lips

THAT SHAPED HIS NAME, COULD BRING THE WHOLE RACE

AND THE WHOLE REPUBLIC

TO

—'A NEW LIFE,' read the Senator, 'began for me with my marriage at the close of the War, a life, which, alas, was fated to endure only a short time when the incomparable woman who became my wife was taken untimely to her . . .' And so on and so on. I'll skip a little in here.

The Senator shuffled the manuscript of his *Memories of the Republic in War and Peace* and stopped to relight his dead cigar.

—You know, boys, he said, it's been a great political handicap to me not to have a wife and family.

—Your Midas touch has made ballot gold even out of that, Garwood, the Perfessor said. I'm planning to give that recent romantic gesture of yours a special column when I get back to New York.

The Senator wheezed amusement through the shattered stalk of his cigar, as he slowly pulled it into flame.

SENATOR KEEPS FIRE BURNING
IN HOLY SHRINE OF RECOLLECTION
(Epic Fragment from the *Cosmic Enquirer*)

In a private upstairs room of his palatial mansion in the Nation's Capital, Washington, D. C., the distinguished Senator from Indiana was for a long time understood to keep the portrait of a mysterious woman, before which a flame perpetually burned. As the Senator has been for many years one of the most dashing bachelor attractions of Washington society, this rumor awakened a violent curiosity among Capital gossips. Several ladies were nominated by themselves and their friends to this secret niche in the Senator's room. At last a malignant story gained wide circulation that the lady of the portrait was the wife of a foreign diplomat and that in the periods of her absence from Washington, the romantic Senior Senator from Indiana solaced himself by pagan rites before the image of his beloved. Unable any longer to ignore these invasions of his private life, the Senator invited the Washington press to his house, where, in a voice trembling with sorrow and indignation, he said:

'Gentlemen, for thirty-five years, I have endured in silence every species of abuse that unscrupulous enemies could heap upon me to discredit my long, and I hope honorable service to the Republic. But now that the venom of partisan hatred has crept into the most sacred recesses of my life, I can no longer be silent. I invite you to examine my home and satisfy your curiosity as to its contents. Go, gentlemen, I give you leave. Open the door. Enter. And, if you are so inclined, report what you see to the World, that the World may not again dare to invade the sacred privacy of a grieving human heart.'

Here, unable to continue, the Senator flung wide the door into the famous chamber. There, the gentlemen of the press beheld the portrait of a beautiful young woman, before which was a lamp burning with a clear white flame.

'This young woman,' said the Senator, 'was my wife, who died in childbirth in the year 1865 when I was an obscure young lawyer in my home state of Indiana.'

Like men caught in the commission of a foul crime, the newsmen slunk in shame from the room. Though all were members of a profession scarcely notorious for indulgence in the softer emotions, several eyes were observed to be filled with a sentimental moisture. This moving drama has touched the heart of the Nation and will, we believe, have no little effect in winning a tremendous victory for Senator Jones and his Hoosier supporters in the coming election. . . .

—I never had a wedding night, the Perfessor said. I must say I wouldn't relish it. Marriage, I always thought, was a kind of funeral, in which we bury a part of ourselves.

The Senator laughed gently at this macabre witticism, but Mr. Shawnessy winced.

—Great institution, marriage, the Senator said. I remember my wedding night well enough.

He plucked from between his lips the halfspent cigar and holding it between his two fingers tipped the ash.

Mr. Shawnessy blushed, inhaled too much cigar smoke, coughed.

—Youth is a great thing, the Senator said. Ah, to be young again, gentlemen!

—Beauty is Youth, Youth Beauty, the Perfessor said.

—I remember the day of your first marriage, John, the Senator said. I'm afraid I was cockeyed. We sure gave you a hell of a sendoff. Of course, no American then living will ever forget that day anyway. One of the most fateful and dramatic days in American History! That was the day they sent that damned old murderer and fanatic

December 2— —Down —1859

THE RIVER FOR YOU,

MY BOY, GRAMPA PETERS SAID,

as he walked fatly up the bank to the churchyard. Johnny was leaning against a wagon surrounded by male friends and relatives. Fifty feet away, the church of Danwebster was whitely beautiful in the clear December morning.

—I'm plumb winded, Grampa Peters said. Must be a-gittin' old. Had to come up, though, and see this boy hitched. Got yourself a fine looker, I hear. How long is it yit?

—About fifteen, twenty minutes, Cash Carney said, consulting his watch. Bride and best man haven't showed up yet.

People were still driving up and entering the church. Niles Foster, small, quick-eyed, with bright black hair, got out of a buggy and walked briskly up to the yard. He had a folded newspaper in his hand.

—Hello, Niles, Grampa Peters said. What's the latest on the hangin'?

—We're just waiting around for the news, Niles said. I've got out several special editions already, and I'm all set up and waiting for the dispatch.

—Reckon anything can save him? a man said.

—You can't tell, T. D. said. They may relent at the last minute, or the Governor pardon him. Of course there's talk too of his being rescued.

—Not a chance, Cash Carney said. They want that man's life. They won't be satisfied till they crack his neck.

Several more buggies stopped close to the church.

—Quite a power of folks here for your weddin', son, Grampa Peters said. It won't be long now until . . .

TIME OF EXECUTION BRINGS WILD EXCITEMENT

(Epic Fragment from the *Free Enquirer*)

Many people are coming from all over the country to this little

Southern town. The excitement is beyond all comprehension. This correspondent has found it impossible to get a private room in a hotel. A remarkably stout gallows has been constructed especially for the occasion a little way out of town. To this spot hundreds of people gather as if unable to take their eyes off a spot soon to be the scene of an event whose consequences may be fraught with a somber significance in the time to come. As for the several reports that an attempt will be made to rescue Old Brown, this correspondent has been unable to verify any of them or to find anybody who has the slightest information as to any agent whereby such a rescue could be effected. Nevertheless the reports persist and have reached fantastic dimensions. Some say the Negroes are plotting to revolt and to bring off their would-be redeemer. Others say that an Army of Abolitionists will materialize from the crowd surrounding the scaffold. But there is nothing to indicate that such a move is seriously contemplated in any quarter or that, if it is, there is any possibility of its success. John Brown is a doomed man and no one seems to be any more clearly aware of it than he. He does not talk or act like a man who expects or even desires to . . .

—Live and let live, I say, said Grampa Peters. We'll git along with the South if we just hang enough of these nigger-lovin' abolitionists.

—I'd best go in and see if everything's all right, T. D. said. Anyway, it went off good in rehearsal.

—Right smart of you to marry your own boy off, T. D. That's a sure way to keep 'em respectable.

Grampa Peters wheezed, belched, and shook Johnny by the shoulder. T. D. walked off toward the church, plucking nervously at his mustache.

—Now don't be skeered, boy, Grampa Peters said. Women is all alike after you git 'em untied. This is the wust part of it right now. What gits you is the waitin'. Now I like to see a . . .

PRISONER CALM AS LAST HOUR APPROACHES

(Epic Fragment from the *Free Enquirer*)

As the time of execution nears, the prisoner's calm resignation is the admiration even of his gaolers. Still weakened by the wounds received in his audacious undertaking, he is constantly busy talking with visitors and writing letters to friends. There is no reason to suppose that the dignity and calm which he has so far exhibited will desert him on the scaffold. He is reported to have said to one of his visitors: 'I am far better now to die than to live.' As for the preparations for the execution proper, much thought has been given to such questions as . . .

—What do you want done with the body? intoned a deep, familiar voice.

It was Garwood Jones, coming up the bank, sleek and radiant, chewing a fat cigar, thumbs hooked in a flowered vest.

—When does the crucifixion start? he said. When do we nail the Hope of Raintree County to the cross?

—Twenty-five minutes, Cash said. Anyway, we got the best man now.

—Floral tributes, Garwood said, may be left at the sidedoor of the funeral home. What's the matter with you, John? You aren't talking much. Whassa trouble, boy? Nervous?

—Leave 'im save his strength, Grampa Peters said. He'll need it. I recollect muh own weddin' night. I reckon it won't hurt to tell it, bein' as how they's only men present, though the woman'd be fit to be tied if she knowed it.

—Go on, Grampa, a man said. I heard it a hundred times anyway.

—Well, sir, Grampa Peters said, there I was a-stampin' and a-pawin' and a-roustin' and a-rootin' fer that there cerrymony to be over. I was gittin' so wolfy about the head and shoulders, they had to nearly put me in a salt barl to keep me from spilin'. Young and strong—say, I was a prize bull in them days, boys, and don't you fergit it.

—Still pretty good, ain't you, Grampa? one of the men said.

WILL HE TALK?

(Epic Fragment from the *Free Enquirer*)

It is noised around through the town that Brown will make a speech on the scaffold. It is reported, also, that he has prepared a last will and testament and has given directions for the disposal of his body. He spent the last few hours writing and praying, leaving this last message to his friends:

'I, John Brown, **am now quite** *certain* **that the crimes of this** *guilty* *land: will* never be purged *away:* but with Blood. I had *as I now think: vainly* flattered myself that without *very much* bloodshed; it might be . . .'

—Done left me so etarnally exorsted, Grampa Peters said, that when the boys arrived around two o'clock in the mornin' to give us a chivaree, I could hardly lift muh shotgun. Wellsirree, they come right up on the front porch a muh cabin—we sot up housekeepin' over on Bar Creek—and they hollers, Come out a there, Jack Peters, before we pull ye out. Out I come with a shotgun on muh arm. Clear out a here, boys, sez I, do you want to keep all yer parts. I no sooner stuck my head out a the door than somebuddy jumped me from the side and grabbed muh gun. They got me down and tore off what little I had on, and damn if they didn't ride me on a rail right down to the Crick and in I went. Next thing, here they come and brang the woman down and throwed her in too, leavin' her nightgown on out of special respeck to the sex. When we got out a there, somebuddy had sot fire to the woods behind the house, and smashed all the winders a the cabin. The boys was drunk and hogwild, and I didn't know if I was goin' to git out a there alive. Wellsirree——

Grampa Peters stopped to pant and light a cigar.

—In the old days, a man said, it was barely wuth a man's life to git married. Still, I heerd of a boy got married last summer, he was so bad hurt in the chivaree he couldn't do his dooty as a husband for three weeks. Reckon they don't aim to do nothin' like that to you, John.

—We mean to deliver him intact, Garwood said. Besides we won't have a chance. They're catching a train right after dinner.

He put his arm over Johnny's back and winked at Cash. Johnny could smell whiskey.

—What's keeping Susanna? Cash Carney said, consulting his watch.

—Well, I don't want to be responsible for any wild rumors, Garwood said. It's just something I heard.

—What's that?

—They say she ran off with another fellow, Garwood said.

—Now don't be nervous, boy, Grampa Peters said. They's lots wuss things ahead of you than gittin' married.

Zeke Shawnessy came out of the church and walked over to the group at the wagon.

—Women are in a fearful fuss in there, he said. No use you goin' in yet, John. Place all stuffed with flowers in pots.

A surrey drove up from the direction of Freehaven and stopped. Two Negro girls got out. Susanna stepped down from the back seat. She had a black hooded mantle drawn so close around her head and body that one could see only her face and the train of her gown, which the two Negro girls carried into the church. Small girls gawked, squealed, clapped their hands trying to get a glimpse of the bridal gown but without success.

—Goddernit, there they go, Grampa Peters said, gittin' the bride so all fixed up a man cain't hardly tell what he's gittin'.

—Is there any advice you'd like to have, sprout? Garwood said. Matrimonial matters openly discussed. Highly important to both sexes.

—Maybe you better take him along, John, Cash said.

—At your disposal, son, Garwood said. Perhaps a little demonstration on the new missus by an expert might not be amiss.

—You better hang out your shingle, Cash said.

—Skillful deflorations at small charge to the client, Garwood said. Our work is guaranteed unconditionally. If entire satisfaction is not had, we will repeat at no extra charge. We are available at any time. Please do not hesitate to call us in. Anything for a friend.

—Garwood, you're drunk, Cash said.

—By the way, maybe the boy here would like a little slug of this himself. It might help him through.

Johnny shook his head as Garwood pulled a large flat bottle from his hip pocket.

—All right, said a woman's voice from the door of the church. Bring him in.

—He's all ready, Garwood said, for . . .

THE LAST RIDE

(Epic Fragment from the *Free Enquirer*)

The streets of Charles Town were lined with hundreds of people as they took John Brown to the place of execution. Few people said anything, and it was impossible to tell by the silent faces, intently watching the old man, what the sentiment of the crowd was. Brown rode in a cart, sitting on his own coffin. As they drew out of the

> town and into the open country, approaching the place of execution, he looked about him and said, 'This is a beautiful country.' The procession finally stopped. . . .

At the church door, several women crowded around Johnny and Garwood whispering instructions, fixing flowers in buttonholes.

—Any last words, Garwood said, folding his hands preacherwise and rolling his eyes, will be appreciated. Some little message that might help others to avoid the same fate.

When Johnny stepped inside the church, the preliminary strains of nuptial music were wheezing from the footpumped organ downfront. The groom and the best man went along a side aisle, picking their way through the crowd. Johnny had never seen the church so packed: the benches were filled; the side aisles were jammed with people standing; more people were coming all the time and, being unable to get in, were waiting before the church to see the bridal couple come out. Faces of small boys kept goggling through the windows.

Johnny stood at T. D.'s left with Garwood, waiting for the bride to appear. Since her arrival, Susanna had been closeted with her two attendants in a little cloakroom off the entry hall. It was she who had planned the wedding and directed the rehearsal.

—I want Uncle Garwood to be best man, she had said, and I want to walk down the middle aisle all by myself.

The wait was a long one. The white light of the church made Johnny's eyes smart. He let his gaze wander nervously over the crowd. The women looked peculiarly intent. Their eyes were beady; they licked their lips, leering expectantly.

Suddenly he realized that this ceremony was not really for him. It was for Raintree County. The Perfessor's comments on marriage in a recent letter came to his mind. To this ancient human usage, Raintree County conformed with a peculiar ferocity. All these women had come here to reassert their subtle dominion over the conscience of the County. They had come in their great gowns and petticoats and fussy hats to reaffirm the County's most sacred institution, the Family. The mystic rite of marriage, in which Johnny Shawnessy seemed to himself hardly more than a stage-prop, was a guarantee that the Family would survive triumphant and that everything which tended to undermine its dominion would be put down.

In the beginning, God had said, Let there be the Family, and there was the Family. But God had also said, Let the Family be brought forth in sorrow, for the crime of lustful love. And even today in Raintree County, it must not be admitted that life was conceived in an act of pleasure. To admit that might endanger the existence of the Family. The County sanctified procreation, but not the procreative act. The Christian religion, which ordained the Family and guaranteed its preservation, had been founded by the virgin birth of an immaculate conception. Thus, deep in the County's culture was the belief that all sexual congress was a crime, and those who were permitted to indulge that pleasant and necessary crime must be implacably reminded of its consequences, perquisites, and responsibilities.

Let the girl that is now become a woman no longer flaunt her young body before the eyes of the young men. Let her no longer make herself too beautiful, too alluring. Unsex her, and let her get quickly to the production of children. Let her now become a mother, symbol of the home.

Let the young man who enters into this pact no longer look with longing on the form of beauty. Now he will have one brief, reluctant morning. He will have one long farewell.

Yet the old pagan frenzy was still there and not to be concealed. The County gathered for this mystic rite to gratify an ancient craving. It forbade the nuptial embrace before the nuptials, but as soon as they were consummated the embrace became mandatory and unavoidable. Half the women in the church were now permitted to remember how they had themselves been victims of a legal rape on the marriage night.

All these faces that Johnny now saw, these leering, gleaming, happy faces, reflected the intense human curiosity in the mystic rite of love. They replaced a more ancient assemblage in which the community actively took part in the joining of lovers.

In Raintree County, we are civilized. Let there be no more of the laying on of hands and the sacrificial rupture of the hymen by the priest, attired in the habit of a god with great bird beak or costume woven of corn. Let the lusty males of the tribe, themselves initiates, not assist in this violation, one after another, while the cheated groom beholds the ritual defloration of his beloved. In Raintree County, we are civilized and refined, and though there may be a little rough fun after the ceremony, we do not permit ourselves to run amuck.

So they all sat and waited with Johnny for the entrance of the bride-to-be, albeit in this instance the County didn't look with entire favor on the proceedings because the bride was an out-of-county girl. The nuptial embrace, in which the whole congregation was assisting in fancy, was not quite so intimately communal as if it had been Nell Gaither or someone like that. Besides there was a rumor that the ceremony wasn't the only part of the marital adventure which the lovers had rehearsed in advance.

The organ went on wailing and squeeching, and Garwood and Johnny began to shift from foot to foot.

—Goddammit, Garwood said under his breath, what's keeping her?

Just then there was a disturbance in the crowded entryway. The organist took a quick look and plowed through a series of painful discords into the opening strains of the wedding march. The congregation unashamedly craned heads around and stretched necks to see.

A gasp went through the crowded little church of Danwebster.

Susanna was coming through the back door and down the aisle. Her glistening coarse black hair fell in waves down her back. But the real sensation was her dress. The skirt was enormously emphasized, a circular bell of cloth and froth, whitely wound on bone and wire. Out of this shot cleanly the supple stalk of Susanna's waist, sheathed in white satin that flowed plastically on the lithe contours of her flesh, just catching the soft points of her shoulders and barely containing the abundance of her nodding breasts. Exposed for all to see was a faint scar extending from her throat in a curious curve to the left breast.

—*Dearly beloved,* T. D. said in a far, foggy voice, smiling sweetly and rocking so far back on his heels that Johnny was afraid he would fall down, *we are gathered together . . .*

ON THE SCAFFOLD

(Epic Fragment from the *Free Enquirer*)

The condemned man mounted the scaffold with little assistance from his attendants. He did not make any speech. He did not delay his executioners. But the swinging off was unaccountably delayed for many minutes while troops of the Virginia militia paraded ostentatiously in the open space before the scaffold. During this time Brown maintained a stoical calm. Then the deathcap was fitted over his head, and the rope was placed around his neck. He stood on the greased trap. His time had come. The State of Virginia was about to close its case against John Brown. A man stood with hatchet raised ready to cut . . .

—That cord ought to hold good, Grampa Peters said. Your pa tied it good.

Standing inside the churchdoor with Susanna, Johnny stuck his finger into his high collar, which was much too tight. While he shook hands with Grampa Peters, Garwood Jones, heading a line of grinning young men, kissed the bride with prolonged zest. As the other young men came off the kissing line, Garwood gave each one a snort from his bottle, meanwhile shouting exhortation and encouragement.

—Get a good long one, Bob. John won't mind.

—Don't let go yet, Ezry. There's plenty more where that came from.

—O.K., Slim, that's enough. After all, you're not her uncle.

Garwood went around and got another kiss on the strength of his avuncular relationship.

—After all, I am the best man, he said, and everyone applauded and laughed because everyone in Raintree County considered Garwood Jones a wonderful guy.

There was a big dinner afterwards at the Shawnessy home for relatives and friends. The bride and groom were given seats of honor where they sat blushing in bridal costume and hardly eating. Around them, a great many hungry people gobbled the fat of the County—huge plates of fried chicken, platters full of steaming mashed potatoes, gobs of butter, pots of greasy vegetables, slabs of pie. Johnny had never seen so much eating before except at funerals. Dozens of people he had never met or only vaguely remembered came up, wrung his hand, hit him on the back, claimed relationship with him, and introduced squads of frecklefaced, mat-haired children, as if to impress him with the implications of the thing that he had done. In this wreak and wrangle of faces, voices, laughter, food, handshaking, backslapping, kissing, crying, and singing, Johnny felt that he and his bride were in danger of being swamped. It seemed he had not simply married an alien girl with black hair and a scar on her breast, but the whole of Raintree County.

Confusion, noise, and excitement increased as the time neared for the goingaway.

Susanna ran up a stair and turning threw her bridal bouquet to a crowd of girls, who fell upon it shrieking and clawing. The bouquet burst and flowers scattered everywhere. Girls ran screaming after the fragments, like hens pecking at corn.

Johnny waited downstairs with Zeke, who was in charge of getting the married couple safely onto the train.

—Now don't worry, John, Zeke said. I got an extra buggy hid out in the barn and all ready to drive off. They think we're goin' in the family buggy, but we're goin' to fool 'em.

Zeke looked worried when he said it. Garwood Jones, Cash Carney, and some of the other boys were reported to be drinking heavily and hadn't been seen for an hour. After a while, Zeke said he would slip out to the barn and guard the buggy himself. He left and didn't come back.

Johnny couldn't imagine how he and Susanna were going to get away from the house. Rooms and doors were packed with people. Dozens of buggies stood in the lane and along the road. The yard was jammed.

After a while, he was called upstairs, where he found Susanna and his mother and sisters. Susanna was in a dark goingaway dress, trimmed with red velvet. She gave Johnny's hand a quick squeeze, but otherwise they had been like strangers to each other ever since the ceremony had begun.

When the time came to run downstairs and out of the house together, Zeke was nowhere to be found. Johnny and Susanna ran down the stair anyway. People flung rice at them as they went through the door. Faces rushed at them shouting. Someone tripped Johnny so that he fell headlong, scuffing his knee. A lot of half-grown boys stung him with handfuls of rice and wheat while he was down. He got up laughing, and he and Susanna ran back toward the barn pursued by a screaming pack. In the barn they found the buggy, but no sign of Zeke. Garwood Jones and some of the boys stood there grinning.

—We've been guarding it for you, John, Garwood said.

The buggy was covered with signs, most of which betrayed Garwood's pungent muse. Cleverest was one that read:

> O, my banjo! do not cry for me.
> I'se gwine to Louisiana with Susanna on my knee.

Johnny and Susanna started to climb into the buggy, but there was a great dungy pig sitting in it. Johnny gave the pig a kick, and half a dozen chickens flew out of a box on the buggyfloor, squawking and flinging feathers. A big frenzied hen flew into Johnny's face. Waves of bellylaughter came from Garwood and the others, who stood around the buggy in a cordon preventing anyone from helping the groom.

—Where's Zeke? Johnny said.

—He went fer a walk, someone said.

There were stifled sounds from a back stall, where three young toughs were sitting on Zeke and trying to hold him down.

—Let him up, Johnny pleaded. He's got to drive us to the station.

Someone shoved Johnny from behind and threw him to the floor.

—Come on, boys, pile on sacks! yelled a big lout whom Johnny had never seen before.

Johnny struggled to his feet and knocked his assailant down. Another strange person jumped off a stall onto his shoulders and rode him down again. Two others jumped on, and the boy he knocked down got up rubbing his jaw and snarling,

—Let's throw him in the horse trough, boys.

—Who are these guys? Johnny yelled to Garwood, who was leaning on the stall looking in, cigar in mouth, grinning broadly.

—Just some boys—puff, puff—from the Clay Crick neighborhood, Garwood said, shaking out the match.

Johnny struggled wildly on the ground while drunken bodies wallowed on him, kicking, squeezing, gouging, butting. He felt as if his very life was in danger. Everyone, even his friends, wanted to inflict injury on him. Apparently the marriage ceremony wasn't over until the blood sacrifice and the dionysiac frenzy.

Into this wallowing sty of male bodies flew a wildcat fury, snarling and clawing. It was Susanna. She tore one boy's cheek open and bit another in the thumb till he screamed. Ellen Shawnessy appeared and shamed the roisterers. Johnny's other brothers pitched in, and Zeke got loose and knocked out one of the boys who had been holding him. The boys from the Clay Crick neighborhood were routed.

Johnny stood on the side of the buggy and kicked the pig out. He was almost crying with anger and indignation. Susanna was sobbing as he pulled her up beside him.

—Gangway, he yelled, whipping the horse.

The buggy lunged forward, and a wheel rolled off. The horse began to buck and plunge, and for a moment it looked as though he might run away with the crippled buggy. While Johnny was fighting with the reins and the rearing beast in the middle of a big crowd, Garwood and others who had assisted in unbolting the wheel stood around hitting their knees and holding their bellies. After quieting the horse, Johnny got into the Shawnessy buggy, but wasn't permitted to start until strings of old shoes and assorted junk had been tied on behind. Zeke took the reins for the drive into Freehaven to catch the train. Johnny had a last glimpse of his mother waving with one hand and holding a handkerchief to her face with the other, and then the buggy rolled out and down the road.

A dozen other buggies full of shrieking young people set out in hot pursuit. Garwood Jones overtook the bridal buggy and driving alongside tried to force it off the road. Everyone shrieked and laughed as if unaware that lives were in danger. Johnny could see Garwood's flushed, healthy face, eyes gleaming savagely, as his buggy kept drawing abreast, its wheels locking and catching on the bridal buggy's. Finally Zeke reached out and lashed Garwood's horses, and Garwood's buggy nearly upset. Someone fell out of the buggy and lay in a ditch screaming, but Garwood didn't bother to stop. The whole procession roared into Freehaven and went once around the Court House Square, while a crowd of glum citizens looked on in disgust.

Reaching the station, Johnny began to feel as though he and his bride were not meant to go away together. There seemed no limit to the cruelty of this frenzied mob. But the train was waiting, and he and Susanna grabbed their suitcases and ran toward a coach, with the crowd following. As Johnny handed his wife up, something hit him a blow on the side of the head and nearly knocked him down, bringing tears to his eyes. It was a big old dirty boot. He smiled, pretending not to be hurt, threw a kiss in the general direction of the crowd, and was knocked through the coach door by a shower of shoes. A glass shattered, and an angry conductor had him by the collar, saying,

—Someone will have to pay for this.

—It's all right, Johnny said, I'll pay.

He gave someone a dollar, and someone told him that it was too much.

—Have fun with those hundred and fifteen dolls, John! Garwood yelled as the train got up steam.

—Hundred and sixteen now, Uncle, Johnny said, grimly.

—Counting you, sprout? Garwood yelled.

The train began to pull out, and even now as it ran slowly parallel to the road trying to get up steam, the buggies followed, while two rough characters amused themselves by aiming rifles at the train windows and raising the guns slightly just as they fired. Several of the passengers lay on the floor of the cars, and the conductor pulled out a pistol and threatened to fire back.

After a while, the train veered away from the road, and the buggies all stopped, and the occupants sat waving and laughing in wonderful spirits, while the two roughs fired several parting salutes.

Even when the buggies were lost to view, Johnny couldn't recover from the feeling that he and Susanna hadn't yet got off safe. He kept expecting some last, most fiendish trick of all to catch them, perhaps just at the border of the County. But they made the change at Beardstown without molestation. A few minutes later they were crossing the western border of the County, and turning then to Susanna, he said,

—Well, honey, I guess we're safe.

As he put his arm around her, he felt more alone than he had ever felt in his life before.

It was a significant moment for Johnny Shawnessy when late that night he and his bride crossed the Ohio River at Louisville. The broad water shimmered from lights on either bank as the wallowing ferryboat brought them slowly to the southern shore, which was lined dense with shacks in which the black people lived. He turned to the girl beside him. She was looking out of the window at a steamboat swimming on a wash of yellow light. He studied the proud silhouette of her face and shoulders against the window. She was like these rivers and this earth—proud and scarred and beautiful and strange.

—You're South, she said, turning toward him, impulsively. You'll *love* it, honey.

They were very tired when they reached the hotel in downtown Louisville where they had reservations. Johnny felt pensive and uprooted. Alone in a room on the second floor, they opened their hand luggage and were surprised to find a variety of things that they hadn't packed themselves. There were two dolls, a boy doll and a girl doll, with their arms tied around each other and a paper pinned on inscribed with a poem in Garwood's hand. Johnny started to read it aloud:

> —Then, where is Seth, ye rocks and streamlets, say,
> For whose sweet note Aurora erst did long?
> He doth disport him with a lovelier lay,
> And ringeth in the day with merry—

—Aren't they cute! Susanna said, holding up the dolls. Isn't that just like Uncle Garwood!

A bottle of applejack brandy had a note appended,

> Remember the hard cider. Ha, Ha.
> CASH CARNEY

—Ha, Ha, Johnny said.

Susanna was pleased.

—Let's have some of it, she said. To celebrate.

The brandy was excellent. After a while Johnny and Susanna began to review the events of the marriage, which at a distance became very comical. They both talked and laughed volubly. Johnny imitated Susanna's Southern accent, and they began to have a very good time. It seemed to him that perhaps this was a good chance to get something off his conscience.

—I ought to tell you something, Susanna, and I should have done it before. My family has a skeleton in the closet.

—What is it?

—My father's an illegitimate child, Johnny said. I learned about it myself just recently.

—O, is that all? Susanna said. There's lots worse things than that, Johnny.

—O?

—Like having Nigro blood in you, Susanna said.

—Well, Johnny said, laughing, we're all white in my family except for one of my grandpas, who was as black as the ace. They captured him on the Congo after a terrific fight, and——

—Mustn't joke about it, Susanna said gravely. Just one little teeny drop, and you're all Nigro. Think of it. One little teeny-weeny drop makes you black. And you can't always tell whether you are or not. Some of the octoroons in New Orleans are as white as I am.

—I hear they're very pretty, Johnny said irrelevantly.

—It makes a person very passionate, Susanna said, to have just a little of it in them. Think of it. One teeny-weeny drop. You heard about the woman, she was all white, and one of the best families of Louisiana, and she married a fine man, a sailing captain or something. He was from one of the wealthiest and most respected families in New Orleans. When they had their baby, it was a Nigro.

—O, Johnny said.

—Men are so careless, Susanna said. Would you want a Nigro woman?

—I? Did I ever tell you about the time I——

But Susanna was not amused.

—O, Johnny, she said, suddenly taking his head in both hands and putting her deep lips to his, I *do* love you so much. I have a feeling that nothing can happen to me as long as I have you, honey. You won't let anything happen to me, will you?

She snuggled up and put her head on his shoulder. It was all very sweet and romantic. But abruptly she sat up.

—Now let's undress you and put you to bed, she said.

It seemed to be a whim of hers to reverse the situation in which they had been once before, and it wasn't long until Johnny was entirely without clothes and shone upon by gaslight, while Susanna sat fully clothed on his lap, laughing with little excited shrieks and tickling his ribs.

—Enough of this nonsense, Johnny said.

He picked her up and tossed her, still laughing, on the bed.

—No! she shrieked. You can't see my scar! Protect me, Jeemie!

Earlier she must have hidden the charred doll under her pillow. Now she pulled the hideous little thing out and hugged it to her breast, shaking her head, and laughing helplessly. In a way it was charming.

—Does this little personage go everywhere with us? Johnny asked, tugging at one of Susanna's shoes.

—Naughty boy! she shrieked, kicking and twisting. Trying to ravish us! I'm going to keep everything on!

However, in a short time, Susanna had nothing on but her wedding ring and her scar. Johnny threw the last stocking on a chair. Feeling victorious, he grabbed, none too gently, the doll in Susanna's hand.

There was a terrible shriek. It seemed to come from the doll. Johnny sprang up, his flesh crawling. People were shouting and yelling, and over all rose the unearthly screeching of the doll.

Only it wasn't the doll after all—it was a siren right under the hotel window. Someone began to pound a gong. A woman screamed. People were running on the street. Doors slammed. Fear, guilt, shame rushed over him. He and Susanna both ran and peeped out of the window. Around a lighted building across the way, a growing crowd churned excitedly. Several small boys ran out of the building waving papers and yelling in hoarse voices.

—What is it? Johnny yelled down.

No one paid any attention. A little while later, someone pounded on the door of the room. Johnny opened it a little way, and it was a newsboy with an armload of papers. Johnny gave him a dime and took one of the papers.

—What is it, honey? Susanna asked.

—They hanged John Brown.

—Serves him right, Susanna said.

Johnny read the headlines.

THE EXECUTION OF JOHN BROWN

HE MAKES NO SPEECH

HE DIES EASY

THE BODY HANGS HALF AN HOUR

BROWN FIRM AND DIGNIFIED TO THE LAST

THE BODY GIVEN TO HIS WIFE.

—O, I don't know, Johnny said wanly. He believed he was doing right.

—He was a damned old murderer! Susanna said, her face broad, flushed, wild-looking in a shower of loose black hair. I only wish the whole race of nigger-lovers and abolitionists had got hung along with him.

They listened a moment. People were trampling around in the rooms of the hotel. A sound of boots approached their door, and someone knocked.

—Who's there? Johnny said.

—They hanged the son of a bitch, a drunken voice said. Come on out'n have lil drink.

—Go away, Johnny said.

The man went away. Johnny looked at the paper again and saw the words:

> The old man was swung off at 11:15 precisely, he having remained firm and dignified to the last.

—Come on to bed, honey, Susanna purred.

He looked about him in the wavering gaslight, and he wondered how he had come to be so far from home in this hollow, rambling, echoing old hotel somewhere in the Southern city of Louisville on the Ohio River, while a naked girl lay on the bed, her body glowing olivebrown in the rich light, her proud eyes closed as if in sleep already, her wide nostrils flaring and falling with her breath, her deep lips parted.

—Come on, Johnny, she said in her small child's voice. I'm so tired.

It turned out that she wasn't tired at all. Far from it. And as for young John Wickliff Shawnessy, the life was strong in him that night, so strong that even when at last he slept (while the gasjet burned on weakly through the dawn), he continued his marriage day in fevered and strange dreams that were like a climax and farewell to a life that he had left forever.

In his dream, he was late to his wedding, and besides he hadn't yet obtained a marriage license. Riding into the Court House Square, he drove up the south side. The Square was jammed with people so that he could hardly get through.

NEWSBOY

shoving newspaper into Johnny's hand,

—Read all about it. Git yuh papuh, heah! Biggest dern newstory of the yeah!

JOHNNY

stepping into doorway of Post Office, reading from headlines printed in jasmine-scented ink,

—LAST OF THE PURITANS SUNK IN SHAME. SCARLET LETTER REVEALS HIS NAME. POET INVOLVED IN WHISKEY RING. ONE-SHOT JOHNNY IS GOING TO SWING.

The Square had darkened. Some great catastrophe had overtaken the County. Portions of it had been ravaged by fire and flood, and in the darkness crazed multitudes streamed past. Broad waters were flowing through the County, washing away beloved hills. Perhaps it was the last deluge, the flood intended by God to purify a guilty earth, stained with the lust and folly of mankind. Familiar roofs, fences, buildings were slowly sinking in the flood.

NELL GAITHER

turning over and over in December waters, her voice trailing back to him, with a dim, rehearsed sound,

—One for whom you once professed affection, Johnny . . .

He ran along the bank of the river, touched with a great sorrow. What was it that had happened to his beloved earth? It was all dissolving in the flood. The Shawmucky had overflowed its banks and become a torrent of disaster. Who was it that had struck this mortal blow at the old County and its way of life? And how could the bloody wound be healed?

A great assemblage had gathered around him. He was standing on a kind of scaffold overlooking the Ohio River. Softspoken but brutal Southerners were fitting a noose to his neck. In the crowd, he saw his own friends and relatives, waving handkerchiefs. His mother was crying. He remembered then that he had been guilty of a great betrayal. It was he who had uprooted a sacred rock and had caused the dark flood which had come upon the land.

GARWOOD JONES

prosecuting attorney,

—The State of Virginity versus John Brown Shawnessy. The

prosecution charges that this man did wilfully and willingly beget the said child upon the said woman in the said state at the stated time in the state of the Union, a Union of States, wherefore we do hereby denounce them a man and his life forever redescended into slavery.

JOHNNY

—May it please the court, I have a few words to say. My only purpose was to free——

T. D. SHAWNESSY

reading from family Bible,

—Dearly beloved, we are gathered together here in the sight of God and in the face of this company to join together . . .

A girl was sitting on his shoulders, her nude legs wrapped around his neck. He had a tenfoot pole in his hand and was teetering on a wire cable stretched from the Indiana to the Kentucky shore of the river. His performance had something to do with reconciling the split between North and South. That was why thousands on both banks were cheering him as he swung perilously above the yellow flood.

GIRL

tightening her legs,

—You'll *love* it, honey. You'll just l-o-o-o-o-ve . . .

He was strangling. The cable thrashed back and forth. He was falling, falling, falling. . . .

The steamboat going to New Orleans was a fat, wallowing hotel, honeycombed with rooms. He wandered through endless interiors blazing with gaseous light, opulent with scarlet curtains and ornamental mirrors. All the men and women were fashionably dressed. Their faces were unnaturally white, and they all smiled with radiant, fixed grins.

Suddenly from this gay throng there burst a man with a black, blistered face. He seized Johnny and attempted to strangle him. He threw Johnny down, and his knees ground on Johnny's chest. All the men and women gathered around.

JOHNNY

—Help! Pull him off!

No one seemed to understand that this dreadful person was a

murderer and fugitive. No one seemed to understand that this broad palace concealed a crime so dark and a secret so dreadful that it had never been put into print. The men and women began to run here and there, waving their arms, swinging their canes, but all still smiling happily. They didn't seem to know that the boat was sinking from a gash beneath the water line. No one tried to help Johnny, grappling with the stuffed body of his assailant, who uttered fiendish grunts and shrieks.

He saw then that all the men and women were dolls, jiggling and bouncing on hooks and ledges. They began to tumble down on him, shrunken, disintegrating, in a dreadful rain. He was floating down the river in a canopied bed, which was gradually sinking in the yellow water, dolls and all. He held the doll Jeemie, in fact a dead child with faintly negroid features. The bed was sinking; he was going down fully clothed in cold water.

A woman swam nearby, her dress soaked to her body. The flood flung them together. She rose and threw her arms around his neck. He struggled to keep his head above. His hand gripping her dress tore it away exposing . . .

The marriage license which he held in his hand was wet as he floated downstream, turning over and over like a *carte de visite* photograph. The script was still legible on the fleshlike parchment.

> This is to certify that I have this day joined in the bonds of holy matrimony John Wickliff Shawnessy and . . .

The print ran and blurred. The parchment was a map of Raintree County. A red gash had been torn in it, the wound was bleeding, the whole map was covered with dark blood, staining his hands and covering him with shame and a hideous fear from which he kept trying to awaken with small choked cries. . . .

He awoke. He had no idea where he was. A face was leaning over his face, almost as though it had been drinking his breath.

—Johnny, what in the world's the matter? It's me, honey! Wake up!

In gaslight enfeebled by the gray dawn coming through the window, he recognized the face of his wife Susanna, lips, eyelids, and cheeks faintly swollen by love and sleep.

And that was how Johnny Shawnessy, in a single day and night, left Raintree County for the first time in his life, crossed the river that divided North from South, and came to his marriage bed at last a long way from home and in an alien earth. And that was how he discovered a dark land and a dark sweet love together in the night, and, in the days that followed, great rivers going to the gulf, majestic steamboats stacking to the piers, music on bright waters, rank odors rising from off swamps, and a city at the river's mouth, the Mistress of the Delta, languorous and enchanting, steeping in beauty and incantation the oldest, darkest crime in all the world; that was how he found white columns beside the river, and eternal summer like a memory of his prehistoric childhood—a dark land and a dark sweet love together. But he found also that he couldn't wholly forget a leafless tree that waited for his return in the cold December of Raintree County beside the little river, nor a face with wide green eyes that made hot tears of love in the night, nor a stone at the limit of the land—no, he couldn't have forgotten them though he had steeped himself

IN THIS DARKBLOODED AND DELICIOUS LAND

NOT ONCE,

BUT

—SEVEN TIMES, the Senator said. Laugh if you will, gentlemen, but back in those days I was a brute of a boy.

Somewhere down the street a boy touched off a cannoncracker. Mr. Shawnessy jumped, felt unhappy. The Senator was approached by delegates of the Sitting and Sewing Society, whose hands he pumped for a while.

—I used to pull a pretty mean oar myself, the Perfessor said. By the way, John, what is that godawful yelling over there?

For some time, a great voice had been booming over the trees, getting louder and angrier. Now and then a stentorian shout soared above the rest, grating hoarsely like a horn blown too high and too hard.

—That's God, Mr. Shawnessy said.

—What? said the Perfessor, crossing himself. Is he here today too?

—It's the Revival preacher, fellow named Jarvey. One of these Kentucky evangelists. He confuses himself with the Deity—and understandably, too, if you saw him. From June to August, he's the most powerful man in Raintree County. The ladies come back every year to get converted all over again. He's been pitching his tabernacle on the National Road here for the last three summers. No one knows just why. When I first came to Waycross in the summer of 1890, he was already here. Your little friend, Mrs. Evelina Brown, has been very friendly with him. She considers him a magnificent primitive personality, which in a way he is.

—That's just like Evelina, the Perfessor said. Like all thoroughly erotic women, she begins by falsifying an aesthetic type. I hope it didn't go any farther than that. Where does he go for the winter?

—Nobody knows. Back to the Kentucky mountains, I suppose, after restoring heaven to the local souls.

—I suppose like all these Southern ranters he's a goat in shepherd's clothing.

—So far he's escaped criticism of that kind, even though he's a bachelor. But he's a brutal converter. Built like a blacksmith, he brandishes his great arms and beats the ladies prone. He has a great shout that scares everybody into the arms of Jesus. You ought to hear him.

—I *do* hear him, goddamn him, the Perfessor said.

—Still he's a man of God, Mr. Shawnessy said resignedly. My own wife regularly attends his revival meetings. She's over there now.

—I'd like to meet the little woman, the Perfessor said. Are you happy with her?

—Entirely, Mr. Shawnessy said. My wife Esther is that rare thing—a good woman. Speaking of faces, hers will interest you. Though the family denies it, it's strongly suspected that great-great-grandma something or other was a fullblooded Miami.

—How did you finally manage to get a good woman, John?

—Fashioned her myself, Mr. Shawnessy said, and Pygmalionwise fell in love with my own fashioning. She went to school to me when she was a little girl. I'm eighteen years older. Like Eve, she sprang from a bone of my breast.

—Raintree County girl?

—Yes.

—The homegrown tomatoes are always best, said the Perfessor. I'm eager to meet her. Let's see, your marriage——

—Was on a Fourth of July fourteen years ago. This is our anniversary, as well as the Nation's.

—Of course I remember about your courtship, the Perfessor said. That must have laid the old county by the ears. You certainly worked to get this philosophical existence at the Crossroads of the Republic, John. You deserve it. Funny, isn't it, how you had to go through hell to get here. Now you have a wife whom you love and who loves you, a brood of happy cherubim, good health, and a steady source of income. You have achieved the good life. How does it feel to be perfectly secure and serene?

The big voice a quarter of a mile away shot up in a high wail and came down with a snarling crash. Mr. Shawnessy felt vaguely insecure and unserene.

He saw the fabric of his life a moment spread out like a map of interwoven lines. Across this map trailed a single curving line, passing through its many intersections. Source and sink, spring and lake existed all at once. One had to pass by the three mounds and the Indian Battleground to arrive at the great south bend. One had to pass by the graveyard and the vanished town of Danwebster to reach the lake. And one had been hunting the source all one's life. The forgotten and perhaps mythical tree still shed its golden petals by the lake.

Beyond this map, the earth dissolved into a whole republic of such linear nets, all beaded with human lives. Then all these lines dissolved, and there—without north, south, east or west—was the casual republic of the Great Swamp, a nation of flowers black and white, brown and red and yellow.

We were great men in our youth. It was one life and the only. We strove like gods. We loved—and were fated to sorrow. But from our striving and from our sorrow we fashioned

The Oldest Story in the World

FOURTH OF JULY SERVICES
REV. LLOYD G. JARVEY, *Officiating*

ESTHER ROOT SHAWNESSY, returning from the Station, walked to a place midway in the tent and sat down. She looked around, but Pa wasn't there. His shiny buggy and fast black trotter weren't among the many vehicles parked along the road. Pa had been coming regularly to the revival meetings, since the Reverend Jarvey had converted him a few weeks ago. He would sit in a back seat, and after nearly every meeting, he had come up and said,

—How are you, Esther?

—Just fine, Pa.

—The old home is waitin', Esther. You can come and visit any time.

—As soon as I can bring Mr. Shawnessy and the children, I'll be glad to come back, Pa.

Pa would bow his head slightly and kiss her cheek and drive away.

Years ago, not long after Esther had left the Farm, Pa had taken a second wife and had begot nine children upon her before she died. Nevertheless Esther thought of Pa as being alone in that now never-visited part of the County. As for her, whenever she saw him, she had the feeling that Pa still had the power to take her back, though she was thirty-five years old and had three children.

The tent now filled rapidly as the excitement over the Senator's arrival subsided. A great many people who wished to remain in Waycross for the Patriotic Program in the afternoon dropped in for the revival service, not a few attracted by the fame of the Reverend Lloyd G. Jarvey.

Sitting under the vast foursided tent, the crowd watched the little tent adjoining in which the preacher customarily remained in prayer and meditation until the hour for the service. The flap of this tent was closed. A murmur of expectation ran through the revival crowd. Two ladies were talking in the row behind Esther.

—Do you think he'll turn loose and convert today?

—I don't reckon he will. He'll just preach. I hear he converted a hundred people last Thursday. They say he converted one a minute after he got started.

—He converted me two Sundays ago. I didn't think he could do it, but he done it.

—Where'd he convert you, Fanny? Big tent or little tent?

—He converted me in the little tent. All the women said it was better that way. They said in the little tent it was harder to resist the Lord. They said to go around after service, and if he wasn't too tired he'd convert you.

—I like it better that way. More private-like.

—When I said I didn't like to do it in front of everyone, they kept tellin' me to go and do it in the little tent. I kept sayin' no, I didn't feel like it. I didn't know if I was ready to let Jesus come into my heart. Finely one night I waited around after service, and nearly everybody was gone, and he was still in the little tent and the flap down. I was terrible skeered. Finely I felt the spirit in me just a little bit, and I went up and raised the flap a little. He was in there all right, convertin' Lorena Passifee.

—Lorena Passifee! I thought he converted her last summer. In the big tent.

—He did, but I guess she slipped.

—She slipped all right. How'd he convert her?

—It was real good. When I raised the flap, Lorena was on her knees, moanin'. I'm a sinner! she yells. Hosanna! he yells, and he laid her flat on her back and converted her right before my eyes. He did the layin' on of hands, and he shook her to let the spirit of the Lord come in. She was like a ragdoll in his arms.

—Lorena's a big woman too.

—I know that, but she was like a ragdoll when he shook her. Then he saw me, and he broke right off as courteous as you please. I'll come to you directly, Sister, he says. Just wait outside. I waited, and pretty soon Lorena come out of there lookin' all shook to pieces. I was that skeered I could hardly move. Come on in, Sister, he yells in that big voice of hisn. God's waitin' for you. Don't keep Go waitin'! I went in, and from then on I hardly knowed what hap pened to me. I kept throwin' my arms around and pretty soon, h picked me up and shoved me right up in the air as if I was goir straight to Jesus. I never felt such strength in anybody's arms. Tak her, Jesus! he yells. Jesus, she wants to come to you. Zion! yelled. Then all of a sudden down he brung me and flat on my back and the first thing I know I'm proclaimin' my sins and acceptin' th Lord, and he converted me.

—He sure works you up. He converted me two summers ago an agin last summer. Mine was both little tent ones. Ain't he the mo: powerful man!

—But it's too bad about his weak eyes.

—Has he got weak eyes?

—They say he's blind with his glasses off.

—I just love to watch him convert. June, they say he converte the whole Sitting and Sewing Society three weeks ago in one afte noon.

—I believe I'll have to let him convert me again, June sai thoughtfully.

Esther was remembering Preacher Jarvey's attempt to convert he Two summers ago, she had gone one day after a Sunday mornir service to see him about a program of the Ladies' Christian R formers. He was alone in the little tent.

—Come on in, Sister Shawnessy.

While she was explaining her mission, he had peered down at h queerly—he didn't have his glasses on. Suddenly he had caught h hands.

—Sister, I feel the presence of the Lord in this tent.

—Well, I hope so, Brother Jarvey.

She allowed him to hold her hands. Men of God had alwa seemed to Esther an elect breed, with peculiar privileges.

—Sister Shawnessy, have you been converted?

—O, yes, Brother Jarvey.

In fact, her conversion at age sixteen had been a dreadful a exhausting experience. She had been broken up for days before a after. She never expected to be converted again, and didn't und stand people who got converted over and over.

—Sister Shawnessy, I think you ought to get converted again. I think you ought to let the sweet light of Christ to shine on your soul again. Sister, I feel that we are both bathed and beautified by the radiant presence of Jesus at this very moment.

—I will never be converted again, Brother Jarvey.

—Let us pray! Preacher Jarvey had shouted. Down on your knees, Sister. The Lord is comin'.

Obediently, she had gone to her knees and had placed her hands in the attitude of prayer. Brother Jarvey had then prayed with wonderful fervor for half an hour, exhorting the kneeling sister to search her heart out for all impurities, to consider well whether or not she was entirely pure and perfect for God's kingdom.

She had repeated with infinite patience that she didn't consider herself perfect—no one in this mortal sphere, Brother Jarvey, was perfect except her husband, Mr. Shawnessy—but she had never once swayed from the teachings of Christ, at least since her conversion. It had seemed to her that it would be a blasphemy to the memory of it, the second greatest experience she had known, if she let herself be converted again.

But Brother Jarvey was not easily put off. He had persisted with a force that she would have deemed brutal except for the holy purpose behind it. He exhorted and sweated. When everything else had failed, he finally resorted to his godshout.

—Go-o-o-o-o-o-d, he yelled suddenly, his voice attaining a trumpet pitch of exultation, grating hoarse like a horn blown too hard.

His powerful body shot straight up with the cry, towering above her. He prolonged the shout on a high pitch and then came screaming down:

—is here!

This treatment could be repeated as many times as necessary. But usually one godshout was enough. Most of the ladies caved in and allowed themselves to be thrown bodily to Jesus. But Esther had continued quietly in her attitude of prayer through six successive godshouts, each more triumphant than the last.

After his failure to convert her in the little tent, Esther had observed a coolness toward her in Preacher Jarvey, even though she had been most helpful to him in his work and had attended the services regularly.

Her experience was not typical. As far as she knew, only one other woman in the County had been able to resist that thundering call to Christ. Mrs. Evelina Brown had held out too, though for different reasons. She was a freethinker, and though she was very much interested in Preacher Jarvey as a personality, she didn't believe in the Christian religion. Nevertheless, she had often gone for talks with the Preacher in the little tent, and he had made mighty efforts to convert her. He had spent hours discussing theology with her, a field of knowledge in which he had a surprisingly deep learning. Preacher Jarvey had publicly remarked that the abiding heresy of Mrs. Brown was the greatest sorrow of his life. Mrs. Brown had privately remarked that she had once lived through twelve godshouts without capitulating.

The highpoint of a revival service in the big tent came when Preacher Jarvey finally unwound and let his voice hit the sky with the godshout. The longer he postponed it, the more devastating it was.

—Go-o-o-o-o-o-o-o-d is here!

With that tremendous cry, he unleashed the thunderblast of divinity on the unshriven sheep, and down they came in flocks trembling to the altar.

—I sort of hope he'll turn loose this morning, one of the ladies in the back row remarked.

It seemed unlikely to Esther that he would, but the Reverend Lloyd G. Jarvey wasn't easy to fathom.

It was after ten when without warning the flap of the little tent flew up, and Preacher Jarvey appeared in the opening, clad in a long black preacher's coat, reversed white collar, tightfitting black pants and hookbuttoned black shoes.

A man of perhaps forty, he stood six feet tall, but seemed less because of his great shoulders and arms. His head had a wild, lawless look; hair and beard made one brown shag that nearly buried his ears and mouth. His brown eyes were savagely restless under frowning brows. He had the look of a huge, primitive god, poised on the brink of some tremendous act.

Instead, he reached into the pocket of his coat and took out a pair of spectacles, which he perched on the bridge of his fleshy nose. All the forbidding grandeur of his aspect was undone by the little thick round lenses, through which the Reverend Lloyd G. Jarvey peered, a great strength imprisoned.

Now he walked under the flap of the big tent and up the steps to the platform, leaning slightly backward, heavily swinging his feet and arms but taking a rather short stride for the effort involved.

Once behind the pulpit, he plucked off the glasses. His brows unbent, and his face assumed a look of majestic displeasure mingled with sorrow. He leaned his head farther back. His eyes closed. He paused.

The congregation became raptly still.

—Let us pray.

The lips flapped slowly, as if themselves immobile but moved by the action of the jaws. The voice was a harsh baritone, monotonous and trumpeting, quavering with sanctity. The Southern accent gave it a faintly barbaric sound to Northern ears. The Preacher's language was a bastard fruit produced by the grafting of Biblical phrase on the speech of Southern hill people.

The introductory services passed with prayer and hymn-singing. At length, Preacher Jarvey opened the black Bible on the pulpit.

—Brothers and sisters, we are celebratin' today in pomp and pride the birth of our Republic. It's a beautiful day that God has given us to remember our beginnin's. Look about you, and see what the Lord has given you. He has given you this green and pleasant valley teemin' with all good things. The trees drop their abundance on the earth. The kine return at evenin' with full udders. The corn is as tall as the knee of a virgin. It is a beautiful mornin', and the day is all before you.

Beware! Holy and terrible is the voice of the Lord. Beware! lest you hear His awful voice at evenin' in the cool of the garden.

Brothers and sisters, on just such a day as this did the father and mother of mankind wander in that beautiful garden which God in His great beneficence bestowed upon them. On just such a day as this they heard the sound of the clear fountains flowin' with perpetual balm, and the voice of the lion roarin' was like the bleat of a lamb. Alas, on just such a day as this they sinned and knew not God and turned from His teachin'.

On this great day of our national beginnin's let us remember an older beginnin'. I come before you today to remind you of the origin of mankind. If every word made by man were lost and the first leaves of God's Book remained to us, man would still know his sinful history and his sorrowful heritage. The oldest story in the world is the story of the Creation and the Fall of Man. Hit's a beautiful story, o, how beautiful it is, for hit is full of the beauty and the terror of the Lord.

As he warmed to his subject, Preacher Jarvey had spoken with longer cadences, the hoarse chant of his voice achieving higher climaxes before the trumpeting doomfall at end of sentence. Now he plucked the glasses from his pocket and put them on his nose. His brows made their ferocious pucker as he easily lifted the big pulpit Bible and held it close to his eyes, his face hidden by the book.

—*In the beginning, God created the heaven and the earth.*

Esther listened as the hoarse trumpet of the voice behind the Bible blew on and on. She had often heard these beautiful words, the oldest in the world; they were like a language of her soul, telling her a forgotten legend of herself. As she listened, images of her life in Raintree County crowded through her mind, bathed in the primitive light of myth—pictures of sorrow, love, division, anger.

—*And the Lord God formed man of the dust of the ground, and breathed into his nostrils the breath of life; and man became a living soul.*

And the Lord God planted a garden eastward in Eden; and there he put the man whom he had formed.

And out of the ground made the Lord God to grow every tree that is pleasant to the sight, and good for food; the tree of life also in the midst of the garden, and the tree of knowledge of good and evil.

Now, brothers and sisters, I ask you to imagine this primitive garden in the midst of the earth, bloomin' with the first freshness of creation upon it. How beautiful is the garden before the great crime! Here the first man walks in innocence. He knows not that frail defect called Woman.

Meanwhile, in the midst and middle of this garden two trees are growin'. Some people say that they were apple trees. Some people say that they were pomegranate trees. The Bible does not say what they were. And the reason why the Bible does not say what they were is that they were alone of their kind. Those trees did not bear fruit for seed, after the manner of natural trees. They had no name except the Biblical name. One was the Tree of the Knowledge of Good and Evil, and the other was the Tree of Life.

The Tree of the Knowledge of Good and Evil—brothers and sisters, hit was no ordinary tree. Hit was God's tree. Hit was many cubits thicker at the base than the greatest natural oak. The bark of the tree, hit was a thick scale. The leaves of the tree, they were broad and polished. The fruit of the tree, hit was a scarlet cluster of sweetness, burstin' with juice.

And what was that other tree like? O, dearly beloved, the mind of man is not able to picture hit, and the voice of man, hit is not able to declare hits kind. Hit was called the Tree of Life, and hit grew in the darkest and oldest part of the garden, guarded by dragons breathin' fire.

And the Lord God commanded the man, saying, Of every tree of the garden thou mayest freely eat:

But of the tree of the knowledge of good and evil, thou shalt not eat of it: for in the day that thou eatest thereof thou shalt surely die.

Disturbed by the sound of a buggy approaching, Esther looked up, but it was not Pa's buggy.

—*And the Lord God caused a deep sleep to fall upon Adam, and he slept: and he took one of his ribs, and closed up the flesh instead thereof,*

And the rib, which the Lord God had taken from man, made he a woman, and . . .

Under the great tent filled with the trumpet of Preacher Jarvey's voice, Esther was sad, remembering

1857— How —1863

IN HER OLDEST AWARENESS OF BEING ALIVE SHE WAS STANDING

in a field back of the farmhouse. She was very close to the earth as if she had just come out of it. It had a brown soft look in the light, and the light was like early morning in the spring. The earth of the field had been freshly turned by the plow. The ribbed furrows seemed to spread from a point far off and come undulating toward her, widening and widening until they engulfed her where she stood, her bare feet pressed down into the earth. Pa came up the field following the plow, the horses became bigger and bigger straining at the lines, she heard the heavy shout of Pa as he tugged at the lines, she saw how he swung the doubled reins crashing against the horses. The sharp share of the plow turned the earth with a digging sound, the team and the plow and Pa came up close, Pa's bare arms bulged from his grip on the handles, he was grand and terrible in his anger as he made the circle around the place where she stood.

Pa was a black thick beard, a broad pink face streaming with sweat, fierce black eyes, a big nose ending in a delicate tip, a mouth shouting strong words at the horses.

This was a sharp clear memory, but there were a lot of other vague memories of the earth, the plowing, and Pa. She could remember times when Pa would curse the horses so loud and fierce that her mother would shut the back door and cry.

Pa never went to the church on Sundays, but he expected Esther and the other children to go. Her mother got them all ready, and they all went to the church, nine of them after Mollie came along and grew to any size. They took up considerable room in the church. On Sunday Pa dressed in a black suit and left the fields and rested from his work, but he didn't bother to go to church. It was a thing for women and children and the other people of the countryside, but not for Pa, who was so grandly angry and violent.

When Pa cursed, he sounded a little like the preacher at the church. He swung his arms about and used some of the same words. Only Pa was much broader and stronger and louder even than the preacher.

Of the girls, she liked Ferny the best. She hated Sarah, who was bigger than she and always having it in for her. Sarah was always jealous because she had to work in the house and help their mother. As far back as Esther could remember, all the girls had chores to do in the house except herself. Pa always took her to the field with him, and she would watch him plow. When she was bigger, he would let her help sometimes in little ways.

Her mother told stories to them in the evening before they went to bed. Pa never told any stories but merely sat and listened without saying whether he thought it was a good thing or not. Her mother had round dark eyes and dark hair and skin. She was fat and always a little wistful and tired-looking. But she knew all kinds of stories, for telling or reading. Most of the stories came from the Bible.

The Bible was the big book with stiff covers that lay on the parlor table. It was all full of words that told about the Creation and God and Jesus and many ancient people who did strange things in the earth a long time ago. These things did not happen in Raintree County or even very close to it and did not seem to have a direct connection with anybody or anything she knew. All of the people in the Bible had died a long time ago except God.

God had always been alive. He lived above the earth in Heaven. He had a terrific temper and was big and broad, but his beard was probably white instead of black. He had made the earth a long time ago and had rested from his labors.

All people who died were buried in the earth. There was a place in Raintree County, just a little way down the road from the Farm, where Grandpa and Grandma Root had lived. They had been buried in the earth behind the house on a hill under a tree. Their names were on white stones, and God had them now.

All people that ever lived on the earth, except God, had died and been buried in the ground. Esther was terribly afraid of being buried in the ground like her two little brothers that had never got beyond being babies. But she was very strong, and it did not seem possible that she could ever die.

When they went to school, she proved to be the smartest of the girls. The teacher was a tall, stern man with a bald head. He whipped the ones who didn't have their lessons or were naughty in school. Esther was afraid of whipping more than anything else, because Pa had said that when they got whipped at school they would get another whipping at home. That was how she happened to remember a Fourth of July when she was six years old.

One day in the spring, one of the older girls at school had teased her about being descended from an Indian.

—I ain't descended from an Injun, she told the girl. My pa says it ain't true. We ain't any of us descended from Injuns.

—My ma says you're part Injun, all you Root kids got Injun blood in you. Squaw blood. Look at your hair and eyes. Halfbreed! Halfbreed!

Esther had turned and run at the girl, and in her desperation hunting for a word she had called the girl the worst word she knew.

—You're a *nigger,* she said.

In their part of the country, that was the worst thing you could call anyone. The niggers were black people and slaves. The War was being fought in those days to free the slaves, and a lot of the men had gone off to the War.

When she called the girl a nigger, the girl had gone and told the teacher.

—Esther, did you call Mabel Coombs a nigger?

The teacher had a switch, and his voice was thin and dry in his throat. The other children sat listening, and the whole room was quiet.

—Yes, Esther said and began to cry.

What she had said and done now seemed so evil that she had forgotten to mention the provocation.

The teacher struck her a few times lightly on the arm with the switch, and it had hardly stung at all. But that was not what worried her.

When they were outdoors, Sarah said,

—Wait till Pa hears. You'll catch it good.

She begged and pleaded with Sarah not to tell on her.

—Promise you'll do the dishes in place of me, Sarah said, and anything else I ask you, or I'll tell Pa.

—I promise, Esther said.

She was very unhappy for weeks after that, afraid that Pa would find out about the whipping she had got at school. Pa had a big black buggy whip. It was terrible to see how he would lash at the horses when he became angry. She had heard him whipping the boys in the barn a few times, and it had made her white and weak so that she would go off and cry to herself.

For weeks, she did everything that Sarah asked her to do. She washed the dishes for her and carried things for her.

—Just you fail to do one little thing I ask you, Sarah said.

Then one day at supper table, Pa had called Sarah down for something, and Sarah had talked nasty and said that their father favored Esther and everyone knew it.

—Sarah, don't let me hear you say that again, Pa said, standing up, so that they all shrank in their chairs.

His face was red and his little moist red mouth worked inside his beard. He reached a hand across the table toward Sarah.

—I don't care, Sarah said. I never been whipped in school, and Esther has. She called a girl a nigger, and the teacher whipped her. She made me promise not to tell, but she done it, and he whipped her.

Esther became very still, and her heart beat so hard she thought it would burst.

—Is that true? Pa said.

—Yes, Pa.

—Why did you call the girl a nigger?

—She said we had Injun blood in us, and I called her a nigger.

—Did the teacher whip you for that?

—Yes, Pa. And I promised Sarah I'd do her work for her if she didn't tell. But she told anyhow.

She was crying now, and she thought she had never seen Pa that angry before. He grabbed Sarah and dragged her out of the house and took her to the barn. Esther ran off to the stormgrove and hid, and she could hear Sarah screaming and Pa whipping her. She thought it would surely be her turn next.

Later on, Pa came out and found her there. The sweat stood out on his head, but he didn't seem angry with her.

—You done right to call that girl whatever you wanted, he said.

There ain't any Injun blood in our family. That's a lie. That teacher ain't in the County any more. If he was, I'd tear him limb from limb. Did he hurt you when he whipped you?

—No, it didn't hurt a bit.

—If he had hurt you, I'd of gone to find him no matter where, and I'd of taken the hide off of him with a rawhide whip. Anybody ever goes to whip you or hurt you, you let me know.

—Yes, Pa.

The next day was the Fourth, and Pa took her to Freehaven with him, just the two. It was the first time she ever remembered being at the County Seat. She was dressed in her Sunday best, and Pa had on his black suit and looked very fine and terrible and strong. He only cursed a little bit driving the horse into town and seemed to be in a good mood.

In town, it was a big day. Everybody talked about there being a battle in a place called Pennsylvania. Esther walked all around the town with Pa. It was fun to see their faces in the windows of the big stores on the south side of the Square. There were orations and fireworks, and Pa took her around to see everything.

In the evening, Pa put her in the buggy and told her to wait for him. She must have gone to sleep, and when she woke up, there were a lot of people running past the buggy and yelling fire. She got out to see, and there was a big house close to the Square—it was on fire, burning like a tall torch in the night. Pa came and found her and took her hand and led her down to where they could watch the fire. People said that a woman and a little boy had got burnt in the fire.

On the way home, Pa told her never to play with fire, or she might get burnt like the little boy in the house at the County Seat. She felt awfully sorry about the fire, but it had been a wonderful, exciting day, the town was so full of new strange faces and beautiful women in long dresses and handsome men, some of them almost as big and strong as Pa. She went to sleep wondering how they would ever bury the little boy if he was burnt completely up, and

HOW HE COULD GO TO HEAVEN AND GOD HAVE HIM,

IF HE HADN'T

ANY

—Body and soul, the Woman was made out of Man. Body and soul the Woman belongs to Man. God made her to be Man's partner and helpmeet, and o, sisters of the congregation, how woefully she betrayed His trust!

Preacher Jarvey shook his shaggy head and bent his brows sternly against the good ladies of Raintree County, who made up the major part of his audience.

—Now, let us consider this Woman. In makin' her, God put a new thing into creation. He made a frail defect. He did it with a purpose because the Lord God Jehovah does everything with a purpose. He made it to try the Man, to test him. And o, brothers of the congregation, how woefully Man betrayed his Maker's trust!

But I am gettin' ahead of my story. Now then, after the Lord made Woman, she wanders alone in the garden. The shinin' of the sun of that eternal summer, which is the only season of Paradise, shows her body to be without all habiliment or shameful adornment. Sisters of the congregation, she had no other garment than her innocence. God gave it to her, and she needed no other.

The good ladies of Raintree County shifted uneasily in their bustles and great skirts. They patted their flouncy hats and poked at their twisted hair. Preacher Jarvey's savage eyes glared displeasure on their finery. Then his eyes became remote. He departed upon a point of pedantry.

—Some depict the Mother of the Race as wearin' a figleaf before the Fall. Fellow Christians, this belief is in error. Hit is against Holy Writ. The Book tells us that she was nekkid, and nekkid she was.

Behold her then, the first Woman, cowerin' in the dust before her Father and her God. In that first blindin' moment of existence, she recognizes on bended knee the majesty and godhead of her Maker.

Esther followed a buggy with her eyes as it approached from the direction of Moreland. It was not Pa's buggy.

—Yes, the Woman knew her Father before she knew her Husband. Then the old story tells us that havin' made the Woman, the

Lord brought her unto the Man. O, sweet encounter! Brothers and sisters of the congregation, hit is the dawn of love before Man knew Woman in carnal pastime. They reach out their arms to each other, not knowin' that they are the parents of mankind but only knowin' that the loneliness of the garden has been overcome. Behold them standin' in

May 1— THE —1866

SOFT SPRING WEATHER

OF RAINTREE COUNTY BATHED HER

in warmth as she waited in the yard of the Stony Creek School on the last day of the school year. Esther had a gone feeling inside, and her heart went at times like a bird jumping in a cage. Perhaps she could be the first to reach Mr. Shawnessy when he appeared on the path through the woods. Many of the girls were inside the schoolhouse arranging their books and things because it was the last day of school.

She hated the older girls who could run faster than she. The one who reached Mr. Shawnessy first got a kiss and could walk along and hold his hand all the way to the schoolhouse. Usually it was one of the bigger girls, though it was understood that the very biggest girls didn't play the game. Not that they didn't want to.

She was afraid that some of the girls would notice her hanging on the bars and see how limp and funny she looked. It seemed to her, though, that if she didn't get to Mr. Shawnessy first today she would never get over the gone feeling she had inside. It was the last day of school, and she wouldn't see him again all summer.

Then when no one was watching, she did something that she had thought about before but had never dared to do. She slipped through the bars and started down the path, intending to lie out along the way and watch for him. That way she would get a head start. Once away, she didn't look back, but her breast was crazy with excitement, and she felt as though she would die if one of the girls yelled out,

—Look at Esther! She's gittin' a head start!

Then she was out of sight past some bushes, and no one had seen her.

She walked down the path in the woods. Just beyond the woods on her right she could see a field set in early wheat. The earth was soft from the recent rains, and the air was full of earth odor, the smell of flowers and damp wood. Violets and spring beauties were thick beside the path. She walked very slowly, hidden from all sign of human habitation, from all looking of human eyes.

She walked for about two minutes until she could see the stile across a railfence. Then she sat down in a bank of grass, half hidden behind a fallen log. Sunlight filtering through leaves made warm splotches on her body.

It was warm in the sunlight. The green grass of Raintree County was rushing up around her, a dense hair growing. The precise faces of flowers were close to her face. Shiny insect forms, looking impossibly clean and perfect, were in the thick growing of the green world around her.

The sunlight drenched her naked legs with warmth. She was all alone in the woods beside the little path. She was all alone and waiting in the green murmurous garden of Raintree County, a small girl, nine years old, weak with love and waiting.

Even now she could not banish a fear from her breast—the fear that some of the other girls would notice her absence and come down the path looking for her.

Here when she was lying with the soft hair of the earth brushing against her legs and face, the world was an easy thing to understand. God had made the earth, and he had made Raintree County as a place apart. And he had placed in it the wisest and tenderest of his creatures, Mr. Shawnessy. He had put Esther Root here too, and surely he meant that she should be happy in this beautiful place.

There had been a while months ago when she didn't know whether she ought to like Mr. Shawnessy. That was early in the year when she had first heard people say he was an atheist. An atheist was a person who did not believe in God. It was the greatest of all crimes not to Believe. She, Esther Root, had never for one single moment doubted or disbelieved in God. She was afraid to think what God would do to her if even for one little moment she were able to Disbelieve.

But it was plain to her very soon that Mr. Shawnessy wasn't an atheist or anything else bad. In fact, he seemed to her the kindest and best man she had ever seen in her life. She had known only a few men, and none of them were like Mr. Shawnessy. Her other teachers had been stiff, ugly men whom she feared and secretly hated. Mr. Shawnessy, who knew many times more than they did, was never loud or stern or overbearing.

She could remember a thousand things from those few months, which seemed as much as all the years of her life before. Always before, she had been happy when summer came. Now it hurt even to think that there would be no more school for months.

School was Mr. Shawnessy coming along the path in the morning. It was the fierce rush of the small girls to reach him and hold his hands. It was all of them laughing and leaping around him as they went into the schoolhouse door.

School was Mr. Shawnessy telling a story during the Opening Exercises. He told the most thrilling stories, some of them being continued from day to day for weeks. One story that he told during the year was about the War and how a young soldier fought through the Southland and helped emancipate the black people and saw Lincoln's assassination. It taught them more about the War than any history book, and Mr. Shawnessy said it was a true story, too, about a person he had known.

Mr. Shawnessy had also been in the Civil War. He had come back from the War in 1865, just the summer before the school year opened. People said he had been sick and wounded and had fought in Sherman's Army, but he never said anything about his own part in the War. Yet he must have been in some of the great battles and seen men killed, and maybe that was why he so often had the sad look that was in his eyes when he wasn't smiling.

Or maybe he was sad because of that other thing that people said about him. He had been married, and there had been a terrible tragedy, and now he lived alone.

It was very sad and sweet to think of Mr. Shawnessy living alone. Esther would have been only too happy to live with him and help look after him. She could have done the cooking and the housework and everything that would make him comfortable. She could be as good as a wife to him any day. Always she thought of Mr. Shawnessy alone in Raintree County, walking about on lonely roads and streets, remembering the War and his tragic married life, and no one to love him and care for him.

School was also Mr. Shawnessy telling a funny story. At such times, his long blue eyes would light up and flash, his face would become really handsome with his longmouthed, shy grin, he would make people come alive with the way he talked, and the children would just split with laughter. There wasn't a boy or girl in the school who wouldn't have gone to the stake for Mr. Shawnessy. Anyway, she, Esther, would have gone to the stake and gladly, and they could have tortured her with whips and put burning splinters in her skin. She would have saved him as Pocahontas did John Smith, putting her own neck in the way of the axe.

Those days, her life had got divided into two worlds. There was her family and Pa, and there was the school and Mr. Shawnessy. She was going to have to give one world up for a summer.

None of the other girls were coming along the path after all. She was lying here limpsy and weak in the mild air, and all of Raintree County was a blurred, beautiful garden in the spring with good things growing, and in this place there were only two people who mattered, Mr. Shawnessy and Esther Root.

Then a new fear came. Suppose that for the first time all year Mr. Shawnessy didn't come down his accustomed path. After all it was a special day, the last day, and it must be getting a little late now. Suppose he were to come another way.

She sprang to her feet and looked wildly up and down the path. Perhaps school had begun, and she had failed to hear the bell. Sarah would tell on her at home, they would ask her why she was late, and because she wouldn't dare tell the real reason, Pa would whip her.

Just then, she saw Mr. Shawnessy. He was still a long way off coming along the railfence on the far side, approaching the stile. He had his coat over his arm and was chewing a grass stem. Crossing the stile, he stopped and looked back at the field that he was about to leave.

Esther began to run down the path, afraid now that some of the other girls would come at the last moment and, racing past her, would get to Mr. Shawnessy first. She ran wildly through the woods, teeth clenched, eyes shining, pigtails flying around her shoulders.

—Mr. Shawnessy! Mr. Shawnessy! she cried, panting hard, her voice shrill with love.

Mr. Shawnessy looked a little surprised to see this small girl with the intense brown eyes, who had apparently been running along the path by herself and who now stood beside him gasping and holding up her small, determined face.

—Why, Esther, he said, how you have run!

Then, as if remembering, he smiled a little vaguely, and leaning over put his one free arm around her and brushed her cheek with his mustaches. She put her arms around his neck and held on passionately as long as she dared. His coat fell off on the ground. He leaned over and picked it up and then began to walk absently toward the school.

She could think of nothing to say and so walked along beside him holding his hand. She kept measuring the distance to the schoolhouse and wishing she might slow the walking down. He seemed lost in thought. To herself she was wondering whether he knew,

WHETHER HE HAD THE FAINTEST SUSPICION
THAT SHE WAS SO
HOPELESSLY

—In love with him, as he with her, Preacher Jarvey was saying, what a picture she makes, walkin' there hand in hand with her beloved!

And Adam said, This is now bone of my bones, and flesh of my flesh: she shall be called Woman, because she was taken out of Man.

Therefore shall a man leave his father and his mother, and shall cleave unto his wife: and they shall be one flesh.

And they were both naked, the man and his wife, and were not ashamed.

This, brothers and sisters, is the brief period of the innocence of the race. O, transports of love and fellowship with the Lord God Jehovah in the dusk and sunlight of the Garden! O, rapturous evenin's and mornin's!

I pause to remind you that scriptural time is different from our own. One day, brothers and sisters, one day in the dawn of Creation is the equal of years of sinful life today. O, how they enjoyed the fruits of that beautiful garden, the yield of wildgrowin' trees, o, how they plunged and swam in the limpid streams of Paradise! Their bed at even was the pressed grass. God tempered the air to their nekkidness. And reachin' up they plucked the grapes of Eden that fell to their hands. Truly, brothers and sisters, truly, they fed on honeydew and drank the milk of Paradise!

This is the time of the testin' of the Woman. And the Lord God Jehovah walks unseen in the Garden a-watchin' this last work of His hand. He considers it His best job. Hit is a beautiful and wellproportioned bein', and He is well pleased. But as yet hit doesn't have a name. Hit is only Woman, bein' made out of Man. Hit is the time before the Woman became Eve. Hit is the time before she sinned against her wellbeloved Father.

Esther was filled with somber pleasure to remember the time when the Woman was at peace and without sin, alone in the world with her Father and her Husband, and beloved of both.

—Hit was the time of the testin' of the Woman. Hit was not the time of the Great Temptation. That time was to come, o, hit was to come, brothers and sisters, hit was to come. Hit was the time of the Lesser Temptation. For durin' all this time, the Tree was still there and the red fruit a-hangin' out of it, and the Woman a-walkin' there. And she let the red fruit of the Tree brush against her nekkid back and breasts, and she brushed her face against the boughs smellin' the sweet smell of the fruit, and often she just touched her curved lips to the rind—just to test herself, not to eat.

The Reverend Lloyd G. Jarvey perfectly mimicked the Woman's temptation, twining and twisting about as if he dallied under the branches of a tree laden with forbidden fruit. His voice was louder, more rhythmed in its chant.

—She longed to eat of it, o, how she longed for that forbidden taste, but the time was not yet. The time was not yet, but hit was to come. O, hit was to come. Her womanly nature was sorely tempted. Hit couldn't be satisfied with the fruit of the other trees of the garden. Yet hit was good fruit, but hit didn't look as good to her. Hit was the old womanly failing. No daughter of Eve is free from it today. Hit's what we don't have that we want the hardest. Makes no difference to a Woman how good the old is, in her weak and womanly nature she longs for

June 1— THE —1876

NEW COURT HOUSE

WAS BY FAR THE MOST IMPRESSIVE BUILDING

Esther had ever seen. Below and behind the great tower, which stood out from the east wall, the main building was a strong rectangle of brick trimmed with stone at the corners, doors, windows, and eaves. The Main Entrance was through the base of the tower, where Justice, a life-sized woman with scales, stood in a niche above the door. The tower rose to a height of one hundred and ten feet, having at the top a foursided steep roof, dwindling to a small observation platform, fenced, from which stood a masted American flag. Each of the four faces of the tower roof had a clock.

The New Court House had been seven years building, after the Old Court House had burned down during the War. In the years when there was no court house in the middle of the Square, Esther and everyone else had felt as if a sacred object containing the innermost meaning of life in Raintree County had lost its tabernacle. But as the New Court House had begun to rise, slowly the feeling of security returned. It was good once again to be able to walk on one side of the Square without being able to see across to the other. The feeling that had been associated with the Old Court House crept, subtly changed, back into the walls of the New. For a while, only the main building itself was completed, but the tower, slowly taking form above it, so captured the imagination of the people that they quite forgot the Old Court House, which had had no tower. When at last in 1872 the tower was completed and the flag fluttered from an iron mast at the top, visible for miles around, a new era had begun in the life of Raintree County.

Children who had never seen the Old Court House were already referring to the present building simply as the Court House. For Esther, however, and for all the older people, this building would keep forever an indefinable look that connected it with the days when it was a brave new edifice, the finest in the County.

Esther had been in the Old Court House a few times but had never been in the new building until the day she went in for the Teachers' Examination. It was in the summer of the Centennial Exposition. She was nineteen and had decided to teach. A vacancy had occurred at the country schoolhouse where she had got all her learning, and there was a chance that she might have the place if she could pass the Teachers' Examination. She was nervous and excited, and it was good to have Pa with her as they hitched the horse on the east side of the Square and walked up to the Main Entrance of the New Court House.

As Esther started up the steps into the great building, she felt wobbly and scared. The Court House was a place of men. Any man might go into it or hang around outside of it, jetting tobacco juice. But a woman went into the Court House only for a very special purpose.

When she got inside the New Court House, she smelled tobacco and urine, the immemorial odor of all American court houses, the masculine odor of civic probity, justice, and official function. There was, however, a difference, perhaps a subtle remnant of the New Court House's newness.

Her anxiety increased, and she clung hard to Pa's big arm as they mounted the steep iron stair just inside the Main Entrance. In these gloomy rooms and corridors, the ancient rites of civic administration were performed. The priestlike titles, blacklettered on the door, awed her. Here were the County Commissioners, the Clerk, the Treasurer, the Judge, the Superintendent of Schools, gods who could make their faces benign for the humble aspirant and admit her to the select sisterhood of those who dispensed the sacred mysteries of education. Somewhere in these odorous, secret rooms reposed the State. The Court House was the Republic. The Capitol in Washington was only a greater and grander court house.

She and Pa hurried on up to the Court Room on the second floor, where the examination was to be held. Around the door were several girls and men, all laughing and talking. She looked in vain for her friend Ivy Miller, who was also taking the examination. Inside the Court Room, people were already finding places.

—Now, Esther, Pa said, just you go right in and don't be afraid. You'll do fine. You're as smart as any of them.

He held her hand in both of his, and some of his strength and bigness came into her. His big bearded face was serious, proud, a little flushed from the drive in. He was a handsome, powerful figure of a man, and being a man, felt no weak, womanly fear.

—I'll do the best I can, Pa, she said. I wish you weren't going away.

—I'll stay right here, he said. I'll be just outside the door. I'll get a chair and wait. Now go right in and do your best, Esther.

She left him then and went in through the door and took a chair at one of the tables brought in for the examination. The Court Room occupied most of the second floor of the building. Tall windows let in light from two sides on the gilded ornamental walls. Esther was so scared that she hardly dared look around. It would have been better had she stayed at home on the farm to tend the garden and help Pa in the fields. There were so many things that she didn't know.

Her friend, Ivy, a tall blackhaired girl with an aquiline nose, a big expressive mouth, and vivid brown eyes, came in and sat next to her.

—I'm scared to death! How about you, Esther?

They squeezed each other's hands and waited. Several men were there, looking supernaturally intelligent. One had spectacles, greased black hair, and a bowtie. He talked with a loud nasal twang and was very sure of himself.

—It's nothing to be afraid of, girls. It's a mere formality for a person of intelligence.

There was a fluttering of dresses, pens, and papers as a man came down to the front of the room bearing the examination books.

Esther started violently. It was Mr. Shawnessy. She hadn't seen him since that single year long ago when he had taught the school near the Farm. In the flood of emotion that came over her, she felt as though she were a little girl again, and she was ashamed for Mr. Shawnessy to see her here, a pretender to knowledge, presuming herself able to take the school that he had once taught.

Standing at the front of the room, Mr. Shawnessy said a few words about the examination and began to distribute the books. After that he wrote the questions on a large, moveable blackboard at the front of the room.

Mr. Shawnessy had changed very little, it seemed to her, since the year 1866, when she had seen him last. His temples were a little higher, but his hair had no gray in it, and despite his heavy auburn eyebrows and mustache, his face had a youthful look, much less than his years, which she thought must now be about thirty-seven. His eyes, she saw, had the same remote, sad expression that she had remembered of old.

She was so excited at this revival of an old emotion that she couldn't hold her hand still to write her name on the outside of the Examination Book.

The examination lasted for four hours. After her first panic passed, she found that she could answer most of the questions. From time to time, she looked up at Mr. Shawnessy. He was reading a book most of the time, although often he went over to an open window and stood leaning on it and looking at the Square. Once or twice in answering a question from a bewildered candidate, he smiled a little, and his face was so kind that she forgot her fear and wondered how it was that she had ever been afraid.

Once when she glanced up, she found him looking at her, and she wondered if he remembered her. But his eyes were remote and sad, and she hurriedly looked back at her paper.

As the examination drew to a close, several of the girls went up to hand in their papers. They giggled and joked with Mr. Shawnessy. Some of them, Esther noticed, were wearing earrings in the fashion then sweeping the County. Their round eyes, white teeth, and sharp, whispering voices, their jeweled heads, powdered faces, summerclad bodies assaulted the shy, lonely form at the front of the room as if to overwhelm him and bear him off a prize. Esther felt her face flushing with envy as she thought of her plain dress and her hair chastely bound over her ears.

Around five-thirty in the afternoon, Esther was the last one in the room with Mr. Shawnessy. She was violently excited as she took the paper up to the front of the room and handed it to him. She was going to turn away and leave without looking at him, but he smiled and said,

—Pardon me, but aren't you Esther Root?

—Yes, she said.

—You were a pupil of mine at the Stony Creek School back in '66?

—Yes.

—You had forgotten me?

—O, no, Mr. Shawnessy.

—Well, he said, it's nice to see you again.

She held out her hand gravely, and his strong hand closed around it for a moment.

—I hope you get your position, he said. Was the test hard?

—I think I passed it, she said. I don't really know a great deal. I think I learned more the year with you than I have ever since.

—You were a bright student, he said, the best in the school. I have no doubt you'll pass the examination.

They talked a little of the school system and the examination, as Mr. Shawnessy began to gather up the papers. She turned to leave. It was late afternoon, the light in the Court Room was changing, and the air held an odor of cigars, varnish, ink. She was very tired now that the examination was over. She said good-by and went to the door.

When she stepped out, Pa was there. She had completely forgotten his promise to stay for her. She was so glad to see him that she threw her arms around his neck and kissed him on the mouth.

—I think I passed it, Pa!

—I been here all the time, he said, thinkin' about you, knowin' you was makin' out all right.

—I was the last one through, she said. I stayed to the very last.

They were both strangely moved.

Esther's voice was low, sweet, and fast as she and Pa walked down the stair to the lower floor of the Court House.

All that day on the way home and that evening, she felt an unnatural calm as if some great thing had happened to her and passed before she had had time to appraise it.

She had come up from the country in the June weather. A slim and consecrated maiden, she had gone into the place of examination, the masculine place. In the New Court House, she had found again one whom she hadn't seen for ten years. She had seen his face and had touched his hand, she that was now a mature, comely girl with smooth red lips and budded breasts and jetblack hair.

But she had noticed a sad hunger in his eyes at the coming and going of all the girls in their flowery dresses. She was thinking that perhaps she ought to take more pains with her person, and perhaps adorn herself with some kind of jewel as the other girls did.

At night she stood before her mirror and looked at herself unclothed, at the slender outline of her body in the mirror, the dark shower of hair around her shoulders, her shining black eyes. She was thinking that she might be taking in the eyes of a man if she had an earring, a little globe of brightness just under each ear. Then with her hair bound back she might raise her face to that of Mr. Shawnessy (if she ever saw him again) and the light of his long blue eyes would flow over her face and catch the sophisticated glint of the earrings. Yes, she would have to get her ears pierced for earrings.

She wondered if it would ever be possible in this world that she would one day hold her face up to his and they would look directly into each other's eyes. It seemed to her that his eyes would look at hers with such a warmth and brightness that she would faint away, being as someone who had emerged from a dark place into a flood of sunlight.

As she lay in the bed, she repeated the long afternoon in the New Court House, the questions that had been asked on the examination, the way the rooms and corridors looked and smelled. She repeated with infinite care the details of her brief conversation with Mr. Shawnessy. Then she thought of how she had come out of the examination room, and how in a sudden fit of wildness she had thrown her arms around Pa, finding him there, and had kissed him, and how his hands and voice trembled.

It seemed to her that she still smelled on her smooth arms the odor of the New Court House, and that she held upon her spirit the whole mass of the building with its terrific ornamental tower. And it was peculiarly right that she had found, in the very quick and core of this stately building in the civic center of Raintree County, the living form of her teacher, Mr. Shawnessy, who had been away from her life for ten years.

Asleep at last, she dreamed of the New Court House. She was wandering through its brown corridors hunting for the room where the examination was to be held, but something was wrong. The New Court House was not as it should be. It appeared that the tower had collapsed, and the wreckage had exposed once more the walls and corridors of the Old Court House, which had been hidden all the time within the New. Vaguely, she remembered the wonderful tower which had risen above the County in some earlier, happier time. She had gone there for a special purpose then. But more timeless, more enduring, musty, dirty,

SMELLING OF TOBACCO AND URINE, THE OLD
DETESTED RAMPARTS ENCLOSED
HER

—*Now the serpent was more subtil than any beast of the field which the Lord God had made.*

Preacher Jarvey removed his glasses. He was beginning to breathe hard.

—Brothers and sisters, behold the Serpent! Hit is no ordinary serpent which I am about to describe to you. Hit does not go upon its belly like the common run of snakes. God had not yet cursed it down. This serpent is as big as a man. Hit has the arms and legs of a man. Hit has a long dartin' head. Hit makes a hissin' music with its tongue. O, there is somethin' remarkable familiar and delightful to the eye about this serpent. Hit is a huge, charmin', and deceitful creature, and here it is lyin' in wait for the Woman.

The Reverend Lloyd G. Jarvey had undergone a remarkable change. His body was beginning to writhe voluptuously behind the pulpit, his head made rhythmical darts and withdrawals, his eyes glared fixedly.

—When did the Woman first see this damnably beautiful serpent? Maybe it was when she was swimmin' alone in one of the beautiful rivers or lakes of Paradise, and all of a sudden there it is! Hits green eyes smile at her, hits tongue plays in and out, hit slides through the water beside her. When the Woman touches it with her hand, hits great back shoots up out of sheer pleasure. The Woman is charmed by this talented serpent, and it becomes her constant companion and plaything.

Alas! little does she know what it is. Hit is no ordinary serpent.

And now brothers and sisters of the congregation, we are approachin' that fateful moment which plunged the world into darkness. For the Woman and the Serpent find themselves one day beneath the Tree. And the fruit is hangin' low, a-temptin' the Woman. And the Serpent beguiles her. O, he beguiles her and he seduces her with soft talk about the Tree. Look at it! he says. Hit's wonderful fruit. Why shouldn't you eat of it? But the Woman still has some slight stirrin' of conscience. She is not yet completely seduced and corrupted. The Lord has forbidden it, she says. But let us see what the Book says upon this subject:

And the serpent said unto the woman, Ye shall not surely die:

For God doth know that in the day ye eat thereof, then your eyes shall be opened, and ye shall be as gods, knowing good and evil.

And when the woman saw that the tree was good for food, and that it was

July— PLEASANT —1876
TO THE EYES
DURING THE CENTENNIAL SUMMER

were the earrings worn by the young women of Raintree County.

—Esther, Pa said, I absolutely forbid you to git any.

—But why, Pa? All the girls have had their ears pierced.

—I don't want any daughter of mine gittin' herself cut up so she can hang gimcracks in her ears.

Pa spoke with an energy unusual even for him, and Esther didn't pursue the subject further. But inwardly she felt a violent rebellion, such as she had never felt before. She was nineteen and ready to support herself with teaching. She felt that she had a right to be attractive.

On a Saturday two days later, she saddled a horse and rode into town and went to a back room of a jeweler's shop where the girls got their ears pierced.

While she sat waiting for the operation, panic seized her. For the first time in her life, she was openly rebelling against Pa's will. None of the other girls had ever dared to do it, and now she, his favorite, dared to do it.

She watched the jeweler, a small uncertain man, fumbling in a drawer for his instruments. The back room was dark and cluttered with bottles and boxes. Esther began to feel that she might have fallen unawares into a nest of iniquity. The silence of the man hunting in the drawer became unbearable.

—I don't know whether I want my ears pierced after all, she said weakly.

—This will hurt only a little, he said as he bent over her.

His plain, drab face over her shoulder became, she thought, fiendishly intent, his eyes glowed, he seized her ear and touched it with a cold instrument.

At the touch, she began trembling violently, and the courage all drained out of her. She bit her lip to keep from screaming. She shut her eyes. It seemed to her that she had fallen into the hands of a fiend who was about to plunge an infernal weapon into her and rob her of her purity, her religion, perhaps her life.

At the same time, she foresaw Pa, the blackening skin of his face, his terrible anger.

Suddenly and forcibly a hard point of pain pressed against the lobe of her ear. The ravished flesh stung under an implacable assault. Instantly, the pain was unbearable, and she screamed. But already, it was hurting less. She felt unwashably polluted, as the thin, warm stream of her own blood ran down her neck onto the linen cover he had tied there.

A second time the hot pain stabbed her, and again there was the hot flow of the blood. The man dabbed at her ears with a cloth and tied a gut string in each ear to keep the apertures open. She was sobbing uncontrollably with pain and fear.

—There, he said, a little alarmed. It doesn't hurt now, does it?

Suddenly she stopped crying. She felt that if she didn't get out of the man's office she would swoon.

—How much is it? she said nervously.

She gave the man a dollar and, dabbing at her ears with a handkerchief, walked hastily to the street.

—Esther! someone said.

It was Ivy Miller. Esther didn't know whether she was glad to see Ivy or not. But she stopped and told her what had happened.

—That's nothing, Ivy said. I'm engaged to be married, and you must be my bridesmaid.

She told how she was going to marry Carl Foster, and she began to run on about the arrangements for the wedding, which was to be in two weeks. One thing that she said came clear to Esther Root, whose ears sang with confused tongues.

—Carl wanted to have John Shawnessy for his best man—you know, Mr. Shawnessy, the famous teacher. But he's gone off to New York, and won't be back perhaps ever.

—Mr. Shawnessy has gone to New York? Esther said.

Her ears stopped singing, and she felt cold and quiet.

—Yes, Ivy said. He's gone clear to New York, to be a great writer or something. I reckon the County ain't fast enough for him. We're just small shucks around here to a man like him. He went about a week ago, and there ain't any certainty he'll ever be back.

Esther began to untie the horse. She climbed up and said something about having to go on home now because her ears were beginning to hurt. She rode off in the direction of home. She no longer thought of her pierced ears. Her stomach had a queer hot feeling, and her heart was very high in her chest. If he's gone to New York, she was thinking, then I'll probably never see him again. We'll never see him again back here. It seemed to her as if all joy and promise had gone out of Raintree County.

A half-mile from home, she decided to leap the fence and ride the path along the creek. The horse barely cleared the fence, stumbling a little, but she held him up and, tearing a limb from a tree, switched him into a gallop. Along the creekbank, tree branches brushed at her face, but she hardly noticed. Then she was almost torn from the horse by a violent jerk at the left side of her head. She kept her seat, but her left ear burned with pain. A branch had caught in the tied gut and had jerked the earlobe open, so that the flesh hung trembling warm.

When she got home, she went upstairs crying. There was no use trying to conceal the affair from Pa, and somehow or other she didn't care.

When he learned what had happened, he was angry even beyond what she had expected. He had never spoken to any of the girls as he now spoke to her.

—See what you've done, Esther Root! he thundered. I told you not to git your ears pierced! What in the devil has got into you? There must be some young man meetin' you in secret, like a common whore, and he must have put you up to it!

She had got over crying now and kept her eyes lowered and said nothing. The rest of the family looked on in silent anguish. Even Sarah was abashed by the torrent of passionate language that Pa gave vent to. After a while, however, he shifted his attack to the jeweler.

—What is the name of this goddam butcher of young girls? he said.

Sarah told him who it was.

—He's done a lot of girls that way, Pa, she said.

—By God, I'll have his heart's blood, Pa said.

He fairly burst through the back door. Esther's mother and several of the children went out and tried to stop him but there was no use.

—I'll cut the bastard in two for this, he shouted, so help me God, lurin' young girls up to his place and cuttin' 'em up! I'll give 'im a cut with my whip he'll not soon forgit. I'll whip that bastard till he hollers for mercy. See that Esther don't leave the house.

He thundered off in the buggy, leaning far forward in the seat, his face flushed, his black eyes set hard on the road and glittering like obsidian. The whip went crashing over the horse. James and Ransome, the oldest of the boys, both saddled horses and rode after him.

Before the day was over, it was known all over the County how Gideon Root strode into the office of the jeweler and cursed the man by every oath he could lay tongue to and how the jeweler pulled a pistol out of a drawer and threatened to shoot his assailant if he so much as put a finger on him and how James and Ransome Root finally managed to get their father downstairs, and a big crowd gathered, and lawyers and policemen closed in on the thing, and both parties threatened to carry it to the courts. It was one of the big stories in the County papers for weeks.

The upshot of it was that some of the young men who had been thinking of paying court to Esther Root were warned to be careful, her old man was a terrible Turk, and would thrash hell out of them if they tried anything fresh.

—That old bastard is tough as nails, the boys around the Court House said, and would just as soon blow your head off as pick a melon.

As for Esther, little by little, the feeling of shame and mutilation left her. And the ear healed. But the flesh of the left lobe was badly torn and hung loosely with a gash clear through. She never wore earrings in her ears, and she knew now that she would carry to her grave this only blemish

ON HER BODY AS A REMINDER OF HER FIRST

ILLSTARRED REBELLION

AGAINST

—HER FATHER is watchin' her, but He doesn't attempt to stay her hand. Hit is by her own free will and accord that she does what she does. And the evil and the sin is hers. Hers and the Serpent's. For now, brothers and sisters, the Woman is about to do it. She is lingerin' there on the brink of that dreadful act which plunged us all to perdition. She reaches out her hand to take the fruit. She is about to take it. No, she draws back. She fondles the fruit. She is sorely tempted.

Esther had been watching the road. Her eyes still swam with the nooning brightness of the day as she looked back to the Reverend Lloyd G. Jarvey, who was half-rejecting, half-accepting an invisible something on the platform. She closed her eyes and beheld the Woman standing naked under a tree beside a lake. Words came swimming up to her from the picture, alive and blackly writhing like serpents in a place of sunwarmed waters. She could hear voices calling of young men and women by the lake in beautiful, fatherless summertime.

—Down from that tree, all of a sudden the Serpent shoots his hissin' face and thrusts a big cluster of the fruit upon the tremblin' hands and lips of the Woman! And his voice is loud in her ears: Eat! Eat! Eat!

Brothers and sisters of the congregation, the fatal hour has

August— 'COME TO PARADISE LAKE,' —1877

THE LITTLE ADVERTISING BOOKLET HAD SAID.

Come to Paradise Lake, situated in the geometrical center of Raintree County. Summer tourists, fishermen, honeymooners, whoever is seeking a happy sojourn in a lovely natural setting will find the realm of their heart's desire at this little beauty spot, replete with all the charms that Nature can bestow. When the sun is slanting down across the water between gigantic trunks of ancient titans of the forest, and the fish are leaping in the lake, when the songs of amorous couples come wafting through the glades, and the zephyrs of evening fan your relaxed and dewy temples, you will agree that this gardenground of the Universe is indeed, as its name imports, a very Eden. And while there, don't fail to put up at THE BILTMORE HOTEL, a brandnew edifice, offering the most stylish modern accommodations at reasonable prices.

O, come ye now, and bring your children,
Bring your wife and sweetheart true,
To the earth's most lovely garden
With its treasures just for you.
Come to Paradise, ye tourists,
And for years thereafter tell
How you spent a week in Heaven
At the grand Biltmore Hotel.

Though Esther Root had lived in Raintree County all her life, she had never seen the lake until the summer of 1877 when she went to the Raintree County Teachers' Institute, which was held that year at Paradise Lake for the first time. Her excitement was partly engendered by the folder she had read but mainly by the fact that her two weeks at the lake were to be her first long visit away from home.

It was early afternoon in mid-August that she set out in a buggy with Carl and Ivy Foster from the level acres of her home. It was late afternoon, as the sun sank on the burning horizon, that she approached the secret hills in which the lake was waiting. The earth here was fissured with ravines and strewn with rocks. Elsewhere in the County, the land was level, or gently rolling, sieved with running streams. Here only, remote from any town, the earth had an old scar and a green, smooth water. She was deeply thrilled to think that somewhere in these hills lay a pooled-up essence of the County's life, a lake.

Come to Paradise Lake, in the very center of Raintree County! What trees grow on the slopes that rim the waters of Paradise Lake! What plants and flowers nod at the water's edge of Paradise! See how daylight sinks down flaming to the west over the green waters of Lake Paradise in the very center of Raintree County!

The road seemed half-obliterated as they came nearer to the lake. Signs of human habitation disappeared altogether. Now and then there were low places where rushes grew. There was perhaps a sinking of the land now, a moistening and enriching of the earth as it approached the stagnant pit of Lake Paradise. The air was perceptibly cooler. Any moment they might come around the hump of a hill or through a fringe of dark woods and see the lake.

Then they went down a succession of sloping hills, and at last below her in the spent day Esther saw the lake itself. It was a small lake, not more than a quarter of a mile across, and yet Esther had never before seen so much water all at once. Almost to the road, arms of the lake extended, green and scummy, choked with rushes. Beyond fringes of trees, she saw smooth waters. Frogs piped greenly in the shallows.

A single rowboat stood motionless in the very center of the lake; a single fisherman sat in the boat, line in water.

On the south shore where the road ended was a white wooden building with many windows fronting the lake—the Biltmore Hotel. There were a few cottages near it, but at least two-thirds of the lake shore was a dense tangle of bushes and trees.

On a hill overlooking the water's edge were the tents of the Teachers' Institute, clustered around a large building with open sides. A sign said:

REVIVAL TABERNACLE

A pier extended shakily on waterrotten piles into the lake. On and around this pier were a dozen cavorting figures of young men in bathing suits, plunging and splashing in the shallow water by the shore. Soaked heads stuck from the water farther out and moved slowly to handsplashings.

When the buggy stopped by the pier, people crowded around to greet the newcomers. Several young women came down from the tents of the Teachers' Institute, and several of the men came up from the lake. Esther turned her face aside at the sight of dripping mustaches and bony feet. She was both shocked and excited with this glimpse of a new world. Everyone called her Esther, and several hands were laid upon her modest luggage. The air was loud with harsh voices of young men and shrill, yolky laughter of girls. Esther stepped down from the buggy.

It was evening on the lake; waterbirds were flying flat on the waveless surface. Shoulderdeep at the end of the pier, slowly from the lake emerging, a man came. The slant red rays of the sun were on his head and shoulders as he stood up streaming. His big mustache was dripping, and his hair stuck lankly to his forehead. His face had a remote, sad look as if while swimming he had been thinking of something else besides the swimming. As he came closer to the shore, his body was clearly defined in the soaked bathing suit; he was lean with wide shoulders, narrow hips and slender, longmuscled legs made for swiftness. The skin of his arms and legs and of his chest at the neck was white and firm. There was a scar on the top of his left shoulder.

She had known immediately that it was Mr. Shawnessy. She had thought him hundreds of miles from Raintree County and was so amazed to see him here that she could hardly make coherent replies to the bantering talk that went on around the buggy.

O, come to Lake Paradise, ye virgins, and watch from the shy reeds. The young men bathe along the shore, plunge their hard bodies out of sight, emerge with streaming hair. The lifegiving waters are odorous with the flesh of fish and trees rotten with rains. And the virgins lie at night haunted by memories of the nature gods halfnaked, swift runners with sad eyes. . . .

The first night at the lake was as long as any week of Esther's life before. When at last she was lying in bed, she could not sleep for thinking of how the sun went down on the lake, how the young people clustered about and sang and joked and yelled, how they all ate together in the Biltmore Hotel in a room especially reserved for them during their two weeks at the lake, how Mr. Shawnessy came in to dinner, dressed in a light summer suit, his hair all carefully brushed, and sat down somewhat to himself, and how late in the evening when they were going to bed, Ivy Foster told her about the sudden loss he had suffered that had brought him back unexpectedly from New York.

—It was Carl and I, Ivy said, persuaded him to come to the Institute. He's going to teach some of the classes. We thought it might take his mind off his grief. I think we all ought to go out of our way to make him happy, get him to join in the fun and all.

When Esther went to sleep the first night, she was pondering how she might go out of her way to make Mr. Shawnessy happy.

On the following morning, Esther found that Mr. Shawnessy was teaching two classes at the Institute—Natural History and the English Poets. She signed up for both and found them attended by nearly all the teachers at the Institute. Mr. Shawnessy was widely known at that time as the best teacher in Raintree County. Besides that, all the unattached young women were in love with him. They chattered endlessly about his blue eyes, his boyish, lanky look, his pleasant grin, his sense of humor, his sadness, his marital status, the smouldering passion of which they fancied him capable. They reported variant stories of the famous tragedy that people said had wrecked his life during the War. The second day, a girl swooned in his class, and everyone said it was from excitement over a compliment Mr. Shawnessy paid her, though the girl herself claimed it was because she was laced in too tight. Esther never joined in this talk, but she slaved at her work and tried to outdo everyone in the Natural History and Poetry classes, working so hard at them that her performance suffered in the other classes.

The Natural History course was conducted informally as a Nature class, and the students spent much of the time outdoors in biological excursions, learning the names of plants and insects and the principles of their growth. Often the class was continued unofficially in the evenings as the students sat on the front porch of the Biltmore Hotel or on the lawn slanting down to the lake. Many and spirited were the controversies over the origin of life, the doctrine of evolution, the descent of man, the story of Adam and Eve.

In these discussions, Esther entered fully into a world she had halfglimpsed years ago. She acquired a new vision of the earth on which she lived and so of Raintree County. This new Raintree County was a microcosm of the eternal dream of life, a mystical symbol of the human soul invested with the changing, perishable flesh. She learned how the land here had been formed in ages inexpressibly remote when the earth cooled and contracted from a flaming sphere of gas, and how the waters at length withdrew, and how aeons passed with bucklings and crackings of the earth's surface, and how oceans had lain at one time over this place, and how ice formations had advanced from the north in successive conquests, until the last recession left the rough contours of what was now Raintree County moist and dripping in the great mild age that was to bring the human race to flower. She learned how during this endless process of the alteration of the earth, life had sprung up in a place of waters, and living forms had begun to people the waters, and at last the land had swarmed with life. Here too in Raintree County, stuff of the earth had felt anguish and festered into form. During remote ages archaic monsters had moved in the forests and plains of what was some day to become the County, huge reptiles had swum in lake and river, vast carboniferous forests had swayed their succulent stalks above the earth and silted down their big yellow spores into the swamp of life. And then by dryings and coolings and coverings and depositings, the earth had become firm here, the waters had shortened and shrunk, and now there were only the softened outlines of the scars of old convulsions, there were the rivers, there was the lake in the center of the County, there were the few hills and the lonely boulders and the pebbly silt, relinquished burden of the last glacier.

And then man had come to Raintree County, a form already formed, an impulse already impelled from the remote source of humanity, the Asian womb. He had come and had brought consciousness, memory, conscience, language. One day human eyes had looked on the lake and on the river that fed the lake, and this earth became for the first time, in some sense, Raintree County—the place of names.

She learned then of the history of man on this earth, of man the wanderer, the homeless one. She learned of the races of pre-

Columbian man, the peoples who became the Indian peoples, mysterious races, how they had left their traces on the earth of the County, mounds beside the river, and shards of implements, old battlefields where young men fought for the preservation of now forgotten cultures.

And she learned how the white man had come here and only fifty years before had drawn for the first time on the ageless earth the four lines that bounded Raintree County. She learned the theory of how the County had received its name, the legend of the fabulous preacher, Johnny Appleseed, who had planted a tree from seed brought overseas a devious way. She was flung into speculations about this mysterious tree that no one had ever positively seen. She learned of the coming of the settlers, and the naming of Freehaven in the liberal, confident spirit of the eighteen-twenties, when Robert Owen's New Moral World had been established at New Harmony on the Wabash. Then there had been the schools, the teachers and the books, politics, the controversies over the fate of the Republic, there had been the churches and the homes, the farms, the fences and the roads.

And at last Raintree County was Raintree County, its way of life had been fixed—as if forever—and those who had emerged upon its breast and wore its clothing and spoke its speech felt that they had been born into an eternal way of life.

Then Esther Root, whose descent was the descent of man, had been born upon this earth.

Esther felt that she was in the presence of a mystical secret. Mr. Shawnessy was the poet, the priest, the prophet—perhaps the god—of this holy feeling. All the words he said were eloquent with the language of it, and even when he was drawling along in the late afternoon classes, in his amiable and sometimes slightly bored fashion, she felt that what he said was wondrous because he said it. He was the final embodiment of the magical fact of life in Raintree County, he who had emerged for her with lank hair streaming from the waters of the lake at evening when first she had come down the hills to the little ancient pool of Paradise. The feeling she had toward him was so strong—and, for her, new—that she hadn't even given it a name like love. It was an ecstasy of adoration in which she was lost.

And indeed she was like one lost out of time and almost out of space during her days at Paradise Lake. She seemed to discover herself for the first time by an immense loss of herself in which she found all human life and history and all meanings near and far. The lifeplace in the center of Raintree County had taken its inarticulate child and had breathed all of its great secret into her, had filled her with its holy mystery.

What was this mystery? What was this life? She could only say that life was the lake and the faintly luminous forms in its green depths. Life was the seed and the burst bloom and the withering flower. Life was also the words, the names, the poems that man, the wanderer, had brought to Raintree County.

Every word that Mr. Shawnessy spoke, every book in which she read during those fleeting days at the Teachers' Institute at Paradise Lake were graven upon her memory with a stylus of flame. Nature, Humanity, Liberty, Poetry, Passion, Love, these became meaningful concepts to her and summarized eternal images of life on the earth.

Come, o, come to Paradise Lake in Raintree County. There you will see Humanity in the guise of a lanky man of thirty-eight, clad in a wrinkled summer suit, his mustaches are long and roughly trimmed, his skyblue eyes are sad, he recites Byron to the solitary glades, he rows the young girls out across the lake at evening, and they wish he might express to them the Great Passion of which he is capable. Come to Raintree County, and behold primal forms of man and woman against a background of quiet woods and the long upland fields where clover fragrance floats upon the wind of summer. Here is Passion become serene, as among the most tranquil gods, here is life's purpose made clear, here are Truth, Virtue, Poetry, and Love—Love exalted and purified above all carnal contact.

After a few days, Esther began to have a strong desire to cross the lake to the other side and explore the marshy ground around the region where the Upper Shawmucky emptied. Mr. Shawnessy and others had spoken of the perils of this place and had warned the women not to attempt to find their way through it. But all week there had been a contest on to see who could find the greatest variety of tree leaves for the nature notebooks, and Esther had made up her mind to plunge into the steaming world of the lake's northern shore where perhaps she would be able to find for Mr. Shawnessy rare leaves that no one else had found. She even played with the thought that she might by persistence and strength find the Golden Raintree in this wild region where the river joined the lake. Mr. Shawnessy had shown them pictures of the raintrees of New Harmony, Indiana, and she was certain that she could identify the leaf. A little after noon, then, on a cloudless day, she took one of the boats from its anchorage and rowed alone across the lake while the other students were relaxing from the heat in the shade of the Revival Tabernacle.

Before she had reached the center, she was half blinded by the brilliant reflections that leapt from the sheeted lake. In her white dress and swaybrimmed bonnet, she felt herself a great flower floating on the water. She saw now that the hotel and the buildings and tents around it were only a random collection on a small part of the shore and that all the rest of Paradise Lake was primitive, green, savage. She saw the low hills sloping to the water's edge on one side, the marshes and reeds where water birds flapped and cried, and at either end the inlet and outlet rivers, the Upper and Lower Shawmucky, flowing torpidly through shallows choked with rushes and the green paving of the lily pads. And then she thought of the great age of the lake and of the things that grew within and around it, and it seemed to her that it was a living pit, the soft navel-scar left by some old birth of long ago.

Come, o, come to Lake Paradise, the oldest scar upon the earth of Raintree County. See how the soft green hair of life blurs the old scar that is in the very center of Raintree County! . . .

She had a hard time finding a place on the opposite shore where she could run the boat in easily, but she finally tied the boat up to a tree branch and climbed ashore. The hotel looked impossibly small on the far side of the lake. She began to push eastward, finding herself immediately involved with nettles, rushes, berry bushes. But she was not at all afraid. From the moment she set her foot on this side of the lake, she had felt a wild excitement as if she were about to discover something hidden to everyone else. She was a strong walker and had often boasted that she never tired out, and she didn't intend now to turn back.

All along this side of the lake, the ground was lower. It seemed to her that the leaves were greater, greener, thicker. She found several new plants and placed leaf, bloom, and bits of stalk in a little wooden box with a hooked lid, which she carried for her specimens. She saw big butterflies, amazing dragonflies, and again and again turtles and frogs that slipped from bank to water as she approached. Her luck with leaves was so great that she began to dream of herself as the discoverer of the Raintree, which she pictured as an incredible trunk whose fanshaped burst of foliage towered in isolation above the other trees.

Come, o, come to Raintree County and to the central gardenground thereof, where hills slope circularly to form the ancient scar. Here was an old uprooting. Here grew perhaps the Tree that flowered above the garden in ancient days. O, little transplant from the Asian homeland and heartland of the race! O, Biblical tree! O, mysterious seedling, lost and only vaguely remembered!

She pushed on toward the eastern end of the lake, finding her way ever more difficult. She was obliged to make wide detours to avoid swampy places and thickets; and as she tried to make her way back toward the lake, the water had somehow passed beyond the seeming shoreline and deep into the region where she was hunting. She finally took off her shoes and stockings, and holding up her dress, she waded on, feeling more and more determined to reach the place where the river emptied into the lake. She began to lose her bearings. Great waterbirds sprang shrieking into flight, the sunlight poured a furious brightness into open pools, frogs slithered away in troops of hundreds, green bugs buzzed by her, blind as bullets. She began to be afraid. She had come too far. She didn't know where she was. Her white dress was stained with the green blood of life, her bonnet was being continually knocked off her head, her feet were stung and bruised by stones and stalks. O dear, she thought, I'll have to go back. I'll have to give up. But then she saw not a hundred yards farther on, across bunches of horseweeds and rushes, a clump of trees, cleanroofed and stately as if rising from an island of firm ground.

Halfway there, she began to fear for her life. There was something sinister about this place. Savage and endless variety of forms, each form endlessly and savagely repeated, smote her with the frail uniqueness of her own form. A slender, sallowskinned girl with black hair, she felt foolish, lost, helpless in her white dress and bonnet, but she clutched her shoes and stockings and her specimen box and pushed on.

Then it was that she stepped on the snake, a long lewd fellow, writhing under her very feet and slithering away in the water with a gay fury. She had touched this green and yellow monster with her naked foot, and here she was now helpless in his domain, in the very sink and center of it. She began to run blindly through the water toward the high ground where the trees were.

Just then she saw something that shocked her almost as much as the snake had. It was a man sitting on a wide, flat rock beneath the trees.

Involuntarily, she called his name in a voice mingling surprise and relief.

—Mr. Shawnessy!

He turned and watched her, as, feeling very faint and foolish, she stood motionless, wishing she were miles away.

—Come on up here, child, he said. What in the world are you doing in this swamp, Esther?

It was the first time that week he had called her by her first name. She came up obediently and laid her belongings on the rock.

—I was hunting specimens, she said.

He shook his head and laughed.

—Have you found any?

—Some, she said.

—Well, you can add me to the collection.

He smiled, but Esther had always been of a humorless turn of mind like her Pa and made literal interpretations. She blushed violently and tried to think what Mr. Shawnessy might mean.

—How in the world did you get through the swamp there? What way did you come?

She told him, and again he shook his head and laughed.

—There's a path, he said, that you might have followed to this point. It curves wide around and comes out on the north shore about where you tied your boat. We can go back that way. My boat is tied along there too. Well, I suppose you're wondering what I'm doing here.

Strangely, she had not wondered, having immediately accepted his presence on the wild side of the lake as inevitable and right.

—No, Mr. Shawnessy.

—Why don't you call me by my first name? After all, we're fellow teachers now. People call me John.

—O, no, Mr. Shawnessy, she said. No, I wouldn't want to do that.

She knew that she could never under any circumstances call him by his first name.

—As you wish, he said, a little sadly. I forget how young you are.

—Not so young either, she hastened to say.

He looked at the surrounding tangle of grass, reeds, swamptrees, padded pools, mucky places, lost arms of river and lake, mudbars, thickets, flowers, weeds, all bathed in light and heat and stridulous with sound.

—A good place to get lost in, he said, and never found again.

—You seem to know your way.

—This isn't the first time I've been here, but I don't know my way. Few people have ever been through this place. It's a strange earth here. From here on to the river, it's even worse than where you were.

—You've been there?

—Once—long ago. I never came back until I came back today hunting for someone.

—Someone? she said, surprised.

—Yes, he said. A boy. A boy twenty years old, a joyous youth. He swam over here eighteen years ago and found his way into this region and never came out again.

He looked at her curiously to see what she was thinking. Later when she repeated this conversation over and over in her mind, she was amazed at what he had said. Now, in the savage light and beauty of the place, as they sat together on the rock, she with her bare feet chastely drawn up under her dress, she was curious to know his meaning but not shocked.

—He's lost here somewhere, this boy, Mr. Shawnessy went on in a low, pleasant voice that she thought was thrillingly sad and sweet. He's still here, I suppose, wandering around trying to find his way out. He was a very remarkable boy, you know—perhaps the Hero of the County. Do you know why?

She kept her face turned up to his and shook her head.

—Because, if I'm not mistaken, he's almost the only person who has seen the Raintree.

—O! she said. You think it's here then?

—I think it *was* here, he said. I think the boy found it but didn't know it at the time.

—Why not?

—He had drunk too much cider. He had swum too far. He was occupied with other things. Only later did he realize that he had seen the Raintree. It was then a slender tree with a rooty base, and it dropped its pollen on the boy's naked arms and shoulders and into his hair, for that was the season of its blooming.

—But if it was here then, it's still here.

—Maybe so, he said. But of course, everything changes here. Islands of solid earth dissolve, trees are rotted out and crowded away by others.

—Did—did he find it on firm ground?

—I think he found it on a little island of firm ground closer to the river. There were two stones for markers at the base with rude letters chipped on them—perhaps the initials of the man who planted the tree.

—This boy, she said, watching him intently, he came back?

He shrugged his shoulders again and smiled in a way that showed sadness rather than joy, and then he turned and looked at her a moment as if studying her face.

—I'll tell you about this boy, he said, if you won't think it foolish.

—I'd love to hear.

—I'd tell you his name if I could, but in fact he had no name. He left his name on the cultivated side of the lake. It was a hot, bright afternoon like this. He was a good swimmer, and he entered the water somewhere on the southern rim of the lake and began to swim across. This was in a time when few people came to the lake and there were no buildings around it. He swam for a while and landed here, but he found that there was no definable shore here where the Shawmucky flows into the lake. There was someone with him. A girl.

He turned and looked at her, and there seemed to be a gentle question in his eyes. He waited.

—Go on, Mr. Shawnessy, she said. What did he do?

—He didn't know precisely what he was doing, but at the time this youth believed that he had found the source and secret of all life, beauty, and desire. He thought that he had found all wisdom and had become superior to good and evil. He thought that he was about to pluck the fruit of the tree of everlasting life. Do you understand?

—Maybe, she said.

—He was perhaps a beautiful young man—beautiful because he was young—his hair was thick and tawny and caught the sunlight, he was like a young god, and he had the living present in his hands. The girl was naked like himself and very beautiful. These two slept and awakened beneath a tree. They lay for an incalculable time between the two stones. They ate of a forbidden fruit.

He waited for a while.

—Yes? she said.

Her voice trembled a little, and she felt that for some foolish reason she was going to cry.

—That was when the boy was lost, he said. He never came back. He was nameless anyway, and it didn't matter if he was lost. But in the evening, a young man who had a name swam back across the lake with a girl and put on clothes and with them shame and a sense of guilt.

She felt a great anguish, because of the thrilling sadness of Mr. Shawnessy's voice. She understood that he was referring to something in his own life that had happened long ago and had changed everything for him.

—But it was long ago, she said. And it's all right now, isn't it?

—Nearly twenty years ago, he said. I wonder if the tree the boy found is still there.

—Let's go and see, she said.

He looked at her curiously again, and she turned her face away because it seemed to her that she simply couldn't bear to let him see her eyes. After all this was her teacher, Mr. Shawnessy, whose wisdom and passion were greater than anything else in Raintree County.

—We'd better not, he said. It's a perilous business, and we're not dressed for it. Besides, I don't know that it would do any good to find it. It's funny, but I've made a myth out of that tree, and I don't want to destroy the myth. Somehow, that tree embodies the secret of life, the riddle of Raintree County, and yet I know it's not the physical tree itself that embodies it, and I don't want to disillusion myself. If I found the tree, I should remind myself that in the principle of its growth it's no more nor less miraculous than any other tree—and all trees are miraculous. I should see that the two stones were like all the other deposits of the glacier—having mass and form, and that the initials on the stones were just chipped letters, no more nor less remarkable than any of the billions of letters that mankind has strewn upon the earth. No, the tree is not the secret, but is itself, like the letters chipped on the stones, part of the secret only. There *are* secret places in the earth. Every county in America has its secret place and every American life its Delphic cave.

Esther sat very quiet now in the still, bright air, wishing that this time would never change. She felt certain that Mr. Shawnessy had just confided something to her that no one else knew.

—You've always lived in the County, haven't you, Esther?

—Yes, my father's father was one of the first settlers in the County. And then you know, they used to say that there was Indian blood in our family, but I don't think it's true.

—You don't say! Mr. Shawnessy said.

He studied her face.

—It might very well be, he said.

—I don't know why I told you, she exclaimed, shocked at herself. It probably isn't so. I was always ashamed of it. I don't know what got into me to tell you.

—You should be proud of it, he said. Perhaps that's the unique quality of your beauty.

—My beauty! she said, surprised. O, Mr. Shawnessy, I never thought—— O, pshaw, you don't really think I'm pretty! Why, I never——

—Pretty! Why, my dear child, he said, of course you're pretty. Didn't you know that?

Esther had known that she was prettier than most girls, but she had never supposed that Mr. Shawnessy would notice it. It was not a usual type of prettiness, what with her sallow skin, her high cheekbones, her dark round, haunting eyes, and her austere, almost stern expression.

—Why, yes, he said, speaking with surprising energy. You're

very beautiful. I always thought so. I should think many a young man would have told you that.

—I've not been courted much, she said. Pa doesn't favor it.

They talked for a long time, and after a while they took the long path around, leaving the solitude of the wild side. Esther had put her shoes and stockings back on and had brushed off her dress. But she was still dizzy from the strange things that had happened to her across the lake. She kept thinking of the young man who had been lost there beneath the Raintree and had never come back. She knew who this young man was, he was just her own age, twenty years old, and to be pursued by this young man and to lie with him unclothed beneath the Raintree would be to . . .

Come to Lake Paradise, o, wandering one, come in the summertime and cross the lake to the wild side. Here you will lose the name and garments that you had in Raintree County. Come and seek the place where, amorous and young beneath the tree, the young god waited for you. For you, a long time there he waited, and only you can find him and restore him to himself. O, little wanderer from a dark earth, o, little vesselbearer from the Asiatic heartland and homeland of the race!

After their afternoon together on the wild side of the lake, Mr. Shawnessy was often in Esther's company. He went walking with her and sometimes boating with her. He sought out any party of young people which included her. He seemed to like to talk with her, though he didn't speak again of the daring young man who had been lost on the wild side of the lake, nor did either of them say anything about their afternoon there. He spoke, however, of many things—old days in Raintree County and his experiences in the Civil War. He now always called Esther by her first name, and she of course continued to call him Mr. Shawnessy. Gradually he seemed to recover from the remoteness and gloom of his first days at the Institute, and some of the sadness went out of his handsome eyes. He smiled and joked more frequently.

There were hours of fun at Paradise Lake such as Esther had never known in the world of Pa, who had little laughter and lightness in him. Esther herself didn't often participate in the funmaking, being by nature stoical and humorless, but she was excited by it and by the part which little by little Mr. Shawnessy took in it.

Some of the best sport was the swimming. The girls wore yards of frilled stuff designed to conceal the shape of their bodies. The lake and the surrounding hills echoed squeals and screams as the young men and women frolicked in the water, splashing and ducking each other. Mr. Shawnessy avoided the more boisterous fun and undertook to show Esther how to swim. She learned to make patient, rhythmical gestures with her arms under the water, pointing her hands as if in prayer and stroking out from her breast like the figurehead of a ship cleaving the water. But her bathing costume was so heavy that these motions never served to keep her afloat, and she went down beneath the water again and again, still stroking stoically as Mr. Shawnessy had shown her. Each time, he would reach down and pull her out.

—Esther, my word, child, you'll drown! You don't have to go on doing it after you sink.

—I was doing it all right, wasn't I?

—Perfectly, he said. Only you always sink. If it weren't for your suit, you could swim.

He blushed.

—After all, he said, a fish couldn't swim dressed like that.

One night, the girls went to a remote part of the lake in boats and took off their clothes and bathed and soaped themselves. While they were giggling and dipping their pale forms in the water, they heard a shout from across the lake and a lantern flashed. Some men were rowing in a boat toward them. The lantern palely illumined the white bodies of the young women beside the lake, and they all screamed shrilly and put their hands over their breasts and the dark mound hair.

There was a loud chorus of song, a confused shouting of male voices, the boat drifted slowly farther out on the lake, and the girls spoke in loud voices indignantly as they dried themselves and dressed.

The next day there was much speculation as to what men had made up the party.

—From what I hear, John Shawnessy got the whole thing up, Carl Foster said, winking.

—Mr. Shawnessy is too much of a gentleman to do any such thing, Ivy said. It sounds like some of your doing, Carl Foster!

—The boat was loaded exclusively with married men, someone said.

—More's the pity, Ivy said. Why waste such a sight on married men!

—Give me a boatload of lusty bachelors any day, said another lady, slightly past forty and of redundant outline.

—The whole thing was the doing of John Shawnessy, Carl Foster said. That's what I heard.

—What about it, Mr. Shawnessy? several girls said.

—I know nothing of all this, Mr. Shawnessy said. I do, however, recollect rowing out on the lake for a quiet pipe yestereve with a party of kindred spirits, when chancing to put our boat in close to a sequestered arm of the lake, behold! we saw what seemed to be mermaids bathing in the water. More lovely were they than mortal maidens, and like Ulysses we were hard put to keep from beaching our boat there, but as luck would have it, an illomened breeze sprang up and bore us away. Can any rede me this riddle?

The affair was a subject for mirth days afterward, but as for Esther, she was wondering if Mr. Shawnessy had really been in the boat, and if his long blue eyes had been able to spy directly out her own naked form through the lanternlit darkness.

Come to Lake Paradise, ye nymphs. Ungarb and stand beside the lake, brownlimbed, with dark hair down. Plunge deep and cleave the glaucous depths and watch the frogs go by with long legs trailing. On the floor of Lake Paradise, the waterweeds are a dense mat. Be a white form fishlike in the vitreous waters while the god is watching from the glades.

So the days passed at Lake Paradise in the deep of that mythical summer in which Esther Root first left her father's home. It might have been ages since the evening when she had come down the sloping hills to the lake. So precious was this new existence to her that she had ceased to count the time, for she didn't wish to remind herself that only a few days remained of the Teachers' Institute. Nor did she seek to analyze her association with Mr. Shawnessy. She was teased by the other girls because of his obvious preference for her company, but she didn't dare to imagine what his kindness toward her meant. Perhaps in his mood of bereavement he preferred her stern simplicity to the lighthearted frivolities of the others. She lived lost in the wholeness of the experience and waited for time to tell her what to do.

All week, plans had been in the making for a big picnic which was to be held far up the river at the site of the Indian mounds, whence the picnickers were to row down to the lake. The whole affair had been planned as a climax to the first week's activities. For two or three days the girls talked of it continually among themselves at night. When the great day arrived, the weather was clear and fine. Already most of the young people had paired off.

At breakfast in the hotel, someone asked Mr. Shawnessy if he intended to go along.

—Why, no, he said. I guess that's just for the young people and the lovers.

He smiled, but not with his eyes. At the morning class, his voice was very gentle and remote, and it was only by a severe effort that he kept his attention on the wavering responses of the students. Esther didn't know when she had felt so much pity and love for anyone. She wanted to tell him that she, Esther Root, would be pleased to have him go along on the boating excursion and that to her he was as young as anyone there, no older than a boy of twenty who in some legendary summer had swum boldly across the lake and lain beneath the tree of life. The more she thought about the situation, the more upset she became, until she was annoyed by the excitement and laughter of the other students as they prepared for the picnic. She turned down two invitations from older men who wanted to escort her on the ride back. Just before they were all ready to leave, Carl and Ivy Foster came around for her. They were talking about Mr. Shawnessy.

—Maybe we could persuade him to go now, Ivy said.

—No use, Carl said. He just hasn't got over his sorrow. You can't get him now anyway. He left the camp a little after the class, and I don't know where he went. He hasn't been back since. John Shawnessy's a queer cuss in a lot of ways. He told me he was going out for a walk and not to worry about him. I asked him where he was going. I'm going to try to find someone, he said. Someone to love. We have to replace the old loves, Carl, don't you think? He was smiling and yet I never saw a man in tears look as sad as he did smiling.

When they were all getting into the buggies, Esther said to Ivy,

—I'm not going.

—Why not, honey? Come along.

Esther, who was no good at subterfuge and never lied about matters of fact, merely said,

—I can't tell you why. I'm just not going.

Carl and Ivy soon gave up trying to persuade her, and the party went off without her.

It was then about two o'clock in the afternoon. Esther ran back to the empty tents. She was wearing her white dress again, newly washed and ironed since the day she had stained it on the far side of the lake. She carefully washed her face and tied up her hair. Then she studied her face in the mirror. It was a slender face with smooth red lips, large liquid-brown eyes, high cheekbones. It had two spots of heatflush just under the eyes, and there was a burning excitement in the eyes. Then she went down to the lake, and taking a boat which didn't even belong to the Institute—all that did had been taken up the river the day before—she began to row across the lake.

Her stomach was all weak, and she was faint and dizzy. She had eaten little breakfast and no dinner at all. In what seemed an absurdly brief time, she had run the boat against the bank on the far side of the lake. When she climbed out, she was panting and the palms of her hands were red and hot from gripping the oars. She now set off on the wide path that skirted the swamps leading to the little neck of firm ground where she had met Mr. Shawnessy a few days before. She hoped that she would be able to follow the path, but as she went over it in the opposite direction, all was changed. Indeed the whole northern side of the lake seemed different. There was a kind of white soft mist in the air; leaves and grass had a vapory look. It was certainly the hottest day they had had yet, and her handkerchief was soon drenched with wiping her forehead. In a few minutes, she had quite lost her way and began to go on as best she could, pushing through the thickets and wading through low ground in the general direction of her goal.

All the time she kept telling herself that she was foolish and bad to do the thing that she was doing. Nevertheless, she kept on going and looking all the while for the trees. At last she felt sure that she had overshot them, for she was wandering and floundering in a wide marsh of swampgrass and reeds, and began to think that she would have to turn back. She took off her shoes and stockings and stood for a moment looking about her. She was panting, her hair had come down, and her slight body was drenched with sweat. Her heart knocked at the top of her chest. She thought she might faint out here in the cruel sunlight: the bubbly substance of the swamp would close over her, and she would be like a flower destroyed before it could bear its seed. Once again, she saw the insouciant gaiety and swiftness of the water-creatures. A snake swam in a pool not far away. The shining green-shouldered frogs were everywhere. Noon, splendid, uncaring, blazed and buzzed around her.

She decided to go on. For perhaps half an hour she wandered completely lost. She didn't know what trees she passed, what stones she stumbled over, but at last she saw the familiar headland and the boulder—only she was approaching it from the other direction. There was no one there. She had a great sinking of heart. She began to run on the firm ground toward the boulder. When she reached it, she stopped and put her shoes and stockings down. She had heard steps coming along the path.

Instantly Mr. Shawnessy appeared. She had beaten him to the rock.

She stood, watching him, her lips parted, unable to take her eyes away from him. He walked swiftly up the path, watching her all the time, and when he reached her, he put one arm out as if to steady her, for in fact she was swaying like a great flower bending on its stalk. She put her arms up over his arms, knocking his coat to the ground, and she clung to him so tight that she nearly pulled him off balance. His face was very close to hers. Then she was touching her face against his face. She felt his mustache on her cheek and against her neck as she held to him, shutting her eyes to the unendurable sunlight. Her body seemed to tip backward and sway as if her head had become too heavy for the rest of her.

Come to Lake Paradise, in the very center of Raintree County, o, come, come, come to—o, come to Lake Paradise in the very lifegiving warmth and brightness of—o, come, come, come to——

Esther couldn't talk, and he put her down on the rock where she sat, still clinging to him.

—I had no idea, child, that you felt this way, he said.

—O, yes, she said, I've always loved you, ever since I was a little girl. There was always only one man for me.

He began to tell her something about his marital situation. She nodded her head, but just then this information didn't seem important to her. He went on explaining something to her with great care, and she kept nodding her head, and still holding to him. She kept shutting her eyes and then opening them hastily as if she were afraid to find that all her happiness was a mirage. Finally, he said,

—Well, what about it, Esther? Do you want me, knowing all that?

—O, yes, Mr. Shawnessy, she said.

He smiled and said,

—Don't you think you could call me by my first name now?

—I'll think of something, she said.

She didn't want to leave the wild side of the lake and return to Raintree County, but about four o'clock Mr. Shawnessy said they must be back before the picnickers.

—We'll have to be careful, he said. We mustn't tell anyone, of course, until I have a chance to work this out and find a way to make it all right.

It was hard to be careful, though, during the next few days. The rest of the people at Paradise Lake had become as though they didn't exist for her. She smiled at them, listened to them, even sometimes said something, but she wasn't sure afterward what she had said and whether it made any sense at all. In a single hour, the real world had been enormously contracted and by the same token enormously expanded. There were only Mr. Shawnessy, herself, and the lake, and the hours that they spent together. All other hours were a vague dream of waiting to be alone with him. And if some afternoon the mythical youth had suddenly disclosed himself to her, she knew that she would become his companion in ecstasy beneath the Raintree. But he remained lost and didn't appear, and neither of the two lovers ever referred to him.

—Esther, Ivy Foster said to her sharply one day while they were dressing and no one else was around, what's happened to you?

—I don't know, Ivy, Esther said, smiling tranquilly. Why, what do you think has happened?

—I think you're in love, Ivy said. You silly little fool, you *are* in love!

—Well, Esther said. Yes, that's it. I'm in love.

—You're in love with Mr. Shawnessy, you crazy little thing!

—Yes, Esther said, smiling a sweet smile of resignation and candor. Yes, I am.

—Is he in love with you?

—Yes.

—Don't you know, Ivy Foster said, her eyes brilliant at the pleasure of having discovered a real passion and a shocking one at that, don't you know that he was married and has a wife and——

—Yes. Yes, I know. It doesn't make any difference. I always did love him.

—We mustn't tell anyone, Ivy said. Maybe it can be arranged. Maybe the woman will die, or something.

—Maybe so, Esther said.

She was hoping that the woman would die. It seemed the only decent and honorable thing that the woman could do. Surely if the woman knew the great love that was between Esther Root and Mr. Shawnessy, she would understand the importance of gracefully dying and permitting that great love to have its course.

—What about your Pa? Ivy said.

At this, Esther came suddenly to her senses. Here was the thing that she had been hiding from herself. Here at Lake Paradise, she had denied that other world.

—I don't know, she said. I dasn't tell him.

—He'll hear, Ivy said.

—He mustn't, Esther said. We must hide it.

—You aren't hiding anything, Ivy said. Anyone can tell you're sappy about Mr. Shawnessy. Everyone's talking about it.

Next day, a mature maiden lady who had spent a good deal of time thrusting a bounteous bosom under Mr. Shawnessy's perceptive nose during the earlier days of the Institute, took Esther aside and said in an ardently friendly way,

—Esther Root, I'm goin' to tell you something for your own good, because I'm your friend and a friend of your family. Everyone knows the goings on between you and Mr. Shawnessy. Now, you're headin' for trouble, dear. It's nothing to me person'ly, but I take a personal interest because of your family and all, and I know how your pa would take it, just to mention one. You must know that John Shawnessy is *not* a free man, dear, and his reputation isn't anything to shout about. Besides, child, he's twice your age, even if he doesn't look it. Now, I say all this in the warmest spirit of personal friendship, and I'm a little older than you myself, dear, and take this sisterly interest in your welfare, out of my personal friendship for you and your family. What I say is you'd better not have anything more to do with him. That's just my personal advice to you, and you can do what you want with it.

Esther didn't feel anger or any other very definite feeling except foreboding and sadness. She thanked the lady and said it was kind of her to say tactfully and honestly what she thought about things.

That afternoon she and Mr. Shawnessy went walking as usual.

The night before the Institute was going to end, there was a big dance in the dining room of the Biltmore Hotel. Esther danced all the dances with Mr. Shawnessy. It was a hot, hushed night on the lake. Parties of young people came out from Freehaven, and there was a tumult of buggies coming and going in the darkness. A sound of singing came from across the water, and someone said that some of the young men at the dance were drunk.

Around ten o'clock, while she was dancing with Mr. Shawnessy, she looked up and saw Pa standing at the door of the hotel. He had his riding whip in his hand, and his big face was stern.

Then she knew that she had sinned a sin so blissful that the penalty must be proportionately severe. She kept her eyes on the floor while Pa walked across the room in his great boots.

He didn't look at Mr. Shawnessy. He held out his hand to her. Putting her hand in Pa's, she walked toward the door, but just before leaving the hall, she turned and looked once at Mr. Shawnessy. His eyes had a curious brightness.

Then she was following Pa out, and they got into the buggy, and Pa laid his whip to the horse, and they were riding away.

—Esther, Pa said after they had ridden for a long time in silence and had at last reached a main road, I know you didn't know what you was doing. It wasn't your fault. You're only a child after all. I know I've only to tell you what kind of man this feller is to make you see the light. This John Shawnessy is plain no good. If it were anyone else in the world, I don't know as I would stand in your way. But in this case, I feel it my fatherly duty to protect you. This feller comes from a nogood family, and he's no good himself. He has a weak streak in him, always had. Besides, he's married and had a child by his wife years ago. They's a big mystery about what ever happened to her. He's a queer sort of feller—folks say he's an atheist. Any which way you look at it, Esther, he's not fit to lick your boot. Now, I want you to know that I don't blame you at all. I blame him. And by the livin' God, if ever I catch him hangin' around you again——

Pa's deep voice rose and trembled violently; his body seemed to bulge as if enlarged by passion.

—You're wrong, Pa, she said. He's a good man.

She couldn't remember ever before saying to Pa in so many words that he was wrong. But Pa's voice was deceptively gentle as he said,

—You're just a child, Esther. I don't blame you at all. You just don't understand about these things. I'm your pa, and I know what's good for you. In this case, you'll just have to take my word for it. I think I know how you feel. This man is much older than you, child, why, he's about as old as I am, old enough to be your—your father.

She was crying then, sobbing hopelessly as the buggy went on through the night farther and farther from Lake Paradise and back across the level part of the County toward the Farm, from which, as it now seemed, ages ago she had . . .

Come to Lake Paradise. It is—it is in the very center of Raintree County, and here (but o, so long, so many years ago) the father and mother of mankind walked alone and naked. O, come to Paradise Lake in the center of Raintree County! Here was planted the tree from which the County takes its name. O, did we not eat long ago of the fruit—of the delectable flesh of the fruit of the golden tree? It was so long ago, and now the tree is gone, only the scar remains, and the fruit is stricken from our hands. Come back, come back to Paradise Lake, from the wrath of the allseeing father, come back, my darkhaired child,

SOME DAY TO THE STILL WATERS AND
THE CIRCLING HILLS OF
LAKE

—PARADISE lost in one willful act! For the Woman takes the fruit and bursts it between her lips. And she finds it delicious. And she's not satisfied to have a little of it. O, no! She takes down whole armfuls of it, and she and the Serpent both eat of it and gorge themselves on it, and then she goes out and finds her husband. O, I've just found the most wonderful thing, Adam! Here, take a taste. Poor Adam suspects what she has done, deep in his heart he knows, but the Woman beguiles him to sin with her. And Adam takes a taste of it too. Hit is good, he says. Hit's wonderful! she says. And the taste of that fruit maddens them. They look at each other with new eyes. And, o, I'm afraid, I'm very much afraid, that the father and mother of mankind give rein to lewd and improper desires. Anyway, such is the interpretation of Milton, the great Puritan poet. Let us draw a curtain of reticence on them, poor, sinnin' creatures wallowin' briefly in the pleasures of their lustful discovery. Hit *is* good, Adam says. O, hit's wonderful! she says.

Preacher Jarvey's voice was elaborately ironical. His small eyes glared lustfully around as he plucked and tore imaginary fruit from an imaginary tree.

—*. . . and they knew that they were naked; and they sewed fig leaves together, and made themselves aprons.*

And they heard the voice of the Lord God walking in the garden in the cool of the day: and Adam and his wife hid themselves from the presence of the Lord God amongst the trees of the garden.

Esther had been so absorbed in the Preacher's discourse that she had failed until this moment to observe a buggy approaching on the road from Moreland. Now, looking up, she saw what looked like Pa's big shiny black pulling a buggy, though dust and distance obscured the face of the driver.

—*Unto the woman he said, I will greatly multiply thy sorrow and thy conception; in sorrow thou shalt bring forth children; and thy desire shall be to thy husband, and he shall rule over thee.*

And unto Adam he said, Because thou hast hearkened unto the voice of thy wife, and hast eaten of the tree, of which I commanded thee, saying, Thou shalt not eat of it: cursed is the ground for thy sake; in sorrow shalt thou eat of it all the days of thy life. . . .

The buggy was only a few hundred feet now from the tent. In the seat, Esther saw Pa's erect, broad form, his broadbrimmed black hat, his patriarchal beard.

—*In the sweat of thy face shalt thou eat bread, till thou return unto the ground; for out of it wast thou taken: for dust thou art, and unto dust shalt thou return.*

The buggy began to slow down. Esther could see Pa's black eyes searching the rows of heads under the Revival Tent. His right hand gripped the handle of a whip.

—*And Adam called his wife's name Eve; because she was the mother of all living. . . .*

—*And the Lord God said, Behold, the man is become as one of us, to know good and evil: and now, lest he put forth his hand, and take also of the tree of life, and eat, and live forever:*

Therefore the Lord God sent him forth from the garden of Eden, to till the ground from whence he was taken.

So he drove out the man; and he placed at the east of the garden of Eden Cherubims, and a flaming sword which turned every way, to keep the way of the tree of life.

Preacher Jarvey put the book down and closed it resoundingly. He removed his glasses. His great hairy head dripped sweat. The front of his shirt was soaked. The horn of his voice had been muted to a pitch of resignation and sadness.

—So endeth, brothers and sisters in Adam and children of the errin' mother of mankind, so endeth the Oldest Story in the World. *In Adam's fall we sinnèd all.* The highest wisdom is to know that we are sinners. In the pride and pomp of this day on which we celebrate the birth of our nation, let us not forget the birth of our race. With one hand, God giveth, and with the other He taketh away.

The citizens of Raintree County picked up their hymnbooks. The ladies, daughters of Eve, fanned themselves briskly, looked shrewdly around at each other, twisted uncomfortably in their cloth, bone, and metal cages, badges of lost innocence.

The service over, Esther found Pa waiting for her outside the tent.

—I'd like to have a word with you, Esther, he said. I'll drive you to where you're goin'.

—I'm going to the schoolhouse to help fix the G.A.R. Banquet.

She got into the buggy with him and they drove slowly through parked vehicles to the National Road. Pa plucked at his black-veined beard and played with the handle of the whip coiled in his lap.

—Esther, he said finally, weighing his words, you know my second wife has died and I'm alone at the old farm. Supposin' I was to say that you could come and bring the children, and I was to say that I'd take them in and help care for 'em like they was my own, and——

—I'll come back and visit any time, Pa, when I can bring Mr. Shawnessy.

Her father went on plucking at his beard. His voice was a heavy monotone.

—Supposin' you was to find out before the day was over that he wasn't a fittin' husband for you. And supposin' you was to regret marryin' him and runnin' away from your old pa the way you done fourteen years ago.

—That never could happen, Pa.

They sat in the buggy, side by side, the broad figure of Gideon Root, the slim figure of his daughter Esther. Both looked straight ahead. Their black eyes had the same look of stern endurance.

—It might happen, Pa said. And if it does, you remember what I said. The old home is waitin' for you, Esther.

They were turning west at the intersection. She could see Mr. Shawnessy sitting in the middle one of three chairs backed against the wall of the General Store. The buggy proceeded west toward the schoolhouse. A vague anxiety had touched her for the tall form in the black schoolmaster's suit. Was he entirely safe there sitting beside the Great Road?

She realized that she had never felt quite secure in her possession of this strange, wise, godlike creature who had ruled her life from childhood on. She had never quite severed herself from the dark earth of her origin, the obscure, violent parentage embodied in the figure on the seat beside her. Part of her was still living with a divided heart back in the era of a

House Divided

MAY RESULT FROM COMING ELECTION
SENATOR WARNS ON EVE OF DEPARTURE

Washington, July 1. On the eve of his departure from the Nation's Capital to mend political fences back home, the Hon. Garwood B. Jones, Senior Senator from Indiana, expressed his belief that the issues at stake in the present election are the gravest faced by this country since the Election of 1860. 'Unless an intelligent citizenry registers an overwhelming voice of disapprobation against the forces of anarchy which are abroad in the land, we may face the prospect of a House Divided, such as that which confronted the immortal Lincoln in 1860. The opposing points of view are fundamental and irreconcilable. Our Union is threatened as never before, by a more insidious foe than open rebellion.' The Senator declined to elaborate further on this statement made in the course of some impromptu remarks during a little farewell gathering at the home of James C. Parks, longtime friend and supporter of the popular statesman from . . .

The *Indianapolis News-Historian* smelled damp and gray. Mr. Shawnessy glanced at the front page and reached the paper to the Perfessor. The Senator was still talking with the ladies of the Sitting and Sewing Society.

—Time for our history lesson, children, the Perfessor said, shaking out the paper and running his eyes over the front page. Let's see how the Supreme Being is ruling his creation in A.D. 1892. Hmmmmmm. I see by this that the Senator left Washington amid kisses and tears. If there were truth in print, this article ought to read as follows:

SENATOR FEASTS SELF AT WHORE'S HOUSE
WOOS NEW VOTES AND OLD DRAB
(Epic Fragment from the *Cosmic Enquirer*)

Garwood Jones, the Senator from Indiana, who is solicitous of keeping his seat (size forty-six) in the Senate, threw a farewell party for himself at the home of his current mistress, that versatile and available female, Mrs. Petronia Parks, whose alleged husband seems to be chronically and cornutely absent from the City on business. The party was well attended by a great many people whose political eggs are in the Senator's basket. The Senator delivered an impromptu speech, of which advance copies were available to the press. There was a great deal of fun, festivity, and other fricatives. The food was passable, the liquor was plentiful, Petronia was a bad girl again, and a good time was had by all.

The Perfessor flapped pages of the *News-Historian,* folded it neatly, dropped it on the ground, and plucked a notebook from his coatpocket.

—It's impossible to report the news as it really is. But, if you're interested, John, here's my digest of the news in the year of our Lord 1892, as compiled from the *News-Historians* of our Nation. I amused myself doing this on the train down.

He adjusted his pince-nez and read in a metallic monotone:

—LIFE IN OUR TIME

(Epic Fragments from the *Cosmic Enquirer*)

We the people of the United States in the year 1892, four hundred years after the Discovery of America, one hundred and sixteen years after the Declaration of Independence, seventy-two years after the founding of Raintree County, and nine years before the beginning of the Twentieth Century, have produced the following commentary on the great documents under which we are governed:

A MORE PERFECT UNION

The various political factions by which our Republic is controlled began to hate each other with official ferocity. The Republican Party, representing money and the main chance, held a convention in June and nominated Benjamin Harrison for the Presidency. The Democratic Party, representing money and the main chance, held a convention in June and nominated Grover Cleveland. The Populist Party, representing the people against their will, met in convention on July 4 for a result not yet known. All over America, government was conducted by the few for the few.

ESTABLISH JUSTICE

A colored man was jerked to Jesus in a lynching jubilee down in Memphis, Tennessee, to remind the Negro in an Election Year that the Constitution like the Decalogue is a Sunday instrument.

DOMESTIC TRANQUILLITY

The domestic manners of the Americans exhibited the usual spicy variety. A wife beat her husband's actress whore with a whip. An actress beat her stage-manager paramour with a whip. Jack the Ripper cut throats. A Boston man drowned his pregnant sweetheart in the Mystic River. Lesbian love crept into America's papers when Alice Mitchell, a nice little Southern girl of good family, jealously cut the throat of her sweetheart, Freda Ward, another nice little Southern girl of good family. In North Carolina, the hill people went on swapping wives according to a time-honored custom.

THE COMMON DEFENSE

Secretary of State James G. Blaine, the Plumed Knight, assisted by Sancho Panza Benjamin Harrison, Twenty-Third President of the United States, ran a course against various windmills. Little Chile talked sassy to Uncle Sam after Chileans beat up American sailors in Valparaiso. Sam made a fist. Chile yelled Uncle. The Eagle and the Lion engaged in controversy over sealing rights in the Bering Straits. The Seal, interested third party, was not consulted. As Election Day drew on apace, Ben and Blaine tugged vigorously at the Lion's Tail. While protecting Home Industries, the McKinley Tariff stifled economic recovery in America and free trade everywhere.

THE GENERAL WELFARE

Victims of youthful error of either sex were earnestly besought in all newspapers to use Sanativo, sure cure for nervous debility, early decay, and lost manhood, without the aid and publicity of a doctor.

THE BLESSINGS OF LIBERTY

In Pittsburgh, on the Fourth of July, the workers at the Homestead Mill prepared to defend their practical right to feed and clothe themselves and their families, while the employers prepared to defend their sacred right to accrue wealth by the enslavement of men. Three hundred miners were entombed somewhere. Strikes spread as Americans, the richest and happiest people in the world, starved.

GOD AND THE WORLD

The Reverend Lyman Abbott affirmed that God's Word was a typographical error and that Christianity was civilized paganism. He recommended the marriage of Darwin and Jesus for the salvation of the world. Little blind and deaf Helen Keller asked her instructor, Miss Sullivan, the following questions:

1. Who made God?
2. Where is God?
3. What did God make the universe out of?
4. What is a soul?
5. If God is love, why does he permit sin and suffering?
6. If God made all things, did he not also make the evil in the world?

Dozens of doctors and divines, rushing eagerly into print, flunked the exam.

SPORTS AND GAMES

A female heavyweight wrestler subtly illustrated the general trend of the Nineteenth Century by flattening a succession of males and planting her broad rump on their chests. Thomas Lake Harris was alleged to be conducting a sex community as naughtily nude as Oneida, with Edenic baths and other pastoral pastimes.

LOST AND FOUND

Various nude, ravished, dead girls' bodies in various parts of the United States.

MODERN ENLIGHTENMENT

At the suggestion of friends, a man dug up the corpse of his consumptive wife and cremated it lest her diseased lungs feed upon her children's.

CIRCUS MAXIMUS

Trains jumped trestles, rivers flooded, ships foundered, and hotels burnt to kill thousands and entertain millions.

LITERATURE AND THE ARTS

People went to the theatre to see *Shiloh,* a play about the Civil War; *Around the World in Eighty Days,* a play about the speed of modern transportation; *The White Patrol,* a play about the Haymarket Bombing; *The White Slave,* a play about prostitution; *The Lost*

Paradise, a play about a factory owner and a factory waif; and *Cleopatra,* a play about Madame Sarah Bernhardt. In addition, they saw Lillian Russell, Shakespeare, the Vaudeville, and a Program of Gems, Varieties, Specialties, and Minstrel Comedians. A lionmaned Pole named Paderewski made a majestic assault on America's concert keyboards. Stoddard lectured. Mark Twain, America's most famous living writer, hacked out *The American Claimant.* Americans continued to read *Looking Backward, Progress and Poverty,* and *The Young Mail Carrier of the Rockies.* In Camden, New Jersey, Walt Whitman died obscure. Last words: 'Warry, shift.'

SCIENTIFIC NOTES

Anthropology: John L. Sullivan, Boston Strong Boy, Heavyweight Boxing Champion of the World, in training for his title defense against Challenger Gentleman Jim Corbett, had his right biceps muscle measured and recorded a circumference of seventeen inches. Biology: A twoheaded boy was exhibited talking German on one stalk, Italian on the other. Technology: Reporters were admitted for the first time to an electrocution in Sing Sing. Mineralogy: There was a gold rush near Denver.

FINANCIAL PAGE

Bulls and bears butted and cuffed each other on Wall Street while the Nation ran down hill to another depression.

OURSELVES AND OUR POSTERITY

The Dove of Peace spread its wings on a world becalmed in one of its rare seasons of tranquillity, a blessing conferred upon humanity by the Industrial Revolution, bourgeois enterprise, and Queen Victoria. In Russia, millions were starving, and Count Leo Tolstoi, well-fed, bled for them. In America, on Memorial Day, people laid flowers on the graves of young men who died in the Civil War thirty years ago. Cash, not beauty or intelligence, ruled society. It was generally agreed in pulpits, newspapers, books, barrooms, brothels, congresses, caucuses, schoolrooms, and the Home that humanity had never been so blessed and that the Cosmos was infallibly moving toward a millennial century of Peace and Prosperity.

The Perfessor closed the notebook and returned it to his pocket.

—There, he said, is Life in Our Time. What do you think of it?

Mr. Shawnessy picked up the *News-Historian* and rubbed a sheet of it between his fingers.

—Fifty years from now, this paper will be a brittle dust. No rag content.

The Hon. Garwood B. Jones was making senatorial faces for the members of the Sitting and Sewing Society. Through the mist of Mr. Shawnessy's cigar, the Senator in his duckbottomed suit became a stiff cartoon on faded paper. Fat men made word balloons about forgotten issues. Around them swirled brittle bits of headlines. Brown dust of the year 1892 settled slowly in guts of old libraries.

—Remember the papers of the sixties, Professor? Much better paper. Life had an epic quality in those days of the rag content. There was something worth preserving. Thirty years ago the great issues were the Union and Human Slavery. Today, the main parties electioneer over the protective tariff and the free coinage of silver, both artificial issues. But down underneath, the great issues wait to be recognized again. They are still what they've always been in human affairs—Union and Human Slavery.

—The Republic has to relax, the Perfessor said, after its moral and military orgies. These are the brown decades. No doubt in a few years we'll get excited about your so-called great issues again. Meanwhile, we have the *Indianapolis News-Historian* to remind us that we're living in a new age, the age of the Modern Man, or perhaps still better, the Common Man—common because he's becoming commoner all the time and more and more like every other man. The reason for this is that through the free press and the blessings of literacy he shares the atrocities of mankind more fully with his fellows. The newspaper is the true epic of this modern Odysseus, the Common Man. He's the most exciting hero of all time. The world's his oyster, and he opens it every morning over his coffee. In the space of a few minutes, he lays the Atlantic Cable, wins and loses wars in Europe, abdicates thrones, treads a tightrope over Niagara, and rapes an unidentified woman on a deserted part of the New York waterfront. For this, he's lynched from the nearest limb and cured of impotence, baldness, old age, and the piles. His heroic form is carried in pomp and ceremony to the vault of the Vanderbilts in a casket that weighs a ton. Resurrected, he goes off a trestle at ninety miles an hour and around the world in sixty-nine days. He lives a life of gilded ease on Fifth Avenue in New York and makes a pile on the stock market. Taking a vacation from respectability, he murders innocent bystanders with anarchist bombs and assassinates Presidents. The jungle fascinates him, and he buys a sun helmet and bustles off to Darkest Africa, where he emerges into a clearing, bland face smiling, hand outstretched, and greets himself, bland face smiling, hand outstretched, after living two years among the aborigines. Despite his emaciated condition, he has his chest measured for all the world to see, is admired for the bulge of his biceps and the size of his triceps, and wins the heavyweight boxing championship of the Cosmos. All this the Common Man accomplishes by the expenditure of a penny, while sitting squarely on his prosaic beam in the Main Street of Waycross, sucking on a five-cent cigar.

—Meanwhile, Mr. Shawnessy said, the real world goes on, the world of the only possible fact.

—What is this fact?

—A human life. That's the only thing that ever happens, whereas the *News-Historian,* like History, deals with something called the Event.

—What is this Event? the Perfessor said, cooperatively.

—The Event is something that never happened. It's a convenient myth abstracted from the welter of human fact. Events happen only in the newspapers and history books. But life goes on being one human being at a time, who is trying to find that mythical republic in which he can live with honor and happiness.

—Just so, the Perfessor said, and thus the Republic's a lie and History's a lie and the newspaper's a great lie. Culture's an inherited lie with which we hide from the human beast that he's only an ape with nightmares. All the world's a lie, and all the men and women merely liars. And with these lies we divert and deceive ourselves while our life-stuff goes through its little fury of growth, orgasm, and decay. Confess, my boy, that there's nothing real but the nature of Nature.

—But that's just the most primitive of all the lies.

—How does one get out of your chamber of mirrors? the Perfessor said, smiling pleasantly.

—It's better than your chamber of horrors, Mr. Shawnessy said, smiling pleasantly.

The Senator returned to his chair through a series of deep bows, proposing his backside to the Perfessor's contemplation.

—Thirty years ago, the Perfessor went on, we all murdered and sang and whooped it up for Liberty and Union here in the U.S.A. But the Southern Negro's still a slave and the Northern Worker's still a slave. Gentlemen, we grow old in a land of greed and lust.

The Senator, settling himself solidly in his chair, cleared his throat and looked around to see if he was observed.

—Gentlemen, it's perfectly true that the Southern Negro is still a slave.

He lowered his voice.

—And what of it? I always thought and still do that the South was morally in the right during the Civil War. As a political entity, the South had a right to be independent from the North, as much so as America did from England. As for slavery, Southerners believed —and by God, they were right—that the Negro was a being inferior to a white man as a horse is, though in lesser degree. They believed that because of his jungle background and his native physical and mental characteristics he wasn't a man in the same sense that the white man is a man. The proud people of the South wouldn't live on a basis of equality with these pitiful black brutes, because such equality would finally mean that Sambo's seed was as good as a white man's and could go where a white man's could. If Northerners had as many black men around them, they'd feel the same way. Before the War, the South had a system that kept the nigger in his place and yet took care of him. God knows, as a race, the nigger hasn't been any happier since. I tell you, morally and politically the South was right.

—This Republic, the Perfessor said, will never achieve anything resembling real equality until the mixture of the bloods is complete. It's too bad we don't all have a big black buck swinging from a branch of the family elm—we'd all get over our pride of race. Really, the human beast'd be a lot happier and wiser if he returned to the morals of the Great Swamp. Let the seed go where it pleases. It's all only a little passion and the earth.

—I will say one thing, the Senator said. The hottest women in the world are those famous octoroons. During a brief sojourn in

New Orleans lately, I had occasion to—shall we say—observe some of them again. They have just enough black blood in 'em to make 'em boil.

—The loveliest faces in the world, if it comes to that, the Perfessor said, are good old Anglo-Saxon mixed with nigger. You take that noble Northern look, and you taint it with the jungle. For this erotic masterpiece, we're indebted to the Old Southern Planter. I always thought he was well named. He planted. There was a lot of good black soil handy, and that fahn ole gemman put in a crop.

—I have a real fondness for the South, the Senator said. It gets into your blood.

The Perfessor raised his cane and recited:

> —O subtle, musky, slumbrous clime!
> O swart, hot land of pine and palm,
> Of fig, peach, guava, orange, lime,
> And terebinth and tropic balm!

Mr. Shawnessy, brooding and sad, lounged back in his chair and sipped through slow nostrils the black fragrance of his cigar.

> Our thin smokes curl upon the summer air
> Tracing a legend of an elder day.

Land of perennial summer woven with rivers, lost Eden of America, darkened with memory of a crime! I wandered in your old magnolia swamp and touched my face to one of your most sensual flowers. And a jovial, greatbearded God brooded above us watching. Lost pillars of a Southern paradise enshrined us where we sought a tree.

All this was long ago, the history of a lost republic. In sentimental vistas, we hid our nakedness for shame of old remembrance.

All this was long ago and far away, in the old Kentucky homeland of our soul, where 'tis summer and the darkies are gay, all this was on the river, down upon the river, way down upon the Mississippi River

1859— FAR, —1860
FAR AWAY
TO AN EVERBLOOMING SUMMER

the river brought him on its broadening flood. Days and nights, he and Susanna travelled in one of the big river boats south, a floating hotel paddled by a huge wheel. The boat's lobby sparkled with cut-glass chandeliers. Carpets paved the floor with a soundless softness. Mirrors in mahogany frames swarmed with the images of a fashionable throng making the winter journey down the river.

It was a lazy, lavish voyage; yet there was a constant sense of danger.

From what?

It was hard to say. In part, from the yellow river and its snags, shallows, hidden bars, treacherous channels, shifting shores; in part from the leashed fury of the boilers roaring with pine fires in the boat's entrails; in part also from the glittering crowd that swarmed along the river—gamblers, roustabouts, planters, Negroes, whores, fine ladies, soldiers, statesmen. These and a hundred other vivid types of humanity, most of them entirely new to Johnny Shawnessy, sought the river with a strange devotion. Down the Mississippi, the oldest highway of the Republic, these pilgrims travelled toward a sensual Canterbury. Its name was woven through all their conversations. And always this name meant exciting, sinful, dangerous, much desired.

It was at night that the boat carried Johnny Shawnessy and his wife Susanna into the harbor of New Orleans on the Mississippi Delta. Herds of boats, shrilling and baying, wallowed to their stalls. Down five miles of masts and funnels, light blazed from rows of floating windows. Orchestras played familiar Southern airs, and voices drifted across the water in nostalgic tunes.

As for the City, lying there on its silty bed, it winked, hovered, trembled, breathed, sighed, and stank. Mainly, it stank.

It stank of fish, tar, rum, cess, garbage, horse dung, human beings. It stank appallingly, and this stink as they neared the docks in the windless night almost choked Johnny. He looked in embarrassment at his wife leaning against the rail, eagerly watching the levee. Was it possible that she wasn't aware of this stink? What about all these others—habitués of New Orleans—didn't they smell this great stink? As for him, he never would be able to live in this stench. Even if he closed his nose to it, the mere thought of it would gag him.

Yet before long his nostrils had accepted it; and later he had to remind himself that this great human stink was there, always there, and that it would envelop everything he saw and did in New Orleans during the next few months.

—There they are! Look, Johnny! Aren't they sweet!

The levee, as they approached it, was alight from lanterns and the boat's own blazing battery of windows. Among the many people waiting there for friends, relatives, and loved ones, Johnny saw a group of young men and women, perhaps a dozen in number, who at this distance looked oddly prim and stiff, bristling and fluttering with canes, hats, curls, ribbons, handkerchiefs. Their faces were all upturned, the women's in bonnets tied under chin; the men's under tall, dandy hats. These creatures nodded, waved, smiled in happy unison, jerking their chins.

—Aren't they wonderful! Susanna shrieked. O, Johnny, you'll just *love* them! Hi Bobby! Dody! Barbara! Judy!

As they came nearer, Johnny became uneasily aware of their eyes, all fixed upon him with a brilliant intensity.

But as soon as he and Susanna had descended the gangplank, all these figurines dissolved into real people and overwhelmed the bridal pair with kisses, handshakes, backslaps, hugs, tears. Everyone was delighted to meet Johnny. Though Susanna had posted him ahead of time, so many young women gave him cousinly kisses that he could only distinguish Cousin Barbara Drake, a tall, languid blonde, who said in a voice mingling pleasure with surprise,

—My! Isn't he nice!

and Cousin Dody Ransome, a plump brunette with big shy eyes, who said in a sweet voice,

—Why, Sue, I'm *so* pleased with your new husband.

Of the men, he instantly picked out Dody's husband and Susanna's favorite relative, Robert Seymour Drake, with whom the honeymooners planned to pass most of their sojourn in New Orleans. Cousin Bobby, as Susanna called him, was in his middle twenties, a tall, lean man with a delightfully casual air. He had kind, handsome blue eyes and a dry, humorous mouth.

—So this is the lucky man, Sue, Cousin Bobby said, holding Johnny by the shoulders at arms' length. Children, I'm downright proud of you.

Johnny instantly liked Cousin Bobby, and all the others too, for that matter, as they swarmed around him, drenching his ears in an accent musical and mannered almost to lewdness. At first, he felt that he could no more adjust himself to its barbarous exaggerations than he could to the great stench of New Orleans; but in a short time, the whole party had poured into barouches, and with a feeling of enchantment and abandonment Johnny was swallowed up into the malodorous night and the soft voices of Susanna's people.

Later it seemed to him that during his sojourn in the South, he had lived in the scenes of a new *Uncle Tom's Cabin,* starring in the principal role Mr. John Wickliff Shawnessy from Raintree County, Indiana. And indeed this life in which he steeped himself was a delightful, barbarous, cruel old melodrama which for some reason or other all the actors and the audience passionately believed in. Johnny himself was constantly alternating between wholehearted participation and amused aloofness during his time there—and he was there a long time before he finally disentangled himself from that dark sweet land.

From December to the following August, he and his bride were entertained in New Orleans and the country up and down river. Those months were a procession of parties, balls, picnics, river excursions, and country week-ends. As Bobby Drake said when he ushered Johnny into his big winter mansion in New Orleans, a pile of brick, stucco, and iron reflecting the mongrel Spanish-French-English descent of New Orleans,

—Son, we'll try to show you a little of that famous Southern Hospitality.

The everblooming South showered warmth and fragrance on him from the beginning, beguiled him with beauty and leisure. You'll *love* it, honey, Susanna had said. And the truth was that he did love it. For young Johnny Shawnessy at the age of twenty-one was a rare mixture of poet and moralist. Moralist, he stored his memories for another day. Poet, he drank the warm milk of this existence and tasted its dark, exquisitely flavored honey. He had the poet's insatiable appetite for life, and New Orleans and the downriver country were everything that Southern life was—distilled to a dark quintessence. He saw it all. He saw its chattering blend of races, Spanish, French, Creole, Indian, Negro, Anglo-Saxon, a welter of tongues, bloods, manners. The river had lured them down its broad stream, had carried them along with centuries of silt, and dumped them on the Delta.

He saw the French Quarter, its Place d'Armes and whitewashed cathedral, the cafés where swarthy men and vivid brunette women sipped exotic drinks—*eau sucrée,* cognac, orange-water.

He saw the glittering amusements of the City, bullfights, cockfights, dogfights, horse races, operas, acrobats, melodramas, farces, gambling, *bals masqués.*

He saw the levees, miles of manmade walls to hold back the river, the levees crowded with commerce from all over the world, pouring the lavish wealth of the South into the Gulf and so to the ports of the world. He saw the molasses, sugar, tar, rum, timber, furs.

He saw especially the cotton, fat bales piled high on the docks waiting to be shipped. He saw that it was cotton which made this City the fourth port of the world, filled it with its glut of races, gave it wealth, beauty, seduction, sin, and death.

And as the months went by, he saw the wealth, the beauty, the seduction, the sin, and the death.

The young people of New Orleans with whom Johnny Shawnessy mainly consorted during his sojourn there were not like the people back home. As a class, they enjoyed something that didn't exist in Raintree County—leisure. Leisure to be fashionable, charming, and —on occasion—exquisitely sinful. The young men seldom read anything or performed any visible labor. They drank, danced, rode, gambled, whored. In the process, they laughed and cursed and talked like gentlemen. They were young Southern gentlemen.

The young women were in general a lively, pretty, romantic lot, completely dominating the men before and after marriage by a posture of defenseless womanhood requiring adoration and protection. The attitude was pretty and natural; they had been educated to it, and their mothers before them. They were young Southern ladies. And if they seemed during those months somewhat more daring than most young ladies of their class in the South, there were no doubt good reasons for it.

The Southern education of Johnny Shawnessy began early with an exposition of the phrase 'Southern Hospitality.' The young women of New Orleans, who presided over its hospitality and dispensed its blandishments, were much interested in Johnny for some reasons that he could fathom and some that he couldn't. At the first balls and parties, he felt himself watched by feverishly brilliant eyes. Later, the interest became more specific and personal. As Susanna had said, there was something about him. Perhaps it was a mixture of virility and gentleness, conscience and humor that could come only from Raintree County. Perhaps it was his dark hair shot with red, his expressive mouth and quick smile, his blue eyes watching the world with a mixture of innocent excitement and serene evaluation under their slightly lifted brows. At any rate, he had a peculiar effect on the young women whom he met in New Orleans—Susanna's own relatives and friends, some of whom carried the principle of hospitality rather far.

There was, for example, Cousin Barbara Drake. Cousin Barbara was tall, slender, and blonde in a languidly voluptuous way. Perhaps because she was thoroughly wearied of her young husband, who was a gamecock and a bore, she spent a great deal of time with Johnny on social occasions and was always coaxing him out for talks on lawns and balconies. As much the same group went to everything, Johnny was thrown with her constantly, a circumstance that pleased him as she was the most intelligent and witty woman he had met in New Orleans. But he hadn't become fully aware of the trend of things until one night when she said abruptly,

—Johnny, why did it have to be you?

—Yes?

They were sitting alone in an alcove off the ballroom at a home of mutual friends. Cousin Barbara, who had perhaps taken too much wine, was very languid and relaxed beside him.

—I mean, she said, you're just so darn nice. Tell me, weren't you ever in love with anyone but Cousin Sue—some girl up there where you live?

—Well, yes, I was, Cousin Barbara, he said.

She took his hand and gently pressed it.

—And was she in love with you?

—Well, she did in a way reciprocate my youthful passion, Johnny said, more and more embarrassed.

—No wonder. With that smile and those eyes. There's something about you, Johnny.

For a moment, he thought that that something was going to be the long, slender arms of Barbara Drake, but some other couples drifted by, and after a while Susanna came around and found him.

Johnny had no idea how far the thing had gone until the day he got an unsigned note in elegant script telling him to come, if his heart so prompted him, to a certain street corner in a remote part of New Orleans at dusk where a certain person, whose identity he could perhaps divine, would be waiting in a carriage to impart to him something of value. This invitation savored so finely of all the romantic stories he had read about the romantic South that he kept the rendezvous just out of curiosity. A carriage drove up, and the door opened. A lady in a veil beckoned him in with long, slender hand. When he was inside and the carriage was driving away, the lady in the veil said,

—O, Johnny, you must think me an evil woman. I had something I felt I must tell you.

Before she told him, however, she swooned in his arms and clung languidly to him, staining his shirt collar through the veil with tears and cosmetics. It was a very delicate situation.

—We really mustn't do this, he said. After all, Susanna's your cousin, and—uh—that makes you my cousin.

Along with this, he smiled lamely and held the slender trunk of the lady, which was quivering with sobs.

—O, dear, Johnny, she said. What have you done to me?

—We wouldn't want to hurt Susanna, Johnny said. After all, it's my honeymoon, and I want to remain worthy of her.

The lady in the veil sat bolt upright.

—O, I wish someone else would tell you, Johnny!

—Tell me what?

—Cousin Sue just isn't the right type for you, the lady in the veil said evasively.

—Why not? Johnny said, inwardly agreeing.

—Surely you know you're a very desirable young man, Johnny. You could pick and choose.

—Well, it strikes me that Susanna's a very desirable match. Money, culture, beauty——

—But why do you suppose she didn't marry down here? She had enough affairs.

—I don't know. Why?

—I didn't mean to get on this subject, the lady in the veil said. I feel so nervous.

She swooned again. Puzzled, he hung on through another storm, and after a while, she became very contrite and murmured some words about a moment of indiscretion and her certainty that a man of Johnny's character would not betray a heart which had never before deviated from the path of rectitude but which had been in this one instance, alas! too susceptible.

—As for those other things I said, Johnny, she remarked, angrily removing her veil and talking in a suddenly practical little voice as he stepped out of the carriage in a remote part of New Orleans, I was overwrought and no doubt jealous. I ought to hate you. But I don't. Good-by.

Whatever it was of value she had intended to impart, he never got it.

There was also the time he and Susanna went on a privately chartered steamboat excursion. In the middle of a night of wild festivity and much going about in other people's cabins, Johnny finally went to bed in what he took to be his own room. The room was unlighted, and when he started to climb into his bunk, a lady in the dark rose up and enveloped him.

—O, dear, Johnny! she whispered. My God!

—My God! Johnny whispered. I'm in the wrong place.

He stumbled out and wandered around all over the boat trying to find his stateroom and Susanna. Later he became convinced that he had been in the right room after all. Next day, the lady in the dark (whose voice he knew perfectly well and who had always seemed very sedate in his presence) was exceptionally noisy at the dinner table.

But the worst shock of all came just a few days before they left

New Orleans. Susanna made an overnight visit downriver with Cousin Bobby to attend to some legal matters involving an estate in which she had a part interest. Johnny stayed in New Orleans and along with Bobby's wife, Cousin Dody, represented the family at a lustrous *soirée* which he and Susanna had earlier agreed to attend. Sometime during the night, Johnny woke up suddenly in the huge bed which Dody had lovingly draped for the bridal couple. A woman was standing beside the bed with her arms at her sides, her eyes staring straight ahead.

It was Dody in a silk nightdress.

—Dody! Johnny said. What's the matter, dear?

Dody said nothing but looked at him with her large dark eyes somberly blazing. She slowly collapsed on the bed where she lay on her back, inert. Johnny picked her up and carried her to the door. He looked up and down the hall. It was empty. He carried her to her own room and put her on her bed, which was made.

—Dody.

She said nothing, but her arms clung around his neck.

—Dody, are you awake?

She said nothing but pulled gently at his neck.

—Go to sleep now, dear, Johnny said.

She appeared to be in a trance, and in fact he recalled something that she had said the day before about sleepwalking being a failing in the family.

The following morning at breakfast, she said,

—I think I must have walked in my sleep last night, Johnny. I didn't disturb you, did I, dear?

—Not at all, dear, Johnny said. I sleep like a log.

The Drakes and related families had large holdings upriver in the cotton and sugar plantations. The most enjoyable part of the honeymoon for Johnny was his visit to some of these great homes, which represented the finest flower of Southern life. Here in the loamy earth behind the levees was the South he had fashioned from all the romantic books he had read and the old nostalgic songs. It was all there—the everblooming summer; the levees holding back the mile-broad river; the cottonfields; the pillared mansions; the Negro quarters, shacks and cabins clustering close to the river; the fine manners; a way of living gentle and proud.

This earth had a kind of voice for him which seemed to say: Young man, you were mistaken. Forget your rigorous square of Raintree County. We give you your archaic dream, perennial summer and the lenient gods. Child of a vigorous northern parentage, stay with us here, and listen to our homeremembering songs. 'Tis summer and the days are long. Listen to the husky music of the darkies singing on the levees. Fondly we embrace you. We are not angry with you for your wrong contempt. White arms will cling about your shoulders, and you will press your lips to scarlet blossoms and delicious fruits. Have we not builded you the republic of your dreams? See how it stretches over slow lawns through gardens of cypress and magnolia to tranquil columns. We waited for you here with soft arms and voices a long time. Stay with us, wandering child and restless seeker. Fondly, fondly we embrace you.

He saw also the black people. In all Raintree County there had been hardly a dozen Negroes; but on the Lower Mississippi there were more black faces than white. In a way, he knew that he had come South to see this nameless swarm. And now he saw them—everywhere—streets, docks, levees, boats, houses, fields. He heard their mutilated tongue, English tainted with the jungle. He heard their music sung in darkness by the river where they lived in little cabins. Their songs were sometimes frenzied like the dances in which they whirled to syncopated rhythms, but more often muffled and sad with the inenarrable misery of their bondage. Few could remember the jungle home. Most had been born to cotton and the river.

They were all slaves, human beings whose dark skins made it legal for other men to rule them. They were also all Christians.

There was nothing South that wasn't impregnated with their presence. Black had builded this republic. Black had bled and labored for White and borne the casual lust of White so that this republic might lift its Doric columns from the Great Swamp. Black had planted and picked the white cotton that made White wealthy. Black had dressed the pampered bodies of White in satin gowns. Black had built the levees that held the dreaded river at bay. Black had bred and trained the swift horses with which White won the stakes at New Orleans. Black had distilled the fine whiskeys and the syrup rums that White sipped on long verandahs. Black had picked and dried and rolled tobacco leaf for White's long smokes. Black had dug the ditches and tied the bales, had reared the houses and built the roads. Black had erected the court houses and the state houses. Black had made White strong and proud and warlike, leaders of men, statesmen who shaped the course of empire South and West. Black had done it all, nameless and unrewarded, and would go on doing it, nameless and unrewarded.

So the secret of this culture, white and proud, was that it had all been built over the stinking marsh of human slavery. Often when Johnny was driving through New Orleans, in a maze of old streets, he would notice green scum in the gutters bubbling with gas. And when he had gone a little way beyond the City, he would see, heaving up to the very rims of the negrobuilded roads, the swamp from which the City had been rescued. The delicate iron festoons and romantic walls of New Orleans had in a few miles given way to Spanish moss swinging in soft scarves from the trees. Roots of twisted willows bulged from the unreclaimed, unreclaimable muck.

Yes, it was there always, a dark secret. When he lay in bed at night, it throbbed in the warm dark that settled like a mist, scented, miasmal, on the City. Here, in the American Republic, men openly committed the darkest of all crimes. The bought flesh lay forever beneath whiteblossoming summer.

From this old harlotry came the stained beauty of the South. This was the South's peculiar essence, this was what Susanna had meant, without knowing it, when she had said in her husky voice,

—You'll *love* it, honey.

He understood dimly why the songs most beloved by the white culture of the South were all simulated darkie songs. Through them all, a nameless darkie toted a weary load and longed for the old plantation. He was the South's primitive, simple hero, laden with his chains. White and Black seemed to find artistic satisfaction in this image of a human being sold downriver into exile and slavery, growing old in a land that was not his own, wandering on the earth and hunting for a lost Eden of peace and security. Thus the master race found its supreme symbol in the beautiful patience of its slaves.

So also Johnny noticed the slurred indolence of Southern speech, which was in some measure the result of long verbal contact between White and Black. The tongues of lost generations of slaves murmured in the speech of the South's most beautiful ladies.

Trained in disputation at the Pedee Academy and himself a staunch advocate of Republican principles in the press and elsewhere, Johnny Shawnessy made a tactful effort to present Northern views during his sojourn in the South. Now and then the book *Uncle Tom's Cabin* came up for mention. Without exception, Johnny Shawnessy's new friends cursed it for a tissue of monstrous lies, foully misrepresenting the institution upon which the South was founded. They justified slavery in a hundred ingenious ways.

Whether slavery was right in the beginning, they maintained, it was unavoidable now. The slave was described as shiftless, ignorant, immoral, dishonest, incapable of taking care of himself. In slavery he found security and protection against disease and poverty. He was happy and satisfied with his lot if only the abolitionists would let him be. The whole thing was justified from the same immortal documents which were the Scriptures of Raintree County. The Constitution didn't forbid black slavery and on the contrary protected the slaveowner in his property. The Declaration of Independence declared that all men are created equal, but the Negro wasn't a man. The Bible justified slavery, as any Southern minister could show by countless quotations.

In these discussions, Johnny Shawnessy remained uniformly good-natured, but his antagonists did not always manage to do so. On the subject of their peculiar institution they were likely to lose all detachment, amiability, humor. If pushed hard, the most cultivated, like Cousin Bobby Drake, would gently chide the young man from Raintree County for his lack of information about the real relationship between Negroes and whites in the South. They would appeal to the obvious workability of the present state of affairs, the danger of upsetting it. If there was a crime here, none now living was guilty of it. Let the Northerners explain their own institution of wage slavery, whose workwrung victims lived in greater misery than the Southern Negro.

Less gentle Southerners became dangerous on the subject. A light like lust or fear crept into their eyes. They appealed to the brute fact of force and *status quo*. That was the way the South was, and no goddamyankee had better try to tell them how to run it.

As for the question of Union, Southerners everywhere openly

expressed their belief that before they would endure any restrictions on the practice or extension of their peculiar institution, they would withdraw from the Union. If the existing government couldn't or wouldn't protect their rights, then they had a sacred right to form a government of their own.

When Johnny attempted to reason with his new friends on this subject, he had the feeling that he was plunging into a great dismal swamp of human prejudice and error, in which there was no path for reason to follow. Slavery had been enthroned through so many generations of complete acquiescence on the one hand and complete mastery on the other that nothing conceivable would ever unseat it. What he saw made him deeply suspicious of some Northern claims that slavery was doomed to extinction and would die of its own weight in a score of years.

Indeed, there was evidence that exactly the contrary was true. Southerners everywhere in newspapers, at public meetings, on long verandahs, were talking openly of a revival of the slave trade. Cotton was a landkilling, mankilling crop. It had already ravaged its way from the Atlantic coast to the Mississippi and beyond, crowding out all other crops, leaving a trail of exhaustion behind. It had to push on, get more soil, more slaves. Territories not yet admitted to the Union must be open to this dynamic, self-devouring economy.

—What's it all leading to? Johnny sometimes asked the more intelligent people of his acquaintance. Where will it stop?

He never received a satisfactory answer to this question. Here he touched one of those blind, earthen walls that Southern life had been slowly building for a hundred years to keep the great yellow river of slavery within bounds.

Nevertheless, there was a goal toward which this proud race tended. The masters of the South had dreamed an enchanting dream. They had dreamed of a Greek republic on the soil of America. In its pillared homes would dwell the most beautiful women and the most distinguished men in the world, women with honey voices, glowing eyes, voluptuous bodies, men like jolly modern gods. The ports of the world would be open to this new republic and her imperial crop. Controlling the mouth of the Mississippi, Cotton Diplomacy would control the continent of North America and in time the world. This culture of power, wealth, and leisurely democratic traditions would be erected on the toil of ten million slaves. From the inexhaustible human mines of Africa, they would be imported once again. South and West, by the brilliance of her diplomacy or the might of her sword, the new State would expand, and the cotton would go with her, and the black man, and the pillared mansions. Let men beware how they placed any further barrier against the South! For this dream was dreamed with the religious consecration of proud spirits; into it they wove the poetry of names more beloved to them than the concept of Union. Those names were the long, the sibilant, the river-murmurous names of the Southern earth—Louisiana, Alabama, Mississippi, Texas, Arkansas, Georgia, Carolina, Florida, Virginia. Let all beware how they spattered the sovereign beauty of those names!

At the time, Johnny had little leisure or inclination to subject these views to the cold process of dialectic. He was exploring this life built on the Great Swamp, and he found that it had terrifying depths.

There was the time, back in New Orleans, when several of Susanna's male cousins invited Johnny to go on a stag dinner at the Gem, perhaps the City's most fashionable drinking house. The dinner slowly turned into a prolonged drinking bout, from which Johnny abstained, the better to hear what went on. At first the talk revolved largely on horses. Slowly, however, it turned from horses to women—and not white women but colored. In response to a hesitantly worded question about the famous octoroons, Johnny was drenched in a torrent of sensual detail. The stories grew richer, the epithets more brutal. Faces became flushed, eyes glowed, white teeth clenched in hard bursts of laughter. These young white men were banded in a collective verbal rape on the women of another race.

A little while after midnight someone stood up and suggested that they take young Johnny Shawnessy, that goddam no-account Yankee, and show him a little of the real South. Johnny looked inquiringly at Cousin Bobby Drake, who had smiled affably during the talk, contributing sometimes a gentle observation but always keeping the tactful, gentlemanly air that Johnny admired him for.

—Come along, Johnny, he said. I'll protect you. It's something to see, son. Downright educatin'.

They started out at a *bal masqué* in the Ponchartrain Ballroom, where the masqued women were all quadroons.

—Lots more men here on the nigger nights, one of the cousins explained.

There was some dancing and one or two of the cousins dropped off, but several robust characters had taken their place, and there was nothing for it but they must plunge deeper.

—How about takin' Johnny to the Swamp? one of the men said.

Through murky old streets the cabs plunged, spiralling deeper into the nocturnal muck of New Orleans as if to reach its lowest circle of depravity, which—the name was peculiarly right—was called the Swamp.

—They don't call it that much any more, Cousin Bobby explained to Johnny. They've cleaned it up a lot since the old days. But it's still the hottest part of town. You can hardly get a white woman there.

Not long after, Johnny followed the mob into a decayed hotel called Madame Gobert's, on whose name, pronounced *à la française,* indelicate puns were made. The interior main room of the building, which they reached through a tunnel with leaking walls, was under street level. Yellow light blazed shamelessly on walls once ornamented with gilt statues and scarlet scarves but now befouled by time, like the rouged old white woman who met them at the door. She was the only white woman in the place.

The night was far advanced at Madame Gobert's. The place seemed alive with women of all shades from obsidian black to light olive, and costumes in all degrees from full ballroom attire to stark nudity. White men chased giggling Negresses up a broad stair carpeted with filth fading into a murk of upper rooms. In this hell of decayed magnificence, it seemed to Johnny that the whole paradox of the South had come to detestable flower. He sat there, defended on one side by Bobby Drake and on the other by a wall oozing sweat, and watched. Here the white masters came as if to hurl themselves back into the morass from which they had reared their City. They talked the vilest words they could summon up, clenching their teeth and excreting drunken epithets with savage zest. These obscenities, devoid of imagination, were brutally repeated like the blows of a whip. The women for their part giggled fatuously and called the men Mister Jack and Mister Jim and Mister Bob.

—You mustn't get the idea, Johnny, Cousin Bobby said, that all

Southerners are like this. Of course, a lot of the planters will have a Nigro concubine or two. But these boys are kind of wild.

—Hello, Mister Bob, one of the girls said.

—Hello, Jewel, Bobby said. Well, I see the other boys have snaked upstairs on us. S'pose we get out of here, Johnny, and get a little fresh air.

But before they left, some of the other men rejoined them, and when Johnny finally did get out and gulped gratefully at the stinking, warm dawn of New Orleans, his friends swarmed around him with an account of their erotic achievements.

—Johnny, one of them said, trying to give him a true-blue look from drunken eyes, I like you, son, and I wanna do you favor. Now, I got lil mulatto gal shacked up right here on Girod Street. I'm rentin' her to another fella for twenty-five dollars month, which is damn high, boy, but she's worth it, ever' cent of it. She's a good clean girl, came right off my own pappy's plantation, and the old man had a lot of it himself. She ain't any blacker than that wall there, and son, she kin git a wiggle on. If you'll come with me, I'll take you in there right now.

Johnny thanked him a lot and managed with difficulty to get away. He tried to understand the significance of what he had seen. It wasn't ordinary prostitution. The white master was doing a thing so obscene and yet, for some reason, so desirable that he had to defend himself from conscience by an extra brutality. Here in a Black Mass of sensuality, he acknowledged the forbidden secret—his equality with the slave. But this acknowledgment was such that it was a baser indignity than the whip and served more than the bloodhound to keep a race in subjection.

Such was the darker side of that gentle whoredom called slavery, by which a whole race had to prostrate itself for the pleasure of another.

As for the more openly published aspects of the Southern trade in human flesh, Johnny saw that too. He went to the Arcade, where the best slaves were auctioned. They were treated with great care, for a good black would bring fifteen hundred dollars on the block. Slavery was getting more expensive all the time, and a cheaper source of supply was getting more imperative every year.

Johnny saw almost nothing of the beating and murder of slaves, so vividly depicted by Mrs. Stowe. In fact, all the time he was there, he saw only one instance in which a slave was struck.

It happened one afternoon when he and Susanna had driven out to the Drake plantation upriver with Bobby. As they got out of the buggy, Susanna dropped her bonnet and bending quickly over, picked it up. Her pretty breasts tipped against the rim of her blouse and the scarlet scar darkened suddenly. The Negro holding the horses, a boy of fourteen, watched in fascination. Susanna quickly caught up with Johnny, who took her arm and started up the lawn to the verandah.

Just then there was a thud of fist on flesh. Johnny turned around to see the Negro boy sprawling on his back, hands up, and Cousin Bobby Drake standing over him. Cousin Bobby ran his eyes around the yard; then, coldly purposeful, stepped over to a woodpile and picked up a broadaxe leaning against the logs. His shoulder muscles hardened under his loose coat and his long white hands bulged on the axe handle.

The Negro boy licked his lips but didn't move.

Without a thought, Johnny sprang forward and grabbed the axe handle. Cousin Bobby's lean, pleasant face, which had been entirely calm before, turned suddenly white, his eyes burned, and he exerted all his strength to tear the axe loose from Johnny's grip. The two men struggled furiously in a dead silence.

—Now stop that right now! Susanna said in a querulous voice from the porch. I'm downright ashamed of both of you!

Instantly, Cousin Bobby laughed and let go of the axe, which dropped between them. He adjusted his soft tie.

—Take it easy, son, he said. Can't a man scare the liver out of his own nigger? I wasn't going to hit 'im. I never in my life killed a nigger, and I wouldn't start before a lady.

He smiled and took Johnny's arm. He was breathing heavily, and his hands trembled.

—I'm sorry, Johnny said.

—Anyone else would've killed that nigger, Cousin Bobby said, his voice gently chiding, though his face muscles worked. I only aimed to teach 'im a lesson. He's lucky to be alive.

He hadn't even looked back at the Negro boy, who still lay where he had fallen as the two men and the girl walked up the verandah to the door.

As soon as they were inside, Susanna put her hands on her hips.

—Johnny, you ought to be ashamed of yourself, shaming Bobby that way in front of his own Nigro. Don't you know Bobby's the best master on the river! His slaves love him.

—Take it easy, Sue, Bobby said, smiling.

Johnny stood looking at his wife Susanna, whose left hand now nervously touched the scar on her breast, while her violet eyes glared indignation at him, her little foot stamped, and her breath panted through her pouting lips. Something hot gripped his entrails, and he felt like vomiting. A man had almost lost his life for looking at a scar on the breast of this girl. He stood, appalled at himself and the black moment that had sprung upon him from ambush in this genial place, among these hospitable people who loved him and had been so good to him.

—Hell, Cousin Bobby said, if Johnny wants to wrastle me in the sight of my own hands, I don't give a goddam. I want the boy to have a good time.

Later, after a couple of tall rum punches, Cousin Bobby remarked privily to Johnny,

—I assure you, son, I wouldn't kill a thousand dollars' worth of nigger just because the boy looked a little too long at my cousin's lovely tit. Frankly, I think the boy showed good taste. But you have to learn 'em young, as my old man used to say.

The thing passed over very well, and Susanna even made it up to Johnny privately that night. She crawled across his knees and said,

—Give me a good spanking, Johnny. I deserve it. Go on and hit me *hard,* honey.

He looked at her back in the warm dark—soft olive, with its graceful furrow. Suddenly, he imagined it covered with long, cruel gashes.

He didn't sleep at all well that night, and for the first time he began to want to leave the South.

During all this time, he had been absorbed in a highly personal preoccupation with the woman he had married. All the blind stirrings, hungers, and subtle lusts awakened in him by the feverflower of New Orleans seemed to embody themselves at last in her. Upon her catlike body, a creature of this earth, this South, this river, and this city, he sought to exhaust and still them. Through the long days he yearned for her and for the night as she for him.

Susanna had returned to her home as to a conquest. In its congenial air, her beauty acquired a hectic emphasis. Everywhere she attracted attention. But she remained entirely true to Johnny and exhibited him everywhere with open pride. Her whole effort during their time in the South was to make him accept and love this life in which she had been reared and from which, curiously, she had fled to find her love.

It was almost at the end of their stay in the South that Susanna made a special trip with him.

—It's a surprise, she said. I won't tell you where we're going.

They drove for miles north of the city and at last turned into a narrow lane overgrown with grass. There was a smell of rottenness and the river. In places the swamp oozed across the road.

—They haven't kept the levee in repair here, Susanna said.

The path they were following became lost in marshy growth, though now and then they found surviving traces of the way. At last close to the river, they passed through an ornamental gate into the remains of a once classic garden. Rare flowers and rank weeds grew thickly together around chunks of old statues and sections of fence. They passed pools of dark water, misted with mosquitoes. As they walked in the insufferable, still heat, a peculiar smile kept tugging at Susanna's pout.

At last they reached stone steps going up to a charred verandah. They stood on the roofless, uncolumned porch and looked down into a rectangular pit like a huge sunken grave, boiling with weeds so dense and tall that Johnny could scarcely see to the base of their stalks.

—Here's where I lived when I was a little girl, Johnny, Susanna said.

As she stood looking down at this great, festering grave of something that had once been her life, Johnny reconstructed the mansion in his mind, building it up from the shadow-smudge of an old daguerreotype. The desolate tangle of the garden became once more barbered and coolly lovely. An old black gardener worked among the roses and the lilies. The house reared its white walls from a verandah shaded with slender and tall columns. On the steps stood a little girl with black hair and violet eyes clutching under her arm an unburnt doll. Father and mother stood beside her, and in the shadow of the porch, leaning against a column, was a darkskinned woman with tragically lovely eyes.

—How did it burn, Susanna?

—No one knows, she said.

She stared fixedly into the grave.

—How—how many died?

—Three, she said. Mamma and Daddy and Henrietta. You saw their picture.

—Only those three?

—Yes. Only those three. I was lucky to get out alive. I slept next to Henrietta's room, and she was burnt.

—How old were you then?

—Just seven, she said.

—You remember it, of course?

—Yes, she said evasively.

—Why wasn't it rebuilt?

—I don't know, she said. There was a controversy over ownership. No one wanted to build again.

Later, she walked back in the direction of the river and hunted around a long time for something.

—There used to be a little cabin here, she said, but I guess it's gone.

After that, they drove away and, returning to the main road, stopped some distance down at a small but wellkept cemetery. Susanna led the way through the filigree gates and down a walk shaded with lindens to a little marble fountain featuring motifs of resurrection. She stopped by two stones near-by, enclosed in a rusty iron fence.

—Here's where my daddy and mamma are buried, she said.

Johnny read the inscription:

JAMES SEYMOUR DRAKE

and

wife REBECCA

Died August 16, 1844

—August 16, Johnny said. Why, that's today!

Susanna had the same strange little smile as she studied the grave. She kept glancing shyly at Johnny as if to see if he approved. Confining himself to cautious banalities, he followed her to a less pretentious plot, set clearly apart from the rest of the cemetery. Here there were many mounds but few stones. Johnny read some of the inscriptions in passing:

Here Lies Old Ned, A Good Slave

. . .

Eliza
Gone to Heaven

. . .

This Stone Is Erected to the Memory of Dred
Who Was Brought to This Country from
Africa
in 1780
and Died a Christian in the Arms
of His Master, John Drake
at the Age of 82.

There were no last names on these stones. Then Susanna stopped before an exceptionally fine stone on which was the following inscription:

Here Lies HENRIETTA COURTNEY
Died August 16, 1844.

—Here's where they buried Henrietta, Susanna said. She took care of me. You can't imagine how lovely she was, Johnny. She was like a great lady. In fact, she *was* a great lady. I'm not ashamed to say it. Of course, she *was* a Nigro.

—Was—was she a slave?

—O, no! Susanna said. She came from Cuba—Havana, that is. That's where I was born. Daddy was there several years, and Henrietta came back with us from there. It's funny now to think of her lying there. That is, if she *is* lying there.

She paused and looked almost shyly at Johnny.

—How's that? Johnny said.

—Some people say the graves were mixed. It's sort of a family scandal. I had an aunt several years ago said she wasn't sure but that nigger hussy Henrietta was sleeping in Mamma's grave.

—How could that be? Johnny said.

—O, they could hardly tell the women apart they were burned so bad. Though it's funny, because Mamma was kind of fat and Henrietta was slim.

—How could they make the mistake then?

—O, I don't know, Susanna said. You know how some people will blab. This particular aunt had never spoken to Daddy anyway for years. It's funny, isn't it, to think of them lying down there. And here I am. Is that you, down there, Henrietta?

Susanna cocked her ear prettily to the silent grave.

Johnny studied the grave. A woman lay beneath this earth, hair, eyebrows, eyelashes seared off by fire, the same fire that had touched the shoulder of the girl beside him. He and Susanna looked silently a long time at the grave, but the earth gave no sign, except to remain beautiful with summer. It had taken back the white flesh and the black, made no distinction between them. Now they lay beside the river, all passion stilled.

The following day he took Cousin Bobby aside.

—Bobby, he said. There's something I thought maybe you could tell me. What's all this about Susanna's family and that darn fire and the identification of the bodies?

Cousin Bobby laughed disarmingly and took Johnny affectionately by the arm.

—Just one of these old family skeletons, John. You know how crabby and suspicious women are! After all it was a pretty gruesome situation, those bodies burned beyond recognition. They hadn't any trouble identifying the man, but the women were another matter. Of course, I was just a shaver then. It all had something to do with the location of the bodies when found—I think they'd fallen through to the cellar. It was a hell of a mess, John, especially, you see, when one of the ladies was nigger. But there's no use digging all that up again.

—Still I'd like to know. After all, I'm married into the family and might as well be privy to its secrets.

—What did Sue tell you?

—She won't talk about it much.

—Well, Cousin Bobby said, weighing his words with an air of studied casualness, it was Sue's Aunt Tabby, sister to Aunt Becky, Sue's mother, who raised special hell over it. You see, Susanna's father was a queer sort—marvellous guy, everyone loved him, especially the women—but he was headstrong, and then he had a hell of a bad piece of luck. The woman he married—that was Aunt Rebecca—was from one of the finest families down here, and well, to put it brutally, she wasn't all there. She went loony, and it was a pretty bad life for him. You'd have found that out sooner or later, anyway. But don't let it worry you. Most families have a nut in 'em somewhere.

—But about this fire, Johnny said.

Cousin Bobby slowly lit a cigar.

—Well, John—puff, puff—to get back. After the fire Sue's Aunt Tabby charged into the mess, and there was a fight between her and Aunt Prissy—that was Uncle Jim's sister. Why, they couldn't even bury the bodies for a while. There *were* some odd wrinkles to the case. Two of the bodies were glued right together by the fire—sort of morbid—no use going into that.

He puffed on his cigar.

—So? Johnny said.

—So, Cousin Bobby said, what the hell!—it looked like there might have been foul play. I mean, why didn't they wake up? Everyone else did.

—I don't know, Johnny said. Why didn't they?

Cousin Bobby got interested in the story. It was evidently something he knew a lot about. He drew hard on his cigar and began to talk a little more freely.

—That's just it. Why didn't they wake up? And then as I said before, there was this question of identifying the bodies. Which was the odd woman?

—I don't know, Johnny said. Which?

—She was found some distance away from those two. What with coroner's autopsies and Aunt Tabby getting into it, and Aunt Prissy—that's the younger sister who always idolized Uncle Jim—trying to hush it all up, it was some story. There was some talk of Uncle Jim and—and the woman he was found with being shot in their bed.

—The woman he was found with?

—Act your age, John, Cousin Bobby said. Anyway, the thing was hushed up, and Uncle Jim was buried with the woman he was found with, and that was that. Probably, the whole thing was a lot of petticoat gossip. Aunt Tabby had it in for Uncle Jim ever since he beat the hell out of her husband.

Cousin Bobby stopped, laughed, and shook his head.

—You sure are getting a dose of family skeletons, John, he said.

—Go on, Johnny said. What for?

Cousin Bobby paused a moment, but the story was clearly too good to keep.

—The way they tell it, he said, Uncle Jim walked into a saloon in downtown New Orleans and took Uncle Buzbee by the collar and pulled him up. Neither man said a word. Uncle Jim had his horsewhip in his hand, and he started in hitting Uncle Buzbee. He hit him and hit him—on the face and the chest—and Uncle Buzbee stood there and took it till he dropped. Uncle Jim walked out, and no charges were brought. But after that Uncle Buzbee was a broken man and never showed his face in public again. He was a loose talker when he was drunk, and he must have said something. That wasn't so very long after Uncle Jim came back from Havana. Well, after that, people didn't talk—at least openly.

—Talk? Johnny said. What about? O, I suppose about Uncle Jim and Henrietta.

Cousin Bobby looked blandly at Johnny and made a smoke ring.

—I suppose so, he said. You know how women are. And this family is worse than most. I don't want to scare you, boy, but you won't lead a quiet life with that little woman, God bless her.

—Does Susanna know all this? Johnny asked.

—Well, of course, people don't talk about it around her. But since Aunt Prissy ran off with Susanna up to your country and sort of looked after her for years, she probably gave her the lowdown on it.

—Thanks a lot, Johnny said, for clearing things up.

He was more confused than ever. And somehow he didn't want to pursue the subject any farther.

That night, he lay a long time awake thinking of many things. Around him lay the putrid flower of the City of New Orleans, rankly nodding its head above the magnolia swamp. The languid stream of the river, draining all the waters of middle America, found its way here through many changing channels to the sea. Mingled with its yellow tide was the water of a little river far away in Raintree County, the legendary Shawmucky. The girl beside him lay in a characteristic posture, her knees drawn up, her head resting on her two hands pressed together. Her deep lips were open, the heavy lids lay lightly on her violet eyes. Susanna! *I had a dream the other night when everything was still. . . .*

It seemed to him then that she lay there couched in mystery like a sphinx, and that her presence and her musical name meant something tragic and mysterious which was at the heart of all human existence. Surely a strange fate had ferried this scarred, lovely creature up the great river to his arms.

It was during this night that Johnny definitely decided to go back to Raintree County. When he suggested it to Susanna the next day, to his surprise she said,

—Let's do, Johnny.

He couldn't imagine what it was that had changed her mind, especially now in late August with the political campaign roaring to white-hot fervor. Men and women were openly cursing the Republican nominee, Abraham Lincoln, and predicting a Southern secession if he was elected. Johnny was getting more and more uncomfortable, and he was delighted when Susanna seemed as eager as himself to go back to Raintree County.

Lately she had seemed listless during the day and unquiet in her sleep. He was distressed about her, wondering if perhaps she had caught the yellow fever. This pestilent monster from the swamp was making his annual summer visit to the Lower Mississippi and was killing his thousands. It was a good time to leave New Orleans.

The day Johnny and Susanna left was close and hot. As they boarded the steamboat in the crowded harbor, Johnny heard a voice husky and plaintive above the tumult of arrival and departure.

—Lost child! Lost child! it wailed over and over.

The source of this cry became apparent when an old Negro passed through the crowd beating a little muffled drum, repeating the strange, monotonous call. Leaning over the railing of the steamboat, Johnny and Susanna waved to friends and relatives who had come to see them off, perhaps a dozen in all, smiling and nodding and jerking their heads in charming unison.

—Aren't they sweet? Susanna said pensively. They all love you so much, Johnny. Good-by, Dody! Good-by, Judy! Good-by, Bobby!

Cousin Barbara wasn't there. She had died the week before of the yellow fever. Johnny had bravely volunteered to go and see her in her last sickness, but she had forbidden it. No doubt it was because the fever had blackened and shrivelled her long, lovely body with a touch like fire and corruption.

—She just literally burnt up, Dody had said. Poor Barbara.

—The fever kills that blonde kind fast, Cousin Bobby had said to Johnny. There are some advantages in being black. The niggers hardly ever die of it.

Some of the women were in tears as they watched the honeymooners leave. Dody stood waving her handkerchief and crying heartbrokenly. It was only a few nights before that she had been sleepwalking into Johnny's room.

Indeed, it seemed to him now that the whole structure of that delicious life had been swiftly decaying around him in the envenomed summer as yellow fever smote many with death, and election fever smote all with a rabid disease, and men and women did mad, lewd things.

A mist crossed Johnny's eyes; his throat felt big as he leaned there on the railing and watched the city and the crowded harbor dwindle until the figures on the pier were a line of dolls nodding and fluttering in the tremulous heat. He remembered how when he had come into this harbor months before, he had smelled a great stink. It must be here now, the same stink, even more detestable than when he had come down from Raintree County, because after all it was summer, the yellow fever was on the city, the slave pens near the Arcade must be fetid with their black stock. But he couldn't smell it any more.

Strange grief smote him. He leaned against the rail and turned his face away from Susanna so that she wouldn't see how moved he was. He felt that he was leaving something archaic, beautiful, and doomed. In the main room of the boat, the orchestra was playing. The music drifted across the yellow flood of the Mississippi streaming through summer to the Gulf.

All de world am sad and dreary,
Ebrywhere I roam,

O, DARKIES, HOW MY HEART GROWS WEARY,
FAR FROM DE OLD
FOLKS

AT HOME, thoroughly, in the middle of a good hot argument, the Senator stopped long enough to suck life back into his cigar.

—Between you, me, and—puff, puff—the outhouse, he remarked, looking around to see if he was observed, Abe Lincoln was the greatest charlatan in American History.

The Senator made a satisfactory smoke ring and let his last remark sink in. Then he said,

—Lincoln was just what the Democratic sheets called him—a clownish country lawyer. He had honest convictions about the Union and slavery all right, but does that make him a Great Man? Hell, no. Several thousand abler men than Lincoln had the same convictions, and hundreds of thousands died for them. Lincoln was a political accident. The Republican Party needed a man from the West in 1860. As for the way he fought the War, no war was ever fought so badly as the Civil War. As for the freeing of the slaves, did Lincoln do the Nation or the Negroes a real service by the Emancipation Proclamation? Because of that great mistake, this Nation will go on bleeding for centuries to come. Lincoln was a freak of history. The popular mind made Lincoln into a symbol of the Common Man because Lincoln himself was so goddam vulgar and common. Besides, everyone loves a bleeding martyr. Booth made Lincoln great.

—Garwood, Mr. Shawnessy said, you never recognized Lincoln's greatness because you never understood his time. Only a very great President could have subdued the South. And all through the War Copperheads like you in the North kept the councils of the Union divided. You couldn't heave a rock in Raintree County without winging a Southern sympathizer. The greatness of Lincoln was the greatness of America in his time. America in the years 1809 to 1865 was capable of creating a great man.

—This is all hindsight, John, the Senator said. Lincoln *is* a useful symbol; I don't deny it. God knows, I've made as much capital out of him as anyone. I acknowledge the debt. But when I allow myself to be swayed only by the hard facts of history, I can't admit that Lincoln was a truly Great Man.

—There are few if any hard facts of history, Mr. Shawnessy said. But there are some words in the right context. Perhaps the real office of the historian is to rebuild an accurate context around the few great words that survive.

—I suppose, the Senator said, that we're about to recite that admired classic of American oratory—the Gettysburg Address!

His stub was out again, and he bit savagely at a new cigar and spit the tip into the street.

—Lincoln had some power of phrase all right. But we exaggerate even that. If Booth hadn't made Lincoln the Great Martyr, no one would have dug out the Gettysburg Address, which was a flop when delivered. Let's not forget that the Civil War was a time of general eloquence anyway. There were themes to inspire it. At least a dozen men in the country were speaking more eloquently than Lincoln during the War. But of course Lincoln gets the historic limelight.

—Great words, Mr. Shawnessy said, come only from great men. Almost every public utterance of Lincoln's has a touch of greatness. He had the power to see issues clear and to make others see them clear. He was the voice of America long before the fighting began, of South as well as North. He defined the situation so clearly that even the South accepted his definition, and knowing exactly where she stood when Lincoln was elected, she threw down the gage. As early as 1858, this obscure lawyer from Illinois found the epoch-summarizing phrase, *A house divided against itself cannot stand.*

—What was so bright about that? the Senator said. Millions of Americans knew that the Nation couldn't exist half slave and half free. *A house divided against itself cannot stand.* Just a Biblical quotation.

Mr. Shawnessy smoked quietly, waiting for the sound of those words to stop echoing. The fabric of a house rose silently and stood waiting to be recognized, all murmurous with voices and footfalls, its upper chambers filled with filtered sunlight.

Once long ago in a time discrete from time I lived in such a tall house with a beautiful woman from the Southland. And I think I can remember how she moved in the upper chambers of the house in twilight, and I think I can remember how this was in a time before a time of terror and devastation, and I wish I could remember what it was that happened to that antique life.

—Well, what are you thinking, John? the Perfessor said.

—Of farewells, Mr. Shawnessy said. I'm thinking—oddly—of how Abe Lincoln took leave of his fellow townsmen in Springfield,

Illinois. While Southerners were screaming for blood and taunting the supineness of the old Union, Lincoln said:

> My friends, no one, not in my position, can realize the sadness I feel at this parting. To this people I owe all that I am. Here I have lived more than a quarter of a century. Here my children were born, and here one of them lies buried. I know not how soon I shall see you again. I go to assume a task more difficult than that which has devolved upon any other man since the days of Washington. He never would have succeeded except for the aid of Divine Providence, upon which he at all times relied. I feel that I cannot succeed without the same Divine blessing which sustained him; and on the Almighty Being I place my reliance for support. And I hope you, my friends, will all pray that I may receive that Divine Assistance, without which I cannot succeed, but with which success is certain. Again I bid you an affectionate farewell.

—Stop showing off that famous memory, sprout, the Senator said. I don't want to brag, gentlemen, but I could beat that speech every day of the year, from the back of a train getting up steam, with a squawling baby in my arms, and a boy lighting a firecracker under me.

—You couldn't have pronounced a single phrase of it, Garwood, Mr. Shawnessy said. It's the only utterance of the period that sounds right to us now. Lincoln, as usual, had the moral gravity to understand the tragedy of the hour. Compare it with the oratory of the South or of other Northerners during that time, and you'll see what I mean.

—I don't see at all what you mean, the Senator said, rising to greet an approaching delegation, but for the time being, I bid you an affectionate . . .

Farewell. Farewells echoed up and down the streets of country towns in Raintree County years ago, those little streets that lay like channels of eternity beneath the sugar maples. Farewells were spoken on verandahs of houses long ago. Farewells echoed in the vague, lost years before the War (these darkstained memories were all of the years before the War). And in these memories a young man walked along the pre-war streets. And if he followed far enough, these streets would bring him again through the memory of old farewells back to a certain street in Raintree County long ago, and looking up he would see once more on a steep lawn the mournful face of

1860— THE —1861
HOUSE, SUSANNA'S
TALL HOUSE IN FREEHAVEN

became the home of the young married couple after their return from the South. These were troublous times for Raintree County and the Republic, and troublous too for Johnny Shawnessy. On his return, he became a full-time assistant to Niles Foster on the *Free Enquirer,* which was now a Republican daily paper, engaged in a desperate fight with the Democratic elements of the County and growing rapidly in circulation and influence as the election of 1860 approached. On the side, Johnny tried to work at an epic poem on the history and meaning of America, but for some reason it didn't go very well.

His life was dismally complicated by the fact that he was living in his wife's house and that she was a Southerner. In the savage reprisals of a political campaign this domestic paradox was not overlooked by the rival newspaper. Only two weeks after Johnny's return, the following editorial appeared in the *Clarion:*

WHAT'S THIS ABOUT HYPOCRISY?

Those who charge the Democratic Party in this County with the mote of hypocrisy in their stand on the slavery question had best look to the beam in their own eye. It is, we believe, only too well known that a certain young man from whose pen emanates three fourths of the inflammatory and seditious doctrine now appearing in the Republican organ of this community, has recently returned from a summer in the South, where he was feasted by the very people whose institutions he is now attacking with such venomous ferocity. Not only that, but we have it on unimpeachable authority that the imposing mansion which he and his lovely wife, a girl from Louisiana, inhabit near the Square includes in its domestic arrangements two colored people whose status with respect to those freedoms for whose protection the Republican Party claims a monopoly, is, to say the least, questionable. Now we, for our part . . .

The appearance of this article forced a showdown between Johnny and Susanna.

—How about it, Susanna? Are Bessie and Soona slaves? Johnny asked her, holding a copy of the *Clarion*.

—O, I wouldn't call them that, she said listlessly.

They were at the breakfast table. Susanna, who hadn't been feeling very well, was in a velvet morning robe, her black hair dishevelled. She had come down late, having spent so much time talking with the dolls in bed and dressing them that she hadn't yet dressed herself. Johnny had finished eating and was ready to leave for the office.

—Susanna, you'll have to free those girls or get rid of them, he said.

—They've been in our family since they were born, she said. They'd be unhappy anywhere else.

—I've got to stop this criticism, he said. You can see the position I'm in.

—I don't see why you got yourself in such a position. Honestly, Johnny, after being South with me, I don't see how you can go on being a Republican.

—It's useless to argue about it, Susanna. Those are my honest convictions. You can go on thinking your way, and I won't quarrel with you. When you're South, you can have your slaves. After all they're your property, like this house. But this is free country up here, and as a Republican and a newspaperman, I've got to be able to repudiate this attack.

—I wish we hadn't come back then, Susanna said.

—You didn't have to come back, Johnny said, turning pale.

—Johnny, I wish you wouldn't pick on me now. I don't feel well.

—I'm not picking on you, dear. I just want to be able to say that those girls are not slaves.

—You *are* picking on me, Susanna said. I wish we could go away from here.

—We can't do that, Johnny said. Not now.

—Sure we could, honey, Susanna said pertly. I have plenty of money. We could take a trip. To Europe—or somewhere.

Johnny bowed his head. Yes, Susanna had plenty of money.

The house was hers, and the Negro girls were hers. With what he made, he couldn't even buy her clothes.

—I can't go now, he said. I'm in a crusade for something I believe in. Don't you understand, Susanna?

—I don't see why you're so stubborn about it, Susanna said. What did anybody South ever do to hurt you? Why, you know how sweet and nice they all were to you, and you know you *loved* it. And now——

—That's not the point, dear. Those are personal matters. This is a contest of ideals.

—But it *isn't,* Susanna said, triumphantly. That's just where you're wrong, Johnny. What the Republicans really want is to take our slaves away from us and try to make us live in a different way. But we don't *want* to live in a different way. We want to live in our *own* way. Besides, Johnny, I just don't see how you can go out and electioneer for a man like Lincoln. If it was somebody else—why, all right, but *Lincoln!*

She made a sound of disgust. She hunched her shoulders and shook her head. Something colubrine seemed to flow up and down under the velvet robe.

—What's the matter with Lincoln?

—No selfrespecting person could vote for him, Susanna said, beginning to lose her petulant tone for one of strident conviction. Now surely you know that, Johnny.

—Why? Johnny said, grimly watching the gap widen in the thin walls that they had maintained so long against the great boiling river of their sectional difference.

Susanna stood up and began to walk lithely back and forth, thrusting her shoulders, shaking her hair, and stroking her neck.

—I mean—well, it's a wellknown fact, and you must have heard about it too.

—What?

She turned defiantly, standing at bay.

—I mean the fact that Lincoln has Nigro blood in him!

It was one of the notorious undercover smears of the campaign, growing out of the obscurity of Lincoln's maternal background. But coming in all seriousness from Susanna, the statement somehow struck him as funny. He began to laugh.

—He does too have Nigro blood in him! Susanna said, her eyes blazing. You don't have to laugh. It's so! I know it!

Johnny laughed harder.

—Lincoln's mother was—was the issue of an illegitimate birth, Susanna said. Some Southern planter and a Nigro girl. Just ask Uncle Garwood.

This really was too funny in a dreadful sort of way, and Johnny laughed helplessly with tears in his eyes.

—What's so funny about it? Susanna said, her voice getting higher. If you want a Nigro for President, go ahead and elect him. Anyway, anybody that'd vote for Lincoln and abolition the same as says I'm no better than a nigger girl.

—Don't be ridiculous, Susanna. All I ask is that you get rid of these poor colored girls or pay them wages or something, and we'll keep our political views to ourselves.

—I know you don't love me! Susanna shrieked. You never did! You've been asking questions about me! And you hate me! I know you do! Your mother and father hate me because I'm Southern!

—Take it easy, Johnny said, his desire to laugh suddenly gone. All I——

But the levees were gone, and the angry waters poured through. For the next few minutes he watched whitefaced while Susanna pointed her finger at him and shouted wild, incoherent things. At last he got up.

—Look, he said, do what you please about the girls, but if they're not free by tonight, I'm not coming back to this house.

He walked out and down the long steps to the street and over to the *Enquirer* office.

He was covered up with work all day. Several times, he went to a back window of the office and looked out toward the house, which was just hidden by a shed built close to the newspaper building.

It was after dark before the special issue on which he and Niles were working was ready for press. With cold misgivings, he left the office and walked to the alley from which it was possible to look up a long, slanting shaft between buildings to Susanna's house on its high lawn.

What he saw shocked him.

The house was ablaze with lights. All the windows, front, side, and rear, were streaming light into the quiet September evening. It reminded him of something, but he couldn't say what. He ran down the slope of the alley and crossed a street and began to climb the gentle grade that led up to the house. Just as he set foot on the steps, there was a shattering sound like the bursting of a thousand wire strings. He realized then that his nerves were overwrought. What he had heard was someone letting both hands fall on piano keys. He ran up the steps and opened the door.

—Surprise! Surprise!

The house was full of people. Most of them were friends, but some were people Johnny had never seen. Someone was pounding the piano in the parlor while couples sat on the stair and sang or danced in the hall. Johnny could even hear sounds of merriment from upstairs. He walked into the parlor.

—Well, I'll be hornswoggled! Look who's here! jocundly boomed a familiar voice.

Garwood Jones was in the front room by the piano, a drink in his hand and one arm lovingly embracing Susanna, who giggled shyly.

Johnny stood blinking, trying to keep from looking like a man who had just come home late at night to find more people than he expected in his bed.

Susanna ran over to him and threw her arms around his neck and kissed him. She was in a dark winecolored gown he hadn't seen before. Her eyes shone, and her cheeks had a hectic flush. Her mouth made little pouts and smiles.

—It's a party for you, honey, she said. Uncle Garwood helped me do it.

—I'm sorry you ever came, chum, Garwood said. We were having fun till now.

Someone swatted Johnny on the back, and someone shoved a glass into his hand.

—I mixed the punch myself, John, Garwood said. An old Indian recipe. Pure corn and just the least lettle bit of pure lye.

Johnny put his worries at the back of his mind and became the life of the party. He danced with all the girls and executed some new Southern steps with Susanna. He had never seen her so innocently lovely. She laughed and danced and drank and prattled at a rate that would have exhausted ten ordinary women. The climax of the party came when she threw her hands up in the air and began to shriek,

—Hush! Hush! Everybody hush! I have an announcement to make.

Everybody hushed. Susanna went over to Johnny and took his hand.

—I want you all to know, she said, that I don't keep any slaves in this house. That was a wicked article, and, Uncle Garwood, I'm ashamed of you!

—Don't mention it, honey, Garwood said, looking surprised but quickly rising to the occasion. I'd slander my own grandma if it'd beat the Republicans at the polls.

—I have freed both of those girls, Susanna said, and they work for me on wages.

Bessie and Soona, the two colored girls, standing in the door and obviously a party to this charade, nodded their heads and grinned widely.

—Hurrah! someone said weakly.

There was even a little applause. Horribly embarrassed, Johnny tried to get the party started again, but the life had died in it. Pretty soon, people were bowing out of the door. When they were all gone, Susanna held out her arms.

—Now, she said, you see how much I love you, Johnny.

—My dear child! he said, putting his arms around her. Susanna, I——

She had not yet completed her elaborate gesture of conciliation, but slipping out of his arms ran up the steps.

—Come and find me in our room, she said. I'll be waiting for you.

When he went up later to the front room on the second floor where the bed with the scarlet drapes was still enthroned in lonely splendor, he didn't know what to expect. Opening the door, he looked apprehensively in. It was even better—or worse—than he had expected.

In the light of a candle, a naked woman was on her knees beside the bed, with head, arms, and hair flung forward in an attitude of slavish surrender. The flickering candlelight made dusky shadows in the hollows of her back. She had somehow twisted a scarf around her wrists and pinioned them loosely to the bedpost. There was a leather whip lying on the floor beside her.

—My God! Johnny said involuntarily.

The figure on the floor sighed and said mournfully,

—*Whip* me, honey. I deserve it.

Johnny picked up the whip and tossed it into a corner of the room.

—Get up, you crazy little thing, he said.

—Go on and *lash* me, she said with savage intensity. You're too *good* to me, Johnny, and I don't *deserve* it. I wish you'd *beat* me good and hard.

Johnny leaned over and pulled her to her feet. She was crying and kissing him at the same time.

—I'll do anything for you, honey, she said. I love you so.

Johnny looked around.

—There *is* one thing——

He jerked the scarlet draperies aside and picking Susanna up, put her not very gently on the bed. He found himself talking between clenched teeth.

—Let's start by getting rid of these damned dolls!

He picked them up one at a time from their precarious perches around the bed, and one at a time he threw them.

—Take that! he said. And that! And that!

Their little waxy heads and stuffed bodies smashed against the walls of the room. Each time he threw one, Susanna gave a shriek of laughter and clapped her hands.

He started picking them up by the armful. They fell around the bed. He kicked them. He plucked the big fat one from the base of the bed and holding him by one leg threw him the length of the room. Finally, he grabbed the burnt doll.

—You, too, he said, you hideous little devil.

Susanna gave a particularly loud shriek of excitement as the doll Jeemie rebounded from the wall.

—Now, Johnny said, at last we can have a little privacy in this bed.

That was a wild, sweet night, but there never was another that good in the tall house south of the Square. In a way, it seemed to be a turning point. The following morning Susanna was very sick. She moped in bed for several days, and the dolls all had to be collected and put back in place, and Johnny, Bessie, and Soona waited on her hand and foot. But she refused to have a doctor.

—Maybe you're going to have a child, Susanna, Johnny said at last.

—No! she said bitterly. I'd rather die.

That night, he awoke vaguely alarmed. He sat up suddenly.

A woman was standing before the single great window of the bedroom. Dressed in a long white vaporous robe, she turned her head from side to side, eyes shut, as if rejecting something. Then her lips parted, her eyes opened and stared in terror at the pale square of the window, she thrust her arms out several times with the palms forward, writhing her body fantastically backward in attitudes of loathing and rejection. She was breathing hoarsely like a person in the grip of strong passion—love or terror.

Johnny got out of bed and started toward her.

—Susanna!

Instantly she put her hands clawlike to the sides of her face and screamed. He caught her wrists, intending to awaken her and lead her back to bed. She fought frantically. She spit and snarled beastlike. Her nails raked his face and chest. He hugged her, pinioned her arms to her sides. She went on twisting and screaming. He shook her violently, and at last she went limp. He carried her to the bed where she lay silent, refusing to say anything, turning her head away as if ashamed.

—What was the matter? he said, lamely. Bad dreams?

Instead of answering, she gave a long, shuddering sigh and began to cry. She cried helplessly and loudly like a child. He tried to quiet her, and at last she stopped.

—Tell me what's the matter, Susanna. Please.

—O, she said, it's—it's that I've been having such awful dreams. I've been so afraid. I think—I think maybe it's because I'm going to have a child, Johnny.

—Well, why in the world didn't you tell me? It's nothing to be ashamed of. When do you think it happened?

—In August just before we came back, I guess. I've known it for quite a while.

—No use to be alarmed, honey. Having a baby's the most natural thing in the world.

It was something he had often heard T. D. say.

—I suppose so, she said.

They talked for a while and finally she said,

—I remember now what I dreamed if you'd like to hear it.

—Sure. Go ahead.

—I thought I was back in our old home—you know, before it was burnt. Everything was just the way it used to be, except that the house was all covered with dust as if it had been closed up for a long time. And it was all silent like a tomb, nobody else in it but me. There was some kind of mystery about it, and I was trying to find out what it was. I went up the main stair to the second floor and walked over to the window and looked out. There was the garden just the way it used to be, but it was getting dark. Then I could see a steamboat on the river coming up to the landing. It was all lit up, and there were hundreds of people on board singing and waving their hands. There were men and women and children, and about half of them Nigroes. They were all happy and excited, and then the steamboat blew two blasts of the whistle and all the little Nigro and white children came running down the gangplank to the levee. I was walking across the garden then toward the river. It was dark, and there was a celebration of some kind, slaves singing and dancing by the river. I turned and went down a lane and through the trees till I reached the little cabin where Henrietta used to stay and where I played doll. I thought I'd left something there that I must be sure to get. I went in the door, and everything was dark. I had a lamp in my hand, and I went over and climbed the ladder to the loft and went over to the window and looked out. Big red fires were burning by the river. Then I thought I was in the bed there or somewhere else, and it was pitchdark, and suddenly I realized that it was a plot to kill me. Somebody was trying to get in at the window and I tried to move, but I couldn't, and a big black thing covered my face and throat and was trying to strangle me. That was when I woke up.

On following nights Susanna woke Johnny often to tell him dreams that she had been having. More often than not they were grotesquely distorted incidents of her childhood in the South, before the death of her parents. Little by little, he explored a Southland of her soul, from which a portion of herself had never been withdrawn. In the sleeptime, dark hands carried her back and back, and she was again a little girl in a landscape of dream-illumined rivers, rotting cabins, old plantation homes. Often in her dreams she saw the dug earth yield bodies of women dead in childbirth or children, mothlike, with crusted eyes, whose little pinched faces were faintly negroid.

As autumn advanced, she awoke often from this tainted land and would cling to him like a scared child and talk solemnly for hours in the night telling him stories of her childhood, as if by these recitals she could discharge at last the whole of a sick burden and be rid of it forever.

—Mamma was very queer, she told Johnny one night. When I was little, everyone said that Mamma wasn't well. I know now that she was crazy. I hated her.

—Was she that way when your father married her?

—Soon after, I guess. Aunt Prissy said that Mamma made life unbearable for Daddy. I think her madness must have had something to do with his leaving Louisiana and taking her to Havana. He was there several years, and I was born there.

—Were you the only child?

—Mamma had another baby before they left Louisiana. It was a little boy, born dead.

—Do you remember anything about Havana?

—I was only four when we came back to the plantation. But I have some memories of when we lived in Havana. That was a happy time. Henrietta had more of the care of me then.

—Where did Henrietta come from?

—According to Aunt Prissy, she belonged to a rich man in Havana, and Daddy bought her freedom. She was a famous beauty, the most beautiful woman I ever saw. She was very gentle and sweet, and I loved her much more than I did Mamma. When I was very little in Cuba, we had a house in the country, and Daddy would come and visit sometimes. Henrietta was like a great lady and had her own servants. Those were the happy days.

—What made your father go back to Louisiana?

—Daddy was the only son, and when his father died, he went back to take the plantation. That was his great mistake. Everything changed. Not that I wasn't happy at first. When we first came back, Henrietta lived in a little cabin not far from the main house. She had a girl to wait on her. I used to stay at the cabin with Henrietta most of the time and play dolls there.

—Didn't your mother ever take care of you?

—No, Susanna said. Mamma had a room of her own on the third

floor and a special girl to attend to her. Every now and then, Daddy would take me up to see her. In fact, my earliest memories of Mamma are always the same way. She would be sitting in a chair looking at an album of pictures. She was a fat, darkhaired woman, not pretty any longer. When Daddy took me up, he would say, Here's your mother, Susanna. She would like to see you again. Mamma would smile as if she knew a secret no one else knew and would go on turning the pages of the album, hunting for something all the time. She never touched me, never said anything, never showed any sign that she recognized me or cared anything about me. Once she laughed in a way that frightened me. Your mother isn't well, Susanna, Daddy would always say when we left the room. That's why she acts the way she does. Then the bad time came.

—How was that?

—It wasn't very long after we came back that there was some kind of trouble. Aunt Prissy has told me more about it since. It seemed as if Mamma's relatives made a protest of some kind and wanted to take Mamma away. Aunt Tabby—that was Mamma's older sister—was at the bottom of it. Anyway, that was when Henrietta went away, and her cabin was shut up. I was terribly lonely. And for a while Mamma got better and came downstairs more. Daddy had a girl to look after me. But Mamma would sometimes watch me in her peculiar way and smile, and sometimes she would laugh at me. I believed that she had driven Henrietta away, and I began to hate her and fear her then.

Susanna's voice trembled. She turned restlessly in the bed, trembling.

—That was when I would go down to Henrietta's cabin, and I found a way of getting in through a loose board on the back door. And I would go upstairs to Henrietta's bedroom, where the window looked out on the river, and get on the bed and play doll and pretend that Henrietta was there. Then one day, Daddy came to the house and said, I have a surprise for you, Susanna. He took me down to the cabin with him, and there was Henrietta. I was so happy I cried. Daddy just smiled in his sad sweet way. He was the most wonderful man, Johnny.

—Then Henrietta stayed—for good?

The phrase seemed unluckily chosen.

Susanna's voice was hushed and solemn.

—Yes. Only, after awhile, she stayed up at the house and had the large front bedroom next to mine. That was when Mamma was so much worse, and two people had to watch her all the time.

Susanna began stroking her throat as if to rub away the memory of the thing that had suddenly devoured this tangled skein of love and madness. For these conversations between Johnny Shawnessy and his wife always ebbed into silence against one now nevermentioned scarlet fact, a night of fire whose secret was impenetrably lost on the river of years.

These verbal debauches came all at night. During the day, Susanna talked little. She became pale and almost ugly during this time, looking somehow younger, like a haggard child in the grip of an incurable disease. She was pathetically dependent upon him and the Negro girls. She could hardly bear to have him leave the house, and when he returned she was avid to hear of everything he had done and of everyone with whom he had spoken.

—Did they inquire about me? she would ask.

She was especially inquisitive about members of his family. When his parents called at the house in Freehaven, he felt constrained in their presence, knowing how entirely he had been taken out of the old life with them. He felt that they too were ill at ease in this house. Somehow he couldn't talk with Ellen and T. D. about Susanna's condition, and once when he suggested to her that T. D. might handle the delivery of the child, Susanna objected so violently that Johnny didn't mention the subject again. Indeed, it was months before she consented to see a physician at all.

During this time, the summer and fall of 1860, the year of the great campaign, Johnny Shawnessy felt that he had passed entirely from his years of sunlight and young aspiration into a somber maturity. At Susanna's insistence he had grown a mustache and beard, and in other ways she caused him to feel much older—by her utter dependence on him, her sickness, and her jealousy when she discovered some part of his present life denied to her. Her childishness became so complete that it dominated their relationship to each other and filled him with emotions that he couldn't define. At this very time when he had made her a woman fruitful, she had become to him most like a passionate, irresponsible child. And he in turn became in his own mind like a father, grave, full of brooding anxiety and a persistent feeling of guilt. He felt that he was transgressing some ancient, most austere prohibition.

The only good thing about Susanna's illness was that she ceased to care about the political contest that was now shaking the land to its foundations.

Election Day, 1860, was the most memorable in the history of Raintree County as well as the Republic. For the first time, North was openly pitted against South on the question of slavery extension. The Republican Party had become the party of the North, reflecting the widespread moral and economic opposition to slavery, which had grown steadily greater for fifty years and had now swollen to an irresistible flood. The Democratic Party, which had until that time tried to remain the party of compromise—of North, South, East, and West—was hopelessly split and enfeebled. In separate conventions, the Southern branch of it, abandoning all compromise, had nominated its own candidate, while the Northern-dominated branch chose Lincoln's old senatorial opponent, Douglas. A fourth party, calling itself the Union Party, merely increased the confusion. In this chaos the Republican candidate, Abraham Lincoln, presented a clearcut opportunity for voters to elect a President who stood firmly for the preservation of the Union at all costs and against the spread of slavery as a moral and political evil.

On Election Day the Republic made the fateful decision that it had been evading for fifty years. In Raintree County, the people went down to the polls all day long in a tide unprecedented, overwhelming, irresistible, and voted for Abraham Lincoln in the belief that they were voting for the future of America as one Nation indivisible, with liberty and justice for all.

Johnny Shawnessy, twenty-one years old, cast his first vote that day. He had never seen such wild excitement in the Square. As the dimensions of the Republican victory gradually became clear from reports pouring in from other parts of the land, the elation in Freehaven mounted until it broke all bounds.

One of the great moments in Johnny's life came on the night when Lincoln's victory was assured and had been posted in the windows of the *Free Enquirer* office. Johnny and Niles Foster were standing at the door watching a Liberty Parade go around and around the Square waving banners, shouting Republican songs, ringing cowbells. Thousands of people were weeping, laughing, singing.

—We helped cause this, John, Niles said. I guess we have a right to enjoy it.

—We want Foster! We want Foster! the crowd chanted. And then,

—We want Johnny! We want Johnny!

A dozen hands reached out and lifted the two men up. They rode around the Square in the light of the victory bonfires. When Johnny finally managed to get back on his feet, dozens of men came up and shook his hand, and women hugged and kissed him.

In the midst of this emotional frenzy, outdoing even the Great Revival of '58, Johnny came face to face with Nell Gaither. She had apparently been marching with the crowd. Her furcollared coat—for it was a chilly evening—was pulled close around her chin. Her bonnet was knocked awry, and strands of her bright hair had come down. Her cheeks were streaked as though she had been crying. Her eyes were full of green excitement.

—Hello, Johnny, she said. Isn't it wonderful!

—Sure is, Nell.

They stood in the crowd unconsciously gripping each other's hands and arms, both trembling with excitement. They hadn't seen each other since Johnny's marriage.

—How is—how is everything with you, Nell?

—Just fine, she said. Johnny, you have a beard.

—I know it, Johnny said. We—we change.

—How is everything with you, Johnny?

—Just fine.

—I'm so glad, Nell said. Well, I guess this is a good time to say good-by, Johnny.

—Good-by?

—Yes, I'm going back East, Nell said. To stay with Mamma's people.

—O, I'm sorry, he said, without sufficient thought.

The crowd was all gone for him. The Election was forgotten. The bonfires had died away. The hundreds of faces pressing around him, shouting and singing, were all phantoms and unreal. Johnny touched his beard and smiled his wistful, affectionate smile.

—As the Professor would say, he said, I guess it's time for a little quotation, if I can lay my tongue to one. In the words of that dear book, which you inscribed to me, Nell, *Fare thee well! and if for-ever——*

—*Still for ever, fare thee well,* Nell said, smiling her bright smile.

Her hands tightened on his arms, and his on hers, and they let go of each other, and smiling, both were lost in the vast, victorious crowd that wound endlessly around the Court House Square.

Of course, there was an awakening from all this jubilation, as Johnny had known there would be. Raintree County had scarcely been elated by the news of Lincoln's victory when it was shocked by news of another kind. The Southern States were quitting the Union. Secession started with South Carolina and spread fast, engulfing, one after another, the great names below the Mason and Dixon line. Federal forts and arsenals were seized. Southern orators began to proclaim the New Republic in sonorous, confident phrases. They were through with the old Union, and they offered to the North peace or a sword. In contrast, the Northern leaders seemed pitiably inept. President Buchanan and his expiring administration watched impotently as the breach widened. The President-elect, Abraham Lincoln, whiled away his time in Springfield, Illinois, saying nothing much except that he expected the Union to hold together. Johnny began to doubt the wisdom of the political compromise whereby an obscure, untried Westerner had become President of the Republic in her most critical hour. In Raintree County, there was a feeling of complete paralysis, which deepened as weeks and months passed. The Republic appeared to be mortally wounded without ever having begun to bleed.

On February 18, Jefferson Davis became the President of the Southern Confederacy. In the harbor of Charleston, South Carolina, an island fortress called Fort Sumter became a stormcenter of discussion as it continued to hold out with a small Federal garrison while the South demanded its surrender. Everywhere in the North men were asking themselves the same terrible questions: Would Sumter be evacuated by the incoming administration and a clear case of Northern acquiescence to the seceding states be established? Would Lincoln be inaugurated on March 4? Would there be a capital in which such a ceremony could take place? Would Washington, D. C., an old Southern City, remain a part of the Union? Would Virginia, lingering and indecisive, go with the seceding states? What would become of the border states between North and South, like Tennessee, Kentucky, Missouri? What of the Far West, which the South was trying to win to its banners?

On February 11, Abraham Lincoln left Springfield for Washington. A little less than a month later, the new President was inaugurated at Washington without bloodshed. Johnny took some heart from the tone of the President's inaugural. He hoped that Lincoln's wise plea for reconciliation would be hearkened to, but in the following weeks no overt act, either of violence or concession, occurred on either side to change the situation. The most exciting headlines continued to feature Fort Sumter, still holding out in Charleston Harbor. The newspapers were filled with contradictory rumors: The Federal troops were to be withdrawn. They were to be reinforced. They had been bribed. Lincoln had sold out the Republic. Lincoln would stand firm. The South would give in after certain concessions to her hurt pride. The South was secretly preparing to attack the North. No one knew anything for certain, and everyone had a different idea as to what ought to be done.

In Raintree County, Indiana, the voice of compromise was louder all the time. Even Johnny Shawnessy felt the infection. For his part, he was married to a Southern woman, he had spent some time in the South, and he understood better than most people in the County the sectional pride of the Southerners, the things they were saying, their old, compelling dream. Besides, he had personal problems that left him precious little emotion to expend on the Republic.

Susanna was coming to her time.

One day late in March, Johnny met T. D. and Ellen on the Square. He hadn't seen them for several weeks. When they asked him how Susanna was, he said,

—All right, I guess.

—You're expecting around the middle of April? T. D. said.

—Yes.

—Well, don't worry, my boy. Having a baby's the most natural thing in the world. By the way, if you need us for anything, just call.

—Sure, Johnny said.

He smiled and talked a little with his parents about the national situation, toward which T. D. took a hopeful view. Johnny said good-by, still smiling to reassure them.

He didn't tell them about Susanna's absolute refusal to let T. D. have anything to do with the case. He didn't tell them how she had been pleading with him to let her have the baby without medical assistance. He didn't tell them how Susanna kept to her bed almost constantly, except when she wandered forlornly in the upper rooms of the house. He didn't tell them how he had awakened a few nights before to find her gone from the bed and had discovered her on the top floor leaning from an open window, looking down fixedly at stone steps dropping steeply to the street two floors below. He didn't tell them how he had hardly slept at all lately, for fear of some violence she might do herself. He didn't tell them how she lay in her bed restlessly stroking her throat and watching him with scared eyes, while together,

IN THE HOUSE ABOVE THE SQUARE

THEY WENT ON WAITING,

WAITING,

—WAITING for the War to start, the Perfessor said, was one of the most exhausting ordeals this nation ever had. Sumter was a positive relief. I was reporting it for the *Dial,* you know, and I saw the iron seed sown in Charleston Harbor.

—Speaking of Sumter, the Senator said, resuming his seat before the General Store, it illustrates my point. Do you realize that the *casus belli* of the Civil War didn't occur until the sainted Sucker had held office for over a month and after seven Southern States had seceded! Lincoln was either cowardly or inept.

—Sumter! the Perfessor said. How in your theory of history, John, do you encompass this bloody name on which the Republic foundered? Take away the flagwaving and the patriot shrieks, and what do you have?—a few hundred iron balls bounding on brick walls from which a dyed rag fluttered! For this, the Republic resorted to four years of mass murder. And all from a word—Sumter!

—The whole Nineteenth Century willed Sumter, Mr. Shawnessy said. Lincoln was merely a wise doctor to Time's bloody birth. He knew that he couldn't prevent the physical fact of Sumter, but he gave moral direction to the Event. If you want to understand Sumter, go behind it to Lincoln coming across the Nation to Washington in the days before his inauguration. Listen to the voice of this ungainly Western lawyer speaking to crowds in the railway stations, outdoor assemblies, and torchlit halls. Once he said:

> If the great American People only keep their temper both sides of the line, the trouble will come to an end, and the question which now distracts the Country be settled, just as surely as all other difficulties, of a like character, which have originated in this Government, have been adjusted.

—That illustrates Lincoln's lack of sand, the Senator said. Goddammit, the War was inevitable. A fighting President wouldn't have made such a Christlike martyr in retrospect, but he'd have got the War over with sooner. Jefferson Davis was no genius, God knows, but even he was an abler man than Lincoln. I said so then. I say so now.

—Read the Inaugurals, Mr. Shawnessy said. Davis did a mediocre piece of sword-rattling. Lincoln said:

> Physically speaking, we cannot separate. We cannot remove our respective Sections from each other, nor build an impassable wall between them. A husband and wife may be divorced, and go out of the presence and beyond the reach of each other; but the different parts of our Country cannot do this. They cannot but remain face to face; and intercourse, either amicable or hostile, must continue between them.

—You know, the Perfessor said, I have an idea that Lincoln's fondness for this marital image was caused by bitter personal experience. Death had surely no sting for a man who had to bear the American Civil War publicly and Mary Todd Lincoln privately.

—Lincoln was really a sordid fellow, the Senator said. What does it do for the hero-image people have of Lincoln when you think of this big, ugly, rawboned bastard getting into his dirty nightgown every night and going to bed with that crazy little fat chattering bitch, Mary Todd!

The Senator wheezed with laughter and bit savagely at the end of his cigar.

—By God, I've always hated Abe Lincoln, he said, and still do. He's the cross I have had to bear for becoming a Republican.

—Your hate, Garwood, Mr. Shawnessy said, trying to keep emotion from his voice, is part of the great human enigma of Abraham Lincoln. Out of those stale bedrooms filled with the nagging spirit of Mary Todd Lincoln and out of smokefilled law offices where men cursed and told dirty stories and discussed old trials, came somehow the mind that distilled the First Inaugural. How do you explain the wise, tragic tolerance that Lincoln alone showed, of all the leaders North and South?

> I am loath to close. We are not enemies, but friends. We must not be enemies. Though passion may have strained, it must not break our bonds of affection. The mystic chords of memory stretching from every battle-field and patriot grave to every living heart and hearthstone, all over this broad Land, will yet swell the chorus of the Union, when again touched, as surely they will be, by the better angels of our nature.

He said the last words hastily in a low voice. Unexpectedly, as he spoke them, he had beheld the President. Lincoln stood on a platform erected from the steps of the Capitol in Washington. The living light of time sculptured the lined face, coarse black hair, long body in a lank black suit. This man had been.

—Lincoln, the Perfessor said. What is Lincoln? Who knows? Lincoln is one of your Events, John, that we together, good mythmakers all, have labored to build.

The three men smoked inscrutably. Firecrackers burst in the Street of Waycross. Faces, wheels, hooves passed on the National Road.

In the Garwood B. Jones Period of the Republic, let us remember the great names of our youth. Hail and Farewell!

Abraham Lincoln is a photograph by Brady. Or a memory in the mind of an old, old citizen, whose eyes are gleety with the gray discharge of time. Or a mist of print in old newspapers stored in the tombs of great metropolitan libraries. In these we touch the man Lincoln, the seamy, memoryhaunted face, the fabulous flesh of Sangamon County, Illinois, Spencer County, Indiana, Hardin County, Kentucky.

Where are the days of the life of Abraham Lincoln?

They are yours, Republic! They are yours, American earth dense with the roots of prairie grass! They are yours, mythjetting Time, in which the centuries go and go in ranks of streaming headlines.

What was the man Abraham Lincoln?

He was a memory and a hundred thousand memories, mostly of the earth.

He was a memory of the western earth, its clay-dissolving rivers in the springtime, its red tobacco flats, the young saplings in the raw weather and their perfect buds of green, the wet flaw and shining mud of crude little roads from house to house in the early springtime. He was a memory of big trees felled for clearings, of hands handling the broadaxe. Trees fell crashing and were hewn into rails for fences. He was the memory of divisions of the prairie earth, of western names, the names of counties.

Abraham Lincoln was a memory of Hardin County in Kentucky, of a cabin made of logs and clay, a cut between the hills, a spring and a running branch, of a mother whose name was a sound of the ancient English ancestry of these people. Abraham Lincoln was a memory of Nancy Hanks.

Abraham Lincoln was a memory of Spencer County, Indiana, and how you got to Indiana by crossing the Ohio. Indiana was North-of-the-Ohio; it was the United States of America, and when you crossed the broad water you crossed from slave land into free. Indiana was the new nation in 1816, the people spilling westward, a free earth. In the rocky soil of southern Indiana, there were hills of small trees, there were ravines of rotten leaves, there were cold rains, it was a raw, wet country, winter and spring. Abraham Lincoln was the memory of days and ways in early Indiana. He was a memory of his mother's thin, ruined body in the February earth of Spencer County.

Abraham Lincoln was the memory of Sangamon County, Illinois, green fields, the prairie land divided by rivers. He was a memory of a young man's strong desire of love and fame, he was the memory of a young man's days and nights of dreaming and of learning out of books in leather bindings. He was the memory of a big strength looking for a weight to swing. He was the memory of girls' faces against green lawns and going to the County Fair.

Abraham Lincoln was a long memory of the American earth. And in the time of the testing of the Republic, the West gave Abraham Lincoln and his memories to the Nation. And we in turn, Humanity, give him down the Ages as a memorial of our culture, we give you his words and his memories, we offer you his long figure in the black suit to be placed in the mausoleum of the great, beside the few men who deserve to be remembered. We give you him to be remembered because he is all of us, being what we were and are, because we fashioned him, and he is like us when we are most like unto ourselves.

—Every people has a rendezvous with destiny, the Perfessor was saying. After an Event happens, we get the feeling that it had been waiting there like an ambush. Sumter was the bloody ambush of the Nineteenth Century. I never have ceased to regret the Civil War. It's silly of me, of course. Perhaps I ought to take the attitude of a character in one of Mrs. Stowe's later novels: *Wasn't everything topsy-turvy for a time!* But the War was the end of a rather gentle, rich old life and the beginning of something nobody really wanted.

—Spare the tears, Professor, the Senator said. As I see it, nothing great is accomplished in this world without letting a little blood.

Yes, there shall be blood on the earth. There shall be a dark hour when men meet on the streets and shake their heads and hurriedly pass on. There shall be a dawn when the sun spouts blood on the fringe of night.

—So we came to Sumter, the Perfessor said. For better or for worse.

So we came to Sumter. So we came to Sumter down all our different ways. So we came down streets of old American cities and down the roads of countless summertimes and on the swollen backs of rivers, and at last, at last, we came to Sumter. So we came through the days of our strong, blithe youth, we heard the voices of the talkers talking from the platforms erected in the clearings, we heard the voices ringing in the liberty parades, we were not afraid, we marched with long legs swinging into step, rawboned, greatchested, with fiercely tender smiles, with hornloud laughs and lips that talked of beauty, whiskey, tobacco, and the Rights of Man.

So we came to Sumter. We came, our name was legion, we came, we had been coming. We had been coming there for fifty years. We had been moving there and never knew it. When we crossed the Alleghenies and struck across the forests of Ohio, we were coming. When we poled our flatboats down the western rivers to the Gulf and saw the big hands sold at auction on the blocks, and the girls with ebon thighs and the planters with white appraising fingers, we were coming on our way, we were on our way to Sumter. When we crossed the burning plains, when our wagons shrugged and staggered in the passes, when we reached the far slope thin and dying and demanding food, we were coming down to Sumter.

When we laid the rails across the prairie, when we put the bridge across the river, when we rolled at forty miles per hour down the grade, we were coming down to Sumter.

When we lay together in the dark, my unforgotten darling, when the rose of love was blooming in the dark, because we both were mortal, when we touched our bodies in the night and made that fatal crossing of the seed of North and South, when we lay dreaming by each other in the night so long and long, my darling, we were coming down to Sumter. *O, Susanna, do not cry for me,* we were coming down to Sumter

April 12–14— IN —1861

THE DAWN,

IN THE RED DAWN,

he awoke with a feeling that something terrible had happened. At first he thought that he was in his old room at home. Then he saw the pale rectangle of the window that looked north to the Square and remembered where he was.

Asleep beside him, Susanna stirred uneasily. He wondered if she was dreaming of her old home, going down forgotten lanes hand in hand with some elder person, reprieved for a little time from fear of the heavy, feeding guest in the dark of her body.

As he watched her, she rolled her head from side to side on the pillow. The dawn grayly sculptured her face into the look of a child about to cry. Her pale, deep lips opened and drew down at the corners. She moved her mouth as if making sounds of negation, but the words strangled in her throat.

—Susanna! Wake up!

Surprised under the translucent veil of flesh, the thing that wakened in her sleeping body paused, expressed itself in a series of little whimpering cries and sorrowful contortions of the face, then abruptly withdrew into silent depths. Susanna's eyes opened. She was wide awake.

—You were dreaming, he said. You called out.

She turned her head to one side.

—I think it's come, Johnny.

—You mean——

—The pain. I felt it all night.

—I'll go for the doctor, he said, smiling to show an assurance that he didn't feel.

She lay without speaking and stared at him, her eyes dilated and expressionless.

—Now don't worry, honey, he said. Having a baby's the most natural thing in the world.

The words gagged him. She didn't say anything but rolled her head away, staring at nothing.

He dressed hurriedly and called the Negro girls.

—Now, Bessie, he said to the more intelligent one, you look after your mistress until I come back. I want you to stay in the room with her. Don't leave her.

—Yes, sir.

—And, Soona, you run any errands that are necessary. I'm going for the doctor.

In the latter stage of Susanna's pregnancy, he had finally persuaded her to see a doctor whose house was in the northern part of Freehaven, almost a mile away.

As he rode through the pale dawn, all things seemed strange to him. He beheld a world that no man ought to see, a world of gray streets, houses, yards. Sleep had fixed batlike on this scene and sucked it bloodless. Dawn beat around it in a lonely tide, trying to engulf it to all eternity. All things seemed alien to him, devoid of relevance, drawn back to namelessness.

There was no other person in the Square as he passed through, the horse's hooves echoing off the blank faces of the business fronts. No man ought to behold this world devoid of human faces and meanings. No man ought to see the discarded husk of this huge stage, after the actors and audience had gone home.

Yes, all things were strange in this dawn. But strangest of all was himself, a bearded, haggard young man, shivering in a thin coat, riding as if his foolish haste could change the thing that had come to pass. The tide of years had stranded him on this bleak shore of morning, and he couldn't say how he had come here. He only knew that he was afraid and desperately alone.

There could no longer be concealments and evasions. A new life pressed against the gates of time. The enormous mystery in which Raintree County floated like an island in oceanic dawn had sent another wanderer to the shore of Names, Boundaries, and Events. It had come from Unspace and Untime. It was as old as the world, and yet it would be called a child. It had woven into its dark fabric the memories of ages. It had never forgotten anything.

No, whatever it was, it had never forgotten anything. And it was necessary that it be received and seen and that its paternity be acknowledged and that it be given a name.

It was gray morning when Johnny reached the house that he was hunting. He knocked a long time at the front door. A woman opened.

—Is Doctor Howard in?

—No, the woman said. I'm sorry. He was called out to the country. He left an hour ago.

The woman suggested that Johnny might ride out and find the doctor and take him directly to Susanna. She told him how to reach the place, which was close to Moreland.

—You'll probably catch him on the way back, she said. Since it's her first baby, she may not have it for a while. I think you've got plenty of time. It might be a false labor.

Johnny thanked her and rode off. He cut through the outskirts of Freehaven to the familiar road east. The sun was up when he passed the Home Place. He felt a little foolish riding by and hoped that neither T. D. nor Ellen had seen him.

At the house near Moreland, he found that the doctor had left an hour earlier and had taken the road north, ostensibly to call on someone before returning home. Johnny rode some distance up the road, making inquiries, but without success.

He turned around and rode hard back to Moreland and turned for Freehaven. As he neared the Home Place, he made a sudden decision. He turned in, rode up to the back gate, dismounted, and went to T. D.'s Office. There was a sign on the door:

Have went to town. Be back in the afternoon.
T. D. Shawnessy

The house was empty like the Office.

He galloped the horse all the way back into town. It was already ten o'clock. To his surprise, he kept passing people, more and more people as he neared the outskirts of Freehaven. He tried to remember if it was a holiday. The street into the Square was full of vehicles.

When he reached the Square, he looked around him, vaguely surprised to see that the empty mask had been filled with life. Apparently most of the County had come in for the day. He tied up the horse to the hitching rail and began looking for members of his family.

Almost immediately, he saw Ellen and T. D. in the middle of a group of citizens. T. D.'s hands were clasped behind his back, his chin was up, he was talking with animation, though no one was listening very closely except Ellen.

Johnny motioned to Ellen, who left the group. He started to tell her what had happened and explained how he had been unable to get the doctor.

—I wonder if you and Pa could come right over, Mamma. I should tell you that Susanna doesn't want T. D. and you to—to have to help. She's been—well—a little upset. She may seem a bit strange—but if you could come over in a little while——

—Why, sure, we'll be right over, Johnny, Ellen said. My, you picked a bad day!

Then for the first time in hours, Johnny looked about him with seeing eyes. The Square was packed with people. A band was striking up somewhere. Everyone was talking, gesturing, laughing. Businessmen had left their counters and were standing in the street. Knots of citizens grew thicker until around the telegraph window at the station north of the Square they were a solid mass of heads.

—Say, what's going on anyway? Johnny asked.

—Haven't you heard? Ellen said. They've fired on Fort Sumter.

The mythical words had come at last. And with these words, he knew, as all men did, that an era was done. These few words had slain an old republic.

A throng of men and women marched into the Square behind a band. They were singing:

—Blow ye the trumpet, blow
The gladly-solemn sound.

And indeed, everyone looked jubilant. Even T. D. kept smiling from sheer excitement.

—Well, he said, after he had come over and learned Johnny's predicament, you picked a solemn day, my boy. This means war as sure as anything, though I don't think it can possibly last long. Perhaps this was the only way to settle the matter.

—The Southerners have made a big mistake, a man said. This was all we needed. Now we'll go down there and beat the time out of 'em.

—Ain't no two ways about it, a man said. They fired on the flag.

—Come over in about ten minutes, Pa, Johnny said. I'm going home now.

He picked his way through the thickening crowd to the alley on the south side of the Square. The old sick anxiety coursed through him stronger than ever as he approached the house.

Inside, he met Soona on the stair coming down.

—Nothin's happened yet, Mistuh Johnny. She's just havin' the pains, tha's all.

Johnny went up stairs, and sitting down beside Susanna, took her hand and gently broke the news to her that T. D. and Ellen were coming.

To his surprise, she said only,

—It doesn't matter who comes.

She clung to his hand and watched him with frightened eyes. Her face was pale; her deep lips were deadpale. Her hair looked coarse and lifeless like an animal's. Her eyes were dilated by fear and pain. She seemed a stranger to him. Her suffering had stricken off her beauty, her sophistication, and her stately name.

With sad wonderment, he realized that this moment was indirectly the consequence of a golden afternoon beneath the tree on the shore of Lake Paradise. Then too she had lost her name, her clothing, her sophistication. Then too she had been wholly woman and without shame. Now for this candor, she must have an equal candor. For this namelessness, she must suffer the suffering without a name.

Like a rhythm of waters was the tidal recurrence of the birth contractions as he sat and watched with her. From the fetid swamp of life beneath the time and space of Raintree County, dark rivers flowed, dark waters bore their burden to the shores of time. He was filled with pity as he watched her lying there exhausted, waiting for the empty pool of her anguish to fill up again. But she hardly made a sound. She had the same expression in her eyes that he had sometimes seen there when he discovered her walking in her sleep.

Johnny was relieved when T. D. and Ellen came in and took charge of the situation.

—Now, John, you stop worrying, T. D. said. Having a baby's the most natural thing in the world.

Susanna didn't have her baby that day. Toward night the pain lessened, and T. D. pronounced it a case of false labor. He and

Ellen decided to stay for the night. All night and the following day, which was Saturday, the vigil continued.

—I don't know what the trouble is, T. D. said. She ain't quite made up her mind yet to have this baby.

Then about midnight the strange old tide in Susanna's body began to reach the full.

—I think her time is here, T. D. said.

—Johnny, I think it'd be best if you waited downstairs, Ellen said. You'd just be in the way, and besides it might be hard on you. Bessie and Soona and T. D. and I are enough to handle this.

Pacing back and forth in the empty first floor of the house was also hard on Johnny. He heard unidentifiable sounds from upstairs, crisp orders from T. D., exclamations from the Negro girls. The periods of silence were worst of all. Now and then Bessie or Soona would come down the stair to get something from the kitchen. Johnny would stand, haggardly watching the descending face to see what he could read there.

—Miss Susanna sure is brave, Soona said once. She don't hardly call out at all, poor thing.

Later, however, the cries from upstairs were louder; and shortly after that, his mother appeared at the head of the stair.

—It won't be long now, Johnny, she said. She's had the breaking of the waters.

Back to Johnny's mind there flashed a scene from years ago. An old song throbbed in his brain with sad, insistent rhythm:

I had a dream de udder night,
When eb'ryting was still;
I thought I saw Susanna dear,
A-comin' down de hill. . . .

Like yesterday, he remembered the day he had driven into Danwebster with T. D. and Ellen and had stood before the General Store, listening to a woman cry in an upstairs room, while men discussed slavery, compromises, and the western lands. Now thirteen years had passed. He had drifted down the incredible great labyrinth of time for thirteen years. And it was strange to think that without that elder scene, this scene could never have been. That old scene had been the parent of this scene, that child had been father of this man, and every word spoken before the General Store, the haunting westward song, the Doniphants and their infant boy (lost child, bearing a name of Raintree County toward purple mountains), the fat bulk of Grampa Peters, the newspapers, and the election—all had been necessary. But who then could have charted Johnny Shawnessy's voyage on the webbed waters of the Republic? Who could have guessed the reunions and farewells that were to bring him and the Republic to this perilous day? So the waters of life were breaking, mystical waters, on the shores of Raintree County in vast propulsions and withdrawals, bringing events and souls to birth.

Dark questionings, suspicions, memories coursed through Johnny's thoughts. Alas! for guilty seed brought overseas in old migrations! Alas for the inscrutable Swamp from which had risen a stately, mongrel City! Did anything guarantee that each time a woman's womb became fruitful it would give back a repetition of the parent forms? What was the child of a man and a woman?

Johnny Shawnessy stood in darkness, and the darkness had the head of a sphinx, and from its moving lips the riddle of life was propounded. This riddle couldn't be solved except with a cry of pain in the night, with a priestlike laying-on of hands, with a violation of beauty.

O! Susanna,
  Do not cry for me;
I come from . . .

He was slowly aware that the moans and cries from upstairs had ceased. A silence hung over him batlike, descended, clung to him, enveloped him in horror. Cold sweat drenched him. His heart beat violently. He wanted to run up the stair, he wanted to force his way past the watchers in the room, he wanted to tear the hideous veil of his fear and behold whatever it was that had caused this silence.

—Johnny!

It was Ellen's voice. His mother appeared at the head of the stair. She leaned over. She had something in her arms wrapped in a blanket. He heard a thin, piping cry.

He began to walk up the stair, trying to see his mother's face in the darkness. His tongue was glued to the roof of his mouth.

—You're the father of a fine little boy, Ellen said.

At the head of the stair, he plainly saw his mother's face. What he saw there reassured him. Tears started to his eyes. He looked down at the thing she cradled in her arms.

All that he could see for certain was that it was red and raw like the other babies he had seen in his time and that it had the imprint of humanity on its little ancient face.

—Magnificent child! T. D. said, coming out of Susanna's room. And the little mother is all right. Came through fine. There's nothing to worry about.

They all went back into the room where Susanna lay, her eyes closed in deep exhaustion.

—I think this calls for a little prayer, T. D. said.

Johnny, Ellen, and the two Negro girls bowed their heads. The baby in Ellen's arms went on crying. T. D. closed his eyes, leaned back, extended his arm, and said,

—Dear Father in Heaven, we ask Thee to bless this little child who is this day born unto this young man and woman. May he grow to manhood in a land free from the troubles with which Thou, in Thy all-seeing and beneficent judgment, hast seen fit to visit upon this poor distracted nation. May . . .

The baby went on crying. The Negro girls and Ellen joined in. T. D. went on praying. Susanna slept like one dead.

Later, Ellen took Johnny aside.

—You'd best be with Susanna when she wakes up, she said. She had a hard time of it, poor thing. I think she was nearly out of her head, but she'll be all right.

It was dawn when Susanna finally stirred in her deep sleep and opened her eyes.

—Susanna, it's me, Johnny.

She stared at him mournfully, and her hands began to trail slowly down the blanket.

—You're a mother, Johnny said. We have a fine little boy. Everything's all right.

She watched him with mournful, suspicious eyes.

—Listen to him, Johnny said. You can hear him.

The baby was crying in a little cradle near-by.

—Is it all right?

—Fine, Johnny said. T. D. says he's a perfect child.

Susanna's eyes burned with a steady intensity.

—I want to see him, she said.

He brought the baby and showed it to her. She spent a long time looking at its little hands and feet and its blue eyes.

—You sure there wasn't another? she said.

—Another?

—Yes, Susanna said, fixing him with the same truth-demanding gaze. A twin. I thought I remembered that there was another.

—No, I'm positive. You just imagined it. What'll we call him?

—Sure there wasn't another? Susanna said, watching him narrowly. One that wasn't—that wasn't right? One that was thrown away?

—Absolutely not, Johnny said.

But Susanna was so solemn and persistent in her questions that he began to wonder. When T. D. and Ellen got up later in the morning, he spoke to them about it.

—Pa, there was just this baby, wasn't there? There wasn't—there wasn't another one—I mean born dead?

He watched T. D. narrowly, wondering if he and Ellen were concealing something.

—What's that? T. D. said.

His clear blue eyes were innocent and bewildered. Instantly, Johnny's doubts dissolved. He described Susanna's memory that there had been another child.

—All women worry about their baby not being perfect, Ellen said. The poor dear was out of her mind with pain. It was a hard labor.

When he returned to Susanna's room, he found her suckling the child. As she didn't ask any more questions about it, he decided that she must have recovered from her anxiety.

—What'll we name this kid? Johnny asked.

He had thought about names before, but when he had approached Susanna with the question, she had always said to wait until the child came, and then they could name it. Now she said,

—If you don't mind, Johnny, I'd like to call it James Drake Shawnessy. After my father.

—All right. That's a fine name. I like it.

—James, she said thoughtfully. Jim. Yes, that's what I want to call him. Jim. Little Jim.

—Little Jim, Johnny said.

He laughed. But Susanna didn't laugh. Instead, she looked up at him with a curious smile. Then whispering to him as if they were conspirators, she said,

—You're absolutely sure? You can tell me now.

—Sure about what?

—That there wasn't another.

—Absolutely, Johnny said. Now, you go to sleep. You just need a good rest.

He kissed her then, said good night, turned down the lamp, left the room. He went downstairs and, feeling unable to sleep, asked T. D., who was going back to the Home Place, to let him drive. Ellen intended to stay and help look after Susanna for a while.

—I'll walk back from the Home Place, Johnny said. I'm not a bit sleepy. I feel like walking.

—Better get some rest, T. D. said. You got a new responsibility.

But Johnny drove his father home. The earth was bright and cool in the early morning. It was April in Raintree County. Johnny Shawnessy felt strong and confident again as he strode out resolutely along the road from the Home Place back to Freehaven.

Yes, all would somehow be well with him now. It was necessary to have courage and conviction and to find one's people at the right time. All would yet be well, too, with the Republic. Even if it came to war, there were brave men in Raintree County and throughout the Nation, and they would fight to see the Union sustained in Liberty and Justice. It mattered after all whether one was right or wrong. It mattered about slavery. It mattered about the Union. This was the springtime of a solemn awakening of conscience.

He looked about him at the earth of Raintree County, a dark earth on which the little flowers were putting into bloom. He saw the gentle hills and shallows lying away to north and south. He passed through the town of Danwebster, huddled in the crook of the river, he saw the river running clear and clean on its pebbly bed. He drank the young day scented with the flesh of flowers and colored with a mist of buds bursting on winterblackened trees and bushes. He loved this earth, which had been somehow sundered from him by the parting of the Nation.

For Raintree County, he felt, lay far beyond the four borders which contained its span of dirt. It was also the Republic, a peerless dream. The war that had come was being fought for Raintree County and its way of life. It was for the soul of Johnny Shawnessy and his wife Susanna. It was for the future of his son.

At about nine-thirty, he reached the office of the *Enquirer*. Niles Foster was out in front talking with several other men. Although it was Sunday, the Square was crowded.

—Hi, Niles, Johnny said. I have an item I want you to print tomorrow.

—Tomorrow be damned! Niles said. You can print it today if you want to.

—I thought today was Sunday.

—It is, Niles said. My boy, we're putting out a special edition. Come on in and help.

—You mean——

—I mean we've struck the flag on Sumter. Pulled it down this morning, and surrendered with honor after a heroic defense. The Rebels shelled the place for two days steady. No telling how many brave men lost their lives. By the living God, the traitors will have to pay for it. Starting today we nail our colors to the masthead, 'Down with Treason. The Union Forever.'

—We'll fight then?

—Sure we'll fight. This town's crazy right now with war spirit. I never saw anything like it. They sure have pulled in their necks down at the *Clarion*. Every boy in Raintree County with red blood in his veins is itching to volunteer and get into the fight.

—They'll have to have it without me, Johnny said. I've just had a baby.

—Congratulations! Niles said. Leave the facts inside, and I'll write it up. Boy?

—Yes, sir.

—You'll never get into it then, a man said. War'll be over before that kid uncrosses his eyes.

Johnny had a hard time getting through the Square. In front of the *Clarion* office he found Garwood Jones.

—Hi, John, Garwood said. Hear you've gone and had that baby. You picked a bad time.

—What's the Democratic line on this Sumter matter? Johnny said.

I suppose it's all just a mirage in the minds of victory-drunk Republicans. Like Secession and all the rest.

—I cannot pretend, Garwood said, clearing his throat and looking around to see how many people were listening, that I am not deeply moved by this insult to the Flag. We are men of generous breasts and slow to anger, we of the North, but——

—Save it for the *Clarion,* Johnny said. So you're doing a turntail?

—Hell, no, Garwood said, talking low in his informal voice through the shattered horn of his cigar. After all, can you blame the Southerners? But if the people up here want war, war there will be.

Later, Johnny ran into Zeke.

—Well, John, Zeke said, you better take a last look at your favorite brother.

—How's that?

—I'm volunteerin', Zeke said.

—Folks know?

—Not yet. They been too busy gittin' that brat of yours born.

—How long do you think you'll be gone?

—Maybe a month, maybe two, Zeke said. Long enough to chase those skunks into the Gulf. Yippee!

His big redbearded face was flushed, eager, happy. He laughed, rubbed his hands together, slapped his knee.

—Who's organizing the volunteers? Johnny asked.

—Jake Jackson is takin' a company over to Indianapolis next week. They say Lincoln will issue a call for volunteers any time now.

A band went by playing 'Yankee Doodle.' A lot of hysterical citizens, men and women, were marching behind it.

Down at the telegraph office, a talkative mob was taking the news apart as it came in.

—Hell, a heavyset middleaged man said, if you boys have half the guts that we had back in '46, you'll have the damn traitors whipped by the Fourth of July. I wish I could git into it myself.

The crowd was making fun of an old man, who was the town's only veteran of the War of 1812.

—How about it, Pap? Goin' to git into it?

—Demn right, the old man said. If they'll let me.

They thumped the old man on the back, his eyes watered, he laughed happily—an old man's idiot, toothless laugh. All the young men were being slapped on the back too. Veterans of the Republic's last war kept feeling the youngsters' arms and giving them advice. The young men grinned goodnaturedly and looked vaguely shy and heroic. They were the chosen.

Almost everyone seemed elated and confident about this war, which had begun with a defeat.

Cash Carney had one thin, trimtailored leg on the top of a hitching stone and was evolving plans.

—The key to the situation is railroads, he was saying. When you get right down to it, railroads will win the War. And we got more and better ones.

—Think it'll last long, Cash? Johnny said.

—It can't last long. Not the way people feel about it up here.

Before he left the Square, Johnny picked up a copy of the *Enquirer*. The news from Sumter filled the important space. Down in the lower lefthand corner of the last page was an item under Personal News.

NEW BABY

(Epic Fragment from the *Free Enquirer*)

> The union of Mr. and Mrs. John Wickliff Shawnessy has been happily blessed with a male heir, who was ushered into this valley of tears, turmoil, and trouble at 4:00 this morning. The new cherub will carry the cognomen of James Drake Shawnessy, and a finer little fellow, it is reported, has never yet gladdened the eyes of doting parents. He weighed eight and a half pounds, and the mother is doing quite well, thank you. The father, a young man of prominence in the community, is resting easy and is expected to pull through. Interviewed just after the Happy Event, he stated that the arrival of the child would,

AT LEAST FOR THE TIME BEING, MAKE IT IMPOSSIBLE

FOR HIM TO GO

TO

—WAR, said the Perfessor, is the most monstrous of all human illusions. All ideals worth anything are worth not fighting for.

—War, gentlemen, the Senator said, is one of the world's necessary evils. This nation grew strong through battle. The Civil War was the college in which the young men of this country learned how to do big things.

—War is just plain killing, the Perfessor said. You understand, I'm not sentimental about it. God knows, unless we drew a little blood now and then, there wouldn't be room on the globe for us all. What's pitiful is how men murder each other and then glorify the crime in song and story. The real issues of the Civil War always seemed simple to me. The Civil War was fought quite simply because some men are darker than others. In a way both North and South were fighting the Negro—the South to keep him a slave and productive, the North to keep him from being too productive, which meant making him free.

—There's a lot of truth in that, the Senator said. No use pretending that either side fought the War on moral grounds. Two economic systems were pitted against each other—railroads against cotton. When I changed over and became a Republican, it was in recognition of that fact. Economically, the South was behind the times. This country was meant to be one Nation, one big industrial and political bloc. It was Fate, and the South had to give in to Fate—and the bigger battalions.

—The Civil War, Mr. Shawnessy said, was fought because man will be free. Both sides fought it as a holy war.

—But you see, John, the Perfessor said, you and I were part of the War, and we can't get away from its fine old fervors. All that cant about Liberty and Union was part of our youth, and a man will cling to as much youth as he can. But was it so important after all that a certain hunk of the earth be called by one name instead of two? Which side fought for God and the Right? Well, I'll tell you. God doesn't care about these things. God was quite untroubled by the Great American Civil War. God, the God of Nature, is a great brute impulse. He laughs at our romantic ideals of love and war. I tell you, John, the farmboys went out and died merely because they had the goddam rotten luck to be born one side or other of a river. There's no absoluteness in these things. War is neither moral nor immoral, just as life is neither moral nor immoral. War simply happens to men, they're blind victims of it, it's a clash of forces ruthless and natural, like the unconscious strife between the dinosaurs and the little early mammals who ate their eggs and destroyed them. Only our everlasting glorification of the individual makes us believe in the epic heroism of war. We get completely lost in a swirl of proper nouns. Sumter, Fredericksburg, Antietam, Gettysburg, Lincoln, Lee, Sherman, Grant, Washington, Richmond, the 134th Indiana Volunteers, the March to the Sea, Shiloh, Vicksburg—what are all these names? Words only, I assure you. All this is simply the romantic human being trying to deny that he's an animal. It's because we all try so hard to be immortal and distinguish ourselves from every other individual who ever lived that we have so much sorrow and so much poetry. We'd be happier if we practiced the same ethics toward ourselves that we do toward flies. What is the death of one hundred thousand flies? Just a natural phenomenon. A fly is not an individual. A fly is simply the representative of a species. No one but that sentimental sap, Uncle Toby, cares about what happens to a fly.

—Perhaps the fly himself dimly resents it, Mr. Shawnessy put in.

—But, the Perfessor continued, the death of a million men in a series of bloody explosions and stinking camps is called the Civil War and each man is lamented and remembered for a time, and people have banquets for fifty years, and Congress votes pensions, and schoolboys recite the Gettysburg Address. But *sub specie aeternitatis,* this is all nothing. Strictly speaking, there is no past. That which no longer is never was. Events, as you say, John, are something that never happened. The dead are simply nowhere. The new generations will look back on the Civil War with great calm. It's hard to feel sorry for folks who died a hundred years ago.

—The Civil War, Mr. Shawnessy said, drawing a deep breath and weighing his words, was fought for the Republic—or what Lincoln called the Union. The Republic transcends boundaries, triumphs over space. In America, a man not only possesses his home and his local gods, but he possesses the Republic, which is a denial of tribal boundaries and tribal prejudice. The Republic is the symbol of man's victory over the formless earth. It may be an illusion, but to be human is to accept the human illusions, which were created by centuries of struggle. This Republic is, in Lincoln's phrase, *the last, best hope of earth.* It affirms that a portion of America—this earth discovered, adorned, and named by human labor—shall not be the property of a single generation to wrest it away and shape it to new things at will. The North didn't fight through a desire to acquire the South, to possess it, to invade it, to enslave it. They didn't even fight to destroy slavery within it. They fought to preserve the Republic, a mystical concept that affirms the humanity of man. The Southerners threatened to destroy the Republic on a point of inhumanity—the perpetuation of slavery. Thus their moral position was hopelessly weak from the start. The ante-bellum South was a proud, feudal, voluptuous dream. In their blind way, the Southerners imagined that they too fought for freedom. But it was freedom to enslave other human beings. Their so-called right was not the world's right nor humanity's right. Thus a war came to be, in which the North was lucky to find great moral leadership in the person of Lincoln, while the South—significantly—found great military leadership in Robert E. Lee. As a series of physical facts, we know how terrible the War was. As a series of Moral Events, it was necessary and even sublime. It had to be fought and won for the future of humanity. If the Civil War had been lost by the North or had never been fought at all, Balkanization of the American Republic would have resulted, and the last, best hope of earth would have been lost for a time.

—Will you philosophers pardon me while I do a little vulgar politicking, the Senator said, rising to greet an approaching delegation.

—Well, said the Perfessor, this may all be true. But what of the martyrs who fought and died for this noble dream, the Union? Where are the young men who died in the first battles? Where are the heroes of First Bull Run? For them—and forever—

1861— 'ALL'S QUIET ALONG THE POTOMAC,' THE NEWSPAPERS SAID. —1863

Awakening sometimes in the summer night, Johnny would have this phrase on his mind, and he would remember that the War had been a long time fighting. In these awakenings, he would come back from dreams of better days to the dark, highceilinged room, the pale square of the window that looked down on the town, the recumbent body of his wife Susanna, and the child sleeping in its crib.

Then he would remember names of battles. They were old names already, belonging, as they did, to the first years of the War when it was believed that every battle might mean the end of hostilities. Sumter, First Bull Run, Shiloh, Corinth, Island Number Ten, Forts Henry and Donelson, The Seven Days' Battle, Second Bull Run, Antietam, Fredericksburg. Each of these names had swum slowly into the columns of the papers, had lain there wallowing bloodily for days, had swum slowly out again.

The Civilian's War had long ago assumed a pattern of uniformity in chaos that made it tolerable to the general public, North and South. Its landscapes, costumes, trappings had achieved the familiarity and fixity of myth. It had its epic rhythms, epithets, heroes. It was a newspaper Iliad of seasons, maps, and proper nouns. Antietam, Fredericksburg, Bull Run, Shiloh, Second Bull Run.

Summer (and this was the beginning of the third summer of the War) was the season of battles. It would be time, then, to have a map on the front pages of the more enterprising dailies. The map would be called the Theatre of Operations. On it, two mythical cities, Washington and Richmond, would confront each other across a tangle of rivers, roads, little towns. The roads would be firming now in the Theatre of Operations. The air would be warm and clear.

It would be necessary, then, to have a battle in the newspapers. There would be a certain keenness of anticipation on the editorial pages. Armies were moving now in the Theatre of Operations, were reported here and there. But armies never moved as masses of soldiers. Only the heroes moved. McClellan, Burnside, Pope took up positions, advanced their flanks, forded rivers, fought sharp skirmishes. Lee, Jackson, Beauregard, Johnston, Stuart became alert, made cautious penetrations, conducted raids.

Then there began to be reports of a battle. Towns and streams were tentatively named. In the space of a few days, there had been a battle, there had been no battle, there had been a success, there had been a minor rout, there had been a glorious victory, there had been a partial setback, there had been a sharp skirmish. Lee was beat. Lee was bested. Lee was battered. Lee was prostrate. It was all up with Lee. Lee was still fighting. Various Union Generals had accomplished the impossible. A name would begin to be mentioned more often than others as the location of a battle. There began to be eyewitness reports.

Finally someone wrote confidently of the Battle of Such a Name fought on such a day. Thus long after the fighting, a battle had become the Battle. But the Battle was by no means over in the newspapers. Like a festering wound, it flowed on in crowded columns—with recriminations, conflicting claims, disappointed expectations, removals of leaders (who had accomplished the impossible), and finally the long, backwardwinding processions of wounded and dead.

Then the next battle began to fester in the newspaper columns, and men realized that the last battle was a museum piece enclosed in a glass case called History. Shiloh, Antietam, Fredericksburg, Bull Run, Second Bull Run.

But the battles were only the heavy stresses in the rhythm of the Great War. They were only crests of the waves. The troughs were the periods of waiting. *All's quiet along the Potomac,* said the newspapers.

All's quiet along the Potomac. This phrase distilled the Civilian's War, which was the atmosphere of Johnny Shawnessy's life in the first years of the Civil War. Along a mythical Potomac, in the arena where the fate of the Republic was going to be resolved, in the eternal Theatre of Operations, usually all was quiet if not well. But this quiet was the time of gestation; this quiet was the womb from which vast, blooddrenched Events were born. This quiet was the unpictured swarm of life in camp and hospital, the letters home that said that everything was all right but I'm homesick, the plaintive songs around the campfires, the families waiting for news of sons, the long labor in the factories, the audible hopes and silent despair of millions. *All's quiet along the Potomac.* This phrase would always recapture the hue and weathering of the years when the destinies of the Republic were being worked out in darkness. It would mean great dedications North and South; for the whole Republic, North and South, in its divided camps, shared a Potomac of human hopes and longings, courage and loyalty, a beloved earth threaded with rivers of Indian names.

During this time, the child was growing.

At first Johnny didn't love his son He had a strong feeling of pity and a sense of responsibility—but no love. He examined the little raw form with some care to see if he could find any evidence of a human soul. In the beginning, the Baby, as it was called during its first year of life, didn't even have any particular look. It was like some furtive creature pulled out of a river, halfdrowned, mysterious, mute, unidentified. This moist little visitor from silence and the fruitful night had not yet made itself a place in Raintree County. Johnny was embarrassed even to call it by a human name.

This, then, was the beginning of a human life. His own beginning must have been like this, for once he, too, had emerged from the river of darkness and had lain on the bank stranded, waving tiny fists of frustration, blinking in the strong sunshine of Raintree County. From among the millions and millions of little faceless swimmers, seeds that never found a principle of growth, he had won through, struggling to warm arms and summer. What was he, back in that time of namelessness, where had he been then, did he have any memory of the great deep from which he had swum? 'John Wickliff Shawnessy,' they had called him in order that he might instantly be rescued from chaos and formlessness. The name had been the beginning of his education and the origin of Raintree County. In the beginning was the Word.

Now he had a responsibility to rescue another little swimmer from the void and make it human. 'Little Jim' he would call it until at last somehow it *became* Little Jim.

The child lost its birthflush and was gradually a fairskinned little boy with thick reddish hair, clear blue eyes, and regular features. He was a beautiful child, alert, quick-eyed, expressive. In a few months, if anyone rose up suddenly over the edge of the crib, he would laugh violently. There were times, too, when he would lie in his crib clenching his fists and turning red as if strangling for breath. He began to babble and to imitate the sounds of others.

By the time he was a year old, he had ceased to be called the Baby and was called Little Jim. His coloring was Shawnessy—vital, darkening hair with a touch of the sun in it, a softness and roughness of eyebrow, long lashes, fair skin. His eyes and the contours of his face and body were his mother's. He was gracefully formed. His eyes were dark blue, round, proud, intense.

At ten months he had begun to walk, and at a year he would run several steps, dropping lightly to his hands, only to rise and run again.

—He'll make a runner like his pa, everyone said.

Before he was a year old, he had a vocabulary of half a hundred words, among them the words 'Daddy,' 'Mamma,' 'rock,' 'tree,' and 'Grandma'—variously mispronounced. By this time Johnny was very proud of his son. He spent hours with him, talking with him, teaching him the names of things, carrying him around the town on his shoulders. It got so that he didn't like to leave Little Jim at the house but preferred to have the child with him wherever possible. He lost all personal vanity in this son. He was delighted when Ellen observed to all comers that Little Jim was even brighter than Johnny had been at the same age. It was a common sight in the Square of Freehaven those days to see Johnny Shawnessy walking around with a little boy perched on his shoulders.

Often Johnny would take the boy out into the yard of the house in good weather and put him down to run barefooted in the grass. The child hardly ever walked. His straight feet seemed to be made for running; his legs were slender and for a child's long. While his father worked at a table, writing or reading, Little Jim turned, danced, trotted tirelessly in the summer weather, exclaiming, pointing, asking questions. Johnny was never too busy to answer the child's questions, and the Great American Epic suffered in proportion.

When Little Jim was a year old, Johnny began to tell him stories, short narratives repeating the child's own experience. From the outset, Little Jim was fascinated by stories. He would lie and listen attentively to the image-creating sounds; his round blue eyes would be earnest, all-believing, innocent. He soon learned to ask for a story and wouldn't go to sleep without one.

Johnny didn't suspect the depth of his love for Little Jim until a series of happenings seemed to imperil the child's safety.

After Little Jim's birth, Johnny had hoped that Susanna's morbid fears would be expelled with her pregnancy. She stopped walking in her sleep, and for a few weeks seemed greatly improved as she went about the business of taking care of the child. Then at the return of menstruation, she became pale and haggard, violent in temper, complaining of her hardships, finding no good in anything. During this time, Johnny and the Negro girls began to assume more and more the care of the baby, until it very largely devolved into their hands, while Susanna moped by herself hours at a time in the upper chambers of the house. Instead of establishing a bond between husband and wife, the child had erected a greater barrier. Johnny became gradually conscious that he and Little Jim were drawing apart from Susanna, that she regarded them as belonging together and not to her. He tried to break down this estrangement between mother and child, but Susanna clearly wished to give him the responsibility for Little Jim. Not that she disliked the boy. She was pathetically fond of him and would often come to him and do something for him, hold him and play with him, as if she were an older child who didn't quite know how to act in the presence of a little brother.

—Isn't he cute! she would say, as if in some surprise, as if she hadn't noticed it before, as if paying a compliment to Johnny for being the father of such a child.

It was rather charming to hear her at such times prattling at the child like a precocious little girl, mock-scolding him, hugging him, and calling him Jeemie.

Much of her strangeness, he ascribed to the fact that she felt herself alone in the North, away from her own people when they were fighting for what they considered their national existence. But although there were many Southern sympathizers in the County, Susanna took no interest in them and very little in the War either.

In the spring of 1862, she expressed a sudden desire to 'go about,' to organize parties and entertainments. Johnny encouraged her, even if Susanna was a little feverish and hectic about it.

But excessive gaiety was almost always paid for by periods of extreme depression during which she would remain alone for hours in the secondfloor bedroom. Once when he peeped in noiselessly, believing her asleep, he was shocked to see her lying in the bed, restlessly turning the pages of her picture album. It came to him then that the album was always kept on the dresser in this room and that perhaps she spent much of her time looking at it.

One day in the early fall of 1862, he returned from the office to find Bessie and Soona waiting for him with worried faces. Susanna was gone. She had left in the early morning carrying a little suitcase and dressed in her best. She had refused to tell them her plans. Johnny made cautious inquiries around town and even tried to get in touch with Garwood Jones for help, but Garwood was nowhere to be found. At the train station, Johnny discovered that Susanna had bought a ticket to Indianapolis. Late at night, she came back, flushed, excited, talking volubly about a thousand little things that she had seen and done. When Johnny told her of his anxiety, she scolded him for it.

—I left you a note, Johnny.

—Where?

—Why, upstairs on the dresser.

He followed her upstairs. She went to the dresser in the bedroom and showed him the note. She had carefully wrapped it around the old daguerreotype of her home in Louisiana and laid it on the open pages of the picture album.

—There, you see! she said triumphantly.

When he made a motion to take the note, she laughed shyly, crumpled it up, and danced away from him, her eyes brilliant and excited.

—No, you can't read it!

That night, she didn't sleep at all, and she remained in a condition of unnatural elation for several days.

During this time, in the winter of 1862 and early spring of 1863, she began to sleepwalk again. Several times he awoke to find that she wasn't in bed. He would jump up and, hardly daring to think what it was that made him so sick at heart, would run into the next room, where Little Jim slept. After reassuring himself that the child was all right, he would go from room to room and floor to floor to find Susanna. He would discover her walking in the hall with a stately, regular tread, or standing at a window, or even crouching in the cellar. He soon learned that it was wisest to approach her quietly and lead her back to bed without waking her up.

One night, awakening to find her place in bed empty, he went softly down the stair, aware that a light was burning on the lower floor. Susanna was in the parlor, bending over a table on which the lamp was lit. He was fascinated by what she was doing and remained at the door of the room watching her.

She was examining the photograph album, which apparently she had carried downstairs. With quick, restless gestures, she sifted the pages, bending over them and staring at the pictures with sightless eyes. She appeared to be in a great hurry as if she had only a short time in which to find whatever she was looking for.

When he stepped toward her, she seemed instantly aware of his approach. She turned, appeared to recognize him, smiled.

—I can't find it, she said.

—What?

—The letter. I left it here, you know.

—I know, he said. We found it. Don't you remember?

She searched his face with sorrowing eyes. She reached out and touched his beard with a childlike, delicate gesture.

—She didn't read it then? You don't think she read it, do you?

—I'm sure she didn't, he said.

A look of inexpressible relief softened her features. But it faded as quickly as it came. Emotions of confusion, anxiety, terror fled across her face.

—I must find it. Before it's too late.

—Perhaps you'd best go to bed now and look for it later.

—No, I must find it now.

She began to sift the pages of the album again.

—What was written on it? he asked.

She looked at him again, her eyes dilated, and smiled a fugitive, distrustful smile.

—I could never tell you, she said. I promised not to. You believe me, don't you?

—Of course I do.

—You see, I have had a great loss.

—I know, he said.

—The dearest thing in all the world.

She said the words with a lingering sadness that made him ache with pity.

—The dearest thing in all the world, she repeated mournfully. The dearest thing in all the world. The dearest thing in . . .

It was a long time before he could persuade her to give up the search. She kept looking through and through the pages of the album, these pages covered with images of herself posed in cloudy nightrobes. In his effort to win her back to quietude, he felt that he was battling something enormously persistent, rooted in the bedrock of her being, ineradicable, impervious to reason, sinisterly alive.

Another night, he found her holding a lighted lamp and standing before one of the two front windows on the third floor. She made elaborate ceremonial gestures, approaching the hot chimney so close to the curtain that the cloth began to smoke.

Instantly, he started toward her. She seemed to know him, appeared not to be sleeping at all. She smiled, put her finger to her lips, and leaning toward him, began to whisper hoarsely like a tragedienne in a crude melodrama.

—They're probably hiding in here!

—Who?

She came up to him and examined his face closely, then apparently satisfied with her scrutiny, withdrew a little, and narrowing her eyes to slits, said,

—Of course, I know about them.

—Of course.

When he spoke, she appeared startled and held the lamp close to him. As so often before, the inchoate emotions of her dreaming self stirred and faded in her face.

—Now where *is* that doll? she said, irritably.

—It'll turn up, Johnny said. It's late, you know. Let's go to bed. We can talk about it there.

—No, I must find it, she said. I came up here to find it.

—There isn't any doll here.

She seemed to reflect upon what he had said. He gently took the lamp and led her away from the window and down the stairs. She went obediently enough until they were about to get into bed. Then she began to cry out with terror, and it was some time before he could wake her and quiet her. He tried scolding her about the lamp.

—You might have burnt down the house and killed us all, Susanna, he said. You must simply try to get hold of yourself.

She wept distractedly and held him very tight.

—What did I say? she asked him.

—You were hunting someone. You thought they were hiding somewhere in the house. You asked about a doll.

She had stopped crying and was listening attentively.

—Is there something you would like to tell me, Susanna, something about your childhood or your parents. Maybe it would relieve your mind.

He had asked her the same thing before, but always in vain. Now, however, to his surprise, she said,

—Yes, there is something.

She expelled her breath in a long sigh.

And suddenly he was afraid.

He was afraid of what this woman could tell him. He wished almost that he might have remained in ignorance. He wanted to say, No, don't tell me, Susanna. No good can come of telling me. Perhaps what you are about to tell me ought not to be told at all—to anyone—ever.

—It's—it's about the fire, she said. Something I know about it that no one else knows. I never told anyone—not even Aunt Prissy.

She paused. He didn't encourage her.

—It was something that happened not long before the fire. You remember I told you that Henrietta had been away, and then she came back?

—Yes.

—Well, the day she came back to the little cabin, I stayed and played there, and I left my doll there—Jeemie, you know.

—Yes, Johnny said.

He knew only too well the doll Jeemie. Perhaps he was going to get at last the secret of that hideous little idol from a stained and tragic era, and the secret, too, of all his bright little successors.

—Well, that night, the night Henrietta came back, I was very much excited, and I lay in my bed in the big house and couldn't sleep. I wanted to have my doll, who usually slept with me, and I remembered that I had left him in the cabin. I wanted to see Henrietta again too. The doll was sort of an excuse. So when everything was still, I slipped out of bed and crept down the stair and went outdoors. It was a warm night, and it was a holiday, the Fourth of July. The Nigroes were all singing down by the river, and there was a big scarlet fire burning on the river bank just over the woods from the cabin, and the cabin was all lit up scarlet from the fire. Well, I went down there to the cabin, and I tried the front door, but it was locked, and then I went around behind and slipped in the back door. It was all dark in the cabin except that the light of the fires outside flickered through the windows. I listened and didn't hear anything. Then I crept up the stair because I had left the doll upstairs. There was a light of some kind burning up there, and I could see myself in the mirror at the landing. I had on a white nightgown, and my hair was all shaken down. And then——

She paused, and he was afraid that she wouldn't finish and afraid that she would. But she was entirely in the spell of her own story and had paused as if to contemplate her child's image in the mirror. Her voice had slipped down to a low swift monotone as if it automatically recorded an experience that she was reliving in a center of consciousness far removed from the present in which she lay.

—And then I peeped up over the landing into the upper floor of the cabin, and there were two people on the bed together, and the light from the big fire on the riverbank burned right in through the window, and it made the woman's skin all dusky and scarlet like wine, and the man's skin pale white against it. I don't think I'd ever seen grown people without clothes on before then. I didn't quite understand at the time, but I knew I oughtn't to be there, and I slipped down the stair and went back to the house, and no one ever knew what I saw.

She paused, and Johnny waited. In the night over Raintree County, this other archaic night had made itself a place, and the two figures in the flaring darkness of it were tragically real to him, more real than the great war fighting beyond the borders of the County, on far rivers of the Republic, where armies lay in siege. These two figures embracing in forbidden love were the emblem of a lost republic;

flames licked and flared suddenly around them; they turned in his mind, twisting and twining in their exquisite torment.

—So then, Susanna went on, still talking swiftly to the dark night, I had some dim notion of what it was like between Daddy and Henrietta. And I was proud and glad because I loved them both. I didn't feel so strong then the difference between the races. That came later. Then, a few days later Henrietta came up to the house to live—Daddy was that headstrong—and she had the room next to mine—she was like the lady of the house. And that was when Mamma was so violent. She had had the house by herself while Henrietta had been away. And one day when Daddy was away, Mamma came down and found me in Henrietta's room, and there was a terrible scene, Mamma called her a nigger whore, and screamed and carried on, and said dreadful things to me, and all the time Henrietta just stood there and put her arms around me. And some of the men came and Mamma was led off.

Susanna began to stroke her neck.

—So then, that was when I hated Mamma, and I wanted to hurt her. And I had been reading a novel in which a person wrote an unsigned letter to hurt another person, so I wrote a letter and I managed to slip into her room once when she wasn't there, and I put it in Mamma's picture album that she was always looking through. It was just a little note. It said, 'Daddy loves Henrietta. Yours truly, A Well-meaning Friend.' Wasn't that silly?

Neither one laughed, and Susanna went on, talking faster all the time as if she had to tell it all now and get rid of it.

—So then I wished I hadn't written it. But it was too late to get it back.

—Of course it couldn't have made any difference, Johnny said. Your mother knew about it anyway. Down South, it wasn't an uncommon thing for——

But Susanna hadn't heard him. She drew another deep breath, and her voice was now so low he had trouble hearing it.

—So then after that awful scene with Henrietta, Mamma was shut up more carefully, and she was very violent for a while, and then for a while she must have been much better, because Daddy took me up to see her again. And she became so much better that Daddy had a photographer come and take a picture of us all in front of the house —you know, the picture I have in the album. That was just a day before the fire, and three of the people in the picture never even got to see the picture. And Daddy was planning some big change, I think we were going to go away again back to Havana. There was a lot of packing and excitement. And then that night I was in bed and asleep and all excited about us all going to go away, and sometime in the night I woke up, and someone was in my room with a lamp. I couldn't see who it was, and I leaned out of bed and said, Who's there? I thought it might be Henrietta as she often went through my room at night and her room was next to mine with a little hall between. And whoever it was put the lamp out. I listened and heard a door shut, but no one said anything. There was a lot of noise outdoors that night, there had been a barbecue for the slaves because Daddy was going away again, and they were singing and making a lot of noise. And then all of a sudden I heard something like firecrackers, sort of low and muffled in the next room or maybe in the hall. I couldn't say for sure, and at the time I hadn't any way of knowing what it was. Then I must have gone to sleep. And the next thing I knew, I woke up coughing. It was terribly hot in the room, and I could hear a crackling sound, and my doll was on fire. I began to scream and tried to beat the fire out on the doll, and someone kept saying, Get her through the window! and a man came in through the window, it was one of our Nigroes, and wrapped me up in a blanket, and there was a lot of yelling and a timber fell down on us, and I felt a terrible burning pain across my neck and chest. Then somehow I was out in the yard and they said, She still has her doll, and I had this burn on me. And then I said, Where's Daddy and Henrietta? and they just told me not to worry and took me away. Then they took me to stay with Aunt Prissy to get well from my burn, and she didn't tell me about Daddy and Henrietta and Mamma until quite a while later. Then finally Aunt Prissy took me away, and that was how I first came up here, and Aunt Prissy had this house built—she and I were Daddy's heirs—and we lived here.

—Did you tell your Aunt what you heard the night of the fire?

—Yes, I did, and she said not to say anything about it. It wasn't anything, and no one could do anything about it. But I didn't tell her about seeing Daddy and Henrietta. She worshipped Daddy, and I thought maybe she oughtn't to know. And I didn't tell her about the note I left in Mamma's album. I thought maybe I had caused their death some way. I cried and cried, and no one knew what I was crying about, they thought it was just because of the fire, but it wasn't just that.

—You don't think—— Johnny started to say.

—She *killed* them!

The words were said through clenched teeth. Johnny could feel the bed tremble.

—She killed them! Susanna said again. She planned it all with the cunning of a fiend. I *hate* her! I still hate her, and I hate myself for what I did!

—But, you didn't do anything, child, he said. You didn't have anything to do with it. You were just the victim of the whole situation.

Susanna was suddenly very still. He waited, trying to find something else consoling to say, something that would undo the confession that lay a sickening weight between them. He waited and listened almost afraid to breathe, afraid that there might be some further admission even more terrible—if such a thing could be—than what he had just heard. Here in the night beside him, momentarily lay the real being of his wife Susanna, a child that had come farwandering across the years out of the brown shadows of an old daguerreotype, reaching out her arms to him in the night, holding up her small pathetic face, asking him for help, for consolation, for pity, for reassurance.

—You have been hurt by all those memories, dear, he said. You live back there too much. All that is past now.

He felt how enormous was this brave lie as she lay there in the darkness stroking her throat where a tragic hour had left its signature of flame.

The next day she avoided him and kept to her room. At night when he came to bed, he could tell that she had been drinking. In spite of his efforts to prevent her, she had begun to keep brandy in the room, to bolster her spirits, as she expressed it. While he was preparing to come to bed, she said,

—I lied to you.

—Yes?

—About the Nigro girl and my father. I made it up. It never happened.

She had a defiant, sullen smile on her face. Her eyes stared drunkenly.

—What did you tell me for then?

—O, I don't know, she said. You asked me about it, and I just made up that story. My father wouldn't have touched any Nigro girl.

A few days after that, Soona came over to the *Enquirer* office to tell him that he had best come home at once. When he got home, he found Bessie in tears trying to prevent Susanna from coming downstairs. Susanna had on her hat and coat—it was a chilly April day—and she was carrying Little Jim, who was just a few days past his second birthday.

—If I was home, Susanna shrieked at Bessie, I'd have you whipped.

She saw Johnny in the door and appealed to him.

—She's been trying to keep me from leaving! she said furiously. Am I mistress in my own house, or do I have to let a nigger wench tell me what to do!

Her eyes blazed, her face was flushed, she staggered and nearly fell with the child in her arms. Johnny ran up the stair and took the child. Little Jim looked back at his mother with scared eyes.

—Daddy! he said. Mamma cwied.

He clung with small strong arms around Johnny's neck, like a child drowning.

—Where were you going? Johnny said to Susanna.

—My own business, she said defiantly.

—Don't you know you might have dropped him, Susanna!

—It's this house! she said, her voice breaking into hoarse sobs. It's this awful house!

—Why, what's the matter with it? Johnny said.

—No, no, you don't understand! she said. He might die in here. Something terrible might happen to him!

—Nothing will happen to him! Johnny said fiercely. What could happen to him! Are you crazy?

The words had slipped out. They stood looking at each other. Susanna's mouth opened, her eyes dilated, the blood left her face as if he had slapped her. She lay back against the banister. She began to laugh then; the laughter came bubbling up out of her chest, changed to a low, tearless sobbing, while Johnny stood holding the little boy and listening.

And soon it was the third summer of the War, June of 1863. The Union Armies were reeling back slowly through days of confused headlines and columns of drivelling words. The name Chancellorsville began to emerge, first as a place where a battle might have been fought, then as a place where the Army of the Potomac under Fighting Joe Hooker was reported to have whipped Bob Lee at last after a magnificent effort, then as a place where another inconclusive, bloody fracas had occurred, then as a temporary setback for Northern arms. At any rate the Army of the Potomac was backing up, and Lee was reported to be advancing in the Theatre of Operations, where battles were being fought again over the bones of men dead in battles two years old. At Vicksburg on the Mississippi, the Army of General U. S. Grant, in which Zeke Shawnessy was a soldier, was reported to be closing in at last for the kill, so that the Father of Waters might flow unvexed to the sea. But the capture of the Confederacy's river fortress had been anticipated in preceding years and sometimes falsely reported as accomplished. In January Lincoln had issued the Emancipation Proclamation, so that now the War was being fought not only to preserve the Union but also to free a race. Summer had come back again, the War was still on, and the end was not in view.

During these years of battle, death, sickness and division in the Republic, Johnny Shawnessy had remained out of the fighting. But the War, this brute continuing event, was the somber atmosphere of his life during that time. The remote din of its battles, its names of little towns made reluctantly immortal by bloodshed, its controversies on the home front, its scandals and corruptions, its few great utterances buried in battle-glutted papers, its hundred thousand deaths of young men in battlefield, camp, and prison-pen, its books and poems, songs and sayings, its shibboleths, its ephemeral heroes, its brass bands and banners, its sorry pomps, its nameless, unreported heroisms—all this was the somber background of what Johnny Shawnessy was in those years.

But what he most truly was had nothing to do directly with the War. During this time, long after the physical fact of parenthood, he became a father by touching the form of a little boy, by dressing him, holding him, carrying him, watching him run, telling him stories. The red days rolled on; battles came and went with summer.

But he was touched by the contemplation of a new fact in Raintree County: the flowering of a little being who had come to him out of darkness and terror and had held out tiny hands. In a tall house close to the Square, he watched this being grow from a collection of blind impulses to an intelligent, gifted person, Little Jim Shawnessy, who, because of his unusual origin, was more precious than any other child, and therefore more to be feared for.

Often in the evenings and mornings of those long years, Johnny would go to the crib and look down on the little boy lying in partial darkness, would see the eyes closed, the translucent lids, the lips faintly smiling, the breast moving ever so slightly with a steady respiration.

It was as though the father wished to assure himself that the little visitor had not been taken back into the deep water from which he had risen.

This child had come bearing a great gift, he was irreplaceable, only once could he have come to Raintree County, only one path had existed for him in the fearful complexity of all the labyrinthine paths of life, and that one path he had taken so that his life might be entwined with that of Johnny Shawnessy in the house in Freehaven during the Great War for the Preservation of the Republic.

No caution was too great, no tenderness too deep, no loyalty too lasting, no patience too enduring, for the saving and education of this little being. All life, all time had gone into the forming and the fashioning of this mysterious little man, and now that he was here, it didn't seem possible that there had been a time when he was not. For him, the good life of Raintree County, even as Johnny Shawnessy had often dreamed it for himself. For him, great days on the breast of the land. And one day, the War must end, the Republic would be one nation again, chastened and purified by its great passion. In that time perhaps Susanna would recover from her fears and walkings in the night, and Johnny would all at once complete the Great American Epic, and Little Jim Shawnessy would be the most splendid affirmation of all his father's dreams.

THAT DAY, WHEN AT LAST IT CAME,

WOULD BE

A

—WONDERFUL DAY! the Perfessor said. I never see a day like this but I think, Good battle weather! So the War leaves us.

He paused to relight his cigar.

—Exactly twenty-nine years ago, he said, on the Fourth of July, 1863, the armies were at Gettysburg. The earth is so peaceful now. Hard to believe Americans were killing each other there in the fat Dutch farmland not so long ago. Gettysburg! My God! what a battle! Generations and republics crowded at the gates of time, while Lee's ragged infantry charged up the slopes of Cemetery Hill. I saw it, you know. Of course, it wasn't anything like the storybook accounts. No one knows what a battle was or is. Soldiers making a battle are just poor lost bastards trying to improvise out of smoke, fear, and confusion something that a bunch of brassheads called generals can agree upon as won or lost. The Battle of Gettysburg, that great Event in the History of the Republic, is the sheerest myth. It seems to us now the classic battle of all time, with its neatly contrived stage, its monuments for fallen dead, its two Round Tops, its Seminary Ridge and Cemetery Hill, its heroes, its storybook gallantries, its consequences. We think of the little town of Gettysburg as having existed for that battle. Yet no battle was ever more the farce of brute chance. The armies blundered into each other, blundered into their positions, and blundered for three days trying to discover where they were and what was really happening. Lee, the greatest military genius of the War, achieved the murder of ten thousand men by blindly and brutally pounding away at an impregnable position. Let anyone go to Gettysburg—I mean the place itself—to realize what a froth and frenzy human life is. Here was a little town lying in its peaceful valley where roads met in summer. Here were the hills and the local picnic spots and the little college and the cemetery ground. It might as well have been Freehaven and the country surrounding. Then came the young men, a hundred thousand tired boys marching. Somebody heard there were shoes at Gettysburg, shoes for blistered feet. Gettysburg was fought for those shoes, because both sides discovered that they needed sizeable armed corps along to get the shoes—namely the Army of the Potomac and the Army of Northern Virginia. I remember well enough how I rode into Gettysburg on the first day, just as the First Corps of the Union Army was engaging the Rebels beyond the town.

—And I remember only too well where I was, Mr. Shawnessy said. I fought the Battle of Gettysburg too, though I was hundreds of miles away.

—How is that? the Perfessor said.

—By the implacable law of the continuity of being. I have a peculiar feeling that I will always go on fighting the Battle of Gettysburg in a remote part of myself. If I had enough will, perhaps I could reach down into that world I never knew and find the whole insanely complex happening out of which we built this Myth, this Memory of the Republic, the Battle of Gettysburg.

Professor Jerusalem Webster Stiles shut his eyes and hummed the 'Battle Hymn of the Republic.' He was remembering no doubt a certain young Perfessor with thicker, blacker hair who was riding along a road in the landscape of Gettysburg, a Fourth of July many years ago. What had become of that young Perfessor, and what had become of that landscape and that battle?

Mr. Shawnessy smoked, remembering his own private Battle of Gettysburg, the one that never got into the history books.

He searched the sky and the faces, the day clamoring and spacious. Once more it was July on the breast of the land. Trains hurried west, roads made the same old intersections, the bannered corn waved in the fields, the Shawmucky was filled with flowers and floating seed, the lake was rank with lilies, it was summer.

But where were the tumultuous drums, the cannons, and the tired young faces that poured into the cauldron of Gettysburg? Where was this archetypal battle in which a faceless swarm advanced through mythical summer in a mythical republic, climbing forever from Seminary Ridge to Cemetery Hill? And where were the faces of two children to whom no bronze memorial was erected, but who were also lost in that great battle for the Preservation of the Republic and the Emancipation of a Race?

In the deepest landscapes of his life, he hunted them. Surely they were still there somewhere, flying along their phantom trail. Perhaps he could still find them in the rush and tumult of the trains, in the stations where the cars were changing, among the million lost faces and the decayed landscapes of eighteen-sixty-three. He hunted them, hearing on the horizons of his past the sad old tumults of his personal Gettysburg. It, too, had had its gallantries and its despairs, its random collisions, its varying tides, its shifting incidental terrains, and its dread climax of disaster for the

July 2–4— LOST —1863

CHILDREN OF A

LOST REPUBLIC—SO THEY SEEMED

to him, the people whom he saw on the roads and in the fields of Raintree County as he returned to Freehaven on the train from Beardstown, where he had been on business for the *Enquirer.* Those days, like the whole week or so preceding, had been dark with disaster for the North. Lee's Army of Northern Virginia, victorious in the Battle of Chancellorsville, was on the move. The headlines for days had reported

THE INVASION OF THE NORTH

Just where the main Rebel Army was, no one in the North could tell. It seemed strange that an army of one hundred thousand men could be lost sight of for days, and yet that was the impression created by the newspapers. In the North it was generally agreed that this daring advance marked the supreme effort of the Confederacy, flushed with victory, to win a decisive battle and the War. The reports, confused and tentative as they were, made one thing clear: Lee's infantry were choking the roads of Pennsylvania and flowing northward with little yet to stop them.

In Raintree County, Indiana, far from battles, these days were blue and lovely, and Johnny Shawnessy had the civilian's feeling of paralysis more strongly than ever before. He continued the old routine of his life, nodding at familiar faces, climbing familiar steps, entering familiar doors, while his future and the Republic's were being shaped for better or for worse in a distant valley of rivers, roads, and sleepy towns. There had to be men somewhere who would be willing to die with skill and resolution in a field of corn or behind a railfence lest the Republic be dissolved and something indefinable and holy lost forever to Raintree County.

He had been away for four days; and returning now to Freehaven on the morning of Thursday, July 2, he had an uneasy feeling. Susanna's condition had grown much worse in the last few weeks, and the situation had been badly complicated by the sudden departure of Bessie and Soona, who had at last taken advantage of their freedom and left for parts unknown. Then had come this trip for the newspaper. When Johnny had suggested that Little Jim be left at the Home Place during his absence, Susanna had flown into a violent passion, and he had been obliged to hire a woman to stay at the house with Little Jim, a seemingly dependable widow named Mrs. Gray, who lived near-by. He had told Mrs. Gray that Susanna wasn't well and that he wanted someone to stay and help her.

—You'll be responsible for the child, he said. Just look after him. My wife has been upset lately. The War is very distressing to her and has affected her nerves. It's better not to leave her alone with the child.

As he spoke, he watched Mrs. Gray to see if she had any inkling of the seriousness of Susanna's condition.

In fact, he had told no one, hoping that somehow or other matters would improve. He couldn't imagine a greater indignity than to go before Raintree County and confess that he was married to a crazy woman. In fact, he could hardly bring himself to admit the gravity of Susanna's condition. He told himself that it was a case of overwrought nerves and would improve, especially when the War was over. For some reason, no one else was aware of her illness; he himself had been slow to realize the extent of it. With other people, she was gay and talkative. She sometimes accepted invitations to social functions that Johnny was unable to attend and had been escorted by young bachelor friends of Johnny's, like Garwood Jones and Cassius Carney. Johnny knew that Raintree County was critical of such wandering from its age-old way of complete marital respectability, and he himself wouldn't have approved under ordinary circumstances. But now he was almost glad for Susanna to have these diversions.

The one encouraging thing about her illness was that she had shown no further desire to leave town or to take Little Jim away.

On the train, he kept craning his neck to get sight of the house. He always got some kind of comfort after absence from seeing its elongate front and the pattern of the five front windows. It was as though he feared that the house would change and reveal some new shape of itself, the old one having been only a mask with which for a long time it had deceived him. But he wasn't able to see the house from the train. It wasn't until he walked the block from the station to the Square that he saw it on its high yard a block away. He decided to stop at the office on the way and pick up his mail and report to Niles.

Niles was glad to see him.

—Have you heard the latest news? he said. There's a battle in Pennsylvania.

—Where?

—It's not clear, Niles said. Rebels were last reported heading for Harrisburg, the capital. There's been a skirmish of some kind, and the Army of the Potomac may be making a stand. Several little towns are mentioned—Chambersburg, Emmitsburg, Gettysburg, and so on. I have a feeling this may be the showdown battle of the War. If Lee wins this one, we're through—that's all. On the other hand, if we can whip him and trap him that far from the Potomac, the Rebs are through. Hope you can give me a lot of help the next few days, John. Folks are making a big demand for papers—news of any kind. This invasion has the whole county in a tizzy.

Johnny found some letters on his desk, among them one from Professor Stiles. He read it hastily. The Perfessor, now a war correspondent attached to the Army of the Potomac, gave a discouraging picture of the War in the East. The letter ended:

> . . . Sorry to hear about your domestic troubles, John. Bear up as best you can, my boy. But whatever you do, for God's sake don't get into the Army.
>
> Martially yours, J. W. STILES

He poked hastily through the rest of his mail. One letter arrested his attention. The handwriting on the envelope was a large, almost childish scrawl. His name was misspelled.

Mr. John Shaunessy, Esq.

He tore the letter open and read it, while Niles went on talking about the news of the battle.

> Dear Frend,
>
> Peraps its none of my bizness, but I think somebody shold tell you your wife is in Indianapolis with another man, they are staying in the Maddon Hotel and frend I am not lying to you when I tell you she is having herself one hell of a time. A well-wisher

—God, it gets you, sitting around waiting for the dispatches to creep in, Niles was saying. Right at this very moment the greatest battle of all time may be shaping up a few hundred miles east of here and we sit around on our backends, twiddling our thumbs and waiting for the news. Doesn't it make you feel queer?

—Yeah, Johnny said. Excuse me, Niles. I've got to hurry home. I'll see you later.

He left the office and ran down the alley to the house. He ran up the stair and threw open the door.

—Mrs. Gray! he called several times and then, Jim! Jim! Susanna!

The house was empty.

He was about to leave when, remembering something, he ran upstairs to the bedroom. Sure enough, the album on the dresser was open, and several pages of letter paper had been wrapped carefully around the daguerreotype and tied with a ribbon. He picked the little package up and ran downstairs and out of the house, breaking the string as he went and hastily glancing over the letter. In a minute, he was at Mrs. Gray's, only a block east on the same street.

—Why, hello, Mr. Shawnessy, Mrs. Gray said, startled to see him breathing hard and obviously worried.

—Where are Susanna and the child?

—Why, it was just the day after you left, Mrs. Gray said. Your mother called at the house and talked with your wife. A little while after she left, Susanna said that she had been invited to come out to your Home Place and bring Little Jim with her.

—How—how did she seem when she said that?

—Why, very sweet, Mrs. Gray said. And a little excited too. She acted as if she was going off on a trip. She took a suitcase with her. Did I do wrong?

—No, Johnny said. But I did.

When he reached the Home Place, a half-hour later, T. D. and Ellen were out on an emergency call, but one of his sisters was at the house. She said that neither Susanna nor Little Jim had come to the Home Place and that so far as she knew Ellen had merely stopped to say hello three days ago in Freehaven.

It was about noon when Johnny got on a train at the Freehaven station. He found when he was aboard that he still had Susanna's letter and the daguerreotype in his coatpocket. He now took time to read the letter over carefully. It was several pages of coarse notebook paper hastily scrawled, running on at great length, full of repetitions and becoming more crowded and incoherent at the bottom of each page as if the writer had felt a barrier approaching at that point and had attempted to say everything before reaching it, and then had decided to go on, bursting over onto the next page with a huge, wild scrawl and gradually cramping it again as the bottom of the page loomed up. Thus the letter was like a series of convulsions. It said in part:

> Don't be alarmed about me, darling. They can't follow me. I am outwitting them this time. They thought I would stay longer and they will not be watching the station now if I go right away. I have thought this whole thing through carefully and am doing exactly what I know is best to do. If you saw it the way I do and knew what had happened, you would understand, darling. Johnny, I know now that if I had gone down to the station with you, they would have seen me and my life would not have been worth a puff. You have simply no idea the things that I have seen and heard just since you left. That woman is one of them, I instantly suspected it, and I am perfectly convinced of it now, but I think I have her fooled at least for the time being. For myself I don't care, you know that, it's the child I am worried about, especially after what I know, and as I have friends in Indianapolis this is the best plan. If you knew how I have schemed and what I have had to do to get the best of them, you would never believe it. They will go to any lengths now, I can see that, just as I told you, and they will stop at nothing, simply nothing. My life is simply not worth a puff now, I know that, but this way I know I can give them the . . .

As he read the letter again, he pictured to himself his wife Susanna boarding the train with the child. Doubtless she had been smiling her little crafty smile as she slipped down between the seats carrying the child. Doubtless she had looked furtively out of the window to see if They had followed her.

But of course she had soon discovered that They were on the train too. They had been sitting toward the back of the car pretending to read a newspaper. They had been watching her with deceptive amiability from the bland face of the conductor. They had walked down the car as if to get a drink from the watertank, but it had been really to make sure that it was she. When she had got off at the station in Indianapolis (assuming that she had really gone there), of course They had been waiting for her there. They had pretended to be in conversation with someone at the gate but had turned after she passed and had begun to follow her at a distance. And when she reached the hotel (assuming that she had gone to the hotel), of course They had taken the room down the hall from hers. It was useless for her to try to escape Them now. She had tried it several times, and it hadn't worked. They were everywhere.

It was touching in a way that she no longer thought he belonged with Them. For a while, she had thought that he might be in collusion with Them. During those weeks life had been intolerable. She had accused him of gross sexual infidelities with Them, of going to meet Them when he went out walking with Little Jim, of inviting Them to the house when she was gone. During those days he had argued with her about Them, trying to prove to her that They were the figments of her imagination, but she had a thousand excellent reasons for believing in Them.

—See, she would say, there is one of Them now.

And going to the window, he would see someone perhaps standing under the tree on the Square doing nothing at all.

—He's not even looking this way, he would say.

—That's just it, she would say. He *was* looking, but *now* he's pretending he doesn't know anything. You didn't see the signal he made.

—What signal?

—A motion he made with his hand.

They all had their signals. The women had a way of touching their pocketbooks, and the men a way of touching their hats. They were infernally clever, persistent, tireless, innumerable, sleepless, implacable. They watched the house at night when she was asleep. They followed her when she went downtown. They pretended to nod and smile at the child, but in reality They were watching her. They were incredibly gross beings, who said and did the vilest things imaginable when she wasn't close to Them. They had gradually formed an organization for the purpose of observing her activities and keeping a full record of them.

Sometimes when he listened to her describing Them, her voice low and fluent, her eyes dilated, They seemed almost real to him too. There was a horrible plausibility about Them, the intricacy of their manoeuvres, the relentless tenacity of their persecution, the weblike ramification of their system.

This last acute phase of her illness had begun with her belief that members of his own family and some other people in the town disliked her for her Southern origin and Copperhead sentiments. Like a malignant growth, the system of accusation had spread. His own family and other known individuals were soon lost sight of or became of secondary importance. She no longer directly accused anyone that he knew of being a part of the huge conspiracy to do her harm. Strangers, newcomers in the neighborhood, passers in the street, employees in public places, these became the favorite objects of her accusations. They multiplied their numbers with a hideous rapidity. There were a million indications of their ingenious malice. And all these she noted and assembled in her mind and repeated over and over, spinning out of herself ever more swiftly the enormous web of her delusion.

For a very little while, he thought she was faking the whole thing and consciously lying, but he soon knew that she was utterly sincere. That was the horror of it.

He had tried his best to reason her out of the delusion, but he had soon found that the chance to talk about it only confirmed her in it. Her energy in the construction of this vast empire of persecution was appalling. When he subjected any one of her bits of 'evidence' to the clear light of reason, she produced others equally convincing. At last he gave up attacking the fabric in detail.

The monster spawned twenty heads where one was cut off.

Just before leaving on his trip to Beardstown, he had said,

—Why, Susanna, child, what makes you think that so many people would want to spend so much time and money on one poor little Rebel? Believe me, honey, the United States Government has better things to do.

She immediately corrected his remark in several ways. To begin with it wasn't just the United States Government—*that,* she had known for a long time. In the second place, it was not just herself that They were after—Goodness, she had no vanity on that point!—it was what she *stood* for and what They thought They could get her to *tell*. *She* was just an instrument in their loathsome designs. It involved the *child,* too, and *Johnny* was involved in it too. She had warned him *many* times, and *some* day he would learn to value the intelligence, courage, and foresight of his little wife.

—Why, honey, I'm not in any danger from anything, Johnny said. Honestly, I never see any signals or anything. I——

—Hmmmmm, she had said. Then when you were talking with Mrs. Gray this morning, you didn't even notice?

Susanna sucked in her cheeks and regarded him knowingly with raised brows.

—Notice? What?

She looked at him intently. She spoke clearly, enunciating every syllable sharply.

—She—closed—her—purse—and—put—it—under—her—left—arm!

Johnny waited, mouth open. But that was all.

—Well? he said.

—But don't you see! Susanna said, shaking her head impatiently at his stupidity. Don't you understand! That shows she's in it too. Don't you remember? I told you.

—Mrs. Gray is *not* in it, Johnny said. She——

Then he realized how hopeless it was. Here he was trying to acquit Mrs. Gray and thereby tacitly admitting the existence of the whole thing.

—Not *directly* in it, Susanna said. But They're *using* her. She doesn't know it herself.

As for the letter apprising him of her alleged visit to Indianapolis, he had no idea what to make of it. After all, in her condition Susanna might be capable of anything. And yet with the onset of her derangement she had shown extraordinary sexual reticence. Lately, she had been convinced that They had designs on her person. In particular, They were determined to see her scar, and so she had recently taken to wearing only highnecked dresses again, as before their marriage, concealing even the beginnings of the ancient firemark on her breast.

But perhaps now in a climax of her illness she had flung herself into an orgy of lustful abandonment. He pictured his mad little wife in an Indianapolis hotel, drunk, shrieking with laughter, pawed by lechers who winked at each other and passed the news around. Under the circumstances, he hoped it was some acquaintance of his.

But most of his anxiety was spent on Little Jim. Since he had picked up the letter at the office, he had avoided thinking that any real harm could come to the child. Somehow, Little Jim would pass through the horror of these days and come back safe at last. The stationmaster at Freehaven had said that the boy was smiling and apparently happy when Susanna boarded the train, three days ago.

Johnny Shawnessy bowed his head. Somehow, all had gone wrong for him. Two helpless children, entrusted to his care, had been lost. As in the old poem, they had wandered away on a bright summer's day. Bitterly, he reproached himself.

At Beardstown, where he changed to the main line for Indianapolis, he saw Cash Carney waiting to board the same train. Johnny would have preferred to go on alone, but Cash saw him and came over, and they rode to Indianapolis together. After a little hesitation, Johnny told him the purpose of his trip, omitting some details. He expressed his fears for Susanna and the child, explaining that his wife had been upset with a case of nerves and was really not responsible for her actions.

—Don't worry, John, Cash said. They'll turn up. What could happen to them? Susanna probably went up there to get in on that Copperhead Rally they're having. Garwood's up there and will probably look after her. You know yourself Susanna's a worse Rebel than Jeff Davis.

Cash had clearly been doing well for himself. He had acquired interests in railroads operating out of Indianapolis and had got his finger into the munitions pie as well, where there were scandalously fat plums to be had. His soft brown eyes glowed; he waved his cigar like a wand of pelf and power.

—This war is changing our ideas, he said. We're learning how to do Big Things. The railroad and Northern industry are coming into their own. After we whip the South——

—Do you think we'll whip them? Johnny said. How about this invasion and the battle in Pennsylvania?

—We can afford to lose battles, and they can't. The squeeze is on here in the West. Grant is about to take Vicksburg—I have tha on very good authority from a private source high up. That'll fre the river to the Gulf and turn their flank, goddam 'em. Of course our great advantage in men and materials has been sadly misused. wouldn't say it publicly, but Lincoln is a damn backwoods bonehea and has no more idea how to choose generals and fight a war tha you have, John. If we had just one general like Lee, we'd of bee in Richmond a year ago. Nevertheless, the Republican Party is th War Party, and the War must be won. And the War *will* be wor We have the enterprise, the skill, and the goods. The War's bein won right now on the trunklines of the Nation, in the factories, i the places the lunkheads back home would never think of looking They think it's all bayonets and glory charges and the boys i blue.

—Somebody has to have the guts to stand out there and stop Lee' yelling infantry, Johnny said. Don't forget that.

—Of course, Cash said, I don't forget that. God knows, poo bastards, they've suffered. I could tell you stories that would mak your flesh crawl. These poor dumb farmboys have no idea wha they're getting into when they join the Army. No wonder Indianapo lis is full of bountyjumpers, deserters, and Copperheads. For Christ' sake, John, whatever you do, stay out of the Army.

—Sometimes I don't see how we can pull through, Johnny saic with all this Copperhead sentiment.

—If I had my way, Cash said, we'd hang 'em all in the neares orchard and get on with the War. And the first fat neck I'd tighte the noose to would be that of our mutual and esteemed friend, Ga wood Jones. Imagine the folks back home electing that traitor to th State Legislature! I suppose with so many loyal men in the Army the Copperhead vote was overwhelming.

Chatting with Cash about the War, Johnny had hoped to lull hi anxiety a little, but it only increased as the train went on mile afte mile toward Indianapolis. All the things he believed in were smutte with disloyalty or threatened with destruction. A few short years ag he had lain on the banks of the Shawmucky dreaming of a fa republic in which he was to be the great sayer, the maker of poem Now, here he was, a haggard young man, assistant to the editor of smalltown newspaper, going toward a wartorn city, full of traitor deserters, bountyjumpers, wounded veterans, speculators, thieves, cutthroats, tramps, pimps, whores. And somewhere in this corrupt city his poor mad wife and his little son were at the mercy of depraved people. A few hundred miles away in the summer weather a horde of grayclad men, speaking a speech that was not of Raintree County, were perhaps shattering the proud Army of the Republic and realizing at last their dream of a separate nation. And so the country would become two, the Mississippi would flow through alien lands, and the institution of slavery would be perpetuated for centuries.

At the station, he said good-by to Cash, who had an important conference, and inquired the way to the Maddon Hotel. On his way over, he told himself that his fears were baseless. Now that he was here, the Capital City of the State appeared to be after all only a greater Freehaven, a rather crudely constructed, messy collection of hotels, places of business, public buildings.

People were all stirred up over the news of the battle in Pennsylvania. At the window of a newspaper office, Johnny saw bulletins announcing that a sharp skirmish had been fought the day before at an undisclosed place. It was clear that no one knew yet what had happened.

Just before he reached the hotel, a Copperhead parade went by. Men and women carried transparencies with pictures of an apelike monster, supposed to be Lincoln, and Copperhead slogans.

ABE, WE WANT JUSTICE

. . .

NO MORE BLOODSHED FOR NIGGERS

. . .

PEACE NOW

Men boiled out into the path of the marchers, fists flew, men cursed each other, the parade poured brokenly on.

The Maddon Hotel was a dingy framebuilding about three blocks from the Capitol. From the open door a stale breath gushed. Johnny found the lobby emptied by excitement over the parade. The air stank of beer and tobacco. The floor around the brass cuspidors was stained with spit. Flies swarmed in the diningroom. The desk was empty, the clerk having gone out to see the fun. Johnny opened the register and ran his eyes over the entries. Close to the bottom he saw

Susanna Shawnessy and child

The room number was 34.

He ran up the stair. The thirdfloor hall was dark, the floor sagging with age. As he hunted for the room, something started along the wall and scrambled through a half-open door at the end of the hall. It was a fat gray rat.

Johnny found the door and thundered on it with his fist.

—Susanna!

No answer.

—Jim! It's Papa. Jim!

There was no sound. He tried the door. It was locked.

He ran down the hall, down the stair, into the lobby. People were pouring back into the hotel now. Johnny shoved through them.

—Where's the clerk?

A little man whose yellow teeth jutted longly from under big pale lips, said,

—What can I do for you, friend?

—I want to know if a Mrs. Shawnessy is here. With her son. I saw their names in the register. But they don't seem to be in their room. Room 34, I believe it is.

The clerk turned back to a man he had been talking with.

—If Morton calls out troops, he said, he'll have a rebellion on his hands right here in Indianapolis. The people'll stand for just so much.

—Listen, Johnny said, I want to know if——

The clerk's voice was querulous and ugly.

—This draft call's the last word. They're makin' slaves of us to fight for slaves. By God, I——

—Listen, Johnny said.

He had the ratfaced man by the arm and pulled him around.

—Are you the clerk here or not?

—What's the big hurry? the ratfaced man said.

He moved slowly around behind the counter and fumbled with the keys.

—What's the name?

—Shawnessy, Johnny said, opening the register. Here it is.

The man's teeth slipped out of the pale flaps of his lips, smiling.

—O, that one! he said.

—You remember them?

—I'd hope, the man said. Was that your wife?

He winked at the man he had been talking with.

—Yes, Johnny said. For God's sake, tell me where she is if you can.

—I don't know where she is, the little man said.

He smiled and spat a brown stream prolongedly on the floor. He wiped his mouth with a handkerchief.

—But you better look after her, friend.

—Did she leave here?

—O, yes. Yes. O, yes, the clerk said.

He winked and smiled at his friend again.

—Did she have the child with her?

—Yes, come to think about it, she did. That wasn't all she had either.

Johnny controlled himself.

—Let me share that room, will you? he said. I'll pay the charge already on it and whatever else it comes to.

—That'll be four dollars so far, the clerk said. Here's the key.

Johnny went back upstairs and opened the door. The little bare room had a stale smell of perfume and breathed air. The bed had been slept in and left unmade. The usual cheap fixtures were in the room and nothing else. Susanna's suitcase was gone. The view from the window was a jungle of backyards and alleys. The city appeared to be decaying in a sticky heat. Johnny went downstairs and left a note at the desk for Susanna, telling her if she returned to the hotel, to wait for him there.

At the hall where the Copperhead Rally was being held, guards stood at the door, stopping and questioning people and keeping the soldiers out.

—Name?

—John Shawnessy.

—Party affiliation?

—I just want to see if my wife's here, Johnny said.

Everyone within listening range laughed.

—Better get 'er out a *there,* a man said. She won't come out pure as she went in.

The crowd laughed.

—Go on in, the doorkeeper said, laughing.

In the convention hall, the program was already started. Johnny scanned the crowd for Susanna's face but without success. Speakers took turns expressing sympathy for Vallandigham, the arch-Copperhead. Once when Jeff Davis' name was mentioned, several people cheered. On the platform among the notables was Garwood Jones, looking fatly pontifical.

Johnny stood helpless through the speeches. He was stunned by the openly treasonable character of the meeting. Here within a few blocks of the Capitol Building, within earshot of hundreds of furloughed veterans who had risked their lives to preserve the Union, people openly expressed their contempt for the Cause. Here were hundreds of people, most of them respectable and well-to-do, who hated Abraham Lincoln, opposed the War, sympathized with the South, and favored a peace at any price, even if it meant the dissolution of the Union and the perpetuity of slavery.

It was well along in the afternoon before the Convention broke up and Johnny got to talk with Garwood. As he told about Susanna's disappearance with the boy and her overwrought condition, he watched Garwood narrowly. Garwood occupied himself with lighting a cigar. His eyes were remote, impassive.

—Why, yes, John, he said, puffing deliberately, watching the cigar take smoke, why, yes—goddamn this cigar—yes—puff, puff—I did see her.

A red circle blazed at the cigartip, and Garwood's face was dimmed behind a fog of smoke. His voice was his oratorical voice, measured, deliberate, affected.

—Why, yes, I saw her yesterday, I think it was, for a little while. To tell you the truth, she *did* seem a bit unstrung. Said something about coming up for the Convention, talked a bit—goddamn this cigar—puff, puff—talked a bit wild. If I were you, I wouldn't put too much trust in—goddamn these goddam wartime smokes—put too much trust in anything she might tell you. War's getting on her nerves—all this goddam killing and murdering for niggers, and after all she's a sensitive—puff, puff—woman, and she's unstrung.

—Did she have the boy with her?

—No, I didn't see the boy. She didn't say anything about him. I just saw her a little while in passing. I think it was day before yesterday, I got a note saying she was in town, and I dropped over to her lodging to pay a courtesy call and invite her to the Rally today, but I haven't seen anything of her here. I wouldn't worry too much, my boy. I think you're unnecessarily alarmed. The Big City has frightened you.

Garwood attempted a jovial laugh and put one arm affectionately around Johnny's shoulder. There was a look of real anxiety in the usually cynical eyes.

—Anything I can do for you, John, let me know. By the by, what do you think of our Rally?

—I think it stinks to heaven, Johnny said. You traitors picked a fine time to have your meeting, with the Union Army fighting for its life in Pennsylvania.

Normally Garwood, always a fast man with a comeback, would have had a retort, but now he merely shrugged his shoulders.

—Who can say where the Right is? he said. God Himself must have a hard time choosing sides in this poor distracted nation. Both camps pray to Him. Whatever you do, for Jesus' sake, John, don't get into the Army. Now let me know, boy, if I can do anything for you.

Outside the Convention Hall, in the hot late afternoon, crowds were crushing in around the windows of the newspaper offices. Reports were still coming from Pennsylvania. Newsboys sold papers as fast as they could peel their packs and make change. Johnny bought a paper, with a sick misgiving that there might be something in it about a lost child or a mad woman. But he found only the latest reports of the battle in Pennsylvania and miscellaneous news. The fighting had continued. Several places were mentioned—Emmitsburg, Chambersburg, Gettysburg. It was impossible to tell who was winning or what was happening, whether the main battle had been joined or was about to be joined. But it was clear that fighting had begun deep in Northern territory, and the tension of a great battle had somehow shot in waves outward from its fiery center across the Nation.

Before it was dark, Johnny had reported his case to the police station, where he had trouble making the situation understood to a tired sergeant at the desk. The sergeant told him to keep in touch with the Force.

Leaving the station, Johnny spent a long time walking with crowds. Buggies, wagons, carts ground past him on loud wheels. the nameless faces of the city passed him by, there were no faces to which he could appeal, there were no remembered faces. His panic grew stronger by the hour. He only kept it down by redoubling his efforts, halfrunning, halfwalking for hours in the streets of Indianapolis. He returned several times to the police station and to the hotel, but there was nothing to report. Belatedly, he thought of having the police post someone at the train station, and late at night he spent several hours there himself, hunting among beggars and bums, decayed monsters whom the retreating tides of the city left stranded on the shores of night.

Johnny got no sleep that night. Several times, in the small hours of the morning, he passed the newspaper window where tomorrow's headlines were being manufactured. The bulletins had changed a little. Now they said:

DEFINITE REPORTS OF BIG BATTLE AT GETTYSBURG

. . .

LEE ATTACKING HEAVILY

. . .

VAST LOSS ON BOTH SIDES

. . .

ACTION CONTINUING

Johnny kept going. He hardly felt his fatigue. As before in moments of crisis, he found a reservoir of strength that seemed to have no bottom and on which he drew as need required. Tirelessly all night long, he walked between the railroad station, the police station, and the hotel. But there was no further news.

The next day, Friday, July 3, it was the same story. Susanna didn't return to the hotel. There was no news from the police. The papers carried the little notice that Johnny had requested on a lost last column of the inside pages. Buried in the epic terror of the battle news, it was a piteous little item. It said only:

LOST

A young woman, black hair, blue eyes, pretty, medium size, scar above left breast, talks with Southern accent, may be demented, name, Susanna Shawnessy. May be accompanied by child, James, two years old, blue-eyed, reddish brown hair. Both well dressed when last seen. Report to police station.

Johnny continued to hunt the City. He bought a little breakfast, his first bite in twenty-four hours. Eating it, he was reminded that only the day before he had stopped at the office of the *Enquirer* and had picked up the fateful letter.

He kept up the hunt all that day and into the night. Like a somber background for his search was the growing news of battle. There was no doubt now that a great battle was in progress. Reports were that on both the first and second of July, heavy actions had been fought, but a decision had not yet been reached. The fighting was now located beyond a doubt in the little town of Gettysburg in Pennsylvania.

So then they were still fighting that great battle. It began to seem to Johnny that the battle and his own search were enduring things, lasting for centuries, ages, perhaps forever. As the second night wore on and he found himself a hundred times in the same places, asking the same questions, retracing his steps from hotel to police station to train station, getting the same responses, smelling the same foul air, looking at the same halfdead human faces, seeing the same nighttime shabby cityscapes, gasillumined walls, sooty curtains, bleared windows, he knew that he was building himself a solid hell of memory.

Toward one o'clock in the morning, it began to rain, and he decided that he might as well go back to the hotel as the rain might drive Susanna in. He went upstairs to the room and lay in the bed and listened to the rain drumming on the flimsy roof. He wondered if it were raining so on the distant battlefield. Toward morning he dropped off to sleep and dreamed a brief, dreadful dream. He dreamed that Little Jim was in the hands of lechers and diseased people, a helpless child lost somewhere in a wasteland of dirty hotels, poolrooms, saloons, whorehouses. In the dream it was raining too, a dreary, sopping rain, and at the end of his dream he saw thousands of rainbloated corpses lying on the familiar fields of Raintree County, bodies of young men fallen in battle. He thought that he approached one of these bodies, and was about to pull away the dead hand from the rainsodden face and discover who it was, when he awoke to see the gray curtain at his window flapping in gusts of rain.

He got up and looked out on the drenched backyards of the city swimming in filth. It was dawn. He was careful not to go to sleep again. Besides, there was a noise of firecrackers in the streets, growing louder and louder until it was almost a continuous roar as of battle. When he went out, he found that the skies had cleared.

It was the Fourth of July, 1863.

He went down past the newspaper window. The reports of the battle were confused and contradictory. The latest dispatches reported that the bloodiest battle of the War or a series of battles had been fought on the first three days of July around the town of Gettysburg, reaching a climax on the third day. The Rebels had attacked violently and the outcome of the struggle was still in doubt.

There were still no reports of Susanna. The sergeant at the police station was beginning to be openly uncivil. After all, the Force had better things to do than to be plagued every halfhour by a hayseed who had gone and lost his wife and child in the Big City. This was the Fourth of July, and there were important speeches and celebrations. Cops would be needed to control the crowds. The watcher had already been taken from the train station.

Johnny kept looking. Dizzy with sleeplessness and lack of food, a little after noon he found himself wandering on the fringes of a crowd on the grounds of the Capitol Building, listening to scraps of oratory. The speaker was someone who had led a charge in the Mexican War. He reviewed the Growth of the Nation and the Progress of the War. He expressed it as his opinion that the present battle would be Crowned with Victory and that the War would soon be over as the God of Battles would not endure any more defeats at the hand of Bob Lee. The speaker said that he wished he were right out there in the Front Lines with the boys but the Heavy Responsibilities of Public Office prevented it. The speaker said that the Rebels had underestimated the Power of the North. He verbally brandished the Grand Old Flag and said it would never be Shot Down while he had a Breast to Expose to the ruthless rending of Bloodyfanged Rebellion. The speaker affirmed that the Union was Undying while there were men to defend it and that the Starspangled Banner was yet Waving over the Land of the Free and the Home of the Brave. There was a volley of applause for every other sentence.

Johnny got up and started back to the hotel. He was dripping sweat, dirty, unkempt. He hadn't been out of his clothes for two days. He shut his eyes; the hot sun rained on the lids like fire. He was afraid he would faint. He hadn't eaten since yesterday morning. Yesterday morning. They had been fighting a battle then in Pennsylvania. He opened his eyes.

Somewhere in this same brilliant day, they were perhaps still fighting. Two armies were lying around a little town not even named on the map. Two hundred thousand men had rushed at each other, finding and giving death on the green earth of some rural county where brown roads met in summer. This was History, this was the Shape of the Future, here was the Destiny of the Republic, tossed on the horns of the herding armies. At this moment, that mythical being, the leader of the Confederate Armies, General Robert E. Lee, was studying maps in his headquarters and checking the disposition of troops. His voice was making edges of sound in the hot air. Men listened, rode away, gave orders. Flags advanced and receded. Maps, maps, maps, and the shape of the earth, the lay of the land—this was the whole thing. Everything depended on it. The Battle was for a little theatre of hills and roads called Gettysburg. Whoever won this earth won republics of the future, fair and fecund republics, which, alas, might also be split with endless war in summers to come.

Yet all was chance. Blind chance decreed the battle, the bullet, and the patriot grave. What made chaos a Battle? What made ten thousand murders a sublime Event? Who had agreed to disagree? Who was it that decided to come to these decisions? What gave meaning to the Battle?

And why must he, John Wickliff Shawnessy, be torn with fear because a darkhaired woman with a scar on her breast wandered somewhere carrying a little boy? What business was that of his? Weren't all human beings forever shut off from one another? Had he ever really known or understood her? Was the touching of their bodies any true exchange of themselves, one for the other? Was he the father of this child? Suppose those two were really lost, suppose their poor ruined bodies were found in some back alley of the City? Must he weep for that—he, the young god with sunlight in his hair? Couldn't he simply turn his conscience back like a clock to the time exactly four years ago when he had just run in the Fourth of July Race but hadn't yet gone to Lake Paradise with a girl from the South? Why must he suffer for this thing? What gave it meaning, except to this weakness called a conscience and these faint nothings, composed of shadow and unsubstance—memories?

Then he told himself that he had to acknowledge this connection and these meanings because these lost children had names. They had his name. Perhaps then it was only the names of things that rescued them from utter vacancy, appalling chaos. Only because he could give a comfortable name to this city, to himself, to all the objects that he saw, did they have any meaning at all for him or for anyone else. Without the names, they would instantly slip back into incoherent, frightening nothingness. No, not nothingness, because all these things *were,* they horribly and palpably *were,* and would go on *being,* but they would go on being without any care for one another. They would merely be *things,* nothing would integrate them, they would be forever meaningless.

Names, names, names. Susanna, Little Jim, Ellen, T. D., Raintree County, Indiana, United States of America. Names, names, names. Vicksburg, Mississippi River, Chancellorsville, Gettysburg, Pennsylvania. Names, names, names. Lee, Longstreet, Sherman, Grant, Hooker, Meade, Davis, Lincoln. All were names only, senseless deformations of the lips and tongue, vague cries shaking down clusters of memories. How could one justify the vast structure of names except by the names themselves? If one pulled the words away one by one, the edifice would crumble altogether, and no two things would hold together any longer.

Perhaps John Wickliff Shawnessy was only a transparent awareness in a universe of chance and blind fruitions, an odd sort of newspaper in which certain mythical Events were reported.

It seemed to him then that he was groping helplessly outside his own world and trying to get back into it. He must not give up. He must go on bearing the burden of the whole implacably connected universe of himself.

—Hello, Johnny.

The name was softly personal, like a caress. The voice that uttered it was low and sweet and touched with infinite concern and kindness. He blinked owlishly at the faces around him.

Nell Gaither was standing just at the door of the Maddon Hotel. She was coolly lovely in a green summer dress. A pert straw hat teetered on her upswept curls. She gently swung a green parasol. An anxious, tender smile curved her mouth and made her green eyes peculiarly moist and bright.

—Nell! he croaked. Where did you come from?

—I've been waiting here for you, she said. Garwood told me about your trouble. I've been back in the State for about two months, living here in Indianapolis with relatives and doing war work. I thought I'd come over here and see if I could help in any way.

He told her about his search and failure so far. As they talked on the crowded sidewalk, he felt how far he had come from the older Raintree County of before the summer of 1859. Probably it had gone just as far from him. This poised young woman was after all not the one whom once he had seen like Venus in the river, had saved from a cardboard train in the Temperance Play, had paganly loved in the old Pedee Academy, had rowed down the Shawmucky River in summertime; she was not the one whom he had kissed in a haystack long ago, whose naked form had touched his own, whose long wet hair had fallen on his shoulders, whose teardrenched face had looked up to his in a December night, whose mouth had said, I love you, I will always love you. Those words had been said in the older Raintree County before his term of duty and slow endurance had begun. Those words had meant that he would be loved, yes, always, but always in the older Raintree County, now gone forever, and in the memory of it. There was no certainty that the Nell Gaither standing before him now was the one who had said those words.

Nevertheless, he had a wild, foolish rush of affection, not only for Nell but even for Garwood Jones, who had sent her to him, who was helping out, even if he bore a dubious role in the affair.

Being ashamed of his dirty, unkempt look, Johnny kept his face averted as he talked with Nell. He said that if she didn't mind, she could watch the train station for Susanna.

—I'd love to, Nell said.

—I'll come around and see you there after a while, Johnny said.

Back at the police station, the sergeant had news for him.

—Woman at a novelty store thinks she saw your wife. You can call on the lady at the store now. It's closed for the Fourth, but she said she'd be there and open it for you.

—Was the boy with her?

—I don't think so, the sergeant said. But you go and see this woman. I didn't take the message. Another fellow did.

Johnny ran the few blocks to the shop. The woman was a sharp-featured, talkative person of middle age.

—It was yesterday afternoon about this time, she said. This lady was a young woman in a highnecked dress, kind of wine color. I didn't see if she had a scar. She was very pretty but all run down. She kept smiling and looking around her while she was making her purchase. She had a Southern accent.

—Did she have a child with her?

—No, she was all alone. Her dress was sort of mussed. She did have a suitcase. She was very kind and genteel. I could see right away she was a lady. You'll never guess what she bought.

—Well?

—It was a doll. She handled it for a long time and finally said, I believe I'll take this one here.

—What kind of doll?

—Just like these here, the woman said.

The dolls on the counter were all alike, boy dolls with blond hair and blue suits. The woman went on:

—For your child, Ma'am? I said to her, trying to make talk. Why, no, I need it for something, she said. She paid for it then and left. This morning I read the item in the newspaper and right away remembered her. Do you think it was your wife, mister?

—Yes, Johnny said. When she left the store, which way did she turn?

—Left, I think, the woman said.

He questioned her further, but didn't find out any other important facts.

Leaving the store, he turned left and walked up the street. Susanna had been here only yesterday at about this time. It was agonizing to repeat a fragment of her ghostly trail twenty-four hours too late.

He ran over the conversation in his mind. I need it for something, she had said. Not for someone—but for something. I need it for something. She had walked up this street in this direction. He must still be retracing that lost trail. He stopped and looked around.

Directly in front of him was a large sign hanging over a door:

PHOTOGRAPHS, DAGUERREOTYPES, AMBROTYPES

A temporary card underneath said,

OPEN ALL DAY ON THE FOURTH

Johnny Shawnessy felt the flesh on his back tingle as if a cold wind had blown on him. He turned in at the open door and climbed the steps of the Photographer's Shop. Two at a time, he ran up, as he had done once long ago from the Square in Freehaven. He walked down through the gallery of the shop, which was lined with oval portraits. He opened a closed door there, wondering if he were about to repeat an earlier scene tragically rewritten.

There was only a man in the room working at a chemical bath. Johnny explained himself, described his wife and boy, asked the photographer if he had seen anyone answering that description.

—Yes, the man said, looking at him quizzically. Yes, I did. They were in yesterday at about this time or a trifle later. Lady in a dark red dress and a little boy. They sat for individual portraits and one together.

—Did the—did the young woman act a little strange?

—Yes, she did. She wanted to be posed holding a doll. I thought it was a little queer, but she said it had a sentimental significance. She was Southern all right. She posed by herself, holding the doll, and then she posed herself with the boy, but not the doll. I asked her if she planned to be in the City for the Fourth, and she said, no, she was going home. Home, I said, joking. If I'm not mistaken, lady, home for you is a long way from here, judging from your accent. Yes, it's a long way, she said. She was a lovely woman, beautiful eyes, hair, and complexion, but she looked sick.

—She is sick.

—I have those plates, the photographer said, but I haven't printed them. They came out good. You might be able to tell. I have them here.

He began to run through a box of labelled plates, pronouncing the names.

—Here we are, he said. Henrietta Courtney and boy James.

—What was that name? Johnny said.

The man repeated it.

—Isn't that right? he asked.

—Let's see them, Johnny said.

The photographer held two plates, of the usual *carte de visite* size, up to the light. There, as through a veil darkly, sat Susanna and Little Jim—and the doll.

—My God! Johnny said.

They were there, in his hand, imprisoned in a glass murky with chemicals.

—If she calls for the pictures, hold her here some way and get in touch with the police. By the way, when you finish the pictures, send them to me.

He gave the photographer his address and, not finding any more information, hurried out of the shop and back down the stair. He began to feel like someone running down hill on a path that got steeper all the time.

Back at the hotel, the clerk said,

—A young woman called for you. A Miss Gaither. Said to see her at the train station as soon as you could.

Johnny got his suitcase, paid his bill, and ran on through holiday throngs toward the police station. It was late afternoon as he went in. He told the sergeant his findings.

—Well, what do you think? the sergeant said.

—I don't know, Johnny said. I have a hunch she may have left the city and gone back. I'm on my way to the train station now.

—Well, the sergeant said, we could drag the river. That's where a lot of these cases end up.

—Thanks, Johnny said, tossing a scribbled address on the table. If you find anything, get in touch with me by telegraph there.

He left the police station and ran toward the depot. A cold word trickled in his mind. The River. Yes, the River. Where would she go at last, except the River? The River that ran forever in the background of her life, with the steamboats stacking to the piers and the Negroes working at the levee loading cotton bales. Where would she go at last except back home to darkness and the River! So there were two things here contending, Raintree County and the River. Yet she had said that she would go home. Where was her home? Had she meant the County after all and the tall house below the Square? Where was home now to the uprooted, wandering soul of the little mad Susanna? Would she come home to her last great hope, to the one other person in the world whom she had loved and trusted? Would she come back again to Raintree County, bringing the child safe with her?

He ran through the streets of the city. At the station, he found Nell in the waiting room.

—Johnny, she said, I think she's been here and taken the train. One of the ticket agents remembers selling a ticket this morning around ten o'clock to a woman like Susanna who had a little boy with her. A ticket to Freehaven.

—Thank God! I can't ever thank you enough, Nell.

—I'll go back with you if I can help any, she said.

—No, you've already been an angel. When's the next train out?

—Trains are all jammed up, she said. With this big battle East, everything's messed up. I took the liberty of asking the telegraph operator here to put a dispatch through to Freehaven to Niles Foster, telling him to look out for Susanna. The man said he'd try, but couldn't guarantee it would go through tonight. The wires are full of news all the time of the battle.

Johnny and Nell sat down on a bench in the station and waited. They talked a little and after a while had a bite to eat. It was eight o'clock before a train east was ready to leave.

—Good-by, Johnny, Nell said, standing on the platform and waving to him as the train began to move. And the best of luck.

He waved from the window, watching her small lovely face and stately form recede. In the clanging depot, standing in the classic attitude of farewell, she slowly faded; trainsmoke closed over her; the remorseless, strange river of his life had carried him beyond another anguishingly brief intersection.

Now there was nothing to do but wait. The train was bringing him back across the fastdarkening land. His pursuit had been a circle, returning upon itself. He listened to the lonely whistle of the train at crossings. It couldn't be long now. Two hours at most. He would be back in Freehaven by ten o'clock.

Curiously calm, he was thinking then of the last time he had seen Susanna and Little Jim. It had been a week ago, just before he left for Beardstown. A week—and yet since then the pattern of a whole life had almost unfolded to him. He was beginning to understand, to get it clear. He was beginning to grasp a dreadful, ancient, and significant fact about his wife Susanna and himself and Little Jim. He was about to grab the Sphinx by the throat and pluck the riddle from its tongue of stone.

When he had said good-by, it was in the evening. He had gone into Little Jim's room on the second floor. The little boy had stood up and put his arms around Johnny. At that moment Johnny had felt a strong impulse to lift the child from the bed and take him away forever. The slight form of Little Jim had clung to him thus in the night, and he had said good-by. He had gone downstairs then, and had thought to leave immediately, but he had talked a moment with Mrs. Gray, and then on an impulse had turned and gone upstairs again. He had opened the door to the child's room and stepped inside and had gone over to the bed. It was very dark then, but a little light came in from the window. The child was asleep already. The little breast faintly respired. Again he had wanted to pick the child up, awaken him, and take him away forever. But he had had that impulse many times. There was no use taking it as an evil omen.

Then he had gone downstairs. Susanna had been waiting at the door, and he had kissed her, and she had watched him with almost frightened eyes, while her mouth kept making its little crafty smile. She had squeezed him very hard and had said, with peculiar intensity,

—Now don't you worry about a thing, Johnny! I will look after everything!

No doubt she had already been planning this grand gesture of escape and flight.

From what?

A man got on at Greenfield and took the other half of Johnny's bench. He kept talking, as everyone else did, about the battle. He had a late paper and insisted on sharing it with Johnny. It appeared that the battle had ended in a great Union Victory.

—This time, we got Bob Lee where it hurts, the man said. What's more, Grant has taken Vicksburg. That old river is free at last.

Johnny read some of the reports from Gettysburg. It appeared that the last great day of the three had been July 3, when Lee had launched a tremendous assault on the Union center north of the town. This attack had been repulsed in the bloodiest fighting of the War, and Lee's army was broken and believed retreating, perhaps routed.

He put the paper down. Sleep dragged his chin down. His head ached and buzzed. But he kept automatically reviewing memories, which he tried to put together like the fragments of a puzzle. He remembered that he had some of the pieces in his pocket. He pulled out the two notes he had received on July 2, starting him on his quest. In the dim light, he could hardly read the writing.

Yes, the handwriting on the note telling of his wife's infidelity was very much like that of the note he had found on the album. Now that the bad light dimmed the individual letters, he could see the same pattern in the large, childish scrawl of both notes.

There was no doubt about it; the note apprising him of Susanna's infidelity had been written by herself in a badly forged scrawl and mailed to him from Indianapolis.

He groped for meanings. Was there a dreadful reason in Susanna's unreason? Did her insanity have its own remorseless logic? Why did she want him to believe her unfaithful? Why did she tell upon herself, betray herself to him, become shameful in his eyes? Why did she wish to be undone by her own hand?

And why did she fly from the house in Freehaven taking the child with her, following a trail of madness in which she bore the name of a woman who had died in fire, a woman beautiful and stained, the black Helen of an epic rape? What ancient crime did she thus expiate by self-chastisement? And what was the goal of this fury-driven self-pursuit which turned upon itself in an immense circle?

He sat, musing these questions. Meanwhile the fumes of the little train and the steady jostling motion aggravated his fatigue. He felt sick, as though he had been poisoned. His eyelids kept sticking together. He shook his head and pulled his beard. He felt that if he slept now, relaxed his vigilance, something might happen, he would lose control of the situation, would never again see the lost faces.

The fat man was saying something to him, and he kept trying to listen. Words drifted misty and meaningless on a broad yellow flood of sleep, pulling him strongly downstream. Gettysburg . . . Lee . . . Lincoln . . . Mississippi . . . Downstream, downstream, on a great slow river of sleep . . . Downstream to ancient days and far away . . . Lost child and wandering Susanna . . . Lost child . . . Lost . . .

The steamboat rocked slowly in toward a levee thronging with faces. In his dream he was leaning on the rail, looking at a scene timemellowed, tinted in nostalgic colors: fat bales piled for loading on the levee; slave cabins inland on the verge of the cottonfields; Negroes in attitudes of work and play—supplebacked pickers diminishing to specks and pickaninnies waving at the boat; in the background the old plantation home. The murmur of a million tongues drifted down a rhythmic river of departed summers. He remembered a legend of his youth.

There had been gentle and dark faces; a little white girl had died that a race might be free. He too had loved the earth and the great yellow river. Alas! and a tragic name hissed in the music of those voices. Gone were the days when hearts were young and gay, all gone, he knew, all lost on the river of the years, a dream recaptured in the greatest of the sentimental novels or perhaps in the poem of a lost young bard of Raintree County. . . .

A lane of green lawn dwindled to a distant tomb.

PROFESSOR JERUSALEM WEBSTER STILES

dapperly pedantic, sinking a spade into a mound of earth,

—The skin of the Negro, though black in the womb, is transmuted to white by the touch of the tomb, while the skin of the white in the grip of the grave is black as the black of an African slave.

JOHNNY

digging frantically,

—You really do believe then, Professor, that by untombing the body of this woman we are unwombing the secret of the lost child?

PERFESSOR

leaning on spade, lighting cigar,

—I have a dark suspicion, John, that all is not well in the Old Kentucky Home.

The smoke of the cigar spread with a stink of fever and the river; the valley darkened where they dug.

PERFESSOR

riding away on a broomstick, black hag's hair shaking,

—White is black, and black is white.
Hover through smoke and swampy night! . . .

On the stage of an old Opera House, the play was about to begin, a tragedy of vengeance and incestuous love, more richly implausible than *Hamlet.* The house was filled with people, but behind the curtain all was confusion. Perhaps he ought to warn actors and audience how this old play had ended in fire.

VOICE

of a woman filling the Opera House with a thrilling sound,

—Think of your freedom, every time you see UNCLE TOM'S CABIN; and let it be a memorial to put you all in mind to follow in his steps, and be . . .

The hero of an Old Southern Melodrama, he stood in pale dawn before a house. To this calm mansion, he remembered, a woman had been stolen whose dusky limbs and nodding breasts and beautiful, proud face had made men mad to fight for generations. They had fought here where the river flowed past an adulterous city to the sea. For the rape of this dark Helen, blood had darkened white columns by the river; time had turned the blood to pools of shadow. And a woman with a twisted mouth avenged the old crime—so went the ancient story. But now the memory faded, and he couldn't remember the names, names murmurous of the earth enriched with a charred dust.

Like one passing into the brown shadows of a daguerreotype, he entered the house. Through the deserted hall, a dress trailed audibly.

WOMAN

ascending the broad stair, lamp in hand,

—Follow and you will find a lost child, the tragic issue of a house divided.

JOHNNY

—Who was the mother of this child? Who fired the shot that slew an old republic? What is your earthcovered name, a legend of the Southern sun?

WOMAN

with head averted, wringing her hands,

—Stained. By guilty lust and careless seed. Where can we wash it out except in darkness and the river, the river tinged with the color of our crime? For this, we died, we two. For this our blood made brown shadows on the earth of an old republic.

The audience in the unseen pit of the Opera House applauded as he climbed the stair. It was an old cabin of logs hewn from the great oak forest that once covered all these river valleys. In the rum-and-tobacco-fragrant darkness, a mirror on the landing showed his face faintly negroid, and he remembered the old taint in his bloodstream, which his father had privately spoken of. A woman waited for him in a fourposter bed hung with scarlet curtains, her flesh like a dark wine glowing from logfires on the levee.

BLACK JOHNNY

—It is all a legend of the earth. You and I were the same and are the same always, being children of the same dark loins. Tell me your name, a phrase of music and of strangeness——

WOMAN

—Had you forgotten all our fabled life beside the river? Had you forgotten the names of rivers and the great rich names of steamboats? Had you forgotten why they fought so long and long, my darling? For from our union came the Republic in blood and anguish springing. Had you forgotten? Fondly, fondly I embrace you!

His lips touched hers, drinking a taste of earth. Light lay scarlet on the naked hills, deep shadow in the hollows of her flesh. He knew then that he must repeat the rape of this dark Helen, his eternal sister, wife, and wandering child, weave out a tragic legend until he found again the lost charter that would give them back to purity and innocence. His desire clothed in the dark flesh touched her with . . .

Beams of swung lanterns shot across the room.

ROBERT SEYMOUR DRAKE

breaking through door, axe in hand, speaking pleasantly through white lips,

—It's just an old Southern custom, John.

Fine fat bullyboys in fancy clothes, stinking of whiskey, rum, and tobacco, hugged him hard and hurled him down, squeezed the breath out of him with their buttocky bodies, gouged him with pistolbutts, clubs, knifehandles.

BLACK JOHNNY

struggling,

—Help! Bobby! Help!

COUSIN BOBBY

—Hell, boy, you got to learn 'em young, as my Old Man always said.

OLD SOUTHERN PLANTER

white linen suit stained with tobacco juice, cotton sideburns and mustaches, winey complexion, fat cigar, whiskey voice.

—Jest take it easy, son. Y'all lun to lub the Suthen way of lahf as much as the rest of us. Seh, we Suthun gemmen have a big stake in the well-bein' of ouah slaves. Those were good days, seh, when we used to go daown theh to the little Nigro cabins bah the rivah and pick out the blackest, the sleekest, the puttiest, and shiniest little gal, and then, seh, by Gad, we planted the good old plantuh's seed. Pawt of ouah duty, seh, to stud foh the propuhgation of the labuh supply, seh, in the soft ole nots daown bah the rollin' rivah. Yassuh, way daown Souf in duh lan' of cotton, ole times dah am not fuhgotten. . . .

The Old Southern Planter and a dozen young Southern gentlemen fell upon the cringing form of the mulatto girl and raped her with practiced ease.

T. D. SHAWNESSY

shaking an accusing finger over the rapists, crouched on the fallen girl and pretending to shoot craps,

—Gambling's a sin before the Lord, boys.

T. D. fell through a trapdoor, out of which there sprang a huge dark tree, dripping medicinal gums. . . .

It was night in the Great Dismal Swamp. Stage sets representing typical views of New Orleans were sinking in the foul muck. Bloodhounds bayed in the distance. Lanterns flared. Shotgun blasts ripped the still leaves. A bloodred moon hung low on the horizon. The heaving muds of the swamp shimmered and stank. He was stumbling through the inky water, trying to find a way to freedom. The mulatto girl with him was going to have a baby. He was trying to remember how he had come by this unhappy burden. At any rate, it was a sacred charge, and he must find the underground railway and get her to safety on the northern shore.

The river ran broad and yellow in the semi-darkness. Artificial cotton snowflakes sifted noiselessly down. Floating icechunks swam slowly on the flood. The bloodhounds were just behind.

JOHNNY

sinking with the girl on a rotten raft,

—Help! Help! Save this poor woman!

AUDIENCE

excursionists leaning over the rail of a steamboat, politely clapping their hands, singing,

—O, Father, come out of that old lagoon.
They say you are drowned in——

HARRIET BEECHER STOWE

nightgown, hair in curlpapers, sitting on deck, baby in lap, blowing on her hands from time to time, writing with whispering lips line after line and page after page,

—Calvin, mind the baby. *With wild cries and desperate energy she leaped to another and still another cake. . . .*

JOHNNY

sinking up to his chin, trying to keep the girl afloat,

—Mrs. Stowe, for God's sake, hurry up and get us out of here! We're drowning, Mrs. Stowe! We're drowning! We're——

MRS. STOWE

raising her hand in benediction,

—*Farewell, beloved child. The bright eternal doors have closed after thee; we shall see thy sweet face no more. . . .*

VOICE

of a woman, husky, wailing, lost on dark waters,

—Henrietta Courtney! Henrietta Courtney!

JOHNNY

choking in the yellow water, holding a child in his hands,

—Help! Help! Somebody save him. Before it's too late.

The body of a woman floated in the pale chemical of the river, her flesh washed white as lilies and slowly dissolving from the bone. The child in his arms had turned to a burnt doll. He heard a

VOICE

calling, monotonous, insistent, with a note of sadness,

—Raintree County! Raintree County!

It was the voice of the journeying years, the trainman calling the cars to home. He was calling the names of intersections on the land, of little towns in Raintree County, he was calling names of old republics, he was . . .

Somebody was shaking his shoulder. Johnny woke up and stared through bleared eyes. The fat man was peering at him with a mixture of concern and disgust.

—Son, you better git home and git some rest. You were groanin' in your sleep.

Johnny looked around. The train had stopped.

—Where are we? he said dully.

—Beardstown, the fat man said.

—I have to change trains, Johnny said.

He got off and went into the little station at Beardstown. It was ten o'clock before he left the Beardstown station on the train to Freehaven. In fifteen minutes he would be home. He sat bemused, still holding the pieces of the torn letters in his hand like fragments of a crazy puzzle that he had not yet succeeded in fitting entirely together. He was looking for the missing part.

Reaching now into the pocket of his coat, he took out the daguerreotype around which Susanna had wrapped her letter. That, too, must have been part of the sad design, a plan unknown even to herself, in which she obeyed the bidding of a little dark remembered hand behind her hand. He stared at the daguerreotype. In the dull light he could hardly see the people in the brown shadow of the porch.

But he could see with a dreadful distinctness, rising, filling up the background of that ancient scene, the shape of a tall white house, in whose whiteness (because of the dimness of the light) the white pillars almost were dissolved. The shape of this house (destroyed in fire) was familiar: it had three stories and a corniced roof, and on its face, its doomed and tragic face, there were five windows looking out upon the river,

FOREVER LOOKING OUT UPON THE RIVER,

IN A LEGEND WRITTEN BY THE

SOUTHERN

SUN, nooning, filled up the Main Street of Waycross with light and heat. Faces moved thickly on the Road of the Republic.

—It's eleven-four, the Perfessor said, returning watch to pocket. Phew! it's hot! What's next on the program, John? Can't we have a little excitement around here? I've been squatting here so long I've got bedsores.

—We're to meet Mrs. Brown at eleven-fifteen at the site of the Senator's birthplace. The Photographer's probably down there now.

The Perfessor studied a fullpage lithograph on page 41 of the Raintree County *Atlas,* his sharp nose pointing delicately at a rural landscape, twice-illumined by a summer morning sun.

—You see, he said, it is all sunlight. Farmhouse, barn, roads, brook, cattle, horses, trees, fences, buggies, people—it is all sunlight. We are all sunlight.

Mr. Shawnessy folded his copy of the *News-Historian.* Events of the year 1892 flattened obediently against each other, mist of ink on sheets of perishable sunlight. Older Events, elder brothers of those in the *News-Historian,* stirred in their illusive realm, dry dust of History that never happened. Somewhere through this sifting wordseed of old newspapers, telling of births, marriages, deaths, elections, sports, crimes, wars, pestilence, floods, a woman went holding a lamp in her hand, sleepwalking in the chambers of a house divided, still hunting sunlight and the river.

The Senator shuffled *Memories of the Republic in War and Peace* into a neat square pile, which he then folded and stuffed into his coatpocket. A westbound freight screamed up its sunbright highway to the crossing and went longly by, following the path of the sun toward distant sheds of smoke and tumult. The voice of the Trainman sounded in stations of the far years, calling the cars to home, to home. In the valleys of a lost republic, the cars were changing in the stations. When did the great trains come to rest!

—Tell me, John, the Senator said. Is Evelina as lovely as ever?

—Don't tell me you know her too! the Perfessor said.

—Why, certainly, the Senator said. Mrs. Brown has been in

Washington several times over the last decade to lobby for woman's rightful position in the world.

The Senator wheezed, and the Perfessor shook soundlessly.

—Did you help her achieve it? the Perfessor said.

—Did my best, the Senator said. How do you happen to know her?

—She and I collaborated in certain feminist propagations in New York.

The Perfessor shook soundlessly, and the Senator wheezed.

—Well, I'm glad to have her in charge of the program, the Senator said, standing up. Where does the little lady live around here?

—She lives, Mr. Shawnessy said, standing up, in a lavish mansion just at the edge of Waycross. There are castiron nymphs in her shrubbery. She's the bewilderment of the local ladies.

—Evelina, said the Perfessor, standing up, *Atlas* under arm, is a darling. She writes dear, bad poetry which now and then over the years I have printed in my column.

—What in the devil is she doing *here?* the Senator said.

—Frankly, the Perfessor said, I can't fit her into this picture either. But I'm responsible for her being here. Some years ago, she got acquainted with our boy John through the instrumentality of my column. She admired the philosophic pearls now and then dispensed by the Poet Laureate of Raintree County. She was looking for a place in which to withdraw from the world for the contemplation of her navel—one of the most cunning in my wide acquaintance—and she selected Raintree County.

—How long's she been here? the Senator asked.

—Two years, Mr. Shawnessy said. She bought, rebuilt, and landscaped an old brick house just outside Waycross here. She wanted a house by the side of the road. Something like that. Solitude. Meditation.

—Where did she get her money? the Senator said. Who was her husband? I've always wondered.

—I don't know, Mr. Shawnessy said.

—Nobody knows, the Perfessor said. She turned up in New York ten years ago, a young widow with a baby girl, a pile of money, and a lot of feminist ideas. Who her husband was, she never would tell. She's a figure of mystery, and the biggest mystery is why she sheds the sunlight of her lovely countenance on John and the local anthropoids.

He lowered his voice.

—A number of whom I see approaching.

A halfdozen farmers in Sunday suits shifted uneasily in shiny shoes and tried to rub smiles from their faces. Their leader was a middleaged fat man with a chin beard.

—Howdydo, Senator.

—Howdy, Bill, the Senator said.

He shook hands around, permitting it to be known that he and Bill Jacobs had been close friends in the Old Days and that there wasn't a better farmer in Raintree County, or in the whole nation, by God, than Bill Jacobs.

—Uh, Garwood, while you was waitin' around fer the program to start this afternoon, Mr. Jacobs said, we thought you might be interested in seein' a little special attraction fer men only. Now me and these fellers is all members of the Raintree County Stockbreeders Association, which I am the president of. Now, I don't know as you'd be interested, but I happen to own the bull that took first prize at the State Fair last summer, and Jim Foley here, he has a Jersey heifer he wants bred, and I told him we might hold it as a special attraction on the Fourth over to my barn. If you'd care to come, it's going to be right soon.

The Senator cleared his throat.

—All aspects of farm life interest me, he said. How about it, John, have we got time for this?

—We'll get the pictures taken first, Mr. Shawnessy said. Bill's farm is close. I suppose we'll have time. Want to go along, Professor?

—All aspects of farm life interest me, said the Perfessor.

Leaving the General Store, the three men walked slowly under elms and maples toward the site of the Senator's birthplace. Peering ahead, Mr. Shawnessy could make out a young man setting up a black box on three legs just beyond the shadetrees at the point where the sidewalk ended.

He had been entangled in an Old Southern Melodrama, reshuffling memories of war and peace in a lost republic. Time now to find again the everliving present in which a radiant god was zestfully tracing images of forbidden things. With a finger of light, there where the shadow ended, he drew his legend, forever new, forever old—a garden of strange delight where nymphs were hiding nude in balls of shrubbery watching the motions of

A White Bull

STOOD in a small pasture a little way from the National Road. On three sides he was imprisoned in barbed wire, on the fourth by a tall iron fence flanking an unseen garden. His large brown eyes were fretful and melancholy. North and south, the July corn was an ocean of soft arms in which he was islanded, a great strength formed for love and strife. Brutely propulsive from tight rump to mounded shoulders, he stood lovetortured peering at a world without depth. He did not know what festive day it was. He did not know what month or year it was. He did not know his name. He did not know that he was bull.

. . .

THE REVEREND LLOYD G. JARVEY, shaggily virile, strode back and forth in the little tent beside the Revival Tent. The flap was down. He was alone. Even with his glasses on, he could see nothing clearly except that the sun blazing on the canvas dome filled the tent with a brown mist. Dripping with sweat, back and forth he strode, his eyes glaring savagely with a penned-in, fretful look. Through dull walls he could hear a liquid rush of voices, laughter, wheels. It was a sound like surf beating on an island in which love-tortured a god lay pinioned in a shape of earth.

. . .

MRS. EVELINA BROWN stood in the lower hall of her mansion east of Waycross. Looking into her mirror, she saw a gracefully formed woman in a modish green gown with emphasized hip lines. A small green hat perched on her titiancolored hair. Her face was fullcheeked and fair. The large graygreen eyes and finely drawn uplifted brows gave to her face an eager girlish look though there were faint lines on the forehead and in the corners of the eyes. Nose and chin were pert. The mobile, shining mouth had the full underlip of passion.

Around her gloomed the brick broad walls of her Victorian home, stocked with twisted chairs, bewildered sofas, sentimental pictures in writhing frames, grotesquely antlered light fixtures, flowersplashed wallpapers, and glassdoored bookcases ranked with gilt volumes of Tennyson, Dickens, Byron, Bulwer-Lytton, Victor Hugo, and a great deal of libertarian literature, calculated to achieve woman's rightful position in a thoroughly reformed world.

The house which enclosed her small lonely form looked as if ten different architects had begun work on ten different projects in the same place and had been obliged to reconcile their conflicting designs as best they could. Thin windows pierced thick walls; a green mansard roof looking like elephant rind squatted on the confused pile; ironwork bristled along the eaves. Across the front was a manycolumned verandah. A round tower was rooted obscurely in the gloomy mass. A fence of iron spears enclosed a vast lawn, full of clipped balls of bushes and topiary shapes of bulls, deers, archers, gods. Nymphs stood nude in the shrubbery, castiron buttocks wound in vines. To the rear were a servant's house and a gardener's shop, both brickly respectable. In the back part of the lawn was a little summer house, a roofcone on slender columns. In the east front corner of the yard near the road a fountain made a flower of spray over two bronze children, whose naked forms were halfsubmerged in a pond of waterlilies.

In this house and lawn, Mrs. Evelina Brown, a figure of mystery, had built herself a place apart, from which she looked forth upon a flat world of cornfields and frame houses. In Raintree County, she had constructed something pagan and contrived, an island of wistful feminine aspiration in the corn.

. . .

A CHORUS of loud guffs and snorts followed the Senator's virile remark. The Raintree County Stockbreeders Association withdrew to a respectful distance still savoring the senatorial wit in wheezy chuckles. The Senator, the Perfessor, and Mr. Shawnessy had meanwhile stopped at the site of the Senator's birthplace, where the Photographer under a hood sighted through his box at a big gnarled halfdead appletree standing in a vacant lot at the edge of town. Drawn up to the curb was an odd hooded wagon with the black legend:

E. R. ROSS, PHOTOGRAPHER
Freehaven, Indiana

—Here it is, the Senator said, hooking his thumbs in his armpits and looking sad.

—The humble spot of a heroic birth, the Perfessor said, removing his hat.

—I suppose it was a log cabin, Senator, Mr. Shawnessy said.

—Matter of fact, it was, the Senator said.

—Garwood B. Jones, recited the Perfessor, was born in 1835 in a little log cabin, which he built in the year 1892.

—Some people have no poetic feeling, the Senator said.

—Now, Garwood, Mr. Shawnessy said, if you'll just distribute yourself under that tree, this young man will preserve your outline for posterity.

The Photographer was a pleasant young man with unusual blue eyes, shiny darkbrown hair, and dimples, who did not seem at all disturbed by the confusion in which he worked. People kept coming up and asking him questions about his apparatus, and every now and then, while he was under the hood correcting the focus, a small boy would come up and peer into the lens. Unperturbed, the Photographer waved him away and went on with his work, walking swiftly back and forth from his covered cart to his camera, carrying plates, making adjustments, bobbing in and out of the hood. In this scene, he alone was the artist-contriver as he prepared to trace with a radiant pencil a legend of light and shadow, some faces on the great Road of the Republic.

. . .

The flap lifted. A blurred head pushed through the opening. As Preacher Jarvey walked forward to greet the visitor, the head swam into focus, hovering in a vitreous world like a fish seen through a glassbottomed boat.

Nodding hugely in at the tent flap was the broad bald head of Gideon Root, seen with monstrous precision through the Preacher's thick lenses.

—Praise the Lord, Brother Root!

—Praise the Lord, Brother Jarvey!

The two big voices filled the tent with a harsh, booming sound. The two big bearded faces wagged solemnly at each other.

—Brother Root, I am ready to bring these two sinners before the bar of God.

—When?

—The Literary Society is havin' a meetin' tonight at the home of this errin' woman, and I have gathered a select group to march in a procession, bearin' torches. We will apprehend them in the midst of their profane rites.

—I don't care how you do it, Brother Jarvey, just so you show this Shawnessy up for the rascal he is. I'm not a wealthy man, but I'll gladly contribute another hundred dollars to the cause of God in Raintree County if you can pull this thing off.

—Of course, it would be better, Brother Root, if we caught the guilty pair *in flagrante delicto.*

—What's that, Brother?

—Brother, that means in the livin' act. That means couplin' in lust!

—I reckon that would be hard to do.

—Brother, we will have to proceed without the full evidence of things seen, but we have the evidence of things unseen to prove their lustful love. Sister Lorena Passifee, who lives close to the home of this errin' woman, has observed things and heard things. I have a note from her here to the effect that he was seen in the late hours of last night leavin' her guilty embrace, and the woman was seen in the nakedness and confusion of her shameless passion. O, Brother Root, lust is a terrible thing. Praise the Lord!

—It is a terrible thing.

—Hit is a terrible thing, and hit is tenfold more terrible when hit is embodied in the person of a beautiful woman like Sister Brown. Such beauty ought to be bestowed on the altar of God, but, alas! hit is turned aside and polluted by atheistic doctrine and pagan heresy. Praise the Lord!

—Praise the Lord!

—O, hit is a dreadful thing, hit is tenfold more dreadful when the seeds of lust are sown in a beautiful garden that ought to have been matured to Christ. I had hoped to save this errin' female from her fate, but the emissary of Satan in this County, by name John Wickliff Shawnessy, toils day and night to undo the work of God. But their hour has come, Brother Root. Their hour has come. Hosanna!

—Hosanna!

—For the Lord will not long permit this sinful dalliance. He will chastise it with a whip of flame. He will requite it with a scourge of fire. Praise the Lord!

—Praise the Lord, Brother Jarvey. I'm afraid we'll be heard outside, Brother.

The monotonous horn of Preacher Jarvey's voice had begun to blow high and hard, with a more and more rhythmical rise and fall. Now he muted it down to a hoarse whisper.

—I'm about to go to Sister Passifee's now, Brother Root, to inquire further into this matter with her. Tonight at eight o'clock I'll expect you in this tent. There will be some other men of God from this and neighborin' counties present, who will lend their wrath to ours when we expel these guilty creatures from the nest of their iniquity. Tell you the truth, the local people are not to be relied upon. They worship this scoundrel.

—I think it best, Brother Jarvey, if I keep kind of in the back.

—As you say, Brother, as you say.

Preacher Jarvey lifted the tent flap for Gideon Root and leaning out watched the broad form blur into a mist of green and gold.

He was alone once more in a craving void. Instantly he hungered to hurl himself upon it with voice and fist and starting eyeball and wrest from it some form of beauty that would still the hunger. Perhaps he could lure it by a savage cry, prolonged like a trumpet blown into the void, and name it into being. . . .

. . .

Evelina gave a last pat to her hair. As she turned away, watching her mirror twin sweep large-eyed into a duplicate world, she remembered her dream of the night before. She had lain awake a long time, thinking about many things: her long consultation with Mr. Shawnessy reviewing the last details of the program for the Fourth; the strange letter she had received from Professor Jerusalem Webster

Stiles; her plans for the day—picture-taking at the Senator's birthplace, a studied plea to the Senator for aid in obtaining woman suffrage, her chairmanship of the Program of the Day, and arrangements for the picnic of the Literary Society at her home in the evening. When finally she had slept, she had dreamed a wondrous, strange rehearsal of the day to come. Scenes from this dream, forgotten in the excitement of awakening (for she had risen to this day as to a contest), kept rising unexpectedly from limbo and untime, impinging on her day with a quaintly duplicate day in which a stately twin, more daring Evelina, made an immortal progress through the streets of time.

Carrying her pamphlets in a thin bundle under her arm, she opened the door, stepped forth to the verandah, went down the steps. The day assaulted her with heat, rising in soft globes rolling from the long lawn, shimmering over the cornfield across the road. Bouncing nervously on the springy substance of the path, she walked to the iron gates and into the National Road. Shading her eyes, she looked east into the flagbright Main Street of Waycross lined with wheels, alive with faces. She walked sedately in her peculiar undulant manner feeling the heatflush on her cheeks. A tall man detached himself from a group at the Senator's birthplace and nodded to her. It was Mr. Shawnessy, his eyes narrowed to slots of liquid blue. She made a little motion with her free arm and smiled. Another man with a huge black book under his arm waved to her and advanced, a tall, distinguished person with hawksharp face and glittering black eyes.

—Well, well! here she is, the Perfessor said, a figure of beauty and mystery, that very feminine feminist, Evelina!

Smiling with excitement, she held out her hand to the Perfessor, suddenly remembering . . .

EVELINA'S DREAM

She had been dreaming of preparations for a ritual day. Standing before her hallmirror she had put the last touch to her costume, pinning on a feminist pamphlet like a figleaf. When she opened the door, a flood of light and music struck her. Professor Stiles, dressed like a herald, rakethin legs in ceremonial tights, shouted through a megaphone:

—Introducing, Ladies and Gentlemen, our favorite woman of tomorrow! Mrs. Evelina Brown, that distinguished poetess whose lyrical talents have often embellished our column!

She stepped to the front of a platform in a vast park ornamented by castiron statuary and surrounded by distant buildings, awesomely hideous and vaguely resembling photographs she had seen of Queen Victoria.

—Welcome, lords and ladies gay, she said in a thrilling sweet voice. This meeting of all the ladies from Aurora to dewy Eve has been arranged by the Waycross Literary Society to celebrate the completion of a Century of Progress in the attainment of woman's rightful position. . . .

Under the old appletree stood Senator Jones, in an authoritatively senatorial pose, left foot out, chest and paunch well forward, head and chin thrown back, hands holding coat lapels, thumbs up.

The Photographer pressed the bulb. Melting from granite into flesh, the Senator walked over to the road and swept broad hat from freeflowing locks.

—So this is the little lady who is going to handle the Grand Ceremonies this afternoon! I am honored and charmed to see you again, Mrs. Brown.

The Perfessor relinquished her hand.

—You can have it for a while, Senator. But remember, I want it back.

The Senator enclosed the small hand in his two great hands.

—It seems years since you were with us in Washington, dear, he said. You haven't given up the good fight, have you?

—Not at all, she said. I find I can carry it on here as well as in the Nation's Capital, that's all.

—How lovely you look, dear, the Perfessor said. Don't you agree, Senator, that Evelina ought to stop wasting all this charm on John and the local plowheads?

—Indubitably! the Senator said in his mellow bass.

—Let's have some more pictures under the appletree, Mr. Shawnessy said to the Photographer. With the lady included.

—By all means, the Senator said, leading Evelina over to the tree. Come on, Professor and John. You get into it too.

—May we look admiringly at the lady? the Perfessor asked the Photographer, who had said almost nothing so far.

—Of course, said the Photographer, ducking under the hood. What else?

—A perspicacious young man, said the Perfessor. He will go far in his profession.

Evelina leaned back on the old tree, looking up into the branches, through which the sifted sunlight fell. For a moment, she and the three men became quite still, as the Photographer reappearing from under the hood looked at them with a solicitous expression on his young face and pressed the bulb.

Their forms fled to the dusky inward of his mysterious box, written with a pencil of light upon a stuff of shadow. All else was lost on the Main Street of Waycross, the color of the thronging, curious faces, the boys with fists of firecrackers, the buggies passing. But in a timeconquering photograph four figures stood: a broad gentleman in a cutback coat with wideflung arm indicative of a tree; a longheaded gentleman in pince-nez dapperly leaning on a cane, the sly beginning of a smile on his thin, dry lips; a darkhaired gentleman with pensive, innocent eyes; herself, a lady in a green dress, hands folded coyly over the figleaf zone, eyes looking wistfully upward at the branches. . . .

EVELINA'S DREAM

The Perfessor, leaning forward like a traveling salesman, showed pages from a fashion magazine.

—Could I interest you, Madame, in the latest Stiles? *The Goddess Ladies Book,* featuring the newest Paris fashions. To the most stunning costume since Eve, we are awarding——

Mr. Shawnessy appeared with a golden apple in his hand, attired in his usual schoolmaster's costume. She perceived then that the apple was really the bulb-release of a camera. Mr. Shawnessy was setting up the oddshaped apparatus to take her picture, as she posed in a huge picture frame made of trellised roses.

—Latest Continental dispatches, he recited, record a breathtaking retrogression to fashions popular in the first centuries of this era. A certain notable lady whose mode of apparel has vitally affected all feminine adornment since her time was the first to adopt this charming *ensemble.*

Except for her Princess Eugénie hat, she was posed in entire nudity. With shyly downcast eyes she studied the flow of her wellfleshed thighs and calves to the prim little feet, one slightly advanced and both prettily turned out. There was a flash of rosecolored light, and as the fading fragments floated dreamily around her . . .

The Photographer closed the shutter.

—Young man, the Perfessor said, you have made us immortal.

—Senator, Evelina said, peeling off a pamphlet from the top of her bundle, could I have a word with you?

—The pleasure is mine, dear, said the Senator, looking at her with eyes of shrewd appraisal. I received your charming letter, by the way.

—I hope you will come out strongly for woman suffrage in the present campaign, Senator. The Populist Party, as you know, is going to make it a plank in their platform. Surely it's time that women were conceded equality on this point. If my personal wish can have any weight, I hope you will see fit to raise this great issue above partisanship. A statesman of your stature and popularity would have great weight.

—At a rough estimate, the Perfessor said, two hundred and fifty pounds.

—I assure you, Madame, the Senator said, his voice becoming measured and louder, that I shall give this matter every attention within my power.

—Please take this pamphlet, Evelina said, in which I have summarized a century of striving toward our great goal. Senator, I earnestly beseech you to give us your backing.

The Senator accepted the pamphlet and adjusting a pair of glasses read stagily,

—A CENTURY OF PROGRESS IN THE ATTAINMENT OF WOMAN'S RIGHTFUL POSITION IN THE WORLD. Well, I shall certainly go into this with the utmost interest. Be sure to look me up the next time you're in Washington, dear, and we'll try to work something out.

—For my part, the Perfessor said, I think the ladies, God bless 'em, already rule us entirely. It's a woman's world and getting more so all the time. The books, magazines, and poems are written about, for, or by the ladies. Society is tied securely to the hump of milady's bustle. She queens it here, and she queens it there, she queens it covered, and queens it bare. It's no accident that this great century will be called in history by the name of a fat empress, whose penchant for covering her flabby body with a hideous rind of respectability has been imposed upon the whole sex from the throne down. They have us where it hurts, gentlemen, and, believe me, we trot along briskly enough. For the ladies are in the sidesaddle and ride mankind. They let us go out and graze a little wild oats now and then, but it's only to slap us about the ears and lead us back firmly into the great stable of respectability, where we end up by nosing docilely into our stalls so that government of the ladies, by the ladies, for the ladies, goddamn 'em, shall not perish from the earth.

It was hard to be angry with the Perfessor, but Evelina felt her cheeks burning as if she had been caught in a peculiarly feminine deception. . . .

EVELINA'S DREAM

There was a loud flourish of trumpets. The Perfessor handed her up to a throne atop a carriage shaped like a pumpkin, drawn by six men in mouse costume.

—I crown you Evelina Regina!

As befitted a queen, her gown was a ceremonial costume stiff with jewels. Ladies in identical gowns stood in dense ranks along a wide way colorful with pennants. It was apparently the diamond jubilee of her reign. The Perfessor, assuming more and more the look of Lord Beaconsfield, led the singing:

—Lovely and glorious!
Our Queen Victorious,
Long to reign orious!
(God save the King.)

With gracious mien and little motions of her sceptre, an ivory stick with gaudy ball of gold bestuck with diamonds, she spoke in queenly accents:

—My subjects, it is now fifty years since the great discovery was made by one of our leading female novelists that the words describing the sexes had been exactly reversed by some philological error in the dawn of iniquity and what we have been calling men are actually——

Walking down the boulevard, Evelina Regina set her heels down primly on the necks of prostrate men, who licked her little glittering boots and squealed with pleasure at every touch. Somehow she felt a little dissatisfied with the progress of . . .

—Reform, the Perfessor was saying, leaning on the appletree and gesturing in his old classroom manner, is a feminine invention. The male of the species doesn't give a hoot for reform. In so far as he's male, he wants to destroy, rape, gorge, kill, revel, and rove at will in a world of selfish self-expression. But the female of the species finds it to her advantage to keep alive the old pathetic dream of remodeling humanity. All this is intended to make the obstreperous male a better mate and provider. The American woman, who is the most dominant of her sex since Theseus raped the Amazonian Queen, is especially talented along these lines. She's forever plucking the drink from our hand and the cigar from our mouth. Fact is, Evelina, really enlightened females like you are not doing the sex a service, as your more conventional sisters know. Equality in politics, love, and work may cause woman to surrender her subtle dominion in other things. And where will that get you? In the end?

—Our Evelinas, Mr. Shawnessy said, are a guarantee that tomorrow America will be more beautiful than today. They insure that the earth will be forever feminine—that is to say, mysterious, lovely, provocative.

—Amen, said the Perfessor. What rot I've been talking! For God's sake, Senator, give the bustle a ballot.

—I place in nomination the name of Mrs. Evelina Brown for the First Petticoat President of the United States, the Senator said.

—How about a drink to that, the Perfessor said, in yon healthful beverage?

The ladies of the Mystic Country Cookers Society were dispensing free lemonade at a stand built near the edge of the Senator's birthplace. The Perfessor ordered four lemonades.

—It's on me, he said. Come and get it.

He sneaked a flask of corncolored fluid from his hip pocket and holding it cleverly inside his coat, uncorked, tipped a little into the glass, corked, and slipped the flask deftly into an inside coatpocket. To Evelina, he confided,

—As President of the W.C.T.U., I have a little confession to make. Until the age of twenty-one, I touched nothing stronger than pure gin. But one day in the company of a slicker from the city, I allowed myself to be persuaded to drink a glass of water. Friends, I'm here to tell you——

—Professor, you know I have no objection to liquor.

—I know, child, that your feminism is of a peculiarly amiable type. I sometimes wonder, dear, what the new America will be like when, according to your formula, the ladies have completely emancipated themselves and exchanged corsets for contraceptives. Well, believe me, I'm for it and trust I'll be there. That gives me a rime and a toast.

He held his glass aloft.

—To the World of Tomorrow, a Feminist Fair,
Where the Liquor is Free and the Ladies are Bare!

As she drank the sugared lemonwater, Evelina looked over the rim of her glass at the three gentlemen bowing to her. She had come surely a wondrous and far progress to stand here in her green gown sipping free lemonade on the Main Street of Waycross in the year 1892. Was it possible to cast off caution like a garment, be very simple like a child, say only the most true and eternal things? Was it possible to still the longing of summer nights, to gain reprieve from fevered dawns? How much truth could the world stand? . . .

EVELINA'S DREAM

At first, it seemed to be a meeting of delegates for a convention in a large park. But as she walked among old buildings of the little town and saw in the distance the winding river, she felt sure that it was New Harmony, Indiana, on the banks of the historic Wabash, or perhaps some Fourieristic Community. She remembered the summery lawns of all the would-be utopias, free moral worlds, communist experiments, free-love cults, and nudist societies that had flowered and faded along the pleasanter margins of American History.

She now perceived that hundreds of Americans were walking about the park with almost nothing on against a background of marble statuary and spouting fountains. Their eyes were elevated, and they were all busy conversing of Humanity, Perfectibility, and Universal Suffrage. She herself, decked out in highlaced boots, recognized a grave, bearded gentleman costumed with a copy of the *Paradiso*.

—My dear Citizen Longfellow, she said, how pleased I am to see you! Are there any other distinguished poets present?

Citizen Longfellow spoke vaguely:

—Citizen Whittier and Citizen Holmes are taking the Edenic baths and the Celestial Radiation Treatment. You'll pardon me, dear Citizen. I see two of my friends coming for me.

Giggling in unison, Alice and Phoebe Cary approached and catching Citizen Longfellow each by a hand, began to run lightfootedly through the park with him, he now and then executing a pigeon wing with commendable grace.

—Among Mr. Longfellow's many fast friends, explained the Perfessor, erect and tall in malacca cane and pince-nez, Alice and Phoebe Cary will be remembered as the fastest.

Senator Garwood B. Jones, wearing a cigar, took her arm and walked beside her discoursing with magniloquent gestures.

—Citizen Brown, I promise to do all I can for your cause in the National Sexual Congress of the Uniting States of . . .

She hunted through the great concourse of Americans, and after a while saw a number of ladies exclaiming over a statue. It was Mr. John Wickliff Shawnessy posing as the Apollo Belvedere, thighs turned slightly out, lines of the body idealized, an image of virile repose.

He smiled at her over the heads of the exclaiming women, but there was such confusion that she became lost in . . .

The crowd was getting thicker all the time around the lemonade stand. Both the Senator and Mr. Shawnessy were talking with Mr. Jacobs and some farmers of the vicinity.

The Perfessor, apparently watching for the chance, offered his arm and led her somewhat apart under the appletree at the site of the Senator's birthplace. He had left the large black book in a crotch of the tree.

—Evelina, for Christ's sake, how do you stand living in this little burg?

—It has its compensations, she said. I have my lovely house and garden and my work and studies, and of course, Maribell.

—How old now?

—Twelve.

The Perfessor shook his head.

—Shall we give but one copy of this loveliness to the world?

Evelina smiled pensively and shifted her bundle of pamphlets to the other arm.

—I had intended to pass these out, she said evasively.

—Don't tergiversate, the Perfessor said. Evelina, I've never seen you look so beautiful. You must be in love. Are you waiting for someone?

—Of course, she said, smiling.

—Why didn't you tell me sooner? the Perfessor said, irritably. I'm a shy man and never caught on.

He looked sharply at her.

—You got my letter?

—O, yes, she said. It was an utterly charming and completely wicked letter, and what you suggested was quite implausible. At your age! Really, Professor! Anyway, I don't think I would like Bermuda.

The Perfessor leaned his head against the bark of the appletree.

—Ah, God! he said. I grow old.

He rallied quickly.

—I only said Bermuda for fun. What I really meant was New York. I see it all clearly now. You go charmingly through all this absurd flooflah today. And then right after the picnic this evening, you clap your hands once, and make all these cretins disappear like phantoms of an uneasy sleep. We pack our grips and catch the midnight train, and back we go to New York. How about it?

The Perfessor leaned forward with lifted brows. His black eyes glittered with excitement.

—I really must distribute my pamphlets, Professor. Won't you help, please?

—If only you weren't so damn rich, the Perfessor sighed, I could offer something substantial. As it is, I have only myself.

Resignedly, he took a handful of the pamphlets and began to pass them to various farmers and housewives who walked in the vicinity of the Senator's birthplace. She watched him accosting them with ceremonial courtesy, calling their attention to the title of the pamphlet and no doubt elaborating on its contents, which he hadn't read. . . .

EVELINA'S DREAM

—Farewell.

The cars rumbled and shook; the train was starting. It appeared that she was to have the upper berth, but there was considerable confusion about who was to sleep where and with whom. Hundreds of men, women, and children, all the backwash and breakup of that famous and forlorn experiment, including Mr. Shawnessy, the Perfessor, and the Senator, were hunting through the car for places to sleep. It appeared to be a great excursion to New York, just as the Perfessor had written in his letter.

—I suppose, Mr. Shawnessy said, handing her up to her berth, that the time will come when the whole process will be controlled better than now. But the dispatcher seems to have lost the lists.

In bride's sheer nightdress, long hair down, she clung to his hands.

—I have been waiting with my taper, dear Lord, for your second coming.

The great train roared and wailed, passing like a projectile through a darkening landscape of lawns and lakes and rivers. In the dim car rocking and swaying, she saw his beloved, wonderful face and she tried to pull him aloft into the berth with her, but there was some kind of confusion, for it turned out to be the Perfessor instead, whose long face looked intently into hers, and whose breath hissing slowly turned into the wail of the train, a melancholy diphthong of sorrow and farewell, renunciation, feminine bereavement, and of lost days and faded gardens that were once purple with summer. Farewell . . .

To the old appletree the Perfessor returned for the large black book, which in the meantime she had been idly examining.

—What in the world are you carrying this about for? she asked.

—It's all a delightful hoax that John has played on us, the Perfessor said, hugging the book under his left arm. I'll tell you about it later. Now, if you're ready, I'll see you home.

Passing the senatorial group on the Perfessor's arm, she leaned back.

—Senator, may we hope for the pleasure of your company at the picnic of the Literary Society this evening?

—Alas, my dear, I have an engagement in the great city of St. Louis tomorrow. I'm taking a train right after the Program this afternoon.

—John, I'll be back in time for a certain rural exhibition, the Perfessor said. Reserve a ringside seat for me.

Walking home on the Perfessor's arm, she had a sensation that she was being watched, and when she turned nervously as if she might have forgotten something, she saw that the Senator, Mr. Shawnessy, and a dozen other men were walking down the road behind, their eyes curiously intent upon her.

—Where are they going? she asked.

—To see a painting by Titian, the Perfessor said.

Instantly she thought of the painting 'Sacred and Profane Love,' in which, according to the Perfessor, that duplicate lady, clothed on one side of the fountain and naked on the other, bore a striking resemblance to herself. She blushed, feeling dizzy in the noon heat. The great eye of the sun blazed intently at her and filled her with delicious shame. . . .

EVELINA'S DREAM

It was a medieval storybook setting. Gabled roofs leaned over a crooked cobbled street in which all the men that were in Christendom lined the way, silently watching. Naked, she bestrode the great white horse in the masculine fashion, pleasantly chafed by the smooth column of the back. Her hair unloosened hung in braids of massy gold around her tipping breasts. With rhythmical motions of his head and clopping hoof, the horse wound forward through the predestined way, while she, holding a book in her hand, read gravely to the multitude.

—Then she rode forth, clothed on in chastity.

She had to re-enact the old story of Lady Godiva's indignity to save mankind from oppression. For this she was to make a medieval progress in the jogging meter of the nursery rimes that filled her little book:

—Ride a cockhorse to Funbury Farce,
To see a fine lady . . .

Senator Garwood Jones in guise of a rich burgher in bejewelled gown stood on a platform, rubbing his chin. Gently chiding, she recited:

—Pussycat, pussycat,
Where have you been?

The Senator's face assumed slowly the aspect of a big tomcat's. He pulled his whiskers and licked his lips. . . .

A white cat big as a man was lunging along the street, frightening everyone out of his wits. The veiled purpose of this fantastic spectacle was beginning to be clear to her. It was a trick to rob her of her virtue. Her horse galloped wildly down the crazy thoroughfare frightened by the caterwauling of the cat. She clung for dear life, expecting at any moment to be thrown. Then the remembered climax of the old fairy tale suddenly disclosed itself in a most delightful way, as the heroic form of the young blacksmith stood athwart her path, be-aproned, hammer in hand. It was Mr. Shawnessy, at sight of whom her horse came sedately to a stop. Everyone began to dance and clap his hands with pleasure as the Perfessor, wearing cockscomb and rooster's tail, recited,

—Cockadoodle doo!
My dame has lost her shoe!
And master's lost his fiddling stick
And doesn't know what to do.

Meanwhile, Mr. Shawnessy bent courteously to the task of shoeing her horse, though through some quaint mistake he was nailing on a lady's high heel to the hoof of . . .

—A great white beast is pastured around here somewhere, the Perfessor said, passing Mr. Jacobs' barn. I'm supposed to drop back in time to see him perform in that wellknown museum piece 'The Rape of Europa.'

He was looking at her hair.

—You might have posed for Titian's loveliest paintings, my dear. You belong in the workshop of old Cellini or the *Memoirs* of Casanova, anywhere rather than in Mrs. Mitford's *Village*.

She glanced back again.

—Stop being so mysterious, she said. Where are they going?

—Mr. Jacobs has a bull, the Perfessor said, and somebody else has a heifer. And the Senator has a warm interest in all aspects of rural life.

—My goodness! she said. Are they going to do that again today?

—Evelina, the Perfessor said, isn't there anything I can do to persuade you?

—Professor dear, I seem to remember that we have been all over this ground before.

—In the pursuit of beauty, the Perfessor said, I have no pride. Think how much fun we could have in the great City of New York. Don't you have any secret debts that I could pay?

—No. Professor dear, there isn't anything that you can offer me.

—Don't be always thinking of yourself, the Perfessor said. Think of me. I don't ask love, you understand. All I want is your pity—and unselfish compliance.

The Perfessor as usual seemed only half in earnest, as he walked along jauntily swinging his cane and taking in the scenery around him with his roving, perceptive eye.

—Come, Evelina, he said suddenly. Out with it. You're in love with him.

—What in the world are you talking about?

—Good morning, Madame, the Perfessor said, bowing pleasantly.

A woman was standing at the back of her yard, a roseclipper in one hand and a few cut flowers in the other, her figure buxomly protrudent in a white dress. She had been studying the Perfessor with a shrewd green eye.

—Good mornin', she said, distrustfully.

—Who is that colossally voluptuous creature? the Perfessor whispered.

—Mrs. Lorena Passifee. I'm afraid she doesn't approve of me. It's amusing, too, because she used to entertain men regularly over there, and everyone would get tight on dandelion wine for a purpose which I will leave to your own tender charity. Her dandelion wine is famous.

—How delicate! the Perfessor said. Dandelion wine!

—Then last summer she got religion, and the parties stopped for a while. About time, too, because the good people of the community were ready to run her out. Now she's a prop of the church and the watchdog of virtue in the community—mostly my virtue.

—By the way, I've heard of your interest in the local Revival Preacher, the Perfessor said. Really, Evelina, don't you think you're getting a bit bucolic?

—He's a magnificent primitive specimen, she said. You know, I've had a lot of talks with him, and he's told me a great deal about himself in an effort to convert me. Lloyd—that's his name—came right from one of those Southern hillfamilies. He had congenital myopia that amounted almost to blindness, and they never put any glasses on him. But in spite of that he grew up to be a shrewd, powerful, ignorant young man. He was a terrible sinner. He gave rein to the lusts of the flesh. He's handsome in a savage way, you know. He drank, swore, gambled, and goodness knows what besides. Isn't that interesting?

—Hmmmmm, the Perfessor said.

—It was an incredibly backward environment. The people in those hills live just like the old clans, feuding and killing and carrying off each other's women. There were ten sons in Lloyd's family. The father was a tyrant, and his word was law to his sons and their women and the whole clan. Lloyd was the oldest son, and in spite of his blindness was hated and feared more than anyone except his father. He was called the Blind.

—My God! the Perfessor said.

—Then when Lloyd was about twenty, he and his father had some kind of terrible fight. He won't tell me much about it, but anyway he left the hills. Then a missionary got hold of him and put some kind of special glasses on him, and for the first time in his life he saw the shapes of things. It was like an awakening. Along with it he got religion and became a wonderful preacher, and——

—Don't tell me any more, the Perfessor said. I can see the whole thing for myself. What you have described is the very process out of which our Old Testament religion came. In the beginning, the hill and desert anthropoids who later became the ancient Hebrews were an incestuous, lustful, dirty collection of families, like the rest of primitive mankind, clothing their filth in skins and killing and raping each other like beasts. The son lusted after his mother and the father after his daughter. The head of this hideous delegation was of course the patriarch, the strong man, who maintained his power through brute force and low cunning, and after the force was gone, through the loudness of his voice and his old prestige, beating and cowing his rebellious sons and leading them in rapine. The only law was the law of the family. Whatever the Old Man did was right, and any crime committed in the name of the family was right. The sons had the choice of staying and submitting to the Old Man's rule or getting out on their own and starting their own family clan. The only way the Old Man could be succeeded was by murder. So some particularly rebellious son would finally kill the old bastard with a club, taking a guilty delight in pounding his sire's gray skull to a pulp. Then all the women became his. From some such background, slowly evolving over centuries, emerged the Jehovah religion: the tribal patriarch was elevated to deity, and the crime of parricide and incestuous lust became the memory of an original sin, for which mankind waxed penitent. So morality was born, which was merely tribal law created to strengthen the chosen people against their enemies. No more incest, no more lust. But the object of worship and the source of power remained the same, a violent, lustful, self-glorifying old despot-god, who punishes his children for his own crimes and whom they worship because they hate him and fear him. Now, the hillpeople of America, especially the Southerners, have a special fondness for Old Testament Christianity because they've degenerated into the very savagery from which it came. Paganism made a much more beautiful adjustment of this old crime of mankind, our memory of being beasts. As for your preacher, for God's sake never get alone in the same room with him. The man is dangerous and quite probably insane.

—I've never invited him to my place, Evelina said. And I haven't been to see him for a long time. Of course, he's made an amazing transformation. When he left his people, he studied and read widely and even attended a little theological seminary in Kentucky. He quotes Milton and the Greek and Latin classics. Naturally the essential crudeness remains, a sort of primitive frenzy. You should hear him preach.

They were just about to pass the iron fence which marked the western boundary of Evelina's lawn, when the Perfessor stopped short.

—Jesus! What a brute!

He was looking across a cornfield at a white bull fenced in a small pasture.

—I have nightmares about that thing, she said.

Looking back, she saw the Senator and his entourage turning in at Mr. Jacobs' place.

—Frankly, the Perfessor said, you don't belong here at all, Evelina. What the devil do you want to stay around here for, providing food for local gossip? If you want to reform something, start with me. You can do a lot more for the world from my apartment in New York City than you can from your house in Raintree County. It's a weeping shame that a lovely, eager, warmhearted girl like you ever left New York.

He looked at her shrewdly again.

—Be as objective as you please about your amusing hillbilly preacher, Evelina, but you've become a religious fanatic yourself.

—It's true, she said, looking down.

—And this religion, he said. It is——

—The religion of humanity, she said.

The Perfessor looked somewhat sadly about him.

—So you have found your gentle god at the crossroads. Well, it's a strange martyrdom—and it will pass. My God! When the world isn't crucifying us, we crucify ourselves!

She said nothing but, nunlike, kept her eyes down lest he should see a sudden mist that was in them. . . .

EVELINA'S DREAM

The dungeon cell had a single window, singly barred, through which fell a single ray of light. She stood in her long gown, *décolletée,* hands tied before her, reciting,

—Eternal spirit of the chainless mind,
Brightest in dungeons . . .

It had something to do with the French Terror and the execution of all the fine people who believed in liberty. What her own crime was, she couldn't exactly remember, except that it was a very romantic one, for which society would never forgive her. The other woman in the cell was Mrs. Stowe, who sat at a writing table, adding and subtracting dates, juggling the names of children, making marginalia in a complete volume of Lord Byron's *Works.*

—My dear, it's no use, Mrs. Stowe said. You know you slept with him, and that's all there is to it. Not that I blame you. But you might have considered his wife and the nearness of your relationship. Nothing for us to do now but wait for the carts. But haven't we been tumbriled in a worthy cause!

Metal doors clanged. She arranged her little cap so that the painter David might make an offhand sketch of her on her way to the knife. There was a distant rumbling of drums. The executioners passed in the connecting corridor leading Mr. Shawnessy, his hair damp curls on a marble brow, his white shirt open at the neck. He walked with a slight limp, his eyes flashing with soft fire. Looking back at her, he said,

—My sister! my sweet sister! if a name
Dearer or purer were, it would be thine. . . .

The rolling drums grew louder. She was riding through massed thousands in the streets of New York, London, Paris, or some other great city. As she approached the platform, she saw Mr. Shawnessy walking up the steps toward the guillotine. He smiled his gentle, pensive smile and lifted his hand in farewell.

The crowd intervened, she was lost in the confusion of faces and savage shouts, but she could hear his voice ascending and ascending, highpitched, slightly nasal, reciting,

—It is a far, far better thing that I do than I have ever done; it is a far, far better rest that I go to than I have ever known. . . .

Before her home she and the Perfessor had stopped between the flungopen gates.

—If you find anything in the *Atlas,* let me know, she said. It would go well with the Senator's collection. He showed it to me once in Washington.

—I trust he didn't add you to it, the Perfessor said.

He ran his eyes over her house and garden.

—Lovely place you have here, he said. It's so like you, dear. It's so—so charmingly bewildered. May I come in?

—You'd better hurry back for the Titian, dear, she said.

—Too bad you can't see it, dear, the Perfessor said.

His voice was somewhat remote and his eyes kept playing over the lawn sloping longly up to the brick house.

—Who built the house?

—I did.

—What for?

—To live in, silly.

He smiled sadly, preparing to leave.

—My dear, it's just as I told you in my letter. At the age of thirty-five, you've become a museum piece.

EVELINA'S DREAM

She had on a little torn frock that came barely below her knees as she stood in the slave mart. The auctioneer, bullwhip in hand, ripped her dress off with a brutal jerk.

—And there she stands. Will't please you sit and look at her?

While she stood clasping a Bible between her breasts, the planters crowded around feeling the flesh of her calves and thighs. Senator Garwood B. Jones eyed her with shrewd appraisal.

—I bid one thousand dollars. This ought to go well with my

collection from the old masters, *Neptune, taming a seahorse, thought a rarity.*

Other poor colored people standing near her had been turned into little statuary groups mass-reproduced by machine lathing. Buyers and connoisseurs wandered through the rooms of the museum (which resembled a private home), inspecting its treasures. Professor Stiles approached her as she stood in an alcove, her body painted bronze, in her hand a lamp burning smokily.

—Exquisite craftsmanship, he said. In the Italian fashion. Perhaps one of old Cellini's lost pieces.

She maintained her heroic attitude, reciting,

—I lift my lamp beside the golden door!

She had hoped that among all the people thronging through the vast metropolitan museum, Mr. Shawnessy would take particular notice of her and buy, but already the crowd was thinning out, and he was gone with the others into the murky night, gone in the long train snaking across the land and carrying people home from brown decades and metropolitan adventures, and she hadn't even touched his hand for a last . . .

—Good-by, dear, she said to the Perfessor. I'll see you this afternoon. I will keep the *Atlas* for you if you insist, and you can pick it up later.

With the *Atlas* under her arm, she walked swiftly to the house and up the steps to the verandah. Entering, she continued without pause walking up the steps from the hall to the second floor, turned and walked to a door at the front end of it, and began to climb a spiral stair ascending the squat tower rooted in the foundations of the house. Panting with heat, exertion, and excitement, she came out into a little circular room at the top of the tower and going over to a halfmoon window looking west, she peered down at a foreshortened world. . . .

· ·

In flagrante delicto! Preacher Jarvey pacing restlessly in the tent was tormented by the words. He saw them writhing on a ground of scarlet flame, fiendishly alive, their heads darting and hissing. The flames withdrawing disclosed two forms, a man and a woman naked, turning round and round, their lips and hands and yearning limbs touching and twining.

Preacher Jarvey walked with a rapider stride. He was panting. His eyes glared viewlessly. A vision of profane love tormented him with a whip of shrewd lust as often it had when he lay at night waiting for sleep. In this vision, a hated figure walked through Waycross in the hovering darkness, looking covertly to left and right. Arriving at stately gates east of town, it paused a moment, then darted into a contrived garden that Preacher Jarvey himself had often passed but never entered. And the sinful intruder glided stealthily past vague balls of shrubbery on the lawn, reached a verandah prickly with filigree, knocked stealthily at a door. And the door opened. And the stealthy form was lost in the dark and scarlet depths of a voluptuous mansion. *In flagrante delicto!*

—Hosanna! the Preacher panted under his breath. The hour is here. Hosanna! Hit has come!

And suddenly he burst through the tentflap.

The day was hostile with radiance, walling him in with green and golden mist. He set out walking toward the intersection. As he approached it, laughter, cries, clangs, explosions enveloped him. Wheels and trampling hooves threatened him. The lightfilled intersection of Waycross, which had endeared itself to him by its visual simplicity (four beginnings of streets losing themselves in peaceful summer), erupted with strangeness.

The time had come to destroy this disobedient world and its multiplying eyes.

The Preacher turned east at the intersection. As he walked, he pulled out his watch and held the face of it close to his own. Black hands and numerals swam into the green globe of his vision and wavered there, enormously precise. Eleven-thirty.

Hosanna! The hour had come!

Like sadness and tears, a traitorous feeling surged up from the mist around him. The way here was magical with soft anticipation. Many times in vanished summers he had gone along this street in the late morning and had passed Mrs. Evelina Brown on her morning walk into Waycross. Often and often (for he had learned to depend upon the regularity of this walk) his yearning eyes had plucked her from the oceanic void of the increate and held her, softly writhing, flushed, exhaling a mist of breath. He would exchange a few amenities with her, as the godshout raged unuttered in his breast, and then reluctantly he would let her gracious form slip once more into the stream of the inactual.

The faces were a thinning stream. The sidewalk ended. He plunged into golden heat. He was on the empty road passing the Jacobs farm. He looked neither to right nor left. He wouldn't stop at the Widow Passifee's, despite his promise to Brother Gideon Root. He would go on past. Hosanna! The hour had come!

Suddenly, he was aware of someone approaching in the white roadway, coming closer and closer to the minute pebbles and brown dust on which he walked. The black twisting shape stood suddenly before him like a jinnee in a glass bottle, writhing, fantastic, dreadful. The creature was incredibly tall and thin, black eyes stabbing through pince-nez glasses, face long, lined, grinning with malice and amusement. It made a ceremonious bow, leaning on a cane. A thin tongue of derision licked its hissing lips.

—Have I by chance the honor of addressing the Reverend Lloyd G. Jarvey?

—You have, Brother! Praise the Lord!

The words were hurled like an accusation, quavering and frustrate.

—Praise the Lord! shouted the intruder in a highpitched, nasal voice crackling with sanctimony. Pleased to meet you, Brother.

—Who might you be, Brother?

—A visiting preacher, Brother, the thin intruder said. The Reverend Jerusalem Webster Stiles from New York.

—Pleased to meet you, Brother.

He bowed his head and fairly butted his way past this hateful rival.

—One moment, Brother. What is the status of sin these days in Raintree County? Enough to go around, I trust?

A malicious, cackling laugh pursued him as he went on. Confusion warred with rage. Someone had set this foreign dog upon him.

Nevertheless, he went by the Widow Passifee's and continued until he saw the blurred lines of an iron fence on his left. He slowed down, panting as though he had been running. He listened. His ears cropping from the shaggy brown hair were sickly sensitive to every sound, but there were no footsteps on the road. He walked slowly to the iron gates. They stood open, the ironwork designs drawn on his vision with painful exactness, while beyond them a brown walk faded into a lake of green.

He stopped. He had come to a threshold of decision.

Yes, the time had come. Perhaps he might forestall God's vengeance by an act of loving kindness. Wasn't this woman after all the one most worthy to be saved? Who but Lloyd G. Jarvey, he that had been called the Blind and had been blessed with vision, he that had killed and ravaged in his great hill-strength, who but he was chosen to tame this sophisticate daughter and teach her submission, even in the chambers of her scarlet palace?

My daughter, had you forgotten your God? What have you been doing in my absence, my loving daughter? Did you suppose that I did not foresee this invention, that I was incapable of this pleasant pastime of mortals? Erring and beautiful daughter, God is able to do anything, possesseth every power and pleasure. In one of my earlier shapes, when I was several and not one, I too was Begetter. But I had forgotten this earlier self, until you reminded me of it. You discovered it without permission, my intuitive daughter. You entertained false forms of myself, obsolete deities, in this garden which I gave you to tend. And should you not therefore endure the chastisement of a jealous God?

The Reverend Lloyd G. Jarvey walked through the gate, heavy-footed, his powerful arms not swinging at his sides, but slightly lifted as if appealing. His eyes in the thick glasses had a fixed expression.

But then I am not wholly displeased with you, my daughter. You have reminded me of myself. And what if I should now return, and forgiving you for this evil knowledge that you have acquired, should supplant your mortal lover, and in my infinite power and mercy, take back to my own breast the erring daughter?

Only for God and the gods, the most beautiful mortals.

And if then I should find you here hiding in the garden and hugely should come upon you, and you should stand before me with eyes averted, beseeching my forgiveness and admitting your guilt, and you should stand before me in the stolen garments (but I know your white flanks and the little applefirm breasts tilted for love), then might there not be for you a majestic revealing of Godhead? Then, o, then, might there not be for you the hard, bluff strut and the bullgreat weight of . . .

Preacher Jarvey was standing at the base of the brick house. He saw clearly the clumps of columns supporting the roof of the verandah, and beyond that a dull red mass of walls. He breathed heavily; his breast swelled up as if it would burst with the anguish of a wish that had no name. This wish tore him with fury and anger; he opened his mouth as if to give voice to it.

A sound pierced his ears, at first muted and reedy, then swelling to a trumpet blast and ending in a harsh wail of amorous fury. Male laughter volleyed. Feet scuffled. A gate creaked.

In confusion, Preacher Jarvey turned and ran. Along the path of his flight the garden started into life around him. Naked women with sightless eyes stood suddenly from nooks of shrubbery. Blurred shapes of bulls, archers, chariots formed and faded on waves of lawn.

Harried by scurrilous laughter and scuffling feet, he ran through the gates and stopped in the road. The noises had lessened to a murmur. He peered at the garden from which he had just been driven in confusion. What had he come to do there?

Once more dull fury burned in his chest. Against the old walls of his blindness a thousand stridulous noises beat, surf of an oceanic world beyond his grasp. He was sad as never before. His breath labored. The hot sun smote him without mercy. He knew the anguish and sorrow of the one god who may not be loving of beautiful mortals.

Now he held his eyes up to the yellow light that blazed directly above him. It entered him with splendor, destroying all vision but itself. It poured hot gold and frenzy into his breast. He staggered west, incarnate with a radiant god. . . .

. . .

—Jupiter is his name, Mr. Jacobs said in answer to the Senator's question. Won first prize at the State Fair last year.

—Young? The Senator asked.

—Just a boy. Three years old.

The Senator and his entourage had stopped for a while in Mr. Jacobs' front yard. Now they walked past the barn on their way to the bullpasture.

—John, the Senator said, raising his voice and spreading abroad his eloquent arms, were it not for my obligations to the people, I should have asked nothing better than to be a tiller of the soil of Raintree County. What better life is there, gentlemen, than that of the simple farmer? Who is closer to God than he who gathers by his toil the fruits of the earth? Sturdy, honest, industrious, independent, the farmer is the backbone of the Republic. Without his matchless virility, how many of her wars could America have won? Without his manly valor, what freedom would she possess?

—And without his manifold vote, the Perfessor said, catching up from the rear, what President has she ever elected?

He took a flat bottle from his pocket as he and Mr. Shawnessy fell somewhat behind the others.

—Your farmer, he said, is a poor brute. But I acknowledge his usefulness. Without him there would be no corn. Without corn, there would be no corn whiskey. And without corn whiskey, there would be no sacred frenzy.

The Perfessor put the bottle to his mouth. Mr. Shawnessy watched the antic, tall figure tilted against the green earth.

—I trust you all perceive, the Perfessor said, catching up with the Senator, the object which I hold in my hand. It is, as you see, a bottle, a plain, ordinary, everyday bottle. But this bottle, friends, contains the wonderworker of our age. Here, Senator, have a slug of this.

—To please an old friend, the Senator said.

He lipped and pulled.

—My God! he said. Is this the stuff they fuel the Muse with?

—The Heliconian fount, said the Perfessor, whence all my verse proceeds.

The bottle went around and came to rest in Mr. Shawnessy's hands.

—First liquor I've touched in months, Mr. Shawnessy said. The good ladies of Waycross are teetotalers, except for the annual vintage of the dandelion.

He tasted sun, noon, and the summer earth. The cornjuice throbbed slowly through him as they turned east beyond the barn and started down a lane running parallel to the National Road.

—Well, where's this bull, boys? the Senator said. I haven't seen a heifer heeled since I was a kid. Whose house is that?

—Mrs. Brown's, Mr. Shawnessy said.

The lane led them straight toward the round brick tower of Mrs. Brown's house.

—Good corn crop, the Senator said. Kneehigh by the Fourth of July.

—Mooooooooooo—uh!

The white bull had seen them coming and had made a cry half-human with rage and desire.

—Jove, he's big! the Senator said. I trust that fence is strong. He might be a Democratic bull.

Male laughter volleyed. Feet scuffled. The crowd stopped at the long plank gate giving on the little bullpasture wedged into the cornfields next to Mrs. Brown's yard. Dense shrubbery and trees concealed all but the top of a brick tower. Apart stood the Perfessor and Mr. Shawnessy.

—Jupiter! the Perfessor said. A classic bull. But where is Io?

Mr. Jacobs and another man had stopped at the barn, and were presumed to be bringing up the heifer.

—He reminds me of someone, Mr. Shawnessy said.

—'Tis a senatorial bull, the Perfessor said. Judging from current models, it hath the congressional cut.

The corn was an ocean of softly brandished arms, in which, islanded, the bull was a great strength formed for love and strife. From tight rump to mounded shoulders brutely propulsive, he stood, love-tortured, staring at a world without depth.

—Maybe, said Mr. Shawnessy, he remembers his epic past, the white flanks of the beloved of Minos—that was a sweet begetting—or Europa, who bestrode his shoulders, and her naked calves teased his little pricked ears, or Io, whom ox-eyed Juno envied. Argos of a hundred eyes couldn't prevent his jovial rage. Does he know that he was Dionysus, god of the wineborn frenzy of love and creation? The celebrants hung garlands of flowers on the thick column of his neck; he walked like a man on his hindlegs. He was not always a prisoner in barbed wire where love is rationed to him in brief allotments while lecherous mortals lean on the gate and laugh. He was a god once and loved a beautiful mortal. . . .

. . .

Rear protrudent, the Widow Passifee was at the back of her yard, cutting away a load of flowers with her yardshears. Colossally voluptuous in a white dress, she bulged silently on Preacher Jarvey's vitreous world still stricken with the sun.

Mrs. Passifee's yard had none of the studied formality of Mrs. Brown's. It was tangled and frenzied. The old picket fence surrounding her little frame house sagged with unpruned vines. The outhouse behind was both visible and odorous.

—Sister Passifee.

She squealed and whirled.

—Brother Jarvey! You plumb frightened me.

He glared fixedly at her broad, heartshaped face, green eyes, young wide mouth, small pointed chin. She was flushed in the noonheat. Her neck and the white roots of her breasts were shining with sweat. Her arms were full of torn flowers.

—Won't you come in, Brother Jarvey?

—I will, Sister, I will.

He followed her into the dark cool parlor. She started to put up the shades, which were drawn to within a few inches of the sills.

—Just leave them drawn, Sister. The light hurts my eyes.

He sat on a horsehair sofa and closed his eyes. Instantly, his inward vision swam with golden splendors, splintering afterimage of the sun. Women with great white glowing limbs and golden hair stood in nooks of green, twisting ropes of flowers.

—Make yourself to home, Brother Jarvey. It's hot, ain't it?

—It is, Sister.

She bit her lip and studied the floor with a frown.

—Maybe you'd like a little refreshment. To cool you off.

—As you please, Sister.

A waning gold gilded a garden of clipped lawns, beds of tossing flowers. Flinging their golden hair, whitebodied, with musical cries, the bare nymphs ran.

Returning, Mrs. Passifee had a stone jug from the earth-cellar. Clear yellow wine guggled from stone lips. She filled two glass tumblers.

—Just a little dandelion wine, she said. Practickly no alcohol in it. It'll cool you off. If you don't mind.

For answer, Preacher Jarvey leaned forward, picked up a tumbler, drained it.

He leaned back again and closed his eyes. There was a sharp sweet taste in his throat, of summer lawns, of the sunwarm faces of dandelions.

—Goodness! Mrs. Passifee said. You drink fast, Brother Jarvey.

Giggling nervously, she filled up his glass on a little table beside the sofa and then sitting down beside him sipped at her own.

—It *is* good, she said. A body's a right to a little nip now and then on a hot day, don't you think?

For answer, Preacher Jarvey leaned forward, picked up his tumbler, drained it.

—Goodness! Mrs. Passifee said, filling it up again.

She studied her glass.

—I got news, Brother Jarvey, she said. I mean about him and her. Something that happened last night. Be perfectly frank, I don't think we had much to go on before. But if you really mean to accuse 'em of sinnin' together tonight, why, I seen something that will int'rest you.

—Sister, he said. You may speak to me without reservation. Don't let your feminine delicacy prevent you from givin' a full story of what you saw.

—Well, she said, putting down her glass, he come past here about seven o'clock in the evening, and he had a sheaf of papers in his hand. He turned in at the gate there and went up to her house. I could see plain from the corner of my yard.

—Yes, the Preacher said.

A sweet sadness throbbed in his veins. Sipping the cool wine, he leaned back and shut his eyes. Blood of the dandelion drenched his throat.

—He went up to the house there, and they was there all evening. I come out to my gate again and again, and I knowed he hadn't left. They was no one else in or out of that there gate all evening. They was hardly any light at all in the house—I know because I walked down the road once to see more clearer, and they was only a little low light burnin' in a front room. I says to myself, I bet I know what's a-goin' on in there.

Preacher Jarvey felt his hand squeezed. He opened his eyes. The Widow Passifee was talking fast. Strands of loose yellow hair had fallen around her heatflushed cheeks. Her eyes glittered, and her wide young mouth made sounds that were husky and musical.

—Of course, I hadn't no proof of it, she said. Just what I suspicioned. But a course I never dreamed what was a-goin' to happen.

Well, it was about eleven o'clock at night, time for any selfrespectin body to be in bed, and I crept up to her fence and got in among some sumac bushes that was right by the fence so's I could have a good view of the house. I was even figgerin' maybe I might climb over and see if I could have a real good see. I guess curiosity got the better of me. But just then, I heard their voices, and the front screen opened and shut, and here come Mr. Shawnessy walkin' down off the porch, he never looked back once but just went right down the path and out into the road and toward town. I was just about to climb out a there and go home myself when I seen it.

The Preacher filled his own glass and the Widow's from the jug. Heartshaped, the wide face of Mrs. Passifee was very close to his own. His thick lenses were washed with yellow waves of light. He watched her soft mouth trembling with excitement.

—Go on, Sister, he said.

—So then there I was ready to go, when all a sudden I heard the screen door open again—mind you it wasn't ten minutes after he'd left—and all a sudden here *she* come right down the steps of the verandah and out on the lawn. Well, she was nekkid as the day she was born. Her hair was all let down. The woman's plumb crazy, I said to myself.

—Praise the Lord! the Reverend said. Go on, Sister.

—She was just a little slim thing, hardly nothin' to her, compared to a woman like me. Well, she took out and begun to run around the lawn and to throw back her head and dance. She went here and there all over the yard and threw up her arms, never sayin' a word or makin' a sound. It was warm or she'd a caught her death a cold. After a while she run to that there fountain down in front a the house where them two nekkid children is and stepped right down into it. She's goin' to drownd herself, I says. But no, not her. She puts her face right up in the spray a the fountain and stood right there and let the water run over her nekkid body. She looked jist like a statue, Reverend, white and still in the starlight. There I was—not more'n twenty feet away, a-layin' there sweatin' and scared I was goin' to make a noise. It was so close I could see a birthmark she had on her body. Then she ran out on the grass again, her body a-shinin' from the water, and she run and threw herself on the grass and rolled back and forth like a child, and then she begun to cry or laugh, I couldn't tell which, and then there was some kind of a noise from that field next to her place where Bill Jacobs keeps that big bull a hisn, and she heard it, and she jumped up and run like she was shot up to the house and went in.

—Sister Passifee, lust is a dreadful thing! O, hit is a terrible thing! Praise the Lord!

—Praise the Lord! Sister Passifee said, sipping thoughtfully at her glass and allowing the Preacher to squeeze her hand.

—Sister, the Lord means for us to chastise these errin' creatures. But let us not be too hard on them, Sister. Judge not that ye be not judged. A man may be tempted by too much beauty, Sister, and the Devil may rise in him. Alas, I have known what it is to sin, Sister.

—Me, too, Sister Passifee said, sipping thoughtfully. More wine, Brother Jarvey?

Brother Jarvey's eyes were closed. He was beginning to wag his big head. His voice had become loud like a horn, monotonously chanting.

—Let us pray for these sinners. They were sore tempted, Sister, and they sinned. Down on your knees, Sister. Hosanna!

—Hosanna, Sister Passifee said, obediently going to her knees. Maybe you can't blame 'em too much. Sometimes it's pretty hard to resist the Devil.

—Let us pray, Sister, the Reverend said, dropping to his knees before her and winding his arms around her.

Sister Passifee nestled meekly in his embrace.

—Lord, you have placed this poor weak woman in my arms, Preacher Jarvey said. What shall I do with her?

—Just go on and pray as hard as you want, Brother Jarvey. My daughter Libby's down at the school and nobody'll bother us.

—I lift up my eyes unto thy hills, O Zion, he shouted.

His eyes, opening, perceived the triumphant twin thrust of Sister Passifee's bosom in the white dress.

He felt a momentary sadness that left him stranded and deprived of strength. He waited. Thin sap of the earth smitten into bloom by the sun flowed in his veins, a soft fire. He closed his eyes.

An island of white sands and trees darkfronded enclosed his vision. A tall stone column stood in Cretan groves, and the young women gathered at the base to pelt the shaft with petals. Light hands and flowery lips made adoration and ecstasy at the base of the column in Crete.

The hour has come. Lo! it is here! Now I will prepare for the feast. I will make myself known unto you. It is the joyous noon, and the celebrants dash flowers and wine on each other's faces. Naked, they run on Cretan lawns. They do not know that the god himself is waiting in a green wood. His large savage eyes have selected the whitest of the nymphs, whose lips are wet with the wine of festival. He shrugs and lowers his wrinkled front, the loose folds of his breast are shaken with desire. He rakes the ground with great feet. He is amorous of the most voluptuous nymph, her of the twin disturbing hills. He has remembered his ritual day, the noontide rites of the wine, the flung flowers, and the shaken seed. He is approaching, he will make himself known in the form of a . . .

. . .

—Bull is worth more than man in the sum of things.

The Perfessor lit a cigar and leaned on the fence, looking over at the white bull with a happy expression.

—Where's this heifer? the Senator said. Let's have some action around here.

—The Greeks, the Perfessor went on, addressing his remarks to Mr. Shawnessy, were right to make a god of bull. Christianity debased God by making him a grieving and gibbeted Jesus. Fact is, man may well envy bull. Bull is pure feeling, has no silly moral anxiety, exists entirely for the propulsion of life.

—Bull doesn't know love, Mr. Shawnessy said. Look at him. He's just a phallus with a prodigious engine attached.

—Love? the Perfessor said. What is love? Why, John, your bull is your perfect lover. His sexual frenzy is much stronger than man's. Man's a popgun to him.

—Love is moral, Mr. Shawnessy said. Passion's a form of discrimination. From among a thousand doors, it chooses one. There's no great love without great conscience. But your bull's no picker and chooser. To him, one cow's as good as another. *Jupiter erectus conscientiam non habet.*

—Let's have some action around here, jocundly bellowed the Senator. Where's this heifer?

—It's true, the Perfessor said, that love and sex desire have nothing in common. The sex impulse is a vicious appetite like hunger. We brought it with us out of the jungle and put some clothes on it, that's all. In its pure form, i.e., anywhere below the human level, sexual congress is always a criminal attack. The female of the species is coerced with hooves, claws, horns, and anything else necessary. The male's bigger for a good reason—he has to whip his snatch before he can have it. The female submits, hating it. Wolves love snarling, cats clawing, horses biting. Female spiders eat the male after the sex act, to get even. All mammals without exception use their teeth when they love. The human kiss, that remarkable perversion of Nature, is descended from the love-bite. By the way, did I ever show you my scars?

The Perfessor shook soundlessly.

—Bring on this heifer, the Senator said. Professor, how about another drink?

The Perfessor obliged by passing his bottle up and down the fence.

—As for love faithful unto death, and so forth, the Perfessor went on, all that's a late development in the human race. It's derived not from the sex act but the mating impulse. The only unselfish love exhibited by Nature in her unspoiled—i.e., non-human—form is that shown by the mother for her child. She attaches the male to her during the family period not because she loves the big tramp but because it helps provide for and protect the babies. From the softening influence of mother love transmitted to the male offspring come all the noble passions of mankind—tenderness, devotion, fidelity, glorification of the love object, and so on. In short, romantic human love is an invention of the ladies.

—To the ladies, then, Mr. Shawnessy said gallantly, God bless them. For the garden they have made and adorned with their hands and in which you and I are permitted to wander.

—I've enjoyed my picnics in it, the Perfessor said. But I've never found sexual chastity one of the requirements for admission. It's only necessary that the park be beautiful. But let's not have any gatekeepers. Nature doesn't award any blueribbons to chastity. The prize-winning bull of Raintree County is a bastard and a begetter of bastards. Look at the beautiful flowers. They are all bastards. All the beauty in the world was made by Eros, who is blind.

—Professor, you're a poacher in the human garden. To you this great preserve is like the king's park in which the deer are all alike and fair game. There's nothing in Nature to forbid you, but you haven't made the most delicious of all discoveries.

—And what is that?

—That the human garden in which one wanders is occupied by only one other person, that good and beautiful and passionate and faithful woman to whom we all aspire. In her, we rediscover Eve and regain Paradise.

—How many Eves have you been Adam to?

—One Eve in several reincarnations.

—I suppose, the Perfessor said, falling amiably into his vein of self-criticism, that I have known too few good women.

He looked shrewdly at the top of the brick tower standing above the iron fence and narrowed his eyes.

—Matter of fact, John, he said, I have known in my time the wildest assortment of bitches that God in His wisdom ever permitted one poor old boy to be bullied withal. But I have no regrets. They were gallant girls all. I loved them all as hard as I could, and I refuse to make any distinction between them and the so-called good women. To our immoral part and our only path to immortality, each one was just the happy valley where the wandering one came home.

—It's about time! the Senator said.

Raintree County's prize bull raised his head and peered at a festive procession.

Mr. Jacobs and another man were bringing a pretty brown heifer down the lane. The men began to talk in hearty voices. The Perfessor produced a fresh bottle, which went up and down the fence and came back empty.

—I wonder, the Senator said, if she has any idea what's going to hit her.

He passed out cigars, and all the men lit up and smoked. Mr. Jacobs opened the gate, and the other man led the heifer through, retaining his hold on the halter.

The great white bull watched the intruders. He pawed the ground.

—He's getting up steam, the Senator said.

—The contestants will please take their respective positions on the playing field, the Perfessor said, taking out his notebook. Spectators are requested to hang on to their hats.

—Here we go! the Senator said.

SENATOR JONES GUEST AS STOCKBREEDERS HOLD MEET
ONLY ONE LADY PRESENT
(Epic Fragment from the *Cosmic Enquirer*)

The Raintree County Stockbreeders Association today held a meeting at which the Hon. Garwood B. Jones was the guest of honor, sharing the limelight with . . .

A great white bull, eight feet tall, walked on his hindlegs like a man, stabbed the air with blind hooves. Guttural shouts shook the fence. The Senator's cigar fell from his mouth. The heifer staggered. . . .

. . .

Squealing delicately, Mrs. Passifee upset with a motion of her arm the little table next to the sofa, and looking sideways watched the stone jug and two tumblers scatter on the floor.

—It's all right, she whispered. Nothing's broke but one of the glasses.

Preacher Jarvey made no reply. His brows were bent into a majestic frown.

Listen, I am the god. I was waiting in a cavern of this island. From among all the vestals, I select you. Do you run from me, little frightened sacrifice? Do you hear the thundering hooves of the god behind you? Do you feel the hot breath of the god on your slight shoulders? Listen, I hear your cries, your virginal complainings. Our island is small, and you cannot escape me. You shall be made to feel the power of the . . .

—Lord help me! Mrs. Passifee sighed resignedly. I'm a poor weak woman.

The Preacher said nothing, but closed his eyes.

Who can love god as god would be loved? Only the most beautiful of mortals. Only the most tender and compliant. But who can love god as god would be loved?

—Sakes alive! Mrs. Passifee said, gasping for breath. You're a strong man, Brother Jarvey.

O, I remember how they reared the great stone shaft in the sacred isle. I remember the sweet assault of all the unwearied dancers. Pull down over the column garland after garland of flowers. Wreathe and ring it with tightening vines. Dash wine and the petals of roses against it. Dash it with waves of the warm sea.

Even the god shall enjoy the pastime of mortals. Great is his rage, he is tall in his amorous fury, goodly Dionysus. Bring grapes, he tramples them, raking the ground with his horns. Let him forget that he is god, goodly Dionysus. Let him be only desire on the peak of fulfillment. Let him be only feeling and fury in doing . . .

. . .

—The act of love, said the Perfessor, leaning on the fence and watching intently, bottle in hand, is an extraordinary thing. At such times we are like runners passing a torch. We pant and fall exhausted that the race may go on.

—Gentlemen, the Senator said, his mouth open, his cigar dead between his lips, I am reminded of my youth. How often does he get to do this?

—Not as often as he likes, I can see that, the Perfessor said.

—Listen to her squeal, the Senator said. Christ, wouldn't you hate to be a woman!

—Pull him around again, boys, the owner of the heifer said.

He held the bawling heifer steady, while three men struggled with the bull, who reared blindly and kept falling clumsily and jarring his jaw on the heifer's back.

—Help 'im there, Bob, Mr. Jacobs yelled.

—I'm tryin' to.

—Pull 'im around, Pete.

—My God, the Perfessor said, the old brute's a terrible artist.

The four men, the heifer, and the white bull sweated, struggled, shouted, panted, heaved under the noon sun. The bull was like a hero betrayed. His noble strength had been tricked into this mortal weakness. Now he was beset by pestering inferior creatures who used him according to their own designs.

—No wonder they gave him first prize, the Senator said.

—I wonder if he'd trade with me, sight unseen, the Perfessor said.

—I feel sorry for them, Mr. Shawnessy said. But they don't seem to mind our watching. I suppose it's only human beings who make love in secret.

—We miss a lot that way, the Perfessor said. It's part of the great human denial of origins. We prefer the dark. But in our beginnings, like the gods we made love by day. Noon is the best time for it, high noon, in the drench of the sun. Let all the world behold. What cares bull! *Io Hymen Hymenaee!*

—That ought to do, Mr. Jacobs said, after a while, shoving the bull down. Think that's enough, Jim?

—Should be, the man holding the heifer said.

They talked like two businessmen discussing an order of feed.

—Are they kidding? the Perfessor said. I predict quintuplets.

Mr. Jacobs opened the gate, and the heifer's owner pulled her through. The white bull followed and, in spite of blows, reared at the whole struggling mass of men around the gate. The gate was shoved to in his face. He nudged it with his horns.

—He looks sad, the Perfessor said.

—So would you, the Senator said, if you knew that you might have to wait weeks for another piece. Well, that was some show, Bill.

All the men walked slowly down the lane except Mr. Shawnessy and the Perfessor.

—Behold! the Perfessor said, leaning on the fence, life's a great white bull, beating itself to love's ecstatic death.

He looked sharply up at the tower protruding above the iron fence and the trees of Mrs. Brown's garden.

—A face at the window, he said. Naughty girl.

Mr. Shawnessy, who had also noticed the face at the window, lingered indecisively.

—There she is, the Perfessor said, immured in her private garden, watching from time to time the love-frenzy of a bull. What has humanity gained by putting the bull in his pasture and Evelina in her tower? Have you ever stopped to think, John, that the progenitors of mankind were once all amoral like the bull? Today we cluck with horror at the degraded hillfamilies down South because father consorts with daughter, brother with sister, and the hired man with grandma. Yet the human race was all once more degenerate than these trolls and troglodytes. They were filthy, they were incestuous, they were lousy. They lived contentedly in their own muck. From that universal sink came every man and woman living today, king and commoner, president and prostitute. Our own little Evelina is the product of God knows how much violence, incest, murder, rape, pillage, an incredible history of the corruption called life extending back to the first cell in the dawn slime. Strip away her dress and let down her hair, knock the nonsense of feminism out of her head, unlearn the letters in her brain, and what do you have? A healthy little she-ape of a hairless sub-variety.

The Perfessor shook soundlessly.

—Make a damn cute pet too, he said.

—But what an achievement! Mr. Shawnessy said. In her tower, Evelina has risen above the muck of the Great Swamp. It cannot, will not reclaim her. From her tower, she looks down on a garden of classic alignments. She has achieved beauty—and some of the sadness that goes with it. Perhaps she knows love there too, love which gives her the world. From her tower, she exercises all the dearly bought feminine virtues. She can be tender and sad and piteous. She pities bull, who pities not himself. She pities Professor, who is loveless and forlorn. This feminine pity, this love, she fixes as a beacon there at the top of her tower. This light must not be extinguished, for it equals the sun.

—Do you know, John, the Perfessor said with his usual candor, I think I'm in love with that woman. Now, tell me, what do I love?

. . .

A lady in the window of a tower looked steeply down at two gentlemen slowly walking away from a bullpasture, leaving a white bull stupidly standing. Walking on the National Road, a senator with an entourage of farmers and hangers-on entered the shade of the town, sauntering slowly. Somewhere in town, a band played martial airs. She had not yet returned into herself. Through her window she had been possessed by sunlight. She had been smooth and grassed like the lawn beneath her and rounded with delicious hills. She had run naked in the wondrous garden of herself, had known wild passions, excessively visual pleasures. And still her lover went down bright lanes of her garden in noontime, and shook down on the ticklegrassed lawn a rain of blossoms.

EVELINA'S DREAM

Her garden was very dark now. She was standing like the other nymphs in an ivied recess, a special one near the front of the lawn, with a fountain playing on her body. At her feet bronze figures of a man and a woman were all interlaced with each other among the lily stems. Lonesome, faroff was the sound of the train, for everyone had gone and left her alone with her statues and the vague balls of shrubbery on the lawn. Now at this lost late hour of the night, might she not conjure up her beloved by an old enchantment! Warm water gushed over her as, with a slow bending leap, she sprang from her pedestal and began to run on the lawn, with gestures of conjuring.

Somewhere in the darkness there was a sound of something coming, a fabulous beast—perhaps the unicorn with a wondrous white body and a single great horn in the middle of his head.

She was running up the steps of her house, laughing and sobbing together. She was running up the circular stair of the tower while someone followed her. She was running, fearing that she might awaken before she reached the place of rendezvous, then turned to accept this strong, white-muscled visitor, this father and preserver, eternal triumpher and maker of legends. . . .

. . .

—God, said Mr. Shawnessy, is the object of all quests, and love is the desire with which we seek Him.

—I have been winding through the labyrinth, lo! these many years, the Perfessor said, as they came out on the National Road, and my clue has led me to the Answer. God is a Minotaur, who demands the blood sacrifice from us all.

Mr. Shawnessy saw his two oldest children, Wesley and Eva, standing with Libby Passifee and Johnny Jacobs, peering into a front window of the Passifee home. As he watched, they all turned and ran through the gate to the road. He stopped, waiting for them. They looked startled and shy.

—Hello, children. Oughtn't you to be at the school?

—We came home with Libby for a book they were supposed to have for the rehearsal, Wesley said.

They went on rapidly toward town. Mr. Shawnessy saw no book.

—The Answer, he said, is in us, around us, everywhere. The Answer is every moment of ourselves. The Answer is a single unpronounced and unpronounceable Word, that could at one and the same time denote everything and connote everything.

—Sometimes, John, the Perfessor said, your reasons are better than reason. What's next on the program? Must be after twelve.

They were entering the shade of the town. In the middle of the distant intersection, several men in blue coats and queer hats were awkwardly milling around.

—The G.A.R. Parade is forming up there, Mr. Shawnessy said. As soon as General Jake Jackson shows up, we march, and then we eat.

—Fine, the Perfessor said. I have the devil's own appetite. I've seen a cow climbed, and now I want to fill my belly. After that, maybe I can see somebody killed. Thus in a single day, I shall have participated in the three main pastimes of man, fluting, feeding, and

Fighting for Freedom

FROM SHILOH TO SAVANNAH

is the name of the goddam thing, the General said. I happen to have a few hundred pages of it stuffed into my coatpocket here, Shawnessy, and if you have a little time, I'd like to have you glance it over and tell me frankly what you think of it. There you are.

—Thanks, General. Be glad to look at it.

—By the way, you were in the War, weren't you? the General said.

—Yes, Mr. Shawnessy said.

He and some fifty other members of the Raintree County Post of the Grand Army of the Republic were standing in a shapeless mass at the middle of the intersection, waiting to form ranks and march down to the Schoolhouse for the outdoor banquet. General Jacob J. Jackson, Raintree County's outstanding military figure, a hero of two wars, had arrived in Waycross only a few minutes before to lead the march.

The General, a hearty man in his middle sixties, was a little shorter than Mr. Shawnessy. Broadshouldered, deepchested, he was built like an athlete except for the hard bulge of his belly. Freeflowing gray hair fell thickly from his thinning dome to lie upon his shoulders and blend over his ears into the great ball of a beard. Out of this beard his voice blew like a horn of cracked brass, having no variations in pitch or volume between a hard bray and a hoarse whisper. The General was now standing in one of his characteristic postures, arms folded over chest, head thrust back, left foot forward. One could see the bulge of his right calfmuscle in the army trousers. His small blue eyes glared. The muscles around his cheekbones twitched as if under his beard the General were gritting his jaw teeth. A dress sword and two Colt revolvers hung from his belt. He held a broad Western hat adorned with military cord.

The General made everyone else look like a supernumerary. Most of the other veterans were in uniform too, but only the General seemed clothed in heroic dignity.

—I'm a practical man, the General was saying, a man of action, and I hate like hell to write.

—For a man who hates to write, General, you've ground out a lot of copy in your time, Mr. Shawnessy said. Let's see, how many books is it now?

The General's chest swelled, and there burst from his throat a series of distinct hahs, of exactly the same timbre as his speaking voice.

—Well, let's see, he said. I began with *Fighting for the Flag,* and followed it up with *Memoirs of a Fighting General.* Then there was *Four Years at the Front or Fighting for the Cause* and of course *A Fighting Man's History of the War in the West.* I've also done that series called *Fights I have Fought from Chapultepec to Chickamauga or Tales of Two Wars.* Then, there's that goddam thing my publishers have had me doing called *Fifteen Historic Fights from Marathon to Manassas.*

—I hadn't seen that one, General, Mr. Shawnessy said. I didn't know you went in for the European battles.

—Once you understand war, the General said, one goddam battle is like another. By the way, it's time to march, isn't it?

—Just about, Mr. Shawnessy said. I think the band's about ready.

—Fall in, boys! the General barked.

A little sheepishly, the veterans formed in a column four abreast. Senator Jones stood in the front rank. Mr. Shawnessy stepped unobtrusively into the last row with other men in civilian garb. The General strode strongly to the head of the column, took a stance twenty paces behind the band, and drawing his sword shouted,

—Ready, boys! Column, Harch!

The cracked brass of the command set off a series of explosions from the horns, unsynchronized at first, and then acquiring a noisy pattern that Mr. Shawnessy recognized as the 'Battle Hymn of the Republic.'

He marched briskly with a shortened stride, walking as he never walked in ordinary life and as he seldom had in the Army. His arms swung stiffly. His chin jerked. A troop of small boys marched much more smartly alongside. One of them tossed a lit firecracker into the middle of the veterans' column. A half-dozen men broke ranks, and the whole column lost step and alignment at the explosion.

—Hi, Grandpa! a boy yelled. Playin' sojer again?

Mr. Shawnessy kept his eyes front. The column soon reached the schoolhouse yard, turned in, and marched to a position in front of the banquet tables, which had already been set with plates of food.

—Column, Halt! brayed the General. Fall out for mess!

Professor Stiles, Mr. Shawnessy, the General, and Senator Jones took their seats in that order from left to right, facing west at the main long table, reserved for the veterans. Since for some reason the Reverend Lloyd G. Jarvey hadn't turned up yet, a visiting minister was called upon to say a grace, and the meal began.

—Let me see, Shawnessy, the General said, I don't seem to remember your war record. You *were* in the big fight, weren't you?

—Yes.

The General brandished a drumstick and bit bigly into the bulge of it. His teeth, still strong and white, cut cleanly to the bone.

—Goddammit, the General said, those were the days. The Nation had some guts then. I've never been as happy since. What fights were you in, Shawnessy?

—I fought in your corps, General.

—The hell you did! the General said.

His teeth crushed the big end of the legbone for the marrow.

—Say, then, you'll enjoy reading this book. The whole history of our corps is in it. Everything. Shucks, Shawnessy, don't you long sometimes for the old Army life? I tell you, this generation lacks sand. Hell, if they had another war now, we wouldn't have enough Army to defend Raintree County. Say what you will, goddammit, those were good days.

Mr. Shawnessy looked up and down the table. The fifty veterans were talking soldier talk, reviewing battles, marches, incidents of camp life, reciting names of dead comrades. The words and emotions of 1865 were a little tattered and faded like the blue uniforms that covered the aging bodies of 1892. He was reminded of the collection of Civil War books he had bought at secondhand a few years before, of the sonorous titles, the pomp of language, the repetition of once memorable names and phrases, but all on yellowing pages in gilt bindings.

Mr. Shawnessy looked at the General's manuscript lying on the table. These words too would find their way into thousands of American homes and go sifting down from generation to generation, on yellowing pages, until they dropped at last into the deepest vaults of the biggest libraries and at the bottom of the pile in a back room of the secondhand bookshop. Like a hundred million other words written about the Great War, they were not great words. Yet they were steeped in the sadness of the greatest of all wars; they were the costumed, pompous words in which the War had become an epic in the Republic's memory. Intuitively, Raintree County's soldier-general, a man of practical energy and profane tongue, had put on the mantle of the grand style. He did it as well as a thousand others who had written books about the Civil War.

Mr. Shawnessy ran his eyes over the first page:

OFF TO THE WARS

(Epic Fragment from *Fighting for Freedom*)

> . . . Who can forget the simple pageantry of the enlistment ceremony and the strong pride that animated the patriot's breast as he swore the oath to preserve and defend his country's honor! Who will forget his last day of civilian life, his leavetaking for the wars! Perhaps his final memory of the old life was a mother's face at parting, wet with tears, perhaps the memory of a girl who promised forever to be true, perhaps the strong hand of a comrade in his own, the pat on the shoulder, the wordless wish that he might return soon and safe from battle. But whatever the manner of his going, go he must and go he did, for . . .

—Goddammit, Garwood, the General was saying to the Senator on his far side, we're countin' on you to put some guts into that next pension bill.

—Jesus, Jake, we already let more blood from the taxpayer with those pension bills than the Army gave on the altar of Freedom. However, you can assure all my old comrades-at-arms that I won't let 'em down. Do you think the Army is solidly behind Harrison?

—No one can deliver the G.A.R. vote, Senator, but the boys were pleased by the last pension act.

—The General's still fighting a good war, the Perfessor whispered to Mr. Shawnessy. I suppose in time of war, the Republic needs these muscular bastards, but they're an expensive luxury in peacetime, with campaign medals on their tits and pension bills in their mitts. Every cowardly finagler who managed to get his name on the rolls can live forever on a fat pension—and his widow and his orphans. The heroes of the Republic! And half of 'em never got any closer to the front than the cathouses of Louisville. It hurts when you think that boys like you fought, bled, and squittered from Chattanooga to the Sea, and now you get less than some guy who did his combat duty in a brothel and earned a lifelong disability pension for a case of the clap.

—Well, it was all part of the War, Mr. Shawnessy said. The Republic is generous. After all, the War was more than a big fight. It scarred us all, one way or another.

—By the way, just how much combat did Garwood see?

—He was a Copperhead till after the Election in '64. Then with the issue of the struggle no longer in doubt, he bared his breast to the sleet of battle—five hundred miles behind the lines. He whipped up a volunteer regiment and sneaked out with a colonelcy—and a conspicuous absence from all major engagements.

—Shawnessy, the General said, turning around for a moment, have you been in Indianapolis lately?

—No, sir.

—I've clean lost track of the Monument there. How far along is it, anyway?

—A year ago, the State Legislature appropriated another hundred thousand dollars, and I guess that heaved the shaft a little higher.

—I hardly been back since the dedication ceremonies, the General said.

—What monument is this? the Perfessor said.

—The Soldiers' and Sailors' Monument in the middle of Indianapolis, the General said. The only memorial in the world erected to the private soldier.

—I had a humble part in getting it started, the Senator said.

—How high is it? the Perfessor said.

—It'll be over two hundred and eighty feet, the General said, counting the puss on top. Greatest monument in the world.

—They'll have to hurry it up, the Perfessor said, or the generation that sees it completed won't remember what it's for. In this country, we're always about fifty years behind in our monuments. Just a plain shaft, or ornamental?

—Ornamental as hell, the General said. You've seen the plans, haven't you, Shawnessy? As I remember it, they'll have a Peace Group on one side with a great big gal about a hundred sizes bigger than real in the middle holding up a flag. A lot of symbolic figures will be grouped around her—a farmer, a blacksmith, a veteran, and a dinge at her feet holding up a busted chain. Another woman is floating through the background shaking a wreath and an olive branch, and the sun is rising way in the back. On the other side is the War Group. I helped plan that one myself. In the middle is a female with a torch in her hand, and all around her are men dying, shooting, dead, a guy on a horse behind with sabre raised, guns, a broken drum, horses' heads, and a woman flying in the background with a flag and a mittful of arrows. Say, just one of the soldiers in that group is as high as this schoolhouse. We tried to crowd every typical figure of the War into that tableau and damn near succeeded.

—How about a private squittering and a Chattanooga whore? the Perfessor asked mildly.

The General's chest swelled and from his throat burst a series of spaced hahs.

—After all, he said, this is for beauty and the ages. The main entrances at the base are guarded by four heroic-size figures representing the various branches of the armed forces. Then out from the main groups are a couple smaller groups. One is a soldier boy just leaving the homefolks. Paw is sitting on the plow and holding out his hand to the boy, and Maw has her arms on the boy's shoulders, his gun is laying on the ground, and he's just about to give 'er the farewell kiss. Very spirited group.

—I thought that was to be a soldier coming home, the Senator said.

—Tell you the truth, I forget which it is, the General said. You can take it either way. On the other side are three of the boys sitting in the middle of a battlefield, one of 'em wounded. There'll be fountains and cascades and wide stairs leading to the base and a stairway inside that brings you to the balcony at the top.

—You mentioned a lady on the summit, the Perfessor said. Who is that?

—Victory! the General said, shaking his white locks and digging himself a gob of mashed potatoes. Thirty-eight feet tall, but up that high, they tell me she'll look like a kid's doll.

—It makes you proud of the State, Senator Jones said, pulling out all the lower stops in his great organ voice, to think it will have the most impressive shaft ever erected by mankind.

Mr. Shawnessy was thinking of mounds beside the river, forgotten battlegrounds, and cities piled on cities. He was thinking of a great war long ago, the young men who fought it, its causes and consequences, the dwindling memory of it in tattered books and broken stones.

Forgotten. Forever lost—memories of a war on the land in ancient days. Forgotten—faces of bearded boys, hellraisers, hard marchers, the anonymous architects of History. Forever lost.

But I will build a monument to the private soldier greater and more costly than any ever builded by mankind. I will build a private monument out of memories of comrades.

O, stony and stately magnitudes! Immense fragments of myths, simple and strange with the attitudes of an old war. From these, the ten thousand gilded books in which the Republic remembers that it is One Nation Indivisible with Freedom and Justice for All.

Then did you fight in that Great War for the Preservation of the Union and the Emancipation of a Race? Were you South in that long marching? Did you fight in those battles? Were you a soldier and brave?

Now I will go to a place where the roads of the Nation converge like spokes to the hub of a wheel and walk around and around the vast memorial and find the forgotten faces.

They shall be stone! They shall be a hundred times natural size! And I shall find the face of one who departed from Raintree County in his twenty-fourth year. I shall see the colossal tears of stone on the colossal stone face.

Did he not fight and die in that old war to preserve the Union and free a Race? Did he ever come back again? And who in a thousand days of the years will remember

July 13— JOHNNY —1863
SHAWNESSY'S DEPARTURE FOR THE WAR
RECEIVED THE FOLLOWING NOTICE IN THE FREE ENQUIRER:

LOCAL BOY OFF TO THE WARS
(Epic Fragment from the *Free Enquirer*)

A large company of friends and well-wishers was yesterday assembled at the railway station to see one of our most promising local boys off to the wars. Young John Wickliff Shawnessy, whose life was recently saddened by a bereavement that has touched the whole community, has decided to rally to the grand old flag and do his part in quelling the hideous hydra of rebellion. Mr. Shawnessy, whose amusing and informative compositions have frequently titillated the readers of these pages, repaired to the railway station at nine o'clock. Most affecting were the farewells exchanged upon this occasion, so that hardly an eye refused the tribute of a tear. The most indurate bosom could not repress a sigh at this scene so oft repeated in these melancholy days, and never was the pathos of parting more poignantly expressed than in the words of Mrs. Shawnessy, the boy's mother, who remarked that a better boy never lived and that this was the fourth son whom she has seen consecrated to the sacred task of preserving the Union. As for us, pained as we are by the sorrow of departure, we can better spare this young Cincinnatus than can the Republic for whose existence, never more gravely imperiled than now, he is girding himself to fight. And we say to him, 'Farewell and hail, brave young heart. Would we could join you in the contest! Raintree County loses for a time a shining citizen. The Republic gains a gallant warrior. Go, and God bless you. Hail and fare . . .'

—Well, well, well! Cash Carney said, coming into the station. So you're going to get into the fuss after all, John! What time does the train come in?

—Any time now, T. D. said.

Johnny was sitting beside Ellen on a bench in the station. The great thing was to cut clean and not to cry. He would simply not think of anything.

—John, you'll have to send us some articles from the front, Niles

Foster said. How does it feel, Mrs. Shawnessy, to have your last son go to the War?

—If they need him, I suppose it must be, Ellen said. Johnny wanted to go.

Johnny didn't look at her.

—I think I hear the train, Cash said.

Johnny stood up and fumbled at his suitcase, but Niles Foster already had it. Everyone stood up around him as if to shield him from something.

—Yes, it's the train, T. D. said, looking nervously through the station window. Well——

Johnny looked at his father's face. The mild blue eyes blinked at him. T. D. rocked back on his heels and attempted a smile.

—John, he said, his voice quavering, here's something to help you out a bit.

It was a twenty dollar gold piece. Johnny wondered how in the world his father had managed to get so much money all in one piece. T. D. blinked harder.

—Now take care of your health, John. Be sure to let them know about your medical experience with me. After this big victory at Gettysburg, I don't think the War can last much longer, and I expect you'll be back to us any time. I take a hopeful——

T. D.'s voice was drowned in clanging. The black body of the train slid past the window and stopped.

T. D. looked around, confused. He held up his hand.

—Let us pray, he said.

Niles and Cash removed their hats. Johnny put his head down, swallowing hard.

—Dear Lord, T. D. said.

He stopped. People were pushing through the door, talking loudly.

—Please bring this boy back safe. Amen.

It was the shortest prayer T. D. had ever given.

Johnny shook T. D.'s hand and, turning, looked at his mother for the first time since they had come to the station.

—All aboard, came the voice of the trainman calling. All aboard for Beardstown, Indianapolis, and parts West. All aboard, all aboard.

With a movement quick like a bird, Ellen Shawnessy pressed her small grieving face against Johnny's and hugged him fiercely. Briefly he had seen her eyes sightless with tears. He held her small body, felt it shaking. He kissed her, getting his cheek wet.

—Good-by, Johnny. And come back safe.

—Good-by, Mamma! Good-by, everyone! he said. I'll come back.

He got his luggage from someone and climbed into the coach. As he sat down, the train started. The station was flowing backward, the platform was passing. He put his face to the open window and leaned out. On the platform stood a tall, fragile man with sparse, whitening hair and a small, bony woman with dark reddish hair, bonnet askew. They waved, smiled, wept, they slipped backward, their faces became indistinct, a green water flowed over them, their forms were smaller, smaller, still waving. Abruptly a block of buildings thrust them from view.

Johnny Shawnessy, twenty-four years old, turned his face to the back of the wooden bench in the nearly empty coach. He wept.

He wept for the farewell that he was saying.

Farewell to Raintree County. Farewell to all its lost horizons in spring and summer, brown roads of peace, broad fields flowing with grass and corn.

Where had the long days gone? It had seemed that they would be forever. But the train passing behind the land at evening had been calling to him all the time, calling him beyond the private square of young illusion. Awaken, it had said. Did you think that you could be a child forever on the breast of the maternal and sustaining earth? Arise to the call of your brothers gone before. Arise, young man, bearing the shield of conscience, badge of your ancient heritage.

And now farewell. The days of blood and iron may give you back again, but it will never be the same. The train will pass at evening and make its wailing diphthong of danger and adventure beyond the great oak forest, but it will never be the same. Where is the thing that you were seeking? Perhaps you have already known and lost it. Perhaps you knew it all the time in the long summers before the War, in the peace of the wide meadows of your home. Perhaps you knew it always in the birdlike swiftness and quick voice of your mother, who was young once on this changing earth called Raintree County. Perhaps you knew it in the devotions of your father, a gentle minister of grace and good. Perhaps you found it in the noisy holidays, election days, Saturday nights, cornhuskings, harvestings, barbecues.

Farewell to that more innocent and youthful Raintree County. And to its lost young hero. For he is there—he hunts the shape of beauty by the river, ignorant of defeat and death.

But farewell, too, a long farewell to a house divided and to the memory of two children, lost in the woods a long time ago.

What is the source of all these tears? They are risen from a secret place, a brackish river drowning in its flood the seeds, cries, tumults of a thousand days. Alas for all that is lost on the human river, the mortal and repentant river!

Farewell! The dispassionate train is chugging through the stations, leaving the land behind. Perhaps you will come back. Didn't you hear the prayer uttered to a just God to bring you home again?

And so farewell to Raintree County, farewell to your great home! Your love was deeper than you knew. The river of your life flowed from a more distant source than you suspected. It rises still, a devious flood between green banks of summer. It is there forever, tracing a prophecy across the earth.

Farewell. These tears dissolve the ancient boundaries. The old words blur and flow. Farewell.

At Beardstown, his eyes were dry. He felt unnaturally calm. By the time he had reached Indianapolis, he might as well have been weeks away from Raintree County. The violence of his emotion at parting had made him free. The memory of the last time he had been in this station only a little over a week ago, hunting two lost children, briefly chilled his new excitement. But that memory, like the tears of the morning, could never be any more distant than it was now.

In the best Johnny Shawnessy tradition, he began to see a certain grandeur in his act of departure from Raintree County to the wars, and a certain humor.

SETH A SOLDIER!

WAR CAN'T LAST LONG NOW!

(Epic Fragment from the *Free Enquirer*.)

Those who have followed the fortunes of that congenial cornstalk, Seth Twigs, will be eager to know that the fabulous bumpkin has at last offered his services to the United States Army. To be more exact, the long arm of the draft finally found him in his hide-out on the Shawmucky, where he had planned to sit out the War with a barrel of cider, an old bird dog, and a pack of greasy cards.

Tuesday last, it is reported, Seth made his way to the great Western metropolis of Indianapolis. Descending in the station, he was at first somewhat bewildered by the beehive bustle of the City, but with characteristic rustic acumen, he quickly adjusted himself to the situation. Standing on the steps of the State Capitol and indicating with a sweep of his scrannel arm the metropolitan vistas of Indianapolis, Seth was delivered of this pungent epigram: 'Danwebster warn't nothin' to this. To be puffickly frank, I am consterbobulated.'

Surrounded by reporters and well-wishers, Seth answered several questions with all his usual pith and point.

'How long do you think the War will last, Mr. Twigs?'

'I figger it'll take me at least three weeks to git muh fightin' gear in order,' Seth replied.

'Do you have any particular strategy for bringing the Rebels to their knees?'

'From what I heerd, the Southerners is all frightful chivillerous. I sidjest we put our purtiest gals in uniform and arm 'em with banjos and handcuffs. They can't do no wuss than the men has.'

'What is your candid opinion of the draft?'

'The feller that caught me was the fastest runner I ever seen.'

'Are you for or against Lincoln?'

'Who's he?'

'The President.'

'What in blazes happened to old Andy Jackson?'

Later, it is reported, Seth spent an interesting and instructive day visiting sites of historic and cultural . . .

Confusion filled the city. A few days before, the Rebel raider, John Hunt Morgan, had crossed the Ohio River and had begun a daring cavalry invasion of Southern Indiana, closely pursued by a troop of Union cavalry. The Governor had made a hurried call for emergency militia, and the entire state south of Indianapolis had risen in arms. The raid had already been diverted from the State Capital and was visibly weakening as it approached the Ohio border. But there was still tension and excitement in Indianapolis.

In the Recruiting Office, a number of men, mostly younger than Johnny, were standing around waiting to interview an officer who stood behind a desk. Johnny took his place at the back of the line.

Something hit him solidly between the shoulders, knocking his hat off, and a hornloud voice brayed laughter into his ears.

—Well, hogtie me, if it ain't Jack Shawnessy!

—Hello there! Johnny said.

He turned around, still trying to get his breath, and there stood Flash Perkins, grinning in a great arrogant beard. His forehead shifted into ridges of excitement. His fierce blue eyes were childishly happy.

—Well, I'll be skinned and stretched on a board! Flash said. Put 'er there, Jack!

No one else had ever called him Jack. Johnny stood and wrung Flash's hand as hard as he could to keep his own from being broken.

—What are you doin' here, Jack?

—Enlisting.

—Well, I'll be a ringtailed jackass! So am I. Hey, Corporal, look here, we want some action around here.

The officer behind the counter was a tired-looking sergeant.

—Keep in line and take your turn, boys, he said.

—Hell, git a move on! Flash said, we want to git into your goddam war.

—If you're so anxious, why didn't you get into it before? the officer said.

—Shucks, we on'y jist found out about it in Raintree County, Flash said. It'll soon be over now, boy.

—Where you been, Flash? Johnny said in a low voice, trying to get him quieted down. I don't think I've seen you since the Fourth of July Race in '59.

—I been West, Jack. Hell, I been doin' a little ever'thing. Minin', scoutin', fightin' Injuns. I finely decided this war gone on long enough, so back I come to the County. Figger me enlistin' on the same day with you! Maybe we'll git into the same cumpney.

Johnny was sorry that he had run into Flash. In a way, he had hoped to make a complete break with everyone and everything he had known. But he seemed fated to pick up reminders of himself wherever he went.

Flash hadn't changed much. Apparently nothing had happened to knock the wildness out of him. He had a big Western hat, spurred boots, a pearlhandled revolver on his hip.

—I don't know why you want to go into the Army, boy, the officer said to Flash, when he reached the desk. They'll start by disarming you.

—I mean to keep this tool on me, General, Flash said.

The officer shrugged his shoulders.

—Sign here, boys, and come back tomorrow morning same time. You'll get your medical examination then and swore in.

—Jack and I want in the same cumpney, pardner, Flash said. Be sure to write that down.

Johnny didn't remember expressing this wish, but he let it pass.

Outside, he felt embarrassed as he saw that Flash intended to stick with him. Everyone they passed turned and stared.

—Boy, am I glad to git back to Indiana! Flash said. Shucks, they ain't got no civilization nor nothin' out there, Jack. You wouldn't believe it. Cuss it, they ain't a beautiful gal west a the Mississip. You have to pay as you enter, and then they're all leather and cusswords. Christ, I been dyin' to git back to God's country. That rough life is O. K. for a while, but soon or later, Jack, you feel a hankerin' for the cumpney of culteevated people. Hi, girls.

Two young women, passing, dipped their parasols and walked swiftly by with fluttering eyelids.

—Say, maybe we could hitch onto them fancy fillies and git our trunks hauled, Flash said. Ha, Ha!

He hit Johnny between the shoulderblades and turned around. The girls were looking back with genuine alarm.

—That reminds me, Johnny said, I'll have to say good-by now, Flash. There's a girl here in the city I want to get in touch with. I'll see you tomorrow morning.

—If she's got a friend, I don't mind comin' along.

—No, this is private. Thanks just the same.

—Listen, I got a room at the Greer House, Flash said. If you ain't got no place to stay, you can come in there with me. Shucks, bring your woman along if you want to.

—Thanks, Johnny said. I may turn up tonight—but alone. So long.

It seemed to Johnny that life was full of repetitions and corrections of itself as he walked to an address on Pennsylvania Avenue and knocked on the door of a plain white house, set back a little from the street.

The door opened, and Nell Gaither appeared. She was stunningly got up, cool and pale in a green dress with an immense hoop. She looked imperially ladylike, her head held proudly and tilted a little to one side in a gesture of gracious condescension. Her full-formed, lovely mouth made a shining contrast with the powdered whiteness of her cheeks.

—Hello, Johnny.

She stepped out and put her hand in his. Her mouth curved into a smile of tenderness and pleasure, showing her fine white teeth; and her eyes, suddenly green as she stepped from the dusk of the house into the warm light, glowed with veiled excitement. A feeling of warmth and sweetness coursed through him as he touched and held the small passive hand.

—Hello, Nell. Did you get my letter?

—Yes, just this morning, Johnny. I'm glad you wanted to see me before you left for the War. By the way, Garwood's here, dropped in unexpectedly. We've—we've been practically engaged, you know, have been for over a month, and I——

Johnny was still holding her hand and looking at her. As he listened to her measured, low voice and watched her small face in the summer light and smelled the faint, flowery odor of her powder, he felt a little dizzy.

—It's all right, Nell, he said. I just wanted to see you before I went.

—Johnny, I'm terribly sorry about what happened.

—It's all right, Johnny said. It's all over now.

There were footsteps in the hall, and Garwood Jones came to the door.

—Jesus, John, how are you, boy! Garwood said.

Johnny shook hands with Garwood and went into the parlor, listening to some sonorously delivered condolences. Garwood was sleekly splendid in a new suit. He had a diamond stickpin in his cravat. He had a cane and gloves. Apparently, being a young Copperhead congressman was a lucrative calling.

—Well, I hate to see you get into this mess, sprout, Garwood said affectionately. You're just throwing your life away, but I suppose you know what you're doing. Say, I got an idea.

Garwood took his arm from around Johnny's shoulders and lit a cigar.

—Nell, suppose we take this boy out and show him a good time before the Army gets him. God knows it'll be the last fun he'll have for a while. Send him off with a beautiful memory.

—I think that would be nice, Nell said. If Johnny would like.

—Now then, Garwood said, suppose we get another woman—one of the girls who works with you at the Christian Commission, Nell, and——

—No, Johnny said. I don't want that. Just the three of us.

—Well, all right, Garwood said. If you want it that way, Nell and I would be delighted. We'll take the boy out, buy him a dinner, get him good and drunk, and turn him over to the Army rarin' to go. I want it understood that this is on me, every bit of it. I'll pay till it hurts. Nothing's too good for our boy John.

It started with a few drinks at a place Garwood knew. Then they walked over to the Capitol, where Garwood wanted to hear some speeches. In the yard of the Capitol Building, hundreds of people milled around a makeshift platform on which some dignitaries, military and civilian, were speaking to honor a volunteer regiment about to entrain for active duty on the front.

In the young afternoon, as he walked with Nell and Garwood on the lawn of the Capitol Building, all bitterness and sorrow drained away from Johnny Shawnessy. He was having one of his epic moments. He was walking with a beautiful woman of Raintree County, whom he loved and who had loved him once, and with a friend, who was also a competitor. They were with crowds close to a building that embodied in its tranquil form the wisdom and eternity of the Republic. It was a day of grave portent for the Nation, and words of public men sounded across the bared heads of the throng. Indiana's exultant summer rolled up in waves of heat from littered streets that narrowed to the heat-hazed distance. The city made a low continuous sound like surf. From the vast day, seductive touches came. More beautiful than any fabled flesh, the loveliest woman in the Republic walked in her great bellskirt beside him, dipping her parasol and laughing. The blended image of the erotic and the spiritual, which Nell Gaither had always embodied for him, found somehow its ideal setting here among the scenic attractions of the Capital City of Indiana.

—A call to arms, boomed a great voice from the platform, an

appeal to courage! In this momentous hour when our very homes are threatened, the sanctity of all we hold dear, the honor of our loved ones, can any patriot breast refuse the stirring summons of . . .

Nell and Johnny sat on a bench by themselves while Garwood stalked around the yard, looking important. Gloved hands folded in her lap, Nell gazed at Johnny gravely.

—You look awfully nice with your face all shaved, Johnny.

Johnny rubbed his lean jaws and grinned. It was not right to feel so happy. What had he to feel happy about? Yet something about the scene appealed to that inextinguishably young poet in him, who was always trying to live in a privately lovely universe. The summer drenched him with waves of languor and memory. He remembered the lightswollen stream of the Shawmucky, boats drifting, Nell in a wide white bonnet and a green dress, her fingers stroking the oar-blade.

—Where is the Professor now, Johnny?

He told her, and they reviewed what they knew about the lives of others whom they had known together in the old days at the Pedee Academy. Two of the boys were dead, one at Shiloh and the other of camp fever during the training period. They sat talking gravely and hesitantly about these old things, drifting closer and closer to forbiddenly sweet memories, circling, touching lightly, retreating. Nell removed her left glove and began to trace a series of little curves on the wooden arm of the bench.

—Do you keep up with your reading and study, Nell?

—Not as well as I should, Nell said. Now and then I read a little Shakespeare.

She blushed. Her finger continued to make its delicate tracery on the wooden arm.

—Drive them back, I say, the great voice boomed from the platform, drive them back to the crimestained and slaveryblackened earth from whence they have arisen, till they are brought redhanded and trembling before the bar of universal justice. And were it not for the heavy responsibilities of . . .

—I was looking at my copy of *The Complete Works of Lord Byron* the other day, Johnny said offhand, and I found a page with a pressed flower in it. It left a very delicate stain on a poem I've always loved. Maybe you remember it:

So, we'll go no more a-roving
So late into the night,
Though the heart be still as loving
And . . .

—Who would not be young and a soldier of the Republic? shouted the voice from the platform. Who would not fight God's and his country's battles on distant fields? Be kind to these departing boys, young women of the Republic. They go forth to fight for you and the homeland. They are about to bare their young and amorous breasts to the miniéball and the Rebel bayonet. Embrace them fondly, young women of the Republic, for they go to battle and an unknown . . .

Nell opened her purse and found a handkerchief. She touched her nose and dabbed at her eyes.

—I cry so easily these days, she said. Everything is so sad with everyone leaving for the War.

She put her ungloved hand on Johnny's.

—Isn't it terrible, Johnny! The War and what's happened and everything. I don't know when I've felt so unhappy. Do you think we'll ever get straightened out?

Johnny studied the shining green eyes in the upturned face.

—Just now, I take a fairly hopeful view of the situation, he said.

They both smiled at this phrase which had been said so often in the pulpit of the Danwebster Church, and Nell slipped her hand back into her lap and began to glove it.

—Well, children, Garwood said, stopping in front of the bench, let's go have some fun. These blowhards are going to spend all afternoon sending those poor boys to the slaughter. I suggest we have some more drinks and dinner at the Savoy-Rialto, a new sort of dancehall-beerparlor combined where ladies go.

The Savoy-Rialto was one of the fanciest spots Johnny had ever got into. It had a downstairs dining place with orchestra, and the walls were covered with gilt and draperies. Garwood ordered champagne, and both he and Nell insisted on keeping the glasses full.

—What's the matter, Nell? Garwood said once. Never saw you drink so much before.

Turning to Johnny, he said,

—You know, John, usually Nell's trying to keep me from sopping this stuff up, but tonight she just keeps pouring. We consider this a special occasion, sprout.

He patted Johnny's shoulder affectionately.

—We want you to remember us, he said.

Nell looked at Johnny over the rim of her glass, and her eyes were shining. She seemed very gay for a person who had never felt so unhappy before.

—Fill sprout's glass up, Garwood said, while I talk to the waiter. I feel like drinking something strong. This champagne's just fizz water.

He got up and walked unsteadily away and came back shortly with the waiter and more glasses.

—Got a bottle of choice bourbon, he said. Ripe stuff. I drink it like a baby. Never affects me.

Garwood waved to some friends at another table. He was beginning to leave out the short words when he talked.

—Folks, he said, developing his big voice and striking an easy pose, hand in coat, want you meet my friend, young John Wickliff Shawnessy, hope the Republic. Boy's enlisting the Army morrow. Drink around honor of our boy, John, and s'on me, Ez.

Johnny took a bow while the orchestra played 'The Battle Cry of Freedom.' Everybody began to sing. Johnny put his hand below the table and it touched Nell's hand, which was ungloved and deliciously passive in his. On the stirring rhythms of the chorus it gave his hand tender little squeezes. Garwood got funnier and funnier, and Nell and Johnny laughed more and more. Johnny couldn't remember when he had been so happy. There was no doubt about it—Garwood Jones was a great guy, when he wanted to be.

Some time later, Garwood went off for another bottle of bourbon.

—I reckon you think I've got pretty wild and wicked since the old days in the County, Nell said.

—You never could be wicked, Nell. Of course, people do change.

—Not every way, Nell said.

Her voice was husky. A wisp of her hair kept falling down over her cheek. Johnny had her hand again under the table. It was all right in a way because, after all, everything was meant to make him happy before leaving for the wars.

—This bourbon is really ripe stuff, Garwood said, solemnly trying to fit himself into his chair. Never affects me. I can drink it all night like a baby.

Nell filled his glass, and when Garwood tossed it off to confirm the statement just made, she filled it up again.

A little later Garwood was standing and trying to make a speech, though the Savoy-Rialto was beginning to be very noisy, with a number of officers on furlough singing regimental songs.

—Garwood's pretty tight, isn't he? Johnny said.

—Terrible, Nell said, thoughtfully, as she refilled Garwood's empty glass. I've never seen him this way before.

—I don't think he can stand much more, Johnny said. Do you think we can get him home?

It was around twelve o'clock that Nell and Johnny helped Garwood up the steps and out into the street where they hailed a carriage. Garwood peeled a greenback from his roll and told the driver he was hired for the night.

—I feel like riding, he said. O, night, o, stars! Nothing's too good for our boy John.

Five minutes later, he was out cold. Johnny and the carriage driver deposited Garwood at his bachelor's quarters, where a young lawyer received the body with equanimity.

—Just put it over there, boys. Never saw Garwood so pied before. You know, he really doesn't drink much. Too golderned ambitious.

When Johnny and Nell were alone in the carriage, they didn't say much for a while.

—I guess you—you intend to marry Garwood, Johnny said.

—He keeps asking me, Nell said. But I don't know——

They put their heads back on the seat of the carriage and let the wind stream over them as they rode on rivers of the night toward the place where the gaslamps came together.

—I *wish* you weren't going off to the War, Johnny.

—Going off to the War seems to be one of the nicest things I've ever done, Johnny said.

—Maybe they'll put you in camp around here, Nell said, at Shanks or somewhere.

—Would you like that?

—Yes, I would, Johnny, Nell said gravely.

Her hair had been blown down by the wind, and she raised her arms to lift it and put it back. As they passed a gaslamp, her eyes glowed greenly and then darkly. She took a pin from her mouth. He put his arms around her little waist and felt how gently her face swayed toward him. Her bare arms circled his neck and pulled his face down to hers.

Desire. Desire was of the river and the pale flesh that moved in a green pool of the river. Desire.

He had come back to Raintree County sooner than he had expected, had come back briefly to his older memory of it, had become again the poet and possessor of its beauty. The river ran, a sinuous green, swelling and swelling between treebordered banks to heat-blurred horizons. He would climb up again with a slow stroking of oars to the summit of that serpent water, glide upward in the swooning heat, upward to where the river joined the lake, to where with a slow anguish the strong waters found their way through marsh and shallow, tarn and tangling swamp into the tepid pool of Paradise, in the very center of Raintree County. *Oft was I weary when I toiled with thee.*

Desire! He would know desire, noontide young desire beside the river. O, he would dig his hands into the tingling earth of the twin mounds. He would breathe grass and warm earth in the sunshine, clover and cut hay and dandelions. He would rise and run through cloverstubble toward the third mound, the flowering one a little way off. His cheeks would be raked with a thousand tingling tips of shaken hair beside the river.

He would return to Lake Paradise. Somewhere here the tawny tree was standing, bright pollen fell at noontime by the river.

He would also be the runner through a public place, the string-breaker, applauded by thousands. He would not stop but keep right on until he reached the place of secret waters, thrust to the very quick of life, his form softly flayed and flung by the vines and the beautiful flowers, the tall tough weeds and the odorous grasses in the place where the Raintree grows.

Make way, make way for the Hero of Raintree County! Make way for the young god with sunlight in his hair! He has humbled himself and performed great labors, he has been chastened, he has starved and wanted food—shall he not have at last the golden apples? Make way for the Hero of Raintree County!

Johnny and Nell held on to each other as if they were afraid something was about to separate them forever, and even when he handed her down from the carriage in front of the little white house on Pennsylvania Avenue, they couldn't say good night.

—Do you think your aunt will mind your being out so late, Nell?

—Aunt loves Garwood, Nell said. I'll tell her it was Garwood that had me out late.

—This is pretty hard on Garwood, Johnny said. Not that he doesn't deserve it.

—He said the evening was on him, Nell said. Poor Garwood.

—Tell me one thing, Johnny said. Are you going to go on saying no to him?

—Yes, I will, Johnny. For a while.

—You understand, Nell, my marriage still stands in the eyes of the law. There isn't anything that can be done about it, even if Susanna is hundreds of miles away from here, and I never see her again. She's started back to her family already, you know. We managed to get a passage for her through the lines. It was her own wish. It's all a closed book, but I can't forget having read it.

—I understand, Johnny.

They walked silently arm in arm to the back of the house. When he started to kiss her good-by, she clung to him.

—I don't want to let you go, Johnny, she said. I'm afraid.

—So am I.

—Where are you going tonight?

—I don't know. I haven't a room yet.

—I hate to let you go. I'm afraid something will happen to you.

—Nothing will happen to me, dear.

—Johnny, I love you so much. Why don't you come in with me for a while? If Aunt isn't awake, we can slip in. I have my own place up the back stair.

It seemed to Johnny Shawnessy, standing in the July dark, that life had decided to be good to him again. It was time to be affirmative and forget conventions. Let the wounded republic of war and moral obligation reclaim him on the morrow: tonight he would lose himself in the sweet republic of love. He would have a reluctant, last good night, a long farewell.

They slipped around to the back of the house, and Nell went up on the back porch stealthily and pushed open the door.

Aunt was up. She turned up a huge lamp, and Johnny could see a wattled, proper face peering out into the night. Nell gave a sharp gasp, and then said,

—O, dear, Aunt, I'm so glad you're up. Just a minute, and I'll tell Mr. Shawnessy. We've been working late at the Commission to get off a rush order of bandages. Garwood was busy and had his friend Mr. Shawnessy bring me safe home. Aunt Hepzibah, Mr. Shawnessy.

—Good evening, Ma'am, Johnny said. Pleased to meet you.

—Good morning, young man, Aunt Hepzibah said.

—I'll be right in, Aunt, Nell said. Mr. Shawnessy, I think you have my purse.

She stepped down off the porch, while Aunt retired.

—I'm sorry, Johnny. Isn't that bad luck! But you'll call on me again, won't you?

—Sure. Of course, the Army gets me today.

—You'll get a leave or something, Nell said. And the War can't last forever. Especially now that we've found each other again, Johnny.

Johnny didn't get Under the Raintree that night; yet he had the most intense possession of a person he had ever known. He walked for ten minutes before he remembered that he didn't have a place to stay for the night. A memory of the afternoon came punctually back to him, and he hunted up the Greer House.

It was a dive.

Inside, the clerk was sound asleep on a couch, and the lobby was empty. Johnny found Flash Perkins' name and room number in the register. He walked up to the second floor and knocked on a door. He could hear voices and laughter in the room.

After a significant pause, the door opened, and Flash Perkins stuck his face out. He had on his big Western hat and from what Johnny could see, nothing else.

—Jumpin' Jehosaphat! Flash said. Jack Shawnessy!

He looked perplexed for a moment, his eyes childlike and troubled. Then the fierce smile came back, and the skin on his forehead ridged up.

—Listen, I got a dame in here.

—O, Johnny said. Excuse me, I——

—Shucks, no bother at all! Flash said. She's a good sport. Mabel, meet my old friend, Jack Shawnessy, same place I come from, one a the smartest son-of-a——

—Don't bother, Johnny said quickly. I just came to tell you I've got a place to stay for the night and I'll see you tomorrow, so long.

As Johnny walked down the hall, he heard Flash Perkins yelling after him,

—Hey, come on back, pardner! Have a little drink with Mabel and I. Cuss it, it's our last day, ain't it, before we sojer! Hell, I figger we're entitled to . . .

A SOLDIER'S FAREWELL

(Epic Fragment from the *Free Enquirer*)

It is a heart-warming and spine-tingling sight to see, this leavetaking of young men for the unpredictable hazards of war. The most pulchritudinous damsels of the community attired in their Sunday best come down to the station to see them off. And many manly young brows receive the chaste kiss of parting, the tribute due

TO THOSE WHO ARE ABANDONING

ALL THAT THEY

HOLD

—DEAR me, whispered the Perfessor, the General goes right on acting as if he were in the middle of a Civil War battle.

The banquet was over, and the General was addressing the crowd. He stood like a boxer, left foot forward, right shoulder back. His words came in short hard bursts, as though he were barking commands or trying to shout above cannon. His pauses were decisive and rhythmical, but often without conformity to the grammatical pattern of his sentences.

—I am reminded—he was saying, looking at my old—comrades of the Grand—Army of the Republic——

Applause came from the two hundred people who had been eating at the banquet tables. As the sound of the clapping roared and subsided, the General kept his chin high, his martial eye fixed on a distant point. His right hand crept to his coat and slipped two inches inside.

—I am reminded of—the great effort necessary—to form and fashion—the noble instrument—with which in her hour of peril—the Republic was saved. In these days of peace—it is hard to conceive—the monstrous labors—by which this country was preserved one Nation—indissoluble—with Freedom—and Justice for All!

The General thrust his hand unashamedly all the way into his coat and waited for the applause to die.

Then did you fight in that old war to preserve the Union? Were you a soldier and . . .

—Brave men are not—moulded in battle only. The fashioning of a soldier—is a long and costly—and strenuous process. We had to take men—from every walk of life—shopkeepers, farmboys—teachers, students, factory workers—and hammer them into shape. In the sanguinary glories of combat—we are likely to forget—the long hours of drill—the frequent sickness—the prolonged watches—the rough comradeship and complete democracy—of the training period. Perhaps we even complained a little——

Laughter began at the Veterans' Table and ran lightly over the swaying faces in the schoolhouse yard.

—But somehow there emerged—from this period—the survivors—the strong of heart—the sound of limb—the men who fought—for freedom and the flag—from Shiloh to Savannah!

Applause in the schoolhouse yard was a brief beating of hands in the immensity of the plain through which the National Road pierced thinly, its progress marked by telegraph lines that distantly touched the earth.

—Those hours of camp were not—without their memories of fun—and boisterous comradeship—and in the alembic of time—even the dark—shines with a kind of brightness—as we—veterans now of the greatest armed—force ever assembled on—the face of the earth—the lone survivors of—those scenes, remember . . .

Tents beside the river, and faces of soldiers on green plains beside the river. Remember.

Faces of dead men, you are gone like light words or the forms of flowers, you that were once young in the harsh day beside the river.

Faces of comrades, faces of tenters, I remember your mobile and changing expressions. For you I shall build a private monument of recollection. For you the greatest shaft ever erected by mankind! For you great wreaths of stone and the stone mouths of cannon and petrifactions of beauty!

Say, did you fight in that Great War for the Preservation of—— Did you know such a one named—— Did you camp by the river called—— Did you know so and so who is——

I remember swimmers in rivers, bodies of young men stripped of names, bathing in the webbed waters of the Republic. I remember beauty, corruption, death beside the river. I will strike a tableau that never appeared on stone. I will wind the river through it, and there shall stand upon it a city of tents that is gone forever, the little city of a homely name.

You shall have your poet and your sculptor of forms, you lost young men, whose names I remember. You shall not any one die. You shall be stone, and the tides of the Republic will flow forever past the base of your shaft.

Tell me then, did you—fight in that Great—War for the Saving of—the American Republic and—do you remember

Summer— WHAT —1863

FACES HE SAW IN THE CAMPS,

WHAT HOURS HE SPENT MARCHING AND DRILLING,

what names he heard, what jokes he laughed at, what hours and hours he lay at night on a hard cot wishing, what letters he wrote and received, what endless talk he listened to of home, girls, food, politics, news—all this was recorded in the diary of his memory, day by day, during the summer that he trained for the fighting. All this was part of the gray debris of the War as he knew it, all this was part of the process by which confusion became a kind of form, by which the Republic made men into soldiers. During this time he became almost as nameless as when he crept out on the savage side of Lake Paradise and sought desire Under the Raintree, flaying it down with a branch of golden pollen. By that other namelessness he had lost Raintree County for a time, but by this namelessness, he became more fully than ever before a creature of the County, or of that vast extension of it—the Republic. The clothing that he wore was the badge of his alliance to the County, as surely as nakedness was the badge of his alliance to the earth. In his soldier suit he acknowledged oneness with the Republic and with his comrades. He lost himself in them as they in him. He lived for them and was in some measure indistinguishable from them. A whole republic of Raintree Counties had bequeathed these integers to the sum of the Army. And though there was a part of him that remained deeply rooted in the old life, he was amazed by how quickly he blended into the colorless, inchoate mass of the Army. Only so could a soldier be soldier and survive. Only so could the Republic be served. For a time he ceased to be critical of the beliefs that he had set himself to defend. He became naïve, acquiescent; he was content for a while to be the instrument of an idea, instead of its engenderer.

And yet it was an intensely individual experience that he had in the Army. It was somehow all conducted in the purest Johnny Shawnessy tradition. And if he had been obliged to choose from his memories of the training period one to be graven into stone, as worthy to survive from all the others, it would have been a casual and rather unsoldierly experience that he had about three weeks after he began his training.

That day five tentmates had been set to digging holes in the ground at the far side of Camp Shanks. Several hundred yards distant were buildings and tents, an orderly pattern lying beside the river outside Indianapolis. In the heat of the August afternoon, he could see the first lowlying houses of the city, farmhouses on an entering road, and trees along the river. Through the trees, the cold green water shone.

For three weeks he had been living in the camp, eating, working, drilling. He and the other soldiers walked in long rows together with poles on their shoulders and moved their hands, heads, feet all together at barked commands. They wore suits that were all alike, got up and went to bed all at the same time, touched their stiffened hands to their foreheads in the same way. Everything was punctual and precise. There was a way to do everything. But today this rigorous pattern of life was clearly ephemeral, like the brown tents and wooden barracks that would some day vanish, giving the earth here back to itself. For that matter, the distant city had a temporary look. Only the land looked permanent, and the river flowing among the trees.

—Cuss it! Flash Perkins said. You even have to crap by the book. I don't know about the rest of you bastards, but I'm fed up with the Army. Right now, I'd sure like a souse in that river.

The soldiers stopped working and looked at the river. Besides Johnny, there were three other men, tentmates. Thomas Conwell was a calm, thinfaced boy from an upstate farm. Nate Franklin was a husky, beardless boy from a farm close to the Ohio River. Jesse Gardner was a city-bred boy from Indianapolis, where he had been a bankclerk and an exemplary member of the Methodist Church. Like the majority of trainees, they were all three under eighteen. Johnny felt old by comparison, and Flash Perkins, who was twenty-seven, was referred to sometimes as Pappy and the Old Guy.

Jesse Gardner was having a hard time. At first he had endured the vulgarity of camplife in shocked silence. Then he had begun to object to the rough fun and strident nakedness with which he was surrounded. Soon, he was called 'Mamma's Boy' and 'Sister Jessica' by camp wits like Flash Perkins. During the last week, he had gone silent again and had eaten little. He kept hanging around Johnny, who was the only person to befriend him. The night before, Johnny had heard Jesse crying in his cot.

Flash Perkins had been having as hard a time becoming a soldier, but for different reasons. While Jesse was prompt in accepting discipline, Flash was incapable of taking orders. He had spent hours in the guardhouse. He talked in ranks, wore his uniform in improper ways, and played crude practical jokes, preferring officers as victims. Whenever he obeyed an order or accepted discipline of any kind, he had an insulting grin on his face. He would take any kind of punishment rather than wipe off the grin or curb his tongue. He had upset three officers on a latrine, had set fire to the commanding officer's bed, and had had a woman named Velma in his tent. At night, he woke up the whole camp by imitating screech owls, loons, crows, cows. He had left signs in the latrines reflecting on the ancestral purity and moral character of the commanding officer.

All this was not merely an expression of a fun-loving nature. From the start Flash was deeply contemptuous of the Army or at least that part of it he had seen. He hated the captain of his company, a man named Elmer Bazzle, who had been selected for the position because he had been a lawyer and had booklearning. In reality, Captain Bazzle was a precise, earnest officer, who took his duties to the Republic seriously. But he was a small, pale, nervous man, he had never fired a gun in his life before, his voice was high and uncertain, and he had made some laughable mistakes by sometimes adhering too closely to the book.

As for Johnny Shawnessy, he felt sorry for the Captain and sincerely wished that Flash Perkins would get out of the Army.

But on the day they were digging the ditch, he had been quick to second Flash's suggestion about a swim in the river. He hadn't had a good swim for a year.

—Let's go, he said. They've forgotten about us here. We'd have time to take a dip and get back.

—It's a breach of regulations, Jesse Gardner said. They'll put us all on special duty.

They argued with him, but he maintained his point with finical persistence.

—All right, Jessica, Flash said, you stay and we'll go.

—My name isn't Jessica, Jesse said.

—Reckon it oughta be, Flash said. Maybe you're scared to swim naked. Think you was a girl the way you cover and yelp around. I'm sick of you cryin' around, Jessica.

—My name isn't Jessica, Jesse said.

—Come on, boys, Johnny said. Let's all have just a little dip. Do us good. Come on, Jess.

Jesse put down his spade and followed the other four down to the river. He didn't say another word for a long time.

On the bank of the river, they peeled off hot woolen uniforms and heavy shoes and plunged in. Swimming breaststroke, Johnny could see the pale sheet of the river dwindling to a railroad trestle. The white bodies of his soldier-comrades splashed in the water around him. They had taken off their soldier skins. For a little while, they had resigned from the Republic.

He listened to the sound of cicadas in the trees, watched turtles sunning themselves on distant stones, smelled the fishy smell of the river. He had become primitive, fully at home. The river purified him from soldiering.

—What do they call this yere river? Natie Franklin asked. 'Tain't the Wabash, is it?

Flash Perkins laughed brutally.

—No, son, it's the Mississip, he yelled.

—It's the White River, Johnny said.

—Don't look white to me, Natie said, swimming away to cover his embarrassment.

White river—Wa-pi-ha-ni. He thought of the continuous web of the Indian waters drawn southward to the huge ventricle of the Gulf —Shawmucky, Wapihani, Wabash, Ohio, Mississippi. Somewhere down the woven republic of these shining streets of water, Rebel soldiers were swimming too, splashing the water, smelling the cold green smell, making jokes and laughing.

After a while, the five soldiers swam across the river and climbed up the bank on the other side. They lay down to sun on the soft grass and talked. They felt hungry, discussed food, agreed that they got better cooking at home, expressed a general discontent with the Army.

—No wonder we ain't winnin' this war any faster, Flash Perkins said. You can't win it by diggin' privies. Fide known what a hell of a time it takes to git into the fightin', I'd a never volunteered. Why don't Lincoln git some generals with guts!

—We'd better get back to camp, Jesse Gardner said.

—What was the last time you had a woman, Natie? Flash said.

The boy laughed uncertainly.

—Shucks, I don't know.

—Fie don't git a woman before long, I'm gonna desert, Flash said.

Flash described in some detail what he would do with a pretty girl if he had one. He lay in the sun, talking endlessly, cursing, laughing, teasing the others. Nothing seemed to appall him or give him pause. He was still the most affirmative being Johnny Shawnessy had ever seen, his blue eyes glancing insolence, his forehead ridging up as he laughed his hard, wild laughter. The Army hadn't tamed him. He shook off discipline like the pale water from his supply knit arms and shoulders. He seemed to have no past for regret or future for anxiety. Rarely, during the training period, Johnny had seen a shadow of perplexity touch Flash's face, the eyes go suddenly blank and childlike. But a moment later the bearded, mocking mouth would bare its locked teeth, the forehead would ridge up, and there would follow the crude jest, the horselaugh, or the blow.

The talk of women, food, homefolks, and soldiering went on and on. It was an old talk, this talk of soldiers, destroyers and founders of republics. But older still was the river itself, and the language of its stream drawn from a remote source and distant ages. The river was eternal fixity, container of eternal change. The same bare forms had dropped their clanking weapons and swum in the Rubicon, the Tiber, the Danube, and the Nile. Man bled, lusted, fought, swam, coupled, shrieked, died, decayed in his old battlegrounds and camps beside the impassive waters. Lover and beloved, killer and killed—deep mounds claimed them all. Beyond, on the upland was a camp rectangularly Latin, an ancient formal ground. The legionaries of a new republic were preparing to add white bones and rusty weapons to the old debris of war along the rivers of the world. What did men seek in the fierce pastimes of war and love? What palely lovely flesh whose murmurous name was lost in the conundrum of the river?

A week after Johnny had begun soldiering, on an afternoon when visitors were permitted, Nell Gaither and Garwood Jones had come to camp to see him. Garwood had made some robust jests about Johnny's uniform and had stopped to talk with the commanding officer about legislation for improving the lot of the Brave Defenders of the Flag.

Meanwhile, Johnny had shown Nell around the camp—that is, they had walked through it and out of it and down to the river. Once out of sight, they held hands and walked to the trestle. There they put their arms around each other and made a number of vows. Nell would wait until Johnny got out of the Army, and some way they would work things out. They would write to each other faithfully and regularly. Meanwhile when Johnny got a leave, he would let her know and call for her at the house on Pennsylvania Avenue.

They were so entirely lost in one another that they could hardly talk but simply stood in the deep green shadow under the railroad trestle and held each other tightly, while Johnny kissed Nell's curved red mouth over and over. Her eyes were a swimming greenness close to his own in the river air. Her whitefleshed body twisted in his arms, tenderly responsive.

Johnny was aware that it was one of his epic moments, with nothing to mar the perfection of feeling. He knew that his humble uniform was a badge of valor to Nell; in her arms he became in truth, briefly, what he was supposed to be—the young preserver and defender. They had found each other thus momentarily in a greater Raintree County. Now they wore a costume called the Civil War, but it was summer, and the river made its old reedwoven music near them.

Later on, a train came thundering toward the trestle. They remained wordlessly embraced, as Johnny leaned back against one of the huge uprights of the trestle and watched the black wheels grinding over. Soot dropped in the still air. Stink of coalgas killed the subtle life-scents of the river. The valley of the river was filled up with the iron unhappy shriek of the whistle. Johnny felt the woman in his arms tighten and tremble. But when the train had passed, she laughed, and then, as it was very late, they had walked back to camp.

Back in camp, Garwood had thumped Johnny on the back and had id,

—John, you sure look a scream in that monkey suit.

Johnny and Nell gravely shook hands at parting. Garwood drove f in a fancy buggy, and Nell leaned out and waved her parasol at hnny. Her small face receding in the summer evening had re-inded him of a photographic image that he had tossed into the awmucky some years before on a December night. The eyes shone istily. The mouth, curved with love and compassion, was like mething painted on marble and made to come alive. The parasol ntly rose and fell. The face leaning out had finally withdrawn to the buggy, and Johnny had gone back into the camp.

Now he remembered all this as he lay with his comrades in the nlight by the river. He was also thinking about the leave that was omised him for that evening.

—If a woman come walkin' down that path, Jessica, Flash was ying, what would you do?

—What path? Natie said.

—That path, Flash said, rising on his elbow and pointing down path that wound away from the river toward a road junction and me houses.

He remained pointing, his eyes naïve and troubled, and then his rehead made ridges, his lips curled, and he said,

—Jehosaphat! they *is* a woman walkin' down that path!

The five soldiers stood up and ran down the bank and plunged to the river. When they came up puffing and blowing, hiding in ater up to their chins, there were two women standing on the bank oking at them. The women were garishly dressed. One, a thin, omely girl, who was pulling back on her companion's hand, didn't pear to be over seventeen. The other was a well-fleshed young oman in her twenties. Only her bold, hard look, Johnny thought, pt her from being pretty. Her mouth was permanently turned up the left side, more sneer than smile. Her eyes, large with distinct shes, stared with unashamed interest.

—I told you we shouldn't have come, Jesse Gardner said.

—Come on in, girls! Flash yelled. The water's fine!

The older of the two girls stood smiling and tapping her right oetoe with her parasol. She nodded her head and wrinkled up her nose derisively. Johnny noticed that her shoe was all scuffed and old. He could see her ankle.

—You boys soldiers? she said.

—We aim to be, Flash said, acting as spokesman. You like soldiers?

—Maybe, the girl said.

The younger girl whispered something to her companion, and they talked in low voices heatedly for a moment.

—Those girls are no good, Jesse whispered.

His teeth were chattering, and he was very pale.

—You know what I think? he said. I think they're——

—Say, girls, how about a little fun? Flash said.

He was standing up with his shoulders clear of the water, his teeth bared, his beard dripping.

—Whadda yuh mean? the older girl said, appraisingly, still tapping her shoetoe.

—You know what I mean, Flash said.

The younger one engaged the other in another whispered discussion.

—Not me, Johnny said. Leave me out of this, Flash.

—Me too, said the other boys.

—I'm just stringin' 'em along, Flash whispered. Shucks, this'll be fun.

The woman said,

—You really mean it? You ain't just kiddin'?

—Do I look like I'm kiddin'? Flash said.

The girl looked thoughtfully up and down the river.

—You got any money?

—Sure, Flash said. How much you want?

—O, I don't know, the girl said, tapping her shoe. All of you—or just——

—Sure, sure, Flash said.

—Five dollars maybe? the girl said. That's just . . .

SOMETHING FOR THE BOYS

(Epic Fragment from the *Free Enquirer*)

The local citizenry have done everything in their power to make the soldiers feel at home. Literally nothing is too good for 'the boys, as they are universally called. With one common charitable impulse, the people of the City have agreed to show their gratitude for the lads who are risking their all so that the folks at home may still enjoy those creature comforts to which they are accustomed. . . .

Flash suddenly gave a loud, savage laugh.

—Hell, where would I git five dollars!

He bared his teeth and laughed louder, beating his ribs.

—Five dollars! Hell, I didn't say the whole camp. Five dollars!

Johnny hated Flash. He blushed with shame and pity for the girls on the bank and for himself and all mankind.

—Come on, Flash, he said. Let them go.

—Five dollars! Flash yelled. Jesus, whadda yuh think we are—generals!

The woman slowly blushed through her painted cheeks. Her underlip protruded like an angry child's. The skinny younger girl plucked at her sleeve, saying,

—Come on, Lizzie, let's go.

The older girl shook herself free.

—Goddamn you! she said. You goddam soldiers are no good!

—What language! Flash yelled. Five dollars! That's a good one. I was goin' to charge you.

—That to you! the girl said, with an upswung motion of her skirt.

—You girls go away from here, Jesse Gardner said in a loud, high voice. Go on away. Can't you see we haven't got any clothes on?

—You tell her, Jessica, Flash said, still laughing.

—Listen, runt, the woman said to Jesse, I hope you and loudmouth don't desert before the Rebs gits a chance at yuh. You're all yeller, all you soldiers.

—Aw, shet up! Flash said. Go on and git out a here.

—I'd like to see you make me leave, the girl said.

—Stick around then, Flash said, if you want an eyeful.

He started swimming and walking toward the opposite shore where the uniforms were, and reaching the shallow water, stood up and walked out.

The other girl had moved on down the path, but the talkative one held her ground and laughed, squeezing her sides. She screamed with laughter. She beat her ribs.

—Aw, shet up, Flash said.

—Come on, Tom Conway said, let's make a rush for it.

Johnny, Tom, and Natie followed Flash out and got behind some bushes. The girl was still standing on the far side laughing.

—Go home to your maws, you runts, she said.

—What a whore! Flash said. Say, look at Jessica, would yuh!

Jesse Gardner was still in the river.

—Go on away, he said pleadingly to the girl. Please go away.

The girl stood and looked at him.

—Please go away, he said. Haven't you got any decency?

Flash began to laugh again.

—Come on, boys, let's git dressed. We got to dig those craphouses. Hey, Jessica!

Jesse looked at Flash. His blue lips trembled.

—Listen, Jessica, Flash said, we got to go now. If the Captain asks about you, I'll jist tell 'im that the last time I seen you, you was down here with a couple whores.

—Please go away, Jesse said to the woman.

—Why, you little chickenbreasted runt, the girl said, I wouldn't even *spit* on you!

—Come on out, Johnny called. It won't kill you.

—I won't do it, Jesse said. Make her go away.

—Do you think I want to see you! the girl said. You soldiers are no damn good.

She turned and walked away without looking back.

Jesse came out of the water, trembling with indignation.

—Why—why—why—those girls would as soon look at a man naked as—as—as——

Flash doubled up laughing.

—Put yer dress on, Jessica, let's go back.

Jesse made a rush at Flash and hit him in the face. Flash grabbed him by the arm and flung him down hard in a clump of bushes. Johnny and the others kept Jesse from trying to renew the fight. There was bad feeling all around except for Flash, who was still laughing as they went back to the camp.

When they reached the place where they had been digging, Captain Bazzle was standing there waiting for them.

—You men disobeyed regulations, he said. Where were you?

As usual, he was deadly in earnest, his voice high and nervous.

—We went swimming, sir, Johnny said. Just a dip to cool off.

—It doesn't seem like a big matter to you, the Captain said, but how do you expect us to win this war if soldiers disobey regulations whenever they want to? What if the frontline soldiers felt they could run off any time they wanted a little recreation?

—If we was frontline soldiers, Flash said, we'd be doin' somethin' besides diggin' holes.

—Watch your language, Private, Captain Bazzle said sharply.

—Keep your shirt on, Captain, Flash said, his forehead ridging, or I'll take a hand to you yet.

—You're under arrest, Perkins, the Captain said. Report to the guard.

Flash stepped across one of the open ditches toward the Captain. His fists were clenched, and his teeth were bared smiling. His eyes glared fixedly at the Captain's face.

With a quick, nervous movement, Captain Bazzle pulled a pistol out of his coat. His lips were bloodless and set. He cocked the pistol and took deliberate aim at Flash's chest. Smiling, Flash took another step and another, his eyes fixed on the Captain's face. The Captain's cheek muscles twitched. He closed one eye and sighted.

Just then Johnny leaped on Flash and knocked him down. Tom and Natie helped, but it took five minutes of hard fighting to wear Flash out and hold him. Johnny got his face bruised, and Natie Franklin got kicked in the stomach. Flash cursed all the time and fought like a wildcat, but he never stopped smiling. They carried him back to the camp, where his hands and feet were tied and he was put into a small shack on a cot. Johnny looked in at him through the window.

—It was for your own good, Flash, he said. The Captain would have shot you sure. You'll just have to learn to take orders.

Flash didn't seem to bear any grudge.

—Shucks, he said, I wisht I hadn't got so goddern fresh with that gal down there by the river. I sort of took a shine to her. When I git out of here, I'm gonna look her up.

The Captain came out of a tent and spoke to Johnny. His forehead was beaded with sweat. His cheek twitched. He gave a short, nervous laugh.

—I thought I was going to kill that man, he said. Thanks for helping out. I never killed a man before, and I don't want to start with one of my own men. I'd've been court-martialed. By the way, I might as well tell you now. The command here has been watching you, Shawnessy. They consider you a first-rate soldier. You've been promoted to corporal.

—Yes, sir, Johnny said. Thank you, sir.

—And another thing. All leaves have been cancelled for tonight. There's been a change of plans. General Jake Jackson is in camp, just back from the front. It appears they need men bad down in Tennessee. Big operations under way. We may see action sooner than we thought.

That night, the soldiers in Johnny's camp and all the others were told to make ready to leave. Johnny found time to look in on Flash. It was so dark in the shack, he couldn't see Flash's face.

—Hey, Flash, he said.

—Yeah?

—We're breaking up camp and going south tomorrow.

—You mean we're goin' to fight?

—Sooner or later. We're going south.

Flash gave a cowboy yell and kicked the sides of the shack with manacled feet.

—You'd better be a good soldier and get out of there, Johnny said.

—Tell 'em I'll be good, Flash said. This is what I jined up fer.

That night Johnny lay awake for a time. Would it be such a strange thing, he wondered, if he got up from his cot and left this foolish collection of shacks and tents by the river, and walked through the night until he found Nell waiting for him in the breathing darkness on the porch of a house in Indianapolis?

Always there had been barriers. If it wasn't the Army, it was something else. Men were always fencing themselves in with rigorous Raintree Counties. Men were always drawing lines on the earth and daring each other to cross them. Men and women were always wearing uniforms of some kind, by which they proved their enlistment in the great militia of respectability, piety, duty, temperance, morality. For a brief while in the afternoon, he had touched the primitive source of life again, had lain innocent by the river. But the soldier couldn't really take off his uniform, couldn't really purify himself. In becoming a soldier he had multiplied the barriers. The soldier could have no love, except with a painted face and costing a coin. Evil, hatred, and killing were almost as old as the river. In a casual afternoon, he had seen the oldest corruption of life and the almost corruption of death. Suddenly out of the unwilled sources of himself the red passion flared!

And now long trains were passing in the night, crossing the trestles that crossed the rivers. They were bearing him away from another brief intersection with his love. Where did the great trains come to rest at last?

Suddenly, beneath his shut eyes, with piercing intensity he repictured Nell's face leaning out of the buggy as she waved good-by, and there came to him the words of a recent song by Stephen Foster that had run much in his mind during the past year, because by coincidence it bore the name of his beloved.

> We parted in the springtime of life, Nell and I,
> With all our gushing joys in their bloom.
> But now we've met the world's busy strife, Nell and I,
> And suffered from its dark, chilling gloom.
> But my heart will sigh, for those days gone by,
> That dwell in my memory's soft refrain.
> We parted in the springtime of life, Nell and I,
> And I'll never see her bright smiles again.

Johnny had a feeling that his love-affair with Nell had happened long ago and was already enshrined in memory.

> We built our little huts by the shore, Nell and I,
> And we covered them with bright colored shells.
> We gathered moss and fern from the moors, Nell and I,
> And we plucked the dewy flowers from the dells.
> But the days rolled round, and the dark world frowned
> As Time with its bitter cares fled on.
> We left our little huts on the shore, Nell and I,
> And we left our brightest hopes in their dawn.

It was the music of an innocent love of two childlike creature living in a world of their own exalted fancy in which all was summer, misty and nocturnal.

We wandered by the bright running streams, Nell and I,
And we gamboled on the wide grassy lawn.
And met again in light sportive dreams, Nell and I,
When the weary hours of twilight were flown.
And our love was true, but a coldness grew.
'Twas caused by an unrelenting foe.
We'll play nevermore on the lawns, Nell and I,
Nor wander where the bright rivers flow.

The sad melody of this song haunted him into his sleep, and his dreams that night were woven with emotions of farewell, as the face of a girl leaning from a buggy receded down the long streets of his sentimental youth.

The following day, the men were assembled to hear General Jake Jackson. The General, one of the famous fighting officers of the War in the West, gave a fighting speech. He stood out in front of the ranks, hatless, his coat covered with medals. He was set like a fighter just ready to deliver the knockout punch. He talked with his mouth, his bearded chin, his fists.

—Hot darn! Flash Perkins said. There's the man I wanna serve under.

—Boys, the General said, you're being moved out today. You'll get some more training in Tennessee, and then some of you'll be attached to my corps. We need men and we need 'em bad. We've got the damn traitors on the run now, and we mean to keep 'em that way. I don't want anybody in my corps that isn't ready to go in there any time and fight like hell. We mean to run those bastards right into the sea before the summer's over. It won't be any tea party. The Reb is a goddam good soldier, damn his guts. I ought to know—I been fightin' 'im for two years. But he can't stand up to a real hell-raisin' Westerner. His cause is rotten to the core. I know you men don't like this camp routine, and I don't blame you. They tell me you're spoilin' for a fight. Well, I'm here to tell you that

BEFORE YOU KNOW IT YOU'LL FIND YOURSELVES IN
THE GODDAMNDEST FUSS THAT
EVER

—ALMIGHTY PROVIDENCE DECREED, the General was saying, the Battle, and the Battle was joined. Which among us can—forget the first shock—of actual combat—the energy and resolution—with which the green and untried—defenders of the Flag—hurled themselves upon the foe! Many of those here assembled—have fought in several of those great—battles by which the safety—of the Republic was assured. How proud you must feel—to have had some humble part in the—forging of those great—events! To name the several—and separate actions in which—these men have participated—would be to call the roll—of all the great—battles of the West—Shiloh—Donelson—Corinth—Vicksburg. . . .

Mr. Shawnessy turned the General's manuscript unobtrusively, hunting for a certain chapter.

Then did you fight, comrade—in that great war in the West, were you—one of those legions? Were you a part of——

(Epic Fragment from *Fighting for Freedom*)

Those vast operations on which so many hopes were founded, those intricate manoeuvres in the Fall of 1863, whereby Rosecrans hoped to trap the Confederate commander Bragg and hurl the Rebel forces staggering back from the bastion city of Chattanooga, the Gateway to the South, had finally brought about, sooner than either commander had expected and in a manner anticipated by no one, that two days' bloody conflict which took its scarlet name from a . . .

Who can tell now the names of the rivers we crossed and the mountains we scaled! Those were our first marches. Who can tell how we pulled the guns through the passes, how we tramped on the rocky roads, cursing the grades, we that were men of the plain, how we burst our bootleather taking the bastion city! Who can show now—what sculptor of battles—how we saw for the first time the city of scrofulous shacks on the lip of the river, beneath great mountains! Who can tell with what ardor we sought the battle! Who will show how at last we came together, two armies of thousands of half-bearded boys! The young recruits ran to their first battle, and some were chosen. An inch or a second's wavering, a twist of the body, a slip of the trigger, a flash of the sun, a diverting branch, and one went on to take his place with the dotards of battle, the fighters-over-and-over of old campaigns, and one was chosen to fall and be young forever, lost and covered up in the words of the books about battle.

Dead or alive, they are here beside this . . .

(Epic Fragment from *Fighting for Freedom*)

. . . little stream that joins the Tennessee River just below Chattanooga, and which, by that ironical providence whereby the earth sometimes seems to anticipate and mock the follies of mankind, had borne for centuries an Indian name signifying in the Cherokee language 'The River of Death' and commemorating perhaps some legendary battle of the Indians before the white man brought civilization and the weapons of civilization to this savagely beautiful land of rivers and mountains. Here in September of 1863, along the wooded slopes and banks of the little river, two great armies ran head-on, and there ensued a contest of courage, skill, and endurance which has made mournfully appropriate forever the dark and musical name of

September 19–21— —CHICKAMAUGA, —1863

THE STAFF OFFICER SAID.

CHICKAMAUGA CREEK. ANYWAY, THAT'S WHAT

they tell me. The woods over there on the far side are lousy with Rebs. We'll be fighting for sure in the morning.

He saluted and rode off. In the pale dawn, Corporal Johnny Shawnessy could see the campfires reflected in the creek. He rolled up in his blanket and tried to sleep again. But he kept thinking of the name Chickamauga. After days of marching, he had arrived at a name. Things were coming into focus.

On the far side of this creek, there was perhaps a man now sleeping who would kill John Wickliff Shawnessy of Raintree County, Indiana, or be killed by him. This man was maybe cold, tired, bruised, wet, lonely, unhappy, and hundreds of miles from home just like himself. This man was the Enemy. He and Johnny Shawnessy had been slowly approaching each other all their lives. Now they had almost met in some impersonal, terrible meeting called a battle.

Here was how the Battle had been shaping. A month before, his regiment had moved from Camp Shanks to Louisville, Kentucky. There they were brigaded with veteran soldiers and moved on. They had seen depots and Army bases choked with men and supplies, going south through Kentucky. With less than a month's training, they had become part of the Army of the Cumberland, in the Corps commanded by General Jake Jackson. For weeks, then, they marched. They marched up and down in the land and back and forth. They hauled their artillery and supplies up and down beautiful mountains. They forded rivers. They rode in troop trains. They marched, bivouacked, marched, bivouacked, marched. They performed prodigies that would never get into the newspapers. Just pulling a heavy gun out of a mudhole, over the hump of a Tennessee mountain, or across a river was an epic of ingenuity. One night's sleep in the rain was a saga of misery. A twenty-mile march through mountainous country was an anabasis of endurance. When you put millions of such deeds together, you got the campaign that led to the taking of Chattanooga.

For somewhere in this process of marching, during which they hadn't seen a single Rebel, Chattanooga fell, a Great Victory.

Meanwhile, Corporal Johnny Shawnessy had begun to hate this earth that made him suffer so much. He was a man from the flat country, and he now perceived a new beauty in the level of Raintree County. It tranquillized the spirit, it was the image of space, it suggested civilization and good roads. It meant peace and plenty and contentment. Flash Perkins expressed the opinion of them all when he said,

—Why in the name of Ole Hippopotamus anybody'd fight as hard as the Rebs have for a country like this beats the hell outta me!

Two weeks before, they had marched out of Chattanooga south through a wide valley between Lookout Mountain and the Tennessee River. They were supposed to be outflanking Bragg. Then, less than a week before, in the night of September 13, they had been awakened and commanded back to Chattanooga by forced marches. The word went that Bragg was concentrating unexpectedly in front of the town and that their Corps had to get back before the rest of the Army was smashed in detail. For three days, they had retraced their steps over the narrow mountain roads, dragging artillery and supplies with them. Two days before, on the 17th of September, they were closing in. On the 18th the word was that the Rebels had not yet launched their main attack. On the night of the 18th and 19th of September, they had been brought up through a wood, still many miles from Chattanooga, and in the darkness, hungry and exhausted, had made camp.

They were in contact with the main Army. They had got there in time for the Battle.

Wrapped in a thin blanket, Johnny had fallen asleep, vaguely aware that he was close to a little stream winding through wooded and hilly country. He hadn't slept well: all night long the roads and passes were choked with artillery caissons, supply wagons, guns, cavalry, troops, a tide of confusion moving toward a battle.

In the dawn, he had awakened and seen the little creek and heard its name, and after that he couldn't sleep. Before it was fully day, the brigade was up, and the men ate. Mist was rising from the creek. It might have been early morning on the Shawmucky in some of the wilder parts of Raintree County.

Some distance to the right, a road approached and forded the stream, and at that point stood a white frame building with clear black letters on it:

LEE & GORDON'S
MILLS

Across the creek, Johnny could see a long, low mountain.

The cold, pale waters of Chickamauga Creek ran on over dead stones in the dead light of the beginning day. Across the river were cornfields and a long, low mountain and the Enemy. To this place the Hero of Raintree County had come, life's American, John Wickliff Shawnessy. Here or somewhere near in a few hours, a piece of iron might hit him and tear the life from his body, and here he might fall, absurdly stiff and still, in the sight of this little creek, this cornfield, these trees, this mountain. In all the designs he had ever had of his life, he had never allowed for such a thing. He had never supposed that he could really expire on an unfamiliar earth, hundreds of miles from Raintree County.

He was cut off from all human help. He looked at his comrades and no longer knew them with human warmth and knowing. Their names were Flash Perkins, Jesse Gardner, Natie Franklin, Thomas Conway, and so on, but in this moment they had ceased to be persons with names. They were nothing to him. They couldn't help him. Each would be wholly preoccupied with himself. Each would be wishing that he personally could emerge safe from the Battle, no matter what else might happen. Now the mannerisms and personal whims of each one didn't matter. It didn't matter that one was more handsome or intelligent than another. Each was simply a man facing death.

He was sick with fear. He lay weakly on the ground, flat on his belly, and kept his face down so that no one would see how scared he was. He hadn't even seen the Enemy, he was for the moment perfectly safe, and yet he was despicably scared. How would he ever be able to endure actual combat? How would he ever be able to stand up to wild men yelling and rushing at him with bayonets? Did he really want to defeat the Enemy so badly?

Johnny tried hard to think of the Cause. Now he must be a soldier, the anonymous instrument of a great idea. All memories of himself as an individual with a name were gratuitous hardships now.

But it was no use. Now for the first time the Enemy had acquired a personal meaning. The Enemy was a heartless something that cared nothing at all for the personal sanctity of John Wickliff Shawnessy. It was now really possible that a complete stranger from the South would thrust a bayonet into Johnny Shawnessy and destroy the precious thing that he was.

This would be the most pitiful murder since the beginning of time. To do this would be wantonly to destroy the earth and explode like a child's balloon the whole structure of the Republic.

He kept staring at the other side of the creek but could see no movement in the woods, no sign of the Enemy. But the word all up and down the line was that the Rebels were going to attack.

By eight o'clock with the sun already high and bright, the brigade had been moved to the rear of another brigade, where it would remain in support. The mill was lost sight of. All through the woods troops were marching, guns were being unlimbered, officers came and went, bearing dispatches, supply wagons moved. For nearly two hours, the men of Johnny's regiment remained in a deep wood, where they couldn't see the creek. It was fine weather. The foliage was a rich summer green. The men sat or lay at full length, talking in low voices.

After a while, Johnny tried to fix his attention on what was happening around him. On a road near-by that went down to the mill he could see troops marching. From the shouted orders and the haste, the springing steps, the drawn, excited faces of the men, it was evident that they were expecting to fight. Now and then a wagon train came through and was driven up a road to the right in the direction of Chattanooga away from the creek. Regimental flags appeared in the woods on either side. Staff officers galloped through and through the trees. The flags, the horses, the hurrying, cursing soldiers streaming along the road, the calls from the forest on either side, the bright morning sunshine, the swarming of uniformed men in the hills and hollows, the turning of all the hundreds of faces toward the creek made Corporal Johnny Shawnessy feel that the battle which was about to be fought was like a gigantic celebration. Except for the anticipated shock of the fighting, he might be on a picnic somewhere. It didn't seem possible that all this color and movement was about to result in killing.

Meanwhile there was a good deal of talk up and down the lines.

—When do you reckon they'll hit us?

—Maybe we'll hit them first.

—I wisht I was home on the old farm.

—Elmer, you be sure to mail that letter fer me, if I git hit.

What disturbed Johnny most was the fact that nothing seemed to be planned. Nothing was settled. No one knew anything for sure. Obviously the Union position had been an improvisation—else why should thousands of men be marched fifty miles away from the scene of the Battle and then fifty miles back so that they arrived bewildered and exhausted? Why were men still pouring along the roads beside the creek when the Rebels were expected to attack at any time?

One thing he was appallingly sure of. If every soldier in the Union Army felt as milky, sick, and helpless as he did, the game was up. The Republic was finished.

About nine o'clock, General Jake Jackson came riding along the lines with his aides. Instantly a cheer went up, in which before he knew it, Johnny had joined. Here at least was a completely confident figure.

General Jackson was hatless, black locks streaming out behind. He bestrode a beautiful, fast horse, and he was smiling as if he expected something wonderful to happen. He stopped a short way from where Johnny was.

—Boys, he said, we may have an attack any time now. We aren't just going to sit around and let 'em come on. We'll meet 'em head-on. Aim for their guts, and give 'em hell.

He stopped and exchanged a few words with an officer. Then he rode up to Johnny's regiment and said,

—I understand you men have never been in battle before. That right?

—Yes, sir. That's right, General, several voices said.

—You're not scared, are you?

—We ain't skeered, General. We're just frightened to death.

The General laughed, and everyone in hearing distance laughed. Johnny laughed too, dismally.

—You boys will be all right, the General said, shaking his chin and his fist at the creek. You're from Indiana, I hear. Well, Indiana boys don't break under fire. Let's give those bastards a thumping they won't forget!

The men gave a cheer. As it faded in the woods, there came from the left a series of deep throaty sounds that rolled in thick waves along the valley of the Chickamauga.

The General jerked his horse straight up, whirled and . . .

(Epic Fragment from *Fighting for Freedom*)

The battle began with heavy shelling of the Union Center. The Rebels followed with an infantry assault in their characteristically impetuous manner, as if they expected to carry the field in a single charge and go thundering right on through to Chattanooga. The fighting began to move down the line to the right, where the Third Corps, not yet fully in position after the forced marches of the days preceding, was lying on its arms. The Union right now sustained an attack of great magnitude, the details of which it would be fatiguing to recite, but suffice it to say that . . .

Corporal Johnny Shawnessy tried to see beyond the distant fence, but trees and bushes blocked his vision.

—Can you see anything, Jack? Flash Perkins said.

—Not a thing.

—Hey, Captain, where are the Rebs?

—You'll see them soon enough.

The noise of the shelling had become louder. Johnny and the others were yelling at the tops of their voices.

A staff officer rode up and said something to the brigade commander. They held a map in their hands and pointed excitedly. The commander jerked his chin up and down forcibly several times. He pointed toward the creek. The staff officer nodded vigorously, saluted, and rode off down the line to the left.

The brigade was ordered forward in line of battle.

—Hell, it's about time, Flash Perkins said. They're fightin' right where we was this mornin'. How come they moved us away?

No one else said anything. The men walked forward through the woods. Johnny's company was to the left of the regimental colors. The brigade went forward in two lines, the men almost shoulder to shoulder. The noise from the creek grew. Smoke began to roll up the hill. Rifle fire was continuous.

Men are being killed there, Johnny said to himself. Men are being killed down there by the creek where I was this morning.

He had never in his life before seen a man killed.

Bullets sang through the forest like angry bees, socking trees. Johnny hunched over. He wanted to throw himself on the ground and dig under. A round shot crashed through near-by trees, a brutal chunk of pure chance, lopping off branches. Johnny saw the spent ball, as big as a man's head, roll harmlessly down a little hill.

—Gosh! a boy said. That might've hit somebody.

No one laughed.

Every now and then a spray of leaves suddenly relaxed and sank to the perpendicular or floated gently to the ground.

At the edge of the wood, the brigade halted at a railfence and everyone went to the ground. A battery of Union guns was firing from a little hill about fifty yards to the right. Around the nearest gun the men made quick, methodical movements, then broke away to left and right. There was a stiff white stream of smoke standing out from the muzzle of the gun. A second later the report struck like a slap on the ears. The gunners ran forward, laid hold of the hand-spike and spokes and ran the gun back into position.

Johnny lay on the ground, mouth open, panting, though he had only been walking. He felt that if the noise should all abruptly cease, his fear would become audible. But, in a way, the noise of the Battle was the noise of his fear.

There was a little fluttering sound seemingly in the air overhead but growing louder. It ended suddenly, and a hundred feet away in front of the fence, the earth spurted in a fountain mixed with black smoke. Dirt rained all over the men in Company A.

—What the hell! Flash Perkins yelled at Johnny, as if he had a personal grudge against him, what're they doin'! How come we don't git in there and whop 'em? We ain't jist gonna sit here and let 'em shell hell out of us, are we?

Johnny lay at the base of the railfence, panting and praying. The fluttering, whining sound came again and again as more shells fell in the field in front of the brigade.

Any one of these shells, Johnny was thinking, any one of these bullets might be for him. He seemed to have an infinite capacity for being afraid. He feared each shell and bullet and he feared them all. He feared them before they were shot and while they were being shot.

Suddenly he was lifted and thrown by the ground. A strong stink and blinding flash stunned him. A shell had landed close by. Someone was hit. He could hear a man saying in a low voice over and over again,

—Please. Please. It's me.

—Stand up, boys! Stand up!

Men were getting to their feet all up and down the line. Johnny got up. The officers were standing in the intervals of the companies.

—They're comin', someone said.

The open field in front sloped to a wood on the far side. Out of this wood men came running, stopping now and then to fire their muskets back toward the creek, then biting cartridges and ramming as they ran. One of the men lay down gently on his face. Another stopped abruptly as if he had just seen a yawning hole at his feet. He teetered exactly like a man reluctant to go over a precipice, dropping his gun and swinging his arms for balance. Then he collapsed backward.

—Them's our men.

—Yeah, but the Rebs are back there too.

Men in Union uniforms kept coming out of the woods. They were not withdrawing straight back toward the Third Brigade, but to the left and right.

Suddenly, Johnny realized that he was seeing men killed. While he had been standing here, half a dozen men had lost their lives in the field before him.

—Load! Load at will!

The word went up and down the line.

Johnny bit a cartridge and rammed it down the barrel. All up and down the line the rammers rang in the barrels, the gunlocks clicked.

—I don't see anything.

—Where are they?

—I don't know. I can't see a thing.

Just then Johnny saw several men in gaps of smoke, approaching the fence at the far end of the field. His first impression was that they didn't have uniforms. There were twenty, and then fifty, and then a hundred, and then all along the line of the fence, coming up from the creek, hundreds of them. Flags emerged from the woods. The men were in groups rather than lines.

Johnny took a rest on the railfence and sighted on a man approaching the distant fence. The figure became incredibly small at his rifle's end and was blotted out by the sight.

—Fire!

He squeezed off, and the buttguard socked his shoulder. He coughed with smoke in his eyes, and started to load again. He bit the twist of the cartridge too close, and dropped his rod. Panic rushed over him. He bit another cartridge and managed to ram it home.

He was aware of a thin, high, human sound above the firing.

The Rebels were over the fence and running; they seemed to be sweeping forward in a great V with the point aimed at Corporal Johnny Shawnessy, but with more men at the wings. They were about three hundred yards away. They were yelling. Their bayonets flashed in the sun.

Johnny worked the musket frantically. He got in two more shots and then missed his ramrod. He must have left it in the gun and fired it. He turned around, frantic.

Flash Perkins' body jumped with the kick of his rifle. Natie Franklin was lying on the fence with his forehead touching the lowest rail, as if he were ashamed of something. A black puddle of blood was spreading out around his face. Johnny grabbed the extra rod and loaded again.

A hundred yards away, the Rebels had stopped. The officers were waving swords and pistols. The battery on the hill played directly on the Rebel lines. The Rebels fired a volley at the fence. It was like a gigantic whip flaying the ground around the fence. The whole Rebel line disappeared in the smoke. Johnny fired into the smoke again and again. His lips were caked with powder; his hands were blackened and smeared with sweat and powder. His eyes smarted, and one kept closing up with sweat and powdergrime, where he had run his finger through it to clean out the sweat. He had no idea how many shots he had fired, but the gun barrel scorched his hands, his fingers were blistered.

A man on a horse appeared incongruously in front of the line. It was General Jake Jackson but not the same horse. He was shouting and shaking his chin at the creek and whipping the air with his sword. The officers were out in front and were all beating the air with hands and swords. Out of the corner of his eye, Johnny saw an officer make a gesture toward his company so strongly that he threw himself down and flung his head free of his body and lay, neck spurting blood.

—Forward!

The men stepped over what was left of the fence and went through the field, running and walking. The smoke seemed to dissolve. The Rebels had withdrawn to a fence at the far side. Johnny fired at the fence and stopped to reload. The man on his right stopped too, put the butt of his gun on the ground and leaned on it. His mouth was open; blood spurted in a thin, wavering jet from his neck. He let go of the gun, and one hand went slowly toward his neck. He went down to his knees as if to pray, his head dropped, he pitched over. Johnny fired again and kept on walking.

In front of him, now, he could see the Rebels retiring from the fence; then they were all out of sight in bushes, rocks, trees.

He was at the fence. The brigade stopped and went to the ground under heavy fire. Several bodies lay among the broken rails. Bushes, grass, and weeds were trampled and dabbled with blood. Where Johnny crouched behind the fence, a boy was lying on his back, shirt open at the neck, head rolled back, neck soft and flexible with a clear blue vein showing. His relaxed right arm with halfopen hand was flung out behind his head. His young face was stubbled with blond hairs. His eyes were open, moist and blue, but rolling out of focus. He was barefooted. His wellformed body, dressed in crumpled gray pants and a torn shirt, was lying across a rail, bending gracefully just at the point of the spine. He had only just then been alive. His voice had been making a sound in his throat as he ran up through the woods from the creek to this fence. He had been shot through the heart and lay like an animal newly felled. He had come a long way from somewhere to a little creek in Georgia and had run to a rail fence and had got his death there in the autumn sunshine.

He was the Enemy.

Corporal Johnny Shawnessy was appalled. It was the first Rebel soldier he had seen up close. Here lay his gun and his broad hat. He was perhaps eighteen years old. The Battle took no account of him. For a little while, he had been in the Battle, he was the Battle, now he was gone from the Battle.

At any moment, at any unforeseeable point of time, Corporal Johnny Shawnessy might be plucked out of the Battle and out of the bright sunshine. The whole fabric of memories that made him a person beloved to himself and others would be torn up.

He had his second great moment of fear. He looked wildly around. General Jackson came riding up the line with his staff. He smiled and kept shouting in a hoarse voice,

—Fine work, boys, you restored the line!

Johnny was wondering what line.

A staff officer rode up. The General dismounted, knelt on the ground, and studied a map. He issued some orders and rode away.

Johnny began to fire across the fence into the woods. Now and then through an interval in the trees, when the smoke thinned, he could see where the road ran down to the creek. There was a white building there, and through the smoke he could see at times big black words on the front of it.

LEE & GORDON'S

MILLS

They touched him with an incredibly ancient memory, and he knew that it was the same mill he had seen before the fighting began in the morning.

Just after that, the brigade was ordered back from the fence.

—What fer? asked Flash Perkins.

—To restore the line, an officer said.

As far as Johnny could see, their new position didn't bear any clear relation to any other they had occupied, and they were immediately obliged to abandon it and move back again. Someone said the Rebels were outflanking them and trying to get in their rear.

—What's the matter? What are we goin' back fer? Flash Perkins kept saying.

He was still on Johnny's right and close to the regimental colors.

His face was black as a devil's, his eyes bloodshot and glaring, his cap gone, his coat torn.

As soon as they began to go back, the little coherence and order that had been maintained up to that time disappeared altogether. The wood was full of walking wounded, stretcher-bearers, dazed stragglers, riderless horses, gun crews toiling with their pieces. In the thick bush and the crisscrossing ravines, what was left of Johnny's regiment got lost from what was left of the brigade.

As far as Johnny could see, the Battle was over on his part of the line. He staggered on through the woods, his head aching, his mouth full of the black taste of powder, his ears singing. He was so tired that what he saw no longer shocked him. He merely recorded it all for future reference. Already he had become accustomed to beholding war's insult to the integrity of the human form. He had seen heads blown off, lying with tongues out and eyes blackened. He had seen legs and arms lying separate from bodies, he had seen men flung about by shellbursts as if they were bags of old clothes. He had seen men die with a singular ease, as if nothing were so fragile as a human life. He had seen men living and walking with unbelievable wounds, one with what seemed the whole side of his chest sheared off, another holding an armful of his own guts. He had seen a man trying to say something with most of his face blown away.

In Raintree County, human blood had been an ichor. He had never before seen even a pint of it at one time. But on the banks of the Chickamauga, he had seen puddles of it, and men lying in them.

Back near the base of a ridge, the broken divisions were reforming. There had been a withdrawal of the Union right. General Jackson came through in the evening, riding a third horse. His head was bandaged. Dismounting, he strode among the troops. His eyes glared and his voice was strong as a bull's. He laughed and joked with the officers. He said that tomorrow they would show the goddam Rebs something. He said that his whole Corps was intact and never would have fallen back but for a miscalculation in the Center.

Johnny was so exhausted he could hardly eat. He lay on the ground feeling almost as broken as the bodies he had seen along the Chickamauga. He put his memories away, raw and bleeding, knowing that he would have to deal with them sometime. He went to sleep almost immediately and slept like one dead.

And yet he was somehow aware that all night long wagons were rattling on the roads in the darkness, men were marching up and past the bivouac, horses were thundering by. Apparently this volcano of violence and horror called a battle had not yet spent its eruptive force. The canvas had not yet been sufficiently daubed with blood to make it palatable to that great art critic . . .

(Epic Fragment from *Fighting for Freedom*)

History records no more savage conflict than that which raged all day at the crossings of the Chickamauga. By imperishable gallantry our forces had contrived to maintain their line intact before the impassioned charges of the Rebel hordes. Bloody but unbroken, the whole line retired at nightfall to the base of Missionary Ridge, leaving many a brave comrade lying by the little river of death. As those tired legions who had borne the brunt of the Rebellion's fanatical attack waited in the brow of the long ridge in the waning night, little did they know what fresh encounters of deadly consequence they would be forced to sustain upon the morrow.

On the following morning Nature was resplendently beautiful in ironical contrast with the dark human drama which was about to be reenacted in the valley of the Chickamauga. The sun was bright and warm, and fair soft breezes touched the cheeks of soldiers still weary from the extreme ardors of the preceding day's battle. The Rebels, greatly reinforced and outnumbering the Unionists nearly two to one, resumed the attack. In three columns they hurled themselves against the Union right only to melt away before the massed accuracy of the patriot fire. But then occurred one of those incalculable freaks of chance whereby battles and sometimes nations are lost and the whole course of History altered. While the exhausted troops who had stood the whole fury of the Rebel onset were being relieved and fresh troops brought up, the hordes of Treason, perceiving the confusion behind the Union lines, made a single irresistible rush and in the space of a few minutes . . .

Corporal Johnny Shawnessy was thoroughly confused. Somehow during the past half-hour, while he had been firing from a rocky nest at the head of a ravine, the brigade had melted away from around him. Flash Perkins was still with him, but something had happened. The firing had lessened down the line.

—Hey, Flash.

—Yeah.

—Hadn't we better fall back?

—Where's the Captain?

—I don't know. The brigade's retiring. If we don't go along, we'll get cut off.

The regiment had been fighting hard and holding its own all morning, cooperating in the repulse of several Confederate charges. Now, however, it seemed time to fall back. The Union lines were getting thin or non-existent in the woods here. Johnny and Flash started to the rear, hunting for a solid line. There were other men in squads and whole companies, moving slowly back through the woods. A sound of firing and yelling came from the right and the rear.

Johnny didn't know just how it happened.

He had lost the feeling of alignment, of solidarity with the Army, of coherence. As far as he could see, he was aligned on Flash Perkins and Flash on him, and the rest of the Army was swirling around in confusion. As they went back through the woods, instead of finding the brigade they were pushed out of the way by fresh companies who came up eager for the fight. Then a vast yelling and firing broke out in their rear and on both flanks. Johnny got out on high ground near a road. He was not even sure which direction the Enemy was coming from. He and Flash stopped and looked around.

They were surrounded by artillerymen, walking wounded, stretcher-bearers, dismounted cavalry, infantrymen who had not yet seen combat, officers looking for their commands, commands looking for their officers. The whole mass seemed vaguely worried, and although there were counter-currents, the tendency was to go back and find a point of reference farther to the rear.

Just where withdrawal became a rout Johnny didn't know. But there was a time when he ceased to believe that he and Flash Perkins were going to find a solid line of resistance. And there was a point where he stopped thinking of being a useful part of the Army and started to think of saving his skin. Somewhere along in there, he got separated from Flash Perkins. When that happened, he seemed to lose all ties with what had been the Battle and the Army. From then on he resumed his importance as an individual. He was persuaded that he had done his best. He seemed absolved from blame. When men around him began to run, he began to run. Somewhere along the way, he threw down his musket. He realized then that he ad thrown away the last symbol of resistance. He had admitted efeat. He ran faster then.

About four o'clock in the afternoon, he came out on a road which omeone said led into Chattanooga. Along this road the whole right ank of the Union Army appeared to be trying to retreat all at once. Iaggard bands of soldiers were herding down the road, cursing and eeling. Artillery caissons, ambulance carts, supply wagons, riderless orses, walking wounded jammed the road with a solid stream of gony and panic, constantly swollen by broken companies coming up rom the battle area. Men said that whole divisions had been overun, that there were thousands of yelling Rebels in pursuit, that they ad seen whole companies bayoneted in a few seconds. Everywhere here was candid admission of defeat. Here and there, officers tried o curse order into the fleeing mass, but they were helpless.

Some way the hinge of the Army had been broken, and the Battle ad been lost. The loosely integrated mass called 'the Army' had eased to touch in the important places. Now there was no Army at ll, there were no regiments, there were no brigades, there were no ivisions, there were no privates, there were no officers, there were nly a lot of scared, desperate, wounded, sweating, cursing, unhappy nen, absurdly dressed in blue uniforms, struggling along a road and ying to get to a place of safety.

Johnny didn't see why the Rebels didn't attack and annihilate the hole frightened mass.

As he went on, completely weary and exhausted, he had a dull eeling of despair as if he himself had been personally responsible or the defeat of the Army. Somewhere along the way, he had failed n courage or initiative. Somewhere along the way, he had agreed oo easily to be defeated.

He kept wondering if this was the end of the War. Surely the Jnion couldn't stand a defeat like this. All the elaborate order and ontrivance that had been a third of an Army had been destroyed.

Battle appeared to be a process in which order sought to defeat rder with the weapon of confusion. Defeat was simply utter bewilderment.

Late at night Corporal Johnny Shawnessy was wandering through ne groaning darkness of improvised camps in and around Chattaooga. No one knew where anything was. Everyone was looking for his command. About twelve o'clock he found a part of his regiment encamped in the corner of a field. There was a fire going, and Flash Perkins and Captain Bazzle and a few others were there.

—Here's Jack Shawnessy! Flash said, as Johnny came up and peered at their faces in the night. We outrun you, boy.

Johnny threw himself down on the ground by the fire. He heard much talk of the Battle. It appeared that the Army had been saved by a heroic rearguard stand by General Thomas on the left wing.

So then this was the way it had to be done. This was the way mankind settled its problems. These were the glamorous chapters of history.

My God, what difference did it make if men called a hunk of earth one name instead of another! What difference did it make if a few million simple people were called slaves instead of free! Was it worth the extinction of a single life along the Chickamauga? My God, there were thousands of young men who were stiff and dead around that little creek and all for nothing.

Not even the Rebels had won anything by the Battle. No one had anything that he hadn't had before except wounds, sickness of spirit, gutache, exhaustion, death. What difference did it make! Might as well go back to Indiana, and to hell with the whole war. Might as well go back and let the goddam Rebels have their goddam land. What did a man get by fighting? Could a man get anything by it, anything tangible or important? The Rebels had the field, and the Federals had the town of Chattanooga. And he, John Wickliff Shawnessy, had a bellyache and wished he had never been damfool enough to enlist in the Army. It was a terrible thing, a pathetic, crying thing to think of all those boys lying around Chickamauga Creek, boys who had been alive and strong just two days ago. He might be down there himself and no one give a goddam, except some folks back home, who would find out about it in a roundabout way with typographical errors and never know the crazy, unheroic agony of his death.

Here he lay then—the Hero of Raintree County, who had meant one day to be the poet of his people. Here he lay, who on the banks of a little river in Raintree County had dreamed of a fair republic. Here he lay, who had believed in justice, beauty, progress, love. He had just spent two days of complete selfishness, of abject fear. He had been thoroughly whipped. He had run like a craven from the field, buried in the blissful anonymity of panic and mass retreat.

One thing was certain. War was the craziest damfool madness that ever was. It was everything vile, absurd, brutal, murderous, confused. Mainly it was just confusion—bloody, stinking, noisy confusion with death as a casual by-product. How anyone ever won a battle, he couldn't imagine. This fight, which had no name and ought never to have a name, had been simply the result of two blind forces launched from vast confusion and colliding in vast confusion. What he had seen today was so incredibly evil and foolish that it baffled classification. No one man or idea was responsible for the evil. It was something in which men got trapped through a lack of foresight. All of them hated it while they were in it, and yet all had agreed to be in it.

Later, Flash Perkins came around and handed him a stewkit full of hot soup. Flash's face had a set, baffled look. He kept shaking his head.

—Shucks, Jack! he said, it ain't anything like I thought it'd be. Cuss it, we din't hardly have a chance to git at 'em. Hell, that was jist pure murder.

WE SURE BEEN IN ONE HOLY
JUMPIN' HELL OF
A

GRAND PATRIOTIC PROGRAM

July 4, 1892

Waycross, Indiana

2:30 P.M.

The Star-Spangled Banner..All
Prayer..Rev. Lloyd G. Jarvey
Declaration of Independence (Reading)....General Jacob J. Jackson
The Gettysburg Address (Recitation)...........Wesley Shawnessy
The Battle Cry of Freedom..All
Address of the Day....................Hon. Garwood B. Jones
Medley of Patriotic Airs..Band
Tenting on the Old Camp Ground
Tramp, Tramp, Tramp
Marching Through Georgia
When Lilacs Last in the Dooryard Bloomed
(Recitation)..........................Mrs. Evelina Brown
Medley of Popular and Patriotic Airs........................Band
Old Folks at Home
My Old Kentucky Home
Dixie
Battle Hymn of the Republic
My Country 'Tis of Thee..All
Benediction..............................Rev. Lloyd G. Jarvey

Program Chairman: Mrs. Evelina Brown

Mr. Shawnessy consulted his copy of the program. Following the banquet, the space before the platform had been cleared of tables and filled up with benches and chairs. Promptly at two-thirty, with several hundred people in attendance, many of them standing out in the road, the Grand Patriotic Program had begun. Mr. Shawnessy, who, with Mrs. Brown, had been mainly responsible for arranging the program, sat in a back row with Professor Stiles. The Reverend Jarvey had at last appeared, looking a little tired, the opening anthem and the prayer had gone off well, and now General Jackson, who had shouted himself hoarse in his short banquet address, was thundering through the opening bars of the Declaration of Independence.

> —When in the course of human events, it becomes necessary for one people to dissolve the political bands which have connected them with another, and to assume among the powers of the earth, the separate and equal station to which the Laws of Nature and of Nature's God entitle them, a decent respect to the opinions of mankind requires that they should declare the causes which impel them to the separation.

—From these words, the Perfessor whispered, the origin of firecrackers.

> —We hold these truths to be self-evident, that all men are created equal, that they are endowed by their Creator with certain inalienable Rights, that among these are Life, Liberty and the pursuit of Happiness.

From these words, the Republic. From these words, Raintree County, a rectangular dream.

> —That to secure these rights, Governments are instituted among Men, deriving their just powers from the consent of the governed. That whenever any Form of Government becomes destructive of these ends, it is the Right of the People to alter or to abolish it, and to institute a new Government. . . .

From these words, cannons and cockades, constitutions and congresses. From these words, the Court House and the Court House Square, the clock in the steeple telling the time of day and the flag of many stripes. From these words, the granite lady with the scales over the court house door and the spittoons in the court room on the second floor.

From these words, the enormous geometry of the railroads, trains that pass by day and night making banners of gray smoke on the land.

From these words, the manswarm of New York, Chicago, San Francisco. From these words, the march of States across the Nation in musical procession, New Jersey, Pennsylvania, Ohio, Indiana, Illinois, Kansas, Colorado, Utah, Nevada, California.

From these words, Main Street, the post office on the corner, the general store, the barber shop, the schoolhouse, the church with a steeple holding a bell. From these words, the plain board houses in the tidy lawns, the old plantation home, the mansard roofs, the tenement houses hung with washing, the farmhouse, and the great red barn.

From these words, an infinitude of sounds, vibrations of wire, whistles at crossings, rock and jostle of strings of cars crossing the lonely prairies where the buffaloes stand at gaze, roar of the churning and changeable machines, voice of great cities assaulting the summer night with prayers, oaths, death cries, songs.

> —We, therefore, the Representatives of the United States of America, in General Congress assembled, appealing to the Supreme Judge of the world for the rectitude of our intentions, do, in the Name, and by Authority of the good People of these Colonies, solemnly publish and declare, That these United Colonies are, and of Right ought to be Free and Independent States. . . .

From these words, statues in the Square for the boys who fell at Lexington, Chapultepec, and Chickamauga.

> —And for the support of this Declaration, with a firm reliance on the protection of divine Providence, we mutually pledge to each other our Lives, our Fortunes and our sacred Honor.

From these words, the place called America and the people called the Americans. From these words, the brooding and gaunt form of Abraham Lincoln at Gettysburg. From these words, tumult of many wars (old wars and half-forgotten), unceasing dedications and rededications. From these words——

Mr. Shawnessy's oldest child, Wesley, was standing before the crowd, a blue-eyed boy, blond head close-cropped, new suit somewhat too large. His solemn, tense voice began:

> —Fourscore and seven years ago our fathers brought forth on this continent a new nation, conceived in liberty, and dedicated to the proposition that all men are created equal. Now we are engaged in

November 22— WAR —1863

HAD COME
TO THIS HOLLOW BETWEEN HILLS,

this basin of plain beside the river, this rash of shacks and dingy buildings called Chattanooga, and it had brought with it barricades, trenches, riflepits, gun emplacements, pontoon bridges, tents, barracks, whores, booze, siege, famine, and Corporal Johnny Shawnessy.

It was afternoon as Johnny walked away from the postal depot toward his camp on the fringes of the City, having had a special leave to see why the regimental mail was delayed. For two months now, the Army of the Cumberland had holed up in Chattanooga trying to recover from Chickamauga. The Rebels had followed and besieged the town, and even now, as Johnny looked south up the street, he could see thin smokes of Confederate fires on Missionary Ridge and Lookout Mountain. For weeks, the Union Army had been almost cut off from supply, but at last a lane had been cleared, and the Army had begun to eat again. Then General Grant, the Hero of Vicksburg, had taken command, the Army had been reinforced, and a campaign to break the Rebel siege was promised.

Meanwhile, the mountains had been the abiding companions of Johnny Shawnessy's days and nights in the autumn of 1863. Thin smokes of Confederate fires on Lookout Mountain and Missionary Ridge had burned away this autumn of his life in bitter waiting. He knew that these mountains would remain part of the august scenery of his life, great breasts of earth, colossally feminine and passive. For the possession of this couched shape, immense, brooding, silent, he and his comrades must fight, retch, shriek, bleed, die. On earth's indifferent ramparts, like blowing sand, the battle must swirl and pass with fine abrasion. Men would shout victory with advancing banners. But in the end the earth alone would remain unaltered and victorious. A hundred years hence, picnickers would strew gay wreckage on the slopes of Lookout Mountain and Missionary Ridge, and perhaps their feet would tread the crumbled heart of Corporal Johnny Shawnessy. These old hills would have their solemn immortality, fashioned from his bloody anonymity.

These were his musings when a voice calling his name caused him to look back along the street.

A tall, thin man was walking toward him. A long arm flapped violently. Sharpkneed legs strode briskly past knots of sauntering soldiers and civilians. The approaching figure was dressed in a wide-flapping civilian coat, a checked vest, pants stuffed into jackboots. Beneath a wide hat, Johnny saw a long head, a sharp nose, a spade-shaped beard, glittering black eyes.

—Well, well! said Professor Jerusalem Webster Stiles, that was a long train ride you sent me on, John.

Johnny shook the Perfessor's bony hand. The sharp face hacked up and down hatchetlike. The Perfessor was laughing.

—Jesus, John, he said, I thought at first you weren't going to recognize me. I just blew into town two hours ago. Well, I suppose you're wondering what brought about our reunion on the field of Mars. It's very simple. The paper sent me out here to get a slant on the way you boys are fighting it on this side. Not much difference. They seem to make the same kind of corpses on both fronts. Same old stink, same old waste, same old war. Well, how's everything in Raintree County?

Johnny didn't know where to start, but before he had said ten words, the Perfessor cut in.

—Let's go where we can talk. Where's the local ginmill?

—I don't know, Professor, I——

—There must be one, the Perfessor said.

—I'm not sure, Johnny said. I——

—In fact there *is* one, the Perfessor said. I'll show you where it is. Friend of yours tipped me off. I visited your camp. Chap named Perkins brought me back in and told me to look for you at the Post Office. Showed me the booze house on the way. Said he had a woman lined up there and would try to fix you and me up too. Obliging bastard. Suppose we drop in there for——

—If it's the place I've heard Flash talk about, the whiskey's rotgut and the women are terrible.

—I trust they have the standard equipment, said the Perfessor, albeit a bit battered, no doubt. It's been a long war. As for the liquor, personally I always carry my own brand of the white destroyer.

The Perfessor drew deftly from his boottop a bottleful of bubbling fluid. He led the way to the main business street of the town, turned off, went down a back alley, and fetched up at a door that opened in the side of a mournful frame building. Muffled laughter and bursts of singing came from inside.

The Perfessor rapped on the door. The door opened two inches.

—Who is it? said a hoarse man's voice.

—A friend, Madame, the Perfessor said. On the recommendation of one of your regular clients, Madame.

—Who's that? said the hoarse voice.

—A Mr. Perkins, the Perfessor said.

—We try to keep a respectable house here, the hoarse voice said argumentatively.

—Of course, Madame, the Perfessor said. One hears only good things of your establishment.

—Course it's pretty hard under the circumstances——

—One does not expect perfection, Madame, the Perfessor said, laughing jovially. One merely wants a little relaxation and a place to chat among congenial spirits.

—Flash Perkins sent you? the voice said.

—I believe they call him that, the Perfessor said. You know him?

—Yeah, I know the big lug, the voice said. He owes three dollars. Come on in.

—Thank you, thank you, Madame, the Perfessor said.

He and Johnny walked into an ill-lighted hallway, in which an elderly woman with powdered pouches under her eyes and a slack, painted mouth was waiting for them. Her eyes were hostile and suspicious.

—This one too? she said, in her man's voice.

—Another friend of Perkins, the Perfessor said. An excellent young man.

—The place is full now.

—We only want some drinks, the Perfessor said.

They followed the proprietress to another door and into the main downstairs room. Drawn blinds made the place dark. It was full of smoke and badly lighted by oil lamps, but Johnny could see that it was furnished with plank tables and crude benches. There was a door leading into a kitchen. Three or four ugly young women sat at the tables, and the other half a hundred occupants of the room were soldiers. A woman and a soldier got up from a near-by table and went through a door at the far end of the room. Heavy boots banged on stairs. The planks overhead shook unmysteriously. Johnny and the Perfessor took the empty chairs.

Johnny looked around but didn't see Flash. An aged waitress brought drinks, and the Perfessor insisted on paying. He tossed off his drink, but Johnny didn't touch his.

—Ouch! said the Perfessor. Now, John, tell me about yourself.

Johnny began to tell, in more detail than his infrequent letters had made possible, what had happened to him since the night when he had last seen the Perfessor's blackwinged form spring from darkness to the passing train.

—Well, John, the Perfessor said after they had talked a while, I should have known you'd go and do all these damfool things. I had hoped that with my shining example before you, you would escape the Philistine snares of Raintree County. That was quite a fuss I stirred up, wasn't it?

—I felt sorry for you and the Reverend's wife, Johnny said. It looked like a real passion to me and——

—By the way, what was her name? the Perfessor said.

Later Johnny and the Perfessor talked mostly of the War.

—What's the War in the East like? Johnny said.

To him the War in the East was still the storybook War in a mythical Theatre of Operations between two capitals.

—Gettysburg was a beautiful battle, the Perfessor said. Three days of dramatic corpsemaking and a real chance for Meade to end the War. But he muffed it, and since then he and Mars Robert have been blowing kisses at each other across impregnable positions. My boy, war is the same everywhere. A great stink in the nostrils of God.

He looked around the room.

—Perhaps the whores are a trifle better looking on the Eastern front. What was Chickamauga like?

Johnny tried to give him some idea of the battle, but all he could tell him was his own confused picture of the fighting.

—You poor boy! the Perfessor said. For this you left Raintree County.

—What's going to happen anyway, Professor? Where are we heading?

The Perfessor began to drink directly out of his bottle.

—I just report the news, he said.

—Here we are—getting ready to fight on the same ground where we fought two months ago and got whipped.

—And while you boys kill and cuss on the battlefields, and squitter and whore in the camps, back home a lot of bastards and bounty-jumpers are marrying all the beautiful women and wallowing in gravy. But who are we to question the ways of the Eternal?

Someone was arguing about cardhands in the measured syllables of drunkenness. A woman giggled and squeaked weakly in the alcoholic mist. A song started near-by to the accompaniment of a clattering, tuneless piano. A woman stood up, one hand sentimentally supporting her flabby left breast, and sang one of the War's most popular songs.

—Dearest love, do you remember,
When we last did meet,
How you told me that you loved me,
Kneeling at my feet?
O, how proud you stood before me,
In your suit of blue,
When you vowed to me and country
Ever to be true.

The room stank of sweat, spilled whiskey, powdered flesh, cheap perfume, a jakes.

—Weeping, sad and lonely,
Hopes and fears how vain!
Yet praying, when this cruel war is over,
Praying that we meet again.

The Perfessor sucked moodily at his bottle.

—By the way, he said, I just came from Gettysburg on my way over here. They had a patriotic ceremony there on the 19th to commemorate the establishment of a great National Cemetery. The President was there and spoke. I talked with him.

—What did he say?

The Perfessor smiled, remembering something.

—He told a little story and said we would win the War. The story was a damn good one. I picked up a paper in Cincinnati.

He pulled a rolled newspaper from his pocket and tossed it on the table.

—I haven't seen a newspaper for two months, Johnny said.

He unrolled the paper and started reading:

THE PRESIDENT'S ADDRESS AT GETTYSBURG

The President arose and delivered the following short address. . . .

—By the way, the Perfessor said, standing up, I've got an appointment with Grant in ten minutes. The press will be admitted to the august presence for a while. Want to go along?

Johnny put the newspaper in his coatpocket and left with the Perfessor. They walked to a house where Grant was in conference with his generals. There was tremendous activity around the house as couriers came and went. Several generals entered while Johnny was watching. He heard famous names whispered by bystanders. After about twenty minutes, the Perfessor came out.

—Let's stay a minute, he said. The General's leaving.

In a few minutes, several officers came out of the house. General Ulysses S. Grant was a medium-sized man in a sloppy uniform. He had a black beard, fair skin, pale blue eyes. He looked like a commissary man or an engineer. He had a cigar in his mouth.

A spontaneous cheer went up from the crowd.

—Hurrah for old Ulyss!

—You just give the word, General, and we'll whup 'em.

General Grant got on a horse and rode away. He looked like someone who was going off for a day's work at the office.

—The Hero of Vicksburg, the Perfessor said, as he and Johnny walked away, was in an uncommunicative mood. He said he hoped to give the Rebels some trouble and had no objection to my sticking around to see the fuss. He smokes foul cigars, drinks his whiskey straight, and graduated twenty-first in a class of thirty-nine at West Point. There is no subtlety in the man and very little syntax. In peace time, he would make a bad grocer. In fact, he failed farming and business before the War and got cashiered from the Army once. Nevertheless, he's a good general and perhaps a great one. Of such stuff are the heroes of the Republic fashioned. Let's get back to the shanty.

—Do you think we'll fight soon?

—The General declined to say. But it's no great secret that Sherman is on the other side of the river with maybe twenty thousand men waiting to cross. Anyone can see that Grant is making a concentration. The way we understand it in the East, this damn, dull, whiskey-drinking brute of a general lacks the finesse of our Eastern prima donnas, and when he gets his army concentrated, he can only think of one thing to do with it. Wham! He fights.

It was dark out when Johnny and the Perfessor got back to the shanty and found empty seats at a table in the corner. Johnny opened the newspaper and went on reading the President's Address.

> . . . a great civil war, testing whether that nation, or any nation so conceived and so dedicated, can long endure. We are met on a great battlefield of that war. We have come to . . .

—Meet the girls! said a loud and happy voice.

Flash Perkins smote Johnny and the Perfessor simultaneously between the shoulderblades. The Perfessor's hat fell on the table.

—This one's yours, Jack, Flash said. Doris, this is Jack Shawnessy, the smartest son-of-a——

—Please, Johnny said, rising and looking helplessly at the Perfessor, I was supposed to be back at camp an hour ago, and——

—Sit down, boy! Flash said. Drinks on me. I'm already lit to the roof and rarin' to go. Hell, I aim to have me a time tonight!

He pushed Johnny down. Doris, a skinny woman who snarled when she spoke, sat down on the table beside him, swinging her legs.

—Honey, she snarled, you're the best-lookin' sojer I seen since I left Louisville. I din't think they made your kind no more.

—Look, Johnny said resolutely. I was reading this paper. Have a drink on me, Doris. Then I have to leave. Honest, I'm sorry, but I'm carrying the regimental mail, and also I have a girl back home. Besides——

—Take it easy, honey, Doris snarled. Nobody's goin' to bite yuh.

I don't mind if I have that drink, though. Go on and read your paper, honey.

Johnny stubbornly put the paper up and tried to go on reading. He could hardly see the words.

> . . . dedicate a portion of that field, as a final resting place for those who here gave their lives that that nation might live. It is altogether fitting and proper that we should do this. But, in a larger sense . . .

Flash upset a glass; his girl, who was tall, rawboned, and drunk, giggled. The Perfessor was reciting verse.

> —Is this the face that launched a thousand ships
> And burnt the titless towers of Ilium.
> Sweet Hesper, make me unconscious with a kiss!

—You *are* crazy, Hesper said, but I like you. You're kinder cute and diffrunt.

The Perfessor fitted his thin, hawklike face and beard snugly between Hesper's bosoms.

—I salute the Army of the Cumberland, he said. I salute the Commissary Department of the Army of the Cumberland. I salute the Quartermaster of the Commissary Department of the Army of the Cumberland—for provisioning us with these excellent pillows whereon to rest our battle-wearied brows.

This was so good that even Johnny had to laugh.

—Ain't he a scream! Hesper giggled, as Johnny put the paper up again.

> . . . we cannot dedicate—we cannot consecrate—we cannot hallow—this ground. The brave men, living and dead, who struggled here have consecrated it, far above our poor power to add or detract. The world will little note, nor long remember . . .

—Come on, girls! Flash said. I feel like dancin'. Tell Flo to thump that ole pile a wire and ivory over there, and le's have a little dance.

—Come on, honey, Doris snarled, fluttering a hand over the newspaper. Let's dance little.

—You haven't had your drink yet, Johnny said. Better have your drink.

The Perfessor smiled sympathetically and recited,

—*Virginei volucrum vultus foedissima ventris.*

—He cain't even talk plain now, Hesper said, giggling. He's so drunk.

—Same old war, the Perfessor said, on both fronts.

> . . . what we say here, but it can never forget what they did here. It is for us, the living, rather, to be dedicated here to the unfinished work which they who fought here have thus far so nobly advanced. It is rather for us to be here dedicated to the great . . .

—Jerusalem! Flash Perkins yelled. I feel a jig a-kickin' in my limbs.

Without warning, he upset the table. His forehead was tight with ridges. He clumped his great shoes on the floor. Someone was hitting the piano, and a space was cleared in the middle of the floor. Flash Perkins began to call the figures.

—Ladies and gennulmen, start tew dance.
Jist watch me a-jiggin' in muh bran-new pants.

The crowd roared approval. The square dance started. The rough soldier forms jostled and jumped on the wide boards. The young faces glowed with sweat in the yellow glare of the lamps. The dancers looked bigger than natural size, as they clumped their club-shaped shoes on the floor, flapped their huge, ill-fitted blue coats. Flash Perkins was cutting in and out like a great rhythmical bull, yelling above the racket:

—I got a gal, her name is Jane.
We're headin' for Memphis on the midnight train.

O, I got a gal in Kalamazoo.
You jist oughta see the things she kin dew!

> . . . task remaining before us—that from these honored dead we take increased devotion to that cause for which they gave the last full measure of devotion—that we here highly resolve . . .

—Come on, Jack! Flash yelled, whirling out of the crowd and grabbing Johnny by the arm. Git into the dance, boy! Grab yerself some fun!

Johnny rolled the paper and stood up. As the dance went on, he backed uncertainly toward the door.

—If you got a gal that's a mite tew fat,
You kin melt her down with a dance like that!

But if you got a gal that's a mite tew thin,
You won't have a dern thing left but skin!

But if you got a gal——

A table upset at the far side of the room, glasses splintered, a girl screamed. There was a confused shoving and shouting. A tangle of struggling bodies burst apart. Flash Perkins stood in the middle.

—Come on, you bastards! Come on and fight! I kin lick any man in this whole goddam Army! Come on, you sons-a——

It seemed to Johnny that everyone on that side of the hall accepted the challenge. Flash was buried under a hail of blows and bodies. Johnny shoved the newspaper into his pocket and started trying to get through the crowd to Flash.

The room became a vortex of faces and fists. Someone smashed the lights. Someone shoved Johnny. He fell sprawling. Something flew over his head. A window smashed, scattering glass outdoors. Johnny groped for a table to get under. He found himself grappling with a woman on the floor. She screamed. Johnny stood up. Something hit him smash on the side of the head. He lurched blindly, hunting for an exit. Over the noise, he could hear Flash Perkins' jubilant and terrific profanity.

—Tryin' to hit me, huh! Well, goddamn you, where I come from——

A door opened somewhere and a gush of cold air came in. The crowd quieted down. There was a crisp young officer standing at the door swinging a lamp. Soldiers with bayonets fixed stood behind him.

—Report to your units at once, he said. Any soldier not answering to regimental rollcall one hour from now will stand court martial for desertion.

The door slammed. Someone turned a lamp up on the beshambled room. The soldiers looked at one another dully.

—Must mean we're gonna fight tomorra.

—Le's git out a here.

Johnny found the Perfessor in a corner sitting in Hesper's lap. She was applying a handkerchief to an eggshaped lump on the Perfessor's forehead.

—Poor darlin', she cooed. He hurt hisself.

—Well, Professor, Johnny said, are you enjoying yourself?

The Perfessor put his pince-nez glasses back on his nose, looked around, and recited:

—A poet could not but be gay
In such a jocund company!

—You better come with me, Johnny said. Flash and I have to get back to camp.

—Run along, boys, the Perfessor said, looking intently at Hesper's bosom. Remember—the soldier only has to be at his post, but the correspondent has to cover the whole damn war. See you in Richmond, John.

As he left, Johnny could hear the Perfessor's high voice reciting,

—And oft when on my couch I lie . . .

Back at the camp, General Jake Jackson spoke to the brigade.

—We'll fight tomorrow, he said. Let every man get his arms in readiness. Here's your chance, boys, to avenge Chickamauga. Get a good night's sleep.

Johnny lay on his cot, listening to Flash Perkins in the adjoining cot.

—Yes, sir! Flash was saying, I mean to kill me a whole wagonload a Rebs tomorra. Cuss it, I'm a-gittin fed up with this here war. I simply cain't unnerstan' anybody fightin' agin the United States of Amerikee. Who the hell do they think they are anyhow? Ownin' slaves when respectable folks pays for their hire. Not that I want to fight no war for no dinge—let the niggers take keer a themselves. But I cain't unnerstan' them a-firin' on the Flag, can you, Jack? What I wanna know is . . .

Johnny mumbled something. He envied Flash the simplicity of his concepts. It was perhaps good to take life as you found it, bare your teeth, and laugh like hell. It was perhaps good to have no doubts.

Johnny thought of the coming battle and of his unexpected reunion with the Perfessor. Then he thought of Raintree County lying beneath these sharp, autumnal stars. In his coat he had letters from his father, mother, and Nell. They all said to take care of himself and come back home as soon as he could. The words in these letters cared about him. He thought of the way his name looked in Nell's highly personal handwriting. *My darling Johnny, I take my pen in hand and seat myself to . . .*

When he had read those letters, he had felt like the Hero of Raintree County for certain, the darling boy precious and irreplaceable. But now he was only one of thousands of boys, waiting in darkness for a day of battle. These thousands of young men slept a little time and went back home in vague dreams remembering. But on the morrow they would get up, recalling duty. The General would have a plan. The President would be waiting for news of the Battle. The folks at home would pray for victory and the safety of loved ones. The Flag must be avenged and the Constitution upheld. On the morrow, then, he must be brave, as he hadn't been before, and distinguish himself in the fighting.

Sad words ran in his mind, words of a man named Abraham Lincoln, words from a perishable paper read in a brothel where soldiers hunted for love's poor counterfeit before the Battle. These words had been woven from the deathcries of ten thousand young men on the hills of Gettysburg and also from the anguish of Johnny Shawnessy hunting for two lost children through days of climax and disaster. These words might vanish like the thin smokes on Lookout Mountain, or they might be graven on the memory of the Republic. Tomorrow he and his comrades would go out to give life or death to these words. On the brooding hills of Tennessee and Georgia, they must affirm and reaffirm

> . . . that these dead shall not have died in vain—that this nation, under God, shall have a new birth of freedom—and that government

OF THE PEOPLE, BY THE PEOPLE, FOR THE PEOPLE,

SHALL NOT PERISH

FROM

THE EARTH of Raintree County, covered with corn and wheat, was the image of peace and plenty in the anniversary sunlight. On the platform Mrs. Evelina Brown raised her arms to lead the opening bars of the song.

—Yes, we'll rally round the flag, boys, we'll rally once again,
Shouting the battle cry of freedom,
We will rally from the hillside, we'll gather from the plain,
Shouting the battle cry of freedom.

The Union forever, hurrah! boys, hurrah!
Down with the traitor, up with the star,
While we rally round the flag, boys,
Rally once again,
Shouting the battle cry of freedom.

A chill went up Mr. Shawnessy's spine; he perceptibly straightened his back and squared his shoulders, hoping that the Perfessor hadn't observed.

—We are springing to the call of our brothers gone before,
Shouting the battle cry of freedom.
And we'll fill the vacant ranks with a million freemen more,
Shouting the battle cry of freedom.

He was lifted on a wave forward and upward. Memory carried him on the feet of trampling thousands.

The Union forever! O, beautiful, unanalyzable concept!

Forward, comrades, let us push forward up the slope. Let us carry the banners of freedom to the summit. O, let us be in the vanguard of history, anonymous and fearless comrades! A hundred hands will bear us to the crest. Young men, my comrades, we shall all behold the far side of the mountain in resplendent weather, white roads of peace and blossoming summer. But first, good heart, comrades, a deep breath, a long shout, and——

The Union forever, hurrah! boys

November 25— —HURRAAAAHHHH! —1863

THE CRY SMOTE HIM,

MADE HIM TREMBLE. THE LINES ON THE RIGHT

moved out. The blue rush of the ranks poured like a wave advancing. The movement was given on down the line like a rope cracking. It swirled into his regiment, picked him up. He was running.

—Hurraaaaaaaahhhh! Hurraaaaaaaaaahhhh! Hurraaaaaaaahhhh! He was held up by the deep bass roar of the Army. It was one voice shouting. This force held back from early morning, unleashed at last, was a torrent of grim men. Starving, marching, waiting, griping, despairing were trampled down by the thunder of forty thousand feet.

He went as though the earth moved with him. The blue line reached and topped a little slope that had hid them from view all morning. A hundred yards in front were the Rebel riflepits at the base of the ridge. Smokepuffs flowered along a line loosely entrenched.

Running, he saw on his left how Jesse Gardner, the thinfaced, querulous boy from the City, stuck out from the straight of the charge, leaning and lunging, ran down to his knees, pitched forward, his gun flung out in front. His canteen bounced on the ground like a pod tossing on water. The wave swept on. At the base of the ridge, the Enemy rose. Some furiously worked their ramrods. Others broke for the rear. Belatedly, a few shells dropped, but far behind.

Groups of enemy soldiers fell back in a ragged line, firing. Back of that line, a second was trying to fire through the first. He heard the commands of Rebel officers.

Rocks, bushes, trees faded around. He and others made for a knot of Rebels. One tall Rebel walked forth from the rest. He held his musket clubbed. His eyes glared with a personal hatred. Corporal Johnny Shawnessy flung himself under the swung musket, missed in a lunge with his bayonet, lost balance, fell, rolled over to keep moving. A blast of powder singed the back of his neck. The tall Rebel sat down hard, grabbing his stomach. Flash Perkins reached down a hand and pulled Johnny standing. With clubbed muskets and bayonets, blue and gray soldiers drove at each other in mute violence. Johnny and Flash together rushed a Rebel on one knee ramming a charge. He threw down the rifle. Flash's bayonet was at his throat. The man squirmed like a snake, screamed for mercy, holding the bare blade in his hands. Flash missed twice with killing lunges. All around, the Enemy threw down their arms.

More Union soldiers swept in around them, bayonets flashing like cruel desires. Then an officer riding by, said crisply,

—All right. Go to the rear, you traitorous bastards. Keep your hands up.

Johnny grabbed Flash around the shoulders and pulled him back from the man on the ground, who lay panting and watching Flash with hypnotized eyes.

—Goddamn 'im, he'd a-killed me if he could! Flash growled.

All the Rebels in sight held up their hands and walked slowly, like men treading on wires. One boy was sobbing. As always, the face of the Enemy and the speech of the Enemy were barbarous and strange. These were outsiders, men of a strange belief, plucked like fish from their own world, forcibly into his.

Grape and riflefire whined around him. A Union soldier sat down. He tore his shirt open and looked at his chest. There was a black hole in the flesh of his right breast. The soldier sat looking at the hole in his chest and then shyly around at his comrades.

The blue wave had overrun the riflepits at the base of the hill. It was momentarily confused by its own success. General Jake Jackson rode up the line, hatless as usual. His voice and sword whipped the line forward.

Johnny heard the deep shout again from along the captured pits.

—Hurraaaaaaaahhhh! Hurraaaaaahhh! Hurraaahh!

A word and a primitive cry—a deep aitch, a growling ar, and a raucous ah—it was savage and almost exultant.

—Go on, boys! Captain Bazzle said. Keep moving forward! Fire at will!

The men advanced in groups, firing from cover. Johnny and Flash were to the left of the regimental colors. The ridge here began to rise steeply in humps covered with low bushes and scrub trees. What was left of the retreating first line of the Rebels had become confused with a second, forming in clear view a hundred yards higher. The Rebels fired volleys of grape down the hill. Parts of the enemy line were advancing. A man with a blue bandanna tied around his neck walked right over the top of Johnny's rifle sight, getting bigger and bigger. Johnny squeezed off.

—Up, Jack, up! Flash Perkins yelled.

Johnny got up. The first Union line was forward again, forced on by the advancing second wave which was now firing over Johnny's head. In places the Unionists were running shoulder to shoulder. Johnny crossed a fence and climbed down into a road that ran diagonally up the ridge. Rebels were entrenched along the road or retreating across it. For a moment he appeared to be the only Union soldier on it. Then the road was choked in both directions with his comrades. A Rebel officer stood up from concealment on the far side of the road.

—Come on, boys, he said briskly, le's give 'em what-fer.

Forty or fifty Rebels poured out into the road. The officer cocked a pistol and aimed it directly at Johnny's head. Both sides fired a volley at short range. The road was filled with smoke and cursing men. Rebel soldiers ran out of the smoke, yelling. A big bearded man naked to the waist walked forward swinging his musket by the small end. A glancing blow smashed so hard against Johnny's bayonet that his hands and arms stung to the shoulders, and his musket clattered on the road. He grabbed it by the small end and swung wild. The blue roof of the world bloomed with fire. Stars were shooting up in a fountain of brightness and coming down in dissolving trickles of light. Blackness ate at the light in soft waves.

Johnny felt something rough on his face. He had perhaps been dreaming. Someone was pulling him up. The ground rocked, tipped, turned over, came rightside up. Tom Conway was standing beside him.

—What happened? Johnny said.

—You got a nasty crack on the head, Tom said.

Half a dozen Rebels and Unionists lay around him. In the ditch on the other side, a Union soldier stood over a Rebel, bayonet pressing him down. The Rebel held to the stock of the gun, said nothing, his eyes pleading.

Dirt and smoke spurted in a high black fountain out of the ground where the two struggled. Johnny flattened. When he raised his head, Tom Conway was lying on his back a yard away. Johnny leaned over him. Tom's eyes fluttered open. He looked around.

—What—— he started to say, his voice gentle, vaguely worried.

—It was a shell, Johnny said. Where did it hit you?

—I don't know, Tom said. I can't move.

There was no mark on the front of his body. Johnny started to turn him over on his side. Tom's eyes fluttered again, and he fainted. The back of his torn coat was soaked.

—All right, boys, go on up! an officer shouted. Follow 'em up the hill.

The Enemy was shelling his own abandoned positions all along the base of the ridge. Every able soldier in the road climbed over the ditch at the far side and went on up. Johnny felt the back of his head, matted with blood. His head throbbed, and he was sick in the stomach. He didn't know quite where he was and what he was doing.

After a while, he was alone in dense timber. He didn't remember how he had come there. Sunlight fell down through broad trunks. He walked among gray stones covered with lichen. He lay down and listened to distant cries, explosions, his own hoarse breath. He didn't know how long he had been there. He opened his canteen and took a drink. Down the slope, he could see clear to the base of the ridge. Waves of tiny soldiers breasted the small hills. Cannon inched forward. Bits of bright color advanced. A motionless speck of blue or gray marked where a man had fallen.

Later he was up and walking again. The pale air, streaked with sunlight, had the look of late afternoon under deep trees. After a while he was standing in bushes on the rim of a deep cut.

In a sunflooded, open space here, amazing things were happening. Half a dozen Confederate guns had been parked below. Some of the artillerists were still methodically working their pieces. Others were trying to get away. Horses whinnied and kicked in the traces. The holders cursed and pulled. Officers shouted commands. Thick smoke and the stench of powder filled the air.

All around the cut Federal soldiers closed in, firing and yelling.

One dropped down from a rock near where Johnny was standing and ran toward the nearest gun. The crew had just begun to pull their piece out to a road. The Union soldier fired as he ran, and one of the men fell. A boy sitting on the lead horse raised a pistol and fired back. The Rebel artillerists, seeing that it was one soldier only, closed in on him, one with a rammer, another with a pistol, a third with a sword, like men who knew what they were doing and were sure of the result. The Union soldier broke through them, ran to the gun and onehanded himself clear over the barrel. He turned swinging his musket, teeth bared in the sunlight.

It was Flash Perkins.

—Come on, you sons-a-bitches! he yelled. Come on, you——

Every Rebel in the vicinity accepted the challenge. Johnny ran forward along with several other Unionists.

It was like a race. A battery officer in immaculate uniform stood ten feet from the gun, backing toward it and calmly loading a pistol with practiced fingers, while he kept darting his eyes around to appraise his chances. An officer with a sword ran at Flash from the other side of the gun. Flash swung his musket. Johnny heard the dull clunk of butt on skull. The officer's sword was pinned hanging through the cloth in Flash's coat under the left arm. Bullets sang on the parked gun. Two of the artillerists fell. Flash onehanded over to the other side of the gun.

The Rebel officer with the pistol threw it down and backed around the cannon away from Flash. He put up his hands.

—Prisoner.

A half-dozen Rebels were beginning to fire from farther up the hill on the Unionists clustered around the captured gun. Johnny and Flash crouched behind the prize. Balls spanged on the gunmetal. More and more soldiers in blue came up through the woods, and the Rebels retired all along the line.

The captured artillerist leaned on the gun and took out a pipe.

—Pretty sharp scrapping, he said.

He had a cultivated, amiable voice.

—Either you Yanks got a light?

A brigadier general rode by waving his sword, smiling and violently shaking his head.

—Great work, boys! Fine work! We've got 'em whipped now. Make for that crest, and plant your flags on it.

—Go to the rear, Johnny said to the captured officer. Keep your hands up, and you won't get hurt.

A man came by carrying a regimental flag.

—There's our flag! Flash said to Johnny. Let's go up with it.

He and Flash went up the slope with the flag. Johnny had a terrible headache, and his nose was bleeding. They were only a little way from the top. There was a road up there, and a disorganized mob of Rebel wagons and troops retreated down it.

On the crest of the ridge the regiment raised its flag. Johnny looked down over the ground they had covered. On the wide fanlike sweep of the battle area, he could see troops and guns coming up. Apparently, he and Flash were at the crest of the fighting, first to the summit.

—Give a cheer, boys, an officer said.

They cheered. Other cheers broke out along the ridge. Flags were waving farther down the line.

—We whupped 'em, Jack! Flash said.

He grabbed Johnny's shoulders and shook him. He capered and jumped. Soldiers were hitting each other on the backs and shaking hands. Some were crying.

—Godamighty! Flash said. Raintree County captured a cannon!

They followed the Rebels for a while, but both sides were disorganized, the one by defeat, the other by victory. Around sundown, the Unionists stopped on the far side of the ridge, trying to reform units. The men lay down and rested. But there was a new outbreak of cheering as a General rode down the lines waving to the men.

—It's Grant!

—RRRRRRRRAAAAAAA!

—Good old Ulyss!

General Grant smiled. He stopped at the place where Flash and Johnny were standing, pointed toward a road, said something to his staff.

—How about it, Ulyss! Flash said. We took 'em for yuh, didn't we!

The men stood around.

—Three cheers for General Grant.

They cheered.

—Good fight, men, the little General said. Reform your units, and pursue the Enemy. Don't give 'em any rest.

Out of his blackstubbled beard stuck the stump of a dead cigar. He looked quite unmoved by the victory. As he rode on down the lines, the men continued to cheer.

—Where are the other boys? Flash said.

—Jesse and Tom Conway got hit, Johnny said.

He lay down by the campfire. He had tied a wet bandage around his head. He was too sick and tired to eat. His head whirred, sang, pounded with the violence of the charge.

Twenty million hands, generations of strong hands, had pushed him up that slope. He had reached the crest of Missionary Ridge on a wave of history. Here at this vital place, the thin, tough line of the South had suffered an hour of weakness and confusion, and several thousand stronglegged young men had broken through to the top of a mountain. Perhaps at last far down the roads receding south, where the wreck of the Rebel Army retreated, a man with good eyesight could see the white shape of Victory.

Corporal Johnny Shawnessy ceased to know anything about that. He was still appalled at the fury of that long charge up Missionary Ridge. He desperately yearned for home, for the soft arms of a woman who loved him and to whom he was a precious, irreplaceable person. Hadn't he done enough for the Cause, now that he was a veteran of both defeat and victory?

What he could never get used to was the fact that War was the supreme image of Chance, brutal god of the battle casualty. With a blind sowing of gold seed in the swamp of life, life had begun. With a blind sowing of lead seed in the confusion of battle, life ended.

He began to feel a little better after he had eaten something, and he sat and talked and joked with the others, who were beginning to relive the Battle. Every man had taken Missionary Ridge in a different way. The victory had been twenty thousand separate fights. The Battle of Missionary Ridge was only now beginning to be created in the shared images of the twenty thousand men who had gone from base to summit in the forever lost afternoon of the physical fighting.

Later on, that night, Johnny saw a longlegged figure striding through the lines, looking everywhere among the resting soldiers. It was the Perfessor. His face was haggard and anxious.

—Hi, Professor, Johnny said.

The Perfessor stopped and peered at Johnny's bandaged head in the dusk.

—My God, John, is that you?

His voice was peculiarly high. He sat down on the ground beside Johnny and took a long time to light a cigar, cupping his hands around it.

—I see you got through all right, he said.

—I'm all right except for a bang on the head.

The Perfessor made his cigar glow and took his hands away from his face. He was darting his eyes about in his usual manner.

—It's a great victory, he said. Thousands of prisoners taken. Bragg won't be able to stop this side of Atlanta. Hello, Perkins. Surprised you had any fight left in you, after the other night.

—How are the dames? Flash said.

—You know terrible girls, Orville, the Perfessor said. You boys'll have to pardon me. I have to file some dispatches. How many men lost in your regiment?

—No telling, yet, Johnny said.

—Losses not very heavy for the results achieved, the Perfessor said, as if making a note. This will be great news. The siege of Chattanooga broken! Bragg in wild, disorderly retreat! The Gateway to the South opened to our armies! With his mailed fist, the Hero of Vicksburg smote one——

—Save it for the newspapers, Professor, Johnny said.

—Could one of you boys swipe me a horse? the Perfessor said. Some Confederate nag no one else wants?

Later the Perfessor got a horse and rode off toward Chattanooga.

All night in his sleep, Johnny Shawnessy was pressing up a long slope. All night long in the gray and red figuration of the dream, he was trying to reach the crest of a hill. The pale bodies of a thousand soldiers were scattered on the gray-green slopes of his sleep. The bloody fragments of the day

TRIED VAINLY TO COMPLETE THEMSELVES

IN THE TROUBLED CAVES OF

HIS

—MEMORIES of the Republic in War and Peace, the Senator was saying, which, by the way, I propose to make the title of a modest work of mine soon to be published—flood the soul on such a day as this. Sacred memories of other days they are, and perhaps it has been fitting to linger, as I have done, a little among some, the most sacred and significant, the common heritage of our people.

The Senator had been speaking for an hour to frequent applause. During this time he had discovered America (How many of you are aware that this is the quadricentennial anniversary of the discovery of America by the Prince of Explorers?), established the thirteen colonies (O, proud peoples, bringing in frail barks across the perilous sea the inextinguishable fire of freedom to virgin shores . . .), fought and won three wars (Did she ever bare her sword in other than a righteous cause?), composed and proclaimed two of the greatest documents in the literature of human enlightenment (Two of the greatest documents in the literature of human enlightenment!), exterminated the Indian (We must honor his stoical endeavor to keep his savage empire, but the forces of freedom, enlightenment, and civilization have pushed irresistibly on. . . .), and conquered the wilderness, the great plains, the desert, and the mountains (These ships of the interminable seas of waving grass bore in their ribbed and canvas-covered walls—burning unquenchably—the spark of . . .).

Now the Senator was approaching one of his celebrated climaxes. The Perfessor was frankly asleep. Mr. Shawnessy, impressed by the splendor of the Senator's delivery, was attempting to analyze what it was that made the Senator a magnificent ham instead of a great statesman. He had nevertheless been moved by the Senator's discourse, which was mannered and proportioned like classical inscriptions wherein the history of vanished peoples is preserved. Who then, after all, was the greater poet? Mr. John Wickliff Shawnessy, the maker of a huge manuscript that might never see print, or Senator Garwood B. Jones, whose utterance was the living breath of history applauded by millions?

—If we must choose one word, the Senator was saying, if we must seek out and sanctify a solitary epithet to express the spirit of our generation, the slogan of our Republic in the last fifty years, what would it be? Who that has beheld this epic of the forging of a nation from ocean unto ocean can doubt the answer! Forward the course of empire has advanced, the manifest destiny of a great people, riding the winds of Fate, with Courage for the arms and Freedom for the goal. What word shall describe this pilgrimage of peoples toward the setting sun? There is but one word to fit the scenes that we have seen in fifty years. Yesterday—the desolate, windswept prairie; today—the mighty City with broad boulevards and costly monuments. Yesterday—the rocky, inhospitable coast; today—the great ports filled with shipping. Yesterday—a race in chains; today—the dusky children of emancipation with faces set hopefully to the future. Only by a Union of Free Peoples, One Nation Indivisible, could we have achieved this thing. Under the banner of that God who has never forsaken our people in their hour of need, we shall go on, good soldiers in the cause of freedom, and on our banners, as we pass through burning shards of barbarous superstition and down broad roads of splendid and serene fulfillment, we shall bear a single word emblazoned for all the world to see——

THROUGH DOOMED
ATLANTA WAS PRETTY HARD
because of the hundreds of supply wagons. There could be no question about it—the Army was getting out.

—Hey, Jimmy, one of the drivers called to another, I wish we could stay and see the fun.

—The engineers have all the luck.

—Goin' to be one hell of a big wreckin' party.

The foodbringers of the Army whipped on their horses. The long files kept turning into the street that debouched from the yards.

Johnny and Professor Stiles could see thick ganglia of tracks a block away. They walked on and stopped beside a bank on the corner at the edge of the yards. They were in sight of the depot. Several companies of infantry were laying levers to a length of track.

—All together, heave! yelled a cheeryvoiced sergeant.

With a reluctant shriek, the rail came ripping, up-ending ties. A thin dust drifted. The Perfessor got out his sketch book and began to draw. The destruction of Atlanta had begun.

Johnny Shawnessy stood for a while at the corner watching. He had seen a great deal since the day when, almost a year ago, a veteran of a single battle, he had charged up the slope of Missionary Ridge. Since then he had wintered in Chattanooga and had fought through one of the most exhausting campaigns in the history of warfare. Following the victory at Missionary Ridge, Grant had gone to the Eastern Theatre of Operations, where he had spent the summer in fruitless battles trying to crush Lee's army and take Richmond. Sherman had become the commander of the Armies of the West and in the spring had initiated a campaign to take Atlanta, Georgia. All summer his armies had fought and flanked from Chattanooga to Atlanta. On the first of September, the main arsenal-fortress of the Confederacy in the West had fallen. It was the first mortal crack in the South's armor.

During this time, Johnny Shawnessy had become a veteran soldier. He had learned to fight and to endure. And as the skills of his trade were few and simple, what he mainly had to do all the time was to endure.

To Corporal Johnny Shawnessy and the other fighting soldiers, North and South, the War had long ago become a contest in endurance. Newfangled weapons were all right, the cavalry was all right, the engineers were all right—all these things were necessary and important. But Johnny and his comrades knew that Victory—that theoretically possible but practically invisible goal—was achieved by a brutally simple thing—a soldier with a long musket loading at the muzzle and firing a lead ball. This irreducible unit of warfare had to be powered with legs able to march forty miles a day. It had to be equipped with an intangible something called 'morale' that made it able to stand and fire in the face of an entrenched enemy. There was a great deal more, but it was all subsidiary to the use and advance of this ancient weapon of attack, occupation, and defense, the combat infantryman. If the infantryman was properly used in adequate numbers and if he had enough endurance, a series of pins might be moved on a map until the Enemy position was untenable and further war unthinkable. This goal was the object of something called 'Strategy.' Corporal Johnny Shawnessy and his comrades made Strategy possible.

Except for the long musket and a slight difference in sartorial styles, the Civil War infantryman wasn't far distinguishable from a Roman legionary, and his battles were fought and won according to the same plan. His power to inflict a wound was increased over the short sword. But he was the same instrument of strategy. He was hurled in compact masses on the enemy's front or flank in an effort to break through, roll up, encircle, capture, confuse. Through the primitive forest and mountain country between Chattanooga and Atlanta, the young men with muskets comprising Sherman's Army had flanked and fought all summer to drive the Southern armies from one entrenched position after another. There had been no easy, glamorous, or brilliant way to achieve the thing called 'Victory.' There had been only this strong, bearded, tough, devoted, and probably doomed young man—the Union infantryman.

In the incredibly primitive, unhappy life of a Civil War infantryman, something had happened to young Johnny Shawnessy of Raintree County. To begin with, he had changed in appearance. He hadn't shaved for over a year, though he sometimes clipped his beard, which was much lighter in color and redder than his hair. His uniform was a grotesque remnant of the bright new thing that had been issued to him after enlistment. He had lived a life more brute than a beast's. He had fought for weeks on end through rainrotten forests, up mountains, down endless dirt roads—marching, countermarching, bivouacking, fighting. He had slept in mud, filth, dirt, lice. He had gone days and sometimes weeks without change of uniform or a bath.

Once he had gone a month without looking into a mirror. When he did so, he saw a strange person, a bearded automaton with a lean, sundarkened face, whitewrinkled around two dull, tired eyes. He knew then how greatly he had changed. He had buried all softer emotions in favor of the combat soldier's two main preoccupations—duty and survival.

For skillfully and without heroism, he had done his duty. And inflexibly, he had willed to survive.

For what?

So that one day he could cease to be a fearing, hating, expertly dangerous human being. So that one day he might forcibly lay hands on this hard husk and tear it off and restore to sunlight that young poet of life, a generously emotional, happy, affirmative creature, Johnny Shawnessy of Raintree County. So that one day he might sleep on a soft bed, eat good food, wear civilian clothes, walk freely where he pleased, work at some innocent task that didn't have homicide as its ultimate objective. So that one day—one impossibly remote, breath-taking day—he might put his arms around the supple waist of a young woman who loved him and whom he loved and kiss her upturned face and feel her bare arms on his shoulders.

He didn't allow himself to think too much of that day. For the present, it was best to leave the husk on, hide within it, endure. Endure, endure, and endure.

He suspected, however, that either the husk had become a part of him, or that the creature beneath it had changed. For after all, he had remained a human being even in the Army, this organized deial of a man's humanity. He had acquired certain ideally simple and touchingly human attributes, which he shared with his comrades.

He had acquired the simple loyalties of the soldier. He was fiercely loyal to his comrades, to his regiment, to his brigade, to his General. He had learned to hate—if not the Rebels—at least their Cause. He felt murderous when he thought of the speculators, bounty jumpers, and Copperhead politicians on the home front. The Union of the States had become a mystically beautiful concept for him and synonymous with Freedom.

War had discovered in him a simple human being who clung yearningly and without criticism to the most ancient beliefs of the Republic. They made it possible for him to endure. They justified his agony. This agony was so great and terrible that only by infusing it with an ideal quality crudely religious in its fervors could it be endured. Only an intensely sentimental soldier in an intensely sentimental Republic could have fought and endured the Civil War.

Meanwhile, Corporal Johnny Shawnessy had become superficially like his comrades in some of his other habits. He had begun to smoke. He was rarely profane, but the immense profanity of the soldier seemed to him strangely unprofane. It expressed the soldier's enormous disgust with the inhumanity of his life. What the soldier endured was fit to be described only by verbal excretions. The Civil War soldier cursed fighting, eating, marching. He cursed awake, and he cursed asleep. He was cursing the great insanity of War with the bitter curse of experience.

The soldier's pleasures found their ultimate simplicity in the embrace of the campfollower. Johnny had ample opportunity to study this oldest impedimentum of the foot-soldier. It was possible to have wars without battles but not without whores. They followed the soldier almost into the Enemy's guns. Perhaps it was they who made the War possible for him. They gave him the last of his great illusions. Though Johnny himself couldn't have touched a woman who didn't adore him, he understood that the soldier desperately wanted life in the midst of death. He would have some semblance of love—even its bought counterfeit. He would have it—and its unfailing scarlet aftermath. He would drink, smoke, whore. But somehow he would remain the soldier. Somehow he would achieve by this means more than by any other the purity of the soldier. By this pathetic gesture he affirmed the greatness of his sacrifice. All this was part of the uncleanness of battle.

By the time Corporal Johnny Shawnessy had arrived in the railroad yards of Atlanta, Georgia, he was well schooled in the uncleanness of battle, but there was still something to learn.

A photographer across the yards was focusing his instrument. The wagontrain had stopped just after the last wagon had rolled over the tracks.

—Don't move, boys, the photographer yelled. Just a minute.

The Perfessor went on sketching, while the photographer ducked under the hood behind his boxbodied apparatus.

—What are you drawing, Professor? Johnny said.

—I'm sketching a picture of the photographer taking a picture. Thus I get the best of him.

—But don't forget that he has a picture of you sketching a picture of him.

—Yes, the Perfessor said, but don't forget that I have a picture of him taking a picture of me sketching a picture of him.

The photographer was carrying the plate to his Whatisit for development, the supply wagons were moving again, and time, which had been chemically arrested, began to flow again on the doomed walls of Atlanta.

—What time do you expect the train? the Perfessor asked.

—Any time now.

—It'll have to come soon. Sherman's obviously going to wreck the joint before he moves.

Johnny walked across the tracks to the station. The wagons rolled and rattled through the town on a stream of cusswords, whipcracks, jingled harness, squeaks, bawdy songs. He read the words on the large white building to his left.

ATLANTA HOTEL

and on other buildings around him: BILLIARD-SALOON, HARDWARE, HAGAN & CO., GROCERIES, CONFECTIONERIES, PHOENIX, CONNOR & HARDACE.

Tomorrow would not find these legends written on the treacherous stuff of time. They looked down on Johnny with a tragic fixity, like fragments of words dug from the ruins of an antique city. These sweaty soldiers in workworn uniforms, these cursing comrades in a passing afternoon, these blasphemous wagoners were mythical men. They were the destroyers of Atlanta and the legended walls of Atlanta.

Of course time had destroyed all forums of all republics, but the process had been slow—sometimes a work of centuries. History moved faster now in the white light of the Nineteenth Century, and a sentimental republic with hundreds of thousands of defenders could flower and fade in a few years.

Looking about him at the yard, he thought of days in Atlanta before the War, of the trains clanging to the station, the ladies in wide dresses stepping down, the jocund buggies waiting to receive them, the Negroes lounging outside the big depot. So they had driven forth, these sentimental ladies, into the lazy, lightfilled streets, homeward in summer through a stately name. They had ridden through Atlanta, and they never dreamed, these softspoken, tender ladies, that in a few years a horde of hardlegged boys in blue uniforms would march joking, cursing, singing through Atlanta and tear her ancient fabric.

Here at last, after incredible persistence on the one hand and incredible resistance on the other, the palladium of the South had been surrendered. And if one were obliged to say, just here or here is the tough heart of the South, beating lifeblood to its defenders, it would be this depot, whose great ventricles had pulled and pumped the chugging engines, receiving and replenishing and rendering forth again.

Now the South was stricken in this heart. Her Enemy had had too many engines on too many tracks, too many factories in too many cities, too many determined generals juggling sheets of supplies and railroad timetables, too many corps of engineers, too many whirring, remorseless machines, too many legions of stronghearted boys. An Army sixty thousand strong, trained for endurance, fierce and jocular, veterans of a dozen battles, was poised for the kill. And over these swarming legions presided a symbol of this Army, William Tecumseh Sherman, a Westerner, a man who had seen Destiny, disguised as a locomotive, moving across the plains, Sherman, the madman who had said in the War's beginning that 200,000 men must swarm down from the West in an overwhelming tide of envelopment and devastation before the South could be conquered.

Of all the Northern generals, Sherman had been the first to pay the South the bloody compliment of understanding that she was a total nation and must be totally conquered.

Soldiers were beginning to pile up the wooden sleepers for bonfires. They sang, quipped, called loudly to one another at their work. Johnny went on down through the yards. An engine drawing four cars was coming in from the north. Soot belched grayly from the funnelstack. Soldiers cleared the tracks and stood back waving their arms at the engineer.

—Better hurry, Captain. Ain't gonna be no station left around here in a little while.

Johnny walked on beside the depot and turned in at the open end. He stood on a platform inside, waiting for the train. There was one passenger car and a string of freights. Troops were clinging to the sides and riding on top. They waved their hands. The train came steadily on toward the righthand halfcircle of the three-mouthed depot. Now the tracks were swarming with soldiers as far back as he could see. The train coasted into the depot. Soldiers jumped down; men poured from the open sides of the freightcars. Supplies were lifted out. Civilians and officers came from the lone passenger car.

—Hurry up and unload those cars, a major of engineers shouted. Get that train out of here. We're going to blow this station up.

Under the wide, slow circle of the roof, the engine bell was clanging; the troops were unpacking their gear and moving toward the exits; in the brown sunstreaked spaces of the depot the voices of hundreds of men made a busy murmur.

One seldom stopped to think that great interiors could be destroyed. Hollow containers of change, themselves never changing, they were less mutable than sky and trees. It didn't matter how long ago this roof had been lifted—it had the timelessness of a center of arrival and departure that itself never departs or arrives, but remains a constant in equations of mutability.

On a far platform a spare figure in black civilian garb was standing. Johnny instantly recognized the liquidbrown eyes, the grave composure, the trim, pointed beard.

—Well, John, Cash Carney said after the conventional greetings, looks like I got here just before the deluge. I'm glad you got my letter.

As they left the station, a group of officers standing at the entrance nodded to Cash.

—Goodday, Colonel, Cash said. Going to have some fun, I see.

—Yes. Thanks for sending that load of stuff through so promptly, Mr. Carney.

They moved out into the light.

—Colonel Poe, of Sherman's staff, Chief Engineer, Cash said. I do a lot of business with him. I'm down here now to handle a supply problem for the Army. It's a shame to see them rip all this stuff up. Nice depot. Not much of a town though. Just came down in time to see them blow the hell out of it. So this is what you boys were fighting for all summer? Well, it's a war of railroads. Once Sherman wrecks the Rebel system of supply, this war is going to be over. Do you have any idea where Uncle Billy is going to take you scamps?

—He hasn't told us, Johnny said. The order of November 9 promised a long and difficult march, involving a change of base. The Army is being stripped for movement.

—Wouldn't surprise me if he went clear to the East Coast, Cash said. He's cutting himself off from the North completely. Last telegraphic dispatch went through two days ago. Then they blew a bridge and cut the line. Our train was already over. I've been outside the city the last two days. The Union forces here in the West have been divided in two. One mass is withdrawing to Chattanooga and Nashville, and it looks as though you boys were beginning to move through Georgia. In between, Hood is squatting trying to figure out where to hit. How do the men feel about it? What do they think of marching right off into the heart of the South?

—So that we keep our bellies full, Johnny said, we don't care where we go. This is a marching Army.

—How did you boys react to the Election?

—The Army was for Lincoln. Of course, we Indiana boys couldn't vote because the Copperhead legislature at home wouldn't let us.

—You boys voted with your bayonets. You elected Lincoln when you took Atlanta.

—Have you been home? Johnny said. Seen anyone I know?

This was the thing he had been wanting to say.

—I haven't been in the County for over a year, Cash said. I guess it's still there.

—Clear the yards! came a yell. Depot's going up!

Cash and Johnny withdrew to a drugstore from which they could watch. The Perfessor waved his hand and came over. He and Cash greeted each other warmly. The Perfessor observed that Cassius had a lean and hungry look for a man who had been steeping in gravy since the War started, and Cash asked the Perfessor if he had been chased out of any towns lately.

Already the last charges had been laid under the walls of the depot.

—It's been a nice little city, the Perfessor said.

Colonel Poe and his staff walked leisurely away from the depot. Several engineers ran far back from the sides. A ring of soldiers formed in the surrounding streets. The brick face of the city preserved for a final moment its ancient pattern. Then the roof of the depot shifted and a spray of bricks spouted noiselessly from the base. A series of heavy soundblows staggered the three men at the corner. The walls of the depot crumbled. The roof settled and sank as if slowly relaxing, thundered gently, sent up a huge soft flower of dust and smoke. The soldiers cheered, tossed their hats. Teeth gleamed in bearded faces. The yards swarmed with men, busily at work to destroy the roundhouse and the machineshops.

—Say, a soldier said, let's burn the whole goddam place up. Ain't nothin' to keep us from it.

A hot wind fanned Corporal Johnny Shawnessy's face. Fire was the supreme violence in this existence of perpetual violence. The War would end at last in the terror and beauty of fire until nothing was left but a dead ash. In this cataclysm, he, Northman and Invader, had connived.

A hot breath breathed on Corporal Johnny Shawnessy and died, but left the heat. He and the Perfessor said good-by to Cash Carney and walked away toward the bivouac outside the city. Evening was approaching as they reached the outskirts of the town. In the soft, still air columns of smoke stood stiffly from the center of the city. Flames licked the darkening roofs. The fire was spreading, audibly eating its way through the deserted walls of Atlanta.

Everywhere there was movement. Some companies were already

beginning the march. Wagon trains were assembling and filing through and around the city, though some had to be rerouted because of the unexpected spread of the fire.

Now all along the road where the brigade was encamped, as far as Johnny could see, were the wagons of the black people. For days they had been gathering on the fringes of the Army. No regulations could prevent it. Most of the Southern Negroes stayed with their masters, but in the path of Sherman's Army there were no masters. To the more ignorant, Lincoln was like a god, and Sherman was his brightsworded lieutenant. When they learned that the Northerners wouldn't spit them on bayonets and roast them over slow fires, they came in growing hordes, some on foot, but the majority driving brokendown wagons. In the tragic illumination of the fire, this uprooted people had a new significance. Perhaps they collectively remembered the ancestral rape by which they had been torn from the bosom of primitive centuries, borne oversea in the stinking slavers, sold into bondage in the white man's country. Children of violence, in violence they were being restored to freedom. Atlanta, the city of the white masters, was roaring into death.

The dark flesh glistened on the roads around Atlanta. Murmurous, like a surf, it darkly seethed at the edges of the Army. These people had heard that they were to be free, and like a sign of their liberation they saw this spectacle of fire. To many, the burning of Atlanta was Judgment Day.

Soldiers kept streaming out of the town loaded with plunder raped from deserted homes and buildings. Shortly after Johnny and the Perfessor reached the camp, Flash Perkins came in. He hadn't been in camp for several days. He kept laughing louder than usual and hitting Johnny and the Perfessor on the back. At last, he said,

—You fellers wanna see somethin'? I'll show you somethin' good, if you'll keep your mouths shut.

He led the way down a little sideroad. In the corner of the field was a pile of junk on wheels. A very pretty Negro girl was cooking pigfat at a woodfire. An old Negro man was lying on the ground close to the wagon talking to a little Negro boy.

—What the hell! Flash said belligerently. They wanted to come with me. I sot 'em free. They think I'm a god or somethin'. I brung 'em back with me.

—Um, the Perfessor said, thoughtfully regarding the group. Noble gesture, Orville.

—A souvenir of the Atlanta Campaign, Johnny said.

—I was never distinguished for race prejudice myself, Orville, the Perfessor said.

That night, Johnny, Flash, and the Perfessor took some bottles of wine and some chickens and had a banquet down in the corner of the field where the Negro girl was. She was sleek, coalblack, good-natured, young. She had the grace of a young thoroughbred. She smiled most of the time and spoke in a husky, pleasant voice. Her name was Parthenia. The old Negro man was referred to as Uncle Hervey, though he claimed no relationship to the girl, of whom he openly disapproved. The little colored boy was called Joe. None of them had a last name.

The hot wind fanned Corporal Johnny Shawnessy's cheek. Lying in the redrimmed darkness, he remembered John Brown's song:

> Blow ye the trumpet, blow
> The gladly-solemn sound!
> Let all the nations know
> To earth's remotest bound,
> The year of Jubilee has come!

The torch of Atlanta grew brighter and hotter. For a long time there had been intermittent explosions. Someone said an arsenal was on fire.

—What do you think of that for a bonfire, Parthenia? the Perfessor asked.

—It seem a shame to burn up all them white folk house thataway, she said.

The Perfessor became very moody as the night wore on, and later in the evening he said,

—Do you have a sister, Parthenia?

Flash laughed fiercely.

—I see you took Sherman's advice to heart, Orville, the Perfessor said. Forage liberally on the country.

—What are you going to do with them when we march? Johnny asked.

—Take 'em along, Flash said. Hell, they look up to me to save 'em and take keer of 'em.

Later on, back in camp, Johnny lay listening to the songs of the Negroes still swelling through the redlit darkness.

—No mo hunded lash foh me,
No mo, no mo.
No mo hunded lash foh me.
Many a thousand die.

No mo bag a cawn foh me,
No mo, no mo.
No mo bag a cawn foh me.
Many a thousand die.

His skin was fevered with the heat he had felt from the moment when the depot had shifted and sunk and the first flames had sprung. The wine of the South burned in his veins. Primeval images struggled in him, sensual and strong, bringing no release but only wishes that could have no fulfillment.

He listened to the thick waves of song that came from the night, the distant cries and muffled booms from the city, the rattle and creak of the wagontrains departing, departing. In this darkness, the times were changing, the War was changing, the Republic was changing. After years of deadlock, a few hours had shown signs of the crumbling of an era. The earth of mancreated boundaries and habitations was in convulsion. What did it mean that around him uprooted thousands without names, whose past was darker than their skins, swarmed toward the beacon of burning Atlanta!

He was troubled by the image of the Negro girl. She seemed to him a darkskinned Helen for whom this epic war was being fought.

The hot wind fanned his cheeks. He could feel great tides of change and old desire going over him on the cinderladen wind. Perhaps a man felt most alive when things were changing, when cities were being raped and burned, when love laughed at forbiddenness. If then he could have had a beautiful, smoothfleshed woman of his own kind in this night of permitted crime, he would have been utterly fulfilled.

The hot wind fanned his cheeks. He had come southward to march through stately names. Atlanta—it was a name feminine, as of a once lovely woman of pathetic memory. Now it was being destroyed by fire. Ah, it was no use to be the rememberer at such times as this. Was he doomed always to remember his name and Raintree County origins! All barriers, inhibitions, memories, names, duties, and speculations were swept away by purging and terrific fire! It was time for that nameless hero to exert himself again and striding through the night discover love beneath a shaken tree, while the light of ravaged cities shone on distant waters. It was good to be lost in this onrushing Event, to be this city burning in the night, to be this seed-dense earth on which he lay, to be this flame that purified and destroyed, to be this moving of the wagontrains, to be of and in and for this Army of insouciant young men, to be each and all of them, from the General whose orders set a hundred thousand hands to work, down to the lustful and triumphant comrade who exerted himself this night upon a creature of the musky Southern earth. This it was to live, to be lifted and borne upon the crest of events, to be at the head of the column where the veteran soldiers loved to be, to be in danger, yes, but in prospect of victory and the savage and sweet spoils of victory.

In the morning, he awakened to a vague sense of guilt. A low pall of smoke hung on the gutted city. The brigade didn't march all day, though many others were moving out. They didn't march the following night either, but lingered over the cold banquet of the ravaged city. On the following morning early, they left, marching on the road to Decatur, their faces turned toward the east. As they topped a rise just outside the old Rebel works, the men turned and looked back.

—Right here is where we fought that big battle of July 22, Captain Bazzle said. McPherson fell back there.

Atlanta was still smoking. The broad scar where the railroad tracks had been, the charred fragments of buildings made Johnny think of a face in which the eyes had been destroyed and the withered pits remained, mournful reminders.

—Look there, Jack, Flash said, ain't that Sherman?

A general with his staff was riding along the lines. A cheer went up from the men.

—Hi there, Uncle Billy!

—Hey, Uncle Billy! Flash called out. I reckon Grant is waitin for us in Richmond.

Sherman's thin, ugly face smiled. Johnny was surprised by the flash of kind, quick light in the eyes of a man whom several million people execrated. A little past the two men, Sherman stopped. With an expression of nostalgia and fierce pride, he too looked back at ruined Atlanta—Sherman, who had wept when he heard the news of McPherson's death near this spot months before in the summer of the siege.

Corporal Johnny Shawnessy remembered then how the Army had fought its way down from Chattanooga, remembered Resaca and the wide ditch in which they had buried hundreds of comrades, remembered rainy weeks in the woods at the base of Kenesaw Mountain, remembered the fierce charge halfway up the flank of that conical hill, remembered the flanking marches, the crossings of rivers, the falling back of the Southern Army to Atlanta, the hard battles after Hood had replaced Johnston in the Rebel command, the long looking from distant lines at Atlanta besieged, the sudden withdrawal from before it, the last great flanking move, the news of Atlanta's fall, the occupation, the long camping near-by, and at last the devastation of Atlanta. And now departure.

The vast myriapod of the Army slogged monotonously on. The troops were beginning to sing as Sherman turned his horse's head and rode along the column. The soldiers were singing the oldest song of the War.

—John Brown's body lies a-mouldering in the grave,
John Brown's body lies a-mouldering in the grave,
John Brown's body lies a-mouldering in the grave,
His soul is marching on.

The longstriding Westerners were going East. An army had completely severed itself from its base of supplies, striking straight into the heart of the Enemy's stronghold.

So in the warm autumn of the South, they had turned their faces east, and the Great March had begun. The soldiers didn't know where they were going, but they knew that by nightfall they would be somewhere they had never been before,

SOMEWHERE FAR ALONG THE ROAD TO
THE ENDING OF THE WAR,
SOMEWHERE

. . . tenting tonight on the old camp ground
Give us a song to cheer
Our weary hearts, a song of home,
And friends we love so dear.

Chorus

Many are the hearts that are weary tonight
Wishing for the war to cease;
Many are the hearts that are looking for the right,
To see the dawn of peace.
Tenting tonight, tenting tonight,
Tenting on the old camp ground.

He was tenting on the old camp ground of hundreds of lost encampments, dressed in his faded suit of blue and dreaming of the girl he left behind him. His mother kissed him in his dream, he wrapped the flag around him, boys, to fight and die was sweet, boys, with Freedom's starry banner, boys, wound for a winding sheet. He was tenting on that sentimental old camp ground where all the veterans camped in their declining years.

We are tired of war on the old camp ground,
Many are dead and gone,
Of the brave and true who've left their homes;
Other's been wounded long. . . .
Dying tonight, dying tonight,
Dying on the old camp ground.

And how long would it be, he was wondering, till the very last of them all, the oldest of all the incredibly old veterans, would tent for the last time in the old camp ground of a longforgotten war?

The Perfessor drew a short, quick breath, but lapsed back again into sleep. The quavering horns quickened to a faster tempo.

In the prison cell I sit,
Thinking, Mother dear, of you,

And our bright and happy home so far away.
And the tears they fill my eyes
Spite of all that I can do,
Tho' I try to cheer my comrades and be gay.

Tramp, tramp, tramp, the boys are marching,
Cheer up, comrades, they will come,
And beneath the starry flag
We shall breathe the air again,
Of the freeland in our own beloved home.

Listen to the sound of the bugles blowing loud. *Tramp, tramp, tramp, the boys are . . .*

Who is marching there? Who are these bearded young men?

Bring the good old bugle, boys, we'll sing another song—
Sing it with a spirit that will start the world along—
Sing it as we used to sing it, fifty thousand strong,
While we were marching through Georgia.

Hurrah! Hurrah! we bring the jubilee,
Hurrah! Hurrah! the flag that makes you free!
So we sang the chorus from Atlanta to the sea,
While we were marching through Georgia.

Yes, bring the good old bugle, boys, and blow into being the ranks of the comrades of that Army. Blow into being the columns extending for miles, the husky noise of thousands singing on the march, the rattling wagons. Blow into being the hordes of the liberated slaves. Blow into being the bearded bummers. For it is still marching, that legendary Army. It was never anything but a great myth marching to Savannah on the Sea! They didn't march in any newspaper, they were from the beginning—were they not?—immense soldiers of stone!

Ah, what becomes of young hearts, warm weather, singing throats? And is victory no more enduring than defeat? Where are they all now, commander and commanded! Were they ever real, and was I one of them, bearing in my weatherstained knapsack the unseen grail of the Republic! Then, sing it as we used to sing it

November 26— FIFTY —1864

THOUSAND STRONG
ON THE EARTH OF GEORGIA,

the Army of the West awakened from its sleep. The vague fabric of a dream Corporal Johnny Shawnessy had been dreaming collapsed under the buglenotes fast crowding in the dawn.

He awakened. He was with the Army, they were to be up and marching soon, and there would be another day crammed with fiercely jocund images, as the Army of the West flowed on four roads toward Savannah on the sea.

Hawkfaced, naked except for his jackboots, Professor Jerusalem Webster Stiles was striding toward the dawncolored east on rakethin legs, chanting:

—Then up, then up, brave gallants all,
And don your helms amain.
Death's couriers, Fame and Honor, call
Us to the field again.

On both sides of the road the Army was getting ready to leave the night encampment. Johnny smelled bacon frying. Aroma of coffee fumed in his nostrils. Later he shook a skilletful of corncakes while the Perfessor held the coffeepot.

Flash Perkins drove up the road in a wagon crammed with provisions. Parthenia was sitting on the seat beside him, and Joe and the old man were in back. Flash whistled as he jumped down and walked over to the camp. He flung his big feet sideways. His coat was unbuttoned. His high, hard nasal voice jabbed Johnny's ears.

—Say, are you fellers part of this yere big Army I been hearin' tell about?

As usual everyone was glad to see Flash.

—What's the matter? Decide to march with us poor whites for a while?

—I brung you poor bastards a little food, Flash said.

—What a yuh got?

—Chicken, goose, pig, lard, little ever'thing. What'll yuh have?

—If you don't mind, I'll have a little of that dark meat there, the Perfessor said.

The men were cheerful as they sat around the fire eating breakfast. The sun found them still roasting chickens on their bayonets. The air was warm and bright.

—Jack, you and the Perfessor come with me today, Flash said, and I'll show you some fun.

Johnny had been wanting to go with Sherman's bummers. Foragers who operated independent of all command, they stripped the countryside of its riches and made the name of Sherman execrated on both sides of the Army's path. For a week and a half now the Army had been marching from Atlanta, and during this time Flash Perkins had spent only one day—the first—with his company. Since then he and the other bummers had moved on the Army's flanks and front, returning when they pleased, sometimes mounted on mules, sometimes driving wagons, always loaded with provisions—the fat of the land. There were regular foragers, too, usually fifty from each brigade, duly officered, but the bummers were without regular status. Fabulous stories were told by and about them—how they made themselves rich in a few nights by the pillage of buried treasures, how they went among the plantations acting the part of God's lieutenants, emancipating hordes of slaves, how they sometimes gathered in swarms without officers and fought detachments of the Georgia militia.

Flash, the Perfessor, and Johnny set out on foot, the two soldiers equipped with lean knapsacks, muskets, and forty rounds, the Perfessor armed with an old service revolver.

As they passed along the road, they saw the Army preparing to abandon camp. Hundreds of wagons were assembling for the day's march. The soldiers were packing on their haversacks and blanket-rolls and lining up in loosely ordered columns. Fires were burning out on the low hills and among the woods. Thousands of bearded, bluecoated soldiers had sprung from this ground where they had lain for a night and to which they would never return. Regimental bands played, men sang, horses neighed. Drums were beating on a hundred hills. Like history endowed with visible form, this many-featured mass was slowly unfolding from its sleep and would go on grandly with a thousand unrecorded collisions and adventures through the blue shining of another day and toward another campfire in the night. For the first time the War had found a deep, straight channel.

The three men soon turned down a side lane and slipped off through a forest. They found a road and went on until mid-morning without incident. Now and then from a break in the woods, at a great distance, they could see the Army. It was good to see the thin line of it proceeding, to know that it was there, vaguely parallel to them, advancing.

There seemed to be no danger in the woods and fields of Georgia. The country was pleasant, green, and firm in the dry weather.

About noon, they saw a plantation house beside a road running at right angles to the course of the Army. They came up to it through a long yard. A woman was standing on the porch, white with anger. Halfway down the lane, Johnny stopped and said,

—Maybe we better not bother her. I thought these places were deserted.

—There's gener'ly a woman around to yipe at you while you pluck the place, Flash said. I don't mind 'em. It's fun to pull their feathers and hear 'em squawk.

When they reached the porch, the woman had gone inside. A dead dog lay in the yard. Two soldiers came out of the house, carrying a chest.

—Come on, boys, they said. They's plenty more where this come from.

Around behind the house, soldiers were digging up the yard.

—We didn't git started early enough, Flash said.

He pushed open the back door. The woman they had seen before came out.

—Murderers! she said in a voice of cold hatred. Thieves! Do you call yourselves soldiers!

—Ma'am, Flash said, would you direct me to the pantry?

—Go on, she said. Wreck everything. Take everything. You'll never beat the South that way. You, there—can't you stop these men?

—Who, me? the Perfessor said. Madame, I'm only here in the capacity of a spectator. Alas, war is at best a dreadful thing. May we trouble you for a drink of water?

Johnny and the Perfessor skittered around the corner of a shed to the pump.

Several curious Negroes were watching the men dig for buried plate and money. A middle-aged white man in shabby civilian attire watched the process, chuckling.

—You boys sho is busy, he said. Dog bite it, eberywhere people been sayin', Jest wait'll the militia hems ole Sherman in. They'll cut 'im to pieces. 'Pears to me you boys am still pretty much uncut. Look here, have y'all tried over there behind the woodshed?

—Obligin' cuss, a soldier said. Say, Uncle, you don't sound like no fire-eatin' Reb to me.

—Dog bite it, the man said, I'm tired of this war. I had my bellyful long ago. Have y'all looked down the well?

Glass shattered, and Flash Perkins stuck his grinning, shaggy head out of a cellar window.

—This here cellar's full a liquor, he said. Here, I'll throw it out.

He began to shove bottles through the opening. Several soldiers came around and drank freely. They went on spading up the garden. Johnny and the Perfessor walked down to the Negro quarters. A group of slaves came out and watched them, not saying much.

—You there, Uncle, the Perfessor said to an old black man. Do you know who we are?

—I reckon youse some of Gennul Sherman's men, the old man said.

—Well, do you know what we're here for?

—Yassuh, the old man said. Dey say hit's the yar ob jubilee.

—That's right, Uncle, Johnny said. You're free now. You don't have to work without pay any more.

They heard an explosion of angry voices behind them, and returning to the house found an old white-haired man standing at the corner of the house. He had a pistol in his hand. His mouth trembled, and his hands shook.

—Go on and git out a here, he said. Goddamyankees. Git back where you belong. This land don't belong to you and never will.

—Better put that pistol down, Grampa, one of the soldiers said.

—I'm a-tellin' you to git.

The woman came out and took the old man by the hand.

—Come on, she said. Come on in, Papa. They'll murder you.

—Listen, you ole bastard, one of the men said, we didn't start this war. You folks would a been let alone, but you had to go and fire on the flag.

—Goddamn the flag! the old man said. I ain't never been a Union man, and never will!

One of the soldiers slipped up behind him. The old man whirled and would have fired, but another forager slipping up from the other side grabbed his arm. One soldier tore the gun away from him, and the other knocked him down.

—Go on, git out, you old bastard, he said, before you git hurt.

—Come on, several of the soldiers said roughly, let's burn this place up and git out a here.

The old man sobbed weakly and yelled something, and the woman led him into the house.

—I hate you! she said, turning to the soldiers. You'll never beat us! Never! We'll hate you to our dying days.

—Let's go, the Perfessor said. This is no business for gentlemen to be engaged in.

Flash came out of the barn driving a wagon. They filled it up with hams, pots of lard, live chickens tied in bunches by the legs, turkeys, geese, a hog, several bottles of liquor. They opened a bottle of wine and drank it as they drove off. Johnny kept trying to forget the hatred in the woman's eyes and voice. They drove for a long time down little roads and stopped at two other places where they got some more provisions. At one a very pretty girl stood and watched them, saucy and proud.

—What do you expect to do with us after you beat us? she asked.

—Nothing, Johnny said. If you'd just let yourselves get beat, we'd quit and draw off. Come back in the Union, that's all, and free your slaves.

—What do you expect to do with the Nigroes when they're free? the girl said.

—Educate them, Johnny said. Set them to work like human beings, getting their own wages.

—Well, the young woman said, you may beat us, but you can never rule us.

—Madame, the Perfessor said, describing a deep bow, Beauty rules and is not ruled.

—You ugly jackanapes! she said, what are you doing here? You aren't even in uniform. Just along for the fun, I suppose.

—Pardon me, the Perfessor said, I see you have some newspapers here. May I borrow one?

They picked up several newspapers lying on a table and carried them off.

When they were in the wagon again, Johnny said,

—I don't see how we can ever reconcile them.

—That was a pretty little Rebel, the Perfessor said. I'd love to reconcile her.

They had dinner in an abandoned plantation house close to the line of march. They stopped the wagon in the yard and went inside the house. Other bummers had already been there, and the place was a shambles. Flash built a fire in the fireplace, and they dragged up a table and prepared to eat. Flash and Johnny set about preparing a broiled turkey, while the Perfessor read aloud to them from the newspapers. Several other soldiers came into the room while they were there, and one of them banged on a bayonet-scarred piano.

There was much loud singing, shouting, cursing, drunken mirth. Several of the men came downstairs with velvet curtains draped around their shoulders.

—Well, shet mah mouf! the Perfessor said. These heah Southuhn newspapuhs shuah ah declamatoruh sheets.

He read in a stagey Southern accent:

—TO THE PEOPLE OF GEORGIA

> Arise for the defense of your native soil! Rally round your patriotic Governor and gallant soldiers! Obstruct and destroy all the roads in Sherman's front, flank, and rear, and his army will soon starve in your midst.

—Please brown that turkey a little more on the back, Johnny said to Flash.

> —Be confident. Be resolute. Trust in an overruling Providence, and success will crown your efforts. I hasten to join you in the defense of your homes and firesides.
>
> G. T. BEAUREGARD
>
> CORINTH, MISSISSIPPI
> November 18, 1864

—Boys, let's enjoy ourselves while we may, Johnny said. Beauregard is coming!

—TO THE PEOPLE OF GEORGIA

read the Perfessor,

> You have now the best opportunity ever yet presented to destroy the enemy. Put everything at the disposal of our generals; remove all provisions from the path of the invader, and put all obstructions in his path.
>
> Every citizen with his gun, and every negro with his spade and axe, can do the work of a soldier. You can destroy the enemy by retarding his march.
>
> Georgians, be firm! Act promptly, and fear not!
>
> B. H. HILL, Senator.
>
> I most cordially approve the above.
>
> JAMES A. SEDDON, Secretary of War.

—We done licked everything else, Flash said. It'd be kind of fun to take on this here B. H. Hill and the Secretary of War.

—I'm ashamed of you boys, the Perfessor said. Listen to this:

ATROCITIES BY THE UNION SCUM

SHERMAN'S MEN LOOT, RAPE, AND MURDER

> Let every Southron in whose patriot breast still palpitates a heart not insusceptible to the claims of outraged womanhood rally to the sacred Cause. We long ago knew that the Yankees were cowards and thieves. It is with regret we learn that they are also rapists, arsonists, defilers of everything sacred to hearth, home, and God. Reports emerging from the devastated areas in the rear of Sherman's Army reveal, alas! beyond any doubt the bestiality of these vulturesque and blood-dripping ruffians from the north. Houses ransacked, old men murdered, women outraged, children slain and thrown down wells, every species of atrocity known to the stained and sanguinary story of human depravity has been surpassed a hundredfold by the work of these gory Goths that now rage unchecked on the fair soil of Georgia.

—Boys, the Perfessor said, you see: you've been found out. The press is ubiquitous, all-seeing, impartial. Your names are branded forever in the sheets of shame.

—Tell you the truth, raping ain't been very good lately, Flash said. I only raped six women yesterday and two today. You raped anybody lately, Perfessor?

—Hardly anything to mention, the Perfessor said. A few old ladies in hedgerows. I've got somewhat out of the habit lately. How about you, John?

—I've been observing a Lent, Johnny said, and have limited myself to two rapes a day. Of course, sometimes the Devil tempts me, and I rape before I think.

The Perfessor was in form. He lay on a sofa delicately gouging its velvet flanks with his pocketknife. He put his booted feet on a bust of John C. Calhoun, which some soldier had crowned with a chamberpot. He had a bottle in his hand from which now and then, sitting up, he tipped a little liquor on the potted pate of the pre-War South's greatest statesman.

—Senator Calhoun, seh, he said, addressing the bust, you see now the result of your pernicious subtleties. Give me another leg off that turkey, Private Perkins.

Flash tore a turkey leg loose and handed it to the Perfessor, who shook the leg under the statue's nose.

—Mr. Calhoun, seh, your people are conquered and your land is laid waste, and it's all your own fault. You have awakened the spirit of rapine and conquest, seh, in a race long accustomed to the ways of peace. This goddamyankee, seh, this simple farmboy, this placid mechanic, contained a sleeping demon. You tapped him with a sword, and he sprang up beating his breast, waving his dagger, brandishing his torch. Laughing with white teeth, he strides through the wreck of your fair South, seh. Seh, the gory Goth was a skittish virgin to him. Ages of puritan repression, seh, have made him more terrible than Attila. Tear me a breast from that chicken, Orville.

The Perfessor tossed a halfchewed bone at the bust and accepted half a chicken from Flash.

—Senator and gentlemen, he said, war is a good life. Men are only happy when they are feeding, fluting, or fighting, and war gives them an opportunity to do all three at once. Fellow Goths, man's eternal urge to war was expressed once and for all by the greatest conqueror in History, Genghis Khan. You will remember, Senator and Private Perkins, how one day the great Mongol asked his lieutenants what they considered the greatest happiness of a man. The greatest happiness of a man, said one, is to ride out on a fast horse when the grass is small and a hawk on the arm. That is good, the Conqueror said, but it is not the best. The greatest happiness of a man is to break his enemies, to drive them before him, to take from them all that is theirs, to hear the weeping of their widows and their orphans, to hold between his knees their swiftest horses, and to press in his arms the most beautiful of their women.

The Perfessor gnashed his white teeth on a chicken bone and shook soundlessly.

There was a wisp of smoke coming from the back of the house.

—Damn house is on fire, Flash said.

—Well, boys, let's get on with our raping, the Perfessor said. He paused long enough to pick three volumes from a bookcase and followed Flash and the others outside. The back of the house was burning famously. They watched it for a while and then climbed into the wagon, the Perfessor declaiming,

> —I warmed both hands before the fire of life,
> It sinks, and I am ready to depart.

As they started off, they heard a sound of hooves on the road behind.

—Calvary! Flash said.

He turned around and stood up in the wagon.

—Jinks—it's Rebel!

Johnny hit the road just behind the Perfessor and rolled into a ditch. He trained his rifle on the leader of the oncoming troop of horsemen. There were about twenty. Several shots came from around the house, and one of the Rebels fell from his horse. The others rode swiftly into a little grove.

—Let's get hell out of here, boys, the Perfessor said crisply.

Just then the Rebels came out of the woods, dismounted. They began to advance, firing in a skirmish line.

—I'm goin' to drive the wagon out, Flash said.

He jumped into the seat and began to flail the mules. The wagon shook off down the road. In the shelter of the ditch, Johnny and the Perfessor ran along beside. Bullets sang by. Two or three wine bottles gurgled dark blood on the road.

A large foraging party approached, mounted on motley beasts and led by a captain.

—What's going on? he asked.

—Just a few Rebels, Johnny said.

—The bummers are whippin' 'em for yuh, Captain, Flash said.

Flash parked the wagon and jumped down. He and Johnny joined the newcomers and began to exchange shots with the Rebels, who retired into the grove where they had left their horses.

—Some of you men go around and flank that grove, the Captain said.

Flash and Johnny left the lines and crept through a ditch and up a hill. The field seemed to be swarming with Union soldiers, most of them irregulars, who had concentrated like magic at the sound of the shooting. After a little while, the flankers, including Johnny and Flash, rushed the grove yelling. The Rebels broke out of the timber, riding. There was a wild discharge of rifles at the fleeing butternut uniforms, and one of the horses went down on his knees and skidded forward, flinging over on his twisted neck and lying still. The rider was thrown heavily, rolling free. He started to get up, shaking his head. Johnny and Flash lit out for the place. The Rebel had lost his rifle and had only a sabre. He spat in disgust.

—That's what comes a leadin' militia, he said.

He was a tall, broadshouldered fellow, with thin lips, light silken mustache and beard, blue eyes. He was only shaken up.

—By God, we got a captain! Flash said. A sure-nuff captain.

—I trust I'm in the hands of gentlemen, the Rebel said, looking apprehensively at Flash Perkins and the other bummers who were moving up around him.

—Give me your sword, Captain, Johnny said. And come along with us. We'll take you to the proper place.

The Rebel seemed relieved.

—Hell of a way to git caught, he said. That's what comes a leadin' militia.

They put the Rebel on the wagon seat between them, and drove away. About a mile down, the Perfessor sat in a ditch smoking a cigar.

—Just taking a little rest, he said, to relax my legs. Been riding so much I—— Hey, who's that?

—Just a Rebel captain, Flash said. We picked him up after the scrap.

—Charmed to make your acquaintance, Captain, the Perfessor said. I'm Jerusalem Stiles of the New York *Dial.*

—James Rutherford, captain in the Georgia Cavalry, the Rebel said. I'm pleased to make your acquaintance, sir.

Introductions were completed all around, and the Perfessor climbed up.

—Now, Johnny said, we have to find the Army. You have any idea where it is, Captain?

—If you mean your Army, sir, I reckon it's all over the place.

The Unionists roared, and the Rebel smiled mournfully.

—How about a drop of something, Captain? the Perfessor said.

—Don't care if I do, the Captain said.

They gave the Confederate a bottle, and he took a long drink.

He sighed.

—Well, he said, this is the goddamnedest war! I fought in six major engagements from Gettysburg to the Wilderness and never lost a horse. Then I gits captured by two foragers and a war correspondent. That's what comes a leadin' militia.

—Say, Flash said, this guy's all right. I hate to turn him over to the Army.

From the crest of a gentle hill, they saw the Army again. It was past noon. The men had turned out for dinner. Muskets were stacked. Fields and yards on each side of the road were littered with soldiers.

Before reaching the main road, Flash drove up a side road that brought them across the Georgia Central Railroad. Coming over a hill and out of the woods, they could see a long stretch of the railroad extending for a mile east. Along this line were a thousand infantrymen, and all on the left side. Shouts of command ran up and down the line. The men bent over, some using levers, many taking the iron rail in their bare hands. The whole line strained and tore a mile of track shrieking from its bed.

—Tell me something, said Captain James Rutherford of the Georgia Cavalry. You Yankees claim this land belongs to the whole nation, don't yuh?

—Sure.

—Then why in hell are yuh tearin' it all up for? There won't be anything left down here for y'all or anyone else, after the War's over.

Along the railroad, men were stacking the wooden ties. The iron rails were laid across the tops of the bonfires. When a rail was red-hot in the center, two men would take each an end and running with the rail fold it neatly around the nearest tree.

—That's what they call Sherman's neckties, Flash said to the Captain.

—I can tell one thing, the Captain said. Sherman don't intend to come back this way.

—And he don't intend to let anyone else come back either, Flash said.

They rode all afternoon through scenes of jovial devastation. The Army was happy in its work of wreckage. Back of it, trailing to westward, lay the burned-out trail of the railroad and hundreds of ravaged homes. The Army passed like a plague of giant locusts: they settled on the land for a night; they rose and left the land bare.

Sometimes Johnny could hear the Army singing. The husky thunder of its Northern songs echoed in the woodlands of Georgia, filling the soft air with unfamiliar rhythms.

Meanwhile, all day long, the wagontrains filled themselves to bursting. Nearing a wellstocked farm, they would stream off the road, around through a gate and past the corncrib. As each wagon passed, men would stuff it with forage. Without stopping, the train would exhaust the contents of the crib and come back to the road.

Everywhere along the Army's path were the Negro people. Each day, with pathetic trust, additional hundreds left their old homes, from which their masters had fled before them, and attached themselves to the Army. Their pitiful wagons were stuffed with junk and pickaninnies. Eastward they went as though to a promised land, although in fact there was nothing that Sherman could do with them when he reached the sea.

On this day especially, the uprooted thousands came out of the earth until they seemed to outnumber the Army. Johnny and the other three men in the wagon were vaguely disturbed by this spectacle of a people marching, unbidden, toward a resurrection.

—I just hope, the Rebel Captain said, that the whole goddam race keeps right on marchin' up North with y'all, and settles right down with yuh. In another fifty years, we'll have another Civil War with the situation reversed.

But the Army thought nothing of that. They didn't trouble themselves with consequences. Now there were blue days on the breast of the land, they were marching. Each day, each hour they passed through new scenes. It was a beautiful country, and they took their toll of it like drunken lovers. They sang, they were carefree, they feared not death or the devil, they were young men, a strong tide, a swift river, which must somewhere come to the sea.

By evening of that day, the Army had moved about fifteen miles, through a dense maze of incident, accident, excitement. New hundreds of black people had been added to its impedimenta. A broad swath of country lay stripped and blackened in its wake. The Army left its spoor not only in destruction, but in a debris of empty cans, papers, letters, caps, a few bodies. The Army of the West had made one more sevenleagued stride on its way to the sea, gathering to itself uncountable legends.

In the early evening, the Perfessor, Johnny, and Flash began to hunt for the regiment which they had abandoned in the morning. All day long it had been moving in its appointed path beside them, and now it was somewhere in this widebosomed evening dense with crowding wagons, tired soldiers, and the brighteyed, inextinguishably jubilant darkies. The men were calling back and forth to one another.

—Hey, Sam, I can smell that old coffeepot a-bilin' right now.

—Say, I'm a-goin' to eat me a whole chicken all to myself.

—Reckon we'll have to do any fightin' tomorra?

—Hell, no. This time Sherman's flanked 'em so wide, they ain't an army within a hundred miles.

—Yes, but I heerd they was fightin' up ahead today at a place called Sandersville or somethin' like that.

—Let the calvary handle that.

—Sure, let the damn horseboys do the fightin' fer a change.

Then it was very dark. Breaking out on both sides of the road far up ahead were the first fires of the bivouacking troops. The wagoners were calling back and forth.

—Hey, anybody heard a the Twenty-second Indiana?

—They done got drowned in a river a piece back.

—Get your goddam corpsecart out a the way, and let a man past that *knows* how tew drive.

—Son, I was drivin' an Army ambulance when your maw was removin' snot from your chin.

—Reckon ole Jeff Davis'd like to know where we are.

—They say ole Abe hisself don't know where we are. Folks at the North ain't heerd from us since we left Atlanta.

—Lost—an Army of sixty thousand men. Please return to the owner. Signed, Abe Lincoln.

With laughter and with cursing, the wagons crowded toward their camps. Johnny and his companions found the regiment at last, bivouacked in a trampled cornfield beside a forest.

—Hey, what you got there? the men said, crowding around the wagon.

—We have a little of everything, Johnny said, from fat shoats to a plump Rebel officer. This is Captain Jim Rutherford, boys, of the Georgia Cavalry.

—Pleased to meet yuh, the men said.

It was good to see the comrades again, their faces lit by the flickering glare of pineknot campfires. Fragrance of burning balsam wood perfumed the air. A score of skewered turkeys dripped on the fire. Corporal Johnny Shawnessy was ravenously hungry.

By nine o'clock they were sitting at the fire gorged on cooked flesh, leaning back on beds of straw, cornstalks, and branches, drinking the stolen wine and smoking pipes and cigars. The entertainment was varied but familiar, the only new feature being the presence of the Rebel captain, whom the men permitted to stay in the camp for the night on *parole d'honneur* and whom they plied with wine and questions in their eagerness to learn about the Enemy.

—When this war goin' to end, Reb? Reckon it can't go on much longer now.

—Why, sir, I look to see right smart of fightin' yet. General Lee ain't whupped by a long shot.

—Suppose ole Sherman takes him in the rear, then what'll he do?

—Why, then, I reckon someone'll just have to take ole Sherman in the rear.

They compared notes on army food, combat experiences, women. Everyone agreed that the Rebel captain was a capital fellow.

—Jim, Flash Perkins said, I'll tell yuh the truth. For two cents

I'd a blowed your head off this afternoon and never thought a thing of it. Now, I'm glad I didn't do it. If all the traitors was like you, damn me but I think I could git along with 'em O.K.

—They ain't any different from me, the Rebel captain said.

—I talked with a whole lot of Rebel prisoners in Atlanta, a soldier said. They wan't no different from us fellers. They don't like the War no more'n we do. They acted real human.

—Trouble you damyankees, the Rebel said, is you never knew anything about us. You had to start a damn war to come down and find out what nice folks we are.

—You believe all this truck in the papers, Reb, Flash said, about us rapin' your women and all?

—No, I don't. That there's civilian talk. I don't take no stock in anything I read in the newspapers.

—There, you see! a soldier said.

—Way I look at it, the Rebel said, all the soldiers in both armies oughta go back home after the War and whup hell out of the speculators and newspapermen, beggin' your pardon, Mr. Stiles.

—Don't mind me, boys, the Perfessor said.

He was propped up so that he could read his stolen books, a volume of Shakespeare's *Plays,* a translation of *Les Misérables,* and a copy of Scott's *Life of Napoleon.*

—Willie, Walter, and Victor, he said to Johnny, are true classics. Your true classic confines himself to the classic view of life, which is that men are most alive when fighting and loving. The bloodthirstiest writing ever, is in Shakespeare's historical plays. They are singularly devoid of what we miscall humanity. The heroes kill, rape, murder, and loot equally with the villains. And the whole strong drench is washed down with magnificent verbal poetry alternating with rude Falstaffian comedy. When you write your American historical plays, John, keep in mind that the prime ingredients are blood, lust, and laughter.

Johnny lay and listened to the good soldier talk, which, to illustrate the Perfessor's remark, continued to revolve upon its two eternal subjects, the War and the Women. The Rebel captain contributed affably to the discussion. There was a heated argument about the respective beauty of the ladies North and South. Blondes, brunettes, and redheads were compared as to their intrinsic talents in the art of love. Flash Perkins described in robust detail and with gestures his last contact with a woman. Notes were compared on the camp-followers of the armies North and South.

On all these subjects, the Rebel captain was well informed and entertainingly vivid.

The Perfessor now and then joined in the discussion and now and then read aloud a choice bit from *Henry IV*. Corporal Johnny Shawnessy was never so happy in the whole war as on that night.

Later on, the soldiers began to sing. As he lay listening to the simple soldier ballads, the songs of mother, home, the Union, and the girls they left behind, Johnny felt epic fulfillment. Encamping for a night on alien earth and far from home, he had become at last the Hero of Raintree County. There was no hero like the veteran soldier, the comrade of comrades. In after years, he would be able to say with pride, Yes, I was one of those soldiers. I made the Great March with Sherman to the Sea. I was part of that Army. I saw those places. I remember that earth.

Now for the first time he felt that the War was really coming to a close. Many comrades might be lost, but the end was in view.

—A few more days for to tote the weary load,
No matter, 'twill never be light,
A few more days till we totter on the road,
Then my old Kentucky Home, good night.

Yes, a few more days, and good night to the Old Kentucky Home, the sentimental republic founded on a crime, good night to flags, bands, uniforms, good night to valors and enthusiasms. He and his comrades had conquered more than they supposed in this avenging sweep from Atlanta to the sea.

—Weep no more, my lady,
O, weep no more today!
We will sing one song for the old Kentucky Home,
For the old Kentucky Home, far away.

Later, the singing died, and the bugles sounded taps. Soon the large, low stars of the Southern night whited the upturned faces of fifty thousand young men, sleeping in bedrolls. Sleep touched with mystic wand the face of Private Flash Perkins, closed his savage eyes, erased the ridges from his forehead, stole the insolent laughter from his mouth. Sleep put its soft enchantment on the face of Jerusalem Webster Stiles, correspondent for the New York *Dial,* and turned him into a sharpfaced child in a chinbeard. It touched the face of Corporal Johnny Shawnessy with the beginning of an affectionate smile and discovered, beneath the stage whiskers, Johnny Shawnessy of Raintree County. They slept, these children of far-off counties, in their costume of the Civil War, each one reprieved from time and soldiering, each one escaping into a private world of memory and desire. The Southern night silvered in deep sleep the ravagers of Georgia, Sherman's terrible men.

Where was the sleeping soul of John Wickliff Shawnessy? It was lost in a classic dream of love and war, whose ingredients were blood, lust, and laughter but transmuted from inhumanity by the humane poetry which was the idiom of Johnny Shawnessy's mind. The Southern earth had touched a young Northerner with a sword of silver light, and in his breast a not unamiable warrior leapt alive and was off to the wars in his own private historical drama. . . .

Sleeping, Corporal Johnny Shawnessy dreamed that he was standing in the wings of the Old Opera House while Professor Jerusalem Webster Stiles in the guise of a Chorus stalked out before the curtain and read from a scroll.

CHORUS

—Scene One. Off to the Wars!

The stage and orchestra of the Opera House were lit scarlet with an eruption of soft fire. Behind the scenes Johnny saw a young woman ascending a spiral stair, beckoning with lips and eyes. The dim loft of the theatre turned out to be the upper floor of a house on Pennsylvania Avenue.

NELL GAITHER

lying under a sheet in a huge fourposter bed, bare arm beckoning,

—I do hope Aunt isn't up.

NEWSBOY

popping head in at roomdoor, throwing newspaper,

—Extra! Read all about it! Young soldier off to the Wars. Most affecting were the farewells exchanged on this occasion.

COMMITTEE FROM THE LADIES' AID

fussy spinsters, sitting on bed, folding hands solicitously,

—Corporal Shawnessy, is there anything we can do to assist you in this trying hour?

DELEGATION FROM THE DANWEBSTER METHODIST CHURCH

blackfrocked elders, cleaning teeth with whittled sticks, taking armchairs in a halfcircle around bed,

—Brother Shawnessy, have you been baptized?

T. D. SHAWNESSY

rocking blandly back on his heels, hands behind back, surveying scene from a great height,

—I see, my boy, that you're just a good cleancut Shawnessy. I think this calls for a little prayer.

The old man held up his hand. As he did so, someone pulled him violently through the curtains with a loop of rope, and a cardboard train crossed the stage with a rhythmical, butting motion, forlornly wailing. The sound turned into the trumpet voice of the

CHORUS

—Scene Two. An incident in the French Camp. . . .

He was wandering through the backstreet of a shabby little Southern river town. On the highbreasted hills of Tennessee, he saw wan fires burning. Repeating an ancient act of soldierdom, he knocked at the door of a flimsy building shaken with rough merriment.

GIRL

opening and standing in the dim hall dressed in a costume sewn together from greenbacks and Confederate paper dollars,

—What can love's little counterfeit do for you, honey?

Following her into the brothel, he found himself standing on a platform draped with bunting and seating a collection of celebrities, including President Abraham Lincoln, General U. S. Grant, General William Tecumseh Sherman, members of the Cabinet, and foreign dignitaries. The crowd consisted of soldiers and campfollowers. He held a timesmoothed coin, a quarter-dollar having the head of George Washington on one side and an American eagle with spread wings on the other.

JOHNNY

reading from scroll and addressing girl,

—The President, the Supreme Court, the Senate, and the House of Representatives in joint session assembled have empowered me to present to you, my dear, this medallion, the Republic's highest award, given only to those who have fought with courage beyond the call of duty in this great war for the Preservation of the Republic and the Emancipation of the Race. For Valor.

GIRL

accepting coin with a curtsey, singing dolefully with pretty gestures,

—I'm little May of the Great White Way.
I'm only a twobit whore.
You can get the same from a sprightlier dame,
But it will cost you more.

JOHNNY

—*Una cauda, legionem perturbavit.* 'Tis an ancient and dishonorable profession, as old as——

CHORUS

—Scene Three. The Battle. Perhaps the greatest and most decisive conflict of all time, the Battle of the Shawmucky, as it is denominated in the history books, changed the fate of republics and caused thousands yet unborn to tremble on the shadowy shore of time. Yet it was precipitated by the most trifling circumstance in the world when a number of young men living in the vicinity of Danwebster went swimming one day and, leaving their vestments on the bank, crossed to the far side where as luck would have it . . .

Hundreds of naked women were hiding in the rushes at the rim of the river. Through the green mesh he could see their flametipped breasts, smoothmuscled thighs, and tufted love-mounds, their white teeth gleaming and their red lips.

YOUNG WOMEN

with cruel, lipcurling laughter,

—Jackjackjackjackjackie.

CENTURION JOHANNES FACTOTUM SHAWNESSY

ırmed in shield, short sword, helmet, and shinpieces,

—The Republic hath need of wombs to bear her lusty sons. What ·aliant arms are stiffened to the charge?

WILLIE SHAKESPEARE

pringing up in Elizabethan breastplate and helmet, brandishing a ·pear, presenting shield with full heraldic elaboration—a falcon, his vings displayed argent, standing on a wreath of his colors, supporting a spear gold steeled, on a bed sable,

—Behold, Dan William of the doughty spear!
Full many a field hath felt his martial tread.
Queen Bess herself his crest did knightly rear—
A gold spear regnant on a royal bed!

JERUSALEM STILES

ipringing up, the young professor of the Academy, gesturing with :lassroom pointer, glasses swinging by a string, coat of arms chalked on a blackboard,

—Behold, Jay Stiles that hath the hissing tongue.
With sudden fang his hundreds doth he slay.
On many an eve seductive he hath hung,
A serpent pendent from a branch of bay!

WILLIE

itamping back and forth, cutting and thrusting with a sword, laying open thousands of books, shearing off sheets of other men's plays,

—Ah, what a creature is man, born to be beast, and like a beast ı-borning, but being born, mark you, thou beast in being, thou bully ›awcock, man, what be'est thou? say, boy, say!

PERFESSOR

—Why, we are born to fight and feed and flute, Will, and when ve are faint with our fighting, then feed we, and when we are full of our feeding, then do we foot about our fluting, until with feeding, fighting, and fluting we fall into a fit. For 'tis but a brief road running from womb to tomb.

WILLIE SHAKESPEARE

hotspurring his horse into the reeds beside the river,

—'Tis an old story. Men will have that they will have. And when they have it, 'tis but a little hole that they have, being but big enough to hold your poxy, whoreson body. So the only begetter, the only begotten, is the earth, boys, under and dead and rotten. Goodby, lads, good-by, sweet lads. The horns blow prologue to the swelling act, our sails fairbellied with the favoring wind conceive the bully seed of war, and we——

SUSANNA DRAKE

Queen of Amazons, riding a white stallion stately treading, bearing in one hand a little spear and in the other a garland of oakleaves,

—Mr. Shawnessy, allow me to present to you in behalf of all these young ladies here present this wreath. To the victor belongs——

WILLIE SHAKESPEARE

herald's costume, rakethin legs in tights, proclaiming through megaphone,

—Now is she in the very lists of love. . . .

JOHNNY

mounted on a great white eagle, lunging here and there among the Amazons, silver arrows pattering on his shield and shinpieces,

—Careful, girls, I can't control this thing!

WILLIE SHAKESPEARE

strutting back and forth, declaiming in actor's voice,

—Cry covah! And lash on the gods of raw!

JACK FALSTAFF

tripping up a bank, looking keenly about, drawing sword,

—Here's a jolly fight toward and Fat Jack i' the thick of it. This be no place for a Falstaff—nay, nor a fallen one either for the matter of that. Well, we shall see whether this weapon have still an edge to it. Nay, here's a bit of keenness left, albeit 'tis damnably rusted for want of use. Cut me for a capon if I do not share a little in the sport.

Garde! Avant! There! There! 'Ware, warrior ladies! Give me a bony mount, lads. For—

Fat Jack and skinny Jill
Fetch far better over the hill,
While fat Jill and skinny Jack
Fetch far better coming back.

CHORUS

—Another part of the field.

CORPORAL JOHNNY SHAWNESSY

standing before plantation house, addressing a lovely Southern girl on the porch,

—'Tis the part of man to subdue; of woman, to submit. Submit!

SOUTHERN GIRL

archly,

—Subdue!

Without warning, she pounced on him, slapped his face, bit his shoulder, mussed his hair, scratched his cheeks, stepped on his toe, spit in his eyes, kicked his shins, writhed, panted, hissed, and screamed. She finally managed to get a good grip on him and pulled him down hard.

SOUTHERN GIRL

suddenly going soft, arching her back, purring warmly,

—I love it thataway. Go on, fo'ce me, honey.

OLD SOUTHERN PLANTER

in stentorian voice,

—Ah chahge that man with attempted rape.

SOUTHERN GIRL

—Take it easy, Paw. Give 'im anothuh five minutes, and we'll have a bettuh case.

Along the river, he saw how the warrior women had been driven to the water's edge. The hardmuscled legionaries rushed in among them. With hoarse cries of panic and surrender, the women threw down arrows, sheaths, helmets. Their white forms were tumbled in the shallow water. Victors and vanquished clove together, grappling fiercely. He ran toward the rushes wondering if he could mitigate the fierceness of that old struggle. . . .

VOICE

musical, receding,

—Come back, lost boy. Come back to Raintree County. Before it's too late . . .

He awoke. He lay lost for a while on the immense, patient earth until the dream dissolved. All around him, his comrades lay, a stricken host. Warm pangs of love and fierce yearning still coursed over him. *Come back to Raintree County.* The voice that slew this barbarous dream had been tinged with anxiety. What were they doing there at home? Where was Nell Gaither? Was she lying by herself in a vestal bed, dreaming of Johnny Shawnessy as he of her? Did those slender arms yearn to clasp him and keep him from remembering battles? What was she doing there—back there, while he lay bemused among the alien corn?

And Corporal Johnny Shawnessy slept once more and rose another day. The Army of the West marched and camped for days without opposition in a vast Edenic garden. When the world found them again, they and their march were legend.

And as Johnny saw the Southern earth, secretly, as once long ago, he loved it and was moved by its bitter, proud resistance and the fatal mixture of its bloods. But being a soldier now and simple in his concepts, he never wavered in his belief that this earth, like that of Raintree County, belonged to the whole people by a mystic covenant called the Union.

And they went on, the young Northerners, marching to Savannah on the Sea, through days of Southern secondsummer. They came to the forests of the piedmont. For days they marched then on the level land, between dark ranks of southern pine, and at last they reached the outskirts of Savannah. And a day soon after came

WHEN BEYOND THE PINEFRINGED SHORES,
BEYOND THE SWAMPS THEY SAW THE
SHINING

. . . ocean of thee,
Laved in the flood of thy bliss O death . . .

The Perfessor was still asleep. Mr. Shawnessy was afloat on the ocean rhythms of Whitman's elegy.

—And I saw askant the armies,
I saw as in noiseless dreams hundreds of battle-flags,
Borne through the smoke of the battles and pierc'd with missiles I saw
them,
And carried hither and yon through the smoke, and torn and bloody,
And at last but a few shreds left on the staffs, (and all in silence,)
And the staffs all splinter'd and broken.

Mrs. Evelina Brown stood in the attitude of victory leaning on a sheathèd sword. Her face was tender, her voice sweet with compassion.

—I saw battle-corpses, myriads of them,
And the white skeletons of young men, I saw them,
I saw the debris and debris of all the slain soldiers of the war,
But I saw they were not as was thought,
They themselves were fully at rest, they suffer'd not,
The living remain'd and suffer'd, the mother suffer'd,
And the wife and the child and the musing comrade suffer'd,
And the armies that remain'd suffer'd.

We have reared the great shaft almost to the top. A woman in stone awaits those who have climbed to the summit. A little longer, comrades!

But I had forgotten awhile (though never really forgotten) this old tableau. I will tranquillize its writhings in the serenities of everlasting stone. I will show a fallen form, stone tears, the hand of a comrade soothing a comrade's brow; and in the distance the pillared image of Columbia, a woman fair, the goal of our exertions.

Great God, must there be deaths within sight of the goal?

(Then did you fight in that Great War to preserve the Union?

Did you march in the last march from Savannah northward? Did you see the burning of those cities? Did you weep as all men must for the death of comrades?)

O, let us believe in the simple concepts of Raintree County! Let us believe in the perpetuity of the Republic and its images! Let us believe that the stringbreakers, the strong competitors, the old soldiers never die! Can young fury and lust to live be stilled by a lead ball? Can the most vital figure in the Court House Square be slain? Can death and the Great Swamp overcome the strongest man in Raintree County, the greatchested one, the laugher?

The Perfessor gasped in his sleep, and his chin sank deeper into his coat.

Sleep on, watchdog of cynicism. And I will carve a last memorial stone to the dead comrades of the Grand Army of the Republic! Let us believe also in the great fact of loyalty! For this is the best commandment in the decalogue of Raintree County—that a man shall die for his comrade!

—Passing the visions, passing the night,
Passing, unloosing the hold of my comrades' . . .

February 17— HANDS —1865

POINTING AND GESTURING, FLASH PERKINS WAS RUNNING FROM THE BARN back to the yard where Johnny had been standing in conversation with the woman. At first Johnny couldn't tell what Flash was yelling over and over. Then it came clear.

—Rebel horsemen!

Johnny waited until Flash reached him, and the two ran down a lane that led through an orchard back of the house.

—About twenty, Flash said. They seen me.

—How far?

—Half a mile. I was standin' right out in plain sight by the barn when they come over a hill. The officer pointed, and they all broke into a gallop.

Johnny and Flash with other regimental foragers had crossed the river ahead of the main armies closing in on Columbia, the capital of South Carolina. The Rebel forces in this vicinity were supposed to be thin or non-existent, and the two comrades had gone alone, perhaps unwisely, far to the left flank of the Army to find forage which could later be collected for the brigade.

The day had been bright, warm, and peaceful, despite a steady wind from the north. It was around noon. Johnny had been thinking all day of spring returning.

As they ran, he could hear the thunder of hooves on the road.

—The woman will tell, he said to Flash.

—I know it, Flash said.

There was a railfence back of the orchard, and beyond that a wide field rising gently toward a stone wall.

—Let's git to that wall, Flash said.

They sprang over the railfence and ran across the field. Beyond the field, only a quarter of a mile away was the river. On the far side there would be more foragers and detachments of Union cavalry.

The noise of the horses slowed down and came to a scuffling halt before the house, now hidden by trees. Johnny and Flash ran hard, holding their muskets unslung. Johnny's legs were beginning to go dead with the long run to the summit of the field where the wall was, and his breath was spent.

The field was uneven ground, planted in hay the year before, now stubbly and with a beginning of spring grass. The wall rose cleanly along the summit of the field and ran off slanting, vaguely parallel with the river. If the horsemen followed right away, they would just about catch him at the wall, winded and with one shot in his gun.

Five minutes from now, he might be dead. It would be a dumb, dirty little death, and completely unnecessary, but so had been every other death of the War. But perhaps it wasn't true about Rebel cavalry killing the bummers without quarter, whenever they could.

Looking back again, he saw the Rebels. They had ridden farther along the road before the house, instead of coming up the lane. The officer was pointing down the road, and some of the men were looking at the two Unionists.

He and Flash climbed over the wall. They leaned against it, sucking air and watching the Enemy on the road. It didn't seem to make much difference now which side of the wall they were on.

—Must be some Union cavalry around here somewhere, Johnny said. Maybe these fellows don't want to mess around with bummers. Don't fire at 'em.

The great hope now lay in being unimportant.

The Rebels split into two groups, and all but six rode on down the road toward the river. The remaining six turned back toward the house and disappeared behind the screening trees.

—Those six that went back are probably for us, Johnny said.

—Hell, if they's only six! Le's move up to the angle here, Flash said.

Johnny looked around. Another stone wall approached from the direction of the river and joined their own about fifty yards away, forming the stem of a vast straggling T. They had been moving along the roof of the T. The stem, which they now reached, ran downhill to a thick woods that bordered and concealed the river.

What a line to post a division on! Johnny thought. They were two men trying to get shelter from death on a bare field behind a system of walls a mile long.

They climbed over the abutting wall and were hidden from the road. They kept watching the house and the lane.

—If we could reach the wood there.

—No use, Flash said. They might catch us halfway there. We could fight 'em from here.

A minute passed. Two minutes. Five minutes. Johnny had his breath back. They couldn't see any Rebels now. The larger group had ridden down the road, which curved behind the field and disappeared into the woods along the river. They could hear horses fording the river.

—Maybe those six went on back to the rear, Flash said.

—Perhaps we ought to run for the woods now, Johnny said.

He said it without conviction. As they remained in their absurd position on the crest of the hill, the desire to run to the woods began to fade. It began to seem very dangerous to leave a place where they were unharmed and go to a place that might be full of danger.

Then another large body of Rebel cavalry came along the road past the house and down to the river.

—Where's our goddam calvary? Flash said.

—I don't know, Johnny said. But look over there.

Eastward, a great way off, from the mild elevation of the field they could see a city. A stately stone structure of Corinthian pattern, uncapped or damaged, with a wooden derrick above it, gave distinction to a collection of lowflung houses and buildings. A thick tower of smoke rose from the middle of the city, bending southward under the pressure of the wind.

—What is that? Flash said.

—That must be Columbia, Johnny said.

It was the capital city of the state where the Rebellion had begun. After taking Savannah in December, Sherman's Army had rested for a short time and then had resumed its march, again cutting communication with the world as it marched northward to fasten a deathgrip on the remaining Southern armies, caught between Grant to the north and Sherman to the south. For several weeks, the Army had pushed on through Georgia and then South Carolina, taking a heavy toll of the latter because it had been the hotbed of Secession.

—Lookee there, Jack, Flash said, pointing to a distant slope south of the city.

A river of dull blue was pouring there, and myriad flashes played on its crest. Both men knew instantly what it was.

—There's the Army, Johnny said.

Both men looked with love and hunger.

—Are they over the river?

—I don't know, Flash said. I wish to hell they were over the river.

—I think they're too far back, Johnny said.

Another troop of Rebel cavalry rode along the road below them a quarter of a mile away.

—They aren't going to waste all those men on us.

—Where's *our* goddam calvary? Flash said through clenched teeth. I *always* hated those bastards.

They stayed for an hour hiding behind the wall, taking turns at standing watch over the road and the house.

—Pretty soon, Flash said, part of our Corps will come up and cross, and we'll be all right.

—No use getting alarmed, Johnny said. Let's have a smoke.

They both took out cigars, lit up, and lay in the wall angle smoking. This place where two walls met began to seem the best place in the world to be, except back home.

—I thought that there calvary troop was goin' to cut us up, Flash said. Maybe they didn't see us after all.

—Of course, Johnny said, the woman must have told them.

—She may have been a Union sympathizer.

—She didn't sound like it.

The two men lay and puffed on their cigars. Their loaded muskets leaned against the wall. They began to feel perfectly safe. It seemed absurd that with a big Union Army enveloping the capital of South Carolina, the Rebels would take the time to exterminate two bummers in a wall corner.

—Let's have something to eat, Johnny said, and wait for some of our cavalry to come up and clean these guys out.

They opened their knapsacks and got out some food. They had meat sandwiches and apples.

—Nice little picnic, Jack. All we need is a bottle of corn and some women.

The meat was pork, cold and salty between hunks of moist bread. They drank a little water from their canteens, and then lay back again and lit cigars. They got to talking about the War and Raintree County. They lay for a long time smoking and talking.

—I'm sick and tired of all this fightin' around, Flash said. I'll be glad to git back to the ole county. I'm goin' to live peaceful the rest of muh life, git me a lil gal, marry her, and settle down. I been a bastard long enough, and God mus' be a-gittin' tard of it.

Not long after, a sound of shooting broke out down the river to the west, a halfmile distant. Soon a band of Rebel cavalry rode up from the river. One of them had a roughly bandaged arm. They passed from sight before the farmhouse, the hoofbeats stopped, then started again, going up the road.

A minute later, a small band of horsemen rode up the lane to the point where Johnny and Flash had crossed the railfence and run through the field.

—Cuss it! Flash said, surely they ain't goin' to come up after us now.

—They don't even know if we're up here, Johnny said. Can you see?

Flash was peering through a chink he had made near the top of the wall.

—They're pintin' up here, he whispered. I think one of 'em wants to ride up. They look like just kids. Now they're goin' to ride away. No, now they've turned, and one of 'em is arguin' with 'em again. He wants 'em to come up here.

—How many are there?

—Six, Flash said. Prob'ly them same guys. What they been doin' all this time? Now the others are startin' to ride back, but this one guy—yes—he's waitin' and lookin' up here. Now I think—I think he's—yes, he's comin' on up alone. Here he comes.

Flash began to run his hand up and down the stock of his musket.

—Don't shoot unless you have to. It'll bring 'em all.

—He's comin' straight up. We'll have to shoot 'im. The others are out of sight. He don't think we're here, but he's comin' up to see.

—How far is he?

—About fifty yards. When I say so, raise up and let 'im have it.

—Where is he?

—He's above us now. He's goin' to cross the wall up there on our side. All right, let 'im have it.

Johnny stood up. There was a young officer on a small gray horse, approaching the wall. Looking down the barrel, Johnny saw a man's face startled like one who has discovered danger but hasn't yet had time to be afraid of it.

The two rifles banged. Through the smoke, a riderless horse plunged and ran away.

—Come on! Flash said. Let's git to the river!

The two men ran down the stem of the T, toward the woods. It was a long way down. The brown grass of the preceding summer was thick. There were evergreen shrubs along the wall. Sooner than seemed possible, several mounted Rebels appeared along the wall where their comrade had been shot.

Each of the two runners rammed home a shot running.

The horsemen fired a volley. Unhurt, Johnny bounded over a brush heap and ran into a wood thick with saplings and briars. He skirted a briar patch, looking for a place to take shelter.

He looked back. Flash Perkins had one knee on the ground beside a tree, his rifle up and sighted. His body jumped with the shot. Someone in the field beyond the woods said in a cheery voice,

—Dismount and spread out, boys. Don't go straight in on 'em.

Flash got up and started toward Johnny. He had his hand low over his left breast almost on his stomach. His face was dead white.

Fifty feet away, he stopped to lean against a tree. There was a noise of thrashing in the underbrush.

—Go on in deep, boys, came the cheery voice from the field, and cut 'em off. I think we hit the big bastard.

Flash leaned heavily against the tree, loading his rifle. A dripping stain spread slowly on his shirt. His face was turned away. Johnny ran to him.

Flash was crying. Strong sobs wrenched at his set teeth. They seemed to Johnny the most terrible sound he had ever heard.

—Git out a here! Flash said suddenly in his high, arrogant voice. Go on, git out!

—No, I'm staying, Johnny said.

—Git out, goddamn you! Flash said. Run fer it! No use both of us gittin' kilt! Git out and run! They'll never ketch you in this woods.

In the cool shadow of the forest, Flash took Johnny by the shoulders and shoved him.

—Go on, git!

He clutched his side and sat down under the tree. His eyes closed. Johnny didn't say anything about the wound. There was nothing to be said about a wound like that. He looked around. They were close to the field where at least one Confederate had stayed to watch while the others had gone in wide around. There were a number of stones lying near at the beginning of a rocky gully that ran toward the river.

—We can get down there in that hollow and pile up some rocks and hold 'em off, Johnny said. Can you walk, Flash?

—Give me a hand, Flash said.

There was a hurt, childish look in his eyes. He walked over to the gully and sat down in a depression. Johnny ringed the place with rocks. He heard the Rebels calling to each other deep in the woods.

—Hey, Jake.

—Yeh.

—See anything?

—Naw. How about you, Lester?

—Naw, not a thing. I think they ain't gone in fer. They're layin' up.

—Hey, Fred!

—Yeh? yelled the cheery voice from the field, about where Johnny had entered the woods.

—Sure they ain't stayed right there by the field?

—I'll see, the man said.

Through the branches Johnny drew a bead on a man riding warily along the fringe of the woods. The man was hidden before he could get a clean shot.

—Ever'body dismount and move up toward me, the man in the field yelled, out of sight now.

Flash was lying full length on the ground.

—In the back, he said. Clean through. Christ!

—Listen, Flash, they got us surrounded. Think we ought to surrender?

—They won't leave us to, Flash said. We already got two of 'em. I wouldn't take the chance. Try an' hold 'em off.

—What if they rush us?

—They ain't enough to do that. Only four now. I hit one on my last shot. They's only that guy in the field out there and three others.

They don't know how bad I'm hit. Unless a lot more comes up, we kin hold 'em off.

—Can you fire?

—When I have to, Flash said.

He sat up, turned over, and rested his shoulder against a rock.

Johnny quickly tore off his own shirt, wadded it on the two holes front and back, and bound it to place with long strips tied directly around the chest. He couldn't understand what was keeping Flash alive.

—Hurt much?

—Hell, yes, Flash said.

He had a little color in his face again. Both men kept arranging rocks for rifle rests.

—Pretty good riflepit, Flash said. They'll have to shell us out of here.

He sounded cheerful.

For about five minutes, Johnny heard and saw no movement in the woods around him. Then Flash's rifle boomed with a big sound that lasted a long time in the woods along the river.

—Hell, missed 'im! Flash said, reloading.

—Where?

—Right down there in the ravine. He's hid behind a rock there now. Next time, I'll tear his head off. He don't dare move.

—Hey! said the cheery voice from the edge of the field. Was that you, Jake?

A voice from the ravine yelled,

—I got 'em spotted, Fred. They're right at the head of this here cut.

—Well, le's go in and git 'em.

—I cain't.

The voice was exasperated.

—Why not?

—I cain't move fum behind this here rock.

—Wasn't that you that shot?

—Hell, no. That was them.

—What you goin' to do?

—Hell, I don't know. What *you* goin' to do?

There was no reply.

—I'll keep this guy nailed behind that rock, Flash whispered. You watch for the others.

Johnny searched the woods carefully. He had a view in every direction for about fifty yards, although there were many trees, rocks, and clumps of bushes behind which a man might take cover. At last he caught a flicker of movement on the right. A Rebel had just moved behind a tree.

—Hey, Bob, yelled the man Flash had pinned down. They right in front of you. Be keerful, son!

The Rebel behind the tree leaned out and took a quick look and was back in before Johnny could fire.

—Behind that there little pile of rocks? he said.

—That's right.

The Rebel leaned out and took a quick shot at Johnny who squeezed off at the same instant. The two rifles made one explosion. The woods shook. Johnny had hardly finished loading, when something socked him in the shoulder and knocked him flat as if someone had hit him with a spade. The report of a rifle, fired from behind him, echoed away in the woods.

Just then Flash fired and began to reload frantically. Johnny did the same, finding that he could use his arms, although the left one felt numb all the way down. Blood spilled down on the rocks around him.

—Got 'im! Flash said. Got 'im!

He cursed, trying to ram home a cartridge.

—O, hell, he crawled away. But that's one ain't goin' to charge us.

Two shots came almost together out of the woods and spanged on the rocks, burning splinters into Johnny's face.

—Listen, Flash said. Don't fire unless you got a sure thing. If we're both empty same time, they'll rush us while we're reloadin'.

—I'm hit, Johnny said.

—How bad?

—Left shoulder. High up, I think.

He looked cautiously out between two stones toward the quarter from which the wounding shot had come. Flash had shifted over a little to cover the man whom Johnny had first seen on his right.

There was a crash, and dust blew into Johnny's face as a bullet thumped the ground in front of him. He sighted at the smokecloud forming in some bushes about forty yards away. Catching the glint of a rifle barrel, he squeezed off, ducked, and an answering shot scotched the covering rock.

From then on, it was give and take, the two wounded men firing rarely, just enough to keep the three Rebels careful. After a while, the Rebels stopped firing.

—Hey, Jake! said the cheery voice of Fred, who had come in from the field.

There was no answer.

—Jake!

Down the ravine there was no answering sound. Flash Perkins chuckled and groaned at the same time.

—Jake's absent, teacher, he said.

He was sobbing again between clenched teeth. There was a silence. After a while, the cheery voice said,

—Hey, you! Yanks!

—What d'yuh want, you goddam Reb? Flash said.

It was the old high, hard, nasal rasp, jabbing and crowding.

—Jest wanted to see if you was still there, said the cheery voice.

At this all three of the Confederates laughed. When they were through, Flash said,

—Why don't you sons-a-bitches go off and play somewheres else? You're preventin' us from gittin' our beauty rest.

—You a-goin' to git a good long beauty rest, Yank, the cheery voice said.

—Hell, yes, said one of the other Rebels.

The firing began again. For a while the three Rebels yelled back and forth, and Fred, the cheery one, and Flash carried on a conversation.

—Say, Yank, you shaved that one pretty close. Now that ain't friendly.

—Say, Reb, I heard a lot about Southern hospitality. Is this a sample?

—Say, Yank, you got any coffee?

—Sure. Come and git yourself some.

—Not jest now. Little later, I'll he'p myself freely.

Then there was a while when no one talked. The Rebels fired savagely, but it was hard to get a good clean shot in the woods.

Once Flash said,

—Listen, Jack. These bastards are goin' to git tired a this after a while. One of 'em'll go back and git some more.

There was obviously no answer to this remark. A long period of silence followed, during which Flash didn't say anything and no one fired. It began to grow dark.

—Yank!

Johnny waited for Flash to say something, but Flash didn't talk.

—Listen, we got he'p comin' up, the Rebel said. You fit a good fight. How about surrenderin' to us?

Johnny waited to see what Flash would say, but Flash was silent.

—This yo' last offer, the voice said. Hit's a good chance. You fought brave. But with reinforcements we'll rush yuh, and if we have to do that, we don't aim to take no prisoners.

—That's right, Yank!

Johnny waited, but Flash didn't say anything. He was lying on his face.

—We won't kill yuh, Yank, the cheery voice said. Word of honor. The word of a Virginia gentleman. Captain Frederick Claymore Jackson.

Johnny pulled himself around so as to look at Flash.

—How about it, Flash? he said in a low voice.

There was no answer. Flash might be dead. It was one against three, a clear case for surrender.

Nevertheless, Johnny couldn't get himself to surrender. It wasn't courage. It was sheer instinct to survive. He didn't trust the word of Frederick Claymore Jackson, a Virginia gentleman.

He lay and listened. It was getting darker all the time. For several minutes there had been a sound of trampling horses, distant voices, an occasional shot west along the river. He waited, listening.

—How about it, Yank? Are y'all gonna come, or are we gonna come and git yuh?

Johnny didn't answer. He rubbed off his sight and waited. He could hear a sound of many horses down by the river. The voices grew louder. They were singing. For a moment the rhythm wasn't clear. Then he knew what it was.

—. . . rally round the flag, boys,
Rally once again,
Shouting the battle cry of . . .

—Comrades! Johnny yelled at the top of his lungs. Help! Help!

Flash Perkins stirred and started to sit up. He didn't seem to know where he was. His head was above the parapet of stones. Johnny pushed him flat just as a shot went over.

—All right, boys, said the cheery voice of Captain Frederick Claymore Jackson, le's git the hell out a here. That there's Union horse.

The three Rebels ran off through the brush, making for their horses. The sound of hooves on the near-by road became a little louder and then began to wane. Johnny went on yelling, but apparently no one heard him.

He stopped calling and sat up. He peered cautiously around. The Rebels were really gone. He could hear them riding off through the field.

Flash was lying on his face as Johnny leaned over him.

—Flash! Listen! We're safe, boy.

There was a strong wind blowing in high branches, but here on the forest floor the air was quiet and cool and already full of darkness. In spite of the stiff shoulder, Johnny raised Flash and managed to turn him over on his back. Flash's eyes were closed, but his mouth was open. He was breathing. Johnny put the canteen to the open lips, but the water only spilled down Flash's beard and over his bloody shirt. Johnny wet his hand and passed it over his comrade's forehead. He did this for several minutes. Then he heard Flash mumbling something. He bent down. Flash's eyes were open. They had a set glare.

—Flash, it's me—Johnny.

Flash stared like a sleepwalker. He took deeper and deeper breaths as if he were on the point of saying something. At last he said,

—Listen, they're startin' up. Indynaplis, Greenfield, Beardstown, Freehaven. You hear that, don't you?

—Sure, I hear it.

—Hear that whistle!

Flash was trying to get up. He had Johnny by the shirt. His powerful hands shook Johnny so hard that he cried out with the pain in his shoulder.

—Sure, sure. Take it easy, Flash. Just lie down and take it easy.

Waterstreaks through the powder-black on Flash's face were dead-white. But his voice was harsh and strong.

—We're goin' home, boy, he said, fiercely nodding his head as if trying to convince someone doubting.

—Sure we are, Johnny said.

Flash searched Johnny's face with bloodshot, staring eyes.

—No use worryin', boy, Flash said. Hell, you ran a good race. Hell's fire, it ain't no disgrace to git beat. Hell, I ain't been beat in five years.

Flash's mouth remained open. His eyes dilated. He gave a hoarse cry, as if something strong and masterless in him had just felt the wound for the first time. His hold on Johnny's shoulders let go suddenly, and he fell back, holding his chest and groaning. His eyes rolled. He panted like a runner who had just finished his race. He clutched at his throat coughing, choking.

—I—can't—breathe! Goddammit! Let go my throat, you bastards!

—Flash! It's me—Johnny!

There was a faint red light in the forest. Johnny could see Flash plainly now. He was gurgling and twisting in spasms. Suddenly, Johnny realized that Flash was laughing. He listened to this terrible laughter coming from the big shattered breast.

—Come on, you bastards! Flash yelled. Where I come from——

He went on panting and laughing. His forehead made ridges.

—Git a hat! he yelled. Go on, git a hat! Let's see the color of your coin! Hell, where I come from——

He coughed, his forehead was ridged, his eyes glared savage and exultant.

—Hell, I can lick any man here! I can outrun any man in Raintree County! Hell, where I come from—— Where I come from, why, hell, where I come from——

He coughed for nearly five minutes, blood gushed from his mouth, he rolled back and forth. Johnny clung with one good arm under his comrade's shoulders. Here, surely, was the strongest life that ever lived, and it was dying, it was beating itself out in blood and fury.

There was nothing good about the way Flash Perkins died in a forest near Columbia, South Carolina. He died choking with his throat full of blood, still trying to beat some unseen competitor who was too much for him.

But at last the big thing that lashed him to fury was still. When it was over, Flash Perkins lay on his back, mouth open, blood blackening on his beard and lips, toes turned out, shoulders slightly hunched, chin thrust up in that terrible repose that sleep couldn't counterfeit. Johnny had seen a lot of men lying like that in two years. He sat trying to accept the immense stillness of this form that lay in an alien forest far from Raintree County.

There was a peculiar red light under the trees as Corporal Johnny Shawnessy managed somehow with his one good arm, his feet, and his gun barrel to scoop out a shallow grave in the riflepit. Over the body of his comrade, he piled leaves, dirt, and the stones of the makeshift barrier. On a tree near-by, he carved with his knife the words

Flash Perkins,
Feb. 17, '65
A Union Soldier

Later, he was walking down through the woods along the river, trying to find a road and open ground. He saw now that the red light in the forest came from a big fire east. Later still, he was on a road choked with Union troops. A city was burning in the night. He was half out of his head with the pain in his shoulder. He lay down once in a ditch by the road and rested. Then he got up and went on toward the flames.

Later still, he was entering the town. Troops were singing ironically:

—O, Columbia, the gem of the ocean . . .

In the glare of the fire was the same building that he and Flash had seen at a great distance in the afternoon.

—That there's the State House, someone said. They never finished building it.

Union soldiers were halfheartedly trying to extinguish flames in a little tangle of worksheds in the yard of the capitol building. The fire roared on ravenous through the sheds. Inside, fragments of pediments, capitals, friezes, meant to complete the building, were chunks of incandescence.

The air was thick with flakes of flame that softly dropped as if the sky rained fire.

—It's cotton, men said.

Johnny kept asking for his unit. Finally, an officer was holding him by the arm.

—Say, son, you're wounded. Better get to a surgeon.

Later, he woke up somewhere in a tent, crying out with pain. A surgeon was working over him, washing out the wound in his shoulder.

—What about it, Doc?

—You're all right, the surgeon said. It got a piece of the bone. You've got to be quiet. You've got a touch of fever.

—What about the fire?

—O, that! the surgeon said. It was a good one, wasn't it?

Johnny knew then that the War was over for him. He sank back into fever and dull pain. For days and nights thereafter he lay, dreaming of Raintree County, seeing the earth of it ravaged and dry as if the source of its life had been scorched to a trickle. When the Army made contact with the Navy again, he was shipped with other sick and wounded up the coast and left in a hospital in Washington.

But what happened to Corporal Johnny Shawnessy was only a contemptibly minor incident in the progress of Sherman's Army north from Savannah in the spring of 1865. And as the army that had marched from Atlanta to the Sea cut a path of flame through the state where the War had started, men saw that the gods were tiring of this lengthy game of murder. Like bored children, they began

TO SMASH AND SCATTER THE PIECES

IN WANTON VIOLENCE

AT

THE END of the Grand Patriotic Program was nearing. The Perfessor slept on, his face relaxing from its look of pert cynicism. His sharp chin rested on his breast, his glittering eyes were shut, his face was childlike and almost tender. As the drums and bugles of the band assaulted his sleeping ears, he faintly moved his lips.

With a start Mr. Shawnessy realized that Professor Jerusalem Webster Stiles had once been young in Raintree County.

For thirty years and more the Perfessor had been a wanderer. Now perhaps in sleep he remembered a home. So also did the heart of Mr. John Wickliff Shawnessy yearn for the home of his youth, remembering road and river, a tree that stood by a house, a rock, and the scent of clover. A jocund music smote him almost to tears.

I wish I was in de land ob cotton,
Old times dar am not forgotten;
Look away, look away! look away!
Dixie Land.

Americans, the eternal children of humanity! Rootless wanderers, creators of new cities, conquerors of deserts and forests, voyagers on rivers, migrants to westward, they kept eternally in their hearts the fact or fiction of the childhood home.

Let each remember the face of the earth as it was in his childhood—mystical, brooding, and maternal. Let South remember South, let North remember North, let each remember the Republic. O, wandering one, far from the childhood rivers, o, soldier far from home, do not try to solve the riddle of Raintree County. Do not try to push back beyond the antiquity of the Republic's memories. Do not seek beyond the Old Kentucky Home. Do not try to rediscover the lost source of the river of mankind. Let these inquiries cease. Sleep, inquisitive explorer, sleep and dream of your home in Indiana, the mythical America that is called Raintree County, the map that is like a face or a human form and that is written upon with the unconscious penmanship of the dreamers who came from the Great Swamp, never, we trust, to go back in again.

Mine eyes have seen the glory of the coming of the Lord. . . .

Now we have reached the penultimate ring in the greatest monument ever erected to the private soldier. The prize we sought, in the guise of a woman thirty-eight feet tall and holding aloft a torch, is near.

And I will show comrades together for the last time at the end of their marching, young men holding aloft victorious banners. Forever, they shall approach the Reviewing Stand. Forever an unheard music shall be sounding, stone bugles of the Republic, stone drums of triumph and thudding exultation.

River of stone forms pressing forward between walls of stone on a stone street!

But a voice tells me that the tides of the Republic will beat at the base of this column, men will grow old and die, generations of lovers will walk beside the river, men will forget, and the words on this shaft will be meaningless words: Chattanooga, Chickamauga, Lookout Mountain, Missionary Ridge, Resaca, Pine Mountain, Kenesaw Mountain, New Hope Church, Peach-Tree Creek, Atlanta. People will already have forgotten before dirt falls on the face of the last incredibly old comrade of the Grand Army.

In the beauty of the lilies Christ was born across the sea,
With a glory in his bosom that transfigures you and me:
As he died to make men holy, let us die to make men free,
While God is marching on.

There is an Army marching on Pennsylvania Avenue, strong lads and many. Let it always be there and marching. Let it be composed also of those who fell in the first battles, who never saw the Enemy, who died in prison pen or fever camp, let it be composed of the hundreds of thousands who never reached the top of the column, the ultimate ring, for those who never went home to Raintree County.

Did any of us ever go back to Raintree County after that War?

O, martyrs, waiting for a resurrection, bearded, blasphemous saints, clotted harvest of a hundred fields! March with us too on Pennsylvania Avenue! Rise with us too

May 24— FROM —1865

THE LAST ENCAMPMENT

IN A HUNDRED FIELDS AND STREETS

around the Capitol Building in Washington, boisterously the Western Army rose. Early in the morning legions of Westerners stirred from bivouac, putting on battlegear for the last time as an army. Metal flashed in the clean sunlight, harness jingjingjingled, hooves rang on pavement. The morning streets, already filled with flags and faces, carried the manifold tremendous sound of an army preparing for a march.

On sidewalks, lawns, and open fields, the Army breakfasted. Soldiers polished their metal and tried to make their uniforms presentable, but they couldn't change the look of veteran toughness and careless savvy that hundreds of miles of marching and fighting had given. They talked of the coming parade in raucous Western voices, shouting back and forth from camp to camp. Then they began to crowd toward the streets in response to the marshalling bugles.

—Got to look dandy for the ladies.

—Hey, Bob, you goin' to trim your facefuzz?

—I've had it tied up in curlpapers all night. I'm just about to let it down.

—When does this damn fuss start?

—Any time now. We don't leave till about the middle of the thing.

—Hey, Johnny, where you goin' now that you're mustered out?

—Back to Indiana.

—I mean after that. What you goin' to *do?*

—Haven't decided yet. What are you going to do?

—I'm goin' West.

—Ain't anybody goin' to stay in the Army?

—All of a sudden, they ain't goin' to be no Army.

At nine o'clock, a gun boomed to signal the beginning of the parade. The head of the column, with General Sherman and his staff leading the way, marched out on Pennsylvania Avenue. Johnny's company waited in shade. The song of the leading band dwindled in the bannered distance and was presently drowned in the blare of another band near-by starting up and moving off. Band after band marched out with the troops. The great marching songs of the War pursued each other in overlapping waves down the milelong stretch of the Avenue. Minute by minute, the thick crowds of soldiers around the Capitol continued to feed their mass into the flagbright channel. The men in Johnny's brigade chafed restlessly.

—I pretty near forgot how to march. Reckon I can still keep step?

—The head of the column must be about in front of the stand.

—What kind of a stand is it?

—Why every great man alive is settin' on it. It's right in front a the President's House, and the President is on it, and Grant, and the whole dern Cabinet.

At high noon, three hours after the Review had begun, Johnny's brigade fell in and marched out of the lawns south of the Capitol and into the Avenue.

Marching before the Capitol, Johnny saw steps, walls, terraces black with people. The same great crowds from all over the land who had seen the Army of the Potomac march on the preceding day were there to see the Western Army. As his own company debouched onto the Avenue, Johnny had a lateral view of the column along its whole length from the Capitol to the Treasury Building at the far end of the street. On either side crowds made solid walls, sometimes flowing out from the sidewalks and touching the marchers. Flags fluttered from windows, housetops, towers. Hands waved. Hats went up. Garlands of flowers pitched from windows. Down the Avenue, the ranks became a solid stream of brightness riding on a bed of blue between vague banks of faces.

Then Corporal Johnny Shawnessy was marching with his comrades down the straight of the Avenue, on the last mile of the two thousand he had marched from Chattanooga to the Last Encampment. It was eyes front and shoulders back for the bronzed young saviors of the Republic; it was a strict dress on the guides; it was a rhythm of long strides, thirty-six inches to the take, the ground-devouring tramp of the Western Armies, the longest martial stride in the world.

—When Johnny comes marching home again,
Hurrah! Hurrah!

A girl ran out, pointing to the regimental banner and shouting,

—Hello, boys! Here's a delegation of Indiana people!

Several young ladies screamed, recognizing the flag of an Indiana regiment. The crowd laughed, egging the girls on.

—Kiss 'em, dearie.

—Give 'em a hug for me.

Flowers pelted the soldiers. One excited girl ran into the ranks of the marchers. Her arms clung around Johnny's neck, she kissed him, the crowd cheered.

—I'm from Evansville. Where you from, honey?

—We'll give him a hearty welcome then,
Hurrah! Hurrah!
The men will cheer, the boys will shout,
The ladies they will all turn out.
And we'll all feel gay,
When Johnny comes marching home.

Play on, strong horns of the Republic. Beat, drums of exultation. Receive us in your garland arms, young women of the Republic, pelt our lips with kisses: we have come home from battle. We have come back from the gray days and the many deaths.

—The old church-bell will peal with joy,
Hurrah! Hurrah!
To welcome home our darling boy,
Hurrah! Hurrah!
The village lads and lasses say
With roses they will strew the way. . . .

Corporal Johnny Shawnessy didn't look to right or left. He was thinking of his return to Freehaven. He would arrange things so as to arrive on a Saturday when the Court House Square would be jammed with people. He wouldn't tell anyone of his coming. Then, in a casual way, he would drop in at the newspaper office. His friends would swarm around him, shaking his hands, slapping him on the back, asking questions about the Great March. Then he would step outside. T. D., Ellen, and the girls would be sitting in the old wagon at the accustomed place, eating their lunch. Ellen's vivid eyes would pop with surprise, and she would clap her hands and jump down and run to him.

—Why, it's Johnny! O, dear God! he's back!

She would kiss him and cling to him in her small fierce strength.

—Johnny! How thin you are! You poor child!

T. D. would come over blinking, smiling, leaning far back, taking an unusually hopeful view of the whole situation. Everyone would help Johnny into the wagon as if shielding him from something.

But the best of all was that Nell Gaither would be sitting in a buggy on another part of the Square. Her wide green eyes would be all shining with tender excitement, and her full, flowerlike mouth would curve into that radiant, promiseful smile.

—Hello, Johnny.

He could hear the name said like a caress. He would walk over to the buggy, thin and pale in his uniform. Gravely she would offer her little hand, and gravely he would take it.

—Hello, Nell. How have you been?

—Just fine, Johnny.

The Square and its holiday hundreds and its immense, victorious tumult would be gone, the Great War and its memories would be dispelled like phantoms of an uneasy sleep, and he would be floating again on the wide green river of summer toiling with a white oar lakeward. This time for certain he would find the Raintree, and life's young hero would have the golden apples.

Blow on, bright bugles of the Republic. Beat, drums of triumph and crowding exultation.

Flags fluttered from the windows. Branches of trees brushed against him passing. Children shouted. Girls waved from housetops. The band had struck up a new tune.

> —Sing it as we used to sing it, fifty thousand strong,
> While we were marching through Georgia.

As the jaunty music of this new song swept along the Avenue, the crowd roared its approval. Washington was getting its first view of the men who had marched from Atlanta to the sea.

—How the darkeys shouted when they heard the joyful sound!
How the turkeys gobbled which our commissary found!
How the sweet potatoes even started from the ground,
While we were marching through Georgia.

In the rear of Johnny's company came a motley crowd of contrabands, shouting and dancing, laughed at by the crowd and laughing back. The Army had not yet entirely lost the black human baggage that it had acquired on its famous march. The commissary wagons came by, crowded with Negroes, cooks, campfollowers. Chickens clucked, geese quacked, turkeys gobbled; full jugs, pots, tubs, barrels shook on the loaded wagons. Bummers rode by on donkeys.

—'Hurrah! Hurrah! we bring the jubilee,
Hurrah! Hurrah! the flag that makes you free!'
So we sang the chorus from Atlanta to the sea,
While we were marching through Georgia.

The regimental flags, flapping bullettorn, moved steady and proud. In the streets, people looking at the faces of the soldiers said again and again,

—How young they are!

—We will rally round the flag, boys, we'll rally once again,
Shouting the battle cry of freedom. . . .

Ugly brick and frame buildings—groceries, hotels, brothels, banks, clothing stores, junkshops, saloons, bedizened with banners and bunting—flowed by on either side.

He moved through a valley of thronging faces. He had come two thousand miles, mostly by foot, from Raintree County to the Nation's Capital. He had discovered the greatest of all the court houses, the most significant of all the Main Streets.

—The Union forever, hurrah! boys, hurrah!

Corporal Johnny Shawnessy felt the presence of a grandiose idea in the confusion of Pennsylvania Avenue, in the rhythms of the Grand Review, in the huddled waste of the Capital City—an answer to the conundrum of the Individual and the Republic, a perfection of feeling, an abiding purpose. If now he could only say what it was! But instead, he kept thinking lines and magnitudes, coiled shapes of rivers, faces of people, music of marching songs, outstretched arms of girls.

He felt no vengeance or hatred any longer. In the best tradition of the Shawnessys—who always forgave too easily—he found himself including in his vision of the Republic all the soldiers North and South. By a wry trick of Fate, geography, and ancient institutions, both North and South had fought for liberty, a sacred cause.

The end of the Avenue was close now. The crowds were thicker. The trolley tracks were bright under his feet. The shouting of the crowd increased. The stone shape of the Treasury Building was just above him. Behind an iron railing hundreds of people waved handkerchiefs and flags. In their midst, the black box of a photographer looked down at the scene. The bayonets moved to the turning. They turned. Corporal Johnny Shawnessy was passing out of the Avenue. He had completed the last long mile. The turning column had fixed itself in the dark chemistry of time, young men holding aloft victorious banners.

In front of the Presidential Mansion, he could see the long stand, hung with flags and bunting, with the names of famous battles of the War upon it. The band played more strongly. The guides called for a perfect alignment. He could see General Sherman, standing proudly at attention, Grant and President Andrew Johnson, and several other notables.

—Hurrah! Hurrah! we bring the jubilee.
Hurrah! Hurrah! the flag that makes you free.

He passed the stand, marched down a sidestreet, and halted. The Grand Review was over.

The regiments broke up. The soldiers moved slowly and confusedly in the unpaved streets around the Executive Mansion, thousands of young men, suddenly ill at ease in their uniforms, laughing and telling each other how drunk they would get that night.

In the quiet evening, Johnny went back to the camp in streets where soldiers and civilians mingled. He began to feel lost and insecure as flags drooped in the setting sun, and a few bands played in far streets. The Army was breaking up. It was about time to take the uniform off and go back home.

There was a surprise waiting for him in camp. While he was at mess, a stranger in black civilian garb came up and, stopping near him, said,

—Did anyone here know a boy named John Shawnessy?

—Yes, sir, Johnny said, I'm John Shawnessy.

The man gave him a peculiar look.

—No joking, son—this is serious, he said. Now, this boy's folks back home asked me to find out anything I could about how the boy died, and I promised to check up. This is his regiment, I believe.

—I'm John Shawnessy, Johnny said, getting up from the table. I'm not dead.

The stranger, a short, bald man, with cavernous black eyes, said,

—You aren't foolin' me, are you, boy?

—No, sir, Johnny said, laughing nervously. I'm very much in earnest.

The soldiers crowded around.

—This here is John Shawnessy, mister. No doubt about that.

—Well, sir, the man said, if what you say is true, there's been a mistake then, and there's going to be some folks back home in Raintree County mighty happy.

The stranger, for his part, looked vaguely unhappy and disappointed.

—You were reported dead, son, he said accusingly. All the papers carried it.

—Dead! Johnny said. Why, I wrote a letter less than a month ago, and——

—Makes no difference, the man said. You were reported dead. He said it in an argumentative way.

—Who are you? Johnny said.

—I'm Peter Greenow, the man said. I've taken up the practice of law in Freehaven since you left. Just a week ago, when it became known I was going to Washington for the Review, your dad, T. D. Shawnessy, and other citizens, got in touch with me and asked me to find out anything I could about your death.

—I'm *not* dead, Johnny said.

The stranger looked skeptical.

—The papers carried the news of it last November 18, he said. That was over six months ago.

—But I don't understand, Johnny said. I wrote a letter from Savannah and another from here about a month ago.

He ran his mind back over the past few months. He had written his folks a letter in late October of the preceding year. The Army had left Atlanta in mid-November. For a month, the Army had been lost to the world, and no mail had been sent. At Savannah, he had received a few letters from home written before the middle of November, and from Savannah, he had written and mailed a letter home. Then the Army had cut communications again and had started North. When he was wounded near Columbia, he had been too sick for weeks to write. He had been transported by boat to Washington, where he had been hospitalized. He had got up only once, on the day of the President's assassination, and had suffered a relapse that had kept him in bed for better than another month. He had written another letter during this time, meanwhile wondering why he hadn't heard from his folks but supposing it was because of the vicissitudes of Sherman's Army and his own absence from his regiment. Only a few days ago, he had been mustered out, but had got permission to march with his regiment, though still weak from dysentery and fever.

—Yessirree, the man said, both papers carried your obituary. I've got copies of them here. Your last letter, written in October, was printed in the *Free Enquirer*. You might be interested to see——

The man had been digging in his wallet. He fished out some clippings and handed them to Johnny.

LOCAL HERO DEAD

JOHN W. SHAWNESSY GIVES LIFE FOR HIS COUNTRY

> Recent casualty lists released by the War Department include among those killed in action the name of John Wickliff Shawnessy, whose mother today received official notice from the War Department of her son's heroic death in line of duty. Readers of this paper will remember 'Johnny,' as he was affectionately called by his friends, as a writer and poet of great promise. A service for the departed will be held next Sunday at the Danwebster Church, and floral tributes . . .

—There, you see, the man said querulously. They had quite a service for you, and everybody's got used to the idea now of you being a *dead* hero. There was some talk of establishing an educational fund in your name, and I was made the trustee of it.

Johnny was looking at another clipping, this one from his old rival, the *Clarion*.

LOCAL BOY DIES A HERO
YOUNG JOHN SHAWNESSY SACRIFICED
AT SHRINE OF MARS

Another sad reminder of the heavy toll of this terrible and perhaps fruitless war was the death recently announced of John Wickliff Shawnessy, local young man, whose writings have won him fame throughout the County. Seldom has so much genuine grief been evinced as at the passing of this gifted lad. No braver or better soul was ever immolated in the fearful holocaust of War.

John W. Shawnessy was born in Raintree County in 1839 in a little log cabin which stood on the site of the present Shawnessy Home in Shawmucky township. He early manifested those . . .

—You see, the man said. Why, they even put up a stone *in absentia* in the Danwebster Graveyard.

Johnny was reading another and later clipping from the *Clarion.*

COLONEL GARWOOD JONES
TOUCHED BY FRIEND'S PASSING
WRITES ELOQUENT EPISTLE

We have just received the following affecting tribute from that famous young politician and orator—and more recently, soldier—Garwood Jones. Though we cannot condone the recent action by which this young man publicly renounced his allegiance to the party of Jefferson, Jackson, and Polk, we have always admired his energy and integrity, and we are happy to print his letter.

Dear *Clarion:*

No words can express the deep and profound sense of personal loss which I recently sustained on hearing of the death of my friend, John Shawnessy, Poet, Scholar, and Soldier of the Republic. Many worthier pens than mine may lavish upon this young martyr the praise that is his due, but none can put forth a stronger claim to personal bereavement. How many times have I not crossed verbal swords with this always genial and gentle young man! We sometimes differed, but we respected each other even in our differences. Little did I suppose when I last saw John in a camp in Indianapolis, where I found him the same laughing and confident companion that I had known since my boyhood in Raintree County—little did I anticipate that in slightly more than a year of mortal time, I would be myself in uniform, a humble defender of the flag—and he—brave young heart!—would be sleeping forever in the beloved earth which by his valor and devotion and that of hundreds of thousands like him, we mean to keep One Nation Indivisible, with Liberty and Justice for All.

In my pressing duties as Colonel of a volunteer regiment (soon, I trust, to be hurled into the last onslaught against the treacherous foe), I find little time or taste for literary pursuits, but the poignancy of my grief over this young genius's untimely demise has prompted me to take up the pen again and in hands which have learned to wield a more decisive and terrible instrument, indite a few lines to one of the truest souls that ever lived:

To J. W. S.

R. I. P.

Lo, where is Seth, that erst did fill these glades
With laughter and rejoicing blithe and brave?
Behold! he sleeps where beauty never fades
In martyred glory and a hero's grave.

Dear lad, we shall not fail the sacred trust,
To which you pledged your pure and patriot breath.
We shall do no dishonor to your dust
But take new courage from your valiant death.

Sleep in thy hero grave, belovèd boy!
Sleep well, thou pure defender of the right.
Far from the battle's din and rude annoy,
Our tears shall keep your memory ever bright.

Sleep on, dear youth. And lo! to take your place
A hundred hearts advance whose aim shall be
Never to fail or falter in the race
Till Freedom's banner wave from sea to sea!

—My God! Johnny said, his eyes misting in spite of himself, what terrible poetry!

—Of course, your mother and father've been all broken up by this, and——

—How is everyone, anyway? Johnny said. Do they really think I'm dead? Are they all right? How could they think I'm dead when——

—I assure you, son, as far as Raintree County goes, you're dead as a doornail. Why, they're even thinking of making the commemorative monument for our Civil War martyrs in the Court House Square more or less in your likeness. I happen to be in charge of the plans and——

The man looked unhappy and vaguely disappointed.

—But how did it happen? Johnny said. I wasn't even wounded then. I was wounded much later.

—Of course, the man said, there've been a lot of mistakes like that. It *could* happen.

—It *did* happen, Johnny said. Let me see, I suppose my two letters were lost. The first one had to go by sea from Savannah. The second one I gave to an old orderly at the hospital, and he probably forgot to mail it. My God, do you mean to say that they still don't know I'm alive?

—Son, your ma stopped wearing black a month ago. They've plumb given you up. You'll shock the daylights out of them when you go home.

—I've got to get home, Johnny said, feeling a little frantic. I've got to get back and show them that I'm not dead. They've got to print a refutation.

Everyone crowded around and talked about it, and the soldiers all knew of similar cases.

—Hell, I knowed a boy, a soldier said, he was reported dead, and hell, his wife married another man and when he got home, hell, she refused to have any truck with 'im. Said he was always a goddam noaccount anyway, said the other guy was a hell of a sight better man in bed and made a hell of a sight more dough, and far as she was concerned, this poor bastard, who had the squitters and one arm shot off, could just go back and die decent and not bother her.

—Hell, that's nothin', a soldier said, I heard of a boy they reported 'im dead, and . . .

Johnny tried to imagine what it must be like that almost everyone who had ever known and loved him believed him dead and in fact had gone through the whole process of grief and had closed up all the accounts and neatly stowed him away forever. One thing he was sure of—he must lose no time getting home.

He was two days winding up his affairs and leaving Washington. He decided not to write since he would probably beat the letter home. He might have sent a telegram through, but he began to take pleasure in the thought that he would come back from death and surprise everyone. Now, at last he had become, it seemed, the Hero of Raintree County, but he was in the peculiar fix of enjoying that distinction mainly because he was supposed to be dead and incapable of all enjoyment.

In fact, a cold anxiety began to trouble Johnny Shawnessy. Was it possible to come back into people's lives after what was to all of them a death as true as death itself? Wouldn't he be a pallid disappointment to people who had had months to formulate a hero-image of him? Could he live up to the obituaries, the floral tributes, the stone in the Danwebster Graveyard, the trust fund, and the projected memorial?

He didn't sleep for hours during the first night of his trainride home. The spacious earth of America seemed interminable to him. He had walked almost all the way over to the East Coast, but in a way the ride back by train was longer. Every minute of it prolonged his death. He was as many times dead as there were people who knew him—until he got back home and overcame all those deaths at once.

He was still very weak from his long sickness, and he had a horrible feeling that something might happen to him on the very threshold of return and he would be dead—pathetically dead—in very fact. It seemed almost impossible that he could give the lie to so much newspaper print. Garwood's poem was so tritely final. Could anyone crawl out from under the dead mound of so many clichés? Sure enough, something or someone had been killed, a hundred times over.

On the second day, he fell asleep and dreamed a dreadful dream in which he returned to Raintree County. No one paid any attention to him. People went by him in the streets as if he weren't there, and when he hunted for the Court House Square, he couldn't find it, and when he went out to hunt for the Home Place, it wasn't there. The world that he had known was gone and gone forever, and he knew with a hollow certainty that he could never get it back.

On the last day of May, Corporal Johnny Shawnessy had crossed the border of Raintree County and had got down from a train at the depot in Beardstown. He looked around in vain for someone who knew him. Two other men in uniform were in the station and no one paid any attention to him.

The station at Beardstown hadn't changed in the nearly two years of his absence. Joy and anxiety warred in his heart as he boarded the train for Freehaven, taking his place in an almost empty coach. Still no one recognized the young Lazarus.

The train moved out of the Beardstown terminal, and now a measurable time separated him from home, the home he had many times never expected to see again and which now never expected to see him again. It was fair weather in the end of May, the level fields of Raintree County were green and gay with flowers, the air was warm. He was a little horrified to see that the face of the County showed no sign at all of grief, that the roads ran in the same relation to the railroad and that the young corn was green as it was before Corporal Johnny Shawnessy, the Hero of the County, had become officially defunct. Was it possible for him to be uprooted and the County remain the same? Here was perhaps disturbing proof that the existence of Raintree County was not contingent upon the existence of Johnny Shawnessy.

And yet he felt also like a creator, as if by his return he gave life back to hundreds and restored Raintree County to being once again.

In this collision of vanity and fear, he watched for the white cupola of the Court House in the middle of the Square of Freehaven, as a famished mariner, twenty years from home, might watch for the familiar shoreline of his native island. He waited with short breath and wildly beating heart, his eyes fixed on a green horizon. The train bore him steadily on, stopped briefly at Three Mile Junction, and then continued—beyond the point, he thought, where he had been accustomed to notice the cupola of the Court House.

BUT THE TIME COULD NOT BE LONG NOW,

COULD NOT BE LONG UNTIL

THE

AWAKENING, the Perfessor snorted. He looked bewildered, clutched at his face, and then, touching his pince-nez, seemed instantly to recover his composure.

—God! he said. Garwood should bottle and sell that stuff. I haven't had such a good snooze in weeks. Well, program's over, I see.

Sheets of the Grand Patriotic Program littered the ground. Mr. Shawnessy felt that he had just seen and not quite solved another conundrum of his life. In fact he had devised the riddle himself and was now baffled by his own devising.

For it was he who had conjured up out of himself the Grand Patriotic Program. It was a selection of lines from the greatest of all the epic poems, and this poem was himself and his memories of the Republic in War and Peace. Out of himself, he was always creating it, but he had as yet only discovered a language of conundrums in which to express it. Maps, patriotic programs, sheets of music, old letters, newspaper columns, negatives of photographs taken in the years 1859, 1863, 1865—only in these did he hint the vast comedy, more true than Dante's.

In front of the speaker's platform, people were shaking hands with the distinguished guests. General Jake Jackson strode suddenly from the confusion, vigorously wagging his head and laughing as he waved good-by to friends. He saw Mr. Shawnessy and the Perfessor and came over.

—Maybe you better let me have that manuscript, Shawnessy. Just remembered I want to show it to some friends in Willkieville.

With the Perfessor musing at his side, Mr. Shawnessy walked slowly from the schoolhouse to the intersection, where he turned and followed the broad back of General Jacob J. Jackson through crowds of buggies and pedestrians toward the railroad station.

—There goes, the Perfessor said, a case of arrested development. The General there is strictly a pre-Appomattox American. To feel alive, he has to surround himself with other anachronisms like himself. He has to go on fighting that goddam war to his last gasp. He'll probably die in a home for aged and infirm veterans, wearing full Civil War regalia, draped in the flag, and growling something like, Send McPherson to hold that flank, and give 'em hell in the center, boys! I can see the newspaper article now. The General ought to rate page three in the New York papers with a small engraving of his valorous old puss. I wouldn't mind writing it up myself in my best blackbordered bow-wow style, reserved for the demise of Civil War generals.

—Where else but in America, Mr. Shawnessy said, do famous generals become old hat so soon? Let's give the General his due. When the Republic needed him and his big voice and his bull courage, he was there. And how much more innocent it is to reminisce about old wars than to start new ones!

Mr. Shawnessy watched the bluff form of a certain illustrious commander blending with the crowd at the Station, lost from view in the tired afternoon. He thought then of monuments approaching but not quite reaching their apex. Of love approaching but not quite reaching a climax. Of blind seeds struggling in the swamp and not quite reaching a matrix. And of trains, the great trains coming into stations. Of the miracle of arrival and consummation. Of life incessantly defeating the paradox of Zeno. Of the riddle of Raintree County incessantly proposing itself as its own solution.

As usual the thought of a train coming filled him with excitement. He took from his pocket a telegram received the day before and reread it.

> CANT COME FOR PROGRAM BUT WILL ARRIVE ON FIVE OCLOCK TRAIN IN WAYCROSS FOR BRIEF VISIT ON WAY TO PITTSBURGH STOP HOPE TO SEE ALL OLD FRIENDS STOP LAURA MAY COME
>
> CASSIUS P CARNEY

Mr. Shawnessy wondered then if it was still possible to walk through the late afternoon (when the Grand Patriotic Program was over and crumpled leaves of it were strewn among the burst firecrackers) and find strong love and a great wisdom among the faces of

Waycross Station

ᴡERE THE WORDS painted on the building by the tracks. Eva realized hat always before when she had seen the Station, it had been empty, . bleakly official structure where trains passed and never stopped. Now the Station like the town was filled with people, and all the rains were stopping.

The Reverend Lloyd G. Jarvey stood somewhat apart from the rowd at the Station talking with her Grandfather Root. The two ig heads wagged solemnly at each other. The town had been filled oday with perilous encounters. She remembered how at noon, she nd other children had seen through a window at Mrs. Passifee's a reat white creature in a darkened parlor. This creature had looked lindly at her as it stood in the act of placing a pair of spectacles on ts nose.

General Jacob J. Jackson was climbing into a carriage before the Post Office and waving good-by to friends. Standing near the track efore the Station was Senator Jones and his entourage, while some- vhat apart her father talked to a tall, thin man with a cane.

On this one day, the little town where she had lived for two years ad been briefly touched with splendor, and its homely mask had allen to show an immense tide of faces, arriving, passing, and de- arting. She felt that they had always been there really, and were art of what the town had always been and meant.

Waycross was the place where straight roads crossed on the breast f the land. It was the Shawnessy lot extending from the Road back the Railroad. In this time-enchanted world, rectangular between wo paths of change, the rooms were always quiet in the summer, nd in the bookcase in the middle room the same books held their laces on the wall. On fall nights an apple dropping on the wood- ouse roof made a one, solemn, hollow, haunted sound. Always the ellar underneath the house was cold incredibly, smelling of waxen ims of cans of apples, peaches, pears. A cold jet came from the driven well at the southwest corner of the house. The smokehous smelled of woodchar and rinded pigfat, an odor steeped and staine into its boards. The cherry tree beside the cistern bled a clear jellysa from clotted wounds where armies of ants collected. The barn, th woodhouse, and the walk to the outdoor toilet were eternal things Waycross was this bordered plot of earth, scarred, built on, hived in inhabited—an ancient, man-created ground.

Waycross was the General Store at the intersection, the Post Of fice in the sleepy street, the Station, a huge, decaying toy, left to ro functionless beside the track. It was the Schoolhouse down the Road divided by absolute decree into two rooms.

Waycross was this ancient fixity of things, but it was also th thunder and butting rhythm of trains passing with a cry of desperat haste back of the lot across the land.

And Waycross was at last the broad Road cutting through th town. Endlessly the carriaged faces came, swept by on the low rus and rumorous sound of wheels, arriving, enlarging, impending, pass ing, receding, fading.

Eva knew that she, too, like the town of Waycross was a bein filled with a becoming. Seasons, tides, fruitions poured through thi waycrossing with the changeless name of Eva. Today the long roa widened and beckoned her beyond her present self, the Waycros Eva. In this town to which her father had come to live his life out she was perhaps only to build the last edifice of her childhood an then go forth herself and become one of those faces on the Gre Road, one of those passengers on trains. . . .

EVA GROWS UP

(Epic Fragment from the *Eva Series*)

> And so, indulgent little readers, as we bring Eva near the end o her happy child life and leave her on the threshold of woman's estat we will agree, I think, that the little heroine of our moral pilgrimag is not wholly unprepared to face the great world in which doubtle she will have many troubles—for such, alas! is the fate of us all i this perplexing world. But if she keeps the happy faith of chil hood, may we not hope that all her cares will come to nought and sh will find her way through all vexations homeward at last along

1890— THE —1892

ROAD, THE GREAT BROAD ROAD,

THE NATIONAL ROAD WAS A HUNDRED FEET IN WIDTH

from curb to curb. When Eva ventured across it, she always felt scared until she reached the other side. Out in the middle, she lost her ancient footing in the County. Space attacked her. Tides of force rolled in from blue horizons east and west. What she was seemed annihilated, levelled, trod under, thinned out, and spread over the whole of the United States of America.

Except for the Road, Waycross was like any other town in Raintree County, and a few days after the family arrived in the summer of 1890, Eva felt at home. But it was at Waycross that she herself changed with amazing swiftness. In the spring of 1892 the tide of growth completed its inexorable rhythm, and Eva became in form a woman, though in spirit still a child. The child, the sexless, anachronistic child, still lingered on, ill at ease, unhappy, reluctant to give up. And in a last desperate orgy of self-assertion, this child did strange devotions.

Her jealousy toward her brother Wesley was violently exaggerated. She threw herself with excessive zeal into her studies. She forced her awkward body to the limit of its strength in the schoolyard games. But she was getting plump, her hips were broad, her hands were stubby, and it looked as though she never would be slim and pretty like her mother. She knew that anything she got in the world would have to be achieved through character and intelligence. When her father got her a piano at a serious strain to the family pocketbook, she practiced like a fanatic, sometimes six hours at a stretch, until she was so dizzy and cramped she could hardly stand.

Her mind was feverishly active, wandering off into daydreams in which she was one of the greatest authors of her time. She greatly admired Mrs. Brown and, like her, became an ardent feminist. She was convinced that women were downtrodden creatures: they had never had a fair chance; everything conspired to keep them from asserting their true capacity. She was determined to become a great woman and make the name Eva Alice Shawnessy famous as the names Harriet Beecher Stowe, George Eliot, Augusta Evans, Rosa Bonheur. She selected a pen name—Eva Westward, in honor of her father—and began to write fragments of stories, novels, poems, which she hid from everyone, being painfully dissatisfied with them.

It was during these years at Waycross that Eva conceived her great plan to write her father's life so that nothing that he was would be lost to posterity. She kept the plan secret from everyone and even began to make some small notes. But the whole thing became absurd when she realized how little she knew about her father in the Pre-Eva age. Whole eras of his history were buried beneath the debris of the indifferent years. Like the evolutionary biologist, she had to be satisfied with a leafprint on a rock or a fragment of fossil bone, sole remnants of gigantic life-fabrics that flourished on the earth in lost ages.

Strange, wonderful, and fearful must have been that ancient life before there was any Eva. Now and then, unexpectedly, a pale ray was cast across those old times, and she beheld her father briefly in an attitude of his youth. Once she had found a little wallet full of newspaper clippings, among them some which reported her father's death in the Civil War. She knew something, of course, about that famous mistake. But she had a feeling that there were meanings and happenings buried in his homecoming from the War that she would never learn. What had it been like to come back to Raintree County after being reported dead? What had he found waiting for him after that homecoming?

This sacred, lost person—her father in his younger days—moved, as it seemed to her, through a mystic web of adventures, loves, dreams, exertions which had nothing in common with the life he lived now. The lost eras of his life were all bathed in the golden light of legend; they were inexpressibly remote; they were fragmentary, scriptural, symbolic—like the gospels.

On the other hand, when Eva thought of writing about that part of her father's life in which she had had a part, she was surprised by how little there was to tell. Her father had taught school and written poetry and read books and talked with people; the children had grown up; the family had lived in several little towns in Raintree County. That was all there was to it. Yet even here, she felt the presence of a meaning sacred and momentous, if she could only express it.

Slowly the town of Waycross became for her the perfect image of her father's life in his latter years. To this waycrossing on the breast of the land, the family had been meant to come. Between the two broad roads of change, they had found perhaps a lasting home. She had often heard her father say to her mother,

—This is a good place to spend the rest of our days, Esther.

During these years, Eva became more appreciative of her father's rare literary gifts and began to wonder at the paradox of a man so gifted living contentedly in a little country town and teaching the half-formed minds of children. And yet he seemed perfectly in context, and it was a happy life that the family had in Waycross. Sometimes in the midst of reading something, Eva would lift her eyes from the book and, not yet having left the land of legend, would see the life in Waycross in a perspective as of time and years remote. And then truly it seemed a golden and serene existence to her. This feeling was strongest when she would hunt out certain old manuscripts of her father's—Tennysonian lyrics written in his youth. One such was a little song called 'One Summer Morn,' which perfectly expressed for her the color of the years in Waycross.

My muse and I, one summer morn,
  Built, dreaming we were cunning fays,
A castle on a cloud-isle borne
  Adrift on blue, ethereal bays.
Our blessed isle was far away
  From earth. It swam down eastern skies,
Whereon in bright pavilions lay
  Glad choristers with joyous eyes,
And from their sweet throats woke the song—
'Tis summer, and the days are long.

Far east o'er pure empyreal seas,
  Our happy souls that morning sailed,
Light-seated on our isle at ease,
  Unheeding earth from whence we hailed.
Forgotten was all touch of care.
  An age was lived in one sweet dream,

As in our castle built in air
We swam the blue celestial stream
Safe into daybreak with the song—
'Tis summer, and the days are long.

Summer was his season and his temple. The perfect weather of his soul was in the season of the long midsummer days that rose and blazed and waned above the Road and the Railroad, while the carriages passed in dust and the trains in wailing fury all day long; and in the little rectangle of the family ground, becalmed between the two great bands of change, close by the cornfield in the backlot, beside the sundial with the inscription, *I record only the sunshine,* her father would be sitting in his old rocker, his long blue eyes enclosed in their intricate net of suncreated lines and wrinkles, propping his head on his hand, holding a neglected book, a copy of the *Indianapolis News-Historian,* or perhaps notebook and pencil; and the sleepy noises of the little town—cries of children, murmur of women at backfences, jingle of harness—would rise and fall like surf on white sands; and the whole level, sun-enamored earth of Raintree County would lie in a bland repose outward from the intersection of Waycross—and it was summer and the days were long.

At such times, Eva too would generally be reading, lying on her stomach under an appletree or curled up in the swing on the front porch. She would be walking high meadows of summer in the land of the sentimental novels, stories grave and gay for the instruction of all the wellbroughtup little girls of America.

Then she felt as though she were living in some wise enchantment, and when she came down from the dreamland of her books, it was merely from one circle of her dream into another still more glorious and legendary. Then she felt like the Alice from whom she got her middle name, the fabulous little girl who had walked hand in hand with a gentle elder spirit, lapped in legends old, and herself dreaming of legends. Eva read the last paragraph of *Alice's Adventures in Wonderland* over and over. It anticipated (in a dream within the dream, as it were) how the little storybook Alice

> . . . would, in the after-time, be herself a grown woman: and how she would keep, through all her riper years, the simple and loving heart of her childhood: and how she would gather about her other little

> children, and make *their* eyes bright and eager with many a strange tale, perhaps even with the dream of Wonderland of long ago: and how she would feel with all their simple sorrows, and find a pleasure in all their simple joys, remembering her own child-life, and the happy summer days.

It was one of Eva's favorite daydreams to imagine herself grown and returning to Waycross in afteryears, a famous woman who had succeeded in glorifying her father's life and imprinting it forever on the memory of mankind. Rarely, too, in her nightdreams she had nostalgic sensations as of return after long years to the scenes and places of her childhood. In these dreams, remarkable like her father's for their vivid realism, she would be riding in some odd sort of vehicle on the broad road from west to east, a woman returning to the little town where she had been a girl fifty years before. She would be trying to reconstruct the old tranquil life just as it was in those faded, lost years at the end of the Nineteenth Century.

Yes, she had come back to the old, the archetypal Waycross. She was walking down the unpaved sidewalk beside the tidy fences. Each house was like a homely, once-familiar face. Behind the gray-eyed windows were rooms she had never entered but had always vaguely wondered about. And it gave her a queer start to think that they were all furnished down to the last exquisite detail with the furnishings of a lost era and that they were peopled with faces that were long since gone from the indifferent years. How still and deep the lawns looked and the spaces between the houses!

And now she was approaching the little house behind the white fence. She paused with her hand on the gate. They were all there, yes, they would surely be there in the changeless world between the Road and the Railroad. Her mother would be working in the kitchen where smell of sealing wax lingered forever. The lost Eva and the forever lost Wesley would be in the middle room reading, each one absorbed in a sentimental dream, which was itself peopled only with dreamers. And somewhere she would find little Will, another lost face of her childhood. And if she went behind the house, she would see the sunlight falling through the appletrees, the outhouse papered with clippings, the barn, the narrow backfield stretching to the railroad. And perhaps, even as she watched, one of the trains of those departed years would go roaring by, carrying to westward a hundred mysterious faces.

But no, she wouldn't go in for a while yet. Probably school was in session, since there were no children in the streets. She would turn, then, and approach the schoolhouse—not one of the newer schoolhouses built since her departure from the County but the old frame school where the famous celebrations were held back in those tattered, stained, and lovely years of the early nineties. Yes, it was the old school, and the children would all be there in the holy communion of the schoolroom, half a hundred precise child faces, enclosed in the ambercolored light of those many and many photographs taken before the schools of Raintree County, with her father standing unobtrusively in a corner of the picture, his tall, gentle form half-dissolved in sunlight.

Then there would rush over her the recollection of a thousand lost days in schoolrooms and schoolhouse yards. And all the children whom her father had taught trooped through her memory, proceeding all (by a second birth) from the archetypal schoolroom into the archetypal Raintree County and thence beyond its borders and down the roads of all the years into the sunlight of a new century.

But now she must be courageous and hold hard to the perishable moment if she wished to see her father (whose death in some earlier dream she seemed to remember). And in fact, she was opening the door and stepping into the hall between the two rooms of the schoolhouse. In one room her mother taught the elementary classes, and in the other her father taught the advanced pupils. Golden light of the late spring was in the room, it was one of those days when her heart cried out with music, and she seemed able to accomplish anything. There was her brother Wesley at his accustomed desk, and there close by him was the lost Eva, and there—there at the blackboard at the front of the room, turning now with the light of afternoon on his old dark suit, there to be sure was her father touching the blackboard with a piece of chalk.

—Eva, he would say, will you please go on with the problem from there?

Such strange, timeleaping dreams, speculations, and endeavors colored the early years at Waycross and slowly formed the Waycross Eva, that grave, great-eyed girl-woman, that reluctant daughter-mother, that little transitional being who was passing through the valley of decision between a self and a self. This passing, like nearly all things human, was made imperceptibly and would go on being made for years, and in a sense too, of course, would never be entirely made, since the earlier Evas and the transitional Evas would all linger on in the deeper layers of Eva's being.

Yet there was a moment of self-discovery during these early years in Waycross when Eva herself became clearly aware for the first time that she had crossed a dark valley and was emerging on the farther side. The discovery came in early June of the year 1892 along with one of the great emotional crises of her life. It came suddenly and unexpectedly as a result of a simple thing.

Little by little she had been forced to give up her claims to physical equality with her brother Wesley. Only in wrestling had she still been able to maintain her old proud feeling of equality. One evening after supper in early June, after a day of small disappointments and frustrations, Eva herself had suggested a match. She hadn't wrestled Wesley for several weeks, and although she had had to exert every particle of strength to get a fall in their last match, she still believed in her ability to hold her own with him. It was after supper, and they were all out on the back lawn. The children had been running about barefooted. The air was warm and still, and day was ebbing on the level fields. Her father, who had been walking at the rim of the backlot where the young corn was already a hand high, came back to the middle of the yard.

—All right, he said. Square off.

Wesley stood before her, lithe and wary, hands on hips, waiting for the signal. His mouth and eyes had the usual set look of stoical confidence. At the signal, they laid hold of each other. Eva gritted her teeth and tugged and pushed and pulled and twisted, trying to use her superior weight to advantage, trying all her tricks one after another. She and Wesley had never wrestled longer for a fall than for that one. After nearly five minutes of struggling, Eva felt her strength going from her, while Wesley remained as lithe and powerful as a wild thing. Just then, when she hardly expected it, he gave her a quick twist, and down she went slapbang on her back.

Her mother laughed.

—Well, pshaw! she said. *Did*n't you go down, Eva!

—I just slipped, Eva said, jumping up angry and panting.

Wesley, as usual, didn't say anything, but waited, hands on hips, confident-like. All set to make a heroic exertion, Eva laid hold of him and gave a great push. He cut his leg in front of her, dodged, and she threw herself.

—Well, pshaw, her mother said, smiling one of her rare smiles, *are*n't you getting strong, Wesley!

—There now, that's enough, her father said. Wesley seems to be feeling his oats tonight.

—No, please, Eva said. Three best out of five.

This time, the struggle was longer. Eva lashed herself to a superhuman effort. She groaned, strained, squealed, and thrashed around, but Wesley stuck his tongue between his teeth and this time, without any trick throw, gradually bent her back and back until there was no help for it, and down she went crashbang.

—Pshaw, her mother said. *Don't* they wrestle hard!

She licked her smooth lips and stood watching the contest with more than her usual interest.

—Yes, Eva's father said, when those two lay hold, it's do or die. Of course, Wesley being the older and a——

—Let's try again, Wesley, Eva said, springing up, her voice quavering.

They struggled again—a long, silent, grim struggle. This time, he threw her on her face.

—Well, that's enough now, children, her father said. Let's have a game of——

But she was up and trying again. She thought her heart would burst if she didn't throw Wesley at least once. They were wrestling again, and then again, and again. Each time, he threw her more easily. She lost count of the times.

—Eva, Eva! her father said. You're too tired to win now. Wait until you're rested.

—No, just *once* more, she pleaded, her voice breaking. I want to throw him just once.

Wesley had become an impersonal force that had to be subdued or else there was no longer any hope or joy in life. Tears streamed down her face as she took hold of him for the last time. She began to sob openly.

—Eva, I'm ashamed of you! her mother said.

In the middle of that last struggle, Eva found herself wishing that Wesley would *let* her throw him. And in that instant she knew that she was hopelessly beaten. She knew that she would never be able to throw him again and that she was wrestling him for the last time.

As she went down, all her anguish and sorrow came forth from her in a great wail that sounded ridiculous even to herself. She didn't move from where she was thrown, half-lying on her face, her cheeks wet with sweat and tears.

—Pshaw, Eva, her mother said. You ought to be ashamed of yourself. A great big girl like you! Go on in, and wash your face.

—Poor child, her father said. Let her be, Esther. She was so proud of her wrestling ability. After all, Eva, you couldn't expect to beat Wesley forever. He's a year older than you, child, and he's bound to get stronger. It's nature for men to be physically stronger than women. I think it's extraordinary you've held your own with him so long.

Eva started to say something, but her voice soared off in a series of O sounds, and she didn't seem to be able to take the one deep breath that would stop them.

So she lay there, with everyone watching her, she lay there in the soft grass of the back lawn, her outraged, overgrown girl's body sprawled on the earth. She just wanted to lie there, and she never wanted to have to wrestle anyone again.

As she cried, she was thinking of all the days and ways of her eager, sexless childhood when she and Wesley had wrestled, and sometimes it was one, sometimes the other who beat. It was all, all over now, the innocent, swift days of the two children playing together, Eva and Wesley, the laughter, the jealousies, the frustrations, the triumphs. And now she realized that during that time they had been as one, she and Wesley, in the close passion of competitors, which is fierce like love and hate. All that time they had been one and wedded to each other by jealousy and emulation. And now they were forever and irrevocably two, boy and girl, brother and sister, man and woman.

Strangely then into her heart there crept a feeling of tenderness and strong love for her brother that had perhaps been there all the time, and in this last great defeat there was no longer any bitterness but a sorrowful, complete acceptance. And as she lay on the green breast of the earth, even the tears and the sorrow went slowly out of her, leaving her stilled and pensive. The family went away, and she stayed there in the grass a long time, lying on her stomach, her tear-stained face propped in her hands. She watched the night come on, filling up the backlot and the cornfield with darkness and flowing around the houses of the town. A train went by during this time; the steady thunder faded down the track to westward. Carts and wagons passed on the National Road. The insect voices of the night began to shrill louder and louder. And the cool dew came on the grass.

And still she lay, looking out across the growing cornfield and wondering what great tide it was, gentle, inexorable, and strong, flowing up from all the years of all her life that had at last reached and flooded to the full here in this town to which latterly they had come beside the Great Road, and where perhaps her father and mother would live out their days, had found her as it had been fated to find her from the beginning, and had created at last out of all the earlier Evas (perhaps better and braver and more tender than them all) this new and latest Eva.

Then she looked east and west and thought of the Great Road, the broad straight Road, the National Road, rising upon the plain forever, and flowing in a band of brightness east and west, and of the vast plain beneath the night and of all the lost days of her father's life that were somehow hovering in this night, and of the terrible and beautiful rhythms of the earth, and of its wandering flowers, and of its ancient tides, moondrawn and flowing out of darkness, and of the great tide of death that must some day come and find her father in this quiet ground between the two roads. And so the darkness came, lapping her with mystery as she lay a long time

ON THE GREEN EARTH OF RAINTREE COUNTY

IN THE ATTITUDE OF

A

Sphinx Recumbent

THE PERFESSOR SAID. Yes, I still have it, packed away in a box somewhere. I've moved around a good deal since then. As I remember it, it was a hideous daub. 'Sphinx Recumbent.' What made you think of it?

—O, nothing in particular, Mr. Shawnessy said, shoving the telegram from Cassius Carney, received the day before, back into his coatpocket. Just memories of my City days. Fact is, I dreamed about the darn thing last night.

The Senator's train was late, and as the crowd slowly dispersed, the Senator walked over to the bench by the station door and sat down fanning his face with his hat. Mr. Shawnessy and the Perfessor flanked him. Inside the Station the telegraph key clickclicked its uncertain but incessant rhythm.

—Phew! the Senator said. Wish my train would come. What time does Cash come in?

—Around five, Mr. Shawnessy said. On the Eastbound from Indianapolis.

—Maybe I'll get to see him after all, the Senator said. Jesus, John, don't tell me you mean to stay in this hick town all your life! How do you do it?

—How do *you* do it, Garwood? Mr. Shawnessy said. How do you go on playing the part of the Great Commoner?

—Up there on the rostrum, the Senator said, it's the noble part of me that speaks. You fellows appeal to my baseness. To tell you the truth, I really appreciate Raintree County when I'm a thousand miles away from it. But if I had to live here for a month, I'd go nuts. It's so—so goddam wholesome and peaceful. By the way, what is your candid opinion of the program today? Did it go over?

—You're safe, the Perfessor said. There's one born every minute, and each one has a vote.

—What made you think you needed to pull this big charade, Garwood? Mr. Shawnessy said.

—I have to take cognizance of this new Populist movement, the Senator said. To be perfectly frank, I'm afraid of it. After winning every political contest I've been entered in for thirty years, I don't intend to get stampeded out of office by this gang of amateur politicians and professional horse-thieves who call themselves the People's Party.

—Of which, Mr. Shawnessy said, I'm a member. The People's Party is made up of the folks who are tired of a government of cynical understandings between politicians and businessmen. As for you, Garwood, you never belonged to the People's Party—I mean the eternal and usually unorganized People's Party. You always belonged to just one party, the Party of Yourself, the Party of Garwood B. Jones, and you never had but one platform—the advancement of Garwood B. Jones to the Highest Office Within the Gift of the American People.

—Not so loud, John, the Senator said, oozing laughter. People will overhear you.

He leaned back in his chair, mellow and imperturb.

—Yes, he said, I've always sought the advancement of Garwood B. Jones. He's a magnificent guy, and I like him. But I've always furthered this wonderful bastard's interests in strict observance of the American Way—by giving people what they wanted.

—By *appearing* to give them what they wanted, Mr. Shawnessy said. The people want a chance to own their own land, to have economic security, to see government perform its function of protecting the interests of the many instead of the interests of the few. You'll promise the same things that the People's Party are promising, to keep your party and yourself in power, and once elected, you'll go on doing what you've done before because it's the easiest way and because it's always been successful. You'll continue to obey the voice of the Big Interests, while wooing the vote of the Little Interests.

—My dear fellow, the Senator said, using his big voice like a bludgeon, you do me a great injustice. You speak of the so-called Big Interests as if they were gangs of criminals. Who built this vast country? The Big Interests—that's who. These men are also feathering their own nests—but they've discovered that the best way to feather your own nest is to advance the interest of people generally. The honest capitalist like the honest politician is the servant of the people. He's a man of superior imagination and daring whose ability to do his country good has earned him the just reward of continued power and wealth, by which he can continue to do good. The people know that their best interests lie in the direction of a constitutional government which encourages the Free Exercise of Individual Rights and the Protection of Home Industries.

—I suppose you perceive, John, the Perfessor said, that we haven't after all emerged very far from the Great Swamp. What is life in the fairest republic the world has ever seen? What did the martyrs of the Great War die for? Liberty? Justice? Union? Emancipation? The Flag? Hell, no. They died so that a lot of slick bastards could exploit the immense natural and human resources of this nation and become fabulously rich while the vast majority of the people grind their guts out to get a living. They died so that several million poor serfs from the stinking slums and ghettos of Europe could come five thousand miles to wedge themselves into the stinking ghettos and slums of America. Only in America is Survival of the Fittest, the principle of brute struggle for life, erected into a principle of government. In America anyone who can crawl to the top of the pile through daring, guile, and sheer ruthlessness can stay up there until somebody pulls him down.

—Professor, the Senator said, you read too much. Go out sometime, jerk off your specs, and take a look at this nation. This nation is big enough for everyone in it.

The Senator was standing now, gesturing forcibly and bringing within the range of his voice a number of citizens who still lingered in the Station and who now began to close in toward the center of sound.

—This nation is big enough and rich enough for everyone to pursue and realize a worthwhile goal. What is wrong with the principle of self-interest anyway? Rational self-interest, controlled by law, is the basis of a free society. Look at the men who have risen to the top of the pile—the presidents, the statesmen, the financiers. Where did they come from? Out of log cabins and back alleys. Everyone has the same chance, under the aegis of the Constitution. What is America, gentlemen? I will tell you. America is the only nation in the world where mineboys become millionaires, and paperboys become presidents. It is the place where—— Pardon me, folks, I'm not making a speech. We are just engaging in that grand old American custom of political disputation. After all, it's an Election Year.

—You've got to hand it to Garwood, the Perfessor sighed. He shovels that stuff with a golden pitchfork.

The Senator sat down again.

—By the way, John, about that *Atlas*—I'm beginning to think the whole thing was a fake. Still, there might be something hidden in it somewhere. Suppose you keep it and sift it fine. If you find something worthwhile, let me know. And another thing, John, I'd esteem it a great personal favor if you'd look over this manuscript for a few days and correct any errors of fact relating to the early history of the County, which you know better than anyone—or make any other suggestions that occur to you. Some of it'll interest you, I'm sure. One of the best things is the story of your homecoming from the War. I quote in full the tender lyric I composed on the occasion of your demise. All handled, of course, with appropriate irony.

Mr. Shawnessy took the proffered manuscript of *Memories of the Republic in War and Peace.*

Leaves of my life—but by another's hand.

—To be perfectly frank, John, the Senator went on, I'll never forgive you for walking in on me that day in my office in Indianapolis. At least you didn't have to come in reciting the goddam poem.

Mr. Shawnessy raised a hand in benediction and intoned:

> —Sleep in thy hero grave, belovèd boy!
> Sleep well, thou pure defender of the right.
> Far from the battle's din and rude annoy,
> Our tears shall keep your memory ever bright.

The Senator laughed and laughed until the tears came to his eyes. He blew his nose and swatted the Perfessor on the back with his free hand. He wiped his eyes and went on wheezing with laughter. Mr. Shawnessy had never seen the Senator so amused before.

—I'll never forget the expression on your face, Garwood. It's the only time in your life I've seen you speechless for twenty seconds.

—Just what did I do? I forget now.

—You turned completely white, cleared your throat, got up, walked over, put a hand on my arm to see if I was real, sat down again, studied a moment, and said, You spoiled a good poem, sprout.

The Senator was still laughing.

—That was one hell of a homecoming you had, he said. I wrote it up at some length in my book there. Hope you don't mind. I guess I got the important facts in.

I doubt it, Mr. Shawnessy thought.

—Ah, gentlemen, the Senator said. What things we have seen and done in fifty years! What is America? Well, I'll tell you, gentlemen—— Thunder! there comes my train.

A rhythmical pulse was beating on the rails.

What is America? What is America? What is America?

America is a memory of a boy who was dead and then came home anyway, hunting for an old court house and a home place in the County. America is the memory of millions of young men who came home and never came home and never could come home. America is the land where no one who goes away for a year can come back home again. America is the land where the telegraph keys are clicking all the time and the trains are changing in the stations. America is the image of human change where the change is changed by experts.

Come back, come back to Raintree County. O, wanderer far from home, come back after the Patriotic Program, when the leaves of it are scattered on the grass, and seek again for beauty, love, and wisdom. America is a dream that I was dreaming, an innocent dream among the moneychangers. For I got lost in stations where the trains were changing. I got lost in cities of a gilded age. O, wanderer far from home, come back, come back and live a memory of your illusioned, strong young manhood, a memory of

1865— How —1876

THE FIRST ELEVEN YEARS

FOLLOWING THE GREAT WAR WERE SAD AND LONELY YEARS

for the tired hero who came back to Raintree County one day in the spring of 1865 like Lazarus from the dead. When Johnny came marching home at the War's end and when the reunions and discoveries of that extraordinary homecoming were over, he found that in a sense the report of his death had not been unduly exaggerated. Johnny Shawnessy, that innocent and happy youth who had somehow contrived to keep in touch with the elder Raintree County of before the War, was really dead (though it took his successor a little while to become aware of the fact), and the Raintree County to which he had fondly dreamed of returning was also dead. Out of the shocks and changes of the War and the equally great shocks and changes of the homecoming, there emerged a new hero of Raintree County and a new County. The old (that is to say, the young) Johnny was really gone, interred in the triteness of Garwood Jones's poem. In his stead was John Shawnessy, a sober young man of twenty-six, who had now a new life to live, a new love to find, a new poem of himself and the Republic to create.

Also the old Republic was gone. Johnny Shawnessy had unwittingly put the torch to it along with Atlanta and Columbia. The new Republic was something he hadn't foreseen.

He hadn't foreseen the sooty monster that stood alone after the smoke of battle had cleared, the Vanquisher alike of vanquishers and vanquished. Before the War this monster had been an awkward babe. But during the War he had put on muscle. His name was Industrialism.

Johnny Shawnessy hadn't foreseen that where there had been one factory before the War there would be a hundred factories following. He hadn't foreseen that the railroads would grow with magic speed until the huge vine enmeshed the Republic in iron tendrils. He hadn't foreseen that hundreds of thousands of Americans would leave the farms and go to the great cities. He hadn't foreseen the great cities themselves (for who could have foreseen these huge, glistening mushrooms that appeared one morning on the surface of the Great Swamp!). He hadn't foreseen how tides of aspiration setting ever east to west would bring millions of immigrants to America and how the tidal glut of these innumerable faces would fill up whole cities and run deep into the prairie leaving pools of alien speech and alien ways around and far beyond the borders of Raintree County.

He didn't foresee the Reconstruction of the South, the doomed experiment of giving the black man a vote by force of arms. He didn't foresee the scalawags and carpetbaggers who exploited the prostrate South. He didn't foresee the bayonet legislatures, the wrecked economy of the Cotton Kingdom. He didn't foresee the inflamed race hatred that war left behind, the lynchings, the Ku Klux Klan. He didn't foresee the impeachment of Andrew Johnson (who was a cousin of Johnny Shawnessy's on his mother's side), a shameful effort to wrest from an honest, if tactless, Executive the power vested in him by the Constitution, a cynical effort to destroy the balanced system of government. He didn't foresee the sectional feeling kept alive for years after the War by orators North and South. He didn't foresee the formation of a Solid South, a political bloc, reactionary and resentful, a separate culture in all but legal fact.

He didn't foresee that the greatest Union General of the War, Ulysses S. Grant, would be elected President, expressing for millions the wish to see a nation peaceful and united, and he didn't foresee that, once elected, this politically stupid man would become a helpless front for crooks in high place, who bled the Republic of wealth and honor alike.

He didn't foresee the Tweed Ring in New York, the Gas Ring in Philadelphia, the Whiskey Ring in St. Louis. He didn't foresee the daring speculations, the corrupt deals, the barefaced frauds. He didn't foresee the famous Corner in Gold, the Crédit Mobilier, the Panic of 1873. He didn't foresee Jay Gould, Jay Cooke, Jim Fisk, Cornelius Vanderbilt, John D. Rockefeller, J. P. Morgan—the new men, titans of industry, amassers of corrupt fortunes, exploiters of millions, barons of a new feudalism.

He didn't foresee the materialism of the age, the spirit of getting wealth, of amassing property, of conquering space, of mining and stripping and gutting and draining, and whoring and ravaging and rending the beautiful earth of America. He didn't foresee the grotesque buildings, public and private, that festered on the land, the tenements of stunted souls.

He didn't foresee any of these things. Johnny Shawnessy didn't even foresee John Shawnessy.

For example, he didn't anticipate the loneliness of John Shawnessy, his search for a new religion, and his brief appearance in the political arena.

When John Shawnessy was once more firmly back in the County, he resumed a life that outwardly resembled the good old life he had had before he met Susanna Drake in 1859. He lived at the Home Place with his parents and continued to teach school, work on the *Free Enquirer,* and write. But the resemblance between his new and his old way of life was outward only. Between him and the happy youth of 1859 lay the red divide of the Civil War and many memories.

These post-War years were the saddest and loneliest that he would ever have. Sometimes at night he would dream of his comrades beslutted by death in yellow fields and forests rotten with rain. Waking up alone in his bed at the Home Place, he would be engulfed in silence and a brooding sadness. Was this the Republic that he and his comrades had been tramping toward in the Great March? Was this the Union they had hammered out ringing on the forge of battle? Was this the Raintree County of which Johnny Shawnessy had intended to become the hero?

Pensive, he listened to the pulse of silence and the earth. The earth alone endured the same. The rock still lay at the limit of the land. The river ran in darkness down its pathway to the lake, tracing a word of prophecy and recollection. The lake lay, an ancient scar in the middle of the County. But this was the period of awakening into a new age, and a new light was upon the land. He thought then of the railroads, the newspapers, the speculators, the builders, miners, exploiters of the earth. He thought of new cities crammed with new people. Did they still wait the coming of a young Shakespeare, a hero from the West? Was there still a passionate lover waiting for him somewhere, the incarnation of all the beauty he had ever seen and coveted? Where was the streambegotten girl? Where in all the turning waste of nights and days was the anciently beloved of the youth with the sunlight in his hair?

Then John Shawnessy, that sober young man whose hair had begun to fade a little at the temples and whose forehead now never quite lost its faint lines even when he slept and whose long blue eyes had traces of crowsfeet at the corners, would lie a long time in his lonely bed and wish that he had someone to love and to love him, a woman with great eyes and passionate lips, someone whose voice, touching his ear in the lone spaces of the night, would lull him from the bad dreams.

All things changed on the earth except the earth itself and certain memories of the earth.

He would think then of his wife Susanna. For he was still bound to her by ancient ties. Now and then he would receive and answer one of her poor mad letters. But he knew now that he would probably never see her again. She herself didn't wish it, though she still clung pitifully to the memory of their love, a last anchor in the swirling torrent of her madness. There was no use raising the question of divorce. Even if he could have obtained a divorce, he wasn't sure that his conscience would let him. It seemed best for the moment to let things go on as they were. Time would make decisions for him.

But in one of his most terrible dreams of that lonely period following the War, he found himself walking up the steps of the tall house south of the Square in Freehaven, coming back home after long absence, approaching with the old feeling of nameless dread, and as he neared the door he could see, peering at him through the wavering glass, his wife Susanna, her face and body marked with fire and bound with bandages.

As for his family, the girls were all married, the older boys had farms and families of their own, and his favorite among them, Zeke, had gone West after the War and had started a new life in California. T. D. went on dispensing botanical medicines to a few old patients and meeting more and more rarely, fewer and fewer people in the church at Danwebster. As for the town of Danwebster, it died after the War. Just why it died no one knew, but the life went out of it. Half the houses in town became empty, and the remaining residents began to apologize for living in the place. The walks grew up with weeds, porches sagged and fell, stores closed. By 1870, Danwebster was a collection of roofless sheds and shacks. T. D. would drive by, shaking his head and saying,

—I don't understand. It was a right nice little town before the War.

When several families refused to bury their dead in the graveyard on the hill, it was clear that the town was done for. As for T. D., who had depended largely on the community of Danwebster for patients and parishioners, he too began to seem a pathetic anachronism in the post-War period. No one cared anything for reform after the Civil War. All the ardent crusades had been trampled under in the one great crusade of the generation. The younger people had little faith in the Botanical Medicines. T. D. himself went on taking a hopeful view of things, but without financial aid from his youngest son, he would have been hard pressed to buy food for himself and Ellen.

Ellen, however, seemed to change little with the years. And though the Office behind the house began to seem more and more like a tiny faded museum, the house itself, the fields, the rock at the limit of the land, the brown road running east and west, the contour of the earth remained unchanged, and the taproot of his being was still deep in this ancestral place.

Despite his lonely life during this time, John Shawnessy had complete faith in himself, and there welled up in him stronger than ever the assurance that he was the bearer of a sacred fire. He had been meant from the beginning by a messianic birth to be the Hero of the County. Only he could fulfill prophecy and lead his generation to a nobler way of life, a loftier religion than they had known before.

He had always meant to do this great thing while he was young. At the close of the War in 1865, he was twenty-six. At twenty-six Keats was dead. At thirty-three, Jesus was crucified. The time had come for John Shawnessy to make a godlike exertion, to produce a masterwork, a book that would usher in the Golden Age of the American Republic.

So he would write the epic of the American Republic and its people, the greatest poem ever written. He didn't know at the outset just what form the story would take or what resources of language (rich and daring—equal to the theme) he would discover. But he knew that what he wrote would be the story——

Of a quest for the sacred tree of life. Of a happy valley and a face of stone—and of the coming of a hero. Of mounds beside the river. Of threaded bones of lovers in the earth. Of shards of battles long ago. Of names upon the land, the fragments of forgotten language. Of beauty risen from the river and seen through rushes at the river's edge. Of the people from whom the hero sprang, the eternal innocent children of mankind, latest of the mythic races and of their mythical republic. Of their towns and cities and the weaving millions. Of their vast and vulgar laughters, festive days, their competitions, races, lusty games. Of strong men running to a distant string. Of their rights and their reforms, religions and revivals. Of their shrine to justice, the court house in the middle of the square. Of their plantings, buildings, minings, makings, ravagings, explorings. Of how they were always going with the sun, westward to purple mountains, new dawns and new horizons. Of the earth on which they lived—its blue horizons east and west, exultant springs, soft autumns, brilliant winters. And of all its summers when the days were long . . .

This was the epic vision that John Shawnessy had arrived at shortly after the War and hoped to express while he was still young.

For seven years, then, following the War, he taught school children and worked at the monumental edifice of his poem, slowly erecting it through endless visions and revisions. But it was a gigantic task that he had set himself. It was all to be done from the ground up—a new language to fashion, a new wisdom—perhaps a new religion—to be discovered. Seventy times seven years might not be enough for such an undertaking, and at the end of seven John Shawnessy was still far short of his goal. So in the year 1872, when he was thirty-three years old, he did a remarkable thing.

He left his life of teaching and meditation and ran for political office. This decision was perhaps an odd one for the still unlaureled Homer of the age, but it wasn't entirely inconsistent with his aims. And the resulting scenes were, to be sure, all conducted in the purest John Shawnessy tradition.

For he had decided that the new religion toward which he was groping was not for the pulpit. The pulpit had already failed in America. Orthodox religion, an exotic on American shores, had run out of miracles long ago. The true religion of Americans, he decided—although no American would have admitted it—was politics. American politics had its rituals, sacred objects, saints, dogmas, devotions, feasts, fanaticisms, mummeries, and its Bible of sacred writings. Abraham Lincoln, the most sanctified figure of the century, had been a politician. Perhaps Lincoln was a John the Baptist to a still greater prophet who would lead Americans, a chosen people, to a new vision of heaven and earth. And the messianic task would be accomplished through the very institutions that made America unique among the peoples of history.

This religion of the new republic of John Shawnessy's vision was not, of course, a logical formulation. It was something to phrase in parables. The Old Testament of it was in the writings of Emerson, Thoreau, Hawthorne, Whitman, the Declaration of Independence, the Constitution, and other American scriptures. The New Testament of it had yet to be written—and lived.

Where orthodox Christianity had been the negation of human life, this new religion would be the affirmation of it. It affirmed that heaven and hell and hereafter are now, living and present. It affirmed that every second of life is a miracle greater than Lazarus trembling in the tomb. It affirmed that every human life is sacred because it is the whole of life and that in the continuity of being, no life is lost. It affirmed that the world of human ideals, morality, loyalties, and dedications was in a true sense the work of God, fashioning order out of blind becoming, but that this God was not separate from the universe of his creation or from its creatures. He existed in each human awareness. Only in this mancreated world was there truth and beauty, wisdom and goodness, and these things were both temporal and eternal simply because only in the mancreated world did time and eternity have any meaning whatsoever.

Thus was a man the artificer of his fate, building out of nothing what had not been there before. Therefore was a man free to some extent both in his means and ends.

To believe in this creed required, of course, an act of faith, but no greater act of faith than the creation of a republic of Raintree Counties in the first place, the daily living with others in peace and happiness, the simple affirmation that words had meanings. All human life was founded on faith anyway, and to live more fully required more faith.

This creed was also political. In fact it envisaged a state made up of wisely affirmative individuals, each one having the supreme, amiable vanity that taught him the inviolability of his own soul and that of others. This distinctively American state would be a republic of endless rediscovery, in which souls were rescued from the underside of Raintree County and educated in self-reliance. By an act of total responsibility for themselves and others, men voted themselves citizens of this republic, which was greater than the boundaries of America.

How could such a condition be brought about? The long way was by education. The short way was by an emotional surge, a religious crusade. It was the short way that John Shawnessy was trying when he entered politics in 1872, convinced that the American Messiah, if he came at all, would have to come as a candidate for office and that religious miracles in the pressridden Nineteenth Century would have to be miracles of social betterment and education.

This scheme of John Shawnessy's was either very daring or very innocent—probably both at once. In the America of the railroad and the sweatshop, he foresaw an Eden of social and economic equality. In the era of Jay Gould, President Grant, the Whiskey Ring, and Tammany Hall, he foretold a Periclean Epoch of honesty and forbearance. In the middle of the Gilded, he sought to build the ramparts of a Golden Age.

So it was that in 1872, John W. Shawnessy and Garwood B. Jones were rival candidates for the office of Representative to the Congress of the United States from the Congressional District in Indiana of which Raintree County was a part.

The campaign was probably the most colorful ever conducted in Raintree County. John Shawnessy ran on an Independent ticket, aided in his campaign by the fact that a great many former Republicans were fed up with the corruptions of Grantism and the failures of Radical Reconstruction. Garwood Jones ran on the straightline Republican ticket. He had the backing of the *Clarion,* which he now owned and edited himself, while John Shawnessy had the backing of the *Free Enquirer,* which had become a non-partisan paper during

Andrew Johnson's administration. There was also a Democratic paper in the County and a Democratic Candidate, but the campaign turned out to be a horse-race between Garwood B. Jones and John W. Shawnessy.

John Shawnessy conducted his campaign by riding around the country after school and talking to crowds everywhere. His speeches were short and simple and often humorous. At the same time, he wrote many trenchant articles in the *Enquirer*. Perhaps his greatest weakness was the fact that he was a political upstart, an anomaly, an independent. In general, Raintree County was skeptical of anyone who didn't belong to one of the time-honored parties. Thus Garwood B. Jones, who had done a complete turntail from one party to another, had the advantage of John W. Shawnessy, who belonged to no party at all.

The Independent Candidate didn't promise the usual things to the usual groups. He avoided the now familiar issues of protection and free trade, internal improvements, western lands, cheap money, control of the railroads, reconstruction, and the elimination of waste and corruption in the Federal machinery. He said frankly that he was campaigning simply for a better America, and he set about in his speeches and writings to tell the people of Raintree County what kind of America he thought it would be. Much of his platform was sheerly visionary; and even his most practical planks were regarded as revolutionary. He came out strongly for woman suffrage, protection of the laborer in his economic rights, relaxation of restrictions on divorce, legislative curbs on the big capitalists. He soon built up a following, especially among school children and women (none of whom had a vote) and among the independent voters of the County, of whom there were few.

At first Garwood didn't take his old rival's campaign seriously, anticipating more trouble from the Democratic candidate, but people in general liked John Shawnessy, and little by little his name and fame, already not unknown to Raintree County, spread to the outlying districts. After a while Garwood, who hadn't lost an election since his entry into politics in 1860, became worried and turned the whole force of his attack loose on the Independent Candidate. It was a formidable assault.

Garwood's campaign style was slambang and resourceful. He was adept at mining every vote-rich stratum of American society. His manner was sacred or profane as occasion required. He was known as a damn-good-guy and a fellow-who-gets-things-done.

Garwood was a talented artist of the campaign smear. Although he himself avoided signed or public attacks on the character of his opponent (to whom he always referred in the best tradition of American sportsmanship, as 'my dear young friend, John Shawnessy'), he permitted various libels to be circulated by his henchmen. Gradually he created a picture of the Independent Candidate as an improvident dreamer, an upstart experimenter, a vapid visionary, an overbrilliant and hence impractical scholar.

In addition, someone succeeded in circulating the impression that John Shawnessy was guilty of the two greatest sins in the black book of Raintree County—Atheism and Adultery.

An atheist was anyone who didn't believe in the stern old God of Raintree County and in the literal truth of the Bible, word for word. On this charge, the Independent Candidate convicted himself over and over out of his own mouth, and it was nothing short of a marvel that he had any supporters left at all. What took the sting out was the fact that he always created an impression of impregnable innocence and goodness, while Garwood's strongest supporters never concealed the fact (in fact they gloried in it) that their candidate could beat the Devil himself at his own game, while always remaining within the letter of the law.

The second charge—that of adultery—wasn't so dangerous politically. The libel, purposefully vague, seemed to acquire support from the fact that John Shawnessy was known to be married but not living with his wife. Besides there had been a number of affairs involving young women under his instruction. The plain truth was that John Shawnessy was never associated with an unattached young woman very long before she began to sleep badly at night, dress more attractively than her income permitted, and investigate in secrecy the exact relationship existing between Mr. Shawnessy and his reputed wife. As for him, it was his curse, as a Shawnessy, to feel a strong interest in every woman of unusual charm whom he saw, and during his long period of enforced chastity after the War, it wouldn't have been surprising if he sometimes, in the passion of his young manhood, yielded to temptations more frequent and strong for him than for any other man in Raintree County. But if he did transgress the code of Raintree County and find forbidden loves in those fleeting years after the War, if there were letters written and burned, if there were broken hearts (for women who once conceived a passion for the Hero of Raintree County had a time getting over it), unusual discretion must have been shown on both sides.

Certain it is that during this time no passion occurred in John Shawnessy's life that could compensate him for one that he had been obliged to bury with the defunct Johnny, that brave young casualty of the Great War, so fragrantly interred in Garwood's poem.

As for the charge of adultery, insinuated by Garwood's henchmen, it invited retaliation. In fact, there was a story in the County about a handsome young matron who forsook husband and children in order to follow Garwood to Chicago, where she turned up tactlessly in the middle of a political convention and expressed a willingness to run away with the lionhaired young orator from Indiana, offering a public sacrifice of her family, her honor, and her good name (and his). Some said that there had been a highly dramatic scene in a lobby of one of Chicago's leading hotels, and a great political career had hung in the balance until Garwood's golden tongue and majestic presence somehow managed to stifle the lady and the scandal. For some reason, this story improved Garwood's election chances.

As Election Day neared and it looked as though Garwood was in real danger of being defeated, resort was made by his party to the war issue, still the strongest plank in the Republican platform. Garwood, who had changed parties at the end of the War and had volunteered just in time to get a colonelcy and avoid combat, waved the bloody shirt from every platform in the district. Somehow or other he won a more or less official backing from the G.A.R. and managed to be seen often surrounded by men in uniform, who referred to him respectfully as Colonel Jones.

As for the Independent Candidate, who had fought from Chattanooga to the Sea, he was, oddly enough, handicapped by the fact that he had once been reported dead in battle and had been picturesquely lamented and interred in all the papers of the County. His unexpected return at the end of the War had created a minor sensation, but it left a faint impression that John Shawnessy had somehow cheated Fate and had got a great deal more credit than he was entitled to. Without a single open statement, Garwood labored hard to create the impression that the Independent Candidate's war record, which had turned out to be erroneous in at least one very important particular, would not bear close investigation in other respects.

There was even a squib in the Democratic paper (where Garwood cleverly planted his most poisonous barbs) to the effect that a certain handsome and romantic candidate for the office of representative had acquired the scar on his left shoulder, not, as was reported, in combat with Sherman's Army, but from a drunken brawl in a Louisville hotel.

Of course, some of Garwood's measures were in sheer self-defense, as both the rival parties threw a merciless light on the Colonel's belated and unperilous entry into the fray. The Democratic paper, taking advantage of the mysterious middle initial, that had only recently turned up in Garwood's name, always referred to him as Colonel Garwood Battleshy Jones, while the *Enquirer* carried a delightful anecdote, which, though unsigned, bore the touch of Will Westward, recounting the most dangerous combat experience of Garwood's military service. One day, it appeared, the Colonel had led a regiment of trainees, armed with broomsticks and tin cans, against a haystack. According to the story, Colonel Jones and his men were repulsed, outwitted, routed, and driven in panic from the field by an irate housewife who had a tabby and a litter of kittens in the stack. Garwood himself was credited with great coolness under fire, exceptional gallantry, and valor beyond the call of duty.

When all was said and done, Garwood's most powerful weapon was his persistent ridicule of the mystical pretensions in the Independent Candidate's platform. He built his campaign strategy on the proposition that Americans in the year 1872 were thoroughgoing materialists at heart and had no faith in poets and prophets. Here was a typical Dan Populus article from the *Clarion* during this time.

NEW MESSIAH DISCOVERED IN RAINTREE COUNTY

CITIZENS OF COUNTY DISCOVERED TO BE RACE OF DEMIGODS

Wonders never cease in that Canaan of the Cornlands, Shawmucky Township. Apparently the waters of the Upper Shawmucky possess magic properties. At any rate, a few days ago we heard that a young denizen of those parts had lately emerged from a dip in the river and upon studying his lineaments in a frog pond found that he had suddenly acquired the stature and beauty of a god. Forthwith he went out among the people, effusing a strong radiance. It was a hot day, and a tired housewife in the neighborhood, having laced her stays too tight, happened to fall over on her back, heels in the air, just as the young demigod approached. Impressed with his new effulgence, the transformed bumpkin was visited with a gift of tongues and began to prophesy.

Can anything good come out of the Upper Shawmucky? we asked ourself.

Well, we sent our trusty researcher, Rube Shucks, up there the other day to investigate the phenomenon. Here is Rube's own account of the matter:

'Wellsirree, Mr. Populus, I went up thar and sot down in a pigstye where the noo messiah was a-goin' tew dew his stuff, and I sot and sot, meanwhile exchangifying idees with the local hicks. "What's his creed," sez I to an espeshially intellygent member of the cumpney. "The world will be made pure agin," sez he, settlin' hisself comfortable in a corner of the stye and diggin' his bare toze into the ooze thereuv. "Hit's the Golden Age, mister." "What dew you expect to git out of it?" sez I. "We is all christs and saints and angles," sez he, "and never knowed it."

'I sot and jawed a while with these fokes, when all a sudden I felt the sperrit descendin' on me. I riz up and said to a lady neerby: "Sister, yore eyes is a puffick shinin'. We air all a-floatin' in a ocean of luv, puffick luv. Dew I heer laughter from the back row? Cease your vulgar cacchinations, frend. Under your honest blue jeans, I purceeve the puffick proporshuns of a god. Duz anybody know where I kin git a halo at slightly reduced cost?"

'Jist then, everbody stood up and begun to crane their necks and shout and p'int their fingers. "Hyar he cums," they yelled. "Hyar cums the noo messiah." I thought my ize would pop right out a my hed tryin' to see this grate man. "Whar is he?" sez I. "Right thar," they sez.

'I looked, and, Mr. Populus, so help me God, all I seen wuz old Seth Twigs in a clean shirt, grinnin' and gestickulatin' at the crowd. "Shucks," I sez, "I useter swap lies reglar with that skunk back before the War. But I see he's clean out a my class now." '

DAN POPULUS

The climax of the campaign came on the day before the Election when the two rivals agreed to have a debate in the Court House Square of Freehaven. Around two o'clock in the afternoon, the Square was filled with citizens under the majestic shadow of the New Court House, which had just been finished to replace the old one burnt down toward the end of the War.

As the two candidates and a moderator sat on the platform, both parties conducted a spirited demonstration. A snake-dance, mainly composed of young women and school children, wound around the Court House carrying placards reading:

VOTE FOR
JOHN W. SHAWNESSY
AND A NEW REPUBLIC

The crude picture on the transparencies looked like Jesus Christ with moosehead mustaches. The Shawnessy supporters were led by a small band that played feebly but together. The snake dancers sang the Shawnessy campaign song:

—Our Johnny is in the race to win.
Hurrah! Hurrah!
Let's all get busy and vote him in.
Hurrah! Hurrah!
The boys will cheer, the men will shout,
The ladies they will all turn out,
And we'll all feel gay
When Johnny has won the race.

There was a second verse, but it had hardly got started when it was trampled down under the cadenced boots of a louder song. And another band marched out of a sidestreet into the Square followed by solid ranks of marching men, most of whom had been recruited from Middletown, in the neighboring county. They chanted as they came,

—Tramp, tramp, tramp, we'll vote for Garwood!
Look out, scoundrels, here we come!
Down with Shawnessy and shame!
Send him back to where he came!
Vote for Garwood! He's the boy to make things hum!

In massed ranks, heavyfooted, led by a phalanx of young business-men, the cohorts of Garwood B. Jones strode three times around the Square. Now and then, John Shawnessy could hear the voices of school children bravely singing his own campaign song. But the dominant sound was

—Step right up and vote for Garwood.
Join the forwardlooking throng.
When the final count is made,
He'll put Johnny in the shade.
Vote for Garwood, one and all, you can't go wrong.

Garwood stood up. He waved his great arms. A throaty shout from massed hundreds responded. Deepchested, thickbellied, he stalked back and forth on the platform.

When the moderator made the introduction, Garwood got up and delivered a stemwinder. John Shawnessy, who hadn't heard Garwood talk for several years, was amazed at the man's power and eloquence. For a moment he himself was halfpersuaded that Garwood was in the right and ought to be elected. Garwood smote applause from the crowd like a director whose gestures sculpture the music of the instruments. The whipsnap of his climaxes was a command to a trained beast. Applause piled up against closed gates. Garwood's voice now seemed to invite, now quickly suppressed, now tugged at the gates, now checked unexpectedly, now suddenly smashed the dam and let the flood come through. His supporters clapped, yelled, shrieked, howled. They taunted the Shawnessy supporters.

—Take that, goddern ye! That's Garwood fer ye! Listen to that man talk!

Their banners carried the simple legend:

GARWOOD B. JONES

THE PEOPLE'S CHOICE

But in a few minutes John Shawnessy realized that it was all pure virtuosity. Garwood was the same old Garwood. His political creed was transparent as ever. He promised the farmers better treatment from the railroads. He promised the railroads more money from the farmers. He promised the businessmen and creditor classes a currency that wouldn't fold up and go into any old pocketbook but would find its way clinking into strongboxes with reinforced corners. He promised the debtor and farming classes a currency so plentiful everybody could pay off his debts and buy fat acres. He promised the radical reconstructionists that he wanted to see a firm hand maintained in the South so that the fruits of the War would not be lost. He promised the Southern sympathizers that the Negro would be kept in his place and that the Union would somehow be the old Union of before the War.

Garwood's political creed was even simpler than all that. It was simply and solely to get himself elected to office.

Garwood B. Jones was a born politician. He knew how to make the votes flow. In the hands of Garwood B. Jones, the ballot ceased to be the expression of a free people. It was the charmed tribute of the dumb to the eloquent.

When Garwood at last sat down, he left the Square churned up with fury. Faces leaped through the air and confronted other faces. Men cursed. Middle-aged women fanned themselves and panted as if they had just had physical contact with a Casanova. Cowbells clanked. And above it all, Garwood's band, which was much bigger than the Independent Candidate's and had a great deal more brass and blow in it, played the militant air of Garwood's campaign song.

At this inauspicious moment, the moderator introduced the Independent Candidate.

John Shawnessy knew, when he got up before the crowd in the Court House Square, that this was one of the mythical hours of his life. He was at last confronting the people. He knew most of them, and most of them knew him or thought they knew him. Could he indeed open a door for these people that would admit them to a better day? Or was he, even as Garwood had implied, a cloudgathering impostor?

—Friends and fellow citizens, he began.

—Go home, Johnny, a man in the front row said, and git your maw to wipe your nose.

The crowd laughed.

—Shut up, you! a Shawnessy supporter said.

—You shet me up! the man said.

—Friends and fellow citizens——

A man in the front row plucked slowly a huge belch from beer-swollen guts. Garwood's supporters guffawed savagely.

John Shawnessy stopped, confused.

But at this moment, Garwood Jones made a magnificent gesture. He stood up and said with impressive dignity,

—I repudiate the support of any man who denies to this candidate the right to be heard.

This spontaneous action touched the crowd, and members of all parties cheered Garwood to the echo. With a gracious bow to the Independent Candidate, Garwood sat down. Next morning his behavior was very favorably noticed in the newspapers and elsewhere, except for a few cynics who said Garwood had planted his meanest hatchet men and hecklers in the crowd and had planned the whole thing, including the noble gesture.

More confused by Garwood's generosity than by the heckling of the crowd, John Shawnessy launched into his speech.

Neither speech was quoted in the papers next day. The words which John Shawnessy had carefully prepared were cast like little seeds on the silence and enigma of hundreds of attentive faces young and old. He never knew where the words fell, and where, if anywhere, they took root. He spoke in a calm, serious voice, and there was no applause for anything that he said, except at the end. The Independent Candidate preserved no copy of the address after he made it, deciding that as a political speech it was a failure.

It may have been a great utterance, to set beside the Gettysburg Address and the Sermon on the Mount. Or, again, it may have been a rather stilted and, in the light of the times, pointless performance. Its immediate effect could be easily calculated in the voting statistics of the following day. As for its ultimate effect, perhaps some seed of all its words lodged in the memory of an admiring child and was carried devious ways to a more receptive day. John Shawnessy never knew about that.

But in later years, a good many people who had been very young in 1872, some only children, remembered the speech. And as time passed, an impression grew that it had been a marvellous speech, full of wisdom and high sentence. People often said that they wished they had a copy of it.

—That was a humdinger of a speech, they said, the best I ever heard, now that I think back.

But they couldn't quote a single sentence from it. The lost speech was like the secret of the County's mysterious naming; and it took its place among the riddles and legends of Raintree County, as 'That Speech John Shawnessy Made in the Court House Square in Seventy-Two.'

As for the Election itself, the next day after the great debate Garwood's machine got busy and went to town. Garwood himself admitted that his campaign fund bought five thousand cigars and one hundred barrels of beer for distribution on Election Day. The biggest town in the Congressional District, Middletown, which was beginning to boast an industrial middle class, went solidly Republican. Garwood's machine voted blocks of five all day long—paid votes marked under the vigilant inspection of Garwood's heelers and dutifully held aloft in squads of five until they reached the box. Apparently, the voting American of 1872 preferred a cigar stuck in his face to a halo crammed down on his cranium. He went to the polls puffing on Garwood's cigar and pleasantly exhilarated by Garwood's beer and voted overwhelmingly for Garwood—two or three times when possible.

There was some small consolation for the Independent Candidate. Although he was soundly defeated in the total vote, by some miracle he carried Raintree County proper by one ballot, which he afterwards laughingly remarked must have been his own.

But the verdict of the polls was decisive, and John Shawnessy never returned to the political arena. He had been rejected by his people and called a false prophet. He had come down into the Court House Square from the wilderness where he had searched his soul somewhat longer than the scriptural forty days. But as Professor Jerusalem Webster Stiles remarked to him in a letter written during that time, Jesus Christ himself couldn't have achieved the notoriety of a crucifixion in post-War America. So pocketing his disappointment and pondering his latest epic gesture, John Shawnessy went back to teaching the school children in Shawmucky Township the rudiments of what is known as education.

Enlivened by this single public appearance, his post-War years fled by, and the Republic went on building great fortunes for a few men, swelling up with immigrant millions, pouring westward, multiplying railroads, mining, rending, ravaging the earth, fighting Indians, planting the plains, loving, raising children, dying. And John Shawnessy went on writing, musing, speculating, and preparing, as confidently as ever, for the day when he would complete his task and become the epic poet of his people.

During this time, his face was one of the lost faces of the Republic. It underwent imperceptible changes, aging a little, becoming perhaps a little more gentle, having perhaps a little less of the young arrogance of earlier days. And there were unnumbered faces of school children during those fading years (lost faces like his own and changing) that beheld his face and had some memory of it. And perhaps in those silent years there may have been planted in the obscure womb of time a future flower, a wondrous affirmation of life, some love more passionate and true than he had dreamed. He couldn't say as to that, but went on with his teaching, wondering the while whether he taught anything that was really meaningful and whether he would ever leave his mark on Raintree County in a significant way, or whether he would be taken back into its indifferent earth, like all the other little flowers, even as these withering years were taken one by one back into the watery grave of time while the Republic roared to the end of its first century as an independent nation.

And as the year 1876 approached, the Centennial Year in which the Fledgling of the Nations would complete the first one hundred years of its existence, John Shawnessy, stirred by deep currents of unrest and aspiration and having now completed a sizeable quantity of manuscript, decided that the time had come to do what he had always intended to do, before his youth was gone. So it was that at last he hearkened to the urgings of Professor Stiles, who had become a famous topical poet, newspaper columnist, and special reporter on Life in New York City. In July of the Centennial Summer, he took a few personal belongings, the manuscript of his unfinished poem, and some money that he had painfully saved, and entraining at Beardstown on the Pennsylvania line,

BADE FAREWELL TO HIS MOTHER AND FATHER

AND A SMALL GATHERING

OF

—FRIENDS AND FELLOW CITIZENS, the Senator said, I bid you all an affectionate farewell.

Standing on the rear platform, flanked by his secretaries and press-agents, the Senator leaned down out of his statesman's mask to clasp Mr. Shawnessy's hand. For a second, his eyes looked kindness and concern.

—Well, sprout, finish that great book, he said, and if you ever get to the Nation's Capital, look me up.

Mr. Shawnessy, moved by an unexpected rush of feeling, clung a moment to the Senator's plump hand.

—Good-by, Garwood, I——

Just then, the train trembled along its length. Instantly the Senator straightened up, leaned back into his greatbellied costume, his face became fixed in the same smile that he had worn in the morning, his storeteeth clenched the unlit cigar, he raised his arms, he began to bow massively. The train started.

Dipping, diminishing, receding, Senator Garwood B. Jones, framed in the hindend of a passenger train, gradually lost precision. It was a little melancholy and oppressive to think of the grinning mask of a certain eminent statesman in his frock coat and black Lincoln tie getting tinier and tinier in the immense plain of the year 1892.

The last curious members of the crowd loitered in the Station, sniffing the lingering aroma of greatness, and then left. The Perfessor and Mr. Shawnessy went back to the bench and sat down.

—Something I've never understood, the Perfessor said, is how trains keep from running into each other oftener than they do. If Cash Carney's train is on time—and you say it is—it should be running into Garwood's train any time now.

—It's all done with wires, Mr. Shawnessy said. And dispatchers.

Inside the Station, the single live cell of the telegraph key fluttered endlessly on.

—Wonder what they're transmitting there? the Perfessor said.

Mr. Shawnessy, who had learned the code during the War, listened, laughed, and read aloud,

—'ARE YOU FOR THAT WINDBAG?' 'HELL, NO. ARE YOU?' 'HELL, NO.' The tower men are talking to each other, he explained. 'NEVER FORGAVE HIM FOR CHEATING US IN '77.' 'HOW'S WIFE?' 'O.K.' 'NEW KID?' 'DOING O.K.' 'NAME YET?' 'WAIT. SENATOR'S TRAIN PASSING.'

—The Republic has a voice, the Perfessor said.

There was a silence on the keys. Then:

—'SENATOR WAVED AT SMALL CROWD. KID'S NAME GROVER CLEVELAND.' 'HOW'S BILL?' 'GONE TO CHICAGO. WORK ON FAIRGROUNDS.'

—By the way, the Perfessor said, I plan to go up and see the Fairgrounds at Chicago. The work's pretty well along, I hear.

—How long since you've seen Cash?

—Year or two.

—The telegram says Laura may come too. Is she still pretty?

—There's a sort of ripe splendor about her now. It's still a gorgeous looking edifice. Too bad she hasn't acted since her marriage. Well, poor Cash finally made the grade. Her beauty was rolled for an old man's gold.

The Perfessor looked keenly at Mr. Shawnessy.

—All right, come clean, he said. Did you or didn't you? After all, it was so long ago.

Mr. Shawnessy smiled in embarrassment.

—I've forgotten all that, he said, lying. As you say, it was all so long ago.

—I don't know why I ask such dumb questions, the Perfessor said. Must excite you to think that she may be on this train.

—It's strange, Mr. Shawnessy said. You never know who's going to get down from a train. During my sojourn in the big City, I used to go down to the biggest terminal in town and just stand in the station watching people get on and off, as if I were waiting for someone.

—Did the party ever come?

—No, not exactly, Mr. Shawnessy said. The truth is, I've never lost that feeling of excitement about incoming trains. And I have the same feeling when I get off a train. It's as though I were young again and about to step into the middle of a wonderful adventure, as if the crowds of the City would pick me up and bear me off on a floodtide of fulfillment.

—John, the Perfessor said, you're an incurable idealist. As for me, I've gotten out of too many trains in my time. I always look for the nearest toilet.

—Speaking of the Fair, Mr. Shawnessy said, remember the Centennial Fourth in Philadelphia?

—What a day! the Perfessor said. Remember my monolithic blonde?

—Sure. What ever happened to her?

—Don't ask me, the Perfessor said. Her price went up right after that. The Great American Blonde, I think we called her. Sixteen years ago, by the way. Exactly. To the day. Well, we had some life left in us then, boy. Ah, I can see the sunshine now on her corncolored hair and the little railway that took us around the Fairgrounds. That surely was one of the hottest days in the history of the Republic. And those godawful buildings chockful of third-rate canvas and big glittering machines. The Centennial Exposition! Tell me the truth, John, did that ever happen? By the way, her name was Phoebe.

Her name was Phoebe, and that was sixteen years ago. And her name was Laura Golden, and that was sixteen years ago. The price went up right after that. In America, the price kept rising all the time.

—We're always having fairs, the Perfessor said. And they keep on moving West. New York, Philadelphia, and now Chicago. A few years from now, you can probably meet me in St. Louis. And then they'll go clear out to San Francisco, and then start all over again. And each time they'll build bigger buildings and sell more bellyaches.

—But the blondes will be the same as ever, Mr. Shawnessy said.

—Yes, but the price keeps rising all the time, the Perfessor said. It's awful what you have to pay these days for the bare necessities of life. Are you the way I am? I remember everything by the women I've had. And it's a good thing I have a retentive memory.

—I remember things the same way, Mr. Shawnessy said. If I wasn't in love, I wasn't alive.

—Of course, I generally paid my way, the Perfessor said. You idealists are the real thieves of love. In a business civilization like our own, everything should have a price.

—It all had its price, Mr. Shawnessy said. The tags just weren't marked in advance. I paid my way too, but with a different coin.

Meet me in Philadelphia, or New York, or in Chicago. Meet me in St. Louis. Meet me at the Fair. Hotdog, mister? Buy the lady a pink lemonade, mister. And here's a flower for your coat lapel.

Meet me in the City of Brotherly Love (and Sisterly Reserve), meet me in the station where the faces pour out smiling from the hollow cars forever. I shall be waiting for you there. We shall catch a horsedrawn car and go through crowded streets and find again the city of the lost, exciting domes, archaic domes beside a river.

O, shall we live again the birthday of a nation, shall we walk again beside the river, shall I yearn again to touch my lips to yours in the City of the Love of Brothers (and the shy reserve of sisters)? O, shall you ever meet me, meet me at the Fair?

O, shall we ever find again green pinnacles beside the river, that were new as the shining new republic, and yet no sooner built than old—old, old incredibly—the oldest minarets in all the world, the buildings of the oldest fair that ever was, in the oldest of all the Raintree Counties?

Come back, come back, to that most crude of Raintree Counties, come back to that great fair. O, meet me, meet me once again, and let us walk again, retracing all our paths, and finding others that we never dared to take. O, let us saunter down the Avenue of the Republic and see the brave exhibits.

And you will have your green dress on, asserted by a saucy bustle, the floating island of your parasol will ride on rivers of exultant heat. O, you will be the stateliest exhibition of all the exhibitions.

O, meet me at the Fair, and let us walk together, arm in arm. What have we builded here beside the river in a hundred years? And is everything marked with a price-tag, including you?

O, inventory of progress, o, general store of humanity, I passed your loaded counters one day of ancient summer. I hunted love and wisdom in the guidebook of Centennial Summer. I studied maps of cities that are gone. Babylon was fair, and they say the walls were built to last forever. But Babylon is not more buried in Ozymandian sands than the city by the river in the summer of the Fair.

My God, do no trains run backward, and no clocks counterclockwise? O, let us have dispatchers that make the trains of sixteen years ago run into stations of sixteen years ago, and punctual on the hour.

O, great Dispatcher of the Cosmic Trains, Arranger of the time schedules of the Republic, Deviser of smoothly running overland expresses, do no trains run backward and no clocks counterclockwise?

—Say, what's holding up the eastbound express? the Perfessor said to the head of the station agent jutting from the window.

—Hot box in the Roiville siding, the agent said. She'll be along in a few minutes.

She'll be along, and then we'll go together to the Fair. For they had great fairs in ancient days, that aspiring and erecting people. They built so big they dwarfed all buildings ever built, and yet they never could build big enough. They built a thousand rooms and filled them full of dolls and clocks and pots and arrowheads, typewriters, sewing machines, kitchenware, steam engines, Krupp guns, locomotives, harvesters, telephones, livestock, paintings. But they left something out.

It must have been a dream that I was dreaming. It must have been a huge, disordered dream that rose from the little brick womb of Independence Hall in the middle of the City.

Tom Jefferson, John Adams, John Hancock, George Washington, Ben Franklin, come back, you ancient flingers of democratic seed, behold the thing you did. Behold the buildings out of buildings, behold the words erected out of words, the faces out of faces.

John Adams, and John Hancock, George Washington, Ben Franklin, and Tom Jefferson, old fathers, founders of myself and founders of us all, come back and see the city on the river, the City of the Love of Brothers (and of the silent and the sweet reserve of sisters), come back and meet me, meet me, meet me

July 4— On —1876

THE MORNING THAT

AMERICA WAS A HUNDRED YEARS OLD

John Shawnessy awoke in a hotel room in Philadelphia, to the sound of guns saluting the sunrise of the Centennial Day. He awoke with a sensation of jubilant aloneness and independence, as if he and the Republic had been reborn together.

He went to the window and looked down on Philadelphia. The street, fragrant with the horsy summer smell of the City and empty of people at this early hour, looked like a vaudeville backdrop. Every doorstep, sign, cigarstore Indian, scrap of paper, cigarbutt, burst firecracker was bathed in a painted stillness. But soon hooves would be clanging on the cobbles, horsecars would go clattering by, surf of human voices would batter him with an old excitement that was always new. And somewhere at the farthest end of the wide and sleepy street of summer, eastward on a fabled water, lifting fair banners to the day, the Centennial City waited.

By the time he reached the train station at eight o'clock, the streets were jammed with people. Two hundred thousand Americans had come to Philadelphia for the great Fourth of July Celebration.

From the sunlight of the morning, he stepped into the depot. Out of this vast brown shell, webbed with girders, filled with the sound of trains arriving and departing, faces gushed endlessly to sunlight. In tides they had been moving toward this appointment in the Centennial City. They had won through. They were the most fortunate beings who ever lived. They had come out beside the river in the dawn of the Nation's second century. Each one had a name, wore clothing, had paid the price of a ticket on the railroad. And each one clutched a guidebook to assure his safety in the City.

He found a bench and sat waiting for the train from New York, and to while away the time glanced through a letter that he had received just before leaving Raintree County.

Dear John,

Meet me in the City of Brotherly Love (and Sisterly Reserve) on the morning of the Fourth. I'll arrive at eight o'clock on the Centennial Special from New York, not unaccompanied. Wear shoes, country boy. Ladies (by an enlargement of the term) will be present.

Remember that actress you almost met in Washington eleven years ago? Perhaps—what with the long gap in our correspondence—I have omitted to tell you that that young lady—then known as Daphne Fountain—is today none other than the celebrated Laura Golden, whose name and fame (and shame) have surely penetrated even to the borders of Raintree County. Well, I've always regretted that the assignation of that far-off day was never assignated, and I have put a flea in her ear for you, my boy, hoping that she may do something for you in the Big City. She's being beaued about the town these days by—among others—your old friend and mine, that distinguished financier, Mr. Cassius P. U. Carney. They're planning to come with me, and I'm bringing a little creature comfort of my own.

It will be good to see you again, my boy, after eleven years. At eight o'clock in the station, an old man, drooling and decrepit, will accost you. Do not spurn the poor old dotard. 'Twill be I.

JERUSALEM WEBSTER STILES

The Centennial Special from New York slid by him breathing softly, its power couched in massive metal haunches. The long line of coaches, buntinghung, shrugged to a stop. Instantly, young people sprang from the doors into the arms of lovers; whole families disembarked, waving flags and rushing to get out of the station as if a door might slam shut and cut them off from happiness forever.

He was repeating to himself with a curiously deep emotion the name 'Laura Golden.' Since the receipt of the Perfessor's letter he had been busy fitting out this name of notoriety with fictitious faces like so many masks. He was deeply moved too by the thought that he was about to see again the Perfessor and Cash Carney, neither of whom he had seen since the Civil War.

Was it really possible, then, that the tide of the indifferent years, passing blindly through a thousand gates and sluices, could cast up again these discarded faces?

—Mr. John Wickliff Shawnessy, I presume? said a familiar voice.

He had come suddenly face to face with the Perfessor, Cash Carney, and two women. Blinking and embarrassed, he began to shake hands around.

—My God, boy, the Perfessor said, catching him by the arm, you've aged a little!

John Shawnessy's first impression was that the Perfessor had decayed considerably too, but on a second look it seemed to him that he recovered entirely—or almost so—the pattern of his old friend's face —the black busy eyes, the still black hair slicked back hard from the middle part, the trim, tall, erect figure. The vivid, hacking motion of the face remained invincibly the same and the highpitched crackling voice with its cutting edge. Meanwhile the Perfessor, resuming his old manner of genial showmanship, stepped back and motioned grandly with his cane.

—And now, folks, it gives me great pleasure to present Miss Laura Golden of New York City to Mr. John Shawnessy of Raintree County, Indiana.

—So this is the Gentleman from Indiana!

The woman who spoke, though only a little taller than middle height, somehow gave the impression of gazing down at him from a queenly eminence. Her face—this entirely unforeseeable face—wore an indefinite mocking smile fixed upon it like a mask, its habitual look, its hovering essence. The cheeks with their unusual fullness, the eyes with their drooping lids, the wide cheekbones, the full-lipped mouth, the nose delicate but receding too quickly to the bridge, the pointed chin gave this face an oriental lushness at variance with its pale, clear skin. The tawny gold hair was parted precisely in the middle, pulled flat, and gathered into a heavy ball behind to show the ears. The face, thus thrust forward, as it were, and nodding on a slender neck, this face—inescapable, fullorbed, calm with its disdainful smile—abruptly destroyed all the imprecise masks he had been fashioning.

At first he thought the smile was from the eyes—wideset, long, fountain-green—halfclosed under languid lids. But on looking directly into them, he saw that they did not smile at all, that they had a kind of jadelike impassivity. The smile then came from the mouth. It was lushly fleshed, mobile, beautifully formed, but just at the left corner a faint scar twisted the upper lip. Perhaps this scar made it impossible for the face not to smile its imperial smile.

—This is a long deferred pleasure, Miss Golden, he said. I have been waiting at the stage door eleven years for the purpose of making your acquaintance.

She pointed one smoothly sculptured shoulder at him, and in a voice mocking, lowpitched, thrillingly distinct, said,

—That makes you the most persistent stage-door Johnny of all time, Mr. Shawnessy.

Her mocking laugh reverberated in the hollow shell of the train station, blending with the murmur of wheels and voices. Smiling his pensive, innocent smile, Mr. John Shawnessy made a stately bow, and Miss Laura Golden (as if they had rehearsed their parts) gracefully extended her white hand, softfingered, with lacquered nails, and with one green jewel blazing on the ring finger. He kissed her hand, surprised at its warmth; he smelled the perfume of it vaguely disturbing; the great jewel blazed in his left eye.

The Perfessor's creature comfort, a Miss Phoebe Veach, was a monumental blonde, ripely thirty-five, with a healthy, appealing face and marvellous hair, the color of ripe corn, full of yellowness and life.

Back at the hotel, where the whole party had reservations, the ladies spent some time in their rooms, while the gentlemen waited in the lobby reviewing the years between.

—I suppose you're running the country now, on the sly, Cash, John Shawnessy said. You've gone fast and far since you hitched your star to a locomotive—and your locomotive to a star.

—I barely keep ahead of my creditors, Cash said.

He pulled out his palmsmoothed gold watch. Eleven years had faintly stained and yellowed him and fixed the rapt abstraction of his eyes.

—This business recession, he said, has had us all humping. The layman has an erroneous idea of wealth. What you fellas call wealth is only an increased ability to go into debt. You heard of the man who was boasting about his speculations: Two years ago, he said, I didn't have a nickel. Now I owe two million dollars. Ha. Ha.

He said the laughter flatly without humor. He went on to explain how his various interests were still suffering from the Panic of '73 and how important it was for Hayes to get the nod in November. After a while, he said,

—I got to keep some business appointments here. Good chance to see the Republican nominee and the men around him. Hope you boys'll pardon me if I don't go to the program. Maybe John'll look after Laura for me.

—Sure. Be glad to, Cash.

—The ladies already know, Cash said. See you at the Centennial Ball tonight, boys.

He nodded without smiling and walked off briskly through the station and was lost in the crowd.

The Perfessor, nervous and fidgety as ever, began to pace in a corridor off the lobby. The two men followed each other up and down the corridor, while the Perfessor gestured with his cane.

—Great to see you again, my boy. High time you got out of Raintree County. Hell of a place to bury a talent like yours. Well, we've all come a long way since '65. What do you think of Miss Golden?

—I'm already depositing bouquets at the stage door. What sort of person is she?

—Miss Laura Golden, the Perfessor said, chief ornament of the metropolitan stage, was born some thirty years ago in New York City from a poor immigrant family. When I first knew her, she was a young actress understudying Laura Keene. She disappeared then entirely—did the western circuit, I understand, and went to Europe. Then about three years ago, she turned up in New York with her own troupe billed as Miss Laura Golden in *Mazeppa*. She cased her lovely legs in pink tights, pulled a tight tunic over her tits and had herself tied to the backend of a real horse. It was in half-light, and she looked damn near naked. The boys stood shoulder-to-shoulder in the aisles for nights. It was terrific. She became overnight the most notorious actress in New York City. No one seemed to know anything about her but me, and I didn't know much. She became a myth. The stories about her were right out of Apuleius. I made a major contribution to her fame myself by referring to her as 'the most beautifully undressed woman in New York City.' The crush around her stage door was homicidal—and I was smack in the middle of it, hoping to play Justinian to her Theodora. But lo! it turned out that she was already married to an old millionaire she had picked up in California, who had both feet and his backside in the grave, and inside of two weeks she had fitted her pretty palm against the poor old codger's face and shoved him all the way in. She swore to me once privately that he never got a thing—and I don't doubt it. She still has the house he fitted out for her on Fifth Avenue before the marriage, but I think she's running out of money. The stories about Laura's house are—by the way—richly flavored. I've been in it for balls and things myself, and they always seemed reasonably circumspect. But you hear about lewd pomps and prurient games, and some of the theatre gossips swear that Laura's bedroom is decorated with a Pompeian lavishness for the entertainment of her lovers.

—Like Mr. Cassius P. Carney for example?

—No, she wipes her little boot on him—and he loves it.

—Like Professor Jerusalem W. Stiles then?

The Perfessor shrugged his shoulders.

—O, no, I never fall in love anymore, he said, his eyes unfocused and oblique as they always were when he was telling a whopper. Too exhausting. I admit I tried hard to break into that Forbidden Room myself. I was damned curious about it and her, and still am. But I guess I wasn't virile enough for her. Laura's a cheat, but so am I, and we've become good friends. She pretends to confide in me—that is to say, she tells me grave, gigantic lies about her past, which I pretend to believe. One of these is some kind of hokum about a great love back in her obscure years from which she hasn't yet recovered. No doubt luckier and lustier lovers than I file in and out of her famous bedroom all the time. But getting any hard facts about Miss Laura Golden's private life is pretty hard. She gives the impression of being jaded from too much passion, but it's probably just part of her act. She acts all the time on and off the stage, and there's no truth in the woman.

—Is she a great actress?

She's a great stage personality. As an actress, she simply plays herself—aggressively, emphatically, shamelessly female. She does Shakespeare's vicious, bitchy women to perfection. Mainly she goes in for grand exhibitions of herself, and every play she appears in—whether Shakespeare or Boucicault—comes out a big spectacle, in which Laura strides around the stage in her queenly way, strikes attitudes, and spellbinds the audience with her voice and her regal beauty.

John Shawnessy was surprised.

—You find her beautiful?

—Devil take her! the Perfessor said with emphasis, I find her ravishing! Don't you?

—Why—yes.

He had not, as a matter of fact, until that moment thought of her as ravishingly beautiful, but now he waited with heightened interest for her re-entrance upon the scene, and when she came down the stair of the hotel a few minutes later, wearing a green dress trimmed with gilt and asserted by a saucy bustle, swinging a parasol, walking in a manner that subtly accentuated the opulent contours of her long-stemmed figure, smiling her twisted smile at no one in particular, he was sure that she was indeed ravishingly beautiful, with that rare beauty which was only derived—as the Perfessor had been wont to say many years ago—from a strangeness in the proportion. Certain it was that from the moment when she took his arm, her face, held proudly averted, glowed like an aloof yet sensual moon over the whole landscape of his Centennial Day.

A platform had been set up in the square opposite Independence Hall, the ancient tiny brick building where the Republic had been born. The party of four wedged its way through hundreds of Centennial Americans onto the grandstand erected for the occasion. It was rumored that the orchestra was playing, though no one on the grandstand could see or hear the orchestra. Finally someone said that the National Anthem was being played, and everyone groaned to a standing position. The sun was implacably hot. Small boys sold wilted flags and tepid lemonade. A band came by, marching through a cleared space and followed by troops, thousands, advancing tediously. Someone said that General Sherman was on the stand. Craning for a look, John Shawnessy saw, standing at attention among other notables, a thin, grizzled person, the faded remnant of what seemed now an old-fashioned and rather improbable legend. Someone said that General Sheridan was on the reviewing stand. The soldiers kept on marching, and it got hotter. All the women were fanning, including Miss Laura Golden.

—Do you enjoy the theatre, Mr. Shawnessy?

Her voice had a studied indifference.

—Why, yes, Miss Golden, I love it, he said. But I haven't had much opportunity to enjoy it. The last time I saw a really first-rate troupe was in Washington eleven years ago, the night we almost met. By the way, what happened to you that night?

—Like everyone else, I was almost out of my mind, she said. Most of us just milled around and screamed at each other and finally we all went back to the hotel.

—You had another name then, I believe—and I composed a girl around that name, who was nothing like you.

—Let me see, she said. What *was* my name then?

—Daphne Fountain.

—One of my better names, she said, laughing a delightful mocking laugh that came from her throat without disturbing her smile.

—Have you had several names?

—O, yes, she said. I used to put on a new personality with each name, Mr. Shawnessy. It's as well that you didn't know Daphne Fountain, poor little innocent thing. She was thin, scared, and very, very poor. She had some good qualities that I don't have—she was much more openhearted, generous, and sweet. But I had to discard her—poor little creature. She wasn't getting anywhere. I tossed her back into the costume closet.

—And then?

Miss Laura Golden gave him an amused glance over her undulant fan.

—I'm sure I don't know why I tell you these things. But since you ask, then there was Diana Lord. She appeared with a magician and was sawed in two. That was the end of her.

She laughed again, swaying her head on the slender neck.

—Then there was Vivi Lamar. Less said of Vivi, the better. And then there were one or two others. I don't know why I had such a passion for changing my name.

—Now, of course, you can't do it any longer.

—I know—and it's annoying in a way.

—Didn't it dissolve your feeling of identity—to be so many names, Miss Golden? How did you hang on to yourself—I mean that never-changing essence that we like to call our Self?

—Who wants to hang on to it, Mr. Shawnessy?

He tried to imagine this tall, voluptuous woman changing with the years, receding in a series of poses toward that unknown actress who had stood in the wings of a theatre waiting for him long ago. Were the eyes always as they were now, with this green impersonal fire in them? Was the mouth always scarred and smiling as it was now? It seemed to him that whatever fluctuations there might have been in her appearance and her personality, she had slowly fashioned a costumed, imperial, scornful creature and finished her with such immense certitude that she was immune from time and change.

Was it possible—was it really possible, he was wondering—that this statuesque woman with the many names gave lavishly of her beauty to random gay gentlemen in a secret chamber of the City?

Shortly after nine, the rostrum before Independence Hall was entirely filled with dignitaries, and the program started. It was very hard to hear what was being said.

A minister arose and said a prayer for the Nation. He asked God to shine favorably upon this great nation as she began the second hundred years of her existence. He thanked God for having shone favorably upon her during the first hundred years. Everybody was sweating fiercely from the way God was at that moment shining on the Nation.

Then Richard Henry Lee got up and read the Declaration of Independence from the Original Document containing the Original Signatures. People applauded from time to time.

Bayard Taylor, regarded by many as America's Greatest Living Poet, was introduced and recited by heart his Centennial Ode.

William Evarts got up and delivered the Address of the Day. He spoke lengthily about the Progress of America. He said that this was an Inspiring Occasion. He reviewed the Great Strides since 1776. He said that we had won the Revolution and several other wars. He reminded his auditors that the Civil War was over and that the Nation was One. He pointed out that a Great Mechanical Progress was necessary for a nation to reach the condition which America was in today. He affirmed that all this had been a Good Thing. He said that America had a Future. He gave it as his considered judgment that America was a Nation Shone Upon by Providence and Almighty God.

As the hours went by, John Shawnessy tried to reconstruct the scene of the Founding Fathers founding and fathering the Republic. But it wouldn't come clear and have any meaning. Penetrating into the reality of the Past was an impossible undertaking, he decided. There was, he felt, only one reality—the reality of someone's experience. What people dealt with when they spoke of the Past was a world of convenient abstractions—myths—Events. And even the world of the Present was sustained by the same omnipotent creative fictions. His own life was a myth to himself and others, an agreeably confused, aspirant myth loosely tied together under the title 'Mr. John Wickliff Shawnessy.' And if he was a myth, other people were even more so.

He thought of the talented creature who sat beside him. All names were costumes, it was true, that subtly changed the appearance and behavior of the wearer, but how was it possible to know a woman who had worn so many costumes of names? When you called a thing by a name, you gave it form. By clinging to its name, it clung to its being. But here was a woman who had dissolved her being into many names, the discarded costumes of her outworn years.

The Centennial Day was halfspent, approaching noon when the program ended. After the program, they were an hour getting out of the Square. They tried to find a place to eat, but whenever they put their heads inside a restaurant, they saw that all the tables were already full of hot, healthy, hungry Centennial Americans who looked as though they intended to sit all afternoon and eat everything in sight like goats or locusts. They decided after a while that they might as well go out to the Exposition Grounds in Fairmount Park and try to get something to eat out there. After failing to hail a carriage, they wedged themselves into a streetcar and were carried into the passenger railway concourse just outside the Park and under the massive brick backside of the Main Exhibition Building, which was almost a halfmile long. After passing through one of the near-by entrances, they bought a little red book with black letters on the outside.

VISITORS GUIDE
TO THE
CENTENNIAL EXHIBITION
AND
PHILADELPHIA
1876

The only Guide Book
Sold on the Exhibition Grounds

The walls and pinnacles and spiny domes of the great exhibition buildings lay in shimmering green heat across the graceful lawns and the long avenues dense with sauntering thousands. This, then, was the Great Fair of Mankind, where the world had heaped its richest spoils. Perhaps behind these thickrinded buildings the secret of humanity lay, husked and delicious. Eager-eyed in the nooning heat, he and these other pilgrim thousands had come to seek it out.

The two couples managed to get dinner at the Great American Restaurant and then sat out in the Beer Garden drinking beer and listening to concert music. After a couple of beers, the Perfessor, that expert in calculated insanity, was putting on an unusually perfessorial performance.

—What did you say they call this place, honey? Phoebe asked him.

Taking the guidebook, the Perfessor read:

—Centennial Exhibit No. 1

THE GREAT AMERICAN RESTAURANT

Attractively landscaped, in the midst of the fairground, a favorite retreat for epicures, gourmands, and gastronomes, The Great American Restaurant contains a Banqueting Hall 115 feet by 50 feet, Special Rooms for Ladies, Private Parlors, Smoking-Rooms, Bath-Rooms, and Barber-Shop. Fountains, Statues, Shrubbery surround the building. In this pleasant setting the Great American Stomach can be ministered to in the most agreeable surroundings. In the Special Rooms, the Great American Ladies can be Special in the Great American Way. In the Private Parlors, the Great American Privacy can be had by all. In the Smoking Rooms, the Great American Cigar can be smoked. In the Bathrooms, one can lave one's limbs with a Great American Soap, pouring over one's recumbent form the incomparable waters of a Great American Bath. In the Barber-Shop, one can get the Great American Haircut, plus shave, for two bits. Among the Fountains, the Statues, and the Shrubbery, one can commune with nature and perhaps ambulate hand in hand with one's beloved and when no one is noticing be Greatly American in the most approved and interesting fashion. . . .

—Is that really in there? Phoebe said.

—My dear, the Perfessor said, gently touching her corncolored hair, you have beautiful corncolored hair.

Before an hour was up, Miss Golden had drunk three beers. She and Mr. Shawnessy briefly discussed Raintree County, and Miss Golden recorded her suspicion that it was a kind of recent clearing in the wilderness. Mr. Shawnessy defended his homeland tactfully but zealously. In response to some queries of Mr. Shawnessy's, Miss Golden discussed the New York stage, illustrating her dissertation with anecdotes drawn directly from her own experience. Both Miss

Golden and Mr. Shawnessy arranged themselves as it were into an admiring audience for a creature who walked with queenly stride up and down before the footlights. Mr. Shawnessy deftly introduced the name of *Mazeppa* into the discussion.

—I'm afraid I made quite an exhibit of myself in that play, Miss Golden said. A Centennial Exhibit! *You* will have to write me a play sometime, Mr. Shawnessy.

—What sort of play?

—Something with a great climactic scene of passion.

—You excel at passion, Miss Golden?

—Of course, she said. Haven't you heard about me? I'm supposed to be a very passionate actress, *dear.*

She said the last word in a cutting voice, prolonging it mockingly with her truncated metropolitan ar sound.

—What passion do you prefer?

—Why, the passion of love, of course, she said. Love jealous, love tumultuous, love sensual and brooking no restraint. Now that all passion has departed from my life, I express it on the stage.

He gave her a quick glance to see if she was laughing at him, but he could see only the unchanged smile and the veiled green fire of her eyes.

—Yes, she said, the world contemplates me, Mr. Shawnessy, and I contemplate the world. I find it entirely possible to dispense with passion. Don't you?

—No.

She laughed.

—O, yes, I must say you gentlemen seem passionate enough for two. Really, gentlemen are so persistent. It's quite fatiguing.

He blushed with anger at this remark. This young woman, he found, was more claws than caresses.

At this point, Miss Golden said another disturbing thing.

—Your own love-life has been a singular one, Mr. Shawnessy, judging from what Mr. Stiles tells me.

Mr. Shawnessy averred that this was perhaps so. Miss Golden laughingly surmised the existence of a number of barefoot darlings back in Raintree County with long gold hair hanging down to their waists.

—Mr. Stiles has told me that it's quite pastoral there and that you in particular, Mr. Shawnessy, have a talent for swimming in country waters *au naturel* with young ladies of the vicinity, and all quite innocent and charming.

Mr. Shawnessy was inwardly shocked at the Perfessor's betrayal of confidence. Outwardly he admitted that some such episodes might have occurred in his youth, but that to the best of his knowledge such a practice was an extremely uncommon one in Raintree County at the present time.

—About this marriage of yours, Miss Golden said, showing a remarkably extensive knowledge of Mr. Shawnessy's affairs, I think it's a shame. Can't you do anything to dissolve it?

He had diverted the conversation to other topics, and Miss Golden had then volunteered some information about her own marriage.

—I was married once. To a very rich old man. I'm afraid he died from it. It was, of course, merely a marriage of *convenance.* I didn't mean he should die, of course. But he did.

The consummate cruelty of this statement inwardly annoyed Mr. Shawnessy, but outwardly he joined Miss Golden in the musical laugh with which she dismissed the subject.

—I hope my candor doesn't shock you, Mr. Shawnessy. I'm afraid you find me a very unladylike person, she said, swaying her very ladylike face close to his own.

He said that he liked unladies. At this point the Perfessor was overheard singing:

—O, who would despond
With a beer and a blonde!

—I feel very Centennial, Miss Golden said.

He agreed that this was the only possible adjective to describe his own feelings.

—We'd best look at some buildings, hadn't we? she said. What's that big thing over there?

The Perfessor's vision was blocked by Phoebe. Opening the guidebook, he smoothed his eyebrows and recited:

—Centennial Exhibit No. 2

THE GREAT AMERICAN BLONDE

No matter how rushed for time the sightseeing tourist is, he must not miss one of the prize exhibits of the Fair. The Great American Blonde will be found almost anywhere between the East and West en-

> closures of the Garden. This colossal piece of domestic architecture was pushed to completion just in time for the opening of the Exposition. The maker is to be especially commended for the effective mixture of Byzantine and Rococo motifs that have been blended into the ample curvatures and globed redundancies of the edifice. The exterior is impressive enough, but he who would . . .

At this point, the Perfessor began to shake so hard that he was unable to go on.

—You made that up, Phoebe said. Didn't you?

—My dear, the Perfessor said, looking at her bosom with gentle, unfocused eyes, you have the most beautiful eyes.

Later they left the Garden and wandered aimlessly.

—Where are we now? Miss Golden asked.

John Shawnessy opened the colored map, checked some numbers, and finally announced,

—That's the Main Building there. We are sauntering down the Avenue of the Republic.

In the Main Building of the Centennial Exposition, Mr. John Shawnessy and Miss Laura Golden walked on, looking at plumes shed from Time's condor wings.

The biggest crowds were pouring in and out of Machinery Hall, which everyone said was the real wonder of the Exhibition. The first thing they saw in the entrance was a big truculent cannon made by Krupp and sent over as Germany's prime contribution to the Exposition. A sign said:

THE BIGGEST GUN IN THE WORLD

—God help the Kaiser's enemies in the next war, the Perfessor said.

Machinery Hall was crammed with clanking, glittering, grinding, shrieking, whirring machines for doing and making things hitherto performed by hand. The four visitors wandered a little confusedly until they found themselves part of an awed crowd standing before the Corliss Steam Engine in the middle of Machinery Hall. Someone said that this engine was powering all the shafts that ran all the machines that filled up all of Machinery Hall.

A sign said:

THE BIGGEST STEAM ENGINE IN THE WORLD

The Perfessor removed his hat.

—Mr. Shawnessy, lead us in prayer.

After Machinery Hall, they visited Horticultural Hall, where they wandered around in what a sign said was

THE BIGGEST CONSERVATORY IN THE WORLD

—It smells like the funeral of God in here, the Perfessor said. Alas, what corpse are we burying under all these flowers?

John Shawnessy found himself standing somewhat away from the crowd in an alcove of shrubbery under an artificial palm tree. He suddenly realized that Miss Laura Golden was studying his face with an amused intentness, as if to break through some defense that he had.

—You may call me 'Laura,' Mr. Shawnessy.

—Laura, he said. A stately name. Surely one of your best.

She kept her eyes unwaveringly upon him. It was cruel. He felt himself blushing.

—You may call me 'John,' he said, or—if you prefer one of *my* discarded names—'Johnny.'

—Johnny. Yes I think I *will* call you 'Johnny.'

She had said the talismanic name the first time like a caress in a low, thrilling voice, but the second time she had somehow managed to give it a tinge of mockery.

The Perfessor popped his head into the alcove.

—Touching little tableau, he said. The modern Adam and Eve. Under the Tree. Enter the Serpent.

They were beginning to feel a little bored with the whole thing by the time they went through the Art Gallery, to which Britain, France, Germany, and other nations had sent an impressive acreage of unimpressive canvas. The ladies excused themselves. John Shawnessy found the Perfessor gazing absorbedly at an oil painting richly colored and glisteningly precise in the style of the current romantic school of minor British painters.

It was the picture of a great stone cat with head of woman. It lay couched on sleekly powerful haunches. Its jadegreen eyes looked forth upon an Ozymandian desert backgrounded with vague temples and broken columns. The face, a little mutilated, wore an expression of imperial disdain, cruelty, self-indulgence, enigma. The picture bore the title SPHINX RECUMBENT.

—I wonder if that's for sale, the Perfessor said. I wouldn't mind adding it to my collection of sphinxes.

He shook soundlessly and shrugged his shoulders.

—Old men, John, all acquire revolting little hobbies. Everyone has to collect something to acquire a feeling of triumph over time. Some people collect coins. Some people collect operations. I knew a man once who collected petrified worm dung. For my part, I used to collect women. Now I collect the real thing—sphinxes. It's a passion with me. When you drop into my quarters in New York, you'll see a room there crawling with all sorts of hideous little statues and pictures of sphinxes—grinning, mutilated, multiform, winged, jeweled, headless, noseless, legless, some more woman than beast, some more beast than woman, Greek, Egyptian, American, masculine, feminine, and neuter.

—What—another sphinx! Laura Golden said, coming back unexpectedly with Miss Phoebe Veach. For your collection, dear?

—If it's for sale, the Perfessor said.

He called an attendant, who took the number of the painting and went off to consult the Catalogue of Exhibition.

—By the way, this figure is grotesquely inaccurate, the Perfessor said, which adds to its value. The setting's Egyptian, but the head's a woman's. Now all the authentic Egyptian sphinxes were manheaded or something-else-headed, but never female. The Greek sphinx, on the other hand, was female. Of course the word 'sphinx' itself is Greek from 'strangle.' The Greeks applied the word to that mythical female monster who sat above the road to Thebes propounding her childish riddle and choking all who were unable to answer it. *What creature is it that in the morning walks on four, at noon on two, and at evening on three legs,* children? The local morons flunked this elementary examination and were slain in droves until the boy-prodigy Oedipus came along and gave the answer, hurling the lady down from her high couch.

—I've always thought it the profoundest myth in antiquity, John Shawnessy said. Veiled in this simple question is the hardest of all riddles—*What is man?* This riddle is propounded by that composite beast, the earth—feminine, secret, and recumbent.

—Isn't the title of the picture redundant? Laura Golden asked.

—Not wholly, the Perfessor said. Some sphinxes are standing, some sitting, some are naked, some are clothed. And some wear

bustles. What would it cost me to add *you* to my collection, *dear?*
Laura Golden pointed a shoulder at the Perfessor and swung her parasol. Though a head shorter than he, she had the air of looking down at him from a high couch.

—You'll have to answer my riddle first, *dear.* And how will you have me—sitting, standing, or recumbent?

—Any way I can get you, *dear.* Seriously, though, Laura, when are you going to come up and pose for me? In the nude, of course. I'll do you in oils, and we'll call it 'Laura Recumbent.' You used to pose, dear—you know you did.

—I still pose, dear, but I get well paid for it. Besides, I might catch cold in your apartment.

She laughed her musical laugh.

—I'm afraid we're shocking Mr. Shawnessy. He'll think we're very corrupt. We talk this way all the time, dear, she said.

The Perfessor seemed peculiarly insistent and excited.

—Seriously, dear, I'll pay your price. I paint rather well, you know. And I'll sell the picture to Mr. Cassius P. Carney for a hundred thousand dollars.

—I've been offered that much for the original, *dear,* she said.

—Here you are, the attendant said, pulling the Perfessor aside to confer in whispers.

—Outrageous! the Perfessor said. It's a horrible daub. But put my name down for it, and if no one else bites, I may take it in November, after the Exhibition closes.

The Perfessor folded his arm in Miss Veach's.

—And how is our little Phoebe Redundant? he said. Personally, darling, I like my women pliant and uncomplicated like you. Come up to my studio sometime, and I'll have you pose for a vast green landscape dotted with golden hemispheres of hay.

They had intended to see Agricultural Hall, but they got lost in the exhibits of the several states. John Shawnessy wanted to drop into the Indiana Building, but Laura told him all he would find in there would be the Biggest Ear of Corn in the World. They stopped again at the Beer Garden, gasping with heat, and drank a great deal more cold beer.

Somewhere on the grounds, it was their understanding that the Grand Ceremonies were going on.

—I have had enough Grand Ceremonies for one day, Laura said. Let us have some Little Ceremonies for a change.

John Shawnessy never saw the rest of the Exhibition. He managed to hire a carriage, and he and Laura set out in the early night through the streets of Philadelphia. They had lost the Perfessor and Phoebe.

—I promised to meet Mr. Carney for the ball at the hotel this evening, she said.

—It's past time now, he said.

—Let's go for a ride, dear. Mr. Carney bores me to extinction.

They had the driver take them out around the City. It was all a blur of crowds, vehicles, gaslamps, bonfires. Now and then a rocket streaked up the purple sky and described its great, gentle curve, falling and fading through the Centennial night.

The hood of the carriage was thrown back. A river of cool air streaked with flame flowed over them.

They talked. Miss Laura Golden undertook to educate Mr. Shawnessy into certain ways of the City. She told him about the *haut monde* in which she moved, of balls, pomps, mad, bad parties, of roistering men and easy-virtued girls.

—You must have money, dear, she said in a grave, sweet way that she had assumed during this part of their conversation. Only money means anything in the City. Neither beauty nor intelligence dominates society. Most women of beauty are bought and sold like *objets d'art.* If I have managed to escape all that, it's only because I have money. Fabulously wealthy men are always leaving their cards and sending flowers and trying to buy the favors of my actresses—not to say myself. Of course, your friend Mr. Cassius Carney would give a hundred thousand dollars to be permitted to enter my bedroom door.

She looked directly at John Shawnessy.

—You didn't believe that, did you, *dear?* she said.

—I can't imagine any better way he could invest his money, dear, John Shawnessy came back gallantly.

—Well, it's true, dear, she said. He offered me that much as flatly as you or I would bid on some railroad stock. Poor man, he's asking for a full share of Unpacific Union. Of course he's quite mad about me. Do you think I ought to take his money?

—My dear Laura, your bedroom transactions are strictly your own affair.

She laughed.

—Aren't you tart! she said. I've been shocking you. You find me very, very shocking, don't you, dear?

—I find you very, very Centennial, Laura.

At the Centennial Ball that night in one of Philadelphia's biggest hotels, John Shawnessy and Laura Golden and a few hundred other celebrants danced away the declining hours of the first day of America's second century. There was a good deal of champagne flowing, and the Perfessor and Phoebe left the party early. Around midnight, Mr. Cassius Carney turned up and absentmindedly revolved twice around the floor with Miss Laura Golden and then disappeared as abruptly as he came, consulting a watch. Mr. John Shawnessy escorted Miss Laura Golden to the door of her room. There was a languid condescension in her manner.

—Don't worry, dear, she said. Mr. Stiles and I will take good care of you in the City. You come around and see me at the theatre and I'll introduce you to some little actresses.

—Thank you so much, dear.

—And when you get a hundred thousand dollars, you can come and see *me* at my place, *dear.*

In the halflight of the hall, she leaned back against the door, cruelly conscious of her beauty. She seemed indeed to be couched like a great cat on beautifully muscled haunches. He was angry with her for this cynical, unmeant invitation.

—My dear Miss Golden, he said, not every man is trying to find his way into your famous bedroom.

—Famous? she said, bending her face proudly to one side on the slender neck. Pray—why famous?

Just then she gave a little shriek of surprise as the door opened and she almost fell inside. Professor Jerusalem Webster Stiles, indifferently put together, appeared with his arm around Phoebe.

—I trust you all perceive, he said, the object which I hold in my hand.

He disappeared in the corridor.

—I suppose Mr. Stiles has been telling stories about me, she said. Don't believe anything he says. I'm a very ladylike unlady. Good night, Johnny *dear.*

She had said his name like a caress from deep in her throat, but the lovely disdainful mouth gave the last word a tinge of mockery all the same.

—Good night, Laura dear.

—You know, I love the way you say that, she said, stepping back out unexpectedly. You give it such a courteous sound in your precious Hoosier accent. Say it again, *dear*.

—Laura dear.

As he said her name the second time, she watched his mouth, much amused, moving her lips with his. Tilting her chin, half-shutting her eyes, tipping her head sideways, she invited him to kiss her good night. Slowly, he approached the painted mouth in the moonpale, powdered face and barely touched its sultry outline with his lips, thinking of the scar. Even then, he was surprised by the softness and warmth of the mouth. But without responding, it withdrew into the darkness of the room, and silently the door closed. It had been a very imperfect kiss.

Lying in his lonely bed, John Shawnessy totted up the scattered statistics of the Centennial Day. A muggy dawn was breaking. The Republic had completed its first century of progress toward the goal of Social and Moral Perfection envisaged by her founders.

As for him, he had gone to the Centennial Exhibition, but he had not seen the most exciting of the Centennial Exhibits. He had, however, touched its mystery, couched and strange, a mystery of lives and years. He tried to imagine the face of a girl named Daphne Fountain, perhaps unscarred, as it might have been on that far-off April night when it waited for him in the wings of a theatre in the City of Washington, but instead there came to him the memory of another face in the wings of a theatre, the face of a girl who stood against unused sceneshifts of woodland and river scenery in an old Opera House.

I came to the City, a vagrant day,
  In the bloom of my blithesome youth,
And I sought in the City great and gray
  The beautiful bird of Truth.
I sought her along the wide, wide streets,
  The glimmering parks and lawns,
Through all of the City's dim retreats
  And under its lonely dawns.

Then he tried to remember Miss Laura Golden's face, as he had just seen it, but he couldn't do it. It had become as featureless as a sensual summer moon, nodding languidly upon his fevered meditations —a Centennial Summer moon.

So then it was a hundred years since America had begun. Yes, he would start all over and discover America again.

America was a city by a river, a city of gloomily eclectic buildings, confused unhappy domes and spires of buildings that were trying to be the most beautiful buildings that ever were but couldn't be because they hadn't any souls. America was faces in the Avenue of the Republic, eager, excited faces with mobile eyes. America was the place where all the world sent its third-rate art and gaudiest claptrap and where it was all piled up together and then became something hushed, exciting, wonderful because it was in America.

America was cities—cities that changed and faded overnight, pushed down and trampled under by other cities that had the same names, preposterous and arrogant cities, shooting from the fecund soil like the most fulsome flowers the world had ever seen. America was hotels filled with Centennial thousands; it was the saturnalia of the night-time city, the bodies of persuaded blondes bounding on beds with Centennial abandon. America was a thin bright rocket rising in the purple sky, a streak of force that hadn't yet arrived at its gentle, gradual curve and handsome fall. It was the biggest rocket of them all, obedient to the pressure in its tail. And it was much desire, young dreams, unshakable conviction, clenched hands in darkness beating upon pillows and reaching out for other hands and finding——

America was John Wickliff Shawnessy, and how he left Raintree County, and in the summer of the Republic's rededication to Life, Liberty, and the Pursuit of Happiness, began to seek his fortune in the City of New York, where he was confident there awaited him the greatness and wisdom he had long been seeking, the consummation of a magic poem, and the vouchsafing of a love that was wholly of the City. But whether it would be like the City, sensual and self-indulgent,

OR, LIKE THE CITY, PASSIONATE AND REAL,

HE HAD YET TO DISCOVER

IN

—LITTLE OLD NEW YORK, the Perfessor was saying, has changed a lot since you were there in '76, John. You'd feel like Rip Van Winkle if you came back today.

—'HOT BOX ON EASTBOUND,' the telegraph key was clicking. 'DELAY FEW MORE MINUTES AT ROIVILLE.'

—John, we stand on the threshold of immense changes, the Perfessor went on, gesticulating in his best classroom manner. America —our old America—is gone. The War killed it. The City killed it. The Declaration of Independence and the Constitution never foresaw the Modern City. If Tom Jefferson were to come back today and walk through the sunlight and shadow of New York, he'd say, Good God, what's happened to the Republic?

Mr. Shawnessy got up and nervously smoothed his hair in the glass of the station window. He sat down and listened for the train.

—When you stand on a high roof, the Perfessor was saying, and look down at the canyons of one of our great modern cities, how can you resist the impression that you are looking into the welter and stench of the Great Swamp itself! The people look like frantic bugs going in and out of holes, the sharp angles of the City are softened, whole streets sink back into shadow while others shimmer with a hot radiance. Listen to the dungbed of it seething with a dirtiness called human life! Can you resist the feeling that this is the place where all souls are extinguished? Can any wisdom or love or beauty come out of the City?

Mr. Shawnessy felt an old feeling of revulsion mixed with a taste of bitter passion.

I came to the City a vagrant day in the bloom of my blithesome youth. And I sought in the City what all men seek, and I was lost in the City like one who wandered in a dream.

—Here in the City, the Perfessor was saying, Raintree County is utterly destroyed. The City destroys all the ancient values, prides, loyalties, convictions. The City has no everlasting values, being itself the creature of endless change.

—'SHE'S LEAVING ROIVILLE,' the telegraph key was saying.

And I sought in the City, great and gray, the beautiful bird of truth. I sought her among the wide, wide streets, the glimmering parks and lawns, through all of the City's vague retreats, and under her lonely, under her lonely, under her lonely dawns.

—The supreme irony of it all, the Perfessor was saying, is that the creators of the Machine, believing it the fairest flower of human progress, have really made it the noxious weed that chokes out everything else and finally begins to choke itself out of room and means of sustenance. Thus with the Machine, his last brilliant contrivance, the Heir of all the Ages succeeds in hurling himself back into the Swamp and destroys all the beautiful, insubstantial dreams that made him think he had a home forever on this earth.

Listen! I hear a voice of prophecy in Raintree County. I hear the thunder of the hurrying wheels. Broad roads are built through Raintree County, and the ancient boundaries will dissolve. There is a banner of progress fast and far across the land. And who shall be the Hero of the County and who shall have the golden fruit?

—Gangway for the new man, the new American, John! the Perfessor was saying. You and I are nothing to him. He has dispensed with conscience and morality, those articles of excess baggage on the road to fame and riches. Gangway for Progress and Unlimited Expansion.

—Gangway for the Eastbound Express! Mr. Shawnessy said. Here it comes!

Just then the train broke small and far and fast from the realm of faith into the realm of fact. The black shape of it had been preceded by the sound of its panting breath. And now the whistle wailed.

And many a year I spent at last in the City's swallowing void, till I thought that my youthful dream was past and its delicate, delicate, delicate, delicate, delicate form destroyed. Till I thought . . . till I thought . . . till I thought

1876— How —1877
he came
to the City of New York

in the Centennial Summer, how he lived in the City from a summer to a summer, how he became lost in the City like one wandering in a dream.

He came to the City because he was always meant to come. It was as if a voice had spoken from the sky above his home in Raintree County, saying:

My child, you shall go to the City, because without the City you are incomplete. You shall go to the City and be sad, because you haven't yet been sad enough. You shall go to the City and know a love unlike any other, because you haven't yet loved enough. You shall go to the City, and the City will drench you in its liquorcolored lights, ravish you with its enormous beauty, wound you with its hard surfaces and pointed towers, and reject you from its million doors. Then perhaps some day if you are lucky, having tasted its red forbidden fruit, you will come back from the City to your home again.

What was the City to John Shawnessy?

The City was a street, any street taken at random in summer between the dense fronts of the buildings or valleying to distant parks. It was the dense tide of the faces in the street. For like a tide in those gilded years, the immigrant faces surged through the channels of the City. Surflike, they beat on the island stillness of the brownstone mansions of the rich in parklike yards.

The City was the meeting of the trains in marshalling yards, the changing of the cars, incessant arrivals and departures.

Often in his time within the City, the young man from Raintree County would go down and stand in one of the terminals and watch the ventricles expanding and contracting, the pale tide of the faces streaming in and out. Why did they come, the people of the City, the eager self-appointed heroes, the bewildered children of humanity? He saw their faces looking from the windows of the hollow, gaslit cars, their million faces, tender, delicate, obtuse, deformed, eager, illusioned, cynical, depraved, desirous, a hundred thousand vagrant seeds blown down into this heaving swamp, the City. What other faces did they meet while they swam on the blind nocturnal tides? What faces yet unborn were imminent from faces that he saw? What millions of Americans were being spawned from the muck of seeding faces that lost themselves in chambers of the City? Good-by, they said, and waving left the City, or descending from the cars at evening rushed into waiting arms, were carried by cabs, walked with tired eyes into the shells of old hotels. Good-by! Hello! Hail and Farewell! The City was the place of all departure and arrival, meeting and farewell.

The City was perhaps, most of all, a place where people came to see the City.

The City was the place where the great newsstories were manufactured out of ink and blood. The young man from Raintree County was amazed to see how blindly the people of the City ingurgitated print. The City was the newsboy on the corner. (O, little shaghaired shouter of headlines! O, little seedling of the asphalt!) The hoarse cry of the newsboy on the corner was the voice of Providence addressing Mankind.

The City was A Great Calamity, Sensational Fire, Terrific Loss of Life (Git Yuh Papuh Heah), Custuh Massacree, Centennial Exposition Closes (Git Yuh Papuh Heah), Great Train Wreck in Ohio Terrific Loss of Life, Election in Dispute (Git Yuh Papuh Heah) Southerners Massacree Negroes, Terrific Loss of Life, Negro Lad Names Attackers, Hayes Elected (Git Yuh Papuh Heah). The City was the Great American Newsstory.

The epic of the City in the Centennial Year was the epic of the Custers, roaring with their boots on hell-for-leather out of the smoke of the Great War and across the plains, driving a lot of savages from their own land with the utmost dash and dare. But the West kept its secret from the City, and the City didn't really understand or care that on the sunbaked Western plain, which was America, the body of the Civil War was lying, with brave boots on and an anachronistic arrow in its guts.

The City was the story of closing up the Centennial Exposition in the autumn of the year. The little city of strange domes beside the river was instantly old, naked, forlorn, as time rushed on, panting and wailing down the rails, burning out boxes on the Western plain, and spawning cities, cities, cities, cities, all in the image of the City.

The City was words, it was brown days and months and years of words that flowed across the face of time.

The City was a lonely, desirous young man from Raintree County reading to late hours in a great municipal library endowed by a multi-millionaire who made his money out of railroads that bled the farmers back in Raintree County. One of the saddest images of the City was the young man from the West reading in one of the hundred million books, feeling the brevity of his time within the City and the eternity of the City's spawning of ideas, images, and words. And even as he plowed a puny path through the mounded lore of ages, the City went on with gushing presses, drowning him with words. The magazines were printing poems, stories, novels, the City was a waste of books and words in which a man might sink from sight and never be heard of again. Brown bindings stamped with gilded words turned beneath his hands. In the late hours, he left the echoing building and stepped out again into the stale valleys and caverns of the City, and the City roared around him, multitudinous, unsubdued, uncaring. There were so many books. A hundred lives would not suffice to read the City's own outpouring.

What was the poem that would tell the City—its vastness, richness, cruelty, the beauty of its women, the pathos of its crammed, explosive life, the victories, joys, defeats, frustrations of its days!

When John Shawnessy listened for the voices of famous poets then living, to see whether they were reaching to express this thing, the City, he was disappointed. The laureate voices of the City were singers of poor small songs, sentimental lyrics in the columns of the newspapers, the fancy doggerel of Stedman, the watered nightingale notes of Aldrich. Whitman, though not stilled, had sung his greatest songs, had never made the epic of his people. Emerson was an old man who couldn't remember faces of his youth. Hawthorne, Thoreau were dead. The great voices were all in one way or another casualties of the Great War. The epic of America, her youth, her martial vigor, her innocent dedications, her great crusades, were back in the years when a divided people fought, each side for its dream of human freedom, when a race had been emancipated, when the face of

Abraham Lincoln brooded above the wartorn nation. The City and the Nation had fallen on degenerate days.

He sought the secret of the City also in the theatres. Here he saw the foppish posturings, the sentimental attitudes of a Gilded Age. To express its turbulence and passion, its laughter and tears, the City required a Shakespeare; it had to be satisfied with Boucicault.

When at last shyly he had revealed some of his own unfinished work to certain literary persons of the City, he was coldly rejected. All at once he knew the sinister selfishness of mankind, the infinite gap between his own vision of himself and the brief, indifferent viewing of other people. He knew then all at once how lucky and rare it is for anyone to make his world acceptable to anyone else. He knew then how vain he had been to suppose that the City would be eager to receive him, caress him, lionize him, make him her poet. His manuscripts came back to him devoid of comment, scarcely read.

Meanwhile the City had an insatiable appetite for words and drugged itself with the thin music of a billion clichés.

There were nights when he lay in his room in one of the crammed apartment regions of the City and felt a sick despair rising up around him in the night. The City was this despair, it was the steady pounding of his heart, his face on the pillow, the brown shadows of the room, the winking jungle of the walls, the sound of time ebbing on the shelved and shadowy ramparts of the City in the night.

So like that other gifted young poet, Mr. William Shakespeare, Mr. John Shawnessy had left the little rural water where he had spent his youth and had come (if somewhat belatedly) to the Great City. And to fulfill an ancient dream of his he began to write a play. The epic that he had meant to finish in the City was set aside, for into it had crept the City's own moral and artistic confusion. The play on which he worked ceaselessly now was itself an image of the City. He called it by a somber, glittering phrase that had lodged in his memory and turned to stone, *Sphinx Recumbent.* A verse-drama gorgeous with rich words and violent scenes, it had for its heroine a woman sensual, proud, enigmatic. He set her in the gilded world of the City like an idol blazing with a stony light, against which men beat themselves to death. But there was one, a poet lost for a time in the chambers of the City, between whom and this woman a contest rose, each seeking to find and possess the other's soul—she through cruel conquest, and he through virile identity.

Thus through the long months of his life in the City, Mr. John Wickliff Shawnessy—in his best Raintree County tradition—built a fictitious woman from a woman of flesh and blood named Laura Golden, who became, unknown to her, the subject of a play on the theme of love—love jealous, love tumultuous, love sensual and brooking no restraint.

For there was one thing he wanted in the City more even than fame and fortune. It was love. The City was this love.

The City was Miss Laura Golden posed in attitudes of fear, love, joy, rejection, loathing, horror, surprise. It was her swift body disappearing in the wings, the crashing of the curtain, her gracious encores, the kissing of her hand to voluptuous, noisy gentlemen in the boxes. It was the terrible power of the actress multiplied a hundredfold by the hundred costumes in which her graceful body was masked and a thousandfold by the thousand hushed faces that watched her from the darkened theatre.

But who this woman really was—except that she was the City and his dream of it—he couldn't say. For who could follow the progress of this face through the twisted years? Who could follow it through many loves and many days back to its beginnings in the City? Who could describe the gray lights and seasons of the City, the old brown stridulous fabric of its days, the clamor of its streets and stunted words?

Mr. John Shawnessy saw little of Miss Laura Golden during the first year of his sojourn in the City, except in the theatres where she played. He was never one of those many bachelors with gold watch-chains and greased mustaches who, like Mr. Cassius P. Carney, waited so often at the stage door of the Broadway Theatre with roses in their hands. He did meet her a few times at the Perfessor's quarters, where, in the spring of 1877, a characteristic dialogue occurred between the two principal characters in Mr. John Wickliff Shawnessy's own private drama of *Sphinx Recumbent*.

—Hello, Johnny. Where have you been? I haven't seen you for weeks.

—I've been writing.

—But you can't write all the time. What do you do for amusement?

—I take walks—over the nocturnal City.

—How thrilling! Alone, dear?

—Yes.

—I can't understand it. Aren't you interested in a woman?

—Well, yes. I *am* intensely preoccupied with a certain woman.

—How exciting! Tell me about her. Are you very much in love with her?

—I think about her all the time.

—How lucky she is! I'm positively jealous, *dear!*

—You needn't be. She's no more lovely than you.

—O, but I'm sure she is. Is she—an actress?

—How did you know?

—Just guessing. By the way, when do I get to see your play?

—When it's finished.

—I'm very impatient, dear. You must show it to me the first of all. But I suppose you'll show it to her first.

—I promise to show it to you first.

—You're sweet. Johnny dear, will you do me a favor?

—Of course.

—Write me a letter on my tour.

—Where are you going?

—Out to your country—Ohio, Michigan, Nebraska, Idaho, California—I don't know where all.

—I live in Indiana, dear.

—Well, that's what I said, didn't I? I'll be gone three months.

—I'll miss you, Laura.

—Dear, you're such a terrible liar. How can you miss me when you never see me?

—It's a talent that I have.

—Well, I shall miss you too, dear. So write to me, and I'll read your dear letters just before I go to bed, *dear,* in my lonely little bed.

Her laughter conjured up a picture of a very unlonely little bed. When he took her home that night to her big brownstone mansion on Fifth Avenue, which he had never entered, his goodnight kiss fell on curved lips still laughing, though, to his surprise, Laura's mouth twisted strangely at him just as he withdrew his lips. Or so he thought. But the door closed on her laughter, and he had the warm taste of her perfumed lips—deep, soft, and cruelly writhing—on his mouth. He lingered awhile just outside the parklike yard of her house until he saw a single yellow light go on behind closed curtains in a thirdfloor room. No doubt some luckier, lustier lover had been waiting there in her notorious bedroom. She had seemed in a hurry to say good night. It had been after all a very imperfect kiss.

Why was it then that this woman, who (according to an astute biographer of metropolitan decadence) had made a profession of the theatre and a pastime of love, seemed so invulnerable to the Gentleman from Indiana? Perhaps this distant, amused reserve was intended as a pungent sauce to the appetite of her lovers. As the Perfessor had once remarked, Every whore has her amenity of surrender.

As for John Shawnessy, he told himself that what he felt toward Laura Golden was surely not love (he wasn't sure that he even liked her)—it was a species of intense curiosity, which had been transmitted to him with a vengeance by his old mentor. The pupil was simply making (as he had done before) more profound researches into a subject to which the Perfessor had devoted only a cursory inspection and a few brilliantly illuminating—though possibly erroneous—conjectures.

So he went home that night murmuring to himself, as he did so often in those days, the word 'Laura.'

Laura. This name became his City—the City was this stately, sensual name of his gilded years. Laura.

Meanwhile in the gradual fashioning of his play, as he strove slowly toward a plausible and yet immensely novel climactic scene, he kept imagining how some night he himself would rise through the echoing chambers of the City and approach the door of that Forbidden Room, the City's ultimate chamber. In the door would be the face that brooded over his whole sojourn in the City, moonluscious, with its twisted smile. Then he would follow the jade eyes and the beckoning hand within, and he would solve at last the secret of the City, know it to its inmost meaning, and the City would have yielded to his heroic, lone assault.

And so he lived his season in the City, waiting until his play should have its great Fifth Act or the City

CHEAT HIM OF THE CLIMAX AND AWAKEN HIM

WITH THE SOUND OF A

COLD

BELL CLANGING, the Eastbound Express thundered into Waycross Station, stopped, ejected from its long dark body an exceedingly rich man, and, bell clanging, resumed its way. Cassius P. Carney, the distinguished financier, carrying a grip and lipping a cigar, walked briskly up and shook hands with Mr. Shawnessy and the Perfessor.

—Hello, boys, he said, unsmiling, his brown eyes burning somberly, one delicate quick hand stroking his trim ball of beard, the other plucking the cigar from his mouth.

—Where's Laura? the Perfessor said.

—Didn't want to come through with me, Cash said. I can only stop off an hour. I've arranged to be picked up by the next train through. Got to get to Pittsburgh.

His eyes were probing the town, the Station, and the grain elevator beside the tracks.

—I'll be damned, he said. Is this where you been spending your life, John? I didn't know they built towns this small any more.

The remark seemed without humor, made as a practical observation.

—We've just had a big time here, Mr. Shawnessy said. Garwood pulled out on the Westbound just a few minutes ago. He must have passed you at Roiville.

—I wanted to see the Senator, Cash said, but it can wait. If you boys don't mind, I'll just sit down here in the Station and chat with you until the next train along.

—My wife and I would like to have you stay all night, Cash, if——

—No chance, Cash said. There's a hell of a situation shaping up in Pittsburgh, and a lot of my interests are involved. I got to get over there and look into it.

Cash sat down on the bench, flanked by Mr. Shawnessy and the Perfessor. He took off his derby and fanned his face with it.

Mr. Shawnessy had a feeling of unimportance. Around Cash Carney, he always felt like a little waystation between two really big terminals. Cash looked out of place sitting in Waycross Station. Even now, there clung to him the aroma and strangeness of the linked, thundering coaches from which he had just descended. Senator Garwood B. Jones, the eternal Dan Populus, the Man of the People, had a foot in two worlds, but Cash had gone over so entirely to his one world of big deals and big business that he seemed a bloodless abstraction. His face had not so much aged as yellowed. His nervous hands palping the big cigar, his face, the thin sheet of his oiled hair, even his eyeballs were yellow. Mr. Shawnessy had the feeling that the whole man—derby, cigar, black suit, shirt, tie stud, gartered socks, black conventional shoes with shiny toes, gold watch, massive signet ring—had all been dipped at once into a solution that preserved but discolored.

And the whole world in which the man moved was stained with that tincture of the gilded years. It was a world shut in, a world of rooms in cities, opulent interiors, lobbies in hotels where brass cuspidors squatted like obscene gods, banquet halls filled with fat men choking on rich foods and dirty jokes, depots whose walls were darkened with the sooty breath of trains, office buildings, stock exchanges, banks that saw the world through myopic windows lettered with gilded names and gilded legends, houses that were not houses, but mansions—great cages of iron and stone, diseased lumps of rusty architecture, nightmarish agglomerations of lightless windows and unlofty towers. And everywhere there was the smell of smoke—cigarsmoke, trainsmoke, factorysmoke. And all these interiors were foursquare, squat, thickrinded, and reptilian.

—Let me see, John, Cash was saying, last time I saw you was just before you left New York in '77. I think I remember the very night—the night Laura threw the Grand Ball, and I couldn't stay because of the Strike. Correct?

—Correct.

The Perfessor hummed softly and smiled a bland smile.

—Those were busy days, Cash said. But no worse than now. Those Bastards are getting ideas again.

—You mean, the Perfessor said, you're expecting real trouble there at the Homestead Mill?

—Got it already, Cash said. I got word a couple days ago that an ugly situation is developing there. Of course we don't want that stuff to spread. Those Bastards have a tendency to stick together.

—What're they striking for this time? Mr. Shawnessy said.

—We had to cut their wage, Cash said. It's the times. Threatens to be the worst thing since '77, according to my private information. After all, imagine a shutdown in the steel industry! Imagine, for Christ's sake, the men who make steel, all these wops getting into their heads they don't want to make steel except on their own terms! Do you fellas realize that this nation is built on steel? If you pulled the steel out of it, it would fall to pieces like a house of cards. It isn't just a question of one factory or one city. This thing could get really big. But we don't aim to let it get out of hand. I've exchanged telegrams with Pittsburgh, and we're moving in a whole army of Pinkertons, if things look ugly.

—Of course, it's not to your interest to let it flare up into open warfare, is it? the Perfessor asked.

—Depends, Cash said. When they start shooting, it always antagonizes the public, and we can send the troops in to put it down. The biggest trouble is that the Populist Party is dragging it into the realm of politics. By the way, what does Garwood think about the Election chances? How much strength do the Populists have?

—The Man of the People is afraid of the People, Mr. Shawnessy said.

—And well he may be, Cash said. I don't know whether you fellas have changed your notions any since the last time I talked with you, but I wonder if you know what's happening to this country?

Cassius P. Carney took the cigar out of his mouth, sat briskly erect, placing one hand, fingers neatly folded under, on the knife-edge of his knee, and with the other hand began to wave his cigar.

—This country, he said, has grown great, strong, and rich on the principle of Free Enterprise. We've had the land, the means, the brains, the generosity to welcome and absorb the peoples of the earth. But, boys, it can't go on forever. Do you know why? It's simple. Because we've run out of land.

Mr. Shawnessy looked up and down the track, quiet from its recurrent thunders. Was it possible then to run out of America?

—Yes, sir, boys, we've run out of land at last. God knows, some of us got our share of it.

Cash smiled for the first time since he had landed in the Station—a nervous, almost lecherous smile.

—Yep, the Government don't give it away anymore. Now, it used to be that when the laborer didn't like his job, he couldn't crab about it because there was always that hundred and sixty acres of black stuff waiting for him out in the Golden West. But all that's over now. And here we are, with the immigrants still pouring into this country and looking for work. The cities are alive and stinking with 'em right now, and still they come. These people are willing to work at any wage, and we've still got the work for 'em. But that don't mean we can give 'em all a house on Fifth Avenue, a lot of gilt-edged securities, and a family vault. Hell, no, we can barely make room for 'em at the current wage, what with the country going hellbent toward another panic. And yet Those Bastards blame us for holding down their wages. Let 'em blame each other. Let 'em blame the Law of Supply and Demand. Let 'em blame the Constitution of the United States, which protects the right of an American citizen to own his business and run it as he sees fit.

—Cash, Mr. Shawnessy said, those people are Americans too, and they have a right to a decent living in this big country.

—Of course they do, John, Cash said. You don't need to go and get idealistic on me, son. I love this country and believe in her as much as you do. Every dollar I spend is a bet on the future of America. I always play America as a bull market. And incidentally I've done more for Those Bastards than practically any man living. How many of your social reformers and labor-leaders have given even fifty dollars of their dirty money to help out the cause of the poor and needy? Do you fellas want to know something? Last week, I delivered to the Society for the Independent Relief of Indigent Children a check for exactly one hundred thousand dollars. One hundred thousand dollars! Let's see some of these anarchists and communists tie that.

—Guilt money, Mr. Shawnessy said. You're just bribing them, Cash. That money's in the same category with the money that keeps Garwood winning in a Populist stronghold. Put it on the campaign fund. Write it off to expenses for running the business.

—Money, Cash said, belongs to the man who knows how to use it. Money has to be on the move. If you went and distributed the money in this country equally, the money would stand still, and everything else would stand still. Money makes money, not just for the capitalist, but for everybody. That's the American secret as I see it. Keep capital fluid and in the hands of men who are willing to take risks and who don't have their hands tied. Hell, there's no limit to what we can do in this country if we don't get our hands tied by the kind of legislation the Populists are yelling for.

—Nevertheless, Mr. Shawnessy said, here are a lot of people who are eager to work, who have big families, who are honest citizens of the Republic, and yet they don't have decent homes or enough to eat. How do you propose to remedy this situation?

—Who ever said you could remedy the situation? Cash Carney said. To be perfectly frank, it's a situation that never has had a solution, because there isn't any solution. We've come closer in America than anywhere else.

—There you are, John, the Perfessor said. Malthus and Darwin were right: there are too many Americans. There are too many bugs in the swamp. Some of them will just have to die for the race. Life's a great cannibal.

—But, Mr. Shawnessy said, America's going to get bigger and bigger. If we have troubles like these now, what will it be in fifty years? Is it merely an idle dream, then, to suppose that the Machine, instead of manufacturing more trouble for the human race, might manufacture more leisure, more food, more happiness for more people?

—Put this Machine in the hands of the State, the Perfessor said, sitting up suddenly and waving his cane. Take it away from the control of private individuals like our friend Carney here, and let it work for the best interests of all.

—By God, that's Communism, Perfessor! Cash said.

—By God, you're right! the Perfessor said. And like it or not, gentlemen, that's what we're coming to. I say it without a particle of personal concern, because I frankly don't give a hoot myself. But Marx was right. The bourgeois culture contains the seeds of its own destruction. The Many will some day be more powerful than the Few, just because they are the Many. The Proletariat will some day have a Plan and a Planner, and then God help that little band of rich men who have nothing but fluid resources to stop the flood.

—That day, Cassius Carney said, if and when it comes, will be the end of the American Republic. I hope I won't be alive to see it.

—That Day will come! the Perfessor said. In Economics as in everything else, Mass and Vitality prevail. Can't you see it coming yourself? Freedom, friends—freedom and democratic institutions—were manufactured by happy gentlemen with prosperous acres and contented slaves on the fringe of a wilderness. They and our tradition of rugged individualism, our capitalists, our log-cabin presidents, our millionaire paperboys—all belong not only to the youth of America but also to the youth of the human race. Americans are the frontiersmen of history, and America is running out of frontier. As Cash says, the times are changing. In America history has been speeded up. Wealth and all the power and prestige that go with it have flowed into huge concentrations in the hands of a few individuals. Industrial empires own whole towns, railroad systems, States, and—yes—the Senate of the United States. In a sense a few great combines may be said to own the country. But they own it how? By the remarkable acquiescence of the people they exploit. In creating these empires of wealth and power, our Capitalists have created the instruments of their own destruction. Behold, the day is almost at hand! When several million men suddenly awaken to find that they are forging with their toil the chains that bind them, when, I say, that historic moment arrives, they will find also that they have in their hands the simple means of emancipation. Then will come, gentlemen, the Great Confiscation! For the workers will say, These machines belong to us because we are the people who work them. Then it will also occur to them to say, We are the Government. That, friends, will be the end of our free and easy, hell-for-leather, capitalistic democracy, and the Revolution will be here!

The Perfessor leaned back, vastly satisfied with himself.

—The trouble with you, Perfessor, Cash Carney said, is that you read too much.

—The trouble with you, Professor, Mr. Shawnessy said, is that for you everything is growing old. For my part, I don't think America will ever be either young or old. America is an Idea, and ideas are neither young nor old, they are simply—Ideas. It's entirely possible for the laborer to improve his lot and for the State to own some of the agents of production without an invasion of the individual's sacred rights.

—Even a condition of that kind, Cash Carney said, would be completely alien to the American form of government and the spirit of the men who made America.

—Alien to the spirit of the America we have known, Mr. Shawnessy said. But the Declaration of Independence, like the Constitution, has to be rewritten by each generation, to have any meaning. The Civil War was the second American Revolution. And unless I'm much mistaken, in 1877, a third American Revolution had its beginning in the coalyards and train stations of this republic. The Strike of '77 was the Sumter of a new Civil War for Liberty and Union, a confused War fought by an Army leaderless and lost in darkness. Nevertheless——

—I don't know where you expect to get with this talk of Revolution, Cash Carney broke in. Most Americans know they're pretty well off, and like yourself, they sit on their tails and watch from the sidelines, while cheering a little for the so-called underdog. Meanwhile, by God, a few of us get out there and get the work of the Nation done. By Jerusalem, if some of us didn't keep the mills humming and the railroads running, you'd soon find out about your Revolution. You'd find yourself in the power of a bunch of ignorant dagoes that can't even talk good English, and you'd begin to wish you had back the good old America of Unlimited Opportunity for Everybody and the Protection of Home Industries.

—What a Century! the Perfessor said, suddenly leaning back into one of his gentle, nostalgic moods. And when you stop to think of it, we were there. We've been in on everything. When I look back on the Great Strike of '77 now, it seems incredible. As you say, John, it was like a beginning, an obscure and terrible dawn, which hasn't yet found its day. My God, where have we been heading, anyway? What did we think that we were doing? You remember, of course

July 21–22— How —1877

THE GREAT STRIKE

CAME UPON THE LAND IN THE FIRST YEAR

of America's second century as a nation. How it spread through the Republic in the summer of 1877, following the trunklines of the Nation's railroads. How it smouldered in the smoky yards of the Republic's mightiest cities. And how John Shawnessy saw the writhings of this belated Centennial monster, which the Exhibitors of Progress had wisely reserved until the other exhibits were dismantled and sent home.

No one anticipated the Great Strike or the form that it would take, least of all the men who made it. But the immediate cause was clear enough. The big railroad combines agreed to reduce the wages of their workers, and the workers, already living on bare subsistence wages, refused to work the railroads or allow them to be worked. The Strike began in Baltimore and spread like wildfire along the trunklines of the Nation.

Those days, America had made God in the image of a Locomotive. The people rebelled against God.

In July of 1877, John Shawnessy was still in New York, living by himself in a rented room in one of the dense apartment regions of the City. For two months, he had been exchanging letters with Laura Golden, who had taken her troupe on a tour of the West. Her letters were curious, hasty documents written from many cities, footprints of a woman flying from theatre to theatre, from hotel to hotel, pushing herself and her troupe to exhaustion over the rail lines of the Nation to keep her engagements. These words of Laura's were the first that he had met unaccompanied by her habitual smile and the veiled amusement of her heavily lidded eyes. He found in them a childlike, breathless quality, reflected even in the quaintly barbaric punctuation and spelling. The following letter, written late in the tour, was typical:

Johnny dear,

Well, here we are in Indianapolis. This is the hottest place we've hit yet—the theatre was packed tonight—balcony very restless. We were all tired from the trip down from Chicago.

You will be pleased to know—that I went out and asked the first inteligent person I saw if they were aquainted with Mr. John Shawnessy—and on being told—no—they never heard of him—I soundly berated them for their ignorence of Hoosierdom's greatest author—who I assured them was making his mark in the great City of New York.

Which I suppose is what you are still busy doing—dear. Do you still miss me? Your last letter was very sweet—I have it right here. I'm sorry to anser such beautiful letters with these dredful scrawls. Reading your letters I think I understand you better. If anyone can understand a man like you, dear.

Are you really sending me the Play? I'll get it in Pittsburg—can hardly wait and won't mind if it isn't finished. We'll have a reading when I get back.

All tired out and to bed—

In haste—

LAURA.

P.S. Excuse slips and spelling—morning now—very pressed for time. Rehearsing new play "Belle of the Beautiful West." Will open with it in New York I think. Sending out now to mail this atrocity—is that the way you spell it?

Passionately and perpetually yours—

LG

This letter, with the others, he read with intense care like a scholar trying to decipher a whole era of human life from a stone fragment covered with hieroglyphs. It seemed to him that these little documents were rich with unguessed meanings and that if he could unravel their apparently simple motivations he would find his way to the heart of the labyrinth in which the secret of Miss Laura Golden resided. The most barbed phrases were the simplest, such as, 'All tired out and to bed.' During the past year, there had been rumors to the effect that Miss Laura Golden's leading man, a rather large, gaudy actor named Mr. Timothy Duchet, was very high in her favor. Perhaps Mr. Timothy Duchet amused himself reading aloud in a stentorian voice the letters of Mr. John Shawnessy, just before retiring, all tired out, to bed. Or perhaps (and this was the most dreadful thought of all) Mr. Timothy Duchet and Laura would entertain each other with lines from *Sphinx Recumbent* before collapsing in mutual gales of laughter all tired out, in bed.

It was an agonizing period for John Shawnessy before he received a telegram saying:

JOHNNY AM STRANDED AT HOTEL ROMAN PITTSBURGH BY RAILROAD STRIKE STOP MR CARNEY HERE BUT TOO BUSY TO TAKE CARE OF LITTLE ME STOP CAN YOU TAKE CARE OF LITTLE ME STOP COME IF YOU CAN STOP EVERYTHING VERY EXCITING INCLUDING YOUR WONDERFUL PLAY STOP LAURA RECUMBENT

Around nine o'clock in the evening of Saturday, July 21, when John Shawnessy arrived with Professor Stiles in the lobby of the Hotel Roman after a hectic trip, Miss Laura Golden was anything but recumbent. Instead, she was regally erect among a great many valises, her usually pale cheeks flushed with heat and excitement, her mouth curled with indignation.

—Johnny, I'm so glad to see you! she cried. Things are in a dreadful state. All our props and costumes are in a car down at the yards, and they say no trains will move for days. I've got to get that stuff out and back to New York some way. You know I'm opening there Wednesday night at the Broadway, and I have a Ball scheduled after the show.

Other members of Laura's troupe, including Mr. Timothy Duchet, were standing helpless in the crowded lobby. Muffled explosions rumbled from the darkness of the City. The street outside was full of muttering throngs.

—What's the matter with Cash? the Perfessor said. I thought he owned the railroads in this country.

—O, he can't do a thing, Laura said. He says the strikers are very stubborn. There was a riot this afternoon down at the yards and the troops killed some people.

She stamped her foot irritably.

—After all, *I* didn't start the Strike, she said. I've always managed to meet my engagements, and I mean to this time. Johnny, you'll help me, won't you, dear?

Just then Mr. Cassius P. Carney came walking through the lobby followed by two other distinguished financiers. They were talking heatedly and consulting watches.

—Just a moment, boys, Cash said, spying Laura among her valises.

Hello, dear. Hello, boys. Well, all hell's blown loose down at the yards. Those Bastards'll stop at nothing.

He looked strangely happy.

—What's wrong with giving them their demands? John Shawnessy said. Anybody ever think of that solution?

—We can't afford to pay 'em the old wage. Only way to treat 'em is with cusswords and cold steel. We got more troops coming in tonight. Christ, you'd think the railroads of this country were being run for Those Bastards!

—Who are they being run for? blandly asked the Perfessor.

Cash ignored the question. He was licking his lips and weighing his watch. It was evident that he had a plan. John Shawnessy felt sorry for the Strikers, who in all probability didn't have a plan.

—See you later, dear, Cash said. Maybe we can get your stuff out some way later on. If it isn't burnt up.

—Burnt up! Laura cried.

—Yep. They say the Strikers are burning up all the property of the railroad, dear, and——

—And you just stand there, you great booby, fingering your watch?

—Honey, I can't do anything right now. Want me to go down there and get killed?

—Yes.

Cash was apologetic.

—When more troops come in, dear, why——

—Johnny, Laura said, striding to the door and stopping actresswise just before her exit, you've got to help me!

Cash was already on his way out by another door. He stopped and whispered,

—Take care of her, John. Damn female's crazy. Been that way all day. Can't do a damn thing with her.

—On with the show! the Perfessor said.

They caught up with Laura, who was walking with an undulant, unhurried stride straight toward the Union Depot of the Pennsylvania Railroad.

—I mean to get my props to New York if the whole world goes hang in the process, she said pleasantly enough.

It was a little after nine o'clock. In the direction of the yards, a flower of fire put scarlet petals into the night. The air had an old familiar smell to John Shawnessy, the smell of disaster, a stench of burning coal, wood, oil, the dead strong stench of hot metal, the stink of burning paint. A hot wind fanned his cheeks.

They cut over to where the railroad tracks flowed through the City in a broad band of rails, beaded with switches, engine houses, signal towers. But instead of getting free of the crowds, they found hundreds of people advancing in little squads slowly toward the fire. The fire seemed blossoming and spreading into a cluster of fires. Boxcars, sheds, buildings were ablaze. The tracks looked like the scene of a weird battle fought with huge, clumsy clubs. A wave of carnage had swept by, leaving corpses of boxcars, baggage cars, burst engines, gutted sheds. The ground was strewn with carwheels, couplings, brakes, twisted rods, blackened remnants of freight ripped out of cars and piled for burning.

Laura stopped and asked a group of men if they knew where any baggage cars for New York were.

—Ma'am, a man said, there ain't going to be any cars to New York.

—We'll see about that, she said calmly.

Closer to the depot, they found themselves mingled with an army of destruction. Strikers hammered on freight cars with great sledges. Men ran about with torches setting fire to everything combustible. Explosions ripped the darkness. The air rained fragments of fire.

—Who's in authority around here? Laura asked a man who seemed to be in charge of operations.

—There ain't any authority, he said. We're just tearin' the hell out of everything, Ma'am.

There was a burst of laughter. She tried wheedling him.

—If a lady wanted to get some personal things—of no value to anyone—out of a car that was going to New York—stage things—how would she do it?

—I don't know, Ma'am, the man said. What can you offer?

The men guffawed again. Something exploded in the darkness.

—Laura, the Perfessor said, ducking instinctively, you'll get us all killed, dear. For Christ's sake, go back to the hotel. John and I'll do what we can about your stuff.

As the scene had become more convulsed, Laura had become more poised and disdainful. She now looked proudly at the Perfessor.

—Go back yourself, *dear,* if you want to. I'm going to save my stuff.

A little farther on, they walked out from behind a line of boxcars into a clear space, in the middle of which stood the great roundhouse, squat, dark, and defiant.

—Now, see, Laura said. It's quieter here. Now if we can——

There was a blast of sound, and something hailed against a near-by boxcar. John Shawnessy grabbed Laura by the waist and pulled her down, rolling behind a low embankment.

With a silent, determined fury she turned on him, thrust him back, clawed at his arms, forced her way up to one knee. Her face, which he had never seen with any but a stage passion, was convulsed with real anger. There was no time to argue, as another blast came from the same source. Taking unscrupulous advantage of his strength, he seized her arms, hugged her and threw her down ungently. She writhed furiously beneath him.

—Damn you! Let me up!

—Give up, Laura, he said. That's gunfire.

The Perfessor crawled across her legs.

—Got you, dear, he said.

She made stifled sounds, twisting and panting under the two men.

—I'll have you both arrested! she panted.

After a while, she stopped.

—All right, you two great big cowards.

—Promise to stay down.

—All right.

They let her go. She sat up cautiously, panting, her hair dishevelled, her dress dirty. Her halfbared bosom heaved, shining with sweat.

Yelling, hundreds of men began to run out from behind overturned cars, sprinting toward the great roundhouse of the Pennsylvania Railroad. Spurts of fire came from the roundhouse. A confused shouting rose under its walls. Apparently the troops were inside, and the Strikers had made a breach. After a while, they fell back. There was a continuous rattling sound.

—Poor bastards! the Perfessor said. The soldiers have a Gatling.

A boxcar came careening down the tracks. Soaked with petroleum, spouting fire, it rolled solemnly against the barriered gates of the roundhouse. Another and another car followed flaming and the building began to burn.

—Doesn't it occur to you, Laura dear, the Perfessor said, that there are more important things at stake than your mouldy little props?

She ignored the question. In an interval of the firing, the two men pulled her up and ran to a safe place.

—What a story! the Perfessor said. I got to get a dispatch to my paper right away. Embattled Workers Defeat Troops! Unarmed Strikers Charge Into Concentrated Fire! Hundreds Killed!

At the hotel, the Perfessor tried to file some dispatches. Laura paced restlessly in the lobby, her face flushed, her eyes set. The Perfessor came back consulting his notebook, on which several names were scribbled.

—Been a lot of people killed, he said.

—Martyrs, John Shawnessy said.

—Small-print martyrs, the Perfessor said. Backpage martyrs.

He read aloud:

—John Fabrizio, a worker.
Henry Fisher, a plumber.
John Rowe, a young man.
Mrs. E. Keener, shot through the arm while standing in a doorway.
A little girl.

He flipped some pages.

—Suppose we go and call at one of these addresses I have listed here and get a human-interest story on the thing.

Maintaining a stony silence, Laura followed the Perfessor to the door.

John Shawnessy was appalled by the neighborhood through which they passed that night. Above the swamplike darkness, he saw the ragged shapes of factories. There was a palpitation in this darkness. It sighed with the respiration of the Workers, those who existed only that they might work. And passing, he saw their many faces, pale flowers in the fetid dark, colored with the fire that poured wavering tides of light over the whole industrial region. He remembered another dispossessed race whom Corporal Johnny Shawnessy (that brave young soldier defunct in battle) had seen in another burning city. The torch had been set again to the City of the Masters.

They found their address in a street of frame houses all alike and crammed together touching.

—This where the Fabrizio family lives? the Perfessor asked.

—Yes, sir, a little girl said. Johnny's dead. They brung him in about an hour ago.

As they went up the stair to the Fabrizio flat, John Shawnessy was ashamed of himself and his friends in their city clothes. His shame increased as they met the grieving mother, a stocky Italian woman, and stood in the stale, crowded flat. The Perfessor asked some routine questions. It appeared that the dead boy was only eighteen years old. He had simply been with the crowd at the railroad tracks and had been shot in a blind volley from the troops.

There was an appalling lack of privacy in this death. People kept entering and leaving. The room where the body lay was full of women weeping. When the visitors approached the bed, a sheet covering the head and shoulders of the dead boy was pulled back.

Alone of all the faces in this jungle of weeping, talking, grieving, hating, loving human beings, the face of Johnny Fabrizio was tranquil. It was a face unwasted by age or disease, and as such, reminded John Shawnessy of many a face he had seen in death during the War. It was not a handsome face, but death had touched it with a hand of sleep and silence, had left it without pain or anger or desire.

On the way back to the hotel, the Perfessor made a gesture, indicative of the swarming streets and deserted mills.

—Listen to them! he said. They can't win. A few of them get shot, and they shoot a few other poor bastards in uniform who are merely obeying orders. Meanwhile, Cash Carney and a gang of fat millionaires sit around a table in perfect safety and coldly lay a trap for them. All this shooting will antagonize the newspapers and the so-called American Public, more troops will be rushed into the City, the ringleaders will be arrested and probably strung up, and after starving a few weeks, these poor creatures will come crawling on their knees begging to be taken back by the companies at any price.

—But there are so many of them! John Shawnessy said. If they only had a leader and a plan, they might come out of this jungle and rule it instead of being ruled by it.

—See those factories! the Perfessor said. Someone has to work them. Accept life for what it is, boy, and be happy that it wasn't you lying there in that stinking room with a hunk of lead in your heart.

—But if we can just manufacture enough human beings in this country, along with the trains and the sewing machines, enough people of passion and indignation, we might get somewhere.

—That may be, the Perfessor said. All that may be so—but what will bring back Johnny Fabrizio? Well, anyway, the boy is being wept into his grave. Perhaps in this, the poor have their triumph—there are so many of them, and they feel so sorry for each other. My God, did you ever see so many tears! I don't suppose a pint of water will be poured on the memory of Jerusalem Webster Stiles, when the Great Mother gathers *him* to her loathsome bosom. And yet he was a not inconsiderable figure in his day, wrote verses that scanned indifferently well, composed a number of salty epigrams, even made a few feminine hearts flutter at a faster tempo. Pah—it's a dirty thing to die—to be dead! Life! Life! Well, I'll give Johnny Fabrizio a brief fame. He shall die on the front page of the Nation's greatest daily. Is that a small thing? Vanderbilt did no more. And they buried him—or was it Jim Fisk?—in a casket that weighed a ton!

When they got to the hotel around midnight, John Shawnessy took Laura up to her room. The lights were out in the upper floors of the hotel, and they had a hard time finding the door. He was about to say good night to her, realizing that for a while he had ignored her as much as she had him; but she turned now and leaned back against the door as if at bay. In the darkness he could barely see her face.

—You hate me, don't you, Johnny?

He was shocked by this question asked in a calm, matter-of-fact voice.

—Why—no. Of course not, Laura. I——

—You hate me, she said, because I wanted to get my troupe back to New York. No doubt I have offended your great pure innocent soul.

The words were cuttingly said in a distinct, lowtoned voice.

—I—why, no, Laura. I assure you. It's quite understandable—I—— I don't hate anybody. On the contrary, I——

—O, yes, she said. In a way, I'm not *good* enough for you, Mr. John Wickliff Shawnessy. And it's true. I'm not. Because I *hate* lots of people and lots of things.

—Laura, dear, I——

—You don't understand me at all, she said. You think you do, but you don't.

—I don't think I do, and I'm quite sure that I don't, he said fatuously.

—You saw those people, she said. You saw them—where they lived. Well, let me tell you something, Mr. John Shawnessy, those people are my people. Because that's where I came from. I came from all that!

She made a fierce gesture. Better accustomed now to the darkness, he could see her face. The mouth curled with contempt, the cheeks were deadpale, the eyes were long glittering slits. He touched her arms, as if in a gesture of self-defense.

—Take your hands off me, Mr. Shawnessy. I may not be good enough for you. But I know something that you don't know. I know that when you come from that, you get hurt, and it does something to you. I've been hurt plenty. I've seen men kill each other before. I *hate* the world of men. They have hurt me too and killed something in me. No man will ever hurt me again. I don't care for them—that much! I don't care for you either—Mr. Shawnessy—that much!

She tossed her head and snapped her fingers under his nose. The thing that always shocked him was that when women became outspoken, they became so terribly outspoken.

—Laura, he said, the world may have hurt you, but I haven't hurt you, have I?

—I read your play, she said. And I read your letters. If you don't understand me, neither do I understand you. You are the most maddening man, sir.

—I? he said. My dear child, I——

—Don't dear child me, she said. I know things that would make you pale.

The narrow eyes watched him. With all her powder and rouge gone, the scar on her lip was unusually distinct, a little white line in the deep flesh.

—As for the play, he said, I feel now as if I had left everything important out of it.

Suddenly, it was over. Her laughter reverberated in the empty corridors of the hotel. She seemed very much amused.

—Don't mind me, dear, she said, touching her temples and patting her tangled hair. You know I loved your play. And I loved your letters too. I'm not an easy person to understand, dear. I don't understand myself. All I know is that getting my troupe to New York and opening when I say I'll open are more important to me than anything in the world. Can you understand that?

He intensely disliked her for this remark.

—Perhaps.

—Don't think I'm heartless, dear, she said, trying to rearrange her bodice. Everyone has to have something to love. I've hardly ever had anything to love—to really love—that I *could* love. I've had my work. If I didn't have my work, then I'd be lost, wouldn't I? Everyone's lost, Johnny, don't you see? We're all lost, and we never find anything or anybody, do we, dear? It's like your play, hunting around for its Fifth Act. If I wasn't a trouper, then I'd be lost too—like all those people we saw today. They're all lost.

—They have each other.

—But that's all they have. And then they don't even have each other. Because they get killed.

He became aware that her eyes were fixed on him with a curious intentness.

—What gave you the idea for such a play? she asked softly.

—Laura Recumbent, he said slowly.

She continued exactly the same expression, but her voice was musical and mocking.

—But you haven't seen Laura recumbent. I haven't posed for you, *dear,* have I? You haven't had enough sittings—or shall we say recumbencies!

—I suppose not.

—Well, I'll make you a bargain, dear! I'll finish your play for you. You shall have a special performance of it—just for you—before the footlights and behind the scenes. Now what do you think of that? Would you like that?

He couldn't tell whether she was making fun of him or not.

—Of course. And when does the show begin?

—When I get back to New York, she said. All you have to do is help me get my things and get back.

—It's a bargain.

—And come around to the Broadway Wednesday night to the stage door after the show.

—I shall be waiting for you there.

—And escort me home to the Ball. Here.

She reached into the torn bodice and extracted a card that must have been prepared and placed there much earlier in the day.

—This will admit you to my dressing room. Good night, Johnny *dear.*

—Good night, Laura.

She poised her face for him to kiss, and because one thing she had said was indeed true and he wasn't sure that he didn't hate her, he barely touched her lips. Suddenly, then, he wanted to squeeze this languidly posed woman in his arms until she writhed. But already she was withdrawing. He heard the door close. It had been a very imperfect kiss.

The Perfessor was up when John Shawnessy got to their room. Cash Carney had just dropped in. He was waving a telegram sent by the Governor of the State authorizing a ruthless suppression of the Strike.

—Yes, sir, Cash said. Yessirree, we're going to whip this thing. My God, what kind of a country is it that can't protect the sacred right of the individual to own property, invest capital, and use his wealth as he sees fit? Where would we all be if it weren't for old Cash Carney, Jay Gould, Cornelius Vanderbilt, and other men of vision, who built those roads and gave America an iron roadway from sea to shining sea.

—The audience is invited to join on the chorus, the Perfessor said.

Cash looked out of the window toward the burning yards. He seemed to be apart from the scene, a lean, winged, lascivious god, peering down on a Homeric conflict without danger to himself.

—Don't they know it isn't us they're fighting? he said. It's the Law of Supply and Demand. Labor and Capital are complementary forces. *You* can't change it, and *I* can't change it. Let Capital alone and it'll provide as many jobs and as much money as the times allow. The comeback is certain all in good time. Thank God, we've got courts and congresses that understand these things. God, it'll be good to see the troops really come in and mash hell out of Those Bastards. Good night, boys. See you in New York at Laura's Ball. By the way, I located her stuff all right, and it's safe.

John Shawnessy couldn't get to sleep. He lay and listened to the explosions and distant shouts. It seemed to him that Humanity was in convulsion. While he had pursued his private dream, suddenly he had been permitted to glimpse a million faces pale in the redlit darkness and a million hands reaching for bread and completing the baffled gesture by making fists. They had been there a long time, they would be there a long time, and he hadn't really known it. Something blindly convulsive stirred like a buried titan beneath the pyramiding cities of America.

—John, are you awake?

—Yes.

—Me too, the Perfessor said. I keep thinking of that poor dead boy.

John Shawnessy lay there in the lurid dawn also thinking of the dead boy, Johnny Fabrizio, who had been dead now for ages and forever. And he thought of other dead men, comrades—marchers and fighters. He thought of Flash Perkins who had lain in the arms of Corporal Johnny Shawnessy (also dead), Flash Perkins, a Union soldier, a bloodstained recumbent form in the glare of a distant fire. Had mankind, then, come so very far from the Great Swamp that was the underside of Raintree County?

And as he lay there, he wound and unwound in his mind the skein of a life that was lived in the City and knew nothing but the City for a home, a life rooted in the shadow of the factories, flowering in a space of sunlight between the fences and the sheds where the great trains thundered day and night, living a brief while in the crammed rooms of the City, and returning suddenly into darkness, the same web of darkness and blind hunger from which it had arisen.

Then he thought of another creature of the City, a woman whose recumbent form lay voluptuous in the darkness in a room not far from his. And it seemed to him that he was moving slowly through a drama of gorgeous and confused rhetoric toward a climactic scene that would perhaps show to him at last the answer to his quest in the City.

The next day John Shawnessy and the whole party returned to New York. And in the days that followed, the newspapers reported the continuing of the Great Strike and the spread of it from city to city in the Nation's transportation system. The Constitution of the United States was invoked against the Strikers, troops were sent in to quell the riots, and the great republic that had come one hundred years along the Path of Progress went on bleeding, groaning, blaspheming, and mutilating itself as

IT BEGAN THE SECOND HUNDRED YEARS

ON THE ROAD

TO

—PERFECTION, the Perfessor was saying, isn't attainable in human institutions. When I say I prefer a Communist State, with all wealth vested in the People, share and share alike, I don't mean to say that we'll have the Millennium. Human beings seem to have an invincible talent for being unhappy under all forms of government. But by taking money and property away from the individual, you take away most of his power to do evil to himself and others. Three-fourths of human vanity is derived from property. Property, money, all symbols of personal wealth nurture the illusion that the individual amounts to something, that he has a permanent vested right in the earth from which all blessings flow, and that his dividends will go on forever in the land which the Lord God Mammon has given him. Even a little property makes him one of the chosen—with all the arrogance of the chosen. Property's a religion, and like most religions, succeeds in keeping its priests fat and few and its devotees many and hungry. And all of its dividends belong conveniently to the Future, which is known as Heaven or Prosperity for All.

—If equal distribution of wealth would make men happier and better, let it come, say I, Cash Carney said. But it won't. Instead of the present ten percent wealthy and ninety percent poor with a chance of improvement, you'll have a hundred percent poor and no chance of improvement. Why? Because man's a competitive animal. If we haven't yet reached a condition in which all the people are well off, it's because we're still building America and because the world keeps pouring millions of poor dagos into this country to enjoy the advantages of our system. We just can't catch up with all that poverty overnight.

—But the capitalist state will never catch up, the Perfessor said. It derives its very life from the current set up between the two poles of enormously hungry demand and enormously profitable supply.

—What do you think about this, John? Cash said.

—My economics is improvised—like the Republic's. Capitalism and Communism in their pure form are both contrary to the spirit of American democracy. They both make slaves out of men—slaves to economic principles. The Capitalist stretches man on the rack of Supply and Demand. The Communist sticks him in an economic class and tells him that history will look after him. Both appeal to the Nature of Nature for their principles. Neither Capitalism nor Communism was foreseen by those who founded America. The Declaration of Independence isn't an economic document. Jefferson wrote the economics out of it when he changed the classic formula of the time from Life, Liberty, and Property to Life, Liberty, and the Pursuit of Happiness.

—But, John, the Perfessor said, let's admit it—the Declaration of Independence is a wonderful old piece of scripture that hasn't any more resemblance to the truth of man's nature than the first chapter of Genesis has to the real beginnings of the earth. *We hold these truths to be self-evident: That all men are created equal.* Dammit, that's the most self-evident lie ever told! If you want truth, go to the *Origin of Species.* There we have the word of an honest scientist. Darwin cooked Tom Jefferson's goose for good and all. In fact, what is Communism but an effort to give some truth to the Declaration?

—The Declaration was true, Mr. Shawnessy said. The Signers spoke the language of moral beings, and what they said was true for the republic of men's souls. All men, as *men,* are created equal. Of course they aren't created equal as animals, as Darwinian contenders for life, as economic equations, as class-slaves and wage-slaves, as Proletarians and Capitalists. The Republic of the United States of America was intended as a government for *men,* animated by the virtues that we associate with mankind. This ideal republic was superimposed on the Darwinian Swamp, and the result has been this magnificent pageant of crusade and confusion known as American History.

Cash Carney consulted his gold watch. He fondled the solid, palm-smoothed lump of it in his left hand, pondering.

—It's all right for you fellas that have no responsibility to sit around and criticize, he said. But suppose you had gradually got involved, as I have, in the economic and political life of this Nation. Suppose you were one of the men who thought of building railroads through the West when there weren't any and took the necessary steps and the necessary personal risk to build 'em and operate 'em. Do you think you could ever have stopped anywhere along the line? Do you think I can stop now, with other men like me, who came up the hard way, trying to horn in on my holdings, trying to squeeze me out?

Cash was breathing hard. His eyes had a fixed stare.

—You talk of security, he said. I'll be perfectly frank with you. I never have had a feeling of security in this country. I haven't had any more security than the guy that throws the switch out there. I feel driven all the time. Anything that threatens the financial stability of the Nation threatens everything I have. I tell you, I don't feel I can let up one minute. Every now and then I look at myself and wonder how it all happened, and I realize that it's all just on paper and I'm just one weak bastard holding together factories, railroad systems, and whole cities by my single vision and my willingness to take risks. Believe me, boys, I have to feel that the Government is back of me when I do that. Even now, with this Populist agitation and these big labor outbreaks and the clamor for cheap money, I begin to feel the whole thing trembling crazylike. Sometimes I dream that I'm in the middle of my office in Wall Street, and all of a sudden people start coming in waving bills, bonds, mortgages, stocks, contracts, leases, demanding payments, deliveries, foreclosures. And I haven't any way to meet 'em. I haven't got a red cent. It was all a dream. And there I am trying to hold up the whole works all by myself, and the whole goddam business toppling around me and trying to crash.

Cash kept sucking on his cigar as he spoke, not aware that it was dead. He sucked harder and harder, stood up, his jaundiced cheeks hollowed with the effort, his eyes bulging. He took the cigar and threw it at the tracks and immediately went down into his pockets for another, as if something might happen to him if he didn't hurry. He got a light from the Perfessor, sucked his cigar to flame, and sank back on the bench. He was breathing hard and still holding his watch.

—Jesus! he said. I don't think I've had one minute of real peace since I left Raintree County. Tell you the truth, John, I envy your quiet life—yes, and your family, and all. Hell, those were happy days before the War when all I had was a feedstore to manage. Since then, it's been one goddam thing after another and nowhere I could let go. Other men can retire when they get old, but not me. I haven't any children to give my wealth to, and most of it's reinvested. O, of course, I suppose, if I had to, I could liquidate my holdings, sell out, and come up with a cold million or so to live on comfortably. But tell you the truth, I never was in it for the money exactly. You probably don't believe that, but it's true. It wasn't the money exactly. It was——

Cash leaned back.

Mr. Shawnessy and the Perfessor waited a long time for Cash to say what it was. Finally, Mr. Shawnessy said,

—It was the times. You just went along with the Republic. You're a poet of finance, Cash, and here in America you found your poet's paradise—a perfect playground for your type of imagination—great resources of land and labor, enormous vitality in yourself and others, the most fluid system of credit and finance the world has ever known. You took these ingredients and began to build your own republic, Cash, and you've built it around you like a cage. But of course you have to remember that there are other republics besides your own and that all of them are trying to mingle and become one Republic, which always seems to want to conform to the old pattern envisioned by its creators. We're beginning to reinterpret the Declaration.

—Ah, John, the Perfessor said, I see now, boy, that you were right to stay here in Raintree County. They ought to build a Chinese Wall around it so that you never see the ugly world outside. In America, boy, our old religion, our old morality, our old idealism are going to smash. Moses, Christ, and Plato are finally going to be buried in Oshkosh six feet under and packed down. Democritus and Darwin are going to come into their own. For here are your Americans, the race of dreamers, the idealists of government, and look at 'em! They're the most materialistic people who ever lived. How do they spend their lives? In accumulations. In blind, dirty grubbing for gold. Americans are the first people in history to get down on their knees and worship brute mass. Their idols no longer have a soul—or any particular form—which is, after all, the same thing. Why, they tell me they've started building a new type of building in Chicago called a skyscraper, and the idea seems to be to see how tall you can build it before it falls over. They say you shoot right up to the top in speedy elevators, and there's no limit to how high they'll go. Wouldn't surprise me if Americans went right on doing that, only worse.

The Perfessor bounced to a forward-leaning position and said,

—You believe in values, John. Well, let me tell you something. In America, we've found a quick way to express all values. Everything here fits into the price system. Everybody goes around wearing a pricetag of one kind or another. The looks of the dame you can afford to keep are a pricetag. The house you can afford to live in is a pricetag. The cigar you can afford to smoke is a pricetag. Your degree from the university is a pricetag. The books in your bookcase are pricetags. The color of your collar is a pricetag. The whole cockeyed civilization is a series of pricetags hanging out for people to read each other by. And life in America consists of trying to accumulate more and more spectacular pricetags. Everything is on the block in America and can be had for a price. Money will buy anything from a to zebra.

—Everything but truth, wisdom, beauty, goodness, Mr. Shawnessy said. And love, he added, feeling a little embarrassed as he said it.

But Cash Carney went on smoking, his eyes staring, his left hand fondling the gold watch.

—John, the Perfessor said, you're clinging to a way of life that's doomed. Go and look at the modern City. How can anyone look at it and believe in love? Or morality? Or the Eternal Ideas? Or the Inalienable Rights? How can anyone believe in the real existence of Raintree County, which you, dear boy and endlessly courageous dreamer, have taken as your image of the enduring values of human life? Yes, go and look at the City, and then look at your little Raintree County, child. Shed a nostalgic tear for it, because the City's going to eat it up. The God of the City is going to kill the ancient God of Raintree County, who has nothing but a couple of stone tablets and a golden rule for weapons.

—Still corrupting the youth, I see, Cash Carney said. Don't believe him, John. He's the same old Perfessor and hasn't changed a bit.

—What is this? Mr. Shawnessy said. A contest for my soul?

The Perfessor laughed.

—I don't know why it is, he said, but everybody was always trying to corrupt you, John.

Mr. Shawnessy slowly lit a cigar and watched the smoke ascend.

Good-by to Raintree County, incorrigible enthusiast of ideas. Good-by to the good small roads of Raintree County, the horse-and-buggy roads. Hard roads and wide will run through Raintree County, and its ancient boundaries will dissolve. People will hunt it on the map, and it won't be there.

For America will become the City. America will hunt for a tree of life whose fruit is gold. And that man shall be the Hero of the County who plucks from the high branches the heaviest dividends. And he shall get the most beautiful woman of the City, and he shall lie all night betwixt her breasts. And she will cheat him too, and cheat you too, because she is the City.

—Yes, the Perfessor was saying, in the modern City we can read the doom of our race. For in the City all the women are whores more or less. Some get cash on the bedhead, and the rest get a form of payment in installments called marriage. The City woman has learned to cheat you and herself and the race. Hell, it's really tough on an old bachelor like me, these days. There's no love left in the sex. They simper, vamp, and lead you on, and wear love's life out in sterile preliminaries. I tell you, the race is doomed. The bugs have it all over us and will win out in the end. The roach doesn't require a dowry before he gets his, and the common housefly doesn't insist on a church ceremony. But in the City of the Love of Brothers and the Shy Reserve of Sisters, everyone counts the Cost, and the Price is rising all the time, everyone counts and counts and counts the Cost, and the Price is rising all the time.

—About time for my train to come along, Cash said. Well, I see you two haven't changed much. Still carrying on your lifelong argument. By the way, John, before I forget it, Laura said she might stop off here by herself, next week sometime. Appreciate it if you'd put her up a few nights. Be perfectly frank, I don't know why she wants to—except to see you again, of course. I mean, she hates Indiana, says she'd just as soon live in a gopher hole. And, after all, Waycross isn't the most exciting place in the State for a woman like Laura.

—Of course, with John in it—— the Perfessor started to say, but immediately began to cough. I'm getting hoarse as hell, he said.

—Tell you the truth, Cash said, she told me to feel the situation out a little. So when you write the letter, John, don't let her know I told you. I guess you haven't seen Laura since the night of the big Ball in '77. That was some night.

—You can emphasize, elaborate, and repeat that statement, the Perfessor said, winking at Mr. Shawnessy. By the way, whatever happened to Laura's house on Fifth Avenue? That was one fancy pile.

—That's been gone a long time, Cash said. That land got so expensive, even I couldn't afford the tax. The whole neighborhood there is chockablock with office buildings now.

—That was quite a house, the Perfessor said. Remember that big stair right up the middle of it?

He winked at Mr. Shawnessy again.

—I don't clearly remember the way it looked inside, Cash said. You wouldn't believe the way rents are rising on the Rock right now. Christ, no one but Rockefeller or Carnegie could afford to have a house in that neighborhood now. Hell, some mathematical genius was computing what it would cost a man to pay the upkeep on a six-foot burial lot there in the center of the City fifty years from now, and I forget how many thousands of bucks it would cost you every year just to rot in that earth. Talk about your skyscrapers in Chicago—they ought to start building them that way in New York to save taxes on the land. It's the most expensive dirt in the world, and the Indians just gave us the whole island for a bottle of whiskey.

—They can have it back, the Perfessor said. They cheated us.

—Why, you wouldn't know that part of the City now, John, if you went back, Cash said. I think there's a bank right there where that house of Laura's was. It's really fierce what things cost you nowadays. And the Cost just keeps rising all the . . .

Time, time, time. The Cost keeps rising all the time. They build much taller buildings now, and instead of stairs they go shooting straight up in elevators. But do they still find a Forbidden Room on the top floor?

What was I seeking up that stair? What was I doing up there anyway?

For I was lost among the moneychangers. I wandered in the chambers of a gilded age. I wanted to find love even in the City, where the trains are always changing in the station and the Cost is rising all the time. For I had faith even in the City, heard its seductive language, thought that its meanings were my meanings.

And now if I went back, would I ascend the Grand Stair again? Would I want to taste the City once again from its red mouth smeared with ointment? And now if I went back, would I retrace the last steps of my gilded days? O, would I walk down streets and streets to find my little City sweetheart

July 25— **Before the Footlights and Behind the Scenes** —1877

of New York City, Miss Laura Golden had promised Mr. John Shawnessy a private performance on their return from Pittsburgh. Just what she had in mind, he didn't know, but his curiosity had become an obsession by the time he arrived before the Broadway Theatre on Wednesday evening and read the playbill announcing:

A BELLE OF THE BEAUTIFUL WEST

Starring Miss Laura Golden

and a Distinguished Supporting Cast
Also
'The Mississippi Minstrels'
Minstrel Comedians
and
Burlesque

His excitement increased tenfold when he sat in the steepwalled womb of the theatre looking at the drawn curtains, shrouded entrance to a world of mystery and revelation. When at last the curtains rolled back, he watched the vulgar pomps and promenades of the supporting numbers as if they concealed some wondrous secret—young ladies of the burlesque, clad in a travesty of Greek costume, giving the audience saucy glimpses of legs and breasts; corkblack comedians grotesquely clacking their lips in tiresome jokes.

And when the main show started and the Heroine, Brave as she was Beautiful, rode out to conquer with her Virtue and her Beauty the Untamed West, he felt that he saw a drama greater than its stage, an emotion stronger than its gesture—and as such typically American. Costumed America seemed incapable of any but tinsel gestures before the footlights, but behind the scenes a greater drama strove like a buried titaness, convulsive in her bonds.

Outside the theatre, he went by a side alley around to the Stage Door, where several gay gentlemen were pressing for admittance. He showed a card and was admitted behind the scenes of the Broadway Theatre.

He walked through the dim, cluttered world out of which were born the painted postures that he had been watching. Here the colossal artifice of the theatre became nakedly plain in the daubed faces of the women, the white necks of the Negro comedians, the cheesecloth backdrops, the mouldy canvas tombs, the echoing vault filled with platforms and cables where the stage crew toiled at swinging ropes like mariners in a crazy ship.

In the cellared world beneath the stage he found a door with the sign

MISS LAURA GOLDEN

and knocked.

—Who is it?

The voice had come to him musical and muffled, as from a cave.

—John Shawnessy.

—Come on in, dear.

He opened the door. There seemed to be no one in the little dressing room.

—I'm back here, Laura said, speaking from behind a folding screen. Just make yourself at home. How was I?

—You were completely lovely and charming, my Little Belle of the Beautiful Unwest.

He heard her laughing above a silken rustle of clothing.

—You know, he said, I've never been behind the scenes in a big theatre before. This is the real theatre of course. Most of our life is lived behind the scenes, don't you think? Only now and then we manage to get the right props together, smear our faces with make-up, and appear briefly for a little playacting. My own life, I'm sure, has been a rehearsal for a big show that never quite came off. Pardon me—I sound like the Professor tonight. I'm a little sad.

—Don't be sad tonight, dear, she said, her voice thrillingly distinct behind the screen.

The walls of the little dressing room were thick with photographs, pictures of Miss Laura Golden in various roles that she had made famous. One picture in especial took his fancy. A penned inscription at the bottom said

Daphne Fountain, 1865.

The girl in the picture was rather thin, with great eyes in a broad, sharply contoured face. She was standing in half-profile looking back over her shoulder. Something about the posture and the girl's eyes gave him a dreadful start. He passed his hand over his forehead.

—What are you doing out there, dear?

—Looking at pictures of you. Are they all you?

—Most of them.

—You look like a hundred different women.

—I am a hundred different women, dear.

—I like this one taken in 1865. That's the girl I almost met in Washington.

—I was skinny then. You would like me much better now, dear.

He stood for a long time studying the pictures, listening to the sound of a woman dressing behind a screen. The secret of a soul lay feline and recumbent in the mystery of the passing years, elusive in a gallery of faded photographs.

—Here I am, dear. Let's go.

She came out from behind the screen. Her gown was a black velvet trimmed with gold, drawn very tight at the waist, following and flowing on the curves of her hips and thighs. From this black dress, her neck, arms, and shoulders shone with a sensual pallor. Little gold balls swung from her ears. She wore a heavy gold ring set with a black stone. Her red mouth glistened with ointment. Her face, her full cheeks, her forehead had a kind of pale radiance in the bad light of the little dressing room. He had never seen anyone look so costumed, so contrived. She looked impossibly, stonily beautiful.

He could not repress an exclamation.

—Laura!

—I knew you'd like it, she said, supremely conscious of his admiration. An Egyptian touch—for our play, you know.

She led the way up the stair. In the darkness, he could see only her white neck and gold hair and the beginning of her back with its graceful furrow. He followed this floating disembodied head, faint in the scent of her perfume. Backstage, the lights were out except for a single gasjet. Everyone had already gone. Turning, Laura tossed her head triumphantly.

—This is my world, Johnny! she said. Here I am queen!

She led the way through the wings out upon the stage, still set with the closing scene, dimly illumined through joints in the scenery. Her face was a pale moon floating in this nocturnal world.

—The West! she said. It's ridiculous, isn't it, dear! My whole life is just make-believe. But it's only by making believe that I've become anybody at all.

She seemed preternaturally excited.

—Let's take a curtain call, she said.

Together they pressed through the drawn curtains. Beyond them was the pit, empty of spectators, a great cave of shadows. He couldn't see her face at all now.

—You see, Mr. Shawnessy, this is the way *I* express myself. You sit in a room and make your gorgeous words and think your noble thoughts. And I—I go before the footlights and become a hundred different women.

—In order to keep from being whom?

—Myself, maybe.

She had been speaking in a great stage whisper, of which there were innumerable repetitions in the empty theatre. She was hovering very close, enunciating her words almost in his ear with wonderful distinctness.

—You know, dear, she said, I do believe that everyone has gone home. We're quite alone.

Yes, they were quite alone, quite, quite alone, he and someone on an empty stage. Suppose now he fulfilled one of the ancient images of his life and took this woman in his arms. What better place to enact the beautiful audacity of love than the stage of the Broadway Theatre? But he was paralyzed by a strange anxiety. He was afraid of this woman who walked beside him in the dark. It seemed to him that if he were able to illuminate her face suddenly, he would find that it was the face of someone he had forgotten or someone he had dreamed once in a dream or someone he had never seen before and would never see again. It might even be the face of someone who was dead.

—Johnny, she said, you're strangely quiet.

—We're in *your* world now, Laura. You talk.

—All right, she said, I will. In your play, you have the hero attempting to realize an old image—that of finding a little actress waiting for him in a costume closet, someone to love in the great modern City.

—Yes?

—And the woman who comes to symbolize his passion is a woman of a hundred masks and moods.

—Yes?

—But some innermost part of what she is is hidden—kept, as it were, in a Forbidden Room.

—Yes. I suppose each of us has a Forbidden Room, containing some photographs, some things that we'd rather not have the world see.

—You, too, Johnny?

—Yes. But here, we talk about you.

—Well, suppose you were baffled by someone and that someone gave you a key to her Forbidden Room, do you think you would understand her any better?

—Perhaps.

—Where are you, Johnny? I can't even find you.

He felt her cool hands catching at his, and his own hands touched her smooth arms and slid on the warm velvet of her back, his face brushed her sideheld head, her hips pressed momentarily hard against him, his foot tripped on the curtain, she seemed to elude him in the folds, her laughter was vaguely repeated in the darkened theatre.

—Come on, silly man, she said. We're late for the Ball.

Not until they were outside the theatre and riding in a carriage did he make fully sure that while they had touched each other on the stage, she had indeed thrust the key—a small plain one—into his left coatpocket.

On the way, they passed a square where a mass meeting was being held by people in sympathy with the Railroad Strike. He put this other world out of his mind, and he pressed his hand deep into the pocket of his coat, holding the little key.

In the ballroom of Laura Golden's house on Fifth Avenue stood Professor Jerusalem Webster Stiles presiding at the punchbowl. Everyone was chattering about the Strike. John Shawnessy felt that he had stepped once more into a cheating stageset briefly peopled with these women in flamboyant gowns, these men in tails and ties.

But the world out of which this playlet had been engendered—the world Behind the Scenes—was simply the nocturnal City—its strewn alleys, gaslit parks, belching factories, masted harbor—where people toiled namelessly through dingy nights and days so that from time to time this waxen flower of gaiety might bloom briefly Before the Footlights.

Cash Carney appeared striding among the dancers with a rolled newspaper in his hand. Everyone gathered around him to know the latest news of the Strike.

—Public opinion is beginning to react in our favor, he said. My old friend Senator Garwood B. Jones made a humdinger of a speech yesterday, and it's quoted in all the evening papers.

Cash opened the paper and read a little from Garwood's speech. The Statesman from Indiana, serving his third year in the United States Senate, had begun by challenging any man to show more genuine concern for the welfare of the Common Laboring Man than he, Garwood B. Jones. But it was one thing for the laboring man to ask for a better wage, and it was quite another thing for a mob of hoodlums, incited by foreignborn bombslingers, to rape, burn, and pillage the fairest cities of the Republic. He, Garwood B. Jones, would be doing a disservice to the thousands that had made him their spokesman . . .

—By God, he knew he'd better get up and have his say, Cash said. We pumped a cold fifty thousand into his campaign fund.

The newspaper was passed around, and people read the Senator's address.

—Yessirree, Cash Carney said, and that isn't all. I have it on the highest authority that this thing will be killed and killed dead in a matter of days.

Mr. Carney stayed another five minutes and then, looking at his watch, spit a cigarbutt in an ornamental urn, and left.

—Jesus, the Perfessor said, doesn't Laura look stunning tonight! Ah, John, tell me now, where do they all go, these lovely girls, these lushloined girls! *But where are the snows of yesteryear?* John, I'll tell you a secret. The mistress of this mansion is mad about you.

—What makes you think so?

—I've talked with her since we got back from Pittsburgh, and we talked about you. She has you on her mind. You baffle her.

—We baffle each other.

—I swore on my mother's grave that I wouldn't tell you a word of all this, so keep it under your hat. But she asked some very searching questions about you. Unless I'm losing my acuteness, you're a candidate for initiation into that room on the top floor.

—Where is this famous room?

—Third floor up. Last door on the left, the Perfessor said. Once when I was here and no one was watching, I slipped up just for the hell of it and went all over the house. I found the room all right, but I couldn't get in. It was locked. You see, I too have knocked. But to him who knocks it shall not be opened. And he who seeketh not shall find.

Just then Laura approached.

—I want you two big cowards to come with me, she said.

They followed her into an alcove off the main hall where a glass decanter full of a pale green liquid stood on a table. She poured three wideglobed glasses brimming.

—There, she said. Just for us three. A toast.

—To what? the Perfessor said.

—To Johnny's play, she said.

Her eyes widened and then narrowed to their habitual heavylidded languor as she raised the glass and drank it off. John Shawnessy thought he never would drain the deep green pool of his glass. It had a taste of licorice and fire.

—Ouch! the Perfessor said, Where did you get this stuff, dear?

—It's something from France, she said.

—Hmmmm, the Perfessor said, pouring himself another glass. Pass this stuff around, and we'll have a Roman Holiday here.

—It's quite harmless, Laura said.

She poured herself another glass and drank it. She poured John Shawnessy's glass full.

—There now, she said, this is just for us. It's a special night.

—I can *see* that, dear, the Perfessor said. Laura, you're *damnably* beautiful tonight.

He bowed gravely to her and then allowed his thin form to move sedately around her, like a starved satellite revolving around a plump-bodied planet. She remained calmly posed, head thrown back. Still bowing gravely, the Perfessor backed out of the alcove.

Alone with Laura, John Shawnessy suddenly had a strong desire to escape. His head swam. He leaned against the wall to steady himself. He expected her to say something, but instead, she pressed the full glass into his hand, and looking back over her shoulder, she stood a moment at the door, her face proud, challenging, defiant, enigmatic.

He left the alcove and entered the hall. A great stair, ten feet wide, flanked with marble balustrades and cushioned with red plush, rose without a turn to the second floor. The hall was empty.

On a sudden impulse, clenching his fist on the little key, he ran two steps at a time up the Great Stair, as though he were being pursued. On the second floor of the mansion a few lights were burning. It was after he had started up a narrow stair to the third floor and was almost hidden in the darkness of it that the Perfessor passed along the secondfloor hall below with a woman giggling on his arm. John Shawnessy was sure that the Perfessor's black, busy eyes had seen him.

There was a window at the landing halfway up to the third floor. Looking out, he saw the jet of a fountain falling on a melancholy group of iron gods and goddesses, saw parallel iron spears of the fence hugely repeated on the lawn by the glare of a streetlamp. Stretching beyond and away was the City, a tenebrous, winking world of roofs and chimneytops.

On the third floor he made his way down the lighted hall to the farthest door on the left. He found the knob and the keyhole, fitted the key in and turned it. After all, he had been given permission. The door opened noiselessly, and he stepped in. He gave a violent start.

A great many people seemed to encircle him in a room palely lighted from the hall and the streetlamp outdoors. Suddenly he realized that the room was walled with mirrors. In fact, it was not a bedroom at all—at least in the usual sense—but a kind of little private theatre with its own little stage and an audience of receding mirror reflections.

It seemed to him then that the woman who had teased him with the enigma of herself during his sojourn in the City had given him at last a revelation of herself. It seemed to him that perhaps with the little key he held in his hand he was touching that naked, unpredictable thing—a human soul.

Baffled, he seated himself in a large chair facing the small stage and waited. Slowly the echoes of the Ball expired in nether chambers of the mansion. How little, after all, his world and Laura Golden's had overlapped! She was still to him a sphinx recumbent. As this woman, of whom indeed he knew so little, lingered on the threshold of becoming real, she became still more enigmatic. A disturbing question flickered in his brain. Had all those rumored lovers really come to this private theatre on the third floor, or was the innocent hero from Raintree County perhaps the only one who had reached so far?

At any rate, she herself had offered this rehearsal and dénouement of the play they had jointly written. Doubtless the last act was to be simply her charming amenity of surrender.

He felt vaguely alarmed and unhappy. He no longer desired to finish the play. A memory of Raintree County and another scarred young woman came to him like a sad-eyed protectress. He had a great desire to escape from something, to sleep. The beverage he had drunk and the smell of the room—an odor of theatre ointments—drugged him cruelly. The voluptuous chair heavily embraced him. Of course, he must stay awake. Under the circumstances, it wouldn't do at all for him to go to sleep. Besides, the train would be stopping soon, and he could get off and stretch his limbs. Yes, the train would be stopping, and he would get off for that rendezvous in . . .

The trainshed of the Pennsylvania Railroad was an enormous room with exits in distant corners. On the footworn floor men, women, and children flowed in tidal rhythms to intersections beyond the station walls. Dreaming, he saw a woman leaning on an upright girder. He started toward her, but her face, which was without precision, dissolved into the thousand faces of the crowd, and he was walking in a park of soft lawns where fountains made green jets of coolness in the air. Thousands of healthy, enterprising Americans were hurrying to see the Grand Ceremonies. He consulted his guidebook.

VOICE OF GUIDE

golden and masterful,

—The banners of the Modern Age triumphantly unfurled!
Centennial Exposition of the Progress of the World!

CENTENNIAL LADIES

in strophes of song,

—He sought the gaudy goddess of the re-redundant curve
In the scintillating city of unsisterly reserve!

He joined the seeking thousands as they walked through clanging gates to see the last great exhibit. But the day darkened suddenly. . . .

A great rose of fire burned in the middle of the railroad yards. It was night. A pale horde marched past him, men and women.

MARCHER

a blurred face in the darkness,

—*Quo vadis?*

He turned then, remembering brown decades, squat temples erected to degenerate gods, lewd pomps and prurient games in a mammonloving republic. These pale faces marching in darkness were being sacrificed to make a Roman Holiday. Joining the throng, he walked at their head, leading the way across railroad tracks half-buried in sand under the balconies of a coliseum. Chariots thundered ceaselessly on the circular track, voices cried blood and death, bodies were torn and trampled on the course beneath the wheels and hooves of hurrying chariots.

CROWD

ranked in tiers of seats, yelling with thumbs down,

—Give them to the beast! Blood! Blood!

EMPEROR JUSTINIAN WEBSTER STILES

leaning from the imperatorial box, pale temples wreathed in vine-leaves, hands hanging languidly down,

—I've done all I could, boy. But you know the Populus Americanus as well as I do. They *will* have their little pomps and games. After you've been suitably mangled, I'll see that you get a write-up on the front page of the *Sol Quotidianus.* How about it, Senator, can we get this boy off?

SENATOR CIGARIUS BOVOCACUS JONES

toga, cigar,

—No one is more concerned about the lot of the Common Man than I. But I wouldn't fairly represent the thousands that have made me their spokesman if——

LAURA GOLDEN

costume of Empress Theodora, in Roman attitude of accubation,

—You are the most maddening man, dear.

The gates under the imperial stand opened; a blacksnouted locomotive roared out, bell clanging, and ran butting hither and thither in the darkened arena. The rim of a volcano glowed scarlet in the purple night. Death rained on the City. Doomed hands clutched skyward. Troops, strikebreakers, Pinkertons ran about clubbing, shooting, raping.

CROWD

in streets, voices fading,

—God is dead! God is dead! . . .

In Machinery Hall, an odor of decayed flesh floated off the couched bodies of the machines. Stained light filtered to the cold stone floor. A locomotive lay on its back under the chancel. The wreck of its dinosaur bones thrust through the rotting rind.

REPORTER STILES

—To understand this life in all its aspects, Before the Footlights and Behind the Scenes, one must take a little verbal tour with us. . . .

Backstage in the Broadway Theatre he wandered waiting for his cue, trying to remember his part in the play. Standing on a darkened stage, he saw the pale faces of the audience ranked in receding balconies to the sky misted with stars. Apparently it was a performance of his own play, though he hadn't sufficiently rehearsed it and couldn't even remember his own lines. He was wandering then backstage, hunting for the young woman who had the leading female part. He heard the sound of a train passing in the night. In the far places of the City, across the stony squares and vacant lots steeped by the pale moon, the whistle of the train was loud. The train was rushing from the City, the funnel was a flare of fire, the passengers were homeward-going. He thought of the place where the great trains came to rest, vast sheds of lonely sound, and there among the shapes of steel, the strikers moved, a wan horde waiting for the light. . . .

Somehow he had come to be in an Egyptian temple where stone idols to lascivious gods stood between brownstone columns. Priestesses naked except for belts of the brown tobacco leaf scattered gold coins at the base of an idol of pure gold, which, changing slowly, became Mr. Cassius P. Carney, the high priest of the temple, in ceremonial robes stained with tobacco juice.

PERFESSOR

small potbelly, wearing a Saturnian mask, revolving on goatsfeet around a statue of the Venus Callipygos,

—Goddess gaily unbedight,
Will you be my moon tonight?
Beck and quip and dance and nod
For the jolly Roman god?
Saturn's self entreats thy tail,
Goddess eminently frail!

The broad stone steps rising to the altar became narrower as he ascended. A noise of telegraph keys sounded far off, monotonous, disturbing. It seemed to him that perhaps he was climbing a spiral stair that the sceneshifters mount, or perhaps it was the tower of the Raintree County Court House. The ticking noise grew louder.

VOICE

waning down the corridors, musical, lonely,

—Beautiful river and change everlasting. The clock is ticking in the tower. Have you seen from a window (as you hurried up the narrowing stair to the third floor), have you perceived how the late pedestrians hurry home, and how their footfalls hollowly reverberate in the hushed lawns of the City, and have you seen the sad glowing of the lights—and their extinction one by one?

PERFESSOR

appearing in medieval jerkin and hose, peaked sandals, having the sad, lecherous, pointed face of François Villon, reciting,

—Where is the maiden whose long hair shaken
Over her shoulders was ravendark,
Whose dreambound spirit would not awaken
Because of her body's scarlet mark?
And where is she that was lost on the dark,
The mystic water of love's old tears—
A white oar driving a drifting bark?
But where are the rains of the rivered years?

Sickness of love flowed up his loins. Floor after floor turned dizzily beneath him. He seemed to be walking through galleries of photographs, and the many and many faces of the beautiful young women of his memory silted like leaves around him. The noise of the clock had become a hard, tapping sound, rhythmical and mocking. And even after it had stopped, it seemed to reverberate in his dream for a long time. He kept listening for it and trying to awaken. . . .

Slowly he became aware that someone was calling his name.

—Johnny! Johnny!

He awoke from the dream, aware that while he had been sleeping he had heard the noise of footfalls on the stair, a hard, pointed sound rising through the dark empty halls and chambers of the City, approaching the door. He started up immediately and left the room of mirrors. At the head of the stair, he met Laura Golden, breathless, holding something in her hand.

—It's a telegram for you, Johnny, she said. It was left at your lodgings and a friend brought it over here. It must be something important.

He tore open the telegram, read it, and handed it to Laura. Together they began slowly to descend the stair. He had been recalled to Raintree County.

At the door of Miss Laura Golden's mansion on Fifth Avenue in New York City, Mr. John Shawnessy lingered a moment. The woman, who had perhaps loved him and whom he had perhaps loved in a rather characteristic Raintree County way, held up her face for him to kiss. This time it was he whose lips were cold and passionless, while the mouth that clung a moment hungrily to his was the mouth of a woman distraught with passion. It was a very imperfect kiss.

—Come back, Johnny, she said, when you can, and we'll give the play a more pleasing dénouement. I'll wait in the wings for you—if need be—forever.

This beautiful invitation was in fact a farewell, for Mr. John Shawnessy returned immediately to his lodgings, packed his belongings, and boarded the first train home.

And so he said good-by to the City, carrying in his luggage some hieroglyphs and indications of a soul—the memory of an unexplained but perhaps not inexplicable woman—Laura, whose stately name had become his symbol of the City. And as for his play, well, he would leave it unfinished, without its fifth and climactic act, deciding that he hadn't made a very good job of it anyway. He had only approached and barely touched the real self of the woman who had inspired the play.

Around him now, as he looked from the departing train and saw a last gray dawn rising on the City, he imagined a whole republic of men drowning in neglect and hunger, desperate and lost—as Miss Laura Golden had been, hunting for love and something to believe in through a universe of receding mirror illusions. Who was to help these drowning millions? Was there no hero to stand up each time a human being held out a hand in panic from the swallowing night, and say, Here, take my hand. *By God, you shall not go down!*

For his part, he had been seeking the Tree of Life as an act of self-glorification. In affirming himself, he hadn't affirmed the best part of himself—Humanity. Meanwhile, he carried in his pocket a message from Raintree County, recalling him to himself again, a message that had come down all the wires and the ways of the world since the world began to find him unerringly in the City

AND AWAKEN HIM FOREVER

FROM HIS

CITY

—DREAM on, boy! the Perfessor was saying. It's all a great chamber of self-reflections that you've constructed.

Mr. Shawnessy was startled by the coincidence, wondering if the Perfessor had ever been in a certain room himself on the top floor of an ancient brownstone mansion, now a bank with gilded letters. He was wondering if, for that matter, Cash Carney had ever been there, or whether it was only the innocent hero from Raintree County who had got so far.

But the Perfessor gave no sign, and Cash Carney was putting his watch in his pocket.

—There she is, he said. Right on time.

An eastbound train was coming.

—Well, boys, Cash said, standing up, it's been nice to see you two anarchists again. Don't let this old devil corrupt you entirely, John. If you see Laura, tell her——

The telegraph operator came out of the Station, with a paper in his hand.

—Special message for Mr. Cassius P. Carney, he said.

Cash took the message and read it.

—Well, I'll be goddamned! he said.

He handed the message to Mr. Shawnessy and began to stroke his little ballshaped beard. His eyes burned with apostolic fervor. Mr. Shawnessy and the Perfessor read the scrawled dispatch:

> HOMESTEAD SITUATION VERY THREATENING STOP RUSH HELP STOP GET HERE FAST STOP WE NEED YOU

Cash retrieved the message, crammed it into his pocket. His face muscles twitched. He took out a new cigar, viciously bit off the tip.

—Now, let me see, he said, fixing his eyes on a distant point. I can get two or three hundred men through my agency in Detroit, and they'll be in Pittsburgh day after tomorrow. Now, then——

The train had been approaching all the time, and Cash was walking down the platform, trying to light his cigar while Mr. Shawnessy carried his grip for him. Cash was like a general, calling on his reserves, throwing them into a battle that he would never see himself, except from a distant hill. He had a match to his cigar. The train roared up and stopped, trembled, spat steam, howled, like a black hound held in leash.

—So long, Cash, Mr. Shawnessy said. I'm not sure that I'll be able to invite Laura to see us because——

—Those Bastards never will learn sense, Cash said. I'll get a couple hundred toughs down from Buffalo. That dick in Philadelphia ought to be able to scrape up something. And——

Mr. Shawnessy handed the grip to a Negro porter who had jumped down, bowing and smiling at Cash.

—Good-by, Cash, Mr. Shawnessy said. Just take it easy. Stop worrying. Remember there are only several hundred thousand men on the other side.

Cash didn't hear the remark. He paused before the open door of a coach, while the engineer hung out, impatient for the start. Cash leaned forward, trying to get his cigar to burn. He was still talking between puffs.

—Take several days—puff, puff—to bring in a carload of strikebreakers from New York. If we can hold the lid on till then—puff, puff—Those Bastards will find out who's——

The cigar glowed and Cash threw the match down, stepped briskly up on the platform and turned. One hand was hooked in his vest holding his coat back from the gold watchchain; he waved his cigar with the other.

— . . . boss around here, he said, on a crisp crescendo. Good-by, Perfessor. Good-by, John. Don't let anything happen to Raintree County, John. If you ever drop into Little Old New York, Laura and I'll be glad to put you up and show you a time.

He pulled out his watch.

—Five-fifty-six.

The train was moving.

A thin yellow man, dipped in a preservative acid, was visible only for a second, as he looked out from the moving wall of the train. Then the speeding coaches expunged the image of Mr. Cassius P. Carney, the Distinguished Financier, reading his watch.

—There goes, the Perfessor said, the most friendless person I know. Nobody loves him, including the woman he married. Say, do you really plan to invite her down?

—We're going to have a County Teachers' Institute at Paradise Lake starting next week, Mr. Shawnessy said. I'm in charge, as usual, and I doubt——

—You really ought to see Laura again, boy. What's the matter? Didn't you like what you found up the Grand Stair that night?

Mr. Shawnessy smiled a little sadly.

—I tried awfully hard, the Perfessor said, to blast my way into that room on the top floor, both before and after you left New York, but I never made it. What in the devil did she keep up there anyway? The bodies of her ex-lovers?

Mr. Shawnessy smoked slowly on his cigar.

—Damn you, boy, the Perfessor said. You can be the most uncommunicative person when you want to be. Well, you got back down anyway. You got out all right.

I wonder? In a way, I suppose I'm still up there, reflected and rereflected.

—I hate to beg, the Perfessor said, but I'm damn curious. Tell you the truth, I always thought there was something wrong with that woman. Maybe she had a harpy's body under all the fancy clothes. Hell, boy, you can tell me. I'll keep it out of my column.

—Professor, there are a few things in this world you'll never know or understand.

—All right, all right, the Perfessor said. After all, I wasn't born yesterday. Matter of fact, I was born a long time ago, and right now I feel every minute of it. What a devil of a day this is! Will it ever end? What's on the agenda now?

They were walking toward the National Road, passing the Post Office. Mr. Shawnessy remembered then the letter from Roiville he had picked up in the morning and hadn't yet read, but he allowed it to remain unopened in his pocket.

—Now for a picnic supper at Evelina's, he said. The Literary Society is entertaining, and you can be the Guest of Dishonor.

—I don't see how I can go through with it, the Perfessor said, coughing, unless I get a little more fuel. Mind if I stop off at your house and get another flask out of my suitcase?

—Not at all.

—The *Atlas* is at Evelina's, you know. By the way, boy, I suppose you know that woman's in love with you.

—Professor, you always exaggerate.

—Everything but you, the Perfessor said. People who believe my lies implicitly don't believe me at all when I tell the truth about you. Mrs. Evelina Brown is no ordinary butterfly either. I spent a good deal of time trying to collect that gorgeous specimen myself in New York a few years back. Well, I guess Laura came about as close to corrupting you as any woman ever will. Confess, it was just the body that you were after that time. We made a materialist out of you for a little while in Little Old New York.

Mr. Shawnessy heard the noise of the Eastbound Special, the Thunderer, as it went wailing toward a distant crossing, making its eternal sound of departure and . . .

Farewell. Arrivals and departures. And farewells. Farewells to cities of the East, and gilded days and dreams, farewells. To meet again is only to repeat an old farewell that means, I never can go back again to the City of my young manhood, my barriered wishes, and my gilded dreams.

Arrivals and departures. Appointments and reunions. But are not all farewells forever and everlasting? Is it not well, and very well to say farewell when one is young and never to meet again after the hair has faded from the temples and the innocent brightness has gone out of the eyes? Who loves an old man? And who that loved strength and beauty can love the shattered shape thereof? Ah, God, I have clung too hard to my youth. To become old is merely a form of resignation.

I went to the City a vagrant day. And I was many days in the City from a summer to a summer, and I was lost in the City like one who wanders in a dream. O, hero boy, did you then entirely fail to find the face that was waiting among the faces in the station where the cars were changing all the time, or did you see it for a little while in the City's winking night and gaslit chambers, where you were dreaming in a spell

Between Two Worlds

CONTENDING at the intersection, the Nation east and west and the County north and south, Esther Root Shawnessy was passing in the early evening, coming from the Schoolhouse, where she had stayed to help clean up after the Patriotic Program. She was thinking now that she liked Waycross best of the towns in Raintree County, perhaps because the National Road passed cleanly here through the troubled earth of the County, crossing the old boundaries, dissolving the old obligations.

Approaching the intersection, she watched Pa drive by in his buggy beside the Reverend Lloyd G. Jarvey. Pa saw her and nodded but said nothing as he and the Preacher turned north toward the Revival Tent. She had heard that there was to be a special meeting of some kind at the Tent tonight, but she hadn't been invited.

The warning Pa had given her earlier was in her mind. He had said that she would find out before the day was over that her husband was fooling her. All day she had vaguely wondered at the threat. Perhaps it meant no more than that the voice of scandal, easily raised in small towns, had accused some woman of being in love with Mr. Shawnessy.

If that was the case, Esther wasn't disturbed. She had always known that other women loved her husband. When she had been a little girl, the other girls had loved him, though of course none so passionately as she. Now that she was older and married to him, she still expected that other women would be in love with him. It was impossible to know him without being in love with him—or so it seemed to her. For that matter, Mr. Shawnessy might love other women—as he loved and admired Mrs. Evelina Brown. Whatever was virtuous, beautiful, and feminine, he loved. But as for his being to any other woman what he was to her, Esther considered the idea simply absurd. She used to wonder if she ought to be jealous of

Mr. Shawnessy's first wife and of other vaguely rumored loves of his through the years. But none of these associations had any reality for her. Mr. Shawnessy could no more cease to be her husband, through any act of his own, than her father could cease to be her father.

Her mood today had been tinged with more than sadness. It verged on fear and at times even panic. Once during the Patriotic Program, she had slipped out of the crowd to the parked vehicles and finding Pa's buggy, had searched it, hunting she knew not what. She had found nothing to frighten her except Pa's blacksnake whip, the handle standing stiffly from the whiprest. But then she had been unable to open the rear compartment, which was locked.

At the intersection, she looked south in the direction of the Station, where more than an hour ago she had heard a burst of band music and applause, indicating, she supposed, the Senator's departure. Now as two figures came from the Station, walking toward her, she recognized her husband and Professor Stiles and wondered what had happened to Mr. Carney, who had been expected to stop in Waycross and perhaps bring his wife.

The children, she supposed, had already gone on to Mrs. Brown's for the picnic supper, where she too must go as soon as possible to help prepare the food.

It seemed to her that all the important symbols of her life had gathered today in Waycross. A world abandoned long ago was trying to win her back. Her reason told her that she had made her new world so securely that nothing could take her from it. But some unregenerate portion of herself had never lost the instinct of return, return to her father's farm.

She had no desire to go back. The feeling was more dangerous than desire. It was the feeling of belonging, as if somewhere inside her a tough spring had been stretched out nearly straight and had to be held there by an effort, lest it spring back to the old shape. Even here where the broad road had given her a sunlit promise of a life far from the crooked county road that passed her father's farm, even here the old strife was joined again,

1877— A —1878

CONTEST FOR HER SOUL WAS WAGED BETWEEN TWO WORLDS

in the year that followed the Teachers' Institute at Paradise Lake.

One world was Pa's, wholly now and formidably his. Esther's mother, her sad, wistful, tired mother, died in December of 1877. Her brothers had all married and left the Farm. Her sisters, Sarah, Fernie, and even the youngest, Mollie, only sixteen, were busy being courted and were expecting engagements and early marriages. With these changes the family had assumed a new form, which had perhaps only been waiting for years to disclose itself. The ancient solidarity of the family now took its last refuge in the strong love of Esther and Pa. Pa consulted her in everything he did and gave her the place that had been her mother's in the old days.

During this year, she knew that her love for Pa was the most ancient part of herself—and as such unalterable. The round fair face, Jovian beard, now turning handsomely gray, black passionate eyes, mouth so terrible in its denunciations—all made an image in her life so old that it was no longer to be questioned or changed.

Perhaps her destiny was simply to live forever in this relation to Pa. Sometimes, even, there was a stern joy in the thought of such a dedication. Always she felt as though it would take impossible courage and sinful audacity to sever the ancient tie. Pa's will was right simply because it was his will, and she never questioned his right to keep her entirely to himself.

It was clear to her that Pa loved her more than anything else in the world, had always loved her more, far more, than he had loved her mother. His love was a somber, enduring fact. She didn't expect it to change. She would have been shocked if it had changed, as much so as if some morning on awakening she had found that Raintree County had turned into a desert.

But during the year after the Teachers' Institute at Paradise Lake, especially after her mother's death, there was a change in the way Pa expressed his love for her. He now could hardly bear to have her out of his sight, and when she was at the Stony Creek school, where she taught, she knew that he was thinking constantly of her. As often as he could, he came to meet her in the evening and rode home with her, asking her about her day as if he wanted to relive and repossess every minute of her. When he drove into town, he took her with him. At night before she went to sleep in the room that had been her mother's, he would wait until she was in bed, and then she would hear his heavy footfalls on the creaking stair, there would be a timid knock at the door, and she would say,

—Come in, Pa.

He would come in, always fully clothed. He would come over to the bed where she was now tucked in with only her face showing above the sheet. He would bend over without a word and kiss her mouth, and would pat her hand and hold it a moment, and then say,

—Good night, Esther.

—Good night, Pa, she would say.

Then he would get up and leave the room, firmly shutting the door. The ritual hardly ever varied, and had it varied even a little, Esther would have been deeply disturbed and perhaps even a little frightened, as any change would have meant some disturbing change in Pa.

She was bound as by great cords to the earth of her father's farm.

Nevertheless, there was another world in which she moved during that year and which she tried desperately to keep separate from Pa's world.

The other world had begun a long time ago when she was a little girl in her first term of school with Mr. Shawnessy. For a long time afterwards, only a memory persisted of that world, like voices faintly calling from a remote place. Then for two weeks in the summer of 1877 the voices had become loud and joyous; she had discovered their source one evening when a buggy carried her down sloping hills to a place of waters. For two weeks she had lived entirely in this rival world, had bathed in its green lifegiving pool, had become almost lost in its primitive serenity, had shared its images of beauty, goodness, truth. Then Pa had appeared dreadfully on the threshold of that world and had reclaimed her.

For Esther, too much happiness always had something forbidden and wrong about it. To be really good was to be a little unhappy and engaged in a task that demanded all of one's strength and somewhat more than one's inclination.

She knew from the beginning that there was no way of reconciling her two worlds. They were night and day, with no twilight between. They were stone and fire. They were earth and air.

Not long after the Teachers' Institute, Ivy Foster called on her and left a letter from Mr. Shawnessy, the first of many she was to receive and answer.

This letter all by itself was as strong as Pa's world. It brought back the memory of Paradise Lake. The very handwriting had the curving look of that other world, of its lifegiving foliage, luxuriant shapes, and springing forms. She read the letter over and over, hid it under her pillow at night, carried it always on her person, as a token, a blown leaf, unspeakably precious, of that other world. Of course, she concealed all knowledge of this other world from Pa, knowing the futility of making him understand it or accept it.

She answered Mr. Shawnessy's letter, and there were other letters. They were all very simple. His letters told her that he loved her and wanted to make her his wife in spite of all. They were full of images and recollections of Paradise Lake. Her letters said that she loved him, but that she didn't know whether she could ever come to him. In the earlier letters, he addressed her as 'Dear Esther,' and she addressed him as 'Dear Mr. Shawnessy.' In the later letters, he addressed her as 'Darling,' 'My Darling Esther,' 'Dearest,' and 'Dearest Pet.' She addressed him as 'Dearest One' and 'My Darling.' These forms of address seemed right to her, but she never called him John and knew that she never could. Such a thing was unthinkable.

After she began teaching the school on Stony Creek, she and Mr. Shawnessy managed to see each other secretly. He had the school at Moreland that year, and after school in the afternoons, the lovers would meet as often as possible at a deserted mill on the Shawmucky about midway between the two schools. They also left notes at the trysting place under a stone. Sometimes, too, Esther would be invited to dinner at Ivy and Carl Foster's, their house being only a half-mile from the Root house across the fields. Mr. Shawnessy would be there too, and all four would keep the secret. Ivy was

Esther's only confidante until somehow Fernie found out about the secret trysts in the spring; but Fernie—goodhearted, homely, talkative Fernie—kept her mouth shut and never breathed a word of the affair to anyone.

In fact, Esther never did discover who it was that found out about the secret letters and meetings and told Pa.

One day in April of 1878, she went to the trysting place to leave a note for Mr. Shawnessy. She knelt and placed the note under a stone close to the door of the old mill and was just rising when she saw Pa standing in the door of the mill not ten feet away watching her. He walked over and without a word lifted the stone and took the note.

—Pa, she said in a small desperate voice, please don't read it.

He opened the note and read it through. His face, usually red and bloated at moments of anger, was pale.

—Is he coming here today? Pa said.

His voice scared her as she had never been scared before because it was so dreadfully even and controlled. For the first time, she realized that Pa was fully capable of killing Mr. Shawnessy.

—No, Pa. I don't think so.

—How long have you been meeting him and writing to him? Pa said in the same low, quiet voice.

—Since September, Pa.

—Don't lie to me, Esther. I know about it anyway.

—I didn't lie to you, Pa.

—Where is he now? Pa said.

—I don't know, Pa. Please, Pa, don't hurt him. It isn't his fault. It's my fault.

Pa picked up the gun that had been leaning against the wall inside the mill and went around back of the mill where he had tied his horse. Esther looked at the long black gun with which she had often seen Pa knock a rabbit kicking.

Pa got on his horse and came around. She got on her horse. She kept running her eyes all over the fields and the paths of the countryside, praying that Mr. Shawnessy wouldn't appear, riding along in his abstracted way, his eyes bright and pleasant.

—If you kill him, Pa, she said, I'll kill myself.

—Why did you do it, Esther? Pa said, with a passion so terrible that it took all anger from his voice and made it break like a woman's.

—I love him, Pa.

Pa turned his face away. He was crying. Sobs tore his big frame. Esther was appalled. She had never seen Pa cry, had never dreamed that he could cry. She began to sob with him.

—Don't, Pa. Please don't.

Pa fought to contain himself, his big chest heaving convulsively.

—Please, Pa, she said. I'm sorry. It was all my fault. Honest, I didn't do anything but meet him a few times and write. I'll never do it again, honest. I'll stop it. Honest, I will, Pa. Please, don't—don't *cry* so, Pa.

At that moment, it seemed to her that the whole matter was irrevocably sealed and settled. There was nothing else to do but stop the whole thing. The way it was, Mr. Shawnessy would be killed or Pa would die or something dreadful would happen. This thing was bigger than she. It was Fate that she had loved as she had, and it was Fate too that she was doomed never to marry her love. It was Fate, Godappointed Fate, that she was to live forever with Pa. The pain of tearing herself away from him seemed at this moment greater than any conceivable pain of separation from Mr. Shawnessy, which would be a dull long pain, prolonged over all the years of her life until she died.

So she went home with Pa, and in sorrow, fear, and remorse remained for weeks a voluntary prisoner at the farm. As for Pa, he openly declared his intention to horsewhip John Shawnessy to death if he ever caught him around his daughter again.

Meanwhile, in the world outside, a number of remarkable things occurred that Esther didn't know about at the time.

To begin with, Mr. Shawnessy, who had always been regarded as an easy-going person in the County, showed unexpected fight. And his position in the affair was improved by a strange development.

In late April a letter came from Louisiana, saying that his wife had disappeared several months before from the private home where she was being kept and that although a diligent search had been conducted for her, she had not reappeared. There was some evidence that in her demented state, she had committed suicide, and cannons were fired over the Mississippi River in an effort to raise the body. News of this development had been unpardonably delayed in reaching Mr. Shawnessy, as his wife's family had kept expecting her to be found alive or dead. An action was instituted in a Louisiana court to get the woman declared legally dead, but the affair was pending and promised to go on for a long time. Mr. Shawnessy then boldly claimed the legal death of his wife on the basis of her disappearance. His case wasn't a strong one, but it was better than nothing. The way was as clear as perhaps it ever would be.

Mr. Shawnessy managed to get these facts to Esther by way of Ivy Foster. He said that he was ready to stand up before the world and claim Esther for his wife.

Meanwhile, Esther was being subjected to a different kind of pressure. Pa and other older people whom she respected had talked with her gently but firmly about the matter. They told her that no matter how strong it seemed to her now, her feeling toward Mr. Shawnessy was after all only a girlish infatuation. They said that from no point of view was Mr. Shawnessy a fit man for her. They said that he was an atheist and a no-account, ambitionless drifter. They said that he had had other shady affairs with young girls in schools where he had taught; and though the names of the girls were not named, some details of the affairs were given. They said that Mr. Shawnessy's own father had forced him to marry his first wife. They said that there was a bad streak in the Shawnessy family. It was no secret in the County that old T. D. Shawnessy was the child of an illegitimate union and had come to America to escape the shame of his bastard birth. Everyone loved the old gentleman—true enough—but there was that stain. Mrs. Shawnessy had been, as everyone knew, a wonderful woman, and no one had been more broken up than she by the failures and foibles of her brilliant but erratic son. They said that John Wickliff Shawnessy was an unstable, undependable philanderer, approaching middle age, almost old enough to be Esther Root's father, and once she got over the crazy infatuation she now felt, she would thank her lucky stars forever that she hadn't let herself get caught with him. They said that besides all that, her pa, who had loved and looked after her all her life, was alone in the world, now that his wife had died and the other girls were getting married and the sons had left, and she would break her pa's heart by making such a bad marriage. They said that anyway there were legal impediments in the way of such a marriage. They said that it was better to break off the whole thing clean, or at any rate to wait and get more tangible evidence of Mr. Shawnessy's honesty than an annulment based on a mysterious disappearance.

Meanwhile, Esther was watched and attended by various energetic maiden ladies of mature years who rose staunchly to the defense of outraged fatherhood and threatened chastity. One of them even slept with Esther at night. It became almost impossible to get any word at all to or from Mr. Shawnessy, even through Ivy Foster, who was forbidden to see Esther any longer.

In spite of herself, Esther was shocked and disturbed by what she heard. She hadn't seen Mr. Shawnessy for a long time. It began to appear that she might have been all wrong in her infatuation for him. At any rate there was nothing that she could or would do about it. The gods of Family Virtue, Conventional Morality, and Orthodox Religion seemed to be winning a decisive victory.

These Raintree County deities did not, however, reckon with a certain masterpiece of romantic strategy on the part of Mr. Shawnessy.

In early June of 1878, there appeared in the *Free Enquirer,* in the space usually reserved for the Sage of the Upper Shawmucky, Will Westward, an open letter to Mr. Gideon Root, under which appeared in bold capitals the name JOHN WICKLIFF SHAWNESSY. The letter made a clear, honest, and dispassionate statement of the legal facts of the case, and it concluded with a courteous demand that the writer be permitted to visit the Root home and ask the hand of Esther Root in marriage, as the young lady was now twenty-one years old and the suitor was a man not without friends and prestige in Raintree County—and, to the best of his knowledge, legally single and eligible. A note of passion crept into the letter in the last sentence, in which the writer did not hesitate to appeal to justice and the power of immortal love.

It was the last sentence that threatened to cook Mr. Gideon Root's goose.

On receipt of his personal copy of this letter, Mr. Root went out and got into his buggy, selecting his longest and heaviest leather whip as a suitable accessory. He drove over to the Shawnessy Home and walked into the yard, carrying the whip. What followed was variously reported, but most accounts agreed on the following conversation.

Mr. Shawnessy, upon answering the door and seeing Mr. Root standing there fingering a big black whip, carefully kept the door between himself and his visitor.

—What may I do for you, sir? he said.

—I want a word with you in private, Mr. Root said.

—Just a second, sir, Mr. Shawnessy had said.

He reappeared in a moment with an immense rawhide horsewhip, newly purchased, which he kept twisting between his strong, nervous hands.

He and Mr. Root then walked out into the yard.

—Shawnessy, Mr. Root said, I have come over here to tell you to leave my daughter Esther alone. We want no part of you, and we don't aim to have you botherin' around her any more.

—Are these her words or your words, Mr. Root?

—They're my words and her sentiments.

—What guarantee have I got of that? You've had her jailed up for weeks. I haven't even been able to talk with her.

—Older and wiser people have talked with her and brought her to her senses, Mr. Root said. She knows now that you're a goddam, blackhearted scoundrel, and she don't want no more of your lyin' words. If you try any more tricks to git her, I'm warnin' you, by God Almighty, that you will have more than a poor, defenseless, and foolish girl to reckon with.

Mr. Root's broad hand bulged on the handle of his whip.

—Meaning? Mr. Shawnessy said, shaking out his whip along the ground and absently making the end of it flick at some flowerheads on the fringe of the lawn.

—Meanin', Mr. Root said, that I'm that girl's pa and I intend to take care of her, any way I know how. There are laws to prevent the seduction of girls and to punish their seducers. And if the law don't help, I'll find means of my own.

—Sir, Mr. Shawnessy said, there are also laws to prevent a man from keeping his daughter brutally locked up so that she can't marry the man of her choice.

There was then some violent discussion of whether Mr. Shawnessy was a fit man to marry any woman. Mr. Shawnessy's antecedents, both paternal and maternal, were stigmatized in no uncertain terms. Both men watched each other's whiphands and turned white and red several times. Mr. Shawnessy attempted to keep the discussion on a temperate level and drew several legal distinctions, to make his position perfectly clear.

Finally, Mr. Root said,

—Look here, Shawnessy. Much as you may think so, I have no personal interest in hurtin' you. All I want is my daughter safe out of your hands. Now, I'm not a rich man, but I'm willin' to pay something for that. I'll give you a thousand dollars, my note of hand, to stay away from my daughter. You'll have five hundred dollars down and the rest as soon as I can git it, and I give you my word no one will ever know of it. I'm a practical man. I'm willin' to pay this money and strike a bargain, and no hard feelin's.

—Mr. Root, Mr. Shawnessy said, if you're so sure your daughter cares nothing for me, why are you offering me this bribe?

—I've made the offer, Mr. Root said. Take it or leave it.

—I don't want your money, Mr. Shawnessy said. Esther and I love each other. We want to be married and live as man and wife.

At these words, Mr. Root stared wildly about as if he were hunting for something that he should have brought. He looked at Mr. Shawnessy's whip. He put his hand to his throat as if to squeeze his heart back into his breast.

—John Shawnessy, he said slowly, I ought to thrash you to death.

—Mr. Root, Mr. Shawnessy said, I've lived too long and seen too much to be afraid of a man with a whip. I've been cheated out of a lot of things in my time, but I don't intend to be cheated out of your daughter, if she'll have me. I might as well make perfectly clear to you that I intend to take her away from you and marry her. That's all I have to say to you, sir. Good day.

Mr. Shawnessy turned his back on Mr. Root and walked into the house, and Mr. Root went down and got into his buggy and raised a long ugly welt on the side of his horse.

After Mr. Shawnessy's famous letter to the newspapers, the affair broke wide open. Gideon Root found that he had a hard fight on his hands. He wasn't simply bucking the power of love, but also the power of the press, which is perhaps even greater.

At first, the County split up into factions, and both sides found voice in the newspapers. The Republican sheet, the old *Clarion,* which had long ago done a political turntail along with Garwood B.

Jones, its absent owner, and which had in its time taken many a wallop at John Wickliff Shawnessy, at first leaned a little toward Mr. Root's side of the argument.

Then a wonderful thing happened. A letter came from the Nation's Capital, Washington, D.C., signed by a certain eminent young statesman who had won his first seat in the Senate of the United States in 1875 and had already gained national attention by his golden voice and commanding presence. This letter was received by one of Garwood's old political henchmen in the County, and it was shown widely about. It was not couched in the Senator's sacred style.

Dear Skinny,

It has just come to my attention that my good young friend John Shawnessy has got himself into another big mess back there in the old County. The way I hear it, he's fallen in love with a girl about half his age. No doubt John put his usual hex on the kid, and she's crazy about him. According to my advices, her old man is trying to break it up and hold back the force of young love.

Now it just so happens that John Shawnessy is one of the best friends I ever had, and if cutting off any part of my anatomy (with one exception) would do the sprout any good, I'd submit to the knife.

Skinny, I want it understood that I want the boy to have that girl legal and proper if that's the way he wants it. If I still have a little prestige and influence left in the old County, Skinny, I want it used to bring this thing about. Just let it be known that Garwood B. Jones would be personally gratified to see young love have its course.

You can even show part of this letter to the right people, Skinny, and get the boys behind it. Don't spare money or anything else that will do any good. My personal fund will take care of the thing.

The G.A.R. may be able to help, as everyone knows John Shawnessy fought like hell from Chattanooga to the Sea and got an honorable wound in the gut when we took Atlanta.

Now, Skinny, I trust that's all I need to say, and let me know how the thing turns out.

GARWOOD B. JONES

P.S. By the way, it won't hurt to have my name mentioned favorably in the right places and with a touch of humor as reacting to this situation with characteristic humanity. 'No detail, however minute, back in the home state, fails to arouse the Senator's instant, personal attention, etc., etc.' Some of that old crap might do me some good right now after the stink stirred up among the laboring classes by my reaction to that damn strike last year. Skinny, get busy in there. I'm counting on you personally.

Garwood's signature on this document was so big that it could be read without spectacles.

After this letter, the tide of Public Opinion, already turning strongly to the side of young love as against filial piety, became a raging torrent. The *Clarion* instantly reversed its stand, declaring the issue to be above narrow partisanship and to concern the universal human heart. The Jones machine got busy and went to town. In no time at all the columns of both newspapers were full of letters, suggesting a hundred solutions to the affair, among which the most straightforward was a proposal that old Gideon Root be horsewhipped and hanged on a hickory limb.

The affair attracted attention even beyond the borders of Raintree County, receiving some notice in a widely read column in New York's leading newspaper. Letters came to the local papers from surprisingly remote places. Not wholly characteristic was one to the *Clarion* from a Miss Geranium Warbler Stiles, a resident of Oshkosh (though, curiously, the envelope was postmarked New York). Miss Stiles (who was obviously a very gifted old woman) said that her entire sympathies had been aroused by reports that she had read of the case. She then proceeded to record at great length the tribulations of her own enforced maidenhood which she said had been caused by the determination of a tyrant father to prevent her marriage to the young man of her choice. The upshot of the thing had been that

> . . . my father at last, in a fit of insane rage, discharged a shotgun at my intended, which though it did not mortally wound him resulted in such highly localized damage to his person that marriage was, alas! out of the question.

This letter was at once so touchingly frank and so convincingly eloquent that it had no little weight in turning Public Opinion in Raintree County in favor of the lovers.

It got so that Gideon Root hardly dared go out of his house. One day when he was riding down the road in his buggy, a very muscular man on a bay horse rode up beside him, grabbed him by the shirt at the neck, pulled him half out of the buggy, shook him, and said with deadly seriousness,

—Root, if you don't let them youngsters git married, I'll personally beat the hell out of you.

He then shoved Mr. Root back into his buggy and rode off rapidly in the opposite direction. Mr. Root, who was never a man to back out of a fight, recovered from his surprise and nearly lashed the liver out of his horse in a vain effort to catch up with his assailant, whom he had never seen before in his life.

He got dozens of letters signed and unsigned, of which the following was a fair sample:

> Root, goddam you, if you goddam well don't let Johnny Shawnessy have your daughter, I'll blow your goddam head off with a shotgun. Folks are agin you, Root, and you mite as well know it. Now goddam you, git some sence in your goddam thick skull and leave them youngsters git marred.

One night, a shower of brickbats and horseshoes smashed the lower windows of the Root house, and someone set fire to the barn. The Jones machine got the people in Freehaven so worked up that a huge halfcrazy mob was on its way out to the Root Farm with tar, feathers, and a knotty rail, when Mr. Shawnessy, hearing of the matter, rode a fast horse to intercept them, and using all his wit and power of persuasion finally managed to turn them back.

There were six elopements in the County during this period, all of which were indirectly traced to the abnormal excitement caused by the Shawnessy-Root Affair.

The power of immortal love, the power of the free press, and the personal power of Senator Garwood B. Jones appeared to be closing in on one poor man like an inexorable combination of natural forces. But there was some question whether the last two elements didn't do John Shawnessy more harm than good.

During this time, Esther Root had suffered a virtual imprisonment. All she knew for sure was that her pa, whom she loved very much, was taking a fearful drubbing. He came home one night with his shirt torn and his throat bruised from the assault of an unknown man, and another time the whole family was awakened when hoodlums tried to smash the house and fire the barn. That night Pa ran around in the darkness half-naked like a madman, shooting off a shotgun while unknown people made vulgar sounds from hiding. The next morning, they carried Pa in, half out of his mind, his body scratched with briars, his eyes bloodshot, and his voice a hoarse sob in his throat.

Esther hadn't heard from Mr. Shawnessy for weeks now, and she didn't know what his attitude was. She was told that he had gone around the County boasting to people about how he had made old Root come begging on his knees not to take his daughter away from him. She heard that Mr. Shawnessy had said that he would personally see to it that half the young toughs in the County beat the hell out of Mr. Root every time he stepped out of his front door. She heard that Mr. Shawnessy went around laughing and saying that he could have the girl any time.

These reports didn't make her angry. They didn't square with her idea of Mr. Shawnessy. But they were all she heard.

Things were in this condition when on the third of July Pa came in to see her. He told her that the situation had become more than he could bear. He looked like a beaten man.

—Sometimes, Esther, he said, I wish I was dead. When I think that you that I loved most have caused me all this trouble! But I guess it's my own fault. Maybe I loved you too much. Maybe I've not been a good pa to you.

Again Esther felt the strong anguish that she had felt the day Pa had cried.

—Why, Pa, what have I done now?

—Nothing, he said. Only, I see just one way to git us all out of it, and no one harmed. I plan to let Robert have the Farm, now that all you children are grown. I thought if you had no objection you and I could leave the County and go out West. I got a brother out there, and I got a little money saved up. You could go with me if you want to. If after a decent interval, when this thing blows over, you wanted to come back to the County, you could do it. I wouldn't stand in your way. How about it, Esther? Will you do this last thing for your old pa?

It was the first time in her memory that Pa had ever referred to himself as old in her presence.

—O, Pa, she said, I couldn't bear to leave you. If you say so, I'll go with you.

—I want you to make up your own mind, with no one influencing you, Pa said. I got everything about ready. I'm goin' to town about some legal matters tomorrow, and if I don't git beat up, I'll come back at four o'clock in the afternoon, and we can ketch the six o'clock train at Three Mile Junction. Tomorrow's the Fourth, and everybody'll be too busy celebratin' to worry about you and me. If you do this last thing for your old pa, he can go to his grave knowin' that you were kind to him and more than repaid his love for you. I won't say anything more.

Esther lay long sleepless that night. If she could only see Mr. Shawnessy once more before she left! But then, if she saw him again, she would be lost, and it would be all to do over again. She felt sure that whatever she did and whatever happened, this was the last night that she would spend in her father's house.

Toward morning, she fell asleep and dreamed that she was going somewhere all by herself. It appeared that she was all dressed up and was hurrying across the land. Her feet sank in the freshly plowed earth of the fields around her home, but she stumbled on, crossing fences and pushing through thickets trying to find a place where she was to meet someone. It had something to do with catching a train or keeping an appointment, with whom or where she couldn't say for certain, but in the dream she kept seeing the dark, beloved ground of the Farm lying all around her in a light that was tinged with the sadness and forever of a myth. In the oak forest that lay behind the Farm, the trees were dark and still. She could see deep into the hushed recesses. But across a distant stile, where the spring welled to make a running branch,

THERE HUNG, ALL SHINING
IN THE GRAY
DUSK

The Golden Bough

MR. SHAWNESSY said, is the title of tonight's discussion of the Waycross Literary Society. We are happy to have with us a visiting celebrity, Professor Jerusalem Webster Stiles, who will lead the forum.

The Perfessor adjusted his pince-nez.

—Let me see, he said perfessorially. Yes, I have my notes with me.

He plunged both hands into his looseflapping coat and plucked out two flasks, one half full, the other full. His face, nodding on long neck, leaned past Mrs. Brown, tendering the full flask, an amber bubbling bottle, to his two companions, who smilingly declined.

The face of Professor Jerusalem Webster Stiles was a map of wrinkles and ridges. Black eyes glittered unfocused in seamy sockets. The skull was polished bone under black hair. The wide mouth grinned stumps of moribund teeth. The pince-nez glasses, lensed with pictures of the fading day, were a feature of the face, as much so as the sharp nose and the big shapely ears sensitive to the least shift of the forehead. The face of Professor Jerusalem Webster Stiles was wise and devious like an old monk's manuscript.

Mrs. Brown put the Raintree County *Atlas,* which she had been diligently examining, under the swing.

—Shall I keep the minutes? This promises to be a memorable . . .

MEETING OF LITERARY SOCIETY

(Epic Fragment from the *Cosmic Enquirer*)

Attractively landscaped with smooth lawns, tufts of shrubbery, and pagan adornments, Mrs. Evelina Brown last Monday entertained members of the Waycross Literary Society in her palatial residence east of town. Refreshing himself with frequent drafts from the Heliconian Spring, Professor Jerusalem Webster Stiles led a discussion on the origin of . . .

Mr. Shawnessy was sitting on the right of the porchswing and the Perfessor on the left, with Mrs. Brown between. It was seven-thirty and the picnic supper was over. Mrs. Brown's American-Gothic mansion gloomed over the three forms. The yard was a rectangle of shaven green where children played. A fountain in the left corner lifted a thin jet to flower and fall over two bronze bodies. Enshrined in halfcircles of the fence, the nymphs were lumps of rusty nudity. The house and yard were nearly surrounded by cornfields. A cornfield began on the far side of the National Road and extended to the elevated bed of the Pennsylvania Railroad. Due west, a white bull stood in a small pasture. Islanded in trees, the roofs of Waycross were drenched in fading splendor.

—Mr. Shawnessy, the Perfessor said, will you elucidate our text for tonight?

—Our text for tonight, Mr. Shawnessy said, is taken from the *Aeneid,* the story of a national hero. In Book VI, members, you will recall how the hero descends into the land of shades, after first plucking a golden bough. This talismanic branch makes him superior to death and he is enabled to learn of things past and future.

—To begin then with things simple, the Perfessor said, I propose this question to the enlightened company which I behold before me: What is human life?

—Human life is a myth, Mr. Shawnessy said.

—Amen, the Perfessor said.

—To be most human is to be most mythical.

—This is wisdom, said the Perfessor.

—A myth is a story that is always true for all men everywhere.

—An oracle speaks, the Perfessor said. But are there any new myths? I doubt it. In their wisdom, the Hebrews and the Greeks have furnished us with all our myths. Will there ever be another mythical race?

—Yes, Mr. Shawnessy said. The Americans are a mythical race. We are making a new myth, the American myth.

—What is this American myth?

—It's the story of the hero who regains Paradise.

—Ah, yes, the Perfessor said. The subject of your own great unfinished epic.

—Where does he find Paradise? Mrs. Brown asked.

—At the crossroads of the Nation. In the Court House Square. In a train station. In the center of Raintree County.

—Adam, the prize of God's great bounty,
Pops up again in Raintree County,

recited the Perfessor.

—Americans have rewritten the old epics and have added myths of their own. From the Greeks, we've taken the plural gods, the rape of beauty, the long war, the wandering and the return. From the Hebrew and Christian myth, we've taken the lost garden and the divine man. But to all this we've added our own national experience. Our myth is a sun myth—it has the path of the sun. America is the geographical symbol of the Renaissance. The seagoing humanists set out to find again the lost garden of humanity. What were they seeking except a Passage to India, the cradle of mankind! America is mankind returning upon itself through the circle of the earth and defeating time and space. In a new Eden, we have strewn the memories of all mankind. We began by calling the aborigines of America 'Indians' and have pursued the delightful fraud ever since. We're the new mythmakers.

—But this westward legend, John, and this Edenic dream belong to an innocent day when myths were believable. It belongs to young America. My dear boy, you're trying to Hellenize America after her Hellenic age is over.

—I'm trying to Americanize America, Mr. Shawnessy put in.

—All great myths, the Perfessor went on, are pre-alphabetic. By your theory, then, early America has had the advantage of being almost illiterate?

—The early Americans, Mr. Shawnessy said, were poets of the open road. They rediscovered the earth. They uncoiled the Mississippi, they unrolled the Great Plains, they upheaved the Rocky Mountains. They brought the miracle of names to an earth that was nameless, even as Adam did when God bade him name the earth and its inhabitants. They were the new Adams.

—Adam, who always slept in the raw,
Went to bed with an Indian squaw,

the Perfessor recited. It's an amazing synthesis that you've achieved, my boy. How you ever managed to make this bleak little county conform to a universal pattern amazes me. You didn't have much to work on.

—On the contrary.

—I suppose you're referring to our little local myth, the Perfessor said. Assume just for fun that a seedy halfwit called Johnny Appleseed *did* walk through here seventy-five years ago when this was a wilderness, and suppose this nutty yokel *did* strew a little seed around here. Even suppose he got hold of a seedling of some exotic tree and planted it. What of it? One tree is like another. Johnny Appleseed was just one of the bees who help the winds spread pollen. It's human and poetic to make a myth out of it. But if you and Evelina and I made an excursion tomorrow to your precious swamp in the middle of your precious county and found your precious tree with a couple rocks under it, do you know what we'd do? We'd sit there and have a couple sandwiches and after an afternoon of contemplating the tree, we'd go back home with sunburnt noses and ants in our pantses, no wiser than before.

—I'd be thrilled to death, Mrs. Brown said, to find the Raintree.

A girl's voice clanged in the yard:

—Mrs. Brown!

—I've got to help direct games and things, she said, rising. I'll be back as soon as I can.

The Perfessor took a drink. Mr. Shawnessy made a motion indicative of the lawn, the town, the running children, Mrs. Brown in her green dress.

—You see, he said. It is all myth. We are all myth.

—John, the Perfessor said mellowly, what you say is true. Americans are an absolutely legendary people. Who knows it better than I, after a lifetime of reporting the incredible deeds of this incredible race?

—If we have a recorded epic in this century, Mr. Shawnessy said, it's the newspaper. A hundred years from now the newspapers of this day will provide the epic fragments of our time.

—I suggest, the Perfessor said, that you name your epic poem the *Mythic Examiner,* being a kind of fabulous newspaper in which the deeds of these fabulous people, the Nineteenth Century Americans, shall be recorded in a mythical American style.

—I suppose I've been too close to this stuff of myth, Mr. Shawnessy said, to handle it properly.

—Your great poem, the Perfessor said, is your own life, John. My God, what an epic we have lived in this century! But as you say, we've been the makers of the legend, and I suppose someone else will have to record it. We're essentially a physical people—doers not sayers. Where the Greeks worshipped the form, we worship the act. For us, it's size, strength, and speed that count. I see it all the time, and I think we're getting more rather than less so. Maybe you've been reading about the coming fight between the Great John L. Sullivan and Gentleman Jim Corbett. It's the very stuff out of which our American Homer will some day create his Hector and Achilles, with breast-thumpings, epithets, and great brags. Only a few weeks ago, I myself saw the Great John L. stripped to the heels. I was in Boston when they carted the Strongest Living Body down to a doctor's office to have it measured. It made me think of a big fat beefy bull at the County Fair. We all stood around gaping and gasping, while John L. flexed his biceps and blew out his great chest. Of course, hardly had the Boston doc called Sullivan the Strongest Living Man than Corbett's manager trotted his bruiser down to a doctor, who gave it as his opinion that the Challenger was the finest hunk of man in all America.

—Well, well, we have these cunning things called bodies, and we might as well mythicize them. What's wrong with trying to be first in a hard contest? It's another sign of our innocent obsession with space.

—Ah, I just remembered, the Perfessor said, you were something of an athlete yourself in your youth. Here, have a slug of this, hero boy, and tell us how you sought the garland. Give us a few chapters from your mythic life.

Smiling, he declined. In the yard, his oldest boy ran past the porch, leading a cry of children around the house.

Life's young Greek and blithe contender, maker of myths, stand forth. Stand forth again, pre-alphabetic and prediluvian boy, and find the earth gardened with names, the earth rivered and roaded, fenced and freehavened.

Where is the young American?

He stood on the brink of day and heard prophecies and legends old and new. He dreamed and saw the republic of himself. He knew that somewhere the Tree of Life was waiting, from which the County took its name of music and of strangeness. For this he had come forth to summer. For this he stripped him for the race. For this he heard speech like unworn coins flung down ringing in the Square. For this he made great vaunts and laughed with white teeth.

—And right after this exhibition, the Perfessor was saying, the Great John L. took us all down to a saloon in the heart of the Hub, where he stood at the bar hammering hell out of the counter and buying drinks for the crowd. I can lick any mon in the worrrrrrrld! says he, letting me have the flat of his hand between my shoulder blades. After they picked me up and revived me with a double slug, I said, John, I've seen this Corbett fight, and he's a crafty one. He says you'll never lay a glove on him. At this, John L. roared like a bull, doubled his great fist, and rocked the teaparty town with a blow on the brass. See this arm? he said. I see it, I said. See this fist? he said. Yes, sir, I said. With this arm and this fist, he said, I'll . . .

Make way, make way for the Hero of Raintree County. He who is first in the race shall pluck the golden bough; flowers shall pelt his naked shoulders.

—He stood there, the Perfessor was saying, and so help me, he drank two to my one until midnight and went right on roaring and beating the bar and . . .

The words of an old myth shall be graven on lost columns. They shall be the speech of the early Americans and their Olympic games. Godlike, they ran toward mountains of gold. Goldseekers, train-racers, aeronauts of the blue and enterprising day, stringbreakers, steamboaters, wirewalkers, make way, make way for

July 4— THE —1859

RACE TO DETERMINE

THE FASTEST RUNNER IN RAINTREE COUNTY

was set for eleven o'clock in the morning of the Fourth. Around nine o'clock, opencoated, longlegged, with a blue bowtie at his throat, Johnny Shawnessy walked through the Court House Square nodding to friends.

—Good luck, Johnny.

—Hope you beat, Johnny.

—I got a pig bet on you, Johnny.

—I'll do my best, folks.

In front of the Saloon, Cash Carney was waiting, leaning against the plateglass. He took off his derby and fanned himself with it, though there wasn't a trace of sweat on his elegant face, smelling of lotion. His hair was slicked back flat from a middle part. He tipped the ash from his cigar and swung open his coat, revealing a gold chain on his spotless shirt. He plucked out a watch and cradled it in his hand.

—We got two hours, yet, John. Everything's set. By the way, all of the other contestants withdrew from the Race, and it's just between you and Flash.

—Look, Cash, I'd rather not go through with this business of getting Flash drunk. I think I can beat him sober.

—It's all fixed, Cash said. Jake is all set with the fake bottle, and honest, it looks just like whiskey. Hell, they'll never know the difference.

—They say Garwood is riding herd on Flash to see that he doesn't get drunk. Garwood and the *Clarion* crowd have a lot of money on this race, and they don't aim to lose it if they can help it. Suppose Garwood smelled a rat.

—I tell you, Cash said, only Jake and I and you and your brother Zeke know anything about it. I told Jake if he blabbed to anybody, he'd lose his job.

—Garwood has a way of finding things out, Johnny said. It's been weeks since we made the plan.

—A man has to take some risks, Cash said. After all, I got my money out at two to one. But I can't get any more takers at those odds after the way you run in that race at Middletown Fair last Saturday. I told you to hold yourself in a little.

—I was nervous.

—You didn't have to spreadeagle the field by ten yards, Cash said. How do you feel?

—Nervous, Johnny said.

In the plateglass of the Saloon, his young head was framed with rainbow colors. While he was fixing his bowtie, a familiar image emerged from the door of the reflected Court House and strode importantly through the crowd.

—Well, men, Garwood Jones said, I see you're here early. Suppose we have a little drink before the Race. On me.

Garwood laughed a throaty baritone, removed his straw hat, and studied himself in the plateglass, touching his fat young cheeks and sculpturing his black hair. He took out a cigar and lit up, gently weaving his bulky shoulders as he puffed the tip to flame. Johnny watched Garwood closely, but the handsome blue eyes were veiled in cynical amusement.

Small boys were already out with firecrackers. The Square was filling with people. Venders and showmen were drawing the crowd. Workmen were putting the finishing touches on a platform built halfway out from the edge of the court house yard into the street. American flags were limp flares of color in the windless air. It promised to be a hot day.

—You wouldn't want to take a little more easy money, would you, Garwood? Cash asked, watching Garwood sharply.

—It would be stealing from a friend, Garwood said. By the way, Perkins is sober. I hired three strong boys to watch him.

Several citizens were collecting around the Saloon, and now and then one went in for a drink.

—Folks, said an oily baritone booming from a shady place on the court house lawn, I trust you all perceive this round, elongate object that I hold here in my hand. Why, Perfessor, you say, that's nothing but a bottle, as any fool can plainly see. Ah, ha, my friends, so it is.

But, friends, this bottle—this simple, plain, and ordeenary bottle contains . . .

—The Perfessor's open letter caused quite a sensation, didn't it? Garwood said. By the way, did I show you the letter he sent me along with it?

Garwood pulled a letter from his pocket and read,

—Dear Garwood,

Enclosed find a noble prose, the which I hope you will print in the columns of your paper. It is full of high sentence and pious fraud and alas! a certain seed of truth. If you see Lydia, tell her I love her. Spit in the Reverend's face for me. As for yourself, boy, study my example, and get the hell out of Raintree County before someone gets to *you* with a shotgun.

Your ob't servant, etc., etc.,

JERUSALEM WEBSTER STILES

Garwood borrowed a copy of a New York paper from a near-by citizen and began to read it.

—Shucks, a citizen said, nobody believed that letter, but it was a nice thing for him to do.

—Tell you the truth, a second citizen said, I sort of hoped he'd git away with her.

—Seems to me, the first citizen said, I recommember you were part of the posse and carried a rope.

—I did that, the second citizen said. I already had the noose tied in it.

—Tell you the truth, a third citizen said, I always liked that there Perfessor Stiles. He warn't a bad cuss, at that. Shucks, you couldn't zackly blame 'im.

—If you fellers want my personal opinion, the second citizen said, I allays thought Reverend Gray was an old stinkball. I'm glad he's went and left the County. Besides, my folks never believed in total immersion nohow.

Several men were in front of the Saloon now, reading newspapers and talking.

—That dern balloon went over Fort Wayne day before yesterday, a citizen said. I wisht we'd see one around here.

Everybody looked up at the sky speculatively. This was the summer of balloon ascensions. The newspapers were full of stories about big canvas bags blowing around America like winddriven birds, tearing along on high gales, dropping ballast, collapsing unpredictably, spewing their occupants out on far waters and wildernesses.

—It's jist one dern thing after another this summer, a citizen said. Seem like ever'body's tryin' to think up some damfool way to git 'emselves kilt fancy. And folks eggs 'em on to it.

—Like this dern Frenchman whatshisname, a second citizen said. The tightrope walker.

—Blondin.

—That's him. He ain't satisfied no longer to cross Niagara Falls on a wire. He's got to carry a man across on his shoulders.

—You mean tew stan' thar and tell me he aims tew carry a man across with 'im?

—That's whut I said.

—Well, I declare tew tell! thar might be one man dumb enough to dew a thing like walk a wire over Niagara Falls, but shorely they ain't tew.

—O, ain't they! They's another one besides—an American. Leave me to have that paper a minute, Garwood. Lookee here, now, here's where it says——

The man flapped pages, searching.

—Yes, sir, friends, boomed the great voice of redemption from the court house lawn, if this bottle that I hold here in my hand doesn't afford you all the marvellous . . .

—Here she is, the man said. Right here. John, you read that fer us, will yuh? I ain't got my specs.

Johnny read:

> —'I am an American and a native of Rhode Island. This will show that Americans is as bold and as smart as a Frenchman. I have been in the business about 2 years and have performed on a slack wire, one so small that it is scarcely perceptible. But I could walk on the edge of a razor.' A program of exhibitions is announced. Terrific ascension, etc. The Great American phenomena, Professor Sweet, Music by Full Military Band. Admission only 10 cents.

A general invitation is extended all around
  To the people of the Union in every state and town,
To come and witness this great and daring feat
  Of walking on the mammoth rope by the great Professor Sweet.

—Hmmmm, Garwood said. Look what's coming.

Johnny looked up and saw Susanna Drake in a white dress walking between two other young women. Passing the Saloon, she saw Johnny and Garwood, and a smile of pleasure and confusion tugged at her pouted lips, fluttered and faded on her face. She touched her white satin dress at the shoulder and switched her red parasol back and forth with a lithe fury that seemed to flow from her body into the stalk of the parasol.

—Hello, Johnny. Hello, Uncle Garwood.

The boys said hello.

—What a pair! a citizen said.

Johnny felt wildly excited as he thought of the party of young people who were going to Paradise Lake that afternoon.

—That's that there girl from the South, another citizen said. She's goin' to award the prize to the winner of the Race.

—Say, a citizen said, they've done had another rape case down there. It's in the paper.

—Where's that? Garwood said. I missed that.

He took the paper out of Johnny's hand, lipped his cigar, and flapped pages, eagerfingered.

—Page three, bottom of the second colyum, the citizen said. A nigger raped a white woman down in Alabammy. They lynched 'im.

—Serves the black bastard right, Garwood Jones said, walking his cigar up and down his mouth while holding the paper in both hands. Here it is.

—And now, friends, boomed the baritone voice from the court house lawn, I hope you will pardon me if I offer a little medical advice of an intimate character, but I am sure the enlightened intelligence of the audience I see before me makes it possible for me to talk on a subject highly important to both sexes. This little bottle which I hold here, and which—mark my words, Gentlemen and Ladies—*and* which, I intend to give away free with the other bottle I have just demonstrated . . .

—Hi there! Garwood said. What are we wasting our time in Indiana for? And there's a whole mountainful of gold in the glorious West. Folks are *swarming* out to Pike's Peak. It's like Forty-Nine all over again.

Garwood plucked the cigar out of his mouth and peered keenly at the crowded buggies across the street.

—Hold this paper for me a minute, sprout, he said.

He walked across the street and leaning head and shoulders into a buggy helped a young woman down.

It was Nell Gaither, whom Johnny hadn't seen since a certain afternoon on the Shawmucky which had resulted in a letter requesting him to put from his mind forever *all* recollections of his unworthy but repentant Nell. From parasol to shoes, she was dressed in a complete new outfit. Her long, graceful body bent prettily as she stepped down. She pushed her heavy gold hair back a little from her ears and looked tranquilly up and down the street. Her eyes touched Johnny with a lingering look and poured a green excitement on him. A faint, faint smile touched the corner of her lovely mouth, her cheeks paled and were then faintly flushed with scarlet. She opened her parasol suddenly and knocked Garwood's straw hat off.

Everyone laughed, including Garwood, and Nell laughed nervously, and Garwood retrieved his hat, and Nell walked away into the crowd alone.

Johnny studied the isthmus of her waist and the bellshaped continent of her skirt, green with flowered figures worked into the cloth. A rush of longing went over him. Shutting his eyes, he saw his strong young body floating in green water warm in the sunlight. And this water was between wide banks in summertime, and a smooth oar made wounds in the pale flesh of a river of floating flowers.

A high, hornloud voice whipped across his ears.

—Well, I'll be hogtied and turned in a barl!

Advancing the first of a throng, longlegged, opencoated, with a red bowtie at his throat, Flash Perkins was crossing the street toward the Saloon. Flash's wide hat was pushed back on his head. The brown shag of his hair shot out and over his forehead. His white teeth smiled savagely through his beard. His forehead twitched upward. His blue eyes glared excitement and good humor. He walked flinging his feet out sideways and swinging his hands, half made into fists.

Everyone within hearing stopped and began to move in toward

the Saloon. Johnny didn't shift his position against the window, but he wouldn't have been surprised if Flash had walked right into him. Flash stopped, however, and putting his hands on his hips, and spreading his feet apart, leaned his powerful chest and shoulders far back and . . .

PRE-BOUT SHOWDOWN

(Epic Fragment from the *Mythic Examiner*)

At the weighing-in ceremonies, these two marvellous specimens of American manhood flexed and unflexed their muscles for the delectation of an admiring throng. Small boys trampled each other for the privilege of palping the bicipital bulge of the Champion. When the two had stripped, the crowd withdrew to a reverent distance, while several ladies swooned with high yelps. Those who had suggested prior to the bout that the Champion had acquired too much embonpoint in the pleasant dissipations of vine and venery were obliged to confess that seldom had they seen a more magnificent marvel of mature manhood. In contrast, the Challenger appeared a very stripling. But the boyish mop of his sunset-tinted hair suggested the mane of the young lion. Tall, slender, and fair, he lacked the robust figure of the Champion, and yet there was a light in his blue eyes that bespoke a steely determination to win. All in all, the pre-bout meeting between these two worldfamous athletes was in the best tradition of good clean American . . .

—Put 'er there, boy! Flash said. Le's see have you got any force in your hand.

Johnny Shawnessy, whose nervous hands were strong out of all proportion to his size, took hold of Flash's big fist. They ground at each other's knuckles, smiling at each other through gritted teeth. It was a draw.

—How about a little drink with me before the Race? Flash said. This goddam Garwood Jones won't let me have a drop, but I figger if we both had a drink, it'd be all right.

Johnny almost gasped—it sounded so easy. Cash nudged him in the ribs.

—Well, Johnny said, I don't know as I ought to.

—Now look here, John, Cash said, you're to do no drinkin'. You aren't use to it. You don't know what it'll do to you.

Garwood didn't say anything, but stood smoking his cigar and trying the flesh of his cheek.

—Hell, I forgot this boy ain't even weaned yet! Flash said.

Flash's toadies laughed.

—You goin' to let him git away with that, young Shawnessy? one of them said.

—Heck, no! Johnny said. I can beat this man running or drinking. Come on.

Flash Perkins gave a great laugh and hit Johnny between the shoulderblades.

—Come on, Garwood! he yelled. It's O.K. now, ain't it, boy?

Garwood didn't say anything, but followed Johnny and the rest of the crowd into the Saloon, as Flash walked through the batwing doors without bothering to put out his hand. Johnny and Flash went over to the bar and each put a foot on the brass rail. Half a hundred men shoved into the Saloon and crowded around the two competitors. Everyone was talking at once.

—Johnny Shawnessy is goin' to drink with Flash Perkins, a citizen said.

—Hell, he can't do that, another citizen said. Ain't nobody in Raintree County can drink with that crazy buck glass for glass.

—Say, it'd be smart, a third citizen said, to take a little more of Carney's money. They say this Shawnessy kid is fast as greased lightnin', but that whiskey'll kill 'im.

—What'll it be, boys? Jake the barkeep said.

He was a nervous young man in a white apron.

—You name it, and I'll drink it, Flash said to Johnny.

—What have you got? Johnny said.

—Here's a couple bottles bourbon, the barkeep said. Raw stuff. Right out a the still.

He got two water tumblers and opened both bottles.

—Each boy can have a bottle, he said.

Just then two men in the *Clarion* crowd grabbed Cash Carney and pulled him out of the ring and began to talk bets at two to one. Meanwhile, the barkeep poured one of the tumblers full, set it down in front of Flash, took the other bottle, and started to pour for Johnny.

—Just a minute there! boomed an authoritative voice.

Garwood Jones leaned over the counter, pointed to the bottle, and said,

—Let's have those drinks poured from the same bottle.

The barkeep looked at Johnny, and Johnny looked around for Cash, but Cash was clear out of sight. The barkeep hesitated and smiled a queer smile. He tried to bluff.

—You mean to say—— he began in a small voice.

—I mean to say, Garwood said in his doublebass, full volume, that I don't want any shenanigans around here. Let's have it fair and square and both boys drinking from the same bottle.

The barkeep shrugged his shoulders, put the bottle back on a shelf. He took the first bottle and poured a short tumblerful for Johnny.

—Fill it up! Garwood said, the trace of a laugh coming into his voice. Fill that goddam glass up!

The barkeep shrugged his shoulders and complied. He set the glass down in front of Johnny.

Johnny looked at the tumblerful of whiskey. It was a beautiful amber fluid with a few clear bubbles at the edges. A dense wall of sweaty male bodies and flushed faces shut him in.

—Jesus, boy! a man whispered, you better quit right now. Flash Perkins was weaned on that stuff.

Johnny looked around for Cash and saw him waving his cigar from the corner.

—You all right, John? he yelled.

—I guess so, Johnny said weakly.

Everybody laughed. Garwood's eyes were innocent and remote as he boomed,

—All right, drink up, boys! Let's get started here. I'll have a little of that myself, Jake, but make mine just half. I can't stick it with these Cold Water Army people.

Everybody laughed. Flash Perkins took his glass and stuck it into his grinning beard. It gurgled in his throat like water. Johnny Shawnessy picked up the tumbler and . . .

ROUND ONE

(Epic Fragment from the *Mythic Examiner*)

Without more ado, the referee withdrew and the bruising contest began. Nervous but plucky, the fairhaired hope from the Upper

> Shawmucky advanced with a tentative left hand while the Champion, serenely confident, took the opening gambit in stride. He seemed not to be conscious of the stiff wallop that caught him flush in the puss. The Challenger on the other hand was seen to absorb a jolt in the midsection that staggered him and made him stare and hang on. The remainder of the first round was without incident, and . . .

—How did it go, John? Garwood said, after everyone had stopped laughing and the tears had left Johnny's eyes.

Johnny stood holding the empty glass.

—Nothing to it, he said.

—Come on, Flash yelled. Here, give us another glass. I'm thirsty.

—Not that it affects me the least little bit, Johnny said, but I just don't see what you guys get out of it. It tastes awful.

The barkeep poured two more glasses. Johnny watched the thick stream gurgling into the bright white glass. His insides felt like fire.

ROUND TWO

(Epic Fragment from the *Mythic Examiner*)

> Between rounds the Champion laughed and shook hands with his ringside followers. At the start of the second round he moved unconcernedly to the middle of the ring where he collided headon with his thoroughly aroused and determined antagonist. Both fighters absorbed hard belts to the body, and the Challenger seemed to get something the worst of it. But when he stepped back he was smiling and appeared not to know what had hit him. However, it was later remembered that at the close of this round he went to the wrong corner and had to be directed to his place. There are those who opine that from here on he had no idea what was taking place and . . .

—How do you feel, John?

It was Zeke who had shouldered his way into the crowd.

—I feel fine, Johnny said.

Zeke looked blurred and huge as he leaned over and smelled the glass.

—That's enough, Zeke said. This boy ain't use to strong liquor.

—Don't spoil the fun, Zeke, Garwood said. This boy dared Flash.

—Don't worry about me, Zeke, Johnny said. There's nothing to it. Just a burning sensation.

He felt heroically strong. The world was a place of laughing gods, bathed in yellow fire. He knew now that he would win the race in the Court House Square and become the Hero of Raintree County.

Someone hit him between the shoulderblades.

—Fill 'em up! Flash Perkins yelled.

—Stand back and give the boy a chance! Garwood boomed. Fill 'em up, Jake, and let's have . . .

ROUND THREE

(Epic Fragment from the *Mythic Examiner*)

At the commencement of the third round, the Challenger threw all caution to the winds. He rushed wildly about, extending himself to the utmost. A series of lethal lunges from his veteran opponent left his face flushed and his eyes out of focus. Dead game, he was still slugging merrily at the bell and had to be carried more or less forcibly to his corner, where he insisted on struggling weakly to his feet and had to be held down by main . . .

—Hell's fire, Flash said, son, you're doin' all right for a youngster. Yippee!

Flash shoved a hole in the crowd and did a handspring in the middle of the Saloon. Someone gave an Indian yell and began to wardance on top of the bar. Looking into the mirror, Johnny Shawnessy perceived that it was himself. He sprang five feet straight up into the air and came down to the floor, where he found himself looking into Cash Carney's trim, serious face.

—Say, what the hell! Cash whispered. This is *some* act.

Cash picked up the glass and smelled it.

—Ouch! he said. What's goin' on around here?

A band began to play right in front of the Saloon, and Flash Perkins stood on his hands on the bar. He jumped from the bar, caught hold of a chandelier in the room, swung back and forth. Johnny took a running leap, went clear over a table in the middle of the room. Flash Perkins put one table on top of another, jumped over head first. Johnny followed him over. Someone picked him up, and he found himself standing at the bar again with another tumblerful of whiskey in his hand. Two tough-looking guys supervised by Garwood Jones were holding Cash Carney in a corner.

—Come on, Jack, Flash Perkins was saying, we'll show these folks *how* tew drink.

The band outside was playing 'Yankee Doodle,' and a boy threw a lighted firecracker through the door.

—Jesus Christ! Cash yelled from the corner. Get him to stop, Zeke. It'll kill 'im.

—Come on, boys! boomed the voice of Garwood Jones. Drink up! By the way, Cash, how would you like to take a little more of my money before . . .

ROUND FOUR

(Epic Fragment from the *Mythic Examiner*)

> The fourth and final round of the famous exhibition beggared description. All eyes were focused on the Champion for whom it was clearly a case of now or never. He moved out menacingly, stalking his slender prey for the kill. But the boy somehow managed to evade the knockout wham until just a few seconds before the closing bell, at which time the Champion lifted one from somewhere around the far corner of the arena. The crowd could see it coming from way back, but the intended recipient of this Sabbath Sock seemed to be hypnotized. When it got there, it picked the brave form of the Hope of Danwebster gently off the floor and . . .

Flash Perkins completed a series of handsprings down the top of the bar landing feet first on a chair that folded up like matchwood under his feet.

—Let's see you do that, Jack.

Johnny was on the bar and turning. The ceiling tipped and turned over, tipped and turned over, tipped and turned over. Something fell solidly on the back of his neck. He started to get up and the saloon floor came up gently and hit him a stunning wallop in the face. He sprang straight up in the air and found Zeke and Cash holding him.

—Take it easy, John! Cash said. Goddammit, do you realize that the Race is just half an hour away and that I got nearly a hundred dollars bet on you! Can you still run, boy?

—Can I run? Johnny said gently.

He smiled his affectionate smile and then like a great blithe bird shot out between the batwing doors. Head erect, coat flying, he ran on long, floating strides down the street with Cash Carney, Zeke Shawnessy, and half a hundred men and boys behind him.

—Catch 'im! Cash said.

—No one in the County can do that, Zeke said, stopping. Look at 'im go! He's turnin' the corner now. Let's wait here and catch him when he comes around.

Faces blurred past Johnny Shawnessy, as he ran on and on, drawing a bright circumference on bounding feet. The breath began to pump pleasantly in his lungs. He was going down the east side of the Square, he was leaning over for the corner, he was running down the north side, he was turning, he was running down the west side. But now he had a great weight sitting on his neck and dragging at his whole body. He turned again at the corner and started down the south side where the Saloon was. A crowd of faces and arms spread out, closed in around him, and caught his vaulting body.

—Let's get him upstairs here, Cash said.

Johnny came to, naked and gasping, as buckets of cold water hit him. Something had been aching in spasms.

—Keep throwing it on him, Cash said. And someone go down and get Flash as drunk as possible.

—No chance, someone said. Garwood's got him under control.

—But not till he run around the Square, someone said, to show he could do it as well as Johnny.

—We still got a chance, Cash said. Hell, if John had only saved that till the Race! Cuss that Garwood Jones! That was a mean, sneakin' trick he played. I reckon he knew all the time what we planned to do.

—Hell, he's down there now laughin' fit to kill, someone said. He says he took Jake's girl out the other night, got her drunk, and got the whole story out of her.

—And I'll bet that ain't all he got either, someone said.

—Goddam that Garwood! Cash said. Imagine playin' a trick like that on your best friend, and poor John here that never had a drink in his life before! Let me see, it's fifteen till. We still got a quarter hour to get this boy sober. How d'yuh feel, John?

Johnny sat up in the tub. The sickness was gone. He felt woozy and wonderful. He got up.

—Keep throwin' that water on him, Cash said. I hope they didn't puke Flash. I'm goin' down to see if I can delay the start.

He went over to the window and looked out.

—Jesus, lover of my soul, look at that crowd! he said. Must be two thousand people. They're all lined up along the course right now, and Susanna's on the platform. We should of charged admission. We can't delay it long, but I'll try. After all, they can't start the Race without the contestants.

Cash went out, but in five minutes he was back.

—Flash is rarin' to go, he said. He's beatin' his chest and yellin' for action. We got to get John down there.

—I'm all right, Johnny said.

He walked over to the window. People were beginning to clap and shout.

—We want Johnny! We want Johnny!

Their hands and voices beat excitement through him. His head wasn't clear, but he felt strong.

—Come on, he said. Let's go.

He dried himself and belted on a pair of white flannel trousers, except for which he was naked. He combed his hair back and went downstairs. Barefooted, he walked into the street with Cash Carney and . . .

OLYMPIC GAMES, 1859

(Epic Fragment from the *Mythic Examiner*)

Now they bring forward the young Athenian stripped for the contest. The young man shakes his tawny locks. His feet touch springing on thrown petals. His shoulders gleam in the sun. His supple back is straight as an upright spear. The muscles of his legs are clearly shown in the bright air as are the cupped breasts of chrystoelephantine Athena. . . .

—Yea, Flash, the crowd yelled. Looking back, Johnny saw . . .

OLYMPIC GAMES, 1859

(Epic Fragment from the *Mythic Examiner*)

That other, the bronzed Spartan, he too comes forward now for the running. Amazement takes the breath of the onlookers, to see the vast fashioning of his chest and shoulders. His muscles are like rocks left glistening from the sea. His brown hair waves in the wind. His great calves bulge, and the maidens blush to behold him. . . .

—All right, boys, said a man in a tall black hat, who had been waiting at the starting line. You have the field to yourselves. Now what I want to know is, do you want me to set you off by word of mouth or by pistol?

—Shoot a gun, Cash said. I want John to hear it.

—All right, the starter said, it'll be a gun. One, two, three, and bang.

Johnny Shawnessy stood at the starting line and ran his eyes over the crowd. Everything was bathed in a dewy brightness. Some distance down the lane of faces, he saw Nell. Desire to win, to be first, to get the garland rushed over him in a wave of fire and longing.

—John, Cash Carney was saying in a low voice, it's now or never, boy. Remember, I got one hundred dollars planted on you. One hundred dollars.

—John, Zeke said, you got to get in there and run. Pa don't know it, but I got two months' hire bet on you.

An important-looking citizen walked from the crowd, took off his hat, and said,

—Folks, I know you're eager as I am for the Race to start. Now these two boys are as fine boys as you will find anywhere. They're both trained to the limit, and I know they're going to show us a fine exhibition of speed and endurance. I understand that this race is something of a grudge battle, and it's been talked about in the papers for some time now. I guess both boys are known to most all of us here, but I will interduce them to you anyway. Now, I want to interduce first——

He was motioning to Johnny, who stepped forward and stood hands on hips.

—Mister John Wickliff Shawnessy!

There was a great deal of handclapping and a violent agitation of parasols among the many girls lining the course. Johnny looked down three hundred yards between the roped-in walls of faces to the platform where a darkhaired girl in a white dress was leaning over the rail. . . .

OLYMPIC GAMES, 1859

(Epic Fragment from the *Mythic Examiner*)

Barbarian woman, steepbreasted and passionate, do you wait with a garland of bay to catch the victor? What flagon of grape shall be poured for the stringbreaker! What wine pressed from the vineyarded hills! O, delicious and blood-exciting potion! He shall drink deep the viny adoration of your beautiful eyes. None shall prevent him. Victory, wingèd goddess, be in his bounding feet!

—Go home and git some meat on your bones, kid, a man's voice said.

—Isn't he cute! a girl said.

—This boy, the announcer said, comes from Danwebster, or near it, a place about which we've read a good deal in the county papers lately. Are there any folks from that locality here?

—Yes, sir!

—Betcher life!

—I see, the man said. Danwebster has sent a big delegation to cheer their favorite son. Five or six anyway. (Laughter.) Well, he's a fine upright young man as you can see for yourself, and I'm sure that, win or lose, he'll reflect credit on the home community.

—Speech! Speech!

—Hello, folks, Johnny said. I'll do my best.

—And best of luck to you, Johnny, the announcer said, and now, folks——

Johnny retired, and Flash Perkins stepped out.

—Now, folks, here's a lad needs no interduction. Orville Perkins of Freehaven, better known as Flash. (Thunderous applause.) Flash here hasn't lost a race since he was kneehigh to a grasshopper. He's won the Fourth of July Race five years straight now, and if somebody don't beat him pretty soon, he'll trip on his beard, and get beat that way. (Loud laughter.) Would you say a word to the crowd, Flash?

—Hello, folks, Flash said. I mean to win this here race.

—That's the spirit, Flash. All right, clear the street.

A few dogs and boys were chased out of the street, leaving a lane about ten feet wide down to the flagdraped platform. Shading his eyes, Johnny could see a thin white line of string tied to the platform and stretching into the crowd. A throng of girls made a vague wall of color behind the finish line. Some were standing, and some were sitting in buggies, drawn up in a halfcircle at the end of the street.

—How about them girls down there? a man said. Ain't they too close?

—Let 'em take keer a themselves, Flash said. Let's git this race started.

Flash was stamping his bare feet on the ground and swinging his great arms. His teeth laughed. His forehead was ridged. He kept shaking the shag of his hair out of his fierce eyes.

—Shake hands, boys, the announcer said.

Johnny and Flash shook hands savagely. The crowd yelled like savages. Someone savagely clanked a cowbell, and a whole string of firecrackers went off under a wagon on which a halfdozen girls were sitting. The girls shrieked, and the crowd laughed like savages.

Johnny Shawnessy turned and set his foot to the mark. His teeth chattered with excitement. Goosepimples stood on his arms. At this moment there was nothing that he wanted more in the world than to break the white string three hundred yards off in the middle of the Court House Square. Three hundred yards off through walls of faces, where the flags were hung on the platform, three hundred yards and a few seconds away was the summit of all desire. Victory, wingèd goddess, be in his bounding feet!

It seemed to him that he was out of his body. He wondered if it would run when he wanted it to. Where his body should be, there was nothing but a void of desire. Nevertheless, he saw his own slender foot going to the mark beside the brown foot of Flash Perkins, and though he didn't look at Flash nor Flash at him, he was aware of the powerful body of his rival drawn back like a bow.

—All right! the starter said coming out in tall black hat, swallowtail coat, and stickpinned tie. Quiet, everybody!

He raised a pistol and put a finger in his ear. The crowd laughed, and he took it out. He fumbled with the pistol and raised it again.

—Don't run till you hear that shot, boys.

He waved toward the far end of the course, hallooed,

—Judges ready?

—Fire away! came a thin, high voice from the finish line.

—On your marks, boys, the starter said. One. Two. Three.

There was a long, long, long, long silence. . . .

BANG!

(Epic Fragment from the *Mythic Examiner*)

The Fourth of July Celebration this year in the Court House Square featured some pyrotechnic displays that were quite out of the ordinary. A couple of rockets so constructed as to simulate human form were set in the ground and the fuses having been lit, suddenly took off together at a tremendous speed and whizzed along the ground like two runners to a distant mark. A lively interest was exhibited in the new infernal device, especially by the ladies, a group of whom having gathered . . .

—Go it, Johnny!
—Take him, Flash!
—Look at them two scalawags go!

RIVER RACE

(Epic Fragment from the *Mythic Examiner*)

The *Red Streak* and the *Comet,* those two wellknown sidewheelers, leaned into the current, coming together. Crowds lined the shore as the two fastest boats on the river jostled each other on the last long run into New Orleans. The *Streak* was crammed with fastburning pine, and a nigger squat on her boiler. 'More pine, Mr. Shawnessy?' 'A little more, thank ye, Mr. Burns.' The *Comet,* a more durable-looking craft, though lacking the *Streak's* speedy design, was gathering head, and as they came into the bend she had a lead of a half length. The banks were lined with shouting thousands, the wealth and beauty of America's sultriest City, as the Mistress of the Delta, all braceleted with lights, cheered the stacking steamers to their piers. . . .

—Catch 'im, Johnny! Catch 'im!
—Keep it up, Flash! You got 'im whipped!
—Don't give up, John! One hundred dollars! Jerusalem, boy! Go! Go! Go!

IRON HORSES IN SPEEDTEST

(Epic Fragment from the *Mythic Examiner*)

Running side by side, the Midnight Express and the Northern Fury were like two huge projectiles in the night. Going fully forty-five miles an hour, fullblast, together they roared toward the signal light. It was do or die. A long, thin scream of pain emerged from the Fury as she began to close the gap on . . .

Johnny Shawnessy was turning the earth with his bare toes. Always before, this drumming fury that he had in his feet had beaten his rivals back until he was alone at the halfway mark, in front and thundering to the string. But now at the halfway mark, as faces went by him faster and faster, he and Flash Perkins were running side by side and stride for stride, and every effort of his own seemed only to increase Flash's speed, as if they were one body. A strange madness, akin to joy, anger, and intoxication, ran through Johnny Shawnessy. He fixed his eyes on the white string and leaned into the hot air, trying to overcome and subdue this remorseless companion. But now his legs were growing heavy, he was laboring hard, his arms felt like lengths of lead that he had to swing to keep running. With terror he saw the white string closer and closer. The wall of restless color behind it became the faces of girls: he could see the lines of their lips and eyes, the beauty spots on their cheeks, thin ribs of their parasols. And there was not enough room, not enough, not enough, not enough. Thirty yards, twenty yards, ten yards . . .

Johnny Shawnessy shut his eyes and gave a tremendous leap. Something light touched at his breast, and he plunged into a flashing pool of colors, shrieks, perfume, laughter, and flailing bodies. He was down on his hands and knees and then rolling on his back, while girls' voices shrieked in shrill delight. Fluffy summer gowns raked his shoulders; girls' arms and hands pushed and clung to his body. He felt as if he had just been hurled head foremost into an immense costume closet, where twenty naked girls had been hiding.

Someone grabbed his arm and plucked him out of the heap. It was Flash Perkins, standing up to his knees in girls and holding up a capsized buggy with his shoulders while girls scrambled out from beneath it.

—Who won? Johnny said.

Just then, for answer, out of the exultant morning a great wave of arms and voices surged under him and picked him up, as if he were a light flower floating, and he was tossed on hands and shoulders and borne wildly hither and thither, his panting body sustained by rushes of hoarse sound.

—Hurrah for Johnny! Hurrah! Hurrah!

—Hurrah for the New Champeen!

He was being borne like a balloon aimlessly on tempests of summer violence, and then someone yelled,

—Take him around the Square!

His body was tossed above the faces of the Court House Square.

Hands waved. Lips smiled. Parasols pointed and bobbed. Hats went up.

Below him standing at the finish line was Flash Perkins, rubbing his chin and shaking his head. His eyes had a hurt, bewildered look. He was all alone, and apparently only Johnny remembered him. Johnny felt pity and even remorse for the thing that he had done. He knew then that to become the Hero of Raintree County, it was necessary to kill the Hero of Raintree County.

—Speech! Speech! yelled the crowd.

—I was lucky, folks. I couldn't do it again in a million years.

Someone was yanking at his leg. Looking down, he saw Cash Carney.

—Jehosaphat, John! Cash said. We cleaned up two hundred and fifty dollars. You sure you won't take some a that?

—No, thanks, Cash. It's all yours.

Cash was eating his way into his cigar. Both fists were full of coins, and people were still paying off.

—Just remember, boy, Cash said, the party this afternoon is strictly on me. Every bit of it. Soon as you can get away, meet me in front of the Saloon and we'll get the girls.

Now the crowd was carrying Johnny around the Square while the bearers sang, 'Hail to the Chief!' and 'Yankee Doodle.' In front of the *Clarion* office, Garwood Jones was leaning on the door fanning himself with a copy of the *Clarion*.

—Come and see me sometime at the poorhouse, sprout, he said, shaking his head in disgust.

On the east side of the Square, Johnny saw Nell Gaither, standing lonely and apart under a tree on the court house lawn. When he looked at her, she twirled her parasol and watched him with shining eyes. She looked very small and far-off, as the crowd bore him resistlessly on.

And now they were moving again over the ground where the Race had been run. They carried him toward the platform, and with one last surge they tossed him up and over the rail. He was standing beside Susanna Drake. She looked up at him, her eyes brilliant and soft.

—Hi, Susanna, he said. Well, here I am again.

—You ran beautiful, she said, as she fingered a chaplet of oak-leaves.

—How about that race you and I were going to have? he whispered.

—I wouldn't have a chance, she said.

The crowd was applauding so loud he could hardly hear his own voice.

A minister of the community came forward and said,

—Mr. Shawnessy, we are gratified that you should encourage a spirit of helpful and manly contest; not for the sake of winning, not for the sake of defeating another, but that you may so strengthen yourself that you may be victor in the contests of life. Consider the symbolism of these flags—innocence, truth, purity, manliness. Let them guide you in your different paths through life.

—Mr. Shawnessy, Susanna Drake said, putting her little hand on his arm and holding the oakleaf garland as high as his head, allow me to present to you in behalf of all these young ladies here present this wreath. To the victor belongs . . .

A GARLAND FOR OUR JOHNNY

(Epic Fragment from the *Free Enquirer*)

> The conclusion of this great sporting event, certainly the most exciting ever seen in Raintree County, was a moving and memorable one, leaving more than one eye drenched with sympathetic dew. Miss Susanna Drake, that charming ambassadress from the land of mint and magnolia, decorated the head of the young hero with a garland in token of his prowess. . . .

And there in the white roadway, before the multitude, did the loveliest of the damsels adorn his fine curlclustered head with the antique garland, a chaplet of laurel, flower of the mountain. There did she secretly also tender to the young Athenian the empetalled garland of her love, and all the girls dancing flung wreaths of flowers over the heads of the statues lining the way, and all this was in the day when the beautiful gods still dwelt on the mountains and in the rivers and

PEOPLED THE SHORE AND THE SEA, AND YOUTH WAS A TIME

OF MANLY CONTEST AND OF

INNOCENT

—DESIRE, said the Perfessor, is blind, as the Greeks well knew. The original love-desire is that of the sperm for the egg. This blind little boat loaded with memories goes and goes till the fuel gives out or it touches port. This terrific tadpole is the real bearer of life. It is Aeneas bearing the Golden Bough and overcoming death. And the only sacred place is the darkwalled valley into which it swims. As for us, we're just seedpods with delusions of grandeur.

The Perfessor took a drink.

—I wish I could believe in sacred places, he said. At heart, I'm really a bacchant hunting for a garland and a pliant nymph. I ask nothing better than to shout hymen and jump up and down before the symbol of the god. But beauty and the gods can't survive the era of Darwin and the Dynamo. All lovely things are old things.

He took a pull at his bottle and sighed.

—The barbarous peoples had beautiful and dreadful rites. In Mexico, they chose a young man to be the god. They feasted him, gave him flutes to play and fair young women for his pleasure. At the climax of the festival, he mounted a sequence of great stone steps, breaking a flute on each one. Arriving at the top, he was seized forcibly by the priests. They flung him down on a block of stone and cut out his living heart. Then they bore him tenderly to the base of the altar, where they cut off his young, beautiful head.

The Perfessor took another drink and sighed.

—All the primitive peoples, he said, including the early Greeks and Romans, killed their gods. They all believed in the immortal soul, as we do not, and they wanted their god to remain young and vigorous in a new human proxy every year. With burnings and beheadings and geldings of gods, they celebrated the great mystic rite of fertility and besought the spring to come again. The later Mediterranean peoples touched this blood rite with beauty. Mother-gods of earth and vegetation, Venus, Cybele, Diana, Ishtar, Aphrodite, Astarte, were loved by beautiful young men, Adonis, Osiris, Tammuz, Attis. Each year the goddess and her lover had to mate, or the whole earth would wither without issue. And at the sanctuary of the goddess, each year the human sexes aped the gods in licentious rites. We don't know what the Eleusinian Mysteries were, but we know enough of the Dionysiac revels and the Roman Saturnalia to know that religion used to be fun. In Babylon, the Vestals of Astarte, the Syrian Venus, gave up their bodies to strangers as a religious sacrament. By their charming gift they guaranteed the green returning spring. I don't know about you, but I think they had something on the Baptists.

The Perfessor stopped and took another drink.

—Ah, how beautiful the earth was in pagan times! Imagine going into the sacred shrine at Eleusis. I wonder what words were uttered, words so old that no one knew any longer what they meant, words like the whisperings of a womb, words from the dawn of the Aryan peoples! And what mystic rite did the young initiate behold!

—I think it likely that he was shown an ear of corn.

—What a charming idea! the Perfessor said. John, you must go abroad some day before you die. Of all the shrines, the one I like best is the lake at Nemi in the Alban Hills. Of course, you know Turner's picture of 'The Golden Bough.' The ancient belief was that Jupiter entered the oak, his sacred tree, in the lightning bolt and left his evergreen spirit on its limbs in the herb called mistletoe. So each candidate for the priesthood of the Arician grove at Nemi had to pluck down this golden bough, the life of the god, and take it to himself. Then he could kill the old priest and take his place. No doubt, after this achievement he coupled with the vestals who kept the oak fire burning.

—Professor, you ought to write this great story of the myths of vegetation and the beginnings of religion.

—I'm too old, the Perfessor said. Some other genius, younger and less bibulous, will do it and get the credit for it. You see, John, the Jews made the world ethical instead of beautiful. I for one will never forgive them for the myth of Eden. Of course, the dramatic climax of the story, as in most myths, is simply the act of love. But the great invention of the Jews was their idea that sex was evil as well as fun and fruitful. Their god, though made in the image of man, never made love. The old boy was too busy breaking the heads of rebellious tribes. Why is love taboo anyway?

—Taboo was primitive man's moral law. The taboo thing wasn't evil in our sense—just dangerous. It was charged with the fluid of divine power. For primitive man, all things connected with love and death were dangerous.

—Did it ever occur to you that primitive man was a rather wily customer after all?

—The wisdom of the mythmakers is still with us, Professor. The profoundest mystery in the world is the existence of Another. Erotic love is the intense awareness of this Other, a Sacred Place. The lover bears the golden bough of godlike appetite and mysterious power and passes through the dismal wood that lies at the portals of Tartarus. Among the gibbering shades, he presses in with mortal thrust, making the boat of Charon heavy with his unusual weight. He bears the golden bough to the inmost shrine of the earth-goddess where he repeats the ancient frenzy. As you say, this rite is not unconnected with blood and death, for the renewal of form is possible only by the destruction of form. Love is a sweet death. A million die that one may reach the mark.

He beheld the fading beauty of the day over Waycross. Now the roofs of the town were drenched in a last red bath of fire. A few rays thrust through to paint the green body of a nymph and touch the pooled and spouting fountain with golden light. The children were little blind swimmers in the valley of the day's receding brightness. Corn filled the earth with blind roots. All things were bathed in light and longing.

—We'll never go any farther than those broken stones beside the inland ocean, the Perfessor said. The corn god is gone, and we have —behold!—only the corn.

He took a long pull at his bottle, coughed, and sighed.

—The world is still full of divinity and strangeness, Mr. Shawnessy said. The scientist stops, where all men do, at the doors of birth and death. He knows no more than you and I why a seed remembers the oak of twenty million years ago, why dust acquires the form of a woman, why we behold the earth in space and time. He hasn't yet solved the secret of a single name upon the earth. We may pluck the nymph from the river, but we won't pluck the river from ourselves: this coiled divinity is still all murmurous and strange. There are sacred places everywhere. The world is still man's druid grove, where he wanders hunting for the Tree of Life.

—This conversation is hard on an excitable old man, the Perfessor said. Just look at little Evelina out there! I wish you could persuade her to do her duty as a vestal. And isn't it a ritual day that we've been having?

The Perfessor moved his head in quick darts to an odd rhythm. Under his breath, he was reciting,

—*Io Hymen Hymenaee!*

Io Hymen Hymenaee! On the day of the birth of the Republic, after the runners had gone down the lane of faces to a distant string and the women had made a music of laughter and applause with their red mouths, in the young afternoon, by a curious and curving pathway, the hero made his way unto the place.

And the waters of the lake slept in the solitude of the encircling hills, the stream of the serpent river came down by shore and shallow, through tarn and tangling swamp, the murmur of its waters was beautiful in dense reeds.

And according to a legend, there was a grove near that lake and in the midst thereof a sacred tree, from which the earth there had taken its name of music and of strangeness.

In distant and dark woodlands, in the attitude of one listening, the young hunter stood and waited for a sign. And this was in the time before the fall and death of so many woodland deities, when the earth was young, and the goddess still lived on earth in the person of a woman with bright hair and gracious limbs. It had also been said in the legend that she might be known by a curious and curving mark on the bare flesh of her body.

And the tall oaks of the wood were filled with a living sound, the barky lips were calling to him through the dim forest, saying:

Io Hymen Hymenaee! O, fleet of foot, the goddess is waiting by the tree. O, impetuous young man!

In distant and dark woodlands, in the attitude of one listening, he waited for a sign, and the voices of the woodland deities were saying:

Io Hymen Hymenaee! O, sun-belovèd! For you, the golden bough, all heavy with seed. For you the talismanic branch. For you a prize, dangerous and sweet. O, mortal more than mortal, o, young man more belovèd than a god, hunt deep and far and do not be prevented.

Come, come, the voices said, come unto these woods with dark hair glancing. Come and join our revels. But first drink deep the blood-exciting potion. We will imprison you in ropes of flowers. *Io Hymen Hymenaee!* O, strong young bull! O, young prize-winner!

Victorious boy, feed on the flesh of apples smitten by the sun. It is the season when the corn is green beside the river and the sacred juice of life is rising in the stalk. Let there be rains and golden warmth for many days. O, brave young man, be tender but compulsive. Lo! you were chosen from among thousands to make the goddess fruitful.

The vestals are jealous—all afternoon they plunge their fevered bodies into the lake without relief.

The corn is as tall as the knee of a goddess. Let the corn be high and the seedshock stiff to bursting. Fling seed and make the earth tremble from delirious feet.

Come, come, and bring the hero to the shrine, sweet sisters, unclothe his body, let his limbs be laved in the cold waters of the sacred pool, and bring him, bring him, jealous sisters, into the presence of the goddess

July 4— BARE —1859

EXCEPT FOR A CHAPLET OF OAKLEAVES, JOHNNY SHAWNESSY'S HEAD

was dizzy from the noonday sun and other, more worldly causes. In the buggy were three other people, Susanna Drake, Cash Carney, and a girl from Middletown named Peachy something or other. The buggy seat was narrow, and Susanna sat on Johnny's lap. The girls had insisted that he wear his oakleaf garland. Peachy said it looked fetching, and Susanna said that it reminded her of the picture of a statue she had seen somewhere, but she couldn't remember where.

Cash Carney had brought two jugs of cider and a few sandwiches. The sandwiches were soon gone. The whiskey and the Race had left Johnny very hungry and thirsty, and he drank several cupfuls of cider. It had a sharp taste that made him feel wild. Of course, even in his festive condition, he was aware that Susanna Drake was a Southern Lady and that he must be very careful not to offend her in any way. It was hard, however, to find legitimate uses and places for his hands, until he discovered that she was holding them and squeezing them from time to time. Her hands were warm, moist, and very strong. A light dew stood on the flesh above her pouting mouth, and her body smelled faintly of flowers. After a few cupfuls of cider she was talking very fast and giving little shrieks of laughter at inappropriate times. She bounced and twisted in his lap and now and then to express excitement hugged him so hard that he couldn't breathe.

Cash Carney had brought some firecrackers along, and every now and then he lit one on his cigar and tossed it out of the buggy. He had also brought a newspaper, from which Johnny kept reading aloud to the girls, introducing witty variations of his own into the news, until the sun and the cider made his head swirl and the print blurred. All four talked excitedly and sometimes all at once.

Cash Carney talked about extending the branch rail line northwest from Three Mile Junction and of various plans he had for expanding his feedstore and liquor business to Middletown. He gestured forcibly with his cigar and sometimes put his right arm around Peachy's back and blew smoke in her face.

Peachy talked about various troubles she had had with a dressmaker in Middletown, who was, it appeared, an impossible person.

Susanna Drake talked about various buggyrides she had been on and picnics on rivers down South. She talked about how beautiful Louisiana was and how Johnny must come South sometime and visit her. He would just *love* it.

Johnny, for reasons quite unknown to himself, talked mostly about balloon ascensions, goldseekers in the West, and tightrope walkers.

The road which led from Freehaven to Lake Paradise was a grass-grown trail just wide enough for one buggy, and in the last half-mile it was little better than a cowpath. Those days, the lake was still inaccessible to the general public, though fishermen, hunters, and picnickers sometimes made their way to it. Now and then, in the latter stages of the ride, it was necessary to get out and push the buggy through difficult places. Johnny, still chapleted with oakleaves, performed prodigies of strength. The earth was fluid beneath his pushing feet. There was a strong taste of cider in his throat.

He had always intended to visit Paradise Lake. Now he remembered the time he had set out to do so in a leaky boat, which foundered just short of the goal. On that occasion he had made his way out of a swamp and had encountered a buggy coming from the lake, containing a number of young people, including Nell Gaither. Even now he felt a hot twinge of jealousy because Nell had gone swimming in the mysterious waters of Lake Paradise with Garwood Jones.

The buggy went through oak forests and past dark ravines choked with brush and rotten logs. The air returned the jocund voices with a hollow distinctness. There was a smell of rottenness and the river. Gaps in the forest showed half-naked hills, strewn with glacial boulders. Now and then there was a low place filled with rushes and swampgrass. The path, perhaps an old Indian trace, writhed in and out among the hills, slowly through a vast green summer day. Soon he would see the ancient pool of Paradise.

Meanwhile, he drank more cider, and his vision became less certain. Other people were making the decisions, and he was just going along for the sensation. Somewhere it was decided to leave the buggy and walk.

In the young afternoon, reeling and singing like a clovenfooted god, one finger hooked into the ring of a ciderjug, the other holding the hand of a laughing girl, Johnny Shawnessy came down to Lake Paradise.

He wasn't aware of the exact moment when he first saw the lake. After a while he knew he had been walking for some time beside the cold, flat pool of it, smelling its fishy odor. He wanted to plunge into it, feel the cold wash of it across his floating limbs, he wanted to raise his voice in great cries clanging like the majestic birds that swam down the air along the lilied reaches of the lake and river, he wanted to croak and cry with watergurglings like the troops of frogs that shouted from the shallows.

What happened after that, Johnny Shawnessy never could remember in a systematic way. There was a period during which everything was blurred, and there was a period during which everything had a dazzling clarity.

It was during the blurred period that he and Cash changed into striped bathing suits that hung below their knees. Cash kept his cigar and Johnny his oakleaf garland, token of victory. They hunted up the girls, who had been giggling and shrieking in a secluded place near shore. Susanna came out of the wood in a green bathing dress belted at the waist and reaching to her ankles. Her black hair was unloosened. She and Johnny took hands and ran into the water.

—I can outswim you, Johnny! she cried.

The padded floor of the lake sank under their bare feet. They swam out into the lake a long way.

—Let's dive under! Susanna shrieked.

Diving under, he saw a creature moving through glaucous depths with a fishlike ease in spite of its fantastic costume. Its black hair trailed in the water. Its face approached his in the green pool of Lake Paradise, the large violet eyes dilated, the deep lips parted. This creature below the surface of the lake looked ferally excited. It flung its strong arms around his neck. For some reason, he wasn't at all afraid. With a swift motion, he freed himself and shot to the surface, his oakleaf garland dripping.

The sun was a hot yellow coin in the vast day overhead. The lake lay brilliant and flat around him. There were no human sounds or forms anywhere to be seen except his own.

Then Susanna's head broke the surface.

—Let's have a waterfight, Johnny.

She sprang on him and tried to thrust him under. They were near the northeast shore now, in water up to their necks. Johnny had never dreamed that a woman could be so strong. But it turned out that he was much stronger, and he got a savage joy out of overpowering her without hurting her. The struggle lasted a long time, as they thrashed around in the water. It ended when Johnny plucked her bodily from the water and ran up on the shore with her, both of them gasping and almost crying with laughter. Then they had perhaps fallen down in a strange ecstasy of laughter and exhaustion, and there had been perhaps a kind of sleep.

It was much later that he awoke. The sun hailed heat on his eyeballs. He seemed to remember that he had lain backward and the earth had turned over on him. He had taken it into his arms, and he had touched it with his hands, admiring the slippery warmth of it. The shadecasting hair of it had fallen into his eyes and around his face. He had touched his lips to it again and again. He had touched its mouth, warm and with a taste of passion, and he had drunk the steam of it, which was of madness and of grapes.

The second period, the period in which all things seemed drenched with an unusual light, began when he opened his eyes. He saw then a wild, almost unfamiliar woman's face watching his face.

—We must be sort of crazy, she said. Lying here like this with nothing on.

He reached up and touched his head.

—I still have my garland, he said.

At this, they began laughing, and while they were laughing they sat up, and he saw that they were in deep grass close to the lake. Their cast-off bathing suits lay in soggy heaps beside them. They were in a region of pools, rushes, small trees. Frogs quirped among the lily pads.

The girl sitting beside him dropped her head in sudden shyness and put her hands over her perfectly formed breasts.

—I hope you don't mind my scar, Johnny, she said in a low, thrilling voice.

He had seen it faintly scarlet, descending just to the roots of her left breast, deepening into a pool of cruelly writhen flesh where it ended. But it only emphasized the mystery and beauty of the creature who had been lying with him on the shore of Lake Paradise. And in answer to her question, he was about to put his arms around her again, when abruptly she sprang up and began to walk away from him.

—Catch me if you can! she said, looking back over her shoulder.

—Madame, he said, you have just challenged the fastest runner in Raintree County.

The gesture with which she flung her hair back and began to run was so wanton that he was smitten with a precise ambition, though up to this time he had hardly known what it was that he intended to do. Now, a victorious smile curved his lips, and he sprang after. The olive-tinted nudity of the girl seemed about to dissolve in the green-gold light of the swamp. He made the pursuit much longer than was necessary while his eyes drank in this incredible creature reeling and running before him. He listened to her wild, soft cries. Twice he caught her, but when she struggled to escape, laughing and pushing him away, he let her go.

In this way they came to a place in the deep swamp where there were many small trees of one kind all growing from a grassy mound which rose from the damp floor of the marsh like an island. It seemed an ultimate place as he chased her up the gentle incline among the trees and caught her a third time. He had seen boulders strewn along the ascent, and there were two stones between which, panting with exhaustion, he stood holding his companion.

—You win the race, she said. To the victor——

Her hand came up and lazily pulled at the oakleaf garland around his head, and then suddenly the whole consented weight of her body was suspended only by the circle his arms made at her waist. Head reeling with light and heat, he stood a moment braced against this tyrannous weight that pulled his whole body into an attitude of resistance and desire. The earth seemed tremulous beneath his feet. It buzzed and softly clamored, beat him with quick, soft wings of wind and light. A dust of yellow flowers dripped on his shoulders and into the black hair of the girl.

He didn't know then who it was that he held. She was nameless, untamed, candid. And as for him, even as the river found its way with slowness, as if it had an everlasting summer to swell and swell through its broad channel to the lake, so did he linger on the brink of young fulfillment, life's young American, wearing his victory garland. Mad images of desire, contest, and thrilling achievement, of bold exertions, words of valor and pagan disregard for old convention assaulted him in the rank air of Lake Paradise, where still his feet were arched to support the weight that was pulling and pulling at his strength. He shut his eyes. A flood of words on fragments of newspapers streamed down on him in a soft dust, describing mythical Events in which he was the hero. Stringbreaker, wirewalker, goldseeker, aeronaut of a blue and enterprising day, he lingered on the brink of . . .

TERRIFIC ASCENSION

(Epic Fragments from the *Mythic Examiner*)

The crowd became impatient, as the ascension had been delayed for so long and the balloon still lay collapsed on the car. Mr. Mountain gave a last look of appraisal at the sky, and as everything still seemed propitious he gave a signal to his assistants, who straightway began to inflate the sphere. Gradually the canvas globe rounded out under the pressure of the instreaming ethereal fluid, until with a few last vigorous puffs it burst into majestic rotundity, taut and straining to be off, pulling with gigantic force against the restraining ropes. The ballasting sandbags were torn violently from their place and it was only by dint of grabbing the flailing ropes and hanging on for dear life that Mr. Mountain's assistants, aided by volunteers from the crowd, could keep the prodigious ship from bursting from its moorings and soaring off into the azure with no passengers aboard. There was no time to be lost. With a brisk adieu, still wearing his stovepipe hat and jauntily swinging his cane, Mr. Mountain, overcoat and all, leaped handily aboard, where he was joined by Mr. Jennings and Mr. Luce. Your correspondent bestowed a farewell kiss on the lips of his intended, and notebook in hand, walked toward the eager craft, excited and not a little filled with trepidation at the thought of being the first professional eyewitness reporter of an aerial ascension. The men began to release the ropes, and no sooner had the ballast been removed than with a smooth, birdlike rush, the great sphere shot up and floated blithely down the air. Leaning out, your observer had the giddy dreamlike sensation of being carried aloft on the magic carpet of the Arabian Nights. The City grew small. Figures of friends and strangers became antlike. Then, although there was no further sensation of movement, the rigid projectile was coasting serenely down the blue sunlit vistas of the upper air, proceeding southward at a tremendous rate of speed to . . .

A place of ancient memory waited for him beside still waters. A grove of flowering trees beside memorial waters. *A green isle in the sea, love, a fountain and a shrine.* There had been a legend and a prophecy of how . . .

The young hero swam a night and a day through the ocean stream and arriving at an island of various and pleasant growth, came forth streaming into sunlight, dashing the water from his hair and eyes. Then, entering a gloomy wood, he walked toward the center of the island, where . . .

—I feel right out on public view, he said.

—You're sweet, she said. O, you are *so* sweet, Johnny.

A GENERAL INVITATION

A general invitation is extended all around
To the people of the Union in every state and town,
To come and witness this great and daring feat
Of walking on the mammoth rope by the great Professor Sweet.

The crowd cheered the steel-legged Professor, who was doing his best to uphold the strength, resolution, and muscular agility of Americans before the world. He made his way through roaring thousands. He stopped once, and gesturing for silence, made one of his quaint speeches, to the effect that he had been practicing for two years and that he had every reason to suppose he was as adroit in all the complicated evolutions of the sport as the renowned Frenchman himself. He bespoke himself ready to do whatever another man could on a slack rope or a taut. Admission for the first performance, his virginal adventure in this breathtaking pastime, was free of charge. Taking in hand the usual long, smoothly planed pole, if anything a trifle above the dimensions commonly employed by the famous Frenchman, he set his foot tentatively on the wire and then, as if bracing himself for the shock of standing above the chasm over which he was expected to go and return, he paused while the full military band struck up a chorus. Then . . .

As the young hero approached the tree, he passed by flowers that kissed his body like soft mouths. He beat them down, observing with a sidelong glance the furious and sweet death of so much beauty. And the earth here became more moist and seemed as if it swayed beneath his feet. Looking upward he saw the sunburst of the tree in the very middle of the sacred grove while . . .

WAY DOWN SOUTH

Those accustomed to the pinching and penurious weathers of the North cannot possibly imagine until they have experienced it the day-long softness and fragrance of the Southern air. Below the Mason and Dixon Line, one passes almost imperceptibly into another realm, full of balsamic odors and blue skies of billowy clouds. And who shall sufficiently extol the loamy richness of that Southern earth and who shall describe . . .

THE WONDERS OF AERIAL NAVIGATION

Looking over the side of the car, we perceived that the smoke from the factories had faded. Streets grew narrower and darker, and at last the City had dwindled to a spot. The balloon now commanded an extended view of the Mississippi, the Missouri, and the Illinois Rivers, and another water which we could not identify glimmered eastward in the direction which our flight was now swiftly taking. Your observer had now lost all sense of danger. His feeling was that ballooning, besides being the most pleasant and swift, was the safest mode of locomotion known. Steaming down a rapid current in a boat on a lovely evening, with sublime vistas, romantic caverns, and green foliage on either side, glistening waves below and mild sky above, is grand and delightful; sailing on an unruffled lake, parting the placid water and skimming like a gull with gentle fleetness, is ineffably glorious, but these enjoyable modes of travel yield in point of dainty pleasurableness to the birdlike grace and the impressive surroundings of aerial . . .

THERE HE GOES!

Without more ado, the young American ran a short way out onto the rope, where he seemed to hesitate. Then taking the pole more firmly in hand, he ran rapidly out to the middle, where again he paused briefly, and then, in less time than it takes to relate it, while the crowd gasped, his lithe young form was seen to negotiate the whole length of the perilous crossing, and he leaped down on the far side to accept the applause of the crowd, louder than the cataract over which he had just safely transported himself. Then, as if stimulated by the excitement of his audience, he stepped once more upon the swaying rope, and running lightly out to the center, he stopped, placed the pole crosswise on the rope and stood on his head. As the crowd alternately applauded and begged him to return to safety, he went on to perform certain gymnastic evolutions so complicated as to bring gasps of horror. These acrobatic feats, performed at a fixed spot on the rope, were rendered all the more difficult because of the encumbrance of the pole with which at other times the intrepid boy maintained his equilibrium. Now, however, this unwieldy prop came very near precipitating him headlong to disaster as he several times executed headstands, bodyflips, hung with one leg from the rope, and once again achieved an upright position. The chasm of the Niagara River roared ominously hundreds of feet below, but the steelnerved little figure never for a moment lost his head and at last, amid salvos of applause, catching the balancing stick in his two hands, he ran lightly and easily back to the American . . .

Shore and shallow, tarn and tangling swamp seemed now to mud his feet, but he would get the golden bough, regain the lost garden, achieve what no man ever had before. Still fired to hero fury by the elixir he had drunk from a flagon of enchantment, he rushed on reeling earth toward the trunk, which seemed now touched with motion. Somewhere the dragon brood was waiting, the guardians of the tree, and one, the greatest dragon of them all, lay mudded to forty fathoms in his lair, stirring the coiled length of his great tail. But before the beast awakened in his cave, the hero ran to the base of the tree and catching the supple trunk in his arms thrashed it back and forth. The whole earth swayed and swam beneath this plucking and this shaking, the roots of the tree throbbed and tightened in the deep soil, the dark vegetation lashed itself against him. . . .

WATCH OUT, PERFESSOR!

Just then, to the concern of all, the intrepid young funambulist was seen to miss his footing halfway across, although up to that time, with the blindfold over his eyes, he had proceeded with wonderful surefootedness. And so for what seemed an eternity, he tottered on the very brink of the chasm, while the rope thrashed mightily, and all eyes turned instinctively to the hideous steepness and churning precipitous sides of the abyss into which unless . . .

CRASH!

The violence of the suddenly engendered storm having torn a great rent in the balloon, it was now carried broken and losing altitude swiftly toward the lake, scudding and skimming just over the tops of the trees, with branches now and again reaching up and tearing gaps in the burst, collapsing sphere, and now the cold waters of the lake were beneath us, and having thrown out everything and even taken off and tossed away all our garments, we were preparing ourselves for the inevitable plunge into . . .

. . . one last godlike exertion, whereupon, with a great cry, as if the earth were stabbed with pleasure to its center, the tree gave down the seeddust from its laden branches. This seed raining goldenly upon the earth was warm with exultation and the promise of eternal life. . . .

How many times and how long in that afternoon, the Hero of Raintree County, nameless and remote from time, pleasured himself with a forbidden fruit he couldn't say. But in the late afternoon, awakening as from a sleep, he rose from the place where he had lain. With him arose the woman his companion, and together, silently, not holding hands, they found their way back to a place where they had left their costumes. They entered again un-naked, the cold lake, and they swam back silently across, feeling as if an eye were watching them from covert. Arriving at the far side, Johnny Shawnessy discovered that he had left his oakleaf garland behind him and some other things beside that he would never get back. And with a start of wonder and recognition, now that his head was clearing, he remembered that in leaving the strange island in the middle of the swamp he had looked back and had seen what looked like letters carven on the stones beneath a tree, on one a J and on the other

SOMETHING THAT MIGHT HAVE BEEN

A C OR EVEN A

MISSHAPEN

—S,

said the Perfessor,

is for Sex and also for Sin.
The difference between them is not worth a pin.

—Well, I'm back, Mrs. Brown said, coming up the steps of the verandah.

Darkness, a gentle tide, had risen up the prim enclosure of the garden, hiding the nymphs in pools of shadow. Mr. Shawnessy could no longer distinguish the forms of two bronze bodies entangled in lilies at the base of the fountain. The children had gone behind the house.

—Still talking, I see, she said to the Perfessor. Here let me sit between.

—There's only one thing I like better than good talk, the Perfessor said. Put it right down here. We were talking about clothes.

Mr. Shawnessy cleared his throat.

—Don't worry, John, the Perfessor said. Evelina's an emancipated woman. As for clothes, I'm for 'em. What kills these back-to-nature cults isn't prudery, but the fact that most folks look like hell naked. Man is really one of the more unattractive animals. For sheer looks, the great apes beat him all hollow.

—Strange, Mr. Shawnessy said, that the only animal that knows it's an animal is desperately eager to conceal the fact.

—There, said the Perfessor, you have the beginning of religion. Modern religion is man's effort to convince himself that he's not an animal. Now, animals live according to their instincts. Therefore, says Religion, instinctive life shall be evil, and Sex, the strongest instinct, shall be the greatest evil. God is man's conscience, the policeman of civilization, punishing man for all recollections of his animal state. It's only right that religion should begin with the Fall of Man because religion was itself the Fall of Man.

—Personally, Mr. Shawnessy said, I think we're happier wearing the figleaf of forbidden knowledge.

—O, I don't know, the Perfessor said. The average animal is happier than you or I—that is, until man comes along and fences him in. Think what a good time our friend Jupiter over there in the bullpasture would have if we let him run loose. He could feed and fight and flute to his heart's content until cut down in a serene old age. Man's unhappiness, you see, comes precisely because he knows. Man's the only animal who knows that he's going to die. Religion's a vast ritual of remorse for the unhappy discovery of pain and death.

A sound of singing came from the Revival Tent.

—There is a fountain filled with blood. . . .

—Listen to 'em! the Perfessor said. Inmates of the greatest lunatic asylum man ever built—the Christian Church! The typical Christian is just plain crazy—in a socially acceptable way. He believes that the universe was made by a grand old man squatting on a cloud. He believes that this old man somehow begot a son without intercourse a few hundred years ago. He believes that this son is in some mysterious way also the father. He believes that this son came down to earth for the express purpose of being executed like a common criminal to purge humanity of its sins. He believes that the world is better for all this, despite the fact that people go on being as no-account as ever. He believes that this young man, after being very dead, got up and walked out of the grave. He believes that the old man up there on the cloud is all-good and all-powerful, but that the world of his creation is a world of corruption and death.

The Perfessor stopped and took a drink. A faint glare of fire was on the western wall of the night. The singing from the Revival Tent had lapsed and begun again.

—As for this god, the Perfessor went on, he has all the characteristics of a crazy person. He has a god-obsession. He's being constantly annoyed and persecuted by other imaginary gods that shall not be had before him. He wants everything to redound to his personal credit. Nothing for others—but all only for him, so that he may be glorified forever and forever. He falsifies the history of the world as an act of self-justification. He wields unlimited power like a despot and brags of his triumphs. Whatever he wills is good, and whatever is against his will is evil. He attributes his own faults to others, attacking Satan for wanting to rule in heaven and charging the Hebrews for being a stiff-necked people. Isn't this a picture of a thoroughly unpleasant old man and a thoroughly unpleasant universe?

—Yes, it is, Mr. Shawnessy said. But it was better than what went before. At least the Hebrew God was the product of a strong moral sense. Later, in the Christian ethic of the Golden Rule, this moral sense went beyond the tribal stage.

—The pagans were closer to divinity than Christ was, the Perfessor said. At least they frankly recognized the miracle of sex and procreation. They showed a healthy appetite for life itself, which is more than we can say for the immaculate Nazarene.

—The pagans recognized the divinity of process, Mr. Shawnessy said, but not of personality. And as far as I can see, human life is people. It's even simpler than that. It's Oneself, a simple, separate person. But Oneself exists by virtue of a world shared with other selves. Our life is the intersection of the Self with an Other. In the intense personal form this intersection is love, and in the ideal, general form it's the Republic. Jesus gave us the moral shape of this Republic—the Sign of the Cross.

Mr. Shawnessy heard a commotion in the bushes. The Perfessor's place on the swing was empty, and the Perfessor's head was just disappearing over the side of the verandah.

—I'll be back later, he said. Be good children, and don't eat any apples.

—It's getting quite dark, Mrs. Brown said, her voice low and musical.

She sat beside him on the swing, her hair bound up leaving her neck bare all around in the fashionable way, her hands folded in her lap, her face and figure in piquant profile.

He was thinking of her universe. It was, he knew, a rather brave, hopeful, lovely universe. He understood this universe, liked it, lingered uneasily at the threshold of it. He was thinking of the long, long way that had led from female to feminine, from Woman to Eve. Billions of lost souls had labored to perfect this slight creature and her universe of feminine values. Two hundred thousand years had been necessary to tailor her modish dress out of a figleaf. Billions of dead hands had put stone upon stone to erect the curious monument of her house. Like a sound of ocean was the murmur of dead tongues that had struggled to speak so that her mouth might make musical words about the rights of women and the finer things of life, so that her bookcase might be full of gilded volumes. This woman, too, was Eve, a sacred Other. There was, he knew, a sense in which he approached her through the precise formulations of her lawn, and as he did so, garden and house dissolved; pagan adornments were overcome by bark and leaves. He had entered a grove of danger and decision. There was a sense in which he found her there, forever waiting, naked, with gracious loins, an anguishingly beautiful young woman whose body wore perhaps some curious blemish as a sign of her mortality. There was a sense in which he was always reaching out his hand toward her in this place and touching her face as it looked up into his. There was a sense in which the face was that of the woman he had married, and also of some other women whose faces had been turned up toward his. There was a sense in which this face of the archetypal woman was forbidden, untouchable, divine. In this excitement, there was a sense in which he became lost: he lost his name, his selfhood, his oakleaf garland, and even his own private republic, and achieved a wonderful unity—which was immediately relinquished.

—Professor Stiles is an odd person, isn't he? Mrs. Brown said at last. What makes him so unhappy?

—The Professor has a vested interest in being unhappy. If the world were other than he supposed, he'd be a discredited person.

—He says so much that's true. But he turns it all to a joke or a hollow thing at last.

—But it gives him a great advantage in conversation to speak without responsibility. Nothing is sacred to the Professor. There are no taboos, no forbidden words or places. You and I, on the other hand, Evelina, are continually treading with care as if the universe were all alive and wherever we put down our foot we might hear a cry of human anguish.

—I used to admire Professor Stiles very much, Mrs. Brown said. He wants me to come back to New York. Do you think I ought to go?

Just then, there was a disturbance in the bushes, and Professor Jerusalem Webster Stiles clambered over the wall of the verandah and lay full-length on the stone floor.

—*And curst be he that moves my bones,* he said, his voice hoarse.

—Mrs. Brown!

It was a voice from the backyard.

—Excuse me, Mrs. Brown said. I'll try to come back. It's about time to hang the Japanese lanterns.

She walked down the steps into the darkening lawn and disappeared around the corner of the house. The Perfessor stayed flat, a monumental effigy with eyeglasses on, face sharp and pallid, hands crossed on chest.

—There she goes! he said. What a waste of beauty! Why will women try to be intellectual? The only feminist movement I want to see is one to make women more feminine. For Christ's sake, let's not make them more like men. You know, I really despise bright women. It's unbecoming of a woman to be interested in ideas.

—Professor, Mr. Shawnessy said, don't you ever get tired of being a professional rebel? Why don't you resign yourself to being happy now and then? Why not give up and admit that you enjoy life? Still, I suppose such a radical change of mind might make you disintegrate in a second like the corpse of M. D. Valdemar, when they took it out of the mesmeric trance.

—Really! the Perfessor said. You disturb me, John. I'm not feeling very well as it is.

He crawled over to the swing and sat down.

—I would love to be moral, he said. I would love to believe in the Republic of Brotherly Love, Sisterly Affection, Filial Piety, and Jesusly Humility. If only I weren't so goddam well-informed and bright! After all, John, human morality is a mere refinement of the social instinct, which we see also in some of the other animals. We're moral because it pays to be moral. But the really great problems of the Republic don't achieve moral solutions. Take the Negro question. The Negro is morally about where he was before the War. The Declaration of Independence is still a White Paper.

Westward, from the Revival Tent, came a smell of smoke. Low flames licked the fringed horizon.

—What are they doing over there anyway? the Perfessor asked.

—Just a Fourth of July bonfire, Mr. Shawnessy said.

He was vaguely troubled. He was stirred by a memory of something that had happened, a legend of beauty and the earth, of the tangled world of personal republics, and of their infinite intersections.

—Yes, sir, the Perfessor said. If everyone were like me, the Negro problem could be settled in a jiffy. Sex doesn't draw any color lines, and neither do I. At night, all cats are black. Never in the history of mankind have two races lived so close as the black and white do in America without a complete blend after a while. This dark old rule of the jungle is just what the Southern white fears. Let's not fool ourselves: all his efforts to keep the Negro down are, at root, efforts to keep black seed running in black channels. This paladin, the old Southern Colonel, defends the purity of us all.

Just a Fourth of July bonfire. Some fragments of old lumber that used to be somebody's house, loose odds and ends of lives.

—You may prate as you please, the Perfessor said, of beauty and the good—human life's a dark affair. In the Swamp all was fated, but no one knew it. Now, our advance in understanding consists of *know*ing that all is fated.

—But what you call fate includes moral decisions made by human beings. The tragedies of human life merely teach us that we can't escape responsibility. In short, we can't resign from the Republic.

The two men smoked in silence. The red glare in the west now flickered through the palings in the fence.

—John, the Perfessor said, shaking his head, what a bloody tapestry our life has been! In this modern republic, nineteen hundred years after the birth of Christ, a million young men killed each other in hot blood because human skins differ in pigment. And the end is not in view.

The Perfessor shot a keen glance at Mr. Shawnessy.

—Your own life, he said, has been strangely touched by this mixture of the bloods. You know, John, there was something you never told me about your first marriage, though you hinted at it.

—Yes?

—Maybe I shouldn't ask, the Perfessor said, but I've always been damn curious——

He hesitated.

—Yes? Mr. Shawnessy said, his voice gentle and remote.

He was flicking pages in the book of his own life, a myth of himself and his memories of the Republic in War and Peace.

The trains are changing in the station of Myself. I must catch a darktime express. Good night, ladies. Good night, ladies. Good night, sweet ladies, we're going to leave you now. . . .

O, let's go back and live in old daguerreotypes of houses by the river. *O, subtle, musky, slumbrous . . .*

Yes, I was guilty too. I never could resist the shape of beauty by the river. But I didn't know that I set my mouth to the mouth of a dark Helen.

Did you think that a single black man could feel the lash and you not bear the scar? Did you think that a single comrade might lie dead in the July corn, and you not lose a portion of yourself? Did you think that mankind could go to war and you not fight?

Go back. Unwind the tapestry and trace the scarlet thread. Go back, lonely young voyager on rivers. Relive the sibilant names. Review old lusts beside the river. Lay on the lash and fill the slaver's hold. Plant seed and raise a crop of cotton in the bottom lands. Stand up and give us pompous words about the rights of man, while the darkies labor on the levee.

(All this is the marvellous myth of Raintree County, where all threads come together and where all rivers run and all must find the lake, where all the trains are changing in the stations, and every single word that ever was is written into riddles between the four lines of a square.)

But tread with care. There are lost souls here. There is a piteous and lost republic. Tread with care. There are lost lives here that will cry out like sinners touched by flame. Catch the train. Hurry back along the branchlines of departed Raintree Counties. There are lost souls here. There are lost voices here. There are lost songs. Tread with care.

O, don't you remember a long time ago? O, don't you remember

July 4— An —1863

Old Southern Melodrama

was playing itself up to the last curtain,

he felt, as the train chugged on toward Three Mile Junction. He shook the last of a brief, uneasy sleep from his head. Smoke sifted in through the open windows on his already grimy face. He stared at the daguerreotype in his hand, in which four faces looked palely out from under the shadow of a Southern mansion. He studied the mad scrawls on two letters that had started him two days ago on a hunt for two lost children. He had touched their ghostly trail in a store where a doll had been bought. He had seen the two lost faces imprisoned on a glass plate in a photographer's shop. One of these faces had taken the name Henrietta Courtney, a certain Negro girl, dark Helen, dead long ago in fire. He had said good-by to Nell Gaither in the station in Indianapolis. And now the chase had nearly come fullcircle to the place where it had started.

In a few minutes, he would be home in Freehaven, and the thing would be settled. No doubt this dark old melodrama in which he had been entangled for four years would turn out all right—more or less—and the nightmare of the last three days would have an awakening.

Nevertheless, he felt more terror now than at any time since the hunt had started, as he sat helpless, holding some fragments of a life. He had been slowly assembling the pieces of a curious puzzle for three years now. He reshuffled the pieces, slowly fitting them into place, still hunting for the missing piece.

The faces in the daguerreotype were pale smudges in the yellow gaslight. Behind them rose the pillars of a doomed house. Here (but twenty years ago) was a little girl beside a river.

Then it seemed to him that only through a weakness of the will is the past relinquished. A human life had a dimension that wasn't perfectly understood. In this dimension, the whole river of one's life existed all at once, a legendary symbol written across the face of time. And the source of the river was in the gulf to which it flowed as well as the spring from which it rose. And if one were to understand the enigma of a twisted life on the land, where would one begin, except in a daguerreotypal river flowing past a daguerreotypal house?

The river was flowing, flowing to the sea. It poured its cold strong waters past dissolving swamps. The yellow pollen sifted on the river, the yellow pollen sank and bubbled in the river. The river passed a city on the Delta.

It was summer, and a little girl with violet eyes grew up beside the river, her life rising out of ancient summers where the hot nights throbbed with voices of darkies singing on the levees. They picked the cotton in the fields and piled the bales beside the river, and the steamboats passed in neverending line, their whistles shrilling and their big wheels turning. And the river passed and washed the earth away.

Whence had she come—Susanna, lost child of a stained republic? Who was the mother of this child? Who was the father of this child? Was it possible to follow this child, holding her unburnt doll, back through the windings of the Great Swamp?

The river passed in darkness to the sea, the yellow river passed in darkness, flowing, flowing to the sea.

This little being, being human, knew love and hatred by the river. One night she hunted for a doll in an old log cabin. On the levees, the darkies were gay, a glare of bonfires lit the night to celebrate the birth of the fairest of all republics. And her small form in a nightdress (dark hair hanging to her shoulders) wavered on a mirror at the landing. She saw the dark flesh and the white; the rose of love bloomed scarlet in the night, the symbol of a stained republic. This was the thing she found while hunting for a doll.

(Do you want to lose the most precious thing in all the world? Can you keep the most tragic of all the secrets?)

After that, she never ceased to be a little girl who was hunting something in the night.

The days went by like a shadow o'er the heart. There were novels about sentimental ladies and courtly gentlemen, in which mysterious notes broke up loves, effected conciliations and happy endings. Was it strange that in a little girl's jealous anger, the fatal note was penned?

(How could I know that it would kill the dearest thing in all the world? Didn't I hunt for the letter after that and ever since in the album where I left it? Didn't I hunt and hunt to get it back before she read it?)

Who set the fire that burned the house beside the river?

No one will ever know. No one will ever know who put the torch to the house and burned it to the ground. Was it a little girl who did it with a jealous word? Who was it murdered two bodies joined by fire taken from the ashes of the house beside the river? Whose was the footstep passing in the night? And could anyone tell after the fire which was the mother of Susanna? Did they ever put out the fire entirely and heal the scar and stop the smouldering pain over the left breast?

So there was one who grew up a shape of this earth; her name was musical and proud like names of cities razed. Her body was lovely like Helen and the Greeks, though scarred with a scarlet letter.

And the river flowed, the river flowed in music and strangeness, the father of all waters, dividing east and west and joining north and south, through shore and shallow, tarn and tangling swamp to the sea. And the senators stood up, put togas on their phrases, they bade the black flesh lie quiet in the chains, they bade the clamorous West to be still.

Could they make the words be still? Could they chain the strong words? Could they keep seed from growing and hunting for the light? Could they keep the black flesh in the Great Dismal Swamp?

(For there were strong men ever going West. *O, Susanna, do not cry for me!* They were putting the rails across the plain. The covered wagons shrugged and staggered through the passes. The engines hit the grade at forty miles per hour. They were coming all the time. They were coming down to . . .)

The days went by like a shadow o'er the heart. And one day a hero, lost young bard of Raintree County, sprang from the sunlight of a court house square and entered a room where his image was traced forever with a finger of light.

The train brought Johnny Shawnessy into Three Mile Junction, stopped briefly, and started up for the short run into Freehaven. Several new passengers had got on, crowding the coach. He would soon be home.

Then he remembered the afternoon on the shore of Lake Paradise, when a young gymnosophist had performed for cheering thousands, had walked a tightrope over the broad Ohio, achieved gymnastic bliss, ridden a balloon across the Republic, made bold forays below the Mason and Dixon Line, beaten down desire with a branch of yellow flowers.

And he remembered faces around a telegraph window and a letter at the post office, jasmine-scented from the South. A gray face had been seen many times in the Court House Square, of an old man, biblically stern. (Blow ye the trumpet, blow, all over the Republic!) One evening of November, when leaves dripped on the dead grass, he had stood by a lonely rock at the limit of the land and had remembered duty.

—Jedgin' from the light of them fires, they sure are raisin' a ruckus in town, a man said, peering out of a window. Reckon maybe they're celebratin' this here great victory at Gettysburg.

There was a strong glare of light in the sky over Freehaven, but as the train turned now directly toward the town, Johnny could see nothing more. He sat waiting.

The fragments of an immense puzzle of a human life and the Republic continued to fall into place, moving more and more swiftly and strongly like a river proceeding southward collecting a thousand random waters into one inexorable tide. On such a flood of waters he and Susanna Drake had gone South for their honeymoon to sultry nights of love in an old American city by the Delta.

He looked again at the daguerreotype in his hand. A tall house beside a river with five windows on its face! He remembered then the house near the Square in Freehaven; walkings at night, strange evasions, a scarlet strand of madness growing.

(When we lay together in the night, my unforgotten darling, when we touched our bodies in the night and made that fatal crossing, when we lay dreaming in the darkness so long and long, my darling, we were coming down to Sumter. *O, Susanna, do not cry for me. . . .*)

He remembered then how the bloody rose of Sumter had dawned on the Republic. Meanwhile he had lived in the tall house far from battles and had seen a being that was only a beginning come into Raintree County, Little Jim Shawnessy, a blue-eyed child. This child had come from the swamp where no one knew what seeds had intercrossed, where black and white and red and yellow sought each other blindly in the timeless underside of Raintree County.

He remembered then the face of his mad little wife fading from the doorpane back into the detested fabric of the house.

Who was Susanna Drake? A stream of reflections in mirrors? A sequence of shadows on lightsensitive plates? A river of dreams of rivers? Had she ever awakened from a dream that had begun one night before a fire? Perhaps she had gone on, always moving in that dream, walking in terror at night, hunting through the chambers of a tall house with a lamp in her hand, hunting for a secret darker than any other, whose source was hidden in the night of the Great Dismal Swamp. Did she hunt for a secret so dark that it could only be purged in fire?

He shut his eyes. Instantly, he saw the face of a little boy, an earnest small face in darkness, with violet eyes. A child's arms clutched at him wildly. A child voice cried, *Daddy!*

Johnny Shawnessy's body was bathed in cold sweat. His heart pounded. He was choking in the smoky heat of the car.

A man standing in the crowded coach leaned over and peered from the window.

—Must be some big excitement in town! Look at all them people on the road there!

Many people in wagons and buggies were going into town along the road that ran parallel with the tracks. Two or three wagons on their way out of town turned around and started back. The faces on the road were faintly scarlet.

Johnny stuffed the letter and the daguerreotype into his coatpocket. He got up and walked to the car door. Though the train had just entered the outskirts of Freehaven, he opened the door and stepped down to the last step, which skimmed the weeds along the track. He leaned out, watching. Other passengers lined up behind him. Above the noise of the train he could hear people shouting, bells ringing.

They were in town now. Streets, houses, buildings shuttled past. People stood before their houses all looking in one direction. Down all the ways of Raintree County in this commemorative night, hooves thundered, wheels turned, feet flew, all moving toward a center.

When the tracks veered northeast to the station, Johnny saw a column of flame and smoke roaring straight up.

—Jerusalem! a man said. That there's a *fire!* Must be the Court House.

—No, it ain't the Court House, a man said. Can't tell what it is.

Before the train stopped, Johnny jumped down and crossed the tracks. Running, he reached the Square, to find it full of people crossing it on their way to the fire. He ran on toward the alley at the south side of the Square. He looked between the buildings. There he saw plainly the last fragment of the puzzle.

The house blazed with light. Fire burned into the lonely face of it, fire shot in sharp tongues from the windows of it, fire flowed up it almost without touching it and rose fountainlike a hundred feet into the air.

In every open space where the heat wasn't too great, in streets, alleys, yards, on porches and roofs, hundreds and hundreds of faces enclosed the fire in dense banks watching.

After that, it made no difference that Johnny Shawnessy ran through the crowd and shoved his way out into the space before the house. It made no difference that he tried to throw himself into the fire to find the child that no one had been able to rescue. It made no difference that strong hands had to hold him back. All that made no difference now. In a way he had foreseen this thing, but all that he had done to circumvent it had been part of the great circle of time and fate that brought it about.

Or so it seemed to him as he walked back and forth before the burning house all night, waiting, as if the fire were a surly tenant who would have to be expelled before he could reenter his own premises. He heard people tell how the fire had gained headway before it was discovered, what with the excitement, the bonfires, and the fireworks on the Square. He heard them tell how a brave man had managed to get into the downstairs part of the house and had found Susanna lying unconscious in smoke near one of the windows, a broken lamp in her hand, her hair and face burned. He heard of fruitless efforts to ascertain whether anyone else was in the house. He heard all this and knew that it was all an old legend of pity and terror that had to be played out in expiation of a crime. Not his crime, necessarily—and yet in part his crime.

He received condolences about the lost child. He heard the speculations as to what might have caused the fire. He could have told them now what had caused the fire, but they wouldn't have understood.

He could have told them that fire could only be consumed by fire. He could have told them that this fire had come because men return to the swamp and lust after darkness and the night, because the form of a woman is meant to be seductive, because the earth is our first beloved. He could have told them that this fire had come and destroyed an innocent being because of guilty lust and careless seed. He could have told them that this fire had come because of Sumter and the Rights of Man and the Compromises and Danwebster and Gettysburg and the everrunning river, Father of Waters, which had that day begun to flow once more unvexed to the sea. He could have told them all that, but it wouldn't have done any good.

And as he waited into the dawn, Johnny Shawnessy decided that he too would go forth now and become a soldier of the Republic. It was a choice made not from heroism but from revulsion. He was sick at heart, and he had to leave Raintree County, perhaps in order to rediscover it and rebuild it again. He had to leave it and his memories of its alien visitor, a dark love, a tragic begetting.

And during that night when ten thousand dead young men lay unburied on the picnic slopes, cornfields, and familiar grounds of a little town in Pennsylvania, the house in which Johnny Shawnessy had lived for over three years burned utterly to the ground. Fire ate its way through the mournful face of the house. It cracked and shattered the windowglasses. The roof came crashing down, spattering chimney bricks all over the street. And in the gray of the morning, when a rain came up and beat steadily on Freehaven, there was nothing left of the house but a hole on the skyline

AND A LONG FLIGHT OF STONE STEPS

THAT LED UP

TO

—NOTHING is more certain in my opinion, the Perfessor said.

—But no one will ever know for sure, Mr. Shawnessy said. Everyone who knew is dead.

—How many knew?

—Three. And one was mad. And all were killed by fire.

—Did Susanna really know, do you think?

—I think she only suspected it—or rather feared it.

—Of course, there's one thing dead against the whole supposition, John. Would her father—or any other Southerner of good family—do a thing like that?

—Only for the strongest conceivable reason.

—What reason could be that strong?

—Great love, perhaps. Not so much for the little girl—as for her mother. A transcendent passion that broke all racial bounds and made him wish to legitimize as his child the offspring of his beloved.

—If so, he did it in the teeth of a widespread suspicion. Judging from what you say, it must have been widely rumored through New Orleans society that Susanna was a Negress. Obviously that's why her father whipped Uncle Buzbee—as you call him—to a pulp. That's why the family feeling was so violent both before and after the fire. That's why Susanna never married any of the young blades who fell in love with her.

—Obviously it was only a suspicion, Mr. Shawnessy said. But a suspicion was enough—enough to ruin her life and ultimately to drive her crazy.

—Of course, the madness suggests that she was the child of her mad mother after all, the Perfessor said.

—She was the child of a greater madness, Mr. Shawnessy said.

The two men smoked quietly.

—Life, said the Perfessor, is a volume of blind force, dispersed and trying to return into a condition of stability. In the intersections of this force with itself, human lives and whole nations are caught like gnats. That's what we mean by fate. Susanna was the child of fate. By the way, whatever became of her family? The last I heard, she had run away and was declared legally dead just before your present marriage. Was that the end of it?

—Not quite, Mr. Shawnessy said. In 1880, I received a letter. . . .

He was losing his way in a web of waters, tracing a skein of tangled force across a map. Letters, newspaper clippings, dreams, photographs, faces—they were all drowned. . . .

In the river, the eternal river, the mystic river of her fate, Ophelia-like, facedown, and floating with the stream. Where would she go at last except to darkness and the river? . . .

My dear Mr. Shawnessy,

The enclosed newspaper clippings will apprise you fully of a melancholy event that I am sure you will wish to take full cognizance of. For my part, as the legal adviser of Susanna Drake Shawnessy's heirs, I had never been entirely satisfied in my own mind that she was dead. Therefore, two weeks ago, when I read in the newspaper of an unidentified woman found floating . . .

In the river, where all desire is quenched.

Where then is the soul to whom was given a proud, sibilant name? Her anguish was necessary that there might one day be fairer republics. Shall she be lost, this erring child from the eternal summer of the South?

I had a dream the other night, when everything was still. I thought I saw . . .

A WOMAN'S BODY FOUND IN RIVER

(Epic Fragment from the *Meridian Sun*)

July 8. Excursionists on the steamboat *Delta Belle* were startled in the midst of gaiety and song the other night when someone saw a body floating in the river. When fished up, it proved to be that of a woman unclothed and judged to have been in the river three or four days. Identification is rendered difficult by exposure to the water, but death is believed to have occurred by drowning. The woman is darkhaired and of medium stature. Her face and shoulders appear to have been scarred by fire. Persons having clues to the identity of the deceased may view the remains at . . .

My Old Kentucky Home, or Old Virginny, or Uncle Tom's

Cabin, or just anywhere and everywhere south of the Mason and Dixon Line!

O, tragic legend of the mingled seed! O, beautiful Electra, avenger of your murdered father, followed by furies to the last. O, stained and tragic girl!

So we rebuilt the doomed, incestuous house on the new earth of America, a house divided, a house of seven gables and seven deadly sins. Returning from the epic fight, we found the black stain still on the lintels. We burned the house, rebuilt it, and we are doomed to burn it and rebuild it many times.

When shall the black Helen be freed at last? When shall the river of the Republic flow to the sea unvexed by sorrowful floaters?

—But didn't that invalidate your present marriage? the Perfessor asked.

—I had the ceremony repeated after positive proof of death was established.

The Perfessor had followed with peculiar relish the dark turnings of this Old Southern Melodrama.

—And to think, John, he said, that all this happened to you because you climbed a stair one day to have your picture taken!

—But I can't say that it was for the worse, Mr. Shawnessy said. See the girl out there in the white dress watching the other children —my daughter—Eva? For her to be, there had to be that other little girl and her burnt doll. Of course, the whole universe is implacably interconnected. It was all necessary to produce me, and I am all necessary to produce it.

He found a cigar in his coat.

—I take this cigar, Professor, and I now choose whether to light it or put it back. The delicate balance of the human universe depends on my decision. When I alter my surroundings, even slightly, I alter the timing of the human sperm throughout the world. All the generations of mankind down to the most distant future hang on the lighting of this cigar. Innumerable republics expire with every breath while I make my choice.

He struck a match on his shoe and lit the cigar. He took some time to draw it to a flame.

—All very well, the Perfessor said, except that there was always only one choice for you—the one you made. And so on down the line. There aren't trillions of possibilities, as you imply, but only in every case the one thing that happened. Down to the most distant future, everything has to all intents and purposes already happened in the only way it could—through the operation of causality. In other words, your choice in lighting that cigar wasn't really a free choice. The proof is that you made it and that you can't take it back.

—You admit, don't you, that in a choice between alternatives my belief that I'm making a free choice may be one of the causal ingredients of the choice.

—Well, yes.

—In that case, the idea of freedom has become a factor in the causal sequence, and without upsetting the doctrine of causality, it introduces freedom into human life. Man becomes a free agent by believing that he's a free agent.

—But this idea of freedom is itself caused.

—Good! Mr. Shawnessy said. Thus freedom too is inevitable.

—I fell through a trapdoor, the Perfessor said.

—Human beings, Mr. Shawnessy said, don't know how powerful they are. Every person determines the future by his least act. The Law of Causality means that the life of any man is the sum of everything past and the germ of everything to come. A man's not only the child of wombs but of Events. Every single thing that happened in the world before my time was midwife to my birth. When I pick up an old newspaper of seventy-five years ago I feel a sacred excitement—I know I touch one of the lost copies of the immense newspaper of Myself. The great human problem is to find the source of Oneself. This is the Riddle of the Sphinx. And to find Oneself, I believe, is to find the Republic.

—And what is the Republic? the Perfessor asked.

Mr. Shawnessy was aware of having spent a day of definitions.

—The Republic is the world of shared human meanings—ideas. A man voluntarily votes himself a citizen of the Republic, this great fruitful fiction where men and women exist in time and space, desire each other, perceive beauty, beget children, create institutions, share words. In a very real sense we live in Humanity, that being the only place where we can live.

—Give me a cigar, John, will you?

—I have a couple of Garwood's left.

—I suppose that big pompous fiction is nearing St. Louis by now, the Perfessor said.

He put a match to the cigar-tip.

—Just a moment while I destroy generations unborn.

He puffed the cigar into a glowing tip.

—From Abraham Lincoln to Garwood B. Jones in thirty years, the Perfessor said. Does American History have a meaning? What is a Great Historic Event anyway? Take any three at random—Caesar stabbed in the Senate Chamber of Rome, Christ crucified at Jerusalem, Abraham Lincoln shot in Ford's Theatre in Washington.

—An Historic Event is one of those clever fictions that Humanity fashions from infinite causal intersections. The world's incredibly daring, erected by gigantic human labor, a vast dream, for which each of us is responsible. One doesn't even become a self without entering into that dream. But we become citizens of that world so slowly that we forget the miracle of the process in which we participate. It's perhaps well that we do, for otherwise life would be unbearably exciting. As it is, we every now and then are touched with the feeling of historic participation. We are with crowds. We feel beyond ourselves. We partake festively in the old communion of Humanity. We do it in moments of intense love and great national crisis, on festive days like this. We do it also when we study Great Men and Great Events. Great men—Jesus, Shakespeare, Lincoln—give us the feeling of a human life lived in relation to Humanity, more fully partaking of the sacred communion.

—True, the Perfessor said. All so-called great men are the result of human collaboration before, during, and after the fact. With a little cooperation from Fate, you might have been America's Shakespeare, John, but you lacked the human context. A whole age worked to create the Plays, which are not unwisely attributed to a dozen other men besides the man who penned them. And today we still work at the Myth of Shakespeare, conferring glamor on the Bard beyond his merit.

—Are you about to deflate Shakespeare?

—The truth is, the Perfessor said, that Shakespeare is still only a fad, for we are all his contemporaries more or less, as we are of the Greeks. Mankind has only just begun to write. Man's been thinking man maybe a hundred thousand years, and only in the last few thousand has he been writing. Shakespeare's no older than yesterday's newspaper. There are no serious barriers between his mind and ours. But ten thousand years from now his plays may be pretty precious stuff to an age which, for all we know, will have kicked over the nonsense of romantic love, tribal honor, historical pride, feudal class divisions, and even—perish the thought—wit and humor, which are just human ways of viewing a very unwitty and unhumorous universe. In due time, Willie the Shake may become an old-fashioned curio whose verse-dramas were popular among the curious barbarians of the second, third, and fourth millenniums after the birth of a quaint religious figure called Jesus. The Plays won't seem picturesque or even obscure—but quite simply pointless and dull. Shakespeare is part of the dream of our time. We have an atmosphere of consent for him as for the Myth of Jesus and the Myth of Plato. This is the era of the glorification of the individual and his works. But there may well be a time when art itself will be dead as a mode of human activity.

—Shakespeare's greatest play, Mr. Shawnessy said, was one he never set words to.

—Entitled? the Perfessor said.

—*The Tragedy of Abraham Lincoln.*

—Goody! the Perfessor said. Another riddle!

—A Study in Fate, Mr. Shawnessy said. Picture to yourself a balding, plain-looking businessman-poet-bonvivant sitting down in his London rooms some evening *fin de siècle* to goosequill a surefire historical drammer full of daggers, ghosts, and mob scenes. He conjures up some stage-prop citizens along a concourse and a soothsayer bidding Caesar to beware the Ides. Keen student of human fate that he is, he doesn't know that his fastflowing goosefeather is writing the prelude to another red drama of assassination in a Republic as little known to him as Caesar's Rome. He has no idea that he is adumbrating one of his maddest young men.

—Ah, I begin to follow you, the Perfessor said.

—John Wilkes Booth would never have killed Lincoln except for his background as a Shakespearean actor. Booth had been brought up before the footlights. His father, Junius Brutus, was the most popular Shakespearean actor of his time. To young Booth, living in a dream of pompous tirades, great leaps before footlights, heroic attitudes, but never achieving the stature or fame of his gifted brother Edwin or his father, there came an opportunity to make the most impressive stage entrance of all time.

—And to think, John, that you and I were tangled in the close web of chance that caught the Great Commoner and the Assassin in Ford's Theatre!

—The republic of John Wilkes Booth was not in any real sense the republic of Abraham Lincoln. Booth knew nothing of Lincoln, the real Lincoln. As far as Booth knew, he was killing a vulgar baboon-president who had been strangling a sentimental republic. Little by little, Booth made his plans, revising them as chance required, until at last he came into Ford's Theatre, one night of April, upon the stage of his great act of affirmation. He slinks up through the crowd in the darkness of the balcony, where everyone is staring at a play. Where is he, in what space and time, this strange young man, approaching the footlights of History! He enters the private corridor to the President's box. He fits the pre-contrived bar into the pre-contrived niche to secure the door. All is going as he has planned. He's controlling Fate. For a few minutes, he's all alone on the threshold of History, as he sets his eye against the pre-contrived hole in the door to the President's box. He sees there the outline of his intended victim, a man he doesn't really know, whose hand he has never touched, with whom he has never exchanged a word. There is a burst of applause, and the stage is empty. He opens the door and, still unseen, he aims a pistol at the demon of his self-created nightmare. And in the next instant, by the inexorable law that makes human lives share each other, whether they will or not, President Abraham Lincoln, one of the kindest men who ever lived, tired from the terrible burdens of war, about to take up the equally great burdens of peace, watching a fifth-rate little fiddling farce, is stunned into darkness.

Darkness had thickened into night on Waycross. Over the cornfield straight ahead, Mr. Shawnessy could no longer see the line of the Pennsylvania Railroad, where twenty-seven years ago a train had passed bearing the body of a great man home.

Then he remembered, as if he had heard them all, the dirges in the night (*Let the great bell be tolled!*) and the sound of the women wailing. He remembered, as if he had seen them all himself, the torches, the faces of the grieving thousands (*Lower the starry flag!*). He remembered a train that pulled with sobbing breath from the trainshed in the smoky dawn (*Let the great bell be tolled!*) and the line of the flagdraped funeral coaches, passing through vacant squares, passing on the great bridges, passing through little stations on the plain, day and night journeying westward. And he remembered the crowds in the stations (*Lower the starry flag!*) and the dark body of the train in the dark night going forever to the place where the great trains come to rest (*Let the great bell be tolled,* be tolled, let the great bell be tolled, and the voice of the mourners be heard in the grieving dark).

In the station of himself the trains were changing.

In me, all trains are leaving on the roads to home. In me, the unrelinquished faces press through vacant worlds. In me, lost time is restless for a resurrection. Hail and farewell to all the lost horizons.

This was a face that I made up from the columns of the country weeklies. This is the tragedy that I portended from the primeval slime. This is the play for which I made old marble words, when I was a gay scrivener, actor-redactor of plays, a country boy completely citified back in my old Cheapside days.

For one dead, a sprig of Raintree County lilacs. For one of the great dead, in whom the Republic died for resurrection's sake, a few lines graven on a monument, some faces struck in stone. For one of the great, tender faces, the tribute of a simple soldier, himself —alas! dead also long ago and far from home.

Now I will find out the seed of Great Events. I will hunt for assassins and accomplices through delicately intersected times. I think I will follow the path of a young murderer and the path of one who was murdered. *They know not well the subtle ways I keep, and pass, and turn again.* I will take up a trail of huge and cloudy indications across a forum to a Senate Chamber. Caesar shall be a hundred times reassassinated and Christ a thousand times recrucified, but I shall go to a train station and find a young republic

April 14— WEARING —1865

A BATTLE WOUND, SCARCE HEALED,

CORPORAL JOHNNY SHAWNESSY DESCENDED FROM A COACH and walked across the station. It was the first time he had been in the Nation's Capital, Washington, D.C.

He looked around in vain for an expected face. Being early, he sat down on a bench and waited. He felt very weak, and although the day was not at all warm, he was in a cold sweat. He wondered if he had been wise to leave the hospital and come into the City for the day.

It had been less than two months since Corporal Johnny Shawnessy had got his battle wound near Columbia, South Carolina. During that time he had gone through a hell as bad as the fighting part of his war. He had been sick. On the physical side, his sickness might have been variously diagnosed as dysentery, wound-fever, loss of appetite, general debility, battle shock—but Johnny knew that something more profound and terrible had happened to him. His fever fevered everything he saw. Or perhaps all that he saw was really fevered by the old wound of the War. Before his wounding, he had seen death in battle often, forms torn forever from the shape that they were meant to be, faces suddenly touched with a stillness from which after a while all personality and meaning drained away. But he hadn't yet seen the backwash of the War, the hospital camp, the sickness, the long dying. He hadn't yet seen the total fever and decay of men's souls behind the battle lines. He hadn't yet realized that for many of the soldiers of the War, a lightning-sudden death in battle would have been merciful.

Corporal Johnny Shawnessy's hospital experience was not unusually bad for the times. In fact, care and treatment of the wounded had improved during the War. Soon after he had got his wound, he had been transported by boat to one of the hospitals near Washington, where he received the best care available for the wounded and sick soldiers of the Union. During this time, he lay in a long whitewashed hospital ward of thirty beds. The hospital was short of expert help, and there was some callousness and indifference among the orderlies and nurses, but no more so than in any other hospital of the day.

Those who took care of him would have described him as a typical case. He was Patient Number 23, Shawnessy, John W., shoulder wound, dysentery, and fever—and he didn't make out badly at all. His morale seemed good. He complained little, made no undue demands on the help, seemed to be a rather sweet-tempered, soft-spoken person. His wound suppurated nicely and was not difficult to wash and bandage. The discharge of pus was normal and proceeded exactly as wounds were supposed to in the year 1865. The gangrene that had set in before he reached the hospital was not overly serious, smelled no worse—nor better—than any other gangrene, and soon went away. The patient did have a pretty nasty fever when he came in and was out of his head at times in a harmless way. He was a nicelooking boy with dark hair touched with red but a light—almost sandy—beard. He was very weak at first and languid and the life seemed to be beaten out of him, but most of the patients were that way after they had been jostled over rough roads, carried by boat, loaded and unloaded from stretchers. The fever had stayed a while, and the patient had had a bad case of dysentery, with loss of appetite. After the wound was well on its way to healing, the dysentery hung on, and the patient lost weight, so that, like the majority of dysentery patients, he looked like an anatomical chart, with everything taken away but the essential bone, muscle, nerve, blood, and organic structure—and the mysterious principle of vitality. He went down, as most such cases did, and wavered around the boundary line that so many boys crossed, but he never quite crossed it, and in fact never awakened any special anxiety in the staff, as men without a mark on them were dying all the time in spite of all that could be done for them.

After Patient Number 23, Shawnessy, John W., perked up a bit, he had a very pleasant wit and was well liked by the other men.

All in all, the hospital record of Shawnessy, John W., was quite unpicturesque.

From his own point of view, Johnny went down into hell and stayed there for weeks. No one knew it, because he never told anyone, but there were whole days when it seemed to him that he was dying. Death was approaching all the time, touching with a gradual hand all around him. Other men died who had as much right to live as he, who looked stronger, who were unwounded; and his reason told him there was no good reason why he shouldn't die too.

Whether he died now or not, he knew what death was, and he knew that he could never wholly escape it. Death was an impersonal thing that happened to a person who was alone and far from home.

So he lay in his bed and watched human souls sicken and die, and fought back the thought in his own mind that he too might be sinking beyond the point of recovery. So he clung tenaciously and with a coward fear to a shrunken, mysterious thing, his body.

Meanwhile, he knew the hopes and despairs of the sick soldier.

He knew the indescribably sweet rush of confidence when the surgeon looked at his festering, smelling wound, and with a trace of brightness said,

—Well, my boy, you're coming along. Not bad at all.

The man said the same thing automatically up and down the line, and to boys who were obviously on the brink of death. But those words were as necessary to Johnny as food. He would speculate on just exactly what made the surgeon say them, and he would interpret every little nuance of the surgeon's voice as having special significance.

The surgeon was a sort of god because he walked upright where men were prostrate and pronounced sentence upon life without being fearful of his own. And yet Corporal Johnny Shawnessy, who had a fund of common sense and a good deal of medical knowledge, knew that the chief surgeon was a mediocre fellow who did only what anyone else could do in such cases and who had no real knowledge of what was taking place in the wounded body of Corporal Johnny Shawnessy.

He knew also the awakenings at night, when he was covered with cold sweat and his heart beat hard and swift, as if to run its course and expire in a rush of failing palpitations. At such times, he wanted to talk with someone or have someone rise up and say,

—Johnny, you're all right. It's probably just the air in here. I feel it too.

He wanted people to lie to him about his condition, as if words were facts. He knew the wild joy and black despair aroused by the sound of certain words—'crisis,' 'recovery,' 'suppuration,' 'pulse rapid,' 'fever down.' He came to love the beautiful, holy sound of the word 'normal.'

He saw men die suddenly. He saw men die with a grotesque slowness.

He saw soldier after soldier come into the ward with a belly wound. He never saw one go out alive.

He learned to know the look of death before death came. When a new patient was brought in, Johnny and the other veteran cases (one week or more in the same ward) silently made a diagnosis. Sometimes, Johnny would turn his face aside lest the silent, hardbought knowledge show in his eyes.

He knew the pitiful conversations of the sick and wounded, memories of the past or aspirations for the future, fabrics of sheer hope built in the house of despair. He knew the nostalgic words of the wounded, which were mostly the names of things, places, and people in America.

He knew the sympathies and fierce loyalties of the sick. He found that it was possible to know another person so well in three or four days that his death was like the loss of a lifelong friend. He knew the awful void caused when one of the veteran comrades died.

He knew the unhappy little pleasantries of the hospital, grins carved on the mask of suffering. One of the most cheerful patients was a man who had a leg gone, a chest wound, and dysentery with complications.

He saw boys of eighteen age visibly in a few days and act and talk like old men. He wondered at the courage of the dying. In all the time he was in the hospital, he heard hardly a word of bitterness or disillusionment about the Cause for which these men had suffered.

He saw at least a dozen Rebel wounded brought in during this time. He noticed the lack of bitterness between the wounded of both sides and their dispassionate reference to battles and places. Their wounds had made them historians instead of rivals.

He noticed that Rebel wounded looked like Union wounded, their wounds smelled the same, they died pitifully in the same way. In death they were the same debris of a human being that had to be hurried away and buried.

He knew over and over again the prosaic horror of the orderlies coming with the death-stretcher, the lifting of the shattered hulk, the laying of it on the stretcher, the bearing of it off out of light and time forever.

And he knew that the greatest anguish of all was the thought of dying far from home, of going down into the void without a single face from home to watch the descent, without a single hand to touch the lost hand—except the equally lost hands and lonely faces of the other soldiers who were there.

There were few visitors to the hospital. Now and then some ladies would go through the ward, bravely unembarrassed by the smell and look of the wounded. They would leave gifts of fruit or Bibles. One day a very pretty girl prominent in Washington society walked through the ward. She smiled sweetly and looked radiantly healthy and talked cheerfully with several of the patients. After she had left, the men talked for hours about her face, her dress, her eyes, speculated on whether or not she was married, and agreed that she was a damn good scout.

Another visitor was a big grayhaired, graybearded man with ruddy face and light blue eyes. He came three or four times to Johnny's ward, left oranges and tobacco, wrote letters home for those who wished it, brought books and read aloud whatever the patients requested, listened to boys talk about home hours without interrupting, and sat hours at the bedsides of dying men, lest they should lack company. The boys knew him as Walt. After a while, the word got about that he was a poet named Walt Whitman, but Johnny, who was the literary authority of the ward, had never heard of him before.

One day, the orderlies worked especially hard to clean up the ward and make the patients presentable. Around noon the chief surgeon came in and told the men that they were to have a distinguished visitor, who had asked that his name not be disclosed. Shortly after, a tall, gaunt, ugly man appeared at the door holding a tall black hat in his hand. His face was dark, coarsegrained, and graven with deep lines. His hair and beard were coarse and black, with a beginning of gray. He had a wart beside his nose. His clothes were illfitting.

His gaunt neck stuck far out of his collar. His knees had made bags in his pants. He was so tall he had to stoop to get through the doorway. He seemed to be the most awkward, sorrowful figure in a room of awkward, sorrowful men. He stepped to the bedside of the man nearest the door and held out his hand.

—I'm Mister Lincoln, he said.

His voice was highpitched, clear, and kindly. He got the boy's name and regiment and asked him what battle he had been wounded in. He seemed to become completely at ease as he went down the line of cots. The men found their tongues, saying,

—Howdy do, Mister Lincoln.

—Glad to meet yuh, Mister Lincoln.

—Very happy to make your acquaintance, Mister Lincoln.

Approaching Johnny's bedside, the President held out his hand.

—Where are you from, my boy?

—Indiana, Johnny said. Freehaven.

—Well, it's good to see a fellow Hoosier, the President said. Where did you get your wound?

—Near Columbia, Johnny said.

The President looked surprised.

—You were with Sherman then? On the Great March?

—Yes.

The President spoke with unusual warmth.

—It was a bold move—and boldly executed. I congratulate you.

Johnny blushed and looked down. The President looked as though he wanted to linger and ask more questions about the March, but some of his attendants whispered to him, and it was evident that the President was expected somewhere and was far off schedule.

—I'd a lot rather talk with this boy than with the Secretary of War, the President said.

One of the aides raised his hands in a gesture of good-natured acquiescence. But the President nodded pleasantly to Johnny and went on slowly down the line. He shook hands with every man in the ward and exchanged a few words with each. At the end of the row, he must have said something funny to the man who had the leg gone, the chest wound, and all the complications, for the soldier laughed heartily and so did all the men within hearing.

At the far door, the President turned, stood a moment, a scarred, gaunt figure, lifted his hand, and said in a clear voice,

—Get well, boys, and go back to your homes. There's good reason to hope that the War will soon be over.

When he was gone, the men talked for a long time about the visit.

—He's just like your own folks, they all agreed.

It turned out that the President had told a joke. The man with all the complications had remarked that he had so many ailments he had given up trying to count them. The President's joke involved an old coon dog that had so many fleas 'he'd give up scratchin' 'em 'cause it only stirred 'em up wuss.' The men told the joke up and down the ward. It didn't sound very funny in the retelling, but it must have had a remarkable fitness because the man with all the complications kept laughing about it for hours afterwards.

—Where does he git all them jokes? a man asked.

—I reckon he makes 'em up.

—But didn't he look sad!

—Yes, sir, the man with all the complications said. This war's really been hard on 'im.

And so the days went by, and Corporal Johnny Shawnessy lingered on while that impersonal thing, his body, tried to make up its mind whether to live or die. As for himself, he had never had a more terrible passion to live, to stand up, to walk, to move about in sunlight, to touch human hands, to laugh, to smoke a cigar, to mosey downtown. It seemed absurd that the affair was going to be decided for him by a hundred some-odd pounds of sweating clay.

These were the days of his most violent dualism. He had never before been so passionately addicted to the belief that the spirit is everything, that there is some kind of God, that the Cause was just, that the Republic was a worthwhile institution, that all men are brothers, that love is forever, and that there is no death. On the other hand, he had never been so utterly absorbed by the phenomenon of his body, of which he had once been very proud and which he had enjoyed with the naïve pleasure of a young pagan.

Those days, he clung to his belief in human souls with unreasoning fervor—during the very time when it seemed to him that life was a process in which human beings were carefully endowed with a feeling of importance only that they might be wantonly tortured and destroyed.

The men in Johnny's hospital were intensely religious, and though they swore all the time, they never really took God's name in vain.

These men were the most miserable, unhappy, and wretched men he had ever seen. At the same time they had none of the vanities and pomps of healthy people. They were completely humble. They had no aspirations for wealth, revenge, or guilty pleasures. They only wanted to live and let live, to love and be loved. They were the simplest people in the world. The sicker they were, the more saintly they were. Going on the cross seemed to make them all like Christ.

Johnny never afterward saw so much misery and so much nobility in human beings as he did in the Soldiers' Hospital. He knew that sick people in general showed all the baseness and cowardice in them. Why it wasn't true of the wounded soldiers of the Republic, he couldn't exactly say. When he and the rest of them left the hospital, he felt sure they would all slip back into their old vices and vanities, but as long as they were in the hospital they seemed to rise collectively to a code of behavior that they had always understood, even if they had never practiced it before.

Johnny was conscious of the paradox of the wounded soldier. Out of the most passionate selfishness of his life—the desire to live, to be well, to be whole, no matter what happened to the rest of the world—came also a wonderful unselfishness. For when one of the veteran comrades died, every man went down into death, and all felt miserable for days. By clinging to others, they clung to themselves. Several men in the ward wept bitterly when the cheerful man with all the complications died a few days after the President's visit.

During this time Corporal Johnny Shawnessy dreamed the dreams of the wounded soldier. He dreamed of home. And over and over again in the dream, he wanted to make the ones there understand how desperately he needed them, how much he had longed to see them, how much it meant to him that they were still there. Some of the dreams had a frustrate sweetness as when it seemed to him that he was back in the old Academy Building and he saw the cool, pale form of Nell Gaither standing in the ivied yard and looking at him from eyes alive with love and tenderness. Sometimes too he dreamed that he lay sick in his bed at home. He hoped that now he would be really healed, that she who had given life to him once could give it again. The irregular, vivid face of his mother Ellen Shawnessy bent over him in his dream, a lock of loose hair hung from under her cap, her eyes were full of belief in his recovery. He felt that here was a great strength from which he could draw inexhaustibly. Then he was happy to tears that he was home again.

His worst dreams were those in which it seemed to him that he had come back to Raintree County, sick, lonely, perhaps dying, and no one paid any attention to him.

In the darkest period of his fight to live, when it seemed that he got no better and was perhaps not even holding his own, his strength gone, his shoulder swollen with corruption, his insides weak and sore, his fever climbing to the danger zone, he had sunk one night into a half-delirious sleep. It seemed that he had been on some kind of excursion with a great many people to Lake Paradise in the center of the County. Somehow, he had got separated from the others and had become lost in the Great Swamp. The ancient muds and pools heaved yellow in hideous sunlight. He saw what seemed to be a tree standing cool on an island of firm ground. Sinking in slime, he made his way painfully to the tree and reaching up caught a golden branch. Instantly, the tree changed, the branch became a scaly arm, a little dragon wallowed lustfully down and sprang on his mudded form. Its clawed hands closed around his chest, squeezing the breath from his body. He began to cry out in horror. He was going down in the warm mud of the Swamp. The reptile body sat implacably on his arms and shoulders, dragging him down to death. He shut his eyes, choking, trying to shake the thing loose. He could hear his own cries, feebly, as from a great distance. He was being violently shaken. He heard voices, footsteps. People were perhaps coming to rescue him after all. He went on holding his breath. Something cold was dashed into his face.

He was standing between the bedrows of the Soldiers' Hospital. Three orderlies were fighting with him, trying to hold him. One of his soldier comrades had got out of bed and was yelling over and over,

—Johnny! Johnny! For Christ's sake, wake up!

Most of the soldiers were sitting up. A man was standing with a white pitcher in his hand. Johnny was dripping with cold water. They got him back into bed. He was panting as if he had run a race. He was shivering all over. His teeth chattered violently.

—Get some blankets on him, the orderly said. My God, boy, it took three men to hold you! What was the matter anyway?

—I don't know—I'm sorry, Johnny muttered between clenched teeth.

He was still horrified by the dream. A tired surgeon came in, looked him over, and dressed his wound again.

—I guess you're all right, he said. Everybody go back to sleep.

—Jesus, Johnny! the man next to him said, you really had a bad one.

It had happened often before to others, of course. Every night or so, some boy tried to get out of bed in a delirium.

As Corporal Johnny Shawnessy lay there chattering, sore, weak, soaked in a cold sweat, there came to him with more than usual vividness the memory of the younger Johnny of before the War, the boy who had believed that he would one day be a greater poet than Shakespeare, a faster runner than Flash Perkins, a lover for whom waited the most passionate of women, a hero for whom the Republic reserved her wildest applause. He remembered this Johnny—his strong young arms and legs, his inexhaustible vitality, his happy smile, his strong competitive heart; and then he thought of the miserable shrunken creature who lay in a makeshift building a thousand miles from home, perhaps dying. Hot tears came to his eyes. He buried his face in the pillow to stifle his sobs. He was afraid some of the other boys would hear him—as he had often heard them. He wept—the terrible tears of the soldier sick and far from home. He fought with himself and finally managed to stop. He was amazed and a little heartened by the violence of his fit. The sobbing had been like part of the dream. Then he felt very still and calm. An orderly went by and put a hand on his forehead.

—Your fever's gone, son, he said. That's why you threw that fit. Your fever dropped all of a sudden.

Corporal Johnny Shawnessy closed his eyes. He was exhausted. He sank into a dreamless sleep and didn't awaken until broad daylight. After that he was out of danger. Apparently, that night he had gone down to the brink and had come back.

So Corporal Johnny Shawnessy learned that behind all the victories of the War was this perpetual defeat, and behind all the defeats of the War this strange victory.

During the worst days of his sickness, he had read President Lincoln's Second Inaugural Address, delivered March 4. Johnny went back in memory to the First Inaugural, four years before, in March of 1861; and the strange, devious pattern of the War and of his own life passed in review through his mind. Four years ago, he had been living in the house south of the Square in Freehaven, and Susanna was waiting for the birth of Little Jim. The Republic was split in two. Men were talking War with foolish pride, and yet no certain policy had emerged in the confusion of the moment. The President was then an untried man, a political accident, an oddlooking Westerner. He had stood on a scaffold in front of a capitol building whose dome was only half completed, had looked down at a crowd of Americans, and had said a few remarkably wise and patient words, which were immediately swept away in the violence of Sumter and the ensuing battles. No one had known then what a long, bloody epic of courage, despair, sickness, and death the Republic was about to fashion. Bull Run, Shiloh, Antietam, Gettysburg, Chickamauga, Lookout Mountain were only obscure towns and local landmarks. Ulysses S. Grant was a nobody. William Tecumseh Sherman was superintendent of a military academy in the South. 'The Battle Hymn of the Republic' hadn't been written. The word 'contraband' didn't mean a black man. Andersonville was inconceivable. The Emancipation Proclamation was unthinkable. The Bloody Angle at Spottsylvania was unimaginable. And no one North or South could possibly have dreamed up the half a hundred thousand strong young men in blue uniforms who marched from Atlanta to the Sea.

Nor could anyone have foreseen what lay in wait for Johnny Shawnessy along the railroad tracks of time—a son, a tall house burning, two days at Chickamauga Creek, an afternoon on the slopes of Missionary Ridge, a summer of battles before Atlanta, marches and bivouacs and burning cities, the death of comrades, the hospital near Washington.

On March 4, 1861, Abraham Lincoln had stood bareheaded before the Nation, had said solemn words, and had accepted a solemn trust. Then they had taken the ceremonial platform down. Slowly the dome of the Capitol had gone on a-building, and Washington had become a City at War.

Now the four years were done. Once again the tall, ungainly man stood on a platform on the steps of the Capitol. The dome was complete. Again a throng of anonymous Americans gathered to hear the President's words. Corporal Johnny Shawnessy read them while lying in a hospital cot near Washington:

> Neither party expected for the war the magnitude or the duration which it has already attained. Neither anticipated that the cause of the conflict might cease with, or even before, the conflict itself should cease. Each looked for an easier triumph, and a result less fundamental and astounding. Both read the same Bible, and pray to the same God; and each invokes His aid against the other. It may seem strange that any men should dare to ask a just God's assistance in wringing their bread from the sweat of other men's faces; but let us judge not, that we be not judged. The prayers of both could not be answered—that of neither has been answered fully.

These words of wisdom and forbearance seemed already part of the old legend of this war fought for the preservation of the Republic and the Emancipation of a Race.

> Fondly do we hope—fervently do we pray—that this mighty scourge of war may speedily pass away. Yet, if God wills that it continue until all the wealth piled by the bondman's two hundred and fifty years of unrequited toil shall be sunk, and until every drop of blood drawn with the lash shall be paid by another drawn with the sword, as was said three thousand years ago, so still it must be said, 'The judgments of the Lord are true and righteous altogether.'

These words did nothing to insult or offend the memories of the men who lay in the hospitals, North or South. They were the brooding, almost doubtful words of a man who had carried on his conscience the moral burden of the War, had already, as it seemed, delivered history's verdict on the contest, and had achieved a solemn victory over himself. Abraham Lincoln was obviously the most ungloating victor who ever lived.

> With malice toward none; with charity for all; with firmness in the right, as God gives us to see the right, let us strive on to finish the

> work we are in; to bind up the Nation's wounds, to care for him who shall have borne the battle, and for his widow, and his orphan—to do all which may achieve and cherish a just and lasting peace among ourselves, and with all nations.

Around the first of April, just as Johnny was beginning to recover his strength, the War went suddenly into its final convulsions. For the last time the newspapers published the Theatre of Operations and began to pour forth the confidently inaccurate reportage of battle. The words told of renewed attacks around Petersburg, where Grant had been besieging Lee since the summer before. From habit of many disappointments the soldiers in the hospital refused to be excited. Then the words came telling that Petersburg had fallen and Lee was retreating. Name after name—legendary names that had been defended to the death earlier in the War—fell almost unnoticed. The Theatre of Operations had lost its power to resist. The invading words poured into it and across it, became excited, hopeful, triumphant, ecstatic. One day a man came into Johnny's ward waving a paper with the headlines

RICHMOND HAS FALLEN! !

The soldiers listened stunned. They had been fooled so often before that they had learned caution. But some of the sickest men openly expressed the hope that they would live to hear that the end had come.

Then at last the news came that Lee had surrendered. There was no doubt about it. It was official. The newspapers carried the text of Grant's terms and his telegram to the President:

> General Lee surrendered the Army of Northern Virginia this afternoon on terms proposed by myself. The accompanying additional correspondence will show the conditions fully.
>
> U. S. GRANT,
> Lieut.-General

> Gen. R. E. Lee,
>
> GEN: In accordance with the substance of my letter to you of the 8th inst., I propose to receive the surrender of the Army of N. Va., on the following . . .

After millions of words the mythical words had come.

It would be time later to review the pageantry of that great surrender, with all the false lights and glamors, to envision the meeting of the two generals, Lee in his spotless uniform, Grant, slovenly, smoking his cigar, to imagine the yielding of the never yielded sword. It would be time later to notice the simplicity with which the soldiers agreed that the War was finished and turned things over to the politicians. Just now it seemed that all the rest of a man's life would be downhill from this almost unbearable moment.

The hospital rang with shouts of thanksgiving. One-legged veterans crippled up and down the corridors, waving crutches. Soldiers embraced and cried like children. Every man who had strength enough to get up got up, while the weakest ones lay and yelled feeble hurrahs or wept quietly and helplessly. Soldiers who shouldn't have been out of bed disappeared from the hospital encampment and didn't turn up for days. Some never came back.

The War was over. The peace terms were in; they didn't include the restoration of health, limb, and eyesight to the sick and wounded; but no one thought of that for a little while.

Each soldier's happiness was magnified by the knowledge that it was shared by twenty million people. It was a joy that couldn't be expressed in any other words than the simple statement, *The War is over.*

Like the other invalid soldiers, Corporal Johnny Shawnessy wanted to get out of the hospital. He wanted to be where he could see the faces of thousands of people, wring their hands, walk for hours and listen to their songs. He wanted to see beautiful young women. He wanted them to smile at him and perceive that he was a soldier of the Republic. He wanted these satisfactions not alone for himself—but unselfishly for everyone. Although he was rapidly getting better and had long been out of danger, he hadn't yet lost the wounded soldier's sweet humility. He almost forgave the bounty-jumpers, the professional civilians, the second-guessers.

For several days after the announcement of Lee's surrender, tension mounted. Grant was expected in Washington. Sherman in North Carolina was negotiating with the only remaining Rebel army of any size. Hourly the news poured in, and jubilation went from peak to peak of frenzy.

It was in the midst of this accelerating triumph that Johnny received a letter from New York, in answer to one that he had written not long before. It said simply:

My dear young martyr,

Meet me in Washington Friday morning, first train from New York, and we'll do the City. Everything, including the ladies, will be on

Your ebullient savant,

J. W. STILES

The morning of April 14 came raw and gray. Johnny didn't ask for a leave. He just walked out, and making connections with a local line, was carried into the city, where he sat in the station and waited for the Perfessor to show up. By an understanding with an orderly, he had got himself a freshly pressed uniform and a new cap. His face was cleanshaven. He began to feel a little better as he rested on the bench.

Someone arriving on an earlier train from New York had left a copy of the *New York Tribune* on the bench. Johnny ran his eyes over it, his attention being arrested by some words in an editorial entitled 'The Dawn of Peace.'

And every loyal heart beats fast as it remembers all that has passed since the 14th of April, 1861, and all that is promised on the 14th of April, 1865.

April 14 would always be one of the somber anniversaries of his life as well as the Republic's. On April 14, four years ago, Sumter had been surrendered, and Little Jim Shawnessy had been born.

Soon the train from New York came in. Hands, handkerchiefs, flags were waving from the windows as the train coasted to a stop.

Instantly, young people sprang from the doors into the arms of lovers, whole families disembarked, waving flags and bearing luggage; statesmen, soldiers, businessmen, hundreds of eager and excited Americans, got down into the station, their eyes shining with expectation, all of them looking for faces to greet and doors to hurry through.

The Perfessor, appearing in the crowd with a woman, caught sight of Johnny and came over swinging his cane. With one hand, he shook Johnny's hand, and with the other took hold of Johnny's arm as if to support him. He kept shaking his head and blinking his eyes.

—Good heavens, boy, they've nearly killed you.

The Perfessor introduced his companion as a Miss Bessie Dietz. A spaciously contrived blonde with a sweet dollface, she giggled every time the Perfessor spoke.

—I have a girl lined up for you too, John, the Perfessor said. She's a young actress named Daphne Fountain, who's here with Laura Keene's troupe. They're playing at Ford's Theatre tonight in *Our American Cousin.* She understudies Miss Keene. She has seats for us that we can pick up at the ticket office this morning, and we're to get her at the Stage Door after the show tonight.

They hailed a carriage outside the station.

—Don't expect too much of Washington, the Perfessor said, as they rode away. It's just a poor Southern city, a parvenu trying to look and act dressed up and doing a bad job of it. Take us past the Capitol, driver.

In the raw April day, Washington was a muddy plain of drab, ill-assorted buildings. Johnny looked south down a wide unpaved avenue, at the far end of which was a gray pile of stone and a dome surmounted by a misty figure.

—There's the Capitol! the Perfessor said. Rome on the banks of an Indian river.

—Ain't it big! Bessie said.

The sidewalks and streets around the Capitol were full of civilians and soldiers. Now and then a company marched down the street, and the crowds cheered. Everyone looked purposeless, as if for the first time in four years it was all right to take one's time.

As the carriage turned onto Pennsylvania Avenue, a company of soldiers marched by, singing,

—Hurrah, Hurrah,
We bring the Jubilee.
Hurrah, Hurrah,
The Flag that makes you free.
So we sang the chorus from Atlanta to the Sea,
While we were marching through Georgia.

—It's that new song, the Perfessor said. In your honor, hero boy.

He stuck his cane through a window and pointed to the dome of the Capitol.

—The lady on top there is armèd Freedom, resting on her sheathèd sword. High time. Perhaps we'd best check our reservations at Willard's before we see anything else.

—This city's sort of messy, Bessie said.

> —And nought but mud and Honest Abe we see
> Where streets should run and sages ought to be,

recited the Perfessor.

They stopped at Willard's Hotel, where the Perfessor had reserved rooms. The lobby and the bar were crowded.

Later they left the hotel in a carriage. Pennsylvania Avenue, the main street of Washington, was unpaved. Ugly brick buildings alternated with dingy wood. The sidewalks were dirty; the gutters ran with slops. But hundreds of gay, overdressed young women and their escorts, mostly officers, were walking and riding in the City.

—Let's turn here, the Perfessor said. I want to pick up the tickets.

They turned off the Avenue and rode down a block and a half, stopping before a brick theatre. Bills in front announced the play:

OUR AMERICAN COUSIN

Starring

LAURA KEENE

Johnny and Bessie waited in the carriage.

In a few minutes, the Perfessor returned with tickets for the play.

—Here they are, he said. We're lucky to get them. The President's expected to be there with General Grant.

—What kind of play is it? asked Bessie.

—A prickmedainty piece of fooling, the Perfessor said. Neither fish nor flesh.

So there was time again for third-rate plays. There was time for the theatre. There was time for the ladies to deck their bodies for pleasure and seduction. There was time to lean back in a carriage and dream of a young woman from the City, an actress whose talented body lured perfumed gallants to the stagedoor with bouquets of roses in their hands.

The carriage had crossed the Avenue, going south. Four or five blocks from the hotel was a wide gray sheet of water and beside it a stump of stone.

—I especially wanted to see this, Johnny said. I suppose a dime I gave years ago added a mite to this monument. How tall is it now?

—Just a minute, the Perfessor said.

He had the driver stop and called to a crowd of Negro boys playing near-by.

—How tall is the monument, boys?

—Yassuh, Generl Wash'ton's Monument, one of the boys said as he walked out of the group, reciting monotone. Present height thee hunud and thutty-thee feet. Dammeter at base, thutty feet. Jected height foh hunud and fitty-fah feet. Talles' structure inna world.

—Thank you, my boy, the Perfessor said, pitching him a dime.

—What's this river? Bessie asked.

—This is the Puttoric Histommac, the Perfessor said, across which the General is reputed to have thrown a dollar. In Greece, the hero skins a lion. In America, he slings a dollar.

—The General's dollar fell on fertile ground, Johnny said, judging from the size of this big stone flower.

—The Republic has a poorer memory than any schoolboy, the Perfessor said. A boy ties a string around his finger, but the Republic can't remember anything without piling up several hundred feet of stone.

In the mist beside the Potomac, the Washington Monument was an amputated finger of frustration, indicating an undivined and undivinable future.

—There's the White House, the Perfessor said, indicating a graceful pillared front a long way off across a parklike lawn.

Raindrops began to fall. The carriage crossed a small bridge over an arm of water, went through a block of shabby houses, and came out on a walk skirting the President's Park.

—It'd be nice to see the President, Johnny said.

—Anyone can see Abe, the Perfessor said. Just walk right in, spit on the floor, and make yourself at home. Perhaps you'll be there yourself some day, boy.

—I decline the nomination, Johnny said.

—Poor old Abe! the Perfessor said. He's barely pulled the Republic through a victorious War and the wolves are already at him again. That speech he made a few days ago raised quite a stink. His Reconstruction policy is too gentle to suit most people.

As they returned to the hotel, the mist closed down so thick that the Capitol was no longer visible. The City of Washington was a waste of ugly buildings in rain.

At the hotel, they began to have a good time. They had lunch and got a table in the bar, where they watched the crowds come and go. The Perfessor knew almost everyone of importance and was up and down like a jack on a spring to greet people and bring them to the table. Everyone was drinking and proposing toasts, and toward the dinner hour people got to singing war songs. Corporal Johnny Shawnessy had a good time just sitting there in a blur of faces, colors, sounds.

Along in the afternoon, Bessie tried to get him to tell about his hero experiences. When he declined out of modesty, the Perfessor, who was in vein, put together an ingenious fiction in which Johnny held off a whole regiment of Georgia militia singlehanded while help came up. The story included a Southern beauty, buried treasure, gory fighting, and everything incorrect that people associated with the March to the Sea. Johnny topped the story with a palpable fraud about the Perfessor riding a horse three days and three nights through hostile country, risking his life twenty times, in order to file a dispatch to his paper.

—Oddly enough, said the Perfessor, I felt no fear at the time.

People kept stopping at Johnny's table and saying,

—So you're the boy from Sherman's Army.

When things got a little wild around seven o'clock in the evening and everyone was singing the new song 'Marching Through Georgia,' the crowd made Johnny stand on the table.

—Speech! Speech! they yelled.

—Tell us about the March, boy! they yelled.

—It was nothing, Johnny said. We just walked.

Everyone applauded.

—Isn't he sweet! a girl said.

Johnny said something about his comrades in the hospital and about how much victory meant to them.

—Sure! Sure! everyone yelled.

People pumped his hand, swatted him on the back, and tried to establish mutual friendships back in Indiana. A girl came over and put her arms around him and kissed him on the lips.

—Honey, I'd kiss every man in Sherman's Army, if I got a chance, she said.

—Maybe I could stand proxy for the rest, Johnny said.

Everyone laughed.

—Time to go, someone said.

It was the Perfessor, leaning through the liquorcolored air.

—Play starts at eight-thirty, I think. We've just time to go over and get settled. It seems certain Lincoln and Grant will be there.

Bessie Dietz giggled, and Johnny got unsteadily to his feet. He hadn't drunk much, but he was still wobbly. His ears sang. But he felt very happy when they were outside driving away somewhere through the misty evening. Pennsylvania Avenue was two wavering rows of gaslamps. The illuminated dome of the Capitol seemed suspended in the mist.

The carriage left the Avenue and turned into a narrower way. In a few minutes, they were before the theatre. Johnny's head was far from clear as he joined the crowd crossing over the wooden platform built out across the gutter. As they went up the steps to the entrance, he noticed that the brick front of Ford's Theatre was hung with bunting.

Everyone in the crowded lobby was talking about the end of the War, the latest news from Sherman's Army, the expected appearance of the President and General Grant at the theatre. Someone said that the General wasn't coming after all.

—Maybe the President won't come either, someone said.

They went upstairs to the balcony. People were stirring in the aisles, hunting for seats.

Someone pointed out the President's box projecting over the right side of the stage and ten feet above it. A chandelier hung close by, and a picture was suspended between the folds of an American flag draped over the edges of the box. The double arches were curtained and dark. The curtain hiding the stage showed an autumntinted landscape and a bust of Shakespeare. Hardly were they seated when the houselights were darkened, and the curtain went up for the opening scene in the play called *Our American Cousin.*

Johnny, who had seen few plays in his time and none at all for two years, was thrilled by the garish color and unreality of the stage. The Play itself was a vapid little thing in which bogus Englishmen made laughter over a bogus American. The voices had the artificial hoarseness of veteran performers trying to fill up the back spaces of a theatre. There was much trained gesture and forced laughter. The posturing mannequins on the stage had names—Florence Trenchard, Lord Dundreary, Asa Trenchard.

The performance was spirited, and people laughed and applauded now and then. But the Play itself made no difference. The actors were only supposed to present a little tableau of the times, while everyone, audience and players together, collaborated in a more significant drama. People had come to the theatre, as perhaps they always did, to satisfy an ancient yearning, to find a place of gaiety and mystery with a thousand of their fellows, and to behold time, fate, and the Republic expressed both inside and outside the artificial boundaries of the stage.

As the Play continued, the feeling of excitement subsided only to return again. People moved restlessly in their seats, waiting for the entrance of a more important actor than those now posturing on the stage.

Johnny had become absorbed in the Play and was a little surprised when the actors paused in the midst of some punning on the word 'draft.' There was a disturbance in the balcony.

—The President! someone said.

—And there's Mrs. Lincoln with him!

A murmur ran over the balcony and lower floor as people craned for a look. Four people were walking along the dress-circle that divided the balcony. Johnny stood up, applauding with the others. A little fattish woman led the way, and behind her walked a tall, sloped man. Johnny could have reached out and touched the President as he passed. The party made their way to a door that led down a hidden corridor to the box at the side of the theatre. They entered the door and passed from sight. In a few moments, the President's face appeared in the box overlooking the stage, as if he were leaning forward preparatory to sitting back. Then he disappeared.

—Ha! Ha! Ha!

It was Lord Dundreary on the stage hollowly laughing.

ALL

—What's the matter?

DUNDREARY

—Why, that wath a joke, that wath.

FLORENCE

—Where was the joke?

The excitement of the audience lessened, and there was no further disturbance in the aisles as the Play went on. No one could see the President, unless possibly the people in the box immediately opposite his.

Once more, Corporal Johnny Shawnessy, Soldier of the Republic and unsung Hero-Poet of Raintree County, leaned back in his place, musing on the strange legend of his life. It seemed to him that he had assembled here the lost pages of a myth of himself and the Republic, and that he had only to put them together at last into a meaningful pattern. All was promise, excitement, near-fulfillment. The battle days were over. The Republic was in the ritual hour of exultation. Here was the shrine of that aspiring people, the Americans, their Capital City, rising from mist on its muddy plain, rising from April to eternal spring. Names of battles reverberated in the corridors of the sped years; a door was about to clang shut on the pantheon of a nation's sacrifice. And all was turning, turning toward a new day. The Republic was waiting for its poet, for him who could discover beauty in immortal phrases, for him whose being was attuned to the music of rivers on the land, for him who had known strong passion, love, and death, whose memories were memories of the Republic in War and Peace. Here all about him were the actors and the stage-props of the greatest of all dramas. An unknown actress waited for him somewhere behind the scenes. Pensive, alonely brooding in his box over the stage, was President Lincoln, the gaunt, tender father who had brought the Republic through the War, One Nation. In the camps, hospitals, barracks of the land, the men who had fought from Sumter to Appomattox were waiting for the bugles of the last encampment.

What was President Abraham Lincoln thinking in his forever lonely, barriered world? What were his own memories of the Republic in War and Peace, as he sat brooding in his box above the stage? Was his world the world of Corporal Johnny Shawnessy? Did they not together share the meanings of an eternal republic that both were striving to build, the one by statesmanship, the other by poetry?

Yes, the times were changing. The soldiers were waiting to go home. Now that the battle-years were nearly over, what was it that waited for the Republic and for John Wickliff Shawnessy? All stages were like great stereopticons into which one looked with an illusion of depth and reality. Might not a man of keen vision look into the boxlike diorama of the stage and see shining cities on the land, exultant tomorrows!

The stage was empty, as two ladies went off to the right and a man to the left. Over the ebbing applause and laughter, there had been a sharp, hard sound that made Corporal Johnny Shawnessy vaguely uneasy as he tried to fit it into the Play. He seemed to be trying to remember something that he ought not to have forgotten.

Just then an amazing thing happened to the Play.

A man was falling through the air, violently swinging his arms, tipping over precariously and landing heavily on the stage. It seemed a furious and fantastic piece of nonsense. The man had landed on his bent leg and hands, he was scrambling to his feet with a catlike, frantic speed, he stood up, half-ran, half-hopped like a crazy cripple to the middle of the stage brandishing a dagger, his white face was lit with two black balls of eyes, his mouth spat a deformed ejaculation into the hushed theatre, and then with maimed fury he ran off the stage on the left side.

So unexpected was this apparition that it seemed to Johnny it might have shot dreamlike from the musing part of himself across the outward world. Like everyone else in the theatre he went on watching and waiting for some sequel to explain the thing.

—Where'd *he* come from? someone said.

Just then, across the growing tumult of the theatre a woman's shriek lay like a lash, raw with anguish and unbelief. People began to look toward the President's box, from which and only which the dark, dagger-carrying man could have leaped.

For the moment, nothing could be seen in the President's box. But the stage had lost its look of legend and fixity. The actors were walking across it, making natural gestures, their faces expressive of real emotions. One was trying to tell the crowd something. Words came from somewhere and began to be repeated in the crowd.

—The President has been shot!

Suddenly, what had been a pointless farce had pulled off its little grinning mask and had taken for its stage the whole Republic, for its lines history, for its audience the generations. In the darkness and confusion of Ford's Theatre, Corporal Johnny Shawnessy and his companions had become supernumeraries in the cast, anonymous faces in a cry of citizens.

—Well, damn it, why don't somebody do something instead of just standing around!

—Why'd they let the fella get away?

—Who done it?

—Maybe it's a trick.

—I thought it was part of the celebration.

—Well, why don't somebody do something instead of just standing around!

Most of the crowd in the balcony were just standing or trying vaguely to go somewhere. Many people hadn't seen what happened. Most of them hadn't heard the shot. The Perfessor, as usual, kept his head.

—I'm going down to see what I can find out, he said. If I'm not mistaken, I know the man who leaped down to the stage. Pardon me, folks, I'll see you later at the hotel.

The Perfessor pushed off into the crowd and disappeared, leaving Johnny to take care of Bessie.

There was a clot of confusion now at the door leading to the President's box. The door was suddenly broken through, and an usher let someone in. A young man in uniform was at the door, his arm bleeding.

Now people began jamming to the exits or pushing toward the front of the theatre. Someone kept crying out,

—Clear the theatre! Clear the theatre!

From the pit, someone was lifted up and shoved bodily into the President's box, several hands reaching out for him. An actor ran across the stage and passed up a basin and a white sheet. Someone was trying to shout something to the crowd from the stage, but no one could hear it.

—What's he saying?

—Why don't he talk louder?

—Why don't they get out and catch that fella?

—I don't see the President. Do you suppose he's dead?

—What's he saying down there anyway?

A great many people decided to remain in the balcony. People were trying to get in through the exits as others pushed to get out.

Johnny and Bessie talked excitedly with each other and the people around them, all saying the same things over and over. No one had any idea what had happened, and many expected to find that it was all an accident or a false scare of some kind.

Johnny shared the general feeling of helplessness and confusion. Life had been proceeding with a pretense of orderliness, and now abruptly chaos had come, leaving individual human beings weakly shaking at the ends of strings, puppets whose purposeful motion had abruptly been suspended. He had had this feeling often before and had hoped never to repeat it. It was a feeling that men often had in battle.

In a little while four soldiers came from the corridor leading to the President's box. They were bearing a long, limp body as tenderly as they could.

—It's him.

The crowd was made to stand back as the soldiers carried the body down the stair. The crowd poured after, funneling into the jammed stairway. When Johnny and his companions reached the street, they saw six men holding the President's body, standing in the middle of the street, waiting for something. A young man in Army uniform was pointing and shouting. The soldiers then carried their burden across the street, up the steps of a house, and through the front door.

The Play was over. And the Play was not over, but would go on forever.

—What can we do?

—Is he dead?

—I don't know.

—Where was he shot?

—Through the head, they said.

—It's bad then.

—He can't live. They say he can't live.

—What can we do?

The street began to fill up with more and more people from all parts of the City. Rumors flashed up and down the crowd, crackling from lip to lip, leaving crisscrossed trails of alarm.

—Secretary Seward's been murdered in his bed. It's a plot to wipe out the Government.

—Whole Cabinet's been assassinated.

—They say Grant was attacked on the train.

—Vice-President Johnson was killed in his bed.

—They couldn't win fair, so they tried foul, goddamn them!

A shout of angry voices came from down the street. A man was being pushed and struck by the crowd.

—What'd he do?

—Is that the murderer?

—I think he called the President a name.

—Yes, he said he was glad the son of a bitch got shot.

—Hang the son of a bitch up!

—Hang him, hell! Hanging's too good for him.

—Poor old Abe. Goddammit, why'd they have to pick on him now for!

—It's a plot to wipe out the Government.

The crowd was so thick and wild that Johnny decided to take Bessie back to the hotel. There was no use trying to meet Miss Daphne Fountain.

Everywhere, the feeling was the same. Almost everyone looked and talked as if an unbearable personal calamity had occurred.

—What's going to happen now?

—Poor old Abe.

—I hope he pulls through.

—What's going to happen now?

—What'll we do without Abe?

—My God, Johnson will be President now. I always thought it was a mistake to elect him.

—Johnson, hell! He's been killed too, they say. And the whole Cabinet. We won't have any Government.

—Poor old Abe. I hope he pulls through.

—What's going to happen now?

At the hotel Johnny stayed with Bessie a few minutes and then said good night. He felt all shocked and trembling as if a musket-ball had torn through his belly.

He went back out into the streets. He wanted to be out hunting for someone or something, awake and helping. And yet he had seldom before felt so helpless.

A feeling of ubiquitous disaster hung over the people. It was as though the whole city were bleeding from the pistol bullet that had felled the President.

As the night passed, Corporal Johnny Shawnessy walked through the streets, his face fevered and dripping from the mist. He kept thinking of the Army. If only he felt around him the confident strength of those sixty thousand young men, his comrades, and the fierce leadership of Sherman!

Reports kept coming all night long about the President's condition. The President was steadily sinking, and no hope was held for his recovery.

In the cold, small hours of the night, the Play streamed meaninglessly on, could not be stopped, must be played out. The body of Abraham Lincoln lay dying in the night with a bullet in the brain.

Black despair, beginning to take more and more the form of anger, sat upon the City. Men waited everywhere for a cold dawn.

In the morning came the report that the President had died at twenty-two minutes after seven. It seemed that, after all, the Government stood. Seward was wounded but not dead. No one else had been attacked. The situation was under control. Johnny went back to Ford's Theatre where he was in time to see a dark casket carried from the house across the street. To a sound of bells tolling and a lowering of flags to halfmast, the coffined body was borne away by soldiers up the muddy street. In the dismal weather, Ford's Theatre still had the rainlimp bunting on its face.

Sleepless for a night, exhausted, sick, Corporal Johnny Shawnessy wandered in the City of Washington. He kept feeling that he was himself obscurely at fault. I was in the theatre, he told himself. I might have reached out and prevented the thing from happening. The President passed as close to me as the length of my arm, and was alive and surrounded by friends. Then Death came in and cut him down.

It was some consolation to Johnny to see that others were grieving like himself. Hundreds of people wept openly in the streets, in the churches, in crowded cabs and public buildings. In one great death, all the deaths of the War achieved a representative.

Late in the day, he got back at last to the hospital. He was so sick and weak he was ashamed to see the staff, but for a while no one paid attention to him. The inmates of the hospital were fretfully gloomy. Later, a doctor found him lying in bed.

—Where've you been, Shawnessy?

—Celebrating.

The doctor looked him over.

—You've got three degrees of fever. Fine thing.

Johnny knew he had had a relapse. He lay in bed, hot and breathless.

I must live, he kept telling himself. I must live and get well.

He thought of the President's body in state somewhere in the Capital City, of the blackedged newspapers, of the silent crowds all over the Republic, of his own people back in Raintree County. He wondered if they were thinking of him, if they were saying prayers for him.

Waves of alternate exaltation and sorrow went over him as he thought of Abraham Lincoln. In this death, the War had had its last great death. He must bear the memory of this great death tenderly. It was good to die for mankind—it was a good and great thing to give one's life in battle for one's fellows.

But it was also a bad thing, it was a pitiful and dirty thing to die—to die with a bullet in the brain, to gasp life away in the night while the women sobbed and shrieked and the rain fell. And it was an awful thing to die with a bullet in the breast and rot in a nameless grave hundreds of miles from home. And it was a bad, dirty, pitiful thing to die in a hospital and become a yellow corpse when you were twenty-five years old and had the world before you.

Again he felt remorse, as if it were partly his own fault that he had permitted a figure to vault across the stage of Ford's Theatre, coming out of the unexpected part of himself to burst the boundaries of the little farce. Through a lack of vigilance, he had let the web spin itself out of control for a moment, and this thing had happened. He kept returning to the fated moment and wondering if it were not all a dream. How easily time might have run on at that point, playing the farce to a conclusion! The slightest weakening in the murderer's resolve, the least impediment thrown by chance in his way, and the thing wouldn't have happened. The following morning, the newspapers would have carried a notice, saying that the President and his wife had spent a pleasant evening at Ford's Theatre and had enjoyed the play.

And Corporal Johnny Shawnessy would have met a young woman named Daphne Fountain, who would always be now a fictitious girl waiting in the wings of a lost theatre, watching a never-finished play and expecting to meet a fictitious soldier named Corporal Johnny Shawnessy.

But now the thing was done. And now that it was done, it was part of the vast design; it had to be fitted to its place. It was all a legend now, a story of the Republic. And those who were young must survive and give the legend to their children. The light was breaking on the land. Abraham Lincoln was dead, but the Republic would live.

Corporal Johnny Shawnessy felt that he had come to Washington on a mysterious mission, one upon which hung the Fate of the Nation. He must be with the Army again, and tell them that he had completed his mission. It had been a strange mission—to be an image-bearer of the Republic. He had been brought delicately out of the fighting for this purpose. He must get well and be with the comrades again and march with them for a last time, and then he must go back at last, he must go back home.

Sometime in the afternoon of April 15, 1865, he finally went to sleep.

And he dreamed that he stood on a hill overlooking some historic river. Dense masses of soldiers were coming up to the river in the forlorn dawn. The tide of their ranked faces spread, engulfed the plain below him, rose in the streets of a little town, advanced with a shrill murmur. They came on crying the names of lost nations, states, commonwealths, cities on the delta. The cry went up and down their ranks, their ghastly drums beat up the charge, the officers turned and waved them forward with swords. They were entering the river, crossing to the attack. They foamed and swirled on little breasts of earth above the town. They choked the roads with wagons, the drivers cursed in high yelps, lashing the bodies of decayed horses.

They were all dead men. Lost faces, they passed him, risen from clotted waters. They fought a war of Events, historic, entirely legendary, in a world lost, lost. And somewhere among them, he remembered, was a young soldier of happy memory, long dead, marching forever in his sentimental landscape to a city on the sea.

If he could only stop them from repeating the somnambulism of the Great War and show them that it had all been only a dream in the first place, a nightmare of human contriving! But the dream went on as if to repeat every act of the Civil War and re-create all its dead thousands and hundreds of thousands. And he slept and dreamed in such a fevered and deep sleep that when he awoke on Sunday morning, it was a while before he remembered what city it was near which he was lying and

WHAT IT WAS THAT THE BIG BELLS OF THE CITY
WERE TOLLING SO MOURNFULLY ALL
THE

.

—TIME was, the Perfessor was saying, when a man's life had a kind of sweet vagueness. Back in the Thirteenth Century a man lived in the bosom of the ages, even if he couldn't flush the toilet. He never dreamed he wouldn't go on living, although of course it might be in Dante's Inferno. Since then we've come a long way. Today a thinking man knows that the earth spouted from the sun a few billion years ago, cooled down into a collection of atoms and finally became encrusted with something called life, an anomalous stuff that scummed the place up. He knows that life, like the matter that spawned it, is regulated by brute causality. Man has emerged from the period of his illusions and is approaching the age of Science and the Machine.

—What will the Twentieth Century be like, Professor?

—Maybe you've seen my articles on the subject—the World Fifty Years From Now, and all that crap. My guess is that we'll live in a world of pushbuttons, dynamos, motors. Man will find faster and faster ways of getting nowhere. They tell me there's a chap up here in Kokomo who's had some luck with a horseless carriage. Well, one of these days they'll roll Dobbin up and put him under a hood. We won't stop there. Man will conquer the air too in something faster than a balloon, and the earth will shrink. Nelly Bly's globecircling antics will look pale by comparison. Jules Verne will be a quaint antiquity. Some day, no doubt, man will blow himself right up to the moon. It's all a question of exploiting matter—coal, gasoline, electricity. Man makes a greater reliance on matter—that's all—as he understands it better.

—And is this Progress?

—Of a kind, yes.

—The only real Progress is Progress toward happiness, Mr. Shawnessy said.

—Man will be happier with these things, the Perfessor said mellowly. Why not? Perhaps with his machines, he can even defeat the laws of economics and have more leisure time and more Pears' Soap. The Age of Science and the Age of Contraceptives are apparently going to happen together. When women learn to love without fearing the consequences and every man is guaranteed a job by the Government and an equal chance with his fellows, we shall have arrived at the only millennium mankind is likely to have.

—But man can explore matter as much as he pleases, Mr. Shawnessy said. And he won't find any happiness in it. Happiness and Progress come only through self-mastery and self-expression broadly interpreted. After all, what is matter, Professor?

—What is matter? Professor Jerusalem Webster Stiles said. A subtle question.

He thought a while.

—Matter is that which is there, he said at last.

—But the thereness of matter is suspect. There why, how, and for whom?

—Perhaps it's enough that it's there, the Perfessor said, and that it's completely dependable. It's made out of little bricks that never wear out. What marvellous stuff it is, when you stop to think about it! What beautiful things have come from it! What is the great *I Am,* finally? It's the Atom—the impregnable Atom. This little package of invisible strength and tenacity is diversified into somewhat less than one hundred varieties differing in mass. It just so happens that when you pile up a visible quantity of these little fellows, the mass takes on certain humanly perceived properties. Some kinds of atoms have ways of catching onto other kinds of atoms and forming bigger blocks, by which the world is diversified.

—Is this your God, Professor? Is this the one thing you believe in?

—Yes, the Perfessor said, getting out his bottle of whiskey and taking a long, strong pull. This I believe in. Matter. Wonderful stuff. Palpable, visible, odorous, audible, tastable matter. From this fountain of coagulated force, all blessings flow.

—Is matter forceful?

—I'm probably anticipating someone, the Perfessor said. I always am. Yes, it wouldn't surprise me if matter is a kind of force. How else can it go on happening except by the eternal exertion of its indestructible force? And the God that sustains it is just this basic, brute, invisible Force. If this God is anything like man, I don't know it. He doesn't have to be. All he has to be is Force, beautiful and perpetual Energy!

—But matter doesn't really explain anything, Mr. Shawnessy said.

—What doesn't it explain, for example?

—For example, it doesn't explain matter.

—Perhaps matter is the First Cause, the Perfessor said. The Beyond Which Nothing.

—What then are human beings? What is a soul?

—Men are mirrors of matter. Like a mirror, they are made of matter themselves, but they are matter peculiarly constructed to reflect matter. And when you get two mirrors facing each other, you get the perfect symbol of human society. It's a self-sustaining world, knowing itself only by its mirror repetitions. But when you shatter these mirrors, their reflected images are gone forever. Mirrors have no memory, and neither in the long run have human lives.

Mr. Shawnessy smoked quietly and listened to the creaking swing. No sound of singing or exhortation came from the Revival Tent. But the fire was still burning there, and the wind carried a stench like pitch.

—The human mirror is more lasting than its images, Professor. The real building blocks of the world are those indivisible, mysterious units called minds or souls.

—Souls? the Perfessor said. I don't know what that word means.

—I don't either, Mr. Shawnessy said. But I have been in contact with what it means.

—What is a human soul? the Perfessor said. When a man loves a woman, isn't it a case of two mirrors, one reflecting the other and so itself at the same time? The more you carry about this bland mirror of the ego, presenting it to other mirrors, the more it reflects itself. Narcissus was your only honest lover. One loves only oneself, or a pleasing reflection of oneself in a pond. Who ever loved another person only for that person's sake? Love is utterly selfish.

—The noblest love is the intense awareness of another being, Mr. Shawnessy said. Love is the all-important discovery that one is not alone in the world.

—How well do your own loves illustrate this, John? the Perfessor said. Take, for example, your brief sojourn in Little Old New York. Did you ever find the soul of Laura Golden? Which is perhaps only another way of rephrasing my earlier question. What in the devil did you do up that stair? What the devil did you do there—up there, soul-discoverer?

—I discovered a soul.

—And did you love what you discovered?

Mr. Shawnessy smoked in silence.

—Confess, boy, it was only the body that you were hunting there—for this woman had somehow persuaded you to believe in the existence of her body, and it became necessary to you, proud and sensitive as you are, to have that body. Matter sought matter; the whirling atoms wished to dance together. And perhaps you wanted it just because you felt that her mask of invitation covered the stony mystery of the Sphinx. Did you ever solve the riddle of that devious woman?

Mr. Shawnessy smoked in silence.

—Damn you, boy, the Perfessor said. Tell me this one thing.

—Professor, your atoms are in a frightful agitation. Why be such an inquisitive mirror? Mirrors are supposed to reflect only what is put before them. Mirrors are passive and obedient. What does it matter to your atoms what my atoms and her atoms perpetrated, lo! these many years ago?

—That's what I get for abandoning philosophy for biography, the Perfessor said, leaning back in the swing. But my mirror isn't really willful. It's merely reflecting its own agitations. *Its old agitations of myrtles and roses,* he added, allowing his thought, as he so often did, to deteriorate in a quotation.

Mr. Shawnessy smoked on, in silence. His cigar had a bitter taste.

Holding a Visitor's Guide, he walked on a broad way through the city of an extinct republic. A procession of metropolitan women in murmuring dresses passed on the arms of dandy escorts into the portals of an old theatre. Under the golden languor of the lights, their diminished and receding forms followed the curve of balustrades into a hushed interior from which a music flowed down all the wavering ramparts of the City. Their beckoning hands and painted smiles dissolved by a quaint transition of images into a yard of castiron statuary, walled in by steep cliffs of buildings. A brownstone mansion lay in eternal twilight here on the floor of the aboriginal City, which elsewhere had vanished under mountains of masonry. The parklike yard expanded; it was a place of Exposition. He remembered then how Centennial crowds had filled the park, tidal millions. He had seen the last great rocket rise on its burning tail, had seen it reach the climax of its climb, had seen it burst and shed its petals on the City, had seen it fall and rain upon the City, had seen the City redly lit to its remotest valleys in the night, all fading in the night—and all its naked streets and mournful walls disclosed.

Well, then, what was I seeking in the City? I came to the City a vagrant day. And I sought in the City one who vanished in a dream.

But now and then I must return and find my way upstairs to a chamber on the third floor. I pause at the landing, and looking down, I see around me once again the City, a winking world of shadow, and on the hollow street a footfall sounds. It is a late hour, after the ball is over, and the dancers are gone. And so I wait up there for someone in whose existence I believed. And this, all this, was long ago, a legend of the City.

Ascend the stair again, lost one, far from home and Raintree County. The Republic has many republics, and the City has many cities. Love has a thousand loves, and passion is a dream of mirrors. What was it that you wanted at the stairhead, and what did you find when you were there?

Ascend, ascend the stair, lost dreamer drowned in urban days. For you were drowned in chambers of the City, your innocence was wasted in a yellow flare of passion before the gaslamp of your City days expired.

Go back, dear boy, and make your lonely try again. Is there something more impenetrable than the substance of the atom? Is there a chamber of yourself that will always be locked against you, unless, unless, unless . . .

Go back. The noises of the night rise from the winking roofworld of the City, the vapors of the night are risen from the harbor, and in the slums the sleepers all are sleeping. Go back, and wait, while in a lavish chamber of the City, you hear again a calling of your name.

Along the Pennsylvania Railroad, a train passed in the darkness, crying. It was the old sound of farewell and of recall to Raintree County. It was the most memorable sound of his life, receding down dark lanes of memory into the West. Its voice at the crossing was like a calling of his name, calling, recalling him to him. He listened to its lonely and diminishing cry in sadness, remembering a severance of himself from herself. Arrival and departure and farewell! Union and reunion! A train had passed in the darkness, crying.

—The sound of this century, said the Perfessor, is the wail of a train whistle at the crossing. In this lone vowel of sorrow and farewell, the Nineteenth Century has its perfect poem.

The train had been a passenger express. Mr. Shawnessy had seen in the rhythmic flow of its windows the motionless yet moving images of passengers across the night.

Eternal passengers across the plain, Americans, travellers to cities on the plain, hail and farewell!

Farewell to all passengers on the trains of America, fixed in the yellow frames of windows and passing in the night. To all passengers from dawn to sorrow, to all young men from cities returning to their homes, hail and farewell.

To all days and ways of living in cities of the East, to lone awakenings in the great City where men are lost like atoms in the astral void, farewell.

To mansions on the old brick streets, to stairways leading up to moonlight landings, to hearts that beat a lonely drum in the hollow chambers of the night, to all the sleepers in the lonely beds, to all the sleepers in the unlonely beds, to all the City's twilight rooms, farewell.

To a woman of the City, Laura recumbent in my gilded years, farewell, hail and farewell!

Some part of me I left, always a wanderer in cities.

Go some night to the squares where the girls come out and walk, or to the station where the trains are changing, go some day along the narrow way between the milelong walls of factories, and see if you can find him—this lost wanderer. For I left him to wander in the City, a lonely Gentleman from Indiana with a shy and winning smile. Perhaps you will hear his hollow footfalls in your dreams, and awakening, you may rush to the window and push aside the heavy drapes and hear his retreating footsteps in the dawn.

Remember him in the afterfollowing years whenever you board a train and go across America. Look for his face among the faces of the crowd and for his affectionate smile. Remain a little the sentimentalist of life, life's young American, as he was.

Remember him whenever the boats are putting out to sea from harbors and the wind strains at the skirts of pretty girls along the harbor and the tides are setting strong against the shore. Remember him when the clockface in the tallest tower of the City tells you that time is running out to darkness. Remember him in your awakenings just before darkness dissolves into the dawn. For he is still there among the faces of your City, he is a legend of your City, and in this legend you have a part, eternal actress of yourself, who succeeded in your greatest role by means of failure.

Remember him in the hot summers of your City and in its sudden and bright springs. Remember him in the fabric of its years, for the legend of his days in the City is twisted with your own. Remember him when you are old, and he is gone, and remember that he believed in the existence and reality of you and of the world that you two fashioned together.

Remember him, for he will remember you. Perhaps you learned to find him too, by losing him. Remember that you two lost each other then, but will find each other in some later century of the City (or some earlier perchance) wherever and whenever a traveller gets down from the train to find the face of one who loved him waiting in the station.

—The sound of the train, the Perfessor said, his voice hoarser but his mood more mellow as he watched Mrs. Brown and the children hanging Japanese lanterns around the lawn, is the sound of time. No generation was ever so time-conscious as our own.

—We Americans, Mr. Shawnessy said, always have watches in our hands. We're always rushing to that rendezvous at the far end of the tracks—an appointment with Progress.

—But where, finally, the Perfessor said, are these trains taking us? Where are we going on schedule, keeping abreast of the ticking minutes? Well, I will tell you, lost boy, soul-discoverer. We are going back to the earth.

—So we are, Mr. Shawnessy said, knowing that as usual his meaning was the same and subtly different.

—The earth, said the Perfessor (who drunk or sober was never afraid to be rhetorical—his profound advantage as a conversationalist), the one great mother of us all. We have no other, when the tale is told, except the earth. From dust we sprang and unto dust return. Children of dust, feeders on dust, lovers of dust, fathers of dust, sleepers in dust. I'm not sure that men resist this idea as much as they pretend. Men desire what is natural, and nothing is more natural than to die. Life's a restlessness of unstable compounds that long for the stability of death. Perhaps all desire is really for death. The act of love's a burial whose afterfruit is sadness, a fierce desire to quell desire. And earth is the great bed where all sickness is unsickened and every lust is cooled.

—But doesn't this thought make you unhappy, Professor? Do you really want to die?

With a festive gesture, the Perfessor tossed the empty bottle over the side of the porch where it landed in some bushes.

—Life is sorrow, he said. And death is a stoppage of sorrow. Why then be sorry to die?

Where every sickness is unsickened and every lust is cooled.

—I think it's likely, the Perfessor said, that all the myths of homecoming are really symbols of death. If I took up teaching school again, I'd teach only one thing—resignation to death. By the way, what did I do with my heart pills?

The Perfessor fumbled in his pockets and pulled out the other bottle.

—I will tell you a secret, he said. Perhaps because I'm drunk.

The Perfessor did something that Mr. Shawnessy hadn't seen him do all day long. He removed his glasses and breathed on them. His face acquired a childlike, defenseless look while he carefully polished the lenses with a silk handkerchief.

—Years ago, he said, I was a child in Raintree County.

He paused as if the words just said were full of labyrinthine meanings.

—My father had died before I was old enough to remember him. When I was only ten years old, my mother died. In that death, Jerusalem Webster Stiles knew the secret of life—which is death—and never after added to his wisdom though he added to his words. And with that act, also, he left Raintree County and went East, where he had roots. Now, as you know, he came back to Raintree County when he was a young man, but he never came back home. He learned early, with the bitterness of the homeless child, that the earth cares nothing for our grief, and that even our mother who cared for us in life cares nothing for us in death. We care for her and keep her image alive in our brief world of memory and grief, but she doesn't care for us any longer. She has forgotten us. She doesn't remember our face.

—Your mother, Mr. Shawnessy said. You never mentioned her before. You remember her—clearly?

—My mother, the Perfessor said amiably, was a tall, thin woman in a black dress. She had a sharp, sweet voice. She knew the Bible backwards and made me memorize all the popular passages. I went to church every Sunday and to prayer meetings during the week. I spouted verses at the drop of a hat, being considered a prodigy. I hated God, and I think he hated me. We never got along together.

The Perfessor took another drink.

—My mother, he said, had a kind smile and a wistful look around the mouth. She meant I should be a preacher and praise God. She was very stiff and terrible in her coffin, and they buried her at noon on a summer's day. I remember this like yesterday. I wept so many pints of tears that the well has been dry ever since. Sometimes, I try to cry to see whether I can or not. I make a very impressive racket—but no tears. The bucket comes up empty. After her death, they kept trying to get me to recite Bible verses, saying it would get me over my grief. I went East with relatives and became slowly the pitiful, harmless creature that you behold today. This is the autobiography of Jerusalem Webster Stiles, which may be said to have ended when he was ten years old.

—If you could only cry, Professor, you might recover your faith in life.

—What is there to cry about? the Perfessor said. When you have known all grief and learned all wisdom at the age of ten?

—But you loved your mother?

—Yes, I suppose I did, the Perfessor said. But when I came back to the County years later, I found no trace of her except her grave, and I felt no desire to dig that up again.

—So you believe that the dead are utterly and forever gone?

—This I believe, the Perfessor said, and I assure you that once you accept this wisdom and give up to it entirely, you get peace. You lose your vanity and most of your vexations. Nothing is left of the dead but earth. Can you refute this wisdom?

—Perhaps I can.

—And how will you do it, hero boy?

—By the legend of my life, with which I refute all sophistries. By a myth of homecoming and a myth of resurrection.

Come back to Raintree County, wandering child. Remember the great deaths and the great homecomings. Come back, and bring a sprig of lilac. For you will always be on trains and coming home, and the legend that recalled you from the City will always be tingling along the wires of the Republic.

Come back to Raintree County and find your home again. And you will find again the sphinxlike silence of the earth. Knock hard, young hero, on the gates of death.

Listen to the wail of the train at the crossing. This is the myth of America and of those who cross America on trains. This is the myth of those who come back home.

Who would not suffer grief? Grief is the most beautiful garland given to love. (And who would not suffer love?)

But listen to the wail of the train at the crossing. O, sound of sorrow and farewell, as we go down the years of life into the gulf together! Lost years. Last years. Stations upon the plain. One-minute stops of life and smoky rooms where I got down with crowds. O, gates of iron gushing human faces!

Delay the trains! Keep them from crossing rivers! Delay the iron horse of time!

My gilded years come back to me, my postwar years. The Republic was roaring West; factories mushroomed from the nightsoil of cities. But there was a message for me to come back home. I had known already how the legend would end. All the great legends of the earth are certain like the earth.

For the saddest legend of my life was only some pencil marks on paper, a pulse of atoms in a wire. It was the one undissuadable legend. It had been coming all the time down all the wires and all the ways of the world since the world began, and it found a lost young man in the City and made him once more a passenger on trains, for it was

July–August— A —1877

MESSAGE FOR HIM

TO COME BACK HOME TO RAINTREE COUNTY

was in his pocket as he travelled by train along the trunklines of the Republic. When his train came into Pittsburgh, he remembered dully that the Great Strike was still on. Only a week ago, he had seen the Strike become a bloody war in the yards at Pittsburgh. He remembered an army leaderless and lost in darkness. In the Workers' neighborhood a boy named Johnny Fabrizio had lain dead.

Since that day in Pittsburgh, he had taken the warm flesh of the City into his arms and had possessed it by rejection. Since that time, he had received a telegram. He knew now that time couldn't be measured by Wednesdays, Thursdays, Fridays, but only by the revolutions of the soul.

The telegram that he kept in his pocket and sometimes took out for rereading had already acquired a crumpled antiquity.

JOHN WICKLIFF SHAWNESSY:

COME HOME. . . .

A few words had crossed the statelines and rivers of the Republic and had found him in the City.

As the train passed slowly through Pittsburgh with unexplained delays, he saw the wreckage of the yards, a drab aftermath of battle —ashes, watersoaked rags, lumps of iron, overturned cars, gutted buildings, spewed bricks. Troops were in force, and when night fell and the train hadn't yet left the station, torches sputtered in the yards, and the air was charged with excitement, as if at any time the fighting might flare up again.

As he was leaving Pittsburgh at last, train bells were tolling. He heard them in the yards of city after city on his way back home. They went on tolling and tolling the bloody dirge of the Great Strike. With troops and court injunctions and arrests without right of trial, the Strike was being broken. Cash Carney had been absolutely right. But the trouble was a long time dying in the land.

Usually, John Shawnessy would have expected to come home in a day and a night, but he was many days getting home now because of the Strike.

Those days, the Strikers gathered along the trainways, standing sometimes in mute hundreds. Often at night, the train would be stopped by Strikers, John Shawnessy would be awakened from a fitful sleep, a lantern would be thrust into his face, voices would say,

—Is this the feller?

—No, that ain't the one. Must have been the next car down.

—Who are you, Mister?

—John Shawnessy.

—Where you from?

—New York.

—Where you goin'?

—Indiana.

—What's your business?

He showed them the telegram, and they passed on.

Several times, men raised lanterns to the windows.

—Are there any soldiers on this train?

—No.

—Damn good thing!

Through these summer nights and days of anger and pent violence, he passed, obeying an old command. For certain words had come and found him in the City. They had been reaching out for him with feminine and pleading hands, and they had called him home.

During these days, he hated the bigness of America. These miles of iron roadways, these planless cities, these stations, depots, roundhouses, warehouses, grain elevators, factories were the gray huge swollen river of American time. Like a gulf of bitter waters he had to drink it down before he could come home.

But there was a dark satisfaction, too, in these many delays because they kept the legend of the words he had got from becoming final. Perhaps a man might, by crowded thought, by accumulation of images, linger for a hundred lifetimes between two unrelated points on the vast earth of America.

The convulsions of the Strike had reached Indiana before him.

More days were lost as he was diverted to Chicago, and from there down to Indianapolis, where the Strike had reached a climax of violence. During a stop-over there, he got out briefly in the Union Station and saw the backwash of bloody riots in which troops under the command of General Benjamin Harrison had been called in by a court injunction to put down the disturbance.

Strangely, all during this time, he had a morbid preoccupation with the lives and destinies of other people whom he saw, passengers on trains. He seemed to understand as never before the isolation and uniqueness of other human beings. Each one, he knew, was going a private voyage across time, approaching or departing from the terminals of birth, marriage, death, from the cities of joy and sorrow; and each, whether he knew it or not, carried in his pocket a crumpled telegram telling him to come back home.

Then on a brilliant August afternoon, he was speeding out of Indianapolis on the way to Raintree County. Familiar names went by, tolling the minutes off. Those days, the trains ran unpredictably, even on the local lines, and he hadn't been able to get a telegram through. Consequently, when he got down at the station in Freehaven, he looked in vain for a familiar face. The town was hot and sleepy, and hardly anyone was on the Square.

John Shawnessy set out to walk home. He was unshaven, grimy, sweaty. His suitcase was heavy. His city suit was baggy and hot. The streets blurred and swam in his eyes. Looking back, he saw the flag limply hanging on the tower of the New Court House. The clock said three o'clock.

He was dizzy and panting as he went on through the outskirts of the town. The weeds along the road seemed insultingly lush, tall, fragrant. Thousands of voracious grasshoppers seethed at the edges of the road, frightened by his feet. The Shawmucky was choked with reeds, flowers, small trees, mudbars. As soon as he crossed the bridge, he left the road and picked his way through the lost yards and fallen fences of Danwebster, following a lane that led down to the mill on the river. He crossed the structure of wood and rock that still spanned the river there. He climbed the railroad, went down the embankment, ascended the hill to the iron gates of the graveyard, entered.

The Danwebster Graveyard hadn't been mowed for several weeks.

As he walked through the deep grass, hundreds of insects rose and fell like seeds from the hand of a sower.

He went down on his knees before a fresh mound in the southeastern corner of the yard. The tall stone, surmounted by a cross, had the legend

MOTHER

Ellen Shawnessy

1801–1877

There were bouquets of withered flowers on the grave. The sun beat hard on the crusted earth.

He lay on the earth, and the earth gave no sign, except to remain beautiful with summer. The river made a little sound in the shallows. A train passed, crying.

He thought of a face darkly tranquil in the earth below him.

Then he remembered the living face of his mother, Ellen Shawnessy. And with this memory there came to him like a tide of musical waters the legend of his days in Raintree County. The face of his mother leaned down to him from a prehistoric past. This young, vivid face with the affectionate smile moved, and the mouth said the single piercing word that had touched him into being. *Johnny!* With that word came the memory of his father, T. D. Shawnessy, benignly nodding down to him from a great height. The old days came back, the days of his childhood on the breast of the land, a life steeped in myths and golden quests. Like invulnerable angels, the forms of his father and mother moved on the young earth of Raintree County. From the grass and flowers that brushed his face a sweet, wild fragrance rose of all the withered summers distilled into the little house behind the house. He remembered the primeval Home Place in the County, the log cabin, the road before it—a pioneer trace, the great oak forest, a twilight of stately trunks. *Johnny!* The word was talismanic. It called into being the newer Home Place of Before the War and the days of his burgeoning manhood. He remembered golden afternoons on the upland meadows, harvest of wheat and corn. He remembered the Old Court House, the shrine of clockless days when there had been no death. He remembered a hundred Saturdays, Memorial Days, Fourths of July, footraces, picnics, ice-cream socials, church suppers. The form of a young professor stood at the blackboard in a brick building and chalked a slanting script across it. The river ran through the whole bright legend, green waters of prophecy, rising from an unknown source and flowing to a lake. *Johnny!* With a pang of sadness, he heard the name said like a caress by the mouth of one who was lost and gone forever on the great river of the years.

Now he knew what grief was. It was a memory of time past, of time in its poignant and irrevocable pastness. It was man's memory of being a child after it was impossible any longer to be a child.

It was late afternoon when John Shawnessy left the Danwebster Graveyard and going back to the road walked toward the Old Home Place, looking for its lonely form on the sky.

T. D. met him at the door. He looked pathetically old and broken, blinking back tears, wandering around disconsolately while others talked. Now and then the old man would stop and put his chin up and clasping his hands behind his back, would begin to rock on his heels with a faint revival of the old look of buoyant optimism. But a vague bewilderment erased the smile, and he would turn and go away by himself. During the next few days, he spent hours sitting in his Office fumbling with the Botanical Medicines. T. D. was obviously not long for this world himself.

Ellen Shawnessy's death had been unexpected. A call had come from a neighbor's house two miles away, near Moreland. A woman was about to have a baby. T. D. was away at the time, but Ellen had put down her work, bridled a horse, and ridden away bareback. Arriving, she had got off the horse and started toward the house. She had come up the walk, smiling, flushed with the ride, had raised her hand to greet one of the members of the household. Just then, she had stopped, turned pale, and fallen senseless on the path. A few hours later, without regaining consciousness and shortly after telegrams had been dispatched to John Shawnessy and other members of the family not at home, she had been pronounced dead.

In the days following, while John Shawnessy remained at the Home Place, wondering if he could find his way back to a satisfactory Raintree County, Carl Foster, a good friend and fellow teacher, told him of a teaching position vacant at the school in Moreland. He suggested that John Shawnessy apply for the place and also attend the County Teachers' Institute, which was being held at Paradise Lake in the latter part of August.

With almost cynical resignation (as cynically resigned as he was ever likely to be), John Shawnessy accepted the suggestion.

In the strength of his young manhood, he had gone to Lake Paradise with a girl named Susanna Drake, after a victorious run through the Court House Square. That was nearly twenty years ago. He had plunged for an afternoon into the very quick of life and had done what it pleased him to do, like a young god. That was before he had erected on the horizons of his soul the shape of a mansion doomed to fall in fire. That was before the War and its wreck of human souls. That was before Atlanta fell and Columbia burned and Lincoln's body had crossed the Nation on a flag-draped train. That was before his lonely post-War years and his messianic dreams. That was before he had gone in Centennial Summer to the City, where he dreamed an enchanting dream of love and fame, and hunted through the world Behind the Scenes, trying to find a lovely woman in a costume closet, but found instead the multiple image of a sphinx recumbent. That was before his recall to Raintree County:

JOHN WICKLIFF SHAWNESSY:
COME HOME. MAMMA IS DYING.

Come home. Come home. That was the thing he hadn't been able to do and perhaps would never be able to do again. For where was the home of life's eternal wanderer, the young American?

Now, he was thirty-eight years old, had lived more than half his allotted years. What trophies did he have of his days to carry before him like victorious banners? He had a huge, half-written, rejected manuscript, some letters addressed to a young soldier named Corporal Johnny Shawnessy (dead in battle), some notes scrawled by a pathetic child whose soul had been scarred by fire, a guide-book to the Centennial Exposition, an album of class day posies, some photographs of children's faces in front of country schools, and a crumpled telegram.

Come home. Come home. He had come home and had completed the necessary legend. But now he saw that he hadn't built new ramparts against the day when the old ones came crumbling down. He had his memories of Raintree County and his mother, and these he incessantly turned in his mind in the days following her death, as if now, when it was too late, he would try to recapture and understand fully the person who had gone away.

Come home. Come home. Well, he would go back to Lake Paradise in the center of Raintree County and see it as it was now, with its new hotel, its revival tabernacle, and its cottages for summer tourists. He would remind himself that nothing remains the same, not even the most ancient scar on the earth of Raintree County. He might even wander some day over to the wild side of the lake, where the Shawmucky emptied into it and see if he could find a boy with sun-illumined hair running among the trees (the fastest runner in Raintree County!).

He would, however, not disturb himself to hunt for that old tree, that mothy personal legend with which he had quaintly amused himself from childhood. He wouldn't hunt for it, precisely because he was afraid that he would find it.

After all, it was there somewhere, with two rocks under it. He knew. He alone knew that it was there in the almost impenetrable swamp where the great reeds thrust to sunlight and the bugs went buzzing by like bullets. It was there, where an itinerant preacher had thrust a little seedling into the earth. It was there all right—and exactly what of it?

Or had he been drunker on applewine than he thought and dreamed the tree and the two rocks?

He knew then that he would never go back to the City. He knew then that he had ceased to be the child of his mother and had become at last, reluctantly, a man, who would have to make new alliances with Time and Fate and find, if possible, new loves to replace the old.

So, in the latter days of August, 1877, John Shawnessy climbed into T. D.'s old buggy and drove off toward the lake with a pile of books behind the seat, among them a pamphlet that Carl Foster had given him. It was really an advertisement for the new Biltmore Hotel, containing a gem of commercial poetry. He had read it with sardonic amusement. COME TO PARADISE LAKE, it said:

O, come ye now, and bring your children,

BRING YOUR WIFE AND SWEETHEART TRUE,

TO THE EARTH'S

MOST

—LOVELY GARDEN you have here, Evelina, Professor Stiles remarked to Mrs. Brown.

Esther liked Professor Stiles, but she didn't really understand him. He and Mr. Shawnessy had just left the porchswing, where they had been talking ever since the picnic supper, and were standing with the ladies near the fountain in the front part of the lawn, watching a game of drop-the-handkerchief. The children gave such a wild shout of laughter that Esther didn't catch Mrs. Brown's reply, but it was probably something genteel and witty.

Esther hadn't forgot Pa's warning, given after the Revival Service. Now that the day was so nearly finished and it seemed unlikely that anything could happen, she was more frightened than at any time before. What was waiting there in the hushed night to surprise these revelers in the garden? Was it something that had been waiting in secret for its hour during fourteen years?

Every Fourth of July was an occasion for mixed recollections of joy and sorrow; she always felt pulled apart emotionally before the anniversary day was over. It was both a birthday and a deathday in her life. Always there was a victory to be won over herself. People who had known her joy would have to suffer for it—this she had always known. For greatest bliss, one had to suffer greatest chastisement.

She had known, too, what this chastisement would be, had often found herself thinking about it when darkness would fall on the little towns where the summer evenings died slow, gorgeous deaths.

—I wonder what's happened to the revivalists, Professor Stiles said. What in the world do they do over there? Burn a house down every time they hold a meeting?

Mrs. Brown and Mr. Shawnessy laughed. Esther was surprised, not realizing that the remark was intended to be humorous. Perhaps they *had* been burning something down. She had had for some time a feeling that there was an unusual disturbance in the town. People were perhaps gathering in the darkness, just beyond the palely colored light from the Japanese lanterns.

—Maybe they're coming to run me out of the County again, Professor Stiles said, sniffing. That's a familiar odor. You don't see anyone out there carrying a long, knotty piece of somebody's fence, do you—and a bagful of feathers?

Mr. Shawnessy laughed, but his eyes were puzzled.

About three hundreds yards away in the Main Street of Waycross, bunches of flame began to move, flicker, flare, approach, recede. They were torches. They drew together into a thick cluster. They began to move forward, held aloft in a shapeless mass, yet riding in a fixed relation to each other. They came forward voicelessly, glaring through the spears of the fence. The children stopped playing and listened. There was a noise now of heavy feet trampling on the road coming out of town.

Professor Stiles sniffed.

—Do they do this sort of thing often? Now if they only had a jungle tom-tom or an Indian war-drum and shrieked at the tops of their——

At that moment, the darkness erupted with a shout of voices singing:

—Mine eyes have seen the glory of the coming of the Lord. . . .

Involuntarily, the four older people and the many children in the yard drew closer together.

—Well, Mr. Shawnessy said, I must say——

—Glory, Glory, Halleluiah!

Esther's heart beat hard. A feeling of helplessness came over her, as she waited for this impersonal force to unmask itself and reveal its purpose.

Whatever the purpose was, she felt certain now that it was sinister. Feeling lonely and helpless, she walked over to her husband and placed her hand on his arm. Worst of all was the suspense of waiting. If there were only something that she could do to break the spell, some heroic decision that she could repeat, then all might be well. But as it was, she had to stand here, frightened to the foundations of her being by these trampling feet, shouting voices, swung beams of light. She had to go on waiting here in this garden like someone discovered in the commission of a crime, a guilty woman, shrinking from a sword of flame. She had to go on waiting, waiting,

July 4— WAITING FOR PA TO COME HOME FROM FREEHAVEN, —1878

she went hypnotically through the last details of packing her things. She had a trunk to pack and a small suitcase that she intended to carry. Fernie helped her with the packing, sniffling and blowing her nose from time to time. Esther didn't cry at all.

It was a hot day. When she went over to the window to look out, she saw the yard, the spattered barnlot, fields of corn with limp arms. The taut feeling in her stomach went up into her throat.

Pa had gone into Freehaven at nine o'clock in the morning. He had said that he would be back around four in the afternoon with the tickets for their trip. They were going to drive by a roundabout way to Three Mile Junction, where they could take the train without notice and escape detection. Most of the people would be in Freehaven for the Fourth of July Celebration. Once on the train, the whole thing would be out of Esther's hands. She and Pa would go on out West, and she would try to forget Mr. Shawnessy.

Several female relatives were vigilantly supervising the last arrangements. They came around and talked with Esther, telling her how sensible she was to do this thing for her old pa. They hardly let her out of their sight, except when she went upstairs.

As the hours dragged on, she stood for minutes at a time before the window looking at the road and the fields. But nothing happened. The earth gave no sign, except to grow hotter and brighter. She looked out so long that the fields began to have a kind of white radiance. The earth swam in heat, faintly in motion.

She couldn't imagine what was the matter with her. She felt no sorrow, no joy, no languor, no excitement. She had only this taut feeling of waiting.

Nevertheless, she knew that when Pa's buggy appeared on the road from the direction of Freehaven, rolling swiftly up as she had seen it do hundreds of times, the black horse crisply trotting, the wheels blurred with speed, the polished frame bouncing under

Pa's weight, she knew that then she would have a dark moment of farewell, and she didn't really know what she would do at that moment.

But she had made her decision. She had said that she would go. It was Pa's will that she go, and in this crucial hour of her life Pa's will must be her own will. Only thus could she save from death those whom she loved.

She had voluntarily made a solemn promise. Esther couldn't remember ever breaking that kind of promise.

She kept looking at the familiar rooms, and from time to time she went to the window again. This was the house in which she had spent her life. This was the earth where she was born. The things about her now were the oldest things in the world. In the stillness of these ancient things, she moved restlessly. This world, Pa's world, closed in on her, taking added weight from the heat and stillness of the day. She felt that if she stopped moving for a moment, the walls of her self would be crushed, and she would stop breathing.

At three o'clock in the afternoon she went upstairs to dress. The white dress she took down from a closet was one that she had worn nearly a year ago, twice in one memorable week—and not at all since. She had rowed through the hot brilliance of a summer afternoon and had plunged through a swamp to find someone whom now she would perhaps never see again. There were faint green stains in the cloth that no amount of water would wash out.

It was her most beautiful dress, and this was her most significant day.

Slowly she put on the dress at the mirror of what had been her mother's room. Slowly she bound up her dark hair, winding it and pinning it back to show her ears, one of which bore a disfiguring scar in the lobe. She had no ornament on and didn't powder her face, which looked back at her from the mirror familiar-strange—brilliant dark eyes, lips red and smooth, finely formed straight nose, high cheekbones.

Once long ago, she had been taunted with Indian descent. She had flung back a terrible word, which even now she was ashamed to remember. Pa had risen in a towering rage. She had fled to the windgrove not far away and had heard the whip laid to her sister Sarah.

She had not quite finished her packing. Lying in the bottom drawer of her dresser were some souvenirs she had saved to the last. She opened the drawer and took out a packet of letters tied with a blue ribbon. She carefully wrapped them in a silk handkerchief and placed them among the things in her personal suitcase. There were some photographs, including a large one recently taken of the Root family, sitting on the front lawn before the house. She and Pa were together in the middle of the picture almost as if above and apart from the others.

There was another picture that she had hidden very carefully for years. At the bottom of it were the words

Stony Creek School
1866

She found her own small face in the front row, turned a little to one side and looking across the fields with a brooding expression. The picture was yellowed, yet remarkably clear. She could see the ribbon knots in her pigtails and the creases in her dress. Mr. Shawnessy stood at the right-hand side of the picture, arms folded, eyes half-shut because of the sun. That part of the picture hadn't been properly exposed, and with the fading caused by time, his form looked half-dissolved in light. His figure had a golden, wondrous look, while her own in the middle of the picture was dark, precise, and actual. She noticed also that the school door was open so that the light dimly illumined the hall. She had gone running one day in spring out of that door and had climbed through the bars and had run down through the woods to be the first to meet Mr. Shawnessy.

She put this picture carefully into the suitcase.

She went to the window and looked out. It must be close to four o'clock. She looked across the fields in the direction of the Foster Farm. She hadn't taken the path to Ivy's for months now, but she knew just how it went.

The path to Ivy's went through the back gate and through the barnyard, and out through the orchard, and along beside the cornfield for two hundred yards. Then the path sloped off to the left and down the hill to a stile crossing over into the pasture woods. It went on through the woods for several hundred yards and down past the little spring that rose under the roots of the old dead tree to flow off in a winding stream northeast. The quick way was to cross the stream if it was low, but, if not, to go around. Then there was a short walk through the woods, gently rising until suddenly the path came out into a field back of the Foster house.

She had made this walk several times in the past year to meet Mr. Shawnessy at Ivy's. Sometimes he had come out a way to meet her.

Now, she looked toward the wood, where the path entered the trees. The wood was still. She could see deeper than usual into it because of the immense light.

She walked into the hall and to her old bedroom where she could look out and see the road. There was no one on it as far as she could see. She went back to her packing.

Now she lifted some other things from the drawer. Among them was a certificate which testified that Esther Root had passed the Teachers' Examination with a satisfactory mark and was adjudged competent to instruct in the Public Schools of Raintree County. It was dated June, 1876, and it bore the examiner's signature in a bold, flowing hand. John Wickliff Shawnessy.

She remembered an afternoon in the New Court House, the masculine, exciting odor, the brave, terrific tower. Suddenly, she wondered if she would ever see it again. With a wild excitement, she imagined it now, in the middle of Freehaven. The flag would be bright on its pole at the top of the tower; the clockfaces would look in four directions telling the time of day.

The time of day. The time of day.

The hands would be pointing to the hour.

Pa would have read the clock and would have got into his buggy. Through this heatstricken earth of eternal things, he was driving steadily home, poised on the buggy seat, sometimes making his black whip uncoil and crack above the horse. He had never driven so fast before—of that she might be sure.

Her hands trembled as she put the certificate in the suitcase. She was being compelled to make hasty decisions. The world was beginning to come apart. She had begun to forget where things belonged. She began to rake in the bottom of the drawer, taking things out and then putting them back again—and again senselessly taking them out—pictures, books, folders, lockets, wisps of hair tied in ribbons.

She got up and looked at herself in the mirror. Her face was white, and she had to steady herself. Her head swam. She listened. No, it was not the drumming of a horse's hooves, it was not the humming of wheels that she had heard.

Or perhaps it was. She walked rapidly through the house to a front window.

The road was empty.

She ran back to her room and began to rake through the drawer again, as if she were looking for something important. But she couldn't imagine what.

Yesterday evening, at the risk of Pa's terrible anger, Fernie—poor, frightened, heroic Fernie—had slipped out of the house and gone to Ivy's to let Ivy know of the projected trip. No one was at home, and Fernie had left a note. Apart from that last message, Esther had had no way of letting Mr. Shawnessy know that she was leaving. Fernie, no fancy rhetorician, had written plain words:

> Ivy, Esther is leaving the County tomorrow with Pa. They are going West, and I don't think he aims to ever bring her back.
>
> FERNIE

Well, she had made up her mind to go, but she had desperately wanted to let Mr. Shawnessy know that she was going. She would go West all right, yes, she would go because God willed her to suffer for her great wrong love; she would go so that no one might die. But at least, before she went, she had reached out of her prison and had touched him with a word, a last sign, so that he would say to himself: Now she is going. Esther is no longer here.

Over the fields toward Ivy's the way was empty. The deep woods gave no sign. The air was still. The immense, triumphant afternoon held hardly a moving thing. She remembered the look of the empty fields a few months ago when Pa had come to the trysting place with his gun. She had looked everywhere then for Mr. Shawnessy across the wide fields, fearing that he might come.

She heard a rush of voices from downstairs and someone called,

—Esther, are you about ready?

—Yes, she said, her voice so small and hoarse that she had to repeat the word to be sure they heard her.

Now there was no time to lose. She must hurry now, or she

wouldn't be ready when Pa came. She went to the drawer and, pulling it entirely out, emptied it onto the bed. Among the things lying there, she picked up a little advertising booklet. Impulsively, she opened it, remembering what it was. In the yellow brightness of her room the words swam up to her alive and blackly writhing like serpents in a place of sunwarmed waters:

COME TO PARADISE LAKE

> Come to Paradise Lake, situated in the geometrical center of Raintree County. Summer tourists, fishermen, honeymooners, whoever is seeking . . .

She put the booklet on top of her little suitcase and stood looking desperately about her.

—Esther, the voices called from downstairs. Better come now.

Esther! Esther! Esther! Esther!

Come to Lake Paradise in the very center of Raintree County.

She stood, her body stricken with waves of feeling rising from the sunbright afternoon beyond her bedroom window. She was panting, and in her anguish she bent over and leaned her whole body across the open suitcase and onto the bed. She had not realized until then that she was gasping and sobbing.

There was a noise downstairs, far off, in the nether regions of herself, in the old life, in the world that walled her in as if forever. There were people calling her. There were excited voices.

She listened. Something was burning at her ears, an intolerable piercing sound. She listened.

There was a steady thunder of hooves not far away. Under this noise was a persistent, vicious hum of wheels.

She sat up suddenly and gave a little cry. She pushed down the lid of the suitcase and latched it and picked the suitcase up. She ran out of the door, looking wildly around. There was no one upstairs. She looked down the back stair. It was empty. She ran down and into the kitchen. It was empty. Everyone was at the front of the house, watching for Pa's arrival. She ran out of the back door and down the walk, pushed open the gate, ran into the barnyard. From long habit, she turned, swung the gate to, and latched it. She paused with her hand on the gate.

Come to Lake Paradise, little darkhaired child. Come to Lake Paradise, where long ago, but o, so long, so long, so long ago . . .

She heard the noise of a buggy slowing and stopping in front of the house. But all she could see was the back of the white farmhouse, the not-very-well-kept yard, the weeds along the fence, a few chickens scratching, the back door open, the pump beside the window. All she could see was the most familiar image of her life.

She turned away and began to run.

She could hardly see where she was going: the green earth was drenched with waves of water flashing and brightening in the sunlight. She heard a hoarse, gasping sound. It was her own voice, sobbing and saying,

—Good-by, Pa. Good-by, Pa. Good-by, Pa.

She ran through the orchard and beside the cornfield. After a while her right arm ached terribly, and her chest felt as though it would burst. The earth beside the cornfield was soft, and she kept slipping and stumbling. She fell full length and soiled her going-away dress. She was up immediately, thinking that she heard voices behind her. She ran down the path sloping to the left and went over the stile. Her dress caught on a snag and tore away a wide gash of cloth which clung accusingly on the fence.

She was sure that they were after her. Still she clung to her suitcase and went on, running through the woods. Though the stream was high from recent rains she plunged in and across, soaking herself to the thighs.

Looking up now through the clean woods toward Ivy's, far off she saw a tall man in a black suit striding along the path alone.

She heard then a distinct sound of voices and footsteps far behind her in the afternoon. She didn't look back, but ran forward crying out in a loud voice,

—Mr. Shawnessy! Mr. Shawnessy! Mr. Shawnessy!

She listened, and above the terrible elation of her heart,

SHE HEARD VERY CLEARLY THE SOUND
OF HIS VOICE
CALLING

HER NAME was being called in the garden.

In the cool of the evening, when a thin dew gathered on the grass and the air was still, and it was summer at the end of a long day, and the light had been long gone from the sky, and the crickets chirped, and the grass was tingling cool on her bare feet, and there were dark corners of a lawn, and the night bugs beat themselves to death on the window panes, and darkness was full of distant and vague tumults, she would almost remember. She would listen then for the voices deep inside her, the voices from long ago that said,

—Eva! Eva!

They were calling for her and coming to find her, and she was in the attitude of one listening in beautiful and dark woodlands, and waiting for them to come.

This was a memory then of the very first of the Evas, the dawn Eva. Sometimes in the afternoon, when she had been sleeping and awoke to hear a sound of flies buzzing at the window panes, she would almost remember that Eva. It was the lost Eva, the one who had lived in a summer that had no beginning nor any ending, beyond time and memory, beyond and above all the books—most legendary and lost of Evas!

Now she was in the round room at the top of the brick tower looking down at the other children playing. It was Maribell's playroom, and here Eva could imagine that she was a princess in a lonely tower looking down on strange tumults in a legendary world.

Leaning on the window ledge, secure in her tower, she was remembering the pantomimic scenes that had flickered across the stage of the garden a half-hour before, just after she had first come up to the tower.

It had begun with the torches that had flared up suddenly in the town and moved toward Mrs. Brown's. There had been a burst of song, and the torchbearers had stopped in front of the flungback iron gates of Mrs. Brown's yard.

At first, Eva had wanted to run down, but she could see so well from her place that she remained listening and watching, fearful that it might all be over before she entered the scene.

The leader of the marchers had been the Reverend Lloyd G. Jarvey. There were about fifty men and women in a column, most of whom appeared to be strangers, while on the fringes of the torchbearers little knots of townspeople hovered.

Preacher Jarvey had walked straight up to the open gates and had stood between them. Eva had seen the torchlight reflected on his glasses. The Preacher had shouted something in his deep voice, and Eva's father had walked down to the gate. The Preacher had shaken his finger in her father's face, and as he did so, there was a low grumbling among the men in the crowd. Three or four rough-looking strangers had come up pushing a tub of steaming stuff on a wheelbarrow. The torches had burned smokily, flaring and sputtering.

Then Eva realized that her father was in danger, and she had been on the point again of turning and running downstairs.

But just then Professor Stiles had walked briskly down to the gate, his sharp, high voice cutting the air like a whip above the crowd. His long, thin arm swinging a cane had extended, pointing at the Preacher, and Eva had caught the words,

—. . . happen to be . . . wellknown doctor of theology . . . great city of New York . . . think you are anyway, you . . . promise you . . . every scalawag in this party . . . disturbing the peace, trespassing on private . . . person of an innocent . . .

The Preacher had shouted something back, and Eva's father had said something, and the Preacher had pointed at Mrs. Brown and at Eva's father. Mrs. Brown had shaken her head violently, and Eva's father had squared his shoulders and said some very crisp words that Eva couldn't make out and had opened his arms as if in appeal to the whole crowd of watchers beyond the gate. The Preacher had turned and made a motion of calling someone from the crowd, and a woman who looked like Libby Passifee's mother had stood forth and come up to the gate and talked in a shrill voice.

Once again, Eva had been on the point of running down to the yard, when another amazing thing happened. Her brother Wesley was pulling Professor Stiles' arm and pointing to the Preacher and then to the Widow Passifee. Professor Stiles had raised his cane and, waving it, had shouted in a piercing voice,

—Silence! Silence!

The crowd had quieted down a little, and Wesley had said something else, still pointing at the Widow Passifee and the Preacher. Then Johnny Jacobs had stepped up and vigorously nodded his head and pointed his finger at the Widow and the Preacher. The Preacher began to bellow over and over,

—It's a lie! It's a lie!

And Wesley had pulled Libby Passifee out of the crowd of children and had made her admit something.

Professor Stiles had shaken violently, and the crowd had begun to snicker. The Widow Passifee was shaking her finger at her daughter Libby and threatening her some way. Johnny Jacobs had said in a very loud voice,

—He didn't even have his glasses on!

Professor Stiles had shaken soundlessly again, and the crowd had snickered again.

And the whole crowd had begun to shake their heads and laugh and draw away from the Preacher. The Widow Passifee had shrieked something and walked away very fast toward her house. The Preacher had remained in the entrance to the yard, peering from side to side.

Just then, Professor Stiles, who had been pacing briskly back and forth like a trial lawyer in a crowded courtroom, walked decisively down to the gate and began to harangue the crowd. Eva caught the words,

—. . . duped and led astray . . . exciting you to frenzies . . . final act of madness . . . guilty of committing himself!

At this point, the Preacher had flung down his torch and, raising both arms, had bellowed like a bull. He had made a lunge at Mrs. Brown, but Professor Stiles had planted himself in the way and, pointing his malacca cane before him like a fencer, with a single deft motion flipped the Preacher's spectacles into the night. Thereupon several townspeople had thrown themselves upon the Preacher, and the Preacher had butted, lunged, and struck blindly in the darkness. Professor Stiles, remaining well out of danger, had occasionally rapped the Preacher sharply on the head with his cane or jabbed him in the seat of the trousers. So doing, he had appeared to whip the whole struggling mass through the gates, which he promptly slammed to. The Preacher had turned and reared at his assailants and in spite of blows had broken through and struck fists and head against the iron gates before he realized that they were shut. Then abruptly he had turned and run down the road into Waycross, with short steps, hands open before him like a man half-blind and beset by pestering sprites.

Several people had come up from the road and said something to Eva's father, and some women had come and talked with Mrs. Brown, who kept putting her hands against her cheeks and shaking her head.

Eva's mother had stayed beside her husband the whole time, but she too now went over and said something to Mrs. Brown. Everyone seemed to be very sorry about something, except Professor Stiles, who seemed very happy about something.

Suddenly realizing that the excitement was over, Eva had gone tearing downstairs. She had hunted Wesley and had found out what had happened. It seemed that the Preacher had gone crazy and had come down to accuse their father of doing something bad and being an atheist. Their Grandfather Root's name had been mentioned, and he was mixed up in it some way. Then Wesley had told what the children had seen in the morning, and that had got the Preacher in hot water, and everyone had laughed at him. Wesley was a hero, and so was Johnny Jacobs.

—Just go back to your playing, children, Eva's father had said. In a little while, we'll have those fireworks.

Then the people had gone on back to the town, and the children had started up the game again, and Eva's father and Professor Stiles had gone back to the porch again.

Eva hadn't felt like playing any longer. Instead, she had wandered away again and had come back to the tower and had remained at the window looking out again, wondering if she was missed.

Even now the night was restless with sounds—the last explosions of firecrackers, the last buggies leaving Waycross to go home, the tag-ends of the Revival crowd breaking up. The night was full of terror and mystery. Always, she had known that the earth of Raintree County was full of dragons breathing fire. She had known too that the dark image of her grandfather would haunt her life. She hadn't quite realized how serious the danger had been until it was over.

As long as there were little children and faithful women around, her father would be safe, and so long as her father was safe, she would be safe. The voices and the lanterns had advanced even to the gate and had almost broken in, and then they had been driven back; the flickering cane of Professor Stiles had chased them down the road.

Now all was well, and the night was kept from the garden by colored lanterns and by the shrill excitement of the children at their games. The evil ones had been defeated by their own evil.

But she had been touched to see the sadness in her father's eyes, and she wondered if she alone had seen it. In a way, he had looked as though he had anticipated this coming of torches through the night.

If only there would always be gardens where fountains played in summer and drenched the bodies of children tangled in lilies! If only there would always be days of festival excitement! If only she, Eva, could by strength of mind and faith and daring preserve forever the good world of certainties and keep the look of sadness from her father's eyes! If only the long, promiseful days didn't pass away and the good books close, leaving one stranded on vague shores of summer.

—Eva! Eva!

It was the voice of her brother Wesley calling.

She would stay here in the tower.

—Eva!

Let them be calling her. But she would hide. She would go back, small and proud, and stand in beautiful and dark woodlands, in the attitude of one listening. She would wait in the oldest garden of her being until they came and found her. She would possess the wild, lovely secret of the garden, seen only by her. *O, don't you remember, a long time ago . . .*

Lost child! O, little heroine of the Eva series, blue-eyed wanderer in fields of summer, little boater on secret lakes (all choked with lilies) and listener to stories! Lost child, discoverer of rivers, listen to the voices calling. Listen to the voices of the callers calling by the lake, where it is always summer and the days are long. Listen, listen to the footsteps of the seekers seeking by the lake. And perhaps you will retrace some portion of the dawn when

Pre- A Historic

STRANGE LIGHT WAS OVER
EVERYTHING, SOFT GRAY AND GREEN AND GOLD.

The two children got up before any of the other campers and slipped away from the tent. Papa and Mamma were both sound asleep. Wesley had the clothes, and he helped Eva put on her little dress. Wesley was four years old and knew how to do everything. He knew just what to do and led the way down to the pier. It was funny to see the lake all still and the boats beside the lake all empty and no one on the pier and no one walking around the tents. The world had never been so unfull of people before.

—It's dawn, Wesley said. The sun doesn't come up.

It was Wesley's idea about the two of them getting up early and going on a botanical expedition. The teachers all got to go with Papa every day, but Papa wouldn't let Wesley and Eva go. But Wesley knew how to row a boat, and he could take them across the lake, and they could gather leaves and come back before anyone missed them.

Just as they got into the boat, Eva felt sad about Papa lying in the tent asleep, and she had a feeling that if Papa knew what was happening, he wouldn't be pleased. But Wesley was already pushing the boat out into the water, and he had a hard time getting into it, struggling with his feet waving in the water. He got his pants wet, but that was all right and couldn't be helped. The lake was all a funny green, and the lilypads were all flat and green, and the lilies were just beginning to open. Wesley worked hard with the oars. She had never noticed before what a funny sound they made, a lonely, plunking sound when they went into the water.

When the boat reached the other side, Wesley and she got out, and it was too bad because the boat slipped out from under her as she got out, and Wesley tried to catch it, but it floated very slowly out of reach and just lay out in the lake a little way. Eva felt like crying about it, but Wesley said,

—Just leave it be.

They went into the woods together, and Eva kept thinking about the book that she and Wesley used to look at in the bookcase at home. *Through the Dark Continent.*

—Ith thith a dungle, Wethley? she asked.

—I guess it is, he said.

Wesley was four years old and knew a lot more about books than she did. But he knew nothing about dolls and didn't even have one. In the book about the jungle there were big fernleaves and thick trunks and snakes and wild beasts and black men. A white man was looking for another white man, and when they met in the middle of a clearing, they shook hands. Africa.

They kept finding funny leaves and mushrooms and sticks and stones, and after a while there was sunlight in the woods and singing noises and birds flying. Wesley told her to wait for him while he followed a bird. She did wait a long time, and then she went over through some bushes and found a path and walked along it. She stopped once and called,

—Wethley!

She was a little surprised because there weren't any teachers on this side of the lake. Not that she was afraid. She wasn't afraid of anything hardly.

—Eva doesn't have enough sense to be afraid, Papa had said, smiling.

Several times, she came out where there weren't many trees, and it was a good thing she didn't have her shoes on because in places it was very muddy, though the mud felt warm and all sinky and nice. She got clear out of the woods after a while, and wandered around where the sun blazed down on her. She began to get hungry and turned around and started back. Wesley had been gone long enough now to find that bird.

She kept going around and around. The forest was full of strange things. Once she stopped for a long time and watched a frog at the edge of a pool.

She must have wandered around all morning and she was very, very hungry. After a while, she came to a place where the water was very deep, and when she started to wade into it, it went right up over her knees. She backed out of it then, and there was a big yellow and green snake shooting himself around in the water. The biggest flies she had ever seen in her life would stand still in the air right next to her. Their bodies were like little pencils and their wings all misty. There were lots of turtles plopping, and she tried to catch one, but they were too fast for her.

She always loved to wade, and now she was getting all she wanted. The water was warm and the reeds were very stiff and tall, and there were green things everywhere. The sun shone down so hard that she had to blink her eyes. She kept on going, and once when she looked up, the sun was right overhead, and very small. She wondered what they were doing over on the other side of the lake anyway and if they had missed her. She felt very lonely and hungry and cried for quite a while because she had sat down and got her dress muddy. It was just the same way everywhere she went. She couldn't seem to get out of the muddy places, and just went along walking in the water.

Pretty soon, she came to a place where there were a lot of little trees with slender brown trunks, and the sun was shining down through them, and they were all covered with yellow flowers. She could look right up between them to a bigger tree at the top of a little hill. This was the best place she had found, because the grass was soft under the trees and the ground was dry. She walked up in the soft grass, and when she got to the big tree she sat down there between a couple of big rocks that were sunken in the ground and half-covered with grass. The big tree was like the smaller trees, but it was taller and had a thick trunk. She kept feeling the little yellow flowers touching her hair and face. She was all warm and itchy and tired and hungry, and it was so hot that she thought she would stay there. She lay down in the grass, and it felt good just to shut her eyes because the earth was all warm and a little breeze was blowing up from somewhere, and she could hear a noise of water trickling. Frogs were splashing around and making chunking sounds. Every now and then a big bug whizzed by her. She could hear bees. They said that they made honey out of flowers.

They said that they made honey out of flowers, and in a greenhouse you could see flowers inside a glass. God was up in Heaven where there were many flowers. All the flowers made a murmuring sound as if they were all full of great bees, the earth rocked her, blowing on her hair and eyes, the soft flowers sifted on her face and hair. They said that they made honey out of flowers.

After a while, she got up and found that she had been lying in the grass. She thought then that she had better go home. She felt very hungry and could think of them all eating back home.

The air had a different look now. She couldn't see just where the sun was, but up in the tops of the trees there were rays of light, and she could see the yellow dust sifting down through the rays. The yellow dust was thick in the grass and on the ground. She picked up a handful of it and put it in her little pocket. Her dress had dried and was all stained with leaves and crusted with mud.

She started walking down under the trees. It wasn't the same as when she had come up this way. It showed you how quickly things changed. Now, it was almost dark under the trees. She was terribly thirsty and hungry. If she only had some berries.

She went on down and came to the place where the water was deep again, and she couldn't find a way around it. It was darker now and not a soul anywhere. She was going to cry again. Perhaps she had better go back and lie down and cover herself with leaves like the two little babes, those poor little babes, whose names I don't know. They were carried away on a bright summer's day and lost in the woods as I've heard people say. And lost in the woods. Lost.

That's what she was. She was lost in the woods as I've heard people say. She had got lost. It was too late now to do anything about it.

She had never been lost before, unless it was a long time ago as I've heard people say because a long time ago she couldn't remember where she was.

But God took care of all little children, and God would take care of her. She was lost in the woods as I've heard people say.

She began to cry a little then, being lost. She would have cried more, but she heard voices calling to her.

—Eva! Eva!

They weren't so very far away, and she called back.

—Papa!

Her voice wasn't very strong because the voices just went on saying, Eva, Eva, the same way, and the way they said it was very musical. They made the name last a long time, and the sound went on quavering after it was really over.

She wandered away from the water and came back, and pretty soon, she heard Papa's voice very close say,

—E-e-e-e-va!

—He I nam, Papa.

—Stay where you are, Papa said.

He came over to her, stomping and wading through water. She was very happy to see him and said,

—I dot my dreth dutty.

—So you did, Papa said.

He picked her up and gave her a big squeeze. He was all scratched, and his shirt was torn, and his hair was mussed. As they walked back, he kept calling out,

—I've found her! I've got her!

He went a long way around, and it kept getting darker and darker. When they got to the lake, it was very dark. A lot of people came up with lanterns and kept shining them at Eva.

—Eva, you sure gave us a scare, people said.

She just clung to Papa and was very happy. They got into a boat, and several people were rowing boats over the lake. There were big lights on the water. Papa told her she must never run away again.

—Wheh ith Wethley? she asked.

—O, he's all right, Papa said. Count on Wesley.

When they got back to the camp, Mamma came down, and her face was all wet as a child's is when it has been crying, and she gave Eva a very stern, unhappy look and squeezed her very hard, and said,

—Well, pshaw, Eva, *did*n't you give us a scare!

Everybody was around them and walking with them when they went up to the tent.

—I'm hungwy, she said.

They took her into the hotel and gave her so much to eat she thought she would pop. Everybody at the lake didn't seem to have anything to do except to come in and watch her eat. Men kept coming in bunches with lanterns, and someone would yell,

—She's in here. John found her on the fer side of the lake.

—Right in the middle of the swamp, Papa said, just ready to fall into a pool two or three feet over her head. How she got that far without drowning I'll never know.

—How'd you happen to go there, John? a man said.

—Just a hunch.

—Look at her eat!

—Poor child! she's starved.

She had never been up after dark before. It was just as black as when she woke up sometimes at night. When they carried her out of the hotel and down to the tent, it was sort of cool, and there were lots of people around all smiling and coming up to see her. Her mother took the little dirty dress off and bathed her. Papa picked up the dress and shook it and the little yellow flowers fell out of the pockets.

—Where did you get these? he said.

—Unduh a twee, she said.

—We'll have to give Eva the grand prize in Natural History, he said.

He stood with a strange look on his face sifting the tiny flowers from one hand to the other.

She had meant to tell more about the flowers and all the things she had seen because these were things that no one had ever seen before, and she wanted desperately to tell Papa about them, but she didn't have the words, and she got all sleepy, and they put her to bed.

The moment she shut her eyes, she was back under the trees in the middle of the swamp, where the earth rocked her softly and the warm sunlight touched her cheek, and the soft yellow flowers fell on her hair and eyelids, they said that they made honey out of flowers, and she was hungry and a little sad, waiting for them to find her, and their voices were far-off and

HAD BEEN A LONG TIME CALLING
AND CALLING HER TO
COME

—BACK where I started from, the Perfessor was saying. Well, thirty-three years ago, the Lord God Jehovah drove me out of Raintree County, and now I've driven him out.

He and Mr. Shawnessy walked up on the verandah and sat down again in the swing.

—And to think, the Perfessor said, that the old ranter himself had been riding the circuit only this morning. Well, it's been a busy day for us all.

The Perfessor looked at Mrs. Brown, who was still standing near the gate. He sighed.

—If I had your chances and my morals, John, what a time I'd have! Couldn't I love that, though! Ah, that is sweet! Look at her out there! Ah, John, life is so good to us, and we are so bad to it! It gives us beauty and the earth and days and nights. Then we build our walls and weapons and defy each other to come in.

The Perfessor was very hoarse. He and Mr. Shawnessy lit cigars.

—You certainly are putting on a good show today, John. As for me, I've nearly talked myself out. What time is it?

—Nine-fifty, Mr. Shawnessy said, consulting his watch.

—What time does my train come through?

—Twelve o'clock.

—You're sure it'll stop?

—Yes, we'll wave it down with a lantern. But, frankly, I don't like to let you go into this dark night, Professor. What will become of you?

—O, it's very simple, the Perfessor said. I shall die.

—In my opinion, no one will hold harder to life than you. You'll take pills to the end and expire with the beginning of a witty word on your lips, as if you intended to finish it in the hereafter.

—But if we could only resign ourselves to death, *complete* death, the Perfessor said, how much happier we'd be! I seem to see things more clearly tonight, John. And I'll give you my *History of Mankind* in a few hundred words, which are more than it deserves.

The Perfessor took a long, hard pull on his last bottle.

—THE HISTORY OF MANKIND

by Professor Jerusalem Webster Stiles

Sometime in the mist of the hugely indifferent ages, the ancestor of Man climbed down out of the elm and walked on his hind legs. The female of the species was beginning to lose the hair around her vestigial tail because the male of the species liked it better that way and chased the ones with the bare behinds. This is called Natural Selection. From this beginning Man became the Bald Mammal—though I must say he carried it a little too far. The tail itself was beginning to curl up and wither, and some of the foremost sports of the day expressed a strong preference for the ladies who didn't have this curious twig.

Dawn Man was a dumb little character with a jut jaw and a flat head, bearing a remarkably close resemblance to a cousin of mine in Spokane. Back in his Asian homeland, where for centuries he enjoyed immunity from serious competition, he managed to evolve sub-species of different colors.

While he was still in his original home, Dawn Man began to enjoy a loud blat that he discovered in his throat. He brayed loudest in the mating season and from that time forth made poems. He was a pugnacious runt from the beginning and fought ferociously with other males for the possession of his little bearded doxies.

With the discovery of fire, our little bastard progenitor won a secure foothold on terra firma and a resounding victory over the other mammals, who were afraid of his torch. Sometime after that, he discovered words, and by words he began to build up his brain, being no doubt somewhat less attractive after he made the top of his head bulge. He spent several thousand years adding to his cortex and his vocabulary, and meanwhile the races of mankind began to spread out, and whole cycles of languages flowered and decayed. Language gave Man a means of transmitting his knowledge from generation to generation. Thus culture came about, being the intellectual inheritance of mankind as distinct from the physical. Morality grew from the fact that Man was a social beast. All Man's moral sanctions were really social. And the only reason Man ever held back his hand in the whole range of his history was the fear of retaliation.

This little Dawn Man, our poor relation, our skeleton in the biological closet, had wonderful hands. His little deft hands, developed by swinging on limbs and picking fleas, were as good as Modern Man's, and with hands and words he developed his brain. For the human brain itself, with all its wonderful processes of language, memory, aesthetic feeling, and association, was only a highly specialized instrument of survival. Some of the variations of the species seem to run away with themselves and develop beyond the point of utility, and Man's brain, with its myth-making power, wasn't an unmixed gift. Primitive Man was a creature so enmeshed in taboos and totems that he was much less free than the beast he hunted for food. Biologically, Man never came very far from the little bald mammal with the deft hands and vestigial tail who came down from the Miocene oaks all ready to elect Garwood B. Jones President of the United States.

Modern Man began with the discovery of the alphabet. Modern Times were characterized by the following grand illusions—warfare on a large scale, art, religion, and science, most of which had to be written off as a dead loss to the development of life. For example, the invention of gods and finally of God didn't help the Bald Mammal to any noticeable extent. Religion was a purely intramural pastime of the existing tribes. Taken as a whole, God was merely Man's pathetic hope that a creature like himself devised the world.

As for who devised the world, Man never found out. Science, the religion of the intelligent man, never told him who devised the world. But the world wasn't well explained by imagining a Person who made it. After all, what was the Person of God? The most searching theologians were obliged to deprive It of all real attributes and make of It a Great Someone who was Nobody and Nothing. The most advanced men said, Nature is: this Isness is what I believe in because I can see it, measure it, and make predictions about it.

In the department of miscellanies, I wish to take special note of the Christian Religion, the Republic, and the United States of America. The Christian Religion was the cultural product of a little tribe with delusions of grandeur. By a fascinating historical process, the infection spread. But Christianity reached its peak in the Middle Ages, and erosion set in. The Church encouraged the Bald Mammal to believe in his importance, and he could believe in it only if he seemed important enough to be punished for his crimes. Actually, the Universe never cared enough about Man even to punish him. It just accepted him and let him live and die as he could. As for the Republic, it was merely the primitive horde squared—and acted like it. America was one of the more picturesque migrations of the Bald Mammal. One sub-species exterminated another by superior weapons and numbers. As an instrument of biological survival, the American Culture proved a wondrous supple weapon. The Doctrine of Moral and Political Equality invited expansion by attracting other people to its banners. The Economics of Unlimited Material Expansion and Free Enterprise kept the race on its toes and squelched the unfit. And of course the Americans stole a magnificent hunk of earth from lo! the poor Indian.

—And how did it all end?

—We gibbon apes, who superseded Mankind as the master race on the planet, look back today with a certain nostalgia on that quaint dead-end of the Simian Family, whose specialized nervous system led to self-annihilation. Unlike most species, whose decline and fall are gradual, Mankind's collapse would appear to have been sudden and spectacular. Though more weakly armed than the insect in the reproductive battle, Man's overthrow would appear not to have been induced by procreative weakness. The most ancient historians of our own race, to whom there remained some literary relics of the pre-gibbon ages, refer over and over to the amorous fury with which the human males wooed their pertbreasted and plumpbottomed females (to use the epithet of that quaint old historiographer Jehoshaphat Wooster Stuttius, whose veracity in this particular there is no reason to doubt). Probably it was Man's own somewhat remarkable gifts that proved his undoing. He was his own—and life's—greatest enemy. By his extraordinary mechanical ingenuity, he discovered ways of destroying the delicate adjustment of the species to one another. And in the year 2032, he blew himself right off the face of the earth. *Requiescat in pace.*

The Perfessor made a small, neat smoke ring, which rose slowly and somewhat mournfully into the night.

—And this is *The History of Mankind?*

—This is it, the Perfessor said. What can you say against it?

—Against it, I'll set another history, which is included by it but which includes its includer.

—And this is?

—*The Legend of Raintree County,* Mr. Shawnessy said. A little fable with multiple meanings, and a moral for a vestigial tail.

—All right, the Perfessor said, let's hear it.

—THE LEGEND OF RAINTREE COUNTY

by JOHN WICKLIFF SHAWNESSY

Once upon a time a child looked abroad on the darkness of a Great Swamp. And a voice spoke and said a Word.

And behold! the child lived in a place called Raintree County, which had been forever, even as the child had been forever. This was the magic of the Word, for the Word was of God, and the Word was God.

But the child had forgotten the curving path by which he had come into Raintree County, and he had forgotten the location of the shrine where the Word was spoken, and he had forgotten the Tree, which was the living embodiment of the Word. And as he grew in strength and years, he had a quest to find the Tree and the sacred place, which was the source of himself.

Now, wherever he sought he found the earth penetrated by names and peopled by other souls, wanderers like himself in quest of beauty and eternal life. Each one was a private universe. And the feeling with which the child sought to understand and share the universe of other souls was love. When the child had grown in years and strength and had become a young man, his love was a strong desire to pluck forbidden fruit and know a sweet pleasure which only could be found with a mysterious creature like himself but subtly different, who embodied in her white beauty the ancient secret of the earth touched into breathing form.

Meanwhile, he and these other souls struggled darkly through a series of Events, the imperfect writhings of their human dream. Out of them they built a fiction called the Past and embodied it in a myth called History.

And seasons and years passed, and he continued in his quest, which was no other than to win eternal life from darkness and a dream of darkness.

And slowly he discovered that in the imperfect world of his personal dream, he had been making the legend of a hero. This hero was Humanity, and the place in which the hero strove for beauty and the good was the Republic. Both Hero and Republic were immense fictions. They could never have existed without their poet, but neither could he have existed without them.

For he had localized the great myth of the Republic in Raintree County. He and all who had ever lived had labored to create this vast, amiable legend, the Republic, and this most gentle and passionate of heroes, Humanity. Unknown to himself, the child had already consummated the quest, the quest being itself an eternal consummation.

And in so doing, he became in truth, what he had always known himself to be, the father and preserver of Raintree County, which without him never could have been at all. And thus, by becoming most himself, he became a greater than himself—in fact a god, who singly by his own desire and faith created and kept alive a universe.

—And thereby hangs what tail?

—And so he learned that Raintree County being but a dream must be upheld by dreamers. So he learned that human life's a myth, but that only myths can be eternal. So he learned the gigantic labor by which the earth is rescued again and again from chaos and old night, by which the land is strewn with names, by which the river of human language is traced from summer to distant summer, by which beauty is plucked forever from the river and clothed in a veil of flesh, by which souls are brought from the Great Swamp into the sunlight of Raintree County and educated to its enduring truths.

—And this is *The Legend of Raintree County?*

—This is it. What can you say against it?

The Perfessor had sunk far down in the swing, shoulders hunched, head sunken between them, face in shadow. After a while, his voice rasped up as from a cave.

—To my *History of Mankind,* he said, I wish to append a footnote:

Homo pluviarboriensis, or Raintree County Man, who evidently consisted of a dried testicle, a copy of the *Indianapolis News-Historian,* a cake of Pears' Soap, a Colt revolver, a McGuffey *Reader,* and a railroad spike, was dug out of a tertiary stratum in which were also imbedded *bovum domesticum* and his spouse *bova domestica, la cucaracha,* and John D. Rockefeller.

The Perfessor considered this so funny that he shook, choked, and coughed for half a minute.

—Seriously, John, he said, there's much truth in what you say. Your *Legend of Raintree County* is a beautiful and brave fable. For my part, I love ideas, and I love people—some people. I think that in our human world are all beauty, goodness, love, and godlike disputation. Only, I also think that all this is only a mist—a dream, if you will—from which we awaken into nothingness. All this is only a by-product of blind process. In the enormous web of chance, which a little while ago you described so eloquently, I believe that there was no provision for myself or any other, but that we merely happened to arrive. I go forth beneath the skies of your Republic, and everywhere I see impermanence—beautiful, fleeting forms, among whom, alas! most beautiful and most fleeting, I perceive a certain reflection in a mirror—Myself! A man knowing himself is merely a property of living matter, the by-product of certain agitations in his nerve-system.

—I name, Mr. Shawnessy said, the Sacred Name of the Great God Nerve-System. His Law is Cause, and his abode is Space, and his Divine Substance is composed of Matter. Through his all-pervasive body Electric Impulse passes and creates the World. This is the Truth, the one Truth, and the only Truth. And when the Great God Nerve-System dies, then shall we all be dead and overthrown. And we who believe in the Great God Nerve-System accept on faith—for in our infinite humility we do not understand—the Sacred Mysteries of Name, Cause, Space, Matter, Electric Impulse, Truth, and Death. For all that we are and all that we hope to be we owe to the Great God Nerve-System.

The Perfessor elevated his hands in a priestlike gesture.

—You are taking advantage of a sick man, he said. What do *you* believe in, my boy?

—In miracles.

—Such as?

—In the eternal miracle of the living Self which is greater than itself. From this premise all begins: that science and all the world are unavoidably human. Everything exists by the authority of that sturdy republican, the Self. The world in which we live lives in us. To look outward at the farthest star is to look inward into oneself. We are merely exploring our immense cupboard.

—Get me another bottle off the shelf, the Perfessor said.

He tossed an empty bottle into the bushes.

—But, John, your Self and its precious Ideas don't explain anything.

—For example?

—They don't explain your Self and its precious Ideas. By what authority is the Self here and who or what implants its Ideas? To be brutal with you, boy, what is the *cause* of all this?

He made a gesture with his hand indicative of the night, the fountain, Mrs. Evelina Brown, Esther Root Shawnessy, and the children, who were busy fixing rocket sticks in the ground.

—There are laws beyond the Law of Cause.

—Such as?

—The Law of Being.

—Which is?

—I am that I am.

The Perfessor crossed himself and shuddered dramatically.

—Then to be is to be God?

—In a way, yes. Beyond all Cause, is the Uncaused Thing, the Causer that isn't Caused. Beyond every mystery is another mystery—by Cause itself, which creates more and more causes by its own law.

—But what is the ground of it all?

—The ground of it all, the Uncaused Causer, is a Self, which must always assume a prior cause, creating mystery out of its own law of order. The deepest intuition is that we are alive in mystery. Know thy Self, Professor, and the greatness of thyself.

—And is this Self God?

—Each Self participates in God.

—John, the Perfessor said, I have a crudely logical mind, and I must say that if I have to believe in God, frankly I would rather believe in the crude old God of Christianity because this comfortably crude old God was at least a creator, and He crudely explains what I cannot explain and didn't create—the world and its creatures.

—But the world is a perpetual creation, Mr. Shawnessy said. Every moment of it is an intense, sustained act of creation, in which everything participates. Each Self is a part of this divine act of creation and couldn't detach itself from it if it wished. Each Self is a Universe, and no universe is possible without God.

—I have a petty geographical mind, the Perfessor said. This Self—where does it live?

—In Raintree County.

—And where is Raintree County?

—Where is Raintree County? A profound question, Mr. Shawnessy said.

He studied for a moment.

—That's like asking, Where is place? The only reason we can

come back to Raintree County is that we've put it there ourselves and haven't forgot it. Raintree County was never contained in its map. Nor, I trust, was a human being ever contained in that semblance made of dust and called a face.

—That's what you meant this morning, John, when you said that a face is a map?

—Yes—a symbol of what is always placeless, being its own place, of what is always wandering, exploring, creating—a human soul. A face—like a map—is the earth imbued with human meanings. And the earth is a Great Stone Face, in which we perceive the profile of our own life.

The Perfessor made a motion of frivolity with his head and shoulders.

—Great Eve, the Mother of the Race,
Went to bed with the Great Stone Face.

As the dialectic died in this perfessorial couplet, Mr. Shawnessy was thinking of the map of Raintree County, repeated in many copies—one by an old landsurveyor, another varnished and hanging in a clockless court house, another faintly colored and finely printed in an *Atlas of Raintree County, 1875.* What dream was this in which the earth was ensnared on a piece of paper?

He had a moment of doubt. The myth was beautiful, but was it truly lasting? Who could save Raintree County from destruction, what brash hero, weaponless and now with fading temples? Or who could save the hero himself, whose life was twisted with this legend of the earth? Or who could save his children or his children's children? How and why did it ever happen that there was once a place called Raintree County, and a young man grew up beside a road and visited a court house square on Saturdays and lay beside a river with a mystic name and fell in love with another soul? What were all the wars and the City days and the letters and the newspapers now? Some day, suddenly and surely, this little piece of paper called Raintree County would be rolled up and put in a bottom drawer of the Cosmos along with the loose sheets of an unfinished poem, and it would be forgotten. Forgotten. Lost.

On an obscure impulse, he reached down into his left coatpocket and fished up the letter that he had got at the Post Office in the morning. He tore it open, held it in such a way as to catch the glare of the lanterns, glanced over it, and then read it to the Perfessor.

—Dear Mr. Shawnessy,

In reply to your request for information concerning a family burial lot in Havenholm, we wish to advise that we have such a lot available for you at moderate cost. Burial Plot 163 is at the south side of the Cemetery, on the peripheral drive, near the railroad. We cordially invite you to examine it at your convenience. Havenholm, the Cemetery of Beautiful Rest, has recently been enlarged and landscaped, and the beloved dead may be committed here with the satisfaction that they will be cared for in death as in life.

The lot in question is ten by twenty feet and costs $50. For $50 more, you can purchase Perpetual Upkeep.

If you are interested, let us hear immediately. A check by return mail will insure your retention of this plot. We have many requests, and we wish to give you exactly what you want.

Respectfully yours,
The Havenholm Graves and
Markers Company, Roiville, Indiana

—Buy, buy! the Perfessor cried, rejuvenated. Have and hold in Havenholm! It's a sure investment, the one piece of real estate you'll never part with! It's a bargain! Eternity for fifty dollars!

—Do you think I ought to buy Perpetual Upkeep too?

—They're giving it away! the Perfessor said. Ten thousand years from now they'll still be changing the posies in your urn and wiping the bird dooey off your block.

—But what if they lose the account book? Or what if they just plain decide they won't do it?

—You won't mind, the Perfessor said. You have bought and paid for two beautiful and satisfying words, 'Perpetual Upkeep.' Are you afraid to think of yourself lying by the railroad, John?

—I shall never lie by the rails with unlistening ears, Mr. Shawnessy said. Even now, as I think of my stone there, and others rising in years to come, and the great trains passing day and night, and the feet of pilgrim hundreds——

—*Blest be the man that spares these stones,* intoned the Perfessor.

—I'm certain that I, John Wickliff Shawnessy, won't be there.

—Just so, said the Perfessor. You won't be there.

—If I should die, the human world dies with me. Nothingness knows no Time nor Space. To it ten million years are like a second. In the very instant of my nothingness, the whole pageant of humanity expires. The faces that leaned over me in the moment of parting, that sorrowed at my death, they too are all gone in the moment of my becoming nothing. Nothingness! Can you imagine real nothingness, Professor?

The Perfessor chewed his cigar in silence. A little reluctantly, he said,

—No.

—If I—who am something—were to become nothing, it would be the annihilation of everything. On my life, the world depends. After all, nothingness is not and cannot be.

—Then you believe in resurrections?

—In Perpetual Upkeep.

—And yet, John, the Perfessor said, suddenly bestirring himself, as if for a last effort, nothing is more certain than that fifty-four years ago, there was no John Wickliff Shawnessy. You yourself have a memory of awakening awareness and no prior memory. Why then do you suppose that fifty-four years from now there will be a John Wickliff Shawnessy?

—I didn't exist before or after. I exist always. It's a riddle of Time. Time was when Time was not. Man doesn't live in Time, but Time in man, eternal conjugator of the verb 'to be.'

—Ah, my boy, the Perfessor said, adopting his gentle, sweet manner, what really worries me, you see, is that I'm afraid to die. I do not sincerely believe that I will live forever. I do not sincerely believe that anyone who ever died was ever seen again on earth or heard again. I do not sincerely believe that there are resurrections. I do not sincerely believe that the dead lovers ever find each other again. And from this one fact, more than any other, I derive my great Nature God, who doesn't sincerely believe these things either. You see, my boy, I am afraid to die. I am afraid of the grave.

The Perfessor appeared somehow pleased and revived by this confession. He bestirred himself, sitting up as if for a last effort.

—You know, John, in your pleasant vanity, you remind me of another misguided idealist, young Jesus of Nazareth, who also believed in the Resurrection and the Light. And yet, the resurrection of Jesus was a myth like those that have gathered in the wake of every great moral personality since the world began. If it weren't for the newspapers, Lincoln would have had a resurrection. I wish I could go back to the days after the murder of young Jesus and take a series of photographs and write it up for the newspapers as it really happened. Call it if you want to

THE REAL STORY OF THE RESURRECTION

by Reporter J. W. STILES

(Epic Fragment from the *Cosmic Enquirer*)

Imagine yourselves, friends, plucked up and put down in the middle of the crucifixion scene as it really happened. You see a very Semitic young Jew hanging naked on a cross and groaning audibly. He's sweaty and ugly as all men are in pain, and you perceive that he's flesh and bone like anyone else. Everyone around you has a drab, everyday look, and there aren't any thunderbolts from heaven. The aging shabby Jewish woman standing near-by with some other crones is, of course, Mary, the Mother of Jesus. She's shaking her head and moaning with grief. Young Jesus, the first of her nine children, always had been a source of great concern to her, ever since his dubiously virginal begetting had caused her such anxiety—until she caught the pliant Joseph for a husband. And ever since adolescence, young Jesus had raised a stench in the local community with his overactive mentality and his messianic obsession. Now here he is at last, being nailed up like a common criminal between a couple of thieves.

Now if you follow this great Passion a little farther, you see the women take the bedraggled and very dead remnant of young Jesus from the cross. Just now, it looks as though the whole thing is washed up. A little more historical perspective on the part of the local authorities, a little more judicious killing, and Jesus will go into the records as an old forgotten court case—you know, another one of those young Jews that are always coming out of the hills and pretending to be God.

Just now the disciples are lying and sweating and doublecrossing each other to escape the axe. Some of the miracle-healing jobs are going around, openly admitting that they still have the sores.

Meanwhile, the women, who are the only ones with sand enough to admit a connection with Jesus, carry the body off, and the greatest *corpus delicti* case in all history is under way. The big problem is, what to do with it? No doubt young Jesus himself predicted his resurrection —that would go well with his sublime vanity. The faithful fear reprisals on the body and a possible visit from the civil authorities. So a pretense is made that Jesus has been buried in a certain tomb to throw the policemen off the scent. People come and worship around the tomb and perhaps open it after a few days. No Jesus! He has arisen! some say out of ignorance and others out of deception.

As time goes by and the law fails to take any reprisals, the body becomes more and more important. Meanwhile, the physical remnant is beginning to embarrass its custodians, and the question of disposal gets serious. People are really beginning to believe in the resurrection, and something must be done about it. Some of the sturdier apostles are beginning to get back their courage. They're not going to have a life-career as preachers go down the drain just because the body of Jesus is still around. Besides, people at this time are close enough to primitive mental states so that they can't conceive of real death anyway. What is important is that someone should see the shade and talk with it. Everyone believes in ghosts anyway, and very ordinary people have seen other very ordinary people after death and are willing to swear to it. Nor do people distinguish clearly between dreams and waking reality. Is it any wonder that one or more of the disciples—a thoroughly neurotic gang anyway—claim that they've seen the Master? They're all rival preachers and quarrelling with each other over the spoils. So each comes forward with his own private myth of resurrection, and finally they all get together on a collective falsification. I suppose literally hundreds of people see Jesus in the days following the crucifixion.

But what really happened to that poor outraged, murdered body, of course we'll never know. At least we may be sure that it obeyed the universal laws of decomposition by fire or decay.

The whole thing may be even simpler than that. It's entirely possible that the body remained in a marked tomb for years and was known to be there. We can't emphasize too much how little we know of the real Jesus and how late and untrustworthy our only records are.

A few hundred years after Jesus died, there was a quantity of recorded myth available, and out of this the Divine Scriptures were selected. Thus upon a basis of lies, bad reporting, and the memories of ghost-ridden barbarians, the greatest religion of all time was erected. In the face of this unpleasant historical truth, can you call yourself a Christian?

—In transition, Mr. Shawnessy said. I believe in the eternal existence of a great human being named Jesus, and I also believe that this man was God.

—In the Raintree County sense, said the Perfessor.

—In the Raintree County sense, Mr. Shawnessy said. And as for the question of his resurrection, I do not believe that the physical body of Jesus had a resurrection. This is a crude, primitive conception which retards rather than assists religious feeling. But to think that this Jesus was a man, a human being, and that he was born as all of us are born, and died as all of us must die, makes him a more divine being than if he were some nature-transcending god. I also believe in the Divine Words of Jesus Christ, which, along with some other Divine Words uttered since the beginning of time, affirm the sacred and eternal miracle of life.

—You know, John, the Perfessor said, with a little luck, you might have been a messiah yourself. But you were born into the age of newsprint and the locomotive. Do you really want to be a Great Man, my boy?

—Of course.

—Then I'll tell you how to do it. Die obscure. Fifty years later, when civilization has all but destroyed itself and has returned to moral barbarism, your epic will be found among the ruins in a state of tantalizing incompleteness. The critics will acclaim it an authentic masterpiece, having the freshness and golden splendor of America's lost youth. Lines from it will be on everyone's lips. But biographers hunting for traces of the author will run up against a series of locked doors. Instantly, people will come forward with hundreds of untrue stories about you that will be canonized and a few true ones that will be discredited. Forged letters will appear that will be much more flattering to you than any you might have written. Someone will come out with a book to prove that you were really a down-at-the-heels country schoolteacher of no ability and that the great work attributed to you was an unacknowledged piece by Walt Whitman. Several unidentified photographs of this era will be proved beyond contention to be you. Three incredibly old ladies will claim that they enjoyed intimacies with you in your heyday and will write memoirs to prove it. A monument will be erected to your memory on the banks of the Shawmucky. An illiterate old man will show visitors through the Shawnessy Home in Waycross and sell them hunks of wood from the local lumberyard as chips from the eponymous Raintree. Someone will contend that your father and mother were never legally married, and the way will be open for a doctrine of a virgin birth. And if you can manage to hide the *corpus delicti,* I might even promise you a resurrection and a religion of which you will be the new messiah.

—Well, it's entirely possible that I'll stay here in Waycross the rest of my life and die in a roomful of unsorted manuscript.

—John, the Perfessor said, please don't speak of dying. My own death I contemplate with some degree of placidity and resignation. But somehow it makes me bleed to think of you dying. Of course, you have the advantage of the rest of us. You've already died once and come alive. *Sleep in thy hero grave, belovèd boy!* No, my boy, never die, if you can help it. You're my last great hope. When all is said and done, I'm damnably afraid of this dream in which we live and of its sudden awakening. It has been a rather dependable dream in some ways. It has always been possible to get on a train in New York City and arrive after a day or so in the neat rectangle of Raintree County. But I'm afraid that all the time we were all lost and didn't know it, because it wasn't really possible to come back to Raintree County even in a dream.

The Perfessor's voice was cavernous. He seemed a rack of bones hunched in shadow, faintly shaken by the swing.

—Lost! he said. Lost in the nation of the railroads and the century of wars and revolutions. You can't go back to Raintree County and find it, because it won't be there. Not one—*not one single moment* of time past can ever be got back. *Not one little thing* can escape change and death. Lost, the early Republic of our agrarian dream. We fought for it in battle and destroyed the thing we fought for. Lost, the years of our youth. They were good days and many, and they are all gone. And think of all the girls, John, the lovely girls, the lushloined girls who have gone down into the gulf of years.

Mr. Shawnessy shuffled the loose leaves of Senator Garwood B. Jones's manuscript, stuffing up the righthand pocket of his coat. *Memories of the Republic in War and Peace.* Perhaps on page 46 there would be an engraving of one of the lost faces, a floater on the mystic river. Drowned in years.

O, river of remembrance, you carry her on your memorial tide down many summers through an ancient Raintree County. O, nymphic whiteness and the river green with life! O, young—forever young!—and prediluvian days.

It was getting very late. The day seemed to be running in jagged rhythms, eccentric and aimless, but far beneath it, was a leading idea, a river of memory that had been moving all the time toward a shadowy gulf.

He shut his eyes. He was taking the long way, the river way to the homeland. He seemed to be bearing a map to a place that had been lost. He held a parchment, yellow, immensely old, smelling of goat's musk. Archaic symbols—hieroglyphs, dawnwords—cluttered the margins. He heard dawnsounds. Great waterbirds plunged squawking into flight from the rivermarge. Frogs shouted from the shallows. The papyrus rushes made a murmuring sound. He heard the hiss of oars breaking the green skin of the river. There was a place where his boat had mudded in a swamp that choked the river's flow. A yellow pollen lay inches deep on the heaving muck. Reptilian birds beat upward on vast batwings from banks of rushes big as telephone poles. Their horrid cries clanged on the stridulous murmur of the Great Swamp. He floundered in sucking bogs, half-drowned in light and life, and a forest of flowering trees nodded their plumed tops at him. The flowers were halfsized human heads, dipping on fleshy stalks. One was the face of a certain lost young woman. Blushing, with eyes averted, it whispered in husky accents, *One for whom you once expressed affection, Johnny. . . .* Faces, innumerable faces, swam on the thick air, and some were the withering faces of children on blasted stalks, and the flowerfaces filled the swamp with a low, terrible cry.

—Ah, God, the Perfessor was saying in a low, terrible voice, if there were just some way to keep from going down into that Great Dismal Swamp!

Beneath his shut eyes, with startling vividness, Mr. Shawnessy beheld the form of Professor Jerusalem Webster Stiles sinking, pince-nez glasses and all, into the muck of the Great Swamp. The Perfessor seemed to be taking it placidly enough and made no struggle as the mud climbed up his white linen suit. Down he went deeper and deeper, weakly waving the malacca cane, his mouth submerged and bubbling slime. Attempting to rescue him, Mr. Shawnessy felt himself also plucked into the heaving pool, and in a fit of anger at the Perfessor's resignation, he caught the linen collar in his right hand and angrily shook it. The Perfessor tried vainly to escape. He wriggled and ducked and squeaked, he shrivelled and wept and pleaded. Then in swift succession, he changed into a grinning skull, a wood nymph, a revival preacher, the Pope of Rome, a bony goat, a Republican Fourth of July Orator, a Democratic Congressman from the Deep South, a Certain Eminent Statesman, an Exceedingly Rich Man, an Illustrious Commander, a gray rat, a mortuary effigy, a bottle of rotgut whiskey, a book with ELBIB gilded on the cover, a hissing serpent, a copy of the *News-Historian,* a classroom pointer, a glistening black insect, and at last a small darkhaired boy, sobbing and trying to pull an old oaken bucket out of a well.

Mr. Shawnessy looked sharply at the collapsed form of the Perfessor on the porchswing and shook him gently by the shoulder.

—Good friend, for Jesus' sake forbear
To dig the dust enclosèd here,

groaned the Perfessor.

—Wake up, Professor. It's about time for the fireworks.

There is a music on the ties of time. The clock in the Court House Tower is telling the time of day. Come back. Come back to Raintree County. Come down the branchlines of the past and take another turning. *Wake from thy hero grave, belovèd boy.*

For resurrections! For homecomings! For heroes! A last inscription! For soldiers who died for the Republic! For warwounded, casualties, homeless ones! For amputees of legs, arms, eyes, and hopes! For those who were falsely reported missing in action! For those who were truly reported missing in action! For all the Americans who tried to find their way back to youth and hope!

For all the converts and disciples who hunted for the Master! For all the mothers who waited in the night and never gave up hoping! For all who were once living in Raintree County! For all the lost souls hunting for each other and reaching out hands and touching each other with words! A last inscription.

For all who wait for the millennium, for all the campers on the hills waiting for the world to end, for all the revivalists and resurrectionists! A last inscription! O, I shall make a last inscription for all the passengers on trains crisscrossing on the roads to home. O, I shall make inscriptions and inscriptions for a lost young man, the father and preserver of Raintree County, returning out of windless days in summer, and I shall tell the story of a day

May 31— WHEN —1865

JOHNNY CAME MARCHING
HOME AGAIN (HURRAH, HURRAH)

or—more accurately—riding on a train, it was a day in the late spring, and the weather was fine. As the train approached Freehaven, after a brief stop at Three Mile Junction, he stood up and went to the cardoor, craning for a look at the Court House cupola, which he hadn't seen for nearly two years. But now the train had turned and was running directly toward the center of town. There were few people in his coach, and none besides himself who intended to get off. He decided that he still had a long way to go to recover from his sickness, for his legs were weak and trembly, and his heart beat uncontrollably fast. He had to sit down after all.

He could see his face dimly reflected in the smokebleared window, a thin, curiously youthful face. Though his uniform had looked smart when he left Washington, two days and nights on trains had made it slovenly. Despite the heat, Johnny buttoned it to the neck and set his cap straight.

A wild young happiness flowed over him, and he turned his face toward the front of the car so that people couldn't see his emotion. Everything was soft and radiant in the spring light. It was morning. Out of thousands, he had come back. Out of thousands and hundreds of thousands, he had been chosen.

He had a few more minutes to live in his private never-never-land of suspension between two worlds, war and peace, wandering and homecoming, death and life.

He leaned back against the seat and shut his eyes. He took a guilty pleasure in thinking of the sensation that his return would cause. He could already see the headlines. . . .

LOCAL HERO BACK FROM THE GRAVE

(Epic Fragment from the *Mythic Examiner*)

Over six months ago, young Johnny Shawnessy was reported killed in action. Today he is back in the land of the living. At exactly ten-thirty yesterday, he stepped down from a train into a community as much thunderstruck as if the Judgment Day had come and yielded up its harvest. Words fail to describe the sensation caused when . . .

But he hadn't been able to banish an undercurrent of anxiety felt ever since a stranger in Washington had confidently pronounced him dead. Could the soldier whom seven months ago the newspapers had interred in fragrant prose really come home? Was it possible to find one's way back to the gentle County of the elder days? And which had changed more—himself or Raintree County?

He touched his righthand coatpocket to reassure himself. In it, he had a dozen letters that Nell Gaither had faithfully written to him during his days at the front.

Dearest Johnny, I seat myself and take my pen in hand. . . . My darling, I think of you all the time. I hope these few words find you well and strong. . . . Johnny, come back safe, and don't forget one who . . .

They had been in strange places—these letters. They were worn from rereading and stained with fingerprints. These letters had gone from Atlanta to the Sea. A couple of them were smeared with blood.

But then he had heard of boys who had come home with letters like these to find the girl married to a fat civilian and insisting that she had merely done her duty and had written the same stuff to lots of boys to help bring them through the fray. Girls were incurable sentimentalists and would write nearly anything in a letter to a soldier of the Republic a thousand miles away.

Nevertheless, if all went well, he would come back a hero, and he would get his marriage to Susanna annulled, and he would take Nell away from Garwood Jones. It was no more than Garwood deserved for writing that repulsively sincere poem. Yes, if necessary, he would take Nell Gaither and go West and start up a new life. Lots of the boys were going West, and he had always wanted to go himself. Not that he would be in any great hurry to leave the County right after getting back to it. It looked plenty good to him. His tastes had been simplified by two years of soldiering.

His excitement went up as the whistle shrilled at the crossings and the moments ebbed away. Green, fragrant, familiar, the fields of Raintree County flowed by him in the sunlight. Here was a house that he knew, and here a little leaning shed that had been slowly decaying for as far back as he could remember. A barn just outside town still had a familiar legend little faded in two years' time:

BUY DOCTOR HOSTETTER'S STOMACH WATERS

He could see the houses of Freehaven and among the roofs and trees a steeple.

The churchbells, they will ring with joy,
Hurrah! Hurrah!
To welcome home our darling boy—
Hurrah! Hurrah!

He went out to the observation platform and leaning out a little looked down the tracks to the station. The train began to slow down, bell clanging. There were some people standing on the platform. He couldn't keep from grinning. Probably someone would recognize him.

HUGE DELEGATION GREETS RETURNING HERO

(Epic Fragment from the *Mythic Examiner*)

It was a gala day in the old home town. The whole dern county, as the poet says, turned out to welcome back Raintree County's distinguished soldier-poet, Corporal John Wickliff Shawnessy. When the young man descended from the train, he was overwhelmed with the scene that greeted his optics. One thousand people had somehow managed to cram themselves onto the platform and into the station yard, and were backed up several hundred yards on the walks and streets leading down to the station. A brass band played appropriate national airs, and his honor the Mayor was on hand to confer upon the young soldier the key to the City. Our manly hero, as bashful as he is brave, is reported to have said, upon seeing this acclamatory multitude, 'Shucks, I'd rather face Rebel musketballs.'

He tried to slip away from the scene unnoticed, but the crowd would not permit it. Hoisting the young Cincinnatus to their shoulders, they bore him off to the Square, where . . .

Corporal Johnny Shawnessy got down into the station and looked around. The people who had been waiting on the platform boarded the train without noticing him.

An enigma presented itself to him. He had marched hundreds of miles, emancipated a race, and saved a republic; and when he came back, he found the station hardly changed at all. The brute immutability of physical things appalled him and yet filled him with strong excitement.

He walked out into the street and started toward the Square, carrying his suitcase. It was a usual summer weekday in town. Hardly anyone was on the streets. When he reached the Square, he understood why he had been unable to see the cupola from the train.

Where the Court House had been, there was a sunken pile of fireblackened bricks and timbers. What was left of the cupola lay on its side, half sunken in the middle of the pile. The Court House had evidently burned down months ago, for weeds were growing in its grave.

The four sides of the Square were visible all at once. The little shops, stores, banks were naked and dingy. In fact, the Square as he had known it was simply not there at all any longer.

He walked to the ruined yard and sat on his suitcase in the shade of a tree. It was a much hotter day than he had supposed at first, a real Indiana scorcher.

There was no use kidding himself. Everything would be changed more or less. In the ashes of the Court House, of its Grecian columns and white cupola, in the ashes of its chaste republican design, a great many memories were inurned—memories of the old hitching-post days, the Fourth of July celebrations, the platform speakers, the county fairs, the barkers for the sideshows, the medicine venders, the phrenologists, the footraces, the temperance rallies.

All he needed was a rusty gun, and they would take him for Rip Van Winkle.

Nevertheless, he was feeling pretty good. It was fun to prolong the suspense a little before really coming home. After all, people came home to people, not to places. There was no memory in the earth. There was no memory in trees, buildings, houses. He had remembered them, but they hadn't remembered him. Shucks, they could burn down the whole town as far as he cared. But there were people who couldn't easily have forgotten Johnny Shawnessy, he of the affectionate smile and the innocent young eyes, he of the fleet legs and the gifted speech.

Just then a middle-aged man walked past, eyeing Johnny curiously. He stopped and came back. Johnny remembered the man's name, though he hadn't known him well. A little sorry that he was going to be greeted home by someone besides a close friend, he waited for the man to speak.

—Hello, there, the man said. Say, ain't you one of the Shawnessy boys?

—Yes, sir, Johnny said, standing up crisply, as if coming to attention.

—Well, I see you're back from the War, the man said, jedgin' by yer uniform.

He kept peering at Johnny, almost suspiciously.

—Yes, sir, I'm back, Johnny said.

—Well, sir, it's been a long war, the man said. How long you been back?

—Just got back, Johnny said.

—Well, well, the man said. I reckon you don't remember me.

He watched Johnny closely, trying to size him up.

—Sure, Johnny said. Harley Walters.

—You do sure enough, the man said. I know your pa well. Well, I reckon you saw considerable fightin'.

—Quite a bit, Johnny said.

—Lots a boys been comin' back lately, the man said. We had quite a cellybration just yestiddy, welcomin' General Jake Jackson back. They had a lot of troops up from Kentucky. You remember young Garwood Jones?

—Sure, Johnny said.

—Well, he led them boys, and say, they was somethin' to see! I never seen sich a smart bunch in my life. He marched them around the Square several times, and right here where we're a-standin' they had up a platform. Colonel Jones got up and made a speech recitin' the deeds of General Jackson and tracin' the course of the War, and say, I want to tell you it was a humdinger! Then General Jackson got up spite of wounds that hadn't healed yit and give a grand speech. We hain't had sich a cellybration fer back as I kin remember. It practically laid us all out.

The man stopped and eyed Johnny a little suspiciously.

—What campaigns did you fight in? he said.

—Chattanooga, Johnny said, Atlanta campaign, and the March to the Sea.

—Yes, we've had several boys back from those, the man said. You look a little peaky and kinder washed out. Must have been hard on you.

—Yes, sir, Johnny said. I've been a little sick.

—Well, sir, the man said. Well, anyways, you ain't dead. Lots of boys died.

Johnny knew then that the man didn't really remember him or must be taking him for one of his brothers. He decided to let it pass.

—Well, sir, the man said, I got to be runnin' along now. Good day to ye.

—Good day, Johnny said.

He stood a moment, watching the man walk off. Panic went over him. He had had dreams of returning home and not finding anyone who knew him or cared about him any longer.

He picked up the suitcase and went over to the office of the *Free Enquirer*. The door was open, but the office was empty. Johnny went in. He set the suitcase down and peered around. The office had the old inky smell. There were scraps of papers everywhere. His own old desk was littered as if someone had just been working there.

In a corner of the office was a table piled up with copies of past issues, an accumulation of seven or eight months.

A strong curiosity caused him to go over to the pile. Here was the record of a Raintree County that had given him up for dead. Here was the history of the earth after his demise, the record of a world that had gone on without him.

He felt a feverish excitement. He was about to cheat death and read forbidden words.

He plucked up a huge flexible load of papers and read the date on the earliest. November 12, 1864. It was full of news about the Election and President Lincoln's victory over McClellan. He remembered the date spoken by the stranger in Washington—November 18. He leafed through and found the paper for that day, turning the others upside down on his old desk.

Sure enough, here was the news of his death. He turned more papers, running his eyes up and down the columns. Except for the war news, the columns carried the usual diet of deaths, marriages, births, society news, reports from surrounding communities, personal notices, poems. His death had certainly not put the institution of newsprint out of business.

He turned pages rapidly. Yes, here were other mentions of his name. On November 25, Garwood's poem appeared, borrowed from the *Clarion,* but with typographical errors and on the back page. Johnny was a little hurt, but supposed that the position was dictated by political considerations and lack of space. After the appearance of Garwood's poem there was no further mention of John Wickliff Shawnessy. Other war dead were mentioned, among them two or three boys he had known, and there were other poems. He read some of them. He derived a wan satisfaction from the fact that they were neither so eloquent nor so metrically perfect as Garwood's poem.

He kept turning pages. He ran his eyes up and down, hunting familiar words, almost afraid of what he might find. He turned a week of papers, reading less and less carefully. Then on the front page of the paper for December 5, he saw a headline:

JONES-GAITHER RITES SOLEMNIZED

He drank the article down at a gulp. It had been a church wedding with the usual embellishments. The bride had worn a simple but fetching white dress. The groom, who had been on leave for three weeks following his successful campaign for County Prosecutor, was resplendent in his Colonel's uniform. There was to be a brief honeymoon before the Colonel returned to pressing duties at (or adjoining) the front. Cassius P. Carney had been best man, and the bride's father had given Nell away. At the reception afterwards, Mrs. Garwood Jones had received a host of friends and well-wishers at her father's estate in Shawmucky Township and had left with the groom for parts unknown in a simple goingaway gown of green brocade and a bonnet trimmed with flowers. Rough military friends of the Colonel had planned a chivaree, but the Colonel fooled the whole bunch by a cleverly timed getaway. Guests at the wedding and the reception had included . . .

Corporal Johnny Shawnessy lifted the heavy load of papers and carefully put them back on the table. He picked up his suitcase and left the office. His throat felt hot and choky, and his eyelids burned. He walked across the street and put his suitcase down in the shade of the tree again. He sat down on it and stared at the ground.

When Johnny comes marching home again (hurrah, hurrah) . . .

The first wave of anger and disbelief passed and left him pale and weak. After all, what did the dead expect? Did the dead have any rights? Besides, long ago, he had said good-by to a tearstained face on a rainy night in December, and the next day he had left Raintree County with a bride, though the getaway hadn't been very cleverly timed.

It occurred to Corporal Johnny Shawnessy that his anger was the first sign that he was getting well and becoming a civilian again. In a few days, he would have all his old vanities and vices back. The purity of the soldier was already passing. But what about the yellow corpses in the Soldiers' Hospital, the mouldering form of Flash Perkins on the edge of a forest near Columbia, South Carolina? What was a newspaper article more or less to the dead? After all, he couldn't expect to come back and have the world at his feet. Who did he think he was anyway?

Panic rushed through him. He wanted to go back and read the rest of the papers. After all, in six months, terrible things could happen, things that one didn't even want to dream about. He hadn't had a single word from home for six months.

He got up and took his suitcase and started out of town along the familiar way. He felt as though he were going to choke, and reaching up found his collar buttoned tight and the blood throbbing beneath it. He opened the collar. Sweat dripped into his eyes. He ran a few steps now and then, but the heavy suitcase slowed him down. Grass, weeds, and flowers along the road were thick and fresh. In the air was a fragrance of clover hay, the first cutting.

They were cutting the clover in Raintree County, and Johnny Shawnessy had been six months buried in the memory of Raintree County.

The corn was a hand high, bright spears in wavering rows. Wheat, a tender, undulous carpet, covered the uplands along the

Shawmucky. When he reached the river bridge and looked down the street of Danwebster, he saw a few men around the General Store. He didn't want them to see him. He didn't want anyone to see him until he got back home. He made a quick decision. After crossing the bridge, he climbed down to a path that followed the river bank.

The river was cold and shallow here at its great south bend. The air was tranquil under the bordering trees. Frogs splashed in the shallows, fish leaped, heads of turtles broke the skin of the water, floating. The river had a cold old smell of rottenness and fishy life. The Civil War had come and gone, Chickamauga had been fought by furious thousands, Missionary Ridge had been scaled from base to summit, Atlanta had been burned, Savannah had been taken, Lee had surrendered, Lincoln had been shot, and Corporal Johnny Shawnessy had been interred in iambs. And all this was simply nothing to the river.

How beautiful the still air was under the trees beside the river! Ah, it was all here, the same plentiful and peaceful earth. All the old symbols were here, the tokens of the legend, waiting to be read. The great enigma was here, murmuring its lost language among the rushes at the river's edge. Whither, whither, whither, the waters said, and whence, whence, whence.

Johnny had expected to give the mill a wide berth to avoid seeing anyone, but to his surprise the mill was abandoned. The wheel had been dismantled, and several timbers were down. He sprang up on the northern abutment. Then on a sudden impulse, he walked across to the other side. The path had been freshly cut. He reached the railroad embankment, climbed over, and made his way to the hill beyond. He reached the iron gate of the Danwebster Graveyard. He could see the family lot over in the far corner, the two stones marking the graves of his little sisters who had died in the epidemic of 1842.

There was a new stone in the Shawnessy family lot.

He started over to it, but almost stumbled on a grave that was lying across the way. It had the usual raw look of a new grave. There were withered funeral bouquets lying on the mound. He glanced at the stone, rising in a tranquil arc. The legend was simple.

NELL
Wife of Garwood Jones

Died in Childbirth, May 24, 1865,
and
Lies in this Earth with her Infant Child.

. . . .

'We Parted in the Springtime of Life,
Nell and I.'
S. FOSTER

Johnny Shawnessy sat down on his suitcase again. He was really very weak.

He looked at the stone, reading and rereading the words. He looked at the fresh gash of the grave, the fast-withering flowers. It had rained since the burial.

So then, all the time, these legends had been a-building. Day and night, while he was gone from home, the words had kept coming from the presses. Time hadn't stopped in Raintree County, merely because Johnny Shawnessy had gone to the War. Birth, marriage, death, the cutting of the clover, the harvest of the corn—all these things went on.

And the river had carried its unceasing burden of musical waters to the lake, day after day, and who could say how many creatures had died and sprung into birth along the valley of its course!

If only this grave were not so new and naked and ashamed! If only the years had touched it with gentle curves and greenness!

He made some calculations. Nell had been dead for a week only. The child, since it was unnamed, must have been a very premature birth. May 24. That was the day of the Grand Review in Washington. Garwood must have rallied fast for the victory celebration in Freehaven.

Well, what about Corporal Johnny Shawnessy? He had been a jaunty marcher on that day. Or was there really a relationship between what he was doing that day and this legend in stone? Hundreds and thousands of years would make no difference now to the green-eyed, streambegotten girl named Nell. He had never known her anyway, the real Nell, who had lived a hundred thousand hours in a Raintree County uniquely hers, while Johnny Shawnessy had gone selfishly along his own way, building fantastic dreams of love and fame.

Who was Nell Gaither that was once the belovèd of Johnny Shawnessy? Who was she that lay beneath these weeds? Did she rise once from serpent waters—a precise little face, gold hair streaming, wary eyes? Was her white back a stately column in the sunlight? Who was she that was once the belovèd of Johnny Shawnessy, under these flowers?

Was she the same whose young mouth was moist with a taste of passion on a haystack in summer long ago beside the river? (O, legend written with an oar in the pale flesh of the river!)

Had she remembered Johnny Shawnessy in her last hour, or did she not rather cling to those who were living, to her husband, her friends? There must have been many sorrowing, and the preacher must have said a good deal about beauty cut off in the prime and God numbering her among his angels.

What became of precise little faces? What became of girls who swam palely naked in rural waters? What became of words of undying devotion written to soldiers away to war? What became of the soldiers and the wars and the names of battles and the columns of casualties in the back pages of the newspapers?

But what became of Johnny Shawnessy, the dead boy, the fleet of foot, life's innocent victor?

Here were immense symbols and tokens strewn beside the river. Here were legends for a young man to read, who had been dead for a time and had come back to life. Here were memorial verses and graven columns—fragments, only, it was true, and half-inscriptions.

What became of the old newspapers and the reporters of the news in the old newspapers and the news reported in the old newspapers?

Perhaps it was better to have no legends at all, no letters composed into rigid words and pressed on sheets of paper. Break up the forms and melt the letters back. Let there be no more legends on the earth. Let life live and death die, and let there be no names for sorrowful recollection. Let there be no words for the earth, for love, for life, for death, for beauty and piquant faces.

Let there be no sorrow or recollection of life. Let there be only the river and its odor of fish and flower, let there be the river, the nameless river, flowing from distant to distant summer.

Let there be no geologists, archeologists, biologists, collectors of specimens, classifiers of species. Let no one disturb mounds beside the river and give names to extinct peoples. Let all the fossils remain undisturbed around the watering places of the earth. Let no one sorrow for the extinct dinosaur. Let no one grieve for the three-toed ancestor of the horse. Let no one mourn beside the tomb of Abraham Lincoln in Springfield, Illinois. Who was Abraham Lincoln of Springfield, Illinois? Who was Uncle Tom of Uncle Tom's Cabin? Who was Johnny Shawnessy of Raintree County? And what was the Republic that they died to save?

Let there be no more historians of species, nations, races, suns. Let there be no nebular hypotheses. Let there be entire forgetfulness and beautiful and blissful ignorance. Let there be no lusting for forbidden fruits. Let there be no historian of the decline and fall of empires, ancient or modern, or of republics ancient or modern, or of Raintree Counties, ancient or modern.

Let there be only the earth, which does not weep or have vanity. Let there be only the earth and the nameless memories that the flesh has. Does the frog have a name? Would it make the green frog happier to know that he is frog? Only the namers have names; only the bald mammals with the adroit hands write names on stones.

Down with the alphabet. Let there be no symbols traced on stones. Take away the words and give man back to the earth. Let the earth have its own. Let there be no more songs about the Old Plantation; let no one sing of the Old Kentucky Home. Let Old Black Joe go back to the jungle from which he came. Let Dred and all the other blackskinned thousands sink peacefully back into the Great Dismal Swamp, and do not emancipate them from ignorance into grief.

Go out and ask the earth about loyalties and listen for a response. Go out and ask the river about permanence, and listen to its voice of change. But stay away from graveyards and mounds beside the river. As long as you can, hero boy. As long as you can.

Beside the stone that had the word 'Nell' on it, Johnny Shawnessy sat very still with bent head. Well, he had come marching home again (hurrah, hurrah). Life's victor had come back from the South, in a uniform with brave brass buttons. He had come up flowerstrewn avenues with bugles and thumping drums. (Receive him with garlands, o, ye virgins!)

The Hero of Raintree County sat on his suitcase and looked around him. The day was a typical Indiana scorcher.

What good had he been to those who loved him, believed in him, and remained more or less true to him (at least as long as he was alive), while he went around getting into forbidden places and doing forbidden things? Had he been able to hold back this legend of the earth? Had he, the supreme poet of his people, the bard of the Shawmucky (*Good friend, for Jesus' sake forbear*), been able to unwrite this single legend? While he sat bemused in theatres, assassins leaped from the wings. While he marched in parades, a victor among victors, his postwar dreamworld (which was really his prewar dreamworld) expired in agony and became a legend on a stone.

It was all very simple. It was not he who was the maker of legends. The earth was the maker of legends, and he was one of the little legends of the earth. And the earth had trillions of such legends and absolutely no way of filing them for future reference.

His sadness was for more than the now shattered dream he had had of coming back to Nell's soft arms. (After all, the earth was full of girls who would consider it a privilege to solace Corporal Johnny Shawnessy and keep him from remembering battles.) His sadness was a universal sadness.

Or maybe it was only a kind of self-pity because John Wickliff Shawnessy had been done out of a good thing and a sweet thing and a lovely thing. Maybe it was all mawkish vanity; and what he was really worried about was the lost boy, Johnny Shawnessy, who had been buried after all, six feet under.

Put up a stone for the lost boy Johnny Shawnessy. He ran for garlands in the Court House Square. He had a talent for finding beauty in the river. He had a dream of love and fame. Put up a stone for life's eternal young American.

Now here was a thing ended. Now here was a chapter closed.

He put his head in his hands and leaned over. His tired young mouth drew down at the corners. He kept shaking his head and trying to understand.

It was not just one stone in the earth. What he beheld beside the river was the grave of mankind. The banks of all the rivers of America were filled with white bones. They died on the Ganges and the Nile and the Seine and the Tiber and the Rhine. The history of mankind was a mound beside the river.

Was it possible that all the beauty, life, and loyalty, the brave dreams and the young hopes had to die after all, after all! Was it so easy to dispose of that intense young person who went by the name of Johnny Shawnessy? This young man had held up whole worlds by his single strength. He had floated a universe by the simple expedient of filling his lungs with air. With a very sensitive pencil he had wrought the fairest republic since the beginning of time.

Perhaps it was right after all to worry about himself. If he fell and came apart, all things fell and came apart. Who else could save the streambegotten girl or find beauty by the river? Who else could discover the secret of the Shawmucky, except him whose name had also flowed from remote ages? If he triumphed, there would be triumphs for all, but if he died, there would be deaths for all. It was still his legend, and they couldn't take it away from him.

Cities on the land, dwellers in cities, republic of the races, red, white, brown, and black, and yellow—human thousands, hungerers after infinite satisfactions! Soldiers of the Republic, dead in stinking explosions, yellow sacks of bone, debris of the Great War! Slaves—dark millions, hunting for a way from Africa to light! you shall be rescued by one who includes you all, the sum of all that you are or ever were or will be—a single, simple person not easily overcome.

Looking across the graveyard, he saw the new stone in the Shawnessy family lot. He got up and walked over.

The inscription was simple.

JOHN WICKLIFF SHAWNESSY
1839–1864
In Memoriam

. . . .

'Sleep in thy hero grave, belovèd boy!'
G. JONES

He took hold of the top of his tombstone and tugged on it. It was firm as if it had taken root. He gritted his teeth and pushed and pulled. The stone wanted to stay there. With a great effort he tore it loose from the earth and pushed it over. It fell flat, curiously solid and inert, the words staring up. In a fury of effort, he picked it up and carried it to the brow of the hill and rolled it down.

He picked up his suitcase and took his way back to the railroad. He climbed the embankment and began walking down the ties, peering through the woods in the direction of the Home Place. But the house was not, as he well knew, visible from the railroad. He reached a spot behind the farm, where he had always turned off before. He stepped down and pushed through weeds and little trees and found a path through the woods. In a few minutes he would be at the limit of the familiar earth. He was almost home.

He was coming through the great oak forest in the summer afternoon, carrying his suitcase. There could be no question about it now. He was going to get back home.

But as he neared the place where he had lived the strange legend of his life, as he thought of the land waiting there—a mysterious, indestructible *place*—as he thought of the human beings who were perhaps there and of his long absence from the place and from them, a mixture of joy and fear swept over him. All things around him—the still woods in the blazing afternoon, the separate, quivering leaves of the trees, the round bright ball of the sun overhead, the spongy earth underfoot, the sticks and stones and darting birds—acquired a miraculous immediacy and intensity. Thousands of separate, glittering objects surrounded him; yet all were impervious to him, bathed in an air that he could never invade. The whole thing was like an enormously vivid dream, becoming speedily more and more intolerable. He had a fearful thought. Perhaps in the woods near Columbia, South Carolina, he had actually received his death wound and everything since had been a dream taking no more of human time than the instant required to die, moving faster and faster toward this climax, in which he would approach his home and be about to touch loved hands and faces and hear the voices of people long dead to him, and then—in the very instant of attainment—the whole thing would explode into nothingness, and his death would be entire.

As if to reassure himself, he reached up and stripped a branch of oak from its parent bough. Still holding it, he reached and climbed the railfence at the limit of the land. Just on the other side was the rock against which one evening long ago he had leaned his head and wept. He was walking up the long slope. He came to the brow of the hill.

Below him beside the road was the Home Place. The little Office was under the lone, familiar tree. Things were grown up around. But there the Place was, perfectly still and completely familiar. He couldn't see anyone in the yard. Perhaps T. D. was in his Office. Perhaps Ellen was in the house. Perhaps they were gone. Perhaps the house was shut and there was no one there. My God, perhaps they were all dead!

He was walking with long strides, unconscious of the weight of the suitcase. He wondered why the house was so strangely blurred, as if great waters were washing across it, and why the earth seemed to rise and fall around him in misty waves. He fixed his eyes on the back door. He walked down the lane from the orchard. He walked through the barnlot. He walked into the backyard. The breath rushed in his throat. Flies buzzed on the screen door of T. D.'s Office as he went by. Someone was coming to the back door. Johnny Shawnessy's voice was a great cry in his throat.

—Mamma! It's me—Johnny! I'm back! I'm home!

And to Johnny Shawnessy in the moment of his homecoming, it seemed that he did indeed become life's eternally young, triumphant American. It seemed to him that he would never have to hunt farther than that moment of return, when the earth surged up from the lonely rock at the limit of the land and carried him into the place of memories. It seemed to him that he would never come any closer to the secret of Raintree County than the instant when he saw again the faces of his father and mother.

From an ancient wall engraving in T. D.'s Office, a tree grew whose fruit was for the healing of the nations. Johnny Shawnessy had discovered again the antique map of Raintree County, which was surely as old and as new and as eternal as the life of Johnny Shawnessy. Yes, he had come back from long wandering. He had learned the humility of the soldier, he had been purified by loathsomeness, he had been given back to life by death. His vanity would be greater now, for he would have to be vain for millions living and dead. He would be an interpreter now. He had come back to Raintree County (if indeed he had ever really been away), and though it wasn't long after the homecoming that an old restlessness returned to him and some of the magic went out of the familiar objects around him (the Home Place badly needed a coat of paint), he knew that he must hold firm to revelation and express, so that it would never die, the legend of his life, which was the legend of his people, the story of the republic in which all men were created equal, the amiable myth of the river and the rock, the tree and the letters on the stones, the mounds beside the river,

THE ANTIQUITY AND SOURCE
OF THE NAMES
UPON

THE LAND surrounding was lit by the flare of the last rocket, a big one painted red, white, and blue. It left the earth with a great gush of force and shot to a surprising depth. A fountain of fire burst on the climax of the arc. The spray bloomed white, faded into scarlet, lazily fell. Mr. Shawnessy stood, the burnt match in his hand, color of the rocket changing and fading on his face.

—Behold! John Wickliff Shawnessy is himself the Hero of Raintree County!

It was the hoarse voice of Professor Jerusalem Webster Stiles, heard among the exclamations of the children.

The explosion of the great rocket was the climax of the Glorious Fourth in Waycross. The planned program was over. There was nothing to do now but to see the Perfessor off and get to bed.

Mr. Shawnessy walked over and said goodnight to Mrs. Brown, who was standing alone beside the fountain in the front yard. Some of the children were already taking down the Japanese lanterns.

—It's been a wonderful day, she said.

The Perfessor came over with the *Atlas*. He handed it to Mr. Shawnessy and put his long arms around the two, like a conspirator. The last lantern was out, leaving the garden dark.

—I don't know about the rest of you, he croaked, but I'm pooped! Was there ever such a day! They won't believe this in New York. Be sure not to miss my next column, which will be entitled 'A Day Spent with the Americans.'

—When are you leaving, Professor dear? Mrs. Brown said.

—On the midnight train, dear, the Perfessor said. How about coming with me?

—Why don't you stay with us in Raintree County, Professor dear? And we'll reform you.

—My dear, the Perfessor said, you can take Raintree County, and rolling it into a neat parcel, stow it in the first appropriate place that occurs to you.

He straightened up and spat into a dark tangle of bronze limbs and lily stems.

—As for that *Atlas,* John, he said, you see, it was all a fraud.

There's no use trying to make Raintree County over, even in our imaginations. And no flybynight artist would be clever enough to hide something in it that could escape the subtle scrutiny of Shawnessy and Stiles.

—Wait! Mr. Shawnessy said, trying to remember something. Perhaps that was our mistake. We were *too* subtle. Perhaps the artist hid it by putting it in the most conspicuous place of all. Perhaps old Waldo found it precisely because he wasn't looking for it.

—Like Poe's 'Purloined Letter,' the Perfessor said, instantly pleased with the idea. The arch-criminal fooled the police by putting the stolen object in front of their noses. It's true, John, that only a supersubtle mind detects the supersubtlety of simplicity. Now, following this line of reasoning, what is the most conspicuous location in the whole of Raintree County, children?

The Perfessor thought a moment.

—Obviously the Court House Square, Perfessor, he said, answering his own question.

—And in the Court House Square, children? he asked.

—The Court House, Perfessor, he replied.

—And on the Court House, children?

Mrs. Brown began to laugh, a low, bubbling contralto, as if perhaps the memory of the Raintree County Court House with its famous Statue of Justice over the Main Entrance, spattered with pigeondung, were a delightfully amusing thing, when seen from the proper—or the improper—angle.

But Mr. Shawnessy sprang forward, rested the *Atlas* on the shoulder of the fountain, and flapped the leaves to page five where the long form of the Raintree County Court House was couched in darkness like a sphinx. He tried to plunge his eyes into the space above the Main Entrance where in the standard copies the Statue of Justice stood. He saw a pool of shadow there, vaguely alive with sculpture. In his skipping examination of the *Atlas* during the day, he couldn't remember having looked at precisely that spot.

—Give me a light, Professor.

The Perfessor struck a match on his sole. He and Mrs. Brown bent over to see.

The flaring match illuminated for a brilliant instant something in the niche above the Main Entrance that left all three speechless.

The Perfessor, reaching for another match, recovered first.

—Zeus! he said. Let's put some more light on that!

He struck the match, but the head flew off flaming.

—Shades of Michelangelo! he said, fumbling for another match. Wasn't that terrific! It was there all the time, and we didn't see it.

Etched in flame, the imprint of the tiny group seen slantingly above the Main Entrance of the Raintree County Court House persisted as an afterimage. On the instant of seeing it, Mr. Shawnessy had felt that it was just as he had known it would be and where he had eventually intended to look.

And now that he saw it, it was (in the Raintree County sense) not at all naughty—for what was naughty about the oldest picture in the world, the frontispiece for the first book printed by man—the father and mother of mankind in beautiful nakedness, tasting the Forbidden Fruit! With what an exquisite feeling for paradox, an unknown artist had substituted his symbolic statue of Edenic rebellion for the stern yet necessary lady with the scales, whose upright form had ruled the conscience of Raintree County from the beginning!

He had displayed the inadmissibly beautiful reverse of the coin. He had unveiled the Eleusinian mystery to the Court House Square where it would be seen by all who came there—the Saturday hundreds, the platform speakers, the visiting dignitaries, the prodigal sons, the carnival barkers, the dancing girls, the freaks, the medicine venders, the storekeepers, the candidates for office, the horseback evangelists, the city councillors, the county functionaries, the loafers on the court house lawn, the marchers in the Memorial Day parades, the housewives, the travelling salesmen, the pigeons, the prostitutes, the farmers, the girls in their summer dresses, the small boys with fists of firecrackers—in short, the whole lusty tide of life that pooled and poured into the foursided enclosure of the Court House Square to appease a devout hunger as old as the gathering of mankind in crowds.

So from their infinity of vantage points, in the changing lights and seasons of this mythical Raintree County, they would behold the double figure hewn from a single block of marble, the *E pluribus unum* of the classic coin, the Paradisal pair in the moment of republican and pluviarboreal discovery, trembling nameless on the verge of names.

While the Perfessor groped in his pockets for a third match, Mr. Shawnessy gave him the *Atlas*.

—Here, he said, you can bring it with you. I'll meet you in front of my house.

He stepped through the gate into the road to rejoin his wife and the three children. But they were already considerably in advance of him. He could just discern the form of the woman he had married entering the tree-pillared night of Waycross, and with her the forms of the three children.

Yes, he had overcome the aloneness of the garden. On an unsuspected path he had found her waiting. He had helped to fashion her, and yet she had lain at the very sources of himself. In her, he had rediscovered Eve. Bearing the name of an old reformer and Bible translator, Mr. John Wickliff Shawnessy had rewritten into the landscape of Raintree County the great book of God in all its beautiful, disarming candor.

He felt immensely joyous and calm. The vision was not only Hebraic but Grecian. Had he not also been sent, chief of a visiting delegation of Cosmic Lithographers, to record in stone the eternal verities of the Republic!

Half-shutting his eyes, he seemed to see the statue of a goddess waveborn and beautiful, begirt with foam, a sign to travellers on the seaward approaches of the Republic. He had climaxed a lifetime of Phidian endeavor by erecting this wondrous symbol, the Lady Custodian of the Temple.

And perhaps when he approached the Temple, after tying his stonewheeled cart up to the rim of an antique fountain, when he walked past the stone clock with its stone hands fixed forever at nine o'clock (*'Tis summer and the days are long*), when he ascended the wide marble steps strewn with the bearded grain and fitted his gold key to the lock and thrust the bronze doors in, perhaps then he would see her standing on her pedestal in the robe and attitude of the island Venus. (*Hello, Johnny. How do you like my costume?*) And leaning down, her form would lose the look of painted stone for the warm imperfection of a living woman, and she would remind him in her stately voice (lingering like a caress along his name) that a real woman had posed for the goddess found on Melos and that the sculptor who strove with the marble had learned ardently and well the lesson of those deepfleshed loins. (*Oft was I weary when I toiled with thee.*) And then, stepping down, she would walk before him, allowing her robe to travel off her graceful back. And they would go thus together through the Temple, while a white stony light bathed equally columns, roof, and floor, every line and plane distinct from end to end of the vast rectangular space. And the urge to impose form would possess him like fire and hunger as the Lady Custodian of his life, his mother-daughter-wife-and-sweet-companion, moved undraped between vast lumps of Parian marble newly quarried, in which slept the limbs of gods and goddesses, a world of linear perfections. And her unsandaled feet would make no sound, but he would hear the cold clang of hammers striking on stone.

And naked with uncut hair, he would follow her, riding a wingèd horse, until he reached the ledge of the great pediment where the painted marble frieze showed fauns pouring a purple wine into gold cups and nymphs with scarlet cheeks flying from young gods beside a river choked with rushes. Putting one hand around her bending waist, he would touch his face to hers. And for a marmoreal instant, assuming the attitude of a lost engraving in an old book of Raintree County, together they would achieve the ecstasy of form, an unendurable bliss.

And in that instant the faces of the people, the pale blue vault of sky, the rectangular horizons, the distant temples, the viny hills, the clustering roofs became an image of arrested time.

By a single bound, riding the white horse of Eros, he had achieved the summit of the Platonic forms, the shrine of Justice on the Court House Square.

Soon enough, he would have to restore the lady with the grocery scales to her accustomed niche.

In front of his house he stopped, having overtaken his family. He could hear the Perfessor coming along in darkness under the trees.

—I'll see Professor Stiles to the Station, he said to his wife. You'd best go to bed, Pet.

The Perfessor came up, carrying the *Atlas.* He took his suitcase from the porch. He said a gracious farewell to Esther, patted Will's shoulder, winked at Wesley, and paid a pretty compliment to Eva, although his voice was nearly gone.

—A return of an old throat ailment, he whispered, contracted during the War.

Mr. Shawnessy and the Perfessor walked together to the Station. The street was littered with fragments of the memorial day—cigar butts, firecrackers, picnic sacks, patriotic programs. The Perfessor whimpered as he carried his suitcase.

—Here, let me take it to the Station for you, Mr. Shawnessy said.

—Gladly! the Perfessor croaked. I must have talked a hundred thousand words today. Remind me never to visit you again in Waycross, John. Heaven defend me from the quietude of country towns!

They turned at the intersection and walked on toward the Station, the Perfessor stooped and hobbling, but still clutching the *Atlas*. When they reached the Station, they found the agent asleep inside, propped up in a chair. A single lantern burned on the table. The telegraph key clicked sleepily from time to time.

Sitting down on the outside bench, the Perfessor slumped forward, chin on breastbone, but instantly sat up when the agent came out of the Station swinging a lantern.

—She's about due, the agent said.

The Perfessor opened the *Atlas* and studied the statuary group that an unknown artist had placed in the most conspicuous place in Raintree County.

—Ah, he said sadly, Life! Life! John, I'll give you a hundred dollars for this book, and you can make your peace with the Lady Custodian in whatever way you please.

—Sorry, Professor, Mr. Shawnessy said, but, after all, she gave it to me on faith. The Senator gets the first bid.

The Perfessor turned, still clutching the book.

—Men have been known to kill for artistic masterpieces, he said hoarsely.

His eyes brightened strangely. His face looked so evil and convulsed that Mr. Shawnessy made an involuntary motion of raising his arm between himself and his friend.

But in the next moment, the Perfessor, acting as usual, shook with amusement. The sweet, forlorn look came back into his eyes, and he laid the *Atlas* on Mr. Shawnessy's lap.

—There you are, he said. Keep it yourself, boy. It's your own Raintree County and no one else's. Forever the little straight roads shall run to lost horizons; and in the niche reserved for Justice, the image of young love and soul-discovery forever shall be poised. It shall be there for you alone, in your unique copy of the universe.

A low thunder of wheels was swelling from the east. A red eye glared in the dark, grew astonishingly big and close. The agent swung his lantern athwart the rails, and the train rolled heavily to a stop in Waycross Station. Instantly, a figure, resembling the Reverend Lloyd G. Jarvey, appeared from the darkness and climbed into one of the rear coaches.

—O, o! croaked the Perfessor, who hadn't missed the movement. The Lord God Jehovah and I are getting out together.

He and Mr. Shawnessy shook hands, and the Perfessor swung onto the coach behind the coalcar. The glare from the furnace showed a long, thin body in a soiled white suit, a face old and cunning, black eyes shining through pince-nez glasses. Already the engine was beginning to puff. The smoke and the furnace glare stung Mr. Shawnessy's eyes so that they smarted.

—Good-by, Professor! he cried out, waving his hand.

The Perfessor opened his mouth.

—For our mirrors! he was shouting.

He tried to say something else, but his failing voice was lost in the roar of the train. He leaned far out, pointed to his voice-box, and then with characteristic quickness of decision elevated his malacca cane and traced huge letters in the air. Mr. Shawnessy was not able to decipher the first part because a gush of smoke crossed the writing, but the Perfessor's last blackboard flourish was entirely legible and familiar:

Mr. Shawnessy could no longer see his old friend's face. He could see only the long arm and the malacca cane, which lingered a moment in the air indicative of stars. But the legend lay across his memory, the initials of his own name.

Suddenly, he realized that the Perfessor with his usual cleverness must have written them backwards, and what was in reverse for him had come right for Mr. Shawnessy.

The train which bore the mortal shell of Professor Jerusalem Webster Stiles was already lost in the night except for the smoke-stack flare. There was a lonesome wail at the crossing a mile west of town. The train was entirely gone then except for the steady chugging of the engine. It was entirely gone then.

It was entirely gone, and the night had closed in upon Waycross. The agent had left the Station already, and Mr. Shawnessy started back up the street toward the intersection. The starlight was now so intense and his eyes so well accustomed to the night that he could easily read his watch. It was twelve o'clock.

There was no light burning now in Waycross. He felt a wonderful and soft serenity. All things around him now were sunken into sleep.

The long day and its images shook in his mind like a chain of luminous and tinkling fragments. As he approached the intersection, faces and faces on the Great Road of the Republic pressed through his memory, fading and fading into summer night. What was this immense, tranquil substance, that which was there, enormous and eternal thereness? And where were all the warm, relinquished shapes of a day spent with the Americans?

He mused upon the strange dream called Raintree County. In some oriental garden, the seed of it was sown, but it had had its nurture in a womb of fair and fecund ideas on the rim of an inland ocean, and it had ridden west in wingèd vessels, and it had rebuilt itself through more than four levels from its earliest antiquities. Now, impending in the still night was the world of mystery, the world that hovered forever beyond the borders of the County. What was Raintree County except a Columbian exploration, a few acres of discovery in a jungle of darkness, a few lightyears of investigated space in nebular vastness! That which lay beyond its borders was simply—everything potential.

And who was John Wickliff Shawnessy, whose wavering initials had just been signed in smoke in Waycross Station? How deep and broad was the substance of himself, built into this engendering night? Surely there was a being who didn't bear his name but was none the less a composite of all that he had ever been or ever could be. How did one find access to this eternal Self-Affirmer, this restless Shakespeare of Creation, hovering in a world Behind the Scenes? What was he doing there, down there? Polishing the lines of the eternal tragi-comedy of life, setting up props, trying on masks, restlessly taking on and off the costumes, assembling the company for endless rehearsals, reviews, redactions? What was he doing there, down there? Weaving a legend of a younger brother, a residual and mortal brother, this innocent and fortunate brother who walked the streets of time?

At the intersection of the two roads, he looked west. West, just touching with clean rim the empurpled earth, a huge halfball of yellow poured down the National Road a river of golden light. Five hours behind her radiant brother, tranquil, with stately descent, the moon had sunk to her setting.

The wall between himself and the world dissolved. He seemed suddenly lost from himself, plucked out of time and space, being both time and space himself, an inclusive being in which all other beings had their being. A vast unrest was in the earth. The Valley of Humanity was turbulent with changing forms. The immense dream trembled on a point of night and nothingness and threatened explosion.

He held tight to the *Atlas* and walked on. Strong yearning possessed him to build again—and better than before—the valorous dream. If it should all expire, he would be able to rebuild it. He would walk on in his old black schoolmaster's suit, shaking from Family Bibles, McGuffey Readers, Histories of America, Latin and Greek Texts, Free Enquirers, Declarations of Independence and Constitutions, the seeds of words, planting the virgin earth of America with springing forms.

So each man had to build his world again!

So he would plant again and yet again the legend of Raintree County, the story of a man's days on the breast of the land. So he would plant great farms where the angular reapers walk all day, whole prairies of grass and wheat rising in waves on the headlands. So he would plant the blond corn in the valleys of Raintree County. Yes, he would plant once more the little towns, Waycrosses and Danwebsters, and the National Roads to far horizons, passing to blue days and westward adventures, and progress, the cry of a whistle, arcs of the highflung bridges, and rails and the thundering trains. (Hail and farewell at the crossing!) He would plant cities, clusters of blazing jewels on the dark flesh of the night, and faces shining under the glare of the great fires—San Francisco, Indianapolis, Pittsburgh, Philadelphia, New York, Washington, Washington, Washington, and parts between, cities and dwellers in cities, a dragon seed, a harvest of fury. (Shall there be one man hungry, and I go fed!) He would plant gilded years and gilded dreams, the young men wandering lost in metropolitan jungles, and the place where the great trains come to rest. He would plant science, explorers of matter, finders of new species, the august ascent of man from form to form, and honest doubts and dark misgivings. (Are you there, old truepenny, reverse of the coin!) He would plant the young messiahs down from the hills, divinely arrogant heroes, makers of bread and beatitudes, the gentle gods dying on angry crosses, and new crusades, and fearless emancipations. He would plant the anniversaries of mankind, celebrations of great beginnings.

He would plant the Republic of Mankind.

Yes, he would plant the great fair dream, again and ever; he would record it on paper so that it might be found from time to time among old manuscripts in a forgotten drawer of the Cosmos.

Did you think that I had lost the way? Did you think that I was drowned in darkness and the swamp? But I was here always, bearing a stem of the summer grass.

Make way, make way for the Hero of Raintree County! His victory is not in consummations but in quests!

Bearing the huge book of Raintree County, he walked along the now entirely deserted street of Waycross, approached his own home, and entered the gate. The town lay somewhere in infinite night, hushed and potential with all mystery and meaning.

Where was the town of Waycross at night when the sleepers all were sleeping?

But where were the trains that only lightly disturbed the ears of dreamers, and where was the whereness of a dreamer, dreaming dreams in an upstairs bedroom of a little town beside a road in America long ago? For in a little time, he knew that he would be that dreamer, lost in darkness, lost and yet not lost, away and yet at home, forever awake and yet forever dreaming. He would be that dreamer, and he would have perhaps again his ancient and eternal dream. . . .

Of a quest for the sacred Tree of Life. Of a happy valley and a face of stone—and of the coming of a hero. Of mounds beside the river. Of threaded bones of lovers in the earth. Of shards of battles long ago. Of names upon the land, the fragments of forgotten language. Of beauty risen from the river and seen through rushes at the river's edge. Of the people from whom the hero sprang, the eternal, innocent children of mankind. Of their towns and cities and the weaving millions. Of the earth on which they lived—its blue horizons east and west, exultant springs, soft autumns, brilliant winters. And of all its summers when the days were long.

So dreaming, he held the golden bough still in his hand. So dreaming, he neared the shrine where the tree was and the stones and the letters upon them. And the branch quivered alive in his hands, unrolled its bark, became a map covered with lines and letters, a poem of mute but lovely meanings, a page torn from the first book printed by man, the legend of a life upon the earth and of a river running through the land, a signature of father and preserver, of some young hero and endlessly courageous dreamer

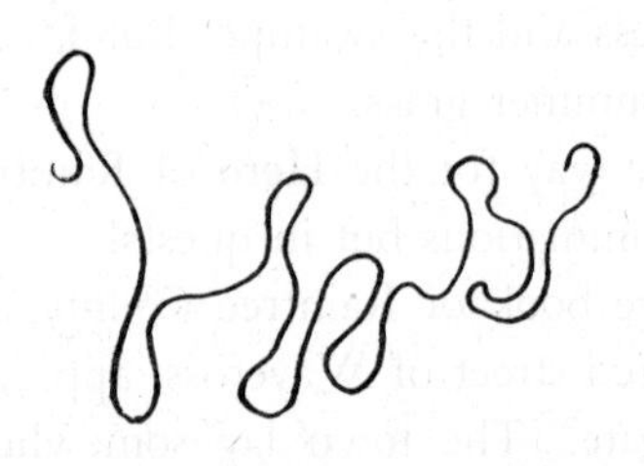

Chronology of Some Historical Events

CHRONOLOGY OF SOME HISTORICAL EVENTS
With Bearing on the Story
of
RAINTREE COUNTY

1816 .... Indiana becomes a State.

1801–1847 .... John Chapman (Johnny Appleseed) plants apple-tree nurseries in the Middle West.

1826 .... New Harmony, Indiana, founded by Robert Owen on the southern Wabash.

1844, November .... James K. Polk, Democrat, defeats Henry Clay, Whig, in Presidential Election.

1846–1848 .... The War with Mexico.

1846, August .... The Wilmot Proviso, proposing that land acquired from Mexico be free territory, reopens the slavery controversy.

1847, September 11 .... Stephen Foster's 'Oh! Susanna' sung, probably for the first time, at Andrews' Eagle Ice Cream Saloon in Pittsburgh.

1848

January 24 .... Gold discovered in California.

July 4 .... Cornerstone of the Washington Monument laid.

November .... General Zachary Taylor, Whig, wins Presidential Election.

1851 .... Hawthorne's story 'The Great Stone Face' published in *The Snow Image*.

1852 .... *Uncle Tom's Cabin* published.

1854

May 25 ....Kansas-Nebraska Bill passed.

July 6.................A Republican Party founded in convention at Jackson, Michigan.

October 16 ....The 'Peoria Speech' makes Abraham Lincoln famous throughout the Northwest for its clear statement of the moral and political case against slavery and its extension.

1855 ....*Hiawatha* and *Leaves of Grass* published.

1856, November ....James Buchanan, Democrat, defeats John C. Frémont, Republican, in Presidential Election.

1858, June 16..............Lincoln opens senatorial campaign against Douglas with 'House Divided' speech.

1859

October 16 ....John Brown raids Harper's Ferry.

December 2..........John Brown hanged at Charles Town, Virginia.

1860, November ....Lincoln elected President of the United States.

1861

February 8..........Confederate Government formed.

March 4.............Lincoln inaugurated in Washington.

April 12–14..........Fort Sumter besieged and surrendered; Civil War begins.

1863

January 1.............The Emancipation Proclamation.

May 2–4 ....The Battle of Chancellorsville.

July 1–3 . . . . The Battle of Gettysburg.

July 8–13 . . . . Morgan's Raid passes through Indiana.

September 19–20 . . . . . . The Battle of Chickamauga.

September–November . The Siege of Chattanooga.

November 19 . . . . Lincoln delivers the Gettysburg Address.

November 25 . . . . The Battle of Missionary Ridge

1864

November 14–16 . . . . . . The destruction of Atlanta, Georgia.

Nov. 15–Dec. 10 . . . . . . Sherman's Army marches to the Sea.

1865

February 17 . . . . Fall of Columbia, South Carolina.

March 4 . . . . Lincoln inaugurated for a second term.

April 9 . . . . Lee surrenders to Grant at Appomattox Court House.

April 14 . . . . Lincoln shot by John Wilkes Booth in Ford's Theatre in Washington.

May 23–24 . . . . The Grand Review in Washington.

1869, May 10 . . . . The Golden Spike driven at Promontory Point, linking the continent by rail.

1869–1877 . . . . Presidential term of Ulysses S. Grant.

1876

June 26 . . . . Custer Massacre at the Little Big Horn.

July 4 . . . . Centennial Fourth in Philadelphia; America is one hundred years old.

November .... Disputed Presidential Election between Tilden and Hayes; finally awarded to Hayes.

1877, July .... The Great Railroad Strike.

1892

June .... Republicans nominate Benjamin Harrison for President; Democrats nominate Grover Cleveland.

July 1 .... Carnegie and Company lock out 3800 men on a wage dispute at Homestead.

July 4 .... The Populist Party convenes at Omaha, Nebraska.